D0275834

'A fine writer . . . a literary event.'

Marion Zimmer Bradley

'A rare narrative talent.'

C. J. Cherryh

'Confirms Mary Gentle's status as a writer of sensitivity and imagination.' *Irish Times*

'A superior blending of SF with Fantasy.' *Time Out*

'Gentle understands both the movement of politics across nations, and the motivations of seemingly insignificant people, and she makes her reader feel both.' Sfsite.com

'Writing of the highest quality, an irresistible combination of unforced style, unbounded imagination and great storytelling.' *Prism UK*

MARY GENTLE

Orthe: Chronicles
of Carrick V

Copyright © Mary Gentle 1983, 1987

'The Crystal Sunlight, the Bright Air' first published in 1983 in
Isaac Asimov's Science Fiction Magazine, Davis Publications, Inc.

This omnibus edition first published in Great Britain in 2002 by
Gollancz
An imprint of the Orion Publishing Group
Orion House, 5 Upper St Martin's Lane,
London WC2H 9EA

A CIP catalogue record for this book
is available, from the British Library

ISBN 057 507287 3

Typeset by SetSystems Ltd,
Saffron Walden, Essex

Printed in Great Britain by
Clays Ltd, St Ives plc

Golden Witchbreed

For my Grandfather
Claude William Laurence Champion
who was, among other things,
a story-teller

CONTENTS

PRINCIPAL CHARACTERS

Lynne de Lisle Christie, envoy
Sam Huxton, marine biologist, head of the Dominion xeno-team:
Timothy Eliot, xeno-biology
Audrey Eliot, xeno-ecology (land)
John Lalkaka, geologist
Margery Huxton, xeno-ecology (sea)
Elspeth Huxton, her daughter
John Barratt, demographer
Dr K. Adair, medical research
Carrie Thomas, xeno-sociology
Maurie Venner, assistant sociologist
David Meredith, envoy

Dalzielle Kerys-Andrethe, T'An Suthai-Telestre, Crown of the Southland,
   also called Suthafiori, Flower of the South
Evalen Kerys-Andrethe, her daughter
Katra Hellel Hanathra, First Minister of Ymir
Katra Sadri Hanathra, his sister, *s'an telestre*
Sadri Geren Hanathra, her son, shipmaster

amari *Ruric Orhlandis, T'An* Commander of the Southland army
Ruric Rodrion Orhlandis, her *ashiren*, called Halfgold

Sulis n'ri n'suth SuBannasen, T'An Melkathi
Hana Oreyn Orhlandis, First Minister of Melkathi
Nelum Santhil Rimnith, Portmaster of Ales-Kadareth

Telvelis Koltyn Talkul, T'An Roehmonde
Verek Howice Talkul, his son
Verek Sethin Talkul, his daughter
Sethin Falkyr Talkul, Sethin's son
Asshe, commander of the northern garrison

Jacan Thu'ell Sethur, T'An Rimon
Zannil Emberen n'ri n'suth Telerion, Seamarshal of Morvren Freeport
Arlyn Bethan n'ri n'suth Ivris, T'An Kyre

Talmar Haltern n'ri n'suth Beth'ru-elen, a Crown Messenger
Achil Maric Salathiel, l'ri-an to the envoy
Aluys Blaize n'ri n'suth Meduenin, a mercenary

Kanta Andrethe, the Andrethe of Peir-Dadeni
Eilen Brodin n'ri n'suth Charain, an intelligencer
Cethelen Khassiye Reihalyn, a minister in Shiriya-Shenin

Tirzael, an Earthspeaker
Branic, a Wellkeeper at Terison
Rhiawn, a Wellkeeper at Terison
Theluk n'ri n'suth Edris, an Earthspeaker
Arad, a Wellkeeper at Corbek

Dannor bel-Kurick, Emperor-in-Exile
Kurick bel-Olinyi, ambassador from Kel Harantish

Gur'an Alahamu-te O'he-Oramu-te, a barbarian woman
Speaker-for-the-People, a fenborn of the Lesser Fens

the Hexenmeister of Kasabaarde,
Tethmet, a fenborn of the Brown Tower
Havoth-jair, a sailor
Orinc, of the Order house Su'nair

PART ONE

CHAPTER 1

Carrick V

A ramshackle collection of white plastic and steel buildings stood at the edge of the concrete landing strip. Beyond the trade station grey rocks stretched out to a startling blue sea. A fine dust sifted down.

I walked away from the ship's ramp and stood on the hot concrete, the pale sun burning down on my head. The light off the sea was harshly brilliant, dazzling; Carrick's Star is nearer white than Earth-standard yellow.

Behind me there was the bustle of the shuttle-ship unloading. I was the only passenger disembarking on Carrick V. On the FTL starship, now in orbit, I'd been busy with hypno-tapes of the languages and customs of the world. Orthe was the native name, or so the first expedition reported. Orthe, fifth world of Carrick's Star, a sun on the edge of the galaxy's heart.

I shouldered my packs and went across to the station. Shadows on Earth are grey. At their darkest they have a tinge of blue. Orthe's shadows are black and so sharp-edged that they fool the eye; while I walked I had to stop myself avoiding shadow-holes in the concrete.

A moss-like plant clung to the rocky soil, and from its dense blue clusters sprang small crimson flowers on waist-high stems. A hot wind blew off the water. There were whitecaps. The arch of the sky was cloudless, the horizon amber-hazed.

Pinpricks of white light starred the sky.

I took a deep breath and stood still. The mark of a world on the edge of the core of the galaxy, these were Orthe's daystars. For a second everything – sea, wind, rock, sunlight – stood out shock-ingly alien.

A man walked out of the trade station, waved a careless hand, and headed towards me. He wore shirt, britches, high boots – and a sword belted at his hip. He was not human. An Orthean.

'Your pardon, *t'an*, you are the envoy?'

9

I recognized the speech of Ymir.

'Ah – yes.' I realized I was staring. 'Pleased to meet you.'

For my part, I prefer aliens that look alien. Then when they ritually eat their first-born, or turn arthropod halfway through their life-cycle, it isn't so much of a shock. You expect it. Humanoid aliens, they're trouble.

'And so am I pleased to meet with you.' He bowed slightly. The speech inflection was formal. 'I am Sadri Geren Hanathra of Ymir.'

His papers authorized him as escort for the Dominion envoy: they were made out and signed by the head of the xeno-team, and countersigned by someone I took to be an Orthean official: one Talmar Haltern n'ri n'suth Beth'ru-elen. Like everything else on this mission, it had the air of being a haphazard arrangement.

'Lynne de Lisle Christie.' It being customary to give country of origin, I added 'Of the British Isles, and the Dominion of Earth.'

He stood well under two metres tall, about my height. His yellow hair was short, the hairline somewhat higher than I expected. As he glanced back, I saw that it was rooted down his neck, vanishing under his collar. Either the custom was to go clean-shaven or the Ortheans had little body-hair. There was none of that fine down that marks a human skin; his – as he held up his hand in greeting – I saw to be smooth, slick-looking, with almost a hint of a scale-pattern.

He was young, with a cheerfully open expression, but with the air of a man accustomed to lead rather than follow.

'Christie. Not a Southland name – but of course not.' He gestured. 'Come this way, I've a ship waiting off North Point.'

Drawn up on the rocky shore was a dinghy, attended by two Orthean natives. The older one took my packs and stored them at the prow. Geren scrambled in and sat at the stern. I followed, less agile. No one offered help. The two Orthean males pushed us offshore, climbed in, and began rowing.

'There is my ship,' Geren turned to me, pointing. 'The *Hanathra*, named for my *telestre*. A good vessel, but not as far-travelled as yours, I think.'

A *telestre* was something between estate and family and commune, I thought. I wasn't sure of the details. Hypno-tapes always give you that feeling at first: that what you're hearing is never exactly what the other person is saying, and that you can never find the right words yourself. It wears off with use.

A sailing ship lay anchored offshore, the kind of craft the Ortheans call *jath*. It was no larger than a galleon, though not square-rigged: triangular lateen sails gave it the rakish look of a clipper.

10

'Have we far to go?' I asked.

'A week's journey, perhaps, if the wind favours. More if not. We're bound for Tathcaer, for the court there.' Geren's smile faded. 'You must realize, *t'an*, you'll be the centre of some attention. You should beware intrigue.'

The word he used was not precisely intrigue, or conspiracy, or politics; it is an untranslatable expression that includes the Orthean term for challenges and games.

'Thank you for warning me. It's kind.'

'If I mean what I say?' He laughed. 'I do. I've no love for the court. I'd sooner sail the *Hanathra*. But don't believe me just because I say so. Take no one at their word.'

It was a taste of that same intrigue. I was certain he did it deliberately and I liked him for it, but it emphasized how much of an unknown quality Carrick V was, and what a series of locked doors I would have to open.

Coming out from the shelter of the point, the dinghy began to rock. The water was clear: the pale green of spring leaves. A fan of spray went up, polychromatic in the white sunlight. We crawled through the troughs of the waves toward the ship.

There was a pause while they tossed a rope-ladder down the hull, then Geren went up it like an acrobat. I looked at the wet, dark timber, and the rushing gap between the ship and the rocking dinghy. The rope-ladder jounced from the rail, rungs rattling against the hull.

The boat rose on a wave crest and I grabbed at the ladder and went up it, swinging dizzily, missing my footing and barking my knuckles. Acres of canvas gleamed and swung overhead. Feeling sick, I got two hands to the rail and heaved myself onto the deck.

A barefoot Orthean woman in shirt and britches leaned over the rail, neatly caught my packs and set them on deck. She and another woman swung out davits, the two men came up the rope-ladder as if it were a staircase, and all four of them began hauling the ship's boat onboard.

The distant island rose and fell gently. I had a last sight of the starship's shuttle towering over the trade station.

'This way!' Another woman shouted and beckoned.

I followed. The deck was crowded with men and women furiously working; I kept dodging out of one person's way only to find myself in someone else's. Masts towered. Canvas blocked the sun, shaken out to snap on the wind.

A door below the poop deck led, by a dark, narrow passage, to small cabins.

'Yours.' The Orthean female opened a door. She wore a corded

11

sleeveless jacket, and her thick black mane was done up in a single brad. Her skin was faintly patterned, and there were webs of lines round her eyes.

In the dim light her eyes seemed to film over as she watched me, and then clear again. The Ortheans have a 'third eyelid', a nictitating membrane like a cat's eye. And something else. I looked at her calloused hands.

Put them side by side with mine and they would be no wider, but she had five slender strong fingers beside her thumb. And thick nails, kept filed down on all but the little finger, which sported a hooked claw.

'Afraid you're sharing,' she said, 'but I'm mostly nightwatch so we shouldn't get in each other's way.'

'Thanks. I'll try not to cause you bother.'

'You think I didn't fight for the privilege?' She had a surprisingly human grin. 'I want something to tell my children about the famous Otherworld envoy.'

'Surilyn!'

The woman's head jerked up. I recognized Geren's voice.

'I'd best get to the helm.' She turned. 'The shipmaster's cabin is there, call *t'an* Geren if anything's too unfamiliar.'

I went into the cabin. It was narrow; bunk bed one side, sea-chest the other. A square, iron-framed port with inch-thick bolts let in green-gold light. I had to stoop. The ceiling – the underside of the poop deck – showed beams a foot thick. There was the constant creak of timber and the lap of waves against the hull.

I sat down suddenly. The ship shook throughout its length, quivered, and settled into a steady pushing rhythm, driving ahead. It was an uneasy motion.

Sitting there, with the blankets rough under my hands and the sunlight sliding up and down the wood, I had a moment of stillness. This was not a starship, not even a sea-going ship on an Earth ocean; the voyage would not end at London or Liverpool or the Tyne. Sadri Geren Hanathra and the woman Surilyn, they were not conceived, born, or brought up on Earth.

I began to accept the fact that here, on this world, I was the alien.

The *Hanathra*, under intermittent wind and plagued by cloud and squalls, sailed on into the Inner Sea. At the end of the first nine-day week Geren told me the season was famous for fogs and summer calms. I spent time below decks, talking to whoever was off duty; and every day I stayed a little longer in the intense sunlight, getting acclimatized.

Zu'Ritchie, the youngest of the crew, had what I took to be a birthmark covering most of his face. He was unusually pale-skinned, and the mark took the form of grey dapples, like fern-patterns on the skin, that extended from his forehead down over his cheek to his shoulder.

'That?' Surilyn said. I questioned her when the boy wasn't around. 'That's marshflower. It only means his *telestre* borders the Fens.'

I had to be content with that. Later, in warmer waters, some of the crew stripped to the waist and I saw that the 'marshflower' extended over his torso. The pattern grew larger and darker, almost black in places. Natural markings, I realized. Zu'Ritchie was not the only one with it, though his was most pronounced; and he was a little teased because of it.

The second shock – and it was only a shock because it was so like and yet *unlike* humanity – came when I saw the rudimentary second pair of nipples that both sexes carried low on the ribs. Most of the women were small-breasted compared to the Earth-norm, their bronze-brown nipples as small as the males'. I suspected that in times past, if not now, the Ortheans had littered a larger number of children at one birth than we ever did.

I watched Surilyn coiling a rope, the muscles moving smoothly under her brown skin. Her black mane was unbraided, and I saw that it rooted down her spine to a point well below the shoulderblades.

My own hackles raised at the thought. Almost us, and yet not us.

I wondered what other, less visible, differences there might be between our two species.

A thin line grew out of the haze and became solid. Surilyn, leaning beside me on the rail, pointed.

'Those are the Melkathi Flats . . . see those hills on the horizon? That's the beginning of Ymir.'

We were not close in to the coast, I noted. No passenger was going to jump ship and slip away . . . Not that I would; at the moment I needed to act through official channels.

'How long until Tathcaer?'

'We'll be in on the noon tide, if the wind holds.'

Carrick V has no satellite and therefore only solar tides, low at dawn and sunset, high at midnight and midday.

'I'm going below,' Surilyn yawned. She squinted at the dawn haze, which showed no sign of clearing. 'Noon. *If* the wind holds.'

'Christie,' Zu'Ritchie called, '*t'an* Geren wants to see you in his cabin.'

'I'll be right down, tell him. Sounds like my holiday's over,' I observed.

'I'm sorry,' the black-maned woman said. 'All you've told us, about the Otherworlds, they were fine stories.'

'But did you believe them?'

She grinned. 'Can't say that I did. But I'll be sure and tell my children.'

'You're going home after this voyage?'

She shrugged. 'The ship's due for refitting, I'll stay aboard. Likely Suan will bring them down from my *telestre*, they're old enough. She's their milk-mother.'

I had no time to press the point.

'Till I see you, Surilyn.'

'Till we meet, Christie.'

I went below and found Geren in his cabin. He straightened up from the map-table as I entered.

'Drink?'

'Thanks.' I smelled the spicy odour of herb-tea brewing. I crossed the swaying cabin to look at the charts.

The first was a single-hemisphere map. There was no indication of what the survey satellite showed in the other hemisphere: a myriad islands, none with civilization above the stone age level. This was a map of the oikumene, civilized Orthe.

It had the look of all old cartography, ornate and inaccurate. There were two continents joined by a long island-archipelago. Most of the northernmost continent was left blank, but its southern coast was filled in with what I assumed were cities, kingdoms, ports – and was annotated *Suthai-Telestre*, the South-land, and so must be our destination.

The southern continent seemed only to be occupied round the coasts. The centre of the land mass had hieroglyphics I couldn't decipher.

'We sailed from here,' Geren said, putting his finger on a group of islands far out on the edge of the map. 'The Eastern Isles, here, and then we—' he drew his finger across and up to the southern coast of the Southland '—sailed so across the Inner Sea, to Tathcaer.'

Tathcaer was marked at a river mouth midway along the coast. A good central base for an investigative xeno-team, I thought – but not if, like the one I was going to meet, you couldn't leave it.

Geren handed me a bowl of herb-tea. He didn't smile when he

14

spoke. 'I hope you'll forgive my calling you in like that, but I wanted to talk to you before we dock in Tathcaer.'

'Geren—'

I thought, would it be better to wait until I reached the officials at Tathcaer before beginning discussions? Geren Hanathra was little more than a messenger.

'No, wait. I must say this.' He sat on the table, oblivious to the swinging lamps and the shifting pale light. 'I don't press advice, usually, but . . .'

'But now you're going to?'

'It's perhaps not wise. You're the envoy, after all.'

I leaned against the table. 'I'd like to hear it, Geren.'

'This, then. I am of the party that supported contact with your Otherworld. I have even met – though not to speak to – those of your people who are present in Tathcaer.'

'And?'

He rubbed six-fingered hands through his yellow mane, then looked sharply at me. His eyes veiled. 'And so I likely know as much about you as any here, though that is little. But I know how you, envoy, will seem to those at court.'

'Yes?' I had to prompt him again. He stood, pacing in that confined space. I wondered whether all Ortheans had that grace.

His eyes clouded again. He had the marshflower also, I saw, faint as a watermark.

'It is not good. *T'an*, they will look at you and say: here is a loose-haired and swordless woman, with a child-face and eyes like stone—'

I laughed, choked on the herb-tea, and coughed myself into sobriety. 'Geren, I'm sorry.'

'I say only how you seem to us. And much of it is custom only.' He faced me. 'I suppose strangeness of dress is to be expected, and hair neither cropped as in Ymir nor in Peir-Dadeni braids – and that you never blink, and lack the witch-finger; well I dare say we look as strange to you. And in a priest's skirt, too, and you are no priest . . . and, Christie, you are young.'

'Twenty-six. Less for Orthe, your years are longer than ours. As for youth,' I said, 'time cures that soon enough.'

He chuckled reluctantly. 'You're not offended?'

'I've come here as envoy,' I said. 'I must be awkward, I must deal with your people as I would with mine. I'll make mistakes, yes, that's not to be avoided, but it doesn't matter. Watching me, you'll see the truth of Earth. I can't bring books or pictures to show you what we're like, all I can do is be. I've come to see – and be seen.'

After a moment he nodded. 'Yes. Of course. *T'an*, it was foolish of me to think that you would not know your trade.'

'I'm no expert.' It was true enough. My two previous appointments had been with established embassies; this was the first time I'd worked alone.

I looked down again at the maps, marked with the imprints of the *Hanathra*'s many voyages. So much I didn't know about Orthe, so much data lost, or mislaid in the rush to get someone – anyone – here. But under the circumstances, that was inevitable.

'But you must promise me you will at least bear a *harur* blade. It is the one thing that will tell against you.'

I was silent. It was not a promise I was prepared to make.

'Christie, I'm thinking only of your safety.'

'I know. I'm not offended.'

'No,'he said, exasperated, 'I believe you're not.'

I left him. The dawn mist hung in pearls on the rail and deck, glistening and cold. Restless, I went below again. I lit the oil-lamp in my cabin, shuttering it in its thick glass casing. The air was damp. Surilyn was asleep. I didn't disturb her.

On the sea-chest lay the traditional paired Southland blades: the *harur-nilgiri*, too short to be a sword, and the *harur-nazari*, too long to be a knife. I picked up the longer of the pair, the rapier-like *nilgiri*, gripping the cord-wrapped hilt. I flourished it, remembering old pirate fantasies, childhood games. The weight was unfamiliar on my wrist. I did not know how to carry it, wear it, or use it. I put it back.

Sadri Geren was wrong. Even if etiquette demanded it I had no business carrying a *harur* blade. That required a lifetime's training, and a lifetime on Carrick V, not Earth.

By noon the haze had thickened into fog, and the wind dropped.

From the deck, the masthead was invisible. The sails vanished into grey moisture. Zu'Ritchie descended from the crow's-nest wringing wet, and reported no thinning of the fog at that height.

'Drop anchor,' Geren ordered.

'How long?' I asked.

'Summer fogs don't generally last above a day or so in these waters.'

'Can't we go ahead anyhow?'

'You're not a seawoman, are you? Despite your British Isles. We can anchor here safely. Further west and we'd come to the mouth of the Oranon River and be drifted south. And there are the Sisters Islands not far south of here.'

When he spoke of the sea you could tell where his heart was.

Then he was not thinking of the court at Tathcaer, or the ship and crew, but only of rocks and islands, tides and currents, and the prevailing winds of the Inner Sea. Some care more for inanimate things than for people. Geren was like that.

'You must guest at my *telestre*,' he said, his face animated again. 'If they ever let you outside Tathcaer, come to Hanathra. If you had the time I'd take you voyaging down to Quarth, Kel Harantish, even the Rainbow Cities – an envoy should know the sea-routes. The Southland isn't all of Orthe, no matter what they say in Tathcaer.'

'I will if I can. How far is it?'

It was unlikely I'd have time for contacts other than the strictly official, at least to begin with. Still . . .

'A good weather voyage to Quarth and Kel Harantish? Perhaps six or seven weeks. A half-year to Saberon, first of the Rainbow Cities, and further to Cuthanc.' He looked up and was suddenly serious. 'Christie, remember I make you that offer in all honesty. If you should need to leave Tathcaer, come to me.'

It was cold on deck, despite the coat I had on over jeans and tunic. I shivered.

'All right, Geren. If I need to.'

By night the fog had dispersed, and for the first time I saw the Orthean summer stars. Carrick's Star lies on the edge of the galactic core. The sky holds thirty times as many stars as Earth's; I stood on the deck of the *Hanathra* and the starlight was brighter than Earth's full moon.

And before the next morning's mist had burned away, the ship came to the estuary of the Oranon River.

CHAPTER 2

Tathcaer

Sails flapped wetly as the ship tacked to come about. The light of Orthe's white sun on the water was blinding. I went forward out of the way, and looked ahead.

To the east mudflats gleamed. Spider-thin shapes flew up from the reedbeds, wide wings beating; their metallic cries came loudly across the water. *Rashaku* – lizardbirds. They triggered a flood of associations. Long-horned beasts grazed the blue-grey watermeadows – *marhaz? skurrai?* No clear visualization came with the terms. Beyond them, chalk headlands retreated down the coast into a distant haze.

There is always some degree of haze on Orthe. Not weather, specifically, but a quality of the planet's atmosphere; the same quality that makes radio transmissions impossibly distorted.

With radio, I thought, I'd've been talking to the xeno-team in Tathcaer by now. No, with radio, I probably wouldn't be here at all . . .

If my predecessor as First Contact envoy had had radio, he might have had the benefit of satellite weather transmissions; might not have died when the Eastern Isles ship was caught in a storm.

'Christie,' Zu'Ritchie paused briefly as he passed me. 'Look – Tathcaer!'

The vast estuary was choppy, and wide enough still to be mistaken for open sea. The ship wallowed. The wind dropped, caught, the sails snapped out – hills and a crag loomed up, and we were driving straight for a harbour.

Two spurs rose up, and the harbour lay in the crescent between them. The early sun shone on the buildings rising behind it, packed closely together. I gripped the rail, dampened by spray, as we came under the shadow of the fortress-crowned eastern spur. Rivers flowed into the harbour from the far side of each spur; the same river, it came to me. The Oranon split some dozen miles upstream to enclose the island that was Tathcaer. An island-city. And the land to the east was Ymir, and the land to the west, Rimon.

The ship glided in between other anchored ships in a forest of bare-masted *jath* and a multitude of smaller craft. Some boats threw ropes and guided the *Hanathra*'s bulk into the anchorage under Easthill. The nearer river was shallow with many bridges while the other outlet of the Oranon by Westhill was wide and deep. I watched the bustling activity.

I have seen cities (not only on Earth) that stretched as far as the eye could see, horizon to horizon; cities it would take a week to drive across. So I could understand why the xeno-team's tapes referred to Tathcaer as a 'native settlement'. Settlement? I tasted the word in my mind, looking at the myriad buildings cupped between low whaleback hills, at the sprawling confusion of white and sand-coloured low buildings. And the bulk of Westhill just clearing the haze way across the harbour, crowned with another squat brown fort pocked with the black shadows of windows. Shouts and cries came from the moored boats, and from the docks beyond.

It came to me that there was more of this city over the saddle-back between Easthill and Westhill. And that, call it settlement if you like, Tathcaer is nonetheless a city.

Geren came across the deck.

I picked up my packs. 'You coming ashore yet?'

'No, I've to see the *Hanathra* safely docked, then report to the court. I may see you there.' He squinted at the quay. Half his mind was on the ship still. 'They're sending a boat. There'll be court officials to find you a place, staff; show you the city.'

The first thing they could show me was a bank, I decided, then I could change the money-drafts that our respective governments had decided were valid. The shipboard holiday was finished, it was back to routine – but a new world is never routine.

I said goodbye to Surilyn, Zu'Ritchie, some of the crew, and Sadri Geren himself. Then I climbed down into a ferry, the rowers bent to the oars, and we glided away from the *Hanathra*. I saw her furled sails and the line of her hull sweet against the river, then faced front as we went into the confusion of the city.

The quay was stacked with crates and cloth-covered bales, and crowded with Ortheans. Back against the buildings (I supposed they were warehouses) stood canvas-sheltered food booths; the smells of cooking were unfamiliar, pungent. Shouts, the squeals of pulleys, the ever-present creak and sway of the ships' masts . . . Dung and other unidentifiable odours came from the harbour.

Long-tailed scavenger *rashaku* yammered over the dirty water. A gang of young children tumbled past. There were children underfoot everywhere; on the foodstalls, in the warehouses, on the moored ships.

I stood on stone paving, between bare masts and high buildings. They were flat-roofed with many-angled walls and, as far as I could see, windowless. I looked round to spot anyone who might be there to meet me. My balance was a little off. That must be the sea: Carrick V's gravity is only an imperceptible fraction less than Earth-standard.

I knew the xeno-team must be in Tathcaer, if only because my first priority was to get them travel permits from the Crown. But I was beginning to wonder if I'd have to find them on my own, when I caught sight of a middle-aged Orthean obviously heading towards me.

'Envoy?' At my nod, he bowed. 'I'm Haltern n'ri n'suth Beth'ru-elen, of the Peir-Dadeni *telestres*.'

The same Haltern that countersigned the travel permit? One of the minor official contacts the xeno-team must have with the authorities, I guessed.

'Lynne de Lisle Christie, British Isles.'

'The Crown sent me to meet you.' He used that informal term for the ruler of the Southland, the *T'An Suthai-Telestre*. 'When you're settled in, we can arrange for an audience. End of the week, perhaps?'

This was said all in one breath. He had a cropped blond mane brushed forward, disguising its retreat into a mere crest, and watery aquamarine eyes. That whiteless stare was forever alien, Orthean. Over the shirt and britches that were common Ymirian dress he wore a loose tunic, green and a little threadbare, with a gold feather-crest on the breast. *Harur* blades hung on worn belts. He had a vague, harassed look about him. If Geren had anyone in mind when he warned me about intrigue, I thought, this is just the type.

'No audience before the end of the week?' I queried.

'There's a residence to be found. Staff. Wardrobe. *Marhaz* and *skurrai*. *L'ri-an*. The Crown would not wish you to come to court before you feel ready.'

Before you've learned not to make a fool of yourself, I translated bleakly.

'After all,' Haltern added reflectively, 'when God made time, She made enough of it to go round, don't you agree?'

*

20

The *skurrai-jasin* slowed on the steep hill. The sky above the narrow twisting passage – you couldn't call it a road – was a star-dotted strip. Featureless walls intensified the heat. *Kekri* flies clustered on open drainage channels. They rose as we passed: long-bodied, thick as my thumb, wings flashing like mirrors as they hummed on a low-pitched note. Some of the walls supported vines, but their fist-sized blue flowers couldn't prevail against the stink.

Haltern, leaning forward, spoke to the driver. The *jasin*-carriage swung left up an even steeper hill, into an even narrower and more convoluted alley.

'Can they manage?' I indicated the beasts.

'Surely. They're strong.' For the first time he used the informal inflection to me. 'They're *skurrai* from Dadeni Heath; that breed could pull twice our weight up a worse slope than this. You see their quarters, that's where their strength is—'

He broke off and glanced apologetically at me. 'I could be a bore about *skurrai*. Beth'ru-elen *telestre* lies close on the Heath, we breed similar stock.'

'They're beautiful,' I said, and he seemed vaguely pleased by the implied compliment.

The *skurrai* were yoked double: reptilian animals with cleft feet and paired double horns, cropped and capped with metal. White sunlight shone on pelts the colour of new copper wire as they plodded up the hill, ruminatively uncomplaining. They stood about waist-high, and they still looked too small to me to be that strong. The *jasin* rattled and jolted on.

I'd seen two or three places that might do as present Liaison Office and future consulate or embassy, but for now I was content to be carried round Tathcaer. It was a large city and I wouldn't cover it in one afternoon, but I wanted to see as much as I could.

'There's one here.' Haltern stopped the *skurrai-jasin*. 'I thought it might prove suitable, though Easthill's far from the Citadel; but you may prefer it that way.'

I dismounted, stiff-legged, not really sorry to be out of the springless carriage. Haltern was unlocking the gate of a blank-walled, two-storey building. The gate opened into a tunnel leading to a central courtyard, but instead of walking through he stopped and unlocked a door to the house.

He wasn't as stupid as he managed to look, I thought. The post of liaison officer and envoy was separate from the xeno-team's first contact agreement, and while it wasn't an important post in itself it might pave the way for full diplomatic contact, and eventually for the opening up of Carrick V to the Dominion of Earth. Therefore I couldn't be seen to favour one faction over another. And to be situated in an obscure part of the city was a fair way to start. Haltern would bear closer acquaintance.

'You're at court?' I asked him, as the heavy wooden door swung open. We entered the mosaic-floored hall. It was cool, smelling of dust and spices.

'In the Crown Messengers. I was in the Peir-Dadeni *tha'adur*,' he used a Dadeni term, 'but the *t'an* Turi Andrethe seems to have loaned me permanently to the Crown.' He smiled. It was a young smile, deceptive. 'Hence my being sent to you.'

The place was smallish: a kitchen and two rooms on the ground floor, three rooms on the first floor, the whole surrounding a tiny courtyard with stables. It was surprisingly light, for all its blank exterior – many windows opened on to the courtyard. Haltern took me round the beam-ceilinged rooms. Old, warped a little here and there, but sound. Thick, flawed glass was leaded into the window. The plumbing was as primitive as reports had led me to expect.

A flight of stairs from the courtyard brought us out onto the flat roof. The heat struck down hard: Carrick's Star is strong in the ultraviolet. The wind up above the city was like warm water. Sweat ran down my back.

Gravelled tar was tacky underfoot. Tubs spilled emerald blossoms, and a lemon-sharp tang cut the air. I walked to the low guard wall.

'I don't think I'll find anything better than this.'

'I'm glad you like it.' Haltern was at my shoulder. 'The others of your people – and there were only eight of them – have laid claim to five separate buildings.'

I could almost fathom his wonder. Buildings seem rarely to be put up singly in Tathcaer – the norm is a sprawling complex centred on a courtyard with a cistern or well. They are used either by members of the same *telestre* or of the same Guild (which, as they say, is a trade-*telestre*).

In front of us the city was laid out like a map. To me it looked congested. There are no streets in Tathcaer. No streets as such, I should say; there are paved and unpaved ways that twist between the various *telestre*-houses, but these are not named. The one exception is Crown Way.

The top of Easthill was behind us, and Westhill was visible across the harbour. In the hollow of the island plaster-walled buildings were yellow and white and pink under the intense sun. Old stone buildings jutted up at intervals, their architecture oddly curved and unfamiliar. The rivers were distant threads, marking the city limits, spanned by bridges and crossed by roads that led away to blue-grey hills. But over the spurs and slopes of the city, past gardens and domes, at six or seven miles distance, a rocky plateau jutted out of the haze. Stone buildings topped the sheer cliff. Beyond that the land went down into northern distances, and daystars shone in a powder-blue sky.

'The Citadel,' Haltern pointed, 'at the end of the island. And see these, below, the House of the Goddess; and the prison, and there—'

He pointed out landmarks: markets, companion-houses and theocratic houses, the Guild Ring, and The Hill – that rich district of the city that houses the *T'Ans* of each province of the Southland: Ymir, Rimon, and Melkathi; Roehmonde, Morvren Freeport, Peir-Dadeni, and the Kyre. I couldn't take it all in at once. At last he was quiet. When I turned to see why, he had the worried expression that seemed part of his face.

'What's it like,' he said, 'out there?'

He was the first Orthean to ask. Perhaps Geren and his crew hadn't truly credited I was alien. Haltern did.

'Some worlds are very like this. Some are very different.' I shrugged. 'What can I tell you? There are so many worlds.'

He shook his head. 'Incredible.'

'Earth—' I stopped. He wasn't the one I should talk to about that. And I couldn't discuss population and famine and taxes and urban decay on an afternoon like this. 'Earth's different again.'

He nodded. 'I'll give orders, have this place furnished tomorrow. One of your countrymen – Eliot, is that the name?'

'Probably.' There was a Timothy Eliot with the xeno-team.

'Eliot has extended an invitation for you to guest with his *telestre*. With his household,' Haltern corrected himself. 'I'll take you there.'

'I thought *telestre* was land?'

'Land, people; people, land – the same thing.' He made his way towards the steps, then hesitated. 'I don't mean to correct you, *t'an*.'

'I'm ignorant of many of your customs. How am I to learn if no one corrects me?'

I saw that pleased him.

'I'll arrange for *l'ri-an* too,' he said. 'Meanwhile, if you'd like to take a late meal, my *telestre*-house is not far from here.'

At first light there was a discordant clamour of bells. I lay half asleep in bed, listening to the varying chimes: near and far, low and high. Tathcaer keeps natural hours, dawn to sunset. Given a choice, I don't.

When I began to wake up properly I took a look at the room. I hadn't noticed much arriving at Eliot's place the night before. Eliot had been out, and his wife Audrey had been hospitable enough to let me go straight to bed. I was still a long way from being acclimatized to Orthe's 27 standard-hour day.

The room was plain: pale plaster walls, the beams boxed in, long drapes to hide the windows and a plain-woven carpet on the floor. All chosen to be as un-Orthean as possible. Xeno-teams are notoriously odd in their methods of adjustment.

I dressed and went downstairs. Voices came from the kitchen. There I found Timothy Eliot at the table, and Audrey Eliot at an iron cooker brewing (by the smell) genuine Earth coffee.

'Ms Christie—'

'Lynne, please.'

'Lynne.' Eliot grinned. He was a solid man in his late thirties, hair thinning on top, wearing a bright shirt over faded jeans. 'I'm Tim. You met Aude last night? Good. Sorry I couldn't be here to welcome you.'

'The rest of the team are down the road.' Audrey brought over a china jug of coffee and a plate of toast. She was younger than Eliot, a bright nervous woman. 'I'll take you round later and introduce you.'

'Thanks.' I found it a relief to be speaking English again. We talked over breakfast. They were a husband and wife team, xeno-biologist and xeno-ecologist, paired with the rest of the team for six years.

'Ten months of it in this hole,' Eliot observed, squinting against the brilliant sunlight flooding the kitchen. Most of the furniture was in plain style again, not like the flamboyant carving and ornamentation I'd seen in Haltern's *telestre*-house.

'Tim,' Audrey said warningly, 'don't prejudice the guest.'

'Oh well . . .' He waved a hand carelessly. 'Lynne's working on our behalf. Isn't that right, Lynne?'

'Not entirely. As the government's representative, I've a duty to be impartial.'

I can never say things like that without sounding pompous, and I could hear myself doing it again.

'But nevertheless, a duty to plead our case to the Crown?'

'Yes, of course.'

'Hopefully you can get us travel permits. *We* can't get them. Damn it, why agree to a contact team if you're going to keep them cooped up in one settlement all the time?'

There was long-term indignation in his voice. It would be harder for them – the sociological half of the xeno-team could at least study in Tathcaer.

I tried tact. 'I think that they don't worry too much about time.'

'That's true enough.' Eliot turned to Audrey. 'One day, and she's seen it; that's the way these aborigines are.'

'You've been on many worlds, Lynne, I expect?' Audrey left the stove to sit down at table. She was wearing a robe with pleats and short hem, something that would have been fashionable about three years ago. I'd brought few clothes: one formal skirt-and-jacket, and jeans and shirts. It's less costly to buy on-world than pay the weight penalty on FTL ships. But xeno-teams are allowed leeway there.

'I was on Beruine, the water-world.' But not for long, I silently gave thanks. 'And then with the embassy on Hakataku.'

'Ah. One doesn't seem to see many women in the diplomatic side of the Extraterrestrial department, somehow.' Eliot smiled, it was meant to be pacifying. 'But I'm sure they wouldn't have sent you if you weren't capable.'

'I'm sure too, Mr Eliot.'

There was an awkward pause. Then Audrey Eliot said, 'What's the news from Earth?'

'The usual, I guess. Squabbles between the PanIndian Federation and post-communist China. I've nothing very recent.' Even with FTL, the trip to Carrick V takes over three months.

'More recent than us—'

There was a rap at the window, and a man walked through the back door. He was in his thirties, dark, and wearing an Ymirian tunic over jeans.

'Hello, Tim, Aude. Heard we had a visitor.'

'John Lalkaka, Lynne Christie.' Eliot served introductions like tennis balls.

'Are you going to get us travel permits, Ms Christie?' Lalkaka leaned against the doorframe.

'Hard to say. I haven't seen the authorities yet.'

'Lord! I hope you can. I'm the last man to criticize ET civilizations—'

I intercepted long-suffering glances between Tim and Audrey.

'—but ten months standard in one settlement! You wait, Ms Christie. Until you've been clanged awake by dawn bells every day for ten months solid; ten months of lousy food and worse plumbing—'

'John.' Eliot grinned and shook his head. 'Give it a rest.'

'*I* miss civilization,' Lalkaka said, not at all offended, 'and when

25

I get back from this mission I intend to spend the next ten months in a rest centre – not at home, but somewhere you can get all the comforts. TV, pre-packed dinners, stereo-tapes ... Bombay, maybe, or Hyderabad.' He laughed, teeth white against his brown skin. 'You wait. A month here, and you'll have your own list to add to mine.'

'I don't doubt it,' I agreed.

'Oh well.' Lalkaka slouched in, sat down, and helped himself to coffee. 'What's the news from home?'

The focus of the world has long since shifted east: Asia holds the twenty-first century's future. Nothing of real importance happens in the declining West. Still, I felt it from Lalkaka and both the Eliots: what interested them was the British Isles. Home.

'Not again!' Audrey intervened. 'Lynne, how about this evening – Tim, you remember what I said?'

He nodded and turned to me. 'We're having a gathering tonight. The team, and a few people from the city. If you come along you'll stand less chance of having to repeat yourself so much.

'Sure. I'll be over at my office for most of the day, moving in, but the evening's fine.'

'You're up on Easthill, aren't you?' Eliot gave me a look that said, smugly, that information travelled fast. 'I'll send a carriage at sunset-bell. You might not find your way otherwise.'

CHAPTER 3

T'An Suthai-Telestre

When I found my way back to the Easthill Malk'ys household, there was a young Orthean waiting for me. He introduced himself as Tasil Rannas n'ri n'suth Methris, cook and housekeeper, and said he would deal with all my supply problems. His *telestre* was a few miles upriver and he apparently had some connection with Haltern's own staff.

The furnishings arrived. Rannas and I spent an hour or two rearranging things, the two downstairs rooms being made up as office and reception, and the first floor as my own quarters. Then Rannas went out to the street-booths and returned with a second (and, by Orthean standards, extremely late) breakfast: bread, fruit, the pale, bitter herb-tea, and whitemeat from the fishmarket – which I suppose, strictly speaking, isn't 'fish': Orthean seabeasts are almost all mammalian.

I retired upstairs to unpack, leaving Rannas to settle the kitchen. His thick accent was all but incomprehensible to me, and I suspected my Ymirian wasn't very good. We communicated in gestures where words failed.

There was little to unpack. Some polyplastic crumple-free clothes; personal effects; the micro-recorder, and the sonic stunner that was one of the few weapons allowed on Pre-tech worlds. It was keyed to my sweat and fingerprint pattern: quite simply, it would not function for anyone else. The department provided it ostensibly as a protection against wildlife. Other uses have been known.

I had also a locked case with credentials, bank drafts, and similar papers; keyed again to my own bio-patterns.

Rannas opened the door. 'One from the court to see you, *t'an*.'

'I'll be right down.' Bells sounded as I left the room, the single chimes for midmorning.

I found Haltern in the office, staring out of the window and humming tunelessly. There was a boy with him.

27

'*T'an*.' He inclined his head. 'Is all well here?'

'You're most efficient, I compliment you.'

Again, the bow. It took the place of a handshake, here where that custom was not common.

'The Crown gifts this household to your office for as long as you need it.' Haltern beckoned the boy forward. 'I've brought you your *l'ri-an*, Christie, *ke* is Achil Maric Salathiel.'

The Ortheans have two neutral pronouns, one for the inanimate and *ke* for the animate. Animals are *ke*, and sometimes the Goddess is, and so are children, though I didn't know why. *L'ri-an* I was more sure of, that was a personal assistant; the word has its roots in the term for apprentice.

He was thin, brown skinned, with a short-cropped black mane. He looked at me sullenly, and then nodded. '*T'an* Christie.'

'Yes. Right. Ah – you'd better go and find Rannas in the kitchen, he'll look after you until we get settled down.' Personal staff were the rule here, and though I was paying a silver piece a day for the privilege I still wasn't happy about it.

'I could have found you an experienced *l'ri-an*,' Haltern said. 'But, Christie, as you're not used to the custom I thought it would be better for you to train *kir* yourself. Fewer disagreements.'

'Isn't he a little young?' But he would be older, Earth-standard, than he appeared.

'*Ke* is *ashiren*, a child, under fourteen. You'll have to stand as foster *telestre*, but that's a formality.' He added, 'The *telestre* is Salathiel, they keep the Westbank ferry. While *ke* is with you, you stand as *s'an telestre*.'

That clicked into place. Geren had said 'landholder', *s'an telestre*, the ruler of an estate. *In loco parentis*. Custom is custom, I thought.

'I need to find a bank,' I reminded Haltern.

He steepled his sharp-nailed fingers. 'You'll want the Guild house at Singing Gold. I'd also suggest you visit the market, you'll want riderbeasts. Maric is capable of tacking up and stabling them, by the way. And—'

'And the court,' I said.

He gave me a wary look. 'I could perhaps arrange a private audience for the beginning of next week.'

'I'd prefer it sooner.'

'Well, I suppose . . .' He shifted uneasily.

'I can't insist, of course. But I'd like to show willing.'

He hesitated, calculating. 'There's the open audience this afternoon, but that's the Fiveday common audience in the Long Hall.

It's not a special reception. There won't be any of the *takshiriye*, the important *t'ans* of the court, there; at least, not the influential ones.'

We looked at each other. He smiled.

'I'll call a *skurrai-jasin*. What was the last bell, midmorning? Then there's time for dinner at my *telestre*-house.'

'I'll get my papers.' I fetched the document case and rejoined him.

'You're wise,' he said as we went out, 'to see the *T'an Suthai-Telestre* without other influence. Tell me, *t'an*, are all Otherworlders as hasty as you?'

'It pays off sometimes.'

The carriage waited in brilliant sunlight. We jolted off over the paving-stones.

'*T'an*,' he said. 'No, what is your Otherworld custom – Ms Christie—'

'I think you'd better settle for Christie.' I'd got used to that on the *Hanathra*. And I could see that Haltern, being the kind of man who makes character judgements, had made one, and I was curious.

'Christie,' he said with that mixture of honesty and formality that is peculiar to Ortheans, 'be wary. When I heard of another Otherworld envoy, I thought – no, never mind, I was wrong. But there will be those among the *takshiriye* who are no friends to you or your world. They can be dangerous. I admit you seem able to handle the job—'

'And why not?' I was too sharp. Eliot's earlier remarks had touched me on a sore point.

'I meant no offence.' He spread his hands. 'How was I to know your court would not send some lordling or hanger-on, or woman who cared for nothing but her own ambition? We've had such from Quarth and Saberon and Cuthanc. Remember, we know nothing of the Earth court.'

Haltern took me at face value, whatever the department's view of my appointment might be. And that, I realized, might be similar to Maric: a young person to be shaped by events rather than be a shaper.

'We don't have a court,' I said, 'we have a parliament. At least, we do have a Queen – Elizabeth III – but she doesn't have the authority that your Crown does.'

'A Crown without authority?' Haltern was incredulous, and more than a little shocked.

I spent the rest of the carriage-ride to the city trying to explain the India-China power axis, the isolated Western enclaves, and the workings of British parliamentary democracy.

His *telestre*-house was not far from the Guild Ring. The *l'ri-an*, a taciturn old Orthean male, served a light meal of salads and herb-tea, in a bright room that faced out into a walled garden. A slender treefern trailed thick purple flowers. Petals littered the flagstones. Haltern and I sat by the open window.

'I use rooms in this place in summer,' he said, in the course of conversation. 'While the court's in residence in Tathcaer. In winter they move to Peir-Dadeni, lock, stock, barrel – and Crown Messengers. Inconvenient, but traditional. And no one is going to argue with the Andrethe.'

'Andrethe? I thought the Crown ruled.'

'In theory.' He sipped the bowl of herb-tea and set it back on the table. 'In practice, no *T'An Suthai-Telestre* would cross the Andrethes of Peir-Dadeni; that I say though it is my own province. It's the only province that swears equal alliance, rather than allegiance.'

'And the rest?'

If Haltern was talking, I was sure there was a good reason.

'From your point of view?' He nodded sharply. 'Peir-Dadeni and Ymir are pro-Earth. Rimon over the river . . . uncertain. Roehmonde's never supported any contact with your Otherworld, nor has Melkathi; but then, nothing good ever came out of Melkathi. Morvren Freeport would trade with the Golden Witchbreed themselves. As for the Kyre, they'll be as remote from you as they are from us.'

'And Tathcaer?'

'Oh, they call it the eighth province sometimes, as being purely the Crown's island. That's why you Otherworlders must stay here in the city.' He shrugged. 'But it's the heart of the Southland, without it the Hundred Thousand would fall apart.'

I didn't recognize the term. 'The Hundred Thousand?'

'The *Ai-Telestre*. Traditionally, the hundred thousand separate *telestres* of the Southland. The provinces are nothing, the cities come and go, but the *telestres* are forever. Goddess grant.' Unselfconscious, he signed himself with a circle over the breast. 'But you must know, Christie. You have an Otherworld *telestre* of your own.'

'No. I'm not a landowner.'

'*Own* land? Goddess forbid! I am not landholder, but still . . . !' He was scandalized. Then the outrage faded. He said carefully, 'But matters are different, doubtless, on Earth?'

'Yes.' I left it at that. He had the courage to admit that other cultures might be different from his own. At the moment, I didn't want to trouble him with just how different.

'Now the Crown has you here, there will not be much attention called to you.' He was subdued. He hesitated, then said, 'I imagine that's why I was sent to you, rather than one of the *takshiriye*. Choosing one would offend the others. If you did but know, it's something of an insult. Had you been, say, ambassador from the Rainbow Cities, there'd have been a delegation to meet you, perhaps with Turi Andrethe or Ruric Orhlandis with them.'

He sat back, fair mane ruffled. His tunic was rubbed bare in places and his boots were scuffed, he was overweight for an Orthean, and approaching the middle forties. It would be easy, I thought, to dismiss him as one more native court official. Easy and quite wrong.

'I'm not that important,' I said. It was true. If nothing useful came out of my time as envoy, the Dominion would wait a few years and send someone else. 'It's also very difficult to make me feel insulted.'

The membrane blurred his eyes briefly, and the corners of his mouth twitched. He chuckled. Outside, bells sounded in the heat.

'Noon,' he said. 'If you're still determined on this audience, we'll go up to the Citadel.'

Crown Way – that one named, paved road that runs from the docks clear up to the Citadel – was crowded. We drove down into the centre of the island where it was noisy, and the road was blocked with *skurrai-jasin* and heavier carts. But going up out of that we came among older buildings and quieter districts, passing under fronds of *lapuur* that were never still, even in that wind-sheltered place. From time to time Haltern indicated landmarks: the theocratic houses of learning, the Wellhouses . . . You needed landmarks in this trackless, signless city.

Shadows dappled the white flagstones as we drove into a square the size of a parade ground. Barracks and prison and the House of the Goddess formed three sides; the fourth was cliffwall.

The crag reared up fifty feet – not a great height, but sheer, grey rock webbed over with blue vines. A zig-zag walk was cut into the cliff face, the single entrance of which we now approached. Solid rock had been carved into a gateway, and a heavy iron grill hung ready to be lowered. I stared up the cliff, seeing a similar gate at the top.

'There's no way but on foot,' Haltern said, dismissing the *skurrai-jasin*. 'We'll go up if the audience is open. Hei, Kyar!'

One of the soldiers at the gateway came over. They were in green and gold uniforms, two pikemen, four with what looked like crossbows. These were the élite, the Crown Guard.

This soldier, with the *harur* blade of an officer, was a woman. She said, 'May I aid you, Haltern of Beth'ru-elen?'

'Is the Fiveday audience open?'

'Yes: pass on.' She stared at me. I suppose I returned the compliment; I wasn't entirely sure hers wasn't only a ceremonial position.

'My thanks. Christie?'

I followed Haltern, nervous now that it came to it. Any off-worlder has that responsibility, that he or she will be taken as the measure of their world. And a lot depended on how this meeting went.

It was a long hot walk up the path. We were in a constant stream of Ortheans, in the dress of every trade and province. Haltern paused once, and I with him, looking back across the arrowhead-shape of the island below. A fresh wind came from the sea, taking the edge off the heat.

We passed through the upper gateway into gardens. Paved walks led to the Citadel itself, looming behind feather-leaved *lapuur* trees. A huge and sprawling complex of buildings – or perhaps one building; with Ortheans you can't be sure. Carved, painted stone-work; rounded towers and secretive windowless walls.

Inside was chill. High ceilings echoed to passing footsteps, galleries hissed with quiet conversations. We came to a hall, a long abruptly-angled flight of steps, and then were suddenly in a long stone-paved room.

'Here,' Haltern said quietly, 'this way.'

Two fireplaces held braziers, coals glowing against the stone's chill. A line of Crown Guard stood down each side of the Long Hall. Sunlight came whitely in through slit windows, falling on tapestries, and on the bright robes of male and female Ortheans.

Haltern led me past conversing groups. Some stared at me: my formal skirt and jacket bore no resemblance to anything Orthean. But I'm not so different, I thought, looking round. Skins varied from satin-black through brown and tan, but there were many as pale as I. Likewise brown-blonde hair, green eyes; these were common; and I was pretty much of average height.

I felt as if I had walked into a room full of half-animals, crop-maned and six-fingered. It comes at some point in every visit to an alien world. Half animal and half human: it was the whiteless eyes, the blurring that might have been a trick of the light and wasn't, that gave the curious subtlety to the Orthean face.

'How long?' I stifled nervousness.

'A little while.' The inevitable Orthean answer.

Banners hung at the end of the hall, crimson and gold, blue and emerald; and over them all the green and gold firecrest of the Crown. The Ortheans, as they came closer to the far end of the hall, took advantage of the benches there to sit and talk. As each one's turn came, they went to stand before the Crown.

I sat in silence beside Haltern, mentally rehearsing Ymirian speech inflections. Then, seeing that he also seemed worried, I hazarded a guess why.

'Haltern, would you call yourself one of the pro-Earth party?'

'Why, yes, I suppose I would.' He looked at me sharply, and then nodded as if confirming an impression. 'You're right, Christie. I was concerned. There are a number of us who've backed this policy against all odds.'

'So have we.'

'Yes . . . yes, of course.'

I could see him calculating. He was given to evaluating people accurately, I guessed. And his support might influence others in favour of Earth.

'After this one,' he said. 'Just walk up and give your name.'

The present speaker was a broad-faced Orthean female in the sash of the metalworkers' Guild. She stood with her arms folded, speaking a language – Rimon, I think – that I didn't comprehend. I missed the sense of the Crown's answer, but the voice was husky, tenor, and – when I could see – younger-sounding than its owner.

The *T'An Suthai-Telestre* was a small woman of about fifty, lean and tough-looking. Her skin was sand-coloured. Her blue eyes and fair lashes gave her the wind-blasted squinting look that professional soldiers acquire. Her braided mane was a shade darker than her skin, and was retreating slightly at brow and temples.

She wore boots, britches, and loose tunic, all in green and thickly encrusted with gems and gold embroidery. The tunic had a quilted look, slashed to show a shirt woven of some iridescent cloth. The same fabric, *chirith-goyen*, lined a cloak that fastened at the throat. This I assumed to be against the Citadel's chill, but it gave her a half-suffocated appearance. As she talked she sat back with her legs extended, the *harur-nilgiri* blade lying across her lap. She fingered the hilt compulsively. Her voice was even and controlled, and the woman metalworker nodded now and again as if perfectly satisfied.

A final word and that audience was over.

It was barbaric, anachronistic and alien; and it intimidated me. I took the few steps that put me in front of her.

'Your excellence.' I managed the bow that custom demands. 'My name is Lynne de Lisle Christie. May I present the respectful greetings and felicitations of the government of the British Isles, and of the united governing bodies of the Dominion of Earth.'

The Orthean woman sat up a little. Her eyes were suddenly bright.

'We are most pleased to receive the envoy.' She gestured, without looking behind her. One of the Guard placed a stool in front of her. 'Come, be seated.'

I obeyed. It was a favour, I could tell by the whispers behind me. Most of the nervousness was wearing off.

She enquired as to my health, the quarters I had in the city, any aid I might need and any difficulties I might be having. I answered as well as I could, remembering to mention Haltern n'ri n'suth Beth'ru-elen; thanking her also for anything else I could think of.

And, both of us having got the formal rubbish over and done with: 'I had not thought to see you here so soon,' she said, in the less formal mode.

'I wanted to present myself to your excellence as soon as possible, so as not to appear impolite.'

'And so you come to the open audience. I like that.' She smiled. 'You understand it was my decision that your people should come here. And my decision that they should have a representative of their own Crown here.'

I agreed, wondering if there might be an opening for a fully established consulate soon.

'I hope,' the *T'An Suthai-Telestre* continued, 'that you will visit more of the Southland. I'm sure you'll receive many invitations. Don't let your duties here keep you from travelling.'

It took me a second to realize what she's said. Then, very carefully, I said, 'With your excellence's permission, I'll accept. Does this invitation extend to my people who are already here?'

'Unfortunately, no. Not yet.' She hooded her eyes. 'Lynne Christie, you will undoubtedly receive invitations from people it would be safer not to visit. My Hundred Thousand are not all willing to befriend Otherworlders. I think it is necessary that they witness what they would condemn. Travel where you will. I'll write you free passes for the *telestres*.'

'So that Earth may witness what she would befriend?'

She chuckled richly. 'Oh, indeed, indeed. So it must always be. Go out and see my people, Christie.'

'The *T'An Suthai-Telestre* is most kind.'

She was apparently satisfied. Then she frowned. 'I permitted a weapon to be brought here. Do you have it?'

I took the stunner from the clip under my jacket.

'Show me.' She held out her hand. A sonic stunner is not impressive, only a grey oval casing with a flat stud on one edge.

She handed it back distastefully. 'It kills?'

'No, your excellence, merely renders unconscious.'

She shook her head. 'Show it as little as possible, there are places it would be taken for rank Witchcraft. Better: find another weapon.'

'Your excellence commands.'

She sat back again, interlocking her claw-nailed fingers, gazing at me.

'You could almost be a woman of Ymir or Rimon,' she said at last. 'It will be hard to keep in mind that you are not, and that you bring such weapons. I am not sure if I should not have preferred you to be a recognizable stranger, at least.'

'Our people aren't so different.' I've sometimes wondered if the department's policy of preferring empaths for diplomatic service is right; it does mean that we identify with aliens, sometimes over-much so.

'Are they not? We shall discover the truth of that, perhaps. But I think we will not speak of it now.' In that crowded hall she asked no questions about Earth. 'I thank you and your world for your greetings. We shall speak again, Christie, you have much of interest to tell me; the audiences must continue, however. I wish you good speed, and the Mother's blessing.'

I backed off, my place was taken by somebody else; and then I felt Haltern take my arm.

'This way. Suthafiori favours you,' he observed as we passed down the hall. 'It won't affect her policy, but I envy you her good will.'

'Suthafiori?'

'The Crown: Dalzielle Kerys-Andrethe. They call her Suthafiori, the Flower of the South; she was beautiful—'

'Haltern. *T'an*.'

I stopped in the doorway to see who'd interrupted. It was a woman. Haltern eyed her with wariness and distaste.

'I introduce myself. I am Sulis n'ri n'suth SuBannasen, *T'An* Melkathi.'

Her accent was one I didn't recognize. She wore a sari-like blue garment, and over that a leather cloak fastened with a silver chain. Her skin was translucently pale, her features fine and hard, and her sleek cropped mane was white. She looked to be at least seventy.

'Lynne de Lisle Christie.'

'The envoy. I hope you like our land, *t'an*. It must be very different from your own.'

'I haven't been here long enough to draw conclusions, *T'An Sulis*.'

When she moved, I saw that she supported herself with a silver-topped cane.

'A pity you may not leave Tathcaer. My own province of Melkathi is worth visiting.'

'Perhaps I will, then, *T'An*.'

Her eyes flicked up. Age had whitened the nictitating membrane and it was semi-retracted, giving her a hooded, hawkish aspect.

'Will you so? Then I will gladly receive you in Ales-Kadareth.'

'The envoy has much to do,' Haltern said urbanely.

'So, yes, of course.' As she looked at him, her smile vanished. 'And she is so young, and so like us. It is unfounded rumour, then, Haltern, that makes these Outworlders out to be some Witchbreed spawn grown cunning with disguise?'

'Your pardon, *T'An* Sulis.' Haltern bowed fractionally. 'Your knowledge of the Golden Witchbreed is doubtless far superior to mine.'

She gave him an unfathomable stare, and turned back to me. 'Perhaps you may visit me yet. *T'an*, I wish you well.'

Once out of the Citadel, the white-hot glare of the sun was a shock. I felt as if I'd spent days underground. An instinctive deep breath brought the unfamiliar faint mineral taste of the wind. Haltern was frowning.

'What's the matter?'

'Nothing. Only that I did not know Melkathi's ruler was at court, nor do I know why she should be at the Fiveday audience.' He sucked his teeth thoughtfully. 'I'd hazard it was chance, but it served her well. Christie, that SuBannasen has no love for Earth.'

'No,' I said. 'Haltern, what about the Golden Witchbreed?'

The scent of *sidemaat* fire-roses and flowering *lapuur* trees followed us down the cliff-walk.

'They were a cruel people,' Haltern said at last, 'and long gone now, though some half-blooded remnants of the race remain far to the south of here, over the Inner Sea, in the city Kel Harantish. They claim the pure blood there, but I doubt it. They need no excuse for their familiarity with treachery except practice. As for Sulis – and I should not slander her or her *telestre* – she is like all of us Southlanders. Prone to see Witchbreed in anything new and anything new as Witchbreed trickery.'

The Golden Empire fell some two thousand Orthean years ago, after a five-thousand-year reign; and the Golden Witchbreed have since attracted all evil legend and conjectured abominations into their history. How much was true, the hypno-tapes couldn't say.

'You'll be suspect, for some,' Haltern added as we came down into the square. 'But you have the advantage that you bear none of their features.'

'Which are?'

'A pale skin that has a shade of gold in it,' he said, 'white-maned and with yellow eyes. They were tall and thin-boned; for the rest, I know not.'

We waited in the shadow of the cliff for a *skurrai-jasin*.

'I was given to understand that the Golden Witchbreed no longer existed.'

'Nor do they, except perhaps for Kel Harantish.' He shrugged. 'That's where you'll have your name coupled, when any doubt you.'

'Do you doubt me?'

'No,' he said. I believed him.

The bells rang for mid-afternoon as our *jasin* carriage came. I remembered I was due at Eliot's house that evening. The *T'An Suthai-Telestre* had put me in one hell of an awkward position.

I wondered how I was going to break it to the xeno-team that I had travel permits and they didn't.

CHAPTER 4

A Dinner at Eastharbour-Salmeth

The *skurrai-jasin* jolted through narrow passages. Hooves clopped a muffled rhythm. There was the scent of *kazsis*-nightflower and dung, a curious sweet-acid mix. The driver, a grey-maned old Orthean female, leaned and spat chewed *ataile* leaves onto the rutted earth. I saw her eyes for a moment as she turned. The membranes were drawn back, the pupils swelled to velvet-black holes.

She had brought a message from Eliot: the dinner was now being held at one of the team's other residences. I missed telephones and a postal service.

The carriage clattered under an archway and into the courtyard of Eastharbour-Salmeth, an hour after the rapid sunset. I climbed down and paid the driver, and stood for a moment by the fountain.

The alien city was hot and quiet, the natives gone home behind shuttered windows and barred gates. Night winds blew. The immense stars of the Core blazed overhead, casting a pale light on the fountain. Roofs stood black against the brilliant sky, fringed with stars so numerous that they merged into clouds of light.

I heard a rising hum of conversation as the door opened.

'Good,' Eliot said, 'you're early. Come in and meet everybody. This is our host, by the way, Sam Huxton.'

'Ms Christie, come in. Please, let me take your coat.' Huxton was about forty, tall and burly and dark-haired. His hospitality was overwhelming. 'This is Margery, my wife – Marge, here's company for you. This is John Barratt.'

Barratt was a sharp young man, who shook hands lightly and then showed a marked disinclination to let go.

'And Adair, and I think that's Carrie over there and—'

'We've met.' Lalkaka grinned at me.

'And Maurie . . . Well, that's all of our team. It won't take us long to get to know each other.'

'Or to get thoroughly tired of each other.' Barratt gave me a smile that made me doubt his sobriety. 'I don't mean to be offensive. Social activities here are – limited. We all know each other very well indeed.'

It was a long room, lit by oil-lamps, shuttered against the brilliance of the night. By now there were Ortheans arriving. Groups split up and reformed, talking, and drinking a pale Ymirian wine. Standard formal reception, I thought.

'Adair,' said a neat and fussy-looking man beside me. He was in his sixties, old for field-work. 'I'm medic here. There are a few shots I've developed that you ought to have, Ms Christie. Can you call on me tomorrow? I'm down at Eastharbour-Kumiel. You're not prone to hayfever, by the way?'

'Not so far.'

'That's good.' He nodded at one of the younger team members, whose name I couldn't remember. She appeared to have a streaming cold. 'This planet is hell for anyone prone to histamine reaction.'

'We'll be out of date at the department,' I said, thinking aloud, 'with the time-lapse. I'll need to catch up.'

'I've done you a faxsheet,' Adair said. 'The usual run of allergies. As they say, don't drink the water. Mind you, the natives are tough, they seem to survive any infection. Don't bank on doing the same. Stay out of sick-rooms. Oh yes, there's a list of foods you should avoid – they don't eat eggs but I'm not sure if that's a taboo or not. You'll have to see the expert, Barratt. Not now.'

The Ortheans stood together, their dark eyes flicking nervously round the room. When they moved, bright fabrics flashed, jewels shone, and *harur* blades clashed on belts and chains. They seemed unused to the Huxtons' idea of a reception, and stood holding drinks and looking lost.

'You probably didn't catch my name,' a middle-aged woman said. I took a second look: she was from Earth, though what she was wearing was mostly Orthean. 'I'm Carrie Thomas, xeno-sociology. Come over here and have a drink. I promise not to say a word – you must be sick of us by now.'

I accepted a glass of the pale wine, feeling like the proverbial bone in a dog-kennel. 'Mrs Thomas—'

'It'd better be Carrie, love, we're all going to get to know each other very well. Too well, if they don't let us out of here.' Frustration appeared on her face. 'Here I am, with the first socially mobile pretech world on record – no caste-system, nothing – and can I get a look at a working *telestre*? Can I, hell!'

She broke off and laughed. 'Oh lord, and I promised I wouldn't bend your ear! There I go. It's the lure of a new face, none of us

39

can resist it. I can see John and Maurie hovering like vultures, waiting to get at you after I've finished.'

I chuckled. 'I'll keep them waiting for a bit, then. Mrs Thomas, Carrie, I mean – you're the first one I've met who seems to have some sympathy for the Ortheans themselves.'

'Ah, you've been staying with the Eliots. And Lalkaka and the Huxtons are the same. Don't blame them. They were keen, a while ago. It's having no opportunity to work. Now me and Adair and Maurie—' here she pointed to the woman with the streaming eyes '—we're not so badly off.'

'Speak for yourself,' Adair said, reappearing. 'For a culture with practically no privacy taboos, they're damned hard to examine physically.'

'Addie would like some nice dead specimens to play with,' Thomas said caustically. 'Fortunately, or unfortunately, the Ortheans cremate their dead. It's the live ones that bother me. I'll give you an example: why is it that the young are called "it" until they're adult? This *ke* pronoun . . . It may be that there's a rite of passage, that they have to earn the social right to gender, but it doesn't ring true. All societies do some division of labour according to sex – all but this one.'

'They tend toward triple and quadruple births,' Adair said, vaguely pursuing his own line of thought. 'I did get a look at one adult male specimen. You've noticed the second pair of nipples? Well, this one – and it may just have been a throwback, I don't know – it had what I suspect is a vestigial marsupial pouch.'

'A *what*?' I said.

'A thick fold of skin here—' he drew his thumb across his belly '—about eight centimetres wide and four deep. I can only assume that at some point the male Ortheans cared for the young.'

'Yes but listen, Addie—'

While Carrie Thomas was arguing with him, I slipped off to refill my glass. A small child in a night-robe appeared at the far door and wailed on a low key. Margery Huxton rushed over to pick her up. They were close by me so I couldn't very well ignore them.

'What's your name?' I asked the child. She was about four, dark-haired, strikingly like her mother. She stared at me in silence.

'Oh, she won't say anything.' The woman set her down and said confidentially, 'It worries me sometimes, but it would be worse if we couldn't bring her with us. But sometimes I think she doesn't remember much English at all.'

'What's your name, *ashiren-te*?' This time I asked in Ymirian.

'Elspeth Huxton, of the British Isles.' Her accent was unfamiliar.

I realized she'd learned her Ymirian by hearing it, not from tapes. 'Goddess give you good day.'

'And to your mother's daughter.' It was the traditional return.

'One of the ladies up on The Hill has Elspeth tutored with her own children. Well, you can't isolate a child, she needs others to play with.' Margery Huxton sighed. I had her placed now, she was a xeno-ecologist and her husband was a marine biologist. She said, 'But I do worry about what she might pick up.'

I felt sorry for her, trying to hold the tide of Orthe back from her door. Then I wondered if it wasn't Elspeth I should be sorry for – she'd have to adapt back to Earth.

The girl wriggled out of her mother's embrace and ran to the door. A late guest bent down and took her hand, exchanging a few words with the child.

This guest was striking: darker than the usual run of Ymirians, with skin the colour of flaked coal, a cropped black mane and a narrow, merry face. I judged her to be in her early thirties. She wore a padded, sleeveless leather jerkin over shirt and britches, marking her as a soldier. As she let go of the child's hand I saw that one shirt-sleeve was empty, neatly folded up and pinned. It was the right arm and her *harur-nilgiri* was slung for left-hand use.

She caught me staring and gave a broad white-toothed grin. The child swung on her arm, and she lifted her up and gave her back to Margery.

'Ruric,' she said to me, inclining her head casually. 'You're the envoy, Huxton tells me.'

'That's right, the name's Christie.' I checked an impulse to shake hands, and then couldn't think what to say. At last I said, 'You like children?'

'The *ashiren*? Other people's, and part time.' Another flash of white teeth. 'Elspeth comes to my household to learn with the others there. It's something to meet a child from another world, after all.'

At that point we were called in to dinner – to the great relief of the Ortheans present – and I found myself between Lalkaka on the one side and Ruric on the other.

The Ortheans' talk was soft and swift. The cutlery laid for dinner seemed to confuse them. They fingered the eating-knives that hung at their belts and eventually tried (with varying degrees of success) to handle forks. Only the dark woman used her own knife. This, with its split point, she used both as knife and fork, eating nimbly with her single hand.

'You're from Tathcaer?' I asked. Her accent was faint, not immediately identifiable.

'I'm from more or less anywhere. Melkathi, the Skulls garrison, Peir-Dadeni . . . I've just come back from Medued-in-Rimon.' She put down her knife to raise her glass. 'Have you been here long?'

'A few days.' I remembered that, as well as the *T'An* households, The Hill was also the location of the barracks. The crippled woman would be a soldier, then, perhaps a retired soldier.

'What do you think? Or isn't that a fair question?'

'It isn't, but yes, I like the city.'

'You're one of the few, then.' She looked round the table, and turned back to me. It was only then, seeing her full-face, that I noticed her eyes. The membrane retracted, leaving them clear, and the whiteless irises were yellow. As yellow as buttercups, as yellow as ospreys' eyes. Sunny and friendly eyes; I felt drawn to her.

'You must come to my household—'

'You must visit Easthill Malk'ys—'

We broke off, having spoken simultaneously, and laughed.

'Ms Christie.'

I made the mental effort and switched from Ymirian back to English. 'Yes, Mr Huxton?'

'Call me Sam. Maurie was just asking about travel permits.'

I nodded. 'I saw the *T'An Suthai-Telestre* this afternoon.'

'And is she willing to raise the ban?'

'She's sending me out of the city,' I was careful in my phrasing. 'I rather think that when she gets reports back, she'll be willing to let all of us travel more freely. It shouldn't take too long now, Mr Huxton.'

'Sod that!' Barratt was explosive. 'More delays, and meanwhile you go buggering about all over the country—'

Carrie Thomas hushed him. I saw the dark woman, Ruric, glance at me with amusement. She must understand some English, I thought.

'It's more of a concession than we ever managed to get,' Adair said. 'I feel it's encouraging.'

Audrey Eliot agreed, sharp and nervous. She said, 'But what about Earth? We only have the three-monthly dispatches. What's the news?'

So I had no further chance of speaking to the Ortheans, I had instead to drag out every item of home news that I could remember. All of them, even Barratt in his half-stupor, sat there like hungry children taking it all in. It made me wonder, empath or not, what my opinion on Carrick V would be in a year or so.

And the Orthean guests, with that singular urbanity that etiquette demands from them, talked quietly of ships due and harvest prospects and affairs back at their *telestres*.

CHAPTER 5

Saryl-Kabriz

In the false dawn the stars fade and the east is dim. Ortheans call it the first twilight. Then comes the pale blaze of sunrise, too white, too brilliant for Earth, searing through the river-mists, opening the day.

The sky was clear, cloudless, the daystars no more than burrs round the horizon.

'It'll rain later, *t'an*,' Maric said, coming in with hot herb-tea in a blue glazed bowl.

'Mmmrghph?'

'Before the noon bell. The wind's south-westerly.'

I muttered something incoherent, and when he'd gone, dragged myself up to a sitting position in bed. The Orthean day was too long. When I woke, I never felt as if I'd had enough sleep.

I rose and dressed slowly, aware that since I should have to keep what clothes I did have for formal occasions, the sooner I bought Orthean clothes the better it would be.

It rained after sunrise.

The report I'd begun the day before looked fatuous in the light of morning. I wiped it off the micro-recorder, deciding to leave reporting until I had a better idea of what I was talking about.

There were numerous messages brought in by the *l'ri-an* of various households, mostly in the form of a couple of lines of script inviting me to dinners and functions, and mostly from households interested in trade. It was too early to have a policy on that – Carrick V not being classified as restricted or unrestricted access, as yet – but I accepted them, to be on the safe side.

About mid-morning, when the rain was clearing, Haltern appeared.

'There you are.' He handed his cloak to Maric, after removing a paper from a lining-pocket. 'Yesterday's weekly broadsheet. The part that will interest you is towards the end.'

The paper was grainy, probably reed-based. The printing was

sophisticated for this level of culture, something of the order of Caxton or Gutenburg. It was one sheet, dated Merrum Sevenweek Fiveday, and it was mostly incomprehensible to me, gossip about people and places I didn't know. But squeezed in at the end was a notice of the *Hanathra*'s return.

'"We announce the arrival of still another Offworlder,"' Haltern read aloud over my shoulder. '"And also draw our readers' attention to the ship's route, which is: passing the Inner Sea close to the Desert Coast, and close also to the city Kel Harantish."'

'Meaning?'

'Meaning Witchbreed. The slur is nothing, but it shows prevailing opinion.'

There wasn't anything I could do about it. I said, 'This broadsheet, this is just in the city, is it?'

'Yes. The church often passes these things for use inside Tathcaer's walls.' His eyes veiled. 'They like to see their effect, before they loose them in the Hundred Thousand.'

'The same applying, of course, to dubious Offworld visitors.'

'I – ah – couldn't say.'

I rubbed the rough paper between thumb and forefinger. It told me things purely by existing. For example, the Ortheans were highly literate. That didn't fit with a culture at this level either.

'You've had invitations, I see.' Haltern hesitated. 'Has there been one from SuBannasen?'

I shuffled through them; there was nothing from the *T'An* Melkathi. 'Not so far.'

'Well . . . Remember what I said. Nothing good ever came out of Melkathi.'

'And if she doesn't remember it,' a voice said, 'I will.'

It was the dark woman from the Huxtons' reception. She'd obviously come in as the doors were left open.

'*T'An*.' Haltern made a low bow. 'I didn't mean—'

'Don't be a fool, Hal.' She grinned and slapped him on the shoulder, left-handed. His pale eyes were veiled with embarrassment. 'I didn't realize Dalzielle had sent him to you, Christie.'

I must have looked as puzzled as I felt. Ruric gave a great shout of laughter. 'Sorry, Christie, I should have introduced myself last night.'

'The *T'An* Ruric Orhlandis of Melkathi,' Haltern said uncomfortably. '*T'An* Commander of the Southland's army.'

'Also called Onehand and Yelloweyes, and a number of things I won't repeat outside the barracks for fear of Hal's modesty.' She turned to me. 'Now you've found out my secret, does that mean I'm not welcome?'

44

'Good grief, no.' I saw she was joking. Army Commander, I thought; and she calls the Crown Dalzielle. Here's another *t'an* come to get a look at the Outworlder.

'I must go,' Haltern said, 'I've business elsewhere. Christie, good day to you. And to you, *T'An.*'

'Come to noon-meal tomorrow?' she called after him, and he nodded.

'He's a good man,' she said. 'Don't trust him.'

Ortheans are capable of that kind of contradictory advice. She approved of Haltern, that much was obvious.

'What can I do for you?' I asked.

'Do?' She walked back and forth across the room, studying it, and gazing out of the window at the courtyard. 'Nothing, that I know of. I came to see if I could be of use to you.'

'Yes?'

She hitched herself up to sit on the arm of the great carved chair, and grinned at me. 'Yes, and to satisfy curiosity, I own to that.'

She was honest. I grinned back. 'I'll try.'

'Coming to the point, you'll be travelling, by what you said last night. And since there's no *skurrai-jasin* outside Tathcaer you'll need riderbeasts, and so – are you a rider?' she interrupted herself.

'I've done some riding.' That was horses. I didn't know what I might be called on to ride here.

'Good. If you haven't yet seen to it, I wondered if I could be of any help to you?'

'Yes, I—'

'Only I don't know your customs. If I offend, say so.'

'You don't, and I could use some help.' Probably I could have arranged it through Haltern, but I wasn't about to refuse the woman's offer.

'Good.' She stood, energetic. 'If you're not busy now, there's a beastmarket down at Beriah's Bridge.'

Outside, the paving stones were slick with moisture. There were no *jasin* carriages in sight. We began walking down the hill towards the east river.

The rain had passed. The tops of buildings were swathed in mist, rolling in from the harbour. When it swirled aside, pale sunlight washed over the white walls of the city. Shadows were blurred, and blue. The muggy air and shifting light seemed to muffle the calls of the street-traders and the rumble of cartwheels. And there was, as there always is, the smell of the sea.

'You must have wanderer's blood,' Ruric said, 'to come so far from your land.'

'Itchy feet, I guess.'

'Yes, I know another like that. My—' here she used a term I didn't catch '—he's a wanderer before all else. I'll travel when necessary. But you, to come so far . . .'

'I suppose it's – a hunger to breathe a different air?' I wasn't certain myself.

'If I had to leave—' she stopped mid-sentence, and her shoulders went back. 'I love Tathcaer. Out of all the Southland, I love the White City.'

Her cropped mane fell in a raven's-wing over her forehead. When she was serious, as now, I could see the thin lines worn into her snake-smooth skin.

'Is it strange to you?' she demanded. 'You, offworlder, do you have cities on your world that you love?'

'Yes, of course.'

'Ah, we are not too different, then.' She was alert, mercurial, and I had the feeling that deeper thoughts were going on under her stream of speculation.

'Will you guest with me?' she asked. 'When you are done with this travelling.'

'Yes,' I nodded. 'I'd like to.'

We went down the hill. The *telestre*-houses, fronting passages with blank walls and barred gates, made me feel again the essential secrecy of the alien city. Having an entry, all these things were open to me, but a stranger could be left to wander the narrow ways, alone and lost.

We passed Guild Ring, that collection of trade *telestres* that has spread and grown until at the very least forty buildings stand connected by bridges, walkways, and steps between their upper floors. All trades are there: goldsmiths, booksellers, cartwrights, saddlers, ship's chandlers, *chirith-goyen* merchants (where we detoured to place orders for clothes), and a multitude of others quite incomprehensible to an alien. The elected Guild Council live there, watching the ebb and flow of trade as keenly as the shipmasters watch the tides.

From Easthill Malk'ys to Beriah's Bridge is perhaps two *seri*, something over two-and-a-third miles. We reached the embankment a little before noon.

The Beastmarket is close by the bridge, an ancient high-walled enclosure. Grim stone echoed to the bellowing and trumpeting of driven beasts, and as we entered I heard the bars of the pens rattle in their sockets.

'They are the *marhaz*,' Ruric said, 'and there are *skurrai* down

46

there. If you take my advice, there's a man who supplies the army's mounts. He's less likely to cheat you if he sees me.'

'Suits me.' The beast-smell was pungent here.

She smiled widely. 'I ought to learn your customs. How do you bargain your Otherworld?'

'In my part of it, we mostly don't.'

Her eyes clouded in surprise, the subtle flick of membrane that passes in Orthean for much body-language.

'Grief of the Goddess, you're Freeporters! Then perhaps I should do it, or you'll pay more.'

'You're the expert, *T'An*.'

'Oh, *T'An*, is it?' Amusement flickered. 'At any rate, I know the *marhaz* traders.'

The *marhaz* were tall and bulky, but moved lightly in their pens in that roofless hall. White sunlight gleamed on their pelts: plush black, cropped white, shaggy bronze. Their lizard eyes were dark and brilliant. The pelt appears similar to hair or fur, but like that of most large Orthean landbeasts is actually composed of thread-thin fibres, very tough and flexible, which resemble feathers in structure. Great tufts feathered their cloven hooves, dung-spattered in the close confinement. Broad bony quarters and deep chests – they were first cousins to the *skurrai*, I thought. Long thick necks tapered to broad-jawed heads, deep-socketed eyes, and feathered ears. And on the forehead, just below the ears, the first pair of horns jutted out. Straight, as long as my forearm, with a spiral grain. Under them was a second pair, no longer than a finger, but equally straight – and sharp. The *marhaz* looked dangerous, heavy beasts.

Ruric chatted to a trader, and I leaned on the pen bars. Close by, a black *marhaz* mare with jet horns rolled its eyes. A grey stood still, coat twitching now and then as it shivered. And there was a striped white and bronze beast, its horns cropped and capped with metal.

'Christie, come down this way.'

I joined Ruric. 'Found anything?'

'Says he has a *marhaz* gelding, *ke*'s quiet.' She eyed me. 'I thought you'd prefer that?'

'You thought right.'

'There,' the trader said. An *ashiren* led a grey crop-horned beast out of one pen. Ruric scratched its pelt, chucking under her breath, and studied its eyes.

'*Ke*'s from Medued,' the man said. 'Two years old.'

The dark woman stepped closer, gripped the pelt in her single hand and pulled herself lightly up, stomach-down over its back and then swinging her leg astride and coming upright. It rolled slit eyes, shifted and stepped back, then stood at the pressure of her knee and heel.

'Medued,' she said. 'Kerveis always was a good trainer.'

She didn't dismount the normal way but lifted one booted foot over the *marhaz* gelding's neck and slid to the ground.

'Well?' She looked questioningly at me.

'If it'll put up with that, I expect it'll put up with me.'

She laughed. 'That's wise. Well, don't tell him yes or no now. You'll need packbeasts, let him show some of the *skurrai* before you talk money.'

The *skurrai* were the breed I'd seen pulling *jasin* in the city. All had their horns cropped and capped.

'*Marhaz* will fight with you, if trained,' Ruric observed. 'A *skurrai* – *ke* hasn't the sense for it.'

By mid-afternoon when we left, I had closed orders for the grey *marhaz*, a black *marhaz* mare as a re-mount, and two *skurrai* mares as baggage carriers. I made a mental note to tell Maric.

'There's tack,' Ruric said, 'but your *l'ri-an* can probably cope with that.'

'I hope so.' At times like these I wonder if one jeep or land rover would violate the no-technology rule that much. 'You're not working on commission, are you?'

When we had that satisfactorily translated, the Orthean woman hooted with laughter.

'Come up for noon-meal tomorrow,' she said as we parted, 'up at the barracks, at Hill-Damarie.'

'Get dressed,' Adair said, 'you're all right. If those shots give you a reaction, come back and see me again.'

I tucked my shirt into my britches. In the Ymirian fashion, everything laced together rather than buttoned; even the soft leather half-boots laced at the ankle. But I was beginning to feel comfortable in Orthean dress.

Eastharbour-Kumiel overlooked the boatbuilders' yards. From this window I looked across warehouse roofs through the clear afternoon to the ribbed hulls of unfinished ships.

'If you're going up-country you'd better take a medical kit.' Adair sighed. 'Young woman, I hope you're prepared to be uncomfortable. Because you will be.'

'I realize that.' I heard the jealousy in his voice.

He turned away, clearing up instruments.

'To be honest,' I said, 'I've wondered why you didn't apply to

48

the department to open negotiations with one of the other nations on this planet.'

'We considered it. It seems this is the biggest political unity on the planet—' he turned, '—and naturally it's the one your people want contact with. So I suppose we don't try the others until things break down irrevocably here.'

Barratt rapped perfunctorily on the door as he came in.

'Something may break down,' he said darkly. 'I don't give the Dominion itself more than twenty years. At the outside.'

He grinned at me, picking me to pieces with his eyes.

'War?'

'Nothing so simple. We've come too far, too fast. And we haven't adapted.'

Adair watched him, worried. Absently, he said, 'It's not that I can't see your point—'

Barratt swung round on me. 'You know yourself how over-loaded the ET department is. That goes for all the member-nations. People are being sent out half-trained, too young, too inexperienced—'

I ignored the implicit slur. Adair took his arm, but Barratt shook him off.

'And for why? Maybe a hundred million stars in this galaxy. Maybe a hundred thousand planets capable of supporting life we'd recognize as life. And – when we do at last, at long last, get the light-drive – how many do we find inhabited?'

No one spoke. We knew the answer. I wondered how long Barratt had been drinking. He was flushed a dull red, almost purple colour.

'All of them,' he said in threnody, '*all* of them. So we go out exploring, trading, forming links and alliances—'

'John, for God's sake shut up,' Adair said.

'—but there's too many worlds and too few of us. It's a strain on resources now. In twenty years it'll fall apart. I'm telling you, it'll be sheer bloody chaos.'

As he went past me I caught the stink of alcohol and sweat.

'Can't you do anything for him?' I asked when he'd gone.

Adair shook his head. 'We need to go home. He needs to. That's all. He's been away too long, with too much time to think.'

I went back to Easthill Malk'ys.

It was almost dark at noon the next day, and the bell chimes came muffled through the pelting rain. I had the hood of a thick cloak pulled up, and still the sea wind drove damp cold into my bones. Below the knee, rain dampened the legs of my britches. The great cold body of the *marhaz* gelding shifted uneasily, hooves thudding on the paved way. Maric trailed behind on the *skurrai* mare.

In common with other buildings, the barracks showed blank walls and barred gates to the outside world. Maric spoke to the guards and the gates were opened. Inside it was like a small village, everything – stables, smithy, kitchens, dormitories – opening into the paved ground in the centre.

Hill-Damarie was at the far end, a fortress within a fortress, stone walls streaming with moisture and vanishing up into lowering grey clouds. Maric leaned up from the *skurrai*'s back and heaved on a bell-rope. Ruric herself unbarred the gate.

'Come,' she said, not with a bow but with that rare Orthean handclasp. 'We have guests, as you will see. It's good that you come so: none outside these walls will have recognized you.'

Maric led the riderbeasts off to be stabled, and I followed Ruric through the high archway into Hill-Damarie.

An old *l'ri-an* took my cloak, and Ruric waited while I dried the rain from me with a cloth. The rooms were high-roofed here, stone groins left undecorated. Thick embroidered *chirith-goyen* hangings cloaked the walls. The floor was paved with a veined stone and covered with pelts. Despite it being midday, the elaborate brass oil-lamps were lit against the rain-twilight.

The Orthean woman opened a door into a small chamber. A fire burned in the hearth, and a table was laid before it. Three or four people who stood by the flames turned as we came in. I was met by Haltern's bow, and a joyful handclasp from a richly dressed young Orthean male. It was a moment before I recognized him.

'Christie, it's good to see you.'

I'd last seen him barefoot, shirtless, shouting curses at the harbour pilot. Now he wore blue *chirith-goyen* cloth, soft boots, and *harur* blades with sheaths embroidered in gold thread.

'Good to see you too, Geren.' He was the same as ever: yellow-maned and open-faced.

'You know Haltern, of course,' Ruric continued. 'This is Eilen Brodin n'ri n'suth Charain, of Peir-Dadeni.'

Brodin was a hawk-faced and sardonic Orthean male in his early forties, with the dark skin of south Peir-Dadeni. His brown mane was braided down to mid-spine, he wore the slit-backed robe common in that western province, and the nails of his right hand were uncut.

'*T'an* Christie.' He gave a very offhand bow.

Ruric excused herself and left. When Geren began talking to Brodin, Haltern came over to me.

'I've heard SuBannasen is leaving the city,' he said thoughtfully. 'So?'

'Carrying news of your intention to travel . . . Well, there was no way to prevent that news spreading, even if you wanted to.'

Ruric re-entered with two more people. One was a cloaked woman. When she put her hood back she was instantly recognizable.

'*T'An Suthai-Telestre*.' Haltern bowed, and Brodin and Geren followed suit.

'Dalzielle will serve as my name, if there are foreign ears,' the Crown said.

An old man stood with her, barefoot, clad in a length of brown cloth that wrapped round his waist and continued up over his shoulder as a cloak. The outline of muscles and tendons showed plain under his snake-textured skin.

There was no taking this one for human: the paired nipples showed bronze against his brown skin, and his shaved mane came down in a black vee-shape between his shoulder-blades. His mud-splashed feet were high-arched, six-toed, claw-nailed.

'Lynne de Lisle Christie.' His voice was resonant. One sharp-nailed hand touched my arm. He gave me a stare like cold water.

'This is the Earthspeaker Tirzael,' Ruric said soberly.

There are two titles given by the church: Wellkeepers, who are the custodians of the theocratic houses, and Earthspeakers – who are wanderers, advisors, students, mystics, a multitude of things of which we as yet have no more than a superficial understanding.

'We are safe, I think,' Suthafiori said, and took a seat at the table close by the fire. She undid her cloak and laid it over the back of the carved chair. 'Christie, sit with me. Ruric, do we all starve?'

'No, *T'An*.' She and the same old man who had taken my cloak served the meal. Then I knew she must have sent the rest of the *l'ri-an* away.

There was an almost tangible air of cabal. Crown, Army Commander, Crown Messenger, representatives of Peir-Dadeni and the church, and one of the most wealthy shipmasters . . . This, I thought, is the nucleus of the original pro-Earth party.

'Does it seem overly dramatic to you?' Suthafiori smiled at me. 'To me, also. But it doesn't always pay for the *T'An Suthai-Telestre* to be seen in certain matters.'

'Am I to speak of this, then?' Brodin leaned forward. He had the expression of a man smelling something distasteful.

'Not in so many words, but if my cousin in Shiriya-Shenin were to hear this hinted at, then well and good.' She added quietly to me, 'Brodin holds the same position for Kanta Andrethe at her court as Haltern does in mine, which is to say, eyes and ears where they are most needed.'

The fire sputtered in the grate, and the smell of rain came in through a partly open window. This was a meal in the Orthean style, where great dishes were set on the table and it was up to the individual to serve themselves, using their own eating-knives. It's not as easy as you might think, eating with only a knife, but I'd thought it wise to practise, and didn't disgrace myself. Conversation was desultory while we ate, but after that when wine and herb-tea were served, I found out what kind of inquisition I faced.

First there was questioning by Tirzael and Suthafiori, seemingly with the intention of discovering everything they could about Earth and the Dominion. They must have gained some facts from the xeno-team, I knew, and would be double checking; so I kept my answers as simple as possible.

Suthafiori leaned back, cradling a glass goblet in her six-fingered hands.

'You understand,' she said at last, 'I cannot support you as far as I would wish. I have to look to the interests of all the *telestres*. And besides, if I go against the desires of the Hundred Thousand they are likely to name a new Crown, and one less friendly to your world. I find myself convinced of my policy, therefore I let you travel – but you must do your own reasoning with them.'

I wondered how many were open to reason. 'Yes, *T'An*.'

Ruric shook her head, taking her gaze from the fire. 'Dalzielle, I'm your reluctant ally, as you know. I say, take the measure of these people very carefully before we admit them to our lands.'

This was the *T'An* Commander speaking, and not the woman. Her yellow eyes met mine.

'Christie's honest, I grant you, but can we judge by one?' She shrugged. 'I've known good men even in Quarth, and how many sea-raids has that city mounted on our coasts?'

'This is old business. We have to deal with the present.' The Crown turned. 'Haltern?'

He was serious, the mask of vagueness dropping from him. 'Since the first contact and the arrival of the Otherworld team, every intelligencer in the Southland has come to Tathcaer seeking news. I say, end rumours, send the truth out. Christie should travel to as many *telestres* as possible. Better we discover the facts, then let these others – Kasabaarde and the like – come to us for news.'

'Oh, I doubt Kasabaarde must come to us for information.'

Suthafiori and the Earthspeaker seemed to share private amusement. Then she sobered. 'Brodin, what word from the Andrethe?'

'That she would welcome Otherworld visitors at the court. Truth told, she's tired of Tathcaer and the Kerys-Andrethe *telestre* – forgive me, *T'An* – keeping this new thing to themselves.' There was no noticeable apology in the man's abrasive tone. 'She will consider your further plans, but does not guarantee support. But I add this myself, *T'An*, there are as many foreign ears in Shiriya-Shenin, being a river port, as there doubtless are in seaport Tathcaer.'

'We hope to make contact with all of Orthe, in time,' I said to Suthafiori. 'From our point of view it's a good thing if they're prepared beforehand, if only by rumours.'

'That depends on what they prepare for.' Again there was a glint in Suthafiori's eyes. 'Geren, how say you on that?'

'There are rumours in the near Rainbow Cities of Otherworld visitors.' He linked his hands, staring at the claw-nails, then looking up. 'As to Kel Harantish . . .'

There was an almost imperceptible stir. I saw Ruric lean forward, and Brodin frown.

'I docked there before sailing to the Eastern Isles, as your messenger directed me.' By his expression, he hadn't liked being sent on the Crown's errands. 'The so called Emperor-in-Exile took care to question me himself. They have a close interest in the matter. I answered as little to the point as I could, and took care not to outstay my welcome.'

A ripple of amusement went round the table, breaking the tension. The Crown signalled for more wine, and the old *l'ri-an* refilled the goblets.

Seeing Ruric and Geren, I noticed their hands lay close together on the table as they talked. One pale and dappled, claw-nails white; the other velvet black with tawny nails. Many-fingered, like great spiders.

My *arykei*, she had said. In the informal inflection that was bedfriend, lover. A wanderer before all else. It was plain in the way their hands touched: Ruric Orhlandis and Sadri Geren Hanathra.

'And you,' Suthafiori turned to me, 'what do your people say?'

'At some point the Dominion has to classify this world, as to the amount of contact that will go on between you and us. Which may be much, or very little, taking into account your wishes and our capabilities.'

The Dominion has a complex structure of classification according to the technological level of a civilization, but I wasn't about to suggest to the Ortheans that they were low-level.

Suthafiori nodded slowly. 'That is our policy with outsiders. It's not our business what is done in, say, Kel Harantish or the Rainbow Cities. Unless it comes within our borders – then we are ruthless, root it out.'

'I have spoken with your kin of "war",' Ruric added. 'Your ways are strange to us. But do you know, if you attack us, you have not one enemy but a hundred thousand. That is our strength in war, and our failing in peace. We have no unity among the *telestres*.'

'There's no need to talk of fighting.' Suthafiori was reproachful. 'But trade, now, that's another matter.'

'It must come through us.' The voice was Tirzael's, cold, and with no deference in it.

'There are medicines and suchlike, things that may aid us.' She was mild but determined. 'If it's to our advantage, it's foolish to prevent it.'

'There are no quick nor easy answers.'

'No. No, there are not.'

After a pause Tirzael said, 'I passed through Medued-in-Rimon on my way here. The talk is all of Witchbreed – meaning yourself, *t'an* Christie, and your kin here. The Wellkeeper there speaks of rumours that the Crown is seduced away from good policy by Witchbreed cunning. If you would stop this talk, then you must be open.'

'The church supports me in this?' Suthafiori pounced.

'Neither supports nor opposes you as yet, *T'An Suthai-Telestre*. Go slowly. Better spend years, even generations, to come to the true judgement than do in haste what cannot be mended. Here is a thing we have not faced before, to open our borders to those from the stars. Yet the stars are the Sunmother's Daughters. *T'an* Christie, your people must be *n'ri n'suth* to us at the least.'

'That is decided, then,' Suthafiori stated. 'It remains only to decide which *telestre* you visit first, Christie.'

'Agreed. Ah, now, wait.' Ruric gave an order to the *l'ri-an*. 'T'An, I have an Otherworld drink you must try, Christie's kin the Eliots sent it to me. Let's wait, and decide the rest afterwards.'

There was some talk of various destinations. Then the *l'ri-an* returned with glazed drinking bowls and a great jug. The acrid smell of coffee flooded the room. Good for Aude Eliot, I thought. Coffee was one of the things I was going to miss on Orthe.

'Try it first,' Ruric invited me, 'give your opinion on how correctly it's been made.'

54

It was hot, and bitter. I took a sip and waited for it to cool.

'What about Shiriya-Shenin?' Brodin asked. 'You take the court there in Torvern, and it is near the end of Merrum now: should the *t'an* Christie travel with you?'

'My cousin is my supporter,' Suthafiori said. 'It's my enemies I would convince.'

'There's the Melkathi faction,' Haltern observed.

I stood to pour out the coffee. Another mouthful was less scalding. I blinked. The bitter taste increased, there was a sudden flood of saliva in my mouth.

'Christie!' Ruric shouted.

A faint ringing or humming seemed to come from the air. I must have moved. Then the stone floor swung out from under me, and I put out my hands to stop it smashing up. Distantly, I heard the bowl splinter as I dropped it. The floor was solid under my hand, but I was sliding down into a pit.

'Don't touch it!'

Geren's voice.

I felt my hands scrape the cold stone. Someone's arm was tight round my shoulders. The whole of my vision filled with yellow sparkles, until I was drowned and dizzy.

'Christie—'

Firm hands clamped round my jaw, forcing my mouth open, and someone thrust blunt fingers down my throat. I spasmed like a hooked fish, bent forward, and vomited copiously.

As my eyesight cleared, and the confusion subsided, a goblet of water was put in my hand. I drank it and was able to stand up. The pain subsided to strands of hot wire in my stomach.

I was between Geren and Haltern, both supporting me. Their fingers burned on my skin. I was hot and cold by turns.

'Are you well?' Geren demanded.

'I – think so.'

'In my household!' Ruric's grip on my arm was surprisingly strong. Her face ran with tears. 'Goddess! in my household – Christie, forgive me.'

Brodin stood holding the jug. His nostrils flared.

'*Saryl-Kabriz*,' he said. 'The odour is unmistakable. *T'an*, I do not know why you are not dead.'

I was able to stand unaided now. Haltern called the *l'ri-an*, and the mess was cleared up. It was only then that I realized someone had tried to poison me.

Someone had tried to poison me: it was only the infinitesimal difference between human and Orthean biology that kept me alive.

I found I was shaking, and took hold of Ruric's arm again.

'Why me? Or was it for me?'

All eyes went to Suthafiori. She smiled grimly.

'There is no one here who does not have enemies. And we are all players in the game. But no, even a fool could guess you'd be asked to taste it, Christie. It was meant for you.'

My head swam. It was not just reaction to the poison. Someone had tried to kill me. And they were taking it so calmly. I met their veiled eyes, aware that these were aliens. Not human. And maybe dangerous.

'In my house,' Ruric repeated. 'Well, I am your supporter, Dalzielle. I suppose to have the envoy die in my house might please your enemies, as well as mine.'

'The *T'An* Melkathi,' Haltern suggested.

'It has SuBannasen's style. And she and I are not friends,' Ruric said. 'But my *l'ri-an* are loyal, I'd have sworn to it!'

'It appears you were wrong,' Suthafiori said gently. 'But let's end this now. Ruric, find an escort for *t'an* Christie back to Easthill Malk'ys, and a physician.'

'Geren and I will go,' she said. 'Dalzielle, you'd better take an escort too.'

'No, I have my own ways of returning to the Citadel.'

With Ruric still apologizing, we moved out towards the stables. I was still dizzy. No one had ever hated me badly enough to want to kill me. I'd been hurt and I didn't understand why.

But I was coming to understand that Carrick V was dangerous.

Puddles covered the yard. The sky brightened, the breeze was cool. Clouds were breaking up, going north on a swift wind. As we entered the yard Maric rode out on the *marhaz* gelding with the *skurrai* on a leading rein.

He saw me and his eyes widened, doubt and shock written across his face. He yanked at the reins but Ruric ran forward and caught his heel and tipped him over. The *marhaz* skittered sideways. The boy hit the paved yard, sprawling heavily.

'What?' I said, bewildered.

'You saw *kir* face,' Geren said. '*Ke* never expected to see you walk out of here alive. Ruric, bring *kir* here!'

She thrust the boy at us. Suthafiori stood back beside Tirzael, her hood drawn up. Haltern held the boy's arms.

'You were in the kitchen,' Ruric said calmly. 'All *l'ri-an* go there, why should you be suspect, you were waiting for the *t'an*.'

'Yes.' His voice broke.

'Let me.' Tirzael came forward and spoke quietly. The conversation was inaudible, and the boy was crying.

'To use children, *ashiren* – !' Ruric swore.

'*Ke* says,' Tirzael came back to us, 'that *ke* was approached and threatened by two men, then given a substance – *ke* doesn't know what, only *ke* is sure it wasn't poison – and told to put it in the *t'an* Christie's drink. Ke saw the foreign drink prepared in the kitchen and put it in that, thinking perhaps one of the *t'an*'s friends was playing a joke on her.'

The yard was quiet except for the boy's crying. It tears me up to see kids cry.

'Of course that's not all of it.' Ruric bristled with hostility. 'No doubt *ke* was bribed as well as threatened, and *ke* knew very well that it was poison.'

Suddenly she pulled the boy's head up and struck him across the face. 'She is *s'an telestre* to you – what were you thinking of!'

'They were going to kill me!'

'I doubt we'd find the men,' Haltern said, 'certainly we'd never trace who hired them.'

Suthafiori touched my shoulder, saying quietly, 'If it were me, I would take that journey that we spoke of.'

'I can't go yet, I've made appointments.' I watched the boy. 'What are – what happens to him now?'

'That's for you to say, you still stand as *kir s'an*.' Ruric's answer was disinterested. 'You could let the city Watch have *kir*, there may be things *ke* hasn't told us. Or send *kir* back to Salathiel *telestre* and they'll punish *kir*.'

'Oh lord.' I couldn't think straight. 'Look, kid – *ashiren-te* – if anyone else comes to you, you come and tell me. All right?'

He stared blankly at me.

'How much were they going to pay you?'

'Five gold pieces,' he said. Ruric made a hissing noise under her breath.

'Right, you work for me till you've paid off twice that, we'll call it done with. Yes?'

Brodin looked the boy up and down. 'You're a fool, *t'an*, you'll have your throat cut inside a week.'

'No,' Maric said, 'she won't.'

He gave me that sullen look that I was used to. You couldn't blame him for being intimidated.

'All right, I know. Go and get the riderbeasts, will you?'

He crossed the yard, making soft noises to call the frightened *marhaz* gelding.

I said, 'I don't propose to blame a child for what's happened here. You find me the man or woman responsible, and then I'll put a complaint before the authorities.'

Ruric sighed and scratched her head. 'You're right. I've got a short temper, I'd have had *kir* whipped raw.'

'You must travel outside Tathcaer,' Suthafiori said, 'and soon.'

'I'm sorry, *T'An*, if I'm going to be any kind of an envoy, I've got to keep the appointments I made for next week.'

'I've to go to Roehmonde next week or the week after,' Ruric said thoughtfully. 'Suppose she comes with me to Corbek, and begins with the *telestres* there?'

'Is that agreeable to you?' the Crown asked me.

I was suddenly tired, and could only agree. My mind was blurred, but it didn't sound a bad plan.

'Then I say goodbye,' Suthafiori said, '*t'an* Christie, we'll meet again on happier occasions.'

I rode home to Easthill Malk'ys between Ruric and Geren, through the rain-washed alleys. The air was cold and the sun too bright, there was the subliminal awareness – now brought into sharp relief – that this was not Earth. We rode without speaking, and Maric came behind on the *skurrai* mare.

Fourteen days later I left Tathcaer.

PART TWO

CHAPTER 6

The Road North

Corbek in Roehmonde is five hundred *seri* from Tathcaer, a good six hundred standard miles through semi-civilized country, riding the *marhaz* on dirt-track roads. And travelling in the last weeks of Merrum and on into Stathern, that season where summer gives way to autumn.

'Given good roads, good riderbeasts and good weather, I'd call it twenty days.' Ruric stood with Adair and myself under the archway of Hill-Damarie. 'For us, not on forced march, and allowing for storms . . . Say twenty-five days. The end of Stathern should see us in Corbek.'

She went out into the yard. It was full with men, women, *marhaz* and *skurrai*. The riderbeasts threw their heads back and bugled fiercely. Chains rattled on the carts, Ortheans shouted, somewhere a child bawled. Dirt skirled on the wind. The confusion was illusory. Stable *l'ri-an* were hard at work, and the troopers had long since got themselves ready, and were now in the relaxed attitudes any soldier assumes at a moment's notice.

I saw Ruric in close conversation with a commander, Kem, a young red-maned male. He strode off shouting orders for the placement of the baggage cart.

'I'll say goodbye now.' Adair shook my hand. 'If you do find out anything new, I'd be grateful if you'd send me duplicate tapes of the reports. How we can be here this long without pinning down the species' life-cycle, I don't know. You may see things outside the settlement that we don't here.'

'OK, doc. Keep an eye on the shop for me, will you?'

He nodded and left. I'd been to all the diplomatic functions requiring my presence in Tathcaer and there were no more duties for me in the city.

It was a blustery day, clouds travelling fast on a southerly wind, a haze on the horizon. Hill-Damarie's stone walls reflected back the early heat.

61

'The *skurrai* are going with the cart,' Maric announced, appearing out of the chaos. '*T'an*, may I ride Oru?'

I wouldn't be needing the black *marhaz* as a remount on this kind of journey, and he might as well ride it as ride on the cart. He was astonishingly competent, for a kid.

'Sure, why not. Is Gher ready?'

'Yes. Thank you!' He grinned, and went to get the grey *marhaz* gelding.

Gher was placid because he was stupid. I was becoming attached to the riderbeast but having ridden him round Tathcaer, getting some of the stiffness out of my muscles, I was still dubious about riding him for days at a time.

I was checking the straps of the baggage roll behind the high-backed saddle when Haltern came by. I had the micro-recorder and the sonic stunner in that pack and I was taking good care of it.

'Be wary,' he advised. 'The Roehmonde *telestres* are strange country.'

I might have dismissed him as a fussy old woman, but it had taken me six days to recover from the *saryl-kabriz* poisoning and I still had a high temperature and a throat like sandpaper.

'You think there'll be trouble?'

He shrugged, then looked up sharply. 'The physician, Adair, he spoke to you of that?'

'No, he just came to see me off.'

I hadn't mentioned the poisoning attempt, though naturally it would go in the report to the department. But that would take over three months to reach Earth. All my decisions would have to be reached unaided and I didn't want the xeno-team butting in. I'd warned them to be careful but I hadn't been specific.

('What happened?' Adair asked when he examined me for my supposed allergy. 'Eat something that disagreed with you?')

Haltern said obliquely, 'At least you're in no greater danger in the provinces than you are in Tathcaer.'

'Under the circumstances, that's not as reassuring as it might be.'

'Come back safe, Christie, and soon. The sooner they let your kin loose on the Southland—' he left the sentence unfinished. The sooner they stop trying to scare off Lynne Christie? I wondered. I should be used to that kind of pressure, having been trained as envoy. Maybe there was some basis for Barratt's gibe about under-trained personnel.

'Goddess give you a clear road,' Haltern said. He raised his hand and waved and was swallowed in the crowd. I realized I was going to miss him and his knowledge and his half-pretence of timidity. I knew he would be about his curious unobtrusive business, eyes and ears in the right places to gather information.

'I think they're ready, *t'an*.' Maric came back leading Oru. He swung himself up into the saddle. I hauled myself up Gher's cold flank.

I was almost beginning to regret the kid. I had to give him coppers, or else he'd be tempted into stealing from me, and he'd be with me until he worked off his fine and his debt – a long time. And now he had started talking to me, I was hearing more about west-bank Salathiel and the *telestre's* chain-ferry than I really wanted to know. But he was tireless and enthusiastic, and I couldn't dislike him.

Ruric walked back with two children clutching at her legs. She handed the dark-skinned pair over to her *l'ri-an*.

'Grief of the Goddess!' she swore good-naturedly. 'Terai, look after the *ashiren*. Christie, we're ready. She's their milk-mother,' she added, seeing me glance at the young woman *l'ri-an*.

A sudden pause produced a moment's hush: one *marhaz* pawed the flagstones, I heard a child crying somewhere outside the walls.

The troopers mounted *marhaz*. Most carried cloaks rolled up and strapped behind the saddles. They wore mail-coats that came down as far as the thigh, and dun surcoats belted over the polished links. They mainly favoured curved *harur* blades, and a few carried winch-bows. There seemed to be no standard uniform except for the firecrest of the *T'An Suthai-Telestre* and the metal rank-badges carried on their belts. They shouted at each other, laughing and exchanging insults, and I found it difficult to picture these men and women fighting.

Ruric kissed the children, then mounted a dark striped *marhaz* and rode up beside me. She nodded to Kem. A small drum-frame was beaten, an atonal pipe wailed and the troop formed up with magical swiftness in ranks of three: baggage carts in the middle of the troop with the *skurrai* packbeasts behind. They moved off behind Ruric and Kem and I.

There's something about cavalry on the move. The hollow multiple sound of hooves on stone, echoing between high walls; jingling of harness, creak of leather, the hissing of the *marhaz*: there's a rhythm to it. I glanced behind at the bobbing heads and wondered what it would be like to face them at full gallop. They'd cut through a crowd like butter, I thought, as we came off Crown Way and down into the city; and I had some intimation of how deadly they could be.

'I'll miss the old city,' Ruric said affectionately. She rode heel to heel beside me.

'And your *ashiren*?'

'Yes, of course – but they're not Orhlandis *telestre*,' she said. 'Herluathis and Iric are being fostered with me from Vincor *telestre*. And my Rodion is being fostered in Peir-Dadeni.'

Down through the narrow passages, just wide enough for the baggage carts, between high blank walls. Past alleys that stank. Past the fishmarkets and the beastmarkets, odorous and noisy. Then out onto the embankment, riding under the shadow of the city wall – twenty feet high and a dozen thick – down to the Sandferry Gate.

'We'll ride ahead when we get out of the city,' Ruric said. 'The troopmaster knows the route I've planned.'

Sandferry is an old stone bridge, with carved piles. The river runs crystal over orange gravel. A fine lace-like yellow weed floats just under the surface.

Ruric reined in to let the troop pass. Gher sidestepped, and skittered in a circle before I could bring him round.

The air was colder, blowing up from the estuary. Downstream, Beriah's Bridge began the south-eastern Melkathi road. Upstream, the city walls followed the bends in the river, and I could see four more bridges. There were fewer people here. It was peaceful to sit and look out over the lush water meadows to the hills of Ymir.

We followed the troop out of the shadow of the wall, into the fierce sunlight, across the bridge.

I turned in the saddle. The city's white walls flashed back the early diamond light. I heard bells, and saw the full sails of a *jath* ship in the estuary, and the pennants flying from the grim Citadel.

I would have ridden a gallop back to the docks, begged a shipmaster to sail me to the Eastern Isles and stayed on that desolate rock until the next ship came from Earth – if I'd been able to foresee what was going to happen to me before I entered Tathcaer again.

'It'll be easy riding this first day,' Ruric said. 'The Hanathra *telestrte* lies about twenty-five *seri* east of here, they'll guest us for one night.'

The troop rode behind and below us as we climbed the track into the hills. They were making good speed, considering that the baggage carts must slow them down.

'Should we wait for them?'

'No. Crown law holds pretty well in these parts.' She managed the striped *marhaz* one-handed, reins looped up on the saddle, controlling it with pressure of heels and knees. Gamble, she called it; a lively sharp-horned beast. 'When we get into rough country the troopmaster will send scouts ahead. But you were thinking someone would try and follow up that poison?'

'It had crossed my mind.'

'I can't say it won't happen.' Her grave eyes met mine. 'There's no knowing the truth of it. Haltern names SuBannasen – though she's gone back to Ales-Kadareth now – and I believe him. But there'll always be such things. We're all players of the game.'

'What reasons do you have for suspecting SuBannasen?'

'My own,' she said shortly.

We rode on in silence for a time, with the heat shimmering over the blue-grey mossgrass, and the lizardbirds calling their metallic notes. It was difficult to tell where dust-starred hill ended and star-dusted sky began.

'Sorry,' she said at last. 'That was a hard year, the uprising in Melkathi, and it's with me still. Sulis n'ri n'suth SuBannasen has her own reasons for hating me and for striking at me through you. And since you're an Offworlder she may prove your enemy too.'

'I was wondering where I came in.' Some of the black resentment in me spilled over. 'I suppose at least I'm having some effect here – no one ever tried to kill me on any other world.'

'No one ever—' she cut off. 'Christie, you must come from a strange world. You bear no *harur* blade, and I've heard you called coward but I don't believe that's true. You have your own weapons. And yet it's so different.'

Gher balked at a slope, and I brought him round and thumped my heels heavily into his ribs. He turned his head and glared reproachfully from wide-set eyes.

The Orthean woman said, 'When I was your age, I'd birthed a child and fought in four uprisings.'

There was a challenge there. Even allowing for the difference between Orthean and standard years she was barely a decade older than me. I grinned. 'Sounds dangerous. I prefer travelling – light years from Earth – and seeing new worlds. Of which, by the way, I've set foot on three so far.'

'Hei! You sound like Geren. He'd sooner sail than fight.'

The track wound on into the hills, chalk dust going up from under the *marhaz* split hooves and whitening boots and britches. The mossgrass made a tight blue-grey carpet. It was high, empty country.

'I'm the same as you,' Ruric said, 'a small piece in a large game. There'll be other *T'An* Commanders after me, and other envoys after you. Which is good. We can't judge a world by you. And you can't judge the Southland by a Roehmonder priest or a Dadeni rider – or even a Melkathi woman.'

The day wore on, and the dust the troop kicked up hung in the heavy air. There was no wind in the hills. It was hot.

Ruric leaned back in the saddle, hooding her eyes and staring directly at the sun. The Ortheans can look on the face of their Goddess; their mysteries are mysteries of the light and not the dark.

'Nearly noon,' she said, with the radiant shadow of the sun still in her eyes. 'We're making good time.'

As we crested the next rise I saw we had only come up over a spur of the hills, and not crossed the hills themselves. They swung away into the north-east, ranging into the distance, hull-backs sharp against the sky. Above them rode the scatter of daystars that Southlanders call *siriye* after the starmoth. They dotted the sky like flour.

We crept across the landscape like flies. Six hundred miles, I thought. And I could drive that comfortably in three days.

The feathery *lapuur* grew up to the foot of the downs like a sea. In the stillness of that day-starred noon, they were a slight but ceaseless movement. As we rode down under the trailing ash-pale ribbons, they shrank back. Thermosensitive. I put up a hand to brush them aside, and the fronds that slid from the *marhaz*'s cool flanks for a moment curled and clung to my skin. An automatic reaction to body-temperature: but I shivered. It's never far, that tension endemic to being on alien soil.

I saw clearings and the smoke of settlements, and fields of grain further off. In some areas they were burning off stubble, but when we came down off the hills the grain was standing heavy and amber beside the road. Ruric leaned down from the *marhaz* to pick a stalk, offering me one of the double-headed ears, and we rode on chewing the bitter kernels and spitting out the husks.

We dropped back after the midday stop for food, and rode with the troop. They were in a straggling line, talking and singing.

'Ceremonial visits are easy duty,' Ruric commented, 'even if it does mean riding to such Goddess-forsaken outposts as the Skulls Garrison. They're alert enough when there's need for it.'

Whoever compiled the xeno-team's language tapes hadn't spent their time round the Hill-Damarie barracks. Their slang dialect was unintelligible, though from the looks I got I gathered the Out-worlder was being discussed. I made a mental note to question Maric later.

About mid-afternoon it began to cloud up, a wind coming from the west. Before long it was raining. A few drops spattered down through the *lapuur* fronds, there was the hiss of a wood in a rainstorm, and visibility shrank to a grey circle. I hastily unstrapped my cloak and put it on, pulling the hood up.

Rain seeped through to thighs and shoulders. I could feel water down my back, and see it dripping off the rim of my hood. The troop closed up, centring round the carts; hoods up and heads down, riding with the rain at their backs. Ruric rode down the column to consult the troopmaster.

The Southland's word for road is the same as their word for boundary. In the main we were following tracks that marked the borders of *telestres*. I watched for a markstone with the Hanathra insignia. The afternoon passed in the curious yellow light of a rainstorm.

My legs were aching and I had a sore backside and I was as wet as I'd have been in a river. Gher ambled disconsolately on after Ruric's *marhaz*. I kept quiet, knowing my temper was filthy. I didn't even want to think how I was going to feel once I dismounted. But God knows you can't enthuse about the wonders of primitive societies and then scream for a jeep when you have to ride a *marhaz* in a downpour. The wind blew gustily. We plodded on. Somewhere behind me, a trooper cursed and spat. I thought about hot food, hot drinks and hot baths.

'How far now?'

Ruric gave the crook-shouldered shrug that was her trademark. 'Two or three *seri*. Not far.'

'Will Geren be there?'

'He's still in the city. Sadri is *s'an telestre*, you'll meet her.'

Not long afterwards we came to a fork in the road, with the Hanathra sign on the markstone. By the time we had ridden across the *telestre* the rain was down to a drizzle. Ruric rode with Kem, and I fell back beside Maric and the troopers.

We topped a rise and I saw the household spotlit by the low sun, against a background of purple rainclouds. At first I thought it was a village, and a sizable one at that; then I saw that each building was interconnected, the main polygonal stone building throwing out wings and offshoots and outbuildings covering several acres of ground. We rode round past storage sheds and beastpens, and under an archway to a courtyard the size of a field. The pale yellow stone, lit by the level westering sun, glowed golden. An antique coping in the centre marked the well.

A crowd of *ashiren* came running up, chattering and screeching, and squat, red-pelted beasts hissed at the *marhaz* heels as they splashed through the spreading puddles. Kem called an order, the troop dismounted and began leading the riderbeasts towards the stables. By now there were adults with the *ashiren*, some helping the troopers, some coming to greet Ruric.

There was a certain respect in the way they spoke to her. She was all ease on the surface, but it was obvious she was known and had a reputation.

'Christie,' she called, coming over.

I threw one leg over Gher's quarters, slid to the ground, and would have fallen flat if the Orthean woman hadn't shot out a hand to catch me.

'Jesus wept!' I bent double, rubbing knotted thigh and calf muscles.

'That was the easy day. You wait until tomorrow.'

I tried my recollection of Ymirian curses. She laughed, pushed me one-handed at the main doors, and then we were out of the rain and in a flagstoned hall. Water pooled round my boots. I straightened, winced.

'We must go round and check their quarters afterwards,' Ruric said, and then bawled at a short stocky woman. 'Sadri! Sadri, is there any hot water in this *telestre*?'

A squat iron boiler radiated heat. Piped through to the bathhouse next door, hot water filled a tank that looked to have been carved from a single granite block. There was the headachy smell of *lapuur*, that fierce-burning firewood.

I sat on one of the underwater ledges, relaxing in water almost too hot to bear. It was bliss. Ruric sat on a ledge opposite, her cropped black mane floating like seaweed. She ducked her head, blinked the water out of her veiled eyes, and massaged the stump of her right arm. It had been taken off midway between elbow and shoulder, a nub of smooth skin and lumpy flesh that was not ugly, only wrong.

'Aches in wet weather,' she said, ducking her head again, and coming up blowing water. 'That I also owe to Melkathi, and Ales-Kadareth.'

'What about Melkathi?' I said. 'I ought to know.'

'The whole business? Yes, you did. Perhaps this wouldn't have started so soon, if it wasn't for that.'

I occupied myself with the gritty soap. Every fibre of me ached. When I looked up, Ruric said, 'I can't explain it without telling you something of my *telestre*, so bear with me.'

'You don't have to.'

After a silence she said, 'I've spoken to your kin. Is it true that on your world people of the same household live apart, in different lands, with no disgrace?'

'Yes, it's true.' I saw she still looked unconvinced. 'Me, for example, I've lived in several parts of the British Isles. In the south, when my parents were alive – they died when I was thirteen – and then in London with the de Lisle half of the family.' Without thinking, I added, 'They never exactly approved of the Christies, but they couldn't refuse to take me in.'

'But they were your *telestre*.' She was watching me narrowly.

'My mother's side of the family. The Christies were never quite good enough for the de Lisles. I suppose I decided to use them, they're an old diplomatic family; but I'm not sure that they didn't use me, turning me into another career diplomat.' I stopped. I was tired, liable to run on.

'What would we be if we weren't driven?' Ruric said dreamily. 'Me, not a soldier; you, not the envoy. This was your birth mother's kin, was it; or your milk-mother or foster-mother?'

'Birth-mother.' Orthean relations are complex. 'Never mind: tell me about Melkathi.'

Her dark face, seen through wisps of steam, was serious and open. It was the turning point (rarely recognized) when she became a person to me.

'You've got the look,' she said, 'I've got it too, I know. That's what it is about you Otherworlders. You're *amari*, motherless. Landless, too.'

'I can see how it would look that way.'

'And my *telestre* . . .' she nodded, making comparisons. 'If we'd had an Earthspeaker to put us right, it would have been different; but the church has always been weak in Melkathi. And Orhlandis is a poor *telestre*, it won't support more than a score living there. So, like you, I think I was one too many. And yellow-eyed, too.

'How it was: my father was a wanderer, shipped out from Ales-Kadareth one spring, came home seven years later with nothing, but the clothes on his back and the babe he carried: that was me. He knew it would overstrain the *telestre* if he stayed, so he and his brother and his brother's sons went to Ales-Kadareth to earn silver. That was the summer of the White Plague. It killed him. It spared them.'

She sat up, rippling the water, soaping her scarred ribs.

'So half my kin were in Ales-Kadareth as *l'ri-an* for the *T'An* Melkathi, who at that time also was from SuBannasen *telestre*. I didn't know or care about that. As soon as I was no longer *ashiren* I came to Tathcaer and joined the army. I should have gone back. But what can you do?'

'Nothing,' I said, remembering.

'The uprising started in Ales-Kadareth. They always do. It's a rebellious city. The Melkathi *telestres* are all dirt-poor. If it was me, I'd change the boundaries, move half the people out, and let the land support the rest – but there's no going against the church.' She sighed, then continued, 'Four years back, I went in with the army, established lines of supply and laid siege to the city. Sure enough the *telestres* began to withdraw support. But 'Kadareth held out. It was bad, four seasons before the siege broke. In the end I wasn't sure if they'd starve before we were wiped out by plague – it was a blazing hot summer, and every disease you can name went through us. I used winch-guns to drop our dead inside the city walls. That opened them up. There was some close fighting before the SuBannasen surrendered – that was when I took a cut in the arm and it turned poisonous. Then I had to judge 'Kadareth by Crown law.'

There was no apology in her tone. Looking at her, I believed she'd done all she said: planned, executed, killed.

'Three of the chief rebels were Orhlandis *telestre*. What could I do? If I spared them, it was injustice. But I hated them. Goddess, how I hated all my kin! And how can you deal with someone justly when you'd like to gut them like a fish? They pleaded. Then they accused me of using Crown law to be revenged on them.'

'What did you do?' I asked.

'What could I do? They were guilty. I hung them on the walls of Ales-Kadareth. And I still don't know if they were right in what they said.'

'Sometimes there is no right thing to do.'

She was quiet, then said, 'But the point of this is, I also had executed the *T'An* Melkathi, who was Sulis's brother. She was *s'an* at that time, but since became *T'An* Melkathi herself. Naturally she'd like to see me dead. This is what you've been dragged into.'

'It would have happened sooner or later. I'm a stranger here.'

'But she'll leave it, you having gone beyond her reach for a time.' She sluiced off the soap, stood up, and climbed unselfconsciously out of the bath to get a towel. Unlike most Ymirian clothes, Ruric's had button and loop fastenings so that she could manage one-handed.

I climbed out and towelled my dripping hair, wiped my face, and found Ruric staring at me. She looked me up and down. I felt myself getting hot behind the ears.

'Not one,' she said. 'Not one scar, not anywhere.'

I almost exploded with laughter.

'Let's go and find Satri,' she said, and glanced at me again.

'Yours must be a very strange world. I wonder what I'd make of it?'

Hanathra *telestre's* main hall was full of people. Besides the household, which seemed to extend family relationships at least as far as sixth cousins, and the *l'ri-an* and the *ashiren* being fostered, there were also the soldiers of Kem's troop.

Oil lamps stood on ledges round the stone walls, and firelight gave some clarity of view beside the six great hearths. It was low-ceilinged, a large hall where pale yellow stone arches held soft shadows. Tables and long benches were set between the pillars. The great crowd that there had been at the beginning of the meal had divided into groups round the hearths, some talking, some singing – Ortheans sing anywhere, given half a chance – or passing gossip and getting city news from the troopers. Kids sat round on soft *wirazu* pelts, pummelling the guardbeasts or fighting or falling asleep. You could see from the colours of the stone that the walls had been rebuilt once or twice, at intervals of several centuries. Where I sat, on a bench inside the hearth-nook that was as big as a small room, the stone was grey veined with blue, old and worn smooth with use.

Maric sat curled up on the furs, staring sleepily into the fire. He was dazed: it was his first time out of the city. Ruric and Sadri sat beside me, talking.

I leaned back, aching, savouring the feel of clean dry clothes and staring up the chimney-shaft at the stars, shimmering in the fire's smokeless heat. It was that point in a journey that brings mild depression, when you look back and feel every inch of the journey, every increasing mile between what's familiar and what's strange. I was the first of my kind to travel into this unknown country. The thought of that – sensed far off down the years, at idealistic fourteen or fifteen – had once fired me to begin a career in the ET department. The reality was at once more frightening and more satisfying.

Ruric shifted beside me, moving the stump of her arm into the fire's heat.

'Does it still pain you?' Sadri was concerned.

'No.'

'You were the best,' she said. There was an expression between them that meant they'd had this conversation before. She turned to me. 'She was the best with the *harur* blades that ever lived in the Southland.'

Ruric's answer was that crook-shouldered shrug. It must hurt

71

her to have that said, I thought, not yet used to the Orthean habit of washing dirty linen in public.

'I don't know about that. You can't make comparison with the dead masters who're gone, or with those who're not yet born – but yes, I grant you, I was the best in my generation.'

There was no pride or pity in her voice. She made it a statement of fact.

'I have still the *harur-nilgiri*,' she added, and her lips quirked into a smile at Sadri. 'Whether my balance is gone or not, you wouldn't like to challenge me.'

'I would not,' Sadri agreed.

The fire crackled restfully, and she eased a log back into the embers with the toe of her boot. The sound of singing came from the distant end of the hall.

Katra Sadri Hanathra was a small woman, no more than four feet ten or eleven inches tall, with a squat round figure. Her skin was fish-pale, and lightly marked with marshflower dapples. Her grizzled red mane was cropped short. She had a wrinkled moon-face, lined forehead, and wideset eyes in bags of flesh. There was no telling her age, it could have been anything between fifty and seventy. She should have been strikingly ugly – and indeed, with the nictitating membrane over her eyes she sometimes resembled a comatose reptile – but she had the same open expression that Geren had, and the same gift of making you feel welcome.

'How's Geren?' she asked Ruric.

'Refitting ships.' There was humour in her voice. 'I think he's got the idea of the Western Voyage again – convinced that if the *Hanathra* can sail directly west for fifty days, he'll find land.'

'He'll be gone a while and come back with nothing, I know him. You,' Sadri said, with her hand on Ruric's shoulder, 'you're his *arykei*. When are you going to become *n'ri n'suth* Hanathra?'

'If we were one *telestre* it wouldn't keep me in Ymir, or him on dry land.'

'I don't ask you for that reason. You've got good friends here. I'd like to see you come home here, instead of to soldier's quarters in some garrison. Don't you agree?' she appealed to me suddenly.

I felt inclined to pretend I knew nothing about it, but that kind of tact has no place there. As Ruric said later, in the entire Southland, there isn't enough tact to fill a bucket.

'It wouldn't work on my world, or at least, not the part where I was born,' I said. 'Perhaps it would, here. You're used to having milk-mothers and foster-children and – I don't know – you seem to hold your children and relatives in common, don't you? It's much narrower on Earth. Either you belong or you don't.'

72

'It's the land,' Ruric said. 'I'm Orhlandis-bred, if not born there.'

'The land wouldn't matter so much for us,' I said, and was momentarily alone, faced by alien eyes.

'You never root the land out of you,' Sadri contradicted.

'Where you grew up as *ashiren*,' Ruric said, 'the first fields and paths and coastline that you ever saw. The household. You remember your house,' she challenged, 'and the rooms, and what was in them, and where you slept?'

'Yes, of course.'

'And the hills,' Sadri picked up the thread, 'and the way the light fell, and the winds, and the river, and the paths through the trees?'

'Yes—'

There wasn't too much like that where I was born. No, but I remember the street and the old bombsites the kids used to claim as their territory; all of it mixed up with life before my mother and father were killed. If I had ever got into adolescence while they were alive, quarrelled and cut free, it would be easier. As it is, I have a child's memories. A child who doesn't remember the faults, only the good times.

'They feel it too,' Ruric said, and I saw her and Sadri watching me.

'Still, you weren't meant for that *telestre*.' Sadri returned to her argument. 'Any Earthspeaker would have told you so. It's no disgrace to be born in the wrong *telestre*, and it's the Goddess's will that you go where you can live best.'

'I wasn't born in a *telestre*.' Something of steel flashed in Ruric's voice. 'As I was constantly reminded. I'm *amari*, motherless, born outside the land.'

'It doesn't matter to us.'

'I *am* Orhlandis,' Ruric said, almost brutally, 'I am of Melkathi, I am a Southlander. What would you have me do, Sadri?'

'I've touched scars. I'm sorry.'

Dusk turned to darkness, and rain drummed on the small-paned windows.

'Maybe one day—' Ruric interrupted herself. 'Yes, Kem?'

'Only a rumour, *T'An*.' His eyes flicked nervously over me, and he looked away. 'The *ashiren* say there was a man here earlier, asking if the Commander's troop were coming here; and as they did not know when we were coming, they could tell him nothing. He rode off, but they can't say by which road.'

I saw Sadri's glance at Ruric.

'Now is that one of Suthafiori's messengers,' Ruric thought aloud, 'or is that SuBannasen or some other *t'an* having us followed?'

CHAPTER 7

The House at Terison

Maric woke me after first twilight, bringing a basin and a jug of hot water. He knew better than to expect sensible conversation from me at that hour and so left me to dress, having told me that the *T'An* Ruric and everyone else were already up.

Every time I moved, I winced. The inner muscles of my thighs seized up, and for a while I seriously thought I'd done permanent damage. I tried to sit on the edge of the bed, yelped, and collapsed back across it. There was no way I could bend. Dressing was a slow process, mostly horizontal.

The other beds in the room – it was more of a dormitory – still bore the warm imprint of bodies. I washed perfunctorily. Unlike the city households, this had a primitive system of flush plumbing. Somehow I'd expected to find the city more sophisticated.

Before I repacked my baggage I took the sonic stunner out and strapped on the belt-holster. The laced tunic concealed it. I didn't want to analyse my motives for wearing it, but it was comforting.

I limped through half a dozen empty rooms, looking for stairs. There were no corridors, room opened directly into room. Grey clouds were shifting outside and a pale light filtered in. The place smelled of dust and old cooking.

Opening one door, I came into a bare room whose walls were covered in old maps. An enormous iron and glass structure stood under a skylight. It was a primitive telescope. The lenses were visibly flawed but it was still beyond anything I'd expected to see on Carrick V. This world might, I thought, be on the verge of some technological revolution. I studied the star-charts: complex for summer, less so for the Orthean winter sky, empty only by comparison.

A spiral staircase went down from one corner of the room and I went down and found myself at one end of the great hall. Ruric sat with Kem and his Second, poring over a map spread among the ruins of breakfast.

'—through Meremoth and up to Brinor.' She saw me. 'Christie, I didn't think you'd be walking this morning!'

'My legs may let me down yet.' I eased gently onto the bench.

They continued their discussion, while I made inroads on the meal. Meat broth, bread, hot herb-tea; then a fruit with what seemed like sour milk on it – but there are very few Orthean land mammals – and finally *rukshi*, land arthropods.

'It wouldn't be a Crown Messenger,' said Kem's Second, a broad-bellied woman called Ho-Telerit. 'He'd have waited, or given word to the *s'an telestre* here.'

'Someone's got their eyes on us,' Ruric agreed.

'*T'An* Commander,' Kem said, 'you don't imagine someone's going to ambush a troop of the Crown's army? We're not thirty *seri* from Tathcaer!'

'If it were to be done, that would be the way to do it. Where least expected. But no, I don't think that.' Her satin-black finger traced a line across the map. 'I think Sadri can tell any inquirers that we've gone the way I planned: Meremoth, Brinor, and Salmar. Meanwhile, let's see if we can take our follower east a ways, and lay hands on him. I'd like some answers.'

'There's a companion-house near Sherahtha,' Kem suggested.

'Right. Let's move.' She stood. 'Who are your best scouts?'

'Perik and Vail,' Ho-Telerit said.

'See if they can pick up our follower.'

Not long after that we left, Sadri riding with us as far as the border of the *telestre*. It was a bright, starry morning, the road muddy with the previous day's rain but passable. Warm vapour curled up from the earth, and with it came the acrid smell of mossgrass and the sweetness of *ziku*.

'The *telestre* is open to you any time if you come back this way.' Sadri sat astride her black *marhaz*. She squinted at me in the early light. 'And remember Hanathra when there are voyages to your Otherworld – if I can't come, then Geren certainly will.'

We crossed another spur of the hills, coming down about mid-morning into wooded valleys. The slender *lapuur* gave way to taller, broad-leaved *ziku* trees. Bronze-red foliage shaded us from the sun as we followed a winding track.

Indigo shadows came up from the darkness of the wood. Then the sun blazed out again, and we were suddenly riding through sapphire light. Under the bronze trunks of the *ziku* grew a darker blue species of the mossgrass. The hooves of the *marhaz* sank inches deep into it, muffling their tread. The depths of the wood were azure, bright as the sea, and over that blue thousandflower-moss blazed the red fire of the *ziku*. Even the troop rode silent, the pace increasingly slightly, a tension obvious in their faces. No *rashaku* sang.

'Before the *telestres*, it was called the old Commonwood,' Ruric said as we came out into sun and farmland again. 'Some say it once marched from the Fens to the sea.'

Maric made casts with a sling as we travelled and brought down a lizardbird that Ho-Telerit commandeered for the noon meal. It was the first time I'd studied one at close hand. Brown plumage flecked the wings and back but the body was scaled. A thin, wedge-shaped head bore serrated jaws. It had four clawed feet.

'*Rashaku-dya*,' Maric said. 'I used to snare them in their treeholes under the Rimon downs. They're good eating, *t'an*.'

It was a long day, and well into the second twilight before we came to Sherahtha. It was a companion-house on the border where three *telestres* met, run by each in turn; a low and sprawling cob-walled building.

'He's been here before us,' Ruric said, coming round to where I was seeing to Gher's stabling.

'The one that's following us?'

'One man can move faster than a troop. And make a good guess as to what road we're on.' She frowned. 'We'll keep in the hills tomorrow, where he'll have to come close to get a look at us, and see if Ho-Telerit's scouts have any better luck.'

We sat by the courtyard window of another shabby companion-house. Outside, the evening was hot and still. Heat soaked up out of the dry earth, shimmered over the fields of stubble where hay stood in small, egg-shaped stacks. They resembled fields of squat standing men. Hills blocked the western horizon. We'd been riding north-east for two days after leaving Sherahtha.

'Whoever he is, he knows his business. And he's lucky,' Ruric added as an afterthought.

'They lost him in the woods towards Torfael, *T'An* Commander.' Ho-Telerit had just taken the reports from her scouts, trailing dispiritedly into the yard.

'How far from here?' Ruric asked.

'Four *seri*. Perhaps five.'

'Mrnm . . . Yes, all right, Ho-Telerit.' She watched the woman stump off. 'I don't like being trailed if I can help it, Christie.'

'So?' I prompted.

She spread the map on the window-ledge. 'We're here on the northern edge of the hills. Corbek's way up here in Roehmonde . . . you see the direct route's still north through Brinor.'

'That's where he'll expect us to go.' He had taken up a shadowy reality in my mind, though no one had been able to give us an accurate description.

'There's a chance Ho-Telerit's scouts have driven him off our track today. We'll go due east, cut across the heathland.' Her widespreading fingers left the map, and it coiled up into a scroll. She scratched at her black mane. 'There's a theocratic house at Terison, we can stop over there and go north the day after.'

I didn't feel half-crippled by a day's riding as I had done at the beginning, but I was tired and dirty and suffering mild stomach trouble from the unfamiliar food.

'How far to Corbek?' I asked.

'Two weeks, maybe twenty days. Which reminds me,' she said, 'how's your Roehmonde dialect?'

'Almost non-existent.' The Southland boasted at least seven distinct languages not on the hypno-tapes. That didn't count dialects – to some degree, each *telestre* has its own individual dialect; the provinces reflect language divisions more than political boundaries.

'I was up there about eight years back, doing garrison duty at the Skulls Pass. I'll teach you if you like,' she offered, 'and if you don't mind speaking it with a Melkathi accent.'

'I don't mind if they don't.'

'They're odd people, the Roehmonders,' she said. 'It'll be interesting to see how things have changed since I was there last.'

Off the hills, the ground was soft peat covered with the low scrub they call bird's-wing for the feathery striations on its yellow leaves. The carts made poor time on the wet track.

'There,' Ruric said, as the sun sent our shadows jogging east ahead of us. 'Terison.'

The terrain was becoming drier and there were stands of silver-barked trees. A speck that I had thought was a copse resolved itself into buildings.

'Goddess,' Maric whispered beside me, 'look at that!'

I shared his wonder: it was different from anything I'd seen in Ymir so far. There were two or three structures clustered together. No wall had an angle in it. Above the ground-floor slit windows the walls bellied out to join with their neighbours and make a single upper storey. The roofs rose into onion-domes. As we came closer, I saw the last sunlight give a gold tinge to the brown brickwork.

'It's an old place, they tell me, but it has a good reputation.'

Ruric clapped heels to the *marhaz*'s barrel-ribs and rode ahead. The dust that was dark on me was grey on her. I saw her reach the outer wall and stop, speaking with someone, and then dismount.

Maric stayed close to me, even when the *marhaz* were taken for stabling. He had his sullen look again. It masked what was almost a superstitious awe of the ancient structure.

It was dark inside the curved entrance arch: brown brick walls and grey stone flags. I stood with Ruric and Kem, accustoming my eyes to the gloom. Several *ashiren* came in while we were there. They wore *chirith-goyen* smocks, with a length of cloth wrapped apron-like round their waists. As they came in they went to the shallow troughs in the stone floor, stood in the water there and washed the dirt from their bare legs and feet. The cloth-apron was used to dry them and thrown into a stone basin. The children gave us bird-bright glances but didn't speak. Ruric seemed content to wait.

The curved arch framed an enamel-blue sky. Palmate leaves the size of dinner plates hung on a vine there, and tiny crimson grapes in fist-sized bunches rested against the bricks. Between us and the smooth arc of the outer wall were strips of cultivated land. A bell began to toll somewhere in the building – comfortingly familiar, after Tathcaer – and a dozen or so older *ashiren* came in. With them came a tall woman and a stocky man.

Ruric stepped forward and bowed. 'Goddess give you good day. Is it possible to claim guest-right for myself and my people?'

'Our house is open,' the man replied. He wore a priest's skirt. 'I'm Rhiawn. This is Branic.'

Ruric gave our names and set Kem to looking after the troop, and we entered the Wellhouse at Terison.

The passages curved and re-curved, the roof was a round arch, even the stone floor was worn concave by use. There were no lamps here, but we passed *ashiren* lighting torches in wall-brackets. There was a smoky tang to the air.

'We've many guests now, at harvest time,' Branic said. She was a head taller than any of us, and had a permanent half-stoop from the nearness of the ceiling. 'Some of you may have to sleep in priest's cells, the guest rooms are full.'

'The roof of the Goddess over us is comfort enough.' Ruric used the formal inflection for that politeness. Obviously there was no preferential treatment here, even for the *T'An* Commander. I was too tired to worry about what they'd make of me.

We came into a round well-lit room filled with tables and benches. The noise warned me before I got to the door: thirty or so *ashiren* yelling and chattering. There were stares when we entered but they soon lost interest. Other Ortheans there looked to be from farming *telestres*.

'You're just in time for evening meal,' Branic remarked, and she and Rhiawn left us to find seats on the crowded benches. The food was served by them, with help from the older *ashiren*.

Perhaps it was tiredness: as I ate, I seemed again to be among the half-animal humanoids that the Ortheans at first resembled – especially the light-boned children with their slender many-fingered hands, and their blurring eyes. A failure of empathy. It was easier with adults, I thought. The harsh-faced Branic, she could have been human. And that woman beyond her, the one so obviously pregnant. And that man—

The man I was looking at turned. His face was horrifically scarred. Maric, who'd followed my gaze, said, 'Goddess! that's an ugly one, *t'an*.'

I hushed him. The Orthean male was fair-skinned and yellow-maned, broadshouldered and tall. It looked as though he'd been burned – all one side of his face was a red-and-white patchwork. By some miracle he still had the eye, bright in its nest of ruined flesh. Where the burn vanished into the hairline, his mane had grown back silver.

I thought about plastic surgery and, as an extension of that thought, Ruric's missing arm; and it brought home to me the fact that Orthe needed us. Culture shock or not. You have to be practical.

The meal finished, the benches and tables were shoved back against the walls and a brazier was lit in the centre of the room. The *ashiren* settled on the floor in groups, talking, some playing a variant of the Southland game called *ochmir*. I saw Rhiawn putting two benches together, and a folded blanket over them, and the pregnant woman lay down there close by the fire. The party with her were bawdy, boisterous.

'Is she all right?' I asked Branic.

'She's come to the Wellhouse for the birth,' the Orthean woman said, as if that explained everything. 'The Goddess keeps an open door. For them, too,' she said as one of the *ashiren* brought wine. 'Runaways, most of them.'

'But don't you send them back home?'

'You can't take a child from its mother,' she said, with the inflection that turned 'mother' into 'Goddess'. 'The land's poor here. We work harder than most of the surrounding *telestres*. A lazy one knows running here won't help. The other *ashiren* must have their reasons.'

But they're children! I wanted to protest, and didn't. The young of the species weren't childlike.

A little later I went with Maric and Ruric to oversee the transfer of baggage to our rooms. These were separate small cells with hard beds, buckets for washing, and a pisspot under the bed. All the residents of the house shared the same discomfort. It was simple, primitive, and (I thought, looking at the worn stone floor) perhaps because of that, it had survived for a good long time.

'I must have a word with Kem before tomorrow,' Ruric said, and we went with her back to the round hall – and walked into chaos.

Most of the people there had given up their various occupations of talking and drinking and *ochmir*, and were paying close attention to the woman on the benches. She cried out once, then grunted, breathing hard. They called encouragement, crowding round. Those closest to her were breathing in her rhythm.

'Jesus, isn't there *anything* they keep private?'

Ruric's head turned. I realized I'd spoken aloud.

'Nothing's private in the one *telestre*,' she said, sweetly reasonable. 'And we're all one *telestre* in the Goddess's house.'

'But they haven't even sent the kids out!'

She looked at me as if I was mad and I shut up. If I was shocked, it was culture shock, or maybe species shock.

'Hold her up—'

'Ready!'

'—be careful—'

The woman didn't scream, but she grunted as if she were being kicked. I saw her head tilt back. A dark-skinned male was gripping both her hands. Branic, kneeling at the foot of the bench, threw blood-stained cloths into a basin.

The woman yelled. The younger woman squatting beside her stood up, cradling a bloody mass. I bit my lip. It was a child, and it was covered in a thick membrane.

The young woman, with a practised gesture, hooked her sixth finger and slit the membrane with her claw. The baby choked and then gave a thin squawl. My throat constricted. It was tiny: much smaller than a human baby.

By the time the woman had washed it – she must be a midwife, I decided – the second and third were born, and free of their membranous cases. I felt sick. It was a shame Adair wasn't there, I thought, he would have appreciated it.

'A three-birth,' Rhiawn said beside me, and pointed at the younger woman. 'Kyar will nurse them until Gabrit's milk comes in.'

Adair had said milk was always late with Orthean females. I had a glimpse of how that bound them in interdependence: there must be large family units, there must be milk-mothers and foster-mothers.

I fully expected the mother to be put to bed, but within a short time she was sitting by the fire, wrapped in blankets. She and the father and the milk-mother were each holding one of the babies, swapping them round occasionally. Branic came back with more wine, and everyone present gave some wish for the future, and before long it had turned into a party.

'Are you all right?' Ruric said to me impatiently.

They were an appallingly tough and hardy species, I thought. I nodded, and took the next mug of wine that passed.

The window was visible only as a dark grey slit. Darkness filled the room. I lay awake wondering how long it was to the dawn bell. The bed was hard. I still wasn't used to that. I'd be glad to get to Roehmonde, I thought. Travel here was dirty and insect-ridden and uncomfortable.

Wood creaked.

Several seconds passed. Simultaneously with my realization that, as the floor was stone, it must be the door, came another noise. A harsh slithering hiss.

I held my breath and willed the blood to stop pounding in my ears. The noise had been the drawing of a *harur* blade from its sheath.

Silence.

Could I be wrong? Of course: nothing could possibly happen here.

The stunner was in its holster, flung down on my bags in the far corner of the room. My belt-knife was there too. And I couldn't pretend, now, that I heard nothing. There was someone in the room.

I sensed movement. Then the window was obscured. All in one convulsive movement I slid out of bed, hurled the rough blanket in the direction of the window, and ran. Something caught me a crack across the shins. I stumbled, grazing my hands on the stone floor, and something whipped past my head and thunked into the doorpost.

I reached up and a red-hot iron bar slammed into my palm. I snatched my hand back, yelling. Silence was my enemy now. I heard distant shouts: I was cold with fear, hatred, relief. And I'd marked myself as a target.

Footsteps.

Definite, slow, shuffling; a little to the left of me. I held my breath and crabbed sideways until my shoulder touched the bed. Flat to the floor, I did a half-roll and reached up to touch the slats of the wooden frame. Safe, safe, safe! If I could keep quiet. Absolutely quiet. Whoever it was didn't have a torch. They expected to find me asleep. Something tickled the length of my forearm. I shrunk down.

'Christie!'

A yell down the corridor. In the room the footsteps went back and forth, then the door creaked, then there was silence. I didn't move. A flickering yellow dazzle appeared in my vision. I wondered if I was going to pass out. Then the edge of the door and the brickwork became visible, shadows jumped, and I realized that someone was running down the corridor with a torch.

'Christie?' Ruric shouted.

I crawled out from under the bed, dust clinging to my shirt, barelegged and feeling vulnerable.

'There – I think there was someone in here.'

'Think? Don't you know?' She jammed the torch in the wall-bracket and came across, grabbing my hand. I yelled. Bright drops spattered.

'I didn't see.' The blood fascinated me. It had run down my arm to my elbow – that had been the tickling sensation. My hand felt as if it had been hit with a hammer. There was a deep slash across the palm. I must have put it up and run it into the *harur* blade.

Ruric abruptly left the cell. There were more torches: Branic, Rhiawn, Maric, and Ho-Telerit appeared. Time disjointed. I sat down while Rhiawn bathed and bandaged my hand, and breathed deeply, and steadied myself against rising hysteria.

My hand was a raw sharp mass of pain.

'You're lucky,' he said, 'it hasn't touched the tendons. You'll keep the use of it.'

He let go of my hand reluctantly, staring curiously at it. Hadn't he seen the difference before? I thought, and laughed shakily. It was my right hand.

'Ruric—' I said. She came back into the cell.

'You've no idea who it was? Were they heavy or light, quick or clumsy? Was it *harur-nilgiri, harur-nazar*?'

'I'm sorry, I – it was too dark – I don't know.'

Branic stormed back in. I hadn't seen her go. She towered over Ruric, furious.

'Your soldiers refuse to let me outside! There are drawn swords everywhere. In the house of the Goddess!'

'Theocratic house or not, it's under martial law.' Ruric was cool.

'I've directed my commander to put guards on all doors, at the stables, and on the outer gate. I want no one leaving here. Ho-Telerit, wake anyone who isn't already awake and get them assembled in the hall.'

Rhiawn left with Branic. I sat on the bed, just beginning to take in what had happened. Ruric seated herself beside me.

'Have you any ideas?' Her hand was on her swordhilt. I saw where her gaze went.

'I don't believe it was the kid.'

Maric looked up, scared. 'It wasn't, *t'an*.'

Ruric didn't look convinced. 'Come along to the hall, Christie, there might be something that triggers your memory. You might recognize someone. No, the *ashiren* too. *Ke* walks in front of me.'

I laced my britches, not bothering to put boots on, and followed Ruric back through the winding passages. Kem met her outside the hall.

It was while they were talking that I remembered the medical kit. It was in the cell. So was the stunner. I wanted the use of both, and I should have remembered before. I was slipping: that annoyed and scared me.

I left Ruric there, going quietly back down the corridor. It wouldn't take a minute, I thought.

I walked into the room and on to the point of a blade.

CHAPTER 8

Assassin

I went down as if I'd been dropped, already rolling, and caught him across the shins. The unfinished thrust took him forward. He fell, twisting. We came up facing each other. It was the man with the scarred face. He had his back to the door, *harur-nilgiri* still in his hand. Unarmed, I fell automatically into the ready position, as if this were a practice bout.

He cut. Incredibly fast. I swayed, let it slide past me. Balance. Too slow. The sleeve of my shirt snagged, the cloth turning red like blotting paper soaking up ink. Adrenalin pounding. Watch the eyes, the eyes and not the blade!

Grey light. Stars. No chance to turn and grab the stunner lying in the cell's far corner. Silver light sliding on metal. The cautious sighting for a skewering thrust. He's angry. I'm unarmed. I've dodged his cuts and slashes: yes, he's angry. Good. And I move right—

Metal skids across brickwork. Panic: *no*! but it's all I can do to back off safely. Out of reach. How long before I'm cornered: not long. Now: the feint, the circling, eye and eye. The ferocity of the dance.

And thrust.

I can't get close and throw him. No chance, not one-handed. (Concentrate: ignore the raw pain there.) He's stronger than I am, can't hold him.

And the razor-edged thrust—

Caught between two walls, cornered. And if I knock his arm aside, the return cut will take me just between the ribs, blunt and hollow-sounding as a butcher's cleaver; and I can't hold him.

Not fear: certainty. You fucked it up, Christie.

Coming for me quick, no place to move to, can't move; taking me high in the chest, is it, or the throat, or—

So I came forward and saw the surprise on his face. Left-handed, not blocking the thrust but catching his wrist, pulling him forward.

The blade slid over my shoulder.

Still gripping his wrist, and the point slammed into the wall. There was a sharp sound clear in the air that – except for hurried breathing – was silent. Ugly: a snapping sound. His hand still tangled in the grip. A moment of numb stillness, neither of us believes this.

He shook his hand free of the guard, dropped the blade, and slammed through the door. Anger took over: utter, cold, and certain. Total: destroying all training and thought. So that I had the door open and was running down the passage, yelling, no, *screaming* with hate; the stunner in my hand and no recollection of picking it up. Running and firing left-handed, but the corridors twisted: I couldn't get a line on him.

He kicked another door shut in my face, and I swung it open – a dead-end room, trapped him. But someone hung on to my arm and shouted, then I was freed and someone caught me a tremendous clout across the head.

'Christie, stop! *Stop!*'

I stood still, shaking, frightened at myself. I hadn't expected to tap such reserves of fear and fury. Careless, I thought. Jesus Christ, use your brains, can't you!

Fear and fury: the time I was beaten up when I was a kid, the time I was followed home by a gang of youths, hugging the street-lit centre of a dark road. The child's fear, and the woman's. And the same snarling reflex: you touch me and I'll fucking kill you!

'He's claimed sanctuary!'

'Ruric?' When I wiped my face, it was wet. Things focussed. The dark woman gripped my arm.

The door opened on a domed room, white plaster walls reflecting star light from a skylight in the roof. The man knelt beside a low circular rim of stone. Light reflected from the well water onto his twisted face. He cradled his swelling wrist. Broken: I saw the jutting edge of bone under taut white skin. His eyes watched me with blank hatred. I raised the stunner.

'You can't kill him, he's under the Goddess's care,' Ruric insisted.

'I'm not going to kill him. Just knock him out.'

'You can't touch him!'

'Don't tell me what I can't do.'

'*T'An* Commander—' Kem came running up and stopped, taking in the situation. I heard others coming. It must have taken a very short time, that clash: the razor-edge of circling metal, and the fear.

It was almost like a practice session back on Earth, unarmed combat against the blows of a wooden staff. There, a mistake meant bruises. And here . . . the shirt-sleeve stuck to my arm, where the hairline cut was already dry. I couldn't seriously believe someone had tried to use a length of sharp metal to kill me.

'He's under the Goddess's protection,' Ruric repeated. Rhiawn and Branic came up, others following them. Kem and Ho-Telerit kept them back.

'You mean to say that because he's standing there – in that room – you won't touch him?'

'In a Wellhouse? I can't. I've gone far enough as it is. Even as *T'An* Commander I'd be in trouble if I did more.' She glanced over her shoulder. Rhiawn and Branic glared at her, stiff-faced. 'Sutha-fiori would back me, but she doesn't need me making trouble between her and the church. She had enough of that bringing you here. No, I think I've got to leave this one.'

The palm of my hand ached bone-deep. I was afraid. Wounds turn septic. Ruric had had an arm amputated for something not much more serious in its beginning.

'I'm not bound by your laws. I won't kill him. But I'll bring him out.'

She didn't let go of my arm. 'If you use Witchbreed weapons in the house of the Goddess—'

'It's nothing to do with the Golden Witchbreed, it's a coherent sound amplifier!'

'I know that. But anyone between the Wall and the Inner Sea will call you a liar. It's a pity you can't handle the *harur* blades.' There was acid mockery in her tone.

'I have no intention of walking in there with half a yard of butcher's knife and you know it.' And it occurred to me that if he'd had time to draw *harur-nazari* as well as *harur-nilgiri* when I surprised him, I might not be having this argument.

'Unwise, in any case: if you upset the church it won't please your government or mine. The man isn't stupid,' she said, loosing her grip on me, 'It was only bad luck that he didn't kill you the first time.'

'*Bad* luck?'

She abandoned her temper. 'His. And our good fortune.'

'I'm glad you think so.'

She looked at the man, who gave no sign that he heard us. 'I'll leave Ho-Telerit and her people here, keep him penned in. He'll either give in or attempt escape, in which case she can bring him along after us.'

'He might get away. At least find out who he is, who sent him.'

She shrugged, but stood in the doorway and asked questions.

He never moved or answered. She came away, signalling to Kem, who placed guards at the door.

'I'd say he's a hired sword, Ymir or Rimon by his clothes – that style of *harur-nilgiri* is south-Rimon. Picked up in Tathcaer and set to trail us, hoping for a surprise kill.'

Now it was finished I was experiencing a tight knot of tension in my stomach.

'Whoever it was, SuBannasen or another, won't try that again,' Ruric continued. 'Not with us ready for it. And we'll have their name out of him soon.'

'So we carry on to Roehmonde?' I couldn't see any advantage in returning to Tathcaer.

'We do. We're formidable enemies, when we're ready.' She smiled at me, not maliciously. 'Even you, *S'aranth*.'

It was an epithet I'd heard the troopers use, but after Terison it had a different tone. Maric translated it as 'swordless' (with the implication it held of being *ashiren*). I remembered what Geren had said, a long time ago: it's the one thing that might tell against you. All Southlanders acquire use-names. Ruric was Yelloweyes. From then on I was Christie *S'aranth*.

I carried the pain of my hand while it healed, but I was disturbed by the violence of the response it had called out of me.

The sedatives could take the pain away, but nothing could make me sleep the rest of the night. After a while, when it became apparent that there was no use trying, I lay and watched the patch of sky visible through the window: the moving stars, the dulling to first twilight, and the gradual unstoppable lightening of dawn.

I felt . . . not afraid, not angry, not shocked or excited: but as if I had been woken up to the degree where sleep was no longer a human necessity. The effects of shock are the same, I think, whether its origins are good or bad.

Terison was lost in the early morning haze. The mist pulled back from the arch of the blue sky. We rode over peaty heathland among bird's-wing scrub and thousandflower-moss. Light flashed off *siriye* webs white with dew. There was a cool wind, a smell of damp earth, and the harsh calling of *rashaku*. The morning was painfully bright, lack of sleep beginning to make itself felt.

'According to the map we can pick up one of the Old Roads north of here. That should speed up the pace.' Ruric's heels dug into Gamble's hide and the *marhaz* edged closer to Gher. In a low exasperated tone she said, 'Sunmother's tits! What's the matter with you? You're acting like a woman after her first fight.'

'I – well, yes, I suppose it was.'

'You're seriously telling me—'

'That was the first time I ever put combat training into practice. Somehow I never expected to have to.' Gher hissed, reluctant to pick his way through boggy ground, and I reached forward and scratched between his horns. 'I don't know how I feel about it. Your people treat me differently . . .'

'You've to expect that.' She was shrewd. 'Up until now they've taken you and your kin for overgrown *ashiren*. Now they know you're the same as us, it's just your methods that are different.'

The man's scarred face stayed with me. That, and the noise that bone makes when it snaps.

'I'm not a violent person.'

'Nor I,' said the Orthean woman, 'and never when it isn't necessary.'

'That's what the *T'An* Commander says?'

She laughed sourly. 'I'm no bloody-sword barbarian. I play the game to keep us out of wars. But when I have to, I can finish one in my favour faster than anyone alive. That's why Suthafiori made me *T'An* Commander.'

We lost some time before noon when the cart bogged down in wet ground, but after that we made a good pace and came about mid-afternoon to stands of *lapuur* trees and level ground. Ruric called a meal break.

'There,' she said as we walked out from under the yellow-green fronds of *lapuur*. 'The Old South Road.'

At first I thought it was only flat land, and then I saw that it ran straight as a ruler towards the low ridges of the north. South, it vanished under the wet earth. A strip of hard ground some thirty feet wide, it made a cutting through the distant ridges.

'The 'Breed made roads where it suited them, and not where it suited the land,' Ruric said. 'Kem won't like travelling on that but I want to make up time.'

I walked over for a closer look. Digging down with a belt-knife, I found some six or eight inches of soil and then rock. When I had cleared enough for a good look, I found a smooth, flat surface of blue-grey stone; a stone that I couldn't begin to scratch with the knife. There was a line too straight to be a crack. Two stones butted together that couldn't be pried apart: this was a paved road.

'Have you finished grubbing about in the dirt?' Ruric asked, strolling back from her meal. 'We're ready to go.'

'Yes. No. How long has this been here?'

She shook her head. 'Legends say since Sandor's time, the last Emperor. I don't know. Way before the fall of the Golden Empire.'

Three, maybe four thousand years. I stood up and brushed the mud off my knees, appalled at antiquity.

'If we—' she stopped, staring back across the heath. 'Ho-Telerit. That was quick. Slow down, woman, you'll have your *marhaz* in a pothole! Wait a minute – only six riders?'

She ran back towards the carts. When I got there, the troopers were dismounting, and Ho-Telerit stood with an unhappy look on her broad face.

'You're swift,' Ruric commented.

'We left only a short time after you,' she admitted. 'We lost him, *T'An* Commander.'

'How?'

'He was missing after the mid-morning bell. My people say he never passed them. I believe them. There's more than one way out of a Wellhouse, *T'An*, especially if you've a priest's aid.'

'Branic,' Ruric said, hand hooked in her swordbelt. 'That flare-tempered, landless woman Branic!'

Ho-Telerit nodded. I said, 'You mean she let him go?'

'Let him? She likely gave him a *marhaz* to go on. And she knows I can't lodge a complaint, things are touchy enough as it is with the church.' She frowned, then shook her head. 'All right, Ho-Telerit. Kem, I want us moving, right now.'

'Was Branic paid?' I was getting as paranoid as an Orthean.

'No, I don't think so.' She whistled Gamble. Maric came over with Gher. 'That was to let me know they don't like *harur* law in a theocratic house. And there's nothing I can do about it. Let's move. The further away I get from these southern conspiracies, the happier I'll be.'

The Old Road took us north for two days, almost eighty *seri* through desolate moorland. On the third day we crossed the Tulkor river where it joins the river Turi. We came into low hills and flame-red *ziku* forests, and turned north-east to follow the Turi up into northern Ymir.

It was strange country to ride through, almost deserted. If it hadn't been for a few cultivated fields I could have believed it uninhabited. We travelled many *seri* before coming across one of the castle-warren-like *telestres*, and long intervals before we passed any others.

I got into the rhythm of the journey: rising at first twilight and riding until the stars rose, with a break at noon to eat. Sometimes we had guest-right and slept in a *telestre*, sometimes in one of the infrequent companion-houses. But as we went further north the troopers often made open camp, setting up tents and lighting fires like born nomads. If there were no *telestres* for supplies, the scouts did more hunting than scouting.

On Stathern Firstweek Fiveday we arrived at Salmar, usually admitted to be the northernmost of the Ymirian-speaking *telestres*. It was the fourteenth day since leaving Tathcaer.

'I like to break a journey,' Ruric observed, as we walked through the fields of Salmar. Hives stood in rows under the sheltering bird's-wing scrub: hives of the *chirith-goyen* clothworm – or at least, two or three of the several hundred varieties of that species. A lot of the northern *telestres* are *chirith-goyen* harvesters and weavers. And if not the clothworm, then the *becamil* webweaver-beetles.

'But I'd not have done it if I'd known. Mother!' She chuckled.

'A five-birth and a three-birth within days of each other – no wonder they're busy right now!'

I pictured the total breakdown that would have produced in any family I knew. But the Salmar community, a *telestre* of nearly two hundred people, was managing nicely.

'It's all right for you,' I said, 'having your kids in quads and quintuplets. We have ours one at a time!'

She was thoughtful. 'I had a single-birth.'

The intense sun shone on the *chirith-goyen* webs. We walked across the mossgrass, back towards the stables.

'How many births, then, would you have in a life?' Ruric sounded startled.

'Without preventive methods? It's been a long time, but . . . my great-great-grandmother was the ninth child of a family of eighteen.'

She stared. 'I wondered how there got to be so many of you.'

'And you?'

'Two births,' she said, 'perhaps three; or sometimes only one. Not all will live.'

That confirmed what Adair had told me. Allowing for accident, disease, and primitive medical standards, I doubted Orthe would ever have a population problem. I made a mental note to add quarantine restrictions to the suggestions in my report.

'I saw Elmet's three,' I said, 'they looked healthy. But three girls at once, that's a handful.'

'There's the father and the milk-mothers to help. She'll probably stand as milk-mother herself to some of the five-birth.' As we came into the stable yard she stopped and faced me. 'What do you mean, girls?'

'They were, weren't they?'

'They're *ashiren*. How can you tell what sex *ke* will be until *ke* are adult?'

That simple. Standing there in the sunlight, with the hissing of *marhaz* and the burning odour of the smithy: I thought, *Adair, you only had to ask . . .*

'You mean your young are born sexed?' Ruric was incredulous. 'Born adult?'

'You mean yours aren't?'

There was one of those silences that ensued whenever we tripped over species differences. Maric passed us, leading Oru, and waved to me cheerfully.

'He—'

'*Ke*'s about a year off change,' Ruric said. 'The *ashiren* usually develop into adults around fourteen, that's why they're prone to sickness about that time. Christie – if your *ashiren* are born sexed, how can you tell when they're adult?'

'There are changes. Nothing that drastic.' I studied Maric, where he stood holding Oru's head while the smith lifted a back hoof. Something in the mouth, the eyes . . . yes, I could see him as a girl. But my first impression of him as male contradicted that.

I could see Maric as boy or girl, but I couldn't do what the Ortheans do, see *ke* as neuter. It was either/or. And, realizing that, I knew why the xeno-team hadn't seen it. It was not a view one ever questioned. Either/or.

Nothing is private in the one *telestre*. And somehow I seemed to have become part of the Southland, while Adair and Eliot and the others remained isolated in Tathcaer.

How can you bring up a child if you don't know what sex it is? Some reactionary part of my mind protested. But I realized the question was nearly as meaningless to me as it would be to Ruric, and I let the subject drop.

After Salmar we left the hills behind. The land was flat and fertile, broken by winding streams, and there were many of the tri-vaned windmills that the Roehmonders use. We rode winding tracks between grain fields now harvested to stubble and stacks. This part of Stathern was fine, but the nights were getting chill. Still going north, we crossed tawny grassland where double-horned *skurrai* grazed, and were two days travelling between amber mossgrass and eggshell-blue sky with only the hissing bellow of the beasts for company. The *telestres* were large, the Ortheans more reserved – or perhaps it was just that my Roehmonde was worse than my Ymirian – but they granted guest-right to the *T'An* Commander of the Southland.

Hills broke the horizon again as we came to the beginning of the Roehmonde forest *telestres*. The *tukinna* are tall and spindly,

91

grey-green, with crooked branches and rosettes of tightly-rolled leaves. Nothing grows under them but mossgrass and goldenfern. The *telestres* depend either on timber or hunting for survival. We made camp in clearings, and kept fires burning at night. The silence of the brilliant starlight was broken by snarls and cries, and the metallic whooping of *rashaku*, but we were too large a party to be attacked.

The slash across my palm healed. I rubbed salve in to make it flexible, and took painkillers when necessary. Perik, one of the scouts, offered me *ataile* leaves to chew. I refused, not being sure of the effect on human metabolism. She and I often rode together, and Maric and another scout named Vail rode with us. There was some discussion about unarmed combat, which I demonstrated, and the finer points of *harur* swordcraft, which she attempted to teach me. We were neither of us good pupils.

Markstones were infrequent but we managed to keep to the right track. Ruric was determined to press on in the good weather. Six days brought us through thick forest to Remoth, where gaunt hills went up towards the east, and we skirted west of them through steep river-gorges. The next night brought us to a companion-house at Temethu beside the river Beruth.

'Look,' Maric said. 'Too far for bow-shot, but I suppose we don't need to hunt now.'

Down between the *tukinna* trees I saw first curving backs, then raised heads, and then – in the instant before flight – grave, spindly beasts as large as *skurrai*. Their back fur was rich brown. They rose on strong haunches, tiny front legs drawn up to their scaled chests; they were almost black against the sunlit goldenfern. I saw them bound away under the trees.

'What are they?'

He touched the brown pelt on Oru's saddle. '*Wirazu.*'

The path curved closer to the river and there was no use talking, the thundering water made it impossible. High, forested gorge walls rose on either side of us, and the daystars were bright in the narrow strip of sky. A fine spray hung over the rocks.

I rode up beside Ruric, Maric following me. He was smart in clean tunic and polished boots. The troop hadn't left Temethu until noon, being occupied with cleaning gear and grooming *marhaz*, and putting on the long-saved last clean change of clothes. Ruric wore a brown *becamil* cloak embroidered with gold thread, and all her rank-badges gleamed on her belt. I'd had to compromise; you can't ride a *marhaz* in a formal skirt. I settled for formal Earth jacket and Ymirian britches.

We crossed the river by a broad stone bridge, riding down a track that was paved where the gorge widened. Clumps of blue thousandflower rooted in the shale. *Tukinna* furred the high slopes, rising out of the damp shadow. The river ran quietly.

I rode, hearing that wine-glass reverberation: wind in the scrolled leaves of the *tukinna*. There was a disturbing metallic taste in the air.

Smell is the keenest way to memory. I paused, and what came flooding back was the heat of summer streets before I was five years old. To recall that warmth, then to open eyes on the pale northern shadows . . .

. . . and realize that river dampness was bringing me the previously-unnoticed odour of *tukinna*, and that the smell of this alien vegetation was identical to the road-tar that melted in yellow Earth summers, and ran in the gutters of childhood.

Even the most basic certainties can change, form again into something strangely new.

The road made a sharp turn north.

It was Stathern Secondweek Nineday, twenty six days since we left Tathcaer, the fastday before the autumn solstice. I rode over the bridge where the Berufal meets the Beruth and entered Corbek.

PART THREE

CHAPTER 9

Hospitality of T'An *Roehmonde*

'Christie?'

'I'm out here.'

Ruric appeared beside me on the balcony. She was wearing one of the long sleeveless Roehmonder coats, unbuckled and showing the rich *zilmei* pelt lining. It was a chill morning, even in the room behind me where the brazier's embers glowed.

'I thought I'd tell you, I'm leaving after the solstice feast tonight. Going up to Path-of-Skulls in the morning.'

'I didn't think you'd go so soon.'

'I want to talk to the garrison commander, Asshe. He's an old friend of mine.' She leaned on the wrought iron balustrade, gazing out over Corbek. 'I want to know what he makes of all this . . . of course, the garrison gets its supplies from the *telestres* north of here, but he comes down to Corbek on occasion. And I've got to make the official visit in any case – the Barrens are quiet, and he thinks the barbarians are planning another series of raids.'

'And Corbek?' That was the crux of it.

'You saw it when we came in! There was always a problem here, even eight years back when I last saw the place, but never – *never* – this bad.'

Corbek lay spread beneath us, its clusters of towers and domes in pale grey stone. Frost whitened the wrought-iron gates and balconies. Carts jolted through unpaved lanes. From here it was just possible to see over gentle slopes to the watermills along the Berufal, and the barges on the Beruth. Thick early morning haze hung over both rivers like cotton wool, the horizon was grey, and it was only at the roof of the sky that I saw pale stars and sunlight. Hidden – but not forgotten, sharp in my mind – were the wooden shacks and mud-rutted slums where the rivers met.

'There are always a few landless men and women,' the Orthean woman admitted, 'and it's inevitable that they drift into cities, I suppose. But so many – and with *ashiren*! What's the Wellkeeper thinking of?'

'What could a Wellkeeper do?'

She swung round, her back to the sheer drop. 'Send Earth-speakers to find out why they left their *telestres*! Find new *telestres* that they could become *n'ri n'suth* to. Apprentice them as *l'ri-an* in the city! What else are Wellhouses for?'

She paced the stone-tiled floor, apparently oblivious that she was barefoot to the cold. Her single hand sought and rested on the hilt of her *harur* blade. When she looked at me again her opaque eyes had cleared, and she relaxed.

'Sorry. Why shout at you, after all? But I don't like to see this, and I wish you didn't have to either.'

'I haven't seen real poverty on Orthe before, no. But I was bound to meet it eventually.'

'Is it so inevitable, then, for you?'

'Yes, I think it is. And I can remember when there were no beggars on the streets of London. Corbek's slums, for all their dirt-poverty, at least function.'

The line of sunlight crept down the face of the bluff, brightening the windows and balconies of the rooms built into the cliff. Our shadows fell sharp and black against the half-circle arch that opened into the room.

'How long will you be away?' I asked.

'Say, eight or nine days riding north, and I'll have to stop over a few days . . . Expect me early in Torvern Forthweek, if the weather's good.' Her preoccupied expression returned. 'I'll send one of the troopers south now, let Suthafiori know how things stand here. Not that she can do much.'

'Maybe I'll ride back to Tathcaer with you,' I suggested as we went into the low-ceilinged room. 'I should have finished here in three weeks' time.'

'Yes, why not,' she agreed.

I never made that ride with her.

The Roehmonders ring their day bells in chimes. The cascade of the sunset bells died away across the city. I finished brushing my hair quickly, standing before the full length mirror of beaten silver. I couldn't help smiling: the deceptive light of Carrick's Star had tanned my uncovered arms and face, but the rest of me was pale. I was piebald. The snake-texture of the Orthean skin doesn't tan.

Formal dress again: dark skirt and jacket, the price for coming to a civilized city. But I was glad to be there, glad not to be on the open road with dirt and bugs and no hot water.

I went down the flights of stairs that honeycombed the cliff, inside and out, to where Maric waited with Gher and Oru. We rode along the muddy lanes to the end of the bluff. It was a *seri* or more to the *T'An* Roehmonde's household. Our breath steamed on the air. Semi-circles of light shone from the arches above us. The last of the season's *siriye* floated in the chill. Ruric rode up on Gamble, coming from the river side of the city, not inclined to talk much.

The descending line of the cliff face merged imperceptibly into the walls of the *T'An* Roehmonde's household, and we turned and rode through a tunnel hacked out of the rock. Coming out of the low arch, we were in the natural amphitheatre formed at the side of the bluff, in a vast courtyard surrounded by domed buildings and round towers. The main doors of the hall were open, spilling light out into the ornamental pools and fountains; and when I looked up past the carved facade of the hall I could just make out the dome of the Wellhouse that crowned the bluff.

'Maric,' Ruric said quietly, as we dismounted, 'you're *l'ri-an* for the envoy tonight in the hall. Just keep your ears open in the kitchens, will you?'

He nodded, taking Gamble's rein and leading the other *marhaz* away.

'What do you think he's going to hear?' I was curious.

'If I knew, I wouldn't ask.' Then she grinned. 'All right. He'll hear whatever won't be said within earshot of the envoy, the *T'An* Commander, or the *T'An* Roehmonde. Which might be useful.'

The game again, I thought. The omnipresent game of intrigue played within the *telestre*, or between *telestres*, or between cities – and perhaps between worlds, now.

'*T'An* Commander.' A plump Orthean male met us, bowing. '*T'An* envoy. Please, come this way.'

He led us through an antechamber and into the main hall. I recognized him from the reception committee of the day before: he was middle-aged, and unusually overweight for an Orthean, with a dark mane receding into a crest. The Roehmonder dress – long tunic, loose trousers tucked into short boots – was topped in his case by a *wirazu* pelt, and a belt studded with gems the size of hazelnuts. His six-fingered hands were clumsy with rings, a beaten silver chain hung round his neck, even the hilts of the *harur-nilgiri* and *harur-nazari* were thickly ornamented. The name surfaced after some digging in my memory: Verek Howice Talkul. Talkul was currently the ruling *telestre* in Corbek.

'Ruric!' An elderly man came forward and gripped her hand, looking her up and down.

'*T'An* Koltyn.'

'Ah, you sober southerners,' he remarked, taking in her plain dress. Her only ornaments were the rank-badges on her belt. 'I give you greeting. You also, envoy. Come: sit with me.'

He leaned on Howice's arm as he walked. Telvelis Koltyn Talkul, *T'An* Roehmonde, was the oldest Orthean I'd seen. His mane was white and sparse, his eyes half-veiled, and the flesh seemed to have shrunk onto his bones. Narrow chin and broad forehead: the Orthean face was not very human, studied in that condition.

'Sit' was a misleading term – the Roehmonders ate reclining on low couches. We made our way between them. Knowing Ymirian, Roehmonder had not been too hard to pick up. Koltyn's pace was slow, he stopped often to introduce other members of the *telestre*. Names filed themselves in my memory. There were over a hundred people in the hall, from *ashiren* to the old. And all one family: brothers, sisters, uncles, mothers, cousins, *n'ri n'suth*: the linkage of a *telestre* is inclusive and complex.

A great firepit was sunk in the middle of the hall, and *l'ri-an* walked on a level below us, turning meat on spits. Howice helped the *T'An* Roehmonde down onto his couch, and we all took couches round him. I noticed a prevalence of brown robes, both Earthspeaker and Wellkeepers. Maric came over with wine for Ruric and I.

'Verek Sethin Talkul,' Howice introduced the group. Sethin was a thin woman, neither young nor old. 'My sister. Sethin Falkyr, her son. The Earthspeaker Theluk. The Wellkeeper Arad.'

Falkyr was a neat cold man in his twenties, Theluk a dark-maned woman somewhat older; and Arad a contemporary of Howice, lean where the other man was stout.

'Theluk?' Ruric said as the *l'ri-an* were bringing round platters. 'I used to know a Theluk n'ri n'suth Edris up at Path-of-Skulls, a few years back.'

'I was your Second one winter, commander – *T'An*, I mean.' The woman shifted, embarrassed for a moment. 'The year the Simmerath nomads attacked.'

'I remember. Eight, no, nine winters back. Yes. And you're Earthspeaker now, and not Edris *telestre*?'

'Since six years ago. I was called. I mostly work down the east coast, but I've come upriver for the winter.'

'For the winter, was it?' the Wellkeeper Arad remarked, and the woman veiled her eyes. The food came round, and I heard Ruric quietly asking Theluk about conditions in east Roehmonde, but didn't hear the reply.

The *l'ri-an* served great steaks of *wirazu* and *zilmei*, with root vegetables and black bread, and later fish from the coast, and *hura* clams from the river. I ate lightly and drank hardly at all, wanting a clear head. There's no Orthean tabu against talking business over a meal, indeed I sometimes think it's the only reason they eat together.

Iron stands held candles by the score, black iron wrought into eye-bending loops and curves. Candlelight glinted on rings and arm-bracelets, on *harur* blades and buckles, and on crystal beads braided into Orthean manes. The stone floor was inset with patterns. It was warm where we were, by the firepit, but people had pulled their couches away from the chill at the doors.

'You had a long journey, envoy,' Howice said, as the second wine came round. 'How long does it take, travelling between the worlds?'

'Ninety days from my world to yours. Our days are shorter than yours, though.' He seemed satisfied. I wasn't going into details of FTL ships – the FTL drive is instantaneous in any case, it's getting far enough out of a star's gravity well to use it that takes the time.

'And to send word to your home?'

'The same.' There's no altering that, until we get a transmitter that works through trans-light space.

'A long exile.' He shook his head, sympathetic.

'I'm glad to be here.'

'And your *telestre*?' Sethin asked.

Orthean questions fall into a pattern after a while – what kind of *telestre* do we live in, why do we live apart from our families, what land do we hold (the term 'owner' passed out of my vocabulary), what weapons do we carry; how many *ashiren* do I have, who is my *arykei*, who is my *s'an telestre*, what is the custom of 'marriage', what is the Earth court like? I talked to Sethin without more than my average number of mistakes in Roehmonder terms and inflection.

There was an odd tinge to her skin, and sepia shadows under her clouded eyes. A little later she excused herself and left, and I saw Howice's eyes follow her anxiously. The old man, Koltyn, appeared not to notice; he was conversing with Ruric. I realized Sethin was a sick woman.

'No doubt we seem primitive to you.' There was an edge to Howice's voice. 'You and your kin who travel off the world doubtless have easier methods of doing things. Mining, for example. There are many forest *telestres* who'd like to hear of your methods of mining metal and quarrying stone.'

'I'm not an expert on that science, I'm afraid,' I said, taking closer notice of the man. 'One of my kin – my colleagues – in Tathcaer would be better qualified to tell you that.'

'Would they come here?' he asked.

'It's possible.' Ruric interrupted her conversation with the *T'An*. 'Once Suthafiori's had Christie's report. I don't agree with it myself, but—'

'You don't agree?'

Howice's pounce was indecently quick, I thought. His layer of charm was convincing, but very thin.

'Don't get me wrong. I approve of Christie.' Ruric grinned broadly at me. 'I even like some of her kin in Tathcaer. But letting her people – who we don't know at all – loose on the Southland, that I'm not so sure about.'

I hadn't been able to change her opinion. I wasn't sure that I wanted too. Orthe was a definite case for making haste slowly, and my reports were being coloured by that fact.

'We've much to gain by meeting Christie's people, I'm sure.' Howice was urbane. 'Though we're poor in Roehmonde, and have besides the Wall to guard, and tribes who envy us and would take what little we do have.'

'There again we come to methods,' the young man, Falkyr, said sardonically. 'Your people have weapons, I would suppose, that put our *harur* blades and winch-bows to shame?'

Howice gave him an angry glare. He was lean and crop-maned, Sethin's son, with something of a detached manner.

'None that we'd bring here,' I answered him, watching the quickly hidden greed on Howice's face. 'It's our strictest law.'

'So you carry no swords between worlds,' Arad's deep voice said, 'and yet you carry news of people who do not live by the Goddess's ways, and that may be fully as dangerous.'

I said, 'I can only tell you the truth.'

'Who said the truth wasn't dangerous?' Falkyr demanded, and laughed.

'Lies, also,' Theluk said softly, looking at Arad, 'and mostly they are dangerous to the liar.'

There was a circuit of hostility between them, Howice and Arad, Falkyr and Theluk; something they were aware of that we didn't know. I caught Ruric's eye. She gave a meaningful glance at Koltyn.

The *T'An* Roehmonde was propped up semi-reclining on cushions, staring abstractedly at the firepit. I put it down to old man's vagueness. Then I saw the thin thread of saliva leaking from the corner of his mouth. The membranes covered his eyes completely.

'The *T'An* sleeps,' Howice said, calling a *l'ri-an* who half-carried Koltyn from the hall. 'You'll excuse him tonight, I know, he is an old man and weary. I'll return in a moment.'

There was a brief hush in the hall as they left, and then the flutes picked up again, and there was singing over on the other side of the firepit, where the *ashiren* sat. Under cover of pulling the benches closer together, Ruric leaned over and spoke.

'Sleeps? That old man's senile! I couldn't put my finger on it till a while back, but when we were talking he thought it was nine years back, and I was commanding the Skulls garrison. Goddess!'

Her expression was pity mixed with disgust.

'He can't know it, can't realize it himself, or he'd renounce being *T'An* Roehmonde. But what's Talkul *telestre* thinking of? They must know he's in no condition—'

She broke off as Howice rejoined the group.

Theluk and Falkyr had been arguing heatedly for some minutes, and it was in the silence accompanying Howice's return that the argument broke surface.

'—nature of the Goddess—' Theluk stopped abruptly, with a glance at Arad.

'The Goddess being incarnate, then, on earth,' Falkyr pursued, as sceptical as I'd ever heard a Southlander be. 'In every generation?'

'Alive, and human,' Theluk said eagerly. 'Sometimes knowing Herself for what she is, and sometimes not aware but living as we live. And as liable to be a Roehmonder as an Ymirian, a woman of Kasabaarde as a man of the Rainbow Cities.'

I was all for staying out of religious arguments, but just then Falkyr gave me a superior smile.

'I suppose, then, that when She's here,' he said, 'She might very well come as an Otherworlder?'

There was an intake of breath from Arad. I swore mentally, cursing Falkyr. It was his way of annoying the Wellkeeper, but I didn't want it rebounding on my head. This was something to stop before it started.

'It's very unlikely, surely?' I said.

'But possible,' he needled Theluk. 'You said She is not always aware.'

'It's a question for the church,' Arad said harshly, 'and I agree with the envoy. In any case, the question is only ever settled with hindsight, after several generations.'

'You can answer me a question without waiting generations.' Ruric, distracting attention, stirring up trouble. 'The slums between the two rivers – eight years ago they weren't there, just a few landless men and women living round the barge-docks. Now there are shacks from the Berufal to the Beruth! What's happening?'

Theluk stared challengingly at Arad and I saw Falkyr watching with hooded eyes. Howice was apparently unaware of the whole discussion.

'The same problem, *T'An* Commander. The landless.' Arad was equally as hostile as Ruric. 'All the rogues and ruffians turned off their *telestres* come down to Corbek, and some ship out to the coast, and some stay and rot. What would you have me do, *T'An*, drive them out with swords?'

'If the *telestres* can't care for their own, they need looking to. In any case, the church has a duty—'

'And has performed it,' the Wellkeeper snapped.

'Are they *all* landless?' she asked, with that particular inflection that means Goddess as well as land. She was thinking of the *ashiren*, I knew.

'If a man or woman leaves their *telestre*, there must be a reason,' Arad persisted with the vehemence of an orator. 'We do not pick out of the dung-heap those who are too evil for even their own households.'

He glared round. People avoided his eye. Theluk looked as though she would have spoken, but then lowered her head.

'People must stay on their *telestres*.' Arad's gaze went past me to where Maric was pouring wine. 'When I was young, the *ashiren* didn't expect to be fostered hundreds of *seri* from home. We weren't made to become *l'ri-an* in other households. We stayed on the land where we belonged, forging the link with the Goddess. Now these rootless wanderers come to Corbek and expect us to take them in. No! Let them rot where they have chosen to be.'

Ruric turned on Howice. 'Does Koltyn agree with this?'

Faultlessly polite, Howice said, 'I'm afraid I can't discuss the *T'An*'s policies in his absence.'

Not long after that, the hall began to clear. Maric whispered that he was staying to help with the cleaning, and I agreed that he should. Ruric went off in Theluk's company, and Howice – I wasn't surprised to see – spent his time soothing the Wellkeeper's temper.

'Sanctimonious landless *amari*!' Falkyr said under his breath. Then he saw I'd overheard and shuttered his eyes. Abruptly he said 'Ride out with me tomorrow. I know the city. And you might as well answer my questions as theirs.'

'I might as well,' I agreed, cheerfully.

*

'I thought you'd gone,' I said. 'The troop has.'

'I'll catch them up on the road. I've sent Ho-Telerit south,' Ruric added, 'but there's something needs doing before I leave Corbek.'

'Maric brought me your message.' I looked behind. The *ashiren* was holding the reins of Gher and Oru, and Falkyr was just dismounting.

'Don't worry about Sethin Falkyr, he'll do as a witness.' She turned, walking up the muddy lane. She wore a blue *becamil* cloak thrown back from her left shoulder, letting the drape of the cloth conceal the pinned sleeve and stump of her right arm. You wouldn't automatically have recognized the *T'An* Commander.

'Did you talk to *kir*?'

'About the *l'ri-an*? Yes.' Maric had come home late the previous night, very puzzled. 'He says they're afraid, but doesn't know of what.'

'Being *l'ri-an* has a bad name in Corbek – and *I* don't know why.'

Ruric stopped where a blank wall was broken by an ornamental gate, waiting for the young man to catch us up.

'*T'An* Commander.' Falkyr was cool, unhurried.

The iron gate swung open, and I saw Theluk in the shadow of the archway. She squinted up at the starbright autumn sky, eyes half-hooded.

'It's nearly time.'

'We're ready.' Ruric caught the challenging stare of Falkyr, and bowed, and ushered us both through the archway ahead of her. We crossed the tiny courtyard, and Theluk pulled open a heavy wooden door.

'Small, for a Wellhouse,' Falkyr commented, 'but a better-known one would not have suited you so well, perhaps?'

'Wellkeeper Uruth, here, is my friend,' Theluk said.

'And so lets you have the use of his house. What it is to have friends,' he said ironically, watching Ruric.

The room was small, domed, the stone walls lime-washed. A slot in the dome let in late morning light. The circle of the well mouth was black. We stood in a luminous twilight, except for one patch of white sunlight that showed dust on the floor, and flakes of lime.

'Who comes before the Goddess?' Theluk spoke formally.

'Lynne de Lisle Christie,' Ruric said.

'Who stands as her second?'

'*T'An* Commander *amari* Ruric Orlandis.'

'Who stands as witness?'

Ruric glanced at him. 'The son of Sethin sees this.'

'I witness it,' Falkyr said grudgingly. 'If you bring me here to see your fool trick, I suppose I can't deny I've seen it.'

'I'm not sure what you're doing,' I said, 'but are you sure it applies to an offworlder?'

'If it applies to those outside the Southland, it can apply to anyone. And there may come a time when you need to answer yes, if they ask you if you've been recognized by the Goddess.'

I couldn't back out. Ruric had that look of abstract determination that meant she was plotting in advance of events.

'It's time,' Theluk said, approaching the well. The black water's surface was motionless.

There was a soundless explosion of light. I flung up one arm against the glare, and when I lowered it the room was pearl-bright with rainbow coruscations. Bells chimed across the city. The noon sun struck down through the slot in the dome, hit the surface of the well water, and dazzled us with luminosity.

'Here is Your daughter from a far—' Theluk hesitated '—a far world. Receive her name.'

Ruric's hand in the flat of my back pushed me forward. Theluk bent and dipped her hand in the well, lifted it dripping clear fire. She touched her wet fingers to my forehead, and both eyes. Momentarily I felt her heartbeat through her fingertips, the difference of her hands.

'The Goddess knows you,' she said, 'Lynne de Lisle Christie.'

'Witnessed,' Ruric said.

'Witnessed,' Falkyr echoed reluctantly.

Outside in the courtyard, I was still breathless and dazzled.

'If you need me, *t'an*, the Wellkeeper here will know where I am,' Theluk said awkwardly to me. She gripped Ruric's hand, and then made haste to swing the iron gates shut behind us.

'You think that will have any practical value?' Falkyr challenged Ruric.

'The point is, it's done, and I'm grateful.' I wasn't entirely sure for what, but her intentions were obvious.

She smiled, yellow eyes hooded. 'Torvern Forthweek,' she said. 'But you can always send a message up to the garrison. Though, knowing you, you won't need to.'

We walked down to where Maric held the *marhaz*.

Gher splashed mud as we cantered up beside the Berufal river. One of the rare autumn rainstorms had swept down the river valley and this was the first time in four days that we'd ridden outside the city.

The road was a morass. Shacks crowded close to it, sprawling wooden structures with board-tiled roofs. Some were old and disintegrating. In other places new, round, box-like rooms had been tacked on, two and three storeys high; staircases wound between them. Clothes hung on ropes strung between buildings. Steam went up into the rainwashed sunlight. The pig-like red guardbeasts, *kuru*, rooted in the dirt. Drab-clad *ashiren* played in the mud, or sat on steps blankly watching us ride by.

'You'd think they'd go,' I said. None of the structures were temporary. 'Why don't they leave?'

Falkyr shrugged.

'This doesn't happen in Tathcaer.' It was my only other point of reference.

'They don't belong.' Falkyr delicately edged his *marhaz* closer.

'To a *telestre*?'

'To anything or anybody.'

I'd been in the Southland just long enough to appreciate how atypical that was.

'Can't they go back to their *telestres*?'

For the first time in the several days I'd known him, Falkyr had no mordantly witty or sarcastic answer.

'There are certain new laws from the church. You heard Arad. We are not to leave our *telestres* without very good reason.' He didn't look at me. 'Having left for no better reason than that living there was impossible for them – they can't go back. And no one follows old custom and takes them in *n'ri n'suth*, or *l'ri-an*.'

'Because they're afraid?' I guessed.

'If it were Arad alone – or even the *T'An* alone—' His head came up and he straightened. 'I'll give my uncle his due: more people are prosperous because of it, because of keeping to their *telestres* and working; it's better for Roehmonde.'

'But some people pay a price.'

His eyes hooded. He smiled. 'There's always a price, *t'an*. Even your world's marvels come with a price on them, I'd say.'

He was formal again, irreverent and laughing; but I'd had a glimpse of an unhappy man. He'd said: leaving for no better reason than that living there was impossible . . .

Was it impossible living with Howice, with Sethin, with the sick old man? I didn't ask. Loyalty is to the *telestre*. He wouldn't answer.

It was Torvern Firstweek Sixday, the day I returned to the *T'An* Roehmonde's household to find another guest. A gaunt white-maned woman, whom I regarded for several minutes before I recognized her from our one previous encounter: Sulis n'ri n'suth SuBannasen, *T'An* Melkathi.

CHAPTER 10

Arykei

SuBannasen was seated in a high-backed chair, her silver-headed cane resting against its arm. Facing her across a small table was Sethin, and a young woman sat in the window seat breast-feeding a baby.

'Excuse me,' I said, 'I was looking for *t'an* Falkyr. Sorry.'

'No, don't go, come in.' Sulis n'ri n'suth SuBannasen beckoned.

'I was just leaving,' Sethin remarked. Her face paled as she stood up. 'You'll excuse me if I don't finish our game, Sulis.'

'Yes, of course.' The old woman sounded concerned.

'It's time for the *ashiren* to sleep, anyway. Jacan,' Sethin called the young woman.

The window of this tower room looked north across the amphi-theatre at the foot of the cliff, high enough to see across the city to where flat plains descended into cold haze. It was unusual in the Southland to have that exterior view. Thick, leaded glass kept out the chill.

SuBannasen watched Sethin and the woman leave. She frowned, shaking her head.

'It's a great pity,' she said, almost to herself, 'and she's a good woman. Will you be seated, *t'an* Christie? Do you play?'

A hexagonal *ochmir* board was set out on the table. It is the perennial game of the Southland, played on two hundred and sixteen triangular divisions of the board with an equal number of double-sided counters.

Unlike our games it is not based on territory but on manipula-tion. The counters are double-sided (traditionally blue-on-white and white-on-blue) and are of three kinds: the *ferrorn*, the *thurin*, and the *leremoc*. They are drawn sight-unseen from a bag in the course of the game. The object – which can take a remarkably long time to achieve – is to have all the pieces showing one's chosen colour.

To turn a piece, it is necessary to place a majority of one's own colour into the minor hexagons formed by any six of the board's triangular divisions. The minority pieces are then reversed to show the opposing colour. Now add to this that *ferrorn* may be placed and not thereafter moved, that *thurin* may be placed and afterwards move in a limited fashion, and that the rare *leremoc* can be moved as desired.

Add also that, as thought will show, the pattern of minor hexagons within the board is a shifting, overlapping one. And that what is on the obverse of a *ferrorn* may not be another *ferrorn*, but *thurin* perhaps, or even *leremoc* . . .

And you begin to see that *ochmir* is a game of labyrinthine and almost limitless complexity. Mobility, not rank; manipulation and not territory: the themes of interdependance and control are central to the Southland mind.

I knew just enough about it to see that Sulis had been winning.

'Thanks, no,' I refused her offer, 'I'm not very proficient at the game yet.'

'I sometimes think it can take a lifetime to master all the intricacies.' She smiled as I sat down opposite her. 'I'd heard you were here, and hoped we'd meet before I left.'

'You've come up from—' I remembered the name of her Melkathi city '—Ales-Kadareth?'

'I had a ship due to sail up the east coast, and then came upriver by barge. I'm a little old for rough travelling on Roehmonde roads – and land travelling is uncertain, they tell me. Besides, the sea is quicker.' There was amusement in her hooded eyes.

'The *marhaz* riding is tiring, yes.' I should have come on a ship, I thought, and then I wouldn't be in danger of becoming permanently bowlegged.

'But I wanted to see you,' she repeated. Her chicken-claw hands closed over the knob of her cane. She leaned forward. 'The last time we met, I was – a little formal, perhaps. Not because of yourself, envoy; but I dislike the company of grubby intelligencers.'

She was genuinely apologetic. There's no proof it was her behind the attacks, I thought. But no proof it wasn't. In this half-civilized land there's no lack of candidates. And yet if it wasn't SuBannasen, who was it?

'I don't know if you have plans,' she went on, 'but after you've finished here, perhaps you'd like to come south with me to Melkathi. I'm here because of my daughter's child Beris – *ke*'s old enough to foster in the Roehmonde court – but I shall be going back towards the end of Torvern Thirdweek.'

'Fostering seems to be out of fashion here, lately.'

'This was a previous arrangement of long standing. Howice . . .'

her brows quirked up. 'I have no mind to let Howice Talkul spoil my arrangements. And Koltyn was my friend.'

Despite myself, I was liking the old woman. But I wasn't anywhere near ready to trust her.

'It's a kind offer, *T'An* Sulis. Perhaps we could talk it over again when you're ready to leave, and then I'll have a better idea of what I'm going to do.'

'Certainly. I hope it's possible,' she said. 'My old bones won't put up with Roehmonder winters. They're bad for the health – so cold. But winters in Melkathi are mild. You'd find it much more comfortable there.'

I wanted to ask: is that an offer or a threat?

She reached out and fingered one of the *leremoc* counters. 'I might even have the time to teach you how to play *ochmir*.'

I came back one noon from riding with Falkyr to find Maric in a state of excitement.

'You've got a visitor, *t'an*.' He was grinning.

I pulled the embroidered hangings back and went into my rooms.

'Hello, Christie.'

'Haltern!' He gripped my arms. I must have knocked the breath out of him, thumping him on the back. 'Hal, I'm really glad to see you. When did you get here? What are you doing here?'

He laughed. His boots were muddy, his *becamil* cloak threadbare; I guessed he'd not long arrived in Corbek. There was some truth to Sulis's jibe about grubby intelligencers.

'You can't have met Ruric's messenger,' I calculated. Ho-Telerit had only been gone fourteen days.

'I met no messengers.' He took a bowl of herb-tea as Maric came back with them. We sat on the couch beside the brazier. 'Suthafiori sent me – the Goddess only knows why it was me, I loathe the provinces – after she'd had a report from an Earth-speaker.'

'That wouldn't be Theluk, would it?'

'Some such name.'

Suthafiori would send Haltern because she trusted him and I knew him. And because, although Theluk had been opposing Arad before I ever arrived, I couldn't pretend my presence wasn't disruptive.

'I'm just going to nose around quietly,' Haltern said. 'But what about you, did you have a good journey up here?'

'Oh lord, you don't know about that, either! We've got a lot to catch up on. And you must tell me how Tathcaer is.'

'Better than the bug-ridden north,' he grumbled.

110

Maric scavenged round the kitchen and brought up food, and we were still talking when the midnight bell sounded, and the boy was curled up asleep on the pelts in front of the brazier.

'Unarmed,' Haltern said as I finished my story. 'Unarmed and against a hired sword!'

Displaying the pink healing scar on my palm, I said, 'I did that too, if you remember.'

'There you are. Normally it takes years of training to be able to cut yourself like that.'

I laughed so hard I woke Maric up.

'I've talked enough, I'm going to bed.' Haltern stood. 'For an envoy, you make a good intelligencer; you notice a lot of what's going on.'

Some of my guesses, then, must correspond with Theluk's report. I said, 'There's one other thing. Sulis n'ri n'suth Su-Bannasen is here.'

'Is she, now? That's interesting. Yes.'

I reminded myself, there are private feuds going on here that you know nothing about, envoy, and they might have nothing to do with you. You might be justified in trusting the *T'An* Melkathi.

'It's possible I'll go to Ales-Kadareth,' I added.

His eyes opaqued. After a moment, he said, 'Have you made a decision yet?'

'I'm still considering it.'

'You know your own job best. But I should think about it carefully,' he advised. 'Yes. Very carefully. Goodnight, Christie.'

There was the usual round of meetings and dinners in Corbek, meeting the *s'ans* from the Roehmonde *telestres*. Often as not, Howice or Arad were there, and there was always a large number of brown-robed priests. I found the Roehmonders asked far less about trade than the Ymirians, and far more about technology. I visited some of the mining *telestres* to the east with Sethin Falkyr. Falkyr seemed to have appointed himself the envoy's companion, but his contribution was mostly sarcasm. When I went looking for Haltern, Maric told me he was staying anonymously in the city. No doubt keeping his mouth shut and his ears open, I thought.

The weather turned cold, with heavy frosts, and the first snow fell in the dry air, powdering the domes. I found nowhere warm in all of Corbek and went round bundled up in one of the long *zilmei* pelts. Falkyr laughed at me for a southerner.

'You and your world of marvels,' he said ironically, one afternoon. We were in his high tower room. He was dividing his attention between teaching me *ochmir* and trying to understand Earth, and as a result doing neither particularly well. 'With engines to take you through the sky, and do your work, and keep you warm – and no doubt bury you when you're dead. What do you find to do with yourselves?'

'Much the same as anybody else.' I moved a *thurin* into a minor hexagon, giving me a 4–2 majority. His two pieces, reversed now and so mine, proved to be *thurin* and *ferrorn* respectively. 'Your move. And when we've got bored with our machines, we come and see how you live – and remember how lucky we are.'

'Are you sure you haven't played this before?' He regarded the board suspiciously.

'I'm sure.'

He got up and crossed the mosaic floor, bringing a wine jar back to the table with him. I refilled my bowl. He came round behind my chair, studying the pieces from my point of view.

'But you are different,' he said, as if completing a train of thought. It was unexpected, then: one hand that lifted the weight of my hair, one hand that stroked the bare nape of my neck. Smooth, instead of the Orthean mane. There was the shock of desire: flesh calling to different flesh. Some of my feelings over the past days were abruptly clear to me.

I looked up and saw his face human, not cold, not sarcastic; only asking – as we all ask – not to be hurt.

I saw him as human: it's the penalty of being an empath – and the reason why, although we're extremely useful to the ET department, they don't altogether trust us. Inside your head you are not man or woman, young or old, Western or Third World. So now I couldn't see the two of us as human and alien, but only as Lynne de Lisle Christie and Sethin Falkyr Talkul.

Falkyr with that brilliant, bitter mind; who moved with all the dangerous Orthean grace, who was born an outsider in his own land; it was inevitable.

'Christie,' he said, 'are we to be *arykei*?'

'That *ashiren* took long enough finding you,' Haltern grumbled. I was surprised to see him there in the main hall. The evening meal was just finishing.

'Don't blame Maric. He had to come over to Falkyr's rooms.'

'Sethin Falkyr? Yes, I've met him.' Haltern's expression underwent a sudden and total change. Then he grinned.

'Is it that obvious?' It seemed that it was. I was cheerful. 'Don't worry, Hal, it's all being done according to the *arykei* custom.'

'Congratulations.' He, like Maric, appeared to regard it as cause for public celebration. Being no Southlander, I wanted it kept quiet.

'What did you want to see me for, anyway?'

'What? Oh – yes.' He became serious. 'There's been a message received from the Skulls garrison. Ruric won't be leaving for a while. She's ill.'

'How bad is it? Serious?'

'Just a fever, from what I've heard, but they won't move her. The *t'an* Howice intends one of his physicians to ride up there and make sure it's nothing bad.'

I was quiet, taking it in; almost guilty to be happy while the Orthean woman was sick.

'Should we ride up there?'

'It's a week's ride . . . if the next *rashaku*-carrier brings no better news, I'll go,' Haltern said.

'I'll come with you.'

But the messages over the next week were good, and Howice's physician arrived at the garrison and pronounced it only a fever brought on by the north's unaccustomed cold after Tathcaer. Haltern grumbled something to the effect that anyone connected with Howice Talkul couldn't doctor a sick *marhaz*, but seemed content to remain in the city.

The first rush of duties being over, I was free to spend time with Falkyr. I avoided Sulis n'ri n'suth SuBannasen on the pretext that I was busy. Sometimes soon I'd have to make a decision, but not yet. Not until I was sure Ruric was well.

Not until I understood what was happening between Falkyr and myself.

Any difficulties we had were habit and not physiology; Adair had been right about that. For the rest, it was the time you spend totally wrapped up in each other's attention, the best time, before doubts and practicality creep in.

And, as it turned out, it was only a very little time.

'Have I leave to go to the city, *t'an*?' Maric asked.

'What? Sure, I shan't need you this afternoon.' I pulled the fur robe tightly round me while I hunted for riding britches. Falkyr and I intended riding out to Delu *telestre* where they bred hunting *kazza*, trackers and killers. 'Have you seen my shirt?'

'It came back from the washroom, I hung it in the closet.'

If I'd had any sense, I'd have found my clothes before I undressed to change. Corbek wasn't getting any warmer.

'You remember the Wellhouse the *T'An* Ruric took me to, before she left?'

He nodded.

'Could you find it again?'

'Yes, *t'an*.'

'Well, if you happen to go that way this afternoon, call in on the Wellkeeper. Ask him if he knows where Theluk is. Haltern wants to know.'

He hadn't been able to find the woman priest for several days.

'I might happen to go that way.' Maric grinned.

'Well, go on, get lost before I think of something else that wants doing.'

He went. I sat down on the bed and began to unlace my boots. A few minutes later I heard footsteps. The curtain was pulled back without any preliminary call. Howice Talkul came into the room.

'Lynne de Lisle Christie, alleged Otherworld envoy—'

I stood up, barefoot on the cold stone, tugging the long *zilmei* pelt round me.

Alleged envoy. Trouble, I thought. And it's big.

There were half a dozen men and women behind him, with drawn *harur* blades. I recognized two of Falkyr's brothers. All had the Talkul face, younger sons and daughters of the *telestre*.

'—in view of the doubt cast upon the status of the alleged envoy, and certain allegations concerning the said Lynne de Lisle Christie and that most abhorred race, the Golden Witchbreed—'

Howice read stolidly from a paper. There was no trace of the polite and friendly man who'd been helpful to the Earth envoy.

'—my pleasure that she shall be conveyed to a place of safety, and there held until a trial may be convened on the matter. Given on Torvern Thirdweek Eightday, under my hand in Corbek: Telvelis Koltyn Talkul, *T'An* Roehmonde.'

Howice let the paper snap back into a roll, and tapped it primly against his hand.

I stood staring at him like an idiot.

'Are you saying you're arresting me?'

CHAPTER 11

The Justice of the Wellhouse

The cells were cold.

Condensation ran down the rock wall. Dim light filtered down through roof-slots, and I saw bars and shadows.

A wooden bench hung on chains from the rock wall. I sat, feet tucked up under my robe, hugging the pelt round me. Bars divided the chamber into several cells, each with their bench and bucket. I couldn't see if there were other occupants, but no sound broke the silence.

Cold struck up from the rough floor, and seeped down through the air slots.

I lost track of time.

Noise shattered the quiet. I jumped up. It was the heavy outer door being opened. I limped over to the bars, legs numb from lack of circulation; and was dazzled by torches. The light was all but gone; it must be evening outside.

One guard unlocked the cell next to mine, ignoring me, and two or three more came in with a man struggling between them. They threw him roughly into the cell, and left. The oily black smoke of torches drifted in the air. My eyes readjusted to the twilight.

'Haltern?'

He got up. We touched fingers through the bars. Good Roehmonder ironwork. He looked unharmed, only a little more disreputable than usual.

'You all right?'

'Yes. I was planning on leaving Corbek, but I didn't go in time.'

'They're not serious, are they?' It was a rhetorical question. Some of my stupefaction wore off. 'How long are we going to be here? Can we get a message out?'

'Perhaps. Christie, it's not good. The nearest help is at the garrison.'

'And Ruric's ill.'

'Or else south, in Tathcaer.'

'Too far. Too long a time to be any use.'

He nodded. 'You have no . . . weapons? Nothing that would free us?'

'Nothing. All my gear is in my rooms.' A thought struck me. 'Maric?'

'I didn't see *kir* when they brought me in.'

'What are we going to do?'

'Wait,' he said.

The cell was small, three paces one way and four paces the other. The bench was barely large enough to stretch out on. We talked for a while, each on our separate benches, and the last of the light failed.

'Don't depend on him.' Haltern's voice came out of the darkness. 'First loyalty is to the *telestre*.'

'He'll find some way to get us out.'

I lay awake, waiting for Falkyr to come.

Pale sunlight streamed down the air slots. I chafed my arms and feet, half-paralysed by cold. It must be early, I thought. I'd slept in snatches, despite the hard bench, but it had been impossible to get warm and my feet had got cold enough to be painful.

Haltern was still curled in a foetal position, asleep. It gave me a chance to use the bucket in relative privacy; I still wasn't used to the casual Orthean attitude.

Then there was nothing to do but wait.

The light moved down the wall and reached the floor of the opposite cell. It lit up dust and dirty straw. Now I was certain one of the other cells was occupied, there had been sounds during the night. When the sun fell directly on the straw the heap shuddered and opened, and a woman stood up.

She took hold of the bars of the cage door, shaking them until the iron rattled and echoed.

Old white scars were visible on her dark skin. Her hands were thin even for an Orthean, all twelve claw-nails bitten back to the quick; and her feet had wide-spreading toes as gnarled as roots. She was naked. As she swung round, pacing in that confined space, I saw her bramble-thicket mane that was rooted down to the small of her back.

Her face was scratched, her mouth crusted with old blood, and her eyes were as expressionless as black glass.

'Goddess!' An amazed whisper. Haltern was awake.

At the voice, she froze. Watching us.

I said, 'Who are you?'

116

No answer. She backed out of the direct sunlight, back against the wall of the cell, fading into the dimness.

'That's no use,' Haltern said, 'she's a barbarian. From over the Wall. They must have sent her down from the garrison.'

We ceased talking as the main door opened. A tall and very thin woman came in, carrying her *harur-nazari* unsheathed. She unlocked the door of my cell. Others followed her, carrying blankets, furs, food and wine and, finally and most welcome, a brazier and a stock of coal.

'You have friends in the *telestre*,' the thin woman said. I recognized her, not from her face but from her expression, she was another of Sethin's children. 'Do not speak of this, if you are asked.'

'Is there a message?'

She shook her head quickly, re-locking the cell.

'Can you take word? Say that—'

The main door banged shut, and I heard the bars being slotted into their sockets on the outside.

I was able to pull the brazier close to the bars, where Haltern could feel the heat, and pass him some of the blankets. It was still cold, but I no longer felt that bone-penetrating chill.

'Your *arykei* is to be commended.' Haltern upended the wine flask and drank deeply. 'It's a risk I wouldn't take.'

I managed to toss a haunch of roast *wirazu* into the opposite cell. The barbarian woman squatted down, ripping it apart with her teeth. No one had fed her, or us, and the hard pain of hunger made it difficult to think.

'I should never have left Tathcaer,' Haltern said grimly. 'Cities are my business. Not grubbing in Roehmonde dirt. Have you got any money?'

'No, not one copper bit.'

'I've some silver. Next time I'll try and bribe them to take a message out.'

The barbarian woman said something, a short phrase. Haltern stopped, mouth open, and stared at her.

'Who are you?' I went to the bars. 'How did you get here?'

There was still no animation in her face, but there was a question in her tone.

'Ymirian?' I was incredulous.

'An archaic form, perhaps,' Haltern said, 'you're right.'

The woman pointed. 'Who?'

'Christie,' I said, and repeated it when she said it back to me. She came forward, wrapping her bony hands round the bars. Her voice was harsh.

'Who is thy friend?' she asked.

'Haltern.' I added, 'he's from the south.'

There was no telling how much she understood. Haltern came up beside me and asked questions, but she didn't reply. Before long she went back to the rear of her cell, ignoring us.

'How long has she been here, I wonder?'

'I don't know. Did I ever,' he went on in a plain attempt at distraction, 'tell you about my *telestre*, Beth'ru-elen?'

I settled back on the bench with three blankets and a *zilmei* pelt round me. 'No, you never did. Come on. Let's hear it.'

I ducked my head, flinching from the white light. There was a hand on my arm, halting me. Automatically I reached out to steady myself, and the metal cuffs cut into my wrists. The guard's hand caught me, and I was able to stand. Half a metre of chain hobbled my ankles.

'Be silent in the presence! Be silent in the house!'

The hum and chatter died away.

A great dome towered above my head, the noon sun falling through the roof slot, blinding me. I squinted. Tall pillars edged the domed chamber. Beyond them were smaller domes, and in those alcoves a crowd of people.

I stood between two guards.

Noon bells cut across the silence; brief chimes echoing in the dome.

The guard pushed me forward. I stepped up onto a raised block. In front of me was an iron grating, circular, some five metres across. I looked down. For a few yards the sun lit the rock sides of the great well shaft. Then there was darkness.

On the other side of the well stood Arad. There was another raised block, this one empty. He stood by a table on which were piled scrolls and documents, conferring with a young Earth-speaker.

Apart from us, I saw no one on the vast, tessellated floor of the dome. My eyes becoming used to the light, I made out how the natural rock amphitheatre was carved in rising tiers of seats, and how smaller domes clung to the sides of the main one. Between pillars I saw a multitude of Orthean faces, surrounding me on all sides.

'I have called you to the Wellhouse to consider a most serious matter.' Without being raised, Arad's voice penetrated clearly through the dome. 'The *T'An* Roehmonde has decreed that this is a matter for the Wellhouse and not the court. I call you all here to judge and witness.'

There were Earthspeakers in that assembly, and other Well-keepers that I recognized from social functons, and *s'an* of the nearby *telestres*. I stood pinned under the spotlight of the noon glare. Peering past Arad I made out members of the Talkul *telestre*, and then all at once saw Howice, and Sethin, and Koltyn himself. The old man nodded at Arad, staring at me with no recognition.

'We witness,' Howice said, and other voices echoed him. Searching along the line I saw Sulis n'ri n'suth SuBannasen, her face impassive.

'The woman you see—' Arad's hand flicked in my direction '—has claimed to come from another world. There are certain things which would seem to support this. In Tathcaer, they believed it. But there are other explanations. There is evidence that she is the product, if not in fact the child, of that most ancient, bloody, cruel, and proud race, the Golden Witchbreed.'

This was what I'd expected, and now it came I was relieved. I said to the nearest guard, 'When may I speak?'

'You?' he stared at me. 'You're not here to speak.'

'What?'

'Keep your mouth shut.'

'But if I'm not allowed a defence—'

The hilt of a *harur* blade caught me high up under the ribs. I shut up. Arad was still talking. We were ignored.

'—having heard her freely confess to such machines and engines as are used on her world,' Arad said. 'Which indeed you have all heard, when she visited your *telestres*, making no secret of it. And these are familiar matters to us, who know how Witchbreed travelled between their many lands riding the air, we who know what weapons devastated the Barrens, we who know the legacy of desolation left to us. We, whose kin swore after that Empire fell, never again to permit such ruin of the earth.'

He was so reasonable, I found I was afraid of him. This was no savage, and this was no audience for my carefully-thought-out pleas for the benefits of science. And if I couldn't get a hearing . . .

'There's no dispute about the existence of other worlds, I suppose.' Arad seated himself casually on the edge of the table. 'The stars being the Mother's Daughters, it were no great wonder if they also had children such as ourselves. Philosophers have often speculated that it may be so, and so it may; but I ask you, which is the more likely? That such people would find out a way to cross vast gulfs, and send this woman here – or that she comes from some untenanted part of our own world; perhaps even a known part, perhaps even Kel Harantish?'

I was surprised by the sophistication of the argument, even

while my spirits were sinking lower. The quiet in the assembly chilled me. I thought, if it comes to it, can I prove I'm from Earth?

'You have the Crown's seal on my documents!' I sensed movement from the guards, but Arad signalled them to stand back. I didn't raise my voice. The acoustics were such that I was being heard throughout the dome. 'I'm an accredited envoy of my world.'

'Not all tales out of Tathcaer are true,' he said, 'and even the *T'An Suthai-Telestre* may be taken in by a liar. Be silent. The evidence will be heard.'

At his signal the young Earthspeaker picked up a document from the table, and stepped on to the raised block.

'The evidence of Kethan n'ri n'suth Renu, physician,' he read. '"On being summoned to tend the *T'An* Commander Ruric Orhlandis, I found her to be suffering from a fever unknown to me. She presently lies ill here in the Skulls garrison. It is my opinion that the illness was deliberately caused, though I cannot say by whom, or why."'

As he stepped down, Arad said, 'The *T'An* Commander of the Southland's army lies sick, and this after – and only after – travelling to Roehmonde in the company of the alleged envoy.'

I missed the evidence of the next two or three, mainly *s'an* of mining *telestres* describing what I'd told them of Earth technology. Ruric? I thought. They suspect me of – that's crazy!

Kethan n'ri n'suth Renu, I remembered, is Howice's physician.

Questions were asked, some by *s'an*, some just from the assembly; and that quiet rational voice went on piling up circumstantial evidence against me. I shifted, easing my back, wishing I could sit down. When word of this got back to Tathcaer, and to the xeno-team—

If word got back. And suppose it does, I thought suddenly, supposing even a garbled version of the truth gets out, what could they do? What could they do in time to help me? Even if it ended in an execution, ultimately there was little that could be done; and I wasn't interested in posthumous justice.

'Evidence of conjecture, perhaps,' Arad said. 'However, I have a last witness, an eye-witness, a man who has seen this envoy – this alleged envoy – use forbidden Witchbreed science. Your name, *t'an*.'

'Aluys Blaize n'ri n'suth Meduenin, of the Mercenaries' Guild in Rimon,' the man said, mounting the witness block; and the light fell on him, and I saw the ruined half of his face and recognized him. The face that had stayed with me from Terison, the hired sword, the nameless killer.

'I see you know him,' Arad remarked in my direction. It was too late to deny that.

'He made an attempt on my life. I'm not liable to forget him.'

'Nor I to forget you,' the man said. I realized I'd never heard him speak. It was a deep voice, speaking Roehmonder with a thick Rimon accent. 'I bear your mark still, Witchbreed.'

He held up his wrist, strapped and bound. I saw the *harur-nilgiri* slung for left-hand use.

'I was travelling east. Our paths crossed at a Wellhouse.' He stared round the assembly, his head up defiantly. Roehmonders have no love for mercenaries. 'We became friends, then *arykei*.'

Blood thundered in my ears. The faceless crowd narrowed down to one focus: Howice Talkul's smile. Plain as words it said: deny that's possible. Just try.

'She has an object about so big—' Blaize held his hands a little way apart '—the shape of a *hura* shell, grey and hard. When I saw it, I asked what it was; she told me it was a weapon. Weapons are my business,' he appealed to the assembly, 'I was eager to study it, she not at all eager for me to lay hands on it. We fought. She carries no sword, nor ever did while I knew her. Her sole weapon was that object. She used it against me – pointed it from a distance – called down forked lightning out of the air. My swordhand was useless: I fled for my life. When I knew where she had gone, it became my duty to warn you.'

As he stepped down, Arad picked up an object from the table. 'This is that weapon?'

'Yes.'

'You have leave to go.' Arad waited, then faced me again. 'You do not deny this is yours?'

'I deny that it does what he says, or that what he says happened took place.'

They'd searched my baggage. What else would they have found? The reports – no, they couldn't play them back, and it wouldn't make much difference if they did. The medic kit. That would puzzle them. And I didn't want to lose it.

Arad displayed it round the assembly as evidence against me.

'I demand the right to speak!' I controlled frustration. Talking was all I could do, and now I was denied even that. 'Have I ever said that Earth is not a technological world? Have I ever denied we use our own science? Tell me how that makes me part of a race that's extinct on this planet! Can't you see I'm different from you? Use your eyes!'

'You're different,' Arad said, 'but such changes were always within the power of the Witchbreed, it proves nothing either way.'

'I'm under the protection of Crown law. This isn't justice.'

'But you are in Roehmonde,' Arad said over a growl of approval from the Roehmonders, 'and this is a Wellhouse, and you are under the justice of the Goddess.'

The guards took me out of the Wellhouse, and we waited in an outer chamber for the larger part of the afternoon. My protests were ignored. I was beginning to accept that.

When I was brought back in the torches were lit and the last afternoon light fell on the black well shaft. I stood at the edge of that dizzying pit.

'You have witnessed,' Arad said to the assembly, 'now judge.'

Eventually a woman came forward onto the floor, glancing back at the *s'ans* and priests.

'It's taken us a long time to confer,' she said hesitantly, 'and we feel the case isn't proved against her, but we're not convinced she's innocent. She may be Witchbreed, and she may not – we can't be sure.'

There was a murmur of approval. I sought out Howice's face. He wasn't happy about it.

Arad, after conferring with some of the Earthspeakers, said, 'This is my word, then. Let her be taken back and confined in the cells. We will search for new evidence. We will hear this again. Is this acceptable?'

I hardly heard their agreement. It was no more than time I'd gained, but it was better than what I'd feared.

I saw the scarred man across the hall. He never saw the sonic stunner, I thought, and certainly he never saw me use it. Someone rehearsed him very carefully with his evidence. Someone who'd previously hired him, and knew to bring him here . . .

Old suspicions flared up, but I couldn't see Sulis now. Going down to the cells again, my mind made and discarded plans. If I could get a message out. If Ruric recovered soon, and returned. If Falkyr—

I didn't see Falkyr there, I realized.

'It's time,' I said, when I'd told Haltern about it. 'Surely we can do something?'

'We can be careful.' He was grim. 'They've given the envoy a hearing, and by the law of the Wellhouse they can keep you in the cells until they decide to give you another one. And wouldn't it be convenient if you sickened and died of the damp-lung sickness, or bad food – or the assassin's sword?'

I woke from a beam of warmth, of fingers knotting in the roots of a short-cropped mane.

The barbarian woman shook the bars, the sound echoing. Her face was turned up to the air slots.

'What?'

She said a word several times, but it was not until I looked up that I understood her. Morning: pale snowlight. She gave the bars a last kick and went back to her heap of straw. She had a tremendous capacity for conserving her energy in sleep.

Our talk never got much beyond the 'who are you?' stage. Neither mine or Haltern's versions of Ymirian and Roehmonder were comprehensible to her.

'What day is it?'

'Forthweek Fourday, I think.' I was pretty sure the hearing had been on Twoday. 'You all right?'

'We're almost out of fuel.' He ignored the question. I'd heard him coughing during the night.

'I can't believe this.' There was no way to work off my anger. 'I can't believe there's no way to protest. And I don't believe that travesty was due process of law!'

'It was informal, and it was Wellhouse custom.' Haltern pulled the blanket shawl-like round his shoulders. 'If it had been Crown law, you'd have been allowed to speak, and call your own evidence. Which, I suspect, is why the *T'An* Roehmonde turned it over to Arad.'

I refuelled the brazier, shaking the ash onto the floor.

'Howice. Not Koltyn.'

He nodded. 'Forthweek Fourday . . . if the *T'An* Ruric is well enough to return—'

'If.' The thought disturbed me. I knew Haltern was wrong, Howice wouldn't order me killed yet. Not yet: he would still be coming to terms with what he'd done – arrested an envoy accredited by the Crown. But if he was able to deceive Ruric about where I was, and if she went on south, *then* he'd think again. He might not be so chary of disposing of the envoy.

It was not being able to do anything that hurt.

Dampness hung in the air. Thin streams of water mizzled down from the air slots, pooling on the stone floor. The brazier held nothing but warm ashes.

The barbarian woman gripped the bars of her cage door, shaking it on its hinges. Monotonous, hopeless: her face with no more expression than it ever had.

'Stop that Goddess-forsaken noise!' Haltern added a curse in Peir-Dadeni. His hands were shaking. He threw the empty wine flask at her, and it struck the bars and skittered into the rain pool.

'Don't shout at her, it's not her fault we're in here.'

'It's not *mine*,' he said acidly.

'Bloody half-civilized savages,' I said. 'All of you.'

The rain eased. Moisture pearled the sleeping-furs. The cold of the iron bars bit into my hands.

'Haltern? I'm sorry.'

We touched hands through the bars.

'So am I. Sorry. These Roehmonders—' he shrugged. 'I thought I was too clever to get picked up like that, at my age.'

'It's not as if you are half-civilized.' I was pursuing my own train of thought. 'The Witchbreed are more than legends. And I'm not trained for post-holocaust societies.'

'Christie,' the barbarian woman called. She was backing away from the bars, watching the main door.

'What—?'

The door swung open. I expected either more of the food and wine that was anonymously supplied to us, or else the *T'An* Roehmonde's guards. Instead, a woman entered and swung the door closed behind her.

'Verek Sethin.' Haltern went to the bars.

'I've little time.' She unlocked the door to his cell, and then mine.

I said, 'Where's Falkyr?'

'With my brother Howice. There is a hunt, this being the Fiveday holiday.'

'He isn't here?'

She looked at me uncomprehendingly. I stepped outside the cell. I didn't want to ask the next question.

'Does he know about this?'

Sethin shook her head. 'My son is loyal to the *telestre*. T'an, you must come with me quickly.'

Haltern was rolling up the less bulky blankets. I watched him. Part of me had stopped thinking.

'She's got to come too,' I said, as Sethin passed the barbarian woman's cell.

Haltern nodded. 'You're right. They'll get out of her what she's seen if she stays here.'

His pragmatism shocked me.

The barbarian woman shied back, then stood still while I knotted one blanket round her under the arms and pulled another one over her head as hood and shawl. She might pass as a Roehmonder. I hoped.

She strode after Sethin and Haltern, blankets tangling her legs. I followed. Sethin had two of my packs waiting in the empty guardroom. We went through long stone passages and up seemingly endless flights of stairs.

'Sethin.' I elbowed past Haltern to speak to her. 'If he didn't . . . who was it saw to it that we were comfortable, down there?'

'That was Falkyr's wish.' She didn't slow her pace. 'He would do all he could for an *arykei*. Indeed, he did much. It was he who spoke to Howice of your recognition by the Goddess—'

'Hell!' How could I have forgotten? I thought. But I had, it had gone out of my mind completely. I suppose I'd regarded it as partly a charming native ceremony, and partly as one of Ruric's good intentions; but it had never crossed my mind, not even in the Wellhouse.

'It would have done you no good to mention it,' Sethin added, 'Howice knew, and Arad knew, and how would it have sounded to say that you were recognized by the Goddess, and that your second presently lies struck down with sickness?'

'But Falkyr—'

'He did what he could, within the law of the *telestre*.'

'And you?' What I wanted to ask was, why are you here instead of him?

'I do what I can,' she said, 'and I don't have strength or time enough to put it to the *telestre*, so I act now, for myself.'

The bluff hung above us. The damp air struck me as warm, coming up from underground. The sun was past noon, daystars were white over the towers of Corbek. We stood in the rutted lane, blinking at the light, breathing the wind, silent for long minutes.

Less than a week. Eight days. And yet it had changed. The trees in the gardens were changing colour: yellow to grey. The air smelled sharply of autumn.

'I'll do no more, and know no more,' Sethin said. 'Go. Leave Corbek.'

She stood in the doorway, the light cruel on the sharp planes of her face. Her eyes were dull, brown-shadowed, and the same colour crept round her pinched lips. Her clothes hung loose from her angular shoulders.

She had that cold and stubborn expression I had often seen on her son's face.

Falkyr. Who was Roehmonder, who was Talkul *telestre* above all else. Much as I'd disliked the thought of my freedom resting in someone else's hands, I'd still relied on him, imagining him working for my release. Now I was betrayed. Not by him. By me: expecting us to think and feel the same way. Thinking I understood the *telestre*.

125

'Thank you.' I took Sethin's cold hands. 'I won't speak of this, whatever happens.'

'In a while, it won't matter to me.' She smiled wryly. 'Have you any word for my son, Christie?'

Under the rationality, bitterness welled up. I shook my head. I couldn't trust myself.

'We're grateful, *t'an*,' Haltern said, 'and the Crown shall hear of this, privately if you wish. And if you'd send word to the *T'An* Ruric?'

'Not outside Corbek. If she comes here, yes.' Sethin regarded me. 'Don't think too badly of us. Arad is honest in what he does, he believes you are Witchbreed and a danger. Even Howice does what he does for us. He loves control, I grant you, and all that goes with it, but in all honesty he believes there are things he can do for the *telestre* that no other can.'

'Then let him wait,' Haltern said. 'When the old man dies, they may name Howice as *T'An* Roehmonde.'

'But then, you see, they may not. And he has waited so long.' Her face closed up and she was cold again. 'Now, go.'

The door shut behind her. I took the barbarian woman's arm, and followed Haltern down into the city.

CHAPTER 12

Flight to the South

'Where are you going? We've got to get out of here!'

'Be reasonable,' Haltern said. 'The alarm will go out when Howice returns – say, sunset, or dawn tomorrow at the latest. He'll send fast riders out to warn the *telestres*. If you can think of a way to get out of the Roehmonde *telestres* by dawn—'

'All right. All right, but what do we do? We can't stay here.'

'That's just what we can do.' He was flushed, alert; freedom filled him with a sudden energy. 'For a time.'

The blank walls of the city *telestre*-houses shut us out. It was slippery walking, the mud was ankle-deep and the ruts filled with rainwater. I kept hold of the barbarian woman's wrist, not trusting her to stay with us otherwise. I carried the packs over my shoulder; they were light, and I was doubtful about how much of my property remained in them.

'Theluk,' I said.

'Go to a Wellhouse?' Haltern said doubtfully.

'She said that Wellkeeper could be trusted, and she's no friend of Arad.'

'If she's still in Corbek . . .' he hesitated as we came to an intersection. 'Yes, but not to stay, that's too much of a risk.'

'You think this isn't risky? Let's get off the streets.'

I might pass for Roehmonder if lucky, keeping my eyes lowered and my hands out of sight. The barbarian woman, swathed in blankets, was already attracting stares. Now we were coming down into the Fiveday holiday crowds. And Haltern laughed. It was ludicrous: but I had to laugh with him, I was out of that filthy place, and that was all that mattered.

The Wellhouse was shut up, but Haltern rattled the iron gates until an inner door was opened, and then Theluk herself came running out.

'Inside. Quick! How did you – never mind, get out of sight.'

In the courtyard she stopped and stared at us, and used one or

127

two expressions I'd heard from Ruric's troopers. She opened the door to one of the rooms beside the Wellhouse dome, then: 'What's *that*?'

The barbarian woman shied back from the door. I could understand her not wanting to go under a roof again.

'Thee will stay?' I indicated the courtyard, and she nodded. Theluk had locked the outer gates.

'Thou and thy friend . . . leave this—?' she used an expression I didn't know, but the comprehensive gesture of her gnarled hand took in all of Corbek.

'Soon, yes.'

I left her sitting cross-legged on the flagstones, blanket put back from her head, face turned to the sky.

Inside the ill-lit room, an *ashiren* rose from setting a fire in the hearth. '*T'an!*'

Maric gripped my hands. I was embarrassed: there was no reason he should be so glad to see me. He fetched food while Haltern sketched out events for Theluk, and I sorted through the packs.

The medic kit was there, half emptied; and some spare clothes and a handful of silver bits. No sign of the micro-recorder. But, at the bottom of one pack, wrapped in a *chirith-goyen* shirt, I found the sonic stunner.

I wish I'd thanked Sethin when I had the chance. There were no half measures for her when her conscience moved her. I hoped Howice wouldn't hurt her.

'There's no going by river,' Theluk said, 'I tried to get passage east on one of the barges, but they want travel permits signed by the *T'An* Roehmonde.'

'East would be best – take ship at the mouth of the Beruth for Tathcaer. Going south, too many *telestres* support Talkul.' Haltern scowled. 'Travel permits in the one province? I never heard of anything so against rule and custom!'

'That's Arad you have to thank.'

'Have we got enough money for *marhaz*?' I was counting my silver.

Theluk shook her head. 'You need also a permit to buy *marhaz* in Corbek.'

Haltern swore, outraged, then said, 'I wonder – a bribe?'

'I've tried. It was only luck I wasn't arrested.' Theluk turned to me. 'You can't stay here, *t'an*. I don't mean to be unfriendly, but Arad knows I oppose him, and they're searching all Wellhouses.'

Maric brought stone cups and a jug of gritty wine. Anxiously he said, 'What will we do, *t'an*?'

128

We're not so much better off, I thought, now that we're out of the cells . . . and that's ridiculous! There has to be a way.

'Can we do it on foot?' I was remembering the ride up to Roehmonde, with Ruric's troopers. 'East . . . or north, to the garrison. Or south, until we find someone who'll credit the *T'An Suthai-Telestre's* authority and not the *T'An* Roehmonde's. It's all that's left.'

'On foot through *this* country—?'

'It's not so mad an idea,' Theluk cut in. 'The weather should hold dry and cold now. We used to take out foot patrols from the garrison in Torvern, and we're a good few *seri* further south here. You're less likely to be seen, more able to hide.'

'If you think I'm walking to Tathcaer you *are* mad!'

The idea wasn't that crazy. I've done survival courses: I was fairly confident we could get out of Roehmonde, but it wouldn't be comfortable. And they would be looking for us. My mind flinched away from the thought. It wasn't until I was free that I knew: no one was going to lock me up again. Ever.

'They'll search the roads,' Haltern protested.

'Go west, where they won't expect to see you.' Theluk bent down and picked a charred stick from the fire, and scratched in the ashes. 'Here's Corbek, and the hills to the west, and the flat land to the north . . . the rivers and the forest to the south. If you were to go west, then southwest, you'd reach the Oranon river, and the *telestres* there are admitted Ymirian.'

'That's over a hundred *seri*,' Haltern said, aghast.

'Six days, maybe seven, given good weather; any trooper can do that.'

She was optimistic, I thought. But she knew the country, she'd been a soldier, she might be right.

I said, 'Maybe you should leave Corbek too.'

'Yes.' She put the stick down, the six-fingered hands linking before her. 'I've had to keep out of Arad's sight. He won't listen to reason, and he's heard much from me lately; I'd be safer out of Roehmonde.'

'You're both mad,' Haltern said testily.

'It'll do until we have a better idea. But if we can't stay here . . .'

'You can't,' Theluk confirmed. 'You'll have to come with me. Out of sight of the Talkul *t'ans*. I know where.'

Waking, I felt excited, anticipatory without knowing the reason. Then it came back: I wasn't in the cells. Apprehension returned. Leaving the city . . . could we do it?

A greenish light hung in the room. It was round-walled, all

wood, even the low conical roof; rough stones were mortared together to make a chimney.

Still as a rock, the barbarian woman stood holding the leather curtain away from the doorway. Her head was up, her hands knotted into fists. The light shone on her unhuman body: the scarred ribs, small paired breasts and lower nipples, the unbroken sweep of smooth skin down to the hairless groin.

'Christie.' Her quiet tone woke nobody.

I got up, pulling the blanket round me, and went to stand beside her. Outside, the first twilight was giving way to sunrise. Ground mist rose over the shacks, hid the river.

'You'll have to come with us,' I said.

'What is thy road?'

'That way.' I pointed west, and her eyes were suddenly opaque.

'I will come,' she said, and turned away.

Breakfast was cold meat and herb-tea, most of our funds having been spent on gear for the journey. I let Maric work out loads and weights; he was more expert.

'There's Gher and Oru still up there,' I said, rolling blankets.

'Go and ask Howice for them,' was Haltern's acid advice.

Or Falkyr, I thought, and was still for a moment. It had a way of going right out of my mind, and then coming over me suddenly. I'd cried, and sworn at his memory, and it still came back.

'Are we ready?' Theluk wore *harur-nilgiri* and *harur-nazari* now, as Haltern did. Maric had a belt-knife. It was habit with me now to wear a short knife, but I carried the stunner holstered under a Roehmonder coat. Spare clothes were worn rather than add weight to the packs.

There's no reason for anyone to stop us, I thought. If they don't look too closely.

The morning air was chill. I climbed stiffly down the outside steps to the ground, adjusting the pack's straps. My boots sank into mud. Haltern and Theluk joined me, and then the barbarian woman – in a Roehmonder coat that did nothing to disguise her angular height, her wildness – and Maric. A hard knot of tension settled under my ribs, eating acidly at my stomach.

We set off on the river road. Narrow passages led between stacked rooms and rickety staircases, where stone chimneys breathed black smoke. *Kuru* rooted in the mud. There was an unidentifiable sour smell. We left the rooming-house – it would be charity to call it a companion-house – behind in the river mist.

This shack town was the first place that reminded me of Earth. It was a transient's town. No one had asked our names. More important, no one had asked about our *telestres*. My purse had been weighty enough to hire rooms. The people here had a restless look, they were drifters and strays; and being Orthean, they took it worse than I did.

Maric's shoulder brushed my arm. 'What to we do if they stop us?'

'They won't. If they do, run and hide. Wait for the *T'An* Commander to get here.' And just how sick is she?

The sun grew brighter. We followed the Berufal upstream, where water mills thundered and rumbled and speech was impossible. Turning north and west took us past the old city walls and out to where the northern roads begin. Walls went past, and lanes and passages; and people walking, and riding *marhaz*, and some with the Talkul insignia. I met no one's eyes. Tension silenced us.

Then we were past the *telestre*-houses, on cinder-track roads. I looked back and saw Corbek's terraces rising behind me, steps and stairs and towers; and crowning the bluff, pale in the morning light, the dome of the Wellhouse.

Haltern let out a long breath, scratched through his thinning mane and grinned. Theluk laughed. It was the first time I'd seen her anything but serious, it made her look as much an *ashiren* as Maric. Maric himself peered round the barbarian woman – we'd flanked her though the city – and gave me a hard look. There was something very determined about the boy: he didn't intend going back to Corbek any more than I did.

'That's the worst over,' Haltern said.

'Don't be too sure.' Serious again, Theluk stopped and rested her foot on a markstone, retying a sandal-thong. 'They've sent out the alarm, you can be certain.'

'We can avoid them in the forests.'

'So let's move.' I eased the pack again, tucking my thumbs under the strap.

And step by step, Corbek receded behind us.

The land was flat, with forested hills to the south of us, a pale mass broken by the blue and scarlet changing leaves of *lapuur* and *ziku*. The air was sharp. It was empty country. A few carts passed us, and one or two *marhaz* riders.

Is it that easy? I thought, as noon came and we turned to roads that went south and west. And tried to ignore the weight of the miles that lay between us and Ymir.

'There's a companion-house on the edge of these hills,' Theluk persisted, 'just a bit further on.'

'You've been saying that since noon,' Haltern grumbled.

It was the fourth day since leaving the city. The second day had been the worst, working off stiffness, but after that we made better time. To my surprise I was enjoying it. The walking was tiring, but not unduly so; the packs weren't over-heavy; and we fell into a routine. Mornings, the ground rang iron-hard with frost, and rime stiffened the waterproof *becamil* tent. The days were clear, skies that pale blue of an Orthean autumn, and the noon sun still had heat. We talked, walking through pale gold light in the hazy short afternoons; and sometimes Theluk scouted the hills to hunt, and sometimes Maric. Cleaning game was messy. The barbarian woman trailed us, staying off the roads. We didn't hurry. It snowed powdery dust on the third morning (and I discovered that *becamil*, as well as keeping out rain, keeps in heat); the wine was doled out more heavily that day, and we went on in breathy white clouds of cheer. That was the day we saw no one at all on the hill tracks, and – searching for water – disturbed a *zilmei* that reared up a good twelve feet, beating the air with wide claws, and was gone in a ripple of grey-white pelt and a hooting, mournful cry. We were more sober, after that. And today, for the first time, turned due south.

'We're still within fifty *seri* of Corbek,' Haltern guessed, 'but we need supplies, we need news – need to know where the search is.'

'You're coming to the end of the land I know,' Theluk said, 'but – ah, there, I was right!'

A low, flat-roofed building sprawled below us on the southern spur of the hill. Thin smoke went up from the chimney. I could just make out *marhaz* in the yard.

'I'll go down,' Theluk offered, 'all Earthspeakers are wanderers, no one will think it strange if I ask questions. Are you coming, *ashiren-te*?'

Maric trotted off down the rough track after her. We went back off the skyline, resting in a dip where the blue thousandflower grew. The barbarian woman coalesced out of the wood's shadows. She was sucking her fingers. They were slimed with blood. She did her own hunting.

'We can't take her there,' Haltern said.

Attempting her archaic inflections, I said 'Will thee stay?'

'Not within walls.'

'You can't trust her. You don't know what these people are like.'

'Hal, what were you planning to do about her anyway? Not take her to Tathcaer with us?'

'There are questions she could answer.'

'Willingly?'

He shrugged. 'We should know what they're planning. A few

132

quiet seasons . . . they may be massing for an attack. It's happened before. I wish I knew where Howice got her.'

'This direction, I think. I've had the feeling as we travelled that she recognizes it.'

'Don't be ridiculous, we're hundreds of *seri* south of the Skulls pass—'

There was crashing in the underbrush. We sprang up, Haltern with *harur* blades unsheathed. Maric tumbled into sight.

'We can go down! Theluk sent me back. She's hired rooms.'

'The search hasn't come this way?'

'Yes, been and passed a day back.'

Haltern sheathed the paired blades. He looked at the barbarian woman.

Tranquilly she said 'I will await thee, and the morning.'

And was gone.

The companion-house, kept by the two *telestres* Ereval and Irys, was not as small as it appeared. It was built into the south face of the spur, with six floors leading down to another set of stables on the main route from Corbek to Mirane. It was not crowded – most of the harvest markets were over by now.

'Shall you risk going south now?' Theluk asked as we ate, and then frowned. 'What in the Goddess's name do they put in this stew?'

'Customers who don't pay their bills, I should think.' Being under a roof restored Haltern's spirits.

'You're a Crown Messenger,' I said, 'send a message. Surely we're far enough away now.'

'Give it another day or two. There are no lines of communication to Tathcaer until we reach the Oranon river, anyway.'

'They're still expecting you to have gone east,' Theluk guessed, 'but give them time, they'll work it out.'

Our rooms were over the stables and grain-loft. The musky smell of *marhaz* got into my head, and I dreamed in the night of riding to the edge of the world. I woke once, and lay awake – paradoxically, now I was comfortable I had time to think, and couldn't sleep.

After a while I realized Haltern was awake too. He watched me. The starlight shone in his eyes, membrane retracted, pupils become velvet holes. He sees me better than I see him, I thought.

Softly he said, 'Did you ever ask him to become *n'ri n'suth* to your *telestre*?'

There was no question of who was meant by *he*.

'No, how could I?'

'Did he ever ask you to become *n'ri n'suth* Talkul?'

'No.' I hadn't known he was meant to.

'Then you were *arykei*, well and good, and it ended perhaps before you were ready; but for the Goddess's sake, Christie – when something's dead, leave it alone!'

Under the hectoring tone there was something very like concern. It kept me from telling him to go to hell.

'It's different customs, isn't it? And misunderstandings.' I was very tired. 'It's all right, Hal. I don't want to discuss it. But thanks for saying.'

'We need you here,' he said, 'and not with your spirit still in Corbek.'

The night was full of noises: *marhaz*, people in the companion-house, and one hunting night-*rashaku* with a call like rusty metal being torn apart. I smelled the chill of frost, and thought with a sudden longing of Tathcaer, and the sun, and how glad – how very glad – I would be when we got to the south.

I came back across the yard from the outhouse, lacing up my coat and shivering. The frost had gone, the morning was damp. From the top of the spur you could see for miles, the southern hills rolling down into haze. I traced the road. It was achingly slow travelling. Would they be willing to sell *marhaz* here, I wondered, or was it too risky to ask?

As I turned I caught sight of movement on the road. Riders. Light flashed from ornamented *marhaz* harness. Too far to make out insignia, or even the number of riders. My spine prickled. All the tension flooded back.

The first rain fell as I hurried back inside.

'Motherless, landless turds,' Theluk said under her breath. 'There they go. That's blocked the south road. Offspring of Witchbreed!'

'Do you think they know we were there?' Maric had a strained look about him.

'The keeper was bound to tell them. Hei, why did they have to come back this way!' She kept her temper on a tight rein. We wriggled down the slope to where Haltern stood guard over the packs. The rain was fine but persistent.

'The main force has gone south, they've sent out scouts.'

'They've guessed what we're doing. We'll have to go back into the hills, and west again.'

There'd been no opportunity to steal *marhaz*. We'd crept out as fast as possible, and as a consequence were underprovisioned.

'Check the path,' Theluk told Maric, and when he'd gone added 'One word: these are north Roehmonders hunting us. I have known them use *kazza* to track down fugitives. We may be grateful yet for this bad weather.'

I'd not seen the hunting *kazza*. We never made that ride out to the northern *telestre*: I was arrested. But Falkyr's voice came back to me. Difficult as *rashaku* to train, he'd said, and difficult as fate to avoid.

'There's your barbarian friend,' Haltern said to me, 'if they take her – and Goddess knows where she is now! – they'll be certain it's us. Then we're finished.'

'*If* they catch her.'

Before midmorning, the rain turned to sleet.

'Christ!' I yelled ahead to Theluk, 'we can't carry on in this!'

I stopped, waiting for Haltern to catch up. I had my arm round Maric; he was huddled into my side, head down.

'Nobody's moving in this,' Haltern panted, 'them or us. Tell that woman we don't all have Earthspeaker's stamina – we've got to get under shelter.'

It was impossible to face into the wind. Frozen rain sliced out of the south. Mud clogged on boots, weighing them down. I felt water seep through layers of coat and tunics, cold against fever-hot skin. Uncontrollable shivers centred in my chest and stomach. Even through mittens my hands were numb; there was no feeling in my face.

'Get under the trees,' Theluk said when she was close enough to be heard.

The *tukinna* blocked some of the wind. I pushed on up the slope after the Orthean woman. The blue mossgrass broke away underfoot, leaving long skids of mud, and I had to let go of the *ashiren* and use both hands to climb. The pack overbalanced me. *Tukinna* bark peeled away wet and black when I gripped the tree boles.

'Come on.' I reached back and hauled Maric up beside me.

Haltern was fifty yards down the slope, labouring. Theluk skidded past me, crabwise down between the twisted trees, and got one of his arms over her broad shoulders She was less protected than any of us: only a Roehmonder coat over her priest's skirt, and sandals, and yet she kept going. As if the cold didn't touch her.

'Further up,' she called, 'in the rocks.'

Water fell in streams from the trees. We were suddenly out of

135

the wind. I scrambled up over ridges of earth, one of Maric's slender-fingered hands gripped in mine. The dim light outlined rocks. Rivulets drained between them, soaking knees and elbows. Twilight became shadow. I stood up. High outcroppings of rock hugged the ridge, split and fissured into blocks.

There were no caves. There were splits that went back into the main mass of rock. We tumbled into one that was wide at ground-level, narrowing as it went up. Damp mud, damp rock, but no wind or sleet.

Maric was shaking as hard as I was. Haltern, let out of the Earthspeaker's grip, pitched forward onto his knees. Theluk leaned against the entrance of the cleft. Her eyes opaqued, then shut.

It was cold. It was frighteningly cold. It hurt. People have died from exposure, I thought, and pneumonia.

It was a long time before any of us moved.

'Fire,' Theluk said.

'Give away our position.' Haltern's eyes opened. 'What would burn? Too wet.'

'Mossgrass. In the clefts.' She looked at me, and I slipped the pack off and stood up.

'I'll look.'

My feet slipped, struck rock; sometimes I fell. I was numb. I pulled mittens off with my teeth, so that I could strip mossgrass out of sheltered cracks. Some brushwood wasn't soaking wet, only damp; I took that too. Above my head the clustered leaves rattled to another onslaught of rain.

When I came back Theluk was using her *harur-nazari* to hack off bird's-wing bushes and pile them against the entrance to the cleft. I dumped what fuel I'd collected inside. Under a makeshift *becamil* shelter Haltern was chafing the *ashiren's* hands and feet. A wine flask lay open and empty.

'He all right?'

Haltern nodded without looking up. I forced myself to go back outside. Theluk had scaled the rockface and was putting brushwood over top of the cleft. Grey veils of sleet fell from the *tukinna* trees. The cold was so intense that it burned. And it was, despite the overcast, bright – the fierce Orthean sun blazed behind the storm clouds.

Theluk dropped down beside me, sure-footed on the mud.

'Shouldn't do this,' she said. 'End of Torvern, beginning of Riardh; it should be dry.'

'It—' I bit down on my temper '—it isn't, though, is it?'

She took hold of my hands. Her bare fingers were warm. Hot, against my numb skin. I stared at her. It was difficult for me to understand the Goddess's priesthood: they were not celibate, they carried weapons, there seemed nothing to distinguish them from other Ortheans. Except that Theluk was tired, not exhausted; cold, but not frozen. And serenely unafraid of this killing weather.

She managed to light the mossgrass with her tinder-box, and build a small fire. We gathered brushwood to dry. Then, in the firelit dimness, we clustered over the tiny flames.

The last wine flask was passed round and emptied.

(What would I take with me? I thought, half-tranced. If I had to do this again. Matches. Compass. Waterproof boots. A good pair of binoculars. Protein tablets. A brain that would keep me from getting into these situations in the first place.)

There were dried strips of meat to chew, and handfuls of the bird's-wing bush's berries. It was not satisfying.

'The rain's got into everything,' I said. 'Clothes, blankets, the lot.'

'Use them anyway,' Theluk fed twigs to the fire. Damp smoke coiled up, sifting out through the makeshift roof. My eyes stung.

'It's near second twilight.' Haltern's instinct for time was not dependent on the visual. 'What do you say, Earthspeaker, will the night be colder?'

Her nostrils flared slightly. The plump face was serious, concentrating.

'The wind to ease . . . the still air to be warmer, but cold towards sunrise. Tomorrow . . . no, I do not know.'

'Is she accurate?' I was too tired to be sceptical. Or polite.

'Most times,' Theluk herself answered.

'If not this time, you'll kill us all. Be sure,' Haltern urged.

'And if I am not sure, what will you do? Go out into the dark and seek Howice's riders?'

'It's the *ashiren*,' I said.

Maric opened dark eyes and said, 'You can't give in, *t'an*, I won't be the excuse for that.'

'When I give in, I won't need an excuse.'

He grinned weakly at me.

'I'll take first watch,' Theluk said.

At first light, there were five of us. Theluk pulled the brushwood away from the entrance and found the barbarian woman sitting cross-legged in the shadow of the rock. She was still wearing the torn Roehmonder cloth, blackened and flecked with *tukinna* bark. I understood none of her brief remarks.

The fire was ashes. We ate the last of the dried meat, and repacked the blankets. The packs were light.

'Weather?' Haltern asked. His thin fingers dug into his neck, trying to shift cramp.

'I don't know. We're a long way out of the land I know . . .' Theluk peered up at the pale clouds visible through the *tukinna*. 'I think it will be dry.'

'I hope you're right.' Sleeping in damp warm blankets had given me stiffness in both legs, and a crick in my neck that meant I couldn't move my head.

'They'll be out looking,' Haltern said. 'We must stay off the roads, try and work south west.'

Maric fixed his slingstones to his belt. 'We might be able to kill something for supper.'

It was slippery walking under the trees. The day advanced, and we travelled over sharp ridges. Weak sun broke through the clouds towards noon. We saw no one. No *rashaku* called. Twice I took the stunner and scouted round with Maric, hoping for game, but we saw nothing. Tracks were days old. We filled the water flasks after midday, leaving the rivers and coming into shallower hills.

Theluk cocked her head. 'Listen!'

We were in open woodland, bird's-wing growing sparsely under the *tukinna*. Haltern stopped, drawing the *harur* blades.

'What is it?'

A high-pitched whining came from all directions. Maric drew his belt-knife.

The first one left the trees as I groped for the stunner. I saw nothing but the movement. The boy screamed. The barbarian woman caught something in mid-leap and went over backwards. A snarl split the whining. Haltern yelled. Theluk's *harur-nilgiri* came free as she slipped her pack from her shoulders.

In that second I thumbed the stunner onto full strength and wide beam.

'Out of the way – *now*!'

Maric hurled himself behind me. I held the stunner two-handed and fired. Awls drilled into my ears. I heard Theluk scream, distantly. On widebeam, there's leakage.

I didn't miss.

I was suddenly aware that there was no sound except my harsh breathing. The whining had stopped. The stunner was quiet. It had been as natural as target-shooting on the practice ranges. Except that it was quite different, and nothing was moving now.

Haltern bent double, convulsed by racking coughs, leaning on the blade that held a corpse to the ground. Theluk sheathed first the *harur-nilgiri*, then the short *harur-nazari*. She turned one of the bodies over with her foot.

Deep red feather-pelt, black markings, no bigger than a dog. Large cup-like ears. A long weasel-body, short legs. A sharp-toothed bone jaw, lips drawn back from a swollen split tongue. The tail was short and not covered by the pelt. Black slit eyes were already dulling over.

Maric bent down, and Theluk swatted his hand away. 'Hei, what—?'

'Don't touch it. That's killpack fever.'

Soundlessly, the barbarian woman was with us. Sorting out memories, I realized that first hand-flick of hers had broken the spine of the beast that attacked her.

The bodies lay in a fan-spread between the *tukinna*, some forty in number.

'Vermin,' Haltern said.

'Let's go. They're sleeping, not dead.' I holstered the stunner.

'At least we know why game's scarce,' Theluk commented as we went on through the watery sunlight.

'They know where we are,' I said, 'and they know what we're trying to do.'

'We've *got* to go south. I don't know exactly where we are, but if we're caught between them and the Fens—' Haltern broke off, shaken by deep coughs.

'Between hammer and anvil,' Theluk agreed.

'I won't go back to Corbek.' My determination frightened me. It was fear: I wasn't going back in those cells.

'We'll fight them!' Maric insisted. 'That weapon you used on the killpack!'

'No. They're riding in companies, we'd never do it.'

The soft rain fell. We'd had three dry days, three days of looping south and barely avoiding the Talkul riders. Now, going north over bare hills, we trudged through mud. Perhaps they couldn't use *kazza*, I thought. Perhaps they'd lost us. We'd seen no one since the day before.

'Markstone!' Maric shouted. The first in days.

'Oeth,' Theluk read. 'No, I don't know it.'

The barbarian woman was missing again. I scanned the line of hills. The rain was easing. There was no sign of her. I wondered if this time she'd gone for good.

'*Marhaz*. Steal or buy, it doesn't matter which,' Haltern wheezed. 'Then make for Mirane as fast as posible, and hope we don't meet more riders than we can deal with.'

139

'We're not left with many choices, are we?' Theluk was gentle.

'I agree. Let's go.' I moved up beside her and when I had the chance asked 'What's he got?'

'Damp-lung. He needs to rest up a week or two.'

Oeth lay below us when we reached the top of the hill. A large *telestre* surrounded by outbuildings and beast-pens, almost a town. The pale sun picked out activity: carts, *marhaz*, people.

Beyond Oeth, stretching west to the horizon, lay the Fens.

PART FOUR

CHAPTER 13

The Lesser Fens

The lush mossgrass went down to clumps of weed, and then to vast beds of double-bladed reeds. Towards the horizon were stretches of standing water. Other species of mossgrass and fungi covered the acres of mudflats: black and purple, blue and green, iridescent as peacock's feathers. As we watched, a patch of sunlight swept across the desolate, flat marshland. Lurid colours flared. Water channels became silver threads, netting the sun: rivulets, ditches, pools, a web of outspreading waterways.

'The Lesser Fens,' Haltern breathed. 'Oh, that finishes it, we must go south now. *Now.*'

To the north and to the south, the hills came down like a coastline to that sea of quicksand.

Maric moved closer to us. 'Is it true – things live there that aren't human?'

Haltern looked at Theluk, who shook her head. 'We keep the edict that was made in Galen Honeymouth's time,' she said. 'We to our borders, and the fenborn to their own. No, I do not know if they are more than legend.'

'It's no concern of ours. We need *marhaz.*' Haltern stumped off down the track towards Oeth.

The main courtyard was a hundred yards across, *telestre* house on one side, stock-pens on the other three. The pens were full, an incredible hissing and bawling and stinking surrounding us; men and women shouting their bids for *kuru* and *skurrai* and *marhaz*, and for sacks of grain. Besides the fruit and bread-fungus stalls there were tables laid out with embroidered *chirith-goyen* shirts and *zilmei* coats; tunics, boots, and belt-buckles and jewellery; and the short curved *harur* blades of western Roehmonde.

'Don't stray too far,' Haltern warned, turning over in his palm what we'd been able to contribute: a few bronze bits, a silver cloak-clasp, and Theluk's sea-ivory knife. 'I'll search out someone less fond of Arad's laws, honest enough to sell for an honest price.'

'Or dishonest enough,' I said.

We walked round the square while he was gone, looking at the stalls where Ortheans wove hurdles from the thin *tukinna* saplings, and watching the professional acrobats and jugglers. Once round then back to wait, trying to look like just another group of visitors to the market. Haltern was gone a long time. Theluk settled down beside a wine stall out of the press of the crowd and Maric and I sat beside her. There was a story-teller behind me, speaking to a gaggle of *ashiren*:

'—said to the Emperor Sandor, "Golden you may be, my lord, and Golden your empire; but because of what I have done, it will not outlast the reaping of this year's golden corn—" '

A man walked past, his hand twisted in the collar of a hunting *kazza*. He did not wear the Talkul insignia. The beast stood hip-high, heavily muscled, the short white pelt marked with blue dapples. The feathery tail lashed nervously. A leather hood covered the square-jawed head, with only slits for the eyes.

Maric yanked at my sleeve, pointing.

Haltern came running through the crowd, pushed past one man, knocked a woman aside, ignoring her curses, and came up to us out of breath and sweating.

'They're here,' he said curtly. 'I saw Howice. And that hired sword, from Rimon. They must have worked out we were being driven here.'

'*Marhaz?*'

'No one will sell—' he glanced over his shoulder. 'We've got to get out of here!'

As we left the courtyard a yell went up from the far side. I heard a strong voice bellow, 'Witchbreed!' Suddenly I saw Talkul's insignia, and ran. Maric darted off towards outbuildings. We pounded through narrow mud-tracks. Haltern was wheezing, Theluk had him by the arm.

Maric shrieked something lost in the din. Then I was clear of the outbuildings, running through thick blue-grey mossgrass that dragged wetly at my boots. Panting, sweating. I slowed to wait for the others. Between the wooden buildings, I saw a man bend down and unlace the muzzle of a *kazza*.

Marhaz dotted the hills round Oeth.

'They put a cordon round the *telestre*.' It was so simple. I should have known.

Haltern, speaking between gasps, said 'Too much. One day. Saw us. Yesterday.'

Maric drew his knife. '*T'an?*'

'Run!'

144

The ground was soft. We out-distanced them, but it wouldn't be for long. As I saw past the southern edge of the *telestre* I stopped, breath heaving, chest burning. There were riders to the south, too.

'Right.' Fear hid under determination. 'Let's go out towards the Fens, see if we can work round, hide.'

The yowling whine of a *kazza* rose over the shouting.

The ground turned to mud and the mossgrass to double-headed reeds, and we halted on the very edge of the marsh. Haltern clung to Theluk's shoulder. Maric went a few steps into the mud, lurched as he sank ankle-deep, and dragged himself back. The mud sucked hungrily at his boots. We stood close together.

'That's it.' Haltern sounded relieved. 'We can't go any further.'

I put my hand under my coat, feeling the hard shape of the stunner. On a tight focus . . . perhaps.

I dropped the *kazza* thirty feet from us. The closest men and women hesitated, the impetus of the mob was lost. I glimpsed riders forcing their way through. Even a powerpack wasn't inexhaustible: I couldn't take them all.

Theluk touched my arm and pointed. There was a speck, coming down from the north over the grassland. A human speck moving with such speed that it was deceptive: she seemed to float.

The barbarian woman. And *marhaz* riders behind her. So they had put a wide cordon round Oeth: I was sorry they were taking her in it.

Now I could see her clearly, running with her head high and her elbows tucked into her sides, never putting a foot wrong. Parallel to the reed beds. A last spurt of effort – wasted, there was nowhere for her to go.

She wheeled and ran into the marsh.

She's killing herself! I thought. She dodged and turned like a dancer, not sinking, not drowning. Following a route visible only to her animal senses, picking her way out across the marsh—

'Come on!'

'You're mad,' Haltern yelled.

'Maric, stay close behind me. Tread where I do.'

The mud was black. Stepped on, it sank. A wash of evil-smelling water submerged my feet. I splashed knee-deep in mud, tore myself out, and was suddenly on firm ground.

The barbarian woman was waiting a hundred yards on. I hoped she was waiting, and not stuck. I picked my way towards her with paralysing slowness.

Water plopped. I looked round. Something splashed into the mud beside me. Theluk wasn't far behind us.

'*T'an*, please. Hurry.' Maric's agonized whisper started me moving again.

'What is it?'

'Winch-bow bolts.'

My back crawled. It was nightmarish: I couldn't move faster than a slow walk. Theluk closed the gap, catching us up. *Marhaz* riders clustered on the edge of firm ground. *Kazza* whined. I couldn't see Haltern, there were reed beds between us. Now I recognized two riders. One was Howice. The other – utterly familiar, forking the saddle as if he were part of the beast – was Falkyr.

The barbarian woman moved again, picking a slow way between water channels. Searching out the spurs of solid ground that must underlie the marsh.

Now the winch-bow bolts fell short.

Step and look, step and test. Reed-mats sagged. Mud stank, gasses bubbling up. Iridescent blue weed masked treacherous ground. The test sunlight was swallowed up in cloud. Grey haze began to creep up from the water.

'Christie.'

I waited until Theluk caught up. Like Maric and myself, she was coated in black mud to the waist. Running had made me hot: now I felt the chill of the Fens.

'Where's Hal?'

She shook her head. 'We can't wait. I don't know what happened.'

'We can't leave him!'

'If they see us, they'll follow – edict or no edict.'

The barbarian woman wasn't waiting this time. It was follow her or be stranded. I didn't hesitate. We picked our slow way across the Fens, she and I and Maric and Theluk. Great flocks of long-legged *rashaku-nai* whirred up round us, until the sky was black with them.

'He's not following.' Theluk had ceased looking behind for Haltern. 'They must have taken him.'

'There's a simpler explanation.'

'You think he's dead?'

I didn't want to believe it, but these Fens were deadly. 'It's possible.'

I realized we were on relatively firm ground. Maric ran ahead to where the barbarian woman had stopped and squatted down. This was almost an island in the fenland, a few yards high, perhaps a quarter-mile long. Thick-boled scrub grew tightly on it, nowhere more than waist-high. The metallic green leaves shone in the evening light.

I saw her digging bare-handed, then the barbarian woman unearthed several large packages. They were bound tightly in something that looked waterproof – greased hide, I guessed. She unrolled one. It was a bundle of fist sized lumps of paste, unappetizing and greasy. Already stuffing it in handfuls into her mouth, she pushed the other pack at us.

'Goddess!' Maric said a few minutes later, pausing in gobbling the fatty mess. 'This tastes foul. How can you eat it, *t'an*?'

'Cast-iron stomach. First necessity for a diplomat. You want to see some of the things they shoved at us on Beruine.' This was meat-based, I thought, and welcome; but water was going to be a problem. We couldn't drink fen water.

'How did you know?' I asked the barbarian woman.

'When—' her arm described an arc from the north-west back towards the hills '—then were many. Now—' her arm swept back, her fist closed and touched her chest.

'You left these? Caches of food?' Getting no response, I pointed north. 'There were many?'

'Dead,' she said simply.

Plain enough, if I was guessing right: a group of her people come to Roehmonde, all but her killed, and now she was returning the same way. Where, I wondered. Over the Wall, Haltern had said, Haltern who wouldn't see if his guess was right or not.

Surprisingly, the scrub burned well. Sap spat and hissed, the heat was intense. Maric joined me in pulling up bushes and dragging them into a shelter and firewood pile.

'Grief of the Goddess!' Theluk's face was stained red by the leaping flames. 'Damp it down, they'll see that twenty *seri* off!'

'Who'll see?' I watched the wood catch. It was more a bonfire than a camp fire. Standing as close as I could get to the flames, I was warm for the first time in ten days. The *ashiren* squatted down beside me. Even the barbarian woman edged closer. 'If they were going to follow, they would have by now.'

'There may be wild beasts.' Theluk was quiet. When I looked at her, I knew why. She was afraid. 'And . . . the fenborn may not be legends. Galen took it seriously enough when he was *T'An Suthai-Telestre*. In four generations no one's broken the boundary.'

Maric looked up dreamily and said, 'The High Hall of the fenborn in Tethi Starsmere is floored with skin, human and Golden. I heard that in a story somewhere.'

'That *is* legend.' As the fire died down, she kicked the outer fragments into the centre. We erected the little tent, damp-smelling, but better than sleeping in the open.

Night came, and the thick stars of the Orthean winter sky shone through the clear air. It was chillingly cold facing away from the fire. A while after dark, the tail of a nebula rose above the horizon. Filmy red and blue, it covered half the southern sky. It took me some time to think, I've travelled past that. Out along the spiral arm, to Earth.

The hills near Oeth still looked close, despite the *seri* we'd come. In the clear morning air I could make out each dip and hollow, white in the early sun, grey in shadow. Coils of mist hugged the fen water. Ice spangled the scrub.

Maric was coughing. Theluk took his head in her hand, peered in his eyes and nose, and down his throat. She patted his arm dismissively.

'You'll be all right.'

He began rolling the tent up. She crossed to me and said, 'Damp-lung. It's not surprising. Why you brought *kir* into this wet country amazes me.'

'I was supposed to leave him for Howice's people?'

'They'd have cared for *kir*.' Watching me, her expression changed. 'Who'd harm an *ashiren*? Who'd dare?'

'Anyway, *will* he be all right?'

'Not unless *ke* gets somewhere warm and dry.'

The night chorus of whoops and cries had stopped at dawn. It was quiet now, a white silence. In the faded blue sky the daystars were pinpoints of light. The Fens stretched out south and west and north, flat to the wide horizon.

Only, in the north there was a line of darker blue about ten degrees up the sky. I couldn't decide if it were low cloud or extremely high hills. As the dawn warmth drew the mist up, I lost sight of it altogether.

'I will not wait for thee,' the barbarian woman said.

'Oh – sure. We go that way.' I pointed south. We could parallel the Roehmonde hills most of the day, I thought, and hope Talkul's riders had lost us when we emerged.

'No.' She indicated north-west. 'That is my way.'

'Damn it, we don't want to go further into this!'

'That is my road,' she said, with the nearest to temper I'd ever heard from her. 'If it is not thy road, go thy way.'

'Theluk!'

But Theluk couldn't argue her out of it either. The barbarian woman was going home – wherever that was – and nowhere else.

'The other side of Lesser Fens, the Great Fens begin, and the other side of the Great Fens is Peir-Dadeni – and that is six hundred *seri*, skirting the marshes, and do you think we can walk six hundred *seri* through this? Can you?'

Eventually she gave up. 'Can we go south alone?'

'Can you find a path?' When that sunk in, I said 'If we lose her, we're stuck, it's that simple.'

'You may have killed us all, coming here.'

'So I may – but that doesn't mean I'll stop trying to get out.'

She turned her back on me. 'Load your pack light, *ashiren-te*, I'll take more in mine.'

My head was hot and heavy and thick. I couldn't stop my nose running, and I shivered continuously. Throat and lungs were raw from coughing. I chewed another of the bitter painkillers from the medic kit. It didn't lessen the pain, but it detached me from it.

Maric, when he coughed, spat pink phlegm. Even Theluk had the wheezing that marks the beginning of damp-lung.

The barbarian woman pushed on as fast as was possible. With all her circling and back-tracking, she was keeping us headed north of west on a direct course. It may have been fever, or empathy, but I was beginning to see the Fens as she must: islands of safe ground, of greater and lesser size, separated by rivers and seas of insect-ridden water.

Two days, or was it three? This was the first night we hadn't been able to light a fire. Fog drifted past us. At the arch of the sky it was silver. Moisture clung to the twisted branches of low trees. We sat among roots, on the highest spot of land in a flooded basin, wrapped in *becamil* blankets, boots almost in the water.

Luminous *siriye* darted past, multifaceted eyes glowing. Odd cries came from the reed beds. Maric leaned against me, sleeping with his mouth open, breathing harshly.

Darkness hit me. It wasn't sleep. There was no knowledge of being unconscious: it was as if time pleated itself. I woke with a headache that threatened to split bone.

An unhuman face stared into mine.

Time slipped again: totally disorientated. When I sat up, I held my head and whimpered. Phlegm loosened, I coughed and spat. Each spasm rocked my head. The pain almost blinded me.

At last I could sit quiet. The relief was incredible. I opened watery eyes. The light was green. Reaching up, my fingers met a yielding surface. Very slowly it dawned on me that I was under cover. The surface was leather. Pegged over – branches? And laying on more of the same: me, and others with me. The face I'd seen – or was that fever-dream? – that cat-eyed and prick-eared face stayed with me, with visionary intensity.

Theluk. Maric. The *ashiren* lay sprawled on one side, looking very young and vulnerable. Theluk's face was the colour of uncooked meal. Both were asleep or unconscious. The barbarian woman was missing. But on the other side of Theluk, a broad-shouldered man lay with his back to me. For a second I thought, *Haltern*! But as I knelt upright, I saw who it was.

Scarred face, the puddingy red and white skin masking half the forehead, cheek, and chin. That's a burn, I thought detachedly. Fair silver-streaked mane. The faint dapple of marshflower on his broad hands.

I saw the hired sword out of Rimon, Haltern said. In Oeth.

Did they all follow? Is he the only one? Why; who?

It was like coming out of anaesthetic, I didn't believe in the reality of the world. I'd had dreams in the dark that were coming back to me now. This might be another. There were long gaps in my memory. That last camp site was more than a day away, I thought.

I slept again.

Light flickered. I rubbed my gummy eyes open. There was a dim impression in my mind of being fed something liquid, and – perhaps of being carried, I wasn't sure.

Light was red, yellow, was firelight, and shadows moved on the sides of a tent. A much larger tent. There was a gap at its apex, and a glimpse of daystarred sky.

The barbarian woman sat cross-legged beside a firepit, feeding chunks of peat and wood to the flames. I moved, sat up, coughed. Physical misery rushed back. It was at the same time stuffy and cold in the tent, and difficult to breathe. I edged over on all fours to the fire.

'Thou?' She touched her throat, and then mine.

My, head ached, my throat was sore, but my lungs had cleared. Dopily I thought, I must congratulate Adair. The shots work. No pneumonia, no pleurisy. Christ. Lucky!

I said, 'Where are we?'

Her answer was unintelligible. I knelt over the fire for a while, and then stood up. My legs were weak. The tent stank of excrement and illness. I made my way over to the flap, gripping the struts for support, and picked at the lacings.

150

There was no warmth from the sun hanging low in the south. The pale sky dazzled me. I blinked. Outside, the chill struck into me. This was high land, a good yard above the water table level: an island larger than most. Scrub and twisted trees covered it. I went a little way from the tent to shit.

The Roehmonde hills were no longer visible. There was nothing, in all the vast circle of the horizon, except the Fens. Across a water channel were more of the dull green tents, blending into the background, and a few figures – I couldn't tell what they were at that distance. Quarantine, I thought. And giggled weakly. Whoever had us didn't want us.

Back in the tent I found Maric awake and huddled over the fire. Theluk was trying to question the barbarian woman. The man – Blaize n'ri n'suth Meduenin, it came back bell-clear from the trial – was muttering in his sleep, and twitching.

'They're fenborn!' the boy said excitedly. 'I was awake, I saw them.'

'Where are we?' Theluk asked.

'As near the middle of nowhere as makes no difference.' I had to sit down before I fell down, I had no resources of strength left. I wondered just how ill I had been.

'What's he doing here?' Maric jerked his head at the man. 'They've taken our packs, *t'an*, and the *harur* swords.'

The stunner was missing too, I realized.

Theluk bent over the fair-maned Orthean, rolling up his eyelids with her thumb. She frowned. Examining him, she sniffed his breath and peered down his throat. The puzzled look vanished.

'He's not sick,' she said, 'maybe a touch of damp-lung, that's all.'

'What's wrong with him?'

'He's *ataile* addicted. For some time, I'd guess. He won't find any in the Fens. Well, if he lives through this, he'll be free of it.'

'If he lives?'

'We ought to kill him,' Maric said. 'While we can. He's followed you to kill you, *t'an* Christie.'

And got picked up the same time we did? I thought. He must have been behind us from Oeth. What drove him to that?

'*Ke's* right,' Theluk agreed, 'we've little enough chance of getting out of here as it is.'

'No, we can't do that.' I had a sneaking regret they hadn't done it while I was unconscious. You can't argue with a fact. And I didn't need active malice on top of everything else.

There was a call from outside. The barbarian woman rose fluidly to her feet and left the tent. I followed her, Theluk holding onto the struts of the doorway behind me.

Fenborn.

He was not human, not even by Orthean standards, which were what I applied. The barbarian woman talked to him, standing on the edge of the waterway.

He was younger than she, slender, with stick-thin limbs, and not much taller than Maric. Pale, dusty-olive skin had, in the wintry sunlight, a bloom of gold on it. Green and gold, changing hue with every movement, as in the weave of a cloth. He was hairless except for a fine black down on his skull, a ridge from forehead to mid-spine. Obviously male. There was something wrong or odd about the jointing of his limbs.

Seeing us, he left the conversation with the barbarian woman and walked over to the tent. His eyes were black, slit-pupilled, half-veiled. As he breathed, I saw light and shadow chase each other over his skin.

He touched my hand (rough snakeskin feel) and snatched his fingers away. There were webs between them, pale dapples down his seamed belly. I wanted to laugh: hysteria. His fingers were ice-cold. He said something I didn't understand, repeated it, and turned away.

The barbarian woman was not having much better luck in making herself understood, I saw.

In one movement the fenborn slid under the surface of the channel, out of sight until the dark-ridged head appeared thirty feet away, at the far bank. With obvious distaste, the barbarian woman waded through the mud and swam after him.

She hadn't returned by nightfall.

We rested four days in that temporary camp. I often saw the barbarian woman among the other tents with the fenborn, though she mostly returned to us at nightfall. She answered no questions.

I wasn't sure at the end of that time if the fenborn were intelligent, or only animals. Their speech had nothing in common with any of the Southland languages, being only grunts. They pegged hides over branches as tents, and gutted the *rashaku-nai* and marsh beasts with stone knives . . . and yet beavers make dams and fieldmice weave nests. The fenborn were equally at home in water or on the low land, or – judging by the pack of young ones – in the twisted branches of the trees.

None of them entered our tent. One came as far as the entrance and had a chittering and growling argument with the barbarian –

she was not much better understood in their camp than she was in ours – which ended in a scuffle. It was not until I studied the fenborn that I realized they had no use of fire. And the barbarian woman had Theluk's tinder-box, and a firm determination to keep the firepit going.

'We can't stay here,' Theluk said towards afternoon on the fourth day. 'They can't keep us.'

Westering light was lilac over the water, and the low trees stood black against the horizon. Wide-winged lizardbirds circled overhead.

'It isn't them – it's that.'

The Fens lay chill under the darkening sky. The days were noticeably shorter now.

'How's the kid?' She'd been caring for him; Earthspeaker duties included medical training.

'*Ke's* well enough, likely to recover if *ke's* kept warm. There's nothing else I can do.'

'The other one?'

'What's he got to do with me?' She was uncharacteristically savage. 'Hunts us half-way across Roehmonde, drives us into this Goddess-forsaken place, and expects nursing? No, not from me. If it's his time, She'll take him; and if not, he'll live.'

Walking the perimeter of our island, we came back to the tent. It was no great distance. The woman stretched, linking her bony fingers; and then dug them into the roots of her mane, kneading the muscles at the back of her neck. She was tense all the time now.

'I don't feel for this land,' she said, 'it's too far from home. Perhaps Arad was right. Too much strangeness – there are some parts of Her that I'll never understand.'

She ducked under the open flap into the tent. I watched the fading light. A cluster of dark blobs in the water resolved themselves into fenborn young. They chittered, darted back to the opposite bank as swift as fish, and became a shrieking, tumbling mob.

'Tastes like *rashaku* droppings.'

'Eat it or starve.'

I woke to hear Maric quarrelling with the scarred man. We had no hot food or drink, only raw meat that could be scorched in the firepit, and a choice between fen water and leather containers of some milky liquid. Meduenin was right: it was foul.

Theluk rolled over, ignoring everyone. I saw the barbarian

woman was missing again. On top of the cold, I was developing some kind of allergic reaction, my eyes and nose streaming, and a skin rash.

'You're dead,' the man said, 'all of you. You may be too stupid to realize it, but you are.'

The jeering note got to me. I sat up. He was propped against the tent strut, hands flat on the ground beside him. Sunlight from the open flap lit his dusty mane, and the red ruin of his half-face.

'You want this?' Maric passed over the leather bag. I sucked the milk, ignoring the taste.

'You were paid to kill.' My voice was rusty. 'Pity you got caught with us. Not too clever, was it?'

He looked pared down to the bone. All through the withdrawal fever from the *ataile* addiction, it had been impossible to make him eat. At one point Theluk had knotted a blanket round him, while he thrashed in delirium. Now he stared, cocky because he was alive. And wondering why none of us had knifed him, I thought.

'I'm going to see you dead,' he told me in a conversational tone.

'What good will it do you? Will it help that if you kill me?'

His left hand was rubbing his right wrist: he snatched them apart as if they burned him. The broken wrist had mended, though not set (Theluk said) as well as it could have been. He had the use of it.

'You won't find them,' Maric put in, seeing him looking round for his packs. 'The fenborn have everything.'

'Fenborn—' he glanced outside obviously remembering something of what had gone on round him. Seen in profile, he was young. Younger than Theluk: late twenties, perhaps, or early thirties. 'Well now: fenborn.'

'My government—'

'Is a long way from here, if I understand right.'

He was not impressed by Earth, by envoys. Obviously not, or he wouldn't have been hired as killer and witness against me.

'Leave it.' I stood up, rubbing my itching eyes, and hunched over the fire. The whole conversation was beginning to seem unreal. Events were hallucinatory. I thought, *how fit am I?* 'Just – leave it. We'll settle it later on. Not here. Not now.'

'Why not now?' he challenged.

There were four of us in the tent, and no one of us fit, but it was still three to one. I admired his nerve, if nothing else.

'Because I don't propose to do the fenborn's work for them. Because if they kill us, they won't leave you out. It's nothing personal – different customs, you might say. Let's call a truce.'

'Is it true you're Witchbreed?'

I shook my head. He sounded as though he hoped I was.

'Law doesn't apply here,' he said.

I was still trying to work out exactly what he meant, when the fenborn came for us.

CHAPTER 14

Speaker-for-the-People

Orthe's pale sky gleamed like water, freckled at the horizon with needlepoint daystars. Pith-reeds spiked up out of frozen mud, brittle white spears. The ground creaked underfoot. Webs of ice edged the open water. The flat marsh went out to an infinite haze.

A fenborn gestured with her spear, and we huddled aside while the tent was ripped down. The firepit was given a wide berth. Two or three of them bent to paw and sniff the leather and struts. Eventually it was discarded, left in the mud. I felt homeless. Sweat, the lingering taint of sickness: it had enclosed a warm and somehow comforting smell of humanity, but the chill air dispersed it.

'What are they going to do?' It was the first time Maric had questioned or complained, though he'd been crying when he thought himself unobserved.

'I don't know. It's all right.' I put my arm round his shoulders, taking him under my blanket. I needed to hold on to somebody. We had the clothes we stood up in, and covers rescued from the tent; that was all. Theluk was barefoot, her sandals lost somewhere. We looked like refugees.

They carried spears and double-tined forks with stone blades and long shafts, and stone axes. Some flint-tipped spears lowered in our direction. I tensed. The barbarian woman appeared out of the mob, gestured towards the water, and a gap appeared in the crowd. I moved hesitantly in that direction. Theluk closed up the distance behind me, her eyes scanning rapidly. Herded, we reached the water.

There was a scuffle behind. I paid no attention. Blaize n'ri n'suth Meduenin cursed, and then was with us again, wiping a bloody mouth.

Flat-bottomed boats were piled with rolled-up tents and fishspears. We sat among damp leather and gutted marsh beasts.

A woman heaved us free of the mud, and we were poled across the deep water to the other side of the channel. Tall reed beds rattled in the wind.

A group of fenborn stepped lightly aboard. I could see six other boats from where I sat, all low in the water. Hides stretched over a wooden framework: I could feel the pulse of the water under me. Theluk sat bolt upright, gripping the sides.

'Can you swim?' Blaize said sardonically. 'It might be easier in the end.'

'They'd kill us.' Maric's eyes fixed on the fenborn, adult and young, who followed the boats, threading paths over the treacherous mud, or swimming and diving in the open channel.

'Quick, at least. There are harder ways of dying.'

'Be quiet,' I snapped. He shrugged.

We passed through deeper channels between towering banks of reeds, yellow-green and still with the husks of red bloom on them. Two of the fenborn stood at the rear of the leaf-shaped boat, digging long poles into the mud. A third sat in the centre, breast-feeding an infant. She had dugs like an old sow. Two others, nearer me in the boat, were trying to keep four or five young fenborn quiet.

One of the litter, about three seasons old, crawled over the tents to stare at us. The dark eyes watched us, nictitating membrane blurring the slit pupils. Broad forehead, pointed chin, and flat ears that came to a small point. The impression was half-human, half-batrachian, but not ugly. A changeling child.

The younger male swept it up and dumped it unceremoniously back in the stern, with the immemorial gesture of adults. Male? I thought. And stared. The belly bulged. Undeniably male, but to all appearances pregnant.

Settled back down again, the younger male and the female had their heads together. I saw him, slender webbed hands at his stomach; and then he was holding an oblate spheroid, and then another. The female took and examined them. They were greenish-white, fist sized, and with a tough flexible covering.

Terison, it came back to me; Terison, and the birth, and the babies born in a flexible membrane. The membrane that must be the last evolutionary remnant of this process.

The younger male was replacing the eggs in his pouch, and the other female giving suck to the child – or was it a different child? I couldn't tell. Ortheans don't pair, they group. This group, I thought, must be one unit; I wonder if it applies to the other boats . . .

'Are you all right?'

I hugged Maric closer, and managed to stop giggling. 'It's just funny, the things I still notice. When there's no need.'

Theluk's knuckles were white with the strain of gripping the boat. She didn't talk, only shaking her head in response to questions. Blaize n'ri n'suth Meduenin had a curious abstracted expression, almost a lost look, and his hands went to his belt-pouch as if he expected to find *ataile* leaves. It was not an addict's search. If he lives, Theluk had said, he'll lose the desire. I thought, he's trying to understand why he doesn't want it any more.

Towards noon I saw the shadow-line on the northern horizon again. It was too hazy for hills, unless extremely distant, but too solid for cloud. I lost sight of it after that, as we came among wider channels and higher islands covered with interlinking trees. Roots hung black into the water, contrasting with the chrome-yellow, plate-like leaves. The water was the colour of jade. *Kekri* flies hung in clouds in the midday warmth, glittering metallic blue and green. Other fenborn came to take over poling the boat. They swam in the stagnant water, catching their food live, and sometimes throwing mudcrawlers or amphibians into the bottom of the boat. No one fed us. I was too tensed up to notice.

I thought, if this is how they took us when we were first captured and drugged, we could be a hundred *seri* from Roehmonde. And if so, and if we do get free – where are we going to go?

Channels and mudflats: the monotony of the flat land bore down on us. The afternoon passed in a daze. The sun stood over my left shoulder. The boats crept on northwards, and a dark smudge grew infinitesimally until I could make out more scrub-covered islands. I began to see more fenborn, some in camps, some standing and watching as we passed. There were no hails. We drifted in a silence that lulled us into apathy, hid fear under temporary boredom.

Trees met overhead, enclosing us in a yellow twilight. Through thin gaps the afternoon sun dappled white on black water. I shook Maric awake.

'What?' He threshed upright. 'Where?'

'I think we're stopping.'

The trees extended roots into the water, black scaly bark covered with scarlet and blue mosses. Fenborn children crouched on the roots watching us, sometimes slipping under the surface and coming up beside the boat. They chattered, and gave high-pitched squeals. The adults grunted and swatted them away. The boat was poled into an apparent dead end, where other boats were moored. The charnel, spicy odour of the disturbed water was overpowering.

Fenborn slid lithely ashore, pulling and jamming the boat between roots. There was no earth visible. The roots and fibres formed a semi-solid mat. Maric looked questioningly at me. I tried to focus, to concentrate; I wished I could see the barbarian woman. One fenborn grunted, jabbing a spear in my direction. I reached out and hauled myself up into the roots, clambering, clutching at branches, and holding out a hand to Maric. Underfoot, the matted roots gave and swayed. Blaize followed, then Theluk. The fenborn chittered.

Theluk shoved me aside, breaking free. Scrambling over roots, clutching branches, hurling herself along the edge of the island – away from the fenborn. Maric called out. The nearest fenborn threw a stone axe with perfect accuracy, catching the Earthspeaker at the base of the skull.

She went forward as if her legs had been cut out from under her, hit the roots, spun sideways, then jack-knifed in a fold that slid her under the black water.

The ripples died.

I stared stupidly at the spot where Theluk vanished.

Two fenborn dived under the water, and reappeared moments later. As they climbed out, a swirl of water showed the soaked cloth of Theluk's coat. It sank again. The fenborn chattered at each other. The spears jerked with an unmistakable command: move.

'She – I – she wouldn't have felt—' I was blank. 'It can't have happened. It – must have killed her, she—'

Maric cried noisily and wiped his face, leaving smears of black mud.

'Do you want to end up with her?' Blaize shoved the *ashiren* forward. The fenborn's incomprehensible order came again. Spears raised.

Theluk. It was impossible to walk over the mass of roots without concentrating on not slipping. I thought of Theluk, and if branches were too weak to bear my weight, and of Theluk: never really known, only as the friend of a friend. Bemused, moving in a dream, under snaking branches and green and yellow leaves; and Theluk, competent, and a private person: *why* did she run, what panicked her?

Now we were surrounded by fenborn, male and female, old and young; with a pack of children underfoot. Barefoot, sharp-eyed, frighteningly silent.

Those seconds: so quick, so casual, if I'd had my head turned the other way I'd never have seen it. Theluk. The slung axe, the folding body. Barely a disturbance. And now wide-eyed and mud-throated down in the tangled roots.

'Christie.' Maric took my hand, and we walked onto firmer ground.

Shafts of autumn sun speared down into the gloom. The tangle of branches lifted, forming a high roof and the tightly woven roots were carpeted with skins. Fenborn sat and stood round the edge of this natural hall. The skins, two and three deep, made for firmer footing. They had a curious dusty gold sparkle to them. In the centre space, on a massive block of blue-grey stone, sat an ancient fenborn. Beside her was the barbarian woman.

I went up to her, pointing at the old fenborn. 'Has she thy tongue?'

'Yes. Little.'

'Then tell her – tell her there's been a murder.'

The silence was broken, the barbarian woman and the fenborn with us all screeching at the old fenborn woman. The assembly jabbered. A child's thin wail rose above the noise. The old woman raised her arms. The noise quieted.

'She is Speaker-for-the-People,' the barbarian woman said. 'Thy friend is dead?'

'They killed her!' Maric, shrill.

The fenborn woman grunted. I stepped forward. She looked down at me. She was dirty, faded, eyes filmed over with whitening membrane. A frown tugged at her forehead. She gestured.

'Show thy hands,' the barbarian woman said.

I put my hands flat on the shoulder-high stone. The fenborn woman put her hand beside them, prodding, counting over the fingers. Her hand was icy. She reached down, touching me on the cheek, staring into my eyes. I held still. There was nothing to do. It wouldn't bring Theluk back if I got myself killed.

A flare of empathy came through the old woman's touch. I knew beyond doubt that she would not order me murdered. It was so certain that I was not surprised when the barbarian woman said, 'Thou and thy possessions are free of here: she says, *Go.*'

'What's she going to do about Theluk?'

There was speech too swift for me to follow, part in the fenborn grunts and squeals, part in the barbarian woman's archaic con-glomerate of several Southland tongues. Behind me, Blaize n'ri n'suth Meduenin swore.

'Never mind the dead,' he said, 'what about the living?'

The barbarian woman argued in the sun-striped twilight. Yells came from the crowd. The blue-grey stone, lit by the white sun, showed intricate carvings on its side. Too intricate for fenborn. Hunger buzzed in my head and settled in a knot of pain in my chest.

'She says, *Go*,' the barbarian woman repeated.

Some of the other fenborn dragged packs out onto the floor. They'd been opened and picked through, some seams ripped, some clothes torn, and a lot of stuff missing. The medic kit was there, but empty. Surprised, I saw the *harur* blades had been left untouched.

I hesitated. It was failing Theluk not to push it further. But what good would it do?

I scooped up half the stuff and Maric grabbed the rest. As we turned away, spears lowered.

'You said we could go!' I called.

'Thou,' the barbarian woman said, 'and I, but not these others.'

Maric gaped. Then Blaize spoke.

'Possessions too,' he emphasized, 'and *ke* is her *l'ri-an*, and I am her hired sword; you must send us with her.'

The barbarian woman translated it. I saw Blaize keen and tense, half his attention on them and half on the discarded *harur* blades. He'll fight, I thought, if this doesn't work.

At last the barbarian woman touched her hands to the fenborn's, and walked swiftly towards us. She gestured us to follow, and this time they let all of us pass.

'Watch your back,' Blaize murmured, 'they've already killed once.'

'I don't need reminding!'

'Pity you didn't remind them.'

I nearly stopped to argue it out there, but we had to keep moving. The fenborn clustered round us. They were overhead in the branches, sure footed; close by, not quite touching.

'I should have talked to her,' Maric said. 'She looked after me. If I'd seen she was scared, if I'd listened, she might not have run like that. Do you think she would have run like that?'

'She misjudged, that's all.' Blaize was less sharp. 'There's no second chances.'

Out from under the trees, to a low muddy shore. The whole western sky was silver and indigo, reflected in water channels, gleaming on mud flats. The rushes rattled. The barbarian woman caught the prow of one of the shallow boats. I dumped the armful of stuff in the bottom of the boat, and Maric copied me.

Why they took us, why they didn't kill us, why they let all of us go – I can speculate, but I don't know. The barbarian woman and

I still had a very imperfect understanding of each other. It was possible they thought the Fens would kill us. Or other fenborn. Or the barbarian woman herself. Or was it some blood-price for Theluk?

'Move,' I said, trying to keep balanced, and the barbarian woman and I clumsily poled the boat out into the middle of the channel. The fenborn watched us in silence. Blaize sat, sorting through the baggage for his own gear. Maric held the edge of the boat, staring back over the stern.

'I suppose it's different for an Earthspeaker,' he said, 'but everyone should go back to their own *telestre* when they die. For the fire. The Goddess is always the Goddess, but – I don't want to rot in these marshes.'

'Nor do I.' It was difficult to keep the boat from grounding. 'We'll stop when we're out of sight. See if you can't get *rashaku-nai* with that sling of yours. We've got to eat.'

The boy was expert with slingstones, and the barbarian woman had a remarkable ability to catch mudcrawlers. Blaize took a turn poling the boat. And I watched for the fenborn. I couldn't believe they'd leave us alone.

Second twilight showed, on the distant northern horizon, the faint shadow of hills.

PART FIVE

CHAPTER 15

Over the Wall of the World

'Can you use these?' I offered Maric Theluk's *harur-nilgiri* and *harur-nazari*.

He said hesitantly, 'I'm still *ashiren*.'

'And I don't know one end of them from the other – you do.'

He buckled the belt round his waist, drew the blades – that simultaneous flourish – and replaced them to make readjustments. I thought how he'd changed. He was skinny, a little taller, and the once cropped mane hung round his face in rat's-tails. But he was not a child. *Ashiren* or not, if he were human I'd have taken him for a young man.

'The packs are light,' he observed.

'Thieving savages.' I knew the fenborn had followed us, watching, to the edge of the Fens. Their light-fingered way with property didn't bother the Southlanders – who weren't particular that way themselves – but it annoyed me. All I'd got left was the stunner, and that only because it had no recognizable use. It was pure chance no one had tossed it in a ditch.

'Christie.' The barbarian woman came over with her arms full of the waxed food-skins. I used my knife to rip one open, and Maric and I ate handfuls of the cold greasy meat. It had been lean going the past five days. Most fen beasts and predators were hibernating.

'Which is thy way now?' I asked her, and the barbarian woman pointed at the Wall.

The five days in the boat had been mild for autumn, hazy skies and mist over the Fens, so it was not until today that we had gained a clear sight of the hills. I was curious: they were surely too low to have shown up so far across the marshes. Then, looking idly up beyond them into the hazed sky, I saw first blue shadow, then what I took for solid cloud, and at last glittering rocks and snow peaks. Breaking from the haze and showing itself clear across the northern horizon was the Wall of the World.

We camped on a low heath just out of the marshes, using the framework of the boat to fuel a fire. Low hills rolled up to the north, covered with a brown-gold mossgrass and outfalls of rock. About six *seri* away the foothills humped up, covered with dark trees; and the base of the Wall fanned up from them.

'You want us to *climb*—'

'There is a path.' Her hands moved narrowly apart. She must have come down that way, I realized. So there must be a pass.

North-east and south-west, the line of the Wall continued. There were peaks, headlands, crevasses striking back into the northern land. But in most places it was sheer rock face, heaved up like a snow-crested wave about to smash down on the Fens. Some gigantic slip-fault. We faced rock cliffs easily seven thousand feet high, and those further off – I squinted in the clear light – maybe twenty or thirty thousand.

'If you're going to have an unknown pass down from the Barrens, this is the place to have it.' Blaize n'ri n'suth Meduenin bent down to fasten his pack. He nodded at the Fens. 'Any barbarian army that can get through that and still manage to invade us deserves to win.'

Maric pointedly ignored him. 'Need we go, Christie? Maybe we could follow these foothills back to Roehmonde.'

'If it doesn't mean crossing fens again. If it isn't a great distance, which I suspect it is. If Roehmonde was any less dangerous than being here.'

He had to crane his neck to see the top of the peaks. 'Is that any better?'

'To be practical – while we follow her, we know there are caches of food along the route. We'll eat. As for getting back to Roehmonde,' I admitted, 'I'm lost.'

'What about him?' He indicated Blaize, who'd moved out of earshot, staring up at the Wall.

'Keep it as we've been doing it. Sleep alternate watches, and don't take your eyes off him.'

We paralleled the Wall all of that day, walking in a mild sun and a south wind from the Fens. Towards second twilight the barbarian woman turned from west to north, rounding a headland that flamed saffron in the sunset. Twenty *seri* away across low hills, the Wall stood black against the west. The crevasse ran up towards the north, so that we were walking with peaks on either side, and the ground was almost imperceptibly rising. We made camp in a shallow dip, burning strips of the brown mossgrass and eating cold rations.

I took first watch. The sun set abruptly behind an outflung spur of the Wall; second twilight was short. Silver light flooded the ground, inking in shadows, leaching the colours from the heath. The others huddled asleep in the dip, out of the night wind. I was alone.

The stars were so close and so numerous that they ran together in blazes of light, webs of blue-white spangled with darkness. The Fens lay hidden under pale fog. This barren land that went up between rock faces was rough-coated, a shaggy sleeping animal. And the Wall itself, the Wall of the World, blocked out the stars like a tide of night.

I came back towards the camp, lacing myself up. It was chill, the mossgrass was crunchy with frost, and the sun put long shadows into the west. The peaks and cliffs of the Wall stood out in minute detail. I paused, looking south over the Fens. Somewhere past them, past Roehmonde and Ymir, hundreds of *seri* from here, the same sun was gilding the ship's masts at harbour in Tathcaer, and now the dawn bells were ringing out over the island.

Light flickered in the corner of my eye. Reflex taking over, I ducked and fell and rolled away. Coming upright I thought, over-reacting, you're getting nervous, Christie. And then I saw the knife at the base of the rock outcrop, and the white scar on the stone. Blaize n'ri n'suth Meduenin came lightly down the slope, *harur-nilgiri* carried in his left hand and *harur-nazari* in his right. The scar made something impossible of his expression.

Can I take him? I thought, and he circled round, and the morning sun was in my eyes. I dropped again, anticipating, and heard the spang of metal on rock: the *harur-nazari* thrown and lost. I backed into rock-shadow. The steel glittered wickedly.

He closed in, and I rehearsed in my mind the methods for disarming attackers, feeling stiff and awkward in the cold air. And he came closer and I shot him.

The whine of high-pitched sound cracked the morning open. I heard Maric shout and then he came tumbling over the slope, drawing Theluk's *harur* blades, and stopped dead. The barbarian woman watched impassively from the top of the dip. I took my thumb off the stud, and the silence was frightening. The stunner was warm, comfortable in my palm.

'Is he dead?' Maric asked.

'I don't think so.' I knelt down and rolled the man onto his back. He was heavy. His arms flopped. I'd never used the stunner on an Orthean. If they were more sensitive . . .

A little blood ran from his ears and nose. But the heartbeat was strong under my hand.

'What am I going to do with you?' I was talking to myself. I left him, melted frost soaking into the back of his tunic, and went to pick up the knives. The blade a few feet from his outstretched hand was a slender Rimon *harur-nilgiri*. Maric eyed the man warily and came to sit on one of the rocks. I had to sit down. I sat rubbing the heels of my hands into my eye-sockets, trying to relieve tension. It was quiet. We were that way for some time; the shadows shortened as the sun rose up the sky, and the *rashaku-nai* hooted mournfully down in the Fens.

'What are you going to do?' Maric asked flatly. 'You – we – have to kill him. Before he kills us.'

It was logic, but I couldn't face it.

'Or we could leave him here. Just – go. Let the land kill him for us.'

'No, we can't do that. I know he's a good tracker. I can't be forever watching my back,' I protested.

'Spoken like a true Southlander.' Blaize's voice was a croak. He hitched himself up on his elbows, watching us.

'What the hell do you think you're playing at?'

'I was hired for a certain purpose,' he said.

'In the Fens you claimed to be my hired sword.'

'In Corbek I claimed you were my *arykei*, does that make it true?'

It made me furious. He grinned, sitting up and shaking his head to clear it. He rubbed his ears. Part deaf, I guessed.

'Of all the stupid . . . and we're miles from Melkathi.'

'Did I mention SuBannasen?' His head was cocked sideways and he was frowning. And watching lips, I realized, and deliberately turned my head when I spoke to Maric.

'Get the stuff packed. I think there's a limit to how long she'll wait for us.'

'Right. What about him?'

'Leave it to me.' I balanced the *harur* blades. I'd keep the throwing knife, I decided.

'You don't have to mention SuBannasen,' I told Blaize, 'I can add up facts as well as anyone. But what difference does it make, here?'

I had to repeat the question. He said, 'I'm a sell-sword. I make my living because I keep my word. Unreliable mercenaries don't get paid.'

'Is that what brought you into the Fens – money?'

He got to his feet slowly. I pushed the *harur* blades over to him. There was no point one of us being unarmed in this wild country.

'You're careless,' he accused.

'No, I'll defend myself when I'm attacked.'

'Oh, that I don't doubt.' A touch of the old acid.

'Shall I tell you one more thing? The damage isn't permanent, I shouldn't think. You'll hear clear by the end of the day.' It was impossible to miss the fear and relief in his eyes. 'But that's once – I can't answer for what might happen a second or third time; you seem to be more sensitive to high-frequency sound than we are. If it happens again, the damage might be permanent.'

He sheathed the blades and then looked at me, weighing up what I'd said. Maric appeared with the barbarian woman, and called to me. She was already turning away towards the Wall.

'You think you can cross *that*?'

'She did.'

'Ah, I see. Sooner than return south, you prefer a quiet death on the rock face. Understandable.'

'Well, never mind mercenary ethics. Am I going to have to watch my back all the time from now on?'

'That's rough travelling.' His gaze still took in the Wall. 'And as I thought before – laws don't apply out here.'

I didn't trust him. But we went on up the narrowing valley, between peaks spidered with snow against a glaring sky.

Walking was hell. The brown mossgrass here grew tough and springy and knee-high. Impossible to push through, it was necessary with each step to tread it down. And it hid potholes, ankle-wrenching rifts in the ground. The first half-hour had me running with sweat despite the icy wind. Old dry shoots broke off as we walked and crept into everything; hair, eyes, shirt, and boots.

By unspoken consent we broke to rest every few miles. I sprawled belly-down and breathless, and thought that if the barbarian woman couldn't wait for us she could go too – but she sensed our temper, I think, and slowed her pace.

At second twilight I raised my head, having been walking all day, watching where I was putting my feet. It amazed me how close the mountains had come. No, not close, I thought. We're already in them.

Miles distant on either side, the great peaks rose up. This rough unforested land they held between them was an ancient geological split – and must be the barbarian woman's pass. We were way above fen-level, and the land was still rising.

Mist gathered over a cold stream bed. The barbarian woman uncovered food and skin tents in a cleft slope that wasn't worth the name of cave. We cleared a space to burn mossgrass, and huddled out of the wind. Sleep didn't come easy. By now we were wearing all the spare gear we had, and it was still bone-chillingly cold. I woke several times to chafe circulation into hands and feet.

If the weather doesn't break, I thought, maybe we stand a chance. If the wind rises . . . if the chill-factor increases . . . if it rains . . .

If we don't get across this pass and down into the country beyond inside a day – tomorrow – then the chances are we won't make it.

I fell asleep without ever wondering what lay the other side of the mountains.

Dawn showed pale rock against a star-dusted sky, all milky shades of blue and pastel grey – soft, it looked; and yet as I saw it I could sense the knife-sharp rock, the razor-edged wind. Here the cold presence of the rock was closely felt: dark, wet, massive and solid. But ahead and all around, scarp-faces reared up into the northern sky. Ten, fifteen, twenty thousand feet in one sheer span. And the blue distance softened them to grey and white.

Dawn, and a long day coming.

The mossgrass grew sparsely as we climbed higher – it was a blessing to walk easy for once – and great broken boulders littered the steep slope. The chill of the rock struck through *becamil* coats; breath was white on the air.

Towards midday the first tendrils of mist crept down off the peaks.

Old brown snow, still frozen from last winter, clung to the northern shelter of the boulders. Sounds echoed. Somewhere I heard water falling.

A hot ache settled itself under my ribs. The air parched in my throat and lungs. Cold and the physical effort shut me off: we climbed each in our own world. The barbarian woman was always ahead, vanishing into the thickening mist and reappearing like a vision.

Putting one foot in front of the other took all my concentration. Mist pearled on my hair, soaking it; my lips froze with every breath. Twice when I sat down to rest I fell instantly asleep, but the cold woke me. Each time it was harder to get up again.

It frightened me that I was so exhausted, so soon. And there was a new sensation I felt but couldn't identify – more a vacancy than an exhaustion – that would have frightened me all the more had I been capable of worrying about it.

The mist boiled and shifted, soaking like a soft rain, and it was a long while before it mattered to me that the slope was now a downward one. I saw a thread of chill water flowing downhill past me, the mist thinned as we came out from under its ceiling, and all of us stopped to look in the long afternoon. The cold eased as the wind dropped. There was no joy in knowing we had crossed the pass, nor any point in looking back: now we could only go on.

'We're lucky,' Blaize said grudgingly as we rested, 'any later in the year and this would be blocked by snow. It must be Riardh Secondweek or Thirdweek now.'

Movement alerted me. The barbarian woman was on her feet again, and picking her way down the long slope. The rock went down into many gullies and long transverse hills. Clear light covered the tundra, pale gold. Even I could see that we couldn't survive here in bad weather, and not very long in good weather either. Nothing grew, and the hunting would be sparse. Here were the exposed ribs of the land, the bones of Orthe. An uncompromising country, we'd have to come to it on its own terms or it would kill us.

The barbarian went ahead, our only guide.

There was a food cache in the valley coming down from the Wall, but half of it was spoiled. Faint white plumes on the peaks became streams in the valleys, noisy and rushing, cold enough to freeze hands. We stayed there, in that air that seemed mild after the pass, for all the next day. We had come down no more than three or four thousand feet – the whole tableland was higher than the fen country.

'Where are you going?' I asked the barbarian woman in as many ways as I could frame the question.

'We are Kirriach people,' she said, and her brown arm swept out towards the north west. That was all.

We're coming to the end of it, I thought. One way or another. There's a limit to how long we can live rough. There's a limit to how long we can go on with never enough sleep – Christ, but I'd like one unbroken night! A limit to how long we can live half-starved. And sooner or later there's bad weather coming. She can survive. She's tough even for an Orthean. But we can't.

I spent most of the day sleeping. Every time I stirred, I saw Maric and Blaize dozing by the embers of the fire. Suddenly there was no question of watching each other. The barbarian woman was sometimes there and sometimes not, seeming unwearied.

Someone shook me, and I opened my eyes to twilight. The sun had set behind the peaks already, flushing the snow pink and saffron. Maric was leaning over me.

'I think she wants us to move. What shall we do, Christie?'

It was a minute before I collected my wits. I blew on my hands to warm them, and looked round for the pack.

'Could make sense – keep walking at night, sleep in the day when it's warmer. Better than freezing to death. Yes.'

'"Make sense"?' Blaize was incredulous. I ignored him.

We went on by starlight, bright enough for us to pick a path. The barbarian woman increased the pace, waiting impatiently until we caught up. A sense of urgency infected us. I didn't know what there was in this land that we should fear. As the night wore on, we tired. The long cold hours after midnight sap the strength. I trudged on beside Maric. We were leaving hill country, coming into flat land. If I'd thought, I might have wondered at the smoothness of the route.

Something angular blocked the starlight. Then the barbarian went in through an arch. A doorway. I touched a wall, wonderingly. Stone. Dressed stone, here in the Barrens.

Yellow light flickered, destroying night vision. A deadwood fire showed the limits of the broken-roofed stone room, and the barbarian woman, crouched down with Theluk's tinderbox. The fire was catching now. Blaize shouldered past me, dropping his pack on the flagstones, and hunched down, cupping his hands for warmth.

Water-skins. Fat meat sealed in waxed leather. I saw Maric slit the stitching with his knife, and was released to join in. We ate like animals, not sparing breath to talk, and soaked dry tongues in water. The wood crackled noisily. The barbarian woman laid strips of mossgrass on it, and it burned low and intense.

I saw her face by firelight, teeth gleaming. She leaned back against the wall, watching the smoke spiral up to the sky showing through the gaps in the roof. I'd thought her expressionless before. Now I could see that the strain had gone out of her face; she was relaxing.

I fell asleep as false dawn outlined the archway.

Something hard was jammed into my cheek. Warm and half-sleeping, I was reluctant to move. The discomfort roused me. I opened my eyes. It was a boot-heel, belonging to the Rimon mercenary. When I moved, I banged my head against Maric's leg. Neither of them moved.

The fire was dead. The barbarian woman wasn't present. By the light through the arch, the sun had been up a good long time.

I picked my way across the floor – over blankets, foodbags, and firewood – and out of the arched doorway. Sunlight dazzled me.

The stone was blue-grey, almost translucent in the light. I went outside to relieve myself. Then I took a bleary look round and realized what I was seeing. This was no isolated hut. There were dozens of buildings in my immediate view, and the wind blew dead leaves down paved streets.

It was a ruined city.

Ruined and deserted, that much was obvious at a glance. The buildings were all of the same stone and all of a pattern. They gave the impression of being curiously incomplete, mere shells. Reaching a crossroads, I saw one way led back towards the snowpeaks – that must have been the road we came in on. But in all other directions, the city stretched away as far as I could see.

I followed paths. Mostly there were triple junctions, and after I'd passed a few it became apparent that the prevalent shape of building was hexagonal. And the buildings lacked that central courtyard that I'd come to take for granted in Southland architecture.

'Christie!' The boy came scrambling after me. 'Goddess! It goes on for ever.'

Knife-edged shadows lay across our path, the straight-edged shadows that only occur in cities. The sun was low in the south behind us. Ahead, there was barely anything left standing. Walls jutted up from moss-covered hummocks. Pale-leafed scrub forced its way between the paving stones. The weather had rounded the edges of the slabs, worn them smooth. The walls might have been carved, once. Further on, open to the sky, there were only lines on the barren earth to show where walls had stood. A great flight of steps went down a slope, beginning nowhere and ending nowhere, grown over with a feathery silver-green weed. We stood on the steps. They were as rounded as if the sea had worked on them.

'It's old,' I said. 'Lord, it's old!'

'It's big.' Maric stared round. The ruins went on north as far as the eye could see. A few miles off were taller structures. I caught myself wondering if it would be possible to explore them.

'I don't like it,' he said quietly, trying not to disturb the silence. 'It's – this is what they warn us about. No wonder the tribes are barbarians. Living with this.'

'We don't know that they do.'

The circle of the horizon, with only a southern snow peak boundary, cupped the ruined city in worn fingers. A wind blew across the desolate land and whined between the jutting walls.

'Let's go back,' Maric said. I agreed.

The barbarian woman was there, and Blaize was arguing with her. She watched him in total incomprehension. When she saw me, she pointed to the north.

'Our road.'

'We can't travel far.'

Her hands moved close together. 'Not far.'

'Days?' I indicated the sun.

A headshake. That was all I could understand. She waited impatiently while we packed all the spare food and water with our blankets. Blaize had the set look of a man dragged into something against his will.

He and Maric were alike in one thing, I thought, as the barbarian woman led us on northwards. Being in a city this size – even one that had been dead several thousand years – bothered them. The parts of the Southland that I'd seen had nothing as big as this.

Before mid-afternoon, we stopped. The barbarian woman led us past shallow dips in the earth that I realized were collapsed underground chambers, and into thick scrub. There she halted, casting about, and hauled a stone slab to one side. Worn steps went down into the dimness.

Inside was cool and dry. Light seeped in from gaps in the ceiling, a ceiling that must have been the floor of a great building but was now masked with the brown-leaved scrub. My eyes adjusted to the twilight. It was a huge hall-like space, stone-floored and with pillared walls. Stacked along the far wall were water-skins, leather food bags, blankets and pelts.

'In every stone place.' The barbarian's voice echoed softly. 'Enough for twelve—' she counted on her bony fingers so that I'd understand her '—twelve of us, for twelve sunsets. We must pass these lands.'

'You?'

'All Kirriach people.'

Maric was walking past the shadowy stacks. He came back with strips of mossturf in his hands and put them in one corner. The floor was blackened from previous fires. The barbarian woman crouched down with the tinderbox, striking flints over dry slivers of wood.

We ate. The short afternoon drew down to evening outside. At last the barbarian woman stood. She went to the steps. There was a cold wind blowing.

'Christie.'

I went over, waiting for her to speak.

'Thee must wait.'

'How long?'

She counted twelves on her fingers two or three times and shrugged. 'I will speak with Kirriach people. Thee must stay.'

'May I not come and speak with them myself?'

'They would kill thee. There is food. Wait. I will come to thee.'

I followed her up the steps. She pointed towards the less destroyed part of the city.

'There is well-water.' She put both hands on my shoulders. 'Stay here.'

'I'll wait,' I said. There was nowhere to go.

She dropped her hands from my shoulders, turned, and loped off into the second twilight. I stood in the cold until I lost sight of her, and then went below.

Both pairs of eyes fixed on me. The man and the boy, both with the same distrustful expression. I squatted down beside the fire.

'We wait till she comes back, I guess.'

'She's going to her people?' Marie asked.

'Let's hope she doesn't bring them back with her.' Blaize was as self-contained and sharp as ever. 'I'd sooner keep my head where it is, and not on a barbarian's lance. But then, considering she's gone south with a band of her own people, and come back alone with two Southlanders and you—'

'She'll have some explaining to do.' I regretted he'd heard Maric and I speculating about her origins.

We waited.

175

CHAPTER 16

Kirriach People

'*How* long?' Blaize persisted.

'You can count, can't you?' Maric added the eighth notch to his tally stick. He'd tried scratching the wall, but the blue stone was diamond-hard.

'How long will you carry on this stupidity? The longer we stay here, the less we'll have to keep us on the journey. It's a long walk back to the Southland.'

'Any time you want to try it, don't bother to wait for us.' Maric went back to stirring broth in the small can hung over the fire on a stick wedged across the hearth-corner. It was the only utensil we'd saved.

Blaize lounged with his back up against the pile of scrub-wood, one booted foot almost in the ashes of the fire. His pale mane was dark with dirt. He was cleaning under his claw-nails with the tip of his knife.

'The first thing we'll run out of,' he went on, 'is firewood. There isn't that much growing hereabouts. Not water, I admit; there's the well. But food, now, and time—'

'If you think we're short on wood, why don't you go out and collect some more?' I couched it as a suggestion. To my surprise he grunted, got up, and went up the cellar steps.

'We – ah – we could pack what food we could carry.' There was a query in Maric's tone. 'We could walk. I don't know where. That garrison the *T'An* Ruric went to – it must be on the Wall somewhere.'

'East of here. But north-east of Corbek, if I remember the map. It's probably a good three hundred *seri*.'

His face tightened. 'We could try.'

'Look—' On the verge of hysteria, I said 'I don't know how to put this. I don't want to start walking again. I don't think I can. All right?'

'I don't want to either. But if we don't, what happens to us?'

'I suppose . . . we might have to stay with these tribes for a while.'

'You mean as prisoners?'

'There's worse things than that.' At the back of my mind was the thought that, the barbarian woman having gone down to the Southland with her own people and returned with three strangers, it might be much easier for her (and who wouldn't take the easy way out?) if she just forgot we were here.

I heard footsteps, and Blaize reappeared with an armful of branches. I hauled myself upright and grabbed the wooden bucket.

'Going to the well.'

Outside there were coin-sized spatters of dampness on the grey stone. Flakes glittered in the air, not rain, not quite snow. The peaks of the Wall were hidden. Massive grey-white clouds hugged the horizon, looking as though their undersides had been soaked in ink.

I levered the slab off the top of the well, and lay flat to dip the bucket in icy water. The wind thrummed on the ruined walls. I sat on the stone slab for a few minutes. Sometimes the cellar walls closed in. I was irritable, partly because I was always hungry, and trapped in a circle of digestive upsets. But partly because I was here, miles from any kind of civilization, in a ruined city of the Golden Witchbreed. And I knew why.

I don't think I was less efficient in Corbek than I was in Tathcaer. But things were different in Corbek. If I hadn't been careless I would have realized what was going on; all the clues were there in Arad and Howice's behaviour. If I'd had more than half my mind on my job. Lover, *arykei*, under whatever misapprehension . . . when it's dead, Haltern said (Hal, I need you here), when it's dead, leave it.

Failure has its own heady excitement. Tried by church court, hunted across half a province – I fucked it up, I thought, but I'm still here, I've survived so far.

That wouldn't last, I knew; as I'd get used to it, it would start gnawing at me.

Falkyr . . . Falkyr at Oeth with the hunters. And Haltern – if he was dead, I'd make somebody pay. If I ever get out of here, I thought, I'll take it to Ruric, to the Crown . . . Ruric: I don't know if she's alive, any more than I do Haltern. And Theluk—

I can face her death now, I thought. I might die that way myself, sudden, unprotected. I don't want to, I'll fight to prevent it, but – it's possible. And if I can accept it for myself, how can I not accept it for her?

*

A dusting of snow fell the next day. Maric called me outside.

'Look at that.' He pointed.

Tracks feathered the snow: delicate claw and wing marks, heavier paws, sinuous trails. The sharp edges of the ruined city were masked.

'I thought there was no game here.'

'Oh, it's here.' Maric was frustrated. 'But I can't get close to it. Everything here is used to being hunted.'

'The tribes, I suppose.' I thought of the barbarian woman, and changed the subject quickly. 'I'll get the water. Can you check the fire isn't going out? It looked low.'

'Right.' He clattered back down the steps.

There was a thin film of ice over the water. I shattered it, kneeling, and then paused. Reflected in the black water: a face. I almost didn't recognize it. It wasn't just that I was filthy, my matted hair cropped back with a knife. I'd lost weight, had hollows under the cheekbones, my temples were sunk in. There was no mask left: I looked afraid.

I dipped my hands in the icy water, shuddering. It was too cold to wash. My old Roehmonder clothes had lost their original colouring, become a uniform mud-brown. Dirt flaked yellow on my skin. Lice-bites made red irritations. I'd torn my last and least filthy shirt up to bandage my feet; chilblains had burst and were running sores.

For pre-tech worlds, you don't have to be too fussy. Nobody likes dirt and discomfort, but put up with it. So he said: my uncle, John de Lisle, minister for the department. That was when I applied for off-Earth postings. I'd always sworn never to use family influence – certainly not the de Lisle family. That noble resolution lasted until I realized how badly I wanted in to the ET department. It wasn't fair; he was the only de Lisle who felt guilty about his family's treatment of mine. When I came asking – and I was qualified – he had to give.

Would I be here? I thought, shivering, still kneeling beside the well. Would I be off Earth without that influence? Yes. Would it have happened this soon? Ah, now, that's another question.

Hearing footsteps, I hastily scooped up a double handful of freezing water and rinsed my face. I choked and shuddered, wiping my eyes on my sleeve.

'Problems?' Blaize said.

'Nothing you haven't got as well.' I pulled the bucket up by its rope handle and started walking back towards the cellar. He fell in step beside me.

'Which one is it?'

'What?' I saw him point, indicating the few daystars still visible in the west. 'Oh. You can't see Earth's sun from here.'

The stone paving was treacherous under a slick coating of snow. I kept my balance with difficulty. The man made no move to help.

'What's it like out there?'

When I looked at him, I saw he was serious. Whether it was that – that he credited my alien origins – or the isolation, or simply that his attacks on me seemed to have been made a long time ago in a different world, for some reason I felt I should be civil to him.

'It's surprisingly similar. Given this kind of star – sun, I mean – and a world at a certain distance from it, all plants and animals and people are variations on a theme.'

The real aliens are the life forms of gas giants, and roving interstellar worlds and close-orbit planets; those we may never understand.

'Like that?' He stretched out his hand: thumb and five fingers.

'That's a minor variation.'

'And you live in high towers, and fly through the sky, and travel in carriages drawn by no animal.' His tone was mocking. 'You begin to make me think they're right, you are Witchbreed.'

'Who are "they"?' He didn't answer. My guess was SuBannasen. We came in sight of the cellar. A thin column of heated air rose from the concealed hearth.

'Why did you come? And what follows you – more 'Breed trickery?' He turned the scarred profile away from me. 'We have our life. It's the one we've chosen. Will knowing your Otherworld make our life better?'

For some mad reason – and this was the man who had twice tried to kill me – I thought I owed him honesty.

'My government talks about mutual enrichment of culture by contact between Dominion worlds. Which is true enough. Not to say that they won't enrich themselves, if a world has anything worth trading or buying. And if they can sell you anything, they'll do that too. There's also medical aid, improved agricultural methods, things like that – which you'll need.'

'We have all we need.' He was stubborn, and as certain as if he could say 'we' and speak for every *telestre* in the Southland.

'How can you say that?'

'We've seen the other. Your way. And it doesn't work.'

He was angry, and less protective of his pride than I'd ever seen him. Shabby, walking with his hands tucked inside his worn coat, ears and nose red from the cold, the mottling of his scar turned blue and purple.

'Because you've had one technological society on this planet that failed, it doesn't mean another will. And it's too long ago—'

His head came up, and all the old acid was back in his tone. 'I assure you, the 'Breed are as dead as their city – but not forgotten.'

He strode ahead. I shifted the bucket to my other hand, blowing on cold fingers, and followed him down into the cellar.

'Here.' Maric took the bucket, and handed me the small can. It was uncomfortably hot, full of the preserved meat boiled down into a broth. 'When you've eaten, I'll do his.'

'You've had yours?'

'While you were outside. What's it like?'

'Cold.'

'There's snow coming,' Blaize said contemptuously.

I settled down beside the makeshift hearth, picking meat lumps out of the can and sipping hot broth. Maric sat beside me.

'I wish I was back on my *telestre*,' he said. 'It was cold by the Oranon sometimes, but not as cold as this.'

'Maybe we should found our own *telestre*. Though this isn't exactly the best place.' It was weak humour.

The membrane slid back; his eyes were bright with astonish ment. 'It took the Crown and church four generations to decide the Peir-Dadeni *telestres* were legal, *t'an*. You might have to wait a while.'

Something Haltern said came back to me: no *telestre* has changed its boundaries since it was founded, there have been no land transactions in the Southland since *amari* Andrethe founded Peir-Dadeni.

'But you must be able to . . . where do people live?'

'Three choices,' Blaize said, across the fire. 'Their own *telestre*. Or *n'ri n'suth* to another. Or landless.'

Maric snapped 'She is not landless!'

'She has no *telestre*.'

'But it's different for them—'

It was at that point that empathy, the xeno-team reports, and gossip came together in my head to give me an image of Orthe. Solid, unchanging, a totally static society. It appalled me, because it was by choice. They'd had the technological knowledge of the Golden Empire and they refused to use it. As I'd realized in Corbek: not a pre-technological society, but a post-technological society.

That put me in a bad position. I was trained for primitive worlds. The department's rule of thumb there was that a non-spacegoing race wouldn't prove a threat to the Dominion, and that one member of the Dominion can't cause major damage to a world.

Inaccurate, yes, but good enough for troubled times. On Earth they called it the Dispersal, this headlong rush to explore space by the FTL drive, and their main problem was holding their own authority together.

But Carrick V wasn't pre-tech, not a world to scan and classify, and perhaps keep satellite surveillance over. Carrick V had had a civilization that could leave ruins like this city.

We've misunderstood them badly, I thought. What kind of a mentality leads a world (or is it only the Southland?) to prefer living in danger, squalor, and disease? That makes Wellhouses and *T'An Suthai-Telestres* suppress all of the knowledge that could improve conditions . . .

I looked across at Blaize. I'd had hinted to me often enough in Corbek that Wellkeepers and Earthspeakers hoarded all kinds of knowledge, including medical – the Witchbreed had been as advanced as the Dominion in that respect. There was no technology now to back up the knowledge, but it could be created. I could live with disfigurement if I knew there was no way to cure it, but if I knew there was a way, and it had been decided to forbid it . . .

On Earth such a society wouldn't hold stable for two generations, never mind two thousand years. It argued a more alien quality of thought than I'd anticipated, seeing humanoids in some respects so similar to ourselves.

'You finished with the can?'

I gave it back, empty. Maric was sulking. Obviously they'd been quarreling while I was lost in speculation. Given the circumstances, one was as sensible as the other.

Blaize was sitting with a wooden case on his knees. I'd seen it before in his pack and assumed from the way he guarded it, it was money or other valuables. It wasn't. He opened it out: a travelling *ochmir* set. It gave a board the size of a large plate. The pieces (in two bags, one for the version of the game with three players) were enamelled with the various script characters for *ferrorn*, *thurin*, or *leremoc*.

It took me back so hard I caught my breath. *Ochmir* games in Corbek's cold towers, that so often were left half-finished while Falkyr and I pursued more important matters.

Blaize gave me a hard look. He said, 'I don't suppose you do anything as civilized as play *ochmir*?'

It would take my mind off the waiting. And any break in the boredom was welcome. Even with Blaize n'ri n'suth Meduenin.

'Yes,' I said, 'I do.'

*

181

The snow came, and lay for a morning before melting. After that it was clear and cold. We left the underground chamber as seldom as possible. But it was necessary to go further for firewood.

Carrick's Star was an ice-eye low to the south. Clouds massed on a north wind. It was glittering, restless weather. Wet stone, far off, shone like silver. I used the excuse of firewood to explore, for as long as I could stand the cold. Seemingly endless, the city offered nothing but ruins. There were obvious subsidences where underground buildings had collapsed, but nothing left of the Witchbreed city except stone. And the three of us camped there, building fires on their tessellated floors, with no protection against cold or darkness – the barbarians were in the city and no mistake, I thought.

A call attracted my attention. The bundle of scrub-wood was difficult to manage. I climbed a flight of shallow steps to higher ground. It was Maric. He brandished the *harur* blades. But it wasn't a warning yell. Something was on the ground beside him.

When I got close I saw it was some species of lizardbird, the jaw long and toothed, the body scaled rather than feathered. Maric's stroke had severed one grey-webbed wing almost completely.

I put the bundle of wood down and took one wing-tip, while he took the other and stretched it out. The full wingspan was over three metres. Hand-sized talons bore vicious claws.

'It attacked me.' He grappled with the body, dragging it towards the cellar steps. 'Over where all the potholes are. I didn't see it. It nearly took my head off'

Blaize never stirred from beside the fire. He eyed the corpse, and Maric. '*Kur-rashaku*. That was lucky.'

'It wasn't luck! I waited until the last moment, then I—' he let go of the lizardbird, illustrating a complex double flourish of blades. His hands were black with blood.

'Lucky for us, I mean. A change of diet.'

For the first time I saw a grave humour in the Rimon man's eyes, but he kept a straight face. To my surprise, he helped skin and cut up the body. Mercenaries' skills, I thought. They were beyond me. I trekked out to the well again.

After the meal we stretched out round the fire. Maric was attempting to clean the blood off Theluk's blades – or his, I suppose they were now – with a rag. Blaize watched with mounting impatience. He muttered something obscure, rummaged in his pack, and threw the boy some of the strips of oiled cloth he used on his own blades.

'Thanks.' Maric was wary.

'Mmmph.' Blaize leaned back into the shadows. When the metal was clean, he said, 'You favour the *nilgiri* too much.'

'Maybe,' Maric admitted.

Like most Ortheans, he was ambidextrous. The shield is unknown in the Southland, and *harur* blades in combination are lethal. And, like Blaize, most can switch the use of the *nilgiri* and *nazari* to either hand.

'You ought to practise.' He intercepted a hard stare from me. 'Don't you worry, *T'An* Outworlder. I'm not about to butcher your *l'ri-an*.'

'I never imagined you were.' Which wasn't entirely true.

'Need exercise, cooped up here.' He took Maric's blades, testing the weight. 'I was arms-tutor to a Morvren *telestre* for a year, once, before I went down to Saberon. Look, try this.'

He set the boy to doing some obscure exercise with the two blades, and then sat down beside me to watch him.

'You want to train?' A half-malicious offer.

'I know where my talents lie, and that isn't one of them.' I didn't plan on being careless enough to be on the wrong end of a Meduenin blade again. 'I'll stay with the less energetic sports. One of these days I'm going to beat you at *ochmir*.'

'Ah, you're thinking we'll be here all winter?'

As he went to retrieve the board and counters, I put more wood on the fire. He could no more help being sarcastic than he could help breathing, it came to me. But for all his bitching, he was pulling his weight. I wasn't sure precisely why.

We drew for the first move, decided by who gains the more mobile piece, and the game opened slowly. It was quiet in the underground room, the noise of the wind didn't penetrate down. Maric ended his blade practice and returned to the fire. It was our central reference-point.

Blaize put down one of the static *ferrorn* to open another area of conflict on the board. I studied the pattern, and moved a *thurin*.

'You can't do that,' Blaize contradicted. 'Only across a line, not across an angle – unless the piece is a *leremoc*.'

'You did,' I protested.

'"All *ochmir* players cheat", that's a proverb. Also. . . .' he bent down, scrutinizing the board, and the firelight made an impossible mask of his scarred face. 'Also, "good *ochmir* players cheat only when necessary."'

'This, then.' I forced a reversal on one of his blue *thurin*, which proved to be a white *leremoc* on the obverse: a considerable advantage for me.

He drew another handful of counters from the bag, weighing them thoughtfully in his palm. His eyes were dark and clear in the dim light. 'I was in Kasabaarde once. In the trade city. That's where I got these.'

'That's not in the Southland?'

'No, over the Inner Sea, down past Bridge Alley and the archipelago. There was some fighting down the Desert Coast. About six years back. Quarth and Kel Harantish, I think it was.'

'You were fighting?'

A shrug. 'I was hired.'

'Is that the way you look at it?'

'It's a convenient way.' He put a piece down. I wasn't sure if it was a legal move; I'd been distracted. By now I was more interested in the conversation. And treading lightly.

'You came home after that?'

'Back to the Southland. As for home – it's a good *telestre*, but I was right at fourteen when I left it. I keep *telezu*, mind.' He referred to the custom of spending one season in the year at the *telestre*. 'When I can. No, that time I was in the Medued city Watch for a couple of years.'

'You sound like me. I move around. But that's less common here, isn't it?' I put down another *ferrorn*.

He moved for a majority in a minor hexagon, which shifted the balance in several of the overlapping hexagon-frames. By the time the implications had worked out to the edge of the board, I'd lost a score of pieces.

'Yes, it's uncommon. I went down the coast to Morvren again, after that. That's where I got this.' His hand strayed up to the burn.

'In a war?'

He laughed. It was loud, natural. Maric opened his eyes, then went back to dozing.

'In a companion-house in Morvren Freeport,' he said gravely, 'in a fight over nothing at all. Ten years overseas, then that. Some *amari* threw an oil-lamp.'

He lifted his arm, demonstrating how he shielded his eyes. The sleeve pulled back and I saw scar tissue from wrist to elbow.

'She won't do that trick again,' he added, touching the hilt of the *harur* blade. 'But I'm getting too old for this game.'

We carried on in silence, playing a game which was not the one he meant.

There were twelve notches on the tally stick.

*

The fifteenth day was bitter cold. Yellow snow clouds massed from the east, but no snow fell.

'It won't be long before it's winter.'

Maric nodded agreement. He hacked another root free with his knife and handed it to me. 'The passes are closed in winter, I've heard.'

'I expect you're right. Let's get back, that's enough wood. It's vicious cold out here.' I realized we'd come a long way from the cellar. The ruins were similar to the eye. I searched for landmarks.

'This way!' Maric called.

'Are you sure?' It wasn't the way we'd come. I followed him. The going was easy, he was keeping to the paved ways. We came up on the hidden entrance from a different angle, so that I didn't recognize it until we were on top of it.

'You're quick,' I said as we hurried down the steps and made for the fire. 'I was lost there, for a minute.'

He threw the wood on the stockpile. 'I'm not clever, it's just that I lived here before.'

My hands tingled with returning circulation. It was a minute before I heard what he said.

'You *what*?'

'Lived in this city. Under the 'Breed, of course.'

'Of course,' I said automatically, and met Blaize's eyes. I couldn't cope with delusions now.

'What's wrong with that? It's a coincidence, I admit, but—'

'You as well?' I suspected them of some elaborate charade.

'No. My memories show me no mountains, when I was in a 'Breed city.'

I rounded on Maric. 'You never mentioned this before!'

'I didn't realize, *t'an*.' He spoke with self-possession, as if it were a thing everyone would know. 'Since we came here, my memory-dreams have been stronger, and matching up with what I've seen. Only I think it must have been a long time ago. The city's larger than I remember.'

I appealed to Blaize. 'Look, I know we're all under a considerable strain—'

'You don't have them, do you?' There was no mockery at all.

'No past-memories?' Maric, frightened, looked at Blaize. That alerted me. This was no joke. We'd been close. Something that would make him turn from me to a hired sword, already proved untrustworthy . . . but a man of his own race.

'He's afraid,' Blaize said, 'because the Witchbreed, also, had no

185

memories of their previous lives. And perhaps no lives to remember. Are you like the Witchbreed in that, you Otherworlders?'

'I can't answer that question before I understand it. Sit down a minute, I want to talk. Maric, for God's sake, I'm not going to hurt you!'

Shamefaced, he sat beside me. 'I know. I know you, *t'an*. But I thought you were – like us.'

'Tell me about it.' I faced both of them. There was that glance of complicity between them, that I had thought meant they were in league. It was for reassurance. This had hit them both hard.

'We live,' Blaize said simply, 'and return, under Her sky. That's all.'

'That's not all – it can't be – how can you be so sure? Oh,' I stopped Maric interrupting, 'I don't doubt you believe what you say. There are people on Earth who believe the same thing, equally honestly. But there's no proof!'

'We remember,' Maric said. 'We can't all be wrong, or else we wouldn't remember the same things, would we? We know about the Witchbreed because we remember being there, being their slaves. Christie, we know.'

'The church . . .' It made an odd kind of sense. Why they weren't given to extravagant funeral celebrations. And Theluk had shocked me, once, when she seemed to approve of suicide. And Maric, who had hated this city when he entered it, was comfortable in it now.

'So you know what a technological civilization is like.' They were both watching me. I had to frame careful questions. If there was one thing the Ortheans were reticent over, it was this heart of their belief. Without the situation we were in, lost in desolate country, I could never have had the discussion at all.

'We know. I told you,' Blaize said, 'we've seen it and we don't want it.'

'But the Witchbreed, are none of them – reincarnated?'

'Yes!' Maric said. 'What about Kel Harantish?'

'No, they're human like the rest of us.' Blaize was sober. 'I've seen them. The 'Breed were exterminated, so it's said.'

'Said? I thought you knew.'

'There are those who claim to have been born after the Fall of the Golden Empire, but I don't believe them. It's too soon.'

I found I was walking up and down the floor. I came back into the circle of firelight. It was feasible. It would work as a superstition, or as a reality – and they were convinced it was reality. It was bedrock to them, I could see that.

Suddenly depressed, I squatted down close to the heat.

186

'If you know you'll be reborn, why put up with *this*?'

There was silence for a time. Blaize leaned forward, his silver-streaked mane falling over his eyes.

'When it comes to it – I won't stay longer than I have to.'

'But to leave everyone,' Maric whispered. 'It means losing all of them, all the *telestres*, everybody. And what kind of a world will it be to come back to? I know the Earthspeakers say it'll be the same, but it's so long . . . and I won't be Maric Salathiel then, I'll be another person, with some of my memories, born into a different world.'

'None of us wants to die.' Blaize was abrupt. Then he lifted his head and looked me in the face. 'Dying with no hope of return? You're a strange people, Christie.'

Bedrock, yes. It was too fundamental a difference to grasp completely. To have that certainty . . . And because of the form it took, for it not to play a vocal part in everyday living, though it shaped the society in which that living takes place. No wonder the Witchbreed were a living threat, even though they were two thousand years dead. Or that the memory of the power of technology hadn't faded, nor the determination never to use it again.

'Perhaps it is the same for you,' the boy said hopefully, 'and you just don't know.'

'I *don't* know. As I'm beginning to find out.' And the more I did find out about Orthe, the more I was depressed by my total ignorance.

Blaize said nothing, staring past the child at me. He was shaken, because he could imagine what it would be like to die without knowing what follows – as much as any Orthean can imagine that. Maric, like the young of every race, didn't quite believe in death yet.

The crackling of burning wood sounded loud in the cellar. The walls gleamed in the red light. I came back down from the opening hurriedly. It was still snowing outside, and snowing hard.

The *ashiren* stirred, mumbled something, and rolled closer to the fire without waking up. I stepped over him and sat down by the woodpile, feeding fragments onto the fire. It was not far off dawn, I thought. Not that it was possible to see any change outside, but it felt close to first light.

I thought, there's no point keeping a watch. Nothing's going to find its way down here and attack us. Nobody's here.

Realization crystallized. We had been abandoned. This was where we'd stay, if we didn't do anything for ourselves. What could be done? Pack and start walking? Not back to the Fens. Look for a pass across the Wall? How far away is that, I wondered, and how far can we expect to travel now, in winter, without supplies? There's no reserves of strength left. It was all used up coming from Corbek to here.

Blaize grunted, and half-started up, one arm protectively over his head. He stared round with no recognition, and sank back. Head resting on his arms, asleep. I knew he had nightmares. Some times his mouth moved soundlessly as though he were shouting, and when he woke he didn't hear what was said to him.

The boy dreamed memory-dreams, becoming more remote from us as time went on. He looked at the city and saw more than I ever could, sometimes smiling and listening to the wind's voices.

Sixteen days. Part of it was hunger: the food was rationed now. And lack of various things in the diet, and boredom, and the thought that we had left it too late now to begin walking anywhere.

Stone walls merged with city streets, ruins became megalopoli. At the same time that I knew I was dreaming, I knew that this was not a Witchbreed city I dreamed of. It had aspects of Earth: London, maybe, or Peking, or Bombay. People lived there who weren't hungry, who weren't cold, who travelled without walking, and talked in a language that was bitterly familiar. And I was another person, one who had never left the safe earth. Dry sobs of self-pity woke me; I can never cry in dreams.

'Christie!' Blaize whispered urgently.

I sat up, confused. Maric lifted his head, frowning, listening.

'Can you hear that?'

'Blaize, I—' The stunner slid into my hand. 'What is it? I don't hear anything.'

My feet were frozen and sore. It took me a minute to stumble up the steps after him. Maric drew his *harur* blades. White light blinded me. I leaned on the ruined stone, rubbing water out of my streaming eyes. Blaize was black against the snowlight, the Rimon blades catching the sun.

'Cover,' he said to me sharply, pushing Maric towards the scrub that concealed the entrance.

'Wait a minute. Wait!' I shielded my eyes. Carrick's Star at dawn, on the new snow, was unbearable. 'What do you think you're going to do? I don't care who it is, it's a better option than starvation!'

He lowered the blades and nodded. Maric hesitantly came back to join us.

I said, 'I still don't hear anything.'

'Over that way.' Blaize pointed. Stark walls were plastered with snow, blocking the view. I strained, and heard something that I couldn't name.

'Let's go and meet them.'

The hired sword looked at me as if I were crazy; and he was nearly right, I'd stopped worrying about danger. He shrugged, accepting it. The boy walked between us, still carrying the naked blades. The stone was glassy underfoot, snow clogged my boots. Soon we were holding on to each other just to keep upright.

I hoped it was the barbarian woman come back, but I didn't care. Not then.

We rounded the highest wall, looking down over a stretch of old road, and came to a dead halt.

CHAPTER 17

The Woman Who Walks Far

A dark-skinned man was riding over the virgin snow, following the unnaturally flat expanses that marked the old roads. Others rode behind him. The sky at their back was eggshell blue floured with stars. The air was clear to the horizon, each snow-covered wall and hillock of the city distinct and indigo-shadowed.

As the riders approached, I saw they wore tunics and thick pelts. The high saddles were cushioned with furs, hung with glinting and flashing ornaments. The riderbeasts were nothing I recognized, certainly not *marhaz* or *skurrai*.

'Goddess . . .' Maric's breath smoked white on the air. He was open-mouthed. Blaize had his hand on his sword-hilt. His nictitating membrane protected his eyes against snow-glare. Our shadows lay black towards the west, towards the riders.

The size of the grey riderbeasts became apparent: two metres or more at the shoulders, and their slender tapering necks added at least another metre. Reins looped down, knotted loosely on saddles, jingling with metal decorations.

'Look, I—' Blaize fell silent, staring west.

Behind the outriders, travelling slowly on the old road, was what I at first took for a sledge. Eight beasts were yoked in pairs in front of it, shaggy white-pelted animals, bulky, with short pairs of horns projecting from their broad foreheads. The vehicle travelled on what were obviously makeshift runners. It was bright against the snow, as bright as blood, crimson as a severed artery. There were people in it. It was bigger than any vehicle I'd seen on Orthe so far, and the shape was odd and familiar: a flattened ovoid, open at the top.

'Don't frighten them,' I said foolishly. 'Don't make them think we're dangerous.'

The first riders reached us, keeping a distance and circling so that we were surrounded. The grey-skinned beasts left delicate tracks in the snow. It didn't seem possible that such spindly legs could bear the body and long neck. The riders looked down at us, silent, dark-eyed. They carried short curved swords, I saw, and metal-tipped lances. Men and women both, as far as I could tell with Orthean faces.

The sledge approached, steam going up from the white beasts' nostrils, runners crunching through the snow. I caught sight of another, smaller, vehicle behind the first, pulled by a team of four beasts, skins strapped down over whatever it was carrying.

Maric said 'There are *ashiren* in that thing, look!'

The team-driver sat on a high perch over the shafts, reins in her hands. Behind her in the body of the ovoid vehicle, fur-clad children crowded at the rim, scrambling up on the high tail fins for a better look at us.

Blaize and Maric exchanged glances.

'Yes,' the hired sword said, 'but it shouldn't travel on the ground, should it?'

'They rode the air, when this was a city.' The boy's eyes were bright.

After he'd said that, it was obvious. It was aerodynamic, a shape I should have recognized myself; but my mind couldn't accept its existence. Not here. Not now.

The shaggy beasts stopped, snorting white jets into the frosty air. The high sides of the vehicle towered over us. Morning sun turned it crimson and gold. A rope-ladder unrolled over the side, and a scramble of *ashiren* and adults came down it, one woman elbowing her way to the front.

Her mane was glossy and her skin oiled. A great white pelt was belted over a supple leather skirt and a curved knife stuck under the jewelled belt. But she was barefoot, and white scars seamed her ribs, licking down between breast and second nipple, familiar on the dark skin.

'Peace!' the barbarian woman shouted. The *ashiren* were silent. She smiled broadly, reaching out to grip my hands. I stared, numb. 'Ah, thy choice was good; I feared thee would not wait. I was sick, and could not come to thee. But now I am here!'

'Thank god for that,' I said; and then we were in the middle of a crowd of *ashiren*, pushing close to touch us, and the riders dismounted and crowded round, gabbling in their archaic tongue. I was dazed and dazzled: after the long silence, it was too much.

'Peace,' Blaize was laughing, 'we could have guessed; not even the tribes bring *ashiren* to a battle, Christie.'

I put my hand on Maric's shoulder for support. He couldn't stop grinning. It was confusion for a while, it seemed everyone had to touch us, finger clothing and flesh, before they believed we existed.

'My brothers.' The barbarian woman pulled forward two young men, who veiled their eyes, embarrassed, and then jabbered at me faster than I could comprehend. 'And this, my sister's *ashiren*; and mine.'

I couldn't pick them out from the other children. Manes were dark, smooth skins black or brick-red except in a few cases – I saw one milk-skinned child with a silver mane. They were curious, forward, self-reliant as all Orthean children are.

'What – I mean, where—?' It was overwhelming.

'Come,' the barbarian woman said, 'and thy friends, also; thou must ride with me.'

It was not until then that I realized she was no plain tribes-woman, but a leader, or chief, or both. She'd never said more than was absolutely necessary; that kind of reticence is easily mistaken for stupidity.

'We have to trust them, don't we?' Maric said.

'Yes. Run and fetch anything you want to bring with you. Quick.'

I touched the side of the ovoid vehicle. It was neither wood nor metal, having a texture that reminded me of plastic. And light, judging by how far it pushed down the snow. The colour was integral. Up close, I could see that it was pitted and worn. How long could something like this exist? On Earth, glass is still found from Phoenician times, plastics from the early twentieth century. But to survive from the Golden Empire – two thousand or more Orthean years, perhaps two and half thousand Earth-standard – that was incredible. Yet it looked to be moulded in one piece, it was conceivable such a framework could last . . .

'Christie.' The barbarian woman held out the rope-ladder.

The team strained, the team-leader whooped, and the vehicle crunched free of the thin film of ice and began to glide. I settled back on the pelt-strewn wooden bench. The barbarian woman sat next to me, one of the many *ashiren* in her lap. Maric sat on the bench below, next to Blaize, his back against my knees. The cold wind took my breath. We pulled the feather-pelts round us. Oblivious to cold, the older *ashiren* screeched and hung over the side of the vehicle.

An old man, who the barbarian woman called from his grey beast to ride with us, spoke a passable Roehmonde. With his interpretations and her accented, antique tongue, we understood each other as far as was possible.

'Thee and I must talk,' she said. 'Thee and Kirriach people.'

At the name, Maric looked up. He said 'The city Kirriach, which was called aKirrik.'

'That is so, aKirrik was the name of this place.' She glanced at the old man.

'He remembers being here,' I said carefully, and their faces cleared.

'Does thy memory tell thee what else was here?' she asked.

He twisted, pointing back eastwards. 'There was another city, S'Imrath.'

She nodded, pleased. 'Simrathan people. That way we do not go, we are enemies. And this way?'

The boy frowned. 'A . . . a river. I don't know how far.'

She looked at the old man, who translated, and she nodded again.

The vehicle bucked slightly on its runners, and we followed the long curve of the road north-west. The snow had been heavier here. Sunlight glittered on icicles hanging from broken walls.

'Thee must talk,' she repeated, intense. Her expression was never easy to read. She spoke slowly, darting looks at the old man to supply her with words. 'I have spoken of – of thy Otherworld. Thy people. Of thy journey here, to the Mother – to the world. Thy speech has been to lowlanders. Now it must be to us.'

I was staggered by how much I'd underestimated her. And yet we'd talked in front of her, Haltern and I, as if she was an animal. The Southland term was always 'barbarian.' For the first time it dawned on me that they might be wrong. And it brought me back to what I'd forgotten, being solely concerned with survival: I was still envoy.

'I'll talk to anyone who'll hear me,' I promised.

'Thee must go soon,' the barbarian woman said. 'Winter is soon this year. The passes will close. Thy friends also must go.'

Rain lashed the terrace. The snow was gone. Grey clouds veiled Kirriach, hiding the river and the distant plains. I squinted out at the slanting water. My eyes were puffy and swollen. Something in the barbarian's diet was causing a histamine reaction, but it was mild. The choice between starvation and allergy was an easy one.

'I've only been here a few days. It isn't long enough to explain—'

In one of her rare interruptions, she said, 'Go, or spend winter here. And then thou must be fought over, Simrathan and Yry-themne and Giryse-Acha will hear of thee, and raid us.'

'Could I not speak to them, as I've spoken to your people?'

'There is no debt between thee and those others. They would kill thee. Or else take thee for Goldens, returned, as stories say they will.'

Wind gusted rain across the terrace, and the barbarian woman reached out to pull the wooden shutters closed and bar them. The stockade walls and beastpens were hidden from sight.

I went with her down the stairs to the main hall. It was similar to the other halls of the Kirriach people: the shell of a Witchbreed building, in which were wooden platforms and partitions and cubicles, and a generation's worth of murals fading on the walls. They had painted in and outlined the worn carvings of the original stonework: symbols and hieroglyphs that, while incomprehensible, teased the mind with the strange geometric relationship between them.

I never saw all the Kirriach tribe in one place to estimate their size; there were always hunting and raiding parties absent. This hall held some fifty people, and I'd talked in at least six other halls.

Maric came up. 'What's happening?'

'I think we're leaving when the rain eases.' I saw Blaize solemnly playing a kind of *ochmir* solitaire by the hearth. 'Tell him, will you?'

The barbarian woman was smiling. Reflectively she said, 'There were those who bade me kill thee anyway, Christie.'

I didn't doubt that. She was not the tribe's leader – I don't think they had a leader as such, all had an equal voice in the argument. But as there was a broad-built man with a bushy mane who was acknowledged expert on the hunt, and another man expert in the preparation of grain and dried meat stores, and a woman in the managing of raiding parties, so the barbarian woman was acknowledged expert on anything that came from 'the lowland' beyond Kirriach.

'But you didn't kill me.'

'If thee was dead, who would carry word of us to thy people?' A lithe shrug. 'And in the lowlands, thee and I . . . but there must be messengers sent to us from thy Otherworld; do not forget, but do it.'

'It may take time.'

'We are Kirriach people. In winter we are here. In summer—' her hand flicked out northwards, towards the great plains, as if she could see beyond the grey stone walls. They spent the fine season crop growing and hunting in the north, returning to the city in the harsh winter, treading a fine line between poverty and starvation. 'Thy people will find us.'

'We'll try.'

194

'And perhaps thee will trade with us? Perhaps,' she said, 'we will trade for such weapons as I have seen thee use?'

A silence spread out from where we stood, as the tribe broke off from eating and talking to listen. Maric and Blaize came over the dirty moss-strewn floor, looking round with concealed anxiety.

Many of the tribe's weapons had a Southland look to them; I didn't need to be told they raided to get them. I rubbed my eyes, cursing the irritation. These were not people to quote Dominion law at, especially the laws about importing high tech weaponry.

'No,' I said, 'and I'll tell you why. You've seen me use this?'

I held out the stunner. The barbarian woman nodded.

'Show,' she demanded.

Some *kur-rashaku* nested in the high roof of the hall. I raised the stunner and sighted on one. The narrow focus of sound produced a high whine. The lizardbird thudded down on the stone floor. As I thumbed it off people drew away, expressions of pain fading, talking and shouting. The barbarian woman's yell produced silence.

'We would trade for those,' she said, 'many of those, and then let Simrathan raid us!'

'Take it.' She hesitated, then did. I held her hand over the stud. 'You saw what I did. Point it, then press down.'

The interpreter was called over and the idea translated. The barbarian woman gripped the stunner two-handed, held it at arm's length, and fired at another of the lizardbirds. Not having my big-patterns, she got no response. Before she could do more than spit and swear, I took the stunner back and threw it to Blaize.

'Look!' I got her attention. 'It's the same for South – for the lowlanders. Go ahead,' I invited him, 'try it on me.'

The eyes veiled, lines tightened round his mouth. It might have been amusement or irony. I didn't underestimate Blaize n'ri n'suth Meduenin; he was capable of that.

He aimed as carefully as if he thought it would work, and thumbed the stud down twice. Nothing happened. The stunner was passed round from hand to hand while all the tribe confirmed its lack of function.

'Our weapons don't work for you.' I hoped it sounded convincing.

'Thy people are cunning,' the barbarian woman said quietly. 'I knew it would not live in my hand, I took it from thee in the wetlands, when thee slept. But it is dead to all: *that* is cunning.'

She might have killed me in the Fens if it had worked, I thought; no matter what debt there was between us over Corbek. (I assumed it was over Corbek, she never made it clear.)

'The rain will end by morning,' she said. 'I will gift thee food and *lahamu* for the road south.'

'We'll go no further,' the old man said in his accented Roehmonde.

'The lowlanders are near. That is thy road to them.' The barbarian woman indicated the ancient stone, all but covered under mossgrass and rockfalls.

The riders of the grey *lahamu* beasts gathered round the vehicle as we dismounted. This was another relic of the Witchbreed, an ovoid whose use I never discovered, fitted with a wooden axle-frame and wheels, and drawn by the shaggy *muroc*. It had been better for sleeping than the cold ground, but rough travelling over the old highways.

Kirriach lay five days to the north. Its blue-grey stone walls, with their curiously fused appearance, were left behind; remote as Earth's pyramids. We followed the thread of a road south until the peaks of the Wall crept up over the horizon, and the air became colder the further south we went. It was rising ground all the way with the mountains ahead of us, until this last day when I realized that we were travelling up between spurs of the Wall itself to a pass.

'Follow the road,' the barbarian woman said, 'and when there is a place where *lahamu* may not easily go, turn them loose. They will return to us.'

I took the reins of the grey beast. It had a musky scent, and a cold reptilian hide. Blaize and Maric could mount theirs without help; the *ashiren* aided me. Even though the saddle was built up at the back, I still had the feeling of slipping; the *lahamu* barrel-body slopes towards the hindquarters.

The riderbeast skittered sideways and I stayed on with some difficulty.

'Christie,' the woman said. She stood up in the vehicle, on a level with me. 'I have thy name.'

'Yes.' None of the Kirriach people gave names outside the tribe.

'I am Gur'an, the fighter; I am Alahamu-te, racer-of-*lahamu*.' She leaned forward, six-fingered hands gripping the rim of the vehicle. 'I am O'he-Oramu-te, the woman who walks far. There is no debt between thy people and Kirriach!'

The *muroc* team wheeled, the vehicle turned on the long road that led away from the mountains; and as they cantered off, the *lahamu* lifted up their long-muzzled heads and belled like hounds.

Mist hung over the damp rocks, glittering where the sun found rifts in the clouds. The air was chill. Dark mossgrass and lichen grew over the old road. Its shape was clear, winding upwards. Scree slopes went up into the cloud. Boulders the size of houses dotted the slopes. Somewhere there was the sound of running water.

'Nearly noon,' Maric said, without sky or sun to guide him. 'We can't spend the night in a place like this, Christie.'

'We could go back to the plains, try the crossing tomorrow,' Blaize suggested.

'Keep going a while yet.' I concentrated on keeping the *lahamu* under control. 'There's time.'

Snow spotted the mossgrass, clinging in crevices of rock. It was a fresh fall. Have we left it too late? I wondered. I dreaded the pass being blocked, or us being lost; I was determined to get where I could see.

If I have to go back ... I don't know if I can do this all over again. We're running out of strength, of time, of everything.

The cloud came down. I pulled the *muroc* pelt round me and tugged the hood up. We rode on, searching out the thin outlines of the ancient road, up among naked glistening rock. Damp cold slicked the feather-fur. The high altitude was winter-cold. The track was steeper now, and the *lahamu* picked their way delicately over lumps of frozen snow.

Pale light made the mist luminous. It was white, pearl, then pale blue; and the sky opened out over us, and I looked back on the mist that lay like the surface of a lake behind me. All the Barrens were left behind under that mist.

Framed in a double horn of snowpeaks, we sat looking south over the edge of the Wall.

'Jesus! You can see half the world!'

Even Blaize was silent. Maric edged his *lahamu* closer to mine.

The vast distance of empty air turned my stomach. Such space, such emptiness. The eye focused gratefully on the land below.

From this height it looked flat, brown and beige and white rectangles fitting into each other in an interlocking quilt pattern. Fuzzy whiteness bothered me until I saw it moving, and its shadow moving over the tiny fields below, and I realized I was looking down on cloud. Dots like clustered poppy-seeds were copses of trees, their infinitesimally small black shadows pooled on the earth. I followed the sweep of the land out to where a lake, long and narrow and impossibly blue, lay in its cup of white sand.

Details became clearer the longer I looked. Not flat land, it swelled here and there into hills, and in some places the exposed biscuit-coloured face of rock cliffs. Thread-thin divisions between the rectangles were paths, roads, tracks. And tiny clustered

197

squares, flat roofs white in sunlight and sides black in shadows, must be a *telestre* . . . so far down.

Distant, panoramic: beyond the lake, hills and more water fading into the blue haze. And beyond that – the pass opens to the southwest – the Wall of the World went down into mountains, white like crumpled bedsheets: the Northern Wilderness and the Kyre. I turned, taking in that vast panoramic landscape, seeing the mountains fade down until the southern horizon shaded off into level distance. I was half-deafened by the drumming wind.

A haze of cloud surfaced the sky, and down over the mountains flat-bottomed cumulus clouds piled up in white masses, and cast blue shadows on the land.

'The Southland,' Maric said. 'Christie, look. We're home.'

'Not yet.' Blaize reined his *lahamu* in close and slid down from the saddle, throwing the reins to Maric. He strode to the highest point of the Witchbreed road, where it made a sharp turn and vanished over the edge.

I dismounted more cautiously. I'd already fallen off the beast twice, knocking the wind out of myself. Like all the *lahamu*, mine had the habit of bending round and nipping your leg or unseating you.

Snow dazzled against the blueness, thin threads of spray blown off the high peaks. Indigo shadows haunted the rockface. The air was thin and cold, and there was a wind here that scraped the lungs. I went over to where Blaize was standing.

Relief surged through me: it was a pass. Far higher than the rift leading up from the Fens, the Wall here dropped a sheer ten thousand feet.

'It has to be the Southland, doesn't it?'

Blaize nodded refleaively. 'There's only one pass so far to the west. This must be Broken Stair.'

A memory of Theluk came back to me. The other side of the Great Fens, she'd said. Peir-Dadeni. One of the Southland provinces. It's true, I thought, it's true, we're safe, we're home.

'There's the road,' he pointed.

It angled sharply right from where I stood, sloping down the face of the Wall, and then doubled back on itself, zig-zagging down in quarter-mile lengths, down to a thread's thickness, ten thousand feet below. It was cut into the rock; in some places the blue-grey stone paving was still intact. Further down I saw where rockslides had flaked away, taking the roadway with it. Passable? Yes, on foot.

'This is where we leave the *lahamu*.' The beasts were mouthing the rock with their long pointed upper lips, searching for edible lichen. Maric clucked softly, affectionately, and they lay down to have their saddle-packs removed. His ability with riderbeasts always amazed me.

'What shall I leave?'

'Take as much as we can comfortably carry.' It was easier to think ahead now. 'We don't have much daylight left, there might be another night in the open before we get to inhabited country.'

He rubbed the *lahamu*'s muzzle. 'Will they be all right, do you think?'

'They'll find their way back.'

Blaize was still staring south, booted feet apart, head thrown back. I wondered if the height bothered him. Height and cold air and silence, and the soaring rock cliffs that went up to either side of us. It was harsh country. He spat carelessly over the broken edge of the road, and came to get his pack.

Chill wind dried the sweat on me. My stomach churned. Sun reflected off the fractured rock. My fingers were stiff and numb with cold.

'Go left . . .' I coughed, throat dry, and reached out a hand to Maric. 'There's a ledge under your foot, there . . . That's it.'

Our hands met, and I pulled him across the gap. Behind him, Blaize spidered across the rock. I kept my eyes on him, ignoring the vast empty spaces of air. Fragments shaled out from under his boots. Spots of brown, half-melted snow clung to the rock, moisture dripping in the shadows. I reached out again and he heaved himself up onto the ruined road, holding my arm.

'Is that the worst of it?' He looked down over the edge; more than I could do. 'Well, maybe. It's a shame your barbarian friends never gave us any rope.'

'I'll try and remember that, next time.'

One of his sharp looks was followed by a reluctant smile.

After that, there were fewer gaps in the road; in places we could almost have walked abreast. The sun was going down behind mountains that lay west and south, still the Wall of the World. The air had been thin on the pass. Coming down, it was like descending into a sea of oxygen. And warm, after the rock's chill. We made our descent at that time when it is winter on the Barrens, but still autumn below in the Southland.

The checkerboard fields vanished from sight as we climbed down. The last remnants of the road disappeared in the foothills that washed up against the skirts of the mountain. Rocky slopes gave way to mossgrass and streams, and brown bushes that had edible blue berries. Maric coaxed a fire out of the tinderbox, and the last of the barbarians' rations were eaten.

Tomorrow is soon enough to cast about for another path, I thought; there's bound to be a *telestre* in walking distance.

'I'll take first watch,' I said. 'Then you, Maric?'

'Yes.' His eyes were shutting despite his efforts to stay awake.

I banked the fire. The others rolled themselves in their blankets. We were out of the wind in a dip between the hills, out of the bitter cold. It was barely sunset. I walked around for a time to keep awake, watching the last light golden on the snowpeaks, and the plumes of falling water.

'Christie!'

I sat up in a panic, shaken out of sleep. Bright cloudy light dazzled me. I couldn't focus.

'What? *What?*'

'He's gone,' the boy shouted, 'he was here for last watch, and now he isn't, he's gone—'

I knelt upright and wiped dew-wet hands over my face, bringing me coldly awake. A headache throbbed behind my eyes. When I'd got rid of the night's stiffness, I staggered upright. The fire was ashes. The packs were open, empty, strewn on the mossgrass. Except one. That was gone.

'He took everything he could carry.' I wanted to kill Blaize n'ri n'suth Meduenin. We had the clothes we wore, the blankets we slept in; that was all. No – he'd left the *harur* blades, the sonic stunner. But only because we slept with them on us, I thought.

'He took the tinderbox.' Maric was crying openly, but it wasn't for that.

I said 'So much for a mercenary's price. He's gone looking for the quickest way back to SuBannasen.'

PART SIX

CHAPTER 18

Shiriya-Shenin

Streams fell in spate from the peaks, so cold their water burned the mouth; water that whitened the skin and was fire on open cold sores. But there was nothing to eat. The foothills of the Wall are barren. Bogs and ponds made the valleys impassable. Sparse brown mossgrass grew between outcroppings of rock on the hills. Maric and I went hand in hand, supporting each other. At the crest of a ridge, we stopped. The boy knelt, leaning against a grey boulder.

I squinted upwards. The cloudy dawn cleared to a blue and silver day, stars freckling the west. Mountains hung gold and white in the sky to either side, the foothills lost in haze. High overhead, *kur-rashaku* circled. Shrill cries drifted down. I had no idea of direction, except to keep the dip of the pass behind us.

Bone-weary, hands and feet swollen, I felt afraid. Hunger made a hard pain under my ribs. How much permanent damage have I done? I thought. And the *ashiren* ... but Ortheans are tough, aren't they?

The earth, damp under my numb hands, became alien soil. The cold air sang. The wrinkled hills might rise up, I thought, vaguely aware that I had fallen; the hills might shake us off their hide, and we be lost forever.

'Riders!' Maric said, head cocked to one side, listening. His voice sounded thin. 'Coming this way!'

We both stood and walked a few yards down the far side of the ridge. An old track ran south. Now even I heard it.

Marhaz scattered mud: horns burnished, pelts shining. The riders wore horn-mail over dun uniforms, slit to mid-spine, braided manes flying. The high-backed saddles' leather gleamed. Bright spears glittered. The first rider reined in so sharply that her *marhaz* reared in a tight circle. She shouted an unintelligible demand. Maric and I unconsciously drew closer together.

The second rider dismounted, unsheathing a curved blade. He

was jet-skinned, a sleek copper mane pulled up and braided into a horsetail on the crown of his head. He was afraid. I saw the membrane of his eyes retract so far that the whites were visible. He glared, repeating words I almost understood.

It shattered the quiet: the shouting, the hoofbeats, the smell of *marhaz*. The Barrens and the Fens left a silence in me. Now I felt the world break and come together, changed.

'I'm Lynne de Lisle Christie, Dominion envoy.' I repeated it in Roehmonder, and a spattering of Melkathan and Rimon, and then again in Ymirian. They stared at me uncomprehendingly. The man peered at us, and abruptly backed off.

The woman spoke sharply and he remounted, clapped heels to the *marhaz* flanks, and scuffed up divots of mud along the track towards the Broken Stair pass.

'Maric?'

'I'm a southerner.' He shook his head wearily. 'But I think she wants us to go with her.'

The spear came down, bright point lowering towards me. We began to walk ahead of the rider.

Walk long enough to get weary, and keep walking after that, and you fall into a curious frame of mind. Movement becomes involuntary. It's a trance state: the earth is very distinct, all physical sensations are exaggerated, the senses reach out to the world. So, following the track with the rider and *marhaz* behind us, I was remembering going to Kirriach – the sheer distance of the flat horizon. The depth of the pale sky. The cold wind and glittering daystars. The moss and rock of the Barrens were part of my mental landscape now. Tired muscles, lightheaded with hunger, feet rubbed raw by stiffened leather boots, one undershirt sleeve ripped loose and tied over nose and mouth against the freezing wind – it merges, becomes part of the sunlight and the silence.

The hills gave way to open land. Rutted earth tracks ran ruler-straight between drystone walls, and the chessboard pattern seen from the pass resolved itself into thin pasture and the stubble of harvested ground. Flat land and straight track: it seemed we walked and walked and never gained an inch.

The plain was deceptive. I came out of a daze to see that we approached rising ground; crowning it was a winding brick-built wall with flat-roofed brick buildings beyond it. Sunlight glanced off lichened walls and iron gates. Traders booths were being dismantled by the gate, and merchants and *ashiren* turned to stare at us. My face felt bare, as if anyone could read my thoughts for the looking. Even Maric was alien.

The place wasn't as large as it first seemed to me, fresh come down from the Barrens. A fortress, not a *telestre*. Colours were faded. Only the steel of sword and axe were bright.

'They'll have someone to interpret,' I said optimistically. Maric gave a subdued nod.

The rider dismounted, speaking at length to a woman with troopmaster's belt-badges. Now, to me, none of the troopers looked clean, and they oiled their braided manes with a pungent oil. When Maric attempted to interrupt, the gate-guards moved forward drawing curved *harur* blades.

I didn't blame them, considering how we must look. A skinny *ashiren* in filthy clothes, mane in rat's-tails, brown skin caked with dirt; and an equally dirty woman, hair hacked short with a knife, boots splitting at the seams. Out of place: this land – ochre and umber, high and infertile – had a feeling of cleanness about it. Or perhaps it was only sterility.

Other Ortheans drifted through the gates for a closer look. Beyond them, inside the walls, I saw a courtyard surrounded by armoury and stores and kitchen. Familiar. The few practice bouts were breaking up, now they had another source of interest. The troopers linked spears horizontally, blocking the crowd from us. Merchants, soldiers, insular hill men, all in brilliant clothes. Slit-backed *becamil* robes, *chirith-goyen* sashes, loose britches and short boots, and slender curved blades. Most had manes braided down the spine but pulled up into a cascading horsetail on the crown of the head. Quartz beads and bracelets gleamed. I watched their bright alien eyes; surprise and distaste shadowing them as clouds shadow the sun.

The crowd began to scatter as an Orthean male came through, giving sharp orders. He was tan-skinned, stout, in his forties. Rank-badges made him a commander. Of this garrison? I wondered. With him was a younger man in the brown robes of an Earthspeaker.

'Well, now.' The commander's accent when he spoke Ymirian was new, but intelligible. 'Who are you, and where do you come from?'

'Achil Maric Salathiel, of Rimon,' the boy said quickly. '*T'an*, where is this?'

'Ai Garrison. North Peir-Dadeni,' he elaborated. 'How is it you don't know, *ashiren*? And does your companion speak?'

'We've come from Roehmonde. I'm Christie, the envoy from – you call us Outworlders.'

'Huroth said she found you up near Broken Stair.'

I was too tired to lie, or to make it sound less incredible. 'We came down the pass yesterday. We came from Roehmonde across the Barrens.'

The whites of his eyes showed momentarily. He gestured the Earthspeaker forward. The young male, not coming close, sniffed the air. Then he went to Maric, looking into his face, thumbing back his eyelids and looking into his mouth and nostrils. I kept still for a similar examination. The Earthspeaker said something and the nearest troopers relaxed, laughing and commenting.

'They are neither of them fit, but the *ashiren* carries no disease. As for the other, *t'an* Shaid, I can't say. I'm not certain the woman is human.'

I saw them note eyes, hands, differences. 'I'm the Dominion envoy. From Earth.'

'If she were diseased,' the *t'an* Shaid said, 'the *ashiren* would be ill.'

'Yes, that is likely.'

'So, not dangerous that way. But in what other ways?'

'She is—' here the Earthspeaker used an unfamiliar term '—with the earth.'

'We're not dangerous,' I said. 'Tired, yes; dangerous, no. All I want, *t'an*, is to get to the Crown at Tathcaer.'

Some kind of recognition seemed to occur to him. 'So you expect to be fed and kept while messages are sent halfway across the Southland, do you?'

The urbane sarcasm riled me. 'I'm the envoy. Haven't you got eyes?'

'I've seen freaks before. If you were that clever, you'd know that this envoy – whatever it was, and I had my doubts – died of the snow-fever in Roehmonde last Torvern. Ah, that's stopped you. We're forewarned: a messenger changed mounts here this morning, and gave warning of suspicious travellers coming down the Kyre. Broken Stair, my sire and dam!'

I didn't have to ask. A 'messenger' with a scarred face, lying to get a riderbeast to take him south.

'He didn't have to do that,' Maric whispered. 'He could have left, he . . . not to us, he shouldn't have.'

'I'd keep you in the cells,' the commander said, 'but that's a waste of supplies. You have a choice: the road to the Kyre or the road to Shiriya-Shenin. I suggest you take one and start walking.'

I realized he was serious. He didn't believe me. He intended to throw us out, back on the road, where footsteps ate up the miles in infinitesimal fractions.

'You listen to me, *t'an*.' My voice sounded disused, hollow. The

206

wind swept dust against the garrison walls. Now there were only half a dozen troopers round us, but I was aware of eyes watching from the walls. Temper made me breathless, dizzy. 'I'm Christie, envoy of the Dominion, which Suthafiori will confirm. This is my *l'ri-an*, Achil Maric Salathiel. Your informant was a hired sword in the pay of the Crown's enemies. I've been hunted out of Roeh-monde, I've crossed the Fens, I've crossed the Barrens and come down Broken Stair – and believe me I don't intend walking one *seri* more! Now either you keep me here until Suthafiori is informed, or you provide me with transport and an escort to go south. One or the other!'

The commander shook his head, more in frustration than any-thing else, watching me with a clear topaz gaze. The Earthspeaker said something in the Peir-Dadeni language.

'Yes. Of course,' the commander said, keeping eye-contact with me. 'It's Riardh Sixthweek. The *T'An Suthai-Telestre* will have moved to winter court in Shiriya-Shenin by now. Two days downriver, Outlander. What do you say, shall I send you there?'

Later, I realized that was the point he expected me to crack. It's easy enough for an imposter to ask to be taken to the Crown when the court is half a continent away.

'Only – two days?' The flare of energy died. I nodded weakly. 'Yes. Both of us. The *ashiren* stays with me.'

He was puzzled; he still didn't believe me. But he wasn't going to risk being wrong.

'You,' he said to the woman who had brought us in, 'take an escort, go down to Shiriya-Shenin on the water-caravan. As for these two, feed them, but nothing else. Let them go to the *T'An Suthai-Telestre* as beggars, if they're so certain of belief. And keep close watch – see they get to Shiriya-Shenin, and nowhere else.'

Because of the plain it was impossible to see the river until we were on its banks. It was wide, even here, and sluggish; a loop meandered up close to the Ai garrison and then drifted away southwest. Broad flat-bottomed boats were drawn up to wooden jetties. Brown water swirled round the piles.

I was tired of being filthy, resenting the commander's spite – it would have cost him nothing to let us wash, at least. Back of that was an irrational hurt. Despite my better judgement, I'd trusted Blaize n'ri n'suth Meduenin.

'I thought we'd done with trouble when we left the Barrens,' Maric said quietly, 'but it isn't over yet, Christie, is it?'

'Nearly,' I said, and he smiled ruefully.

A damp cold hazed the flat horizon. Traders were loading the

207

boats, lashing crates to the rails. Bundles bound in waxed cloth filled the holds past deck-level. Six or seven boats were moored together, painted in rainbow colours, beaked rudders jutting from the river. Ortheans shouted in the Peir-Dadeni tongue.

We were pushed aboard the last boat, then ignored while the troopmaster had a long, incomprehensible argument with the crew. I sat down under the deck awning, leaning back against the bales in the hold. Maric, sighing, eased himself down beside me.

I must see if I can make that woman understand me, I thought. What did the commander call her – Huroth? Meanwhile I can at least unlace these damn boots.

And in that moment between sitting down and bending forward, I fell asleep.

A sour taste furred my mouth. Cramp caught me as I moved, grunting, and opened my eyes. I lay skewed against the cargo bales. Water hissed against the hull, inches from my head. Some-one had thrown a blanket over me and – I raised my head, wincing – over Maric too.

The garrison escort squatted on the other side of the deck, playing *ochmir*; and the traders sat on cushions under the steers-man's awning.

Midday sunlight reflected brilliantly from the smooth water. When I sat up I saw we had come out of the plains. There were low hills to either side – brown, sparsely vegetated, dotted here and there with *marhaz* and *skurrai* herds and sprawling *telestre* buildings. Some of the slopes were terraced. Perhaps it was only that this was the time after harvest, well into the dead time of winter, but it looked a harsh land to me.

'Christie?' Maric sat up, blinking; then relaxed and scratched his matted mane. 'I thought . . . I've still got the flask here, do you want a drink?'

It was unwatered wine. I coughed. The sun, I realized, was in the wrong position. 'Have I slept the day round?'

'Not all of it. Remember last night?' Seeing my blank look, he added 'The *telestre* we stopped at, where the herds of wild *skurrai* were. You woke long enough to eat.'

It was true, the ravenous hurt was eased. 'I guess I wasn't as awake as I looked.'

A shadow fell across us. Maric looked up. '*T'an* Huroth.'

'Troopmaster,' she corrected, squatting down by him. She avoided looking at me.

'Salathiel *telestre*?' she said at last, in accented Rimon.

'Tathcaer westbank. We run the ferry.'

'Yes. I thought I knew the Salathiel face. I've a sister who's *n'ri n'suth* Lyadine now, I used to visit them there.'

'You'd have passed us on your way up the Oranon, then.'

She grunted. When she did meet my eyes, it was with her own veiled.

'You have your *ashiren* well versed in *kir* story.'

I said, 'You don't believe he's lying.'

'Ah. Well.' She stood. 'You're going where you wish. Isn't that enough?'

The boats kept to the eastern side of the wide expanse of water, passing terraced hills. Every scrap of earth was hoarded. I watched the narrow ochre strips pass, seeing the pale stone walls retreat back up from the river's edge in steps. Noon shadows pooled black under the occasional isolated *tukinna* tree. *Telestre* buildings were stone-walled, stone-roofed. It was land worn down to the bone, a land that had been scoured clean.

Ribbons of sunlight stretched like tapes from the broken cloud cover, sinking into the silty river. The sun never got as low in the sky as I was used to in the British Isles, but nevertheless the pale star was hanging close to the southern horizon. Southward the river valley wound between shallow hills, diminishing into golden haze.

Huroth talked a little and some of the traders spoke Ymirian, so I got some idea of where the water-caravan was heading. Shortly after noon on that second day the river curved westward. We passed a burning-ground, flat cremation stones set in a valley close to the water, and I guessed we must be close. Then the river turned south again into higher, hillier land, and I saw the city.

The river is narrow here, between hills that rise up steep to either side; mossgrass turning from summer browns and blues to winter's ochre and umber. I saw *tukinna* trees in clefts so deep their crooked branches hardly reached up to the open air. And then, ahead, was Shiriya-Shenin. Ridged hills went up from the eastern bank. For a moment I thought – map changed to territory – that every hill had contour lines on it. Then that they were stepped, like pyramids. And then I saw that these cone-like hills were terraced, the low walls following every fold and dip and ridge. In all that massive natural amphitheatre that holds an eastern meander of the Ai river, there is not one yard of uncultivated soil.

Shiriya-Shenin sprawled on the plateau a little above the river, brown as the hills surrounding it, long and low and cornered with ziggurat towers. As we came further round the bend in the river, I saw how far it stretched: a city larger than Corbek, larger even than Tathcaer.

Numerous docks and jetties were crowded with the last of the season's riverboats. We came under the city wall, glowing honey-coloured in the winter sunlight, loaf-shaped bricks gleaming with thick glaze. Squat towers spaced along the walls opened slit windows on the river-side.

The crew of the water-caravan steered the boats in, taking ropes thrown from the dock, and each vessel was moored. Huroth curtly directed her troopers to guard us, and went ashore.

Finally we were herded off the boat. The wooden dock was hard underfoot. I found it difficult just to walk. Maric groaned, held my arm, and cursed under his breath. Huroth beckoned us forward.

Between two ziggurat towers, great painted wooden gates stood open. Stone plinths on either side supported statues of *zilmei*, painted very lifelike: one on all fours, ears flat against the wedge-shaped skull, showing tusks in a snarl, the other rearing up and clawing the air, head back as if to give out its whooping cry. So it was that the *ashiren* and I came into Shiriya-Shenin by the great Fifthwall *Zilmei* Gate.

Muddy streets were flanked by boardwalks at the rivergate. It was an effort to walk. The troopers jostled close, afraid of our vanishing into the crowd.

Don't you worry, I thought as we stepped on to brick-paved ways further in. We're not going to escape, no indeed.

I plodded on behind Huroth. Even Maric, Orthean and *ashiren*, was at the limit of his endurance. Damp wind chilled between blank-walled *telestre* houses, whipping down narrow streets – and they really are streets, I thought. The same secretive houses faced inward to courtyards with pools and cisterns, but they were set out on a grid system. *Kur-rashaku* wheeled and perched on flat roofs, their harsh cries sounding over the crowded passages.

It was not only that these people spoke a different language – they seemed alien even to Corbek and Tathcaer. The *ashiren* ran barefoot, ceramic beads woven into braided manes. Adults sported uncut six-clawed hands. There was not a street in which you could not hear singing. There were no bells. Cages hung by the gates, and squat-bodied lizardbeasts gripped the bars with spatulate fingers and sang shrill warnings.

At each wall – the city has outgrown its boundaries four times – Huroth showed authorization at the gateways, and wrangled interminably with the city Watch. From Fifthwall to Firstwall took most of the afternoon.

At the L'ku Gate, guards clustered round a brazier, stamping their feet against the cold. Beyond them lay a warren of single-storey buildings, yards, raised walks and hexagon-shaped halls: the old Firstwall city founded by *amari* Andrethe. Huroth argued with what I gathered were aides and ministers of the *tha'adur*, the Peir-Dadeni court. Eventually, half asleep on my feet, I interrupted in Ymirian. Someone must understand.

'You,' I said, picking out a pale gold-maned Orthean at random, 'tell the *T'An Suthai-Telestre* that the Dominion envoy is here.'

He gave the slight inclination that passes for a bow in Peir-Dadeni. He was not young, a tall Orthean in scarlet slit-robe with sash and rank-badges and curved Dadeni blades. The diamond-scale pattern of his skin was more pronounced, changing with the winter. One six-fingered hand rested on a *harur* blade. Gold flashed. Like many Ortheans he had the atrophied remnant of webbing between his fingers, and the thin sections of skin were pierced with gold and quartz studs. Orthe's streak of the barbaric.

'Cethelen Khassiye Reihalyn,' he introduced himself measuredly, speaking Ymirian with a south Dadeni accent. 'You understand, these things take time.'

'I understand that Suthafiori will lose little time in making her displeasure known, if this is kept from her.'

'That is easy to say.'

'Then say it to her!' I snapped. 'I haven't come halfway across the Southland to stand waiting at the gates of Shiriya-Shenin.'

'It's true, *t'an*,' Maric said to him. 'We have come across the Barrens from Corbek. The Otherworld envoy lives; it is for the *T'An Suthai-Telestre* to know this as soon as possible.'

'Keep guard on them. Wait here.' Khassiye's gaze flicked over us before he went back through the Firstwall gate, and I saw subliminal recoil. Well, we're not pretty, I thought, but we're alive, that's something.

City sounds quieted. Smoke went up grey into the second twilight. The Nineday fast would be broken now, I could smell evening meals cooking. My gut contracted: I was hungrier than I knew. The streets were emptying, and oil-lanterns were lit and hung over *telestre* archways.

'I've had enough of this,' I said.

'They might kill us if we scare them,' the *ashiren* said thoughtfully, 'considering where we've come from. I never heard any good of these northern lands. Best to keep quiet and wait, *S'aranth*.'

'We'll go in under guard,' I said to Huroth, 'but I'm going in to find someone who knows me, or we'll be here all night.'

She was no keener on being kept waiting than I was, and the

211

troopers wanted to spend what time they could in Shiriya-Shenin before they returned to garrison duty. She endured the remarks of the city Watch only under protest.

'Yes,' she said, 'it was commanded we take you to the *T'An Suthai-Telestre*, not stand outside the L'Ku Gate. You there, stand aside! Goddess! they're under guard, aren't they? Stand out of the way.'

There was no troopmaster present, so she outranked them. I'd counted on it.

The garishly-painted gates had lost their colour in the twilight. The city smells dispersed on a cold wind. A light rain began to fall. Windows shone yellow in the low mass of brickwork that was the Firstwall city. The gateway was a tunnel: footsteps echoed as we went through.

One gnarled *tukinna* grew in the centre of a hexagonal courtyard where shallow steps went down to a covered well. Lanterns hung at intervals shed yellow light on the brown flagstones. I saw the same expression on Maric's face that I must have had on mine – intimidated, overpowered by the age and arrogance of the secretive walls. Diamond-slit windows lined the low flat-roofed buildings.

Huroth strode past tree and well, her back stiff with tension. As I caught up, intending to speak to her, a woman in a green *becamil* cloak came out of the far building. Silhouetted against the open doorway, then resolving into recognition. The cloak's hood was thrown back, disclosing cropped black mane, gaunt dark face. She moved abstractedly, head down, left hand tucked under her belt. The cloak hung flat from her right shoulder. I almost didn't know her: she must have been desperately ill, I thought.

'Ruric!'

Her head came up and her face went blank. The yellow eyes veiled, then became clear. Am I that different? I wondered, seeing how very slowly the recognition came. But it came.

'Christie? Grief of the Goddess, *Christie*!'

Then we were embracing, swaying in the rain and twilight; and she was laughing and pounding me on the back in her single-armed embrace. She put me back to arm's length, and we grinned foolishly at each other. Her gaze took in Maric, the Ai garrison troopers.

'Wha'?' She shook her head ruefully, and wrinkled her nose. 'Goddess, Christie, but you stink!'

'I have an excuse for that. A number of excuses. The Fens, the Barrens . . . this is my escort from Broken Stair, by the way.'

She shook her head again, still grinning. 'I have to hear this.

And so does Suthafiori . . . You – troopmaster – I want your report. Christie; dear Goddess, what a story!'

I rescued my knife and the sonic stunner, but the rest of my clothes and gear had to be burned. Their state was unbelievable, even to me. I peeled off wrappings from sore hands, and when I finally did remove my boots and the makeshift bandages, two or three nails came away with them. Open coldsores smarted in the hot bath water. I spent a mindless, comfortable time in near-scalding water, ridding myself of scurf and dirt and lice; it took four baths to go from black-brown to scrubbed pink. *L'ri-an* took me to a set of rooms in the quarantine hall and a woman came to clip my hopelessly matted hair. It was cropped shorter than an Ymirian's. I sat in front of the hearth, wrapped in a soft robe, listening to the rain beat at the narrow windows.

'Christie?' Maric came in, belting a *chirith-goyen* robe round him. His skin was pale tan again, the winter scale pattern quite distinct. 'It's quieter in here. All these people . . .'

'Hard to take, yes. We'll get used to it, I suppose.'

He shuttered the diamond-shaped windows. The small room was warm, lamps and firelight bright on the tapestried walls. It would have been easy to sleep. Maric sat by the fire, cradling a wine jug. Clean clothes were laid out on the bed, and I limped across to dress.

Maric leaned forward, running fingers through his mane in the fire's heat. 'Will you braid it when it's dry, *S'aranth*?'

'Sure, in a minute.' No Orthean can reach properly to braid its own mane, and his had grown long enough out of the cropped style to go in Dadeni braids. The implications of that came home to me: in these close-knit communities an Orthean is never without brother or sister, parent or offspring, to perform that simple task.

I'd put my shirt on and was lacing up my britches, when I heard the door open.

'Now it starts, I suppose. Questions. I—'

A middle-aged Orthean came in, fair mane wet, rain darkening on his shoulders. Coldness hit me. For a second I was deaf and blind with a surge of adrenalin, back in the marshes, back in Oeth.

'I came as soon as I heard.' The grip of his six-fingered hands was dry, firm. 'You're not hurt?'

'No, I . . .' Easy tears blinded me. I blinked clear of them, grasping his hands to keep back hysteria. 'No, we're all right. Hal, it's good to see you.'

There was no need to say more. We had entered into our old

friendship as soon as he walked into the room. I remembered Ruric saying, He's a good man, don't trust him. I didn't know about good – he had all the Orthean addiction to intrigue and untruth – but I could trust him.

'Now,' he said as we sat by the hearth, 'now let Howice and SuBannasen lie to the Crown: we've got them!'

'They're here?'

'The *T'Ans* travel with the court. But Howice is here for the Crown's inquiry into Corbek. *T'An* Ruric and I,' he said, 'she got down to Corbek about the time they dragged me back there, we've been stirring scandal ever since. But I never thought we'd have a witness back from the dead.'

I laughed with him. Then, 'Does that mean I've been reported dead, to Earth?'

'Your people were notified, yes.'

'That's going to cause some bureaucratic confusion.' It was a difficult concept to translate. Then, making the connection, I said, 'If Howice is here, does that mean Falkyr is?'

He nodded, eyeing me warily. 'Somewhere, yes.' A pause. 'Sethin's dead, and the old man Koltyn; which makes it difficult for us.'

Relief, sorrow: I didn't know what I was feeling, or for whom.

'What happened to that barbarian woman?' he said avidly. 'And – where's Theluk?'

Now I knew I was back in the world again, and I took the weight of it. Maric was looking for me to answer.

'The fenborn killed her,' I said. 'Theluk's dead.'

CHAPTER 19

Echoes of Corbek

Towards the end of that week I attended the inquiries (having spent most of the intervening days asleep). There were two, called quickly because of the speed with which the scandal spread through the city: an inquiry into the report of my 'death' in Corbek, and into the hiring of a mercenary assassin by person or persons unknown but widely supposed to be SuBannasen *telestre*. I had hopes of uncovering a multitude of injustices.

Both courts being there – the Dadeni *tha'adur* and the Ymirian *takshiriye* – the inquiries were presided over by the *T'An Suthai-Telestre* and the Andrethe, and given in both languages. The Andrethe's investigator turned out to be Cethelen Khassiye Reihalyn (who made no mention of our meeting at the L'Ku Gate); and for the Crown, the First Minister of Ymir. Despite lines of age, his face was familiar. I was not surprised to find he was Hanathra *telestre*, Hellel by name.

'How much do I have to say?' I asked Haltern as we filed into the low-roofed hall on the second day.

'Very little. You'll be called on to affirm the statements you've made.'

Haltern was working with a knife-faced man I recognized. He'd been at the disastrous dinner at Hill-Damarie: Brodin n'ri n'suth Charain. I eased back on the carved wooden seat – it was near one of the hall's ornamental iron braziers – and rested my feet on a cushion. There was still no way I could get boots on my swollen feet, they looked and felt like slabs of raw meat. So I had them bandaged and swathed in several pairs of stockings.

'For *telestre* Talkul: Verek Howice!'

The Orthean stood, was acknowledged, and came forward. He wore Roehmonder dress, dull against the bright Dadeni robes, and he was just as I remembered him.

The light through the lozenge-shaped windows dazzled me where it fell on the mosaic floor. The Wellhouse, the cells: it came back with a bitter taste. Clear-eyed and guileless he looked across the hall at me. The shock of hatred was like cold water. I loathed him. No, that was unprofessional. Nonetheless . . .

He said, 'Can I be blamed for the actions of an old man and a mad Keeper?'

They couldn't shift him from that defence.

'Koltyn was an old man,' he said, soft voice clearly audible through the Hexagram Hall. 'Now it seems he was a senile old man. I could deny that I realized it, but it wouldn't be true. We all knew. He was an old man, but he had been a good *s'an* to us, and it would have broken him to know that he was no longer capable. We – let me be honest, we imagined he would soon die. We didn't know he could do so much harm before he did. We kept him as *s'an*, we obeyed him as *s'an* – both wrong, perhaps, but wrong for the right reason.'

It went down well with the Ortheans.

'Lying little shit!' I said under my breath. In English.

'Yes,' Haltern whispered back, recognizing the tone, if nothing else. 'But how are we going to prove it? Koltyn's dead, and Sethin.'

And Theluk, I thought. It doesn't leave much credible evidence.

'Arad,' Khassiye Reihelyn queried. His six-fingered hands flashed gold as he gestured. 'What of him?'

Howice shrugged. 'The church in Corbek is asking that very question, and I can't anticipate their answer. All I can say is that I think he was misguided, but he believed in what he did.'

At that point I realized that this inquiry was anything but a foregone conclusion. Here was I, worn raw from Howice hunting me across Roehmonde, but pinning him down . . . it was going to be harder than walking across the Barrens.

It broke up inconclusively again, and I sat there while the hall emptied. Eventually I limped across to the ornamented fireplace to be introduced to the Andrethe, who sat there talking with Ruric and the Crown.

'Envoy, be welcome.' Suthafiori studied me as if there was some change apparent. I sat down. I'd seen her the day I arrived, but didn't remember making too much sense at the time. 'For a dead woman, you look well.'

'Andrethe,' Ruric used the formal inflection, 'this is Christie *S'aranth* of the British Isles.'

Kanta Andrethe was mountainous, her coffee-coloured flesh enclosed in a blue and gold robe belted with a wide *chirith-goyen* sash; the robe split down the spine to show her brown mane in elaborate braids. Her arms were hams, her legs tree-trunks. But her face – unveiled raisin-eyes in wrinkled flesh – showed an odd mixture of maternalism and shrewdness.

'Outworlders, is it? I'm not convinced. Some adventurer out of Saberon or Kel Harantish.' She gave me a very direct look. 'My dear, I don't apologize, I like your style.'

'I also make no apologies, excellence, that I come from a greater distance than Kel Harantish or Saberon. May I present the greetings of the governments of the Dominion to the Andrethe of Peir-Dadeni.'

She hesitated, then gave a snorting chuckle. 'My sire and dam! Yes, you may.'

A l'ri-an came in to rake the fire into life, and serve bowls of hot herb-tea.

'The SuBannasen awaits your inquiry, T'An,' Haltern said to Suthafiori, 'but there again we are robbed of witnesses.'

'The Meduenin hired sword,' Kanta Andrethe's black eyes veiled. 'He is here. With Sulis, Brodin tells me.'

'So arrest him,' I said, rather too bluntly. Meduenin in the city – no, I didn't want to think about the past.

'Ah, he will have closed the contract by now if he is wise, and then there is no questioning him.' The Andrethe glanced at Brodin, who nodded. 'But still, we do know what Sulis n'ri n'suth Su-Bannasen did in Corbek.'

'Yes, bribery; and how?' Suthafiori's head lowered as she stared at her linked hands. 'Melkathi is poor, and she has spent gold on this. Where did that come from?'

'Who knows? But it went to Howice,' Ruric observed, 'he could tell much, if he would.'

'If! Mother, yes, if he would.' Kanta's heavy head swayed from side to side. 'And if Corbek is questioning that Wellkeeper Arad . . . we will see.'

At her gesture the l'ri-an brought forward a table. A map of the Southland telestres was inlaid in enamel on its surface. (The sheer permanence of political divisions impressed me – coming from a world where atlases are liable to be out of date almost as soon as they're printed). Haltern and Brodin conferred. The women studied the map, slender fingers pointing. The Andrethe wore gold studs between her plump fingers. Brown, massive, a woman ruling a province the size of Ymir, Melkathi, and Roehmonde put together. Beside her, silvergilt and slender, the Crown seemed almost childlike.

'Melkathi, Roehmonde . . .' Suthafiori touched Ymir, that lies between them. 'There are quarrels between telestres of Ymir and

Rimon that might be revived. And you say the SuBannasen fosters *ashiren* at Corbek, envoy? Yes . . . but Morvren Freeport will not fight the Crown, nor you, Andrethe, nor the Kyre.' She was grim. 'On your Otherworld, envoy, what would this mean?'

'I'm not sure. War, perhaps.' There was no literal translation. 'If they attacked . . .'

'Raiding, you mean?' Ruric sipped from her tea-bowl. 'Then they'd have the whole Hundred Thousand in arms. No, Su-Bannasen's not stupid, nor is Howice.'

The Southland's standing army puzzled me at first, being no more than the few thousand necessary to man the garrisons at Ai and Tathcaer and Path-of-Skulls. Then I realized that Southlanders are trained fighters from *ashiren* onwards: a force which is, by nature, defensive.

'I'll tell you, Dalzielle.' The Andrethe rolled back in her chair, fixing her gaze on Suthafiori. 'Next year, yes, comes Midsummer-Tenyear? Well, then. When it comes to naming the Crown again, how many *T'An*s will you have that favour you?'

The small woman nodded. 'If the *s'an telestres* should name the SuBannasen again for Melkathi, and Howice for Roehmonde; and if those two gained the support of Rimon, say, or Morvren . . .'

'Then you have lost the Crown, and must go back to being Dalzielle *telestre* Kerys-Andrethe. Last Tenyear you were lucky, that was the year you beat the barbarians at Skulls. This Tenyear – this is the year you brought Golden Witchbreed back to the Southland!'

'Your pardon, *T'An*,' I said, 'we're not Witchbreed.'

'It's what they think you are that matters.'

Ruric widened yellow eyes. 'Oh I agree, Andrethe.'

The woman snorted. 'So, all that's gold may not be Witchbreed, I'll grant you that.'

'Should there be a different Crown, that will cause problems for you and your people, envoy.' Suthafiori paused. 'But I think you need not be concerned. I am Crown, and mean to be so after Midsummer-Tenyear.'

It was after the midday gongs sounded across the city that I left the Hexagram Hall.

It can drag on all through winter, I thought. Howice is as slippery as a fish. And will it be any better with SuBannasen?

I walked through the passages to the Hall of Mosaics, meaning to go and check on the progress of the Crown's inquiry. A group of Ortheans were talking, brightly illuminated by the hall's coloured glass windows. I avoided them. One drew his sword to demonstrate a stroke and parry. A Roehmonder *harur-nilgiri*, I noted; the group were mostly in Roehmonde jackets and loose trousers. Cropped manes had rock-crystal beads knotted down to mid-spine. Then the sword-wielder's head went back as he laughed, and a familiar voice made some barbed comment. He sheathed the blade, turned, and saw me.

'Christie,' he said soberly. 'I heard you were here. I'm glad you're well.'

Sethin Falkyr, Falkyr of Corbek.

Was that only last autumn? I thought. It seems years ago. Was that woman really Lynne Christie?

'I heard about Sethin,' I said. 'I'm sorry.'

'When the sickness was advanced, she came to me,' Falkyr said, 'and asked what a mother may demand of her sons. So I made it painless. Death was easy for her. May we meet again.'

It was the traditional acknowledgement of death. It wouldn't have surprised me to hear that Sethin had taken her own life, but it shocked me that she had asked Falkyr, and he had done it, and seemed to regard it as a mark of favour. How close were we? I wondered. How far did we ever understand each other?

'Koltyn should have done the same,' he added, 'but She took him at the beginning of Riardh Secondweek.'

An awkward silence fell. There was nothing in his expression to say that we had ever been *arykei*.

'And you, you're well?' I asked.

'Yes. I travel with *t'an* Howice now. Who knows, I may become one of the *tha'adur*.' Something of the old sarcasm sounded in his voice, but his eyes were veiled.

When it's dead, someone said to me, then leave it. We'd been joined in nothing but flesh. Looking back, I couldn't recognize us in the two people standing here.

'You're thin,' he said, 'you should rest. They tell me you crossed the Barrens, that's hard country. When you're well, perhaps we'll ride out round Shiriya-Shenin.'

'Perhaps, *t'an* Falkyr, but I am kept fairly busy here.'

We parted bewildered on both sides.

It drew on towards Orventa, the winter season. I took rooms in Firstwall, not far from Ruric. There wasn't a two-storey building in Shiriya-Shenin, with the exception of the ziggurat watchtowers; seen from the nearby high ground it resembled its own terraced hillsides, each long low line of *telestre* buildings forming a step up from the river. I could have done with less walking in the interminable maze of passages. Not until the late season storms struck did

I appreciate the advantage of being under cover, as a wind came upriver that would have stripped any tower off the hillside.

Rain lashed the lozenge windows, the last snarl of a storm, and Haltern walked into my rooms. I was attempting, again, to write out a report in longhand.

'Where are we today, then?' I asked cheerfully. It wouldn't surprise me to hear they'd moved the inquiry yet again.

'Nowhere.' He crossed to the window and looked out at the failing rain. 'They've closed the Corbek inquiry.'

'They've done *what*?'

'Closed it. It's finished.'

I heard shouts in the courtyard outside. *Ashiren* beginning the celebrations for the end of Riardh, and for winter festival.

'So what happens to Howice?'

'Nothing. He's left, gone downriver; plans to get back to Roehmonde before winter makes travelling impossible. Most of his *t'ans* have gone with him.'

'Shit!' And a few other English expressions.

Haltern shrugged. 'Arad must explain Corbek's poverty, and that is church business. All Howice did he claims his *s'an telestre* ordered him to do. No, by spring Howice may be *T'An* Roehmonde himself.'

I remembered Sethin. 'And then again – he may not.'

There was a pause.

'I see you're busy with the *t'ans* here,' Haltern added, 'but spare us a little more time, Christie. I need to call you for the inquiry on Sulis n'ri n'suth SuBannasen.'

CHAPTER 20

The Answer of SuBannasen

'We won't get many more boats downriver before the freeze.' Ruric hitched her cloak one-handed round her shoulders. A keen, damp wind blew off the river, and the sky was heavy with unshed snow.

'I want to get a message to Tathcaer – get them to pass word on to the Earth ship that I'm not dead.'

It is a curious fact that it is quicker to travel the nine hundred *seri* down the Ai and the eight hundred *seri* up the Rimon coast by ship than it is travelling the mere five hundred odd *seri* across Dadeni Heath and north Rimon on land. Especially the way Southland roads are in winter.

The river dock was half deserted, the warehouses shut up, the shipping *telestres* closing down for the day. Maric was with me. Neither he nor I wanted to walk far.

A raw cold came up off the grey water.

'How about it?' I asked Maric. 'You want to send a message to your *telestre*, let them know you're all right?'

'Yes, I do.'

'Or do you want to take the message in person?'

His head came up, his eyes were bright; there was no need to ask if that was what he wanted.

'I'm still your *l'ri-an*.'

'Of course. I'll send my message to Tathcaer by you, then you winter over at Salathiel. I'll be downriver again in the spring.'

'It's good of you. But I'll stay here if you want me, Christie.'

'This is most convenient for both of us, I think. Though I suspect I won't find out how much you do until I have to do it myself – and I don't know one end of a *marhaz* from the other. Speaking of which, do they take riderbeasts on the riverships?'

'They do,' Ruric put in, 'and I have your two in my stable still, Christie, I brought them back with me from Corbek. There was no one else . . .'

'No, of course not. Can't have you walking, though,' I said to Maric, 'so you'd better keep Oru, and take one of the *skurrai* for baggage.'

He thanked me, grinning.

We turned to walk back along the dock to Fifthwall's Silver Gate. When the boy was a way ahead, Ruric said, 'You should call in on Salathiel in the spring – explain to the *s'an telestre* why an *ashiren* comes home with *harur* blades and a *marhaz*.'

'Did I do wrong?'

'No.' She laughed. As we came to the Silver Gate she looked at me seriously. 'You're still going to need a *l'ri-an* this winter. Will you do me a favour?'

'Sure, what?'

'My *ashiren*, Rodion. Will you let *ke* do it?'

Even Ruric isn't above using her *telestre* to keep an eye on the envoy, I thought, but at least it's a friendly eye.

'Yes, of course.'

'It might not be easy,' the Orthean woman warned, 'but you do need a *l'ri-an*, and Rodion needs something – I'm not sure what.'

The SuBannasen trial – because that was what it was turning into – continued into Orventa at the usual slow Orthean pace. I attended, fitting appointments with *s'an* and *t'an* of the court into my spare time, and studying to become reasonably fluent in Peir-Dadeni. The envoy was becoming known in Shiriya-Shenin.

'Rodion?' It was towards the end of a cold morning. 'How long ago did this message come?'

Eventually the *ashiren* slouched out of the back rooms, eyed me up and down, and said, 'Not long.'

'Well, couldn't you have given it to me? Now I find out they want me at the inquiry again!'

Ke shrugged. Gawky, long-legged, this one was all adolescent, and well past the age for an *ashiren* to become adult.

'I didn't ask to be your *l'ri-an*, S'aranth.' The use-name had all its old insolence.

There was some expression in *kir* face that reminded me of Ruric, but that was all the resemblance. Pale mane braided to mid-spine, slick diamond-patterned skin with a flush of gold to it, and tawny-gold whiteless eyes . . . *ke* was very much as the Witchbreed are always described. The other *ashiren* called *kir* Rodion Halfgold: an intimation that somewhere in *kir* ancestry was Witchbreed blood (but I was also told that interbreeding between Ortheans and that extinct race was never possible). Whatever the truth, it didn't make *kir* life easy.

222

'Find Haltern, tell him I'm on my way.'

'Yes, *S'aranth*.'

As Rodion left, I realized something. I'd always seen *ashiren* as either male or female. Even Maric, who a year from now might be man or woman, I saw as a boy. (Once I came on them together, bent over an *ochmir* board, and – before I recognized him – saw Maric as a lean dark-maned girl.) But Rodion was neither, not in appearance or behaviour. In Dadeni robes, *ke* might be female, in Ymirian dress, male; and since those were purely Earth preconceptions I had to disregard them. I was forced into use of the neutral pronoun, and it was becoming natural to see all *ashiren* that way. I found it unsettling and a little frightening.

Ruric met me in the entrance to the Hexagram Hall.

'Inquiries!' she swore. 'If it was up to me I wouldn't inquire, I'd slit SuBannasen's throat. I hear they want our evidence again?'

'For all the good it'll do, yes.' The old woman's defence so far consisted of a flat denial, and an invitation that anyone prove any of their accusations. Which was proving remarkably hard to do.

I saw Rodion out in the courtyard; *ke* ducked *kir* head and scuttled off.

'Is it any easier?' Ruric asked.

'Not so's you'd notice.' I was truthful. 'That child thinks it's got a grudge against everyone.'

'That's my fault,' the Orthean woman said, yellow eyes half veiled. 'My Desert Coast mother must have come from Kel Harantish, I think, and the Witchbreed blood's strong there.'

'*Ke* must be – what, nearly fifteen?'

'Yes, and still *ashiren*. That doesn't help. When I was fifteen . . .' She shrugged as we entered the main body of the hall, taking seats by the *T'an Suthai-Telestre's* table. 'That was the year I came to Tathcaer, worked in a companion-house to save money to join the army. Straike was in the same house. Oh, he was proud, you'd think he was the first boy to father an *ashiren*. And the first year in the Guard is theory and study, I was able to keep Rodion with me.'

'He had that colouring?'

'Straike? No. Redhead, and pale as I am dark; I'd hoped Rodion would take after him. I got him to join the Guard. Bullied him, really. He was my Second all through the Quarth raids.' She paused. 'When he died in Melkathi, I had Rodion fostered up here. It isn't easy for a Halfgold anywhere.'

I saw Khassiye Reihalyn and Hellel Hanathra in one of the Hexagram Hall's many alcoves, and then Brodin passed me; and Sulis n'ri n'suth SuBannasen. The hall was crowded. I was aware that Haltern and Brodin had their own systems of intelligence; many of the seemingly unimportant members of the *tha'adur* and *takshiriye* brought information from other parts of the Southland. Of necessity, I would be ignorant of much that went on.

One face briefly glimpsed in the crowd was familiar. Fair streaked mane lit by sunlight falling through lozenge-windows . . . Blaize n'ri n'suth Meduenin.

'Ah, you're here.' Haltern, emerging from another of the alcoves, interrupted my thoughts.

'Is there new evidence against SuBannasen?'

He smiled, as non-committal as an Orthean can be, and exchanged polite formalities with Ruric.

The air in the Hexagram Hall was chill, despite the fires of slow-burning mossturf. Shiriya-Shenin's river mist combined with the smoke to make a dense fog and the thin winter sunlight vanished. *L'ri-an* lit oil lamps. The yellow glow added to the claustrophobic atmosphere. All but the centre tables were now occupied.

Aliens, I thought again. It was more noticeable in Shiriya-Shenin: their slit robes, curved pairs of blades and manes braided with ceramic beads, their habit of going barefoot on tessellated stone floors.

'I hear the Andrethe is tired of the delay,' Ruric said, 'and so's Dalzielle. I – yes, Oreyn, I saw you: hello.'

The man nodded acknowledgement and passed on. He was old, thin and white-skinned. The Orthean mane receded from his forehead and back from his ears, leaving a cropped crest. Narrow forehead and bright eyes gave his face a singularly insect-like appearance. With his slender six-fingered hands linked before his chest, he resembled nothing so much as a praying mantis.

'Your *telestre*?'

'Hana Oreyn Orhlandis,' she said quietly. 'The last of Hana's birth now alive. He was brother to my father. And now his place is as SuBannasen's first minister.'

'But you said – the uprising—'

'Orhlandis and Ales-Kadareth have always had strong links,' she said wryly, and laughed. 'They won't change that for one member of the *telestre*, even if she is *T'An* Commander.'

Suthafiori and the Andrethe entered the hall, talking, neither taking their places at the central table. I despaired of the Orthean sense of time. A buzz of talk rose. Ruric leaned over and questioned Haltern in a fierce undertone.

'Envoy.'

An old woman's voice. I stood, looking round, and saw that it

224

was SuBannasen herself. She was in the nearest alcove. Oreyn Orhlandis left her side as I went over.

'*T'An* Sulis.' I found it hard to be impolite to the old woman.

She was seated on a window bench, by a glazed ceramic wall that showed a pattern of stars. Her hands shook faintly as she poured wine from a flask into glass goblets.

'Drink with me,' she said, friendly, peremptory, as I sat down beside her. 'It's a shame you never came to Melkathi, *t'an* Christie.'

Her pale eyes, hooded and alert, gazed past me into the body of the hall. Oreyn was in conversation with another Melkathi man – Santhil, was it?

'I wish that I could have visited you, *T'An*.' For a moment, seeing the humour and sadness in her face, it was the truth. 'But I think, perhaps, not now.'

'No. They'll find some excuse,' Sulis said. 'Some excuse to take Ales-Kadareth from me. Ten years ago I would have fought . . . but I'm tired. Perhaps I shall go home to SuBannasen. Come, Christie, drink to the *telestres* we've left.'

It was the honey-thick wine of south Dadeni. A familiar scent rose from it – much clearer to a human, I think, than to an Orthean. I knew it now. Certainly there was less of it in the wine than there had been at Hill-Damarie, but it was unmistakable: *saryl-kabriz*.

The old Orthean woman smiled.

'Thank you, *T'An* Sulis.' I put the glass down untasted. 'Forgive me, I must go back to my place now.'

She picked it up, swirling the contents thoughtfully. It was impossible to resent her, though I had every right.

'I will play you at *ochmir* if you ever do come to Melkathi,' she promised. Then – the inquiry being opened by Suthafiori – she made her way to her seat in the hall.

And there was no shifting her from her defence. No proof of bribery in Corbek: Howice had his own reasons for being absent. No proof of hired assassins – even Haltern couldn't break the Mercenary Guildhouse's code.

She'll do it yet, I thought. Goddammit, she will, she'll do it like Howice!

I realized that I was far from safe in Shiriya-Shenin, for the winter, with SuBannasen.

On my way back across the courtyard I saw Blaize n'ri n'suth Meduenin again. He nodded civilly. '*T'an* Christie.'

The sky was yellowing. A cold wind scoured the yard, swirling the fog, and I was instantly back in the ruined city of Kirriach, smelling bad weather coming.

'You've got a brass nerve,' I said.

'*T'an*?' He appeared puzzled.

He must know I still carried the stunner. But he knows I'm envoy, I thought; and self-defence – he's not going to give me an excuse.

'You've got here quicker than I thought.' He grinned, showing teeth stained with *ataile* juice. His eye membranes were retracted, the pupils enlarged. 'You must have been in Shiriya-Shenin before I closed contract.'

'With SuBannasen.'

Another toothy smile. 'I'm not obliged to say.'

An Orthean proverb says of someone that their word is as good as a sell-sword's, and it's a compliment. And also, I suppose, a necessity.

'If I were you,' I said, 'I'd get out of Shiriya-Shenin.'

'That's wise advice, but I won't take it.'

'If I were Orthean, or prepared to use Orthean methods—'

'Why?' Genuine surprise showed on his scarred face. 'In the Barrens there's no law, but in the Southland I had a contract to keep. I'm a hired soldier.'

'Hired for assassination?'

'Kill one, kill many – it's the same job.'

There was no answering that. I said, 'You could have killed me easily at Broken Stair.'

'I could have done it, but not easily. You recall I've had experience of your Outworld weapons. I preferred not to take the risk, and that cost me fee-money; but it would be strange if I couldn't find another employer in Shiriya-Shenin.'

If I was angry, it was more at myself than at him. He was acting morally, according to Southland custom.

'You might need a hired sword yourself,' he said blandly. 'Not all your enemies are as cautious as my previous employer. I'm open to contract, *t'an* Christie.'

'Go to hell!' There was no translation for that, but he understood the tone. Seeing him walk away I thought, no, it's culture shock, I should be used to this by now.

'You wait,' I said, and he turned and faced me. 'Suppose I say, you stay in Firstwall and keep your ears open, tell me anything I should know about, and I'll pay you a retaining fee?'

I half expected him to be insulted. Instead he looked at me as if I'd finally done something sensible.

'Better hire me for more than that, or they'll know I'm your intelligencer. Call me your weapons tutor, *t'an*, I've done that before.'

'No other contracts while I employ you.'

He inclined his head. 'The price increases for that. Yes.'

I wanted to laugh. It had just occurred to me to wonder how I'd justify this to the ET department's financial section. It was hardly textbook envoy's behaviour. Doubtless any department psychiatrist would tell me I was heading for paranoia. I don't know any psychiatrists who've been hunted the length of the Southland.

'All right,' I said. 'All right. Where are you staying?'

'Down in Fifthwall, the Mercenaries' Guildhouse.'

'I'll find you space in my rooms here,' I decided. 'Maybe weapons training is no bad idea. Who knows, I may need it.'

The SuBannasen trial was abruptly reconvened a little after winter festival. I arrived at the Mosiac Hall with Ruric and Haltern just as the Crown was taking her place at the centre table.

'Well,' Suthafiori said, 'what now?'

Khassiye Reihalyn approached her table and bowed. 'There is new evidence to be heard.'

'On this matter of assassination?'

'On a different matter,' he said; and the hall, which had been resigned to the tedium of more endless wrangling, was loud with chatter and then quieted.

'I thought it better you hear this.' Kanta Andrethe for the first time used the formal inflection to the *T'An Suthai-Telestre*. A milky membrane slid over her eyes as she watched SuBannasen.

Suthafiori nodded and gestured to Khassiye to continue. He called forward another of the Melkathi men.

'What is your *telestre*?'

'Rimnith,' the man said calmly. He was in his middle fifties. 'I am Nelum Santhil, Portmaster of the city of Ales-Kadareth.'

'Santhil Portmaster, do you recognize these papers?'

He took them from Khassiye Reihalyn, scanned them briefly, and then raised his head. 'I do. They are lists of cargo for ships entering the port of Ales-Kadareth over the past three years.'

Unlike the previous days with their long-winded formality, this session was short and to the point. Ortheans favour group discussions and argument carried to great lengths. This degree of straightforward questioning argued a crisis.

'And these, also, do you recognize?'

He took time before answering. 'Yes. These are the true cargo lists for those same vessels, signed by the *T'an* Melkathi.'

I could see SuBannasen where she sat on one of the front benches. She made no movement, but she seemed to lose colour.

'You are aware that there are discrepancies between the two?'

'I am,' Santhil said, 'that is why I made them known to you.'

Khassiye signalled, and the man returned to his seat. Both sets of documents were passed to the Crown. She went from one to the other, the Andrethe sometimes pointing items out; and all that time there was no sound in the hall.

'They have in common, these ships, that all came from or called at the port of Kel Harantish.' Suthafiori's voice was quiet. 'It seems to me, Sulis, that you were less than wise in taking – gifts – from the Emperor-in-Exile.'

'Does that say I did?' She fussed with her cloak, then settled with her bony hands clasped on her stick. A gold-rimmed goblet stood on the bench beside her. I thought, gold is the heart of it. And remembered them asking where she had got gold for her bribery.

'This is your seal,' Suthafiori said, 'and this is your name put to it, and this your *telestre*'s marksign.'

'Let me see.' The old woman peered at the papers when Khassiye gave them to her. I saw her expression fade, seeming to lose direction.

'That is your authority,' Suthafiori repeated.

SuBannasen folded the papers, handed them to Oreyn Orhlandis, and sat back silently. But she's old, I thought suddenly, and she might – she just might – have authorized things without checking them. And if that's true, she has too much pride ever to admit it.

'Do not be so swift to call me traitor,' she said at last. 'If I took gold from Kel Harantish why would I keep such evidence to betray me?'

'Perhaps to make that very excuse,' the Andrethe put in.

'Do you deny it?' Suthafiori asked.

The hesitation stretched into silence. The old woman cleared her throat, sipped from the goblet, and said, 'It may well be true, and if it is not – it will serve.'

The small, gilt-maned woman leaned back, her unblinking gaze fixed on Sulis. 'I must house you in the Kuath-Re,' Suthafiori said, naming the Secondwall prison.

'Wherever the *T'An Suthai-Telestre* pleases.' The old woman's expression was serene. She lifted the goblet again, and drank wine.

Our eyes met. I knew then, remembering the drink that she had offered me, that I was not mistaken. Her gaze was amused, half regretful, and totally without fear. The impulse to stop her faded.

228

It's her right, I thought. She put the goblet down empty, reached for her stick, and walked slowly out of the hall between the guards.

'I don't trust that woman,' Ruric grumbled under her breath. 'Vermin don't lose their poison when they grow old, and she—'

A stir outside in the lobby: I heard the confusion of voices that I'd been waiting for. Ruric sprang to her feet. Through the doorway, a press of people blocked my vision. I saw the silver-topped cane laying on the tiles, trodden underfoot. *Saryl-kabriz* has that virtue, that it acts instantly.

CHAPTER 21

Winter in Beth'ru-elen

Messages continued to arrive, though the last ship had gone south and the river was frozen. The Dadeni Wellhouses train a species of *rashaku* as carriers, and the bird-relay serves the length of the Ai river. Duplicate authorization papers came from Tathcaer, with a promise of medical supplies as soon as spring thaw came, and with the news that a message contradicting my demise had been sent off on a ship to the Eastern Isles. I used bank-drafts to replenish my finances and, set up with *marhaz* and wardrobe and offices, began meeting Ortheans again as the Dominion's representative. In short, I was much as I had been in Tathcaer.

Except that, even to myself, I wasn't recognizable as the same woman who'd come to Orthe the previous summer. It wasn't just physical appearance, being worn bone-thin. The ground under my feet was shifting.

'Won't thaw before mid-Orventa,' Ruric observed, looking out of the glazed lozenges at the falling snow. She put a *ferrorn* down on the *ochmir* board to open up another area of conflict. From where I sat by the fire, sorting through the bundle of messages, it looked likely to be a long game – it had lasted five days, on and off, already.

'*Leremoc*.' Haltern reversed her piece, having gained a majority. 'Did your kinsmen leave before the freeze, *T'An* Ruric?'

'Oreyn's on his way to Ales-Kadareth to tell the *s'ans* they've to name a new *T'an* Melkathi.' She leaned back in the low chair, hand rubbing the stump of her arm.

'Who'll be named?' I asked. Most of the other communications were from downriver *telestres*, inviting my presence in the spring. 'Do you know?'

'It's sudden, *takshiriye* and *tha'adur* are both here, not there; we've left the game a little late for the playing. Still,' Haltern observed, 'I shall be interested to see the outcome.'

'Not that Rimnith man, Santhil,' Ruric studied the board. 'If he'd betray one *T'An*, he'd betray another. It wouldn't surprise me if it were an Orhlandis ... yes, Hal, I know what you think about Oreyn, and I agree with you, but he is popular in Melkathi.'

Haltern's pale eyes veiled. 'Is that necessarily a recommendation?'

Ruric chuckled.

It was pleasant to be there with them. Empathically, it felt right. And recognizing that, I saw the truth; and stared into the mossturf fire.

I thought, I'm afraid of Orthe.

Afraid of being taken over, irrevocably involved. And I don't know Orthe, only the Southland, and that's a dangerous bias ... If it was up to me I'd terminate this mission now. Get another envoy to take over. He wouldn't have my contacts or experience. But then he wouldn't be so personally involved.

Even with Falkyr I never considered resigning as envoy and trying to make a life here on Orthe. But it's coming closer, that desire – and it's impossible. If only for the fact that I've spent my formative years half a galaxy away from Carrick's Star; there's no way I can be an Orthean.

'I'm in a bad position here.' Ruric's long clawed fingers hovered over the *ochmir* board. 'Christie, do you want to come and make it a three-handed game?'

'What? Yes, sure. Just let me finish opening these.' I picked the wax seal off the last paper and unfolded the outer wrapping. Not English, but the curling script of the Southland. I studied it, less happy with the written than with the spoken word.

' "Kasabaarde",' I deciphered.

'What?' Haltern sat up.

It was a city on the second continent, on the far shores of the Inner Sea: I couldn't trigger any more hypno-details.

I was in two minds about doing it but I needed the information, and so handed the parchment over to Haltern. 'What do you make of it?'

It was quite short. He read it aloud. And for once the mask slipped, and I saw the avid curiosity of a very clever man.

' "To Lynne de Lisle Christie, envoy in Tathcaer and now in Shiriya-Shenin: greetings.

' "When the time comes that you must take ship, let it be to the Brown Tower in Kasabaarde, there to meet and speak with –
                                        – The Hexenmeister." '

'Who or what is that?' I asked. 'And to know that I'm in Shiriya-Shenin ...'

'He has his methods,' Haltern said, 'and the time can't be until after the thaw. It's uncommon . . . I know of no direct word out of Kasabaarde for some years, but I think this is genuine.'

'So?'

'So,' he said, 'when the Brown Tower calls you, Christie, you can be certain it's wise to go there.'

But there was other unfinished business, as I found out when I accepted Haltern's invitation to guest at the Beth'ru-elen *telestre*.

The eastern slopes of the Shiriya-Shenin hills are grown over with *hanelys*, the tanglebush: stems as hard and angular as wrought iron grow up to three metres high, and the twining branches form an impenetrable roof. A comfortable morning's ride through *hanelys* from the city lies Dadeni Heath, and Beth'ru-elen *telestre* on the edge of it.

The *marhaz* stepped high over fallen barbs and thorns. Branches shoot down roots at intervals, so that a whole hillside might be one plant. Almost no snow had penetrated through. As the sun rose higher, snow and ice began to melt a little, and I saw the sky through ice-glazed gaps in the *hanelys*. The *marhaz* belled as drops spotted them. Rodion's mount skittered down the hillside. *Ke* rode lightly robed, not bundled in furs like me, and left *kir* white mane unbraided. Even Haltern tended to avoid *kir*. White and gold: Witchbreed. Well, I had thought to do *kir* a favour bringing *kir* out of Shiriya-Shenin and trouble with other *ashiren*.

We came out from under *hanelys* over on the next ridge and Haltern reined in, pointing. 'There – Beth'ru-elen.'

Where the plain sloped down, a vast tract of bog, heath and moorland stretched flat to the eastern horizon, rough contours hidden by the dimpled snow. Thin plumes of smoke rose from a fold in the land, where flat roofs were visible. We rode down, the *ashiren* far ahead of us.

'Beth'ru-elen,' Haltern said again, softly, and then smiled. 'The church's *telestre*, they say.'

'Is it?'

'There's some truth in it. Beth'ru-elen *Ashirenin* founded it, and many Beth'ru-elen go into the church – my mother was Well-keeper for Kyrenden.'

The *marhaz* negotiated a slope treacherous under snow, high-stepping and tossing their horned heads.

'I've heard you called Priest,' I said. It was in much the same way as they called Ruric Yelloweyes or myself *S'aranth*.

'I did train for the church.' He was thoughtful. 'With my *arykei*. Hanat was born L'Ku *telestre*. He became *n'suth* Beth'ru-elen. That was a good time, we were young, I could see us Earthspeaker and Wellkeeper together . . . but he died, and I had no heart for the church after that. Perhaps I never did have.'

'I'm sorry.'

He unsnapped one of his belt-ornaments. The Dadeni robes and pelt changed him, he seemed more alien, less devious, than in Tathcaer. The worn pendant opened to show an etching of a young male Orthean's face. Careless, sardonic, an adventurer.

'Hanat,' he said. 'Twenty five years ago. We have each our griefs. But there is always the *telestre*.'

We came in sight of the *telestre*-house as he spoke. Beth'ru-elen has all the antiquity of Firstwall, but without that city's quality of intimidation. Multiple linked buildings, bronze and flame-coloured bricks bright in the morning light. Snow clung to the roofs. Following the track round we passed long low brick halls and barns, and beastpens. *Marhaz* bugled, and our borrowed mounts answered them. A warm beast-smell was on the wind. An *ashiren*, not more than four or five years old, picked up the hem of its robe and ran shrilly towards the main gate.

Rashaku wheeled overhead, fluttering in and out of the bird-cotes, fluting their weird water-pipe songs. Somewhere a hammer clanged on an anvil; weaving shuttles hummed. *Kazza* prowled, white pelts invisible against the snow, blue summer markings fading. They were muzzled. Slit eyes watched us. I shivered, caught Haltern's glance, and knew we shared a memory.

Guardbeasts hung in cages by the gate, squat-bellied and chirruping loud warnings. Their azure eyes followed us as we rode in under the arch.

'Hal!' A young man hailed him. A crowd collected as solidly and imperceptibly as salt crystallizing: old men and women, young ones, *ashiren*, babies being carried. The babble of voices confused me totally. The Beth'ru-elen have accents varying from incomprehensible southern to impenetrable northern Peir-Dadeni.

I slid down from the *marhaz* and scratched the beast's cold hide between its horns. It nipped at my arms. A tiny *ashiren* pushed its head aside, grabbed the reins, and led it towards the stables. Snow was trodden into slush in the paved courtyard. Sparks from the smithy were orange, gold, sputtering on the stone. A spring-fed pool bubbled in the centre. I smelled cooking, heard voices; the organic machine that was the *telestre* ticking over.

'*S'an*, this is Christie.' Haltern's use of the respectful inflection was for once, I judged, genuine. 'Christie, Arak Haike, our *s'an telestre*.'

Haike was the young man who'd met us: surprisingly young,

with the Beth'ru-elen fair colouring, tending to the obese. His arm was bandaged.

'Come inside,' he said, 'there's food. Christie, you are welcome.' He saw Haltern's questioning look, and rubbed his arm. 'This I got from walking too close to a colt *marhaz*; still, we've an Earth-speaker here to care for us – yes! I almost forgot. Christie, it was known you'd be coming, and this one said he would wait to see you. I believe you have business with the Corbek Wellhouse?'

Beth'ru-elen's Earthspeaker courteously offered me a medical examination, and I was curious enough about Southland healing techniques to accept.

'Change the dressings on your feet again tomorrow,' the old man said. 'The nails should grow back, and the skin become a normal colour – this I would say for one of my own people.'

I re-laced the leather slippers. Beth'ru-elen's tiled floors were hard. However accurate this old man might be – and I didn't doubt that he was, with his own species – I missed Adair's diagnostic machines, micro-recorders, and allergy shots.

'Thank you for doing this.'

'Shall we say professional curiosity – for us both, *t'an* Christie.' He seated himself on the window-couch. Thick glass behind him distorted the snowlight. 'You have done much, though, and should rest.'

'I'm not planning anything strenuous.' What I worried about were deficiency diseases, malnutrition, exhaustion; and for these I had only the traditional Orthean cure. Time.

He looked shrewdly at me. He was a neat man, age showing about his mouth and his crest-mane. '*T'an*, you're young, so far as I may judge you're healthy, but I must warn you that you're approaching your limit. You were nearly six weeks living rough, you tell me. You have to build up resources.'

From Corbek to Shiriya-Shenin it had been five weeks and seven days, Torvern Fifthweek Fiveday to Riardh Sixthweek Two-day. Seven or eight weeks Earth-standard: it felt longer. And I knew it was that season, dry and cold, that had let us live. Summer's fever, winter's storms; they would have finished us.

'I'll be careful,' I said. '*S'an* Haike said that you wanted to speak to me. What's it about?'

His face changed to an expression as clear as cold water. 'I have had messages from Corbek. We must have the death-words for Theluk, and the *ashiren* cannot give them, nor the hired sword. We must have that for the Edris *telestre*. They will have their grief.'

'And you won't?' It was unfair comment, but he was stirring up something I didn't want to see.

'Nothing ends,' the Earthspeaker said, turning to look at the sun through the glass, open-eyed to that pale blaze. 'Some say we spend our other lives in fire, visible here only as the face of the Goddess. That other order of being has its echoes here, its links and connections. We are a small land in a sea of fire, shot through with that invisible flame. She'll come scoured free by that fire, come again; knowing, breathing, living. No, we do not grieve.'

Ortheans burn their dead and cast the ashes into rivers: fire and water mark their passing. None have more of a grave than Theluk has.

'Tell me how she died,' the old man said. 'We will pass the word to Edris, and they will remember. You cannot give her the passing of fire, but this you can do.'

But I never knew her . . . and then thinking back, I realized I knew more than I thought.

'She was a brave woman,' I said, 'though having been a soldier at the Skulls garrison, I suppose that was never in doubt. She opposed Arad, Wellkeeper in Corbek, though he had great influence there. She had sense and endurance, she travelled up from Roehmonde's east coast, and knew then that the only person who would heed her was the Crown. Many of us benefited from her messages to Tathcaer. And she was generous: I don't believe she was afraid to stay in Corbek and face Arad, I think she knew Haltern and Maric and I wouldn't get out of the province without her help. When she died, it was because she was faced with fears that were special to her – even legends of the fenborn offended her – and she preferred to risk her life on the chance of getting free. She was tough, but she had less feeling for the marshes than for any part of the earth. She had the right to take the chance that she did. And it was only chance that it failed.'

The old Earthspeaker was quiet for a time, then he nodded. 'I have it. That was well done, for an Outlander. It is a good word to take to Edris, and a true one.'

It was only after he'd gone that I began to appreciate the custom. Much of the weight of Theluk's death was lifted from me.

The guesting custom at Beth'ru-elen was that visitors worked. Being singularly untalented, I usually ended up gathering and chopping *hanelys* wood, or washing dishes, or mucking out the *skurrai* and *marhaz* pens. There were always two or three Earth-speakers at the *telestre*, and I often saw one in the main hall practising the common script; those *ashiren* who felt an interest copied her. It was some time before I realized this was as close to formal education as they got, and joined in.

It wasn't difficult to live at Beth'ru-elen, and ride back to Shiriya-Shenin on business. Nor difficult to find an excuse for not riding back – snow and hail and rainstorms were frequent. The *telezu* custom that Haltern was following, spending this season on the *telestre*, was elastic enough to include the envoy.

Orventa is the longest season, twelve weeks from winter to spring festival. Towards the end of that time I had become fluent in two or three of Peir-Dadeni's complex dialects, including the southern. Back at Shiriya-Shenin's Firstwall library I studied books on Kasabaarde, memorizing fragments of that language. I had no orders to make contacts outside the Southland – but I'd been contacted myself, and it might pay to follow that up at a later date.

And that Orventa, at Beth'ru-elen and in the city, I began to play *ochmir* in earnest. It hurt. It reminded me of Falkyr, of the Barrens city, of that dead woman Sulis n'ri n'suth SuBannasen; and of the malice against the envoy that was, like the Southland in winter, only quiescent. Maybe that's why I played it with such intense concentration. With Ruric, with Haltern, with Rodion, Blaize Meduenin – anyone. It has a resonance with the Southland: the *ferrorn* static like the *s'an telestre*, the *thurin* mobile as the *t'ans* are, and the *leremoc* rare and powerful as the *T'An Suthai-Telestre*. The areas of conflict shift, what is yours may at any moment be reversed and prove to be playing against you.

I learned a little: how to think ahead, spot the patterns, remember what hieroglyphs the reversed counters hid. Most of my games still ended in an avalanche of reversals spreading out from some minor lost hexagon, but a few were hard-fought. I was learning.

Orventa in closed Shiriya-Shenin is a time for indoor pursuits to flourish: plays are written and performed, *arykei* courted, weapons tournaments are devised, and there are the inevitable marathon games of *ochmir* that last the nine-day-week from Feastday to Fastday. Gossip, satirical songs – and scientific experiments, under the close eye of the church.

After I'd seen steam and clockwork mechanisms, weaving machines, gun-powder and primitive electric motors, I decided that the Southland could have an industrial revolution any time it liked. And after I'd seen the devices dismantled and ignored by their inventors, I understood why they would not. The ghost of the Barrens hung over Shiriya-Shenin, and what I had learned of past-memories came sharply back to me.

In Orventa Eightweek came a slow thaw that isolated everything, and caught me at Beth'ru-elen. The rivers were in flood, the roads impassable. It was Orventa Tenweek before things dried out enough to make travelling possible.

I added more laboriously handwritten pages to the report I was compiling. It was difficult to pin the Ortheans down to an official view of the Dominion. Individual views, yes, from Ruric's acceptance of mutual kinship down to the anonymous stones shied at me in backstreets. But no one would commit themselves to a coherent policy I could pass back to Earth.

The winds turned southerly, the air warm. I rode back to Shiriya-Shenin through slopping mud, Rodion with me. *Hanelys*, black all winter, broke out in a fur of tiny scarlet flowers. The brown dead mossgrass, scuffed up, disclosed new grey-green spring growth. *Kekri* flies in hoards hummed on a pitch that would shatter glass. The terraced slopes round the city were thick with new shoots.

Expectancy was in the air.

'Duined wants an appointment.' Rodion sat down at my desk as *ke* sorted through the pile of messages. 'Downriver man, wants to talk about trade.'

'Much good it'll do him. Make it for Fiveday. What else?'

The tawny eyes flicked up. 'Berun n'ri n'suth Sarsyan again.'

'What does she want?'

'She wants to be your *arykei*, of course.' The *ashiren* grinned. 'You can't blame anyone for being curious, *S'aranth*.'

'Can't I, though?'

'Here's something.' *Ke* read briefly. 'A note from *t'an* Haltern, dated noon. A meeting in the Andrethe's Hall – they've had news through from Melkathi about the new *T'An*.'

The hall was large, built of yellow glazed bricks. A double row of forked pillars supported the low ceiling. The lozenge-shaped windows had hanging curtains of silver discs on cords, twisting and flashing in the spring sunlight. It was still wet outside. Muddy six-toed tracks crossed the geometrically patterned tiles. Silver bead curtains hung in the doorways, fastened back in the spaces between the pillars. A raised platform at one end held padded backless chairs. The wall behind me was patterned with the spiral symbols of the Goddess. The hall was filling with *tha'adur* and *takshiriye*, but at the moment the platform was empty.

Rodion was missing, as usual. I couldn't see Haltern or Ruric, so was pleased when I did find a face I knew.

'*T'an* Brodin.'

'Christie. You have heard the news, then?' He drew aside to let several *t'ans* pass.

'Melkathi have chosen their new *T'An*, yes. Do we know who?'

'No, this has been kept secret until the Crown should make the announcement.' He shrugged. 'Myself, I would say another of the SuBannasen *telestre*.'

That was news I didn't want to hear. 'Not Oreyn Orhlandis?'

'I doubt that—' he broke off. 'Here they are.'

My position close to the pillar commanded a good view of the now crowded platform. The Andrethe stood with Suthafiori and many of the *takshiriye*. One of the Crown Guard beat on a drumframe, and the talk died.

'Hear me!' Suthafiori's voice penetrated effortlessly to the back of the hall. 'I call you together, you of the Hundred Thousand: hear what I say and carry the news. The *T'An* Melkathi is named.'

The drum beat once and was silent.

'The symbol of Melkathi is returned from SuBannasen *telestre*.' Oreyn Orhlandis stepped forward with a plain silver circlet in his hands, and gave it to the Crown.

'Called for Melkathi, called by the *s'an telestres*,' Suthafiori said, 'is *amari* Ruric Orhlandis.'

'What?' Brodin said, his usual poise gone.

'Ruric?' I was astounded. 'Lord, I knew she said Orhlandis, but – good grief!'

The first buzz of surprise broke up into the scattered hissing and hand-beating that is their applause. I saw Ruric then, walking with her dark head up and her shoulders taut. A night-blue cloak draped her. She wore a single silver *harur* blade. The *tha'adur* and *takshiriye* drew aside and she stood alone before Suthafiori.

'*Amari* Ruric Orhlandis,' Suthafiori said in the formal inflection, 'do you accept the office named?'

'I accept the office of *T'An* Melkathi, laying down all other offices I now hold.' There was no detectable nervousness in her voice.

'*Amari* Ruric Orhlandis, *T'An* Melkathi,' Suthafiori pronounced. 'By the power of the earth that we all return to, by power of fire and water through which we pass, I bid you take this outward symbol of the Melkathi *telestres* and bear it well. Their kin are your kin, their wishes your wishes, their welfare your own.'

'I receive this into my care,' Ruric answered, 'holding the land as the hand of the Goddess on earth. I will act to each *telestre* as if it were my own. This shall endure until the *s'an telestres* revoke it. Be it so, in Her name.'

'In Her name,' the Crown said, and placed the silver circlet on the dark woman's head. Against the black mane it caught the light and blazed like a star.

It was some time later, during the celebrations, that I finally got to speak to Ruric.

'*T'an* Melkathi.' I managed a respectable bow.

'What? Christie, you—' her dismay vanished. 'Sunmother's tits! I thought you meant it.'

'How about that?' I said after we embraced. 'Now I have to bow three times before speaking, and watch out for the assassin's blade.'

'Lackwit Outworlder,' she said goodnaturedly. Haltern was beside her, his pudgy features fixed in a smug grin. She gripped his shoulder hard.

'You and Oreyn, you've left me a job – Melkathi, grief of the Goddess! And I suppose I shall have to live in Ales-Kadareth, and let Asshe have the Guard.' She pointed Asshe out to me, a grim, grey-maned little man with a bantam-cock air. 'He's Skulls commander, I dare say he can handle it. Mother! I wish I thought I could handle Melkathi.'

Haltern, I thought, and Oreyn, and who else? Hal's a Crown Messenger, no need to ask if Suthafiori supports this.

'You'll manage,' I said.

'*S'aranth!*' Rodion yelled.

I came out of the *jayante* courts sweating and rubbing bruises. Blaize's efforts to teach me the use of Orthean weapons had largely been a failure, simply because Ortheans fight ambidextrously and I remained obstinately right-handed. The only weapon I showed any promise at was the *jayante*, a short, weighted quarterstaff, and I practised with all the more determination for knowing that the single remaining power pack for the stunner was half exhausted. Blaize's bruising enthusiasm I put down to revenge.

'Well?' I said.

'The Andrethe wants you,' *ke* said, 'in the Crystal Hall.'

'What does she want now?'

The *ashiren* shrugged. Kanta Andrethe monopolized the Dominion envoy in the same spirit that she studied new animals in her menagerie. I sighed and headed back to my rooms to change. Halls, corridors, courtyards: and never a place in all the Firstwall warren to be private.

'Where's my knife-belt?' I demanded, hurriedly lacing on a clean *chirith-goyen* shirt. 'Have you seen it?'

'I expect someone took it,' *ke* said, 'I'll try and get it back.'

Dadeni has no word for 'steal', only less welcome inflections of the word for 'take'. When it comes to property, all Ortheans have a very imperfect idea of mine and thine.

In Dadeni the coinage consists of metal discs or beads threaded on cords, traditionally worn round the neck or waist. I'd had to adopt that custom in lieu of a wallet, after mine went missing. As for my property – that refined itself down to personal documents, reports for the department, and the stunner, all of which I kept in a pack; and the only way I could keep Rodion's fingers out of it was to tell *kir* it was dangerous. True, in a way. If *ke* pilfered those from me, *ke'd* be in as great a danger as *ke* was ever likely to be.

I turned over a few pillows, books from the Firstwall library, but couldn't find the knife-belt. I gave up: I'd have to be informally dressed.

The door of the Crystal Hall was ajar when I arrived. I knocked – never having been able to break the habit – and went in. Spring twilight filled the chamber, the quartz windows gleaming. No lamps were alight. The braziers were red embers.

Did Rodion tell me the wrong place? I wondered. There was a sharp familiar scent in the air.

The Andrethe had her back to me, sitting in a chair facing one of the dying fires.

'Excuse me, excellence . . .'

She made no sign that she heard me. She was leaning back, one fat arm over the side of the chair. Asleep, I thought, now how do I do this tactfully? As I stepped round her, over the dappled furs, the spring light shone on her dark face and red-and-white robe. Her fingers held reflected red firelight, streaming on the furs and stone flags; and the smell came up in a wave.

Firstwall's kitchens and slaughterhouses.

Not a red robe. A white robe, sopping red from shoulder to lap to hem. Running like water, soaking into the furs. Grey cold air, and the stink of blood and faeces. Blood dripping from her curved fingers, covering the gold studs. Her open unveiled eyes stared at me – she must be alive, she moved! I thought. And then realized it was illusion. Not breathing, not blinking. Jammed under her chin, amid rolls of flesh, a knife-handle kept her head back. There shouldn't be so much blood, blood shouldn't be so thin –

Jack-knifed forward, acrid liquid spilling from mouth and nostrils; I heard noises from the corridor. Then the room was full of people shouting.

CHAPTER 22

Berani's Lament

Ruric's single hand shook me. I tried to tell her it was unnecessary. I knew what was happening.

'I found her,' I said.

'Found her? Killed her!' Brodin stood by the chair, hands red, tears streaking his face. Good-natured lampoons linked he and Kanta as *arykei*, I hadn't credited them until now.

'Is that your knife?' Khassiye Reihalyn demanded.

'I – yes, I had a knife taken: Rodion will tell you—'

'I expect *ke* will. Being Halfgold.'

Suthafiori was there, Hellel Hanathra was there; I didn't remember seeing them come in. I wanted to avoid looking at the dead woman.

'Listen,' Brodin faced Suthafiori angrily, 'this thing comes to you, it says: I'm from another world. And you sit there and you believe it! Even when you hear the truth you don't believe it. Witchbreed! Look at her *l'ri-an*, look at her companions—'

'I know your grief.' Ruric bent over the body, studying it with a clinical detachment. 'I'll say I didn't hear that.'

Someone's gone to a lot of trouble to make me look guilty, I thought. I felt dizzy. 'Why should I do this?'

Brodin ignored me, still speaking to the Crown. 'Leave Dadeni without the Andrethe, now, when she's most needed – she was your equal, now who is there to prevent you? They call you mad, believing in other worlds. You're not mad, no. And not above using Witchbreed to further your own purposes.'

'Mourn the dead later, and I will join you.' Suthafiori spoke mildly. 'If I have been mistaken in these people, it will be seen. Keep the envoy under guard.'

'Your pardon,' Khassiye interrupted, 'I've arrested her already under Dadeni custom.'

'And I under Crown law,' Suthafiori said. 'Ruric, take her. Khassiye, I give you acting authority for Shiriya-Shenin until this is over.'

It was quiet outside the Crystal Hall.

'Go back to your rooms and wait,' Ruric said. 'I'll find Asshe, get him to send a couple of guards along in a minute.'

'I didn't do it. You know that.'

Her yellow eyes glinted. 'I know. If it were you, she would have had a broken neck – *S'aranth*. As for being a true Outworlder . . . if you're a liar, you're an exceptional one, none of your stories contradict each other. No, the guards are for your protection, Christie. When this is known, there'll be many won't wait for the trial to decide on their verdict.'

Unconcerned faces passed me. How long would that last? Time's deceptive, it was only a few minutes later in that spring afternoon. Alone now in an alien land – news wouldn't take long to get out, would it?

Someone already knew. The killer.

Blaize n'ri n'suth Meduenin stood up as I entered my rooms. 'I've heard some disturbing rumours—'

'Too late, as usual. I don't know what I pay you for.' A kind of manic hilarity suceeded the numbness. I acted purely on instinct. Took the ET report from my pack, handed it to him. Unlooped a cord of silver coins from my neck. Gave them to him.

'Take Gher from the stables – *don't* let anyone see you – and go overland to Tathcaer. Give the report to the xeno-team. You're a Rimon man, you must know the country. *Go.*'

He didn't ask questions, just took the cord of money and slipped out. I picked up a hooded *becamil* cloak, the pack, and then the *jayante* in its backstrap. I might have been expecting this, I realized suddenly; this or something like it. All my personal belongings were in the pack. It was only necessary to pick it up and leave.

No one gave me a second look. I pulled the cloak on while I crossed the muddy courtyard. If I could beat the news to Fifthwall, leave the city—

'*S'aranth*,' Rodion called, 'where are you going?'

I touched the *jayante*. But fighting would attract attention, and I couldn't fight *ashiren*. The goldskinned face was bland. *Ke* hasn't heard yet, I thought.

'Come with me.'

Envoy and *l'ri-an*, that was a familiar enough sight in the streets of Shiriya-Shenin. Wind flayed my face as we came out from under the Firstwall L'ku Gate.

'Are there riverships leaving today?'

'It's Fiveday holiday . . . but yes, I think so. Why?'

'I'm leaving the city,' I said. A route sketched itself in my mind, familiar from maps. Down the Ai river to Morvren Freeport, then up the Rimon coast to Tathcaer. Safer to be on the Crown's island – if I could get that far. If nothing else, Tathcaer had ships for the Eastern Isles. For Earth.

'I'll come,' Rodion said.

'You don't know why I'm going. It's too dangerous to involve *ashiren*.' If I'd been thinking, I wouldn't have said that.

'Is it my fault I'm *ashiren*? I'm your *l'ri-an*, and I'm coming with you. If I stay, they'll make me tell where you went.' *Ke* eyed me. 'Why do you have to leave, *S'aranth*?'

Secondwall, Thirdwall, and still the Watch passed us through. And now we were lost in the Fiveday holiday crowds round the markets.

'Because I don't propose to be locked up again, certainly not for a murder I didn't commit.' And because it's too easy for one minor Dominion official to just vanish, I thought, and because the Southland has nothing resembling justice.

Kir eyes widened, clearing. 'Murder?'

I pulled the cloak's hood up, protecting against the wind and prying eyes. People jostled past.

'You come,' I said. 'When I get far enough downriver, I'll pay your passage back here. You'll bring messages from me to the authorities, saying what I'm doing and why. By that time it won't matter. You do what I say, Rodion.'

Ke looked as though it was difficult to take in the facts. Uncertain, now, whether *ke* wanted to accompany me.

'I'll do it,' Rodion said. '*S'aranth*, you have to keep me quiet one way or another. This is the best.'

Fourthwall, Fifthwall, the ziggurat towers squat against the sky. The city opened out to grey gleaming river. Cold water lapped at the wooden piers. Now it was a matter of chance, finding out if there was a ship going downriver. Leaving immediately, I thought, looking back at the city, imagining the alarm going out even now.

The rivership's hull sliced through brown water. Twigs swirled in the wake. Brushwood clumbered the bank, left behind from the spring floods. I leaned against the rail, facing away from the people on board.

'The shipmaster wants half-fee now,' Rodion said. 'Where do we want to go to?'

'Where's a large river *telestre*, one that has many ships calling?'

'Kepulanan,' *ke* suggested. 'Hassichil. Pel'shennin.'

'Hassichil.' Unknotting a cord, I counted off silver coins. 'Tell the shipmaster that your *t'an* suffers pain from an old wound, and will likely stay in her cabin for most of the trip.'

'They'll wonder,' *ke* said, 'and when the word goes out, they'll remember us. *S'aranth*, what did you *do*?'

'Nothing. Do what I say.'

Twilight drifted blue over the terraced land, mist rising on the reed-choked banks of the river. I kept the cloak's hood up and avoided meeting anyone's eyes. Below, in the tiny cabin, I discarded the pack and *jayante* and lay back on the bench-bed.

'*S'aranth*,' Rodion said, 'are you sick?'

Ke thought *ke* was on a voyage with a madwoman. I closed my eyes, feeling Rodion's gaze burn into me. Not mad, I thought. Maybe a little unstable at the moment – but not mad, no indeed.

'Where is this?' It was nearly second twilight, a day downriver from Shiriya-Shenin.

Rodion peered at the markstone by the landing stage. 'Baharu-bazuriye.'

'Go down and get my pack. See you're not noticed.'

Beyond the landing stage, masked by giant reedbeds, rose the flat roofs of a large *telestre* house. Town-sized, with warehouses and companion-houses. Good. One of the trade *telestres* – pottery, glass, *becamil* and similar – who'd be used to travellers.

Rodion followed me off the rivership into the crowd at the landing stage. No one saw us go. There's a good chance they won't miss us here, I thought, then they won't know where we disembarked. They're expecting us to go to Hassichil . . .

'Are we staying at a companion-house?' Rodion asked.

'And have them remember us?'

'Where, then?'

There were market stalls set out under *becamil* awnings round the *telestre* walls. I saw no uniforms of the Crown Guard or Andrethe city Watch, but that meant nothing. Will this count as Wellhouse business? I wondered. If it does, they'll send the news out on the *rashaku* relay. And there's no chance of outdistancing that.

'The market first. Blankets and provisions.' I thumbed the cord of coins. No, not poor yet.

The twilight faded quickly. I kept on the move, spine prickling with apprehension. The companion-houses were small, both were likely to note and remember us. I wanted somewhere crowded enough to be lost in. I retraced my steps, back down muddy tracks near the landing stage. There was an alternative. Long, low warehouses stood untenanted, some half-demolished by the winter storms. One door swung open when I pushed.

'It's going to be cold,' Rodion objected.

'The beginning of Hanys. It shouldn't freeze.' I laid out blankets under the soundest-looking area of roof. Rodion unrolled the spare cloak on the wooden floor. I was asleep before *ke* finished muttering complaints.

Wood scraped as the door opened.

Rodion was up and moving and the door was opening and someone came in and *ke* struck once, bare-handed, without even time to draw *kir* knife. Then someone grunted and fell heavily, Rodion was standing wringing *kir* hand, and I staggered up and pushed the door to.

I limped back. The cold had numbed my feet, woken me six or seven times. Now I felt disorientated.

The Orthean wore drab Dadeni work-robes, and he – no, she – lay on her back, a thick slug of blood creeping from her nose, in a vile parody of sleep.

I must have stood just looking at the woman for several minutes. Sleep froze my mind. That blur of movement – but violence is always quick, unexpected. I blotted out memories of Shiriya-Shenin.

She breathed shallowly, damply, on my palm. I wiped my hand, rolled her eyelid back with my thumb, the whiteless eye was opaqued by the nictitating membrane. Her skin was rough, winter-patterned. One outstretched hand twitched, claws scraped the hard wood.

What did you come here for? Tools, a place to be private, what? Was it just another misty chill morning, and did you step in here a moment out of the wind? And now all changed, in the fraction of a heartbeat, forever different.

'*S'aranth*, what are you doing?' Rodion was at the door, with the pack and cloaks.

'She might need medical attention—'

'She'll come to in a minute,' the *ashiren* said. '*S'aranth*, we can't stay here!'

It was true, there was no way out of it. Rodion looked at me anxiously and without a trace of regret.

The dark blood – darker than human – was stilled, drying. And I left her there, hurt; not without a second thought, it's true, but what use is thought without action? I never sent help, I never spoke of her. I still regret that.

Outside, river mist hid us from casual eyes. Carrick's Star was rising, saffron over the eastern plain. The tracks confused me in the half-light. After a few minutes – seeming like hours – I found the one that followed the river south-west.

'Do you know how far until we come to another *telestre*?'

Rodion shook *kir* head.

'Until the next landing stage?'

Another headshake.

'Then we'd better keep walking.'

Double-bladed reeds hid the river's edge. As the sun rose higher it shone on the desolate land a few *seri* to the west. Then, as light filled the vast dome of the empty sky, smoke trails went up from the opposite bank. Sails of early riverships showed white.

'I'm hungry,' Rodion said. 'We should have bought more food in the market.'

'The next place we see,' I promised. Thinking, how long since I ate? On the riverboat before Baharu-bazuriye . . . yes, once yesterday. Not today.

My mind closed down to narrow focus, only aware of the rough track. Winter had left it rutted, pocked with deep holes; obviously none of the *telestre* road-gangs had come this way yet. I felt dimly sorry that Rodion should be hungry and tired – *kir* eyes were showing their whites with sleeplessness – but I was riding some adrenalin-high, and feeling nothing at all.

That day was long, and I couldn't have foreseen its ending.

The morning sun was warm. A chill wind rattled the new growth on the reeds. No one passed me. I searched ahead, trying to pick out the hearth-smoke of a *telestre*.

'*S'aranth . . .*'

'What?' I snapped irritably.

Without hysteria, but with complete determination, Rodion said, 'I have to sleep.'

'Now?'

'I shouldn't—' *ke* blinked, rubbed *kir* forehead, and without any warning pitched forward. I caught *kir* as *ke* slammed into the earth, the warm heavy body limp in my arms.

'Rodion?'

Dirt clung to grazes in *kir* golden skin. Hunger, was it, or fatigue? But the scale-pattern skin was rough, damp to the touch. When I thumbed *kir* eyelids back the membranes were retracted, the eyes rolled up to show half the whites.

The wind blew, and *rashaku* fluted, too high to be seen. Blood drummed in my ears. I slapped *kir* face lightly, holding back fury – I couldn't afford delay now! Had I asked to have an *ashiren* with me?

Ke didn't wake. I abandoned all but my pack, hoisted *kir* over my shoulder, staggering – *ke* was all but adult height and weight –

and plodded on down the road. There had to be a *telestre* up ahead.
There had to be.

A cluster of small buildings hugged a landing stage. Noon sun
made me sweat. Rodion's body was a dead weight. Truly? I
thought, close to panic, but then I felt *kir* ribs moving with shallow
breaths. I might have come two *seri* or three, in fits and starts. I
was ready to collapse myself.

A man left the yard, halted, and came running.

'Can you help—'

He helped me to lower *kir*. He was a dark Orthean, with broad
shoulders under his work-robe. All his attention was on the
ashiren.

'How long has *ke* been this way?'

'Up the road – a way back—' I couldn't get my breath. 'Is there
a physician? An Earthspeaker?'

He nodded sharply, scooped Rodion up in his arms, and I
followed him in through the door of the *telestre*-house. For a time
I had no strength to do anything. One of the old women gave me
a wine flask, while shouting to an *ashiren* to fetch the Earthspeaker. I found myself in a side room, while the man who carried
Rodion was putting *kir* into a cot-bed by the hearth there.

Rodion's head rolled from side to side, making guttural noises in
kir throat. Midday sun came through the narrow window and
gleamed on gold skin and pale hair. I heard muttered comments.
And kept my hood up, hoping that *kir* appearance as Halfgold
would keep them from seeing I was Outworlder.

'Is *ke* late coming to this, *t'an*?'

An ebony-skinned male in Earthspeaker's robes examined
Rodion, holding *kir* six-fingered hands in his.

'Late?'

His pale eyes unveiled, hearing my accent. Disguise doesn't
depend on concealment but on attitude. Not to look him in the
eyes, not to think differently from an Orthean.

'You're Outlander,' he said.

'Yes, from—' the lie came seamlessly '—the Desert Coast. But
the *ashiren*?'

'*Ke* has come late to the change,' he said, turning and giving
sharp orders for blankets. An old woman returned with them and
a double handful of herbs. I sat in the shadow by Rodion while
the Earthspeaker set them boiling in a pan over the hearth. The
ashiren twitched, eyes half open, mumbling inaudibly.

If *ke* dies? I thought suddenly.

The Earthspeaker cleared the room of people and tied the

curtain shut. He brought the steaming pan over to the bed, and while I held *kir* shoulders he bathed *kir* with the infusion.

'Now cover *kir*,' he said, and we wrapped *kir* in pelts. 'It's hard when it comes late, but over sooner. One way or the other.'

'Will *ke* be all right?'

He shrugged. Noting cloak, pack, and *jayante* he said, 'You must break your travels here until it is over.'

Noon declined towards evening. I heard others come in, voices beyond the curtained archway, but we were not disturbed. Sometimes Rodion thrashed in pain, so that it took the Earthspeaker and myself all our strength to hold *kir* down. At last *ke* appeared to sleep.

'Now we wait. Will you eat with us?' the Orthean asked. 'Or if your customs demand you eat alone, Outlander, I will have a meal sent to you.'

'Thank you, yes, if you will.' There were many Outlanders on the Ai, that river they call the highway of Peir-Dadeni. The Earthspeaker's tone had all the insular Southland dislike for the Desert Coast.

'Where are you from, *t'an*?'

'Kasabaarde.' It was the only Desert Coast city I knew the name of, besides Kel Harantish. And that, with Rodion Halfgold there, didn't rate a mention.

'You are not bound to wear your masks always, then?'

Masks? The lie came as easy as breathing. 'Not outside the city. You are a traveller also?'

'On the Ai. I'm Pel'kasir,' he said, 'from the Hassichil Wellhouse. You know Hassichil?'

I shook my head. Fencing with him, not easy. 'We may have seen it from the ship, coming upriver.'

'To Shiriya-Shenin?' he guessed.

'My companions go there. I had a fancy to follow on land and join them there. But now . . .'

'The change is under way,' Pel'kasir said. 'If *ke* passes midnight, it will be well.'

I dozed as the evening wore on. Rodion's cries woke me. Pel'kasir soothed *kir* again with the herb-solution. I tried to keep the pelts over *kir*. The silverwhite mane matted, coming loose from its braids. Tendrils clung to the rough skin surrounding the tawny eyes. *Ke* stared without seeing me.

Sometime in the late hours *ke* lapsed into a deep trance-like sleep.

'It's over,' Pel'kasir said with relief. He drew the pelts back, wiping the infusion over newly-smooth skin. 'There'll be internal changes for a while yet. Some days rest. Don't move ... yes, *ashiren-te*, yes ...'

There was not much to see. A swelling round the upper pair of nipples, the genital slit more pronounced. But it was an unmistakable change. Pel'kasir drew the furs up over the gold-skinned shoulders, and the tawny eyes opened and knew me.

'Ah, she will have *ashiren* of her own someday,' the Earthspeaker said, brushing the mane back off her forehead. The expression in his eyes might have been envy.

'*S'ar*—' a smile shone out, then her lids came down. She slept again.

'Now you may sleep,' Pel'kasir said. 'She is safe.'

'Thank you.' Exhausted, I had no words for gratitude.

'She should not be moved for several days.'

'No. No, we'll stay here.' I stood stiffly. 'Is it possible to borrow paper and a writing-stick? I must send word upriver so my companions don't worry about us.'

The Earthspeaker nodded. 'Many boats pass here; one will surely take your message in the morning.'

Morning came: I hadn't slept. The urgency of getting downriver was obvious, and I was acutely impatient.

'Where are you for?'

'Downstream.' The Orthean woman leaned over the docked ship's rail. 'Lei'eriel *telestre*.'

'How far is that?'

She stepped back to avoid two of the handlers stacking bales of *becamil*-wrapped pottery. 'Forty, maybe fifty *seri*. Well, Outlander, are you coming?'

'Yes. Wait.'

'Not long!' she called after me.

Rodion was sleeping when I left her. I took pack and *jayante*, pulling on the heavy cloak. Her face was untroubled. I knotted a cord of silver and copper coins round her wrist, and re-read the short message I was leaving her.

Rodion –
    I intend going on as planned. When you are well, continue on to Shiriya-Shenin. You will have much to tell our companions there. But do not on any account go before you feel ready. I have left you enough money to pay for food for two weeks. Hoping to see you fully recovered when we meet again,
        – C
        Hanys Firstweek Sixday.

249

You'll take the hint, I thought, looking down at her. And by the time you get to Shiriya-Shenin I'll have taken ship from Morvren, and by then it won't matter. No one will blame you for anything.

I got aboard the rivership while they were loading water casks. No one saw me go. Mooring ropes were cast off, a distance of water opened between ship and landing stage.

Maric had taught me not to take *ashiren* where I went. Granted Rodion was adult now, but this might prove more dangerous than the journey across the Barrens. There, there was only the land to fight. Now I faced the Orthean game, directed against me alone. And I was no expert player.

With the landing at Lei'eriel, I began to come out of the trance of panic that had surrounded me since Shiriya-Shenin.

'Outlander?' a young woman said. 'You'll have come to see Berani's Watchtower, then. They all do.'

The gates of Lei'eriel *telestre* stood open. The woman was sitting in a low chair, robe unlaced, feeding a baby. Two others kicked on the *zilmei* pelt spread at her feet. They were bare to the afternoon sun. Thin down marked their spines. To me they looked tiny, lizard-like.

'You can just see it from here.' The woman pointed towards the western hills that were closer to the river here. I squinted, could just distinguish angular lines.

'Is that the actual tower?' It seemed a safe thing to say.

'Yes, the one in the "Lament".' One of the *ashiren* rolled over, its mouth squared and it began to howl. She scooped it up, putting the other one down on the feather-fur. 'Sssh . . . Terai, *ashiren-te* . . .'

'If I go up there, will I be able to get a boat downriver this evening?'

She frowned, humming under her breath. The child squalled. She sang ' "Thousandflower, bird's-wing, and sweet mosseye; sweet wine and sour wine where tall ships go by . . ." oh, you brat.'

It dribbled milk on her shoulder. She pulled up the hem of her robe to dab it dry. 'There're no downriver boats till morning,' she added, having thought. 'Most Outland folks stay over here.'

I took a room and – more to keep myself out of sight for the afternoon than anything else – walked the two *seri* up into the hills. They were desolate, stony, flecked here and there with brown mossgrass. A path had been hacked through stunted *hanelys*. It was dusty walking.

From the Watchtower knoll I saw the Ai valley laid out below me. Eastwards was fat land, pasture and newly-ploughed grain country, growing on the river's silt. Terraces had been replaced by irrigation channels. Downriver the view was blocked by a spur of these hills. Rounding the knoll, wind blew dust over cracked flagstones.

The remains of the brickwork ended abruptly on the scarp side. There had been rockfalls. A ring of the outer wall was standing. The steep western scarp fell two or three hundred feet to a plain, desolate as the hills, that stretched out to the horizon.

Berani's Watchtower . . . yes, one of the wailing atonal Dadeni songs mentioned it, I remembered at the court. I'd paid little attention.

The sun reflected off something in the western distance. At first I took it for water, but it didn't end as water does. Where it touched the brown heath – seven or eight *seri* out on the plain, I estimated – it ended in streaks. Sharp edges, like cat-ice on a puddle, like splinters. With the sheen of volcanic glass. Then the sun cleared the haze, and all that horizon blazed with unbearable light.

I walked round the ruined tower, blinking the spots out of my vision, and came to where a newer stone had been set up. Common script was cut into it:

'Here was Berani's Watchtower, where of old they kept lookout across the Glittering Plain towards the danger that lies in Eriel.'

Orthe defeated me. I admitted it then, confronted with my ignorance. I sat down on old steps. Nothing was left of the hall but a depression in the ground. My back against sunwarmed brick, I looked down at the Ai.

Berani's Lament. Bits of it returned to me. There was a flavour of betrayal about it, though whether Berani had been betrayed or betrayer I didn't know. A flavour of treachery. Very apt, I thought.

So I let my mind go back and touch what it had been avoiding for days. Kanta Andrethe's butchered death. Somehow I needed to grieve. I let the release come, weeping. For her. For Brodin, that bereaved man. For myself. If there was self-pity, now was the time to get rid of it.

Self-pity. Haltern: why couldn't he have helped me? Ruric. What did she mean: *if* you're a liar . . . and the arrogance, expecting me to wait, unguarded, for Southland justice. The old childish complaint: why didn't somebody *do* something?

Feeling faintly disgusted, I wiped my face and relaxed back in the sun. Whatever: the events at the Andrethe court had occurred.

Now it was up to me to deal with it. Haltern and Ruric had been caught as flat-footed as I had. No one's fault.

Yes. One. The killer. Could I speculate who it was? Another of the SuBannasen? Howice? An enemy in Shiriya-Shenin? No, that was part of the game of intrigue: it could be any one of a hundred people . . .

What to do now, though? Tathcaer's still the safest place for an Outworlder to be. Is Suthafiori still supporting the Dominion? I wondered. If not, ships to the Eastern Isles might be hard to come by.

Lord, Christie! I thought, laughing to myself. A few weeks ago you were planning to stay on Orthe, and now look at the panic when you think you might have to . . .

I woke when the sun had moved off the wall. A blue twilight hung in the river valley, and lanterns glowed like *siriye*. The sky was clear, purple in the west, star-speckled in the east. For a minute I was anxious that I wouldn't be able to see my way back. Then I realized I only had to wait out the second twilight, and Orthe's stars would be bright enough to show me the path.

CHAPTER 23

Freeport

A watery haze hung over the river, softening the edges of riverboat sails and the last, dimly visible ridge of south-Dadeni's hills.

'I go no further south,' Dennet bawled. She was a leathery-skinned Orthean woman from south-Dadeni, running her tiny boat between there and the Morvren *telestres* with a crew of two *ashiren*.

'How far to the city?'

'About two *seri* down that way – you'll find a ferry to take you across.' She turned and spat *ataile* over the side, and yelled at the child on the tiller to bring the craft in to the landing stage.

Landing stops dotted this eastern bank of the Ai, mostly where tracks from distant *telestres* came down to the river. The far bank was invisible in the haze. Here the Ai runs out into estuaries and sand-bars and backwaters, the great river spidering out between flat slabs of lowland to the sea. I breathed deeply, catching the warm sparky tang of the ocean. It was subtly different from seas round the British Isles, less salty, less harsh. A warm wind blew off the land. *Rashaku-bazur* screeched. The water turned yellow and brown with the sand of Orthe's solar tides.

Southern latitudes. I thought us a good two hundred *seri* south of Tathcaer. I'd caught the spring weather, running downriver into it. Now it was Hanys Thirdweek, still liable to rainstorms, but hot.

The *ashiren* unloaded crates on to the jetty. *Marhaz* were visible on the upstream road and one of the riders waved a greeting. I paid the woman, mostly in coppers – it wasn't wise to appear too rich.

'There's unchancy folks in Freeport,' she said by way of farewell. 'Goddess give you a safe journey.'

'And to your mother's daughter, Dennet.'

I set off walking on the southward track, but stopped after a few minutes to take off the thick *becamil* cloak and strap it on top of my pack. The *jayante* settled awkwardly beside it.

Siir choked the riverbank. I walked between the thick, grey-silver stems. Like *hanelys*, it hugged the ground. Great trunks thick as a man's body grew up a metre or so and then looped over to lay along the earth, winding among other *siir* stems. Rosettes of chrome yellow leaves grew on the sunward-facing side of the stems. Bread-fungus hugged the ground under them, together with spring flowers, blue and purple and white. Down on the sandy earth of the river's edge were carpets of the black-centred flowers with ragged orange petals that Ortheans call City-in-Flames.

Close by a junction of tracks, a man was fishing.

'This the right way for Morvren Freeport?'

He looked me up and down, grunted, and waded back to his net. He muttered something about Outlanders that I didn't catch. Some Southlanders' tolerance stops dead at the *telestre* border.

Over the water, I began to see roofs shimmering in the haze, and the tall vanes of windpumps. There was no high land. If it had been clear, I could have seen for miles. I walked on. The pack straps chafed my shoulders. Apart from sweating in the unaccustomed heat, I had an allergic rash from the river's eternal diet of *hura* stew and bread-fungus. It seemed to last forever, walking over that flat land.

Approaching the coast, I found myself in company with *skurrai* carts and *marhaz* riders, and men and women walking in towards the city. No one paid me any attention, except for the inevitable glances that labelled me as Outlander. Morvren Freeport was clearer now, visible across a stretch of water. It looked to be built across several of the flat islands out in the estuary. Low, biscuit-coloured buildings rose above jetties, where many small boats were sailing. All the traffic on this bank was heading down towards a cluster of wooden shacks.

Eighteen days from north Dadeni down to here. Going south-west all the time, between fat eastern lands and desolate western hills. Days and days of sailing past *ziku* and *lapuur* forests. Days and days of south Dadeni's wealthy river-meadows, thick with grazing *skurrai* and *marhaz*. It was too early to get a passenger ship clear down to Morvren, so I boat-hopped. Sometimes on cargo ships or slow barges, sometimes on tiny boats like Dennet's. Once or twice I saw Crown Messengers. More often I heard *rashaku* relay gossip about the Andrethe's death. But I was ahead of it, travelling incognito, the cords of money growing lighter round my neck, the stunner close at hand.

I thought, *What am I doing here?*

Travelling down the Ai had been good. Conversations with shipmasters, landholders, traders, in company with those who collected orders for glass, forgeware, grain, cloth . . . Dadeni waking from its winter stillness, re-forging the ancient linkage of trade and barter that connects all the river *telestres*. Unknown among them, travelling unrecognized on an alien world . . . that was adventure in the old sense! Even as I laughed at the thought, I enjoyed it.

Only now I was coming to a city again – and I was beginning to share the Orthean fascination with, and distrust of, cities. I had to enter the Freeport to get passage on a ship. To where, though? Tathcaer might be no safer than Shiriya-Shenin. The longer I was out of sight, the more chance they'd find the real killer . . . or would they? They were convinced it was me. And I couldn't function as envoy until the matter was settled.

I shouldered through the crowd, blinking in the heat. Sheds and stables edged the river, and a disreputable-looking companion-house. Carts queued on a slipway where a floating platform berthed. Smaller ferries were plying for hire. It didn't take long to find one willing to take me across the water.

Ship's fees and companion-houses eat away at cash. I might still have enough to book passage for the nine hundred *seri* up the coast to Tathcaer. Certainly I couldn't afford to stay long in the Freeport.

The boat rocked in the deep channel, the rower's stroke strengthened. Spray tasted metallic on my lips. We docked at the end of a long jetty. This was a walled city: sunbaked brick to a height of two metres, with one main gate choked by carts, and several smaller ones jammed with pedestrians. Men and women in sandy-coloured uniforms guarded all the gates.

They were checking papers. By the time I saw that, there was nothing to do but go forward.

'Permit,' a tall woman demanded, eyes veiled against the dust stirred up by the carts.

'My companions have them.' I made a vague gesture back at the river. My accent puzzled her, I saw. 'In two, three days, they come. I wait in the city.'

'Shadow take all Outlanders,' she said, barely under her breath; and then as if explaining to the slow-witted, 'No permit – no go into the Freeport. Go back. Wait. You understand me? Wait until your people come with permits. Then you come in. Understand? Sunmother's tits!'

I bowed, said something in English that didn't match the polite tone in which it was said, and backed off. She was watching me. I hung round a ferry queue until her attention was distracted, then slipped off to look at the smaller gates. They were guarded too.

The Crown's permits were useless. They'd remember Christie's name – they must be already on the look-out for it.

'You have trouble?' A pale-maned *ashiren* regarded me gravely. 'You want to enter Freeport, Outlander?'

'Go in the city? Yes.'

'I know a way,' the *ashiren* said. *Ke* wasn't more than five or six. 'A broken part of the wall. For a silver piece, I'll show you.'

Reluctantly I unknotted one and handed it over. The *ashiren* slid off *kir* seat on a mooring bollard and glanced round.

'I'll see if the way's clear. You wait here.' *Ke* vanished into the crowd. I waited. The pale sun blazed, unsoftened by the heat-mist. All but the brightest daystars were masked.

It took me longer than it should have to realize that the *ashiren* wasn't coming back.

I tried two or three more gates with no better result. Then – as I heard midday chimes from inside the walls, and began to smell cooking – I came to a shabby, land-side gate, deserted but for two troopers playing *ochmir*.

'I come in,' I said hopefully, with a worse accent than usual. The older of the two women slouched upright.

'Papers,' she said idly. I repeated my story. The younger woman also stood. Her face was masked with marshflower dapples, and raisin-dark eyes glowed.

'No papers? Maybe we can make an exception, Caveth.' She nudged the older woman with her foot. 'Of course, there's a fine you'll have to pay.'

'Fine?' With a show of reluctance I brought out a cord and began to count coins.

'And the tax,' she added, 'the – ah – tax on Outlanders entering the Freeport.'

'Steady, Zilthar. Even Outlanders aren't that stupid.' The older woman's south-Dadeni accent was thick. Southlanders, finding you can't speak their tongue, tend to assume you can't understand it either. 'Keep it low or she won't pay.'

'Some Seamarshal's guard we are.' Zilthar grinned briefly. 'That'll be five silver pieces, *T'An* Outlander.'

'Suppose they find out?' Caveth worried.

'Who'll tell? This one can't even talk properly. What—? Have I to count it out for you?' She bent over the handful of silver and copper I was offering her. 'Three . . . four . . . five; there.'

'Is that right?'

She looked at me, highly affronted. 'What do you think I am – a thief?'

As I went in under the brick and plaster arch I heard her add 'What does it matter, Caveth? When they throw her out under the nine days law she'll—'

The rumble of carts drowned her words. I went on into the Freeport. The *telestre* houses were low and sprawling, pale plaster reflecting back the glaring sun. Their walls had no windows except for slits on the first floors. Windpumps rose out of the dusty air like broad-petalled flowers. Creepers flowed down from rooftop tubs, crimson-leaved, bright with spring growth of blue and white blossoms. Through open archways I saw sunken pools, mosaic courtyards, Ortheans sleeping in the sun after the noon meal.

None of the streets were straight, so I was at the docks before I saw it. A brisk wind, still cold, blew whitecaps on a sea that stretched endlessly south. After all the long and land-locked winter – the sea.

Islands formed a sheltered harbour here. I saw how the Freeport hugged every scrap of land above water. Ships were moored along the quay, painted sails furled. *Jath* ships from Ymir and Rimon, some others from the Melkathi peninsula; some I didn't know. Ortheans pushed past me, Southlanders and others. Dialects and foreign tongues assailed my ears.

Back of the *chirith-goyen* cloth warehouses I found a companion-house willing to serve a late midday meal. *Skurrai* mare's milk and cheese, and the tough-fibred bread-mushroom. Tired, hot, I sat under the street-awning and drank cold herb-tea.

Ships for Tathcaer, that's next, I thought. Assuming the Portmaster isn't on the lookout for one Lynne de Lisle Christie. Assuming I can afford passage.

If Tathcaer's safe . . . at least I can talk to Eliot and Huxton, I reflected. Set diplomatic processes going. If the late Andrethe's *telestre* don't assassinate me, that is. Lord, how did I get into this mess! What I need now is someone who knows the country . . . I didn't realize how easy it was being made for me, travelling with Ortheans.

'Are there rooms here?' I asked the keeper of the companion-house.

'Maybe. Where's your permit?'

'My what?'

He looked suspiciously at me. 'Haven't you registered with the Wellhouse yet? You'd better, before one of the Seamarshal's guard stop you.'

'I don't understand. I've only just arrived.'

'You register. They give you a pass. It's good for nine days. Then you must go back to your *telestre* or Guild – but I forgot, you Outlanders don't have that.' He sniffed. 'You'll have to leave the city at the end of the week, then. But I can't take anyone without a permit. My *telestre* wouldn't allow it.'

'I'll register,' I promised, and received copious directions to the nearest Wellhouse. I paid and left, taking care to avoid that direction. The church would be looking for Christie.

Someone who knows the country, I thought as I stepped over the covered channel that served as the street's sewer. Someone to know custom, be an extra pair of eyes to warn against assassins; someone who – a sell-sword, yes! The only question is, can I afford to pay one?

I began enquiring the way to the Mercenaries' Guildhouse.

'There is the list of the Guild members presently in the residence,' the Guildmaster said. 'Not all are available for contract, of course.'

She was a tan-skinned woman, strikingly beautiful despite her obvious age. A scar licked up from the corner of her mouth to her eye, giving her a sleepy, sardonic expression.

'You'll have the Seamarshal's permit,' she added casually, 'for an Outlander to hire a mercenary from the Hundred Thousand.'

'Mmm . . .' I studied the list of names on the parchment, mentally cursing Morvren's paranoid Seamarshal. A number of men and women passed through the low-ceilinged entrance hall. I couldn't guess, from looking, which were mercenaries and which were not.

'You're looking for a bodyguard?' The Guildmaster had the air of one trying to be helpful. 'Or one skilled in certain weapons—'

'This one.' I realized I'd interrupted her, but it couldn't be helped. I didn't believe what I was reading. She peered over my shoulder.

'That one's not presently available for contract.'

'I know. I'll wait.'

She shrugged. 'He's in the city, I believe. You may wait in the courtyard, *t'an*, if you wish, until he returns.'

Sand grated underfoot on the tiled floors. Windows laid narrow strips of white sunlight across the interior gloom. The courtyard was roofed with a cloth awning; benches stood by the walls, and desultory weapons practice was in progress in the centre square. I took a seat on one of the benches. The burst of enthusiasm sparked off by the entrance of a potential customer faded, as they saw I wasn't interested.

I didn't wait long.

He came into the courtyard with the familiar light tread, agile for his build. I saw him momentarily as a stranger would: a broad-shouldered Orthean male, not tall, in old mail and scuffed leather boots, worn *harur* blades at his belt. Fair mane, silverlock, and the appalling mottled scar: Blaize n'ri n'suth Meduenin.

'I've been looking for you all day,' he said as he sat down beside me. 'Saw you at the gate, but then I lost you.'

'So much for disguise.'

'I'd know you anywhere,' he said simply.

Can you buy loyalty? I thought. Or am I being obtuse again? Ortheans!

'You couldn't have known I was here,' he added. 'What brings you to Duvalka's Guildhouse?'

'Planning to hire help to get me to Tathcaer. What interests me is what you're doing here, Meduenin.'

He nodded. There was dirt ingrained in his pale skin; he had the look of a man driven hard.

'I got as far as Afrual before the Crown's riders turned me back.' The pale eyes opaqued, cleared. 'Truth told, I think they thought I was you – riding your Gher, they knew the tracks. I went west to avoid them, couldn't break through. When I got as far as Charain I sold the beast to an Earthspeaker travelling north – I owe you that money – and came down on a rivership. Saw you as I came in this morning.'

'How close are they?'

'Close enough,' he admitted. 'They'll be hunting you all the way to Tathcaer, and further.'

'With nothing friendly in mind, I'd say.'

Scar tissue contorted. It was a moment before I recognized it as a smile. 'The consensus opinion is for slitting your throat without benefit of trial – which would suit a number of people very well.'

'You thinking of anyone in particular?'

'Whoever killed the Andrethe.' He sprawled back, tucking his hands under his belt. 'Someone *knows* you're innocent, Christie. At the moment you've been convicted by popular opinion, but if it came to a trial it might not look so convincing. Safer if you were dead.'

'Do ships go from here to the Eastern Isles? No, forget I said that. Blaize, do you have any idea who's behind this?'

'Anyone of the *tha'adur*, the *takshiriye*, or the people in from the Dadeni *telestres*.' He looked up. 'You think I should have warned you. It's what you hired me for. But there was no whisper of it until that last day, it must have been planned at a very high level.'

SuBannasen's dead, I thought, with the ambiguous pang that

remembering her death always caused me. And Howice is in Roehmonde . . . but that doesn't rule him out. Who else?

'It's no excuse,' Blaize said. 'I did all I could. Don't you believe that?'

'What?' My train of thought vanished.

'After Broken Stair – but you never will credit a sell-sword's word, will you?' He grinned, the scar turning it into something merciless.

'Is it important that I believe you?'

He was silent a while. 'I take your gold, deliver what you require me to deliver to Tathcaer. No, what do I want with belief?'

This from a man who twice tried to kill me. So why was I feeling guilty?

'I don't doubt you,' I said slowly, trying to think it out. 'I wish I could be as certain of other people's honesty as I am of yours. You're honest where you're paid.'

He took it as a compliment, eyes veiled, embarrassed. After a pause he said, 'What will you do now?'

The *jayante* dug into my back. I eased the strap. 'I still want that report to get to Tathcaer. Is it safe to try and board a ship?'

'Safer for me, I'm an unknown in this. But I may have led them down on you here, they'll be watching.' He shrugged. 'You'd have a better chance if we were together.'

'And you'd have a worse one.'

'You hired me, didn't you?'

'That may be the most ungracious offer of help I ever had. Thanks.'

He laughed briefly. The courtyard was emptying, and the bells sounding for evening.

'Where are you staying?' he asked.

'At the moment, nowhere. Seems you need a signed permit to breathe in this city.'

'The problem of being a Freeport – if you let everyone in, you have to know who they are. You can stay here, Christie, I'll speak to the Guildmaster.' He stood up. 'You'll have to make a decision soon. There isn't much time.'

'There never is,' I said, 'and what there was has just about run out.'

'That's the Portmaster's office.' Blaize pointed down the quay towards a three-storey building. Despite the cold spring rain, the entrance hall was full and the crowd spilling out into the open. 'We should have come earlier.'

'You've been here before,' I remembered. His knowledge of the city was accurate, taking us from the Guildhouse across several ferry-channels to this outermost island.

'Best I go in,' he said. 'They might have your description.'

'If you can get in. Looks like a longish wait.'

One of the quayside awnings sheltered us. Rain pocked the sea. The pale plaster buildings across the water had a luminous sheen, and a distant spire was alternately veiled and revealed by low cloud.

Blaize touched my arm and indicated a ship. 'That's a Saberonisi vessel, look. From the Rainbow Cities.'

A party were going aboard, their faces caked with blue and scarlet paint, thread-thin chains girdling their dark robes. Saberon I dimly remembered from maps, several thousand miles south.

Despite the rain, there was no atmosphere of impatience in the crowd. A steady trickle of people came out of the building, and just as steadily we edged towards the door. The midmorning chimes sounded.

An eddy: people drawing back instinctively, others peering forward. I heard raised voices, a note of excitement. A group of people were leaving the Portmaster's office.

'Freeport, yes,' came a snatch of conversation behind me, 'but there are limits on who should be let in—'

Two, three, five of them: dark robes over bronze scaled tunics, high-arched feet bare, thin-hafted throwing spears strapped across their backs. The movement of the crowd left me close enough to touch them as they went past. The sea wind blew in their white unbound manes, where bronze and gold pins were tangled. Their skins glowed dusty gold. The brilliance was such that it was a minute before I realized they walked on the same dung-spattered paving as the rest of us, through the miasma from the dirty harbour. They were dirty, tunics foodstained; unintelligible voices harsh. Brown eyes flickered haughtily over Morvren's people. I had expected golden eyes. Some of the bleached manes had dark roots.

'Halfbreeds,' Blaize said in my ear. 'Kel Harantish. Wait here.'

He was gone inside the building, while the crowd's attention followed the Harantish people along the quay out of sight.

By the time he reappeared, I was edgy for no good reason. Perhaps a reaction to the Goldens. We retired to a dockside companion-house for an early dinner, discussing Blaize's news.

'There's two would take passengers,' he reported, 'and two that want deckhands. That we might try, if you've ever done any sailing. All those leave before the week's end.'

'I'm no sailor. What are the passenger fees?'

I listened to him recite figures. This division of the companion-house (a restaurant) was clean and well-lit compared to most of the Freeport. The rain had lessened, and intermittent watery sunlight shone through the stained glass windows.

A hand tapped my shoulder.

'What the—'

'No harm, *t'an*; I would speak with you.'

Alarm faded, replaced by a new disquiet. The man was dark-skinned, wearing sailor's britches. Off one of the docked ships, then. Yes, the accent was foreign. The sun laid white bars across his scarred ribs, nipples, corded throat. A soft leather mask covered his face from mouth to forehead. His dirty mane was roughly braided.

'What do you want?'

'Give me your hand.'

'I think not.'

The lips curved, smiling. Something darkly transparent blocked the mask's eyeholes. I couldn't see his eyes. But he saw mine.

He said 'I have a message from the Hexenmeister, to the woman not born of this world.'

Blaize had *harur-nazari* in his left hand; I hadn't seen or heard him draw it. I put my hands out of sight under the table, feeling the sonic stunner under my tunic.

'The Hexenmeister?' I recalled, then, an earlier message.

'It is this,' he said quietly. ' "Envoy, spring weather is uncertain travelling. If you take ship, be aware that you are welcome at the Brown Tower." That is all.'

'Wait,' I said as he turned to go. 'How . . . how did you find me?'

'All who left the city this season carried such a message.' Another eyeless smile. 'If you were here, you must come some time to the office of the Portmaster. From there I followed you.'

'Do you know who I am?'

'I know the signs to recognize you, and the words to compel your attention. The Tower told me. *T'an*, I have no other answers.'

He left, and I became aware that my hand was clenched on the stunner. It left a white impression when I released it. Blaize sheathed the *harur-nazari* and let out an explosive breath.

'Sunmother! Is the Hexenmeister interested in you now, Christie?' He sounded awed. 'Kasabaarde's an unchancy place, and not to be trusted. If I were you—'

'Yes?'

'I'd settle this mess before I got into another one.'

Being a companion-house, more or less anything was available. I requested parchment and a writing-stick, and they were brought to the table.

Twice this place called Kasabaarde had found me with a message. Even for curiosity's sake I wanted to know why. Besides that . . . I tried to get my thoughts into coherent form. It would be wise to leave the Southland for a time. Wise to diversify, the more contacts the Dominion had on this world, the better. Particularly as we weren't very welcome in the Hundred Thousand at the moment.

Or is that rationalizing cowardice? I thought. Am I just plain scared of going back to Tathcaer? Yes, true. Not that that makes my other reasons any less valid.

I scribbled furiously, folded the sheet of parchment, and sealed it with wax. When I looked up it was to see Blaize leaning back and scuffing his boot on the floor, seething with impatience.

'Are we going to Kasabaarde?' he demanded.

'I am. You're going to Tathcaer. You can take this letter with the report, it's an update to let them know what I'm doing. Naturally you won't deliver it to anyone except a member of the xeno-team. And should anyone ask, you don't know where I am.'

He grunted, then nodded. 'Now you're thinking like a Southlander.'

The spire became a pylon-shaped building jutting up out of the sea into a clear sky. As we came closer I tried to judge the height, revised my estimate upwards several times when I saw the buildings clustered round its base. Skyscraper height at the very least. No, larger. And – when the sun gleamed on it – it showed the blue-grey fused stone that meant Golden Witchbreed.

'Spire Gate,' Blaize said laconically, 'lots of island ships put in there.'

Coming closer now, and it was neck-stretchingly high. The ferry boat berthed in its shadow. Now I could see it was not simply a featureless tower. A third of the way up, a thread-thin structure jutted out horizontally. It went south, straight as a die, over the sea; and every so often a support pillar soared up to seamlessly join it.

'Dear god,' I said, 'is that a *bridge*?'

The Meduenin man grinned. 'Rasrhe-y-Meluur,' he said. 'Otherwise known as Bridge Alley. I've been along it as far as Goldenarch and Stonefire. They say you can get clear to Kasabaarde.'

'Kasabaarde—' Which must be, if memory serves me, on the long side of two hundred *seri* distant.

'It's covered,' he said, rounding his hands to indicate a tube-shape, 'but not safe. Shall I ask round the ships?'

'What? Yes, do.'

Presumably it followed the chain of islands, the Kasabaarde Archipelago. To construct it argued an engineering skill not just staggering, but – for it to exist intact thousands of years – plain frightening.

Eventually I reached agreement with the master of an island ship, not much larger than a fishing smack, but willing to carry passengers down the Archipelago. Being in a hurry, I paid more than seemed strictly necessary. Freeporters, perhaps because of their contact outside the Hundred Thousand, have a clear idea of personal property. The ensuing casual dishonesty reminded me sharply of Earth.

'You could hire someone else to take that report to Tathcaer,' Blaize said. His eyes veiled in the bright sunlight. I had my pack, the *jayante*; there was nothing to do but go aboard.

'Who else can I trust?'

He reached out and gripped my hands, nodded once, and then strode off down the quay. And I went on board the *Mosshawk*.

Going south, spring comes all the faster. Each of the islands we put in at seemed to boast a greater amount of new-leafed *siir* and flowering *lapuur*. Hanys and the first weeks of Durestha often bring storms sweeping in from the Western Ocean, but the *Mosshawk* had a voyage of such balmy uneventfulness that we had nothing to do but watch the Archipelago glide past in daylight, and the starfire swirl in our wake during the cloudless nights.

The *Mosshawk* carried three passengers besides myself: a Desert Coast woman on her way to Quarth, and two men robed head to foot in scarlet who spoke no intelligible tongue. Being Orthean, they gambled. The cabins were cramped and dark and we spent our time on deck, well forward out of the crew's way, playing *ochmir*. After the first couple of days there was nothing new.

South, into warmer waters. Stopping over to pick up or deliver cargo, wine and pottery and seedling plants. It was shirt-sleeve weather when we made brief excursions onto the islands. And the sky grew paler, and the sun hotter, and all the time the pylons of the Rasrhe-y-Meluur cast their unbroken shadow on the ceaseless waves.

Slow travelling, the last few days of Hanys and well into Durestha Secondweek; but one morning I woke to white acid sunlight, and a dark line in the south.

'The coastline of Kasabaarde,' the Desert Coast woman said.

CHAPTER 24

The Brown Tower

The sun flashed off a sea like broken glass. A grey-green fuzz covered the nearer coastline. Sepia mountains haunted the far south, desolate moonscapes and deserts that might have been anything up to fifty *seri* away. We sailed in towards a tall pylon marking the end of Bridge Alley, Rasrhe-y-Meluur.

Blobs of colour swam in my vision. I retreated below decks again, rubbing reddened, irritated eyes. My skin, already tanned, peeled. The hazy days had been bearable; with the protective haze gone, there was no avoiding the searing light of Carrick's Star.

If this is what it's like in Durestha, I thought, I don't want to be here in Merrum.

Wood creaked, waves hissed; gaps in the decks let through sunlight like molten metal. By the time I'd packed, the ship had docked and the other passengers were disembarking. I paid the shipmaster the remaining half of the fee and went ashore.

The land was utterly flat. Carts rolled down a wide quay that was inches deep in fine white dust. I tasted grit on my tongue, the metallic taste of Kasabaarde. The Desert woman and the two red-robed Ortheans were ahead of me at the pale mud-brick wall where several gates opened into the city.

'You wish to enter the trade city or the inner city?' the older of the Kasabaardeans asked the Desert Coast woman. They spoke the trade-tongue mentioned in the books I'd studied; I could just about make myself understood in it.

'The trade city,' the woman said.

'Pass, then.'

The books had been full of information on the trade city. Of the inner city they said nothing, except that the Brown Tower was there.

'You wish to enter the trade city?' The Kasabaardean studied me closely. 'Or the inner city?'

'The inner city.' The accent was manageable.

A young man barred my way with a staff. The group had the tan manes and bleached skins of the Desert Coast. They wore short, rope-belted tunics, and were barefoot.

'Touch the earth,' the Kasabaardean commanded. She had albino dapples down her bare arms, and on her hands the veins stood up with age. Like the others, she was masked.

As was the custom, I knelt to put both hands palm-flat on the dry ground, and then stood. Another woman offered me a bowl. Grey, ceramic, half full of water. They watched me expectantly. I took a small mouthful, hoping I'd avoid any infection. It had a flat taste.

'Have you edged weapons?' the woman continued the ritual.

'No – yes, a knife.'

'That shall be returned when you leave,' she said, taking it. The staff no longer barred my way. Under the mask's edge, her mouth smiled. 'The *jayante* you may keep with you. A welcome to you. I will take you to the inner city gate.'

'I'm looking for a companion-house,' I said as we walked beside the wall. The sun on the white dust and brickwork was painfully bright. 'Or somewhere I can stay.'

'You may stay among any of the Orders.'

'Somewhere cheap. I don't have much money.'

'You will not need money.' Her dry voice might have held amusement. It was difficult to tell, with her eyes hidden. 'In the inner city, all food is free, and all drink, and all clothing and shelter.'

Fitting my steps to her slow pace, we came to a squat gatehouse.

'For Kasabaardeans, you mean?'

'No, for all. For any who come here.'

'You mean anyone can just come here and ask, and get fed and housed?'

'Yes, certainly.'

That's impossible! I protested mentally. We entered the gatehouse. After the sun outside, I was blind. Vision clearing, I saw the Kasabaardean woman handing my knife over to another man. This was a weapons store. The man was jotting down an inventory of my possessions.

'What is yours, you may keep,' the Orthean woman said, pulling off her mask. So it was protection against the sun? I wondered. She had an angular face, and clear-water eyes. 'What is ours – you may leave with no more of that than you may carry on your back or in your stomach.'

I shook my head. Yes, she was amused. She must have had this reaction from strangers before.

'It's not—' I couldn't insult her, so began again. 'Don't you get people coming here and living off you, and not doing anything to earn it?'

'Is that so bad?' She bent over the list the man was making, and indicated I should open my pack. There was no option. She continued, 'All may live here, though none grow rich. That is for the Orders to do in the trade city. We will house you, feed you; if you wish to work in fields or city then you may. If not, then do not.'

'People can't just do nothing!'

Her veiled eyes watched me. Seeing me as an individual, I thought suddenly, not just another stranger.

'Why not?' she said softly. 'Perhaps if they do not toil, they learn some value from the Orders' teaching. Or find some clear vision of their own. Time is what we give, for self-searching or for idleness. And we give choices.'

'I still don't see how you can do it.' I was looking for the catch, as Southlanders and Outworlders do.

'The fields feed us, we have rivers; such wealth as the Orders have comes from trade and taxes. To stay here costs nothing. To pass through, much. And all that comes from the Rainbow Cities and Desert Coast must pass us to go north, and all the Southland must pass us on their voyaging, and there is the Rasrhe-y-Meluur besides.' Her thin lips moved, smiling, her eyes were bright. 'My Order is Su'niar, if you wish to go there. Tell them Orinc sent you. Or there are other Orders, Cir-nanth and Gethfirle, Thelmithar and Dureitch. But it would be a pleasure for me to talk with you further.'

My pack was returned to me. The woman replaced her mask over her loosely braided mane.

'Yes,' I said. 'My name's Christie. Where is – Su'niar?'

'Along past Cir-nanth Way, anyone will tell you.' She pointed from the doorway. As I left she said, 'Christie, what's your business here?'

'The Brown Tower.'

I left her staring after me.

After the weeks on the ship, my legs weren't steady. I walked on into the inner city, adjusting to the solidity of the world. The white light leaked through my slitted eyelids. The heat sucked strength. Sweat dried immediately in the dryness. Ortheans jostled me, many in Kasabaardean robes, many from the other lands of this second continent. I heard a babble of talk.

Low domes lined the curving streets, windows ebony in the expanses of white and sand-coloured plaster and bricks. Broad cartways gave way to narrow passages. Cloth awnings stretched across the alleys at roof-level. Bead-tapestries sheltered doorways.

Perhaps because it was impossible to see more than a few streets ahead at one time, the city seemed to go on forever. Occasionally I glimpsed the distant peaks of the desert land. Sometimes a road opened on to the brilliant sea. But the curved roads and passages had no discernible pattern. Between my version of the trade-tongue and people's attempts to give me directions, I was soon lost.

Vaned windpumps glittered as they turned. They jutted above the domes of this one-storey city, the only landmarks. Coming at last to a broad roadway, I stopped almost in the shadow of the vanes. The road surface sparked up light, dazzling noon fragments. Somewhere I heard water running. Then, as I walked out among the crowds on the scored, worn surface, I saw that the water was underfoot. A covered channel, roofed with semi-opaque blue-grey stone . . .

The last pylon of the Rasrhe-y-Meluur towered in the north. Witchbreed again: another of Orthe's communities flourishing in the ruins of the Golden Empire. I thought of cold aKirrik in the Barrens, Kasabaarde on the searing equator. Not mere archeology, this, you couldn't separate Orthe from its past.

A number of Ortheans were sitting outside one building, their backs to the curving dome wall, in the shade of an awning.

'Where is this?' I asked carefully.

A few looked at me. Like all I'd seen, their eyes were permanently shielded by the nictitating membrane. One trickled dust from hand to hand. It was quiet.

'Thelmithar,' one said at last.

Inside was cool, dim, spacious. A man with blue threads woven into his rope-belt came over to me.

'The food is almost ready, do you wish to come down and wait?' Hunger, thirst; they had been masked by the newness of Kasabaarde. I nodded. He led me down steps, into wide underground rooms where a few Ortheans already sat at tables. I smelled cooking. The light was diffuse, reflected down from the outside world by mirrors. One wall was blue-grey, half transparent, water moving there in the cool shadows.

Black hard bread, some unnamed fruits, and watered wine; and a stew that seemed to consist mainly of fungi. I ate slowly, watching the Ortheans that were there. Some were unmasked Kasabaardeans, some from other Desert cities, one looked as though she might have been a Southlander. As I was leaving, a fight broke out between two of the Desert men. No one attempted

270

to interfere. Pausing on the steps, I watched while one beat the other unconscious. Then I went up into the searing light.

It wasn't possible just to walk out. Something in the back of my mind howled *thief*! While I hesitated, the same man returned from the street.

'Is there something else you desire?'

'No. Yes,' I contradicted myself. A certain freedom made itself felt. And a desire to test to the limit. 'A mask, one of those with the eye-shields. And can you tell me how to find Su'niar?'

'I'll take you there,' he said, returning from a storeroom with the mask in his hand. It felt suffocating at first, then ceased to be noticed. The dust-shields gave the world a sepia tint, but at least I could see comfortably.

The sun declined, a white-hot coin in a pale sky.

The face was thin. You could see the skull's shape under the tanned skin. And the eyes, half white, hard as marble; like nothing on Orthe. And laughing. I laced the mask on, turning away from the mirror.

Good grief, Christie! I thought. What did Blaize say? Finish this mess before you get into another. The department won't like this messing about with 'primitives' on the second continent, not while the Southland's like it is . . .

And anyone who stands there laughing at themselves in a mirror is in no position to question anybody else's sanity. Not even someone who calls themself Hexenmeister, and sends messages halfway across the world. Who's crazy – the one who calls, or the one who answers? What do I *say* to him, I wondered.

I went upstairs. Orinc was in the outer room, sweeping the tiled floor clear of the ever-present dust. Her movements were lethargic. It was that time when afternoon becomes evening.

'Why hurry?' she asked, seeing me masked for the streets. 'Stay here in Su'niar a while, child.'

'I'll be back,' I promised. 'Tell me how I find the Brown Tower.'

'Between Stone Gate and the gardens,' she said resignedly, and loosed the bead curtain behind me as I stepped out into the street.

Rounded shadows patched the streets, blue and soft. The furnace-sky cooled, minute by minute. Crowds dispersed, seeking food and shelter for the night in the houses of the different Orders. I went down by way of the seaward wall, walking until I came to a sandstone-block gate, and then turning back into the city towards the gardens. Scrub vegetation grew by the pools, ash-grey and milky blue leaves quivering in the light breeze. Creepers covered a wall on the western side of the gardens, and over it rose the broad square shape of the Tower. The arch in the wall had no gate. Beyond it I saw courtyards, fountains.

A man stepped out of the archway and spoke. When he saw I didn't understand, he repeated it in the trade-tongue.

'What do you want here?'

'Is this the Brown Tower?' Now it came to it, my guts were snake-knotting.

'Yes.'

'I've come to see the Hexenmeister.' Then it hit me where I'd seen that dark otter-sleekness before. Webs marked hands and feet, the skin was green-gold. In spite of the masked face, there was no mistaking it – this was one of the fenborn.

'The Hexenmeister?' he said, unconsciously arrogant. 'Why?'

'I don't know. You'd better ask him.'

He hesitated, staring at me. At last he said, 'What – who are you?'

'Christie.' At last the laces of the mask unknotted and I was free of it. 'Envoy from the Dominion.'

The evening's brilliance stung my eyes. He made some gesture I didn't recognize, ritualistic and formal.

'Outworlder,' he said, 'be welcome: you are expected.'

I left the sunlit courtyard, the flickering brightness of the fountains and the scent of grey-gold creepers, entering into the shadow of the Brown Tower.

Set into the soaring brown brick wall was a metal-studded door. The fenborn touched one of the studs and it glided open. We stepped through into a dim hallway. The door slid shut and a sourceless light sprang up, illuminating smooth walls and floor and ceiling. I touched the wall. The pale material had a slick feel, warmer than stone.

'Come,' the fenborn said.

Weights and pulleys? And the lighting, concealed mirrors again? As we passed through several doors and along corridors, I realized I was grasping for explanations. The place had the look of high technology about it. Another door slid open at our approach.

It was a library. Bookshelves from floor to ceiling; never since coming to Orthe had I seen so many books in one place. The dusty scent of old parchment filled the air. Evening light fell on woven mats, a blocky table and chairs. There weren't even bars on the windows.

'You're careless,' I said, still stunned by the contrast between city and Tower. 'Anyone could come here—'

'If you had not been desired to enter, you could not even have passed the gardens.' An old man came from behind one of the bookshelves, and placed the scroll he carried on the desk.

'Hexenmeister,' the fenborn said. 'Christie, the Outworlder.'

'Ah. Thank you, Tethmet. Leave us now.'

Like most Kasabaardeans he was a head smaller than me, and bent with age besides. His hands were bird-claws, his skin a diamond-pattern of wrinkles, and his mane gone except for a crest from forehead to spine. A brown sleeveless robe covered his tunic.

'You are the alien?'

'You want to count fingers? Yes, that's me.' I tucked the mask under my belt, and then had nothing to do with my hands. Nervous, fingers twisting together; I wanted to laugh. 'But anyone who can send me two messages across half a world, sight unseen, knows enough about me for my liking. Now I'm here, suppose you explain who you are, what you're doing, and what's so important I have to travel two hundred *seri* to get here?'

His puckered mouth wrinkled and a wheezing sound issued from his chest. I realized he was laughing. Using both hands to support himself, he lowered his body into a chair.

'What do you know of me? I don't wish to reiterate details you may already have.' He spoke fluent Ymirian, possibly choosing that because I still have that accent.

'Know? I don't *know* anything. The books say plenty about the trade part of the city, nothing about the Brown Tower. As for rumour – no one seems sure in their own mind if this is a good city to come to, or a bad one. And for yourself, Hexenmeister—'

'Yes?' he prompted, still short of breath from laughing.

'That you dream no past-dreams because you're immortal, that you see all that passes in the world, that the archives of the Brown Tower hold all knowledge.'

'Such superstition,' he said mildly. 'Well, you and I have much to speak of, envoy, and I will tell you why. I know much of what passes in the known lands, because most news comes either here to this city, or is heard by my people who travel. And it has been the custom – since before Tathcaer was a city – that they bring such news to me. The archives hold much knowledge, but not all. No, not all. And as for the other, that is answered more simply: yes, I am immortal.'

'I'm sorry, I don't believe that. I can't.' It hurt me to be rude to the old man. He had a kind of stillness about him, a solidity, that made it diffcult to believe he was only a mad old man living in the ruins of Witchbreed technology.

'You *must* believe,' he said. 'Or else you'll believe nothing I tell

273

you. And what I tell you may affect the relations between our two worlds. I know you've seen much of the Hundred Thousand, but do not suppose that they can speak for all Orthe.'

'And you can?' The sharpness was unintentional.

His white-filmed eyes met mine. 'You see, you have no proof that what I say is valid. So, though I don't normally deal in personalities, I think I must prove to you what I am.'

He eased forward in the chair, lifting himself with the weight on his wrists as the old do. I automatically moved to help him. His warm hand closed over mine, a many-fingered grip, and then he was standing upright.

'If you will lend me your arm . . . thank you. Lynne de Lisle Christie – and what is the correct usage: *t'an* or landholder, or something from your own world?'

We moved towards the door at his slow pace, and it opened to let us through.

'Christie will do,' I said. Wondering, is it beam-operated? Or – no, it can't be; not even Witchbreed technology lasts forever.

Along a diffusely-lit passage, passing more doors. Slow, at an old man's speed. His weight, leaning on my arm, was considerable.

Another door opened. We stepped into a small chamber, and the door slid shut. There was pressure underfoot, a sickness in the stomach; I realized we were descending. Then it stopped, the door opened, and we walked into another and slightly larger room. The light changed quality. The air felt dry, cool. Then a section of the opposite wall split and slid aside.

'That causes you no fear,' the old man said, 'you have seen such things before. Well, it is not to be wondered at, coming from the stars.'

An elevator. A sterile air-lock. Cool air hit me from the room beyond. Disbelief paralysed me. Kirriach was awesome enough. But Kirriach's safely dead, I thought, and this . . . he said: if you had not been desired to enter . . . Lord, what kind of defences does a place like this have?

'Christie?'

His warm grip on my arm was the only link with reality. Veiled eyes looked up. His skin was webbed with fine lines, the crest-mane thin and wispy. Not a strong old man.

'Seems Witchbreed technology isn't as dead as it's thought to be.' My voice croaked, dry.

'The Brown Tower has stood for ten thousand years,' he said softly, impossibly. 'And hasn't been above borrowing Golden Empire technology when needed. Machines fail, you see. Even these. Though not for a time yet, I think.' He took a few unsupported steps into the room, resting his hands on the edge of metal casings. 'These are precious to me beyond all price, their like is not to be found in the world today.'

A long windowless room, underground. Banks of machinery – I presume it is, I thought – and screens, and cubicles like sarcophagi; and less recognizable objects. Quiet, chill, a subliminal hum.

And one object was familiar. I went forward, examining the table and the headrest – shaped for Ortheans – and attachments that might be electrodes; and connections to other banks of what might be computers . . .

'That is known to you?'

I stood up, sighing. 'I don't know. Chance resemblance, I expect. Except that certain things are common to all worlds – including the laws of science. We have something very like this for teaching under hypnosis.'

We struggled with respective vocabularies, not sure if we were talking about the same thing. All the old man's words were unfamiliar. Kasabaarde, unlike the Hundred Thousand, has a technical terminology included in its language. Some things we certainly misinterpreted.

'You have heard,' he said at last, 'of those of us who possess a perfect memory?'

'Yes. Some humans have that.'

'These transcribe, store, and transfer such a person's memory intact to another person.'

That isn't possible, I thought. Even we can't do that. The hypnoteachers might pass as a prototype of that – a primitive prototype – but if it's true . . . what level of technology did the Witchbreed have?

'So you can record memory.'

'Record and transfer to another person. And that person, also, to another and another.' He smiled. 'With no loss of detail, down through the generations.'

'Someone said to me once—' it was the Desert Coast woman on the *Mosshawk*, I remembered '—"the Hexenmeister has a peculiar kind of serial immortality". No one in the Southland mentioned it.'

'Oh, I am not approved of in the Hundred Thousand.' He gave an old man's chuckle. 'If I hold a hundred generations of memory, then where are my own memories of past lives? No, I am not liked there, but then there are very few who know.'

'It's not immortality.'

'Not for me,' he touched his thin chest. '*I* am not immortal, but the Hexenmeister is. Look.'

He laid his palm flat on a cube-structure. As I watched, it cleared from the centre, as if viscous compartments became transparent. Evening light glimmered in what must be the outer courtyard. A girl was sitting on the fountain's rim, her arms cradling a child perhaps a year old. She was pale-skinned, tan mane braided with beads, wearing the brown robes and rope-belt of the Brown Tower. Just past *ashiren*, not more than sixteen. Her face was unsmiling, bent in concentration over the child that played with her six-fingered hand.

'There is one of this generation's,' the old man said. 'She has many of the memories stored in her mind. Another few years – when I die – and she will be the Hexenmeister. And she'll remember speaking with you, Christie, remember this moment as I do. Since there's no difference in my memory and hers, then she will be me – as I am all who went before me.'

The cube darkened, precipitating me back into the cool room. The evidence of alien technology surrounded me.

'Now do you see?' the Hexenmeister asked. 'Kasabaarde is the oldest city in this world, and I am the oldest person. I know this world. Perhaps I am the only person who does. So when Orthe comes to deal with other worlds – I am the only one qualified to speak for us.'

CHAPTER 25

The Golden Empire

'That's all very well, but—' I realized I was pacing, and came to a halt in front of the old Orthean male. 'It's incredible! What real *proof* do you have?'

He spread his hands, indicating the Brown Tower in all its undeniable existence. 'If it were proved to your satisfaction that these machines act as I claim?'

'I don't have the technical training to prove or disprove it.' And where this was concerned, I thought, it might puzzle a few Dominion scientists to prove anything.

He sat down slowly on one of the metal fixtures, watching me. When his eyes unveiled they were black, bird-bright. Seeming to change tack, he said, 'The Southland is for the most part against contact with your world, I believe.'

'The majority? I don't know. And that may change.'

'They fear technology, the Witchbreed come again.' Slowly he shook his head. 'And all the danger that entails, though it's only a danger to them because they still desire it.'

'And Kasabaarde doesn't?'

'We are perhaps poor in material wealth, but there are other kinds of well-being. If I were to ask you your beliefs?'

'I . . .' It floored me. 'Beliefs?'

'Of the spiritual.'

'I don't know . . . agnostic, I suppose.' The department favours that, as being less likely to be offended by other worlds' religions.

'There are answers to be looked for,' he said, 'in the mind and soul; that is our choice in Kasabaarde. And you may believe what you will, or nothing at all. That is why these—' the protective hand on the machine '—don't touch us, as they would the Hundred Thousand, or Kel Harantish. We have all made our choices. Now we face this new thing, your world. That brings other choices.'

'You,' I said, 'do you believe in a god? The Goddess?'

An expression crossed his face, it might have been surprise or satisfaction. 'You are god, Christie. I am god. So are we all.'

I was lost. Kasabaarde's orientation is radically different from the Southland's. An envoy would have a different job here.

'I – excuse me – I'm still not sure just why I'm here.'

'That, you may discover after you've spent time in the inner city. But as for why I requested you to visit me, that's simpler. The main business of the Brown Tower is knowledge. I want knowledge of your world, Christie. Of Earth and the Dominion.'

I shrugged. 'That's my job. I'll be glad to tell you all I can.'

'Language is inadequate,' the old man said. 'Perhaps we misunderstand each other more than we know.'

'Isn't that inevitable? At first, anyway.'

'Not necessarily.' He stood, his hand grasping my arm for support. 'It will be obvious to you, I suppose. I wish to record your own memories, Christie, so that I will know your world. And, as trade is the mark of Kasabaarde, I am prepared to offer you access to some of my own memories of Orthe.'

'Why do you doubt him?' the fenborn said as we went through the corridors.

'Do I?'

'Yes – or you would not speak the way you do. None of us would.' A note of outrage crept into his voice.

Stick-limbs, slit-eyes, the cool snake skin . . . it was incongruous here in the dusty, scorched south, to see a fenborn in the robes of the Brown Tower.

'Tethmet, how did you get here?'

He manipulated a fixture on the wall, and the outer doors slid open. The round roofs gleamed white beyond the gardens, white in the starlight; and the pungent smell of night-blossoming creepers drifted in.

He said, 'When I was young, men caught and caged me; took me down a great river to show for their sport. When I grew old enough I killed them, fled down the Rasrhe-y-Meluur – *he* found me.'

The sky was a silver blaze, bright stars merging. Without the mask, the city was as clear as daylight.

'You'll come back,' he said.

'I promised to give a decision. I will do, when I've thought it over.'

As I crossed the courtyard the fenborn stepped out of the Tower and called after me.

'Christie – he knows how it is to be a stranger, and an exile. You should believe that.'

Kasabaarde's streets are dangerous, even by clear starlight. Meditation, as Orinc says, turns some to wisdom, and some to idleness and violence; I had no desire for trouble. But in that rootless city there was no need to return to Su'niar. Other Orders were closer at hand.

Days passed, scoured by dust storms from the high lands, dry as a furnace. On the sixth day after my visit to the Tower, the wind swung round to the north. Bitter rainstorms whipped in off the Inner Sea, turned the dust in the streets to ankle-deep mud, and the Ortheans retreated to their dry underground dwellings. Vicious and short, the storms passed. Steam rose from the streets. And the sun blazed, and the grit drifted down from the High Desert . . .

I waited for the Hexenmeister's summons to the Tower to give him my answer. And tried desperately to think what answer I could give.

'Put that down,' Orinc said, exasperated.

Orinc's *ashiren* took the two covered buckets from me. It was a few hot yards' walk down to the street-pump and back. I sat down on the inner room bench beside the old woman.

'I like to be doing something.'

'Su'niar doesn't accept payment,' she said, and then chuckled and coughed, dust in her throat. 'You Outlanders can't do nothing, can you? You've to be fidgeting and working, and – ach! go out and sit under the awning. Do nothing. Then you'll see.'

'See what?'

Her mouth quirked under the edge of her mask. 'Can I tell you? No. If it could be told, it wouldn't be the true illumination. You must find out.'

Her insistence drove me out at last. I sat on the steps, masked against the acid sunlight, the awning's shade falling across me. Dust was warm under my bare palms. As always, a scatter of Ortheans were sitting with their backs to the dome-wall of the Order house. Some muttered, some sang, some stared; most were filthy, and all were incomprehensible. The trade-tongue was frowned on in the inner city.

Assuming it's true, I thought, and assuming Witchbreed technology can be adapted for human use as well as Orthean – how dangerous would it be? Physically, mentally, politically? The problem is simple, do I do it or don't I? I'd be a fool to do it. And a fool not to.

It's beyond my brief as an envoy. Have I the right to pass on information about Earth? But then, have I the right to refuse a chance to get information about Orthe? It's what I'm here for. And I don't know, in either case, quite what information will be gained, or what it will be used for . . . and there's no one I can ask.

Daystars were half-invisible points of light over the domed roofs, the glare of Carrick's Star drowned them. I moved as the shadow moved. Some tightness inside me I identified at last as terror.

I thought, if Kasabaarde is important, the department will condemn me for not getting all data when that's possible. If it isn't, I'll have been wasting time on trivialities – according to their way of thinking – and giving away facts about Earth's defences. So it's a no-win either way. That's assuming shock doesn't kill me – even with the hypno-teachers they have to be so damn careful . . .

Durestha's spring days lengthened, and I learned Orthean patience, waiting for the summons to the Brown Tower.

The young woman lay in the cubicle, head resting back on a mobius-strip tangle of machinery. I watched her face alter with emotions that were centuries dead. Tethmet held her baby, and it mouthed fruitlessly at the front of his tunic. The Hexenmeister sat upright on another cubicle's edge, bird-bright eyes watching.

When she was lifted free of the machine, she took the child and left. Old tears ran unchecked down her face.

'Well?' the old man asked.

'Yes,' I said. 'Now.'

The cubicle was slick under me, with a sensation unlike metal or any plastic. A hum that might have been sound or vibration surrounded me. I closed my eyes, sick. Panic told me this was a mistake, this trusting to an alien science. But it was too late.

There was a sensation that – if it had lasted any longer than a micro-second – would have been intolerable agony. There is no way to describe how that feels: as if the closed confines of the self had opened and become infinite, and the mind fragmented into pieces in an ever-expanding maze.

Total fear: I grasped in panic at some remembered snatch of conversation, and what happened then happened with all the force of synaesthesia—

Pain.

*

280

—sitting opposite me in antique armour with a double-bladed axe at the belt. He – or was it a young woman? – has the dark skin of a northerner; thin, ash-brown mane cropped short, long-fingered hands clasped in her – or is it his? – lap.

'You will allow me to leave?' Direct eyes, unveiled. 'You'll understand I'm in something of a hurry, being what I am.'

Ashirenin, I realize, not recognizing it at first because of its rarity. *Ke* is aged around twenty-seven or eight, by *kir* face. And still unchanged, unsexed, un-adult.

There are those who remain *ashiren* long past the time for change. When the change to male or female comes, usually no later than the mid-thirties, it invariably kills them.

'You are from the Freeport?' The word from the Order house where *ke* stays is not detailed.

'From Morvren, yes. I've friends there, as well as enemies.' *Ke* smiles. 'Good friends. Andrethe. Lori L'Ku. We may go upriver – they say there's wild country there that could be tamed. If you let me leave your city, master, that's what I'll do.'

'And you'll tell them what you've learned here?'

Kir eyes are bright with amusement. 'What have I learned, master? Tell me.'

Sunlight filters through the window, patches the slick wall. It is quiet enough to notice the subliminal hum that is the heartbeat of the Brown Tower. This library room holds the smell of old books, of dust. The *ashirenin* sits facing me, with a similar quiet serenity.

'You have been speaking in the Order house of Thelmithar.'

'Some have listened,' *ke* admits.

'Saying that the Southland's church is false, that the church of the Goddess was set up only to prevent the rule of technology.'

'The second, yes, but not the first. Is it not true, master?'

'That Kerys Founder had such a purpose in mind? It may be so.' And I would like to know where *ke* learned that, but truth has a habit of coming to light in Kasabaarde. 'It is not my concern—'

'Then let me go.'

'—except so far as I have the friendship of the *T'An Suthai-Telestre*.' I watch *kir* face. 'Will you return and tell the Hundred Thousand their belief is a lie?'

'Most know what I know, master, or suspect it to be true. But no, that is not what I'd tell them.'

'What, then?'

Kir expression lightens, serious, but with an undercurrent of laughter. *Ke* leans forward intently. 'I'll tell them that Kerys, telling lies, came at last to tell the truth. The Goddess is, and we are the

281

Goddess. The earth is. The stars are. Life is. What else should we require?'

Ke has found something in one of Kasabaarde's Orders, or in the inner city, or in the air itself: it's visible in *kir* face. I feel loss, because I'll never wholly understand it.

'I haven't long, master,' *ke* says. 'Not with the Hundred Thousand to preach to, and all the church for my enemy. Will you let me go?'

'I am not *T'An Suthai-Telestre*, to exile you from the Southland. You have your own destiny. Leave Kasabaarde. I confess I was curious, hearing from Thelmithar of this Beth'ru-elen. But I will not stop your leaving.'

'But is the Hexenmeister ever curious without reason?' *ke* asks wryly, in that archaic accent. Beth'ru-elen *Ashirenin* stands, with a last glance round at the imperishable walls of the Tower—

An instant's agony. The ancient sunlight fading now, and further falling into other reality:

speaking to a messenger. The man finishes talking, returns to squat by the fire, warming his broad hands over the flames.

'Gone into the High Desert.' He raises his head, fire-dazzled, looking to where the edge of the plateau rises against the stars. Around us, Kel Harantish burns. Wind brings ash, and skirls of dust. Men and women shout. The last fugitives are discovered, their screams hoarse.

'Not all, *s'an* Kerys. You have won a victory here.' Wondering, as I speak, how true that is.

'Have I, master? We have the city, but what use is that? I shall not keep it. We have a few of these half-breed Golden, but not the leaders.' He stands, walks a few paces into the star-lit, fire-lit darkness. Then, turning, 'Tell me, master of Kasabaarde. Tell me they won't build their cursed city up again, tell me there'll be no 'Breed science discovered again on the Desert Coast.'

'As to that . . .' Our eyes meet; his are humorous, thinking of 'Breed science in another city: Kasabaarde. 'I cannot promise, *s'an* Kerys. What is done in Tathcaer and the Hundred Thousand you may command. I have but a small city, and no warriors to crusade against Kel Harantish or Quarth or Psamnol if they rediscover 'Breed trickery.'

Some of his Seconds are here to consult him. I wait while they speak. They avoid looking at me. Kasabaarde's reputation is not entirely wholesome. Kerys returns, rubbing his hand across his eyes. Night darkens as the fires fail. He holds his cloak round himself. Desert nights are cold.

'It must go no further. This—' his arm sweeps out to include the ruins '—is the first step on the road, and the road ends where? At the Glittering Plain? In ruined Elansir? With the Hundred Thousand as dead as Eriel? No, master. We remember that destruction too well, and it must never come again. And – I do not believe we can choose, take what's good and leave the bad.'

'Another way, then?'

His face is shadowed, but the voice is clear. 'I can keep all 'Breed science out of my Hundred Thousand, make it forbidden by the church; I can begin to find that other way, yes. But what of the Desert Coast? If I forbid such weaponry, then we're defenceless. I'd let Kel Harantish do what it wishes in its own borders, why not? But would it end there; what would we do, finding them at the gates of Tathcaer? You cannot send swords against weapons that melt stone.'

'So you'd keep 'Breed weapons for their attack? And they, likewise, for yours?'

'And there is the road again, and destruction at the end of it!'

The stars are blotted out over the city by the pall of smoke. Flashes of blue light and sharp explosions mark the destruction of hoarded Golden technology. Kerys beckons. I rise and walk beside him, over pavements cracked by heat. The acrid smell comes on the wind, and the sound of flames. This garrison city: shattered with explosions, obscured by drifting smoke, and choking with the stink of burning – and worse.

'Easier to follow the Golden way and hope to avoid their end. Harder to make our own way. But still, master, we must try. And if we have not the weapons to defeat 'Breed technology, then we must do it by cunning and misdirection and stealth.' He smiles. The humour is genuine. 'Our ancestors deceived the Goldens themselves. Surely we can outwit this so-called Emperor-in-Exile.'

'It would be no advantage to Kasabaarde to see the Golden Empire come again.'

'Nor any advantage to Kasabaarde's Hexenmeister.'

'That too, *s'an* Kerys. I cannot control Kel Harantish, but I think it unlikely that any Desert Coast city would ally with them, no, and no Rainbow City either.'

'And this is done – how?'

'They must trade, *s'an*, and they must pass Kasabaarde. And we are always open – to those who abhor Witchbreed and all their works.'

Kasabaarde's power now is an accident of geography: to reach the Southland ports from the Desert Coast, ships must sail up the coast to Kasabaarde, re-provisioning, and then on up to the

Archipelago. This is not to say that certain ships can't sail across the ocean to the Eastern Isles and thus directly to Ales-Kadareth – only that such ships must use all their hold-space for provisions, and thus cannot trade. Ships that go that way are passenger ships, or warships. Warships have no need to reprovision at Kasabaarde: another welcome accident.

Kerys stops, one hand on my shoulder. 'We too must trade. But we are a rich land. I think we could survive without Kasabaarde's blessing if we had to.'

Conscious of the pressure of his hand, of being alone and far from my people, I am careful in answering.

'Would you have to, s'an Kerys? There has always been friend-ship between the Brown Tower and the White City.'

'Kasabaarde and Tathcaer, yes. Yes.' His hand moves, links into his belt beside the *harur* blades. 'Sometimes, master, I wonder if we are wiser trusting you than we were trusting Kel Harantish.'

'Would you be here otherwise?'

'Perhaps, and perhaps not.'

He does not look much, this man, to have pulled order out of the long chaos after the Empire's fall. A tan skin, a brown braided mane, and whiteless sea-blue eyes; the diamond-patterns of care incised deeply on his skin. But to see him move, act . . .

And he will create the *telestres* out of chaos, the church out of necessity, and be remembered not for what he did, but – in the manner of legends when past-dreams have not yet made them clear – also for what he might have done. I alone will remember, and know.

'You may trust Kasabaarde,' I say, 'for as long as I am Hexen-meister of it.'

By his glance, I can tell that some rumours have come to his ears. And Kel Harantish burns—

The birth-pains of antiquity:

'—cheated me!' the voice echoes in the vast hexagonal rooms. 'And so I destroyed him.'

Turning from the shattered instruments of glass and copper, I watch Santhendor'lin-sandru. A few sphere-lights glow blue, bob-bing in the still air, clustering to follow him as he paces. Others are only blackened sphere-shells, burnt out and clinging in the upper angles of the halls. Tenebrous darkness webs itself into those corners of translucent grey stone.

'Cheated you, Emperor?'

'I gave him everything!' Santhendor'lin-sandru faces me. Tall and slender, gold-skinned, his unbound mane like white fire. Yellow animal eyes in a face so beautiful that it is desecration for it to look angry, greedy, petulant – as it does now.

'How long did he work, and feed me promises? How long?' The cold-toned voice speaking the liquid, multisyllabic tongue of Archonis. 'And for nothing! So that it comes down to this, you cheat me no longer, Eyr'ra Thel Siawn. Never, no, never again.'

He steps through the vast span of the window-arch, seemingly into void; but a chill shimmer of air supports him, the bubble-field that keeps out the bone-cold northland wind. Archonis lies like a well of light, holding in its stone hand the Six Lakes and the river that flows through them to the inland sea.

'And did he fail, Emperor?' Which, I realizel is what I've come to discover; having spoken with Thel Siawn before that erratic genius's death. Was he allowed time to complete his work?

'He brought me nothing!' The beginning of that hysterical anger to which the Emperor is prone. His back to the sprawling city, he throws out an arm, animal-graceful, pointing into the blue glow of the wrecked chamber. Precise machines lay warped and shattered. 'All this I gave him! The first beastman to lay hands on the old science – irony, that! – so that what we created becomes itself a creator . . . and *nothing*! Am I to be put off, delayed, lied to?'

Behind him, Archonis's lights burn in the crepuscular northern night. Strings of sphere-lights; the hills above the lakes are speckled, freckled with blue, the sky beaded with towers of light that drown a skyful of stars. And for all that, the light is like a single sphere in a great dark hall: it serves barely to illuminate the edges and lower storeys of the city's cyclopean architecture.

Low towers border the nearer lake. Black beads line the rims, like shrivelled fruit. Severed heads. Closer, and you would see how many are wind-dried and dessicated, how many yet bleed.

I follow Santhendor'lin-sandru back into the chamber. The stone echoes as we walk: the brush of footsteps, the low hums and clicks of machinery, the roar of distant flyers in the night sky. There is a taste of dust in the air, despite all that the force-fields can do. A taste of chill, as if the lake-mist could creep inside.

'So Thel Siawn is dead.'

The angel calmness returns to his hawk-face. 'But I should never have trusted him. They are nothing more than animals, these beastmen, they never will be. Never let them into your bed.'

He watches me, and I am careful to give nothing away.

'*You* are some kind of friend to them, I've heard.'

'Friend? No.'

But I know now that Thel Siawn did succeed. Succeeded, and

made use of Santhendor'lin-sandru's desires. Perhaps he was the genius I call him. Certainly he in his short life made more use of the old sciences of biology and gene-sculpting than we have since the Arrival.

'Cousin, you are quiet.'

It smells dry and arid here. Sphere-lights tingle on the skin, the links of metal-cloth slide as I walk. No scent-fountains play. And it is free now of that rank mustiness that no scent-fountain can ever disguise, that of our creations, the beastmen, the slaves.

'It occurs to me . . .'

'Well?'

'You allowed him experiments sculpting viruses, and it is true that many cures for beastmen's sicknesses have come from here. And yet – if that were not all? If there were diseases here to harm *us*, and they were let loose on the world?'

Which is an irony he might appreciate, if he ever knew, having bedded Thel Siawn and thus almost certainly begun the long spreading of a sculpted virus and a certain effect.

'I shall have these halls decontaminated, cousin; and – for your excellent advice – you may stay here and oversee the work.'

There are tendrils of darkness in the city, patches of shadow on the massive stone. Or do I dream, and is Archonis still as he sees it: the brilliant beating heart of the cities of the world, the fountainhead of the infinite sun of Golden rule?

Santhendor'lin-sandru will sire no more children, nor will any whom he beds, nor any whom they touch – spreading out from the middle lands to all the reaches of the Empire. They will turn on each other when they know, fight bloody wars; the Elansiir will be desert, this a barren wasteland of dead cities; the north will become the Twilight Shore, and Eriel pass to leave only a glittering plain. Sterile, this Empire, and terrible its passing.

'There is something else we might do, first.'

'Kyrianshur'na-rian, yes.'

There are places in the south, I've heard, where a Golden woman might find refuge, beyond the Rasrhe-y-Meluur. And we will need refuges when the last of us – long-lived as we are – fall into the hands of Thel Siawn's people.

His embrace is cruel, rapid, welcome. When I leave him I will bear a gift he knows nothing of. In the slick angles of the hall I see our merged reflection, Golden woman and Golden man, and Thel Siawn's ghost with us for ever.

Santhendor'lin-sandru, who in the beast-tongue is remembered as slavemaster and roadbuilder, and as Sandor, the Last Emperor.

*

Pain:

And I am not made up of these brief interruptions, these turning-points, however vital. I am the sum total of thousands of winter days walking the sleeping fields, of summers in the ships on the Inner Sea. Uncounted thousands of days: eating, sleeping, working, coupling; and coming at last to the Brown Tower. These unnoticed days touching the earth, under the changing sky; these made me.

And I am the constructed beastmen, offspring of Golden and fenborn; and all their long descendants in the south. And I am Witchbreed, in the infinite summer of the Empire; a golden richness that lay on the world uncounted thousand years.

In the cold reaches of my memory there is more:

—stars visible even at noon. Our shadows fall blackly to the pole of the world. The fierce sun that parents this world makes life impossible for us at the equator.

Wind rustles the vegetation. The others of the Set are down by the water, overseeing the servitors. I scuttle towards them, hesitate, then pass them and go on to the hilltop.

The pillars of the henge gleam in the sun, the capstones black and dead. I pick my way over the mossy ground to the centre of the circle and rear up into the rest-position. Empty archways surround me. Through them I see lowland, river, distant hills, and the few of us who remain alive.

I have seen these archways when they glowed, each one opening to a separate world, a jewel-box of landscapes, skies, stars and seas.

– It's useless, Keeper –

The Second has followed me, glitter-eyed as she has been since the catastrophe. I answer gently.

– There are too few of us, we cannot activate the Set. No one will pass through. The worlds are closed to us –

Claws strike chitin, she is grieving.

– Singer is dead –

– It is better, I think –

Emergencies happen, accidents happen. But to lose First, Third and Fourth in one contact; to have the Flyer and the Focus mindless, and the Nightsearcher and the Singer dead . . .

– We'll never be a Set again, Keeper. We're on this world for good now, aren't we? –

– Yes –

– And our lives? –

There is no kindness in untruth.

– We're too far from the centre to reproduce. This is all there will ever be of us. But even this far from the centre, our lives will be long –

– Longer than we wish? –

– Perhaps so –

She shivers down her whole length, and turns to watch the few of us that are left: the Favoured, the Breathstealer, the Shadower. And, of course, the servitors.

– Will the servitors adapt to this world, Keeper? Will they breed? –

– I think so. In any case there is life closer to the equator, biped humanoid, very similar to the servitors. We can adapt them to our needs –

– That is good. I would not spend my last aeons alone –

The light, the cool wind, the scent of running water; all are strange to me. I wonder how long it will take for them to become over-familiar.

– We must leave the histories here –

She clicks scorn, her faceted eyes brilliant in the sun.

– Who will find them, Keeper? Who? We are the only travellers. The servitors have no mind-talent. They cannot contact, or connect. None will follow us. None will find us. The worlds are numerous as dust-specks in a sunbeam –

– Nevertheless, I am Keeper. The histories will be preserved –

A servitor comes stilt-legged up the hill, calling us to feed. Small, thick-limbed, wingless; its maned head on a level with mine. Will we change them to live on this world? I wonder; and will they, with their swift generations, outlive us at the last?

Having no power of contact, it bends its jointed stick-thin limbs to approximate the gesture of respect. It has jelly-eyes, with little intelligence in them, but evolution can play strange tricks and flukes. Strange if they were to survive, and raise up empires after we are gone. Eyes like beads, yellow as suns that – I am reminded – we will never see again. I drop out of rest-position to scuttle down the hill . . .

Micro-pain: rejection: fear.

—slick walls, semi-metallic, and the carefully hoarded remnants of technology that remain in the Brown Tower. Moving stiffly, I sit up. The air is cool. There are levels under this, I know, down in the bedrock below the inner city. And above these protected walls the scorched dusty streets of Kasabaarde: I should like to walk in the open now, though I still hold the tactile memory of mossgrass . . .

'Christie, hear me.'

When is this? I wonder. No time feels like the past when experienced. There is only ever Now.

'Are you well?'

A fenborn beside me, mask removed. Were the fenborn ever in Kasabaarde, or is this somewhere else? No, I know his name: Tethmet. The expression on his face is jealousy. And the old man – the Hexenmeister?

How can there be two of us?

He says again: 'Christie?'

'I think . . . I'm not sure. Is this another memory?' I rub my temples, trying to shift the pain. 'When am I going to wake up from this one?'

The fenborn hands me a bowl of liquid; hot, sweet, and stinging. It scours my throat. The physical sensation is an anchor to reality. The old man watches me anxiously.

'That is an effect I didn't anticipate, I am sorry. Believe me, you are out of the machine. This is your direct experience, not my memory.'

'Your memory? Not my memory?' My body aches: bones, joints, tendons, muscles. Looking down, I see unfamiliar hands clasped round the bowl. Stubby short-fingered hands, skin burned dark by Carrick's Star. 'How long . . . how long did it take?'

'It's noon,' the fenborn says, 'you began a little after sunrise.

The old man reassures me. 'Not long, though it seems long to you.'

Details are coming back to me. My head clears. There was something else, wasn't there? Yes. 'You said you wanted to record my memories.' Aware of tension that is fear. 'We'd better get it over and done with.'

'Not necessary, Christie. It was done while you were here.'

'Already? I—'

'It's done,' the old man says. It takes the incomprehension on the fenborn's face to make me realize the words are English. And the old man is looking at me with an expression at once unfamiliar and known, that I have seen before.

In a mirror.

CHAPTER 26

The Players of Ochmir

The sunlight outside the Tower's entrance dazzled me. I blinked water out of my eyes, blinked again – and realized I expected that to dim the brilliance, wanting human muscles to do what they couldn't: bring a third eyelid down. Hastily I put on my mask.

'I need you to come to the Tower again,' the Hexenmeister said. The shadow of the archway hid his face. But the voice, the phrasing, it was too familiar. 'What I know about your world, I find I need explained to me. Perhaps it's the same for you?'

'Yes, I – I'll come back, yes.' Tense, nervous, I waited for something – a needle of pain, maybe, that would wake me to a different reality?

'Be easy,' the old man said. 'It fades, after a time.'

I promised to return, and left him. Walking across the gardens, I was still conscious of unease. Peripheral memories haunted me. Pale-robed Ortheans passed me in the dusty streets, and I stared after them.

I know how it feels to be you, how you carry yourself, veil your eyes with darkness; how fear raises hackles down your spine, stiffens clawed hands. How you breathe and walk, I know.

The walk back to Su'niar was long. I felt uneasy in my own skin.

There were no writing-sticks or parchments available in the Order houses – they're not considered necessities of life – so I paid toll and entered the trade city. It was necessary to make some kind of a report before I lost all the details; I don't have the Hexenmeister's eidetic memory. Grasping remembered visions is like clutching at sand.

Back in Su'niar, while they were strong, I wrote them down. The sexless, illuminated face of Beth'ru-elen, in the days before Peir-Dadeni was founded; Kerys and burning Kel Harantish, at the Southland's birth. And the Golden woman's stark insanity, uncounted ages past in the last days of the Empire. And the

Keeper. Whatever it was. Spanning the ages – but that was rationalization: it felt like yesterday, like today.

Examined from a human point of view, they were often incomprehensible. Memories, like dreams, have their own internal logic.

Stone tubs stood on the flat roof of the tower. Ash-grey and violet-leafed shrubs grew in scarlet moss. Between them were benches, under awnings, and it was possible to sit and look out over the round domes of the inner city to the harbour. Haze hid the daystars.

A humming sound broke the silence. The Hesenmeister glanced at the small dome in the center of the roof-garden. It split open to disclose Tethmet on the lift-platform. The fenborn came towards us, with his usual stare of disapproval for me, and handed a message to the old man.

'This might interest you, Christie,' he said, reading slowly. 'The T'An Suthai-Telestre and the takshiriye have returned to Tathcaer . . . Durestha Firstweek, yes, three weeks back.' He smiled. 'News travels slowly. Sometimes.'

'Any news about the Andrethe's murder?' If they'd caught the killer . . . sudden excitement seized me.

'No, nothing of that. As to the rest of this,' he glanced up at the fenborn, 'say I shall come down to the meeting hall in a short time.'

The fenborn bowed and returned to the lift. I realized I was picking the scarlet moss off the tub beside me. Fragments littered the slick surface of the roof.

'Don't worry,' the old man said, 'they'll discover the killer. She was the Andrethe, she had her guard. She was in the Crystal Hall where she met with her intelligencers – the only time she would be unguarded. And it must have been someone she knew and trusted, else she'd have fought.'

'You're pretty sure I'm innocent.'

'You forget,' his hand tightened on my arm, 'I was there.'

There wasn't the same cross-identity that there had been directly after the transfer, but the closeness still shocked me. When his grip loosened, I stood and walked towards the edge of the roof. The atmosphere shimmered. Sweat dried immediately in the dry heat. I rubbed the back of my neck, where the sun beat down – cropped hair wasn't long enough to be protection. Phantom sensations plagued me: I expected to scratch clawed fingers through the thickness of the spinal mane. Down in the inner city the streets were quiet, but I saw dust rising from the carts in the trade city.

The same scattered crowd sat under the street-awnings. The

individuals changed, but there were always people there. Why not, when the Orders fed, housed, and clothed them? I pulled robe-sleeves down over sun-blackened arms. It was an awkward feeling for me, being a head taller than anyone else. It marked me out: that and my Outlander appearance, and visits to the Tower. And I no longer expected to be different.

The city is a disconcerting place to live. I stood a while longer, looking out over that city where all beliefs are possible: a place of mysticism, idleness, violence, and vision.

'Come inside,' the Hexenmeister said. 'I have a meeting to attend that will also interest you.'

He was painfully slow when he walked. At last we reached the lift-dome, and the light of Carrick's Star gave way to the diffuse illumination of the Tower. I couldn't tell precisely where we stopped; my acquired knowledge was sketchy.

Several of the brown-robes came up to give the Hexenmeister messages. He acknowleged them, continuing towards the meeting hall. It was as bare and functional as all Tower rooms, apart from the old man's quarters. Tethmet supervised the setting of chairs round an oval table, and the provision of herb-tea.

'Let them enter,' the Hexenmsister said, taking the carved chair at the head of the table.

A group of people came in. I recognized Ymirian dress – uncomfortably hot, I thought, and then realized: the Southland, here? Several in Crown Guard uniforms ranged themselves either side of the square-arched door. They were weaponless. The main party entered: a tall woman with a curiously familiar face, some others I'd seen at court, all attended by the Tower's brown-robes.

'Dalzielle Evalen Kerys-Andrethe,' Tethmet announced. '*T'an* Evalen, you are in the presence of the Hexenmeister.'

'Goddess give you good day—' the well-known accents of Ymirian. And the face of this young woman was Suthafiori's, thirty years ago. She looked at me and stopped.

'You have met the Dominion envoy?' the old man inquired.

'I have with me some who have,' she said grimly. 'Haltern!'

He looks harassed as ever, was my first thought. And I'll take bets that he hated every minute of the journey. And coped. And heard every rumour between Tathcaer and Kasabaarde.

'Hal.'

He looked uncertainly at the woman, then at me; then stepped forward and gripped my hands. I thought, has my reputation sunk *that* low?

'I had no news of you after Morvren Freeport. To find you

here—' he shook his head. '*T'an* Evalen, this is Lynne de Lisle Christie.'

It wasn't just the heat that was making the Southlanders uncomfortable. Evalen's narrow fingers linked in her belt by the empty scabbards, and she stared round at the bare brown walls of the Tower before she spoke. Bright clothes that suited Tathcaer were anachronistic here.

I missed Tathcaer's white stone walls, and the northern sea; missed them more than I would have thought possible. The Desert Coast's hot season grated on me.

'Master,' Evalen said, 'you'll understand my reluctance. I refuse to discuss the business of the Hundred Thousand in the presence of the Andrethe's murderer.'

He gave an old man's wheezing chuckle. 'I can answer for nothing else, *t'an*, but of the Andrethe's murder, at least, she is not guilty.'

The woman looked, looked again: a perfect double-take. Exclamations from the other Southlanders were quickly hushed. She said, 'You're telling me she didn't do it?'

'I know she did not.'

An incredulous grin spread over Haltern's face. He looked from the Hexenmeister to Evalen Kerys-Andrethe, and his hand came down on my shoulder in a congratuatory slap.

'Perfect,' he said under his breath, 'perfect!'

'If the envoy didn't do it, who did?' Evalen demanded.

'That I do not yet know, or I would have sent word to your mother.'

Recalled to her duties, she executed a formal bow. 'The *T'An Suthai-Telestre* sends her regards and greetings to you, master.'

He acknowledged that, and gestured at the table. 'If you will be seated.'

She took the chair at the foot of the table. In the confusion as the Southlanders arranged themselves, she leaned across to me.

'I apologize, *t'an*, for what I said. News of this hasn't reached Tathcaer, and I still believed—'

'That's all right,' I said hastily. 'We'll discuss Tathcaer later, if that's possible.'

'Of course.'

When I could speak to Haltern without being noticed, I said 'Will they credit it in the Hundred Thousand, just on the Hexenmeister's word?'

'It carries weight with some. Though not in Peir-Dadeni, you'll find.' He pushed a six-fingered hand through his pale cropped mane, blinking worriedly at me. 'And they'd be better pleased knowing who is guilty, if the envoy isn't – but a clever move, nonetheless.'

I smiled.

He said 'You've changed.'

He didn't seem displeased. I wondered what he saw, shrewd as he was.

'Meduenin said he left you at the Freeport,' he added. 'I thought we might find you somewhere on the Desert Coast, though not here.'

'You've spoken to Blaize?'

'He's with the rest of *t'an* Evalen's company, back in the trade city. Your young *l'ri-an*, too.'

'Rodion's here?' I want to talk to them, I thought. 'Listen, Hal, what's all this about?'

He shrugged, amused. 'The Hexenmeister seems to require your presence in our discussions, and the Southland commonly humours his eccentricities. If you stay, Christie, you'll hear.'

Not like this I won't, I thought. Formalities between the Hundred Thousand and the Brown Tower are lengthy and formidable, and Evalen seemed determined to plough through all of them. The Hexenmeister's interviews were short – I tended to forget quite how old he was – and if they weren't finished soon, I could see nothing constructive being done before tomorrow.

'So what does Suthafiori want with the Brown Tower?'

Haltern's veiled eyes resolved into clarity. 'What anyone requires of the Hexenmeister – knowledge. Knowledge of Kel Harantish. It's apparent now that SuBannasen wasn't the only Southlander taking gold from the Emperor-in-Exile.'

The meeting reconvened after the noon meal (and after the old man had slept for a while, I think). This time it took place in the library, being less formal, and a lot of the Southlanders' tension vanished on finding they were not underground, and had windows open to the sunlight. It could have been any library in the Hundred Thousand, that room, and no one surrounded by books could fail to be reminded of the Tower's reputation for knowledge. The old man set his stage very carefully.

Afternoon sun illuminated the table, and the tea-bowls and fruit and sweetmeats. Tethmet stood behind the Hexenmeister's chair, watching us with the silent dislike for strangers that many of the Tower brown-robes had. His devotion to the old man was fanatical. Evalen bowed as she entered, and motioned the two Southlanders with her to sit at the table. Both took notes throughout. Haltern joined us, leaving the unarmed Crown Guard outside the chamber. The door slid shut behind him, and he flinched.

'Now,' the Hexenmeister said, 'what does Suthafiori say to me?'

'You'll have heard of unrest in the Hundred Thousand,' Evalen said, with complete confidence that he would know as much about the Southland as the child of the *T'An Suthai-Telestre*.

'Yes, and – if I may say this, Christie – much of it centred round this matter of other worlds.'

Evalen nodded. 'It's natural there should be those for and against the matter. But if it were only that, the *T'An* Suthafiori would not need to fear the loss of the Crown at Midsummer.'

'The loss—' I broke off at the Hexenmeister's gesture.

'It has always been the policy of your land not to obstruct the opinions of the Hundred Thousand. If they do not desire contact with the Dominion . . .'

'If that was all it was!' She glanced at me. 'And even so, if the Southland wants nothing to do with Earth, that's not to say Earth won't go to other lands on Orthe. Isn't that so, *t'an*?'

'That's so,' I agreed.

'Saberon, Kasabaarde, Kel Harantish even,' she elaborated, 'all willing, for their own reasons. And there's the Hundred Thousand left to come in rag, tag, and bobtail after the crowd, on Earth's conditions and not our own! Because it *will* come, we can't ignore it. All we can do is try and control the speed of it.' Her hands caught the sunlight, skin gleaming with a grainy quality. Faint marshflower-dapples were visible on her bony wrists. 'Whatever eventual relationship there is between our worlds, envoy, the changes should be introduced gradually. Perhaps over generations. That's always been the way with change in the Hundred Thousand.'

'I can't say yet what the Dominion's policy will be. It's part of my job to gain information to help them decide.' They'd pay lip-service to sociology, I thought, but the truth of it was that Orthe was a backwater world, and liable to remain so. Or *was* that true, with the remnants of Golden technology left here? 'One thing occurs to me, *t'an* Evalen, and that's medical technology.'

The Hexenmeister said, 'There is much you have that we need desperately. Most knowledge was lost when the Witchbreed fell. I grant there are physicians, the best of them in the Southland's church; but fevers and pestilence, wounds, sickness, childbirth . . .'

Steam coiled up from the bowls, and the scent of *arniac* herb-tea permeated the still air.

'If you have aids against such things on your world,' Evalen said, 'would they be acceptable to us here?'

'High level medicine demands high level technology to back it, *t'an*, and your church may object. Unless you'd keep it on a basis of trading for medical supplies . . . but that brings me back to my original point,' I said, 'which is that Orthe isn't a densely-populated world, and any Earth disease you have no immunity to could prove very serious.'

The old man nodded. 'Another year of the White Death could reduce us to Barrens savagery, and who's to say there aren't such plagues on your world.'

'Therefore you need restricted contact with the Dominion. Ideally Orthe should have some kind of quarantine.' That was a familiar concept to the Southland, at least, and I saw Evalen nod agreement.

'And for that you must have a Crown who supports Earth,' she said. 'Suthafiori bid me say it need not be her, but in truth I think there's only she that can do it.'

'It's not my business to fight Suthafiori's battles for her,' the Hexenmeister said testily. 'The Tower doesn't interfere outside Kasabaarde's walls. If she's to be named Crown again, then let the Southland name her.'

'If it was the Southland alone, I shouldn't be here,' Evalen persisted. 'Admitted, there is a strong faction who hold out for no contact with Earth at all – Howice *T'An* Roehmonde for one, and Thu'ell *T'An* Rimon, and perhaps the Seamarshal of Morvren Freeport.'

He chuckled. 'I know the Hundred Thousand too well to be concerned over a few of the *T'Ans*. The *telestres* are quite capable of going off and constituting themselves a new Crown and *takshiriye*, and leaving you and Howice and Suthafiori looking silly.'

'That is their ancient right,' she said stiffly, over the laughter that went round the room. Then, as she relaxed, genuine concern showed on her face. 'Yes, I think – I hope – most are opposed to Earth out of their own convictions. But some aren't, master. There's evidence that much of that party's support doesn't come from the Southland, but from Kel Harantish and the Emperor-in-Exile.'

It was quiet enough to hear boots grate on the smooth floor as one of the guards fidgeted. The Hexenmeister's eyes became bright. 'Now is that so?'

'Several minor affairs point to that city.' Evalen watched me, still speaking to him. 'It occurs to me, master, that if the envoy is guiltless of the Andrethe's death, that too might find a home in Kel Harantish.'

He lowered his hand as if to strike the table, touched it softly instead, and swore archaic oaths under his breath. His fingers moved blindly, following the grain of the wood. 'Now that's not proved.'

'Not proved, but likely?' she appealed.

'It must be looked into,' he said absently. 'Yes . . . Harantish behind a Southland conspiracy? You know your own people, *t'an* Evalen, is it likely?'

'I would have said nothing was less likely,' she admitted, 'nothing – unless it was visitors from the stars. So, one being possible, why not the other?'

'That's supposition, not fact.'

'I have details that my people will give you later. What Sutha-fiori asks is this, master: knowledge of Kel Harantish's affairs, and, I'm now forced to add, knowledge of Kanta Andrethe's murder. Will you help us?'

'I'll see what may be discovered.' He was sitting hunched up, mouth puckered with weariness. A tendril from his crest-mane strayed down towards the veiled eyes, deep in their nest of wrinkles. His hands shook. 'I'm not convinced of Kel Harantish's involvement; you must show me your evidence.'

I got bogged down in the talk of corruption and past scandal that followed. Names and places were familiar to me – but not from my own memories. I nibbled one of the edible fungi, with its pepper-and-spice flavour. It tasted subtly different. My standards of comparison were Orthean.

And I thought about Sulis n'ri n'suth SuBannasen, and treachery, and the game the Hundred Thousand play that isn't *ochmir*.

Evalen was stocky for an Orthean, broad across the shoulders. Her mane, growing out of a short crop, lay damply against her brown skin. Most of Suthafiori's gestures found a muffled echo in her – the way she sprawled back, fingers linked, slurring an Ymirian-accented version of the trade-tongue. But the blunt plodding manner she had was all her own, and concealed a surprising, if slow, intelligence.

'We'll continue later, master, if we may,' she said. 'I'm at your direction, of course, but I should see my company settled in their quarters. Tomorrow?'

He inclined his head. 'The Tower will investigate further, *t'an*. And the envoy, also, will stay in the city? There should be further discussions concerning Peir-Dadeni.'

'Of course,' I agreed. As things stood, Kasabaarde was still safer for me than Tathcaer.

*

I walked back with Haltern as far as the gate to the trade city.

'You'll stay with our company?' He squinted at me, in the glare of that long spring afternoon.

'No.' I saw an expression on his face that was half personal disappointment, and half professional curiosity. 'It's more practical at the moment, the way my finances are, if I stay in one of the Order houses.'

He laughed. 'You know we'll loan you whatever you need.'

'I know, but I'd as soon not be in debt. In any case . . .'

'Yes?' he prompted.

'Not being practical, there are still reasons why I'd like to stay in the inner city.' I couldn't frame them, somehow. But I found the words that made sense to Haltern: 'Your Beth'ru-elen stayed here, after all.'

CHAPTER 27

News from Tathcaer

His fair-maned head towered over the crowds as he came up the covered street, obviously searching for something. He was barefoot, the white dust crusting on his skin. Empty scabbards hung at his belt, and his shirt was unlaced. I saw him pull it off and sling it across his shoulder. Paired nipples showed under the dust that grimed him. His mane straggled out of a crop-cut, rooted down his bony spine. Eyes alert, nictitating membrane closed against the bright evening light.

Even in that city of masks, he left his scarred face uncovered.

'Christie!' he called, coming over and dropping down on his haunches beside me on the Order-house steps. 'Sunmother! What are you doing in this madman's city?'

'Waiting,' I said. 'You took your time. Haltern tell you where I was?'

'If I depended on *him* to know what's happening—' he stopped. 'I forgot, he's a friend of yours.'

'Mmm. What do you reckon on him?'

'Haltern n'ri n'suth Beth'ru-elen?' He shrugged. 'If you played *ochmir* with him, you'd never be able to catch him cheating.'

It might or might not be a compliment. It was certainly true.

'So how's Tathcaer?' I asked.

'I saw your *t'an* Huxton, he took your package. And I think kept silent that he'd had news from you, it wasn't known in the city when I left.' Blaize sat on the steps, removing a leather pouch from his belt. 'He sends this to you. There's a letter in your own tongue, he'd not send a message by word of mouth.'

Huxton had obviously written at a near-hysterical pitch of anger. He wanted to know where I was, what the hell I was doing there, and in any case I should stop it and get back to Tathcaer at once, and for god's sake have a good explanation for what happened in Peir-Dadeni. I read it and chuckled. Whether the head of a xeno-team had technical superiority to an envoy or vice-versa was open

299

to doubt, and I was going back to Tathcaer only when I considered it safe.

'I've another message,' he said.

'Who from?'

'The *T'An* Melkathi Ruric Orhlandis.' He rubbed the bridge of his nose with his fingers, eyes tightened with concentration. 'She says, The envoy's supposed murder of the Andrethe is a major scandal in Tathcaer now, and will be until after the naming of the new Crown. There have been attempts on the lives of some of Suthafiori's party. Advise you to stay overseas until the matter's settled, and the killer found.'

'Mmm . . .' Investigating the pouch further, I found cords of silver and bronze beads. That was one worry off my mind. 'Is she well?'

'She seems so, yes.' He gave a scarred lopsided smile. 'As to that about Suthafiori's party, that's true enough; there have been assassins sent against Orhlandis and Hanathra. All failed. And, being a known associate of yours, I found no employment myself until *T'An* Ruric hired me to travel with Rodion.'

If Tathcaer was that dangerous, I could see why Ruric would want Rodion as far away as possible. Although, being Orthean, she'd also use Rodion as her eyes and ears on the *t'an* Evalen's delegation.

The Meduenin looked tense. I said, 'What's the matter with you?'

'Me?' He seemed surprised. 'Nothing.'

'You think all of Evalen's party are trustworthy?'

'Yes, that's safe enough. As far as it's possible to tell.' One of the Su'niar Order brushed past him, going into the house. He moved aside quickly. The curved shutters were going up in the street as the evening shadows lengthened. Like most Orders, the Su'niar lived on the house's lower floors, but slept in the ground-level domes. Blaize said, 'Why do you stay here, Christie?'

'That's the second time I've been asked that. I like it here.'

'It bothers me,' he said, and I remembered he'd been in Kasa-baarde before. 'No decent food, no music, and crazy-headed luna-tics for company. No, give me the trade city every time.'

'I admit I could stand a drink and a good game of *ochmir* from time to time.'

'No *ochmir*, not in the inner city. It's under ban. You'll have to come to us for that.'

'I will,' I said, affectionately. He was sitting with shoulders hunched, hands linked between his knees. 'Blaize, I'm glad you're here. I wish you'd tell me what's worrying you, though.'

He lifted his head. 'Christie, can I ask you something?'

'You can ask me anything.'

He still hesitated. Then at last said, 'Your *l'ri-an*, Rodion.'

'You've seen her more recently than I have.'

'I suppose I never took much notice of her at Shiriya-Shenin – her being *ashiren* – but now coming from Tathcaer, she's . . .' he moved his hand helplessly, searching for words. 'I didn't think I'd ever . . . but she's so young. And now I . . .'

I thought, she's still a child! But that was a human attitude, and my instincts now were for the Orthean.

'Are you *arykei*?'

He didn't answer directly. 'I can't take her back to Meduenin, even if it is my *telestre*. And how will it look if I come grubbing round Orhlandis to become *n'ri n'suth*?'

Looking at him, I was conscious of a regret that I'd sent him to Tathcaer. I felt as if I'd been shown a possibility and had it denied, all in the one moment. Rodion . . . ah well.

'How would it look?' I threw the question back at him.

'It'll look like some out-at-elbows mercenary come cap in hand to the *T'An* Melkathi's *telestre*, that's how.' One hand rubbed his scarred face. 'Christie, what do I do?'

'What does she say, herself?' Then, seeing his face, 'You've spoken to her, haven't you? Blaize, have you told her any of this?'

'I was waiting – I don't know what I was waiting for.' He sounded angry with himself. Then his eyes cleared. 'You're close to me as any kinsister. If you get the chance, will you talk to her? Don't say anything about . . . just see what kind of a woman you'd take her for.'

'Sure,' I said. 'You think I'm the one to judge?'

'You're the one I'm asking.'

'All right, all right. Shall I see you up at the Tower with Evalen and her people?'

'Not if I can help it.' He stood up to go. 'I wouldn't enter the Brown Tower for all the gold in a Mercenaries' Guildhouse. See you in the trade city, Christie.'

The discussions resumed on Sixday, again in the Tower's library. The *t'an* Evalen brought Haltern with her, as a scribe; and the Hexenmeister kept Tethmet-fenborn by him.

'Regarding Kel Harantish,' Evalen said when the formalities were over, 'and the matter of the Andrethe's death, it seems to me that the solving of the one would do much to counteract the influence of the other. If the envoy were *proved* to be innocent –

301

and the killer found – that would remove much of the prejudice against Outworlders, and so make it more probable that Kerys-Andrethe retains the Crown.'

'You'd be well-advised in any case to discover the real murderer,' the old man said, and the sly humour in his voice went unnoticed.

'So,' Evalen went on doggedly, 'can you help us, master?'

'I know a little of the matter.' He proceeded to outline events as he (or rather I) had seen them. It wasn't something I enjoyed recalling.

My seat was opposite the window. Chill air drifted in, with the scent of *arniac* flower on it. The sun had barely risen. I couldn't see it, the window faced west, but the light sent damp shadows across the city's straight roads. Far in the distance, beyond the domes and the last pillar of the Rasrhe-y-Meluur, the pylon tipped with gold, a blue haze hid the High Desert. Soon the sun would burn all the coolness out of the air.

'I'll say this,' the old man observed, 'that if it were done by order of the Emperor-in-Exile, then he could hardly have chosen a better victim than Kanta Andrethe. She was loved beyond the Peir-Dadeni *telestres*.'

Haltern inclined his head respectfully to the old man, then to Evalen. 'Your pardon, but it was not so in one case. SuBannasen *telestre* have no cause to love her, and though Sulis is dead, there are still others who bear the name. Remember, the Kel Harantish gold came by ship to Ales-Kadareth; SuBannasen is close to the city.'

'They'd not risk it now, not with the Orhlandis named *T'An* Melkathi,' Evalen objected. 'But . . . I wouldn't like to say that Witchbreed gold isn't still finding its way to the Hundred Thousand.'

'Could a SuBannasen have murdered the Andrethe?' the Hexenmeister wondered aloud. 'As revenge for Sulis's death. And then seen an opportunity, and put the blame on the envoy?'

Evalen frowned. 'You said the killer would be one she trusted. She'd never trust any SuBannasen so close, then.'

Haltern said, 'She sometimes saw her intelligencers in the Crystal Hall. That's why there were few guards, so they could come and go secretly. That might have been known to someone, and so they could come upon her when she was unprepared.'

'Now, was it planned or unplanned?' The Hexenmeister shifted in his chair, and the fenborn bent over him and tucked the pelt close round his knees. At a quiet word, he left the room. The old man continued, 'By that I mean, was it a chance killing, and the

302

blame afterwards put on the Dominion envoy because that was convenient? Or was it deliberately planned to discredit Christie's people?'

There was some speculation, inconclusive on both sides. Tethmet returned with bowls of hot *arniac* tea. While we were drinking, I had to go over all the circumstances of my last day in Shiriya-Shenin.

'Someone knew your movements,' Haltern said. His hands cupped a blue glazed bowl, steam coiling over the surface of the crimson liquid. 'Someone knew you were at court, not at Beth'ruelen, and that you were close at hand in Firstwall.'

'You saw the body?' the Hexenmeister said suddenly to Haltern.

'Yes. I was present when it was examined.'

'What were the precise nature of the wounds?'

Haltern's eyes clouded, cleared. 'The knife had been driven into the throat, severing the great vein—'

'Whose knife, is it known?'

'Mine,' I admitted, 'it went missing some time before.'

'Planned, then,' the Hexenmeister said over the talk, as they realized what he meant. 'Planned beforehand to discredit the envoy. What other injuries were there?'

Haltern gave him a curious look, as if he had not expected that question. 'The skull was bruised, there were scratches and contusions on the arms, and some claws broken on the hands. It was assumed she fell when she was struck with the knife, and then perhaps was dragged to the chair where she was found.'

I sipped from the tea-bowl, then put it down. Nausea made me dizzy.

The old man scratched absently at the thin crest of his mane. He seemed shrunken with age, especially in the company of tall Southlanders, but he dominated the room with his presence.

'Could it not also have been,' he suggested, 'that she was struck first on the head? And if so, and if that did not make her unconscious and she fought her attacker – there were other injuries, you say – perhaps she was only killed as a last resort. Perhaps,' he said into the quiet of that morning-chill room, 'she was only killed because she recognized the woman or man who struck her.'

After a moment Evalen said 'For what purpose?'

'I know Southlanders, and the Peir-Dadeni. I do not think anyone she trusted to come to the Crystal Hall would normally have killed her. After all,' he said, turning to me, 'if the envoy were found to have attacked the Andrethe, that would have been sufficient to turn many against the Dominion.'

'What reason could they possibly give?' I was bewildered. 'I've no more reason to attack her than I had to kill her.'

'They would have believed it,' Evalen stated. 'All Outworlders are crazy – pardon, *t'an* Christie, but that's a popular view among the ignorant – and they would not have lacked people to credit the story.'

The Hexenmeister roused himself from his thoughts. 'So. We have a murder possibly done on the spur of the moment, but since it's done, it can still be blamed on the envoy. So they must have Christie there in that room within a very few minutes. They call you to the Andrethe's presence—'

'No one called me,' I said. 'Rodion told me I was wanted . . . Rodion! But she couldn't commit murder!'

Haltern shook his head. 'She was *ashiren* then, and that was a blow needing full strength.'

'Perhaps they planned to call you,' the Hexenmeister continued to speculate. 'Then who comes? The Halfgold, the envoy's *l'ri-an*, who can be trusted with a seemingly innocent message . . . yes, it could have happened that way.'

'Meduenin said—'

'Yes!' Haltern set his bowl down with a clatter, turning to Evalen. '*T'an*, there were assassins sent against Orhlandis *telestre*, as you know. It was assumed they wanted the life of the *T'An* Ruric, but maybe that was wrong. It could have been *t'an* Rodion.'

Her pale brows came together. 'Why has she never spoken?'

'She may not realize what she knows.'

'That's quickly answered, then.' Evalen called one of her guards. 'Find Ruric Rodion Orhlandis and bring her here. Now!'

One of the brown-robes accompanied the guard out.

It took time to find her. The fenborn brought fresh bowls of *arniac* tea, while the company discussed those *telestres* that had had representatives at Shiriya-Shenin that winter.

Apprehension turned me cold. I don't believe it, I thought. I don't believe I'm going to find out the answer. And if I do, will I like the answer I get?

The sun dispersed the haze, and pale buildings reflected back fierce light. I leaned against the edge of the window. We were high up. Among the domes and alleys, the broad covered canals formed a grid, bright in the morning sun. The air felt dry, motionless. I thought about Shiriya-Shenin, about the Fifthwall docks where the north wind could snatch the breath out of your mouth and leave you gasping. And here – still Durestha Forthweek, the beginning of spring – sweat collected in every crease of flesh, and the day's heat reflected back from brick walls to glare in unprotected eyes.

I heard a stir outside, and made my way back to my seat. The doors slid open and the guard and brown-robes returned.

Blaize n'ri n'suth Meduenin followed them. Unarmed, light-footed, tense. I saw him glance once round the book-filled room, eyes wide enough that the whites were visible, and then he stood back against the wall by the door.

Of course, I thought. Hired to guard her, so he has to come.

Rodion halted in the doorway. The fenborn drew in breath, even the Hexenmeister stared. I hardly recognized her. Only six weeks, I thought, marvelling. The first time I'd seen the swift Orthean change from child to adult.

She had her mother's slender wiry frame and alert attitude, but the poise was all her own. The fine silver mane was cropped in Ymirian style, framing her high angular face, and her yellow eyes were wide. A sleeveless tunic laced over Ymirian britches, and empty *harur* scabbards hung at her belt. Taller than when I'd left her, sleeping out the fever of the change; narrow-hipped and high-breasted as Orthean woman are, and with something entirely new in the way she carried herself.

The memory brought fear so strong I could taste it: Sandor's hawk-gold face. Evalen, Haltern, the Hexenmeister, did they also have that resurrection of ancient memories? Inhumanly beautiful, a Halfgold more than ever the image of the Witchbreed.

Then she looked round nervously, swallowed, and it became apparent that we had to do with a young Southland woman and nothing else.

'Rodion,' the Hexenmeister said gently, 'I have some questions about the Shiriya-Shenin court that you can perhaps answer.'

'Yes, master,' she said dutifully, curiosity and fear mingled in her voice; the effect of the Hexenmeister's reputation outside Kasabaarde.

I stared at the table while he asked her innocent questions. I didn't want to look at her, be accused of prompting her; I wanted to hear the truth. *T'an* Evalen waited quietly, betraying no impatience. Haltern sat with eyes hooded, studying her urbanely.

'—you told Christie that the Andrethe wanted her.' The Hexenmeister paused and, almost as an aside, said, 'Who gave you that message, by the way, do you remember?'

'Yes, I remember,' she said with the untempered honesty of the young. 'I met him outside the Crystal Hall. It was Brodin n'ri n'suth Charain.'

CHAPTER 28

Havoth-jair

The air was still.

Ridge-backed lizards crawled on the stones at the edge of the road, basking in the heat. Their movements were abrupt, thin tails flicking like whips. Our footsteps grated on rock. As we approached, their ridged crests rose, opened, and became wings, and the whole flock skittered into the air. Wings hummed in the silence. Then there was nothing but the noise of footsteps and the rustle of cloth.

Blaize looked up at the hazy sky. 'There'll be no wind today.'

'Nor tomorrow, nor the next day, nor the next.' Rodion's voice gritted with irritation. 'How long are we meant to wait?'

'As long as it takes.'

'If there was a wind,' I said, 'you wouldn't be walking the country round Kasabaarde, you'd be on the *Child of Methemna* and halfway back to Tathcaer by now.'

'Ahh.' She made a disgusted sound, and shrugged. 'Conjure up one of your magic ships, *S'aranth*, fly us home.'

'I wish I could.'

The road led between irrigated fields, where pale green *del'ri* already had half its height. Dusty crimson *arniac* shrubs grew among the slender knobbed *del'ri* stems. The land was flat, and the road – the beginning of the great trade routes down the Desert Coast – was raised only a few inches above it. Across the miles of *del'ri* fields, the crags and dunes of the High Desert shimmered in the heat. Shining mirages of water patched the road ahead, only to vanish as we came closer. Kasabaarde glimmered, small in the distance.

'I'll check ahead,' Blaize said. The dust of a train of carts was visible, coming from the city. He increased his pace.

It was mid-afternoon. The days were lengthening now. I'd never had any problems coping with the extra hours of darkness – perhaps because I was so starved of sleep before I came to Shiriya-

Shenin – but the extra daylight hours proved wearying. I usually slept an hour or two around noon to compensate. Besides, it was too hot to do anything else.

Rodion walked without speaking. Was she thinking of Brodin, I wondered, hawk-faced Brodin a murderer? One of the Andrethe's intelligencers, yes. But – he was Kanta's *arykei*. And his grief had been real.

The *jayante* strap tightened across my back; I eased it. Sweat ran under the mask, but the sun was too bright on the road without it. Rodion also went masked, and outside the city wore *harur-nilgiri* and *harur-nazari*.

'*S'aranth . . .*'

'Yes?'

'What did you feel like,' she said, 'the first time you killed someone?'

Blaize was a diminished figure on the road ahead, and the dust-cloud was drawing closer. It'd be safer to wait and let him check them out.

'Let's rest for a minute.' The rock was hot under me. Rodion hitched the *harur* blades back out of the way and sat beside me, still waiting for an answer. I said, 'Tell me how it happened.'

'In the street. Four of them.' She pulled the mask down and rubbed her face tiredly. When she looked at me, her eyes had the deep colour and clarity of a baby's. 'The guards killed one, and Meduenin – my sire and dam! he can fight – he killed one and disabled another; and I, I killed a man. It wasn't two streets away from Orhlandis *telestre* house up on the Hill. It was . . . crazy. Just like weapons practice. I kept expecting him to get up and say, No, you don't do it that way, your wrist should be higher. But he kept throwing up blood and then he died.'

The shock I felt was muffled. To an Orthean, it was not unusual for a child to kill. Yet it was Earth perception that saw her as a child; and cultural reactions against murder lie deep.

'How do you feel about it?'

'I didn't want to do it.' She shook her head. 'He was going to kill me. I was so afraid! I never gave him a chance, I was so scared. And that's wrong, he should have been questioned.'

'Everyone's afraid,' I said, and she nodded. She didn't ask the original question again; maybe she only needed to say how she felt.

'Where I come from,' I said, 'we don't teach children to fight.'

'Then how do they learn to defend themselves?'

'They don't. Well, they do. They don't need to!'

307

She laughed, throwing her head back, and slapped the rock with her open hand. 'S'aranth!'

'I just wish you didn't make it sound so logical.'

She stretched lazily and stared down the road. Blaize was just visible, walking back in company with the traders. Their images wavered. I heard lizards chirruping in the distance. Heat struck up from the rocks.

'It's safe.' She pulled up the mask to shield her eyes again, and stood and brushed dust off herself. 'We'd better go.'

I'm getting suspicious as a Southlander, I thought. I'd been assuming, as they had, that there could be danger on any open road. In Tathcaer, maybe. But here? No, that was just Blaize n'ri n'suth Meduenin: a hired guard has to make the assumption of danger.

There was no shade, and my mouth was dry. It's time we got back to the city, I was thinking; and then Rodion spoke.

She nodded at Blaize, still a good way off, and said, 'What's he like – is he a good arykei?'

'What?' Startled, I said, 'How the hell should I know?'

'You're arykei, aren't you? At Morvren, everyone says.'

I managed not to smile. 'Everyone's got it wrong, then, for once. He's close as a brother, but he's not my arykei.'

'Ah.' She scuffed at the loose rocks as she walked, and then raised her face to the sun. Eventually she looked at me, a smile visible under the edge of her mask, and looked away again.

The carts rumbled past, drawn by the plodding sand-coloured beasts the Desert Coast call brennior. Their short flexible snouts quested blindly from side to side, the musty smell of them hanging in the still air. Blaize came out of the dust-cloud and offered a water flask to us.

'Traders aren't waiting for a wind,' he announced, 'they're risking the land route south. Might be some time before we get back to Tathcaer.'

Ships crowded the harbour. Frustration hung over the trade-city like a sandstorm, and tempers were short in the heat. We came in by the eastern gate, paying toll to enter as we'd paid toll to leave.

'Don't go back yet,' Rodion said. 'Evalen's quarters aren't far, S'aranth, come and visit.'

'Sure.' I'd as soon have been in the inner city's quiet. The trade city was crowded down here at the waterfront. Ramshackle, drystone barns hugged older, domed buildings. You could see that there had been Order houses here once, when the city was larger.

'I'll beat you at ochmir,' Blaize offered.

'I might surprise you there.' Now there were awning-covered streets again, narrow and winding, and we left most of the people behind. Entering the shade was for a minute like entering cold water, and then as hot as before. High curves of buildings shut out the sun, and any breath of air.

Blaize said something I didn't catch. When I turned, he wasn't there. Several streets converged here. I saw Rodion step back, both hands flashing in the cross-draw of *harur* blades. Then earth gritted under my hands and a wall slammed into my shoulder, and I got up on hands and knees without knowing I'd been knocked down. Someone grunted. Boots scraped on the hard earth. The *jayante* was in my hands, its hard weight comforting. I struck out. Something caught the side of my head, and I blinked water out of my eyes, and was blinded by sunlight: mask gone. The scuffling was punctuated by an abrupt cry. Something struck at me too fast for recognition, and the *jayante* caught the upper arm as I aimed, but I fumbled the blow that would paralyse the leg and he – she? – scuttled back into the shadow clutching one arm. A short curved blade lay on the earth, leather-wound grip dark with sweat.

Blaize stood up from bending over a sprawled body. Rodion shouted, high-pitched and harsh as a bird. Footsteps clattered past me. The stunner was in my hand and I sighted, fired – there's no charge left, I thought – but a brief sound split the air, and the running figure skidded forward onto knees, hands, face; and was still.

Rodion stood holding her arm. Dark blood welled and suddenly ran black between her fingers, dropping on the dusty street. Her indrawn breath was sharp.

'Christie – ' Blaize glanced at me, sheathed *harur-nazari*, and went after the one I'd shot. He turned the body over, felt the throat, and smiled.

My hands were shaking and cold. I had to lean against the wall a minute before I could put the stunner away. The *jayante* lay a few feet away from the sprawled body.

There were more than two, I thought, searching the confused minutes for the memory of how many had run. It was only then, after it was over, that I began to know what had happened.

Blaize stood up, supporting the unconscious body of the attacker on his back. Rodion was panting hard, swearing and close to tears.

'Evalen's people—'

'No.' I cut Blaize off. 'I know where we are. Come with me.'

Rodion held onto my arm as we went. It was not far to the gate. As I'd hoped, it was Su'niar's Order on guard.

They let us through, dishevelled as we were, Rodion bleeding from a slash low on her side as well as from her arm, and Blaize with the unconscious assailant over his shoulders. A little way into the inner city I heard a scuffle behind me, and someone slammed between me and Rodion. She cried out with pain. Blaize ran past, vanishing in the narrow darkness of the alleys.

'Where—' Rodion's breathing came harshly.

'Come on.' I took her unwounded arm.

Blaize rejoined us, out of breath, scarred face unrecognizable with anger. He shook his head mutely. When he could speak he said, 'I didn't think he'd recover – not so soon—'

'It's lost power.'

'I should have made sure.' His tone was chilling. 'Christie, where are you taking us?'

'There,' I said as we came out into the gardens, and with my free hand pointed at the Brown Tower. Blaize grunted, but didn't object. Seeing Rodion's head hanging down, her feet stumble, I picked her up and carried her the few yards into the Tower. Blaize came behind, both *harur* blades drawn.

I am not naturally a brave woman. Having been attacked, my one idea was to get to the safety of what was undoubtedly the most impregnable structure on Orthe.

'You're all right?' Haltern asked again.

'Few bruises, that's all.' Experimentally I flexed one arm. Several muscles felt as though they'd been pulled in those hectic minutes. I saw Rodion, now with her wounds salved and bandaged, talking energetically to the *t'an* Evalen. Blaize stood with them.

I tried to reconstruct it in my mind, searching for details. They'd waited for us. Blaize had spotted them first, I think, and yelled for us to get back to back; and it might have been him or the first attacker who bowled me over. Were there three or four of them, and how had they been dressed?

'They were from the trade city,' I said. 'That won't be much help to you, Hal.'

'It won't be up to me.' His thin fingers picked at a worn place on his belt. 'They must be desperate, Christie. Try and kill you in the Hexenmeister's own city? They should know better than that.'

'They won't get another chance. We'll stay in the Tower until the *Child of Methemna* sails.'

'All of you?' His gesture included Blaize and Rodion. 'I don't like to say this, but I think you should be very careful, even when you get back to Tathcaer.'

I grinned. It was a light-headed reaction to the attack: I just felt good to be alive. 'Kasabaarde's full of people who don't feel safe in Tathcaer, isn't it?'

Tethmet-fenborn entered the library, stopped for a quiet word with Evalen, and then came across to me.

'The Hexenmeister requires your presence, envoy.'

'Yes, of course.' I stood up, still shaky. Evalen and I followed Tethmet to the meeting hall. Blaize supported Rodion, who was becoming drowsy from the herbs given to her.

The old man looked up. '*T'an* Evalen, good. Christie, I believe we have one of your attackers.'

So soon? The Hexenmeister's spy system was impressive, I thought.

Brown-robes brought in a struggling Orthean in torn shirt and britches.

'Is this one who attacked you?'

'I . . . can't say for certain. I'm sorry. It happened too fast.'

'Could be.' Blaize took another look. 'Can't say more than that.'

The abrupt tone wasn't meant for rudeness. This brown slick room was no comfort to a Southlander. Even in the days of the Golden Empire, it came to me, the Witchbreed kept much of their power secret from their slaves; Blaize would have no past-memories to soften the shock of the Tower.

'*T'an* Evalen?'

'I know her,' Evalen answered the old man. 'She's one of the *Child of Methemna*'s crew. Are you telling me she—'

'*T'an*, why have they brought me here?' the woman interrupted. 'I've done nothing, tell them to let me go!'

Her accent was Desert Coast, clipped and slurred, all the emphasis different when she spoke Ymirian. She had the bleached skin of the Coast, and a rough dark mane coming down from complex braids; I suppose she was in her forties.

'My people found her running from the Landgate quarter where the attack took place. She has a mark on her that could be from a *jayante*.' The Hexenmeister nodded, and one of the brown-robes pulled up the woman's torn sleeve. A bruise was already yellowing, darkening.

'I fell earlier,' she said, '*t'an*, let me go back to the ship.'

'If you're innocent you have nothing to be afraid of,' Evalen said. 'No one will harm you if that's so; no, not the Hexenmeister himself.'

That dogged defiance in the heart of the Brown Tower touched me. Evalen was nervous as Blaize, nervous as any Southlander.

'But she was there,' Rodion said clearly. 'I saw her. She fought with *S'aranth* and then she ran away.'

'Are you certain of this?'

'Yes. Certain.'

The Desert woman said hastily, 'If you must hear it, *t'an* Evalen, it is this: I was in the Landgate quarter, yes, and I saw the attack happen. I said nothing because I – well, because I didn't go to help them. I don't know why. Afraid, maybe. There were many of them. And then I ran because I thought I should be blamed for that.'

Evalen frowned.

The Hexenmeister said, 'Will you let me question her?'

At that there was a silence, and the white membranes slid down over Evalen's bright eyes.

'I'm not wholly sure of her guilt.'

'Then be sure. I can uncover the truth.'

'I have heard,' she said with her still-veiled eyes on the Desert woman's face, 'that those whom you – question – are not unchanged by it. Some say it's possible to recognize them forever after, because of what they become.'

'*T'an*, you can hurt her greatly and she will perhaps tell you the truth, and perhaps a lie. I will hurt her not at all, and to me she will tell only the truth. But—'

'But?'

'But it is true she will be changed.'

The subliminal hum that underlies the Brown Tower intensified the silence. Cool air, with only the odours that the Southlanders brought in from outside – dust, spices, the sea. In artificial light, in that windowless room, the claustrophobia was almost tangible.

'Havoth-jair, I *must* know.' Evalen turned from the Desert woman to the old man. Her eyes cleared. 'You will question her, master, and I will witness it.'

'No,' the Hexenmeister said, 'you may not be there, *t'an*.'

'If I'm not, then you don't take her! How do we know what – ' she broke off. 'Pardon me, master. There are those who will say she was forced into a lie, not the truth. I must be here and see it!'

About that time I realized that, whatever he might conceal from the Southland, the Hexenmeister wouldn't hide this from me. Because I already knew.

'*T'an* Evalen, would it be satisfactory if I were to witness the interrogation on your behalf?'

She could hardly insult the newly-proved-innocent envoy; besides, her mother trusted me. And though I wasn't from the Southland's point of view the best possible witness, it was plain from the Hexenmeister's expression that I was the only witness they were liable to get.

312

Unexpectedly, Evalen smiled.

'Yes,' she said, 'we would agree to that.'

We went down into the maze of the Brown Tower among the masked brown-robes, the Desert woman pulled roughly along. I walked behind, the old man's hand on my arm. And we came to a familiar entrance, and a cool dry hall lit with faintly blue iridescence, and sarcophagus-machines.

I thought, I don't want to see this.

After sending the brown-robes away, the Hexenmeister turned his attention to the Desert woman. She stood with her arms across her body, hands clutching her upper arms.

'Havoth-jair,' he said, 'of what city?'

'Quarth.'

'That is a lie. I know when you lie. You know of me,' he said, and there was nothing frail or old about him. 'You know who makes the law in the city of the Brown Tower.'

'Don't try to frighten me,' she said harshly, in the Desert Coast tongue. Wrinkles showed round her eyes when she looked at him, membrane-covered as if she stared at a bright light. She was not young. It showed in the way she slumped.

He was mild. 'Tell me how you came to do this thing, Havoth-jair.'

Terror forced her words out, though you wouldn't have guessed it to look at her. But I'm practised at making the paralysis of fear look like the stillness of relaxation, and I know when someone else is doing it.

'I was bribed,' she said at last. 'Someone saw I was on the *Methemna* with the Halfgold, I suppose. They offered me money to kill the Orhlandis and the Outworld envoy. It was easy enough to find others to help me.'

He only watched her.

'Give me protection, master,' she said. 'There are names I might remember, but not under sentence of death. Keep me out of that and I'll tell you.'

She was aware, I think, that he could force any information out of her; but she had a streak of toughness that made her bargain even on the edge of desperation.

I wanted to say, can't we accept that? Can't you let her walk out of here unharmed?

And I couldn't say it, there were too many good reasons against her. Sometimes you play and you lose. The Desert Coast woman lost.

The Hexenmeister shook his head.

*

The brown-robes gave her *arniac* tea and would have forced it down her, but she gulped it hastily, the whites showing all round her tawny eyes. In a few minutes she fell into a semi-conscious state.

'What do you think you will see?' There was amusement in the old man's voice.

'Very little – but it will convince *t'an* Evalen.'

They took Havoth-jair and laid her in the slick coffin of a machine. There was little enough to see. One part of me shuddered at the thought that I had been where she was now. But willingly, I thought. That makes the difference, doesn't it?

And one part of me knows the technique, its limitations and its dangers, knowing that to rip the unwilling mind apart in search of memory is possible, but its effects are unmistakable. Which would have been more reassuring if my knowledge hadn't come to me through the technique itself. But that way paranoia lies.

'You're going to hurt her,' I said.

'It will not be painful.'

Aphasia, amnesia, blackouts, idiocy: and all the possible symptoms of brain damage.

'Suppose she's innocent?'

'Then I am sorry for her.'

Before second twilight we returned to the meeting hall, brown-robes leading the quiescent Desert woman.

'Havoth-jair.' Evalen stood, watching her. 'Of what city?'

'Kel Harantish.'

Evalen blinked, looked at the Hexenmeister, then returned her attention to Havoth-jair.

'You admit to the attack.'

'I was sent to kill the Orhlandis woman and the envoy.' Her eyes, half-veiled, were calm. So was the voice. Peaceful. Not angry, not afraid; as if nothing could touch her now.

'Tell me,' Evalen said.

'The Emperor-in-Exile had me sent to the Southland, me being of his household and having visited it before. I've sailed before, so it wasn't hard to gain a place on the *Methemna*. I knew I should be taken if I attacked the Orhlandis on the ship, so I waited until we reached the city and I could hire mercenaries to help me. Then I waited until she and the envoy met.' Calm, rational speech.

'Are you the only one sent out from Kel Harantish?'

'That wasn't told to me.'

'Why were you to do this thing?'

'That, also, I wasn't told.'

I shifted, easing one bruised leg. It was strange, the woman had attacked me, it was probably me who'd struck her with the *jayante*; and yet because I didn't recognize her face I couldn't connect her with the attack. Reason told me she'd done it, but I had no gut hate-reaction.

'She should testify to this,' Evalen said thoughtfully. 'In Tathcaer, master. *T'an* Rodion, *t'an* envoy, it were better for you if justice on this should be seen in that city.'

'Would she be safe in Tathcaer?' It was a little late to worry about 'safe', I thought guiltily.

'You!' Evalen demanded, 'is your face known in Tathcaer? Would any recognize you in the Southland?'

'I've been to Tathcaer before.' Havoth-jair's tongue ran on easily. 'And to another Southland city, Ales-Kadareth. Three times in the last two years we took ships to Melkathi, ships ballasted with gold; that was a gift from the Emperor-in-Exile. What he had in return for his gift, I know not. Harantish gold goes to the Hundred Thousand; it was on such a ship that I came to the Southland this spring.'

'*This* spring?' I said involuntarily.

'Gold for which *telestre*?' Evalen demanded, but the Desert Coast woman only shook her head. Her face was untroubled. 'Well, they would not tell her, I suppose.'

I said, 'That should have stopped when SuBannasen died. Haltern thought it didn't. Someone has taken over from Sulis.'

'The *T'An Suthai-Telestre* should know this,' the Hexenmeister advised. 'And, if *t'an* Evalen's wise, she'll take this woman to Tathcaer and guard her as if she were her own *ashiren*.'

Excited argument broke out among the Southlanders, each trying to shout over the other voices.

'Stay for this,' the old man said, laying his clawed fingers on my arm, 'and then come to me again. I must speak with someone, and the envoy should be present.'

315

CHAPTER 29

The Emperor-in-Exile

The sunset gongs sounded distantly from the trade city. The gates were closing. The evening air was motionless, soaked with heat. I stood in the Tower's roof garden, watching the sun go down in a welter of silver and lilac. There are no long twilights on the Desert Coast. It was the kind of sky that makes you look for a thin new moon in the west, but here there was nothing but the white dots of stars. *Arniac* and rockmoss sent their night perfumes into the dusty air.

I had to get out in the open; the Tower was making me claustrophobic as any Southlander. And Evalen's methods of questioning Havoth-jair were more openly violent than the Hexenmeister's, and not something I wanted to watch.

The lift-dome slid open and the fenborn stepped out onto the roof.

'He wants me down there.'

'If you will,' Tethmet said distantly.

The city lay silent, domes catching the sun's last glow. I crossed to the lift, and the fenborn stood aside for me to enter.

'You live here,' I said as the halves of the dome slid up and shut out the evening. 'Do you like it, Tethmet?'

His webbed hand touched the switch and the lift began to glide down. The timeless, sourceless Tower light illuminated his masked face. At last he said, 'I don't remember the Great Fens now, except in past-dreams. He's here, and never leaves. What else can I do?'

Just as the lift stopped, far below ground level, he said, 'Are they still the same? He said you crossed the Fens. Have they changed?'

His thin body was tense. Muscles moved along his pointed jaw.

'How would I know?' That was a lie. His urgency impressed me. 'They haven't changed. Don't ask me how I know. They're the way they have been for thousands of years.'

Not until the tension left him did I realize how long he'd been waiting to ask that question. The lines round his eyes relaxed, and for the first time I saw a fenborn smile. It was fierce, a predator's joy.

He said nothing more, but led me through the maze of corridors until we came to a closed door. I heard voices, and a continuous sound under them that puzzled me. As the doors slid open I recognized it as running water. Tethmet followed me in.

It was a large room, pale-coloured, with a multitude of pelts and tapestries thrown down to cover the floor. The Hexenmeister sat hunched up on a low chair, with Evalen and Haltern on a couch beside him. Rodion sat cradling her arm, white-eyed with the effort of keeping awake; and Blaize stood behind her with his hands on the back of her chair. A vociferous argument was taking place.

I went down the steps between two crystal tanks, where blue and crimson fish swam. Another tank took up the far wall; there was a cascade-fountain running noisily. The air was cool, damp in comparison with the city, and the light shaded into green over the pools.

'Envoy,' Evalen called, 'let's hear your opinion on this. I say we must return to Tathcaer as soon as we get a wind and can sail. You'll come with us, and Rodion Orhlandis, and the woman Havoth-jair: and all shall be told to the *T'An Suthai-Telestre.*'

'That were best done soon,' Haltern said as I came over. 'You're rumoured to be dead, Christie, you and the Orhlandis here. If we don't stop that story it'll spread as far as Tathcaer, and then it must be denied before they'll hear you.'

'Dead?'

'In the attack. They have the Orhlandis carried bloody into the Tower and dying of her wounds—' he looked at Rodion, who grinned back at him '—and as for her companions, they were slain by an assassin in the Tower itself. Someone's heard of the woman Havoth-jair being brought here, I think, that's where that began.'

'And if it ends in the Southland—'

Evalen was interrupted gently by the Hexenmeister. He turned his gaze on me, veiling humour. 'There is the matter of getting to Tathcaer.'

'One way or another,' I said, pulling up a stool and sitting beside Rodion. 'I don't care how, I'm going back. With all due respect, I can't function as Dominion envoy while I'm under suspicion of murder. Rodion's evidence against Brodin n'ri n'suth Charain should be presented as soon as possible, and I think I should be there.'

The Hexenmeister inclined his head. 'And if Brodin n'ri n'suth Charain has taken bribes from Kel Harantish?'

'That evidence should also be presented to the Crown.'

'He would not be the only one who has done so, I think,' Evalen said soberly, 'but this may serve to drive such traitors underground, or – if he speaks – condemn more with him.'

'You miss my point,' the old man said. 'All this has its head in Kel Harantish. The Emperor-in-Exile knows you're in Kasabaarde. Indeed, the Desert Coast being what it is, he likely knows all the city's rumours as soon as I do. I mean that you may have an unchancy voyage to Tathcaer, and a grim welcome if you arrive.'

The cascade of the fountain was clearly audible in the quiet.

'I have a small company of guards,' Evalen said. 'We hoped to travel unnoticed. They won't send ships against us – Kel Harantish remembers the last time Southland warships went up against that city – but I'd be surprised now if there were no hired assassins. Those we can defeat if we take care, master.'

He didn't comment, only looking at her doubtfully.

'I don't like the idea of making myself a target,' I said.

'I assure you, envoy, I'll bring you safe to Tathcaer.' Evalen was determined. 'We've talked all this out, what else is there to say?'

'How safe will we be after we arrive in Tathcaer?' I asked Haltern. 'And how long will it take to bring Brodin to trial? Once this is known there'll be no point in anyone trying to kill us, but how long before it *is* known?'

He spread his hands. 'Who can tell?'

Blaize leaned down to hear something that Rodion said, then straightened. '*T'an*, suppose we didn't return on the *Methemna*? Suppose we travelled on another ship and kept our arrival at Tathcaer secret?'

'Good enough if it could be done,' the Hexenmeister said doubtfully, 'but with Harantish agents searching for you?'

No one else is going to suggest it, I thought, so it's going to have to be me.

'Suppose they weren't looking for us?'

Very sudden and shrewd, the old man said, 'How would you solve that?'

'It's happened to me once, more or less. Listen, if those rumours weren't stopped, but confirmed; if we're reported dead officially? That would stop anyone bothering about us. And then return to Tathcaer in secret, as Blaize says.'

Confusion broke out, all of them talking at once. The old man leaned back in his chair, eyes hooded. Clever as sin, I thought, he knows me, and he knows it sounds better coming from me.

'—hear about it in Tathcaer!' Rodion thumped her chair with her good arm, then looked shame-faced. 'Sorry, *t'an* Evalen; but if they hear we're dead, and believe it – my mother—'

'Some things must be endured,' Evalen was compassionate. '*T'an* envoy, I hear what you say. A good suggestion. And then we would take the woman Havoth-jair on the *Methemna*, as we should do if you had truly been killed? Yes . . .'

'They'll be looking out for her, unless she's thought dead too. She could travel with us, I suppose.' And just how did I propose to travel? I wondered.

'What, guard her all the way to Tathcaer?'

'Where's she going to escape to?' I was angry, a little disgusted. Nothing I could have done would have prevented the way they treated her, but I should have tried. 'Between us and Kel Harantish, we haven't left her anywhere to go. Didn't you promise her protection if she gave evidence in Tathcaer? Well, then.'

'If she comes with us, we can be sure at least one witness will get through. I'm not fool enough to have you travel all in the one party—'

'As Dominion envoy—'

'Peace!' the Hexenmeister said. We were quiet then as if we'd been children. He stood, and Tethmet-fenborn took his arm. Then the flare of anger faded and the sense of antiquity, and it was only an old Desert Coast man who smiled at us.

'This was a long day,' he said, 'and you, Orhlandis, are wounded; and the *t'an* Evalen has a company to care for – I will send brown-robes to let you through to the trade city, Evalen – and as for decisions, they can wait on the advent of a wind. No ship leaves Kasabaarde till then. And even I cannot call up a wind for you.'

Evalen chuckled aloud at that and Haltern smiled. Blaize gave Rodion his arm to grip as she rose.

'Say nothing,' the old man advised, 'and I will tell you what rumours go out of the city, and then we will talk again.'

I was about to follow the others out, when he signalled for me to stay.

'Have you eaten?' he asked when the room emptied, and when I said no, he sent the fenborn out for *arniac* tea and *del'ri* flour-cakes. The water ran musically in the background, and the fish made constant slow sweeps through the tanks under the green and golden light.

We talked while we ate, mostly about Earth. Not the Dominion, not the governments, but how it feels to grow up under a different sun and a different sky, and how people get on with the business of living their own lives.

319

'I know so little,' he said at last, 'and I understand less.'

'All I can say to that is, what you've learned from my mind may not be true anyway.' I swallowed the last of the *arniac* tea, draining the bowl. 'I'm not a liar, master, but all you have is one person's view of Earth, and not even all of it, only the parts I know. If any of the xeno-team ever come here, they'd probably give you a completely different story. I don't understand Orthe, even with what you've told me, and you've seen more of your world than I ever will of mine.'

When he looked at me, I remembered he knew everything about me. That should have been frightening. The reason it wasn't, I think, is because not being human he couldn't judge humanity.

'Have you rested?' he asked. 'There is one more thing, as I told you, and you should be present. First, though, I ask you to undertake never to speak of what you see or hear.'

'That's not something I can promise. As envoy, I have to report fully.'

'Well then, say that you will report it only to your own people, and then only if you believe it to be necessary.'

That seemed fair enough. I agreed. He stood and gathered his robes round himself, and walked slowly to the fountain. There he thrust one arm under the surface of the water and remained that way for a minute. As he withdrew it, the far wall split soundlessly down the middle and the room opened to twice its size.

That part of the room was dark. I followed him into it, away from the underwater light, and a dim blue luminescence grew up round us. It centred on a great block of some transparent substance that stood on a dais. A golden light pulsed in its crystal depths.

His face was shadowed, the eye-sockets full of darkness. He said, 'That will call him out. I set it after I heard of the attack this noon. Now . . .'

His hands moved on a panel on the side of the dais. Then, as in the block that had shown me the view of his successor, the clear surface began to fill with images.

'Where—' my voice was husky.

'There are no others left but here,' he said, 'and in that ancient city, Kel Harantish. And this transmits nothing now but my voice, though perhaps that is as well: I keep my face hidden from him.'

The image was complete now, of a room very similar to the one we stood in. Three-dimensional, exact. Something bothered me. This degree of power – whatever the nature of the energy source – should have shown up like a beacon on the satellite survey of Carrick V. Had they missed it, skimped it, suffered a transmission failure? The atmosphere was badly suited to wave-transmission (or I should have been in contact with the xeno-team, legal or not). This shouldn't be here, I thought.

In that other room were geometrically-patterned carpets, and candle-stands whose holders were shaped like beast-skulls. Candlelight and the ruins of technology. An Orthean bent over the panel, so that at first I saw only his bleached loose-flowing mane. Then he straightened up and his face became visible. Narrow chin, broad forehead, and half-veiled eyes the colour of wet sand. And he was no more than nineteen or twenty.

'Dannor bel-Kurick,' the Hexenmeister said, 'you who call yourself Emperor-in-Exile, attend.'

The Orthean male glared at us – no, not at us, at what must be a blank: he looked clear through us. And he was beautiful. He had the presence, that quality the Goldens in my memory possessed. The ability to inspire fascination.

'Show yourself,' he demanded.

'I choose not.'

'Then I choose not to speak.'

'Your assassin,' the Hexenmeister said quickly, and the hand that bel-Kurick reached towards the controls hesitated. 'One of your spies. She had much to say before she eventually died.'

Dannor bel-Kurick laughed. His voice had a pure tone. He said, 'Is it war? I'll fight you, old man, I'll fight you gladly.'

With that I recalled the face of Santhendor'lin-sandru when the Golden woman brought the Empire down. Dannor bel-Kurick was a poor second to that, though he might pass now Sandor was forgotten.

This halfbreed, this Halfgold, I thought; this Witchbreed *boy*, is he the cause of all this?

'I make no quarrels with the Emperor-in-Exile,' the old man answered. 'But I remind him that his city Kel Harantish is a city of exile, and was no city before the Empire fell but only a desert garrison.'

The boy turned and seated himself, lounging back in his chair. Whether he knew he was seen, or whether his actions had that theatrical quality even when he was alone, I don't know.

'Well?' he said shortly.

'Only this: you survive on trade. Kel Harantish has always lived by it, and if I give the word you may die for lack of it. Can you eat rocks and sand?'

In the mind's eye I see shells of towers obscured by the dust of an arid land. The sea like fragments of molten metal. And over the towers, blocking the sky, great whale-backed dunes, sharp-edged and shifting with the wind. Kel Harantish between two seas, the tideless salt water and the sand. Even water must be imported.

Bel-Kurick said measuredly, 'If you set foot on Harantish land I'll come west and burn your port, whether it cost me this city or not. I can still do that. I have allies in the south. I have my army, my ships.'

'I know. I know. Do you think I don't know the Golden Witchbreed?' The amusement was plain in the old man's voice. 'You're not Sandor, boy, whatever you think—'

'I am Golden!' He stood, staring with blind, uncanny accuracy at the Hexenmeister. 'I am of the line of Santhendor'lin-sandru, and I am Emperor! How many lies have you fed me, old man, telling me I'm nothing but a hollow man ruling a dying city? How many times have you tried to steal my throne? There's a price paid for power here that you never paid, old man, never in your lives. I know that.'

'That's true,' the Hexenmeister said, too quietly for the words to be transmitted. His face in the shadows showed pain, and a compassion I couldn't account for.

Dannor bel-Kurick sank back into the chair. 'One must be true Golden to gain the throne, and so I made myself as Goldens are. Anything else I crushed. Now will you tell me I did that only for northerners to call me Witchbreed? Emperor-in-Exile is Emperor still.'

Emperor of what? Kel Harantish with its empty name and half-breed lineage, its power to inspire fear and contempt in equal measure? Emperor of craftsmen and mercenaries scattered across all the southern continent, simply because the city must trade to live. Dannor bel-Kurick: obsessed inheritor of a tawdry past and a tawdry future, ready to ally with anyone and anything promising him military aid – and to betray the rest of Orthe without a second thought. He was a little mad, even for an Orthean.

'What I have to say is simple.' The Hexenmeister paused. 'Will you hear me?'

'Will I ever not?'

'This, then. Your assassin who killed the envoy and the Orhlandis – she spoke of ships that went north to the Hundred Thousand, ships that carry gold.'

'What of it?' the boy asked tiredly.

'Nothing. But if I hear of any more ships from Kel Harantish in Tathcaer, then something.'

There was a pause. Without much hope the boy said, 'And perhaps they won't listen to you, Quarth and Psamnol and

Saberon and the rest; perhaps they think it is time we joined together and broke your stranglehold on the Desert Coast!'

'And if I close the port to those who trade with Witchbreed? I ask again, Dannor bel-Kurick, can your people live on rock instead of bread?'

The cube faded to clarity.

'Let him have his temper,' the Hexenmeister said, 'he's stubborn, that one; cruel and wilful and cunning, but I could find it in my heart to be sorry for him. The Witchbreed glory is past, and he has the shadow of it only. Harantish is a desolate rock. He must take his hand from the Southland now for some years, now that they know he acts against them.'

'Will he stop the ships?' For a word, I thought, a threat?

'He has no choice. Kel Harantish is vulnerable, he can act only at second-hand; now that's finished.'

Does bel-Kurick fear the Brown Tower more than he hates the Southland, I wondered; and will he do more than hide his conspiracies with more care? As for allies in the south . . .

The Hexenmeister rested his hand on my shoulder as we went back into the brightly-lit part of the room, as if he were tired. I doubted it.

I said, 'I thought you weren't given to acting in other people's affairs?'

'That was the past,' he said, 'and this is the present, and now we have contact with your world. The first new thing that's come to me in centuries. Evalen is right, this affects all Orthe. And I believe, Christie, I am the only person who has the right to act for all of Orthe.'

Dim artificial illumination shone in the tiny room. I was far below ground here, down in the brown-robes' quarters, and I could have wished for a window open on the night.

I lay on a block that seemed a solid extension of the wall. Its surface gave under me, accommodating my weight. It should have been easy to sleep, but instead I was awake and restless. The light never changed. I had no idea how long until dawn. Time passed. A cool stream of air passed through the room but despite that the temperature was high.

They might just as well have buried me, I thought. And if I'm meant to be leaving Kasabaarde tomorrow, I need sleep. Damn.

Part of it was fear. The Tower was familiar to me only through false memories, which made it very easy to take it for granted. But the substance I lay on was not fibre or metal, nor did it have the tactile slickness of plastic. The light was sourceless to human eyes

323

– though it seemed to me in memory that Orthean vision encompassed a greater range. Make a conscious effort of realization and it was frightening.

Because if the energy source here didn't register on a satellite survey, one possible conclusion was that it was something we hadn't programmed a satellite to recognize. Something we were entirely ignorant about.

There'd have to be a report made on that, and on everything I'd seen in the city. The department would take a keen interest. What kind of interest? I wondered. There was Witchbreed technology here, yes, outlasting its makers. But how much notice would the department take of the inner city, the Order houses of Kasabaarde?

I thought, I don't want to leave yet. If it was up to me, personally . . . but if I don't get back to envoy's duties soon, there won't be time to finish before I'm recalled to Earth.

Su'niar, Thelmithar . . . for all that they fed, clothed, and housed their Order, the only thing the Order houses really gave away was time. Time to sit under the street-awnings on the dusty steps, time to think, or time simply to exist. I had no illumination to match Beth'ru-elen or any of the mystics. Only I had learned to ask questions, and not to ask them, and to reach some kind of – is it balance I mean? And I would like to have known what happens to a human left in one of those Orthean sanctuaries.

I heard movement, and wondered if Rodion was awake. When I got up and went to see if her wounds bothered her, I found her room empty. I thought about that for a while. Then I went back to bed. She was safe enough.

'Havoth-jair is a witness for the Crown!' Evalen lowered her head, bull-stubborn. 'Also, she's one of my ship's crew. You say you can give us protection in your city, master. I'll undertake to protect Havoth-jair outside of it. I'm taking her to Tathcaer.'

The Hexenmeister was seated in the library, close by the open window. A breeze had come up with the dawn and not fallen yet.

'Perhaps it's better,' I said.

'She's a Southland sailor, but born on the Desert Coast – I cannot keep her in the Brown Tower either way. Very well, *t'an* Evalen.'

Blaize and Rodion stood together, talking quietly. Outside the *telestre* Southlanders aren't demonstrative (inside the community is another matter) and their affection was low-key. Sometimes she touched his arm or his hand was on her shoulder. What was obvious was their closeness, eyes hardly leaving each other's faces, and the joy that came out in sudden muffled laughter.

'*T'an* Evalen,' Rodion said, becoming serious, 'may I ask you to do one thing? When you get to Tathcaer, tell my mother that I live. I know the lie's necessary but don't let her believe it longer than she has to.'

Evalen nodded. 'If necessary I'll ask *T'An* Ruric to keep the secret until you reach the city – but you may be there before we are, the winds are treacherous in spring.'

I would have asked her to inform the xeno-team I wasn't dead, but if they knew, pretty soon everybody else would. Huxton and Eliot and Adair . . . they hadn't developed the sheer paranoia necessary for Orthean affairs.

If I get back to Tathcaer, I thought. This won't be easy.

'As for leaving the city,' the Hexenmeister said, 'I can perhaps help you there, envoy, but we'll speak of it later. *T'an* Evalen, I release the woman Havoth-jair to you. My people will bring her secretly to your ship.'

Before they left, I spoke to Haltern.

'Take care,' he said. 'Sea travelling is an uncertain business at the best of time, and in Durestha . . .'

Any journey on Orthe was a momentous undertaking, it was true. Less safe, less sure than on Earth. Natural hazards might be a bigger danger than conspiracy.

'I'll meet you in Tathcaer. We'll get this whole thing settled. Hal, watch out for yourself.'

The wind blew dust against the Tower's impervious walls. Clouds came over from the southwest, hiding the daystars. Evalen's people were arguing over something with the brown-robes.

'It's bad news to be taking home,' he said, 'and Charain's a south Dadeni *telestre*, and Brodin a good man. I know him, Christie. To go back and do this – it's hard.'

'You're Peir-Dadeni; what about Kanta Andrethe?'

'Yes,' he said. 'That demands justice. And for the envoy, too. Goddess give you a good journey, Christie.'

'My people have packed supplies for you,' the Hexenmeister said when I rejoined him in the library. Behind him, through the window, the shadows of clouds glided over the domes of the inner city. He was alone. Tea-bowls, scarlet with *arniac* dregs, cluttered the table. A forsaken atmosphere clung to the room.

'What ship do we take?'

'Yes, ships . . .' He coughed, pinched the bridge of his nose, and then sighed. With an old man's preoccupation with comfort, he tugged his dark robe more tightly round his shoulders. 'There is one way you can leave the city and be certain you're not seen, Christie, and that's to go by way of the Rasrhe-y-Meluur.'

I remembered the line of pylons that had followed us south, their great shadows distinct on the waves. 'Is it safe?'

'As far as the first waystation, Firerock, and you might take an island ship up the Archipelago from there.'

'Ask the others,' I said, thinking of Blaize's competence. 'If they'll agree, I will.'

They came back from saying their farewells, Tethmet with them; and, though dubious, they eventually agreed. The old man took us into the centre of the Brown Tower then, to a lift that went down for so long that I began to wonder just how far below ground we were going.

The light had a different quality where we disembarked, a harsh blue luminescence. Dry, cold air circulated. Rodion shivered, pulled Blaize's arm around her, and grinned toothily.

Doors opened into a small chamber containing only two benches. Brown-robes brought us packs and water bottles, which Blaize proceded to check expertly. There was some discussion with the fenborn. Then we joined the old man, the doors slid shut, and what I realized now was a kind of monorail began to move forward. The acceleration was smooth. Blaize and Rodion both flinched, and I saw their hands link.

Beside me, the Hexenmeister said, 'What do you think, Christie, when you see this?'

He probably knew what I thought better than I did. 'That Orthe's is a very ancient civilization.'

He looked at me quizzically. 'Us, or the Hundred Thousand?'

'All of it. Odd to realize it now, after all this time. It isn't the popular idea of an advanced race.'

You could all but see him sorting through archetypes in borrowed memories: high technology, controlled emotions. His face furrowed, eyes veiling, then he nodded.

'They advance beyond the Witchbreed method. No one makes land yield like a Southlander.'

But you don't expect an ancient race to be dirty-handed, I wanted to protest. You don't expect them to kill – or if you do, it's with world-destroying weapons: nothing so simple and bloody as a yard of razor-edged metal. And yet they're not simple.

'It's their own choice,' he emphasized softly.

'I'm not arguing.'

The fenborn sat silent as ever, and I wondered if he was thinking of that flat, watery country in the north. Blaize and Rodion took no notice when the old man spoke. At first I thought they were too taken up with each other to notice, but then I realized the Hexenmeister was using a Desert tongue unintelligible to them. And I'd been able to answer. The implanted memories had gifted me one thing, then.

A long time later the car began to slow, and eventually it came to a halt. Then there was a jolt and it began to rise vertically, a car that became a lift.

Rodion flexed her arm, grinned ruefully, and allowed Blaize to help her strap the pack on her back. I watched them, the man and the young woman. Their reaction to attack was alien, Orthean: they picked themselves up like children after a scuffle. For a hired fighter I could understand it, but Rodion . . . yet she was alert, restless, eager to be on the move; and it wasn't a day ago that someone tried to kill her. While I—

The reason I remembered so little of the attack is that I was blind with terror. All my reactions had been instinctive, fear drove me to fight. Even now, with it safe in the past, images haunt me. Not Havoth-jair, or the way a *jayante* jars against bone. The man that I saw only for a second, the man Blaize killed. I still see him. On his back, dead arms raised stiffly over his face, specked all over with red. Fixed in that attitude of pain. Holding his arms up to ward off an injury that had already put him beyond hope.

'I wish you all well,' the Hexenmeister said as the car at last stopped. 'Leave the Rasrhe-y-Meluur before you come to Rimrock, at the latest, it isn't possible to keep the way safe any longer.'

'Orhlandis thanks you,' Rodion said formally. Blaize nodded stifly, still not at ease with the old man.

The doors slid open and we stepped out onto a blue-grey fused surface. I thought, Kirriach's stone. Air buffeted my face. It was cold. A great high space opened round us. Thin sunlight speared down into the depths ahead. Echoes rustled, and somewhere water dripped into pools. There was a sharp, open-air smell.

Rasrhe-y-Meluur. Not below ground, then, but above it: the car had brought us up the pylon to the beginning of that great bridge.

'You will not need torches,' the Hexenmeister said, 'you can reach Firerock before nightfall.'

From where we stood, the fused stone floor curved out and into distance, and in the crepuscular light began at last to curve upwards. And that rising curve of stone soared up into the dimness, and up until it was lost in mist and distance. And to the other side, also, the stone ran out to the edge of vision and then swung up in a great curve to hidden heights.

Ahead, a vast shaft of light fell down into the darkness, hiding the view beyond. When I stepped forward my boots splashed in the edge of stagnant water. The air smelled suddenly of rot. The dripping water echoed. Then I felt a cold wind, and I stared up and saw the mist that moved in the heights of Rasrhe-y-Meluur. It was not mist. Across and up and through such a vast distance of space, I saw that what moved were clouds.

The shaft of light burned silver, then white; and I thought some part of the giant tunnel must have fallen in until I saw how straight-edged the shadows fell. And I saw then that there were apertures in the stone, high enough above our heads that they appeared mere slits, but in reality big enough to pilot a flyer through – high enough for the clouds to drift in.

Rodion, boots clopping through the water, took a few steps forward. It grew deeper, and I realized we would have to follow the sides of the Rasrhe-y-Meluur. Clouds obscured the light, and I saw what lay ahead. That great circular shaft, rank water flooding it like a sea; and the broken and time-worn stumps of buildings jutting out halfway down from the clouds . . .

The sheer size of an enclosed space has an effect of its own – witness any cathedral. But *this* . . . Something in the human mind feels that it's wrong for anything constructed to be so large. A cave, or a river canyon, or the pit of a volcano: they inspire awe. But something as large as the Rasrhe-y-Meluur inspires fear. For it to be man-made is wrong, and for it to be made by aliens is simply frightening.

I saw in memory more real than vision what had filled this shell. How the Rasrhe-y-Meluur had been divided into upper and lower hemispheres, where we stood now housing the hidden machinery, and the top segment housing the multiple rails of the transport systems and the great hexagonal towers of the Witchbreed. The apertures blocked by force-screens, the controlled indoor 'weather' . . .

Now only the tubular shell remained, scraps of stonework jutting out halfway up its height, and the lower level rotting in acidic water. This that had been Rasrhe-y-Meluur, the city of the triumph of the Witchbreed, astounding in its ruin.

'Send no word to me,' the Hexenmeister said, 'I shall know whether you come safely to Tathcaer or not. Envoy, give my greetings to your people.'

The old man coughed, and Tethmet took his arm. The doors slid shut on them, the fenborn and the stooped man in brown robes. We were alone with echoes and chill twilight.

The three of us began walking. The perspective of the Rasrhe-y-Meluur moved with us, now dim, now sunlit; and it seemed that we walked a day and more than a day without moving at all. Only the floodwater grew deeper, and the stone slick with lichen and treacherous, and the seabirds called and called.

It was only then that I wished I'd thanked him properly, that old man, thought of things I should have said, because I was unlikely ever to see him again. But much of me remains in the Brown Tower, and much of the Hexenmeister travels with me still.

PART EIGHT

CHAPTER 30

The Edge of Summer

More than three weeks travelling: thirty days from Kasabaarde.

Storms kept us on Firerock for a time. Then by island ships up the Archipelago, never out of sight of land; and after that the long run out to Lone Isle. I hoped for news of Evalen's ship there, but no one had seen it. A calm kept us fifteen days. And then the *Ahrentine Star* took us to Perniesse, first and southernmost of the Sisters Islands. From there we island-hopped, mostly on fishing boats: Perniesse, Valerah, Iraine's Grave, Little Sister, Ahrentine itself; and then across the last strip of water to a bay between the white headlands of Rimon. Blaize, being a Rimon man, judged us only a few *seri* then from the estuary of the Oranon.

Riders passed us towards noon, as we sat up on the hillside away from the road. Blaize paused, unwrapping provisions.

'That's a Rimon *telestre*.' He gazed down at the *marhaz* and the cloaked riders. 'Hezreth or Makhir, I'd say.'

Rodion took two of the bread-fungus loaves and passed one over to me. 'At least we know we're on the right road for Tathcaer.'

The bronze riderbeasts were bright against the mossgrass of the valley. Their feathered hooves were clogged with yellow mud, and they plodded on until a turn in the road took them out of sight. The air was humid, and the blue mossgrass – still damp from the night's rain – gave a wet scent to the day. Carrick's Star was bright as glass.

I chewed the tough bread-fungus slowly. It had the smell of sea mammal clinging to it, having come from the boat that brought us from the Sisters Islands.

The other two fell silent. He sat against the bole of a *ziku*, resting his head back against it. Small muscles bunched in his jaw, the milky nictitating membrane slid across his eyes: he was chewing *ataile*. She gave him a slanting look but kept quiet. It was a point of argument between them. Her brown-dyed mane flopped over her forehead as she bent down to reach inside the pack. Once she stopped and gazed at him with an expression I couldn't identify. She sat beside him, close but not touching, and drew her knife and began to trim her nails. Without opening his eyes, he put his arm round her.

What am I to make of them: Aluys Blaize n'ri n'suth Meduenin, Ruric Rodion Orhlandis? One minute close to me as brother and sister, the next removing themselves lightyears into an alien humanity. The eternal problem of the empath – however close you come to a world, it's never as close as the native-born; but it's possible to draw so far from your own society that you strand yourself between the two. Out of that tension comes the work of envoy, diplomat, xeno-team. And I am Christie *S'aranth* more than Lynne de Lisle Christie.

'There's more of them.' Rodion pointed down at the road. 'All the *s'ans* going to Tathcaer . . . I don't remember the last naming, I was too young.'

'You'll remember this one.'

She laughed. A brisk wind came up the valley between the Rimon Downs, and the smell of rain came with it. She reached up and pulled down the new, seamless leaves of the *ziku*, rubbing the scarlet buds between her fingers.

'The edge of summer,' she said dreamily, 'when everything grows. That's what we used to call it in Peir-Dadeni, the last few weeks of Durestha. Spring's earlier here. It must be getting on towards the end of Seventhweek . . . It's good that we're home.'

'Will we get to Tathcaer before night?' I asked Blaize.

'Not if we don't start now.' He stood up, spat *ataile* juice behind him, and picked up his pack. Rodion sheathed her knife. She looked troubled.

'I wonder what news they've heard.' She frowned. 'If my mother – I don't know what I'm going to say to her.'

Getting here had taken all my attention. It was only now, a few *seri* from the city, that I also began to wonder what I was going to say.

Cold mist drifted up from the river, blotting out the fierce light of the stars. The pitch-torches on the slipway flared yellow and black. We kept on the edge of the crowd. *Marhaz* bugled and hissed, shuffling their hooves while they waited, and their riders shouted noisily to each other. Every second or third person wore the gold circle of a *s'an telestre*. Over the light-streaked water a darkness rose, massive as the hills, speckled here and there with lanterns: Tathcaer, the city, at last.

A team of *skurrai* dragged a creaking wheel round, and out on the water the torches of the ferry-platform were visible. Chains lifted taut from the river, dripping water that flared orange.

An ancient woman collected the ferry tolls. She was brown-skinned, with only a thread of mane left on her head, her face as whorled as a fingerprint. I unknotted a cord and slid off a silver piece, all the time staring at her familiar features.

'Salathiel *telestre*!'

'What?' Rodion said. Blaize lifted his head, then nodded sharply. I went after the old woman.

'Excuse me.' I caught her up close to the boat-sheds. 'Is there an *ashiren* here, Maric Salathiel?'

'Oh, yes. Yes. Maric!' she called, then added, 'not an *ashiren*, not since Orventa. Maric – someone to see you!' She sniffed disapprovingly. 'One of your Outland friends.'

'Who is it?' A figure came out of the sheds into the torchlight: I recognized the voice.

'Me, Christie, but keep quiet—' I stopped.

With that part of me that was Orthean, I expected it; recognized in retrospect those subtle changes that take place before the end of *ashiren*.

The voice was the same, and the face was Maric's, brown-skinned and black-maned with the old sullen expression giving way to a grin. But – and I could recognize it now – Maric was no longer *ashiren*. A patched tunic pulled tight over small breasts, she was broad across the hips where, at her belt, hung the paired *harur* blades of Theluk's that I'd given him – *her* – before Kirriach. It's hard enough to tell any Orthean's gender, but Maric had come out of *ashiren* a young woman.

'I knew you'd come back! Are you going to the city?' she said. 'Christie, I'll come with you; just let me tell Everil I'm leaving.'

'No, wait, not tonight. I'll send word—' I'd been prepared for a mental shift, to think of Maric as female if need be; what was much harder now was to think of her as adult. '—I'll send word from the city. That is, if you decide you still want to act as my *l'ri-an*.'

'Yes, of course.'

That sounded determined. Salathiel didn't approve of the envoy, I guessed. And Maric was still a very junior adult in her *telestre*.

'You got back from Shiriya-Shenin all right?'

'Yes. I've got your *marhaz* here, shall I bring *ke* with me when I come?'

'Good idea, yes.' The ferry was coming into shore, and the crowd beginning to press forward.

'I told them you didn't do it,' she said. 'Why should you harm Kanta Andrethe? I told them.'

Her tone demanded reassurance. I gripped her shoulder. 'Keep telling them – but not that you've seen me here. I've got to go. Take care.'

'I will.' She grinned as I left. 'They said you were dead. I never believed that either.'

It was a cold crossing.

The river ran fast and deep and the ferry inched through the water, Ortheans calming nervous *marhaz*. I stood between Rodion and Blaize at the crowded rail. The city loomed above us. As white as spectres, *rashaku-bazur* flew silently overhead.

'What will you do?' Blaize asked. 'I should take the Orhlandis to her mother, if the *T'An* Melkathi's in the city. That's safe enough for a Crown witness: besides, it's what I was hired for.'

Silvered water gurgled where it sucked round the piers of the dock. A warm wind came from the city, and the smell of frying oil, fish, and dung. The ferry rocked.

'The island's subject only to Crown law – that still means I'll be arrested the minute I present myself to Suthafiori, there's nothing else she can do. It may well be the safest place, but I can't say I like the idea.' Corbek was in my mind then. 'Anyway, it's too late to do anything tonight.'

'Come up to the Hill,' Rodion asked. 'I want to see my mother. She'll advise us. We can go to the Citadel in the morning.'

Has anyone seen us arrive? I thought. Who knows we're in Tathcaer? No, it's a very small chance that we've been seen.

The ferry shuddered, halted, and I saw the front ramp lowered. The crowd pressed forward. It was difficult to keep together. The stones of the dock were hard, uneven, slick with river moisture. Light dazzled from the open doors of the companion-houses. Ortheans shoved past us, shouting; and I was for a moment separated from Rodion by the cold shaggy flank of a *marhaz*.

'If you're going to the Hill, be careful,' I said when I got back to her. 'First thing in the morning I'm going up to the Citadel. You be there. I think the sooner we see the Crown, the better.'

'Where—' she stopped. 'Yes, I agree.'

If Blaize had any doubts, he was keeping them to himself. He said, 'This isn't the safest city for Outworlders. Be careful who you trust.'

It hurt to be called an Outworlder in a city and among people so familiar to me.

336

We parted there, they heading along the western shore of the island towards the Hill district. I went in towards the heart of the city. It was late, but the streets were still full of people. Companion-houses stood open, light from the courtyards spilling into the gaps between *telestre*-houses. The atmosphere was carnival. But as I went on, *telestre*-house walls rose up and all I had to see by were the stars. A thin river of light showed between the rooftops and I fumbled on. The passages stank of rider-beasts and sewage.

Midnight bells chimed. Cold, tired, I stood in the darkness and listened, eyes stinging. Tathcaer. It felt like coming home. Hadn't Ruric said it was the heart of the Southland?

Coming home to be lost, I thought sourly, having come two or three *seri* from Westbank. How can you cross half a world and then get lost trying to cross a city? Hell, have they never heard of street-lights?

Eventually I saw torches and headed for them, and came out on the quay with the harbour in front of me and Easthill and Westhill rising against the stars. That enabled me to find Eastharbour, and I wandered the narrow passages searching for Eastharbour-Salmeth. All the blank walls and bolted archway gates looked the same.

How long am I going to go stumbling round in the pitch-dark? I wondered; and then at last recognized where I was. It wasn't the *telestre*-house I'd been looking for. I couldn't care less.

I slipped the *jayante* out of its strap and hammered it on the gate of Eastharbour-Kumiel. The banging echoed hollowly. After I'd been pounding for some time – and it was bitter cold by then – there was a flicker of lantern-light behind the gate.

A very badly accented Ymirian voice shouted, 'I've told you I won't be called out at this hour of the night! You'll have the door down—'

I heard the bolts being undone. I tried to brush some of the mud and dust off my cloak and boots, without success. One half of the gate opened. Was I recognizable? I wondered wryly.

'Doctor Adair,' I said, and he lifted the lantern up and hung it on the bracket beside the gate. He had an old *becamil* cloak flung over sleeping robes, and he blinked at me for several long seconds.

'Good God!' he said at last. 'Lynne Christie?'

Outside the windows of Adair's cluttered room, the sky began to lighten. The end of first twilight: soon they'd sound the dawn bells. I rubbed my eyes, wishing I'd had more sleep. Adair had insisted on an immediate medical examination. He – or rather, his Orthean *l'ri-an* – loaned me clean clothes. I'd washed, and eaten, I should be fit. And it was all wrong to me: to travel all this way and come home a stranger.

'Well?' Huxton repeated. He drew a breath and yelled, 'What the fuck do you think you've been *doing*?'

'You got my reports.'

'Reports? Oh, that's what they were meant to be: reports?'

His voice was harsh, blaring. Getting my mind round English again after so long was hard enough. Seeing the two of them was strange: hard-eyed and hard-voiced people with squat hands and sleek caps of hair; towering giants.

'You realize you put a stop to any chance the team had of getting outside this settlement?'

'That's debatable,' Adair interrupted.

'Debatable, shit!' Huxton didn't sound as if he'd been awake long. 'Where do you think we've been this past year?'

I said, 'The *T'An Suthai-Telestre* – '

'It's your business to deal with the native authorities,' Huxton said flatly. 'If you can't do it, they should have sent someone who can.'

'Screw you!' I said. 'Don't talk to me about natives – go out there and talk to them! And when you do, mind your back, you're very likely to find a knife in it!'

He glared at me, and then sighed. 'Well – I had two reports of your death—'

I said, 'We're not easy for them to assimilate, Mr Huxton.'

'No? They seem to have assimilated you without much difficulty.'

'Meaning?'

He looked at me. 'Meaning whose side are you on, Ms Christie?'

'*Really*, Sam!' Adair slammed his hand down on the table.

I grinned. 'Do you know how much like paranoia that sounds? I think you're learning – you'll understand Orthe yet!'

He ignored the second comment, but the first cooled him down. Almost apologetically he said, 'You've changed. I wouldn't have known you.'

Huxton would calm down, I thought; he would probably even work with me in the future, but he was never going to regard me as trustworthy. It wasn't something I had the time or inclination to worry about.

Dawn bells shocked the *rashaku-bazur* off the dockside roofs.

'I must be going,' I said.

'You *can't* go to the native authorities,' Huxton protested. 'It's nothing more than lunacy! Stay here with the team, Ms Christie, and present your evidence in writing. Going to court in person would be extremely ill-advised.'

'I'd sooner go than be fetched,' I said. The thought of Sam Huxton repelling a troop of Crown Guard on my behalf was engaging, if impractical. 'Besides, it demonstrates goodwill.'

'It isn't long to the recall date,' Huxton added. His chin was rough with stubble. A much-worn one piece suit covered his burly frame. All his movements were jerky; he hadn't the cat-glide that Ortheans pick up in weapons training. 'Don't risk your freedom of movement.'

'You can testify you've seen me,' I said. 'You've got my report, you know where I'm going, and if you don't hear from me soon then kick up a fuss, I'll need all the help I can get.'

The cords of money were light now. I slipped them round my neck, under my tunic. Should I take the *jayante*? No, though I felt odd to be separated from it. I straightened my knife-belt and picked up my cloak. The light at the window was brighter.

'We'll get it settled,' Huxton said. 'Don't worry.'

He was under strain, carrying responsibility for the team for all this time, and he looked tired. A year ago there hadn't been that weariness.

'There's a *skurrai-jasin* here,' Adair said from the open doorway. 'Though where my *l'ri-an* found it at this unearthly hour, I'll never know. I've made this up for you, by the way. Medical supplies. Take the capsules with meals, they should help combat allergy and fatigue.'

'Thanks.' I took the leather wallet he held out. 'I should see you pretty soon, I think.'

Crossing the courtyard I thought, you should have said something to reassure them. Their job's hard enough without the envoy making trouble.

The relief I felt at leaving their presence was frightening. Decent enough people, but I wasn't comfortable with them. Other worlds mark you: not all the scars are visible.

Despite the early hour the *skurrai-jasin* had difficulty getting up Crown Way through the crowds. *Rashaku-bazur* yawped in the high air. Blue haze rimmed the buildings, yellowed on their sunward side. The wind was fresh. On its crag, the Citadel rose out of rivermist as if out of cotton-wool. High windows flashed back the sunrise. In the great square below the crag the mist billowed and curled, shot through with sunlight.

Sudden fear touched me. Something must go wrong now, now that I'd come so far, and with so much luck on my side.

I paid off the *skurrai-jasin* and began walking across the square. Morning noises jarred: *marhaz* hissing, *rashaku-bazur*, shouts from the barracks nearby. There were fewer people here. The gates of the great Wellhouse stood open, and fountains sparkled in the courtyards beyond. I walked past, towards the bottom of the zig-zag way and the guarded gate-arch. Remembering: here is where it began, in the common audience. To see and be seen . . .

Three or four Crown Guard stood in the shadow of the gateway; one looked up as I came closer, a woman with troopmaster's badges on her belt. She called something over her shoulder, and Blaize n'ri n'suth Meduenin came out of the gatehouse.

'That's her,' he said. 'Hello, Christie. Rodion's just gone on up, I said I'd wait for you.'

'Sure. Let's go.'

The troopmaster detailed off another four of the Guard to accompany us. Protection or arrest? I wondered. We went up the zigzag way, from mist into sunlight.

'How'd it go?' I asked.

'We found the *T'An* Melkathi's place on the Hill. The *T'An* Ruric wasn't there – I don't know where she is at the moment – but we stayed there overnight, and then came along here.'

The city and the estuary lay below us, and the sun dazzled off the morning sea. Our shadows went long into the west. The Guard took us into the Citadel by a different gate than I'd used before.

Ortheans, I thought. Immediately after meeting Adair and Hux-ton, Ortheans had seemed the small lithe people I'd first seen: cropped manes, claw-nailed hands, and whiteless animal eyes. Now I saw them as familiar, with memories that weren't entirely mine.

We came by various ante-rooms into a high-roofed chamber, where tall slit windows let light in from an inner courtyard. A group of people stood arguing with such vehemence that they didn't notice our arrival.

'She's here!' Rodion said, her arm linked round a dark-skinned woman; and the woman turned and pushed her black mane back from her face with her single hand.

'Sunmother!' Ruric exclaimed, 'the only time I'll believe you dead is if I see the body burned! Christie, what's this about Dadeni—'

'And the ship,' a man rumbled. Ramrod-straight back, white crest: I recognized old Hellel Hanathra, Ymir's First Minister. 'The *t'an* Evalen's company?'

'They haven't reached here yet?'

'We were delayed,' Rodion interrupted, 'maybe they were too.'

'With your permission,' Ruric said perfunctorily to Hellel. 'Clear the hall – Romare, take word to the *T'An Suthai-Telestre*. Troopmaster, guard the entrances here.'

She sat back against the table, fingers knotting up the empty sleeve of her shirt that had come unpinned. 'We've been up all night, Suthafiori and I – this naming's an unchancy business. My sire and dam! Then you turn up.' Ruric's eyes strayed to Rodion, who was talking to Blaize. Her brown-dyed mane showed silver at the roots. 'I hardly knew her when I saw her, Christie.'

Hellel Hanathra stayed, but the other members of the *takshiriye* left the hall. Crown Guard stood at the doors, *harur* blades drawn. Then a woman came in, and Rodion and Blaize made formal bows, and I followed.

She looked older, mane more silver than gilt, lines scored heavily into her face, translucent, diamond-patterned skin stretched over hard bone. Her whiteless blue eyes were keen as ever, and quietly amused.

'Has the Mother given you back to us?' Suthafiori said, 'or is there a simpler explanation?'

'There's an explanation, *T'An*, but it isn't simple.'

She laughed briefly, and settled herself in the great carved chair at the head of the table. Ruric said, 'There's something you ought to hear, Dalzielle. About Peir-Dadeni.'

Rodion and I told it between us. What sounded plausible in Kasabaarde had a hollowness about it in Tathcaer. I was aware of the growing silence. But when I'd finished I knew there was still, in all the uncertainty, that one fact: that Brodin spoke to Rodion Orhlandis outside the Crystal Hall. That remained, and demanded explanation.

Suthafiori said, 'This is that Brodin n'ri n'suth Charain who is now first minister for Turi Andrethe?'

'That's the man,' Ruric confirmed. 'He was an intelligencer, if you recall, for Kanta. Well . . .'

'Well, we have suspected her intelligencers.' Suthafiori linked her fingers and leaned back. 'Albeit without proof, but that in the main because of the supposed guilt of the envoy – I must hold you under Crown arrest, Christie, but I think you know that.'

I nodded. She continued, 'This must be investigated, this and that other matter of Kel Harantish, which must wait on the *Child of Methemna's* return. *T'An* Hellel, be good enough to take the Guard to the Andrethe's apartments in this Citadel: bring Brodin n'ri n'suth Charain here to me.'

Hellel bowed and left. We were all silent. My stomach was tight. Rodion, one hand on Blaize's arm, sat between him and her mother. She wouldn't look directly at anyone. Ruric's narrow dark face showed nothing at all: she must be working out the implications.

'Would that you'd come sooner,' Suthafiori mused. 'Seventh-week Eightday . . . and the solstice and the naming only twelve days away. Still, that may be to the good. If a trial's held, the news need go nowhere but across the island, every *s'an* of the Hundred Thousand must be here by now.'

'Will you try him?' Ruric asked.

'Both of them,' Suthafiori said. 'If nothing else, the envoy's innocence can be established. The word from the Brown Tower has weight. And if the man's guilty, then well and good; and if not, the murderer's still to find. But there's little time for any of it.'

There were footsteps outside. The double doors opened. The acting first minister of Peir-Dadeni came in flanked by four of the Crown Guard, Hellel Hanathra behind them. Brodin wore no *harur* blades, nothing but a richly-embroidered *chirith-goyen* robe, and his sharp face was dazzled with sleep.

'*T'An*,' he began, and then his eyes went to Rodion and to me, and he was silent.

I saw his lean face and I knew I was right, Rodion was right, the Brown Tower had the truth of it. His eyes were feverishly bright as he faced Suthafiori. His hands gripped the back of the chair, knuckles jutting whitely. I have never seen a face so ravaged by grief and guilt.

As it dawned on him what was happening, the strain left him. He seemed to be welcoming what was happening to him. I thought, Yes, you want to be caught. You killed her. And you can't live with it.

'You are held under arrest,' Suthafiori said, anger tempered by his obvious suffering. 'The charge to be answered is the murder of Kanta Andrethe, how say you?'

'Yes,' he was dazed. 'She – my *arykei*, I—'

'Do you confess it?' Ruric was sharp.

'I did it from my own ambition.' That was a mumble. He breathed deeply and raised his head, his eyes on Suthafiori. 'I killed her and I'm sorry for it – more than you could ever know. I killed myself with her.'

'So, and did you also attack Orhlandis?' Ruric was on her feet, hand clamped on Rodion's shoulder.

'Peace, *T'An* Melkathi. That can wait.' When Ruric resumed her seat, the Crown continued. 'Brodin n'ri n'suth Charain, you may have what aid from advocates or Wellhouse that you desire. You will be confined in the Citadel until Durestha Eighthweek Firstday: that day the trial begins.'

'Yes,' he said, and after that nothing more, standing still and quiet as if he might shatter at a touch.

'Remove him,' Suthafiori said, and as he went out added to Ruric, 'A full trial in the presence of all the *T'Ans* of the provinces – then let them say what they like, they have no excuse against my Outworlders now.'

'And if he didn't work alone, if Kel Harantish gold is at the back of it, and others like SuBannasen?' Ruric demanded.

'We'll see what else he'll confess to,' Suthafiori said, then turned to listen to a man who'd just entered. Her intent expression lightened.

'Here's good news,' she said, 'Romare brings word: the *Child of Methemna* is sighted at the Sisters Islands.'

CHAPTER 31

Broдin n'ri n'suth Charain

A short time later Romare brought another man in. He was elderly, brown-skinned, his mane shaven down to black fur: I knew him from somewhere. He wore the skirt of an Earthspeaker.

'There must be no suspicion of my hand in this,' Suthafiori addressed us generally, 'or else I'd keep you in the Tathcaer prison under Crown law. Earthspeaker Tirzael, will you consent to take all witnesses in this matter into the Wellhouse?'

'If it be all of them,' he said. 'I've heard the Charain man has to do with this: him too. And they must live by custom, no weapons, no word, no contact outside the House.'

'May I send word to my people, if that's the case?' I saw Suthafiori hesitate before she agreed.

'Yes . . . yes, they should know where you are.' Her irritation with Tirzael faded as she spoke to the Orhlandis woman. 'Ruric, Rodion, I'm sorry to part you again so soon.'

'At least I'll know where she is,' Ruric said drily, and a little unsteadily. 'There's no safer place than the House of the Goddess.'

'What of your hired sword?'

'I'm witness to the attacks on Orhlandis,' Blaize said. 'Make what you will of that, *T'An*.'

'Confine them all,' she said to Tirzael, and then to us: 'It's for three days only, you'll be free after the trial – all of you who are innocent.'

They took us down from the Citadel to the square, and to the Wellhouse.

Passing through the archway into the courtyard, I managed to pin down the sense of déjà vu. There was the same atmosphere as in Su'niar, Gethfirle, Cir-nanth, any of the Order houses of Kasa-baarde's inner city.

Tirzael dismissed the Guard peremptorily. To us he said, 'Now I must take your weapons.'

Blaize slipped the buckles of his sword-belt, giving *harur-nilgiri* and *harur-nazari* to a young woman beside Tirzael. Rodion bristled, but took off her blades. I'd left the stunner with Adair.

'And your knife,' the Earthspeaker said to me.

'It isn't a weapon.'

'All the same.'

I felt naked without it.

'Now you are free within the walls,' he said. Brodin, who had stood silently by, followed him as he walked off, and I saw them enter the great central dome of the Wellhouse.

Blaize saw me watching. 'They can't deny it to him. Let's find the kitchens – I haven't eaten since last night.'

Is he afraid of us? I wondered, looking after Brodin. It might be doing him an injustice. He was south Dadeni, and as likely to be a religious man in search of temporary peace or consolation.

Like Hill-Damarie the place had kitchens, stables, and smithy all within its walls. Gardens and courtyards extended for a considerable distance, and bird's-wing bushes grew, and tall feathery *lapuur*.

Late in the morning I went back to the courtyard close to the gate, restless and curious. There was nothing to do but wait, and the very waiting ruled out the possibility of a serenity like Kasabaarde's.

Many of the Goddess's people were there, barefoot, shave-maned, and wearing priest's skirts: a length of brown cloth wrapped round the waist and knotted over one hip. The ancient tiles were tracked over with muddy footprints. None of the Earth-speakers or Wellkeepers spoke, though some stared curiously.

So I was there when another party came, the Crown Guard and some others in sailor's dress, and I recognised *t'an* Evalen at their head. She had the Desert Coast woman Havoth-jair with her, and Haltern. I saw Tirzael coming, and went over.

'How's it going?' I asked Haltern.

'Seas like mountains,' he said palely, 'I've not recovered yet. We were two weeks in Quarth harbour waiting out storms, or we'd have been here before you. Christie, is there anything you need?'

'If you're doing favours, you can keep Sam Huxton up to date about what goes on—' I was interrupted by Tirzael, who parted us fiercely. He took Havoth-jair from Evalen, and hustled the others out.

'You,' he said when they'd gone, 'make no sacrilege in Her house.'

'I was marked for Her once,' I said, with a sneaking satisfaction at the amazement on his face. 'In Corbek, in a Wellhouse.'

And there was that other Wellhouse in Corbek, and Arad's

mockery of a trial, and nights in cells that I didn't want to remember. I wondered then how Crown law would differ from Wellhouse justice.

Nothing in the House of the Goddess changed except the light: white sun in the day, fierce stars the next night. Blaize retreated into silent watchfulness. Rodion fretted like a *kazza* in a cage. Havoth-jair kept herself apart, too untouched by the world to be normal.

My one attempt to talk to her that day failed. When I finally did get her to respond:

'I don't want to know,' she said in thickly-accented Ymirian. Though it was a warm day she was shivering. 'What's one stranger more or less to me? If I'd killed you, at least I'd be able to go home to Kel Harantish.'

'You want to?' With all I'd heard, that astonished me.

'It's what I knew.' She had her back to the courtyard wall, sitting and staring up at the intense sky. 'What do I know about conspiracies, other worlds? Nothing. What do I want to know? Even less. And now I'll never—'

She trailed off, and went back to stirring patterns in the mud on the ancient cracked tiles. I left her. The hostility was plain. Sometimes she had a bewildered look, as if she knew something was wrong but not what it was. I knew she blamed me. I should have been obliging and died in Kasabaarde . . .

I took care never to turn my back on her.

'Tomorrow,' Rodion said, kicking her boot-heel against the leg of the table. 'Tomorrow. Land's destruction! how can you just *sit* there?'

Only we three were left in the kitchens. The Goddess's people had eaten, and gone about their business. Afternoon light slanted through the slit windows, gilding the brown bricks and tiled floor.

'You got a better idea, I'll hear it.'

She glared at Blaize. The brown dye had washed out and left her mane a sepia colour, pale against her gold-dust skin. 'There's got to be something we can do!'

'Waiting's a talent. Develop it. No,' he said, 'sorry, *arykei-te*.'

She stood up. Her hand brushed back, the automatic Southland gesture to check the presence of a *harur* blade. Their absence irritated her.

'Sit there until you turn to stone,' she said, 'much good may it do you.'

Her shadow blocked the door for a second, then I heard her

heels rap across the court. Someone spoke to her, and I heard her snarled reply.

'Well, kinsister,' Blaize said wryly, 'what do you make of that?'

'I think she's very nearly as nervous as I am.'

He smiled briefly. 'There's no point raising dust when all you can do is wait. I learned that a long time ago. Christie, you don't think it's something else wrong with her?'

'Like what?'

He searched for words, then said, 'Maybe it looks different to her now, in Tathcaer. Not the way it did on the road and in Kasabaarde.'

His unscarred profile towards me, he looked younger; but under the vulnerability there was more than just physical strength.

'I thought you and she were good *arykei*.'

'We quarrel sometimes. It's the way of things. I thought, I hoped . . .' On the table, his hand closed into a fist. 'We should be *n'ri n'suth*. Meduenin, Orhlandis, doesn't matter. Christie, she's young. She wants to do all the travelling and fighting and having *arykei* that you do when you've changed from *ashiren*. Where does that leave me? I've hired out over half Orthe, and there isn't one place I'd go back to.'

After some time he said, 'Well?'

'Mmm? I was thinking about Hakataku. Where I was last; that's a world that's mostly agricultural,' I explained. 'Dirty, and the food was rotten, and you had to walk everywhere. Only what I was thinking: when I got back to Earth I swore that's it, no more, that's the last time I ever go off-world. Ever. Then Carrick V came up, and you wouldn't believe how fast I jumped at the chance. Incredible, it was, for someone who was never in her life going off-planet again.'

'I've been doing this longer than you.'

'Not much longer, I shouldn't think; and what's that got to do with it?'

His head went back and he laughed, tendons cording his throat. 'Ahh, you may be right, at that. And there's nothing to be done until this trial's over. I'll take my own counsel: patience.'

I want patience, I thought. But I want it *now*.

Rodion was sitting on the edge of the great fountain, looking out through the main gate. The Goddess's people wouldn't interfere unless we attempted to leave. I sat down beside her, trailing a hand in the chill water. Many people were visible in the great square; there was much coming and going, and what looked like tents or booths being set up. It was no cure for impatience, to sit there and be aware of being in a backwater.

347

Rodion flicked her claw-nail thumb on the water's surface. Crimson fish scattered. She said, 'I wish I was back in Shiriya-Shenin.'

That was unexpected. 'Why?'

'Oh, I don't know . . . I was there four years, you know. A lot of the time I liked it. Even being called Halfgold, that was only a few people.' She shrugged. 'I suppose I'll get used to this place, and Orhlandis.'

Something in her attitude was at odds with her speech. She was holding down joy, excitement, surprise. What fear made her conceal it? I asked myself.

'What will you do, now you're not *ashiren*?'

'Learn policy,' she was succinct. 'With an Orhlandis as *T'An* Melkathi, what else? If I stay Orhlandis.'

Under short pale lashes, her eyes glanced up.

'And Meduenin?'

She sighed, stretching her wiry body. Reflectively she said, 'Yes. Meduenin. I don't know the Rimon *telestres* . . .'

'Does it have to be one or the other, and no alternative? No, don't tell me: it does. I know the Southland. But you'll travel, won't you?'

'Where I come back to is important too.'

'And Blaize?'

'Is important, yes. Yes. I have to make a decision soon, Christie.'

She seemed more adult as the days passed now, not just in body but in mind and thought and gesture. I said, 'Should you hurry it?'

'It's later than you think,' she said, exuberance surfacing in her eyes. With a mixture of joy and concern that was wholly Orthean, she added, 'I have to decide which *telestre's* best suited to bring up *ashiren*.'

'What – soon? *Now*?'

She laughed. 'I knew since Ahrentine, I'm carrying children. Christie, keep it silent until I decide – it isn't fair to say until I know what I'm going to do. The *ashiren* belong to Orhlandis. They might not permit me to be *n'ri n'suth* Meduenin – if that's what I decide to do.'

'You'll tell Blaize.'

'Yes, if Meduenin's to be involved . . . *S'aranth*, what are you thinking?'

The child, or children, would belong not to the father, not even to the mother, but to the entire *telestre*: I had seen that at Beth'ru-elen.

'I won't tell anyone before you do,' I said. 'You're a Southlander, you'd better solve this one yourself.'

*

348

Eighthweek Firstday, the day of the trial. I was awake long before first twilight, and heard an escort arrive. They'd gone again before I'd dressed, and I realized Brodin had gone with them, taken to the Hall of Justice before dawn.

At midmorning-bell they came for Rodion, and then shortly before the noon-bell took Blaize; and I was left to wait.

Clouds drifted over, solid as castles, and the sky was paleh and star-freckled. Noon passed. Nothing moved in the Wellhouse grounds but shadow and sunlight. A sea-wind was stifled between the buildings. I thought, Are they going to call me today? Because if not—

I saw a stir at the gate, Crown Guard uniforms, and went over before Tirzael sent for me. There were eight Guard beside the troopmaster. How much trouble are they expecting? I thought. And realized I wasn't even certain where the Hall was.

We left by another gate, passing into the narrow passages between *telestre*-houses that clung to the foot of the Citadel crag. Twists and turns confused me. Then, before the Hall was even in sight, we hit the crowds. Native Ymirians, Melkathians with sari-robes and serrated knives, Roehmonders hot in high-necked tunics; all rubbed shoulders with Rimon men and women, robed Dadeni, Freeporters, and even Ortheans from the Kyre. The Crown Guard formed a wedge with me in the centre, and we pushed on through.

Over the heads of the crowd I saw a sprawling building, ancient and familiar. Brown brick walls followed a succession of curves, and above the first two or three metres swelled up into an egg-basket of domes. Old, this Hall of Justice, old as Terison.

The crowd didn't lessen as we went in under the round archway. A passage opened for us. Many there were *s'an telestres*, I saw, and many were children. A surprising number were just past being *ashiren*, in their sixteenth or seventeenth year.

Beyond the antechamber, the Ortheans were sitting packed together on the tiled floor. An unexpectedly wide space opened up: the multiple domes were supported on brick pillars and the building was one great hall. It was loud with conversation, restless with the vivid gestures of Southland argument, and as the Guard brought me through towards the centre of the hall, many of the *ashiren* and young adults began that sibilant hissing and beating of hands against the floor that signifies Orthean applause.

The troopmaster, a small dark man, observed, 'You have a following with the young ones, *t'an*.'

'I didn't know.' I had no time to think about it.

Under the central dome, eight thrones stood in a semi-circle, hacked out of black rock and covered with pelts and cushions. Between the arms of the horseshoe was a stone block, only a few inches higher than floor-level. All but one of the thrones were occupied: Suthafiori leaning over to talk with Ruric, Hellel Hanathra listening to a man in the brilliant sashed robes of the Kyre, sleek and bright-eyed Howice Talkul *T'An* Roehmonde deep in conversation with a man and woman I didn't recognize. Facing the thrones and completing the circle was a horseshoe-shaped stone bench: the Ortheans here had divided into two seated groups, some talking, some consulting books and parchments.

Haltern n'ri n'suth Beth'ru-elen beckoned me to sit beside him on the bench.

'How's it going?'

'They're still hearing the Andrethe *telestre*. Turi's doing most of the talking.' He indicated a brown-skinned woman close by me on the bench. 'Charain *telestre* aren't pleased, but what can they say: the man's guilty.'

In Haltern's eyes Brodin was already condemned. I saw him then, on the far end of the bench, flanked by Crown Guard. His hands moved like restless, independent animals. His face was motionless, the pale marks of dried tears streaking his skin; and he seemed oblivious of the moisture that from time to time seeped from his eyes.

A bell chimed. The talking died, silence spreading through the Hall until the only sound came from the street crowds. Suthafiori leaned back, steepled her six-fingered hands, and nodded to Haltern.

'We'll hear the Dominion envoy next.'

'Pardon, *T'An Suthai-Telestre*.' The big man next to Howice spoke. He was a giant by Orthean standards, something over two metres tall and bulky with it. His mane had a long crop.

'Thu'ell *T'An* Rimon, I hear you.'

'This, then: the woman here – the envoy – was accused of this same murder. What chance that her evidence will not be false?'

The woman pointed out to me as Turi Andrethe stood, answering from the bench. 'For this reason we do not, ourselves, accept *t'an* Brodin's confession of guilt on its own: we bring evidence from the *tha'adur* of Shiriya-Shenin. If you and these others assembled decide that despite motive, despite confession, *t'an* Brodin is not guilty – then is the time to look again at the envoy's evidence.'

Thu'ell subsided, rumbling inaudible comments.

I went to the stand and told of events in Shiriya-Shenin,

sometimes being questioned by Turi Andrethe and sometimes by the Charain people. Towards the end of it I mentioned Morvren and the Freeport. The woman next to Howice leaned forward. She was pale-skinned, with a great unbound mane flaring crimson over her blue robe. A small child sat between her feet, playing with the ship-embroidered hem.

'And from Freeport you went – where?'

Accent, dress, and position: she must be Seamarshal of that port, I realized. 'To Kasabearde, *T'An.*'

Voices died, Ortheans exchanged troubled glances. Turi Andrethe stood.

'Envoy, will you tell us what took place at the Brown Tower.'

In the silence I heard *ashiren* fidgeting, a baby whining.

'Much took place there, *t'an*, but as to this matter: the Hexenmeister declared himself satisfied of my innocence – the *t'an* Evalen Kerys-Andrethe will confirm that.' It was a strange thing to carry weight in a court of law, I reflected. 'I may add, it was the Hexenmeister whose aid helped uncover the evidence you hear.'

That more or less ended it, though Charain made a desultory attempt to trip me up on small details. They weren't too interested in the Dominion envoy, either as envoy or as murder suspect. Being dismissed, I returned to the bench; and then saw Blaize and Rodion seated on the floor in the front of the crowd, and joined them.

'We will hear the *t'an* Brodin,' Suthafiori said to the Charain.

There was some hesitation, the man not being able to stand, while they brought a chair to place in front of the *T'Ans.*

'We judge the dispute between Andrethe and Charain,' Suthafiori said formally. 'You are accused of killing Kanta Andrethe, third of that name, in her city of Shiriya-Shenin. Do you understand?'

'I hear you,' he said quietly, rationally.

'What say you?'

'Yes,' he said. 'I killed her. You've heard the truth.'

The man in Kyre robes signalled, and Suthafiori nodded. In badly-accented formal Peir-Dadeni he said, 'Even in the mountains it was known, *T'An* Andrethe had her *arykei* among the *tha'adur*: why would you kill her?'

Brodin nodded to himself. 'Kelveric *T'An* Kyre, you have known ambitious men. She – knew certain things of me. *Arykei*, intelligencer . . . with her gone, there are ways for a clever man to become minister, perhaps even First Minister.'

'And for that you murdered her?'

'I have said so.'

One of the Charain woman stood, saying 'T'Ans, our brother is sick—'

Ruric asked recognition from Suthafiori, then said, 'If you would have become powerful in Shiriya-Shenin, would it not have suited you better to remain the Andrethe's *arykei*?'

Brodin shifted uneasily. 'She knew – my life wasn't always guiltless.'

Dark-skinned, pale-eyed; Turi Andrethe came forward again.

'I will ask *t'an* Brodin to listen to this and account for it. The body of Kanta Andrethe, when discovered, showed marks of having fought against an attacker. Not only that, she was struck first with the intention of stunning her.'

'She had been a trained fighter,' Brodin interrupted, highly agitated. 'I knew it would be difficult. I killed her. Why else would I kill her?'

'Why? Yes: why?' Turi surveyed the seven *T'Ans*. 'In Shiriya-Shenin last Orventa we heard Sulis n'ri n'suth SuBannasen, we heard of her guilt; taking gold from Kel Harantish. What more likely than, before she died, she used that gold to good effect – good for the Emperor-in-Exile? I say that Brodin n'ri n'suth Charain killed Kanta Andrethe not for his own advancement, but solely and simply because he was paid to do so.'

Brodin shook his head rapidly. 'I swear by the Goddess, by my hope of Her – SuBannasen paid me for nothing, not for murder, not for any intelligence: I never took gold from her!'

Haltern stood up beside Turi. 'T'Ans, there is another witness you should hear, it touches closely on this matter.'

'Call your witness,' Suthafiori said. 'Charain, look to the *t'an* Brodin.'

They surrounded the hawk-faced man. I saw one of them offer a wine-flask.

Haltern's witness was Havoth-jair. The Desert woman spoke of gold ships from Kel Harantish; those that had gone to Sulis n'ri n'suth SuBannasen, and those that sailed for the Hundred Thousand long after she was known to be dead. It seemed that the half-idiot stare, coupled with the knowledge she had been in the Brown Tower, profoundly affected the Southlanders.

'Sulis was not the Hundred Thousand's only traitor,' Haltern said. You could sense the disapproval radiated by the crowd.

'I'm no traitor, I'm no SuBannasen either.' His voice barely under control, Brodin rapped out: 'I've told you I killed her, what more do you want of me?'

'You have never taken Kel Harantish gold?'

'I received no gold ships from the Emperor-in-Exile.'

It was an evasion. Watching Brodin, I realized he wasn't far off total mental collapse.

'Nevertheless, there is a conspiracy, there are traitors to the Hundred Thousand.' Haltern's certainty echoed in the Hall. I'd never seen him so positive. 'You are a confessed killer. Now confess why it was done.'

'I've told you! How many more times?'

'It was unplanned, no other person had a hand in it?'

Brodin's eyes went to Suthafiori. '*T'An*, how often must I say it?'

Sudden and shrewd, Haltern added, 'And will you swear, in the name of the Goddess, that you have never been paid in Kel Harantish gold?'

Brodin shrugged. 'What need to swear?'

'A great need. Swear that oath: you never took the Emperor's gold, you were never part of a conspiracy to blame the Andrethe's murder on another – let us hear, *t'an*.'

A long silence. Brodin looked this way and that, from the *T'Ans* to Turi Andrethe to Charain *telestre*. I remembered him sequestered in the Wellhouse. The silence lasted. It became obvious he would say nothing. You could feel the crowd turning against him, without a word being said.

'You will not swear?' Haltern persisted.

Brodin at last looked up and said, 'I've said all I have to say here, I'll take no oaths for your pleasure.'

Haltern resumed his seat. Turi Andrethe said, 'There is nothing else we can ask him.'

Eighthweek Twoday I spent in the Wellhouse, with Rodion and Blaize and the Desert woman, while the *T'Ans* debated the case between themselves. Tirzael Earthspeaker had charge of Brodin. He never spoke after his final words in the Hall of Justice. And the next day we were called back to the Hall again.

'Hear me,' Suthafiori said. The crowd's noise died. If anything, there were more people packed in than there had been on the first day. 'Hear the word of Thu'ell *T'An* Rimon, Ruric *T'An* Melkathi, Hellel Hanathra, First Minister of Ymir; hear the word of Howice *T'An* Roehmonde, Emberen Seamarshal, and Kelveric *T'An* Kyre.'

Brodin sat with the Charain *telestre*. One of the men put a hand on his shoulder. Brodin never moved. His eyes were bright, showing their whites.

'For the first accusation, of the murder of Kanta Andrethe, Brodin n'ri n'suth Charain is confessed and proved guilty.' She hesitated. I saw she disliked the whole affair. 'That has the lesser penalty, death. For the second accusation, of a conspiracy with agents of the Emperor-in-Exile, we can reach no decision. By ancient custom we have a season of time before the penalty is carried out. Our word is this: Brodin n'ri n'suth Charain, being condemned to die for Kanta Andrethe's murder, shall be held and put to the question on this matter of conspiracy. Sentence of death will be carried out publicly in the season of Merrum.'

Brodin's face looked as though someone had blown chalk-dust over it. The Charain *telestre* were arguing with the Crown Guard surrounding them, and the hubbub as the crowd spread the news made speech impossible.

I suppose I'd been deceived by the way Southlanders spoke of their Goddess into thinking it wasn't something they took seriously. But here was Brodin n'ri n'suth Charain, already a dead man for the Andrethe's murder, who would not excuse himself under oath to Her. And what he risked by it wasn't simple execution, but being tortured until he broke and confessed.

Confessed to what? I wondered as the Hall emptied. Whatever it pleased the *T'Ans* he should confess to?

Death and pain to an Orthean are lesser penalties, that's a difference in species and culture. But what I thought after Brodin's trial was that there was no more justice in it than in that travesty of a hearing I'd undergone in the Corbek Wellhouse.

CHAPTER 32

S'aranth

'It's not finished,' Haltern predicted, 'no matter what that thing says.'

The Fiveday broadsheet ran to three pages, most of it devoted to Brodin's trial. I spread the second sheet out on the courtyard tiles. Maric came out of the kitchen with another jug of herb-tea, and put it down on the table beside Haltern. He – she – had come back to Easthill Malk'ys after I sent her a message on Fourday.

'Listen to this,' I said. ' "We anticipate also the early confession of Brodin n'ri n'suth Charain to a like charge with Sulis n'ri n'suth SuBannasen, namely, trafficking with the Emperor-in-Exile and receiving bribes direct from Kel Harantish." '

'But did he?' Haltern drained his tea-bowl, wiping his mouth fastidiously. 'I know – I thought I knew the man. I worked with him. He hadn't the mind of a planner. He's a follower, not a leader.'

'Meaning there's someone who was behind him, someone still at large.' It hadn't taken much thinking to reach that conclusion. I weighted a corner of the large, unwieldy broadsheet with a rock. 'Hal, tell me if this makes sense. SuBannasen's intention was always to have the envoy killed, therefore that was the Harantish Witchbreed's intention also. That accounts for the poison, for assassins, maybe even for Corbek. But the Andrethe . . . that's different. That wasn't designed to have me killed, that was done to discredit me, and therefore the Dominion. That was done to break down relationships between the worlds.'

Haltern nodded. He had the distracted look that meant he wanted to conceal what he was thinking. 'So?'

'So whoever took over from SuBannasen has ideas of their own – and I can't see it being Brodin, that's all. It doesn't fit, not with that kind of man, you're right.'

'Mmm.' He reached down and snared one sheet, shaking it out

and studying it. 'You may be right, I couldn't say . . . are you going to the ceremony?'

'When is it?'

'Noon.'

'I don't know if I'll have the time. Every *s'an telestre* in Tathcaer seems to want to meet the envoy, and I've got to see as many of them as I can. I'll try and make it.'

'There's not too much to this one – just the *T'Ans* giving up their offices, and the *T'An Suthai-Telestre* giving authority for Tathcaer over to the *T'An* Commander. You've met Asshe?'

'When he took over from Ruric, yes.' I turned the broadsheet again. It was cool now, just after dawn; later in the day it would be uncomfortably hot. Easthill Malk'ys was small, cramped, and dark – or so I thought, after my travels. The city was bursting full. Streets were mired with dung, and the stench of the drainage channels was unbelievable. The most common overheard remark in Tathcaer was, No wonder it only happens once in ten years.

'At least the press supports us,' I said. 'Looks like Earth's in favour, for once – what are you grinning at?'

His eyes veiled, amused. The mask of innocence slipped from time to time. 'What the press supports isn't the Dominion, but *S'aranth*. Those schemes against the envoy rebounded when you were proclaimed innocent – for the moment, anyway, Christie *S'aranth* can do no wrong.'

'Bloody hell! My god, Hal—'

He wheezed with laughter. 'If you could see your face! Don't argue with it, Christie. It won't last long, but it'll help you while it does.'

They don't have the exact term, but Crown Messengers know all about public relations.

'I'll talk to the xeno-team,' I decided, 'see if I can't rope some of them in and take the heat off. It's only simple questions need answering.'

Shadows were shortening, the sun that touched Easthill and Westhill now descending into the city. *Rashaku-dya* flashed black and bronze, their chirruping clear in the high air. I heard Oru shift in the stables, scuffing the straw and hissing softly. Scents were clear after the dampness of the night, musky dung and fading *kazsis* nightflower and the sharp tang of herb-tea.

'Has Ruric seen this?'

He peered over my shoulder. Tucked in a corner, the name had caught my eye:

'News from the Lu'Nathe: Southland ship *Hanathra*, shipmaster

Sadri Geren Hanathra, wintered over in L'Dui; reprovisioned and departed Hanys Firstweek on second attempt at Western voyage.'

'That, yes. It didn't please her.' He stood, brushing his close-cropped fair mane into some semblance of order. He was as shabby as ever, unlikely to be noticed in the busy city.

'I must get back to the Citadel. Christie, I don't have to tell you, do I? Whoever's behind Brodin has lost their gold-supply, their freedom of action, and they won't look far to blame it on someone. Be careful.'

'I will,' I said. I meant it.

Noon announced itself from the bell-towers. There was no time to attend ceremonies. I managed to get down through the crowds to Eastharbour-Salmeth and see Sam Huxton, who turned out to be nearly as busy as me.

'Do you realize—' he reached over and flicked the recorder off. 'Do you realize we've got slightly over four weeks to the recall date? And I have to have everything up to date and collected—'

'So do I, Mr Huxton, and for various reasons I'm having to do half a year's work before Merrum Forthweek.'

'Various reasons?' He rubbed the bridge of his nose. He was trying not to smile. 'Yes, you could put it that way. Well, what can I do for you?'

'You can lend me anyone in the team that you don't need for a few days. Let them come up to Easthill Malk'ys and handle some of the simpler interviews.' Best to be direct, I thought. The very fact that I had to come to him for help would make him amiable.

'Anyone I don't need—!' He made an incomplete gesture at the pile of tapes scattered over the table. 'In bio-readings alone . . . never mind. All right, Lynne. Carrie Thomas is pretty well finished, I think, and so is John Lalkaka; tell those two I said they should help you.'

'I'll do the same for you someday.' I got up to go. The pseudo-Earth decor of Eastharbour-Salmeth made me uneasy.

'Not me,' he said as I left, 'this is the last time I'm going off-world. Aboriginal pest-holes.'

I walked down with John and Carrie when we finally closed Easthill Malk'ys for the day. Down the narrow passages between overflowing *telestre*-houses, walking in the long golden evening. The companion-houses were open, and we stopped to drink pale wine in a dusty courtyard, John's thin brown fingers darting to emphasize a point as he spoke, Carrie sprawling her elbows on the table and grinning.

'Four weeks,' she said. 'Thirty six days. Then home.'

'If you don't count three months FTL.'

'The first thing I'm going to do when I'm back on Earth—'

I stood. They looked up, barely noticing the interruption.

'I've got to get back. You'll come along again tomorrow?'

'Sure,' Carrie agreed. 'Anything's better than listening to Sam bitch at us. We'll be there.'

I began elbowing my way through the crowds. Occasionally someone spoke to me, and I acknowledged it. I didn't know them, but after the trial the envoy's face was familiar to many.

Ortheans crowded the *telestre*-houses, slept in courtyards and roof-gardens and public parks. An encampment of tents had sprung up on the east bank of the Oranon river and when the wind came from Beriah's Bridge you could smell them. Tradition kept the city from total breakdown, the *telestre* tradition that guests should do their share of the work, so that the *s'ans* cooked and served food, unloaded ships, cared for *ashiren*, drove *skurrai-jasin*, cleaned the passages – did anything that required their labour.

Crowding doesn't suit Ortheans, not in a city. There were few killings but many fights. I witnessed some: the brief vicious scuffles that by tradition end at first blood-letting. Thieving went on without much notice being taken of it, Ortheans not regarding it as serious. I had to keep a close eye on Easthill Malk'ys to prevent them walking off with souvenirs. In the streets I was aware of *T'An* Commander Asshe's troops, but their presence wasn't obtrusive. The atmosphere was festive.

The companion-houses overflowed with custom. Warehouses, previously stored full to bursting, emptied in a rush. Ships in the harbour lightened as their loads poured onto the island. The Guild-Ring stayed open for business from the dawn bell until midnight.

It being a naming, I'd expected the general talk to be of *T'Ans* and the Crown. But these were *s'an telestres*. What I heard as I passed groups in conversation was: the drought in southern Melkathi (dry spring succeeding dry winter), new varieties of grain, Rimon's schemes to make the Oranon a passable waterway above Damory, Morvren's coastal trade, the Peir-Dadeni programme for breeding *skurrai*, *zilmei* hunts in the Roehmonde forest . . .

Almost as an afterthought, they each made their way up to the booths in Citadel Square to name their choice of *T'An*.

That's the split, I thought as I climbed the last hill slope to Malk'ys. *S'ans* and *telestres* on the one hand, and cities and conspiracies – the game – on the other. And yet they're both integral to the Hundred Thousand . . .

The climb left me breathless. Second twilight was coming on, the shutters in the courtyard closed, and I could see Maric had lit the oil lamps. She came out of the archway to greet me.

'There's someone waiting to see you.'

'Good grief, not another one! Didn't you say to come back tomorrow?'

'No, I didn't think I should.'

I followed her into the *telestre*-house, decided we'd better have herb-tea and be social, and went into the room I was using as an office. A small woman in a light *chirith-goyen* cloak stood at the window. She turned. Dalzielle Kerys-Andrethe, Suthafiori.

'Ah, Christie.' She shed her cloak, taking a seat by the hearth. There was no fire, the evening being mild. Maric brought herb-tea, grinned at me, and retired.

'*T'An Suthai-Telestre*.' To cover my surprise, I began to serve tea.

'Oh, there is no *T'An Suthai-Telestre* – not until the solstice,' she said, smiling. 'And any Orthean may call on the Dominion envoy, yes?'

'Yes, of course.' Fencing, guessing: why was she here?

'Yes . . .' Her fingers hooked in her belt, she gazed up from under fair lashes. There was still a hint of winter scale-pattern in her skin. She gestured for me to sit down.

'There are ships newly into harbour,' she said. 'Some Desert Coast, some Rainbow Cities, Saberonisi and the like. You will see them, will you, if they visit the envoy?'

'Naturally, *t'an*.'

Membrane clouded her eyes. 'You favour a slow contact between our worlds – what did Evalen call it? Restricted, yes.'

'There's a danger of infection.' She took that at more than face value, I saw. 'If you're asking me what my recommendation will be, I'll have to say I think this should be a restricted world with a small permanent station of Dominion people.'

'That's wise, yes. I hope your *t'ans* agree.'

'I can't tell you what the final decision will be.'

'No.' She watched me with all the unconscious authority of the *T'An Suthai-Telestre*. Abruptly she said, 'There's another vessel in harbour, one from Kel Harantish. Ambassadors – or so claimed – from the Emperor-in-Exile. Asshe thinks one ship's crew is no hazard to the city. But likely they'll ask to see the Dominion envoy. Were I you, I'd be too busy.'

'If they come, I'll see them. Taking all precautions.' It might do to have company, I thought, Lalkaka and Thomas, and perhaps Maric and Blaize. Facing witnesses, what else could the Harantish do but talk?

'It would be better if you didn't see them,' she stated.

'*T'an*, I think I should make something clear. Any conditions of contact with this world – however restricted or quarantined – apply to the whole of Orthe. Southland, Desert Coast, the Barrens, whoever.'

'Kel Harantish too?' She was grim.

'We can't be partisan,' I said, seeing the anger she was holding in.

'Harantish Witchbreed! Give them technology, and then – and then beware.' Her gaze held mine.

'If Carrick V's restricted, that means no importing high technology.'

'Laws, rules, I've heard that before – and you,' she said, 'are not the only Outworlder we'll have contact with.'

'Anyone else will say the same.' It took a very short time for me to realize that this was the *T'An* Dalzielle Kerys-Andrethe, Flower of the South, probable next holder of the Crown, and some thirty years my senior; and that I was a junior representative of a very distant world.

The tension broke when she laughed. 'You stiff-necked woman, you're as like Ruric as if one mother bore you. The times I've had that same stubborn look from her . . . ! Well, let be, let be; we'll speak of it again after midsummer.'

When she'd gone, I sat shaking for a few moments. The woman was a pussycat on the surface, but underneath – it wasn't to be wondered at, hadn't she been *T'An Suthai-Telestre* for twenty years?

The courtyard of the Mercenaries' Guildhouse was all but empty. Two women spun the double-bladed pikes of south Melkathi, hugging the scant midday shadow. Blaize n'ri n'suth Meduenin, in britches and an old leather vest, circled with a younger man. *harur-nilgiri* and *harur-nazari* caught the sun. Bare feet scuffed the tiles.

'Peace!' he said, breaking off when he saw me. The younger man bowed. Blaize came across, sheathing paired blades.

'Are you free for an afternoon?'

'Usual rates.' There was nothing sardonic in his tone; he was serious about his business.

'Sure. You might not have to do anything. I just want you looking as though you might.' When he consented, I said, 'You're not up at the Hill with Rodion?'

'She asked me to give her time to make a decision.' Under his scale-pattern skin, alien musculature shifted. 'Let her decide soon – there's enough offers going in this city now to keep the whole

Guild working for a year. Ahh, what am I saying?' His glance held complicity, humorous resignation.

'Don't be in a hurry,' I said. It was as much of a warning as I could give.

'That seems satisfactory.' The Harantish ambassador leaned back in her chair. Her gold eyes surveyed the room without ever seeming to watch any of us. 'But this trafficking with your Other-world – comes through the Southlanders, eh, their island here?'

'At the moment, yes, but not necessarily in the future.' I went through the usual explanations about restricted contact between the Dominion worlds.

Blaize stood at the door, relaxed and expressionless, hands clasped on the hilt of his drawn *harur-nilgiri*. The ambassador's gaze took in his mottled half-face, the worn leathers of the Mercenaries Guild. She was not surprised by his presence. John and Connie shared a desk over the far side of the room, working on some of the tapes and talking quietly. Maric managed to find some of the *arniac* tea popular along the Desert Coast, and when she brought it in I saw she wore Theluk's blades:

'Not impossible you'd trade with us, then?' the ambassador demanded.

'Trade? I can't answer that at the moment, ambassador, not until my government finalizes its decision. But certainly there can be contact between our two cultures. If the Emperor wishes—'

'Ach!' She scowled. Her dark robe shifted, and under it was the glint of scaled bronze mail. The face under the unbound white mane was not young, though with the snake-gold of the Witch-breed skin it was difficult to tell. 'Dannor bel-Kurick is a fool, I'm sorry I ever bore him. When you have your answer, *S'aranth*-envoy, send it to Kurick bel-Olinyi; I will see it is heard.'

'Ambassador, you realize I'm unable to give guarantees—'

'Yes,' she said, and to Maric: 'My carriage is outside? Good. *S'aranth*-envoy, one word to you.'

Whether she was deliberately uncivil or whether it was Harantish custom, I didn't know. I stood, giving her a formal bow. 'Ambassador?'

'There's a certain Tower,' she said, for the first time in that long afternoon sounding neither threatening nor evasive. 'Only this, *S'aranth*-envoy: do not believe all you hear in that Tower. Nor all you hear of us.'

She left, going down towards the harbour in a closed *skurrai-jasin*. Blaize followed me out into the steep hill passage.

'I'm glad to see the back of that one,' he commented. 'Kinsister, you're well-spoken in the Desert tongues, did you learn them in Kasabaarde?'

'In a way,' I said, and wondered for a minute what else I'd learned in Kasabaarde, and what price I'd paid for it.

Sixday passed, and Sevenday, and the naming went on. I was seeing no one except *s'an telestres*. On the evening of Eightday Haltern called, walking up to Easthill Malk'ys as second twilight gave way to starlight.

'They want an official Dominion representative there on solstice day,' he said as he sat down beside Maric. 'The *t'an* Suthafiori suggested you, but I can ask Huxton if you're too busy.'

'I'll take a day off.' I wouldn't miss it for a gold clock; certainly I wasn't about to let Sam Huxton oil his way into my place. 'What's going on up there? I haven't had time to ask anyone.'

He picked among the remains of the evening meal, helping himself to a crust of the dark bread. 'It all waits on the naming.'

There was a question I didn't want to ask, but I asked it anyway. 'And Brodin, what about him?'

'He said nothing, nor ever will.' He chewed bread, swallowed; then glanced at me. 'No, you won't have heard, will you? It was only discovered at noon. Brodin took the *T'An Suthai-Telestre's* verdict on himself. He poisoned himself in his cell. He's dead.'

CHAPTER 33

Midsummer-Tenyear

Solstice day:

'You're *late*, *S'aranth*.' Maric paused. 'Is that what they wear on Earth?'

'Yes – but it doesn't look like this.'

The clothes, having been in a chest for the better part of a year, smelled of preserving-herbs. I stood while Maric tilted the mirror, and looked at my remaining formal gear. The skirt hung loose at the waist, the jacket was tight enough across the shoulders to split the seams.

'Oh god. So much for the Dominion representative.' I stripped off. A loud hail came from the archway below.

'I'll get it.' Maric ran; I heard her clatter downstairs.

I dressed again. *Chirith-goyen* shirts were fuller in the sleeve than when I'd last ordered clothes in Tathcaer. Nearly a year? Yes. Clip-fitting britches tucked into soft leather half-boots, laced up the calf. A brown *becamil* tunic over that enabled me to wear the recharged stunner holstered at the small of my back. I didn't trust bel-Olinyi and her ship from Kel Harantish. And there was the unknown person – perhaps to remain unknown now Brodin was dead – with every motive to resent the Dominion envoy.

Maric came back in as I was buckling the knife-belt.

'Message from *t'an* Carrie,' she waved a folded sheet of paper, 'and the *skurrai-jasin* is here to take you up to the Square.'

'Already?' I stuffed the paper into the sleeveless tunic's inner pocket. 'Let's go, then.'

A black, crop-horned *skurrai* pulled the open carriage down into the city centre. The driver was a young shaven Earthspeaker; she said little, concentrating on bringing us through the crowds. All the *telestre*-houses we passed had their gates wide open, and Ortheans in festival dress thronged the courtyards. A sea-wind cleared the stench of dung and drains. Towering cumulus glided overhead.

Avoiding Crown Way – too crowded to pass – we came among the narrow passages and multiple junctions of the Eastside. A ribbon of blue sky was visible between the high *telestre*-house walls, pricked with daystars. The closer we got to Citadel Square, the more dense were the crowds. To my surprise I saw the brown-skirted priests directing the flow of people. Only a few of Asshe's guard were present. The *skurrai-jasin* approached the Square from the Wellhouse side, and Earthspeakers directed Maric and myself along to the front Wellhouse steps.

'Christie – over here!'

Ruric stood under one of the awnings that shaded both steps and Square. As she stepped into the sunlight, her cropped mane glittered like a starling's wing. In the shade, Rodion's silver mane gleamed. Blaize, back in the shadow, signalled a greeting.

'Thought you weren't going to get here.' Ruric gripped my hand. She looked tired but happy.

'Have I missed anything?'

'No. It's just beginning.'

Unbleached cloth cast a sepia shade under the awning. The Saberonisi flanked us on one side, and the Seamarshal's guard on the other. Maric elbowed in next to Blaize, said something inaudible but cheeky, and the scarred man gave her a short answer. Knowing him as I did, I could see he was holding back laughter. Was that some memory of Kirriach?

'I can't find – ah, you're here.' Haltern, harassed as ever, joined me on the steps. Still sheep-dogging the envoy, I thought, privately amused.

Horns blared, drum-frames banged.

Citadel Square quietened, the crowd focussing its attention on the House of the Goddess. Crown Guard stood by the closed gates, feathercrests and belt-badges glittering. At that signal they turned and began to push the double gates back.

Thin pennants hung from the awning-supports, unrolling on rare gusts of wind. I could see the whole Square from where I stood. The entrance to Crown Way was choked. The Citadel gate was barred and guarded. Under the awnings, the crowd was at first glance a blur of colour: green, scarlet, blue, gold, white and earth-brown. Resolving it I saw *s'ans* in robes and bright tunics, *harur*-blade hilts shining, some with young *ashiren* sat up on their shoulders. Near me were a scatter of city tradesmen and merchants and young adults from the Artisan's Quarter. A woman in Merce-naries' Guild leathers and another with the plume-mane of a Dadeni rider shared a flask with one of the Quarth ambassadors.

'Now we'll see,' Haltern said quietly.

Sun glared back from the windowless white masonry. Through the open gates of the House I saw cool fountains, the great dome. A party of Earthspeakers came out onto the steps. A grey-maned Orthean in Guard uniform accompanied them: *T'An* Commander Asshe.

The priests beat a rapid tattoo on metallic drum-frames. A horn blared. No melodic fanfare, but a call as raucous and raw-edged as a hunting horn. An immediate silence fell.

'All hear, all hear!' Asshe's hoarse voice penetrated to the far corners of Citadel Square. 'Let all who hold land by the gift of the Goddess hear this!'

One of the priests – Tirzael? yes – came forward, holding a sheaf of parchments. The sun shone under the high edge of the awning, illuminating him. Midmorning bells sounded, and he waited out their chimes before he spoke.

'Listen and hear. These are the *T'Ans* of the Hundred Thousand, called to their offices by gift and desire of the people, called to be crowned this day in the House of the Goddess.'

At first I took it for an echo, then I realized that priests stationed at the edges of the Square were relaying his words out to the city.

'Called for the Kyre,' he announced, 'Arlyn Bethan n'ri n'suth Ivris!'

A growl of approval went up from the Kyre men and women scattered through the crowd. A surprisingly large number of those insular *telestres* were represented. I saw a plump pale-skinned Orthean woman go striding up the steps, bow to Tirzael, and sign herself with the circle of the Goddess.

'Called for Morvren and the Freeport – Zannil Emberen n'ri n'suth Telerion.'

A louder cheer for the flame-maned Seamarshal, and a buzz of speculation; the Seamarshal's guard near me seemed resigned rather than enthusiastic.

'How do they know to come?' Maric said, leaning between me and Haltern. Her young face was flushed, her dark eyes glittered. 'How do they know who'll be chosen?'

'Technically I suppose it could be any one *s'an* of the Hundred Thousand. Practically . . .' Haltern shrugged. 'I don't suppose there are more than two or three dozen likely names.'

'He's a cynic,' Maric objected, grinning at me.

'What game do you think they've been playing for the last half year?' It was an irritated question. Haltern's eyes were fixed on the priests at the Wellhouse gate, as if he could force them to announce the names he wanted to hear. 'I have a feeling, Christie, this is the most important Midsummer-Tenyear we'll see in a long time. Maybe the most important in my lifetime. I hope they know why . . . We can't afford to ignore the Dominion. Not now.'

'Called for Peir-Dadeni,' Tirzael continued, 'Cethelen Khassiye Reihalyn.'

Pale-skinned, gold-maned; as he went up the steps in his rich robes, gold flashed from his studded hands. Shiriya-Shenin: Fifth-wall. Beside me, Maric grunted in disgust. She remembered Kanta's first minister.

'My sire and dam!' The Dadeni rider near me froze, flask halfway to her mouth, her face a mask of astonishment. 'Khassiye? The man's nothing but an upstart river-man—'

Ruric's narrow features creased into a smile. 'And I dare say he'll be *n'ri n'suth* Andrethe before the season's end.'

'Called for Roehmonde – Verek Howice Talkul!'

'Oh ho,' said Ruric sardonically, '*there* goes a man who expected the *s'ans'* call.'

The crowd parted to let him out on the steps. Howice, hot in gem-studded tunic, loose trousers tucked into *kuru*-leather boots. After the new Roehmonder fashion, he wore *harur* blades cross-strapped across his back. Rings gleamed on his fingers. If there was any Orthean I distrusted and thought dangerous – and perhaps more than dangerous – it was that sleek, plump Roehmonder.

Ruric's thin fingers worked, knotting the loose sleeve of her shirt. She dusted her plain britches. Wryly she said, 'And now we find out what Melkathi thinks of my work this past season.'

'Or how clever Hana Oreyn Orhlandis is.'

Her gaze met Haltern's, and she nodded. 'Oh yes, he'd like my place, I know that.'

There was some delay, the priests conferring in a group; and then Tirzael stepped forward again into the sunlight.

'Called for Melkathi – *amari* Ruric Orhlandis!'

Loud cheers and hissing applause came from the people round us. Ruric shoved her fingers through her mane, tugged her sword-belt straight, and strode down towards the steps. The applause followed her.

Rodion pushed past me, ran after the dark woman, and caught her arm. Ruric stared, listened, then pulled the girl into a hard single-armed embrace. A roar went up. Rodion came back flushed and grinning, as Ruric mounted the steps to the Wellhouse gate.

'What was all that about?' I asked.

'*S'aranth*, I said I'd tell her.' She took Blaize's hand, as he stared bemusedly at her, and announced loudly, 'I'm carrying your children.'

He snatched her up with a whoop. The Ortheans nearest to us crowded round and congratulations were offered to her, and wine-flasks. Another very pregnant woman hugged her. The rowdy celebration was hushed by the Saberonisi, who regarded everyone with disdain. Quiet came, not in time for the next announcement, but I recognized the Rimon man from the trial: Jacan Thu'ell Sethur.

Haltern's hand closed over my shoulder, tightened. His face was tense. The mask of bewilderment slipped; I saw him then as a clever man bitterly concerned for his world.

'Now,' he repeated.

'Called for Ymir,' Tirzael bellowed. Heads turned, talk stopped. 'Called for Ymir – the t'an Dalzielle Kerys-Andrethe!'

The sound was frightening. Spontaneous, raw, wordless: a mob-roar from thousands of throats. Wrenching breath from the lungs, vibrating in the air: I stood deafened for long seconds before I knew it was a massive roar of approval. Haltern stood shaking his head and laughing, as unrestrained as Maric who was jumping up and down. Blaize and Rodion tightened their embrace.

Six of them stood on the Wellhouse steps. Dalzielle Kerys-Andrethe walked to join them, across the dusty square between the awnings. The sun put the awnings' shadow across her path, so that she was one minute a woman in cloak and mail, the next a flare of silver. A short stocky Orthean in her fifties, moving easily, harur blades jangling in the quiet. She climbed the steps and the cheering broke out again: Suthafiori, Flower of the South.

Small bright figures surrounded by brown-skirted priests, they stood for a while to acknowledge the crowd, and then went into the Wellhouse. The bells chimed for noon: I hadn't realized how much time had passed.

An immense relaxation went through the crowd, and the noise level fell to conversational. I saw blankets spread on the flagstones in the sepia shadows. Flasks were opened, food-packs unwrapped. Ortheans sat in groups, talking, eating and drinking, some playing ochmir. The celebration that had begun round Rodion started again, she and Blaize becoming the centre of much attention. I sat down on the steps besides Haltern.

'That's it,' he said, 'it's up to Her now.'

'I'd have thought this was the time you'd be worrying. You've no proof they'll choose the T'An Ymir as Crown, have you?'

'Nobody chooses.' Seeing me puzzled, he said, 'You remember how it was with the Earthspeakers at Beth'ru-elen? That's how it is now. All seven of them will talk with the Earthspeakers and

Wellkeepers, and in time one of the seven will know who is fittest to be *T'An Suthai-Telestre*. Yes, I hope it's her, I believe it must be, but . . .'

But these are Ortheans, I reminded myself. And psychology has a home in the theocratic houses, if not under that name.

'It's not a matter of ambition now. To be chosen *T'An*, yes, that's in the game.' His inflection gave it every connotation of intrigue, cabal, influence. 'But to be *T'An Suthai-Telestre* . . . you must know yourself well enough to name yourself.'

'How long do we wait?'

'We'll know well before evening.'

A *rashaku-bazur* sailed across the square, swooped and clung to the top of an awning-pole. Its wings beat wildly for balance. Sunlight shone through the white feathers. Double tail-plumes flailed, the scaled breast gleamed. Harsh cries echoed back from the high walls.

Looking round, I saw bel-Olinyi and the Harantish delegation and, on the other side of them, John Lalkaka and Adair. The rest of the xeno-team had got there – I saw a bewildered Tim Eliot trying to understand bel-Olinyi's remarks – with the exception of Sam Huxton.

'Oh god.' I fished Carrie's crumpled message out of my pocket and unfolded it. It read:

Tathcaer, dawn.
   Lynne –
   Just heard there's a ship called in from the pick-up point, with someone from the department on it. Sam's with him now. Think maybe he's a replacement; guess the report that you were dead got home before the message cancelling it.
      – Carrie
   PS: His name is David Meredith – mean anything?

'What's the matter?' Haltern asked.

'As if I didn't have enough trouble.' I gave him the paper, then realized I'd have to translate it – but he was following the mecho-type print with one clawed finger, translating under his breath. It didn't pay to underestimate him.

'If he hasn't got up to the Square by now, he's not coming,' I guessed. 'Well, I can wait.'

'I hadn't thought your people would send a ship so soon.'

'They'll have detoured him off some other route, I expect.' I managed to catch Carrie Thomas's eye and signalled, message received. She nodded. 'We'll both go back on the xeno-team pickup, Fourthweek.'

'Fourthweek? Yes, of course. I hadn't realized it was so soon.'
He handed the message back. Eyes veiled, cleared; his smile held
less irony than affection. 'I'm sorry you're going.'

'I'm sorry too.'

'If your people are going to have a station here—'

Rodion, leaning back from a lower step, interrupted. '*S'aranth*,
you're not leaving already?'

'Not for four weeks.'

'We'll be back from Meduenin before that,' Blaize said.

'Are you coming back?' the silver-maned young woman asked.
Her face was concerned, uncomplicated. '*S'aranth*?'

'If I can – yes, I will.'

'It would be best,' Haltern mused; then spreading his hands,
shame-faced, said, 'Yes, but it's not simply policy, Christie.'

'All right, I believe you.'

And will I be back? I wondered. Permanent station, that needs a
promotion, but I may be in line for one anyway now. It's not what
I'd visualized, but . . .

You start off and you think you're going to do the big things,
the spectacular alien worlds, the big embassies. Maybe you do.
Then you get caught up in some little detail – and it turns out it's
not little. It might not be that grand, but it's going to take you the
rest of your life to sort it out.

Carrick V: Orthe. Barbaric, yes, complicated too: a post-technological world. All I'd learned about it only emphasized how ignorant I still was. But the people . . .

'Christie.'

I snapped out of thought, saw Blaize on the step below. Maric
and Rodion were further down in the crowd, Maric introducing
her to a group from Salathiel *telestre*. They shone and glittered, that
company, with gems and *harur* blades, looking like something
between a festival and an armed camp.

'You want to play *ochmir* while we're waiting?' Blaize had the
battered old set we'd used in Kirriach, still with him. Ruined flesh
made his face impassive as he glanced at Haltern. 'You too?'

Haltern gave him a look that was all Crown Messenger, then
shrugged. 'Yes, why not.'

We played three-handed *ochmir* on the step of the theocratic
house. For that game the counters' permutation is between white,
blue, and brown; the winner being the first to get all 144 faces up.
I turned a *leremoc* up early in the game, lost it to Haltern, but
remembered where it was and forced a reversal on him. The three-
handed game moves quicker – instead of a four or five-counter
majority in a minor hexagon, a three will serve to force reversal –

but if anything takes longer, because of the shifting alliances between the players. I gained a notable advantage when, a nearby scuffle distracting Blaize and Haltern, I took the opportunity to flip over a number of counters to show my colour (including three *thurin* and another *leremoc*). The game went in my favour after that.

The afternoon lengthened. Rodion took us up past Hill-Damarie to Hill-Melkathi for a late meal, and we returned to find nothing changed. By the time the midafternoon bells rang the crowd had swollen again, filling Citadel Square to overflowing and blocking the wider passages of the Hill, and the narrow alleys behind the Wellhouse.

'*T'ans*, Outlanders.' A young Earthspeaker came along the steps to us. 'Will you come to the gate, please.'

We reached the gates as they swung open, passing through into the great courtyard where the fountains sparkled in the sun. Saberonisi, the ambassadors from Quarth and Kel Harantish and Kasabaarde, the xeno-team, the *telestres* of those chosen *T'An*, their *l'ri-an* and *ashiren*; and after us all the Ortheans from the Square. The great dome rose up white against a star-specked sky, a sky that glimmered with *rashaku* on a high wind. I saw Blaize's face, scarred and sardonic, and wondered if he too was thinking of Brodin n'ri n'suth Charain. A year is a long time: what would Brodin have done in Hill-Damarie if he'd known he had only a year to live?

Earthspeakers ushered us through the archway and into the dome.

My eyes had difficulty adjusting from the brilliant sunlight to the dim interior of the dome. Half-blind, I made for a seat, and found myself between Rodion and one of bel-Olinyi's Harantish Witchbreed.

Vast iron trees of candles stood at intervals, the myriad white flames illuminating packed tiers of people. The light was mist-pearl. The dome soared up, alabaster-pale. A column of sunlight fell from the roof-opening like molten metal on the polished rock floor.

All the foundations of the dome had been hollowed out, so that people entered at ground-level and went down the carved tiers of rock on ancient worn steps. It was amphitheatre-shaped: here on the top tiers we looked across vast space to Ortheans entering from the archway. Below, in a carved circular space some thirty feet across, the black well-mouth opened. The afternoon sun illuminated a few yards of the shaft and a wide area of the floor.

I saw the seven of them, bright among the Earthspeakers and the Wellkeepers: Emberen and Thu'ell laughing at something

Howice said, the Kyre woman talking with Khassiye Reihalyn, Ruric absently massaging the stump of her arm while she listened to Tirzael and Suthafiori. The acoustics were good enough to hear them speak; if not for the clatter of people coming in, every word would have been clear.

Rodion leaned forward, tense. Her thin fingers interlocked. 'She must know. She's the only one that can do it.'

'Suthafiori?'

She nodded. I saw her swallow. It suddenly seemed a remote chance. How many of the seven favoured contact with the Dominion? Not more than two, perhaps three. One firmly against: Howice wouldn't have changed. The others? Ortheans like generations to come to a decision.

The Harantish man beside me shifted position, with a brief comment to bel-Olinyi. His mane showed black roots, his unveiled eyes were a warm brown. Witchbreed? I thought. Rodion, her gold eyes intent on the wellmouth, was a closer image.

Metallic drumbeats left silence in their wake

'Let the Hundred Thousand hear.' The old Earthspeaker pitched his voice to carry. 'These are called to the office of *T'An* in Her sight and in yours. Bethan n'ri n'suth Ivris, do you accept the office named?'

'Laying down all offices I now hold,' the Kyre woman said, 'I do.'

As each was named and swore the Goddess's oath at the well, a priest brought forward the silver circlet that was their outward symbol of rule. Now there was no applause, no cheers, no noise; only an exhalation of breath at each oath.

'You hold the provinces,' the old priest said at last. 'Their kin are your kin, their desires your desires, their welfare your own. Listen and hear! Older than the provinces are the *telestres*: the Hundred Thousand.'

Tirzael came forward to stand by the old man. In his hands he carried a plain circlet of gold. Unadorned, undecorated, seeming to draw into itself the light of sun and candles.

'It is no light thing to wear it,' the old man said. 'The Crown of the Southland. Who trusts the Goddess for strength to bear it? Who will name themselves *T'An Suthai Telestre*?'

No sound in all that space: all attention focused down on the loose grouping of people at the well-mouth.

What holds them back? I thought. Howice stirred, one gold-heavy hand loosening the neck of his tunic, but didn't speak. What stopped his ambition? The silence lengthened. The priests waited. Tirzael held the Crown between his palms.

371

Brodin came into my mind again. The hawk-faced man, murderer, who would not lie under the Goddess's oath. There was the dichotomy: between intrigue and philosophy. So that at the heart of Southland government there is this public honesty.

'Will none of you speak?'

Two shook their heads briefly, an involuntary gesture: Ruric and Emberen.

At last a voice:

'I speak. It is no light thing, to be the hand of the Goddess on earth; but with Her power it becomes possible to endure and enjoy. Unless Her *s'an telestres*, Her Earthspeakers and Wellkeepers, revoke it: I will hold the Southland's Crown.'

Her gilt-maned head came up to survey the tiers of people. A stocky aging woman, the badges of Kerys-Andrethe gleaming at her belt; the black mouth of the well behind her.

'By your will,' Dalzielle Kerys-Andrethe said.

Tirzael stepped forward and placed the gold circlet on her head. A single voice broke the silence:

'*Flower of the South!*'

Against all precedent, but others took it up; her oath-taking was not audible for the shouting. It spread out from the Wellhouse, out to the courtyard and the Citadel Square. A great bell pealed out.

Out of time, spreading from the Wellhouse out to the farthest parts of the island, out of rhythm, wildly and joyously, all the bells of the city rang.

CHAPTER 34

Night Conference at the Citadel

Celebrations continued well into the night.

From the Stone Garden you can see all the land north of the island, and the lazy curves of the Oranon like plate-silver under the stars. Flat water-meadows stretch away, only at the horizon is there a hint of hills.

The talk stilled for a moment, I heard the sound of broken water at the foot of the Citadel crag. A cry of nightbirds came from the garden, cool in these hours after second twilight, and the scent of *kazsis* nightflower was persuasive. The Citadel itself – towered, windowless, rearing up into blank domes – blocked any view of the lower city. But Tathcaeř would not sleep: the alien city was noisy with shouting and singing, the Ortheans feasted and danced and made love; all the *telestre*-houses kept their doors open.

Rodion and Blaize sat at a table with some of the Shiriya-Shenin *tha'adur*. She brushed her silver mane back, laughing. He sat farthest from the lantern, his face in shadow.

'Will she stay Orhlandis?'

Ruric gave her crook-shouldered shrug. 'Who knows? I've told her to visit Meduenin – she might as well see his *telestre*. I won't keep anyone Orhlandis who wants to change.'

We passed them by, walking on down a narrow flight of steps towards other tables.

In the Stone Garden the natural rock of the crag is shaped into steps and platforms, into screens and pillars. Hollowed out into dew-ponds full of sparkfish, polished into domes that are grown over with thousand-flower and mossgrass, the Stone Garden of Galen Honeymouth stands at the northernmost point of Tathcaer.

The silhouettes of domes and archways were fringed with stars, with clouds of light. Tables and couches were set up on the platforms, under coloured lanterns that were no more than decoration in the starlight; and there was a profusion of food and drink. The Ortheans, according to custom, moved from table to table during the festivities. Haltern said a night's observation of the shifting groups gave a clearer picture of the Hundred Thousand's policies than anything else. I remember someone once told me that *ochmir* originated in the cities.

'That's the new one, isn't it?' Ruric hesitated, looking towards a table below us. 'What's the name—'

'Meredith,' I supplied. Sam Huxton was introducing him to Suthafiori. I heard his accent, the way his inflection altered in the course of a single phrase. 'Was I ever as bad as that?'

'Until you came back from the Desert Coast.' Ruric grinned widely.

'Thanks a lot, *T'An*.'

'Maybe not *that* bad, then.' She laughed.

'I guess I'd better go down and meet him.'

'I'll be with the Melkathi *s'ans*,' she said 'Good luck.'

Mosses covered the stone screen, their colours visible in star and lamp light. Blue, scarlet, yellow and green. Dew-ponds glittered. I went down the steps, past grey rock polished, faceted, cut away to show seams of white marble and black basalt. The garden was loud with talk and laughter, with the atonal songs of Peir-Dadeni and the Kyre. The scent of crushed mossgrass rose from underfoot.

'Mr Meredith? I'm Christie.'

I'd caught him leaving Suthafiori's table. He paused, the lantern light falling on him. A broad man, dark-haired, somewhere in his late thirties or early forties. Like most Offworlders he struck me as slightly absurd. He shook hands: at first I didn't realize what he intended. He had a strong grip.

'Pleased to meet you,' he said, 'though I admit it's a somewhat unexpected pleasure.'

'I'm not as dead as I'm reported to be, you mean?'

'Something like that, yes.' Impatience underlay his good humour. 'The department diverted me here from the Parmiter's Star system – now I find it's not necessary.'

'Communications aren't the most reliable thing round here. But I wouldn't say it wasn't necessary.' I steered him towards a deserted table on the edge of the Stone Garden. We sat down. 'At the moment I've got a workload that means I'm having to second personnel from Sam's – from Mr Huxton's team. If you can handle some interviews, we might get a report finished before recall date.'

He nodded. I poured bowls of herb-tea, the scarlet *arniac* of the Desert Coast. It wasn't until then that I noticed the odd look he gave me.

He said, 'You seem to have fitted in remarkably well, Ms Christie.'

'Call me Lynne, please.' It wasn't politeness. Lynne Christie and Christie *S'aranth* were two different people in my mind, I wanted to keep them that way. 'Yes, I suppose you're right, Mr Meredith.'

'David,' he said. There was a remnant of Welsh in his accent. He sipped the *arniac*, and looked at it unbelievingly. 'I've seen some of your reports.'

'There's another, but it's not complete. You can play it through.'

No one was in earshot, but I was aware we were watched. *S'ans* passed at a distance. The stars blazed over the Citadel. A faint mist rose: river-fog forming below the crag. The lanterns were haloed.

'They read like the worst kind of microfiche novels,' Meredith said. I realized he meant the reports.

'Life's like that – at least, it is here, David.'

'Yes.' He eyed me thoughtfully. The team would have given a fairly strange picture of Lynne Christie, I guessed, since they took me for a lunatic or worse. Meredith was old enough to have been born before the FTL discovery, to have come to this career late. A grade 6 envoy, Huxton said: that meant capable of dealing with high-tech worlds.

'Carrick V's more a post-holocaust rather than a pre-tech world.' He cupped the bowl between his palms, swirling the liquid. 'Not that you can be blamed for that of course, Lynne, just another example of the department acting on insufficient fieldwork.'

What about Kasabaarde? I thought. No, that wasn't in the report yet. Time enough later to tell David Meredith about that.

'When you're de-briefed—'

'The exposure principle, we used to call it on the training courses.' I grinned at him. 'Like, you expose someone to a culture same way as you expose film to the light – bring them back and develop them and there's your world.'

Meredith laughed. 'There's truth in that. Some.'

'Sam will have given you the details of this society?'

'As far as that goes, yes.' Some obscure emotion crossed his face when he looked at the nearby Ortheans. 'Obviously there's classification to be considered. I don't know if you've decided on your recommendation?'

'Restricted.' I elaborated, 'There has to be quarantine – what we have here is practically zero population growth, and an unknown degree of susceptibility to Earth diseases—'

'I'd have thought that a good reason for a medical aid programme.'

'Which brings me to the other reason.' I hesitated. How to put it simply? 'We have an extremely narrow margin of acceptance here. It's a cultural thing, they like to take decisions slowly, over a

375

period of years. If the world's restricted to minimum contact it gives them time to adjust to the Dominion.'

'To grow until they have that capacity?' Meredith's prejudices were showing. 'I admit, at first glance it doesn't seem this world has much to offer the Dominion.'

'I'd've put it the other way myself – the Dominion doesn't have much to offer Orthe. Except medical technology, of course, and that comes within the terms of a Restricted classification.'

His eyebrows quirked up. 'You'll report to the Classifications Board, of course.'

'What's policy these days?' I felt uneasy. 'Remember, David, I've been off-Earth for eighteen months.'

'I think you'll get your classification,' he said. 'There was a spate of Open classifications – someone got it into their heads we were discriminating against non-tech worlds – but that died down when they saw what cultural damage was being done. Carrick V will count as non-tech, because of this anti-science religion and elite that's in power.'

One thing bothered me (and it didn't bother me as much as it should). In my reports on Witchbreed technology I'd gone fully into their past achievements, mentioned what remained in Kirriach, and the communications devices in use in Kel Harantish. What I never reported fully were the devices used by the Hexenmeister of Kasabaarde.

It's unimportant, not worth mentioning, it doesn't worry me— And it should do.

Kasabaarde has left dreams in my head, visions of Orthe's past that come back with all the force of reality. Sometimes I wonder if that's all the effect it had. That's an old city: unchancy, as the Southlanders would say. Kasabaarde and Kel Harantish using the Hundred Thousand, perhaps, as an arena for the continuing battles of the Golden Witchbreed ... How widely might that conflict spread?

'*T'an* envoy.' Emberen Seamarshal nodded as she passed us, arm in arm with one of the Earthspeakers. I acknowledged her absently.

'I don't like to see it myself,' Meredith added, 'I believe a world should be allowed to progress. But with the current hands-off attitude no one will interfere.'

I wanted to deny what he said, and yet from his point of view it was true. Even the remnants of technology in Kasabaarde and Kel Harantish didn't alter that. What did, what made him in error, was the mental attitude behind Orthean custom – and that I didn't have the right to explain. For that he would have to speak to an Orthean.

The scent of *kazsis* nightflower and mossgrass was overlaid by the cool smell of the river. It was chill. The Orthean festival would continue, they weren't so affected by cold. And overhead the summer stars were fierce.

Remembering Eastharbour-Salmeth, so long ago, I said, 'So tell me – what's the news from Britain?'

The first few weeks of Merrum stayed fine: long sunny days cooled by a sea-wind. Huxton's team were bringing their work to a close, and John and Carrie came up to Easthill Malk'ys as often as they could. Meredith's presence meant we weren't as overworked as before, and we worked quietly towards the recall date. *S'ans* came, and – now that the naming was over – Earthspeakers and Wellkeepers too, all wanting to hear about the Dominion.

If I had doubts (and it may be only hindsight to think that I did), I ignored them.

Because there was Tathcaer: the White City, in summer. Waking at first twilight and hearing the water-carts come down Easthill, the clopping hooves of *skurrai*, the water sluicing down the steep paved ways. Dawn on the roofs, then, flaring into gold and drying the passages, shining on the blank walls of *telestre*-houses. Even at that hour there was no need to wear a cloak as I walked barefoot down to the fishmarket at the quay for breakfast. Feast-days, fast-days, holidays: it was no hardship to work. Meredith, like the Eliots with whom he was staying, adopted the custom of a midday siesta. I liked to spend mine on the flat roof of Easthill Malk'ys, among the tubs of *kazsis* and *sidimaat*, dozing under an awning and looking down at Tathcaer. And the long afternoons blazed on, rung in by bells, and Carrick's Star went down over Rimon and gilded the sea out to the Sisters Islands, and the city rang with bells at second twilight. And then there were the stars.

So for that time I managed to dismiss the thought of Brodin, of SuBannasen, and of their living successor. To forget *saryl-kabriz*, the Wellhouse at Corbek, the death of Kanta Andrethe. The malice that prompted that was only hidden, not destroyed. I saw bel-Olinyi still in the city, her ship docked under the shadow of Easthill, and wondered which *s'an* it was that Kel Harantish had sent gold-ships to in the spring. Kel Harantish and the Golden Witchbreed: they were at the back of everything.

I should have known the game wasn't over yet.

*

377

Blaize and Rodion arrived back from Medued-in-Rimon towards the beginning of Merrum Thirdweek. I was at the *T'An* Melkathi's house on the Hill when they got there.

Rodion was astride a copper-striped *marhaz*. She wore loose white robes, and over that one of Blaize's leather vests, the top few holes laced. Her belly was round, already protruding.

She grinned at me. 'There must be at least four, don't you think? Hello, Christie.'

Blaize caught her as she slid down in a jingle of Rimon bracelets and coin-cords. Her *harur* blades were slung across her back, as the custom is for pregnant Southland women. Two others rode with them: a merry woman with a straggling blonde mane, and a man whose unblemished face was startlingly familiar.

'Aluys Feryn, Aluys Ryloth.' Blaize introduced the other two members of his three-birth.

'Come inside.' Ruric linked her single arm with Rodion's. 'You'll guest here, I hope, Meduenin?'

Feryn and Ryloth both dismounted and bowed. We went back into the house. Maric was there, and I saw Haltern had arrived; there would be others coming as the long evening continued. John Lalkaka, and Carrie, and maybe Adair.

We drew together as the recall date approached, wary of wasting time now that we had so little of it.

Shadows flickered in the wide hall. Ruric and I sprawled by the fire, distant from the others; she with her booted feet extended to the flames, slumped low in her chair.

'Ah, Goddess!' she said. Her eyes were half-hooded, her chin rested on her breast; only the curve of her lips showed amusement. 'What a year, what a Shadow-haunted year . . . a few more weeks and I'll have to go back down to Ales-Kadareth, be *T'An* Melkathi . . .'

'You're complaining?' I heard laughter from the other hearth, where Rodion was holding forth to Blaize's brother and sister.

'Complain?' She chuckled. 'Well, maybe I was getting too fond of the game to be *T'An* Commander of the army . . . but Melkathi! Now that's a game worth playing. Between the *s'ans* that support Orhlandis, and those that hate it, and the SuBannasen and their supporters . . . Knife-edge work, that. You'll have to come down and stay in 'Kadareth sometime. In Orh—' she yawned massively, arching her back, stretching her arm '—in Orhlandis too, if you feel brave enough. Strange place, Melkathi.'

'That's because it's run by strange people.'

'I sometimes think you Outworlders have a very obscure sense of humour.' Her expression struggled for solemnity. 'Me, I don't see the joke.'

'That's because you're a savage living in the ruins of a once-great technological society.'

She laughed uproariously. 'That Meredith!' she said at last. 'He should remember his tongue's not unknown here, before he calls us that! Another of Huxton's breed, that one.'

'He's OK.'

'I can't say I – oh, are you going?' she hitched herself up as Haltern came over.

'I have to go to the Citadel.' He glanced at me. 'If I can borrow your *l'ri-an*, Christie? I may want to send you word later.'

'If it's agreeable to Maric, sure.' Now is that further business with Suthafiori? I wondered. I was expecting to meet with the *T'An Suthai-Telestre* again before I left Orthe.

Ruric saw him to the door, and on her way back spoke to Rodion. She and the Meduenin went off to see to their quarters. Ruric dropped back into her chair beside me.

'It may be court business,' she said, using the inflection that makes *takshiriye* mean government. 'There'll be more of that before you go – when is it, now?'

'End of Fourthweek.'

The nictitating membrane slid back from her yellow eyes. 'Christie, will you be coming back?'

'If my people send me here. They'll want some representation on Orthe.'

'Don't avoid the issue. Will *you* be back?'

Lapuur wood burned steadily in the hearth, warming the stone walls that were cold even in summer. Outside, muffled, I heard the sunset bell.

'I can ask you this,' I said. 'Maybe I couldn't ask anyone else. Is it ever possible for an Outlander to fit into the Hundred Thousand?'

'You're asking me because I was born Outland?' She was thoughtful. 'It's true I'm careless of Orhlandis, more than a South-lander should be, but that doesn't mean I don't have the affinity. Truthfully, I think this is my *telestre* – Tathcaer. I've been coming here since I was *ashiren* and I always end up coming back. But am I a Southlander or an Outlander? I don't think I know.'

She pulled herself up, stood and stretched in front of the fire. Yellow light danced on her obsidian skin. The shadowed angles of her bones were wrong, humanoid more than human.

379

She said, 'Meredith calls us a backwater world – no, quiet, who's complaining? For him it may be true. Not for us. But you, is this where you want your career to be?'

'I can do it. Liaise between Orthe and the Dominion.' I watched her: the narrow-chinned face intent, the animal whiteless eyes veiled. 'Maybe I can do it better than a lot of people could.'

'Yes, to be *S'aranth* is a happy accident here and now: good for both worlds. But that isn't what I asked, Christie. Is this where you want to spend your life?'

Here? I thought. Here is a long cold way from Earth, from home.

'Orthe means a lot to me – and I don't know more than a fraction of it. I think the place suits my temperament.' I shrugged. 'And you mean a lot to me, I think you're my closest friend here. And there's Hal, and Blaize; and Rodion and Maric – I've been lucky, very lucky. I just don't know . . . an Earthspeaker told me once that what I really wanted was to have been born here.'

'Oh yes,' she said, and nodded, and looked down at me with veiled eyes. 'I know how that feels. But you're *S'aranth* and I'm Yelloweyes, we're known now. Someone should have warned you, Christie, you come here and the place changes you; something of you always stays behind when you leave.'

Rodion called her then, and she smiled and went to see what the woman wanted. I watched the flames, the shadows.

The ship would leave for the Eastern Isles at the end of Fourth-week, the uncertain sea-voyage from Tathcaer. And then by shuttle to the waiting craft, ninety days standard-time to Eatth. Classification is always a slow business, and there was no certainty they'd send me to a manned station on Carrick V. Possible, yes; certain, no. If they did, it was a long time coming back . . .

A tempting voice in the back of my mind said: let David Meredith go back and deal with diplomatic bureaucracy. Surely I can trust him to do it right. Can't I? Wouldn't it be better if there was a continuous Dominion presence on Carrick V? And who better than Christie *S'aranth*?

Voices echoed in the *T'An* Melkathi's house. The *l'ri-an* came to light the oil lamps and refuel the fire. From the arched windows I could see across the courtyard, through the gates to Tathcaer down the Hill, dark under the rising stars.

I thought, Yes, I'll stay.

Shortly after the midnight bell, when Ruric and I were still talking, there was a hammering on the outer door. The *l'ri-an* admitted Maric. She bowed hurriedly.

380

'Talmar Haltern n'ri n'suth Beth'ru-elen requests that you come to the Citadel,' she said.

'Now?' Ruric looked surprised.

'Yes, *T'An*, if you will.' She glanced at me. 'He said also, Christie should come if she desires to.'

Ruric scratched the roots of her mane, pulled the laces on her shirt. 'Damn intelligencers can't conduct their business at a reasonable hour . . . Yes, I'm coming.'

I pulled on my boots, Ruric grabbed a blue and silver *chirith-goyen* cloak against the night's chill, and we went out into Tathcaer, under the brilliant Orthean stars.

Maric led us past the Crown Guard, up into the Citadel, up through innumerable passages and galleries into the new wing and past more guards to a small richly-furnished chamber in a southern tower.

There was Haltern, harassed-looking as ever, deep in conversation with Suthafiori; and Evalen Kerys-Andrethe with the scribe Romare, and a dark man from Meclkathi who I remembered to be Nelum Santhil, Portmaster of Ales-Kadareth. Ruric frowned when she saw him there.

'So: you're here.' Suthafiori glanced at us, and we took seats round the table by the candle-stands. Haltern spoke quietly to Maric, who left. As she closed the door, I saw there were Crown Guard outside.

I sat between Evalen and Ruric. Haltern stood at the opposite side of the table, shuffling papers.

'Haltern, this is your doing?' Suthafiori said.

'*T'ans*, *s'ans*, I beg your pardon for the suddenness of the call, and for the lateness of the hour. Nevertheless, I have urgent news.'

He seemed reluctant to continue. Evalen and Santhil looked intently at him, Suthaffori frowned. Ruric rubbed at her forehead with slender fingers.

'There is this to be said,' Haltern went on, 'we have not reached the end of conspiracy.'

Suthafiori nodded. 'We never imagined Brodin n'ri n'suth Charain acted solely for himself, but he – wisely, perhaps – went beyond reach of our questioning.'

Haltern's veiled eyes watched us. This is bad, some instinct told me.

'And the Witchbreed,' he said, 'there was a discrepancy there: gold was still being taken from Harantish agents long after Sulis n'ri n'suth SuBannasen's death.'

'That's true,' Ruric said, 'what's the connection?'

Evalen cleared her throat. 'He means we have a traitor among the *s'ans*. It may be so. But there's no proof, Haltern, is there? The dead cannot accuse.'

'They can speak, *t'an*, if they are given time.' Again he hefted the papers, as if weighing something less material than parchment. 'This came to me tonight by way of informers. It seems there were other copies, but those miscarried or were prevented, I don't know. But what is addressed to me commonly comes to me – sooner or later. Will you let the dead be heard?'

I saw Evalen and Suthafiori and Ruric look at each other. Then Suthafiori nodded consent.

' "Confession of Brodin n'ri n'suth Charain," ' Haltern read, with no trace of the dramatic. ' "Given this day Durestha Seventhweek Sixday in the Crown prison of Tathcaer, and made because I fear for my life, not from Crown or church, but from another who I will later name." '

Here Haltern looked up and said, 'The details you may study later, they are much as we supposed; he was employed first by SuBannasen and then – but if I may I'll pass to where he names the traitor.'

'Read,' Suthafiori said harshly.

Haltern thumbed and folded papers. 'Here . . . "On my return to Shiriya-Shenin I was again directed to endanger the life of the Offworlder envoy, this time by a mock attempt on the life of Kanta Andrethe. This is the worst that ever befell me: that I was recognized in the attempt, and so to save myself must turn pretended murder into reality. After this I quarrelled with my employer, but confess I was cowed by threats. Also, gold was given me, which I believe had its origin in Kel Harantish. Now I am justly accused of murder, to which I confess; and of conspiracy, of which I am also guilty." '

Haltern read quietly, in the formal phrasing of the Peir-Dadeni tongue.

' "And I do here affirm and swear by the name of the Goddess that all I have done, I have done on the express orders of the *T'An amari* Ruric Orhlandis, once *T'An* Commander and now *T'An* Melkathi, first named Onehand and Yelloweyes, and now and forever after to be named murderer, conspirator, and paid traitor to the Hundred Thousand." '

Suthafiori laughed shortly, incredulously. Nelum Santhil bowed his head. I think it was a full minute before any of us looked at Ruric.

'Deny it,' Suthafiori said, 'I believe you, Ruric, I'll have this liar killed—'

The woman eased back in her chair, smiling sardonically. Her bright eyes glanced round the circle of faces.

'I've evidence,' Haltern said, 'or I'd not bother to make the accusation. There is Santhil Portmaster of Ales-Kadareth, who received and passed on to you gold from the Emperor-in-Exile; there are the Crown Guards Ty Damory and Ceran Gabril who let their old *T'An* Commander visit Brodin in his cell shortly before his . . . suicide. And there are those who saw you in Shiriya-Shenin, I think, *T'An*. Do you deny it?'

'No,' Ruric said, 'I do not.'

She was within a foot of me, the vibrant breathing warmth of her body, the energy of her eyes. She kept her hand flat on the table and made no move towards her sword.

'You?' I felt dazed. 'That was you?'

Evalen stood and made a sign. Four Crown Guard entered and stood by the door, out of earshot.

'Now let us talk,' she said grimly.

Ruric, with all the calm of the professional soldier, reached out and flicked through Brodin's confession.

'That, I didn't expect,' she said idly. 'You understand he was not such an innocent as he would have you believe?'

'Innocence!' Suthafiori said tautly. 'You speak of innocence!'

'But it is true in most of its particulars.' Ruric let the parchments fall. 'Well, what now?'

'I don't believe it.' Evalen stared at her.

'I'd deny it, but I know my friend's efficiency too well.' Here she inclined her head ironically to Haltern.

'Then let us hear the evidence.'

I sat stunned. Santhil spoke, and the Guard were called to testify. I don't know if I listened. No one was going to dismiss the incredible reality of her guilt.

In one of the pauses Suthafiori said, 'Ruric – how could you do it?'

It was naked hurt, what we all felt: this was personal betrayal. Ruric did not reply.

I thought about Orthe, what had happened to me: the murder, the long pursuit across wild country, across the sea . . . because of this woman I trusted. This woman I'd believed was one of the friends that only come once in a lifetime.

'You lied to me,' I said. 'Everything you did was a lie.'

'Ruric,' Suthafiori broke in harshly. 'In the Goddess's name, I have a right to demand your reasons! *Why?*'

'I suppose it started in Roehmonde . . . no, it was longer ago than that.' The dark woman shook her head, looked suddenly tired. Her eyes sought Suthafiori's face. 'You know I've been against this Offworld presence from the beginning, since I met the *t'an* Huxton and his people. Then I went north in Christie's company – I knew SuBannasen and Howice planned something, but I didn't interfere. When I came back and saw what an effect one Earth woman had on that province . . .'

'Roehmonde,' I said bitterly, 'was that you, too?'

'No, that you may leave at SuBannasen's door, and Howice's. After that – and you must remember, Christie, I thought you were dead – after that, I joined in with the anti-Dominion faction who supported SuBannasen, and I met Harantish agents in Tathcaer that autumn. And in Shiriya-Shenin . . .' she shrugged, not looking at me; arrogance kept her gaze on the Kerys-Andrethe woman. 'Christie being alive, I saw SuBannasen brought to trial. Orthe couldn't defend her own. So I took over SuBannasen's contact with Kel Harantish, and determined to have the Dominion envoy disgraced.'

'Kanta's death, *was* it a mistake?' Evalen demanded.

Ruric ignored her. 'You know how that ended. Brodin and I fell out when he sent assassins against my *ashiren* Rodion, so I saw no need to defend him. But he might have betrayed me.'

'You killed him,' Haltern said.

Suthafiori bowed her head for a moment. When her voice was steady she said, 'You were *T'An* Melkathi, you could have named yourself Crown . . . grief of the Goddess, a Witchbreed agent Crown of the Southland!'

Ruric smiled. Regretfully, as if at lost opportunities.

'And had you done with them, or are you still their agent?' Suthafiori shook her head. 'Ah, no, why? Why, Ruric? It's senseless!'

'Senseless? No.' At last she looked at me. Our eyes met, and I looked away. She stood, in blue and silver, the candlelight like honey on her black skin. She was tall, gaunt, an ageing woman carrying herself with crook-shouldered balance.

'What happened, happened as I've told you. The reasons—' she looked at me again. 'Christie, if you'd been scared off by poison or by prison . . . no, but we'll speak of what occurred. My intention was to discredit the Earth envoy, and the Dominion—'

'Why not kill me?' I asked bleakly.

'What use would that be? They'd send another. I wanted us rid of you and your world.'

Slow, amazed, Suthafiori said, 'You never agreed with me on that, but I didn't imagine you traitor because of it.'

'I'm no traitor!' Ruric flared. 'All I've done, even to murder, I've done for the Southland.'

'Even to taking Harantish gold?' That was Haltern's barb.

'I see no reason not to take my enemies' gold, if I can use it for my friends' good.'

That coolness silenced everyone.

'If you'll have reasons,' Ruric said simply, 'they are these. Earth will destroy us. Either it will change us out of all recognition, or it will destroy the land itself. We've all heard of the Dominion's fire-weapons. *T'ans*, there has never been a weapon in history too terrible for use. No matter how awesome, they have been used. We have for witness the Glittering Plain, the deserts of the Elansiir. Do you think Earth will hesitate to use her weapons on us? As I love the South – I love it more than life – so I have tried to protect it.'

Stubbornly, Suthafiori said, 'You can't turn back time.'

'Can you not?' Ruric shrugged. 'But it seems we have the Golden Witchbreed come again. Oh, not that poor remnant walled up in Kel Harantish. But you star-travelling, land-owning, fire-weaponed Earth people – are you not the same breed as Golden?'

There was silence.

'*S'aranth*?' Evalen prompted.

'There are superficial similarities between that civilization and Earth,' I said carefully, 'and I can't deny that we have terrible weapons. I do deny that we would ever use them – least of all on a world with which we have such friendly alliances—'

'Oh, you are different,' Ruric said regretfully, 'not all your people are Christies, though. I've studied your people who studied us. I begin to know the Dominion by its kinfolk.'

'We'd never do it.'

'Never is a long time,' she said, 'and while we're a backwater world with nothing desired from us, perhaps we're safe from war. But even then, not from change. You are utterly unlike us, and when you come here we can't help but alter. And if we're ever found to have something that Earth requires – why then Goddess help us, Christie, because no one else will!'

I couldn't answer her.

Ruric said, 'I'm a soldier. I know the odds. The Southland can't *fight* Earth. I saw that a long while back. I thought that an envoy disgraced as a murderer might hold back the tide – might even give us an excuse to break off relations with the Dominion. But you've a gift for survival, Christie.'

'Do you excuse yourself?' Evalen asked. 'You've broken every law and custom in the Southland, there *is* no excuse!'

'I'm right,' Ruric said, 'but yes, there's no excuse for failure.'

Suthafiori called the guards. 'Confine her in the outer chamber. Let none come to her, and let her speak to no one.'

Ruric walked out untouched between the soldiers, leaving silence in her wake.

'Goddess!' Suthafiori said at last. '*T'an*, she may yet spoil things between our worlds.'

'Worlds? No.' At that moment I wasn't fond of anybody there. 'She forgets one thing: the Southland isn't all of Orthe. We'll deal with others if we have to.'

'I don't think she cares, so long as you touch no part of the Hundred Thousand. And yet it would come to that in the end. We are one world.' She put her hands to her temples, rubbing six-fingered hands through her sandy-white mane. 'Excuse me – I'll call for refreshment, *t'ans*, we have work to do. There's much we must discuss and decide before the morning.'

CHAPTER 35

The Legacy of Kel Harantish

'You cannot keep it from them!' Asshe stopped his pacing, turned and faced the *T'An Suthai-Telestre*. The grey-maned Orthean was edgy, claw-nailed hand resting on his *harur-nazari* hilt.

'What good will it do my *T'Ans* to know they have a traitor among them? After such a year as we have just had?' Suthafiori sighed. 'No, Melkathi must have a new *T'An*, but the fewer who know why, the better.'

The *T'An* Commander shook his head. 'And the Orhlandis?'

'Yes, the Orhlandis . . . Haltern, I think you had better find Hana Oreyn Orhlandis for me.'

Haltern left the chamber. Candles and oil lamps guttered unnoticed in first twilight. Dawn was lightening over Ymir, lost in river-mist.

I still couldn't believe it. It was a fiction, a bad joke – but it was true, and I might have suspected it long ago. I trusted her. The betrayal hurt.

Evalen was talking to Asshe, trying to persuade him. Suthafiori stood and walked to stand beside me at the window. The courtyard was grey below us.

'I'm sorry you should witness this,' she said, 'though I agree with Haltern, it's your right. You've suffered from her conspiracies.'

'She shouldn't have done it.' Not to us, I meant. She had lied, killed, but most of all betrayed the trust put in her.

'You look on the game differently.' The pale eyes veiled. 'But I agree. Melkathi may be a poor province – but she should not have gone to the Witchbreed for help.'

'What do you expect from an *amari* and a golden-eyes?' Evalen was bitter. She and Asshe began arguing again.

'No, that's not it . . .' As a thought struck her, Suthafiori called the scribe. 'Romare, send word for the Harbourmaster to come to the Citadel. Tell him I want the Harantish ship kept in port.'

387

Now the dawn brightened, so brilliant a silver as to bring tears to the eyes. Carrick's Star was fiercely white. Daystars peppered the arch of the sky. The city came clear of the shadow.

Amari Ruric Orhlandis . . . living in a world that was violent, precarious, unpredictable, herself marked and crippled. After that illness at Path-of-Skulls, she must have come back to Corbek feeling she was running out of time. Seeing the chaos those *telestres* were in, and all that change caused by one Earthwoman. Could I understand Ruric?

I felt close to her because she was the most 'human' of the Ortheans. That in itself was wrong. Did she fall prey to an Earth disease that most Ortheans are immune to – impatience? The Golden race never dreamed past-dreams, did the golden-eyed woman never dream them either? Did she believe that this is the only life there is, the only chance to act? Maybe that's what we had in common, the alien woman and I.

I must understand her, I thought. Nobody does anything like this without a reason. I must try to understand why.

A short time later, Haltern returned.

'Oreyn Orhlandis is not in the *T'An* Melkathi's house,' he said, 'nor are any of the Orhlandis *telestre*. I've begun a search.'

'None of them?' Suthafiori took her seat at table again, thin fingers resting on Brodin's confession. '*T'An* Commander, tell your guard to bring in Ruric Orhlandis, I will question her.'

He left. Shall I go? I wondered. I knew I didn't want to see her again. But I shouldn't go until the *T'An Suthai-Telestre* dismissed me. I rubbed my eyes, shook my head to clear it. I'd been awake all night; the last sleep I'd had was yesterday noon.

The waiting continued. Suthafiori, growing impatient, sent one of her *l'ri-an* after Asshe. Gradually, talk died down. Then Romare entered the chamber.

'The Harbourmaster attends you, *T'An*, and sends a message: the Witchbreed ship sailed at first light this morning.'

'Shadow take it!' Her fist crashed on the table. 'Have they heard – Haltern, find Asshe, find the Orhlandis woman; I want to know just how many Harantish agents there are in this city!'

At that moment the door opened, admitting Asshe. For once the arrogance had gone out of him.

'She's gone,' he said without ceremony. 'And half an army detachment with her. I've questioned the nightwatch. They say she left before first light. They had no orders to prevent her going. She went down Crown Way to the docks.'

The small woman covered her eyes for a moment, then looked up. 'She was their *T'An* Commander . . . I should have left her with the Crown Guard. Romare! Bring the Harbourmaster in. I want to know what ships are ready to sail. Asshe, bring the Guard – she's gone with bel-Olinyi.'

Then, incredibly, she laughed. Laughed bitterly and shook her head. 'Only she could do it. Only Ruric.'

In the frenzied activity that followed, I didn't wait to be dismissed. I found Maric, borrowed Oru, and rode the *marhaz* as fast as I could towards Easthill Malk'ys.

''Morning, Lynne—' Meredith hesitated, then shut the office door behind him. 'What's the crisis?'

'Is it that obvious? Hold on.' I finished what I was writing. I could have made a tape, but tapes can be wiped. David Meredith sat down, watching me. I said, 'You're early.'

'I'm getting used to the time-scheme.' He was keenly aware that something was wrong.

I finished writing and glanced round the office. It was as informal now as any Orthean place of work, the tables piled with papers and broadsheets as well as tapes, graphs pinned to the wall-hangings beside old illuminated maps, haphazard cartography beside satellite-survey prints. Stained tea bowls were piled on a chair, from when the last *s'an* had visited me. I was going to miss the work I'd been doing here.

'I haven't got much time,' I said, 'so here's the way it is. This is my resignation from the post of envoy—'

Meredith protested, but I overrode him. '—and as you're here, that means you're now the official envoy for Carrick V. I'm just a private citizen, as of now. What I do is my own affair, and doesn't reflect on the Dominion.'

As I moved towards the door, he stepped in front of it.

'I don't know what you're getting mixed up in, Lynne, I don't want to know. But I'll say this. Don't. It won't help this world, it won't help Earth, and it certainly won't help you. Don't be a bloody idiot.'

'You're right. Don't think I don't realize that.'

He relaxed fractionally. 'Now will you tell me what's going on?'

'You'll hear. I'm leaving Tathcaer. I don't know when I'm coming back. What I do know is, I won't be able to go as envoy. And I have to go.'

'What about the recall date?'

'What about it?'

He read the paper, looking for a moment as if he didn't intend to move. Then he folded it, put it in his pocket, and stepped aside.

'I'll make this public if it's necessary.' There was a faint emphasis on the last word.

'Thanks.' I stopped. 'Thank you, David.'

He said something as I went out. It might have been *good luck.*

Down on the quay, at this early hour still in shadow from the Easthill, I found Asshe's men embarking on a Morvren trader. It was a broad-hulled *jath-rai* ship, nothing more than a coaster. Pushing through the crowd, I at last found someone I knew: Evalen Kerys-Andrethe.

'What do you want, *S'aranth*?' She was busy with messengers from the Harbourmaster and the Crown.

'Permission to sail with you.'

She frowned. The stolid face showed indecision. I should have asked Haltern, I thought, or even Suthafiori, they'd understand.

'I can't take a foreign envoy,' she said.

'David Meredith isn't asking to come.'

There was the subtle flick of nictitating membrane that might mean amusement. She was not as slow as I'd taken her for, this Kerys-Andrethe woman.

'Find the *t'an* Haltern,' she said, 'he's somewhere aboard. But take care, we sail as soon as possible, and can't turn back to land passengers.'

I went aboard, dodging the crowd: ship's crew and Asshe's soldiery settling down together. The harbour smelled dank and salty, fish-heads floating in the green water. Scavenger *rashaku-bazur* dipped and wheeled in the cool air, riding the wind.

The sails of bel-Olinyi's ship were still visible on the horizon when we put out from Tathcaer. Behind us, from the fortresses on Easthill and Westhill, the heliograph flashed warning messages towards the Sisters Islands and the south.

'This wind won't last,' a voice was saying. 'There's a calm coming.'

'When?' Haltern answering, frustration in his tone. The inflections of Ymirian, alien, liquid, but nevertheless respectful. When I opened my eyes I saw he was talking to an Earthspeaker.

I'd reached the state beyond tiredness that morning and found the light too bright. My voice was high and hoarse from talking through the night, and the skin across my forehead tight with a semi-permanent headache. My concentration had odd lapses in it.

Must have lapsed now, I thought, sitting up on the hold-cover. But the white sun was high, it was past noon. I'd slept.

'Where are they?' I went forward to stand beside Haltern at the rail. The rhythm made me stagger, hesitate as the deck swayed.

With a firm grip on the rail it was better, I could watch the bows cut the swelling water, see the fans of rainbow spray.

'There,' Haltern pointed. It was a speck against the sunlight and the rolling water, barely visible to a human eye. We were no closer.

'Damn it, can't we go faster?'

'You can't hurry the sea.' His voice was quiet under the creaking of wood, the belling of sails.

A faint coastline was visible to the north. The sun's light, dipping on the water, flashed and dazzled me. I thought, not for the first time on Orthe, What am I doing here?

'Come below and eat.' Haltern's clawed hand rested on my shoulder for a minute. Wind ruffled his sparse mane. He was still the same secretive man, but even he couldn't conceal how this had shaken him.

'Hal – what will happen to her?'

'Let the Mother judge her,' he said, 'I can't.'

We ate sparsely, with Asshe and the shipmaster and *t'an* Evalen, to whom Suthafiori had given command of this makeshift expedition. There was little talk. The day wore on.

The turning-point came in the late afternoon, out of sight of land. I wouldn't have realized if Haltern hadn't told me.

Bel-Olinyi's ship lost a little time, or else the shipmaster managed to coax more speed out of the Morvren *jath-rai*. The sails were visible and the dark spot that was the hull. Only the two ships, under a stainless sky, daystars masked by high haze. Then the lookout shouted.

Two other specks were visible ahead of the Kel Harantish ship, and then I saw another off to the south, and what might have been a fourth. Ships that scarcely appeared to be moving, answering the heliograph messages, cutting off the way to the south. Ruric's bad luck that there were ships in sight of that call.

After a little while it became apparent that bel-Olinyi's ship was changing course, and that we were drawing closer to her. But not close enough.

The Harantish ship fled north and east towards the Melkathi coast, and we followed.

The ship's boat grounded and the crew shipped oars. I went over the side after Evalen and Asshe, splashing through shallow water. The flat sands stretched out, lapped by thin waves and ripples, silvered in the west as sunset approached. The sand sucked at my boots. A failing wind feathered the water, and brought from somewhere the smell of burning.

Another boat lay beached a hundred yards away, now empty and abandoned. Far out, where the shallow water shelved, bel-Olinyi's ship was anchored close to the Morvren *jath-rai*. And, walking towards us across the deserted beach, came an Orthean woman I recognized as bel-Olinyi herself.

Asshe gave orders to the Guard with him. Another boat was rowing the long way towards us from the Morvren craft, presumably reinforcements. He ordered the winch-bow holders to cover the woman's approach.

Haltern came up, eyes veiled against the light. 'Don't trust her, *t'an*.'

Evalen's eyes were turned inland, towards the low dunes and flat expanses of yellow mossgrass. A mist was coming up, so that it was not possible to see for any great distance.

'We must be east of Rynnal Sands . . .' she mused. 'The 'Breed doesn't matter, it's obvious the Orhlandis has gone inland. *T'An* Commander! Send your scouts to track their party. Be wary of ambush.'

Asshe nodded curtly. 'They may make speed, *t'an*, and not be concerned about us. If we've passed Rynnal, we're not far from Orhlandis itself.'

A look passed between them. Evalen said, 'Try and stop them reaching it. We'll follow you.'

Two of the Crown Guard brought bel-Olinyi forward. One carried the spear and knife that she surrendered without argument. She loosened the scarf at her throat, pulling it free of the laces of her bronze scaled mail, and surveyed us with composure.

'*T'an*.' She inclined her head to Evalen, then to me, speaking in her gutturally-accented Ymirian. '*S'aranth*.'

Evalen said bluntly, 'Where is she?'

'Your countrywoman? I wish I knew.' Her mouth tightened. 'I think I must speak to your *T'An Suthai-Telestre* when I reach Tathcaer again. It is not fitting for an ambassador to be kidnapped at sword-point—'

Haltern swore. Evalen continued stolidly, 'You claim that you were forced?'

'The woman comes aboard, her people are armed – what am I to do when my life is threatened? I did what she told me. But rest assured, the Emperor-in-Exile shall hear of this.'

'Oh yes,' Haltern said softly, temper for once uncontrolled. 'He surely will! So the traitor is betrayed, and you have clean hands, do you, Witchbreed?'

'Quiet.' Evalen's eyes hooded and narrowed, her six-fingered hands clenched into fists. 'You – troopmaster – take this woman to the ship, tell the shipmaster she is under my protection. And do you tell your own people, bel-Olinyi of Kel Harantish, that you will indeed return to Tathcaer. As soon as I have finished my business with Melkathi.'

'We'll never do it.' Haltern sounded depressed, as if he were still ashamed of his outburst before bel-Olinyi. 'Not in these mudflats, when we don't know the land; we won't come up with Ruric Orhlandis.'

'There'll be light for a while yet,' I said.

The long hot dusk of Merrum wore on towards sunset. What I took to be yellow mossgrass was the ordinary variety half-killed by drought. Light gleamed on ridged expanses of silt, dried waterways, and sand-marsh. Lizardbirds spiralled down, shrieking like rusty metal, settling into dry reedbeds that rattled like bones. The desolate coast stretched out to either side, losing itself inland in dunes and hillocks.

Evalen had brought her people to order, adding those men and women who had come ashore from the other ships. About three hundred, I estimated. Now she was sending scouts ahead of us, so that she would be informed where Asshe and Orhlandis were.

'The night should be clear,' the brown-robed Earthspeaker with her said as we approached. 'Wait out the second twilight, and travel on; I can give some aid to guide you.'

'Go at the front, Lishaan; we'll start now.' Evalen spoke with the formal inflection. Seeing us, she added, 'Keep with the main body. It's possible we'll be attacked.'

Sand stuck to wet boots, clouds of insects followed us as we trudged through the mossgrass-covered dunes. The marsh *rashaku-nai* began to roost. Walking was tiring, irritating. Haltern gazed, pale eyes unveiled, as we faced the flat land that lay back of the shore.

'Those might be Eirye Hills . . . or Vincor, if we're further southeast. *T'an*,' he said to Evalen,' she may not stop at Orhlandis.'

'Why not?'

'Her *telestre* may furnish her with a guard and with *marhaz*, and it's not impossible to get down the coast from here to Ales-Kadareth. *T'an*, a person might lie concealed in that port for some time, and perhaps take ship—'

'To Kel Harantish?' Evalen shook her fair-maned head. 'It must not be allowed.'

Haltern caught her arm. 'She is Ruric Onehand, Yelloweyes of Melkathi, she has friends. If the *T'An Suthai-Telestre* were to judge in haste, and regret that later—'

'No,' Evalen said. 'I won't let her go. She must be judged. If it were my decision – she was my friend also, Haltern, but I'll bring her back to Tathcaer. Excuse me: I must send messengers ahead to warn Asshe of this.'

They're ambiguous, I thought, in their loves and in their hates. But not me – no, not me, I want to see her answer for what she's done.

Threading a way between bogs and mudflats, we came at second twilight to a *telestre*-house on higher ground. Torches set by the open gates illuminated the ancient, mortared stone walls.

'It is Vincor,' Haltern said, as we ate. Evalen was conferring with Asshe's scouts, and the sullen men and women of the *telestre*. 'We'll wait out second twilight here.'

The dusk was warm, and I fell asleep where I sat in the courtyard; not waking until the bustle of Evalen's leaving disturbed me. She and the Earthspeaker Lishaan took those men and women who were able to travel quicker, leaving her Second – a dark Peir-Dadeni man – to bring the rest on later.

'She'll try and keep Orhlandis from the Ales-Kadareth road.' Haltern eased down beside me. 'Rest now, there won't be time later.'

As when I'd first come to Orthe, I was getting used to catnapping wherever and whenever I could. So the next time I woke, insect-bitten and with aching legs, it was in full starlight. Two men were speaking with Evalen's Second. One had an arm roughly bandaged, seeping blackly.

'We'll take the border-path to Orhlandis,' the Peir-Dadeni man said. 'The *T'An* Commander Asshe was ambushed, but *t'an* Evalen's people came up with the Orhlandis company and turned them from the 'Kadareth road; now we are to make all speed to Orhlandis *telestre*.'

Starlight leached the colour from the land, from the stunted *lapuur* that edged the water channels, from the mossgrass that crumbled like ash underfoot. The way was winding, difficult to follow, crossing channels by plank-bridges. After the first we found broken down, the Ortheans carried a set with them. Orhlandis had tried to delay Asshe and Evalen, I thought.

The warm night at last grew chill as the stars faded to first twilight, and we waited out that time until dawn. So light came and showed us still in the flat water meadows, seemingly no closer ro the distant high ground that didn't deserve the name of hills.

We came up on higher ground, following tracks through meadows where mossgrass was dying on acres of cracked mud.

Skurrai raised their heads as we passed, all hide and bone under shaggy pelts. Stunted *lapuur* clung to the borders of the dikes, where *kekri* and *siriye* hovered in clouds over the mud. The pale sun rose from the haze, the air already warm. Then we came up on the spine of a ridge and I saw another high-walled *telestre*-house ahead. Two of Asshe's men appeared out of nowhere with drawn *harur* blades, and led us on to where Evalen was camped.

'*S'aranth.*' She was civil but preoccupied. 'Haltern, good. I'm going to speak with Orhlandis; you as Crown Messenger should come with me.'

'She's under siege?' Haltern glanced at the distant *telestre*-house. He brushed futilely at the mud that spattered him. None of us, after the night's travelling, were in a better state. 'Christie, you speak with her as well, we might still end this without fighting.'

'I'd as soon do it with words. These *telestres* were built to stand against the sea-raiders, it will be bloody work to bring her out of there.' Evalen looked at me. 'She may hear you.'

'I doubt it. But I'll come.'

It was an effort to begin walking again. The hot air was motionless. I followed Evalen and Haltern. The tracks were dusty, winding through stands of *lapuur* and *saryl-kiez* bushes, crossing wide dikes. When I looked behind, the landscape seemed empty. Yet there were two or three hundred armed men and women there. As we came closer, we were softly challenged.

'Go forward,' Evalen told one of Asshe's people. 'Say we'd speak with them.'

The woman laid down her swords and walked towards the *telestre*-house, holding up empty hands. There were none of Evalen's company closer than this, bowshot-length.

Sun cast the shadow of the walls towards us. It was not a large building – it was so small that it surprised me, no more than high walls and a squat tower at one of the obtuse-angled corners. I made out stout gates barring the entrance under the tower. Surrounding the walls was a moat all of thirty foot wide. A single causeway led to the gate.

'There's the obstacle,' Evalen said. 'This Shadow-sent drought has left only mud; Asshe had a man near sucked down trying to spy out a place to attack. You've to cross that in the open, no way to surprise the defenders; and then with no scaling ladders, you've to attack the gates direct – we'd take it by weight of numbers, but not easily.'

'She was *T'An* Commander,' Haltern said, 'and knows all about sieges in Melkathi, *t'an.*'

The messenger's shouting brought movement on the walls, but

little answer. Eventually a winchbow-bolt buried itself in the dry earth at her feet, and Evalen called her back.

'Why should she speak with us, *t'an*?' Asshe appeared, cat-silently. 'I've posted the Guard at all points now, she's surrounded.'

A frown settled on the woman's high forehead. 'We'll wait. She may try to break out. And she may be more willing to speak when she realizes she can't escape.'

They set up tents back where the cover of *lapuur* was thicker, and I shared rations with Asshe's company. The day grew hotter. Evalen and Asshe spent much time with their heads together, planning attack. My stomach went cold when I thought that might happen. Haltern was restless, and we made one wide circuit of the country round the *telestre*-house, from the marshes to the *lapuur*-choked low hillocks inland. He spoke little. The sun blazed down and the daystars gleamed, and we went back to the shade of the tents. A tense atmosphere kept us from resting. A *rashaku-nai* that flew up suddenly in the noon silence fell with four winchbow bolts in it.

Towards evening Evalen sent another messenger to the gates, but with no result.

We waited. Asshe set the night guard-posts. Tension rose: I could see they expected a night attack. But the night was clear, the starlight made everything visible, and Orhlandis remained blank-walled and quiet.

We waited.

'Who's that?' I indicated the group of Ortheans in drab robes who were speaking to Evalen.

'People from the nearby *telestres*.' Haltern eased into the shade of the *saryl-kiez*. If anything, this second day was hotter than the first. 'They want to know what the *t'an* Evalen's doing.'

'Will they help?'

'In Melkathi?' His eyes blurred. 'At best we'll get indifference, at worst – well, Orhlandis is a Melkathi *telestre*.'

Fear transmuted into resentment, into hate. The blank walls of the *telestre*-house shimmered in the heat, mocking me.

'Why doesn't she *do* something?' I demanded savagely.

Haltern had no anger in his voice. 'What can she do?'

Twilight came on the second day, and we waited.

Dreams merged with waking: shouts, darkness, and confusion. *Becamil* cloth flapped in my face, I was out of the tent and into the warm air. Yellow sparks flared across my vision.

396

'—*fire!*'

Another flight of sparks: I stood, head back, watching with all the concentration of a child at a firework display. Sleep blurred the image of rockets trailing down, sinking down and still burning—

Flame ran through the dry mossgrass and *lapuur*, red sparks went up into the windless night.

'Fire-arrows!' a man beside me shouted. I was at the centre of a group of robed Ortheans – the other *telestres*, it must be – chattering questions, wiping sleep off their faces, buckling on sword-belts and lacing robes. Evalen had been trying to gain their aid.

A company of Guard ran past. The camp was in uproar, like an over-turned *becamil* hive; frantic, shouting, panic controlled but present. I blinked in the flickering light. One of the tents hissed up in flame.

'You!' I grabbed the arm of a middle-aged Orthean woman. 'How close is your *telestre*?'

'A few *seri* north—'

'Get your people, bring them here. Now! Help fight the fire.' She stared blankly at me, and I shook her. 'Don't you realize how dry it is – the whole countryside could go up in flames!'

She was silent for a few heartbeats. Then as the din and shouting came closer, and I heard the crackle of burning wood, she gave a quick nod and ran off towards the back of the encampment. I saw her mount one of the scrawny *skurrai* there, kick bare heels to its flanks and ride off at breakneck speed. Starlight showed her the trail.

When I turned back, half the sky glared red.

The speed of it shocked me. I saw silhouettes of tents, then they blackened, crisped, curled – nothing but leaping flames. Showers of gold sparks went up. *Saryl-kiez* underbrush snapped as it burned. Dark shapes of men and women tried to beat out the fire, but as I watched they abandoned the effort. Another flight of fire-arrows soared from the *telestre*-house, then rolling smoke hid it.

Ruric?

Who couldn't take a siege, who was going to burn us out—

I scouted back, trying to circle round the fires. The *lapuur* was dry as tinder. Shouts faded. The fire was a dull roar. I was running, eyes dazzled, night-vision lost, finding the trail by luck and star-light; running as if I wasn't tired, as if I could run all night.

A dike blocked my way. I ran frantically along the edge and across a plank-bridge. Shallow water gleamed in the middle of the silt. Once across, I could turn and look back.

There is fear, and then there's terror. Standing there, heaving air back into my lungs, I knew the difference. With terror there is no fear, because there's no possibility of facing (say) the fire. There's no decision to make. You run, that's all.

A few moments later I came to a group of soldiers, and stumbled to a halt. I was about to ask them where Evalen was, when I saw Haltern there.

'You're all right?' He broke away, facing me.

I had no breath to speak, and could only nod.

Blackness blotted out the stars, darkness with a flaring red curtain at the foot of it. The smell of burning drifted to us. The air was no longer still, an intermittent wind fanned the flames.

'Move out!' Haltern ordered. 'We'll join the *t'an* Evalen at Rimnith.'

Within a surprisingly short time the soldiers were making an orderly way along the trail. I looked back. Flames crackled, rolled twenty foot into the night air, seething in smoke, orange and gold fire.

'She's broken siege,' Haltern muttered as we went, 'she's got her distraction, we can't stop her now – I hope the fire traps her and all her Shadow-haunted *telestre*! Just let her try and seek refuge anywhere in the Southland—'

He had no more breath to speak. We were running now. Behind us, the fire spread as fast as water flows.

Fine black ash-flakes drifted in the air. I coughed, throat raw, the breath rasping in and out of my lungs. The ground in front of me was soft and black and hot. Charred stumps of *lapuur* jutted up. Wisps of grey smoke still issued from the ground. The ashes were too hot to step on, even in stout boots.

I walked back across the dried watercourse and the turned earth, came to a knoll and sat down. My palms were blistered with shovelling and digging. From here I could see the line of dikes that had been turned into firebreaks. Ortheans were scattered along the edge of the burnt earth, sitting, or standing and talking, or just staring at the noon sun. The smoke that had mushroomed up to cover the coast was dispersing. Carrick's Star was a sepia disc, seen through the acrid pall.

They had it worse on the higher ground, I thought. Weariness blurred my eyesight, but I could see the stands of *lapuur* and *saryl-kiez* that grew there, some still sending up plumes of black smoke. I meant to go and look for the people I knew, but thought I'd sit a while longer.

The distant *telestre*-house of Orhlandis stood, a blackened stump, stones brought down by the heat. Gutted. Ash and desolation surrounded it. There'd been no way to put out the fire, it had barely been contained. Only the dikes and lack of vegetation made that possible. Evalen's people and the nearby *telestres* had thrown all their effort into fire-fighting.

Where's Ruric? I wondered. I was too tired to lie to myself now. No, I didn't hate her. I might hate what she'd done, but not her. If she'd managed to get away, if she sailed overseas from Ales-Kadareth . . .

I got up and walked slowly back towards Rimnith, another small *telestre* on the edge of the blackened acres. Ortheans passed me, giving tired greetings. They were dirty and exhausted. I joined those in the courtyard, taking drinks from the well there.

Haltern found me while I was washing my face in a bucket.

'What do you think?' His gaze went through the archway to the burned land.

'It should be watched. It might still be burning underneath.'

He grunted assent. I wondered what was the matter with him. But it was the general atmosphere, there was more depression than could be accounted for by a fire, especially one that had been sucessfully contained.

'Hal, what is it?'

'Evalen's sending parties out to search.' He sounded as though he hadn't heard me. Then: 'She fired her own land. Burned her *telestre*. The stinking golden-eyed—'

'Hal.'

'You can't know,' he said. 'What it means. To do that – the 'Breed are land-destroyers, the Golden Witchbreed, and she—'

'When we came here, you were all for letting her escape to the port.'

He was silent. Then he said, 'The *T'An* Commander's found a *telestre* willing to sell us *marhaz*. You'd rather ride back to the ships?'

'Given the choice, yes. Let's go and see about it.'

I didn't mention Ruric again. Empathy and memories: yes, I could sympathize with what he felt. But then . . . Ruric. I heard enough talk from the Ortheans to know that Haltern's opinion was general.

Evalen was in Rimnith's small main hall, and as the members of her company straggled in she arranged for them to eat and then go out on patrol.

'She may be making for the coast again.' Asshe's grey-maned head was bent over a map. 'Or inland, hoping to hide.'

'You!' Evalen leaned back in her chair, shouting at a man who stood in the corner of the hall. 'Where did she go?'

'I don't know.' The man was sullen. It took a minute for me to see past the dirt and recognize the praying-mantis face of Hana Oreyn Orhlandis. 'I'd tell you if I knew – believe that, *t'an*.'

Evalen grunted. There were others under guard there, some with the Orhlandis face, and some in army gear. I recognized faces from my trip to Roehmonde: Ho-Telerit, and a red-maned male. So they'd abandoned Ruric, or she'd abandoned them . . .

'Have you messages for the Crown?' Haltern took the papers Evalen indicated. 'How long will you stay in Melkathi?'

'Until I've made a thorough search. Let the other ships escort bel-Olinyi's ship back to Tathcaer with you, the Harantish woman has many questions to answer.' She raised her head and saw me. '*S'aranth*, I'm glad to see you safe. Will you stay here, or return with the ships?'

I felt bitterly tired. Nothing had been accomplished by my coming to Melkathi, and as for Ruric . . . Patrols were already skirting the edges of the fire. I thought it likely they'd find her in there. If she'd got out, I thought, they'd have found her by now.

'I'll go back with Hal,' I said.

In the event they found me a copper-coloured *marhaz*, very docile, and I joined Haltern's small party. It was mid-afternoon by then. The rocking gait of the *marhaz* was oddly soothing. I trailed along behind, the sun hot on my head, half asleep. The sky was powder-blue, dust from the earth track mixed with floating ashes . . . the smooth dry meadows, broken by muddy dikes . . . beyond that, beyond the *rashaku* that wheeled over the sandflats, the soft-edged blueness of the sea. . . .

The *marhaz* stopped. I jolted awake.

Hooves rang on the hard earth. There was a scuffle. I saw the half-dozen Guard vanish into a thick copse of *lapuur*. Haltern rode to the edge of the dike, by the plank-bridge. Sunlight shone on his drawn harur blades. I kicked the *marhaz* and it lumbered into a trot.

The feathery *lapuur* fronds blocked my vision. I swung down from the saddle and plunged into the copse. I was aware that Haltern followed me. I heard cries from deeper in.

'Landwaster! *Amari*—'

'—fired her own land—'

'—against the Goddess!'

Haltern shouldered past me into a clearing. 'All right, all right, *leave* her! I said leave her, Goddess rot your guts!'

There was a *skurrai* standing with its head down, cropping at the mossgrass that grew between *lapuur* and watercourse. Beside it, anonymous in shirt and britches, stood Ruric Orhlandis. Her clothes were smeared with ash, only the *harur-nilgiri* she held was bright. The dark mane fell over her high forehead, the narrow-chinned face was watchful. Her eyes glinted.

The Guard spread out, giving each other room, drawn *harur-nilgiri* and *harur-nazari* in their hands. Violence ran like an electric current, sparking in the air. Four men, two women, each face distinct, then merging into an animal gestalt. Ruric half-crouched, eyes flicking towards the dike. No way out. She was *s'an*: they hesitated. But she destroyed the land . . . The possibility almost realized: the unspoken desire to attack—

'No,' Haltern said quietly, his voice shattering a silence like glass. 'You there! Disarm her. If any of you touches her, I'll have your guts! She's going to Tathcaer, to the *T'An Suthai-Telestre*. Now move!'

Then he looked Ruric in the face. Something unspoken passed between them. Her thin lips parted, showing white teeth in a curious smile. The tension went out of her crook-shouldered balance. Sunlight flashed as she opened her six-fingered hand, letting the blade fall.

They hustled her off roughly, binding her arm behind her back and drawing blood cruelly. Haltern took no notice of that. I went back to find the *marhaz*, leading them after the party.

'I thought she might . . .' Haltern glanced at me, then ahead. 'She had that last escape, to make them kill her.'

'Not Ruric.' Perhaps if she'd been ordinary Orthean, not golden-eyed; if she'd had faith in more than one life – then she might have done that.

A wind feathered ashes from the burnt land. The heat of the sun was like a blow. We went on, taking Ruric Orhlandis back to Evalen, back to Tathcaer, back to whatever justice there might be for an ally of the Golden Witchbreed.

CHAPTER 36

Exiles

Tacking back up along the coast of Melkathi, it was not until the dawn of Fiveday that we docked in Tathcaer. Westhill's fortress windows glittered in the sun, Easthill was still in shadow. I stood on the dock while the ferries brought Evalen's company from the ship. The solid earth swayed. I'd got accustomed to the sea's motion again.

'They're sending the Witchbreed,' Haltern observed, watching the Kel Harantish ship's boat approach. Then, turning away, made a formal bow. '*T'An Suthai-Telestre.*'

Suthafiori, dismounting from a *skurrai-jasin*, nodded briefly. 'Is the *t'an* Evalen here?'

'She's bringing the Orhlandis.' Haltern pointed.

'I've heard—' the small woman hesitated. 'Rumours out of Melkathi, the city's full of them. A burning. Is it true?'

'It's true.'

Her eyes narrowed, anger snarled across her face. 'Was it her? Was it Ruric?'

'She's said as much: her people confirm it.'

'The fool, the yellow-eyed freak—' fist hit palm, then she was calm with an effort. 'So that's the truth of it. Send Evalen to me.'

Suthafiori went back to sit in the *skurrai-jasin*.

'The way she says it, you'd think it was the worst thing Ruric did.'

Haltern shook his head. 'You're Outworlder, Christie. To intrigue is one thing, but to desecrate the earth . . . The Orhlandis was my friend. But you can't expect a Beth'ru-elen to approve of a *s'an* destroying her own *telestre.*'

'It's not destroyed.'

'The land will grow again, eventually, but the continuity's gone. A *telestre* can't live if its *s'an* betrays it.'

He went to meet Evalen. I watched him go. No, he couldn't feel any other way than he did. Land, history: more important to

402

Ortheans than any individual person. I could feel it in me too: empathy with the earth.

Evalen spoke to Suthafiori, calling Asshe to her; and the Guard brought the Orhlandis *telestre* on to the quay, with Kurick bel-Olinyi and two other Kel Harantish Witchbreed. After a short discussion, Suthafiori drove off; and the company followed her on foot.

We went between the Guildhouse and Harbourmaster's office, under the great arch and up Crown Way. The city was empty in the half-light. The paved way went in a straight line, over the saddle between Easthill and Westhill, down into the city itself, then rising up until I saw the Citadel, catching early light. I imagined that our destination, but Evalen directed the company through the open gates of the House of the Goddess.

The great courtyard was empty, the fountain echoing loudly in the desolation. A warm wind lifted my hair, brushed my skin, brought for a moment the scent of cut mossgrass and a lifting of the heart. Then, as the company entered the Wellhouse dome, I saw Blaize n'ri n'suth Meduenin. Only a sick resentment stayed with me, that such things as the Orhlandis betrayal should happen.

'Christie,' he caught my arm as we went down to the lower seats, 'they've taken Rodion. Goddess! she's hardly more than *ashiren*, she knew nothing of this—'

'How did it happen?'

'She had a message from Ruric – a few days back, this was – telling her to leave the *T'An* Melkathi's house; being her *s'an*, what else could she do but obey? We'd planned to visit Meduenin again, but they took us on the road there. Christie—'

'Wait,' I said. 'It'll work out. They can't blame a kid like her.'

I took a seat down at the front, close to Haltern, Blaize with me. I saw the *t'an* Evalen frown. There were few enough people in the space under the dome, and most were Earthspeakers and Well-keepers. Some of Asshe's soldiers guarded about thirty men and women in the sari-robes of Melkathi, and there were other soldiers with them.

Maric reappeared. 'Christie, the *t'an* Evalen asks if you aren't fatigued, and wish to return to Easthill Malk'ys to rest.'

I wiped blistered hands on ash-stained britches, amused. 'Tell the *t'an* I'm grateful for the thought, but my duties as observer compel me to remain and witness this.'

The brown girl smiled. 'I'll tell her.'

Evalen might appeal to Suthafiori to have me thrown out, but I didn't think so. All there was to know about this affair, I already knew.

403

Seats round the edge of the floor were crowded. I recognized Hana Oreyn Orhlandis, then silver-maned Rodion – her head bowed, her six-fingered hands clasped over her swollen body and Tirzael Earthspeaker among a group of brown-skirted priests, and Evalen and Romare with Suthafiori herself.

Their bright clothes and sheathed blades shone in the gloom. The long shaft of morning sunlight fell from the roof-slot, illuminating vast spaces of dusty air, leaving the upper tiers of seats in half-light; then shone on dark skin, fair manes, complex braids, on sharply-angled ribs, brilliant eyes, scuffed robes and quick-gesturing hands.

The black mouth of the Well drew my eyes, and it was across that void that I found myself staring directly at Ruric Orhlandis.

She inclined her head.

They had not handled her gently. Her mouth was swollen and crusted. The filthy shirt was torn, so that you could see the black mane rooting down her spine. They'd left her arm free, and she picked unconsciously at the knotted empty sleeve, massaging the stump of her right arm; but a chain hobbled her ankles. Lines were incised in the reptilian skin of her face, drawn lines of tension.

Evalen spoke first, then Asshe; and Suthafiori and the priests listened in silence to their recounting of events in Melkathi. As always, it was the skirted priests that impressed me as alien: ribs sharp as a ship's hull, paired nipples, cropped and shaven manes. The Orhlandis *telestre*, when they spoke, could have been taken for human. It was the old deception of Carrick V.

Of the soldiers that fled with Ruric, only Ho-Telerit spoke. She faced Suthafiori, broad hands tucked in the belt that strained round her waist.

'Conspiracy's one thing. I'm a soldier, and when Onehand – when Ruric Orhlandis was *T'An* Commander I was content to follow her. So also when she left Tathcaer.' The woman shifted her feet. 'But I'm no destroyer of the land, *T'An Suthai-Telestre*, I'm no burner of the good earth. And in Melkathi, when she saw we wouldn't obey her order, she fired the first arrows herself. Some of the Orhlandis did, also, but none of us. And if we'd known it would end so, we'd not have left the city.'

'It is late in the day to make excuses,' Suthafiori said. Turning her attention to Kurick bel-Olinyi, she added, 'Something you would be wise to bear in mind, ambassador.'

The Harantish woman stood. 'She forced control of my ship!'

'That I don't doubt, Witchbreed are noticeably careless of their tools when they have no further use for them. No, I do not think you would have helped her willingly.'

'There's been much said of conspiracy,' bel-Olinyi put her bleached mane back out of her eyes. 'Consider: where has the tale come from? From the Brown Tower and the Citadel, both no friend to the Emperor-in-Exile. You offer me no recompense for the loss of my ship to Orhlandis—'

'I'll offer you this,' Suthafiori said, 'the rest of this day to leave Southland waters, and my own ships to pursue you to Kel Harantish if you're tardy.'

The Harantish party left then, and there was some consultation between Suthafiori and the priests before she spoke again.

'I've heard all,' she said, 'and now I'll give judgement.'

Ruric's head lifted. 'For Witchbreed gold – or Melkathi land?'

'Hear me!' Suthafiori's voice cut through the noise. 'This is my word: there is no Orhlandis *telestre*.'

Sound rose in confusion, perhaps protest.

'No Orhlandis,' she repeated. 'For the land, let it lie until it heals, and then be divided between the *telestres* that border on it. For the people . . . such as are *ashiren*, if they have no other *telestre* they prefer, I will take *n'ri n'suth* into Kerys-Andrethe. No blame lies with the *ashiren*.'

A baby cried and was quieted, two women bent weeping over another child.

'For the soldiers, and those Orhlandis who are of age, this: you shall be exiled outside the Southland for the space of a year, and then return to such *telestres* as will take you *n'ri n'suth*, or to the church.' Her eyes flicked across the seats. 'For Hana Oreyn Orhlandis, who was co-conspirator, the lesser penalty of death.'

Beside me, Blaize n'ri n'suth Meduenin stood. His scarred profile was toward me, I couldn't decipher his expression. '*T'An Suthai-Telestre*, you have one there who is blameless.'

With her gaze still on Orhlandis, Suthafiori said, 'They are adult. She is their *s'an*. It was their responsibility, all of them, to see that she did nothing to harm the *telestre*.'

'What about the unborn?' Passionately convincing, he pointed to Rodion. 'Will you have them, blameless, born outside the land? *T'An*, what will you say to the *ashiren*?'

'This, then: let them be born in the land and taken *n'ri n'suth* into *telestre* or church, and after that let the mother serve her term of exile. And,' she said softly, 'I did not say, hired-sword, that she should go into exile alone.'

He sat down heavily beside me. The small fair-maned woman rose and crossed the floor, with all the Orthean grace, to stand looking up at the place where Ruric Orhlandis sat. The dark

Orthean female stood, the chain between her bare feet striking sharply on the stone.

'Well, Dalzielle?' she said quietly.

'And so it comes to this . . .' she shook her gilt head slowly, Dalzielle Kerys-Andrethe, Suthafiori, *T'An Suthai-Telestre*. 'What did it ever matter that you were *amari* and golden-blooded? You were the best with a blade, the truest friend—'

'Has that changed?' Ruric demanded. 'I played the game with a little outside help. Melkathi's a poor province, and what did the *T'An Suthai-Telestre* ever do for it? Less than I. And I was *T'An* Commander, and *T'An* Melkathi . . . but you'll throw away the help I could give you, just for a few *seri* of earth. The day will come when you'll be sorry for that, *t'ans*.'

'Hear me,' Suthafiori said. 'You will not die, you will be exiled from the Southland for as long as you live, and you will have the exile's brand on your face – I will put it there myself! Ruric-*amari* you will be called, and if you set foot in any of the Hundred Thousand, then the rest of your life will be spent in the dark cells under the Citadel.'

The yellow eyes watched her steadily. 'I think you'll regret this.'

'Take her,' the *T'An Suthai-Telestre* ordered, 'or I may kill her myself.'

I didn't watch her go.

'You have no business going off to god-knows-where,' David Meredith said irritably. 'We must leave here by Fourthweek Seven-day at the latest, and it's Fiveday now—'

'I was acting as observer, that's all.'

'Observing what, for Christ's sake?'

'I've been asking myself that.' I suspected two reasons for his lousy temper: Huxton would have been getting at him in my absence, and, now I had finally got back, I wasn't telling the full story. 'How I'm going to make a report on this, God only knows. It's just one of those things, David, you know how it is.'

He stared absently at the map of the Southland that was tacked to the office door: the mosaic pattern of the Hundred Thousand, the wilderness beyond the Wall of the World – and is the barbarian woman still in Kirriach? I wondered – and the enigmatic symbols marking that vast area of fused rock, the Glittering Plain.

'I do know how it is,' he said at last. 'Difficult to explain in the department, those bastards who've never been offworld.'

His tone was bitter. I looked at him curiously. I'd tended to forget, seeing him only as an unwelcome arrival, that anyone in the department has their own offworld-caused eccentricity. What's Meredith's? I wondered.

'There's some points I have to clear up with the Eliots, I'll be down there most of the afternoon.' He dropped a crumpled paper on my desk. 'As far as I'm concerned, no report's needed; I've been standing in for you while you were sick. But don't pull one like this again.'

After he'd gone, I uncrumpled the paper. It was my pre-dated resignation. I sat staring at it for a long time before I finally tore it up.

'Christie?' Maric put her head round the office door. 'What's the matter – are you sick?'

'Sick to death of something. I'm not sure what.' I left off picking the bandages on my blistered hand, and stood up. I ached. 'Let's have some tea. No, sit still, I'll make it.'

She followed me back into Easthill Malk'ys's kitchen, where a low fire burned in the old iron stove. She was still the same youngster, I thought; seeing this plump brown-skinned Orthean female, and in my mind's eye the sullen scared kid that Haltern brought to be my *l'ri-an*. Hill-Damarie, Corbek, and the Wall . . . and now she wore Theluk's *harur* blades, and behaved with that frightening confidence that young Southlanders have.

'What will you do?' I asked. 'Go back to Salathiel?'

'Not yet.' She reached over and set out the tea-bowls. 'I've been talking to Haltern n'ri n'suth Beth'ru-elen. He might keep me at court, he says, in the Crown Messengers.'

Her dark eyes whitened with membrane: was that amusement or disquiet? One spidery hand slid to a blade-hilt. 'He says I've had experience.'

My hand shook, pouring tea; I laughed outright. 'Now that's a man you should listen to. Yes. If it's what you want?'

'I think so.' Her manner was hesitant. 'But I'm not part of the *takshiriye* yet . . . I don't know if I should tell you, Christie.'

'Tell me what?'

'In the Wellhouse today.' A supple shrug. 'I'm no friend of the Orhlandis, why I should carry her messages . . . she asked if you would come to her. I think she'll be in the Citadel now. I didn't know whether to tell you or not.'

'Always tell me these things.' The midafternoon bell sounded then, thin and clear over the sunlit city.

'Will you go?'

'In a while you can saddle Oru,' I said, 'I'll ride up and speak to them at the Citadel. I suppose I owe her that.'

*

'She's made some petition for you to visit her, I understand.' Evalen folded her arms. Light from the slit windows silvered her mane, shone in her eyes like glass. The Citadel's stone struck chill. '*S'aranth*, it wouldn't be permitted to a Southlander, and perhaps no Outlander, but my mother and the Orhlandis . . . if you wish, you can speak to Ruric-*amari* for a short time.'

'It's her wish, not mine; but yes, I'll speak to her.'

'Romare will take you,' she said, calling the scribe. 'Take care you do no more than speak with the traitor.'

The young scribe led me down stone steps and passages, where the polished grey rock ran with condensation, and breath smoked on the chill air. We passed barred doors, going down spiral steps cut into the rock of the Citadel crag, and small chambers where guards warmed themselves round braziers and played *ochmir*. I was searched, politely but thoroughly, before being taken to another guardroom on the lower levels. Ruric sat there at a table, and rose when she saw me.

Five Orthean guards were there, Romare stood by the door, it was a small room with no privacy. Veiled, curious eyes watched us.

'I didn't think you'd come.' Ruric was as I'd seen her in the Wellhouse, except for a bandage that covered her high forehead. She hesitated, then pushed one stool at me, and reseated herself.

I remained standing, at a loss for words.

'What the hell do you expect me to say to you?'

She eased back against the wall, breaking into the familiar smile. I wanted to hit her. She made me realize how much affection I still had for her.

'I've a fair idea – Dalzielle's said most of it, and what she didn't say, her daughter and mine more than made up for.' She brushed the black mane away from the bandage, looking at me self-consciously. What Suthafiori said came back to me: branded exile.

It was awkward to stand. I sat down opposite her.

'I'm leaving tonight,' she said. 'There's a ship that'll take me to the Desert Coast. And you're going to the Eastern Isles?'

'Sevenday. Hopefully to coincide with the shuttle.'

'"Shuttle".' She echoed the word, strange in an Orthean accent. 'That's a further exile than mine.'

'I've done nothing to prevent my coming back. All right, that's unfair, I know. No,' I said, 'Why am *I* apologizing?'

She chuckled briefly. There was a restlessness about her, her eyes moving round the windowless cell. Almost to herself she said, 'I wish I could see the city.'

'I don't believe it,' I said. 'All that time we were going to Corbek, and then in Shiriya-Shenin, and now – I mean, I can't take it in.'

The nictitating membrane slid over her whiteless eyes and she was animal, alien, unfathomable.

'Why did you come to Melkathi?' she asked.

'I wanted to . . . I don't know.'

'My errors aren't your concern.' Her single hand, corded and dark, strayed to her empty belt. She shook her head. 'I'd have found it easier with Huxton for an envoy, or Carrie, or that physician Adair.'

'Tell me something,' I said. 'Did you order Kanta Andrethe killed, or was Brodin telling the truth?'

'That poor Charain man . . .' She lifted her head. 'Don't they say chance is the last player in any game? Well, it's true.'

The silence was broken by Romare's dry cough, and the click of counters where two guards squatted by the brazier.

'Why did you ask to see me?'

'I wanted to know if you'd come. You understand me, Christie, better than my own people. Did the goddess birth us on the wrong worlds, do you think?' She smiled wryly. 'Worlds – and this a small one among many, yes. But all the same . . . I'm going away now, and even if they send you back, we won't meet again. So goodbye is what I wanted to say.'

'What will you do?'

She looked startled. 'I've lived by my wits since I was *ashiren-amari*, I won't starve now.'

Romare signalled that time was up. I stood. A thought came to me. 'Have you considered Kasabaarde?'

'The city of the Brown Tower? I wouldn't be welcome, I think.'

'The Hexenmeister doesn't concern himself with the internal affairs of the Southland. Or so he told me.'

'Envoy,' Romare said from the doorway.

'I'll consider it. There are many cities on the Desert Coast,' Ruric said with a thoughtful smile. I remembered she had been willing to go with bel-Olinyi. 'Goddess give you a safe journey, Christie.'

I couldn't tell how genuine the Orthean woman was. And so I was escorted back out, and searched again, and left the Citadel for air and sunlight; and it was the last time I saw *amari* Ruric Orhlandis.

And on Sixday:

'I'm not sorry to go,' Rodion said. 'Meduenin's a good *telestre*, and Ryloth will be milk-mother . . . Feel.'

She placed my hand high up under her breasts, and I felt the skin shiver; a movement wholly unlike a human baby kicking. She smiled. Her mane was not braided, the wind blew it about her veiled eyes. Golden eyes. Leaving Tathcaer, she took obstinate care to look as much a Witchbreed as she could.

The *marhaz* cropped the mossgrass a little way off. Here in the dell where we'd eaten lunch, thousandflower grew azure under stunted crimson *ziku*. The day was hot. Maric and Blaize were talking quietly, and I saw the young woman touch her *harur* blades, and heard Theluk's name.

'I never thanked you,' Rodion said. 'For the Ai river *telestre*.'

'There's nothing to—'

'That was my life. And in Kasabaarde . . .' her golden eyes cleared. 'I don't know, Christie. When you left Shiriya-Shenin, I wanted more than anything else to go with you. I wanted to travel. Now, after Riardh, I won't have a choice. And I don't know if I want to leave the Southland at all.'

'It's only for a year.'

'And in good company, I know. Travelling's uncertain,' she said, 'but I think I'll return, and you will, I know. We'll meet in Tathcaer.'

'I hope we do.'

The young Earthspeaker who travelled with them to Meduenin came and sat by us. He had the same serenity that I remembered with Theluk.

'Ruric-*amari*, also, will return.' Rodion said deliberately.

'She will return,' the Earthspeaker agreed mildly. 'Let the Goddess's fire heal her, burning that other fire out of her spirit; she'll live on earth again, *t'an* Rodion.'

'That's not what I meant.' The woman was sullen. A cloud shadowed us, going over the Rimon Downs on a west wind, and when the sunlight returned, she spoke. 'I've heard people say your Earthspeaker past-dreams are nothing more than memory, memories of people that once lived, passed down to us as Ruric-*amari* passed her golden blood to me. Nothing more.'

'Do they seem like that to you?'

'I don't know. You,' she rolled over on the thousandflower moss, facing me again. 'You don't past-dream, *S'aranth*, you have no *telestre*, no links with the earth – what's the Goddess to you?'

'I don't know, Rodion.'

The Earthspeaker linked his thin fingers, digging his claw-nailed feet into the moss. 'You were marked for the Goddess, *S'aranth*.'

'You heard about that?'

He shook his head. Shadow darkened his shaven mane: clouds passing. 'It's obvious.'

I said, 'I still don't know what it means.'

'Nor me,' Rodion said, 'and you live like this, you Outworlders, but I'm not used to it.'

'As for having no *telestre* – they call us the Landless,' the Earthspeaker said, 'because we leave the *telestre*, and we're the only ones who do. In the church there are no *telestres*. Having no land, we have all of it. It's only holding a small area of it that means the rest is lost to you. That's to be remembered in exile: owning nothing, you have all.'

Oru was straying, I saw, and Maric too deep in her own talk to notice. I excused myself and went to catch the *marhaz*. It was a relief to be out of a conversation I didn't understand. That Orthean certainty . . . not afraid of death because they know they'll return, not afraid of pain or disease because suicide is no sin. Living history and dead technology, the paradox of Carrick V.

I looped Oru's reins over a *ziku* branch. The *marhaz* lowered its head and butted me gently, hissing, and I scratched it behind the cropped horns.

Blaize and Maric, as well as talking, were engaged in playing *ochmir*. I watched them, lying under the stunted *ziku* with the board between them, and thought of Kirriach. That wilderness of snow and stone . . . and now the heat-haze shimmering on the Rimon Downs, and the wind-borne scent of wild *sidimaat*.

Blaize glanced up, his mottled red and white face twisting into a smile. He stared open-eyed at the sun.

'Time we were moving.' His broad hands swept the *ochmir* counters into their case, the game forever unfinished. 'You'll ride on further with us, Christie? You can still get back before sunset-bell.'

And Kirriach might have been the best time, I thought, when there was only the land and the cold to fight, and no Orthean or human malice.

'Yes,' I said, 'I'll ride with you.'

'I don't know what I've forgotten,' Carrie Thomas whispered, 'but you can bet your life it's something vital.'

'Everything all right, then?' Sam Huxton eased past us, not waiting for an answer. The long gallery was crowded now, at this farewell audience.

Carrie shifted uncomfortably, adjusting her uniform jacket. 'Lord, but I do hate the formal side of this job!'

'I could do without it myself.'

'I don't trust Ortheans to pack my data-tapes anyway . . .' she subsided, as Huxton struggled through a farewell address in badly-accented formal Ymirian.

Sevenday was proving so busy, I'd hardly time to realize we were leaving. Easthill Malk'ys had been packed and emptied by the midmorning bell – due to help from David Meredith, who I now saw in conversation with Evalen Kerys-Andrethe – and then we had no time for anything except hurrying to the Citadel.

'They could've brought the shuttle down on one of these off-shore islands easily enough,' Carrie added. 'God help us if the boat sinks.'

'It's a ship, and – barring typhoons – we'll be OK.'

'That's a comforting thought.' She was sardonic.

A *jath* ship would take us to the Eastern Isles, the *Lyadine-Southwind* on its long journey down to Saberon and Cuthanc. And where was the *Hanathra* now, I wondered, and Geren? Still sailing west towards (if the satellite surveys could be believed) the shattered island-remnants of a great continent?

I put the memories aside and went forward to speak with Suthafiori, taking her final messages for the Dominion authorities. These were formal leave-takings, conducted with that style and sly humour that are the mark of the Orthean mentality. Dalzielle Kerys-Andrethe: complex simplicity.

'This, I hope, is not the last we shall see of you,' she said at last.

'I hope not, *T'An*.'

She wore *chirith-goyen* summer robes, her mane caught up in Dadeni braids; thin *harur* blades slung from her belt. Nothing marked her as *T'An Suthai-Telestre*, unless it was the shadow in her eyes.

'*S'aranth*,' she said, 'if your people accept our terms, bring the news to us yourself. The Goddess give you a safe journey.'

We went down from the Citadel to the *skurrai-jasin* in the square, Huxton and David Meredith, the Eliots, Carrie and Adair, John Lalkaka and the others. The light glowed on the dome of the Wellhouse, on the blank-walled *telestre*-houses, on the white paving stones of Crown Way. Pausing for Maric to catch up, I saw Haltern waiting in the last carriage, and joined him.

We passed through the crowded alien city, under a blazing star-ridden sky, the heat reflecting back from the high walls.

'It's a strange time we live in.' Haltern watched the scurry and bustle as we approached the harbour. 'Outworlders in the South-land . . . you realize, I suppose, it's the largest single change we've had to face since Kerys founded the *telestres* – since the Golden Empire fell?'

'Ah, but you take change slowly.' I knew stories of Earth were going out towards the Rainbow Cities and the Desert Coast, to the unknown lands beyond the Barrens. What would it be like on Carrick V, twenty years from now? 'You take us, we've had the star-drive less than a generation and it's tearing us apart, it's too much, too soon. But we'll adapt. We're good at that.'

'Oh yes.' Amusement flickered in his eyes. 'We're *n'ri n'suth* cousins at least, Earth and this world. Christie, will your people accept our terms?'

'Limited contact? I think so.'

But would they? There's Orthe's technology to be considered, I thought: the dead ruins, and the live remnants in Kasabaarde and Kel Harantish. How will they classify Carrick V, knowing that?

'There's Kel Harantish,' I said, not mentioning Kasabaarde. I know just how ambiguous a reputation that city has in the Southland.

'The Witchbreed, yes.'

The *skurrai-jasin* came over the brow of the hill and headed down towards the quay. Haltern brushed his sparse mane out of his eyes, blinking in the sea-wind. I followed his gaze: the *Lyadine-Southwind* lay where bel-Olinyi's ship had had its moorings.

He said, 'Whoever it is that holds the throne of the Emperor-in-Exile, it means trouble for us – perhaps for your people too, being so closely allied in their minds with the Hundred Thousand. That's part of the game. But if the Witchbreed sully us in your eyes—'

'You know I can't say what their decision will be. But that won't affect it.'

He nodded slowly. The *skurrai-jasin* were pulling up now beyond the office of the Harbourmaster, where the double-masted vessel was docked, lateen sails furled: the *Lyadine-Southwind*. Waiting on the noon tide.

'You know Suthafiori is giving you the opportunity to return.'

'They may not choose to send me.'

He stepped down out of the carriage beside me. 'More sensible, though, to send someone who's known and trusted; someone who knows their business.'

'Meaning that, having got me nicely trained, you don't want to go through it again with anyone else?'

'You know that's not—' he broke off, laughing, pale eyes as clear as glass. Shabby, ordinary, passed over in the crowd; and yet he can add recruits to the Crown Messengers, accompany the *T'An*

Commander on military expeditions, keep a watching brief on an Outworld envoy. I wonder if Haltern n'ri n'suth Beth'ru-elen isn't the most remarkable Orthean I've met.

Maric leaned over the side of the *skurrai-jasin*. 'Christie, I'll miss you. Will you be back?'

'I think—'

But what I'm thinking about are the Eastern Isles, and how the shuttlecraft towers against the dusty sky, there where the warm tideless seas wash over the rock. Ninety days travelling between here and Earth, here and home. Time to get used to the Dominion, after close on eighteen standard months away. I adapt back at frightening speed, I know: to headaches, industrial stink, racketting noise, and blank, empty skies; and to warm homes, good food, soft beds, all the benefits of technology. Time to get over that first desire to be home. And time to realize *amari* Ruric Orhlandis, see her in perspective. After that, I can make a decision.

'I think,' I said, 'sometimes you have to go away to come back.'

Huxton called something from the dock steps, where the team were going aboard; I saw David Meredith waiting with him.

I embraced Haltern and Maric, and went aboard the *Lyadine-Southwind* with the other Outworlders. Sunlight flashed off the dirty harbour water. The shouts and smells of Tathcaer came clearly to me, and the city shone white under Carrick's Star.

The noon bells rang.

Ancient Light

ACKNOWLEDGEMENTS

Many people have contributed to the writing of this novel, but I would like to thank, individually, the following, without whom *Ancient Light* would not exist: David V. Barrett, who provided the music (especially *Redgum*) and much else besides; Eda Field, who sent me a portrait of the Orhlandis, from Australia, and who asked the right questions; Liz Foulger, for allowing me the benefit of her extensive medical knowledge; Daphne Watson and Tony Warren, for the inspiration of the chapel at Milton Abbas; Sarah Watson, who read the earlier part of the novel aloud, and commented honestly; Sylvia Witherington, for her friendship and support.

CONTENTS

PRINCIPAL CHARACTERS

Lynne de Lisle Christie, special advisor to the PanOceania Company
Douglas Clifford, Earth envoy on Carrick V
Molly Rachel, PanOceania's Company Representative
David Osaka, Company Commercial Liaison officer
Pramila Ishida, Company Administrative officer
Rashid Akida, Head of the PanOceania research team
Dinu Machida, climatology
Chandra Hainzell, xeno-biology
Jan Yusuf, xeno-demography
Joan Kennaway, medic
Ravi Singh, xeno-physicist
Corazon Mendez, Commander of the Company Peace Force
Ottoway,
Jamison, ⎫ lieutenants, her aides
Stephen Perrault, acting head of the PanOceania Liaison Office on
    Earth

Dannor bel-Kurick, Emperor-in-Exile at Kel Harantish
Calil bel-Rioch, the Voice of the Emperor-in-Exile
Pathrey Shanataru, aide to Calil

Sethri-safere, of the *hiyek*-family Anzhadi, a leader of mercenaries
Jadur,
Wyrrin-hael, ⎫ members of Sethri's *raiku*
Charazir-hael,
Hildrindi, of the *hiyek*-family Anzhadi, a *keretne* mystic
Feriksushar, of Hildrindi's *raiku*

the Hexenmeister, of the Brown Tower of Kasabaarde
Tethmet Fenborn, of the Tower
Annekt, a Kasabaarde trader

Haldin Damory, a mercenary of the Medued Guildhouse
Branic, her aide

Haltern n'ri n'suth Beth'ru-elen, a politician of the Hundred Thousand
Blaize n'ri n'suth Meduenin, an ex-mercenary
Nelum Santhil Rimnith, T'An of Melkathi province
Cethelen Khassiye Reihalyn, the Andrethe of Peir-Dadeni
Howice Talkul, T'An of Roehmonde province
Bethan n'ri n'suth Ivris, T'An of Kyre province
Geren Hanathra, T'An of Ymir province

Bekily Cassirur Almadhera, an Earthspeaker
Achil, an Earthspeaker
Jaharien Rakviri, s'an of Rakviri *telestre*
Haden Barris Rakviri, his *arykei*

Roxana Visconti, WEBcaster for the Trismegistus WEB
Mehmet Lutaya, WEBcaster for the Ariadne WEB

PART ONE

CHAPTER 1

Rooms Without Doors

The alien settlement merged with the desolate earth on which it stood, half a mile away. As I stepped down from the shuttle's ramp, I couldn't help thinking: *Is this the great discovery?*

Nothing but cleft and gully and hillock surrounding me; rock and stone and dust. To the south were cliffs, and a hint of mountains in the haze. And to the north, the Inner Sea.

The hot, bright winter light washed over me, shattering into dazzles on the sea. Too sharp and subtle, this white sun, Carrick's Star – and the pressure of the world underfoot, gravity slightly different . . . All but imperceptible in these equatorial regions, Orthe's daystars shone. Orthe: Carrick V, whose sky is full of the Heart Stars, that cluster at the galaxy's core.

Then the smell hit me: an odour of heat and rock and rank water. That is the most ancient sense, and it bypasses rationality. For one second I felt hollow in the chest, as if I had been punched under the ribs, and I thought, *Orthe, this is Orthe, I remember—*

And then, like seeing a face once so familiar, that now you can't name, ten long years reasserted themselves and I thought, *I don't know this world at all.*

Which is unfortunate, girl, because that's what they've brought you back here for.

As if she were a mind-reader, the representative of the Pan-Oceania multicorporate Company said, 'You were never on this southern continent, were you, Lynne?'

'Once,' I said. 'Briefly. But that was a good few hundred miles west along the Coast from here. At least there they could scratch a living out of the dirt.' And, looking round, I thought, No species should be able to survive here, this land is sterile as a moon—!

On other continents of this world, things are different.

The Pacifican woman left the shuttle-ramp and walked over to join me. The scrape of her boots on rock was louder than the lapping waves.

'The Earth-station on the northern continent must have more extensive records.' She glanced across at me. 'Do you want to stay in the ship? You look as if the heat's too much for you.'

I glared at her. Molly Rachel's total lack of tact is something I find disconcerting and pleasing in about equal measures. Only the young can be so honest.

'Molly, you think this is bad? You want to be here in the *hot* season. And shall we assume that a few years' difference in our ages doesn't make me either decrepit or mentally deficient?'

'Or even bad-tempered?'

'Oh, very witty.'

I don't know why I like this woman when she irritates me so much. No, that's a lie. What I do know is that I have to dislike her, because I dislike what her people are going to do. And – God help me, being special advisor to her Company – her people are my people too.

Molly Rachel craned her neck, looking at the nearest settlement-structures. 'I still find it difficult to believe we've found any kind of alien technology here. Either relics, or functional.'

'*I* don't believe it's functional—'

Orthe's technological past is dead. The Golden Witchbreed are a dead race, perhaps as alien to this world then as we are now . . . and the high-level technology they had was destroyed, millennia past. Not without consequences: witness this desolate land.

'—but I know what you mean, Molly. This is a post-technological world, and pre-tech and post-tech societies don't look that different on the surface. Primitive. The difference—'

'Maybe there isn't much difference anyway. If the Ortheans allowed the necessary infrastructure for technology to decay, it's no wonder they're reduced to *this*.'

I winced. She didn't notice. Orthe is more than this, I silently protested. Much more. But do I want the Company to realize that?

'Maybe things have gone too far,' I said, 'and then it won't matter if we *do* find a few artifacts that still function. Unless we're very lucky, that won't tell us the nature of the alien technology that built them.'

And what if the artifacts that the xeno-archeology team found, so recently, tell you no more than the shells of ancient Orthean cities, that Earth has had ten years now to study? Or the ruins of the Rasrhe-y-Meluur, dead these three thousand years? What then?

'Maybe the Company needn't have come here,' I suggested, but she shook her head, negating that.

She stood silhouetted against Orthe's pale blue sky: Molly Rachel, tall, angular and black, with a mass of fine-curled hair, and the flattened features of her Aborigine mother. Like most people from Earth's Pacific Basin area – Asia, India, South America, Australasia – she is possessed of a certain impenetrable self-confidence. It comes from knowing that history is on your side. And since Earth's economic centre shifted there, we all take good care to be on the Pacifican side.

Dear God, I thought, was I ever that young? But come to think of it, she's thirty, and I was four years younger than that when I first set foot on Orthe.

A world must be vast, one thinks, taking in cities and mountains, ancient civilizations, strange skies and suns. But it shrinks. The whole bright gaudy carnival shrinks to a coloured dot in the night sky. And feels to me now like an achievement of youth, recognized and remembered, but put aside for other things.

A warm wind blew off the sea: sparky, salty, electric. Carrick's Star dazzled. The world touched me, alien and unfathomable, too real to be safely locked in a memory.

'One of us should stay here with the shuttle,' Molly said. 'David Osaka, or you?'

'David. The multicorporate's seconded me here to be advisor. Let's say I need a refresher on some points of alien culture.'

The woman gave me a shrewd look. 'I've studied your old reports. Let's say wild horses couldn't keep you out of *that* settlement.'

I laughed, but it was wry humour. Here, in the early light of the sun, the native settlement towered above us.

It is a settlement without streets or city walls.

Flat-roofed stone buildings clung together. Five- and six-sided, like the cells of a beehive; three storeys tall. All faced us at ground level with blank white walls; windows were fifty feet above us, black slots. Squinting up, I could see where wooden steps led from one roof level to another, and from there two or three different stairways led to different roofs, and in turn from them to others . . .

Long shadows fell towards the west. I saw no movement on those roofs. Multiple layers of a celled alien city, a city like a scatter of sun-bleached dice.

The first exultation of arrival faded. This is not the same world and I am not the same person – and the reason I'm here is not the reason for which I would have chosen to return.

'Shall we go?' Molly Rachel said.

'Sure.'

The morning sun glittered on the sea, and the white buildings shone, embedded in the rocky coast, and I took a sudden sharp breath.

Once I might, just *might*, have believed I would come to Orthe again. But I should never have believed this – that I would come to this backwater settlement on the shores of the Inner Sea, to the rumoured and disputed last stronghold on Orthe of the race called Golden Witchbreed . . . to the city of Kel Harantish.

A metallic note rang out. Flying rock-splinters stung my ankle.

I exclaimed sharply; simultaneously Molly said, '*Wait*—'

Nothing but silence and sun.

'That's close enough,' she observed. 'We'll consider ourselves warned.'

A white chip scarred a boulder just ahead, and the sun picked out a metal dart that lay in the rubble. My heart hammered. I felt foolish, tricked. And at the same time irritated by the young woman's confidence.

'Some of the xeno-archeological teams have had this problem,' she said.

'I've read the same reports that you have.'

She gave me a very straight look.

Heat made movement an effort, slowed thought. The half-mile walk from the shuttle exhausted me. Now I looked up from the broken ground to the blank walls of the city that rose up like cliffs. I tasted dust on my lips. Walls and rock seemed all one colour, as if the sun had bleached them together for uncounted thousands of years; vertical slabs that leaned over us.

A foot scuffed rock.

'Lynne—'

Movement drew my eye: a humanoid figure that bent to pick up the fallen dart. Swift and economical action – but disorientating: the human eye reads alien musculature as *wrong*. As the figure turned, I saw the crest-like mane growing long on the narrow head and down the spine. Skylined, the proportions of his limbs subtly different from the human. I saw bleached skin with an almost imperceptible scale-pattern, as six-fingered hands gripped a crossbow-like weapon.

For a moment his glance caught mine, an almost triangular face, wide at the brow, narrow at the chin. His whiteless eyes blurred now with the movement of the nictitating membrane, that third eyelid of the Orthean race. A glance unfathomable and clear: ophidian.

Without the slightest forethought, I said, '*Kethrial-shamaz shan'tai.*' A greeting and offer of hospitality, in a northern dialect of the language of the Desert Coast. And it was nothing to do with thirty-four days shiptime spent revising Orthean culture, but with that overpowering shock of familiarity.

The Orthean male didn't speak, but wound and reloaded the bow. A small group of Orthean natives appeared from the deceptive gullies. Molly Rachel walked forward until she could talk without raising her voice, and in a southern Coast dialect said, 'Give you greeting. You need not fire on us, we're not armed. Our weapons are in our ship.'

That's a nice blend of conciliation and threat, I thought. Now why not try the Orthean for 'take me to your leader'?

Despite the heat, I felt cold. In the northern continent's settlements, I might know what to expect. But even there, time has passed. Here . . .

Orthean faces turned first towards the harbour, and then to the shore where the shuttle was visible, regarding it without detectable change of expression. There was a silence that made my mouth dry. They stood each a little distance from the next, and, as far as it is possible to read the signs, were both alert and afraid.

'There are just the two of us, at present,' Molly Rachel added.

I saw two Orthean males and three females, with dyed-white manes that lay lank over tunics, and what looked to be a brown metal scale-mail. These carried winchbows. A fair-maned female leaned on a thin spear, her exposed lower torso showing the paired nipples of vestigial second breasts.

If I could read their faces, I would be terrified, I thought.

'Give you greeting, *shan'tai*.' A sleek, plump male stepped forward. Light glinted from his brown skin. His mane was braided elaborately, and chains and belts wound round his tunic-robe, but for all that, there was something indefinably seedy about him. Like the others, he stood a good handspan shorter than Earth-standard.

More comfortable now, I stepped up beside Molly. '*Shan'tai*, this is the representative of the Earth multinational corporate Company PanOceania—' at least half of that had to be in Sino-Anglic and not Coast dialect '—who is called Molly Rachel. Our people have visited your city, a half-year ago.'

The Orthean male seemed confused. I put it down to my imperfect memory of tenses.

'Our people came to study the ruins of the ancient Witchbreed civilization,' Molly Rachel said. '*Shan'tai*, I believe we have business with the authorities in your settlement. We have come entirely without threat, and dependent on your goodwill. When will it be possible to discuss these matters?'

I mentally crossed "assistant interpreter" off my list of duties.

While the plump Harantish male spoke to his companions, I said: 'You're fluent enough, aren't you? Hypno-tapes?'

'No. Hard work,' the young woman said, without taking her eyes off the Ortheans. 'Hypno-tapes scramble the brains.'

There are times when I wish they'd known that ten years ago; it would have saved a lot of us time, trouble, and subsequent analysis. But I forbore to mention that. What she didn't say was, *Am I doing this right?* and what I didn't say was *Jesus Christ I hope so*.

The Orthean male turned back to us and said, 'I believe you should speak with the Voice of the Emperor-in-Exile. These guards will see that you truly have no weapons. Then you may enter the lower city.'

Molly Rachel let out a breath, momentarily relaxing; then she craned her neck to look up at the pale walls. The tension returned. Half of me thought, We've got closer than even the xeno-archeology team, they didn't get into the city itself. And the other half thought, This is Kel Harantish and I don't want any part of it! But that was the half that could remember the rumours and superstitions of an alien race.

'Do you want to go back to the ship?' the Pacifican woman asked.

It seems to me – though no doubt it's an illusion – that kids her age get through because they don't know enough to fear. And because they don't believe in luck.

'I'll come,' I said. 'The sooner this is proved a wild-goose chase, the sooner I can go home.'

'You've *seen* the artifacts the team brought back. I don't believe the Company is wasting its time trying to analyse this technology – there must be some profit—' she broke off the long-standing argument, frustrated, as two of the Ortheans came to body-search for weapons.

Orthean skin is fine-textured, dry, warm; the beat of a different pulse beneath the surface. That brief touch brought back, shockingly abruptly, how it feels to dig fingers into the depths of a rooted mane. . . .

Dislocation of reality paralysed me for a moment. Air pressure and sunlight: *wrong*. The air rasped drily in my lungs. Daystars were pinpricks in the arch of the sky. But more – this heatstricken moonscape is not the Orthe of my memories, not this barren rock and sterile sea, without even the sound of an insect. I felt twice-exiled from expectation.

'This is a weapon,' the plump brown-skinned male said, holding Molly's belt-communicator in his delicate hands.

'It's not a weapon, it enables me to speak with my ship.'

The nictitating membrane slid over his dark eyes, and flicked back. He said, 'I could imagine circumstances, *shan'tai*, in which that would prove as deadly as a winchbow. But keep it, if you will.'

I had walked perhaps fifty yards closer to the city before I identified that gesture and tone as amusement.

Here the ground was smoother. I looked up, dazed with heat, to see the outcrops of buildings recede away and back, like chalk headlands. At the base of the nearest sheer wall, wooden platforms were being winched down on ropes.

Molly said, 'There isn't *any* native vegetation or forestry. God, you don't realize what that means . . . didn't you say in your old reports that this place survives entirely on imported goods? What's funny?'

'You remind me of me,' I said. 'It's the sort of thing I used to notice. Generally when about to embark on something horrifically dangerous . . . At the moment I'm just worrying about whether those rope and pulley contraptions are as unsafe as they look.'

The young woman sighed, a little self-consciously long-suffering.

I saw how the nearest buildings stood separate, roofs on a lower level than the main mass. Rope-bridges, just visible, were slung across the narrow crevasse between this cluster and the city proper.

With a scrape of rock, the wooden platform grounded. We stepped on. The ropes creaked, and I caught Molly's arm to steady myself. The dark Orthean male got on with us. I reached out to touch the sheer city wall, and it was smooth under my palm, not yet fully warmed by the morning sun. Then the platform lifted and swung free.

'Pardon?' Molly Rachel said.

'Don't mind me – I can throw up quietly.'

As we inched higher, I saw how ancient bedrock cropped out on this coast, worn down to this Harantish peninsula and a crescent scatter of islands that the sea could not erode. Far out on the water were sails, lost in the molten white glare.

'You come in trade-season,' the dark male said. 'Ships commonly come in Wintersun – if not commonly such ships as yours.'

'*Shan'tai* . . .' Molly left a demanding gap.

'Pathrey Shanataru,' he supplied.

'*Shan'tai* Pathrey, our archeological team didn't report any contact with the city authorities here.'

'The Emperor-in-Exile has no love for your people,' Pathrey

Shanataru said. 'He did not see them. He will not see you. You will meet his Voice.'

'Who is Emperor-in-Exile now?' That alien title comes to me with no hiatus of memory: *K'Ai Kezrian-kezriakor*, the supposed lineal descendant of the rulers of the Golden Witchbreed.

Pathrey Shanataru said formally, 'The present heir of the blood-line of Santhendor'lin-sandru is Dannor bel-Kurick.'

'I think – I've met him?'

Pale sea and sky blotted out: for a second I felt dizzy and half blind—

some subterranean room, a chamber lit by candles set on rough iron stands. Candlelight and . . . the ruins of technology? He is bending over a panel or cube of some material. And then he lifts his head . . .

That face that is half child and half old male: Dannor bel-Kurick. Wide-set eyes veiled by nictitating membrane, white mane rooting down his spine; and faded skin whose reptilian texture has in it a hint of dusty gold . . .

'How could you meet him?' Molly asked me in Sino-Anglic. 'The archeological team said the local ruler doesn't leave this settlement.'

The Emperor-in-Exile leave this paranoid fortress? No. But—

'I . . . may have seen a picture, I suppose.'

She nodded, minimal curiosity satisfied.

I was suddenly uncomfortable, and pushed the thought away. That is ten years ago. Still, such a clear mental image of that face, and something *almost* there—

The wooden platform lurched to a halt, level with the flat roof. I stepped unsteadily on to plaster-roughened stone.

Surrounded again by guards, we were ushered across one roof and up a flight of wooden steps. Square penthouse-structures stood on each roof. As I stepped inside, under the low arch of the nearest, the sudden shadow blinded me. When I could see again, the plump male was already descending a rope-web that led down through a great open trapdoor. Molly Rachel followed him. I paused.

Ropes are easily cut, trapdoors easily barred.

But I hesitated because of a much more mundane fear. I may have grown less agile than I once was; I have grown no greater liking for looking a fool.

Those Ortheans that carried winchbows remained on the roof. I climbed cautiously down, and found myself in a spacious room. Pale light slotted in through narrow windows. With some relief, I saw that a further trapdoor opened on descending stone steps. By the time our party had gone down two more floors, I realized

430

something else: there were no interconnecting doors between individual buildings.

'Given the level of technology here,' Molly Rachel observed, 'this place must be impregnable.'

Paranoia, I thought. To take Kel Harantish, you would have to take each building, individually, and from the top down. That partly solved a question long on my mind: how a settlement so hated and feared could remain undestroyed.

The male, Pathrey Shanataru, paused at the foot of the next steps. '*Shan'tai*, here you will meet the Voice of the Emperor-in-Exile.'

Molly nodded, walking in front of me as we entered. This room was windowless, a silvery light reflected in by concealed mirrors; the air was hot and still. I heard someone move.

An Orthean woman rose from where she sat cross-legged on a mat by a low stone table. She was tall for a Coast Orthean: some five foot and an inch.

'*Kethrial-shamaz shan'tai*,' she said, her voice oddly accented.

I could only stare.

This world's rumour says that the Kel Harantish Ortheans claim Golden Witchbreed blood. My memory, prompted by shiptime study, said, *But that race is extinct – surely? And Kel Harantish's claim, propaganda?*

Small, thin, electric: her skin was pale as stone-dust, in the room's dim light holding a faint glimmer of gold. Her white mane seemed so fine as to float on air, a breath of fire. I looked into her narrow-chinned face. Her eyes were yellow – buttercup-yellow, capriped-yellow, unnatural as flowers. She wore a white tunic girdled with thin gold chains, the tunic badly stained at the hem with spilt herb-*arniac*.

—*stone arches that open upon depths, and that narrow face with coin-gold eyes, and the scent of charnel-halls*—

With an effort, I shut the mental image out. Hypno-tape data thrown up by the chance firing of synapses, that's all; fragmented and confused by hypno-erasure and the passing of ten years. Maybe after a while I'll get used to it.

Molly Rachel said, 'Thank you for consenting to see us, *shan'tai*.'

Orthean ages are difficult to judge: this women seemed younger even than Molly, but that might be deceptive.

'Pathrey told me that an offworlder ship had come. And that you would speak of what your people found in the Elansiir mountains.' She seated herself again, and gestured for us to do the same. There was a stone table beside her that stood only a few inches above the floor, and on it were ceramic bowls containing a hot liquid. Droplets of steam coiled in the air, and there was a sharp strong scent: *arniac*-herb tea.

'The Company's archeological team brought several interesting artifacts to light in this area.' Molly cupped one of the bowls in her pale palms. 'Unfortunately it was at the end of their projected stay, so they couldn't complete their work.'

'Complete?' queried the young Harantish woman.

'Establish if the artifacts were from the old technological culture, the Witchbreed.'

I saw Pathrey Shanataru, who was kneeling down beside the Voice of the Emperor-in-Exile, hesitate momentarily at that word.

The woman linked claw-nailed hands. 'Pardon, *shan'tai*, but that is the name that superstitious barbarians give us. We are the Golden.'

Molly Rachel passed a ceramic bowl over to me. I was vaguely aware of her covert scan, and her nod that it was not poisoned. Crimson liquid steamed: the bitter *arniac*-herb tea of the Desert Coast. Taste and odour were utterly familiar. That hot drink scalded my mouth, brought back names and faces – memories of what this Harantish woman would designate the 'superstitious barbarian' northern continent, and that long year when Kel Harantish and the Emperor-in-Exile had seemed as much Earth's enemy as enemy of the Hundred Thousand.

'Earth may at some time in the future be interested in Golden science—'

The Orthean woman interrupted Molly: 'More "archeology"?'

'A more complete investigation.'

The nictitating membrane veiled those chrome-yellow eyes. 'Well now, *shan'tai*, do you know what that might mean?'

'I'm aware that certain cultures on this world are technophobic. Earth has no intention of importing technological knowledge. This is still classified as a Restricted world.'

'What I meant, *shan'tai* Rachel, is that there have always been those who, since the Golden Empire fell, desired to build it anew. If they could not find the key to the lost science of those "artifacts", how will you do so?'

'Artifact' is an interesting word. It doesn't have the implications of dysfunction that 'relic' does. I thought it time to interrupt, and disabuse the Voice of the Emperor-in-Exile of her ideas of ignorant offworlders.

'I understand that not *all* knowledge of Witchbreed technology is lost. Doesn't Kel Harantish maintain the canal system on the Desert Coast, keep it functioning?'

Molly Rachel said, 'The Company is also very interested in the

432

canals. We understand their construction dates from the time of the Golden Empire.'

The Harantish woman shrugged. The humanoid frame admits of many variations. I watched the movements of alien musculature: the sharp-hulled ribs, thin limbs, the long-fingered hands and high-arched feet. Those signals that stance and gesture send are oddly muffled, uninterpretable. She looked at me: 'You are not new to this world, *shan'tai*. What is your *hiyek* – your name?'

'Lynne de Lisle Christie,' I said. 'New to the Coast, *shan'tai*.'

Molly leaned forward. As she spoke, she unconsciously hunched down, and I realized that with her height – she topped the two Ortheans by a good ten inches – she must feel giant-like.

'Naturally there would be the necessity for discussing trade privileges.' She slightly stressed the final word.

The brown-skinned male, Pathrey, leaned over and muttered something inaudible to all but the Harantish woman; she, for the first time, smiled, and briefly touched his arm.

'Why, yes,' she said; and then to Molly: 'It seems you offworlders have new ways of negotiating. You've quarantined us for ten years, and now this?'

Molly smiled. 'What I say is of course subject to an Earth government's approval.'

No kidding? They *will* be pleased to hear that . . .

And then I thought, Sarcasm would become you better, Lynne, if you weren't Company-employed yourself.

Pathrey Shanataru said, 'The northerners have been content with quarantine. What will you say to them, *shan'tai* Rachel?'

'That depends on how it concerns them.' Molly, without a word, implied the addition *If it ever does* . . .

Old habits die hard. With the Pacifican woman playing conciliator, it left me the perfect opportunity to ask awkward questions.

'If the Emperor-in-Exile has no intention of negotiating with us, is there any point to this?'

Pathrey Shanataru leaned forward as if to speak, and a mere gesture of the nameless woman's hand silenced him. Beginning to interpret Orthean expressions, I thought there was real fear on his face. For an instant it became real to me, this position of power: the Voice of the Emperor-in-Exile.

The young Orthean female rose and for a time walked back and forth, without looking at anyone.

Dropping back into Sino-Anglic I said to Molly, 'Are you going to push this much further now?'

'I'll push as hard as I have to.'

Pathrey Shanataru was kneeling beside the stone table, his gaze fixed on the Orthean woman. I wished desperately that I were reaccustomed to Orthean expressions.

I said to Molly, 'I don't think you realize what a destabilizing factor Earth is.'

The Harantish woman stopped, and then turned with a dancer's grace and balance. She spoke rapidly: 'I'll see others close to the Emperor, later today. Pathrey, convey these *s'aranthi* to a place where they may rest until then—'

Her bare feet scuffed the stone steps, and she was gone.

'What – ?' Molly stood.

Pathrey Shanataru looked apologetic, almost embarrassed. He rose to his feet. 'Pardon, *shan'tai*. I will show you to more comfortable quarters.'

Molly looked at me, and I shrugged.

The dim silver twilight and heat were oppressive; to climb the steps – even if only towards the scorching sun of the Coast in winter – felt like liberation.

As we stepped out on to the flat roof again, Molly said, in Sino-Anglic, 'Do you think they know we've got Witchbreed artifacts that may well turn out to be functional?'

Before I could answer, Pathrey Shanataru spoke. In badly-accented Sino-Anglic he said, 'Do you know who put them there for you to find?'

Stunned, I made to frame a question, but the Orthean male stepped aside and gestured for us to precede him down rope-webbing, into the entrance of the next building. Molly swung down, I climbed more slowly, and then I turned to Pathrey Shanataru.

We were alone.

The trap door fell shut above us. I heard the click of lockbars sliding into place.

CHAPTER 2

The Spoils of Kel Harantish

At midday everything stopped except the fighting.

Running footsteps sounded on the roof. The trap door vibrated, but stayed closed. I felt each sound, deep inside; a physical ache. There was a distant clash of metal.

'What the hell was that?'

Molly Rachel, from where she clung to the rope-webbing, leaned across to the narrow window. Her arms shook with the strain.

'No,' she said at last, dropping lightly down. 'I can't see anything but the sky.'

The light of Carrick's Star slotted down from the high windows like bars of white-hot iron. Outside, it would be unbearable for human eyes without protective gear. Inside, the heat robbed any desire for movement.

I sat with the small comlink in my lap, the case open, trying to manipulate the receiver-amplifier. Static crackled in the hot twilight. My fingers were clumsy. That ache of tension settled in my gut.

Molly squatted down on her haunches. 'I don't think it's the comlink. It's the atmospheric interference. Communications are hell on this world.'

'After ten years, I'd've thought you'd've solved that one.'

'Talk to the Company about my shoestring budget, why don't you.'

The heat made me dizzy, made all movement exhaustion. I wiped sweat from my face. From outside came a cry that might have been pain or triumph or something quite other.

The comlink's static resolved into a voice.

'Here.'

Molly took it. Her tone was sharp. 'David? What's the situation there?'

'. . . shuttle's secure. A few . . . groups from the settlement. You want me to take any action on that?'

'Negative. Not yet. Stay secure.'

David's voice suddenly came through loud, Sino-Anglic accent plain. 'Are you going to put in an official complaint to the native authorities?'

Molly looked at me, and then up at the trap door, and for the first time smiled. 'I don't know if the "authorities" now are the same ones that existed this morning. Why we had to arrive here just in time for a palace revolution . . . Can you contact the orbital ship?'

'Negative. But we expected that.'

'Sure. Contact me again if the situation changes.'

She flipped the comlink case shut. One dark hand rested on it for a moment, as she stared blankly into the middle distance.

I said acidly, 'As for being "just in time" for a palace revolution – I doubt there would have been one at all if we hadn't arrived. Whichever faction supports contact with Earth, we've made it worth their trying to take control here . . . I thought that was likely, when we were kept away from the Emperor-in-Exile.'

The air was hot, stifling. The trap door that led down into the lower building was also locked. Claustrophobia ran a close second to hunger and thirst.

'It's like you said, Lynne, we're a destabilizing factor,' the Pacifican woman agreed, 'but that's inevitable.'

'Is it? – No, *is* it? Molly, you tell me. PanOceania doesn't *need* to be here—'

She stood, rising to her full height, took a few steps and then swung round: 'Tell me what *you* know about it. You were envoy here for eighteen months, and that was ten years ago! For God's sake stop acting as if you owned the place. And if you'd like to get off my back for five minutes, I'd feel a whole lot better! I don't hear anything from you except criticism. And if I want advice, which is what you're here for, all I get is—'

'Is what?'

'—is you acting like a sulky three-year-old. You're paid to do a job here. For God's sake, Lynne!'

'Shit,' I said.

I thought, Dear God I'm too old for this, what am I doing here, I don't have to take this—

Midday silence is oppressive; the ear needs birdsong or human voices. There was not even alien sound. Two of us, in the heart of a violent city. Sometimes it's safer for one to come alone, one is easily missed. With two . . . well, then, an example can be made of one of them, the least valuable. What price a Company representative here? I thought. What price a special advisor?

'This place unsettles me,' I said.

The young woman still stood looking down at me, with fading anger. I felt ashamed of half-hearted apologies.

I said, 'You're doing what I used to do here, as envoy. And maybe doing it rather better. So.'

'So tell me something I don't know.' She gave me a brat's grin, and sat down again, long legs folding under her.

'Sorry. It's because of having been First Contact with this world. I know that if it hadn't been me, it would have been someone else, but . . . there's a responsibility. Maybe a guilt.'

The white square of sunlight had moved on the dusty floor, falling now to illumine the corner of a low stone table. Molly leaned back against the wall. She watched the narrow slot of sky. Then she turned her dark, dazzled face towards me.

'Not guilt. A world's too big for one person's responsibility.'

I've lost the ability to balance fear against result, and gamble. This angular young woman has it still.

'It's . . .' I searched for words. 'It's as if I'd stepped back into the past, to my year on Orthe, and it was being repeated in a minor key. The same theme, but somehow darker.'

'Ah, but those days, the Dispersal – it was a bit unreal. You could touch worlds and hardly change them. It isn't like that now.'

Her tone carried the conviction that her present time and 'the real world' are identical.

A shadow flicked across the falling sunlight, and another, and another; perhaps a dozen Ortheans passing the window-slot, unseen but for that. Voices on the roof above us were muffled.

That accented voice sounded again in my mind: *Do you know who put them there* . . . No! I thought, we have to hear more from Pathrey Shanataru. Who is it wants the Company here that badly?

Is it those people who are fighting now; is it that woman, the Voice, who's in favour of Earth? Or was she bluffing? I don't know. I don't know. We're blind, here.

I said, 'I feel as if there's something important that I ought to remember.'

Molly's expression changed, so that I recalled she was the Company representative of PanOceania; a thing I have difficulty always keeping in mind.

'Something that could help us now?'

I shrugged.

She said, 'There are gaps in your old reports.'

'How do you mean, gaps?'

'When they've been on alien worlds, there are always things that people don't say. You don't say more than most. I know you had a very bad reaction to hypno-tapes. I wondered if it affected your memory.'

That directness hurt.

For an unguarded moment, all the self-doubt and fear that made up that 'bad reaction' hit me again. Memory *is* identity: lose the one and you lose the other.

'It's possible,' I said. 'I don't know. Okay, no more three-year-old stuff. But I do find this world more disturbing than I thought I would, when I agreed to come back.'

From somewhere above came a scream, choked-off; and footsteps that ran into silence.

Molly laughed, wryly. 'I don't find it all that reassuring myself.'

White light hardly shifted on the dusty floor. Orthe's day is twenty-seven hours, E-standard; a slow time passing – but even fear rests. Not so long after that, I looked across and saw that the Pacifican woman had slumped into the obtuse angle of two walls, and was soundly asleep.

They won't take one of us, I thought.

But it's been done before.

Sudden light, the grating of stone: the trap door flung back. Many harsh voices resolved into one: '*Shan'tai* – come from there.'

Molly started up. The pattern of the fibre-mat had imprinted on her arm, and she blinked and rubbed at cramped shoulders and neck. To give her time to collect her thoughts, I climbed with some difficulty up the rope-web, and stepped out on to the roof.

White fire dazzled. I fumbled shields over my eyes and the world turned sepia. Voices were loud. I blinked away after-images, and at last began to see through blood-haze to the afternoon light of Carrick's Star.

Molly appeared beside me. '*Shan'tai*, you owe us an explanation.'

Five or six young Ortheans jostled us. All were armed – spear or winchbow or curved hand-blade – and tension was plain in every glance over the shoulder, every sudden movement. Is that residual? I thought. Or is fighting still going on?

One male had an arm bandaged, and the blood that seeped through was black.

'Come with us, *shan'tai*,' he ordered.

'But the Voice of—'

'Move!'

I stumbled after the Pacifican woman, herded across that roof. We were enclosed in the group. The male followed. His face was masked against the glare, and I thought, Yes, I've seen those masks on another part of the Coast; north, in Kasabaarde—

Molly gripped my elbow. 'Problem?'

'No, I – it's the heat, I think. I'm okay.'

I barely noticed as they escorted us across the fibre-rope bridges to the main city. Like the vibration from a bell struck long ago, the name repeated in my mind: *Kasabaarde, Kasabaarde.*

And I wasn't even there that long, though God knows they helped me when I needed it – Kasabaarde: that city that is toll-gatherer of all trade between the two continents (standing far to the west, where the Archipelago meets the last habitable strip of the Desert Coast); that has, besides, an inner city of mystics and madmen; that has also, at its heart, the Brown Tower of the Hexenmeister . . .

Molly sucked in her breath. I followed her gaze.

This wider roof was bleached by the alien sun. A scent came off it. Not unpleasant, a little sour; but I suddenly realized it came from liquid that soaked the rough plaster surface, two great stains that were dark, dark-red, black.

'Is ship-contact a possibility for us now?' Molly said.

'I'd give it a fifty-fifty chance.'

'Okay. If that's as good as it gets.' She unconsciously straightened, towering over the Harantish Ortheans.

They took us into the warm shadow of a larger roof-house, and we descended through another trap door, down into a twilight that smelled of dust and herb – *arniac.* Without pause, they took us down steps; one flight, two; down into lower levels, three and four and more, and the mirror-directed light brightened. I tried consciously to deepen shallow breathing. My legs were beginning to ache badly.

On the next floor down, the pale sandstone gave way to blue-grey walls. A semi-translucent substance as cold to the touch as metal or stone.

'In the northern continent there's a wasteland called the Barrens—' Momentarily I was far from these silver-dim warrens, in winter air and desolate tundra. 'There are ruins of ancient Witchbreed cities. They're built of this, *chiruzeth.*'

'I've read the same reports you have,' Molly echoed, smiling without malice.

'They were my reports,' I said; and then, 'Jesus Christ!'

This level was spacious, one vast subterranean hall that stretched out in perspective, lit with the sheen of reflectors from the roofs high above. To me, the ceiling felt low; Molly actually had to stoop. Water-channels ran beside the nearer wall, and the air was cool and sweet.

'This place is a junk-heap,' Molly whispered, sounding momentarily closer to thirteen than thirty.

Mirror-light is deceptive, distances blur. The hall's long perspectives were tenebrous with glints of silver. Bright tapestries hung against the *chiruzeth*, between the great low arches groining the walls; tapestries that hung four and five layers deep, but still showed great rents and patches of decay. Threadbare embroidered cloths were scattered underfoot. Metal gleamed in the shadows.

The spaces between the arches were so cluttered that one could only walk down the centre of the hall. The guards escorted us there, between two rows of iron candle-trees, sparsely furnished with tallow candles. Junk had spilled from the arch-spaces. Carved stone chairs, swords; great bales of metal-cloth, the links now frail with rust; broken fountains, crystal tanks starred with shatter-lines, and mirrors set in *chiruzeth* frames, and old discarded implements of crafts and warfare . . . I had a sudden image, totally incongruous, of a child's rocking horse abandoned in some dusty attic; the children long since dead and turned to dust.

'There could be *anything* in here . . .'

I said, 'You expect to reconstruct Golden technology from *this*?'

Molly looked at the Ortheans at the further end of the hall. 'At the moment, that's the last thing I'm worried about.'

The guards pushed a way through the crowd. Ortheans: lithe, quick-limbed, ophidian-eyed. Their close scent surrounded me. We drew stares and whispered comments. A female half turned, hand on knife; a male spoke softly over the shoulder of another; one pulled bright robes aside as we passed. With sudden memories of the north, I thought, But there are no children present.

With the presence of children there is, sometimes, more safety.

'Can you see Pathrey Shanataru or that woman, the Voice?' Molly asked quietly. Even Sino-Anglic might not be a refuge here.

'Not a sign of either.' That made me certain: whichever faction they were, the opposition is in power now.

We found ourselves isolated in the space between the crowd and the arched end of the hall. The guards took up station behind us. The great archway-space made a frame, deliberately dramatic, for the Orthean who sat there in a tall carved *chiruzeth* chair.

'Give you greeting, *shan'tai*,' Molly Rachel said.

Above the Orthean male's head, spheres of light clung to the *chiruzeth*. As I watched, one drifted a few inches lower. It glowed . . . a shadowless light, the colour of lilac and lightning.

Dannor bel-Kurick. Something in the light keyed memory. When this thin, tense-looking male had a child's face, hardly more than a boy, I *did* see him – but not in person. I saw him through a viewscreen.

'I did not command *s'aranthi*-offworlders into my city,' he said.

For a moment, metal-gilt and gems confused the eye; then it became clear that the jewels were polished pebbles; the gilt, green verdigris. There was an underlying scent of decay. Molly's gaze went continually to the one genuine treasure in that heap of trash, the light-spheres, globes no larger than a child's fist. I recalled one, identical and soon dysfunctional, in the research labs of PanOceania.

She said, 'My people will demand explanations, *shan'tai*. The imprisonment of Earth personnel—'

He blinked, a slow veiling of citrine eyes. They were so pale they seemed to have a light behind them. There was little of that boy-Emperor in this haggard man.

An elderly male, standing beside the carved chair, spoke smoothly: '*Shan'tai* Rachel, what else could we do? You were in danger from the fighting. Not intentionally – but accidents happen. This was for your protection.'

'We would have been equally well protected on our ship.'

'You could have stayed with your ship and not entered the city,' Dannor bel-Kurick snapped. Then he said, 'What other Coast cities have you been to?'

'None as yet, *K'Ai Kezrian-kezriakor*.' She stumbled, giving him his title.

'Not to Quarth or Reshebet or Maherwa?' His tone, that had been hectoring, became quiet. 'Or Kasabaarde?'

A pulse of adrenalin hit me. To recall Kasabaarde now is to recall shelter, the Brown Tower there a refuge from a hostile world – and to recall that Kel Harantish is Kasabaarde's traditional enemy. I must have had some expression intelligible to alien eyes, because Dannor bel-Kurick looked straight past Molly Rachel to me.

'You are not a stranger to Kasabaarde, *shan'tai*.'

'I've been there. Many years ago.'

'Those who have been there bear always a mark.'

A certain tension was plain among those in earshot. The Emperor-in-Exile made an irritable gesture, and the men and women round him drew back instantly.

To my surprise, he turned back to Molly. 'What do you know of Kasabaarde, *shan'tai* Rachel?'

The Pacifican woman shifted her stance, still slouched down to

441

avoid hitting her head on the archways. I caught a quizzical expression on her face.

'I know it's a small settlement with a reputation for being a centre of religion and trade.'

'And otherwise?' He looked at me.

'A centre of – news.' I chose the word carefully. 'The Archives of the Brown Tower there are said to go back over many years. I always understood them to be equally interested in present-day history. Which they collect from many sources.'

'*S'aranthi*, I think you have forgotten much. The Tower has a hand in all conspiracy, plot, and cabal on the Coast; and in the barbarian north, also. Now I wonder if they draw offworlders into their plans? I wonder, *shan'tai*, if you have not come from them to us.'

Tension stopped breath. That's the only question he wants answered, that's the reason nothing's been done to us—

'We haven't been to Kasabaarde; we don't have plans to, at the moment,' Molly said. 'All our business has been with this settlement, *shan'tai*; I'd hoped to continue that.'

She was young enough for the truth to be plainly discernible in her voice, and I was glad of it; I've dealt with too many equivocations ever to be that honest in appearance.

Dannor bel-Kurick leaned back in the carved chair. That strange lilac-blue light fell on his face, casting violet shadows on his pale mane. His thin six-fingered hands picked at the folds of his tunic. When he spoke, he sounded infinitely weary.

'You know we have long had Kasabaarde for our enemy. I do not know you, *shan'tai*. But if you know that city, you will have heard the Tower disseminate lies about us. If you have only heard of Kel Harantish from them, you have heard little truth.'

The Pacifican woman said, 'Our business is with you.'

Her face was guarded, but she couldn't keep from looking at that treasure-junkheap that cluttered the length and breadth of the hall. I think she looked right past the faces of the Ortheans who watched us.

'You have no business here now.' He smiled, sudden and unwilling, and for a moment I saw Dannor bel-Kurick young again: mercurial, cruel, unpredictable.

'*Shan'tai*—'

'I have ordered a guard to take you to your ship,' he said. I went cold. Caution and hatred contended in his voice: I couldn't tell which would win. Then he said, 'I will give you a message to take to the rest of your people. Kel Harantish is closed to you now. If one of you *s'aranthi*-offworlders enters the city, now or ever, I will have you instantly killed.'

442

CHAPTER 3

An Echo of the Lightning

'I call it fucking incompetent!' David Osaka shouted. 'The stuff's *in* there, and you get us banned from the settlement—!'

'If I hadn't got in, you wouldn't know for sure that it was there!' Molly Rachel slapped the palmlock as she passed, and the port irised shut. 'There are still the canals. And the northern continent.'

Inside the shuttle, light was a soothing green. There was the subliminal hum of systems on stand-by. I dropped into a reclining seat beside David Osaka, feeling the padded comfort enwomb me.

He stood, now coldly angry. 'That stuff is the only reason we're here. The Company – '

Molly Rachel rubbed her temples. 'You didn't expect to walk out of there today with it, I hope? There have to be preliminaries. Remember, this is a technophobic culture.'

David Osaka leaned over to adjust a scan-screen, kneeling on a seat. His fair hair had grown long enough to fall into his eyes, and now he tucked it back behind an ear with a characteristic gesture. Then he looked over his shoulder at her.

'Molly, it was a stupid thing to do, going in under those conditions. The risk . . . You think the Company's name is enough to protect you? This is some backwater world that's hardly heard of Earth, never mind the multicorporates.'

I said, 'That's something of an exaggeration, David,' and they both ignored me.

'It's going on report,' he said. 'It's not just yourself you're risking, it's the Company's future here.'

'Unless we come up with something concrete, the Company won't *have* a future here. I didn't bust a gut getting a team together just to look at some post-holocaust agricultural muck-heap – if it wasn't for the chance there's something *real* here—'

She broke off, and took the navigation-comlink seat, fitting her long legs in with some care. Shuttles are too cramped to quarrel in, we are all within each other's space. She tapped desultorily at touch-controls. 'Communications systems out again?'

David grunted, leaning over the console. 'About sixty per cent of the time. As far as I can make out, it's the background interference again.'

I said, 'We always put it down to some quirk in the solar radiation here. It could be looked into, when you – when we – take time off from the commercial interests.'

'If it weren't for the commercial interests, PanOceania wouldn't be on this world.'

David brushed fair hair back again. A slight, wiry man, with a smooth-skinned face, and folds of skin at the corner of dark eyes; I would have put him around eighteen, I knew him to be a decade older. He had that kind of sexual attractiveness that becomes plain in movement. When not angry, he can be both charming and amusing.

He touched the console, converting one of the screens to 3D-cartographic. 'Carrick V.'

A globe formed, turning slowly. Figures superimposed over it: mass 0.93465 E-standard, gravity 0.9482745 E-s, atmosphere . . .

Travelling against the sun: a scatter of islands showed up, and then the slow revolution brought continents over the slope of the world.

'You really think there's something here?' His voice lost its sharpness. 'You know the odds against it?'

Northern and southern continents connected by an island archipelago, all but enclosing an equatorial sea.

Molly Rachel said, 'There's evidence, here. It's not been possible to investigate fully *all* the worlds the Dispersal found—'

'Wouldn't be possible even if every woman, child, and man on Earth took a world each,' I put in.

'—why shouldn't something be tucked away in a dirt-poor settlement on a post-holocaust world? Why shouldn't it be here?'

' "It"?' I queried.

David added, 'And even then, it has to be something we haven't found on half a hundred other worlds.'

Molly leaned forward, watching the map's population-indicators fill in: round the shores of that Inner Sea, and further inland on the northern continent. She touched a key.

'Desert Coast,' she ordered; and then, 'I don't mean artifacts. That's toy stuff. I mean some science based on a totally alien perception of the universe, something we couldn't create on our own . . .'

'And what d'you think you'll do with it when – if – you find it?'
I asked.

The light from the screen shone on her blunt features, gleamed in her hair. I recognized a hard ambition in her.

'Maybe there's – I don't know. Simultaneous communication, so we don't have to spend days waiting for FTL-drones between worlds. Trans-galactic stardrives, cures for mortality, who knows?' She grinned. 'Whatever it is, better we should have it than NuAsia or any of the other Companies!'

'And you personally would settle for a fat promotion?'

'Be ungrateful to refuse, right?'

In the screen, webs of lines shifted. A perfect illusion: the God's-eye view of this world. It zoomed into the southern continent, cutting out all but its northern coast, that strip of barely habitable land some few hundred miles long, bordering the Inner Sea . . . West to east, names came back: L'Dui and Lu'Nathe, Kasabaarde, Quarth, Psamnol, Reshebet. And here, on the hook of the eastern-most peninsula, farthest from the trade-routes, Kel Harantish. The backwater settlement of a backwater world.

I said, 'I've a feeling that Kel Harantish would have found something, if there was anything to find. They're the only ones here that would go looking for it.'

Memories of that treasure-junkheap were plain in her face.

'And just maybe they *have* found something. God, I wish I could get back in there with a full research team!'

Her intensity bothered me. It didn't seem to worry David. But he's Company, himself.

Molly sent the narrow-view north from the Desert Coast, over the representation of the Inner Sea, and even to scale it was long minutes before the sea gave way, first to the Eastern Isles, and then to Lone Isle. And then, long moments after, to the coast of the northern continent.

'I want to get in touch with the Earth representative before we make another attempt here. There was something in his report about political negotiations in progress now, between the Desert Coast and the northern continent—' She touched other keys, frowned. 'Navigation back-up out as well?'

David said, 'I've made contact, but not reliably. I wouldn't advise night-flying without it. Not in an old model like the QKN-40.'

I think it's standard practice these days for an orbital ship to broadcast a complex system of navigation aids over any non-tech world; it makes piloting a shuttle no more difficult than piloting a groundcar. It also means you don't have the on-board equipment necessary to do without it.

The woman studied figures. 'It's much faster, but it's a waste of fuel to go back up to the orbiter . . . If we stay on-world, we'll have to do a night stop-over on one of those groups of islands. Dave, can you punch a transmission through and let the others know?'

'I'll get on to it now.'

I said, 'I'd stay on-world, if it was me.'

'Mmm. There's something to be said for that, psychologically.' She rested her chin on the heel of her hand, gazing at the screen.

I tried to see it just as that – lines and beads of light, neatly-scripted Sino-Anglic names, figures, latitudes . . .

'I've notified them,' David said.

'Okay. Lynne, what's the settlement the British government envoy will be in? Didn't they change it from the original first contact?'

'Northern continent.' I indicated a point about midway along the coast of the Inner Sea, a river-port in temperate, fertile latitudes. 'That was my original base, Tathcaer. The records say there's been a move west along that coast, here, to Morvren Freeport.'

She nodded. 'The government envoy, Clifford. From what he reports, over the last decade there have been considerable changes in the northern continental culture.'

No cold recitation of names can hide them: Tathcaer, the city where first I came to negotiate with the Hundred Thousand – with Dalzielle Kerys-Andrethe, and Haltern, and the Orhlandis woman. And Morvren Freeport, a city seen once, ten years ago, on the run for a murder I didn't commit . . .

Changes. Reports are sketchy, don't see what I would see. *What* changes? The Desert Coast is nothing to me, I hardly know it, but I know the Hundred Thousand *telestres* of the northern continent, I've been over them on foot or by riderbeast, honoured or hunted, I know the Ortheans of the Hundred Thousand—

Fierce impatience fired me. To have come so far, to be so close; no room now for other considerations, nothing now but urgency – how have you changed since I've been gone?

David began routine flight preparations. Molly flicked the screen back to exterior-view.

The winter sun's dry heat gone, temperatures plummeted. The Coast's rocky landscape glittered now, thickly furred with frost.

Once, in a room where alien sunlight shone upon the still surface of a well, an Orthean woman marked me with light and sacred water, for her Goddess. I thought it then either a charming irrelevance, or some obscure privilege. I know now it is neither. It is a responsibility. For all the years gone by, this alien world and I still have business with each other.

Luck held. Flying north and west across the Inner Sea, late afternoon of the next day brought the shuttle away from unbroken cloud-cover, into clear weather over the coast of the northern continent.

Land shone grey and blue in the viewscreen, furred with a moss of forests; silver-thread rivers thirty thousand feet below. Nothing showed it to be inhabited country. And yet every acre down there is accounted for, I thought. A great jigsaw of interlocking territories – the *telestres* that are (in human terms) estates, farms, communes, communities . . . And are in Orthean terms the heart and centre of kinship, and love of the Goddess's earth. They have been so for two thousand years. What changes might there be?

'I've got an intermittent signal,' David Osaka reported. 'Standard code. Must be a landing beacon – hell, we must be right on top of them!'

'I thought this world was Restricted, no hi-tech?'

He shrugged. 'Don't ask me. Ask your government's envoy.'

Did I imagine an emphasis on *your*?

'One has to be reasonable,' Molly added. 'Is it enough to bring us in, Dave?'

'It's as good as we're going to get. Activate crash-straps.'

Linking the web across myself, I saw land swelling from a blue bowl to a misty plain, indistinguishable from the sea. The shuttle thrummed and lurched, losing height rapidly.

I felt new enthusiasm. Kel Harantish and that room without doors: I could put that behind me now. Let me get back on firm ground, with the Company administration and the government envoy. That's a system I know how to work. I can *do* something there.

The shuttle levelled out, and then switched into hover-mode. I watched a sea too pale for Earth, and white stars in the daytime sky. For the first time since my return, I felt confidence.

The port irised open. A blast of cold air and rain rushed in. A break in the mist showed water, the estuary shore, and blue-grey moss-grass uprooted by the landing. We disembarked. Rain drizzled, warm and sparky, leaving a tang on the tongue. Clouds shifted, bright, echoing Carrick's Star beyond. Wind drummed in the ears.

'I'm not landing blind again,' David swore.

'We were coded to this area, but I don't see—' Molly Rachel turned her collar up against the drizzle. '—where . . . ah.'

Morvren Freeport is built upon islands, across the massive estuary of the Ai River. Walking round to the other side of the shuttle showed us a dock-shed, and ferry, and a figure who left that shelter and walked towards us. It was human, and I let him speak to the Pacifican woman, and then: 'Douggie!'

We embraced, and then stood back to look at each other. I thought, How dare you look this young?

'It must be, what, five years?'

'Six,' Douglas Clifford said. 'I heard about Max. I'm sorry, Christie.'

I've never managed to answer that one satisfactorily. 'So am I' seems flippant, though it's true; 'thank you' is no acknowledgement of grief.

'Yes,' I said. 'You're looking well, Doug. Offworld agrees with you. And you're the government's—'

'Peripatetic representative,' he said, relishing every syllable. Douglas Clifford: a short, slightly-built man in his mid-fifties, with bright eyes and grizzled red hair; dapper even in these conditions. 'I've got a six-world circuit, two months on each. It's good to see you again. You should have come back to the Service to visit us.'

'With this?' I touched the PanOceania logo on my shoulder. 'I'd have been as welcome as the plague.'

'Can we get out of this weather?' David Osaka protested.

'I have quarters in the city.' Clifford indicated a nearby island. When the shuttle was secured, we walked down to the water. Spongy mossgrass gave way to mud, and an uncertain footing, and the rain-haze quickly cleared. Across the narrow strip of water, I saw pale walls, long low buildings. Like shadows, tri-vaned sails of windmills stood locked and still.

I smiled at a memory. 'Do you still have to pay to get in and out of the city?'

For answer, Clifford slid metal beads from a thong, handing them to an Orthean in the ferry-shed; a cloaked and hooded figure.

The ferry was a wooden platform with canvas stretched over wicker hoops; I walked uncertainly down the floating jetty and on to it, gripping the near rail. The two young people huddled under the canvas, Molly with her head ducked down; and after a word with the Orthean male, Clifford joined us. A cold day. I tried to place the season – Orventa Eleventhweek? Twelfthweek? Late winter, anyway.

'How many Earth personnel on-world at the moment?' Molly asked.

'None, I think, not since the Richards brothers left. They had an archeological dig up in the Barrens,' Clifford said.

'We paid a visit to a Company archeological site on the way here – Kel Harantish.'

Douglas Clifford looked at her with a certain stillness. Yes, I thought. Circuit world or not, you know Orthe . . .

'You went to Kel Harantish?'

'That's right.'

He let the challenge in her voice pass. Chains clanked as the wooden platform pulled away from the jetty. Choppy water tugged us seaward. I held the rail tightly, looking out across that level expanse of water; and it seemed odd, in that flat country, to look *up* at the Freeport's walls.

David Osaka, glancing back at the small island we'd left, asked, 'Is that the only available landing site?'

'The locals are touchy about land. So yes,' Clifford said, raising his voice over the sound of the sea. The fresh wind blew in his face and made him squint. He watched Molly, not the boy.

'I'm beginning to wonder if your Earth-base is in the most advantageous position,' she said. 'The Desert Coast has more to offer.'

'That depends on what you're looking for. The Hundred Thousand is the largest political entity—'

'I'm looking for Witchbreed technology. Not agricultural societies in cultural decay. I need somewhere for my research team to set up a base – I've got to get the demographic people down soon, and the basic equipment.'

Wind whipped hair, drove cold spray into cloth. The ferry platform shuddered as it was winched into the quayside; I saw the turnpike-winch was powered by squat reptilian quadrupeds, copper-coloured beasts with cropped horns. *Skurrai*. The sour smell of their dung was overpowering.

'If I may say so, this world is still nominally under the guidance of the British government. Restrictions are still in force as regards the importing of technology.'

She watched Clifford, and there was no compromise in her expression. 'I have authorization for what I'm doing. You can rely on the Company's being responsible—'

'Of course,' he said mildly. I winced.

'I need results,' she said. 'I need them fast, if I'm to get the funding to stay here – and I need to stay, because I'm certain there's something here for the Company. More likely on the Desert Coast, but possibly here. So if you'll set up a meeting for Lynne and me with the local *T'An* or *T'An Suthai-Telestre* or whoever—'

He said, 'There is no *T'An Suthai-Telestre*. Nor is there a *T'An* of Morvren Freeport.'

'There isn't *what*?' I demanded loudly.

The platform grated against stone steps, and I followed David up to the quay, treading somewhat unsteadily; then I swung round on Doug, as we stood among deserted, canvas-covered bales of cargo.

'Douggie, what the hell are you talking about?'

'The *telestres* don't have a central authority now. Or local leaders. It's a little difficult to explain. The system of administration has been in abeyance for some years.'

'Cultural decay,' the Pacifican woman repeated.

I thought, Christ, you've been quiet enough about that in your reports. And I guess her kind of comment is the reason why.

The rain passed, and every moment the other Freeport islands grew more distinct: Northfast, Little Morvren, Southernmost. Day-stars made brilliant points of light in a silk-blue sky. One sound underlay all conversation: the ceaseless beat of the waves, driving back sand into the estuary. There was a smell of rotting vegetation, *siir* and *hanelys* that, having died upriver, was now swept down on rain-fed winter floods.

I thought of that small, pale-maned Orthean woman, Dalzielle Kerys-Andrethe: *T'An Suthai-Telestre* in the white city of Tathcaer. If those days are gone . . . what could have caused it?

Not cultural decay. Orthe is never so simple to comprehend.

I heard David Osaka's sharp exclamation, and looked up to find him staring south across the estuary. He said '*That* . . . ?'

'That,' I said, 'is the Rasrhe-y-Meluur.'

Chill wind made my eyes water, squinting south across the islands and multiple channels of the Ai river estuary. And there, six or seven miles away, on the last outcrop of the mainland . . .

The winter air is pearl-blue and grey, so close in colour that the massive *chiruzeth* structure hardly shows against the sky. A great spire, or pylon, its sides reflecting silver light; so vast that the passing clouds cast shadows on its surface. I had forgotten the sheer size of it, greater than PanOceania's hiveblocks back on Earth.

It is a hollow ruin. A *chiruzeth* shell.

The simplicity of its line is broken once only, where a thin bridge-structure juts out, soaring straight across the Inner Sea to where (dimly visible in haze) there is another spire, and then another . . .

One should see it so. I was grateful to the cloud-cover, because for some odd reason I hadn't wanted to look down on this from the air. Bridging the waters on which its shadow falls, this that was once both highway and air-hung city of the Golden Witchbreed . . .

And once, on a sailing ship, I travelled beside it for the full length of the Archipelago, from Morvren across the Inner Sea to Kasabaarde – two hundred miles and more. Just to look was to feel the sheer weight, the massiveness of these ruins.

'The satellites picked that up on low-orbit.' Molly sounded stunned.

'That was the level of technology here,' I said, still looking at that shell. 'Five, maybe ten thousand years of it.'

As if by common consent, we turned away. Paradoxical as it may seem, the Rasrhe-y-Meluur is somehow too *big* to be seen. The mind rejects it.

Molly Rachel, as she turned to the first buildings of the Freeport, said, 'Isn't it tragic that these people should have lost all that?'

I said, 'That's a matter of opinion.'

CHAPTER 4

Old Friends

We entered Morvren Freeport by a side gate.

'There must be *somebody* I can speak to,' Molly protested in exasperation. 'Lynne, what would you advise?'

That hour called second twilight was on the city, when the light of Carrick's Star fades, and the stars have not yet their full strength. I turned my collar up against the cold as we walked through muddy alleys, away from the docks.

'It's difficult. When I was here, the *telestres* named a *T'An* – an administrator, of sorts – for each of the seven provinces. It cut the legwork down.'

The provinces are more language-divisions than political territory.

I saw Molly blink, apprehending the sheer size of the Hundred Thousand: a hundred thousand communities, autonomous units, communes, nation-states – whatever label you care to put on them. I have known them be of as few as fifty, as many as five thousand Ortheans.

'Someone here once said to me, "If you attack us, you have not one enemy but one hundred thousand".' I put out of my mind the Orthean woman who had said it, and added, 'If that applies equally to negotiations – God knows how you're going to speak with each individual *telestre*!'

'With difficulty,' she said: a flash of mordant humour. 'I don't have several centuries to spare.'

The alleyways opened out to avenues. Molly spoke in Sino-Anglic, not especially quietly, and heads turned as Ortheans recognized offworlders.

With a sensation of shock, I met the eyes of a dark male, then two young females, and then an elderly woman in a slit-backed robe, mane braided down her spine. That Orthean stare – clear as ice. Outrageously egotistic, the thought went across my mind: *Do you remember me?* I smiled at that.

452

Ortheans of the Hundred Thousand are taller and stockier than Coast Ortheans, and these wore *harur*-blades glittering at the belt or slung across the back. They turned away. I heard talk begin behind us, in the soft Morvrenni language.

Molly said to Clifford, 'Is there *no* part of the administrative system still working?'

'If you give me time – I've just come in from Thierry's World; you'll appreciate that I've hardly had a week here myself—'

'I want to speak to someone now. Not tomorrow morning. Tonight.'

One elegant brow went up in one of Douglas Clifford's more theatrical mannerisms. He has his own brand of self-mockery, does Doug.

'While my government is more than willing to give the Company every assistance—'

The Pacifican woman said, 'Tonight would be convenient; I've other business for tomorrow.'

He looked up at her, blandly unhelpful, and then he smiled.

'In that case, you'd better see – hmm – the Almadhera. Now.'

David Osaka caught my eye, and I believe I had a very similar expression to his. Visions of a warm Residence and food vanished from my mind as Clifford glanced round, and then led off up a wider avenue. The mud was pale, crunching underfoot where river gravel had been thrown down to help traction. Here in the shadow of the blank-walled buildings the wind was bitter cold, and I looked through gateways into courtyards, seeing the yellow glow of lamps being lit, and smelling the cooking-fires for the evening meal. This hour left us all but alone on the streets.

I said, 'If there's no local authority, who or what is the Almadhera?'

Clifford's gaze slid across to me. Diffidently, he said, 'There is no official *takshiriye* – not without a *T'An Suthai-Telestre* to lead it – but the Freeport's the only place now that trades outside the Hundred Thousand, so it does have a kind of unofficial *takshiriye*. The Almadhera is one of its members.'

He used the southern term for the Court of the *T'An Suthai-Telestre*, that I have so often used in Tathcaer.

Now we were coming to buildings three and four storeys high, with slot-windows lining the top floors. The land was flat. With no view of anything beyond, the city seemed tall, overwhelming.

'Can this person speak with any authority?' Molly sounded bewildered.

'She's one of – well, I call them "the Morvren triumvirate".'

Clifford's brown eyes twinkled. 'She's all the authority you're liable to get.'

Multicorporates and national governments agree as well together as cat and dog. Without any surprise, I thought, It's going to be a rough night . . .

'Here we are,' Clifford said. 'If I might offer one word of advice: the Almadhera's political status may be slightly dubious, but she *is* an Earthspeaker in the church of the Goddess.'

As he went up to the closed gates of a courtyard, Molly dropped back a pace.

'I think he's giving us the runaround. What do you make of this?'

'He's no more anxious to help the Company than any government envoy – but I wouldn't underestimate this person. Not if she's an Earthspeaker. I used to convince myself that I understood the political system here. I never *did* convince myself I understood the church of the Goddess.'

The gates swung open, disclosing a small lantern-lit courtyard. Dusk had fallen without my noticing. Now the stars were coming to full strength: the billion stars that make up the galaxy's core, flowering in Orthe's night sky. By that hard light, I saw a child at the gate. It was no more than five or six years old; unsexed, as all the young of the species are, being *ashiren*, genderless, until their fourteenth year.

'Give you greeting,' it said. 'Enter and be welcome.'

Frost was beginning to glitter on the flagstones as the child led us across the courtyard, which was surrounded on three sides by inward-facing rooms, and up an outside staircase to an entrance on the first floor. A coin-bead curtain swung back in my face; I pushed it aside, and stepped into a wall of heat and noise.

The room was wide, low-ceilinged, with shallow curved ribs supporting the roof; and it was full to the roof with clutter. I thought, But the place is full of *children*—

Silence spread out from where we stood.

As they stopped what they were doing and turned to stare, I counted seven *ashiren*. In that ill-lit room there was something disturbing about their sharp gestures and rapid speech. They could be human, until an opaque glance or clawed hand became briefly visible. Manes clinked and glittered, woven with crystal and ceramic beads.

'What's all the fuss—' An Orthean female entered, from where the room continued round the L-shape of the building. Her arms were full of scrolls, books, and papers. She walked between the braziers that were set on the stone floor, dumped the armful on one of the many couch-chairs (dust flew: a stream of papers slid to the floor), and came to meet us, smiling broadly.

'*T'an* Clifford – and more of you? What are you here for? – Cethelen, put the *siir*-wine on to heat! All right, the rest of you, that's *enough*.'

They ran. Bare feet scuffed the stone floor, there was the susurrus of flowing robes. Two *ashiren* brought out cushion-mats, dragging them close to one of the braziers; and I saw that the couch-chairs – as well as the tables, and most of the floor space – were piled with scrolls, papers, and maps. An older *ashiren* looked round the corner of the room at us, and scuttled back.

The Orthean woman whacked at her crimson robe, raising a cloud of scroll-dust. She grinned. I put her in her sixties; a short, brown-skinned female with a tumbling scarlet mane.

As Clifford introduced us, she said, 'I take it you arrived on that ship we heard? And came straight here? What's so urgent, *t'ans*?'

She used the word with the inflection that can mean either 'strangers' or 'guests'. Molly Rachel gave me a look that said *Earn your keep*. Better the special advisor should look a fool than the Company representative.

'Goddess give you greeting and fortune, *t'an* Earthspeaker.' I spoke in Morvrenni.

She responded automatically: 'And to your mother's daughter.' The dark eyes clouded and cleared, this time showing humour. 'So you know how to talk to Earthspeakers, do you, *t'an*? That's not as common as it might be among *s'aranthi*.'

We followed her example, sitting on the cushions by the brazier.

'I used to know some of your church, *t'an*, and some of the *takshiriye* – but that was many years ago. That's also part of the problem. We're from the multicorporate Company PanOceania. If I didn't know better, I'd say we needed to talk to somebody in authority. This being the Hundred Thousand, what I will say is that we need to talk to people who can get word out to other *telestres*. We have questions to ask.'

It was quite a bravura performance, considering the circumstances, and I saw Molly Rachel look chagrined, and Doug grin to himself.

'When were you here before?'

'About ten of our years ago – that would be, what, just over eight years by your reckoning.'

'I . . . see. Yes. It's true there have been changes.' Her six-fingered hands glinted as she reached up to take a goblet, and I saw there were gold studs set in the webs of skin between those narrow fingers.

Clifford said, 'I thought it best to see you, *t'an* Almadhera, since news has a way of coming to the Church before the rest of the Freeport. I thought it might work the other way about. Communication appears to be essential.'

A small *ashiren* handed me a goblet that spilled a hot green liquid, and I surreptitiously wiped my cuff. It was disconcerting to find a half-dozen children curling up on the mats round us, watching us intently. Molly Rachel drew more attention than anyone. It was her height.

'What is it you want to ask the *telestres*?' the Almadhera said.

I let Molly field that one.

'We're here for trade,' she said, partly uncertain, partly challenging. 'Naturally, since this is a Restricted world, regulations still apply. However, our Company has been given a licence to import a certain amount of non-technological goods.'

The Orthean woman tucked her feet up under her. Then she sat still. In that stillness I began to recall the church and its priests – who are mystics and craftsmen, warriors and philosophers, farmers and poets.

'No,' she said.

Molly, startled, said, 'What?'

'*T'an s'aranthi*, if you trade with us, what's the price you're asking? I've spoken with Clifford here often enough to know something of your world – and besides, I know our history. All you *s'aranthi* are ever interested in are the abominations of the Golden Witchbreed – am I right?' The woman paused just long enough for Molly to fumble and stutter, and then said, 'Yes, I am. *T'an*, there's nothing of that Empire left in the Hundred Thousand. We ceased to need such things long ago.'

The oldest-looking *ashiren*, a black-maned child of ten or eleven, spoke. 'That's the first time I ever heard *you* say what the Wellkeepers tell us to say.'

The Almadhera protested, 'I'm not just giving you the Wellhouse orthodoxy. I believe it's true.'

'Just because there are *s'aranthi* here, you don't have to suddenly like everything the Wellhouses say.' The child stared up at Molly Rachel. 'I'm Cethelen. I think we ought to let you trade with the Freeport. Everyone else does, why not you?'

Molly opened her mouth and then shut it again. I caught Doug's eye at just the wrong moment, and he and I and David desperately failed not to laugh. The *ashiren* looked at us in some bewilderment.

The Almadhera chuckled. 'You should talk to some more of us. I'll send these out with messages, it won't take long. We'll heat some more *siir*-wine, too. Have you eaten?'

456

David's heartfelt negative prompted a scuffle of action among the younger children, who fled down inner stairs to the kitchens. I saw him and Molly put their heads together, and I didn't have to overhear them to know what they were saying – *these Ortheans are crazy* . . .

'You must have been one of the first *s'aranthi* we saw.' The Orthean woman stopped, an almost comical surprise on her face. 'Grief of the Goddess! You're that Lynne Christie, Christie *S'aranth*? The Kerys-Andrethe's friend?'

And it was not until then that I made the connection: the nickname *S'aranth* become the generic term *s'aranthi*, 'off-worlder' . . . I shivered. And then grinned at the black irony. When I first came here I was called *S'aranth*, 'weaponless', because I didn't carry the *harur*-blades that Ortheans do. To have that become the name for hi-tech humanity—!

'Christie *S'aranth*,' I confirmed bleakly. Did I avoid the realization?

'Dalzielle Kerys-Andrethe called you that?'

'No, it was Ruric Orhlandis—'

She and I looked at each other. The scarlet mane fell forward, masking that narrow-chinned alien face. She stared down at her claw-nailed hands, and then back at me.

The gaze was as cold and clear as water: that mark of the Earthspeaker, their difference from other Ortheans.

'There is no Orhlandis *telestre*. There was no Ruric Orhlandis, only a woman branded traitor and land-waster and exile.'

I wanted to say *Yes, I know*. Who knows it better than me? I forgot that I shouldn't mention—

But my face was burning red, and I couldn't speak for embarrassment. A fair-maned *ashiren* refilled my cup, and the clear green liquid was hot to taste, and spicy: fermented juice of the *siir*-plant.

'I'm sorry,' I said. 'I knew her very well, and it isn't easy to remember now what I should and shouldn't say.'

'No . . .' The Almadhera was thoughtful. '*T'an* Christie. *S'aranthi*. That's very strange. For you, too?'

'Very strange, for me.'

I found that I liked this untidy, forthright Orthean woman, while still being aware that there were intonations and expressions in her that I was blind to.

'There'll be others here soon,' she said. 'Still, there's someone here you ought to see. Round that way – I'll keep your colleagues entertained.'

You want to even up the odds, I thought. Since Douggie's half on your side – if 'sides' are what we're talking about here.

'Sure,' I said, and left them talking, as I made my way to the end of the room and round the 'elbow' of the L-shape. An *ashiren* who lay asleep on a couch-chair (sharing it with a pile of maps and books) flicked one membraned eye open as I passed.

Small-paned windows shone with starlight. This part of the room was darker, the light coming from a great fireplace; and there were deep chairs there, in the shadows and embers.

A low table held a carved hexagonal board, cut by triangular divisions, on which scattered groupings of triangular counters lay.

'He's beating you,' I said to the *ashiren* Cethelen, who was seated on one side of the *ochmir* board.

'He cheats.'

'He always did. Hello, Hal.'

Cethelen stood to move a lamp closer, and I stopped. Ortheans live longer than we do, and stay longer in their young and mature phases; old age is a swift and ravaging decay.

'I thought I recognized your voice,' said Haltern n'ri n'suth Beth'ru-elen.

I saw a fair-skinned male, plump, dressed in the plain robes of the church. He was all but lost in the cushioned chair. The yellow-white mane was a mere crest, the eyes in that triangular face permanently half webbed over with nictitating membrane.

'Hal, I'd expect to find you round corners, listening to other people's conversations.'

'While you try and bully poor Cassirur Almadhera?'

His hand was dry and hot, the grip not strong. I kept hold of that six-fingered hand as I sat down by him in another chair. For a time, nothing was said. There was a brilliance in that half-blind gaze.

'It *is* you. You look well.' He chuckled, a fat and healthy sound. 'And young. Though I'd wager you're not. Are you surprised at the way I look?'

That mixture of slyness and honesty is essentially Orthean. It brought back so many memories.

'Yes, I am.'

'Nothing but time, *t'an S'aranth*, and age – all the Beth'ru-elen age early. It's in our family.'

To shut my eyes was to bring him back: Haltern, fair-maned, harassed, sweating; a deceptively competent man, no older – then – than Doug Clifford now.

That voice, no less strong, said, 'You've proved me wrong. I always said you wouldn't come back. And now you come in company with traders?'

'I did intend to return. I got posted away. Maybe I didn't try as hard as I might to prevent that. There was a lot to come to terms with, afterwards, and then – well, then there were other people.'

He nodded, slowly. The firelight shone on his skin, the faintest scale-pattern visible; on whiteless blue eyes. For all his frailty, that intelligence was undimmed.

'I'm glad you came back,' he said.

'Hal . . .'

Deliberately picking up on other matters, he said, 'Are you really with a Company? From what Clifford's said of them in the past, I find that difficult to believe. And a Company that's chasing Witch-breed technology?'

'It's a long story, but "yes" and "yes" are the answers to that. And if it comes to it, what are *you* doing here?'

'I like the company of Earthspeakers. I was always of a contemplative frame of mind, given to meditation – ah. Now *that's* Christie.' He grinned, and deep lines shifted in his face.

Having snorted incredulously, all I could say was, 'This place is as peaceful as a madhouse, and you're about as "contemplative" as—' Similes eluded me.

He took a goblet of *siir*-wine from Cethelen, reached over to move an *ochmir*-counter, and under cover of getting the child to stir the fire, switched another two counters to show a colour favourable to him.

What did Clifford call it – the 'Morvren triumvirate'? Now I wonder . . . 'You associate with this Almadhera a lot, do you, Hal?'

'Associate?'

'I'm told there's no *takshiriye*. No official *takshiriye*.'

He slid gracefully over that, saying thoughtfully, 'It was about six years ago; none of the *T'Ans* could name themselves *T'An Suthai-Telestre* after Dalzielle Kerys-Andrethe died.'

Reading that in records, I had been sad, a little shocked: she wasn't old. And when she was (to use the common tongue) Crown, Hal was a Crown Messenger; the first of those intelligencers that I ever met.

'After that, the provinces rubbed along well enough; and the *T'Ans* mostly returned to their own *telestres*.' He set his goblet down carefully. 'That's not to say they won't name a new Crown, if they see the need for one.'

'The lack of one is confusing someone I know,' I said, thinking of Molly, and the likely reaction of the other Pacificans.

'I can see that we have to talk – or is it still Douglas Clifford that I should speak with?'

Noise came from the other part of the room. I guessed there were people coming in.

'I haven't had time to talk with Doug myself . . . He and I know each other from way back. And every time he's looked at me since I got off the ship, I've seen him thinking the same thing – what the hell's she doing with a multicorporate?'

'What *are* you doing?' Haltern asked waspishly. 'More to the point, what are you doing with them on Orthe?'

'Minimizing damage,' I said. 'Or at least, I hope to.'

'Is Witchbreed technology the only interest they have in us?'

'As far as I can make out.' You can't expect a Pacifican Company to learn from a 'post-holocaust' world.

There was a pause. I thought I ought to go and greet the newcomers, but he stopped me with a word: 'I can't help but think back. Christie, do you remember what Ruric Orhlandis once said? "You are utterly unlike us, and when you come here we can't help but alter. And if we're ever found to have something that Earth requires—"'

'"—why then Goddess help us, because no one else will!" Oh yes. It's something I've never forgotten. That's why I'm here. That's why I *had* to come.'

He blinked, that old male, in the fire's yellow light; and as I stood to go, touched my arm. With that I knew we had – somehow – resumed an old friendship; not unchanged, no, but still there.

'Hal, what happened to Ruric?'

'She died, on the Coast. It was many years ago.'

I'd heard, by Service rumour, but I wanted him to say it. Records can be wrong and she was only one woman in what was – for those not involved – only a very minor political incident, on a primitive world. The record might have been wrong.

'Are you sure?'

His gaze, alert, was that of an old spymaster. There was the automatic, professional pause before he spoke.

'I made certain to enquire. And I had word, also, from the servants of the Hexenmeister – *you* have good cause to remember the Tower's veracity.'

Ten years ago I met that "serially immortal" (as the Ortheans term it) custodian of the Tower and the Tower's Archives, the Hexenmeister of Kasabaarde; an ancient male whose investigations cleared me of the accusation of murder. Hal and I, we were deep in that together.

'Will you . . .' I offered him my arm, to rise, but he shook his head.

'Later.' He had a covert smile, that meant there were other conversations he wanted to overhear. 'Yes, we must talk later. Go and meet the others now.'

I left him playing *ochmir* with Cethelen (unsurprisingly, he was winning) and walked back round into the main part of the room. If anything there were more *ashiren* present than before, older children who'd act as messengers.

Molly, rising to stand beside me, said confidentially, 'Things are moving fast. Some of these people are just opportunists, they want a piece of what the Company has to offer, but there are a few that are genuine. One in particular. See that one there, by David?'

The other Pacifican was talking with a group of male and female Ortheans, seated beside a brazier with the Almadhera and Doug Clifford. One youngish, dark-maned male had winterscale skin splotched with those mottled patches that Ortheans call 'marsh-flower'. It made his features seem large, crammed into a small face.

'Don't be so sure these people want what the Company can offer. What about him?'

'His name is Rakviri. He's prepared to take us out to his *telestre*, tomorrow. And by the description he's given me, there's something there worth investigation.'

'Christ, things *are* moving.'

She said, 'They've had ten years to think about it, Lynne.'

The room was crowded now, but I detected an air of expectancy, as if not all the unofficial *takshiriye* were yet present. That was confirmed when the cords of the bead-curtain swung apart, and an Orthean male walked in. He pulled off his cloak, under which he wore the britches and slit-backed shirt of Rimon province. Two *harur*-blades – the *harur-nilgiri*, that is too short for a sword; and *harur-nazari*, too long for a knife – were slung from his belt, the hilts worn with use.

'You know him?" Molly said.

'Oh yes.' I shook my head in wonder. 'Lord, two old friends in one evening? First Hal, and now—'

I took an instinctive step forward. It seemed at first that he stood half in shadow, this stocky male with the cropped yellow mane, but the shadow that lay over half his face was a scar. A burn. I saw a whiteless blue eye, bright in ruined flesh; and as he turned, his other profile was a lined face, looking not a day more than forty.

'Blaize n'ri n'suth Meduenin,' the Almadhera said.

'Blaize!' I held out both hands. I couldn't keep the grin off my face.

His expression changed. I thought, Good God, have I altered so much, don't you recognize me?

Without taking his eyes from me, he spoke to the Almadhera:

'Your *ashiren* brought me the name. I thought it might not be true, but I see that it is. I shall have to leave.'

One hand rested on the hilt of a *harur*-blade, that gesture so familiar; and all I could think was, After all these years he still speaks Morvrenni with a Rimon accent.

And not believe that cold tone.

'Blaize—' I took my hands back, colouring like an adolescent.

The Orthean woman spoke to Blaize, Doug Clifford to the Pacificans; I attended to neither:

'We really need you to talk to these *s'aranthi*—'

'—highly advisable to speak with the Meduenin—'

It might have been a smile that made something grotesque out of his scarred face, or some quite alien emotion. There was an authority about him that was new, and plain in the way he spoke to the other Ortheans, and I felt cold, faced by that impenetrable anger.

'How *you* can come back here—' Blaize Meduenin turned to the others. 'Cassirur Almadhera, *t'an* Clifford; I'm sorry. I refuse to engage in any discussions while this woman is present.'

CHAPTER 5

The Customs of Orventa

A morning wind blew across the flat roofs of the city, fluttering cloth-robes hung out to dry. Windvanes rumbled, ceaselessly turning. Few Ortheans were out in the wide avenues, but I could see bright dots moving down on the quay, where (far off and silent) the sails of a *jath-rai* flapped, the crew hurrying to catch low tide.

I leaned on the rim of the brick parapet, on the flat roof of the Residence. My only clear view – since all the buildings are on a level – was seaward, through a gap between them. I saw the outlines of two other Freeport islands, Little Morvren and Southernmost one behind the other, each with their windvanes and Watchtower and low Wellhouse dome; clear as glass images. The top of the Rasrhe-y-Meluur was hidden in cloud.

'I'll be glad when I get adjusted to local time,' Molly Rachel called, coming up the steps that led from the Residence's inner courtyard to the roof. She was kneading the back of her neck with strong fingers.

'You do adjust – sleep a couple of hours midday.'

She yawned, wide-mouthed as a cat. 'Lynne . . . is Douglas Clifford as much of a fool as he likes to make out?'

I chuckled. 'Not by any means.' And when she looked enquiringly, added, 'I used to know him well. And also, he and Max were colleagues, when they were both groundsiders – sorry: both in the Home Service, I should say. Of course, I didn't see Doug as often as I might; I was offworld a lot of the time.'

If I hadn't been offworld then Max—

Such pain is unexpected. I thought I'd given up that false guilt long ago, knowing that accidents don't fail to happen just because people stay on one world together. It would have made no difference if I'd been on Earth.

News had to come to me on Parmiter's Moon, six weeks after the event. When everything else is gone, that fact remains: I wasn't there. I wasn't even there to see him buried.

Molly Rachel leaned on the brick parapet beside me and looked down. I could smell the morning meal cooking, down in the ground-floor kitchens.

'You can see what's happening here, Lynne. For all that Clifford says, it's obvious. This culture's falling apart. When the lines of administration and authority go down, what's left?'

Local Residence reports mention Watchtowers that stand empty; the Seamarshal's palace boarded up. Now the sound of dawn gongs came across the roof-tops. How do I tell her? It isn't the cities that are important, it never was.

'I've *got* to justify being here, Lynne.'

'How long will home office let you carry on without results?'

She squinted up at the high dome of the sky, and the daystars that lay thick as frost. Crowsfeet laced the corners of her eyes. Because she's Pacifican and young, I tend to think she's uncomplicated. That's always an error.

'It isn't home office. If *I* think the outlay isn't justified . . . I can't bleed resources for no return, it's got to benefit us all; that's the way the Company works. I *know* there's something here. All the hard evidence points to it. But if there's functional Witchbreed technology, we ought to be picking up readings from power-sources—'

Was that a turning-point, could I have pushed her to a negative decision then? Smaller things have discontinued missions. But all I did was suggest, 'Perhaps we do pick up readings, and can't recognize them. Maybe it's something we can't program the analysers to recognize.'

'Just possible,' she conceded. 'Then the Company really would be on to something. When you were here – but that's ten years ago. With the speed of cultural decay here, they might have lost even the few artifacts that *do* exist, by now. Wouldn't that be ironic? Two or three thousand years since the Witchbreed culture fell, and we arrive ten years too late . . .'

'Molly, you do say the damnedest things!'

She had to laugh at that. She raised her head, looking towards the estuary and the sea; taking stock.

'And now?' I said.

The wind drummed in my ears, cold, but with the promise of thaws. Morvren Freeport lies in more southerly latitudes than Tathcaer. Spring will come sooner.

'I'm going along the coast, inland, to that *telestre*. Rakviri, the name is. That's what happens now.'

'We've only been here yesterday and today!'

'There's no point in wasting time,' Molly said. 'Unless the *telestres* are different from this technophobic city, the Company won't be interested in the Hundred Thousand. But in any case, I don't want anyone getting in ahead of us. We're not the only multicorporate that could find Carrick V attractive.'

The Pacifican woman turned, looking at me speculatively. I must be slow this morning, I thought, what's she leading up to? The light was behind her, and full in my face; deliberately so. I'm too old to be foxed by tactics like that.

'I think I have to ask,' she said, 'since these people have influence with the *telestres*, and we need access to the *telestres* . . . What was all that with Blaize Meduenin?'

'Molly, you needn't feel any concern. It won't affect Pan-Oceania's relations with the Hundred Thousand.'

'Don't patronize me,' she said amiably, 'and don't be so bloody pompous, Lynne. I'm head of mission; I need to know. What's the explanation?'

'I don't see why I should be expected to understand the Orthean mind when I don't even know how the human mind works.'

'Lynne—'

If ten years age-seniority gives nothing else, it gives an ability to shut kids up. I stopped her mid-sentence with a look.

'I'll get it sorted out,' I said, and crossed the roof, went down the steps, and never heard a sound from her.

That determination carried me out into the chill of the street, and across the city, walking briskly from the Residence to where Cassirur Almadhera had her quarters. I found no adult Ortheans there, but an older *ashiren* directed me down towards the quay.

The sky was hazed, a high milky blue, and the air had a thin clarity. The human body senses difference: sunlight too thin, wind too cold – still, this day felt like the beginning of Spring season. I walked down between biscuit-coloured walls, remembering how late Hanys in Morvren Freeport is hot and glaring and harsh, and how *jath-rai* from this port sail out to all the coasts of both continents.

The wind whipped the estuary into choppy waves. I felt the spray, shivered; looking up the quay and down. A few coastal *jath-rai* were moored down towards the Portmaster's office, and there were more across the channel in the docks of another Freeport island. Ten years ago I stood here and saw Kel Harantish traders leave (but Morvren Freeport has always had an odd reputation). Ten years ago I was running blindly south, in good company, to what I didn't then know would prove a refuge and a sanctuary: Kasabaarde's Tower . . .

I turned to walk along beside tall warehouse frontages, and stopped.

He stood in the open arched entrance of a warehouse, one thin, strong finger jabbing at the Orthean male he spoke to. The other claw-nailed hand rested back on the hilt of *harur-nilgiri*. Sun illuminated his yellow mane. I noticed that he now habitually stood so as to put his half-scarred face in shadow.

Blaize you bastard—

Anger made me hot and cold. The thought of our last meeting was like a slap across the face.

The younger male saw me. '*T'an s'aranthi*, give you greeting! Have you come to speak with the *takshiriye*? This is Blaize n'ri n'suth Meduenin, if you don't know him.'

'I do have a passing acquaintance. Two assassination attempts on my life, wasn't it? And an occasion when you gave false evidence at a trial?'

A brazier burned in the warehouse entrance, and I stepped up to warm my hands at it, giving him back stare for stare, not displeased to have said that in front of witnesses. The young male inclined his head, and precipitately left.

'I won't speak with you.' Blaize Meduenin turned to follow.

'You *will*.' I put myself between him and the quay outside, too furious to consider danger. As I have cause to know, Ortheans have no scruples about violence. 'I won't be treated like this. None of us can afford personal quarrels. I . . . can be professional enough to forget your behaviour last night.'

He stopped. That pale gaze raked me up and down. What does he see now – an alien: a tall woman, blonde hair flecked white, thinner than health demands? I never could read mirrors truly. And I was so much younger when we crossed the Barrens . . .

The wind blew his mane across his eyes, that yellow mane cropped in the Rimon style, that grows out silver where the burn-scar is. Plain slit-backed shirt, boots, britches; all dusty with warehouse chaff. And *harur*-blades at his belt. Still a fighter. And swordfighters in their middle years are dangerous: experience replacing strength, doubt replacing confidence.

He met my eyes and smiled, quite deliberately. And said, 'I'd thought there could be no worse betrayer of the Hundred Thousand than Ruric Orhlandis. But what would even she say now, that kinsister of yours, if she were living? To see you as you are?'

Using the dead woman's name was such deliberate malice that I could escape the hurt of it. Only to fall prey to memory: *You* used to call me your kinsister, Blaize Meduenin.

Cold air cut through warmth, and the smell of burning *lapuur-*

wood in the brazier. Ortheans shifted crates in the interior of the warehouse, and *ashiren* outside the nearby companion-house chanted an atonal rhyme, but it felt as though we two were alone.

'I don't understand you.' Frustration choked me. 'And what I do understand, I don't like. I was prepared to be reasonable, *more* than reasonable – you humiliated me—'

He took a few steps towards the entrance, looking out at the docks and bare masts of *jath-rai* ships. Then he turned to lean up against the mud-brick arch, with that automatic gesture that swept *harur* blades out of his way. His pale eyes cleared. A stocky Orthean male, fair-maned, ageing; still carrying himself with a fighter's grace. Age, as it does with some, made him more solid, more himself.

'Are you so certain you're right, to be afraid of Earth?' I meant it to sting. He shrugged.

'I know what the Witchbreed were. How their engines devastated this world. And I know how like them you offworlders seem—' He broke off. Then: 'I'll negotiate with Clifford. With the Company, if the *takshiriye* must. I've had to negotiate with all kinds of people, here, over the years – even Dannor bel-Kurick's Harantish Witchbreed. But *not* with you.'

'Because I'm doing what I'm paid to do? Be reasonable—'

'*I* took Guildhouse oaths, and served who paid me! I never pretended moral necessity to mask it.' His voice was loud with disgust. Someone in the warehouse called his name. He ignored it. Carrick's Star brightened, casting the shadow of the archway at my feet, striking fire from the harbour beyond.

'I remember your mercenary "ethics"! How ethical was it when you abandoned me in the wilderness at Broken Stair? And Maric with me, and *ke* no more than a child – I thought then, you're nothing but a paid killer. As if what happened before we were hunted out of Roehmonde hadn't told me that!' Anger left me breathless: 'Don't play soldier-turned-statesman with *me*. You may be in the *takshiriye*, but you still don't have any conception of the wider issues over the personal—'

He shrugged, almost sullen. 'SuBannasen *telestre* paid me and I made two attempts to kill you. And it might have been better for Orthe if one of them had succeeded. Is that view wide enough for you? Impersonal?'

'This is pointless. Just pointless.'

He didn't shout. Razors hurt no less if gently applied. I wanted to sit down, I was shaking; there was nowhere in the dusty warehouse entrance to sit.

'And childish. What do you want me to say? That I should have left *you* to die, when we were being hunted through the Fens? Blaize, for God's sake!' My voice echoed in the vaulted roof. I tried to speak with more restraint. 'I'm here because there have to be negotiations between the Company and the Hundred Thousand. The Company would have come here with or without me, so don't blame me for it!'

He pushed himself away from the wall, stepped in front of me. Automatically, I tensed; aware of physical power. That silver-seamed burn made something unreadable of his face.

'Does the Company trust you – *S'aranth*?'

'Why the hell do you think I'm here?'

He picked up the less obvious implication. 'I know why you *think* you're here.'

' "Think"?'

Sardonic, he said, 'You think you can play both hands in the game. Be a friend, while being an enemy. Mercenary ethics, *S'aranth*? You report to the Company on *t'an* Clifford. Advise the *t'an* Rachel. The *takshiriye* hears these things. With your experience of us – the Company must find you very useful. If not trustworthy.'

His feet scuffed the stone flags. I felt his presence; the warmth of the brazier. Caught off-guard and all the more angry because of it, I said, 'What else can I do?'

His reply was instant, and bitter. 'Go back eight years. Tell me *then* that restricted contact means restricted as long as it pleases Earth, and then no longer. Tell me then what your coming here meant!'

He reached out, rested one claw-nailed finger on the Pan-Oceania logo on my shoulder; a heavy pressure. I wanted to grip that hand, impress on alien skin some vestige of my pain. I couldn't speak.

Blaize said, 'I've been offworld. I've seen what the Companies do on other worlds. I've seen what they've done to *Earth*, grief of the Goddess!'

'That's what I'm trying to prevent, you stupid bastard—'

'You're Company,' he said, implacable. 'While you're in the Company, you'll do what they tell you.'

Ten years ago I would have been with you, and with Hal; discussing government and Company and what we might be able to do to cushion culture shock. And now I'm not. It hurts.

I said, 'The only way I can act as some kind of restraining influence on the Company is to stay *in* the Company. The governments can't do a thing. And maybe that means I have to do some things that aren't wholly defensible, but that's the way things are – there isn't any other way. Don't tell me you're part of the *takshiriye* and never do anything you can't justify!'

He let his hand drop back to his side. My shoulder ached.

'*S'aranth*, I've heard that from mercenaries – "my Guildhouse ordered me to do this".' Blaize rested a hand on the hilt of *harur-nilgiri*. 'The answer's easy: leave that Guildhouse. Don't say your hands are dirty but it isn't your fault! You like to think you're playing both sides – S'aranth. You're not. Like goes to like. You're offworlder. You're Company. And I was a fool, eight years ago, to think different!'

'You don't have the right to say that to me!' Then I stopped, and turned away. I stretched my hands out again to warm them at the brazier. Don't take the past away from me as well.

Why can't we all of us get back to the way we were? That's the perennial vain regret. The last time I came to the Freeport I was on the run, but at least I knew I was innocent of the accusation against me.

'*There isn't anything else I can do!*'

Somewhere voices shouted, and winches creaked; and the smell of cooking came sourly from the companion-house a few yards away. Stone was cold underfoot. I tucked my hands up under my arms and shivered.

'It's a fine profession,' Blaize Meduenin said. 'You can leave your mistakes behind you when you leave a world. No one can tie you to the reparation of error. *We can't leave.*'

I couldn't look him in the face and that made me furious.

'You're not my conscience. You don't know the world I live in, but I do, and I know how to handle it, and I don't need facile, simplistic judgements!'

His voice came quietly from the interior of the warehouse behind me. 'Christie, *you* can't use ignorance as an excuse. Not you. Goddess, I was with you from Corbek to Shiriya-Shenin; I know that you know Orthe! I'm not Haltern, I don't understand doing what's wrong for the right reasons. When you were here before—'

'You speak as though it was yesterday.'

'Yes, I do.' I heard him sigh heavily. There was the quiet rasp of metal, as he shifted his stance, from the harness of *harur*-blades. 'Grief of the Goddess, Christie, why come back? With a Company like this one? If you could stay away eight years, you should have stayed away for good.'

It was as if he spoke his thoughts aloud. Very Orthean, that merciless honesty – and I call myself human. When I put that mental distance between us, I could turn and face him: 'What you say is unforgivable—'

One word from him and I would have lashed out, but he only looked at me, that half-scarred face with a kind of innocent gravity in it. And pain. I sighed.

'I usually handle matters better than this . . . Do you remember when we found each other, here, the first time I ever came to the Freeport? You were hiring out your services from the Mercenaries Guildhouse. I've – grown used to thinking of you as the one in a morally indefensible position.'

'Do you seriously think I'm not?' He grinned, twistedly, and stepped out on to the quay. And then looked back at me. 'Because I tell you not to bring Earth technology here, not its harm, nor its benefits. I can say that for the *telestres*, the Hundred Thousand. We don't need you. I can't say it for all of Orthe – but I do, *S'aranth*, I do.'

He turned away, squinting up at the buildings and the pale daystarred sky. Because there was nothing I could say to that, because I saw no hope of response or solution, I walked away into the cold Freeport morning; walking to find Molly Rachel where she was negotiating a journey to Rakviri *telestre*.

Two hours and ten miles later, on the dirt-tracks of the Hundred Thousand, the *skurrai-jasin* swung eastwards, and I rested my arm on the carriage rail and shielded my eyes with my hand.

'That Rakviri male wouldn't say much about the old technology last night—' Molly Rachel was thoughtful '—because Cassirur Almadhera is in this church of theirs. This technophobic church. I wonder, will that matter less on a *telestre*, or more?'

'More,' I said.

The reptilian quadruped *skurrai* hissed, raising their narrow muzzles and pointed lips. Winter sun gleamed on their harness and metal-capped horns. The wooden *jasin*-carriage rocked and jolted. Open carriages are cold, the driver had bundled us in the black-and-white featherfur pelts of the *zilmei* carnivore. I fastened my coverall tighter at the throat, and flicked the temperature-control in the weave.

Molly huddled in the pelts. 'There's a point on any Restricted world, when I'd swap all my principles about cultural contamination by hi-tech for a warm seat in a groundcar . . .' And she grinned, exhilarated by the thought of possible discoveries ahead.

We drove past grey boles of *siir*-vine, thick as a man's thigh, that hugged the earth. Ahead, shapes resolved out of haze and glare.

Grey stone, white stone; buildings with flat façades, and windows that – though copiously ornamented – are no wider than slots: difficult targets for winchbow bolts. Many buildings, all linked. I looked ahead, down through long colonnades, seeing how each block was joined to the next. Rooms, halls, courtyards; pens for *marhaz* and *skurrai* . . . an interconnected warren of buildings, the whole thing the size of a village.

The *jasin* rattled into the courtyard. A great number of Ortheans were passing in and out of the buildings and yards, so we were partly concealed by the crowd. I glanced up, seeing a sky that glowed pale blue, freckled with daystars. As we dismounted from the carriage, a flock of *rashaku-bazur* rose up from the cornices of the surrounding halls, the scales on their breasts glinting, the beat of their wings like gunshots. They wheeled and flew seaward. Their cries were metallic, out-of-tune bells.

An *ashiren* came to lead the *skurrai*-carriage away. Molly turned, boots crunching on the sea-gravel that floored the yard. 'Now where – ah. That's him.'

A dark male pushed his way through the bustle. I recognized the patch-marked face of the night before.

'Haden Barris Rakviri.' He bowed. Barris, the child of Haden, of Rakviri *telestre*: so names go in the Hundred Thousand.

'*T'an* Barris,' the Pacifican woman acknowledged. Then: 'I understood you to say there was a Witchbreed-technology artifact here that we can see.'

His dark gaze flicked sideways at me, and I saw humour there. Her directness made me wince. It made him amused.

'Several artifacts,' Barris Rakviri said, 'but I doubt that I can bring you to more than one. Still, that should be sufficient to begin with, I hope?'

As a comment, it silenced Molly Rachel completely. He beckoned, and we walked towards a near entrance of the main building; walking briskly, because of the cold. Cages hung from the round-arched entrances, and in them squat lizardbeasts gripped the bars with spatulate fingers, and whistled a shrill alarm. The male Orthean glanced up, and silenced the alarm with a gesture.

'You must meet the *s'an* Rakviri,' Barris said. 'It is tradition.'

'And then—'

'And then,' he confirmed. I saw what I hadn't noticed in Morvren, that he dragged one foot; it had a slight deformity. He was not as young as I'd thought him. His mane was fine and dark, braided down the spine, where his slit-backed coat showed crystal beads in the braiding; and he carried a stick of *hanelys* wood, partly for ornament, partly (I thought) for support.

As we came to the entrance, I said, 'What's all the rush and bother here? Isn't it a bit early in Orventa to begin trade-voyages?'

'We're shipping food east to Ales-Kadareth; it's urgent, there's famine in Melkathi province.'

'Who ordered the *telestre* to do that?' Molly asked. I could see her thinking of authority-channels.

Barris halted momentarily, leaning on his stick and looking up at her. 'The Kadareth *telestre* asked us. Would your Company have to be forced to do such a thing?'

You can't translate "order" into Morvrenni without it having that implication of force. Nor, indeed, into any other Orthean language with which I'm familiar.

We passed a group of five or six Ortheans standing in an antechamber, and entered a long hall. Barris Rakviri glanced round.

'Wait here. I'll find the *s'an* Jaharien.'

Molly opened her mouth to comment, and then her attention was caught by the hall. It had the air of a place hastily abandoned; I guessed all but a few Ortheans were helping with the food-ships. A few *ashiren* were still present. They glanced up with no great curiosity.

'Lynne—'

'*Don't* say "this *telestre* is about to have an industrial revolution". Please.'

She stepped forward, feet planted squarely on the wood-tiled floor, raising her head to gaze round. Light shone on her dark features, in the silver-dusty air. She had almost the expression she'd worn in Kel Harantish.

Books, scrolls, and manuscripts lined the walls. There were low work-tables and benches the length of the hall. And there, tossed down carelessly on a hand-drawn map: an astrolabe. Next to it stood an orrery, finely made, planetary circuits corresponding to no known solar system. One low table held what might have been a powered loom, a length of *chirith-goyen* cloth spilling from it. I saw one *ashiren*, fair mane falling about its face, engaged in some machinery with cogs and pendulum; the other group of older *ashiren* had lenses mounted in a frame and were trying to focus the light from one window to burn a scrap of paper.

Molly Rachel reached out to a table, and with one finger spun a wheel: pistons moved smoothly. A spirit-powered engine, no larger than a child could carry . . . She stared up and down that winter-lit hall, and then she nodded.

'You reported something like this. That winter you spent in

472

Shiriya-Shenin, in the north. This is their custom when travelling isn't possible.'

'For Orventa, winter season. They do this – and they fight, and make poems, and plays, and have *arykei*, lovers—' Which are old memories. 'The first time I saw it, I thought "industrial revolution". And then at the end of Orventa, the spring Thaw Festival, I saw every last machine broken up, melted down . . . It's their amusement, this.'

'And the Wellhouses police it?'

You want to believe that, I thought. Because that will mean you'll be able to bribe the *telestres* with Earth tech – oh, Molly! 'The Wellkeepers couldn't make them do it if they didn't already desire to.'

Barris Rakviri reappeared, his halting footsteps easily recognizable. 'I can't find Jaharien, he may be down at the bay.'

'Then perhaps you yourself could show us the Witchbreed artifacts,' Molly Rachel said.

And in case you're wondering, t'an *Barris, that wasn't a suggestion . . .* I wanted to throw my hands up; monomaniac determination is one thing, discourtesy quite another. But Barris inclined his head urbanely, and greeted one of the younger *ashiren*, asking for *siir*-wine.

'*T'an*, I have to be a little careful. For you to see such artifacts . . . The *s'an* would not object. But to think of trading them to offworlders—' Barris gestured with his stick at the remaining Rakviri Ortheans. 'Were I Jaharien in such a case, I should fear the *telestre* naming a new *s'an*. So you see, we must be circumspect.'

'And the church?' I said.

He smiled wryly. 'Ah – the eminent Wellkeepers, the worthy Earthspeakers . . . *T'an*, they fail sometimes to perceive necessity. To learn, one must give up something. I would be willing to give, or rather trade, what Rakviri has.'

Molly frowned. I could see it puzzled her, this attitude of *telestre* Ortheans: neither technophobe nor technophile.

Some memory stirring – perhaps the implicit comparison with the Desert Coast – I said, 'And the Hexenmeister in Kasabaarde? It always seemed to me there was some influence on the Wellhouses from there.'

The 'marshflower' that dappled his skin made his expression difficult to decipher. He said, 'They say the Hexenmeister lives out the world from age to age, there in the Tower. What can he say to us, who live, and pass, and live to meet again?'

473

It was that effortless Orthean transition from material to mystic. Many things are spoken in the *telestre* that you won't hear said in the cities.

As if fumbling for a landmark, Molly Rachel said, 'Could you call the Kasabaarde settlement a political force here, as it is on the Coast?'

'No . . .' He turned as the fair-maned *ashiren* tugged at his sleeve, the child holding bowls of *siir*-wine. It spoke quietly to him: something I couldn't catch.

'Is he? I'll go, then. *T'ans*, please wait; Cerielle will bring you anything you need.' He went towards another exit, a narrow curtained archway; dragging footsteps fading. The *ashiren* remained staring up at us for a moment, and then in a comically adult manner shook its head and walked away to the group at the further table. This is the generation that has grown up with knowledge of offworlders: obviously we are no major sensation.

'What the hell—!' Molly Rachel frowned. 'Well, I suppose you did warn me. Barris . . . His attitude seems to be that what we're doing is halfway between heresy and, oh, stealing a museum exhibit . . . These people! This might be a major commercial proposition. Can't they take it seriously?'

Having drunk the hot *siir*-wine, I put the bowl on a nearby table; and we walked the length of the hall, and turned to walk back. Winter light fell through slot-windows, the pale brick walls here showing three foot thick. There were *becamil* cloth-hangings; *zilmei* pelts on the wood floor. Sounds echoed. I kept my voice low.

'There always were a few Witchbreed relics in the Hundred Thousand. But I'll tell you now, Molly, you're not going to deduce the ontological basis of Golden science from a handful of defunct toys.'

'If this is a blind alley, I still have to check it out. I know I shouldn't have got us thrown out of Kel Harantish.' Self-condemnation roughened her voice. 'That was our first chance and I handled it badly – too eager to get in. We'll have to get back there, Lynne. But, with respect, you don't know what we might find in the Hundred Thousand, with a full research team. It may not all be defunct.'

Being true, that irritated me.

'While we've got a minute,' she added, 'you've had a chance now to sound Douglas Clifford out. What can we expect from him?'

'Firm support of the status quo: keep Carrick V a Restricted world. He doesn't like multicorporates.'

'Jesus, the Service! – but I can short-circuit that, we're not obliged to have him present on all occasions.'

'It might be politic if we did. Why cause friction – until it's necessary?'

She stopped, resting her hands on the back of a couch-chair lined with the grey-and-white featherpelt of the *zilmei*. I waited.

'I'm not going to have time to attend to all the little details,' she said. 'Suppose you handle liaison between the Company and the Service, Lynne?'

Good grief, I thought. 'You know I was Service myself, once.'

'Then you'll know how their minds work.'

There was a challenge in her sudden, direct gaze. I don't appreciate amateur manipulations of my loyalty. But nor do I turn down an advantageous position when it's offered.

'Why not?' I said. 'In a strange way, it's what I've been doing, groundside, for the past four years.'

The light in that hall shone silver against black shadows, glinted on metal in one corner where a complex structure of mirrors, prisms, and lenses projected up to a skylight-dome. Scrolls lay at its foot, scribbled over with notations of star positions: the milliard stars of day and night sky.

Frustration exploded in the young woman's voice. 'How can they live like this! Like primitives!'

The Hexenmeister of Kasabaarde once said to me, *I don't wish to take away machines, only take away the desire to use them so badly*. I said, 'The *telestres* have had two and a half thousand years to think differently about technology.'

'It's ludicrous!' Caught in this momentary lull, she seethed with impatience. 'And I intend – *there* he is; at last. Lynne – '

From the far end of the hall, Barris Rakviri entered; a short male beside him; in green and white robes, that I thought must be the *s'an* Jaharien. With them—

I put a restraining hand on Molly's arm. With the two Rakviri males walked a middle-aged female Orthean, short and brown-skinned and with a curling scarlet mane: the Earthspeaker Cassirur Almadhera. The three of them slowed their pace, suiting it to the halting steps of an elderly figure, all but smothered in *zilmei* travelling coats, who walked with his arm through Cassirur's. Haltern n'ri n'suth Beth'ru-elen.

And with these two of the Morvren triumvirate walked six Ortheans in the plain robes of Wellkeepers and Earthspeakers.

CHAPTER 6

A Far-Off Cloud

A terrace, covered in with sheets of clear glass, faced southwards. Musicians played the complicated music of south Morvren, as chill and intricate as frost on a window. Noon lay white on the flat land beyond, scoured down by coastal storms to a tangled network of *siir*-vine and scrub-*hanelys*, under a powder-blue daystarred sky. The mossgrass was losing its winter brown, growing through a pale azure. Carrick's Star was warm through the glass. And the glass held also the reflection of the Orthean female who walked beside me as we leisurely paced the length of the terrace.

'You should, after all, take time to breathe,' Cassirur Almadhera said. 'None of you offworlders will do that.'

'I didn't expect to see you again so soon after last night, *t'an* Cassirur.'

Urbane as that was, I saw it provoke a flicker of humour in her; but when I glanced from her reflection to her face, it was gone.

She said, 'I hear that you offworlders have been to Kel Harantish.'

Hardly necessary to ask where she'd heard it: Douglas Clifford.

'That's no secret, *t'an*; we deal with Orthe as one world—'

'We won't trade with you.'

At that interruption, I stopped. We looked at each other. She was a flare of colour on that pale terrace: scarlet mane braided down her spine with crystal beads, green-and-gold slit-backed robe, gold studs set in the skin-webs between fingers and high-arched toes. Age hardly touched that sleek brown face, those whiteless eyes.

Dropping civility and diplomacy together (because I judged it safe to do so), I said, 'For God's sake let's sit down and talk this over. You don't strike me as someone to do the Wellhouses' dirty work for them, but I can't think why else you're here.'

'I suppose I am here for God's sake, though She'd say it was for mine . . .' Cassirur Almadhera inclined her head, and moved towards one of the long tables on the terrace, where a spirit lamp stood ready to heat *siir*-wine. Her hands were steady as she lit the flame. 'We won't trade with you for the same reason that we won't trade with the Desert Coast or the Rainbow Cities—'

'You do trade with them.'

'Nothing of *this*.' Her emphasis took in all the customs of Orventa; the group at the far end of the terrace engaged in constructing a complex mechanism that might (I thought) be a water-clock.

'I know the Hundred Thousand are under the impression only they can be trusted with even this much technology. Cassirur, tell the Wellhouses you can't use the same techniques to deal with multicorporate Companies.'

In a measured tone, she remarked, 'You don't strike me as someone to do the Company's dirty work for them, but I can't think why else you're here.'

That touched me on the raw. I'm here to act as a brake, I thought. A shock-absorber.

'Seems to me we're in a similar position.'

She did grin at that. 'Hal told me you weren't like the young one there.' She waved a hand vaguely down the terrace at another table, where Molly Rachel sat with Barris Rakviri and the *s'an* Jaharien.

'Cassirur, I'm probably more like her than I am like you. And it's her generation that represents PanOceania here on Carrick V. Co-operate a little?'

She shook her head, not in negation but in wonder; a gesture at once weary and graceful. 'But that's strange, to have one generation so different from the last.'

We're not Ortheans – who will tell you (if they speak of it) that they are born remembering all their past lives upon this Goddess's earth. I said, 'We have no past-memories, *t'an* Earthspeaker.'

Speaking her title reminded me of how unlike other Earthspeakers this woman seems. Yet as we sat on the *zilmei* pelts that covered the stone bench, breath smoking on the chill air, scenting the tubs of indoor *kazsis*-vine, I began to sense something of that odd perception that belongs with Earthspeakers and Wellkeepers.

She said, 'But you *have* past-memories, Christie. I know the look of one haunted by them, and you are.'

She was grave, leaning forward to warm her fingers at the spirit lamp; dark eyes holding a brilliant clarity.

'I . . .' Not memories of past lives, I thought wryly. Fragments of old hypno-data, possibly. 'When I was here last, we used to say that you have past-memories of past lives, and we have *dreams*—'

there was no term for it in Morvrenni '—visions of sleep. Yes, I dream. But not – haunted.'

The soft hissing of *siir*-wine as it boiled recalled me to that cold noon, and I took the metal jug and tipped hot wine into ceramic bowls. The Almadhera cupped her six-fingered hands round the bowl: that immemorial gesture of seeking warmth.

I said, 'The Wellhouses won't trade with Earth. What about the *telestres*? Will they?'

She was not to be caught by such tricks. 'All hundred thousand of them? Christie, how could I know? Still, we've had eight years' knowledge of Earth, and seen no great necessity to trade with you before.'

'That was then. This may be different.'

She leaned back against one of the metal struts that supported the terrace's glass cover. Then she trailed one claw-nailed finger down the condensation on the surface, which rang thin, high, and clear.

'Considering you're no stranger to Wellhouses, Christie, you haven't asked a question I'd expected.'

Siir-wine's heat was welcome. The pepper-spice taste carries fewer memories for me, it wasn't in season the last time I was in Morvren. And the last time I was in Morvren . . .

'I know your Wellhouses have contacts outside the Hundred Thousand, if that's what you mean. Dalzielle Kerys-Andrethe, when she was Crown, had a link – albeit tenuous – with Kasa-baarde.' I tried to judge from her expression whether I was on the right track. 'How far will the church follow the Tower's advice? And how far will the *telestres* follow the church?'

Her face showed that paradoxical mixture of awe and friendly contempt that the *telestre*-Ortheans have for Kasabaarde. 'Don't speak of the church in one breath and the *telestres* in another, we're the same. We've gone our own way, always, in the Hundred Thousand.'

Somehow the discussion had got away from me, out of my control; and that rarely happens. Cassirur Almadhera was tough, but that's my job. I thought, It shouldn't faze me like this.

'When I was in the Tower—' I broke off, meeting her eyes.

'Haltern said something of that. Few have ever been further than the inner city of Kasabaarde, but he, also, entered past that and into the Brown Tower . . . I wonder your Company doesn't go to Kasabaarde. Although you would find it no different from us,' Cassirur said thoughtfully, 'with some few relics of the Empire, but no great desire to use them. We've moved beyond the days when there could be an Empire—'

'There's no Witchbreed technology in the Tower; none, none at all!'

Her startled expression told me that I'd interrupted. There was a cold silence. I tried desperately to think of a way to smooth it over, regain that rapport struck up between us, but I couldn't formulate explanation or apology.

'You and Haltern Beth'ru-elen will know more of the Tower than I,' she said, retreating into Morvrenni's formal inflection.

I sat dumb, watching her.

I didn't know, then, what it meant, that blank confusion in my mind. I only sensed trouble, like a far-off cloud. And I didn't know that I would be diverted from simple ambition to ease culture shock on Orthe, into something far more complex and momentous. I could only look into her cool and whiteless eyes.

Distant gongs clashed. A general movement began among the Ortheans on the terrace, summoned to the kitchen-halls for the midday meal. Cassirur Almadhera nodded, and excused herself, and went to join them. I still sat, until Molly Rachel's voice recalled me; and then I rose, a little stiff with the cold, to walk towards the kitchens with her and Barris and the *s'an* Jaharien Rakviri.

Lamps hung suspended from ornamental brickwork. The kitchens were vast warrens, round-roofed brick halls warmed from the open doors of ovens, and smelling of cooking – the last dried provisions of Orventa, the first sea-harvest of spring. Several dozen Ortheans settled into this hall alone. We got curious glances, a few friendly comments, but I took no notice.

I know what's next on the agenda, I thought.

And sure enough, as that *zilmei*-swathed figure ensconced himself in a couch-chair, the half-blind bright gaze of Haltern n'ri n'suth Beth'ru-elen found me. He beckoned me across to his alcove. Even if he hadn't planned to have the Almadhera soften me up, he was much too old a hand to see me shaken and miss the opportunity to question me.

'Give you greeting,' I said, a little sardonically, and pulled the end of a bench across so that I could sit down beside him. 'Cold for travelling, isn't it? And ten miles in a *skurrai-jasin* is wonderfully bracing . . .'

He smiled, leaning back, basking in the warmth of an oven door six yards away. The windows here were roundly arched, and set with an amber glass, so that winter's pale glare was transmuted to warmth, and the light fell on his lined skin and crest-mane like a benediction. A faint and permanent tremor showed in those six-fingered hands.

He let the talk from the other tables mask his voice. 'Journeys end in—'

'Diplomat's meeting?' I suggested.

'I was about to say, in hot food and good company.' The nictitating membrane slid across his eyes, still pale and clear blue. 'Such concern with motives! Such suspicion . . . I like to travel in the company of Earthspeakers, especially when of so liberal a mind as Cassirur; and since she'd determined on visiting her Rakviri friends . . .'

'Give it a rest,' I advised. 'I may be getting old, but I *do* remember your profession in Tathcaer.'

'There's no office of Crown Messenger now; nor will be, until we've named a Crown again.'

'You haven't arrived at Midsummer-Tenyear. But you'll tell me that ceremony won't stand in your way?'

Some of the younger Rakviri brought food: *rukshi*, and bread-fungus, and the early shoots of the *hanelys*. His fingers shredded a piece of breadfungus, crumbling it to release the sharp lemony smell.

'I confess I don't clearly see how we shall deal with PanOceania,' he said. 'Christie, don't take it amiss if I heartily wish you gone – all of you.'

I made an attempt to look mortally offended, and he chuckled; a thin, asthmatic sound. Then, more seriously, he said, 'I do conceive of a future when, since we can't be manipulated, the Company may leave us. To do anything else under present circumstances, you would have to use force. And if young Rachel is a reliable clue, that would require some very concrete evidence before PanOceania would risk it.'

'And perhaps not even then.' I took some of the breadfungus. 'Which presupposes we won't find concrete evidence.'

'Indeed it does. You presuppose, however, that there's something to find.'

'Indeed I do . . .'

Such half-humorous, half-bitter fencing is what I miss among groundsiders, on Earth; to come back to it now is to enter the element natural to me. But like any *ochmir* player, one can prize the game more than the conclusion. That's always a mistake.

'Well, we have our own business,' the old male said philosophically. 'The Coast is troublesome again, and, having no *T'Ans* nor *takshiriye*, we must make the best of that and send some of our Freeporters to talk with them. In the spring, to Kasabaarde.'

'There's been fighting with the Coast?'

480

'The last few years have seen sea-raids on the Melkathi *telestres*, and the city Ales-Kadareth, and on trading ships on the Inner Sea.'

His bird-bright eyes flicked up; the glance aware of names from the past: Ales-Kadareth, Melkathi . . .

Now I could look across and see Molly Rachel talking with Cassirur Almadhera. The red-maned Orthean's head went back, an unrestrained laugh sounding above the general noise; Molly addressed some remark to the *s'an* Jaharien, and she and both of them laughed again.

'Hal, if we're talking about wishes, I'd wish to have the situation as it was ten years ago: nothing demanded of Orthe, nothing we wanted.'

Some sudden perception made me see this for what it was, a lull, paradisiacal by its very ordinariness. We won't talk so easily again, I thought. What I do here, now, supersedes what I did then. And so I tried to imprint on memory those Orthean faces, the bright robes, the rich food; Molly Rachel the centre of attention, all wit and good humour; and the old male with me, Haltern Beth'ru-elen, decade-old memories round us like a benevolent haunting.

'It troubles you to be here,' he said.

'I'm here because you need someone who can see your interests as well as ours.'

'Which, of course, you don't trust any but Lynne de Lisle Christie to perceive . . .'

That was so like Molly Rachel's opinion, and so accurate, that I winced. It may be vanity, I thought; does that make it any the less true?

'I'll tell you something, Hal. Molly Rachel doesn't know how to deal with the Hundred Thousand – but she doesn't *have* to know. The Companies aren't under any necessity to understand alien worlds. They don't need to. Come a little way to meet us. Or you'll get steamrollered.'

The metaphor I used was not quite that one, but the inference was equally plain. Haltern rubbed at his half-covered eyes; and blinked.

'Threats?'

'Hal, if in your advanced state of wisdom and contemplation, you fail to recognize a friendly warning—'

He spluttered a little, that old male; and the light shifted on his winterscale skin as he smiled. The great arches here were open to the cloisters outside, so we sat between oven-heat and frost-sharp air; and the scent drifted in of *hanelys* and *siir* and the warm musk of *skurrai*.

481

'Rakviri is a beautiful *telestre*,' Haltern said. 'My eyes aren't good enough now, but you may have noticed: from the south terrace you can see the beginning of the Rasrhe-y-Meluur.'

That great pylon, soft blue against a pale blue sky, almost lost. Bridging two continents: ghost-image of that past Empire.

'We're not the Coast,' he added, following the connection. 'We don't scratch out a living between rock and bitter sea. You have no – what's a suitably technological metaphor? No lever, to move us all with. Now on the Coast it's the water of the canals, and that lever's been held for two thousand years by the Harantish Witch-breed; do you contemplate taking it from them? I confess I would, were I PanOceania, which the Goddess forbid.'

The entertainment value of seeing Haltern n'ri n'suth Beth'ru-elen play at devout old alien, laboriously reinventing the metaphors of a technological society, is high. If entirely unconvincing. I heard what he said: *Go away*, and *We have negotiations in progress with the Coast, do what you like with Kel Harantish*. And I wished that I had access to his memory, instead of PanOceania's data-nets.

'You could make an argument for there being a lever to the Hundred Thousand,' I said. 'The anti-technology ethic. And the Wellhouses being in control of it. For example, *you* know the *T'An Suthai-Telestre* spoke to us of them and Kasabaarde—'

What curiosity can gnaw a man, even (or especially) a man like Haltern, so long used to knowing the secret side of all events? He said, 'You know more of Kasabaarde's influence than I do – and you an offworlder. You know more of the Tower.'

'The Tower had enough influence to contact me, sight unseen, that winter in Shiriya-Shenin—'

It's slipping, I thought; I'm losing it again: why?

A smell issued from one of the nearby alcoves, where slaughtered carcasses were hung up to drain. Until now mere sensory background, now with that thought, that blood, memory within an instant became concrete—

Spring twilight fills the Crystal Hall in Shiriya-Shenin, the quartz windows gleaming. The Andrethe of Peir-Dadeni has her back to me, sitting in a chair facing one of the dying fires.

'Excuse me, Excellence . . .'

She is leaning back, one fat arm over the side of the chair. Asleep. As I step round her, over the dappled furs, the spring light shines on her dark face and red-and-white robe. Her fingers hold reflected red firelight, streaming on the furs and stone floor.

The smell—

Not a red robe. A white robe, sopping red from shoulder to lap to hem. The stink of blood and faeces. Blood dripping from her curved fingers. Her

open unveiled eyes stare at me. Jammed under her chin, amid rolls of
flesh, a knife-handle keeps her head back—

Nausea: more acute than I thought memory could cause.

You should thank God for Kasabaarde, I thought; Lynne, if the Tower hadn't cleared you of the Andrethe's murder . . . Dear God: old memories!

As if his memory paralleled mine, Haltern reached across to rest a hand on my arm. 'That was a bad time for us all.'

'Are you certain Kasabaarde isn't a lever? Don't forget, I've proof of how highly the Hundred Thousand regards the Hexenmeister's information. *You* believed it instantly when he told you I hadn't killed Kanta Andrethe.'

'To begin with, I know Lynne Christie.' His warmth metamorphosed into curiosity. 'And I have often wished I had all the Kasabaarde traders to bring *me* intelligence of what passes in the world, as the Tower has. That's not all the story, though, is it? The Hexenmeister spoke as if—'

'As if he was there,' I said.

'And yet there's no memory or past-memory of the Hexenmeister ever leaving the Tower.'

'That's the truth,' I said. 'And very wise: if I had what's in there, *I'd* stay in the Tower. It must be the most securely defended structure on two continents—'

' "What's in there"?'

'What?'

'I have often wondered,' he said.

'I don't understand.'

If he laughed, it was at himself. 'Because you and I have both faced that serially-immortal Hexenmeister . . . and while Hexenmeisters live and die, there's but one same Hexenmeister in the tower; my memory—' he gave it the inflection that included memory of past lives '—tells me this is so. But not why. Christie, you know my curiosity!'

'Hal, I really don't understand what you're talking about.'

He frowned, and his claw-nailed hand closed over mine as if he were trying to reassure or comfort me.

'If it troubles you so much, I'll say no more. I'd thought, since you spent time within the Tower, and left it so changed, that you might have spoken often enough with the Hexenmeister to gain some knowledge I don't have. Don't be distressed.'

'I don't know what you mean.'

'Christie—'

I stood and walked across to where Molly Rachel sat among the uncleared bowls and platters, temporarily separated from Cassirur and the Rakviri. She looked up as I approached. A comlink was open in her palm.

'What have you been saying to the Beth'ru-elen?' Molly asked, glancing across at the place I'd just left. 'He's not too happy about it.'

When I concentrated, I could stop that fine perceptible shake in my hands. I looked back at Hal. No memory of a farewell – did I really do that? I thought. Did I just stand up and *go*?

I would have returned, but Cassirur Almadhera slipped into that seat and began talking quietly with the Beth'ru-elen.

'I've been trying to get through to Morvren Freeport,' Molly said, replacing the comlink at her belt. 'Communications are going to be erratic here, to say the least of it . . . David Osaka says the shuttles are coming down from the orbiter.'

Whatever reaction I have to being back on Orthe, whatever version of hypno-psychosis or offworld syndrome this is, it shouldn't be allowed to affect my job. With that thought, it was as if my mind returned to a sharp focus. I thought, I'll make an appointment to see the Psych people sometime this week. Until then, I'll manage.

'What about the Witchbreed artifact here?'

Molly nodded. 'That's priority. Sometime over the next couple of hours, we *must* find a way to talk to Barris Rakviri on his own.'

CHAPTER 7

Heirs of an Empire
Long Passed Away

With that new mental clarity came an appreciation: *we're close to being out-manoeuvred here.* With no *T'An Suthai-Telestre* or *T'Ans* now, it's the Wellhouses that watch offworlders – and they don't want Earth tech at all. And the *rashaku*-relay will have taken the news out . . .

'How does this sound? I'll talk to *s'an* Jaharien,' I said. 'For one thing, it might give you a chance to get to Barris.'

'And?' the Pacifican woman prompted.

The kitchen-halls began to smell stale with old cooking. Light fell through amber glass on to the few Ortheans left drinking *siir*-wine and talking. Not that they ignore offworlders, precisely; it's a kind of self-sufficiency they possess.

'And – I might be able to persuade Jaharien. I don't know. Because my name carries weight here?' I shrugged. 'Molly, understand me. I want you to see, as soon as possible, that nothing here in the Hundred Thousand is useful to the Company.'

The black woman rose from the chair in one smooth movement. Something tireless in her, both physical and mental.

'You'll help because that's your job. If that means using the *S'aranth* name, then do it.' Her gaze was not on me, but searching for Barris. She said, 'You're as much a part of the Company as I am.'

Kites flew on the cold wind; yellow, scarlet, and viridian against the daystarred sky. Streamers fluttered. The glittering curves of the glass terrace formed a looming backdrop to all these small courtyards. I walked with the *s'an* Jaharien beside white walls, hearing the hiss of penned *skurrai* and the larger *marhaz*. The cold kept me alert – it was that hour in early afternoon when I needed sleep.

Even in spring, Orthe has too many daylight hours for human comfort.

'*S'an* Jaharien . . . your *telestre* isn't much impressed by offworlders, is it? But then, I suppose you've had time to get used to us.'

'Ask instead, how many of us are capable of seeing what it means to have offworlders here.' He spoke sardonically, with the slurred Morvrenni river-dialect. I guessed from his broad shoulders and rope-scarred hands that he sailed either Ai River ships or coastal *jath-rai*.

'Perhaps you underestimate the people here.'

'*T'an*, perhaps I do.' The wind blew his short, unbraided mane forward, and he put it back with one claw-nailed hand. 'Barris tells me – he is my *arykei*, and should know – he tells me I think no other but myself capable. And that's why I am *s'an*. And that's why I see *s'aranthi* here, and doubt our wisdom. Your *t'an* Molly Rachel, she sees nothing but her desire.'

'That I'll admit is true.'

Sea gravel crunched underfoot as we walked down the colonnade, and the kites made bright curves in the alien sunlight. Frost still lay in the shadow of the gate-arch, where we passed through into another courtyard. I shivered. And wondered what angle of attack to try next.

'The Beth'ru-elen speaks of you,' Jaharien said suddenly. 'Is it true – *are* you that Christie, Christie *S'aranth*?'

His voice was wiped momentarily clear of the cynicism that seemed his natural idiom.

'I'm Christie,' I said.

His head turned towards me. I saw the slow glide of nictitating membrane: a gaze darker (and somehow deeper) in those unveiled, alien eyes. The edge of his robe hissed on the gravel path as we walked.

'When Barris told me, I called him a liar; the *S'aranth*—' Jaharien stopped abruptly. One six-fingered hand sought the hilt of *harur-nilgiri*, as if for comfort. Now, on those alien features, I could recognize a kind of awe. Even though I'd been counting on something like it, it disturbed me.

Words came from him in a spate: 'So many Orventa tales of you! – that year, that first year; the Crown, Suthafiori; Kanta Andrethe, and Wellkeeper Arad, and Sulis SuBannasen—'

Even in that unguarded enthusiasm, he left out the name of Orhlandis.

'—and the first meeting with offworlders; you and your kin in Tathcaer—!' He shook his dark-maned head, laughed at his own

486

capacity for being impressed. 'Pardon, *t'an*. You must have heard this often since you came back to us.'

Enough to conceive of it as an influence, that *S'aranth* name. Nonetheless, I felt embarrassed. 'There were a lot of us on that first contact team, not just me.'

'But you were the first to come to the *telestres*.'

We walked on. It was too cold to stand and talk. There was a soft discordancy: the clash of bright *harur*-blades belted at his hip.

'I went to *telestres* and Wellhouses,' I carefully reminded him.

'Corbek-in-Roehmonde. The tale is that the Wellkeeper there had you imprisoned, but you escaped to Shiriya-Shenin and had him brought to trial.'

I heard no resentment in Jaharien's voice. No indication that he would support church against offworlders, regardless.

'And does Cassirur Almadhera talk about the *S'aranth*, too?' I asked. 'I don't have to wonder why an Earthspeaker's in Rakviri, do I? Jaharien, I'll say something I shouldn't, but it's for my peace of mind . . . what *will* it do to the Hundred Thousand if we trade with you for Witchbreed technology?'

Jaharien Rakviri had an expression almost of delight. This dark male, a handful of years younger than I; looking at me wide-eyed as any *ashiren*.

'I'd always thought Christie *S'aranth* would ask such a question. *T'an*, pardon me; you don't need to ask that, you know already. It won't do anything to the Hundred Thousand. No more than burning Orventa's machines at Spring Thaw Festival, and building them again next winter.'

His voice had triumph in it. With some self-disgust at the manipulation, I thought, I've obviously lived up to the public image. Does the mask of Christie *S'aranth* still fit? What have they made my name into while I've been away?

Jaharien went on impetuously: 'Earthspeakers, even Cassirur; they're overcautious. You and *t'an* Rachel . . . I think you understand us. Barris was right. There can be no great harm in this. If I allowed it, and didn't believe it safe – I should deserve to have the *telestre* name another *s'an* in place of me.'

I glanced across at his unguarded expression. It's a little late to feel – what? Ashamed? *Don't make me into something I'm not.* Don't let me persuade you against your judgement. I feel as though I'm here on false pretences.

'You know the telestres,' Jaharien added. 'I have some confidence in my powers of judgement, *t'an*. And in yours.'

We turned a corner, passing under another arch, returning towards the crystal façade of the great terrace. My fingers were white with the cold. Carrick's Star blazed.

Against all professional instinct, knowing it might lose me what I'd just gained, I had to protest. 'For all you've heard about the *S'aranth*, I . . . oh, I'd have made a better anthropologist than diplomat; I did better work up in the Barrens than I ever did in the Hundred Thousand *telestres*. In Melkathi I failed – but if you know that story, *s'an* Jaharien, you know how it ended.'

'*S'aranth*, Rakviri isn't Orhlandis.'

He pronounced the name of that Melkathi *telestre* with a kind of arrogant condescension. What I meant for honesty, he took as self-deprecation. No way to get rid of that *S'aranth* name.

As we came under the bright reflections of the terrace, I thought, I've made you trust me. All the easier because you're arrogant, and being impressed catches you off-guard. Christie *S'aranth*.

For a long, vertiginous moment, I wanted to turn him against me. If *S'aranth* is the key to the lock, I don't want to go through the door.

Molly Rachel said, *You're as much a part of the Company as I am.*

'Come with me,' Jaharien said. 'We'll find Barris, and your *t'an* Rachel. I'll take you to where we keep the relics of the Golden Witchbreed.'

I said nothing. I followed him inside.

Somehow, although I know the Orthean mind, I expected more concealment. But Jaharien led us through the sprawling *telestre*-house to the unguarded entrance of a small hall, the ground floor of an octagonal tower.

'Here?' I said.

Jaharien pushed the bead-curtain aside. Barris Rakviri's cane tapped on the echoing stone floor as he went in. Molly Rachel followed, gazing up at the glass mosaic ceiling, in this room where the air smelled of dust and the light is always pale.

'What about the Earthspeaker Cassirur?' I asked, letting the curtain fall back into place behind me.

The Pacifican woman gave neither of them the chance to reply. '*S'an*, you said – functional relics.'

A look went between the two Orthean males, the opaque glance of some shared past-memory. Barris small and thin, leaning on the *hanelys* stick; and the burly Jaharien at his shoulder. Both dark-maned, pale-skinned; in heavy Morvrenni robes.

'How long has Rakviri kept Witchbreed relics?' I asked.

'There was a lost time after the Empire fell. Out of it came the *telestres*. Since then, *t'an S'aranth*.' Jaharien's membraned gaze was blind with two millennia.

In this octagonal room, one wall held the entrance, another an embrasured window; and all the others deep alcoves, set back into the masonry. I could hear the voices of *ashiren* in the courtyard outside.

Molly, impatient, said, 'Then can we *see*—'

Jaharien's gaze cleared. Our eyes met. I saw in him the first intimations of doubt. He put one claw-nailed hand on Barris's shoulder; spoke equally to the younger Orthean male and to Molly Rachel: 'This isn't to be done lightly. The *telestres* . . . offworlder, we don't forget. In four days, at the Festival of the Wells, we'll burn the devices created through Orventa. *This is why.*'

Barris moved away, rejecting the older male's urgency. The marshflower dapples made a sneer of his expression. He leaned the *hanelys* stick against the wall, and went to the nearest alcove, which stood some three feet above floor level. I saw how he tugged his dark *becamil* over-robe about himself, as if he felt cold.

Without looking back at us, he said, 'We're free of the Empire. There are none of the Golden Witchbreed now but in past-memory. Nor will we ever become as they.'

For all her mask of professionalism, Molly Rachel's long-fingered hands were trembling. I thought I felt something of the cold that touched the Rakviri.

Since the Witchbreed Empire fell . . .

We are not Witchbreed, said that nameless Voice in Kel Harantish. *That is what superstitious northern barbarians call us. We are the Golden.*

Since the Golden Empire fell, and all its cities: Simmerath, aKirrik, Archonys (that brilliant beating heart of Empire); since that great alien culture fell, and all its works . . .

'I have no memory to help me in this,' Barris said. There was something bitter in his tone. 'The Empire didn't allow its slave races such knowledge.' The alcove held copper and glass, woven into a fine mesh cage; and the patchmarked Orthean reached into small ceramic pots, touching the metal with several substances.

'*Ashiren*.' Barris turned his head; that dark gaze like a blow. 'We're *ashiren*, playing in the ruins. The Witchbreed could do this merely by bending their will to it, and I . . . *S'aranth*, I play *ashiren*-games with herbs and metal ore.'

He stepped aside, and I saw that the glass and copper mesh cage enclosed a globe of *chiruzeth*. Was it a trick of light, or was that blue-grey substance faintly luminous?

No illusion. A faint light, the blue-pink colour of lightning. Molly's hand closed over my arm.

'Bel-Kurick,' she whispered. Remembering the haggard face of Dannor bel-Kurick, Emperor-in-Exile, in Kel Harantish. But this light was faint, fading . . .

cold high walls, webbed with darkness; the smell of dust, and musk, and the stale air—

'I thought, in Kel Harantish, one responds to it with more than just visual perception.' She spoke in Sino-Anglic, in a tone of suppressed excitement. 'Did you feel it? Like a touch, a smell. It's some pan-spectrum broadcast, not just visible light.'

Revulsion touched me. 'If we can perceive it, it might damage us.'

She was oblivious. 'If we can perceive it, we might be able to understand it. Lynne, we might!'

The *chiruzeth* globe's colour faded to an inert blue-grey. I almost wanted to touch the masonry of the alcove and feel if the light had *stained* it – absurd. But I feel what makes Ortheans fear Witchbreed relics. The echo of a dead power. And is this what I thought I could keep the Company away from?

'It's necessary!' Barris's voice rose, and he stepped back, glaring at the older male. Jaharien paused.

'If you must,' he said finally. Jaharien looked at me, then. More *s'an* Rakviri than admirer of the *S'aranth*. Here where Witchbreed relics were more than a name, I could see him realize how I'd used the public legend. His expression was cold.

The next alcove held a shallow bowl, wider round than human arms could span. Roughcast iron, still jagged here and there from the forge, and with a scar of orange rust on one curve. Barris Rakviri reached up to a niche in the back of the alcove, repeating his first procedure, and another sphere-light began to glow and illuminate the cold masonry.

'Jesus!' Molly said loudly. I echoed her, involuntarily.

What I had taken to be fragments of *chiruzeth* in the iron bowl were not broken pieces. The blue-grey substance *flowed*. A viscous movement began wherever that lilac-and-blue illumination fell on the *chiruzeth*, and an answering translucent depth gleamed in that substance that moved with the tropism of plants, of living matter. The mass moved. The iron in the bowl's scarred interior flaked away, turning to brown-and-orange rust, and decaying into the very air . . .

'Energy transfer,' Molly whispered. 'Christ, will you look at that!' There was no fear in her voice. Wonder, greed, joy; but no terror.

The *chiruzeth* darkened to a dull grey; began to build itself up in complex shapes. All breathing ceased, and all sound. When the device it formed stood complete, part solid, part moving to the pulse of that strange energy, only the lace-like shell of an iron bowl remained.

In Sino-Anglic Molly said, 'You told us they were soft-sciencers, the Witchbreed. Look at it . . . What would you call it? Analogue-DNA? Living crystal?'

'Gene-sculpting?' I suggested. Still lost, still awed.

'Something between living and inanimate tissue.' Her eyes shone.

'If they patterned the structure – genes, viruses – and then . . .' Then some transfer of will, that Ortheans now could only mimic by chemical or biological stimulus-triggers.

Molly leaned closer to the relic. The dimensions of it twisted the eye. I saw curves and angles and solids within that polyhedral shape, but I didn't know what they *meant*. And so perhaps I didn't truly see them.

'How does it function?' she asked.

'You mean, will it function for *s'aranthi*?' Jaharien was leaning against the door-arch, idly keeping watch. 'I do believe it might – you have a persuasive manner, you offworlders.'

That casual tone held black irony. I expected it: still it made me uncomfortable.

Barris Rakviri, oblivious to what Jaharien implied, said, 'It holds images of the time of the Empire.'

I thought, I'm not afraid of what it could show me. Witchbreed cities: cyclopean architecture that, for all the myriad sphere-lights, was never more than one-tenth illuminated; sky-flyers, scent-fountains, metalmesh cloth. Nor do I fear the sight of the Witchbreed, those long-dead faces with coin-gold eyes. Ten years ago I looked on the millennially-old image of Santhendor'lin-sandru, called Phoenix Emperor and Last Emperor . . .

But I am afraid of what unshielded exposure to alien technology might do to me.

'We'll trade for it as it stands,' Molly Rachel said. She tucked her hands under the belt of her coveralls. In Sino-Anglic she added, 'I'm having nothing to do with that outside laboratory conditions.'

'That's the first sensible thing you've said since we came here.'

It was the alteration in her expression that warned me, an instant before all else was utterly changed.

Instead of light, the *chiruzeth* device radiated blindness; a blindness as brilliant as forked lightning. Where it fell on my skin, it had a velvet touch. A scent filled the air: nothing ever known before.

'Stop this—'

As if I could perceive with some sense that was not sight, I saw Molly Rachel, Jaharien, Barris Rakviri. We moved through a vast chamber. No knowing how great: only the age of it was a weight, a pressure. Walked at a slow pace, bearing a burden . . .

Metalcloth robes slide with a dull hiss over a chiruzeth floor. The air is burningly chill. Sphere-lights illumine only the base of cyclopean pillars, carved with patterns that are intricate, stylized or naturalistic variations on one theme only: the death's-head . . .

'———— ——— ————— —————'

Molly's voice, chanting. Language incomprehensible. She walks on bare high-arched feet. Her mane is a pale cloud of flame. All the dimensions of bone and muscle subtly wrong: wrong as the skin that has the sheen and depth of gold. Her robe is patchwork enamel, black-and-white. She paces slowly. In her arms she cradles a cup, a globe, a ragged staff.

Her eyes are yellow gold.

Nightmare, this movement that cannot be stopped, as we pace towards the darkness ahead. A greater darkness, visible negation, anti-light.

'———— ——— —— ————————— ——'

'—— ————————— —— ——— ————'

Jaharien paces in hooded robes all the colours of sunset. His gold-skinned hands outstretched: in one a twin-bladed sword, in the other some deadly construct of chiruzeth and onyx and gold.

Behind him, Barris moves at a slow processional pace, his arms raised to carry a bier. Whitefire mane, yellow eyes. My shoulder aches to the same burden. My mouth moves to the same incomprehensible chant.

'———— ——— ————— —————'

'———— ——— ———————— ——'

The burden set down where a circle of thrones stand on a dais. Our chant in many voices passes from throne to throne. Over, in, around us: that brilliant blackness.

The burden set down: a slender alien body, pale as ice against the dark: a woman of the Witchbreed. Gold skin blotched with pus-yellow, blue-green: the colours of corruption. Lowering that burden, soft and heavy in my hands, to a raised slab of chiruzeth.

'——— —— ————— ———'

'———————— ————————— ———'

'——— —— ————— ———'

The chant continues. Celebrants, we stand. There is a knife on the chiruzeth, at the feet of the corpse. I see on alien lineaments the stirring of ritual appetites. Whose hand will lift the knife; whose hand will cut and divide the flesh?

Surrounded by these faces: faces of the imperial Golden bloodline: she who stands beside me, they who flank the body; even (discernible yet in corruption) that dead face: gold skin, white mane, and coin-gold yellow eyes.

That radiant shadow working on me, like a splinter of metal working inward to the heart: what realization might come when it pierces? Death's bright shadow—

—gone from that pale octagonal room. Sunlight shone on the human face of Molly Rachel, on the two Rakviri males. The masonry of the wall was cold under my hands, where I leaned back for support. And the most banal scent possible brought the world back to me: the pepper-spice odour of *siir*-wine.

I thrust images out of my mind, and, determined to take some initiative, managed to say, 'Give you greeting, *t'an* Earthspeaker,' to the Orthean woman standing in the doorway. She held back the coin-curtain with one hand; in the other she carried a jug and bowls. Scarlet mane, green slit-backed robe.

'Trouble?' asked Cassirur Almadhera, letting the curtain fall behind her as she entered. She was encumbered by the jug and bowls, and put them down on a low table by the door. 'Hal thought he or I could find you, and I thought you might need *siir*-wine—'

Without more than a glance, she gestured with one claw-nailed hand. The *chiruzeth* device lost energy. In moments, it was inert, blue-grey; could have been nothing more than some eye-twisting nightmare sculpture.

Earthspeaker, part of me thought; and another sceptic voice, barely recovering wit to think, said, Showmanship. She waited outside until it had – what? – finished its cycle, gone quiescent? And then she made an entrance.

'*S'an* Jaharien,' she acknowledged. 'I've just met with Mezidon, she's looking for you. Some problem with loading the food-ships, I believe.'

The burly male looked across the room at me. Traces of shock and revulsion remained in his expression, but what I chiefly saw was an odd kind of satisfaction. That offworlders had been shown Witchbreed technology? That the experience had left one of us, at least, shit-scared? That experience of trauma—

Whose hand will take the knife, under that bright shadow?

When he saw me then, what did he see?

'Thank you, *t'an* Earthspeaker.' Jaharien turned and left the room, his footsteps echoing. Barris looked as though he wanted to speak, but only grasped his *hanelys* cane and limped after the *s'an*.

Cassirur said quietly, 'Look to your friend, Christie.'

Molly Rachel still stood balanced lightly on the balls of her feet, eyes fixed on a non-existent horizon. The flat, dark features were distorted, as though she squinted against some light.

'Is that *siir*? If you give—' Finding that an insistent gentle pressure induced her to move, I steered her to the low table, and took the bowl that Cassirur held up. 'Molly, can you drink? Try.'

She drank quite naturally, wiped that long-angled wrist across her mouth and put the bowl down, and then caught at the edge of the table.

'Lynne—'

Cassirur, having almost to stand on tiptoe, brushed black curls aside to touch the woman's brow. Molly pushed her hand away. The Earthspeaker nodded. 'You'll manage. *T'an* Christie . . .' Both her hands gripped my shoulders, fingers covering too wide a span for human body-instincts. Then the nictitating membrane slid back from her eyes.

'I see an old tale's true,' she said wryly. 'You have been in Her Wellhouses, and marked for Her, and She has received your name. Count yourself lucky, *S'aranth*. It could have been much worse.'

Molly Rachel rubbed her hands across her face. Then she let her hands fall and I saw the quite unconscious check: comlink, CAS-IV, wristlink-medicall. 'I don't like mysticism.'

'I say only that Christie's been marked with the water of the Well of the Goddess.'

In Sino-Anglic, the Pacifican woman said, 'Superstitious barbarians!'

The Almadhera shook back the sleeves of her robe, and began to pour more *siir*-wine. I saw those whiteless brown eyes were full of laughter.

'Not barbarians, *t'an* Rachel, surely? We've treated you with all hospitality. As for superstitions . . .'

'Please.' Molly Rachel shook her head. '*T'an* Cassirur, forgive me; I don't think I know what I'm saying.'

'As for superstitions, to be marked for the Goddess means only that we meet, and part, and meet again; and do not forget.'

Molly ignored that. 'It's all mysticism. It's technology I'm concerned with.'

'*T'an* Rachel, when I speak of the Goddess it embarrasses you.'

'Oh, I . . .' Molly shifted her stance. 'The way it is on our reports, your Kerys Founder set up the church after the Empire fell, so that no technology would ever be allowed into the *telestres*.'

'And you will find it reported also, I think, how the mystic, Beth'ru-elen *Ashirenin*, came to find that lie a truth?'

I recall that Hal's *telestre* is said to have been founded by that remarkable Beth'ru-elen, who made a genuine religion from what began as a politic philosophy.

Molly Rachel crossed the room to look at the *chiruzeth* artifact: the congeries of globes, solids, lines, curves, angles. 'Technology isn't good or evil. Only what it's used for can be that. And if the Witchbreed were insane enough to make a technological society into some barbaric, disgusting, cult-ridden—'

She broke off, nodded abruptly to Cassirur, and said, 'I must talk to Barris and Jaharien. Excuse me.'

In the silence after the curtain clashed behind her, Cassirur Almadhera said, 'One forgets. At her age . . . yes, it would frighten her. We, on the other hand—'

Image: figures filled with light too bright to look on, phosphorus-brilliant; that vulture-feast and then a transformation . . .

'It frightened *me*. It still does. I don't comprehend it.'

In repose, her features began to show their age. The Orthean woman said, 'Don't you recognize it? Or is it too strange? They fell in love with that bright shadow, Death.'

'Cassirur—'

'And it frightens me, Christie, because it is so akin to Her realm; Her fire that permeates this world like breath, Her fire made flesh in we who meet, and part, and meet again; and do not forget. But for the Golden there was nothing but this world. And so, imagining some final cessation, they worshipped it. To be out of the world, to be nothing—'

In her voice, I heard the beat of that litany of death; those untranslatable words echoed in the cadences of her speech. I took a bowl of *siir*-wine and drank, and fumbled as I set it down, spilling the green liquid as the ceramic crashed to splinters on the stone floor.

'I'm sorry; I feel – I'm not well—'

She was businesslike, abruptly all Earthspeaker. 'Is it with you still? Speak it aloud, then. You need to. Those of us who remember such things, we need to speak of them.'

A solid truth: might not that language, left unrecognized, control; like a dream forgotten but never resolved?

'To be out of the world . . .'

I picked up the litany, straining for words, knowing how far I failed: 'To go into that bright shadow, to seize on nothingness; willing to leap into the abyss – to love it more than life. Not to reject Her, but to love the bright annihilation *more* than Her. To be hollow with the longing for it. And burn all up in one final self-consummation . . .'

'More,' Cassirur demanded.

'The highest achievement: to reach after it, the only voice made incarnate flesh; to praise annihilation – pain that becomes joy, as cold can seem to burn. Holding it all for one instant within mortal compass, a glory of annihilation . . . Go willingly, joyfully, to meet it; consumed in that brilliance – to choose that bright shadow Death and die, and go into utter nothing . . .'

And it was true, to voice it was to divest it of its splendour. If only because I'm so bad at it, I thought; and then I could relax, even laugh with the Orthean woman.

'I don't have the words – I'm an empath, you need a poet.'

She put back tendrils of mane from her angled brown face, the wisps scarlet against her claw-nails. Her smile faded. 'That's the mere image of the Golden Witchbreed. What would you do if you had our living memory? The slavery of millennia, to *that*.' Passion roughened her voice on the last word.

And strangely enough, it was that that restored the human perspective to me. There are enough problems in the present, now I know for certain there is technology here that the Company will want. I stretched, fingers in the small of my back; and then shrugged. 'It's in the past, Cassirur. It *is* only an image. Will it hurt Rakviri to be rid of it? Trade with PanOceania won't make the Hundred Thousand into another Golden Empire, I know that as well as you do.'

'Do you want me to reassure you, Christie?'

'I wish *somebody* would.'

She chuckled at that, some release of tension visible in the line of arm and shoulder and high-arched ribs. 'Ah . . . It's bad that these matters divide us. We could have been friends, you and I.'

'Are we enemies, then?'

In the Freeport, in that room crowded with the *takshiriye*, she had seemed an Earthspeaker; here, she seemed all politician. One of those who have always to yearn towards the different parts of their divided natures.

'I *fear* the Golden Witchbreed. That Rachel-*ashiren* may be right; I'm nothing but superstitious. Christie, I fear them, whatever name they come under.'

'I'll talk to you again,' I offered. 'If you'll speak with me. Cassirur, we need goodwill on either side. Whatever happens.'

She briefly gripped my hands, her skin warm and dry. 'You have that . . . I must go. It's not in my interests to let your Rachel talk too long alone with Barris and the *s'an* Rakviri, is it?' And she gave me a grin that dropped ten years off her age, and strode out.

Earthspeaker, *s'an*, Wellkeeper, *takshiriye* . . .

The *chiruzeth* artifact gleamed in the depths of the alcove, and for a moment I couldn't think of the manipulations of influence, or of what assistance PanOceania might need; how near or far we might be from a trade agreement. That pale octagonal room was cold, and the alcove held the only shadow.

A coldness: a bright burning shadow . . .

And Cassirur Almadhera doesn't fear it because it's repugnant to her. She fears it for the same reason that momentarily overpowered me: that the bright shadow is so easy to look upon and love.

PART TWO

CHAPTER 8

War Damage

Carrick's Star was setting in all the colours of frost and fire when I at last brought Barris Rakviri, alone, to the great terrace. Molly Rachel turned from staring out through the curved shells of glass. Some disquiet showed in her expression. She put it from her.

'Do we have an agreement?'

'We've got a price,' I said. 'Knowledge.'

The Pacifican woman looked at Barris, his pale skin warm in the citrine light. Her brows raised. 'What do you want to know?'

'Everything,' Barris Rakviri said.

There was an intensity in his tone that shocked me. I am not used to hearing such need in any Orthean voice; it belongs to races who have no assurance of reincarnation.

Molly said, 'I'm not sure I understand.'

'He wants access to the data-nets. Unrestricted access.'

The terrace was all but deserted now. A temporary, hard-won privacy. Somewhere towards the far end, a musician fingered some intricate, cold song. Molly Rachel's gaze returned to Barris, that small and dark-maned male, whose chemical-stained hands were clasped atop the *hanelys* stick on which he leaned.

'Good God, the things these people hear about . . .' She went from Sino-Anglic to Morvrenni: '*T'an*, if you want to learn about the inhabited worlds, you could apply to leave Orthe.'

A tone of condescension came into her voice. 'Yours is one of the species that suffers offworld syndrome, I know; but you could have a short time—'

'Be fair,' I said, 'I've known humans have offworld syndrome too.'

She looked at me thoughtfully. I put it down, then, to my being defensive about Ortheans.

The dark male said, 'Does it matter what you call it, *t'an*? We live, under Her sky. We are part of Her, and we cannot live away from Her.'

501

According to records, there have been eighty-seven Ortheans who, unofficially, and at one time or another over the past ten years, have been offworld. Of those eighty-seven, sixty-eight returned to Orthe within a half-year – the unanimity is almost frightening. But then the other nineteen . . . the other nineteen *died*. Not by illness, or accident. Not even by their own hand. But died like feral animals that can't live out of the wild.

The Pacifican woman said, 'Some of your people have lived offworld.'

'For a very short time, *t'an* Rachel. I need to know more than I could learn that way.'

'I'd like a word,' Molly said, with an apologetic glance, drawing me a few paces from Barris. Cold radiated from the glass of the terrace now, glass that darkened and distorted our reflections.

In Sino-Anglic I said, 'This is a Restricted world; how can you open access to the data-bank network?'

'Is that all we can offer?'

'It's all he's interested in.'

She frowned. 'It's a Restricted world, it's not a Closed world.'

And now we're on dubious territory. As simple as the stone that triggers an avalanche: if Rakviri is successful, then other *telestres*—

'Don't do it. Irrespective of the law, or Company policy; don't let Barris Rakviri loose on unrestricted data-networks. I don't say one person can make a great difference to anything here, but all the same. . . .' And I wonder: when the customs of Orventa demand that reinvented technology be destroyed – does Barris Rakviri regret it?

'We have to take some risks.' Molly raised her voice, drawing Barris into the conversation. '*T'an* Barris, this is going to take some negotiation with my Company, but in principle it doesn't seem an impossible request.'

Principles? I wondered. Maybe this is my first opportunity. If I leak the news to home office in advance, and maybe to the government, through Douggie, they'll protest – I hope. How else do I put a hold on culture shock, except by delay?

'*T'ans s'aranthi.*'

Jaharien Rakviri walked on to the terrace. His step was soundless. Several other Rakviri were with him; males and females with dark manes and opaque eyes. Not Cassirur Almadhera, though; nor Haltern n'ri n'suth Beth'ru-elen.

'*S'an* Jaharien.' And I wondered how much he'd heard. This one we'd better take with dignity, I thought. Since I judge dignity is about all we're going to be left with . . .

He looked at Molly first, and then at me, not hiding his satisfaction.

'It seems I was wrong.' There was a kind of joy in his abnegation. He stood brushing shoulders with the younger males and females, and they crowded close. 'Wrong to let you come to this *telestre*. *T'ans*, I gave you guest-right. I revoke it. Leave Rakviri. That's all I have to say.'

At this hour? How are we supposed to travel to Morvren? Skurrai-jasin across desolate heathland by night – impossible!

I was proud of Molly Rachel. She made none of those protests, only inclined her head slightly, after the Orthean manner, and said, 'We'll leave now, *s'an* Jaharien.'

The discordant music from the end of the terrace rang in the cold air. There was a smell of cooking, at this hour of second twilight. Frost formed on the glass. Jaharien tugged his dark robe more closely round his burly shoulders.

'You'll leave in the morning,' he said.

Judging by Molly Rachel's face, she didn't like that humiliating charity any more than I did. She said, 'Thank you, *s'an*.'

'In the morning,' Jaharien said, 'because I won't ask any of this *telestre* to put themselves in danger by taking *skurrai-jasin* to Morvren at night. No other reason than that.'

He turned his back on us and walked away, the other Rakviri Ortheans walking with him; and the hiss of their bright robes on the stone floor died away into silence.

We left when Carrick's Star was a searing white line along the eastern horizon. I saw Molly exchange a few words with a sullen Barris Rakviri. When she climbed into the *skurrai*-carriage beside me, she was too preoccupied to talk. I didn't see Cassirur or Haltern – And that's probably just as well, I thought. It would strain my professional courtesy, to say the very least.

As the *skurrai-jasin* jolted down the rough track, Molly Rachel swore. She sat for a moment with head bowed, arms resting on her knees, skin dark against beige coveralls; and then she straightened, sighing.

'God*dammit*—' And glanced sideways at me, and shrugged. 'That's two. Two chances gone: Kel Harantish settlement and this *telestre*. How many more chances am I going to get?'

Two unsuccessful attempts at getting functional Witchbreed technology . . . I can't think of it in Company terms, now.

'You talk as if it was just machinery—'

'That's *all* it is.' Her face went blank. 'It may be based on some

503

alien perception of the universe, it may not; either way, *it's nothing but technology*. Get that clear.'

There are unbidden memories in my mind: the dead images of a long-dead race.

Deliberately businesslike, Molly said, 'We're going to have a couple of busy days. I've been in contact with Pramila Ishida: the team will be coming down from the orbiter now. And I've *got* to have something I can give them to work on.'

As long as there are Ortheans blocking the Company from Witch-breed technology, I thought, I don't have to take any decisions. But what happens if – when – we find someone who'll co-operate? What do I do then?

Orventa Twelfthweek Eightday: the Freeport city streets are white with frost. Walking up from the Portmaster's office to the Residence, I smelt on the air the hot sharpness of burning *lapuur*-wood in street braziers. Four days. Four days now, and the alien beginning to be comfortable, to fit like old clothes – or is it clothes I've outgrown?

Sun shone through the *hanelys*-creeper. Its iron-black sharp stems linked the walls of *telestre*-houses, forming a canopy over-head. A few wild *becamil* had made a nest in the right-angled junctions of the plant. For a moment there was no sound but their high-pitched humming. Then, as the avenue opened out into a square, I heard a noise.

Skurrai being harnessed to stout carts stamped and hissed. The larger *marhaz* raised their snake-muzzles and cried. Ten or fifteen Ortheans, mostly young males and females, were working; strapping loads on to tri-wheeled carts with rapid effi-ciency. The winter sun brought steam rising from the mud, and shone on crates and *becamil*-cloth sacks. I stepped back as a cart rumbled past, and felt its heaviness in the vibration of the earth.

'Give you greeting,' I said to a small, pale-maned female, as she turned from watching the cart on its way to the docks. 'What's happening here, *t'an*?'

Whiteless eyes were slowly lidded. Then her gaze cleared. She nodded, and rubbed dirt from her six-fingered hands.

'*T'an s'aranthi*,' she acknowledged. 'I'd heard there were off-worlders in the 'port again – Brovary! Tallis! *you overload that and I'll* – that's better.'

A winter haze made daystars into ghost-images, blotted out by a swooping flight of *rashaku*.

'We're sending a *jath-rai* coaster along to Ales-Kadareth in

Melkathi,' the Orthean female went on. 'Last year was a bad harvest for them. I doubt this year'll be better.'

The names bring back a summer long gone, and words spoken by – Ruric Orhlandis.

'Someone said to me, once, that, if it wasn't against all custom, Melkathi province should be made to have half the number of *telestres* that it does have – and then it might be able to support its population.'

'You know Melkathi?' She pushed a wisp of mane away from her face with the back of her wrist. 'I'm Mezidon, by the way, Anrasset Mezidon Rakviri. Yes, there's some truth in what you say.'

'There's no truth in it at all!' a new voice interrupted. 'The *telestre* boundaries haven't changed in two thousand years, nor should they ever!'

I turned, to see a young male Orthean leaning against a crate. He wore boots, britches, and sleeveless slit-backed jacket; and *harur*-blades on shoulder-baldrics.

He demanded: 'Who are you, to say what Melkathi's *telestres* should do?'

He's young, I thought. Not long out of *ashiren*. A thin, intense boy; with satin-black skin and a cropped red mane. When he shifted off the crate and walked towards us, he had the controlled grace of a *harur*-blade fighter.

'Give you greeting,' I said, amused. 'My name is Lynne de Lisle Christie, *t'an*.'

His stunned eyes met mine. A sudden pulse of adrenalin made me cold. Even an offworlder couldn't mistake it: his face came alive with hatred.

'*T'an* Asshe is here from Melkathi to assist with the relief ships.' Mezidon glanced back and forth at us both.

'Oh yes,' the boy said, 'this – animal – knows Melkathi. And Melkathi knows *you*, Christie *S'aranth*.'

The people nearby stopped loading carts and stared, hearing his voice. Mezidon Rakviri looked embarrassed: 'Asshe, I'm sure the *s'aranthi* meant no harm; and it's a thing we've often said about Melkathi ourselves.'

He ignored her, his eyes fixed on me. 'Shall I tell you who remembers Christie *S'aranth*? I'll tell you. Those who were there when Sulis SuBannasen died by poison, by her own hand. Those who were there when *T'An* Commander Ruric Orhlandis burned Orhlandis *telestre*. When the *T'An Suthai-Telestre* Suthafiori declared Orhlandis not to exist, and scattered its people across all the Hundred Thousand—'

'And that has what, precisely, to do with you?' I asked.

He stared at me with an adolescent defiance I was hard put not to laugh at. And then with his next words it wasn't funny at all: 'My name is Pellin Asshe Kadareth – now. I was *born* Pellin Asshe Orhlandis.'

But you could only have been a baby—! When Suthafiori declared all Orhlandis children must be adopted *n'ri n'suth* into other *telestres*. You could only have been a child. But I can't comprehend the loss, for an Orthean, of land he has lived on, in past-memory, for a hundred generations . . .

'*T'An* Ruric burned Orhlandis,' he said, anger sharpening that unlined face, 'but you made her do it!'

His arrogance and ignorance caught me on the raw.

'*T'an* Asshe, let me tell *you* something. You don't have the right to hate me, or to say one word about Ruric Orhlandis. You never knew her. *I did.*'

'You made her betray the Hundred Thousand!'

I have memories of her, that dead woman; she with her black skin and mane and yellow Witchbreed eyes. That narrow, merry face . . . *T'An* Commander and travelling companion, friend to the envoy; she who had Shiriya-Shenin's ruler killed and the envoy disgraced for it. And I see her trapped and filthy in the burning Melkathi heathland, remember her branded exile in the prison in Tathcaer, and even I cannot say, that was not justice.

'*T'an* Asshe . . . she could do nothing but what she did, believing as she did. It could have been any *telestre* that happened to. Yes, and it could have been any offworlder.'

Twenty or so people were listening now, others having come out of the Rakviri city-house; Mezidon Rakviri winced whenever Orhlandis was openly mentioned, and the others grinned broadly at scandal.

'You were the first,' Asshe said. 'Well, I will revenge Orhlandis on you, *t'an S'aranth*, if I do nothing else with my life. It's a gift of the Goddess; who could have thought you'd return?'

The sun cast his shadow on the cold earth, that thin dark boy. Violence was in him, savage and ridiculous and entirely pragmatic. To be hated so bitterly hurts. I wanted to laugh, to cry. Empathy rose strongly in me: looking into unveiled eyes I could feel the heft of sharp metal, feel how hard this frost-bitten earth would be to fall on; taste blood . . . At the same time anticipated how these Rakviri would disarm him before he could attack; and, standing in that winter light, I wanted to put my arms round him and hug him like the boy he was, say *It isn't her fault, she hurt you as badly*

506

as she hurt me, she's dead now, it was all ten years ago. The empath's sense of multiple possibilities. As so often, it left me incapable of any action.

'It's not advisable to make threats, *t'an* Kadareth.'

The voice startled me out of immobility. I looked round, amazed, at the stocky figure of Blaize Meduenin. And belatedly thought, That's the connection between four days ago and now: he must be the one of the Morvren triumvirate responsible for getting Rakviri's ships to Melkathi . . .

'I knew Sulis SuBannasen when she was *T'An* Melkathi.' Blaize's mouth twisted in wry humour. 'She hired me to kill the Earth envoy – the *S'aranth*. And it was her choice, when her plotting with Kel Harantish was found out, to go to the Goddess as she did. As for the *T'An* Commander Ruric – boy, you know nothing of that year.'

Pellin Asshe said sulkily, 'If not for the *S'aranth*, *T'An* Commander Ruric wouldn't also have turned spy for Kel Harantish; I'd still live with the earth I loved.'

The fair-maned male frowned, his scarred face bewildered, surprised into defending me: 'It was not done at the *S'aranth*'s direction.'

'She was the cause!'

'We were all the cause.' Nictitating membrane slid down over the Meduenin's eyes. 'Don't waste your blame on that, boy, when it's now you should worry. Work to see it doesn't happen again.'

Pellin Asshe never took his eyes from my face. 'I spoke in anger, *t'an* Christie, forgive me. I mean you no harm.'

My legs felt momentarily unsteady, and I reached to grip Blaize's arm; hard and muscled. His eyes cleared, watching the boy walk off between the carts. Loading resumed. I looked at Asshe's retreating back and thought, *I wasn't afraid – until you apologized.*

'I'll see he goes back with the *jath-rai* to Kadareth.' Blaize looked at me, all but shuffled his feet, and then unwillingly smiled. There was an ironic awareness of our last meeting. 'What else was I to say – *S'aranth*?'

The years have deepened the creases in that scale-patterned skin, have faded the blue-purple burn scar; but there is still the same Blaize Meduenin who hunted the envoy, helped her across the Wall of the World, abandoned her in the wilderness, and became in later days kinbrother to her kinsister.

Caught between then and now, I felt the knot of acrimony inside me loosen a little. If I were to talk to you now, what could we say to each other?

He turned back to the loading; and I left, feeling relief and resentment in about equal measure.

I walked on into the city-island's interior, to the Residence; passing through that small *telestre*-house's courtyard, and up steps to the first floor. Inside, lozenge-shaped windows cast patches of sunlight on the walls. The light emphasized the dust, and the air of a place that is shut up ten months out of the twelve. David Osaka was sitting at a table on which stood an old model data-net, tinkering with the display in the holotank, and studying the offprints pinned on the wall above. I paused beside him.

'Is the comlink with the orbital ship working now?'

He shrugged. 'We're having to use a heavy-duty infrared laser system for ground-to-orbit, and put the ship in geosynchronous orbit.'

'Dear good God! Use industrial lasers for comlinks?'

He leaned back, brushing the fair hair out of his eyes. He has the impatience of the young, I thought. Or is it that he picks up my dissatisfaction here?

He said, 'We're having comlink problems all over – on-world and ship-to-ship. Can't bypass the background interference except under the most local conditions. But all this government equipment is outdated. We could end up using *shuttles* for communications.'

The coin-cords rattled as Molly Rachel pushed through the curtain in the door-arch. She nodded a greeting to me; picked up on his remark: 'We don't have that big an energy-reserve; the situation is ridiculous. Dave, see if you can find Doug Clifford, will you? I want to know if government records can shed any light on the problem.'

'Sure.'

As he left, she padded across to the window and stood gazing out. 'Clifford's spending far too much time over at the Almadhera's quarters.' She ticked off names on her long dark fingers: 'Bekily Cassirur Almadhera. Haltern n'ri n'suth Beth'ru-elen. Blaize Meduenin. I know he claims they're influential people here . . . I don't think the Company can rely on him at all.'

I said nothing. The daystarred sky shone beyond the thick glass. Distantly came the rumble of *skurrai*-carts, voices calling, the metallic tones of *rashaku*. Now on the verge of spring season, Hanys, when *jath* and *jath-rai* are fitted out for trade-voyages . . .

'Any word from Rakviri?' I thought, She won't have given up on Barris that easily.

'Nothing. And no approaches from other *telestres*.' The Pacifican woman turned, hearing human voices, and footsteps coming up from the lower rooms. 'You're only just in time for the meeting.'

The Residence's upper rooms began to fill. Faces I'd become familiar with on the ship out from Earth, the Company's research scientists – and now, as I took my place round the table with them, they seemed curiously stolid, graceless; eyes forever wide and staring, thick-fingered hands, manes shaven . . . that double image that comes with being an empath, and seeing through eyes that are never entirely your own . . .

And then they came back into focus. Pramila Ishida, the Representative's aide, quiet-voiced and round-faced; and beside that young Asiatic-featured Pacifican woman was a tall black medic, Joan Kennaway. An older, sharp-faced Pacifican woman, Chandra Hainzell, seated herself on a couch-chair with two more men from Research: Dinu Machida and Jan Yusuf. Beside them, stiff-spined and looking as though he hated every minute of this, I saw the head of the team, Rashid Akida.

'I realize this face-to-face meeting is unusual,' Molly Rachel began, 'and that none of us have comlink-access to the resources of our departments right now. That's the first point I want to raise – have we got anywhere analysing the communications interference?'

A sea mist was pressing against the windows, and the damp air was not warmed by *lapuur* and *ziku*-wood braziers. I could see on the faces round me the longing for a Pacifican environment: heat, light, technology. I wouldn't have turned it down myself.

David Osaka came in at that moment, Doug Clifford following; and there was a small disturbance while other tables were shoved together, and people's seats rearranged. Two or three of the younger team members sat cramped in window embrasures. It's a far cry from an all-screen holo-image conference.

'We're discussing comlink problems,' Molly said. 'Dinu?'

Dinu Machida, a stocky Sino-Indian, spread a printout across the two tables. 'First, I'll have to deal with weather patterns. You can see the problems we're having with satellite surveys. The interior of the southern continental landmass is more or less permanently covered with cloud. Also, considerable areas on the northern continent: here, and here . . .'

Far north of us. Into the Barrens, and beyond, where I've never travelled.

'You've tried infrared,' Molly prompted.

'Naturally. Comes up featureless. It's—' He looked round, obviously itching for a holodisplay-tank. 'Can I explain the seasonal climate pattern? Take this "Coast" area on the southern continent.

A steady influx of winds from the sea, bringing a corresponding monsoon season, then a steady outflow of air from the centre of the continent, and consequently a very long dry season—'

'Hold on,' I interrupted. 'Dinu, I can see a few other people as bemused as I am. For the non-specialist – what are you saying about the climate? And what does it have to do with communications?'

He brushed black hair out of his eyes, and sighed. 'The Coast area is an example. It's too hot for its latitude. There's a climate anomaly, and it's far from being the only one.'

I caught Doug Clifford's eye then, and began to think: I know what this is leading towards . . .

'At a guess,' Dinu continued, 'I'd say the land surface of the interior has to have an extremely high albedo, to reflect back that amount of solar radiation; hence the greenhouse effect and the cloud-cover . . . There are only two geological areas that have that high an albedo – a reflective surface. Deserts and ice fields.'

Molly Rachel said, 'You don't get that many ice fields on the equator . . .'

When the general laugh died down, and she'd grinned appreciatively, she said, 'Desert, then. How does that tie in with the atmospheric disturbances in communications? Doug, is there anything in your records that illuminates this?'

Doug Clifford let the silence grow. A small, neat man; his hands clasped in front of him and resting on the table. All that self-mocking theatre was curbed now; I saw no humour on his face.

'Not desert, in either case,' he stated; and with a nod of acknowledgement to me, said, 'You'll have seen reports on an area north of here, that Ortheans call the Glittering Plain. You forget that this isn't a "primitive" world. It's a post-technological world. Post-holocaust, to be accurate. I suspect that what they call the Elansiir, in the centre of the southern continent, and the areas north of the Barrens, are fused bedrock. War damage. Plain and simple devastation. You will, I think, find that there is more than one contributory factor to the communications interference, but that the root cause of it is that damage, done in a war that destroyed this civilization's high technology. Three thousand years ago.'

Ten years ago I stood on a scarp, north and west of the Freeport—

The sun reflects off something in the western distance. At first I take it for water, but it doesn't end as water does. Where it touches the brown heathland, it ends in streaks. Sharp edges, like cat-ice on a puddle, like splinters. With the sheen of volcanic glass. Then Carrick's Star clears the haze, and all that horizon blazes with unbearable light.

—overlooking what Ortheans call the Glittering Plain.

The silence that ensued in that upper room had a curious quality, because when someone from the Old World says that to a group of Pacificans, it inevitably raises certain historical tensions. And because the thought of damage great enough to change world climate on Orthe is awesome.

The discussion shifted, moving on to the first results from the demographic team's surveys, and it wasn't at all subtle how Douglas Clifford was excluded – Doug and, to a degree, myself. Inevitable. But none the less, it disgusts me.

When I could slip out (a short absence being advisable) I went down to the kitchens to boil *siir*-wine, and taste the acrid hot liquid. Clifford's *l'ri-an* – Ortheans apprenticed by their *telestres* to this temporary duty – clustered round the ovens, cooking, talking, playing *ochmir*. I heard the midday gongs sound while I was there, and stayed to eat, and to play three-handed *ochmir* with a young male and an *ashiren*.

'Need any help up there?' the young Orthean male said, as I conceded the game and stood to leave.

I smiled at that. 'All I can get.'

He scooped triangular counters back into the *becamil*-cloth bag. 'I hear you may be getting a message from Rakviri *telestre* soon.'

Chilled, I thought: Jaharien wouldn't change his attitude – would he?

'And where did you hear that, *t'an*?'

'I heard it in a game.' His inflection could have applied to *ochmir*, but it had all the Orthean connotations of intrigue, cabal, challenge, and art.

When I came back into the upstairs chamber, the thin-faced Rashid Akida was on his feet.

'You're giving us the go-ahead on Carrick V?' he asked Molly. 'Good. How soon will we have an on-world base?'

Pramila Ishida leaned forward. A slight woman, much the same age as Molly, and with an air of deference – she glanced at the Company Representative before she spoke: 'The local humanoids seem reluctant to lease any territory to us, even on a short-term basis. This is a problem area. It's riddled with traditional and religious prohibitions.'

Molly nodded. I thought she might bring me in on this, my knowledge being intended to cover such gaps in this ill-documented culture, but she ignored me. She put her long fingers through her hair, pushing it back from her face, and glanced round at the assembled team.

'I may be able to solve that one, if I can swing a small addition to budget. We could bring in one of the unit-construct bases the Company uses on water- or foul-atmosphere worlds. With a sealed-environment base, we can anchor offshore in the river estuary here. End of problem.'

You have to admire the thinking behind that. Even if the casual "small addition to budget" is a chilling reminder of PanOceania's financial power.

Rashid Akida's chin lifted. In his thirties, he spoke with the gravitas of a man twice his age. 'If I may suggest . . . all things considered . . . looked at fairly . . . is this where you ought to base the team? If we could return to the Kel Harantish settlement—'

Molly cut him off. 'That's not possible.'

And then I knew what she would say next. It's the obvious move for anyone looking at Witchbreed artifacts – even if they are defunct. The canals. The canal system on the Coast, that Kel Harantish controls.

'The Desert Coast canal system is an example of Witchbreed science.'

'The evidence is ambiguous,' Rashid Akida protested. 'Are you certain this isn't just a charming irrelevance?'

He indicated a data-tank offprint.

'From what I gather, the canals were built *after* the war, and the damage that occurred then. A brave attempt to set up irrigation after the climate changed. But the system is unfinished; it trails off *here*, to the west . . . and in the east it comes within forty miles of the Kel Harantish settlement and – stops.'

Molly leaned back. Her long fingers moved, rubbing against the grain of the *tukinna*-wood table. 'The archeological team reported the canals were Witchbreed constructs, and that should be enough to make us investigate.'

Time to be obstructive under the guise of being helpful, I thought. 'I know why you haven't suggested it before, Molly. Primarily because it may or may not be functional in any sense that we can understand. And, secondarily, because there are local political difficulties.'

Pramila Ishida spread out a demographic survey. As always, her eyes were lowered. She said quietly, 'The Coast area is a poverty-line culture. They have a long history of raiding this more prosperous northern continent. My local contact here says this has reached such a point that negotiatory talks are being set up in a Coast settlement. The Company naturally wants to avoid on-world political conflicts.'

And who's been talking with the *takshiriye*, then? I thought sardonically. With Douggie and the Morvren triumvirate . . .

The aquiline Chandra Hainzell said, 'Isn't the northern continent a more likely place to find functional technology? If this poverty-line Coast *had* tech, they'd be using it now.'

The sea mist began to clear, a watery sunlight shining through the lozenge-crystal windows.

'It isn't that simple,' I said. 'You've heard about the areas of war damage – I know we can't survey them accurately because of the interference, but I'm of Doug's opinion – and you must remember: these people have a very clear memory of where technology can lead. Where it did lead, in their case.'

Molly nodded. 'Lynne's right. These people . . . they're not technophobic, as such. There are Witchbreed artifacts in the *telestres*. It isn't that they can't use technology. They *won't*. I've a strong feeling they could build up a hi-tech civilization in a couple of generations, if they wanted to, but they won't do it.'

Frustration showed on her dark, smooth features. Then she shrugged: 'The reason's obvious. Pramila says this northern continent is prosperous. Fertile. There's a low population, too; they don't need hi-tech. Or, I should say, they don't need it with the urgency that these Coast Ortheans obviously do – if that's a poverty-line culture, the Company's got things to offer them, and that's where we come in. We trade with them.'

For Witchbreed technology?

Oh yes, that's PanOceania; and I'd wondered how long it would take the Rachel woman to put that at the top of her list of priorities.

'I've got continuing investigations here,' Molly concluded. 'Either way, whichever continent we concentrate on, I want results. I want to get an FTL-drone off through Thierry's World *soon*. The quicker reports start getting back to home office on Earth, showing progress, the sooner we'll be officially established here.'

Jan Yusuf, a wiry and suntanned man of indeterminate age, said, 'The fact that there's alien technology still extant here *doesn't* necessarily mean we'll be able to analyse it.'

Rashid Akida verbally leapt on him. I stayed for a while, listening to conversations as the meeting broke up – listening, I suppose, for something more than blinkered interest. I didn't hear any. When I saw Molly go out, I followed her down the outer stairs and into the courtyard. The sea mist clung, pearl-pale, to the roofs. The *kazsis*-vines that clung to walls were beginning to bud, and to bear the nodules that incubate *kekri*-flies. After the talk and claustrophobia of that upstairs room, it made me want to run and shout like a child.

'Shit!' Molly Rachel said. She put her hands in the small of her back and stretched, arching; and then pushed her fingers through that mass of dark frizzy hair. She squinted up at the mist-blurred roofs of the Freeport. 'For God's sake, can't you keep Clifford under control?'

'You didn't go out of your way to conciliate him.'

'No . . .' She took a breath: *kazsis*, the dung of *kuru* rooting in the mud beyond the archway gate, the brackish dockside water. I looked past her to where a Pacifican – I recognized David Osaka – stood in the street with one of the kitchen's *ochmir* players. Was that the *l'ri-an* I spoke with earlier?

'You had a quarrel with Blaize Meduenin,' she said. It wasn't a question. She tucked her hands under her belt, an oddly Orthean gesture. 'Lynne, you understand these people. You know what makes them angry, what makes them laugh . . . I think I'm beginning to see it myself.'

'No one ever fully understands the alien. It's not possible. That's a hard saying, but it's true.'

With a startling perception, she said, 'But no one ever fails to understand a part.'

I looked up at the young woman beside me; her black angular height, that direct gaze.

She said, 'All we're going to take from them here is something they don't use, don't want – that they're afraid of. They don't need Witchbreed technology.'

I don't agree with why you're saying it, but . . . 'That last is certainly true.'

David Osaka walked into the courtyard, glancing back over his shoulder. He said something to the Pacifican woman.

Molly frowned. 'I can't see everyone who just walks in off the street.'

'He mentioned the name of Rakviri *telestre*.'

'Send him in. You go upstairs and keep the meeting going.'

I sat back on the wall of the cistern, waiting; but the Orthean who entered the courtyard was not what I expected.

'Achil,' the Orthean male said. 'Earthspeaker. Give you greeting, *t'an s'aranthi*.'

He stood barefoot in the muddy courtyard, looking at Molly, and finally at me. He was thin – almost as thin as a Desert Coast Orthean – and dark-skinned, and his mane was shaven down to gold fur. Impossible to tell his age. Brown cloth was knotted at the hip, a garment that didn't cover his back, where the shaven mane went down to a vee at mid-spine; nor the sharp-angled ribs and

514

paired dark nipples. *Harur*-blades hung from a plain belt. His eyes were wide-set in that narrow-chinned face.

'What can I do for you, *t'an* Achil?' Molly asked.

It was a shock to meet those unveiled eyes: clear as water. His expression changed, but whether it was amusement or disquiet, I couldn't tell.

'I have spoken before with *s'aranthi*,' he said. His high-arched feet were bare; he seemed oblivious of the cold wind.

The Pacifican woman waited.

'*T'an* Rachel, you have visited the Desert Coast?'

Her gaze flicked across to me, an exasperated look that plainly said: *Is there* anything *they don't find out?*

'Briefly,' she confirmed. '*T'an*, I understand that you've come from Rakviri *telestre*; if there's a communication—'

'I have also spoken with the Earthspeaker Cassirur Almadhera, and with Barris Rakviri.'

Now the Pacifican woman was quite still. 'Yes?'

'You must understand, *t'an*, our place is with the land. With the earth. We are born of it, care for it, return on it. Protect it.'

Return on it. . . . Sharp and real, I saw again the ruined city of the Barrens: heard that scarred mercenary talk of past-memories, of once-lived lives. Except in extremity, or among Earthspeakers, it is rarely spoken of.

' "Protect",' the Pacifican woman echoed. There was a hardness in her tone. 'What does this have to do with Rakviri and my Company?'

Something in her voice crystallized a realization. You don't like the Ortheans of the Hundred Thousand, I thought. Just don't like the culture. I wonder if you know that?

Achil said, 'We have – long memories, I believe your people would say. And we know why we mistrust all Witchbreed science.'

'Meaning?'

'To be plain, *t'an* – our history is not your business.'

I looked over at that slight figure, standing in the mist-filtered sunlight; caught a glimpse of some private, tragic humour . . . and decided the pun was both bilingual and deliberate.

'And Rakviri?' I said.

'I have been travelling down the Ai River, from Wellhouse to Wellhouse, and came to visit Rakviri some few days past.'

'That isn't what I asked, *t'an* Earthspeaker.'

For all efforts to anchor discussion in the practical, I could feel the atmosphere change. One forgets – because inexplicable – the very real effect of an Earthspeaker's presence. Now I felt the cold wind, heard the creak of windvanes and *skurrai*-drivers shouting in the street outside; all with a sharp intensity. At the arch of the sky the mist was gone. Daystars shone like a scatter of flour. Carrick's Star was bright. A *rashaku* called.

The Orthean male stepped forward and touched claw-nailed fingers to Molly Rachel's forehead. She flinched. He stared into her face.

'*T'an s'aranthi*, there are those who say time is not the same for us as it is for you. It may be that we remember our future, not relive our past. Seeing what you bring to Orthe, I have thought, perhaps, that there never was such a race as the Golden Witchbreed – until now. That you, in our future, are the Golden Empire that we foresaw . . .'

Molly stared back at him, silenced.

'Then who left all those ruins laying around?' I asked, acidly.

The Earthspeaker Achil laughed. Head thrown back, delight in the sound of it, but still a certain bitterness there. '*T'an* Christie, give you greeting; the Almadhera said that I should like you.'

Molly Rachel said flatly, 'Why have you come here, *t'an* Achil?'

His head went up as he heard human voices from the first-floor windows. The light made the planes of his face harsh, animal, alien.

'Why, to tell you this, *t'an* Rachel. Barris Rakviri is come into Shalmanzar Wellhouse for a time, as our custom is. And certain things that he kept with him in the Rakviri *telestre*-house have also come into Shalmanzar's keeping. And will stay there. And I think that the Wellhouses will not, at this time, willingly admit *s'aranthi*.'

'Damn them!' the Pacifican woman said, as soon as he had passed the archway gate. 'If there's one thing I don't need, it's alien cult-religions—'

She slammed both hands palm down on the rim of the cistern, the noise of flesh on brick like a gunshot in that small courtyard. A *rashaku*, startled into flight from the roof, swooped into the watery-blue sky.

I quoted an old Service cliché. 'When diplomacy meets religion – diplomacy doesn't stand a chance.'

'It's a pity you couldn't charm that Earthspeaker with the *S'aranth* name, the way you did Jaharien Rakviri—' Some remnant of shadow left her eyes. She made no mention of Barris, or that pale octagonal hall. 'Lynne, I'm sorry.'

'I suppose the *S'aranth* name is as much a liability as an asset, now,' I said. 'And . . . Earthspeakers aren't like other Ortheans.'

516

For a second it's as if the sun-warmed stone of yard and buildings encloses me; as if I stand at the bottom of a well.

Molly Rachel raised her head, shutting her eyes briefly, and then gazed at the clearing sky. 'I need to be here myself and push for access to *telestres*. But we also need to open up the Coast area on the southern continent. I can send someone down ahead of me—'

'I'll go.'

I can't stay here in the Freeport. I have been trying to say that Orthe is strange to me but it isn't. It's as if I'd never been away – and I have, I'm not Christie S'aranth now, to think so is dangerous.

And then there is Blaize Meduenin . . . I need time to think it through.

Molly narrowed her eyes, studying me. 'You don't really know the Coast. Still, none of us do. It's not a well-documented area. And you *can* handle Ortheans.'

Not 'well-documented', no. Carrick V is a neglected world. . . . Above me now in this pale stone courtyard are daystars. The sky is full of the Heart Stars that lie on the edge of the galaxy's core. Look up: it is a crowded sky. Each world of those millions is crowded with life, and we, humanity, we cling to those Home Stars nearest Earth, and can't pay attention to every backwater world that falls within our domain . . .

Until something unique is discovered.

The Pacifican woman turned towards the steps, going to the upper floor. The shadow of the house wall was cold.

As I climbed the steps with her, she said, 'I want to get a foothold on the southern continent. Before things get complicated there. There are these talks coming up between the Freeport *takshiriye* and the Coast settlements . . . I've got one of the canal settlements in mind for contact – remind me: you haven't seen the latest data on that.'

She paused, then: 'Yes, you go down ahead of me. We've had two chances at viable Witchbreed science, we can't afford now to miss the third. Lynne, I'll be relying on you.'

CHAPTER 9

Canals

When I was in the Service, it used to strike me how closely our missions approximate the shapes of our lives: born out of the ship-womb into a world full of incomprehensible experience, no sooner gaining a kind of competence than called out of that world again. Flying down to the Coast held something of that feeling – cold ice-thin air outside the ports, the blue-purple of the stratosphere, and Orthe an ochre shadow thirty thousand feet below.

I flicked the holotank-image from exterior-view to Records, and then had to lean forward while Pramila Ishida went past to take the pilot's console with David Osaka.

And I could do without having Pramila along, she's a direct conduit of information back to the team—

How can I hope to cushion culture shock, faced with something like *this*?

The departed archeological team left a message-capsule in orbit, and it was only days after landfall that the team had got round to deciphering its last image. I leaned on the rim of the holotank, studying it – a close shot of an inland Coast city. It was ill-resolved, taken from a shuttle overflight. Satellite surveys are no better, the area being comparatively close (in continental terms) to the southern continent's war devastation. I wondered briefly how the research team were doing with their plans to override the atmospheric interference.

And if Molly hadn't been determined on the canals already, this would have brought her running! Jesus, I thought. If I do my job, I'm helping the Company to move in on Orthe. If I *don't* do it, I'll be out myself. And if this fulfils its implications . . .

Three-dimensional and miniature, the holotank held a barren landscape. Five canals cut straight lines through the desert. The shot had been taken towards dusk: Carrick's Star reflected back amber from the water surfaces. And where the canals would have intersected, a great cylindrical pit gaped in the desert, a pit big enough to land a starcruiser in; and in its terraced walls, tiny humanoid figures moved . . . the city, Maherwa, according to the archeologists' report. To whet the Company's appetite still further, it lies thirty miles inland from the Inner Sea, and only sixty miles to the west of Kel Harantish.

Doug Clifford, emerging from the shuttle's rear compartments, came and sat in the holotank's other viewseat. He smiled.

'Out of communication range with young Molly? She'll miss hearing how obstructive a government envoy I am.'

'I'd like to have read your last FTL transmission to Earth,' I retorted. 'Especially what went in under "Christie, L. D.".'

'Ah, well – one has to say certain things.'

'Doesn't one . . .'

He leaned back, looking at me over steepled fingers. There was a certain affectionate mockery there that I would have missed, badly, had it been absent.

'I find it interesting that a government representative is permitted to come on this mission . . .'

He left that invitingly open, but I declined to comment. 'Special advisor' is a flexible designation; the duties of 'liaison' are not always specified; and if I choose to let Douggie Clifford take a close look at the Company's *modus operandi* – that's my responsibility. The multicorporate's presence has to be counter-balanced somehow.

A little sourly, he said, 'Why should a multicorporate Company worry about a national government, after all? Britain's nothing more than a client state to PanOceania.'

'That's an exaggeration.'

'I believe you've been out of the Service too long. If I were to call you a groundsider—'

'You could end up walking back to Morvren Freeport.' I gave due consideration to the Inner Sea. 'Or swimming.'

He chuckled at that one, eyes bright. 'I must say, I do prefer offworld service to my groundside days.' His gaze flickered, going round the small cabin, passing over David and Pramila at the pilot's console. 'Lynne, just what *is* it you do with the Company, now?'

'You mean when I'm not being hauled out of my Company department and booted off to the further reaches of the galaxy as a special advisor?'

'Something like that.'

'I'm a groundsider. No – quite genuinely, Douggie. On Earth, I run the department that liaises between PanOceania and the British government. After all, if you want to regulate the relations between a multicorporate and its 'client state', that's best done from the inside, wouldn't you say?'

'Which side of the inside?' He grimaced, primly displeased by his own phraseology.

'Sometimes even I'm not sure.'

He twinkled. The irony doesn't escape me – I balance affairs between PanOceania and the government much as I once did between Earth and Carrick V. It's the same job.

The shuttle thrummed, wallowing in the thin air. Clifford leaned back. 'I thought you seemed a little confused. Now let's see – PanOceania won't entirely trust you because you're British-born, and we won't entirely trust you because you're contracted to PanOceania. I don't envy you your position, Lynne.'

'I'm a professional outsider. I'm used to it.'

I keyed the holotank to images of the Desert Coast. Lines, contours, symbols. But I watched that bland, round face.

'Of course, Orthe won't ever have major trade status, even with the Company's presence here.' His tone was deliberately dismissive. 'We've run several Health and Agriculture Aid programmes here, but for no return. The place is uncooperative as well as uneconomic.'

'True enough.' I noted he couched it in terms that would appeal to the Pacifican woman. Aiming to have it get back to her. 'It's not me you have to persuade, Douggie. By the way – Molly Rachel is of the opinion you spend too much time with the Freeport Ortheans. She thinks you're unreliable.'

'I do hope so.' He was almost demure. Then: ' "Unreliable"?'

'They used always to say Service people were prone to going native,' I said. 'Which, being empaths by profession, isn't too surprising.'

'You know as well as I do, we're trained to put Earth's interests first.'

'Which I suppose accounts for Service tendencies to emotional confusion. And our – your – reputation for instability, unreliability, and hypocrisy—'

He straightened, met my gaze. 'I don't know that you're entitled to say those things now.'

'Since I left the Service? Possibly not.' Still testing the water, I said, 'You don't think I mean you? Two months out of twelve on-world, that isn't long enough to go native.'

'Nor is eighteen months, ten years ago?'

'Thank you, Douglas.'

Neither of us was entirely unserious. That's a kind of barbed joking that the Pacificans wouldn't understand. I thought I'd better pay some attention to the record-abstracts on the holo, and so watched the tank for some minutes. Clifford went back to making notes on his personal memlink.

The holotank showed networks of canals, some mine-workings, and seaports; all in that narrow ribbon of land between the Inner Sea and the first mountain range of the Elansiir. There was no data for the Elansiir wasteland itself, under permanent cloud-cover; and precious little detail for anything else. I went back to the archeology team's report, running the image-loop of Maherwa over and over, concentrating on the 'floor' of the pit. Small, badly-resolved, there was none the less a structure of some sort there – it stood out by its size and isolation.

And it might be purely ornamental, and it might be anything, but it *might* be what the archeologists suggested: an entrance to the canals' maintenance system . . . I went back to the government archives. And came up with nothing.

'You haven't been exactly extensive in these reports.' I glanced up at Clifford. 'Most of them are second-hand sources. As far as the south-east Coast's concerned, you might just as well have said "Here Be Tygers" and "Terra Incognita".'

He protested, 'There's a lot on the languages.'

'That's no help, without knowing the context they're used in.'

Doug Clifford frowned. 'You seem to have forgotten a great deal. The social context is well sketched-in, at least in these areas here—'

Pramila Ishida leaned back and interrupted: 'We're coming up on the selected landing site. Can I put us down close to the settlement?'

Tactile memory washes over me: the hammerblows of heat on the roofs of Kel Harantish, only ten days ago. Spring season here, but so great a change from spring in the Freeport. Climate anomalies . . .

'Yes, take us in,' I directed. 'Coast Ortheans don't have the taboo on land. Put us down a tactful distance from the settlement itself.'

She nodded, almost absently, and I saw her lean over to speak to David. He frowned, and they remained with their heads together for some moments.

The vibration of the flight changed subtly.

'Nobody's paid that much attention to the Coast until now,' I said.

'The Coast Ortheans didn't have anything that anyone wanted.' Doug raised his eyebrows: a self-mocking play to the gallery. It occurs to me that, without the nihilistic sense of humour that he often displays, D. Clifford might not be on what is, after all, considered a fifth-rate Diplomatic posting.

He said, 'I did go to the northern areas of the Coast a few years back. Round Kasabaarde and the islands. Lynne, you may contemplate, at your leisure, what it's like trying to cover something the size of the Hundred Thousand when there's no central authority. I've had to spend a considerable amount of my time there.'

'Mmm; sorry—'

The typical fate of backwater worlds: under-staffing, lack of interest, neglect.

'—but I still wish there was more in records.'

He scratched at his grizzled hair, that was turning quite grey over the ears, and looked at me quizzically. Douggie's always been prone to capitalizing on that fifteen years' difference in our ages.

'I'll tell you something, Lynne. *You* want to treat this trip as a First Contact. A fact-finding mission. Things aren't like that any more. There aren't any purely academic questions, or answers of purely hypothetical interest. Where you go, the Company follows.'

The shuttle thrummed throughout its length, and for a split second lights and holo-images dimmed.

'Go for the crash-straps,' Ishida said, 'we're coming in.' She hooked a viewscreen down to helmet her eyes; flicking switches, bringing David in as pilot-standby.

Exterior-view in the holotank: the horizon a haze, where an immense plain of land at last loses itself; the sky luminous, pale blue; Carrick's Star diamond-brilliant. Fifteen hundred feet, rapidly descending, and everything unreal: perfect scale-miniatures – ridged brown land; that multitude of browns, oranges, ochre, white. Hummocks of wrinkled earth beginning to rise: the foothills of the Elansiir mountains. Beyond them, splintered silver in the cloud haze. And the shuttle a tin box. How does it shut out the world so well? The world so real ... Aware of being held, suspended, from some mythical skyhook-point . . .

Thirty miles distant, the glimmer of the sea. A wonder: this country, that was irrevocably "inland", is from this height coastal. Canals are thin ribbons, every curve distinct as map contours. No sight of any city, but I know how easy it is to lose that on aerial-view.

I fastened the crash-straps across me, turned to speak to Doug. The shuttle swung down into a landing-pattern, curving off to the left. A long and gradual curve, a tightening curve—

I didn't shout. Conventions hold, even on such occasions, perhaps because such occasions aren't easy to recognize as they happen. I glanced at the land below, at Ishida, at the girl again; and the shuttle wasn't slowing, was speeding up.

Her fingers moved rapidly over the controls. 'We're coming in too fast,' I warned, levelly as possible; she shouldn't have her attention distracted now, and I wanted to scream, *Pull out! Get us out of here!*

A slow turn, pushing me hard into the seat; insistent pressure throwing me away from the direction of the curve. Why did I think, before I ever flew, that I wouldn't feel that downward pull? *Nothing* between me and the earth. Empty air. Most of the human body is water: as the shuttle banked, I felt it answering gravity, surging like the tide.

Made speechless; thinking, *Stop this fucking thing*—

The shuttle plunged down, still on the curving trajectory, and the image in the holotank abruptly cut out. Fast; faster. Acceleration pushing me back into the seat; a hot fear swelling in my head, feeling as if my skin enclosed an infinite pressure. At one and the same time thinking We're crashing this is it and I always knew this would happen and but I'm not really afraid – why aren't I? Gravity pressed me back, pinned me down. The shuttle bucked and rumbled underfoot; a terrible grinding sound; I couldn't breathe.

The slide, that uncontrolled plunge –

Something hit the underside of the floor. The cabin jolted violently. I heard a crash, only felt the skidding sideways – both hands gripping the seat – and violent braking threw me forward, back. And then a juddering halt.

'*Christ!*' Douglas Clifford said.

As if that were a signal, everybody began to move and speak. I wrenched at the straps, forced co-ordination, and stood up. The exit irised open. I stumbled out, on the heels of David Osaka.

'—what—'

'—we're down, we're—'

'*Jesus* Christ!'

Silence, then realization, then speech.

A hot wind hit my face, and I stumbled over shale underfoot; slippery, dry, and treacherous. Open air; sky above. My hands were shaking, but only slightly. The white dolphin-shape of the craft . . .

'You wouldn't know we'd hit a thing!' David: amazed, exultant. 'You wouldn't know—'

'What—'

Standing safe, I can look, can ask: where did we cross that momentous barrier between safety and danger? When did a normal day become abnormal?

There's where we hit, jolting over a shale slope, rutted and grooved with crevasses (*if we'd hit there*) and a stone tor (*did we come that close to—?*) and the shuttle, there, drunkenly slewed at the foot of the shallow rise.

David and Pramila clung together, each pounding the other's back, panic and rapture indistinguishable on their faces. Doug said again, 'What—?'

An expected sharp panic wasn't there. I shook a little, soon stopped; felt a kind of floaty sensation, and then an acute nausea.

They fell in love with that bright shadow, Death—

Cassirur, we can understand them better than you ever will.

Only for an instant, then natural human fear reasserted itself. And shock: I shouldn't be able to feel such alien emotion.

Empathy is no prized gift.

'Lynne!'

'Uh—'

'All navigation systems cut out!' Pramila Ishida said, at last moving from David's embrace. 'Total freak conditions – we were flying *blind* the last few seconds.'

She grinned, all deference and all quietness gone. Her sallow face was shining with sweat. She made no attempt at self-justification, very sure of herself. In these situations, even the guiltless protest their innocence.

A hot silence, nothing but sun blazing on the earth. My eyes stung, the alien light too harsh for unprotected human vision. Through tears I saw our four black shadows on the shale. Brown shale, speckled with orange; prism-shaped pebbles, flat leaves of rock . . . sharp focus. Pinned sweating under that incandescent dome of the sky, dry-mouthed, hollow, I felt a change: *Orthe* for a moment become only *Carrick V*. A separation, a betrayal.

'Christ!' Doug repeated, his face grey.

That second when the shuttle sank away from under me, that long dive, like a hawk's stoop, is sensation imprinted into cells, not conscious memory. I remembered, as it happened, a feeling almost of satisfaction: This is the worst that can ever happen, and it's happening; nothing in the future can be as bad as this. And, paradoxically, *knowing* I wouldn't die.

Static electricity sparked from clothing, from hair. Round the rim of the horizon, heat-lightning flickered continuously. I turned to speak to Doug and I couldn't; throat muscles paralysed, tongue thick in the mouth. That *knowing* is only the refusal of something living to believe that it can die.

*

And we get from here to Maherwa – to anywhere – *how*? This shuttle's grounded.

Between fear and self-pity I thought, It was going to be so simple. Fly a shuttle down to the canal junction nearest Kel Harantish, visit the settlement, ask questions—

Now we're stopped before we've begun.

Impossible to stay outside, unprotected, in the heat; but the shuttle's cabin was claustrophobic. I sipped flat liquid from a water-bulb, and leaned up against the frame of the open exit-port. Hours had passed. It felt as though it should be midnight, but Carrick's Star was only declining into late afternoon, light still harsh. I ran a finger under eyeshields to clear dust, and looked out at a sepia landscape.

The earth was golden. Not a thing moved on the wide plain, no animal, no insect. There was no cultivated land. Nothing but dry earth. Only in the north-west, round Kasabaarde, are there ridge-backed lizards, and the packbeasts called *brennior*, and fields of *arniac* and *del'ri*.

'Here,' Doug said, passing a belt-holster across. I fastened it round my waist, and drew the CAS-IV sonic stunner – it's one of the few handguns that look impressive on pre-tech worlds. And, being keyed to human biopatterns for use, is not often a two-edged sword.

'The orbiter got us located yet?'

He shrugged. 'Not yet. Pramila says she can get through to them about thirty per cent of the time.'

I rested a hand on the butt of the CAS-IV – Coherent Amplified Sound was originally developed to be a communications device, not a weapon. Technology is mutable.

When I glanced behind me, I saw Pramila Ishida still leaning over the comlink; David with both hands on the back of her chair, talking loudly. Such self-possession.

'It's a miracle there are settlements here at all.' Doug surveyed the landscape. The neck of his coverall was unfastened and he picked at it with oblivious obsession. 'We didn't by any chance cross the mountains, get into the wasteland beyond? It's hardly believable that there are cities here.'

I said, 'We ought to move.'

'We're not in any immediate danger.'

'That's what's so misleading, Doug. We can talk to the orbiter – some of the time – but that's a fragile link. Think of them trying to locate us without it. In the middle of all this. We've got food and water here, no problem; but look out there. How far away is the nearest settlement?'

He rested his hand on my arm for a moment.

'Douggie, it's okay, I know what this is. Because of what happened, it – well—'

'Makes one aware of how much depends on chance?'

'*Everything* . . . Dave and Ishida, they don't believe in luck. When you've lived long enough to know how much is . . . is dependent on . . . what happens, outside your control, in a few seconds.'

'I'll tell you this, Lynne.' The level sun made him squint, even with eyeshields, as he stared out at the plain. 'I'll tell you. I've finished with weighing-up and judging and – the rest of it. From now on I'll do whatever comes along, to get PanOceania off this world. And off any world in my circuit. But *you* know that already.'

With the last words, he looked at me; that small, bright gaze serious. The implied invitation was plain, and I was within an ace of taking it up . . . And knew, as I felt that infinitesimal hesitation, that it meant I wouldn't. 'If I did that, I'd be useless here. You can't stop a thing like this, not once it's been put in motion, but the effect can be cushioned. The way things are, that's what we have to settle for. Reachable goals.'

Doug, unusually direct, said, 'But when young Rachel tells you to go to the Coast and find a foothold for the Company, you do it.'

Pramila Ishida called out. At the same moment that Ishida exclaimed, David pointed.

'There – what is it?'

The level plain was made sharp and clear by the westering sun, behind the shuttle. A flake of brighter gold moved, changing its shape. And by some sudden comprehension that changing shape became a wide triangle, not altering itself, but emerging from behind what must (the eye now saw) be a ridge in the plain. It rippled, taking the wind. A hundred yards distant? A mile? Still partly obscured by the ground—

'It's a sail,' I said. 'It must – a canal . . .'

'I'm getting heat-sensor readings,' Pramila Ishida called. 'At last. Lynne, there's life out there.'

A figure moved at the base of the sail. All things to its scale: now I saw the craft was some two or three hundred yards distant, still partially concealed by a ridge of earth.

'David, you come with me; Pramila, keep the shuttle secure.' I didn't give Douggie the option. I walked down the ramp, hesitated, drew the CAS-IV and then reholstered it. I don't like to carry even stun-weapons.

'They might have scouts,' David Osaka said, catching me up. 'The reports say the Desert Coast *hiyeks* are hostile to each other.'

Hiyek translates literally as 'bloodline'. It carries all the implications of family, lineage, inheritance.

'From what I used to hear at Mercenaries Guildhouses, the Coast *hiyeks* are almost permanently involved in some petty war . . .' Treat it as familiar and maybe the boy will forget the hair-trigger violence in Kel Harantish. The rest of the Coast is no safer.

Our footsteps were loud on the shale, soft on the earth. The heat leached all strength, muscles ached; and I paused for a moment to look round. The shuttle was a white humpbacked shape behind me. The sail glided slowly north. Now we were climbing a long shallow slope, losing sight of all but that and the daystarred sky.

'Hail them, David, will you?'

The Pacifican broke into a trot. A few moments later, I reached the top of the ridge. So deceptive: it was no more than a fold in the landscape. A scant few feet below me, a stone wall marked the rim of a canal. The water was pale azure, reflecting sky and shoals of daystars, in a channel some thirty yards across, and travelling north in a curve so gradual it appeared straight.

David shouted again.

'They've seen us,' I said. I watched the sail altering, sending the low flat barge in towards the bank near us, and realized, They've had time to prepare to stop. That means they do have scouts – and where are *they*, now?

Deceptive land. Memory of Kel Harantish: the whiplash sound of winchbow bolts. I took a step towards the approaching barge. What do we have to protect us? Not weaponry: that's just a sign for them to read, since we're so few . . .

Our difference. Earth's name. Apart from that, only wit and words.

'*Kethrial-shamaz shan'tai*,' I called, as if there was nothing more to be thought of than courtesy. 'Give you greeting.'

CHAPTER 10

Upon Such Fragile Links

Two young Ortheans leaped from the deck to the paved walkway, fending the barge with ropes and hooks. They were armed. Hooked knives hung from their belts, winchbows were slung across their backs. They went barefoot, in much-mended britches; pale manes braided into protective mats on head and spine. One of them kept her gaze on me, eyes permanently veiled against the glare.

A young male Orthean stepped to the ship's rail, looking down. 'Are you what they call *s'aranthi*? Offworlders?'

I stepped down on to the walkway, on to pale, dusty, hard-packed earth. At close hand I saw the barge wasn't made of timber but of riveted metal plates. Sails hung from between metal hoops shaped like wishbones.

'Yes, we're offworlders. Is this near Maherwa?'

The dialect of the south-east Coast is not so different from other Coast dialects, a little easier to follow, if anything. I was aware of David Osaka close behind me, with drawn CAS-IV handgun; of the mixture of languages in which comments were being made on deck. I hazarded a guess, before the young male could answer: 'Are you mercenaries?'

He nodded. 'Under command of one from *hiyek*-Anzhadi.'

'Then tell your commander I want to talk.'

Another Orthean male, this one seemingly in his thirties, left the group and came down to the rail. Unlike the others, he had the bleached skin of the Desert Coast. Dust patterned in the creases of the *meshabi*-robe belted round his narrow hips; his mane – cropped at the front, braided down the spine – was yellow. As he turned to shout an order back at the crew, I saw the vee of his mane, the arched ribs and paired nipples. Then he moved with a loose-boned ease, vaulting the rail and dropping down to the walkway.

'I heard there'd been *s'aranthi* on the Coast, but not here. What do you want?'

'How far is the city?'

He didn't answer. He stood lightly, relaxed, as if capable of instant action. His white robe was torn, patched in several places, and belted with a length of chain, from which hung a hook-bladed knife. Seen close, he had a thin, almost gaunt face; wide-set eyes and a fox-jaw. And then the nictitating membrane slid back, disclosing eyes the colour of wet sand, and for one second he looked at me with a wickedly amused and conspiratorial grin.

'More than a day's journey, *shan'tai*, but that shouldn't trouble you with the "ship" you have.'

'What's your name, *shan'tai*?' I had to ask something to gain me time to think.

'Sethri-safere of *hiyek*-Anzhadi.'

In the *hiyek* nomenclature that translates as "firstborn of a triple birth, child of firstborn of twins"; which shows the priorities of the Coast, if nothing else.

'I'm Lynne de Lisle Christie, this is David Osaka.'

'Give you greeting. And the other offworlders with you, the female and the old male?'

I looked at him for a while.

He said quietly, 'There is a war just finished, *shan'tai*, between *hiyek*-Anzhadi and *hiyek*-Rythana; and so I do not travel without knowing what lies before me.'

I said, 'I want to talk to some of the Coast *hiyeks*, Sethri-safere. I'll talk with yours, provided it's understood that we come peacefully, and intend to have it stay that way.'

'Talk of what?'

'Trade?'

Again that movement of the nictitating membrane; and he put his head a little to one side, gaze going beyond me to the Pacifican. He said absently, 'So I address you as—?'

'Christie.'

'*Shan'tai* Christie.' He returned the full force of that brilliant gaze to me. 'To be truthful, Christie, the city is probably less than a few hours' journey north. You could reach it tonight, but I doubt that you want the city just yet. There's a *siiran* of *hiyek*-Anzhadi that we'll reach very soon. Why don't you come there, with us?'

'What's happening?' David said in Sino-Anglic. 'Lynne, I can't follow half of what he's saying.'

Impolite, but it did at least inform me – if I read him rightly – that Sethri-safere had little understanding of Sino-Anglic.

We couldn't reach the city tonight, not with a temporarily

grounded shuttle . . . A small part of me noted that the literal translation of *siiran* is "enclosed garden" or "shelter". We need shelter on this hostile Coast. The orbiter can track us, but we don't have supplies for a long wait.

I briefly repeated the conversation to David Osaka.

He said, 'What will happen if we refuse?'

Light caught the burnished hull of the canal ship, and I squinted up against the glare. The sails had metal slats, capable of being turned to catch or release the wind, and lithe figures swarmed to alter them. Faces lined the rail, watching us. Young, armed Ortheans; eyes veiled, cautious. I looked back at Sethri-safere.

And he also is in hostile territory, the territory of a just-fought war. I wish I knew, are offworlders a liability or a prize on the Coast?

'They'll keep us under surveillance,' David guessed. Involuntarily, he glanced back towards the shuttle. 'If they wanted to take us for interrogation . . .'

'On the other hand,' I said, 'an ally would be very useful in the city.'

As David Osaka keyed a channel on his wristlink, I turned back to the yellow-maned Coast Orthean.

'*Shan'tai* Sethri, it would be helpful if you could wait a few minutes. One other person will be joining us. And I must talk to my own people, through my ship.' Which I don't want to risk trying to move, but I'd as soon you didn't know that.

The yellow-maned Orthean smiled, with a look that said *consider me warned*, and I thought, It's good to talk to someone who understands a precaution without having to have it explained.

In the formal mode, I added, 'We're pleased to accept your invitiation, *shan'tai*.'

'And even more pleased not to spend the night in a wasteland full of wild mercenaries . . .' Sethri grinned. His tone made it collusive, a joke shared only by the two of us, and I thought, Yes, you're one to watch – and don't you know it.

I turned to go back to the shuttle, and found David Osaka leaning on the low wall that rimmed the canal, absently digging at the stone-plaster surface.

'Something interesting here,' he said in a casual tone, putting the fair hair back from his eyes. Equally casually, I stopped beside him.

Where he had chipped away the pale plaster, and where he had dug with his boot-heel in the packed earth of the walkway, there shone the unmistakable blue-grey opalescence of *chiruzeth*.

*

It was not a long journey.

The Coast is a different Orthe. Brazen sky, daystars hardly visible; air like the breath of a furnace. Chains ratchetted loudly as the barge's sail collapsed. I saw David take the opportunity to speak into his wrist comlink, look both pleased and startled, and not in my direction. So Pramila Ishida's still in range on the shuttle? That's mildly reassuring, I thought, wonder how long it'll last?

Doug Clifford joined me at the barge's rail. 'Is this a way-station of some kind, do you think?'

A cluster of low, flat-roofed buildings stood back from the canal. They were small huts, all but indistinguishable from the surrounding hillocks and ridges. As we came closer, I saw Ortheans. All carried blades, winchbows. Like the mercenaries, they were ill-dressed; the metal the only thing pristine. The place had the air of an armed camp.

'Maybe we should have tried to make the city,' I said.

We docked, and the barge's holds were opened; anonymous bundles were unloaded, with much shouting from the Guildhouse mercenaries. By the languages, most were from the northern continent: Melkathi and Rimon by my guess. Some wore that dress, and some the same metal-belted *meshabi*-robes as the Coast Ortheans. There were some languages I couldn't quite place . . . the Rainbow Cities? The Storm Coast?

I walked down the gangplank, the others behind me. Sethri reappeared on deck, hailed us cheerfully, and jumped down to join us on the dock. He looked around and then shouted, 'Jadur, you idle sack of guts!'

Another male ambled across the quay, taking a drink from a water-can, which he tucked back under his arm. He looked to be much of an age with Sethri, and had a tan skin and copper-coloured mane, what could be discerned of it under a layer of dust. *Kekri*-flies settled on his eyes. He blinked both membranes to dislodge them.

'Everything's under control—' He saw David Osaka, and gaped, and then visibly realized that there were three of us. 'Sunmother's tits!'

With some satisfaction, Sethri announced, 'This is Jadur, he's one of my *raiku*. The barge can handle itself; I'll take you in. The rest of Ninth *raiku* should be here too.'

Live contact is preferable to hologram records. *I want to hear someone who lives in it define it,* I thought, and queried, '"*Raiku*"?'

'"Bonded group"—?' Jadur-safere frowned, and tried for Old

Anglo terms that must have come to the Coast with the first demographic teams: ' "Wives"? "Husbands"? "Families"?'

'In the north they would say "*arykei*", bed-friend,' Sethri added.

In the data-net they say group-marriage. But that is what it is, not how it feels. We walked on. Jadur held out his flask to me: '*Kethrial-shamaz*, offworlder.'

The phrase snapped into focus – 'share our life'. As I walked, I looked at the arid rock, the canal's water under the pitiless sky. Stepping outside the formal role, I said, '*Shan'tai* Jadur, can you afford to share it?'

Jadur glanced over at me. The hot breeze lifted his coppery mane, and his dark eyes veiled whitely against the dust. With too-casual bravado, he said, 'Share. It's *hiyek*-Rythana's water. My brother-in-*raiku* Sethri has made certain many of them have no use for it.'

And then he grinned, piratical, and slapped the hook-knife where it hung at his chain-belt. 'By next season we'll be at war again, for water or *siiran*, but don't let that concern you – what's one mouth more amongst so many of us? You drink, *shan'tai-s'aranthi*.'

The water tasted tepid, from having been in a metal flask in that sun. Not until I had drunk did I realize that I was also passionately hungry.

The earth was trodden down here between the dock and the small buildings, and the heat of it struck up through the soles of my boots. A chain-line of mercenaries were passing the cargo towards the huts, they and the place looking about equally shabby. As we approached, I saw a middle-aged Orthean woman supervising: small, with beige skin and a gold mane, and wearing the hook-bladed knife of the Coast. She shouted at the mercenaries with an authority very like Sethri's, hailed him without levity, and her expression went a degree or two further towards severity when she saw Jadur.

'*You're* here, are you?'

Jadur caught one of her six-fingered hands and touched it to his forehead, a gesture I hadn't seen among Ortheans before.

'*Hiyannek*, beautiful one, when will you let me be one of your *raiku*?' He stepped back as she swatted him.

'When the Sunmother brings harvest twice a year—!'

Sethri pushed the copper-maned Jadur aside. 'Feriksushar, here are offworlders come to talk with the *hiyek*.'

The female's gaze went from him to us, and back to him. There was almost contempt on those blunt features. 'I'd sooner they'd met with those of the *hiyek* who are respectable, not one who commands mercenaries. Still, it can't be helped.'

Sethri avoided my eyes.

'Sunmother be your friend,' the woman said formally to me, and added in atrociously accented Sino-Anglic, 'We are welcome you to us.'

'I'm Company representative for a group of Earth traders,' I simplified; giving our names.

Feriksushar looked from me to David Osaka and Doug Clifford, and still in Sino-Anglic said, 'And these are your . . . your husbands?'

'Er – regretfully, no . . .'

Doug grinned and put his arm round my shoulder. David Osaka looked rather more worried than I thought quite tactful. In fact, considering a brief but interesting episode on the ship out from Earth, less tactful than he had any right to be.

'I'm so sorry,' the woman, Feriksushar, said politely. 'I was *kei-raiku* myself for some while. Please, come inside.'

As we walked up to the nearest hut, Sethri-safere recovered himself enough to ask her, 'Which *raiku* are running trade this season?'

'Twenty-Eighth, Third, Seventeenth, as well as Twenty-First.' She glanced over at me. 'Sethri is Ninth *raiku*. I'm Twenty-First. Arastari and the rest of my *raiku* are in Maherwa now.'

The hut's entrance was low and narrow. I added the number of Ortheans visible, the apparent housing-room, and concluded that, like Kel Harantish, there would be underground installations. Which accounts for why satellites have never told us much that's useful about the Coast, I thought.

'Do you want anyone to stay outside?' David asked quietly. 'I could ask to be shown the docks.'

'Yes. That might keep us in comlink-range of the shuttle for longer. I'll go down in. Doug, what about you?' And when I caught Doug's mandarin stare, added, 'You're not Company, I can't give you orders.'

'I believe I'll see what the inside of a *siiran* looks like.' He switched to what would be unintelligible to David Osaka: Oldworld Anglo: 'If you tell these people about the grand and glorious benefits to be had from trading with PanOceania, I'll tell them the other side of the story.'

'Douggie, don't let me offend you, but there are times when you're a liability . . .'

I followed Feriksushar and Sethri under the arched entrance, seeing inside (as I pulled off the eyeshields) a flight of steps spiralling down below ground level. Doug muttered, rubbing his eyes. I felt muscles relaxing, knew I'd unconsciously been hunched up against the impact of Carrick's Star.

We descended the steps, going deep underground. The air became warmer, but not with the parching dry heat of the land above. This was humid, and smelled of dank earth. Sunlight began to be replaced by reflected mirror-light. Bare feet scuffed the stone steps. Going down, still: sweat sprang out, and I wiped my face. The light from below brightened. Sethri looked back and smiled. The steps made a right angle and ended abruptly, and the passage opened out.

For a moment we jostled together. Total confusion swept round me: Ortheans milling near other entrances; shrieking *ashiren*; mercenaries stacking cargo. It took a long second to absorb the impact of what I was actually seeing.

The eye was taken up immediately to the bright roof of this underground chamber, thirty feet above our heads. A long, flat expanse of semi-translucent substance, shimmering with rainbow lights; and from it fine streams of water ran in channels, down into tanks of earth. Walls, ceiling, floor: all cold and seamless *chiruzeth*. Garden-sized tanks flanked pathways, vanishing into distant perspective. Tall knobbed *del'ri*-stems rose two metres high, near to harvest; and the crimson leaves of *arniac* grew in profusion.

'*Shit!*'

Doug, at my elbow, murmured, 'I couldn't agree more . . .' in a casual tone at odds with his blank, amazed expression.

There were two levels of chambers set back into the *chiruzeth* walls. Looking carefully, I could see where wall corners were rounded instead of sharp, but not by design – by erosion. Two and a half thousand years after the Golden Empire's fall . . . And I looked up into that opaquely-lit space, smelling the stink of used air, and realized that the roof of this vast structure must somehow be underneath, and a part of, the *chiruzeth* base-channel of the canal.

As my eyes grew accustomed to the rippling light, I saw how the water for the tanks ran sometimes in open channels, and ran sometimes within the substance of the *chiruzeth* itself, moving back *up* into the main channel of the canal. I thought, This is seawater, something must purify it before it reaches the earth-tanks and the plants, something must make it circulate . . . functional *chiruzeth*.

'This wasn't our *siiran* until Wintersun-10. Sethri and the mercenaries took it from *hiyek*-Rythana in the war,' Jadur said. He and the older woman, Feriksushar, went to clear away the crowd. I saw them answering excited questions.

Doug Clifford walked forward to the edge of the nearest *chiruzeth* tank and buried his hands in the earth. It was as if he needed that touch to convince him of reality. I followed, splashing through mud and water that pooled on the *chiruzeth* floor.

'How . . . how many of these *siiran* are there?'

When I looked for Sethri, the shabby yellow-maned male was leaning against the wall. He met my gaze. There was something almost protective in the way that he watched us – seeing us as naïve aliens? As prospective allies? Enemies? That maturity that he had seemed to lose under Feriksushar's contempt returned to him.

'Too few for all the *hiyeks*, *shan'tai* Christie.'

Still stunned, I walked to stand beside Doug, oblivious to the curious stares from the crowd.

'Ten years' contact with Carrick V, and no word about this?' Douggie shook his head, incredulous. 'I had imagined the canals to be like the Rasrhe-y-Meluur, only a *chiruzeth* shell. This . . .'

'You're right. The silence is positively deafening.'

I touched the cold *chiruzeth* tank, aware of the smell of warm, wet earth, of *del'ri* growing, and scrub-*arniac*. The contrast made me dizzy. That gleaming blue-grey material, eroded by time; force-grown vegetation; and the shabby, malnourished Ortheans of the Coast . . .

'Who would conceal this?' Doug asked, and then answered his own question: 'the Kel Harantish Ortheans, of course. They maintain the canals, they have the monopoly of technology. Earth science might upset the balance of power.'

Pathrey Shanataru wants it upset, I thought. And so does the Voice. Kel Harantish is divided, there's a faction that wants contact with Earth . . . 'Dear God, what got started when someone managed to plant one Witchbreed artifact where an archeological team could find it!'

Clifford brushed earth fastidiously from his fingers. 'Undoubtedly. And how many times has that been tried and prevented, I wonder, in the past ten years?'

I felt curious glances from the *hiyek*-Ortheans; was aware of Sethri-safere's hawk-poised patience. What might these people want from us . . . ?

Sethri put one six-fingered hand to the *chiruzeth*: 'Do offworlders recognize this? A "Witchbreed abomination", some call it. We could not live without it.' He smiled, briefly. 'That, and Kel

535

Harantish, who keep it living. *Shan'tai* Christie, all the great *hiyeks* exist between Kel Harantish's power – and the power of Kasabaarde.'

The light shone from the ceiling, from the walls; made his young face angled and alien. Dust in that yellow mane, *meshabi*-robe stained with travel; a beggarly commander of mercenaries. And yet he's testing the extent of our knowledge, I thought, and he isn't slow to do it, either.

Deliberately bland, Doug said, 'You have the crops and water that Kel Harantish must have to survive. Some might call it a fair exchange, *shan'tai*. And then, on the other hand, Kasabaarde is only a small settlement, primarily interested in regulating trade between the two continents. Why should the *hiyeks* fear Kasabaarde?'

The young Orthean male laughed. He stood lightly, one hand on the hilt of a hook-bladed knife; and self-confidence came off him like a glow. 'Say "this *hiyek*" or "that *hiyek*", the *hiyeks* have no unity! We have been fighting each other since the Empire fell, and left us in this wilderness.'

He sobered, and the nictitating membrane slid back from those tawny eyes. The humid heat made me dizzy, and slightly sick; symptoms that are often indistinguishable from fear.

I said, 'It's true the Tower has some authority on the Coast. I saw that last time I came to this world. Ten years ago, the Hexenmeister stopped a war between Kel Harantish and the Hundred Thousand, by threatening to close the Coast seaports to their ships. But what does that have to do with these *siiran*?'

'Without *siiran*, this land would be empty.'

Sethri reached across the *chiruzeth* rim of the tank, squeezed earth in one claw-nailed hand, and let it drop. Behind him, tanks of green *del'ri* stretched in diminishing perspective.

'We live in the ruins of what is past, here. Live and starve! Even for that we depend upon Kel Harantish – depend upon their knowledge of the past, and those whose mere shadow the Harantish Witchbreed are: the Golden. And Kasabaarde *condemns* us for it—'

He spoke with such passion and speed that Douggie looked bewildered, losing track of what he said; and I had no time to analyse a moment's fear: *I remember this too well.* Put that aside, face it later.

Sethri took hold of my arm above the elbow, a strong and painful grip.

'If you know the Tower, *shan'tai*, you already know how they hate the Witchbreed abomination above all things. The Tower

536

won't let the *hiyeks* build again – we're barely suffered to live as we do! The Hexenmeister of Kasabaarde keeps us as we are!' He visibly recovered the self-possession he'd lost. 'You offworlders, you'd call it a . . . a spiritual authority that the Tower has. Speak to my brother-in-*raiku* Jadur, or to Feriksushar, and they'll tell you we can live no other way. We have been born to no other way for two millennia.'

I looked at him until he loosed his grip on my arm. There was no apology in his face. Young, violent, impulsive . . . Some touch of the old professional empathy made me think, There's more to you than that.

'I've waited for offworlders to come to the Coast,' Sethri said. There was an arrogance about him that was entirely unconscious. 'I know other *raiku* in *hiyek*-Anzhadi who are of my mind. I don't speak for *hiyek*-Anzhadi alone. There's a double stranglehold on us, Kel Harantish and Kasabaarde, and we have to break it.'

'That's plain speaking,' I said.

He grinned, with all the Orthean addiction to open conspiracy and cautious foolhardiness. 'It's more than that, it's rash. But now you offworlders have come to the Coast, matters will move with speed. As they should.'

When the filtered light ceased to dazzle, other things beside *chiruzeth* became visible in the *siiran*. I looked down at *ashiren*, their faces thin, all eyes; and saw how half the garden-tanks were barren, not sown with any crop. The unloaded cargo now proved to be *del'ri*-grain, and was being doled out by Feriksushar in scant handfuls. It's not merely human prejudice, I thought, this is a place that's badly overcrowded.

I thought of Molly Rachel, back in the Freeport; tasting the sharp irony that it should be me to find exactly what PanOceania is looking for. Functional Witchbreed technology.

Doug, white about the mouth, said, 'From the point of view of personal safety, don't you think our position is a little exposed?'

The palms of my hands were wet. I heard the clatter of blades, where mercenaries unloaded cargo: armed mercenaries in a *siiran*. Orthean factions – those who want to use human technology, and those who want to keep it off Orthe at any cost. Those who abominate Witchbreed science, and those who want to revive it, or to keep its remnants to themselves . . . Few friends to Earth, and many enemies. And at Kel Harantish, ten days ago, there was the ricochet of a winchbow-bolt . . .

I raised my wristlink, keyed for open-channel.

The Company can't know what effect it might have here, won't see anything but the canals. It's true that Witchbreed science doesn't affect the Hundred Thousand, but here – here it's life. And subsistence-level life, at that. Oh, I can see why the Brown Tower is (like the Wellhouses) against the old technology; it's the ruin of this continent in old wars that has made the Coast so barren. I can see why the Hexenmeister is determined there should never be another Golden Empire. But what about this shit-poor, fight-against-starvation *hiyek*—

'If we'd known the poverty was this bad . . .' Doug glanced at me. 'You're calling the Company.'

'They'll come, irrespective of what I do. And if I don't report, Pramila or David will.'

It will have to be a relay: to David outside the *siiran*, to Pramila in the grounded shuttle, to the orbital ship and then to Morvren Freeport. Upon such fragile links, we depend.

'Look at it from the practical point of view,' I said sardonically. 'The more widespread the knowledge, the less personal danger to those of us who are here first.'

I didn't hesitate. I saw Jadur returning, with the woman Ferik-sushar and other Ortheans; and despite his stare, despite being watched with keen intensity by Sethri-safere, there in the chaos of *del'ri*-grain distribution and children shrieking, I opened the com-link channel and sent out the alert.

Sethri waited until I finished.

'I'll take ship for Maherwa soon,' he said. 'Come with me, *shan'tai*. Word will have gone out. You offworlders may find it safer, now, to be moving targets.'

CHAPTER 11

The Legacy of Kasabaarde

Activity on the Coast is impossible for several hours around midday, and so extends well into second twilight and the night. A few hours later, the metal barge sailed north under a sky blazing with the Heart Stars, on a cold canal that reflected back the silver brilliance.

'Cities are supposedly neutral territory,' Doug offered. We shared a *del'ri*-fibre blanket, huddled on the deckhouse bench. I nodded.

'I hope you're right . . .'

Sethri crossed the deck, leaving David Osaka talking with the copper-maned Jadur of Ninth *raiku*. An older male walked beside Sethri. Although he had the pale skin and mane of the Desert Coast, I was somehow reminded of the Earthspeaker Achil.

'This is Hildrindi-*keretne*,' Sethri said.

The elderly male had a thin face, the skin about his pinched mouth shadowed with illness. I said, '*Kethrial-shamaz keretne*. Give you greeting, Eldest.'

Doug Clifford shot me a puzzled look. I couldn't account for it – wrong dialect? If I could remember which language I'm speaking, I thought, things would go better. Coast speech is beginning to seem like second nature . . . My vocabulary translated *keretne* as "eldest", but that doesn't refer to biological age. It's wordplay: *keret* can mean "truth" or "memory".

'You know *keretne*?' Sethri frowned.

'I know that you—' I bowed to the faded, elderly male '—carry the remembered history of your people, as Earthspeakers and Wellkeepers do in the Hundred Thousand.'

'Their memory is of the mind,' Hildrindi said, 'ours is of the blood. Give you greeting, *s'aranthi*. You will meet other *keret* in the city. We will have much to say to you.'

He inclined his head, and walked on across the deck, bare high-arched feet soundless on the metal. There was a pause. Then Sethri took his gaze from the distant *keretne*, and rested one hand on my shoulder. I felt the indentation of claw-nails through the cloth.

'I came to give you some advice, *shan'tai* Christie, if I may. There'll be mercenary companies in Maherwa, now the fighting with Rythana is done. Why not hire one for your protection?'

'Oh my God.' Doug shut his eyes for a moment, and then smiled with an unshakeable public face. 'Indeed. Thank you . . . Lynne, if there's a company from a Guildhouse, one could do worse. I've learned to trust their code, over the years.'

'It could serve as a visible warning,' I speculated. Also, paid mercenaries hear (and repeat) things that wouldn't be said in front of offworlders.

There is a time to dispense with subtlety. It would be ridiculous, if I didn't have the whole weight of Earth's name behind me, and if we weren't stuck in a hostile wilderness; and as I did it, I thought, It may be ridiculous anyway . . . but I don't underestimate the Orthean capacity for violence.

I stood, letting Sethri see the holstered CAS-IV, letting that remind him by implication of the shuttle, and Earth. 'We're not entirely defenceless,' I said.

Thinking, *Douggie don't laugh*. A pair of middle-aged adventurers, both of us would be better with desk jobs; I can be excused for attempting the bravado of the young, can't I?

I saw, by starlight, Doug Clifford look up, and give me an anxious and encouraging nod.

Six hours later we docked at Maherwa.

Water lapped at the *chiruzeth* steps, where the canal came to an apparent dead end. Stepping from the deck, my legs felt unsteady. Doug joined me, and we followed Sethri-safere, walking towards a sheer edge and a void.

Above, the dome of the sky was half pearl, half indigo; stars temporarily hidden. Dawn on the Coast is rapid. Already there was enough light to see the city.

The *chiruzeth* fell away vertically at our feet. I stopped, catching hold of Doug's arm. Across a space of air, shimmering with the beginning day's heat, the far edge was visible: a cliff-face, curving round. To look down into that vast circular pit made my head swim. The emptiness pulls . . . I dragged my gaze back.

Ten yards to my left, the cliff-edge split, a paved road going down; spiralling on a long curve to the flat canyon floor. As it descended, it ran beneath overhangs until it became a part of the cliff-wall. Set further back into the sides of the pit were the arched entrances to *chiruzeth* rooms . . . the eye following that curve down and away. Vast as a meteor-crater, but with the shaped edges of Witchbreed construction, this pit-city of the wasteland.

Dawn became a brazen flare in the east, flooding the world with white light.

'Come down,' the yellow-maned Orthean said.

I felt a slight breeze, and smelled cooking-fires, as we set foot on the paved way. Walking down, heat sucked all energy away, put a rim of perspiration under collar and cuffs, even with the tempera-ture-weave adjusted. Then we passed into the shadow of the overhang. The tunnels and archways were crowded with Ortheans: small, slightly-built, with bleached skins and pale manes, and the *meshabi*-robes belted at the hip, woven with metal-fibre patterns. They stared. I smelled the musty-spicy odour of the crowded city, tasted the gritty dust. All the time I was aware of the yawning emptiness at my right-hand side.

Douggie glanced back; I caught a glimpse of David Osaka, and the *keretne*-Orthean following.

'Satellite images give no idea, do they? This is . . . impressive.'

I bit back a comment, seeing Doug Clifford's face. It showed that fear of isolation that makes the mouth go dry.

Young *ashiren* crowded closer now. Dirty lengths of cloth veiled the rooms set into the cliff-wall; beyond them were cluttered chambers. Babies whined. A child ran past me, limping, and I glimpsed ulcers on the stick-thin limbs. An anonymous voice hissed '*Witchbreed!*', and a group of young males laughed and fell silent as we went by.

None of us spoke. It was a long walk. I said nothing until we had come nearly to ground level, on the opposite side of the pit to the dock. Dawn put a curved shadow across half the flat expanse of the pit-floor.

'Is that—?' And then I couldn't finish the question.

The shadow fell short of the only structure to break that flat expanse. Holo-images had given no clue to its size – it was as large as the grounded shuttle.

A dome or half-globe rested on a tier of circular steps, and where the edge of the dome met the steps, I could make out the deeper darkness of an entrance. A carved archway. Three squat pillars were set at equidistant points round the dome, and set back into the steps, so that they touched the dome-wall. The top of the pillar nearest to me was broken. There were carved statues on the other two, but erosion and dawn light left no detail – only a hint of claws, wings, scales. At one time, quite plainly, all the surfaces had been painted: scarlet, yellow, and blue. Now the paint was chipped and peeling, *chiruzeth* showing underneath it.

On the facing edges of the steps, on the door-arch, and round the base of the pillars, are carved stylized and alien representations of death's-heads. I stood in the dawn light and was chilled. The Golden Empire, worn down by time and wasteland erosion, still incarnate among its poor and shabby inheritors.

There was light enough now to see that all around that enigmatic structure there were guards armed with spear and winchbow. And they wore the brown scale-mail of Kel Harantish.

'Surely this has to be the Company's primary objective,' Pramila Ishida said, as we turned into the entrances of the lower level rooms. 'These people must want to trade. They're so poor.'

Evening of the next day: I'd decided to risk lifting the grounded shuttle the short distance to Maherwa. Now I had Pramila here, and better comlink equipment. I led the young Asian-Pacifican woman towards the inner chambers, where Douggie and David Osaka were eating with the Ortheans, an evening meal of *del'ri*-bread and *arniac*-tea.

'You go through.' I stopped in the outer room. 'I've something to do. I'll join you.'

The low-ceilinged room was partially lit by mirror-reflected light. The walls were plaster-covered, stained in bright patterns with metal oxides. This room was full of outlanders, some in Melkathi robes, some – despite the heat – in Rimon boots and britches; out of place among the *hiyek*-Ortheans. All of these northern continent Ortheans wore *harur-nilgiri* and *harur-nazari*; and were mostly stretched out on the padded benches, drinking fermented *del'ri*-grain and playing *ochmir*, and talking in a patois of Rimon, Melkathi, Morvrenni, and four or five different Coast languages.

I halted beside a female Orthean. '*T'an* Haldin, isn't it?'

She was lying on a bench, legs up on a table, booted ankles crossed. 'Haldin Damory, of the Medued Guildhouse. Have you made your mind up yet, *s'aranthi*?'

'A contract,' I said. 'Guard duty. And no other contracts taken on while you do it.'

She grinned lazily. 'That costs more.'

So Blaize Meduenin once told me. When I think of him, I wonder that I trust mercenaries at all.

'I'll pay.'

Whoops, yells, appreciative comments and a few raucous jeers – her fellow mercenaries approved. They were all young, not one over twenty-five; and all had that savage, laconic, and utterly careless attitude towards violence.

Haldin, hands resting on the hilts of *harur* blades, said, 'Guard duty . . . does that apply to *all* you offworlders here?'

I made a mental note to repeat that question to Doug; he has the sense of humour to appreciate it. 'All,' I said firmly, and we closed the contract. I thought, I'm not sorry to be doing this where *hiyek*-Ortheans can see and know. Another precaution.

I walked through into the inner chambers, pushing past Ortheans, most of whom had *hiyek*-Anzhadi patterns woven into belt or headband or *meshabi*-robe. Some light still entered the unshuttered windows. The last evening breeze brought the smell of dried-dung fires. Clusters of glass bells hung from every window and door-arch, chiming softly. I sat down between Doug and Pramila, on one of the fine metalwork benches, padded with *del'ri*-fibre matting; and drank the acrid *arniac* while Doug and David talked with Ninth *raiku*, and imagined schemes of advantage behind every friendly, curious, or indifferent Orthean face.

I should steer this in the right direction, I thought. *Can you help us with access to the technology here? If not, are you useful as a way back into Kel Harantish?* That's all the Company needs to know. But . . . But?

The young Asian-Pacifican woman beside me stirred, restless. Then she raised her head, looking me right in the eye. 'Lynne, these people are *starving*. The children show all the signs of chronic malnutrition. I've been talking to some of them – there hasn't been a *siiran*-harvest brought in without a war for the last nine years. Lynne, these people *need* a Trade&Aid programme!'

The outburst surprised me; not something I expected from this small, sallow-faced girl. No, I realized guiltily, and you didn't expect her to object to this, because she's Company. As if being in a multicorporate made you blind . . .

'It isn't that simple,' I said.

'Isn't it?'

'You set up Trade&Aid, feed these people, and you'll send the birth-rate up,' I said. 'The *siirans* will be even more overcrowded, they'll overflow. Instead of harvest-wars, you'll have fighting all year round. Soon the cities won't be neutral territory, and the *ashiren* won't come into them, to group into *raiku*.'

I sipped at the *arniac*, cupping the metal bowl between my hands. 'Then there'll be dozens, hundreds of *kei-raiku* people here. Do you have any idea how that will unbalance this culture? The *raiku* are self-supporting groups, everything – trade, crafts, ships, the *hiyek*-bloodline itself – is based on that group. Break that up and you'll have changed these people out of all recognition!'

Pramila, looking stunned, said, 'Did the Ortheans here tell you that?'

'No, I—'

am under the starry sky of Dustsun, standing with my four companions, before the keretne of the hiyek.

"By this blood—"

The metal knives cut. I put my gashed hands in turn to those of my brothers and sisters in raiku, feeling the flow of memory between us.

"—rediscovered, bind us together—"

The rock cold under bare, high-arched feet; meshabi-robe a scant protection; but joy warms me, I have found my other sharers in truth—

'Lynne?'

What the—?

I shut down the flood of vision, concentrated on Pramila's face. 'I'm saying that leaving these people to starve is cruel, and changing their world out of recognition would be cruel; what kind of cruelty should we prefer?'

Voices interrupted as the small room began to fill up with *hiyek*-Ortheans. Sethri, with Jadur and the others of Ninth *raiku*: the twin sisters Wyrrin-hael and Charazir-hael . . . Feriksushar and a crowd of others, and the *keretne* male Hildrindi . . .

What happened? Is it so easy to think like a *hiyek*-Orthean? Frighteningly easy.

'Bad news?' Doug Clifford asked, as Pramila moved over to talk with David Osaka.

'What? – No, sorry; I was thinking of something else.'

'You've surprised me,' he said, under cover of the general noise. 'I don't have anything like your grasp of the Coast culture, and I've been here – well, the Hundred Thousand—'

'The Hundred Thousand isn't the Coast.'

That round face was bland. 'Lynne, there's no need to bite my head off. There would be much on hypno-tapes, I suppose, that never got transcribed into data-net holo-records. It's a pity, in some ways, that we can't use hypno-tapes now.'

'If you'd been through the Psych programmes that I have, to undo the damage—'

'Oh yes. Quite. Not a serious suggestion.'

If I could talk to anyone, it would be to Douggie . . . but I held off. Held off and thought, Am I ill? If it's a recurrence of that trouble I had after the hypno-tapes . . . but it isn't like that. In Morvren I thought, It's as if I'd never been away from the Hundred Thousand. And I have the same feeling here. I know how the *hiyeks* function, what life is like in the *siiran*; every language falls familiar on my ears. But I *can't* know. Ten years ago, I never even came near the *hiyeks* of the Desert Coast . . .

David Osaka, leaning forward intently, finished giving the standard advantages-of-Trade&Aid speech. He glanced over at me. *Yes* it's my job and yes, it'll get back to Molly Rachel that I'm not displaying proper enthusiasm on behalf of the Company. Too bad.

An *ashiren* stood, slender and pale-maned, and reached up to close the metal window-shutters, excluding the night air. Another child brought fresh *arniac*. There were a dozen or so Ortheans here I could put names to, far more that I couldn't. Now the mirrors began to reflect starlight into the chamber, bright enough to read expressions on alien features. Sethri-safere pulled a metal lattice shutter across the door-arch. Through it, I saw Haldin Damory and her troop still in the outer rooms.

'. . . and if we do go to war with *hiyek*-Nadrasiir, the fighting will end when the rains come. *If* the rains come.' The woman Feriksushar glanced up from her conversation with David Osaka. She looked at me. 'Your *shan'tai* Clifford has said we will not benefit from trade. That it would change us. That we would become like Earth.'

Pramila frowned. When I caught Doug's eye, he was entirely unrepentant. I thought, The Coast is not the Hundred Thousand . . . and we sit here and drink *arniac*, eat *del'ri*-bread; relying on hospitality that *hiyek*-Anzhadi may not be able to afford.

As much to myself as to Feriksushar, I said, 'If you have Trade&Aid here, it *will* change your lives. I don't know. Before, I was in the Hundred Thousand, and to them one can say "stay free of Earth" because they don't need help. I don't know if we can say that to you.'

Glancing past the gold-maned female, I saw the pinched face of Hildrindi-*keretne*. When I mentioned the Hundred Thousand, I saw a hatred as brief as it was impersonal.

'That said – I have to be honest. All PanOceania's help will come with a price-tag attached. This time it's access to the Witchbreed technology, the canals. You'll have to decide whether or not you can pay that price.'

A heated discussion broke out. Jadur, seated on the floor, leaning back between Sethri's legs, looked up and caught the arm of his brother-in-*raiku*, speaking urgently. Wyrrin-hael leaned across to speak to her twin, white mane falling across her eyes. Each of the *hiyek*-Ortheans in the room seemed determined to out-shout the others. I saw Pramila lean forward to speak to David, and Feriksushar (in a gesture that passed unnoticed) take Hildrindi's *arniac* bowl from his hand that shook with weakness.

'We can't trade in Witchbreed abominations!' the *keretne* said.

Jadur lurched to his feet. '*Shan'tai* Christie, we fight our wars with mercenary troops and weapons. Weapons from offworld would aid us. Will your Company trade for them?'

Shit, I thought. That's a question I hoped I wouldn't hear.

In the days when my government controlled relations with Restricted worlds, I could quite genuinely have said, We have a policy forbidding that. Now the multicorporates have the same policy, but I fear how flexible it might prove to be.

Before David or Pramila could express an opinion either way, I cut in: 'I'm not convinced that you *can* offer access to the canals, *shan'tai* Jadur.'

He scratched awkwardly at his mane, and sat down again beside Feriksushar. 'It would have to be secretly . . . with danger . . . perhaps not even then.' Forced to that honesty, he looked away, discomfited.

When Hildrindi spoke, it was with an effort. The nictitating membrane opaqued his pale eyes. 'The *keretne* will not agree to this. We listen to the Brown Tower, and to the Hexenmeister; and the Tower will not have *s'aranthi* weapons or *s'aranthi* engines on the Coast!'

'There is this,' Sethri-safere interrupted. 'While we live in this arid land, we will always be in debt to someone. We have merely a choice of creditors. Kel Harantish, or Kasabaarde, or – *s'aranthi* offworlders.'

Voices were raised again, and I leaned back against the cool wall, watching. Sethri made himself heard: 'Listen to me! War between *all* the Coast *hiyeks* is coming. It can't be avoided now. We'll be fighting before the end of Wintersun. The only choice is whether to have war to our advantage, or to our enemies'.'

Claw-nailed hands gestured, one of the males I didn't know stood up, shouting; Charazir-hael drew the hook-bladed knife from her belt, but Jadur restrained her. The stocky Feriksushar was on her feet. A tall male, blustering, shouted, 'Give us weapons, we'll free ourselves of the Harantish Witchbreed!'

Another male looked up lazily and said, 'There are no pure-blooded Witchbreed now. Our *ashiren* have gone to Kel Harantish, their *ashiren* have come into our *raiku*—'

'If you have 'Breed blood in your *hiyek*, no need to accuse us of the same filth!'

Sethri-safere came and sat down on the bench beside me. I saw Doug had gone – and then saw him talking with Pramila. The yellow-maned Orthean grinned at the violent reaction.

'That's stirred them up. They don't trust me, because I've

commanded mercenaries, and that's a dirty job. But it does mean I know what I'm talking about.'

War between the *hiyeks*? 'Who are your enemies, Sethri?'

Nictitating membrane slid over his tawny eyes. He said, 'When your Company comes offering to trade, all the Coast *hiyeks* became each other's enemies.'

Some cold professionalism in me ignored the implications of what he was saying; merely thought, Thank God for someone who understands the problem.

'Suppose I tell you – and it's true – that there's a strict prohibition on our bringing in Earth weapons technology?'

No matter what we might be offered in exchange?

He looked down at strong, narrow fingers, spread on the weave of dirty *meshabi*-cloth; the claws trimmed back on all but the sixth finger.

'Christie, anything is a weapon. Say you trade us a cure for crop-blight – there's a *hiyek* that will grow strong, have many *ashiren*. A *hiyek* that will be able to pay to send mercenaries against other *hiyeks*, to seize what *siiran* it needs to feed that number.' He shrugged. 'Which means that the three or four most powerful *hiyeks* at the time will band together to fight that one, and then fall out among themselves when the war's over . . .'

Sethri-safere. An attractive face, with a deceptively open look that owed much to fair mane and brows and nothing at all, I guessed, to temperament.

'You have an answer?'

He turned his head slightly so that no one should see what he said, and it was an automatic gesture: he was more than used to concealment, he revelled in it. I thought, You should have been born in the Hundred Thousand, a player of the game.

'There aren't answers. Maybe we can adapt. If *raiku* can be allies, then why not *hiyek*?' The skin round his eyes crinkled, bare evidence of amusement. 'I've little talent for sowing or harvest in the *siiran*, the city trade bores me, commanding mercenaries is a regrettable necessity – but I *can* persuade *raiku* into seeing things my way.'

His hand was cool on my arm, dry, with the swift Orthean heartbeat felt through fingertips on my skin. I thought, I trust self-interest even more than expediency – you want to break the stasis the *hiyeks* are held in, but even more, you want it to be *you* that does it . . .

'Christie, you see, I'm honest with you. Who else is to help me to that leadership, if not *s'aranthi*? And who else but me would be willing to help *s'aranthi* get what they want from the ruins of the

Golden Empire?' His smile was warm, mocking, collusive. 'I mean to make a friend of you, Lynne Christie.'

An hour later I left the crowded chamber, going out to stand in the cool night. A boot-heel clicked. I glanced down the paved way, under the overhang – the mercenary, Haldin Damory, lifted a hand in reassurance, and stepped back into the shadows.

I looked out across the pit-floor of Maherwa. The Heart Stars shone bright enough to cast shadows from the dome-structure and pillars, and illumine the distant figures of Harantish guards.

And word will have gone back to Kel Harantish. That's the obstacle – or should I be grateful that there is an obstacle?

All the Coast hiyeks exist between the power of Kel Harantish and Kasabaarde, Kasabaarde—

I swung round, and hit the *chiruzeth* wall hard with the heel of my hand. Vision trembled at the edge of consciousness. A tide of memory that will flood over me, sweep away all that is Lynne Christie—

What *is* it? What's happening to me?

'Lynne.' Doug Clifford's face was in the shadow, but concern was plain in his voice. 'If there's anything I can do . . .'

'Let's leave Pramila and David to it,' I said. 'The mercenary troop have a few bottles of *siir*-wine; let's have a drink, and catch up on what we've been doing since – where was it? – Melhuish's World.'

And Doug Clifford, with urbane tact, agreed.

Four days later, Wintersun-28, word came through on the comlink of Molly Rachel's imminent arrival.

All through the intervening days, *raiku* from Anzhadi and other *hiyeks* poured into the city: groups of three, four, or five Coast Ortheans; some elderly, some still *ashiren*. The speed of communication amazed me, until I saw the heliographs flash across the flat, barren landscape; and as for their mobility – travel along the waterways is, like sea travel, faster than most forms of land travel in low-tech cultures. By Wintersun-28 there were Ortheans in Maherwa from as far up the Coast as Quarth, all of two hundred and fifty miles away.

And by Wintersun-28 I had grown used to sleeping three hours at midday, and six at night, to fit into *hiyek* life; and to carrying on PanOceania's business while armed mercenaries guarded the door.

'We'll go up and meet the shuttle,' I said. Haldin Damory stood, and joined me at the door. The dirty *del'ri*-cloth curtain had been looped back, to let in morning light, and the noise of squabbling *ashiren* on the paved way outside.

'Are you interested in a warning?' the young female swordfighter said as we left the inner chambers.

Nights in Wintersun have still a bitter cold, but the frosts were passing. Now first twilight had gone, and Carrick's Star as it rose left half the city in deep shadow. Haldin paced beside me, alert; dark curled mane carelessly braided up. She wore a horn-mail coat, and one six-fingered hand rested lightly on the hilt of *harur-nazari*.

Four days is long enough to hear rumour, gossip, intrigue. I slowed as we passed an area where the overhang was deeper, going further back into the cliff-face, where the stalls of a market were being set up.

'Warning?' I said.

'I'll tell you a fable, *t'an*, and you draw the moral.' She glanced at me. 'Meeting you isn't the first time I've heard the name of *S'aranth*. When I first came to the Coast as a mercenary – oh, I was an *ashiren*, no more – there was a Commander, a woman of the Hundred Thousand. An exile. She was crippled, she'd lost an arm.'

The young female's face was serious. Is she old enough to remember that long-ago summer in Melkathi?

'I'd heard, yes. Ruric Orhlandis died, in exile.' I don't think my voice was quite controlled.

Haldin Damory said, 'Ah, but that's it, *t'an*, she didn't die – she was killed. An assassin killed her, in the trade-quarter of Kasa-baarde. And now draw the moral: I hear talk in this Goddess-abandoned hole, and I hear there are still people who'd willingly see offworlders, *and* friends of offworlders, killed. That death was a long time ago, but things aren't different now.'

Shall I ask what she said about the *S'aranth*, those many years ago? Ask: was she bitter, driven into exile from her beloved Hundred Thousand, did she hate me for the part I played in that? No. Whatever was said, I can't change it now.

'There,' Haldin Damory said. She dropped back a pace, and I saw her check by line of sight that two of the other mercenaries were not far from us; and then I saw what she'd seen. A head taller than any of the Coast Ortheans, walking where the sun cast a shadow on to the paved way from the overhang, and entirely alone – Molly Rachel.

'Lynne!' she called. She looked past me. 'Are Pramila and David here? Has Rashid arrived yet?'

'No. I wasn't told he was coming.' I stood and waited for her. 'How were the Barrens?'

'We kept to high-level aerial survey. The readings didn't tell us much. Then I got your transmission. Lynne—'

Of all the tribal Ortheans I met in the Barrens, I can remember only O'he-Oramu-te, the Woman Who Walks Far. In that place of tundra and Witchbreed ruins, will she even be alive now?

'—this place!' Molly scratched through loops of her tangled black hair, and slowed that long-legged stride. She stared out across the pit, at the opposite cliff-wall honeycombed with chambers. She pulled down eyeshields, blinked. An *ashiren*, two or three years old, stopped and stared up at this dark giant; and then ran when Molly smiled at *kir*.

'I must say, we've been marking time,' I said. Thinking, Don't ask me why, Molly, please.

She stepped close to the edge of the walkway. At her feet, a sheer drop; empty air, and then – isolated in the centre of the pit-floor – that *chiruzeth* dome and pillars.

'It was the last act of Empire,' I said, unwillingly sharing her fascination. 'The generation that saw the Elansiir destroyed, built this. But they destroyed themselves, fighting; left only the Ortheans . . .'

'That's it, that's what we've got to have.'

We turned to go back down the walkway, Molly ducking to avoid catching her head on the *del'ri*-cloth awnings of the market stalls. Ortheans pointed as we went by, commenting in a variety of Coast languages. There was the ring of hammers from a metal-worker's stall nearby.

'Can the *hiyeks* help us get into that?'

I glanced up at her. 'It's the incredible balance – Kel Harantish with the technical knowledge, the *siiran* with the food and water. I honestly don't know whether you'll get the *hiyeks* to risk it.'

'It all comes back to Kel Harantish,' the Pacifican woman said.

'And I don't think you'll get back on negotiating terms with them in a hurry.' That pleased me: the thought that I don't have to block the Company here, circumstances will do it.

'Lynne, whose side are you on?'

'Ah, now, if I knew that . . .'

'Joking aside. I know Doug Clifford's against ninety per cent of what we're doing here. It's you I can't make out.'

'You've been talking to young Pramila.'

'I've been talking to *you*.'

Sunlight dazzled me, shining into the walkway. I put my eyeshields back on. The market stalls wouldn't stay open long, it was rapidly becoming too hot. I looked out at a steel-blue sky peppered with daystars.

Deliberately putting her off, I said, 'It's a barter economy here. They exchange promissory notes on the next *siiran*-harvest. Taking into consideration they pay mercenaries too, it's no surprise there isn't a *hiyek* on the Coast not chronically in debt. Of course, Kel Harantish uses that to stir up dissent. The last thing they want is for the Coast families to unite . . .'

Molly looked down, shook her head, watching me. The light made silver curves of her round features. She walked with one hand always near the CAS-IV holster.

'They use mercenaries because there's a taboo on personally attacking the bloodline, and all the *hiyeks* are more or less inter-related.' Which the Pacifican woman would know; but it was only an attempt at distraction.

The crowd was thicker here, and we were stopped at the edge of a group of *ashiren* watching glass-blowers at work. Molly and I stood for a moment looking over their heads. Groupings of *ashiren* that would, when their city time was over, become *raiku*.

'*How* do I get into that?' Molly gazed out at the *chiruzeth* dome and pillars, and the guards. Then she looked down at me, and with an abrupt change of tone, said, 'My father was of the Masai. My mother was Aruna. *She* had a choice. She could die alcoholic, because the old life couldn't be lived, or she could take. She *took*. She went to the University of Melbourne, and then to Tokyo. Lynne, sometimes cultures change. It's that simple.'

I listened hard, and I heard nothing at all defensive in her tone. I said, 'Change imposed from outside.'

'It comes to the same thing.' She squinted up at the brilliant sky, and fingered the eyeshields that hung round her neck. 'My mother taught me what she learned when she was a burri – a baby. Sooner or later one culture goes under, so you don't give up, you take. These people here, the *hiyeks*, they're capable of learning that.'

The crowd thinned a little, and I walked on. Aware of Haldin Damory and the two mercenaries, never far away. That honey-combed cliff towered above. I walked slowly towards the Pacifican quarters further round the curve of the wall. After a few seconds, Molly Rachel's long stride caught up. She walked beside me.

'You're looking tired.' Concern in her voice, and something else; something inflexible. She said, 'Lynne, if you want to go back up to the orbiter, not just back to Morvren-base, that'll be all right.

I'm certain that you've found what we want, here – if I can get to it. And I won't need you in the negotiations. This isn't your specialist area.'

I can't believe that I didn't see this one coming.

'There's no necessity for me to return—'

'—immediately. No, of course not. You could just as well go in a day or two, Lynne. Go with Clifford, when he goes back. That'll be in the very near future.'

The sun was a brilliant glare, drowning daystars. I stopped to wipe my forehead, and try to control uneven breath. I ached. Angry with myself: I won't let myself be used and thrown out!

'Molly, I think you'd benefit, still, from having the advice of someone with experience of the area—'

'But you haven't. Not of the Coast.'

Worn flagstones were hot underfoot, too hot to stand still for long, and so I walked on, thinking, Douggie isn't going to like the news of his imminent departure, and I—

I can't be a restraining influence on the Company if I'm not involved in Company negotiations.

A wind stirred the dust on the city floor. It rattled against the *del'ri* awnings. Three young *ashiren* pushed between Molly and me, running; thin limbs and ragged *meshabi*-robes.

Morvren Freeport, the orbiter, and then what? A ship back to Earth? Because there's no need for a special advisor if you know as much – or as little – as she does about the Desert coast and Kel Harantish . . .

I licked my lips, tasting dust. On an optimistic estimate, two days, to save my position here?

'*T'an* Christie.'

Both of us turned. It was Haldin with one of her mercenaries, a crop-maned male. The male said in accented Rimon, 'I have a message, *t'an*, passed to me to give to the *s'aranthi*. There are people here who wish to speak with you.'

Molly frowned. 'From other *hiyeks*?'

Haldin Damory snorted. The mercenary spoke with the sardonic humour of the young: 'They *say* they're from Quarth, come down the Coast by *jath-rai*. *T'ans*, if you were to ask me, I'd say they come from a different port – from Kasabaarde. Or if they don't, that's where their report will go back to. Kasabaarde, and the Brown Tower.'

CHAPTER 12

Dreams of Gold and Silver

What I'm doing here sickens me.

That thought came quite suddenly, following the Pacifican woman under the *chiruzeth* overhang, back along the walkway. It felt cooler. I pulled off the eyeshields.

No, I thought. It's the self-deception that sickens me. While I stay here, I have to act for the Company. What good am I doing Orthe? What good am I doing myself?

Molly Rachel's stride took her ahead, and I followed, climbing the gradual incline. The mercenaries checked doorways to inner rooms. I stopped for a moment, short of breath. White sun glared from the city's far wall, where figures moved like flies, and I trudged on again, higher up, further round the pit-wall.

If it wasn't me it would be someone else—

That's no excuse. It never was.

And I had to smile, thinking, These qualms of conscience have come only when I'm on the verge of losing my post here anyway.

Shadow lay under the *chiruzeth* overhang in a black curve. My lungs burned with the effort of climbing. Haldin Damory glanced back, with a look of concern. At intervals the overhang widens out – or rather, goes back deeper into the rock cliff itself. The Pacifican woman stopped in that shadowy, low-roofed space; staring round at the featureless archways. No wind stirred those ragged *del'ri* curtains.

'*Shan'tai* Haldin.'

Haldin approached her. I stopped, gratefully, a few paces away. Young *ashiren* playing pebble-games scattered as they saw us. I caught sight of one child's thin cheek marred with a raw ulcer, another with suppurating membraned eyes.

Just maybe I'm right about the Hundred Thousand; we could trade with the *telestres* for Witchbreed technology and it wouldn't change their lives. But here – how can we *not* trade, not change? Knowing what culture shock, what disruption; still . . .

The close heat and shadowed twilight made me dizzy. Aching, hot; all the discomfort of alien air, protein, gravity. And ten years less resilient now.

Molly Rachel said, 'One of you fetch Pramila Ishida, I want her here for this, and—'

'Doug Clifford,' I put in, saw her hesitate, then accept.

When I came to Orthe I thought I knew what I had to do, if not how to do it. Now I don't even know what I should be trying to do.

The Pacifican woman said speculatively, 'Traders from Kasabaarde?'

'From the Hexenmeister,' Haldin said. '—S'aranth?'

In the dream, a woman stood before me. She had the bleached skin of the Coast, and a rough dark mane coming down from complex braids. In her forties (and I younger, then). And held between brown-robed servants, her shirt torn, her eyes unveiled and so wide that the whites were visible.

I spoke to that ancient Orthean male, the Hexenmeister, who stood beside me: 'I have heard that those whom you – question – are not unchanged by it. Some say it's possible to recognize them forever after, because of what they become.'

'T'an, you can hurt her greatly and she will perhaps tell you the truth, and perhaps a lie. I will hurt her not at all, and to me she will tell only the truth. But—'

'But?'

'But it is true she will be changed.'

That subliminal hum that underlies the Brown Tower intensified the silence. Aphasia, amnesia, blackouts, idiocy; all the possible symptoms of brain-damage – oh yes: changed.

The woman looked at me with a desperate appeal. I couldn't even recall her name.

'Yes,' I consented. 'Question her, master.'

The Hexenmeister of Kasabaarde watched me with black, bright eyes. And I dreamed that we went down into the maze of the Brown Tower, among the masked and brown-robed servants, to a cool dry hall lit with faintly blue iridescence, and sarcophagus-machines.

'Havoth-jair!' I cried as I woke, stumbled; Molly Rachel caught my arm, and Haldin's mercenary turned swiftly to survey the low-roofed space. The sky beyond the overhang was molten brass. The air stifled. Loud voices echoed back from the walkway.

Not dreaming (but it has, I remember, been a recurring dream for many years); not dreaming, but caught between one step and the next into memory—

False memory.

'It wasn't me! I didn't give him permission to question her.'

554

Bewildered, I found the young woman's arm round my shoulder, half supporting me. 'Her name. Her name was Havoth-jair.'

Rachel looked down at me, frowning. 'Are you all right? Can you stand? Good. Lynne . . . you're not going to like me saying this, but I've seen this coming on.'

I pushed her hand aside, still unsteady. Her skin was slick with sweat. Details of the dream were already fading.

'Lynne, it's on your record. You had an extremely bad reaction to hypno-tape implants. Now you're where everything triggers off those old implant-data memories. I think you'd better go back up to the orbiter. The help you've given has been invaluable, but I won't make you stay here and crack up.'

Her words had a slight reverberation: sounds echo between these *chiruzeth* walls. *Chiruzeth*: cloudy blue-grey. I want to sit down, I need a drink – I'd even drink their fermented *del'ri*-grain. I need to know what's happening to me.

When I rubbed my forehead my hair was plastered down with sweat. Pulse hammering: rapid and unsteady. I walked a few steps, hearing the echo of my boot-heels. The vast emptiness beyond the edge of the walkway shone bright: sun and dust and air. I turned, facing – as I must – that young woman.

What hurts most is that her concern is genuine.

'It isn't that—'

Suddenly and simply, I knew two things. The first and more obvious: it was no use remonstrating, I would condemn myself out of my own mouth. And the second was that this was *not* hypno-tape psychosis.

I've been through that, I thought. I'd recognize it again. I'm in a mess, sure, but that isn't the reason – thank God

A laugh bubbled up, uncomplicatedly cheerful. Unreasonable to be so happy, knowing that – but I do know; I've had long enough to know how I function. With a macabre humour, I thought, I may be having hallucinations, blackouts, false memories, and paranoia, but it's okay. If it isn't that identity-destroying reaction to hypno-implants (I dread that above all things) then it's *okay* . . .

Something of that must have come through in the way I laughed. Molly Rachel looked at me dubiously and said, 'I could be wrong.'

'Believe me, you are.' That irrational joy was still with me. I saw, further down the walkway slope, the approaching figures of Doug Clifford, Pramila Ishida, and David Osaka, with one of Haldin's mercenaries. 'We seem to be all here. Shall we go and talk to these traders from "Quarth"?'

Haldin Damory indicated one of the curtained archways. Molly blinked.

'I . . . er . . . well—'

I beamed, walked past her into the inner room close by, so dazzling her with bonhomie that she didn't tell this troublesome woman she had no right, officially, to be present. There are advantages to being thirty-eight and in one's right mind.

Inside, in mirror-light that cast strange shadows, a group of five Ortheans were seated round one of the low metal tables. I let the Pacificans crowd in behind me, and Molly do the standard introductions. Five of them, four males and one female: none of them old.

A thin Orthean male rose to his feet. He wore a plain brown *meshabi*-robe, and carried no weapon; what was visible of his pale mane was shaven down to white fluff. And he wore a mask. A half-face mask, with some translucent glass or crystal in the eyeholes. Such masks are common on the Coast in summer – and in Kasabaarde all year round.

When he had introduced himself as Annekt, I said, 'Quarth? Give you greeting, *shan'tai* Annekt; I think you're out of your way. I think you mean Kasabaarde.'

Molly Rachel winced at that high-handedness. The Pacificans froze in the action of seating themselves round the low table. Doug Clifford coughed.

Only that curved pale mouth visible: the thin male's face was unreadable.

'We've sailed by way of Kasabaarde's trade-quarter. Many do.' Annekt's voice was husky, with an indeterminate Coast accent.

'And when you sail back, what will you say to the Hexenmeister of Kasabaarde about Company offworlders?'

Molly seized my elbow. 'Sit down!' she hissed. I had little option, and half fell on to one of the padded metal benches.

The Orthean remained standing for a moment. I saw that his long six-fingered hands moved nervously. And then I saw answering small gestures from the seated traders. Communication.

'You're quite right,' Annekt said mildly, 'that all the traders of the Coast commonly bring news and rumour to the Tower in Kasabaarde. I shouldn't wonder but that the Hexenmeister knows of your arrival here.'

Molly glanced round, momentarily helpless. Pramila settled in next to her, and David Osaka seated himself awkwardly on the end of another bench. It was a shabby room, the painted images on the plaster chipped and fading. I saw Doug Clifford exchange a greeting with the other traders and sit down.

The lattice grid of the inner doorway opened, and Haldin Damory re-emerged. She gestured. One of the young mercenaries served *arniac*-tea, handing the bowls to us, but placing them on the table before the Kasabaardean traders. Molly passed her wristlink over her bowl, and I saw Haldin stiffen – an insult to a mercenary's efficiency, to check for poison.

I pitched in again: 'No doubt the Hexenmeister recalls offworlders from when I visited him before – unless there's a new holder of the title. Ah, I forgot. That wouldn't make any difference, would it?'

I wanted this faceless young Kasabaardean male to respond to that needling tone, but only Molly Rachel got irritated.

'Lynne, if you don't mind!'

Annekt said, 'No, *shan'tai*, the Hexenmeister will still remember offworlders. Memory dies not, though we are mortal, and there is always a Hexenmeister in the Tower.'

There was a loud crash. Haldin Damory threw down a ceramic bowl. In a high, tight voice she said, 'No! The Hexenmeister has no past-memory, no *true* past-memory, only some heresy brought about by Witchbreed engines and devices—'

My stomach went tight at the tension of the silence that followed. For a mercenary to lose control – she and the masked young trader stared at each other, poles of power and tension, until at last she turned, spat, and walked out, her boots loud on the *chiruzeth* floor. She curtly directed one of her mercenaries to guard the outer door, and strode off out of sight.

'*Shan'tai* Annekt, I can only apologize.' Molly passed a hand through her tangled black hair, and glanced at Pramila and David. 'If we could perhaps continue this discussion in a calmer frame of mind . . .'

'Of course,' the Kasabaardean male said. He reseated himself. One of the other traders signed something on claw-nailed fingers that made him smile.

How far can I push this? I thought. Ah, since Molly's trying to get me out anyway, I doubt it matters what I say now.

'*Shan'tai* Annekt.' I got his attention. 'What does the Hexenmeister want with us? Is it merely curiosity?'

The male didn't answer for a moment. Then he reached up with both six-fingered hands and undid the lacings of the mask. He put it on the table, and wiped his face – a thin-featured face, under that shaven white mane, with green eyes brilliant against the pallor of his skin. He smiled.

'*Shan'tai*, if you're so well informed, tell me why it should be anything else except simple curiosity.'

Doug Clifford leaned forward, resting his clasped hands on his knees, unexpectedly coming to my rescue. 'It's in our Service records that the Tower's influence stopped a war, once. As I understand it, the Tower threatened to use its influence and cut Kel Harantish off from trade with the rest of the Coast – starve them, in fact. Kasabaarde seems well placed to control the flow of trade.'

The green-eyed male blinked. That shaven mane accentuated the alien proportions of his face: broad forehead, narrow jaw. He said, 'Stopped a war? An exaggeration, *shan'tai*.'

I said, 'If not a war, certainly a very nasty hostile incident.' And why not mention it all? I thought. There's no one in this room now who'll be offended. 'You may not recall, Annekt. It was some eight years ago. The Harantish Witchbreed were financing rebellious factions in the Hundred Thousand *telestres* – SuBannasen, Charain. Orhlandis.'

The male shrugged thin shoulders, looked at me helplessly. '*Shan'tai*, I'm only a trader. If I carry word to the Hexenmeister's brown-robes . . . well, all Coast traders do that. I know little. There will be word sent to you, I doubt not, if the Hexenmeister of Kasabaarde would hear more of you.'

David and Pramila had their heads together, muttering. Doug Clifford appeared to be examining, with absent-minded interest, the patterns of reflected mirror-light on the shabby walls.

Molly Rachel, in Sino-Anglic, said, 'Lynne, we can do without mentioning spies and informers from some cult-ridden settlement in the north. I think we'll consider the subject closed.'

The talks went on after that in much the usual Pacifican manner. Molly conducted affairs, bringing in Pramila and David for logistic and technical support; and the five Orthean traders asked the standard questions about the standard Trade&Aid speeches. Only the unmasked male looked at me, from time to time, and then the nictitating membrane slid back from those apple-green eyes.

The room grew hotter, the air more close; and about the time I judged there'd be a mid-morning break, I edged round until I could speak to Doug Clifford.

'What's all this about, Lynne?'

'Did you know you were leaving for the Freeport today or tomorrow?'

Not what he expected: at first bewildered, then that affable public expression vanished. 'I'm still government representative here!'

'I know.'

Molly said something I didn't catch, there was a scuffle of people rising to their feet: the time well judged. As we went out I said, 'Douggie, we should talk.'

A square of sky was visible through this outer room's window, daystars obscured by a haze. Anzhadi-*hiyek* had given Clifford rooms high up on the city wall. The air was hot and heavy with the promise of rain. The end of Wintersun. I collapsed into one of the padded *del'ri*-fibre chairs, wiping my forehead. Doug crossed to where he kept a flask of the fermented *del'ri*-grain spirit on a low table, poured two bowls, and lifted one in silent acknowledgement of exhaustion.

'Jesus Christ, Douggie, I'm getting too *old* for this!'

He seated himself in a chair beside me, smiling with squirrel-cheeked bonhomie. 'You're not fifty, my girl. Just wait. You don't know what being tired is.'

'What a pair of old wrecks we are – eh?'

Humour faded. The light beat in and hurt my eyes. There was the constant stickiness of sweat, and that undefined irritation that is the precursor of many minor ills. A few months on the Coast, I thought, and what little stamina I have left will be gone.

'I mean, too old for offworld service. Douggie, I swear I don't know how you do it.'

He sipped the acrid *del'ri*-spirit. 'I do it – used to do it – by never getting involved beyond professional limits. Lynne . . . but if I'm being shipped back to the Freeport, it's academic. Thank you for the warning, by the way.'

'Probably the last time I'll be in a position to give one.'

Noise filtered in from the walkway outside, and the shadows of passing *hiyek*-Ortheans fell briefly on the *del'ri* curtain of the archway. There was a smell of cooking, and dung-fires; a last burst of activity before the midday cessation.

I said, 'It's all falling down behind us like dominoes – a palace revolution in Kel Harantish, the *telestres*, the Wellhouses, the *hiyek*-wars . . .'

Doug said grimly, 'Reports *are* going back to Earth.'

I thought, I came here to talk; how do I raise the matter that's important? That sudden influx of confidence, of energy, now gone. I don't have the reserves of strength I had at thirty. Eroded by heat, by exhaustion, by the sheer pressure of demand.

'I thought, when I came here with the Company, that I could *do* something. I really thought that, you know?'

'You've kept the Company's policy within restricted limits.' Doug raised a thoughtful eyebrow. 'Very restricted, if one were to consider, say, Melhuish's World – or the European Enclaves.'

559

He smiled. It warmed me. He's the only one here with the same knowledge of the Company that I have, the same objections to their methods.

'All the same, the problem isn't that simple.' I wiped sweat off neck and forehead. 'Life here – this is subsistence-level, here on the Coast. Sometimes not even that. Is it right for us to be isolationist?'

He shrugged, a gesture that meant he wouldn't consider arguments. 'It's the life they've chosen.'

'Chosen? What choice?'

I pushed myself up out of the chair and went to loop back the *del'ri* curtain, hoping to coax some movement of air through the door-arch. There was none. This room was small, like all Maherwa's rooms. I looked across the narrow walkway at sunlit space.

'Maybe I can persuade Molly I'm still useful,' I said, a little whimsically. 'If I say I'll go to Kasabaarde, perhaps, with the traders? But she doesn't need that if she's got the Witchbreed technology she's looking for.'

He crossed one leg elegantly over the other. 'Lynne, as an old friend, let me ask you something. How long are you going to keep running?'

'Until I know what I'm running from, what I'm running to, and *why*.'

'I'm worried about you. I've been worried about you for some time.'

The low ceiling of the room was claustrophobic. I moved to stand by the window, and felt a feather-breeze of humid air. You want my help against PanOceania, I thought; Jesus, Douggie, that isn't it, that isn't what's important now!

'It's like this,' I said carefully. 'I've admitted to myself that there's a problem. I've got some sort of balance back, but I can't hold it, I'm up one minute and down the next. I get . . . wiped out, by memories. If I don't go on and find out what this is, I'll lose that balance, and that's the finish. But if I *do* find out the cause . . .'

Doug put his bowl of *del'ri*-spirit down on the low table. 'Find out what, precisely?'

'Everything I see now triggers off memories. I think that something was done to me, a long time ago. There's something about it that I can't remember, but I'm afraid to, because if I do remember, then I'll . . . well, make myself a target.'

He looked startled. 'Target for whom?'

'I don't know!'

Doug came and stood beside me at the window, and looked out

at the Ortheans on the walkway. Without turning his head to face me, he said, 'Lynne, this is classic hypno-tape paranoia. You think you have knowledge acquired by some arcane method, but it all comes out of old research data. You know what this is! And as for laying yourself open to attack—'

'It isn't just me. It's all the offworlders here. I *know* that sounds paranoid, but . . . and you never saw Havoth-jair.'

'Who?'

'She was a Harantish woman who spied on us in Kasabaarde, when Blaize and Hal and Evalen Kerys-Andrethe were there with me. She was behind an attempt to assassinate us. We let the Hexenmeister's people question her – break her.'

Why can't I get her out of my mind? I look in this old city's polished metal mirrors and I see her face.

'Douggie, don't tell me to go and see the Psych people.'

He looked at me, indecision in every line of his face. 'I may have to. I know—'

'Know what?'

'What happened to you after Max died.'

The wall was cool against my back: *chiruzeth* under the painted plaster. I looked at Doug; could still see from the corner of my eye the city outside.

'I fell apart. Some of it was Max's death and, yes, some of it was reaction to hypno-implants. I see that now. At the time I thought it was all Max. All right, Doug, I was out for a year, hospitalized. But I do still know what I'm talking about!'

Sincerity isn't always an advantage. I saw how the effort I put into convincing him was making him doubt still further.

'Let's leave it at that,' I said. 'It isn't something I can prove. Not yet. This isn't just some ex-Service woman going crazy. There's something behind it that's going to affect us all.'

I pushed through the *del'ri*-cloth curtain, and went out on to the walkway. Slow anger began to burn, and I strode down that long curve, heading toward the city-floor; not looking back to see if Doug called me. I will not be doubted! I thought. If *I* think I don't know what I'm doing, that's one thing; but I won't have anyone else saying it!

The ridiculousness of that dawned on me as I came to the foot of the walkway. I couldn't help chuckling, but I didn't know whether to laugh or cry . . .

Five or six Ortheans pushed past me. As they went into the cliff-wall chambers, I saw they wore brown scale-mail and carried winchbows, and so must be the Harantish guardians of the dome – I stopped dead and stared. A small, dark-skinned male was last

561

in the group; a plump Orthean male who wore armour uneasily, as if it were the last thing he was used to. He had a cropped black mane. It was as he vanished into the inner rooms, and I realized that I had last seen that mane elaborately braided, that I thought in shock *Pathrey Shanataru*!

I took a step in that direction, and then hesitated. Pathrey Shanataru, and the nameless woman who had been Voice of the Emperor-in-Exile, had vanished in Kel Harantish's "palace revolution". To see him here, now, and obviously in disguise . . .

No, I thought. This wants thinking out.

I entered my quarters, to find Haldin Damory sitting on the bed. She stood, with that apparently effortless movement of the sword-fighter. *Harur*-blades clashed. She wiped six-fingered hands on the thighs of her britches. Embarrassment brought the nictitating membrane down to cover those brown eyes.

'*T'an*, I – I'll understand if you want to call our contract void.'

'What?' Then I realized: the incident with the Kasabaarde traders. 'Oh, no; no, I don't.' I sank down on the nearest metal bench and pulled off my boots. Then I glanced up, surprising a look of gratitude on the young Orthean female's face, and recalled that all her troop depended on the contract too.

'You've been in a Wellhouse, *t'an* Haldin,' I guessed.

She stood with her booted feet a little apart, balanced lightly: swordfighter's stance. That tangled dark mane was falling from its braids. Shabby, stubborn, a hired killer; and yet . . .

'The Hexenmeister mocks us,' she said, almost sulkily. 'I shouldn't speak of it outside a Wellhouse.'

'I was once marked for Her, in a Wellhouse.'

If I keep saying that, some manic hilarity assured me, someone someday will tell me what it means.

She said, 'He mocks us. If his memories are nothing but Witch-breed trickery, passed down from one Hexenmeister to another, then our past-memories . . .' She paused, the nictitating membrane sliding back from her dark gaze. 'As I grow older, I remember more. *T'an*, I don't truly believe our past-memories are deceptive. We have lived before, under Her sky, and we return; we meet, and part, and meet again, and do not forget.'

That change from doubt to certainty would be inexplicable if she were not Orthean.

'I don't want to cancel the contract,' I said finally. 'There is something I want you and your people to do. Before mid-afternoon if you can. Certainly before tonight . . .'

*

The sky clouded over. The drop in ambient temperature was amazing. I could sleep now, I thought; at last, sleep through midday. But I don't dare sleep.

Feriksushar had said, *When the rains come*, and the rains would be a monsoon, I guessed, and not far off now.

Two hours passed before I heard Haldin Damory's cheerful voice ring through the outer room. I turned away from the window as she entered, pushing the *del'ri* curtain aside.

'I've found him,' she announced. 'What's more, *t'an*, no one else knows I found him; not *hiyek* nor *s'aranthi*.'

'Ah, good. Is he amenable to a meeting, here?'

'He – they – they're here now, *t'an* Christie.'

They? I wondered, and followed her back into the outer room. 'Give you greeting . . .'

'*Shan'tai* Christie.'

The sleek, plump male bowed, his brown face beaming. He looked little different from when I'd seen him in Kel Harantish; only that cropped mane, and his face slightly thinner.

'Pathrey Shanataru,' I acknowledged. Then I turned to his companion. 'I'm sorry, *shan'tai*, I never did learn your name.'

That whitefire mane was dyed sepia now, and some brown stain had been used on her gold-dust skin. She was in a plain ragged *meshabi*-robe. Still she gazed at me with luminous yellow eyes, this small Orthean woman who had been Voice of the Emperor-in-Exile in Kel Harantish.

'My name is Calil bel-Rioch,' she said softly. 'I'm glad you came looking for my Pathrey Shanataru. I want to talk with *s'aranthi*-offworlders.'

A kind of silence surrounded her, that made the noise and jostle of the mercenaries outside these rooms meaningless. Meeting that yellow gaze, I shivered. *A wordless chant, a ritual feast* . . . And then she smiled, and was only a young Orthean woman, stripped of the pomp of Kel Harantish.

'If you didn't recognize me,' Calil bel-Rioch said, 'that's because I have no wish to be killed by the Emperor-in-Exile's spies. I've come here to find allies. I want to talk to you and *shan'tai* Rachel and *shan'tai* Clifford.'

Names, too? Now that's interesting.

I said, 'I need to know something. Have you come here with the intention of trading with the Company?'

Calil looked at me thoughtfully. 'I may no longer be Voice, but there are still those of a like mind with me in Kel Harantish. I understand your Company is anxious to trade with the Harantish "Witchbreed".'

The last word had a very curious intonation, part mockery, part self-contempt. The small woman gazed out of the window, at that enigmatic structure of dome and pillars, black in the sunlight on the floor of the Maherwa pit.

'I once served my years among the guards,' Calil bel-Rioch said, 'and I have friends, still, amongst them. Friends who are all the closer since I rose to be Voice—'

'But you're not the Emperor's Voice now.'

She turned to face me. Nictitating membrane slid down over those yellow eyes.

'*Shan'tai s'aranthi*, they know *me*, whether I am Voice or not. What you offer me, I can guarantee to them. I have friends who, when their turn comes to guard Maherwa, will open doors to me; and to PanOceania too, if I so desire.'

Pathrey Shanataru added, 'Some say we have in Calil bel-Rioch a closer bloodline to the Last Emperor Santhendor'lin-sandru . . . There are those of us who follow bel-Rioch, not bel-Kurick.'

'We'll trade,' Calil said.

And just that simply and undramatically, it became clear to me. This is the final point at which I have the chance to make a decision. All the time Kel Harantish was hostile, the likelihood of getting into the canal system was small. With renegade Harantish, though—

Up until now, circumstances have acted to slow the Company down. Now I either take Calil bel-Rioch along to Molly, like a good Company employee, and let it all go on from there, or I . . .

What?

And if I don't, if I take *that* path, then maybe I'm stopping any chance of Trade&Aid to the Coast, help that the *hiyeks* desperately need.

That simple: in a small, shabby room overlooking the cylindrical pit that is Maherwa; among mercenaries and *hiyek*-Ortheans, a little after the furnace-hours of midday. That simple: what do I *do*?

Calil, with a pure and pitiless curiosity, said, '*Shan'tai*, I think you not unfamiliar with my city. Why fear to deal with us? You have had dealings with Kel Harantish before.'

Did she mean that visit with Molly Rachel? Her words keyed memory, took me back to heat and dust and how, as I stood by that city, I heard from Pathrey, for the first time in ten years, the name of Dannor bel-Kurick, then and now Emperor-in-Exile—

I am standing beside a great block of some translucent substance. The Hexenmeister lays his palm flat on its surface. It clears from the centre, as if viscous compartments become transparent.

'Where—' My voice is husky.

That old male, the Hexenmeister, his face is shadowed, the eye-sockets full of darkness. 'There are no other devices like these left but here, and in that ancient city, Kel Harantish.'

The image forming in the block is clear now, and through it I see a room. In that other room are geometrically-patterned carpets, and candle-stands whose holders are shaped like beasts' skulls. Candlelight and the ruins of technology.

And an Orthean – his face framed by a bleached mane: narrow chin, broad forehead, and half-veiled eyes the colour of wet sand. And he is no more than nineteen or twenty.

Dannor bel-Kurick.

I recall the face of Santhendor'lin-sandru, Phoenix Emperor, when the Golden woman brought the Empire down. Dannor bel-Kurick is a poor second to that, though he might pass, now that the Last Emperor is forgotten.

This halfbreed, this Halfgold, this Witchbreed boy—

'I make no quarrel with the Emperor-in-Exile,' the old male says. 'But I remind him that his city is a city of exile, and survives on trade. Can you eat rocks and sand?'

A communications device. A viewscreen. This degree of power – what-ever the energy source – ought to show up like a beacon on satellite surveys of Carrick V. Did they miss it, skimp the survey, have a trans-mission failure?

'Your assassin, Havoth-jair,' says the old male. 'She spoke of ships that went north to the Hundred Thousand, ships that carry gold, to subvert telestres . . .'

'What of it?' the boy asks tiredly.

'Nothing. But if I hear of any more ships of Kel Harantish in Tathcaer, then something.'

Defeat visible on that young face.

'I am Golden!' He stares at the Hexenmeister. 'I am Emperor! How many lies have you fed me, old man, telling me I'm nothing but a hollow man ruling a dying city? There's a price paid for power here that you never paid, never in your lives!'

The image fades to clarity.

'Let him have his temper,' the Hexenmeister says, 'he's cruel and wilful and cunning, but I could find it in my heart to be sorry for him.'

One thing bothers me (and it doesn't bother me as much as it should). In my reports to the government on Witchbreed technology, I went fully into their past history, mentioned the ruined cities in the Barrens. I never mentioned the communications devices used by the Hexenmeister of Kasabaarde.

It's unimportant, not worth mentioning, it doesn't worry me.

And it should.

It should!

Sweat sprang out on neck, brows, palms. I met the gaze of the young Harantish female. Nictitating membrane slid back from eyes as yellow and clear as honey, with pit-black pupils that reflect a star of white light.

A friend's eyes in a stranger's face . . . In desperate pain, memory overwhelmed my sight. The dark face of the dead woman Ruric Orhlandis. Yellow eyes that laugh in that thin face, raven's wing of mane falling over the high forehead; she astride *marhaz, harur*-blade slung for lefthand use, right sleeve empty and pinned up – *amari* Ruric.

Ah, Ruric, why is it that you're dead and your betrayal isn't?

Memory threatens again, the tide of the past, and if giving in to it is desertion—

We'll trade.

That simple: what do I do?

If it's desertion, then I can't help it. Ten years vanish as if they were so many minutes—

It is night, in the Citadel, in Tathcaer. The small room is candlelit, and crowded. Here are Haltern n'ri n'suth Beth'ru-elen, Crown Messenger; and the Crown herself, Dalzielle Kerys-Andrethe; and others, too. And Ruric.

Our eyes meet, and I look away. She stands, in blue and silver, the candlelight like honey on her black skin. Tall, gaunt, carrying herself with a crook-shouldered balance.

'My intention was to discredit the Earth envoy, and so also that world.'

I ask bleakly, 'Why not kill me?'

'What use would that be? They'd send others. I wanted us rid of you and your world.'

And Dalzielle Kerys-Andrethe, called Suthafiori, Crown of the Hundred Thousand; slow and amazed: 'You never agreed with me on that, but I didn't imagine you traitor because of it.'

'I'm no traitor! All I've done, even to murder, I've done for the Hundred Thousand.'

Haltern (young, then): 'Even to taking Harantish gold?'

'I see no reason not to take my enemies' gold, if I can use it for my friends' good.'

Ruric within a foot of me, the vibrant breathing warmth of her body, the energy of her eyes. Keeping her hand flat on the table, making no move towards harur-nilgiri. The calm of the professional soldier: T'An Commander, T'An Melkathi.

'If you'll have reasons,' she says simply, 'they are these. Earth will destroy us. Either it will change us out of all recognition, or it will destroy

the land itself. As I love the Hundred Thousand – I love it more than life – so I have tried to protect it.'

I say, 'We'd never do it.'

'Never is a long time,' she says, 'and while we're a backwater world with nothing desired from us, perhaps we're safe from war. But even then, not from change. You are utterly unlike us, and when you come here we can't help but alter. And if we're ever found to have something that Earth requires – why then Goddess help us, Christie, because no one else will!'

Ten years dead, that voice; and she lived on a little longer, branded exile. Ah, that's no life.

'I knew—' My voice was thick. 'Knew a woman who had Golden blood, and dealings with your city, Calil – what did it do to *her*? What will it do to me?'

Haldin Damory's voice said sharply, 'Christie!'

Images faded, like water soaking away into sand. I saw the tan face and dark mane of Haldin Damory. No sign of Calil's yellow gaze . . . I was sitting on one of the *del'ri*-padded benches, without any idea of how I got there. One of Haldin's mercenaries stood at the door, *harur*-blade drawn.

'Ahhh—' I stood, swayed. If it were a physical pain I could bear it, could cry out, scream; but not this, this *fear*, this void that suddenly opens underfoot, that—

'*T'an*, please, be quiet!' Haldin Damory caught hold of both my arms. Her grip was strong. Her dark eyes veiled. 'What is it? Are you poisoned? What?'

My throat felt sore, I must have cried out. When I could focus, I saw no one but Haldin and those half-dozen other young males and females, her mercenaries.

'I said you were ill. I got the Harantish Witchbreed out, in case they . . .' She let go of my arms. 'Was it them?'

All I could say, stupidly, was, 'Havoth-jair.' The words that Haltern Beth'ru-elen spoke to me in Rakviri *telestre* came back with preternatural clarity –

'*—since you spent time within the Tower, and left it so changed—*'

So changed.

What is it I can't remember?

I dreamed that we went down into the maze of levels under the Brown Tower, to a cool dry hall lit with a faint blue iridescence, a light the colour of lilac and lightning; and there, there were alien machines that had the shape of sarcophagi . . .

And when she left the Tower in Kasabaarde, to come with us and give evidence in Tathcaer, she was little more than a zombie; Havoth-jair, whom the Hexenmeister put to the question—

I knew, with a cold certainty, exactly what I had to do. I fumbled in a belt-pouch for coins valuable in the Hundred Thousand. That cold metal touch threatened to overwhelm me with memory, memory of once sending Blaize Meduenin on a mercenary errand. Hadn't I said, days ago, *As if it were my year on Orthe repeated, in a darker key?*

Haldin Damory took the coins doubtfully. *'T'an . . .'*

'You're still under contract to me. Leave half your troop here in Maherwa – I want that woman, Calil bel-Rioch, I want her kept away from the Company people here. Don't kill her, mind. I never said murder. Keep her away.'

A fair-maned Medued mercenary said, 'We'll try, *t'an*.'

'And you, Haldin.' I held down the tide of synaesthesia, the visible and sensory memory that threatened to flood my mind. 'You bring the rest of your troop. You're my escort.'

'But, *t'an*, where?'

I had no guard on my tongue, thoughts spoken aloud: 'If I let Molly put me on a shuttle, I'll be back on the orbiter, on my way back to Earth – no! I can't leave now. Not like this, not without knowing *why* . . . There are canals, boats, *jath-rai*. I've travelled Orthe before. Haldin, you keep me alive, you hear? That's your contract. Asking questions isn't your business. And I'm leaving Maherwa *now*.'

PART THREE

CHAPTER 13

Violence and Vision

I woke from a deep sleep, thirsty and hot. Light shone in through a round-arched window. The air smelled damp. Voices sounded in distant rooms. A *del'ri* pallet on which I lay scratched against my skin. I stared up at the ceiling: the white plaster and hairline cracks.

Something flopped down on the *del'ri* mattress.

'Max?' I said sleepily.

When I turned my head I saw a tiny face, narrow-chinned, with a short pale mane. A child, no more than two or three seasons old. *Ke* yawned, showing teeth; then lay down on the pallet, curled up against my back; a small lump of heat, breathing with a rhythm that is not human.

I should know something from this, I thought. A child so trusting, the air that smells of rain. Before I could work it out, I fell into sleep like a stone falling down a well.

Waking clear-headed, as from long convalescence.

First one note, then two or three more, then a chorus: the thin tintinnabulation of *rashaku* lizardbirds. The air felt wet and mild, and somehow full of energy; sparky wth ozone and the smell of the sea. The window was a hoop-arch in a curving white wall. Morning put soft blue shadows across the ceiling of the dome, ten or twelve feet above my head. I rolled over on the *del'ri* pallet, and saw a young Orthean male sitting on a bench by the doorway.

His dark crop-maned head was bowed. He sat with booted feet splayed apart, leaning forward, with his six-fingered hands clasped together between his knees. Sleeveless slit-backed jacket showed his bony torso. He wore straps for *harur*-blades, but no blades.

'God give me strength!' I said, sitting up. 'Should I know you, *shan'tai*?'

The air was warm on my skin – I realized I was naked: coverall,

571

CAS-IV, wristlink; all gone. A dirty *meshabi*-robe was my blanket.
I pulled it over my head, tied the belt slowly.

'Sent t'check,' the young male said. His dark mane stood in a
cut crest. No more than sixteen, seventeen? Barely out of *ashiren*.
His surprisingly deep voice slurred a Morvrenni dialect difficult to
understand.

'What?'

'T'check on you. 'S difficult, *t'an*. You keep moving round the
Order Houses.' He stood. 'I'll get Damory.'

Order Houses?

I stretched, feeling the *meshabi*-robe slide across my skin. Aches
slid awake as I rubbed the last sleep from my eyes. I looked up at
the boy: 'I think the traditional question is "where am I?" – but I
know *where* I am. Try: how the hell did I get here, and *why*?'

He muttered something inaudible and, when I queried,
repeated, 'You ordered it, *t'an*. I heard you.'

'Who are you?'

He had dark eyes, far apart and slightly slanted: nictitating
membrane slid down to cover them. 'I'm Branic. Haldin Damory's
troop.'

The tiled floor was warm underfoot. I stood, walked to the
window, leaned on the wide sill. The sky was a pale blue, in this
dawn hour still freckled with daystars. A haze silvered the high
arch of the sky. Damp shadows fell towards the west, lying on the
white earth, the white dust. *Rashaku* called.

Pale, rounded domes rose up from the earth, here with scarcely
an alley's space between them, and some doors were shaded by
awnings on rickety poles, and some had only a flight of low steps
and an archway. A group of four or five Ortheans sat on the steps
of this dome. There was no talk among them. One rocked back
and forth, back and forth. Three had their faces masked. As I
watched, another Orthean male came out on to the steps and
began to brush away the dust with a broom. His *meshabi*-robe was
clean, the rope-belt woven with coloured thread.

'The inner city . . .'

I have known this, even in my sleep. Kasabaarde's inner city,
that breeds within its walls philosophical violence and brutal
vision. Why did I think I needed to come here, of all places on
Orthe?

'The Order Houses of the inner city . . . And this is Wintersun
what?'

The boy grunted. 'Not Wintersun. Wintersun's over. It's Storm-
sun-18.'

'Shit!'

'I'll fetch Haldin – '

'I'm coming with you.' I glanced round the small chamber again. It was bare. Through the arched exit, I could see the steps that went down into the underground rooms – but that would be equally fruitless. 'They didn't even have the decency to leave my boots, the little thieves—'

No translation for that last word in his language. The boy, as we walked through to the outer chamber, said, 'I 'spect someone's using 'em, *t'an.*'

I almost laughed; held it back. The Orthean male sweeping the outer steps stood aside to let us pass, and bowed slightly. I hesitated, turned to Branic, and held out a hand for his cord of coins.

The Order House male smiled. Standing on the top step, his head was just level with my shoulder. He looked at the coins I offered.

'You do forget,' he said coolly, 'though we told you when you came here. This is the inner city. By ancient custom, here you may eat and drink freely, and freely be sheltered. The Order Houses will clothe you,' he said, and I smoothed down the wrinkled *meshabi*-robe. 'This is not the gift: the gift of the inner city is time. And that breeds violence and vision, idleness or wisdom.'

Yes, I remember . . .

Branic looped the cord of coins back over his neck, and signed himself on the breast with the circle of the Goddess. He turned away without a word. I followed. The customs of the inner city are difficult to follow: my instincts screamed *criminal*!

Earth was damp under my bare feet, and the dawn wind mild. I briefly worried about mundane things: sickness, infection. And then thought, *Stormsun-18!* with utter incredulity. The boy began to walk down winding alleyways, going towards the dawn, and I followed him, hard put to keep up with his pace.

As we came out into an open space, and saw a high wall before us, I said, 'Branic, where is Haldin?'

'Trade-quarter. All of us.'

I stopped. The wall in front of me was high, as high as the dome-roofs, and built of massive sandstone blocks. About thirty yards away, it widened. A low gatehouse was set into its twelve-foot thickness. Most of the Order Houses here looked deserted.

'No. Tell Haldin to come into the inner city, to me.'

He scratched at his cropped mane, and his hand automatically fell to where the hilt of *harur-nilgiri* would have been, at his hip. 'I can't – she won't – they make you leave weapons at the gate-house! She won't come in unarmed.'

'She has no business to be outside, she's still under contract to me.'

The boy's eyes cleared, then veiled. 'Are you well? Then you're well enough to pay us.'

I did laugh then; stood in the dawn sun with the scent of *kazsis*-vines in the air, and laughed until I was weak and breathless, and had to grab hold of the boy's shoulder to keep my balance. He looked affronted. I clapped him on the shoulder, sniffed, and managed not to laugh again.

'I don't know why they send idiots like me to places like this . . . Branic, please don't agree with me.' That got a flicker of humour from the boy. 'Tell Haldin Damory she must come in and see me, now. I'll be at—' I dredged memory for decade-old names '—at the Order House Su'niar. That's near the Seagate. Tell her that I can't leave the inner city now. It's the only place where I'm safe.'

He left, but for that moment I hardly noticed he had gone.

There. All other problems set aside, Company and government, Coast and Hundred Thousand; all else secondary now, because there – I see it clearly. Between the low white domes, over the stunted fronds of *lapuur*, in the heart of the inner city. That small and squat building, surrounded by gardens, built of dark bricks and no more than two storeys high: the Brown Tower.

A bowl hit the wall: ceramic splinters flew. I ducked down. The tall female still stood with her arm upraised. A dark-maned *ashiren* shouted something unintelligible. Then both turned and fled up the steps from this underground hall, one maybe in pursuit, maybe not; and quiet fell again. A fair-maned male on the next bench drew a splinter of clay from his hand, and stared with fascination at the trickle of blood. Mirror-reflected light shone on the benches, on the now almost empty hall.

'Goddess!' Haldin Damory came down the steps from the entrance-dome. Her claw-nailed hands clenched, went to her empty belt. She grunted, and all but fell on to the bench beside me. 'Goddess, it's hot up there! So you can talk sense again, can you, *t'an*? I thought Branic was joking.'

A young female with Su'niar Order House's colours woven into her rope-belt brought over a jug of *arniac* and more ceramic bowls. With no expression of surprise or distaste, she then fetched a broom to sweep up the broken bowl. She paid no attention to the fair-maned male's injury.

'How long is it since we left Maherwa?' I asked. 'It must be more than two weeks.'

'Twenty-five days,' Haldin Damory said; sipped the *arniac*, and made a face. 'What I wouldn't give for good Morvrenni *siir*-wine . . . Yes, you look well. As far as I can tell, with *s'aranthi*.' And she grinned.

'I am "well",' I said. Knowing as I spoke that it was true, that somehow – at some level below the conscious – I could hold it all in balance: memory, vision and the past. I haven't resolved the problem, but I've learned to live with uncertainty.

'You picked the right time,' Haldin said approvingly, as she leaned back against the wall, and put her booted feet up on another bench. 'Our contract runs out in two days. I'd thought of just taking you up the Archipelago, to Morvren Freeport, whether you liked the idea or not – your people in the Freeport might have given my Guildhouse a reward!'

She chuckled. She would have done it: bundled me on to one of the coast *jath-rai*, like any other piece of cargo.

'But I don't want to leave the Coast right now,' she added. 'There's going to be a *beautiful* fight, *t'an*.'

Her enthusiasm was unselfconscious, unashamed.

'There were going to be talks . . .' That memory came clear, unbidden. I blinked in the soft mirror-light. Why, it's gone, I thought. That fog in the head, synaesthesia; gone. I am I, and I know what I know, and the rest is – under my control . . .

I smiled at Haldin. 'Talks between some of the Coast *hiyeks* and the Hundred Thousand, I remember it being talked about back when I was in the Freeport. Has that happened yet? Or is it over? Or what?'

She put the curled black mane back from her eyes with one sword-calloused hand, and her dark gaze cleared. 'Now that's sensible, *t'an*, that's knowledgeable. That isn't the puling babe I've had to nurse from Maherwa to Kasabaarde.'

Her words hurt. I stood, and walked a few paces to where the underground hall's ornamental pool lay still and gleaming. Under water, the soft gleam of *chiruzeth*. The water's surface showed me a thin face, with dirt ingrained in the tanned skin; hair bleached by the Coast sun. I dipped my fingers in the water and rubbed at my skin, but the paleness round my eyes remained. Of course: I would have been wearing a mask to travel . . .

Clear, now, these memories: the metal decks of *jath-rai* and canal ships, too hot to walk on in the noon sun. Flat land where only the water moves: no *rashaku* fly, there are no clouds. Only heat-stricken earth. Brown and umber, ochre and black, white and grey. A sea as bright as broken glass. Descending into *siiran*: the curiosity on pale-maned faces. Midday rests and midnight travel, and I do not recall ever speaking; not to Haldin, not to the *telestre* mercenaries, not to the Coast Ortheans, whose bright robes are worn and patched, who live crowded under the earth, hiding from that inhuman heat.

Twenty-five days, heat building to monsoon; all the thousand *hiyeks* between Maherwa and Kasabaarde; north and west, four hundred miles. *And for the last twenty-five days, I've walked in a dream.*

Now I'm free of it, I must act.

'So many *jath-rai* in the harbour settlements.' I turned to sit on the rim of the pool, facing Haldin. 'Stormsun isn't the best season for trade. Why so many ships?'

Haldin stretched her lean arms restlessly. Her six-fingered hands moved to the *harur*-blade harness. Ten years ago, when I first came to Kasabaarde's inner city, they took my belt-knife at the gatehouse. I had been living an Orthean life long enough to feel the lack of it.

'I'm not a Crown Messenger,' she said dourly. 'Not even a *S'aranth*'s Messenger, if there was such a thing. I fight, I don't spy or collect intelligence. But it's simple enough. Those *jath-rai* are warships. The *hiyek*-families are going to massacre each other, just for a favourable glance from your Company.'

That thought seemed to cheer her.

'They mustn't fight. Jesus wept! Molly will have the Company's Peace Force in to protect our interests—'

No longer "our" interests. Not any more.

Haldin said, 'The great *hiyek*-families are in Kasabaarde now, talking with us, and with each other. You wait. They've been here all of Stormsun. I give it nine days, outside, before they fall out. Then I'll pick a likely side for my troop, and . . .'

Again, that grin. Difficult to hold the thought: what this woman looks forward to with such enthusiasm is *harur*-blades and winch-bows and – for all the bloodless chessboard strategy of mercenary wars on the Coast – inevitable casualties.

'In Morvren Freeport . . .' It seems longer than a month ago. 'It isn't just the *hiyeks*, is it? I've heard talk. What will you do, Haldin, if the Coast *hiyeks* attack the Hundred Thousand?'

Haldin hooked one booted foot up on to the opposite knee, gripping her ankle with thin six-fingered hands. She shook her head with lazy cheerfulness.

'You mean invasion, instead of just raids? Ah, it'll never come to that. There's no chance of it. The *hiyeks* can't be allies for long enough. They never have. Cuirduzh is going to fall out with Thelshan, and Pelatha with Anzhadi, and . . . you take my word on it, *t'an S'aranth*. We've only got to keep them talking for a few more days. Then it'll all fall apart.'

'And if it doesn't?'

Haldin put long fingers through her tangled mane, and looked at me with good-natured superiority. '*T'an*, it will.' She paused. 'Is there anything else, before we end the contract?'

There were footsteps and voices in the dome above, but no one came down the steps. I dabbled one hand in the pool and watched the ripples, and then glanced at Haldin. At least part of her expression was contempt. But she's seen me all those days between Maherwa and here, I thought, and so there'll always be that certain amount of contempt. When I think back to then, I could agree with her.

'Two things you can tell me, *t'an* Haldin. I seem to remember . . . did I ask some of your mercenaries to stay behind in Maherwa?'

'To discourage the Harantish exiles. Shanataru and bel-Rioch.' She shrugged. 'You wouldn't have them killed. They didn't frighten. Don't you remember Ty and Gabril caught up with us at Quarth? Said the two Harantish had at last got speech with your *t'an* Rachel.'

When each visual image, each sound, each smell, plunges you into a flood of memory – no, one can't tell what is happening from what has happened.

'How long have I been here in Kasabaarde?'

'Two days.'

She grew more tense moment by moment, it was visible in the taut line of her back. I have known Ortheans who refuse to enter the inner city of Kasabaarde at all. There is no place on Orthe remotely like it – not even Kasabaarde's Tower.

'Let's go outside, shall we?' I led the way up the steps, out of the dome, and into the air.

The noon air felt hot and heavy with storms. We stood under the *del'ri*-cloth awning. The haze thickened to cloud. Heat-lightning flickered over the dome-roofs, and as we watched, raindrops fell like metal bullets to spatter in the dust. Within thirty heartbeats the dust was mud, rain falling in rods, and springing up again a foot high in spray.

I asked, 'Do you know where the envoy Clifford is now?'

'He's here.' The female raised her voice a little, to be heard over the drumming rain.

I smiled ruefully. 'I've been something of an idiot . . . I thought I had to do it all on my own. Someone once said to me: a world is too big for one person's responsibility. Or even many people. But we're all there is. I *do* have friends. We'll have to see what we can do.'

Haldin frowned. '*T'an*, I don't know what you're talking about.'

'Just thinking aloud, that's all.'

The rain eased quickly. Rings spread and faded on the alley puddles, where the last drops struck. Haldin peered out at the sky, moved down the shallow steps; and then spun round as the Su'niar female came to the archway behind her.

In accented north-west Coast dialect, Haldin muttered, 'Your pardon, *shan'tai*; here, take this—'

The Order House female shook her head, smiling a gentle refusal of the coins offered. Haldin turned abruptly and strode away. As I caught up with her, she glanced back at the Ortheans who sprawled by the Order House, and as if she spoke to herself protested, 'But people can't just do nothing!'

That was my instinctive reaction when I came here, ten years ago. I let her walk a little further and then said, 'Where's *t'an* Clifford now?'

'One of the Order Houses near Westgate; Cir-nanth, Gethfirle; I don't know.' Membrane veiled her eyes, though the clouded sky was not bright. '*T'an*, you don't need mercenaries here!'

'Medued Guildhouse can owe me the two days' service,' I said. 'Leave when you need to, *t'an* Haldin.'

She walked away, with no other farewell, heedless of the rain's last drops that soaked her mane and tunic, hurrying back towards the inner city's wall and gatehouse, where she had left *harur-nilgiri* and *harur-nazari*. Going back to where people can't just do nothing. What she hadn't said, but what had been plain in her face from the moment she entered the inner city, was, *This place is a mad-house!* Certainly it's inexplicable, I thought. What will PanOceania make of it?

I turned and began walking briskly through the muddy alleys, going towards Cir-nanth and Gethfirle and the other Westgate Order House. I passed several Ortheans gathered under one of the *del'ri*-cloth awnings. One called out, accent thick, hostility apparent. I walked on, heart hammering.

The alleys widened into avenues, still lined with low white domes. *Kazsis*-vine budded on the curving walls, and an ash-blue plant grew along the base of the domes. *Rashaku* called. Despite the cloud and heat, the ground under my bare feet was cold, and when I looked down I saw the scratched translucent surface of *chiruzeth*, the underground canal waters dimly visible beneath.

And this too was a city of the Golden Witchbreed.

At the end of that long avenue I stopped a young, white-maned Orthean female. 'Are there *s'aranthi* here?'

She looked up with veiled eyes. 'Oh yes, *shan'tai*. And some of them wear Orthean faces.'

She walked a few yards and then knelt down, and began to wipe the mud from the steps of the nearest Order House with bare six-fingered hands.

'Lynne? *Lynne!'*

Bemused, I swung round; and before I knew it, Doug Clifford gripped my hands and then hugged me (which seemed to surprise him rather more than it did me). The twenty-five days since I'd seen him had wrought changes; Carrick's Star had tanned that lined skin, begun to bleach the sandy-red hair. To Service coveralls he had added Orthean boots and a belt-knife. Now he stepped back a pace and looked me up and down, still the same small, neat man.

'Lynne, is that you?'

'Ah, I see – the difficult questions first, eh?'

He snorted, shook his head, regarding me with wonder. I thought, This is one of the few times I've ever seen you speechless.

'Haldin Damory told me you were in Kasabaarde,' I remarked. 'Why the inner city, though? Or is that because of these talks between the *hiyeks* and the Hundred Thousand—'

'Jesus Christ, woman! You've been gone for a month, the Company's got you on the missing persons list, and now you come back and ask *me* questions!'

The livid sky shed a few drops of rain, but he took no notice. Faces appeared at Order House entrances, made curious by the sound of a foreign language, and this man so plainly *s'aranthi*. He frowned. Then he shook his head again, helplessly.

'I don't believe it! The difference between the way you were then and the way you are now – Lynne, why didn't you let me know where you were? Of all the irresponsible, *stupid* actions . . .' He paused, recovering a little of his natural reserve. Then he added: 'You have no idea what I've been afraid of for you. Which is somewhat imperceptive of me, I don't doubt; I seem to recall that in your Service days you made a habit of going walkabout.'

'It was stupid,' I said meekly. 'It's nice to see you too, Douggie.'

He fixed his mouth in a prim line, then laughed. 'Why do I even try?'

'Let's take it that was a rhetorical question.' I linked my arm through his. 'Can we talk inside? I think it's going to rain again.'

Doug Clifford looked appealingly at the heavens. 'She vanishes for a month, and then she turns up out of nowhere and talks about the weather. Why me? What did *I* do to deserve her?'

I could do nothing but laugh, still knowing he used that humour to distance himself from some very real emotion. We walked a few yards to an Order House, and entered the dome. The rain-twilight gave an odd luminous glow to the walls inside. In the underground chambers there would be no mirror-reflected light now, and so we sat in the ground-level chamber. An Order-robed *ashiren* brought *arniac*.

Clifford walked to the window, and looked out. That self-observing theatricalism vanished.

'David Osaka and the Ishida girl are here. Or do you know that? Have you seen them? I wasn't aware that you would attend these talks.'

'Or that I'd been in any condition to do so.' I side-stepped the questions: 'I could say the same thing to you.'

His face was turned away, I couldn't see his expression.

'The Rachel woman gave me a choice. Stay out of the Company's dealings in Maherwa, or find myself recalled to the next world on this circuit. So I came here, to Kasabaarde. I should have had to attend these talks in any case. Or so I tell myself. The Company's busy in Maherwa. You know the Harantish have let Rachel put a research team into the canal system?'

Fear at last realized into reality: it made me go cold. I had a vision of that dome and pillars, of Calil bel-Rioch's golden-eyed face. No need to ask which Harantish. Does she want the Company as an ally, or is she just hitting back at the Emperor in Kel Harantish?

'Have they come up with an analysis?'

'Lynne, I'd be the last to hear.'

A flash of lightning illuminated the low dome, and a moment after, thunder crackled. The warm spring air blew chill. Another of the north Coast's brief tempests. Clifford walked back to the low table. I saw him scrutinize my face.

'Are you sure that you're all right?'

'If you mean, do I still have someone else's memories in my head, the answer is yes. What I've done by going walkabout, as you call it, is learn to control them. Instead of having them control me.'

I expected disbelief, was braced to see that look on his face. Instead, he nodded slowly. Those bird-bright eyes were thoughtful.

'I've had a scan through your old reports. Lynne, I still think you're misinterpreting something that happened to you, but – I could be convinced otherwise.' Doug smiled. 'One sees much, in the Service. Don't underestimate my ability to comprehend the alien. But I need to know what did happen to you. And then I need more evidence than – forgive me, Lynne – merely your unsupported word.'

Warmth and relief swept through me. I wiped my hands on the dirty *meshabi*-robe; I hadn't realized my palms were sweating. Searching for words, in the instant between intention and speech, I made a controlled recollection of memory; held down sound and vision until it was mine to use.

'Douggie, I'll tell you how it was. It begins with the Hexenmeister, in the Brown Tower—'

There is a room lined with shelves, on which rest scrolls and parchments. Evening light falls on woven del'ri mats, on a table, and chairs. A library? Yes, this could be any library-room on Orthe; and the summer breeze that drifts in is soothing – but through the window-arch I see the last spire of the Rasrhe-y-Meluur, that stands outside Kasabaarde, that is a millennially-old reminder of the Golden Witchbreed.

There is a room in the Brown Tower that is like a library because it is a room (the only one) that is sometimes seen by outsiders. It is designed to reassure, to allay fears of long-dead technology. I stand in that room. Before me, in a chair by the cold hearth, is the Hexenmeister of Kasabaarde.

Like most Kasabaardeans he is a head smaller than me, and bent with age besides. His hands are bird-claws, his skin a diamond-pattern of wrinkles, and his mane gone except for a crest from forehead to spine. A brown sleeveless robe covers his tunic.

'What do you know of me?' he asks.

I say, 'I know that you dream no past-dreams because you're immortal, that you see all that passes in the world, and that the Archives of the Brown Tower hold all knowledge.'

These are all stories Ortheans have told me.

'Such superstition!' he says mildly, amused. 'Well, you and I have much to speak of, envoy, and I will tell you why. I know much of what passes in the known lands – because most news comes either here to this city, or is heard by my people who travel. And it has been the custom, since before Tathcaer was a city, that they bring such news to me. The Archives hold much knowledge – but not all. No, not all. And for the other, that is answered more simply – yes, I am immortal.'

'I'm sorry, I don't believe that. I can't.'

'You must believe, envoy. Or else you'll believe nothing I tell you, and that could affect the relations between two worlds.'

He eases forward in the chair, lifting himself with the weight on his wrists, as the old do. I automatically move to help him. His warm hand closes over mine, a frail, many-fingered grip. He stands.

'I think I must prove to you what I am.'

We walk along a diffusely-lit passage, slow, at an old man's speed. His weight on my arm is considerable. We pass a door that opens, slides shut behind us as we step into a small chamber. There is pressure underfoot, a sickness in the stomach. We are descending. Then it stops, the door opens. A great hall. The light changes quality; the air is cool, dry.

'That causes you no fear,' *the old male says.* 'Well, it is not to be wondered at, you come from the stars.'

Disbelief that paralyses. I think, Kirriach was awesome, that city in the Barrens, but Kirriach's safely dead; and this . . .

'The Brown Tower has stood for ten thousand years,' *he says softly,* 'and hasn't been above borrowing Golden technology when needed. Machines fail, you see. Even these. Though not for a time yet, I think.' *He takes a few unsupported steps into the hall, resting his hands on the edge of metal casings.* 'These are precious to me beyond all price, their like is not to be found in the world today.'

An underground hall, banks of machinery, screens and cubicles like sarcophagi. Quiet, chill; a subliminal hum.

'You have heard,' *he says,* 'of those of us who possess a perfect memory?'

'Yes. Some humans have that.'

'These transcribe, store, and transfer such a person's memory intact to another person.'

Is my disbelief so apparent? The hypno-implants might pass as a primitive prototype – but no, such a thing isn't possible!

'And that person, also, to another and another.' *He smiles.* 'With no loss of detail, down through the generations.' *And touches his thin chest.* 'I am not immortal, but the Hexenmeister is. In a few years, when I die, there will still be a Hexenmeister. Who'll remember speaking with you, Christie, remember this moment as I do. Who will be me – as I am all who went before me.'

'It's incredible!' *I realize I'm pacing; come to a halt in front of the old Orthean male.* 'What real proof do you have?'

'If it were proved to your satisfaction that these machines act as I claim?'

'I don't have the technical training to prove or disprove that.'

'And language is inadequate. Perhaps we misunderstand each other more than we know.' *He reaches out, grasping my arm for support.* 'It will be obvious to you, I suppose. I wish to record your memories, Christie, so that I will know your world. And as trade is the mark of Kasabaarde, I am prepared to offer you access to some of my own memories of Orthe. I* know this world. Perhaps I am the only person who truly does. So when Orthe comes to deal with other worlds – I am the only one qualified to speak for us.'

Assuming it's true, I think, and assuming alien technology can be adapted for human use as well as Orthean – how dangerous will it be? Physically, mentally, politically? I'd be a fool to do it. And a fool not to.

And then there is a memory of days spent in Kasabaarde, that long-ago spring. Dry, dusty days. Held back by fear: it's beyond my brief as envoy, have I the right to pass on information about Earth? And pushed forward by knowledge: if Earth deals with this world, it must know this world. It must. I must.

Daystars, half-invisible points of light over the domed roofs, the glare of Carrick's Star drowning them. White dust, and heat. And I was alone, and not yet thirty, and I did it anyway.

'Have you rested?' the Hexenmeister asks, some days later. 'That's well. We can begin. First, though, I ask you to undertake never to speak of what you see or hear.'

'That's not something I can promise. As envoy, I have to report fully.'

Now I can hear the irony in his tone, that I never heard then. You knew, old man. Of course you knew.

'Well then, envoy, say that you will report it only to your own people, and then only if you believe it to be necessary . . .'

The cubicle is slick under me, with a sensation unlike metal or stone. I know it now – chiruzeth. There is a hum that might be sound or vibration. I close my eyes, sick with panic. Closed in alien science like a sarcophagus, a tomb.

I feel a sensation that – if it lasted more than a microsecond – would be intolerable agony. No way to describe how it feels: as if the closed confines of the self fragmented into pieces in an ever-expanding maze.

Total fear: and I struggle, his memory happening to me with all the force of synaesthesia, entangling, inescapable.

Pain, memory, memory not mine: and I am a mirror shattered into a million pieces, a million lives.

CHAPTER 14

Exiles

Outside the window-arch, rain slants across a slate-blue sky. A sky that seems too bright to human eyes. Carrick's Star glares whitely beyond the clouds.

'It wasn't that I couldn't talk about it,' I finished. 'It was almost that I couldn't *think* about it – even to myself. I knew I'd been in the Tower, but my mind kept telling me it was unimportant, trivial, to be forgotten . . . I couldn't even think in terms of being mentally blocked, let alone blocked by something someone had done to me. All I could do was remember someone else whose mind had been tampered with by the Hexenmeister. Havoth-jair.'

Doug Clifford drank from his bowl of *arniac*, grimaced, and paused to pick a fallen *kazsis*-bud out of the scarlet liquid.

'Lynne, I find myself somewhat at a loss . . . I might go to the Tower, myself, I suppose. Send a message in to the Hexenmeister's people. I *am* still government envoy to Carrick V.'

Qualified support, but support none the less. I would have thanked him, but tension made my mouth dry. I stood to pace the Order House's confined floorspace, too restless to sit still.

'Douggie, assume for the moment that I'm right, what will the Hexenmeister do when he knows I'm here?'

Doug said lightly, 'If you had to choose a place to be, you've picked the right one. I dare say even the Tower won't be too eager to interfere in the Order Houses.'

The inner city is separated from the trade-quarter of Kasabaarde by a wall and a millennially-old rule of amnesty; and from the Tower that lies at its heart by a few strips of garden land and a vast gulf of philosophy.

'. . . which, I suspect, is why the *hiyeks* are holding their peace conference in here. That reminds me, Lynne. While I'm busy, you'd better contact David Osaka or Pramila Ishida, hadn't you?'

A touch of malice in those last words. I am still Company-employed. And besides, you don't have dealings with Ortheans for long without picking up the respect they have for the Tower. Clifford, I thought, you're rattled. And who can blame you?

'You're right,' I said mildly. 'I'll find them. Douggie, when you speak with the Tower, remember one thing. It's what I told you at Maherwa. You're not doing this to help one person who's been badly affected by some kind of alien technology. The Hexenmeister told me once that he was the only person with the knowledge to speak for all of Orthe – and if I'm right, and he is, then with a situation as precarious as this one, we're going to *need* someone with that knowledge.'

Walking through the inner city towards Westgate, I came, between one Order House and the next, to the edge of a crowd. I pushed between male and female Ortheans, in brightly-coloured *meshabi*-robes. Some sat on steps, on benches under awnings, or on woven *del'ri* mats. The scarlet, blue, and emerald-dyed *meshabi*-cloth was patchily coloured, often frayed. A deafening hum of talk beat against me – *hiyek*-Ortheans gesturing unrestrainedly, heads together, gathering in groups. I passed some that clustered round a spirit lamp, boiling *arniac*, while an old male in Order House robes looked on worriedly.

It was difficult to pick a way between the seated groups. Heads turned as I passed. Manes braided with crystal beads flashed in the sun. Being a head taller than most *hiyek*-Ortheans, I drew the eye; and some called comments, and I answered noncommittally and walked on.

A few desiccated *lapuur* trees occupied the wide empty space near the Westgate's gatehouse, their ash-grey fronds uncurling by reflex under the heat of Carrick's Star. Pramila Ishida was standing under one *lapuur*. An Orthean stood with her.

Two together: a contrast of fair and dark. The dusty yellow mane of Sethri-safere was thrown back as he laughed – no way would *you* miss being here, I realized – and there was an answering smile on the sallow, round face of Pramila. She wasn't speaking to him, but into her wristlink. Then she saw me, and stared in complete amazement.

The young male followed her gaze. His tawny eyes opaqued, then cleared, and a smile twitched one corner of that wolverine mouth. His white *meshabi*-robe was dusty, and (this being the inner city) no hook-bladed knife hung at his belt.

'How's Molly and the Company these days?' I asked. He had the grace to look disconcerted.

'*Shan'tai*, I haven't seen her – I'm here with the south-Coast *hiyeks*, for the talks. I've got them together without slitting each other's throats, that's an achievement, wouldn't you say?'

We spoke the Maherwa dialect with a fluency that I saw Pramila couldn't follow. I met Sethri's gaze. His insouciant humour had an edge. *I mean to make a friend of you*, he had said, and proceeded to ingratiate himself with Molly instead. When I spoke, it was with malice.

'Some advice, Sethri, if you like. When you're on your way up the ladder, don't kick the rungs away behind you. You're going to need them, coming down.'

He placed one hand on his breast, bowed slightly, with a rueful amusement. 'Forgive me if I underestimated you in Maherwa, *shan'tai*. I have much to learn.'

'Not that much.' I switched to Sino-Anglic, and to Pramila, who still held up her wristlink, mouth open in silent bewilderment. Before she could speak, I said, 'Is that Molly on the comlink? Tell her I apologize for my unavoidable absence. I was taking advantage of an opportunity that arose.'

Pramila made as if to speak, stopped, stared at me with total incredulity, and then said, ' "Opportunity"?'

'To investigate the political climate among the influential *hiyek*-families on the Coast—'

I always say, if you're going to tell a big lie, do it with style and a smile.

'—I knew the *hiyeks* would be meeting the Hundred Thousand here, for talks. I thought Molly might want a wider view of the Coast culture than just the area around Maherwa. There is over four hundred miles of inhabited land, you know.' I paused, and stepped into the scant shadow that the *lapuur* provided. '*Is* that Molly you're talking to?'

Pramila Ishida stared at me for a full thirty seconds. Then she said absently, 'No, it's David, we've grounded the shuttle outside this settlement. "Opportunity" . . . but there was no report! We haven't known where you were, what you were doing—'

'I see . . .'

When I like, I can use all the old Service noncommittal urbanity.

'That's most irregular . . . Yes. I'll have to have words with certain people when I get back, I can see that. If you weren't aware – good grief, Molly must think I've gone completely insane! I must get on the comlink to her. Perhaps I'll come out to the shuttle with you. I need to use a shuttle's resources in any case, pick up a supply of protein and vitamin supplements . . .'

'I can't go yet. I have to help Sethri-safere set up additional venues for the talks.' She rubbed a hand across her forehead, tucked a strand of black hair behind her ear. She was sweating. And not greatly fooled, I thought, by a more than threadbare excuse.

'Molly *will* want to speak to you,' she said. 'She may think it better if you return to Maherwa, or the Freeport.'

She wore a CAS-IV holster on her belt, the comlink connected her to the shuttle: this small and somehow compact figure standing in the noon heat. It was an odd contrast with the stunted *lapuur*, the white mud that was cracked and drying, with Sethri and the Ortheans at the nearby Order Houses.

'Maybe you'd better patch me through the shuttle and the orbiter,' I said. 'I'll stay in the city for the talks. Who's here?'

I could see her internal debate: how much to tell this unreliable, eccentric woman – who is, however, still special advisor to Pan-Oceania on Orthean affairs.

'*Hiyek*-Anzhadi, Pelatha, Thelshan.' She paused. 'The Freeporters, the *takshiriye*. I think there are some Ortheans from the Kerys-Andrethe *telestre*, and the Telmenar Wellhouse. And Meduenin; there are Meduenin here.'

There would be. A knot of tension began to form in my stomach. For a moment I fiercely resented that. Don't I have enough to concern me, without having Blaize Meduenin continually on my mind? The tension remained, no effort of will able to dismiss it. And we shall meet, I thought. It's inevitable, both of us here. God damn it. Some part of me was outraged that my peace of mind should depend on anyone but myself.

And then with resignation I thought, That settles it, girl. When your sense of humour vanishes, you *have* got it bad . . .

Pramila Ishida said uncertainly, 'We're acting as neutral arbitrators. With all the Coast people and the Freeporters here, some of the Houses are saying they can't provide food for them.'

The inner city's Order Houses finance themselves from the tolls and taxes all traders pay to enter and leave Kasabaarde's trade-quarter. It gives the inner city a deceptive appearance of inexhaustible wealth. Looking at the crowds round us, I thought, But it wasn't designed to cope with *this*.

'You'll want to talk with the heads of the Order Houses, and the *hiyek-keretne*.'

So easy, to slip back into the Company frame of mind. But half the memories I call up about the inner city are not mine. And all I can think now is, *How long until Douggie's message to the Tower gets an answer?*

'I'll give you a hand here,' I said. 'Let me talk to Molly first, though.'

Pramila keyed in a contact through the wristlink. I wished briefly that I could get out to the shuttle. YV9s may be old models, they do at least contain clean-up facilities and spare uniforms. Then Molly Rachel would see in her comlink a neat, middle-aged woman, smart in PanOceania coveralls and logo; hair bleached, skin tanned, otherwise no trace of that month's journeying from Maherwa . . .

Who are you fooling, girl? I came out of the daydream: dirt-stained, hair straggling, barefoot, with only a threadbare *meshabi*-robe to keep off the sun – but still, I thought, I have the presence now to convince Pramila I'm in authority, and *that* didn't happen before.

'Here.' The Asian-Pacifican girl handed me her wristlink, and stepped aside out of earshot, conferring with Sethri and – Jadur, is it? – of *hiyek*-Anzhadi.

The 'link cleared, showing in miniature the interior of a grounded shuttle, and the Aboriginal woman's face. Stark light from an open port made her squint, put specks of brilliance in that black hair. Her coveralls were stained with dust. There was a rim of dirt on her face, marking the edges of just-discarded eyeshields.

'It *is* you,' she said grimly.

I said, 'I must apologize for being out of contact for so long. Quite inadvertently, you understand—'

'Bullshit!' Molly Rachel interrupted. 'If I had a spare hour out of the twenty-seven, I'd shuttle up to Kasabaarde and find out what the hell you've been doing. You're advisor to PanOceania, Lynne. The Company's interests are your interests. And your tin-pot government's, tell Clifford!'

She took a breath.

'I ought to have you shipped back to Earth on the first ship out of Thierry's World!'

' "Ought to"?'

She glared, and then wiped her forehead, and looked absently at the pale dust on her dark fingers.

'I ought to bust your ass, Lynne. *You* know that. Just be grateful I don't have the time. Things are happening here.'

The tiny image of her face showed exhaustion, and a febrile excitement that might mean success. But now is not the time to question her.

'Lynne, are you all right? Pramila said you seemed . . .'

'In my right mind? Yes. I intend to check with the Psych people on the orbiter later on, but yes.'

'So it was offworld syndrome. I'm relieved. There's enough going on here.'

I could glimpse, through the open port of her shuttle, the bleached moonscape of the south-east Coast. I faced that Pacifican smugness, hating for a moment that all their answers are (for them) easy.

She sighed, shook her head. 'Lynne, *why* are you so bloody unreliable? I can have you offworld tomorrow – I was going to, I still can; but I could use your help, with Pramila and David, on condition that I know where you really stand on Carrick V.'

'Were you ever in any doubt?'

'*You* were,' Molly said. 'Now you know, and we both know, that you want the Company off Carrick V. Fine. Work for that. Just tell me if you're still willing to give specialist advice. And if I listen to it, I'll bear the rest in mind.'

Why do I underestimate her? God knows it doesn't pay.

Then she laughed. I had to laugh, too. We'd be watching each other. Watching ourselves. But maybe we have a *modus operandi.*

'Call me again later today,' Molly said, 'and we'll talk it through. There isn't time now. We'll talk. Lynne, it's good to have you back.'

The wristlink image blinked out. For a moment I was shamed by her honesty. And then I thought of the Tower, of memories that are not mine, and of Havoth-jair.

How many hours now until there is an answer from the Hexenmeister?

Stormsun-18 wore away to evening, and a hot and humid twilight. I slept a few of the afternoon hours at the Order House Thelmithar, and then came out to sit on their shallow steps, and drink one of the last flasks of *del'ri*-spirit that the House had.

Evening's citrine light shone on a group of us. A tan-skinned female from a mid-Coast *hiyek*, two thin and languid males who claimed origin in the Rainbow Cities, and an older male who didn't speak.

—that same citrine light, a Coast evening ten years gone: I see an Orthean girl sitting on the rim of a fountain, in gardens of stunted arniac *and* lapuur, *her arms cradling a child perhaps a year old. She is pale-skinned, tan mane braided with beads, wearing the brown* meshabi-*robes and rope-belt of the Brown Tower. Just past ashiren, not more than sixteen. Her face is unsmiling, bent in concentration over the child that plays with her six-fingered hand.*

'There is one of this generation's apprentices,' says that old male, the Hexenmeister. 'She has many of the memories stored in her mind. Another few years – when I die – and she may be Hexenmeister. And she'll *remember speaking with you, Christie, remember this moment as I do. And she will be me. As I am all who went before me—'*

The memory is small and hard and clear, like a brightly-coloured pebble that I can take out and examine, and now put away. Because I have learned that it is only memory, not madness. I wondered if Doug will hear that an Orthean female is Hexenmeister now. Could the old male still be alive, after all this time?

When Doug came to Thelmithar an hour or so later, the Rainbow City Ortheans had left the steps, and I sat alone. Second twilight gloomed: Carrick's Star set, the Heart Stars not yet visible. I poured a bowl of *del'ri*-spirit for Doug. The act needed concentration.

'I've seen the Tower servants, the brown-robes. They listened politely enough.' He sat down beside me, loosening the neck of his coveralls, and wiping sweat from his forehead. 'Then they talked for some while, without actually saying anything. I'm told the Hexenmeister will consider an answer . . . Are you going to suggest to the Company that there may be alien technology in Kasabaarde?'

I sipped more *del'ri*-spirit. The effect on human biology is slightly hallucinogenic.

'The Tower must be wondering the same thing.' I grinned crookedly at him.

And the Tower has nothing to protect itself except secrecy – and reputation. No weapons, no troops, only a few defences within the actual walls. Nothing to protect that fragile, ageing machinery that he said cannot be replaced. Except Kasabaarde's reputation. Have I made myself a target?

'Douggie, I wanted to talk to you. Wanted to say this at Maherwa, but I didn't have it straight in my mind. I ought to hand in my resignation to PanOceania,' I said, 'but I won't. Not yet. Not until I've got everything useful out of them that I *can* get out of them.'

Twilight blurred the dome-roofs of the inner city. To the north, just visible, the tip of the last spire of the Rashre-y-Meluur was illuminated by the vanished sun.

'I hope you meant what you've said,' I added. 'Or I'm going out on a limb for nothing. But I'm still going. I can't condone what the Company's doing on Orthe. I'll act as a source of inside information as long as I can – which won't be long, if I know Molly Rachel – and then I'll quit, and carry on here, outside the Company. God knows what I can do, but I'm going to try.'

Doug leaned back against the dome-wall, and took a long drink

590

of the fermented *del'ri*-spirit. He said shrewdly, 'And then you want a bolt-hole to run to. Government Service.'

'If I don't get that, PanOceania can deport me off Orthe. I'd find ways to stay, but I need a position of influence.'

He chuckled wryly. 'You're joining me.'

'A little late in the day. Believe me, Douggie, I know that.'

'And I don't know all of your reasons, do I? No, and you don't know all of mine.' He raised the ceramic bowl in a salute half ironic, half sincere. 'Welcome to the conspiracy.'

I shifted over to sit beside him, sharing the flask of *del'ri*. The last light faded from the Rasrhe-y-Meluur. We talked for a while, quietly. Lamplight spilled from the arch of an Order House further down the alley, and voices were raised inside; the thin wail of a metal flute rising over the din. A humid, sweaty evening. Above, the Heart Stars began to blaze like silver fur.

We sat side by side, he with the collar of his coveralls unfastened, that grizzled red hair slicked up as close as it ever comes to disarray. Behind me, an Order House male lit lamps. Yellow light shone from the door-arch, limning the edges of the steps, and the alley dust rough with the print of bare feet. It shone on Douggie's bowed shoulders, and the small curls of hair at the nape of his neck. I thought, I want to touch that soft, creased skin – here, where air and twilight and gravity are not Earth's. Here, a very long way from home.

I said, 'I took a look in records, back in the Freeport. Sophie's where, now? Arminel-III?'

'On Thierry's World. She's doing xeno-biology research there.'

He got up slowly, heavily. And then remained on his feet for a while, looking up at the Heart Stars. *You're warned: I mentioned her name.* I saw his profile silhouetted against the brilliance. He hesitated and then seated himself again, on the step beside me. The place where he had been half leaning against my shoulder felt cold and unprotected.

I put the bowl of *del'ri*-spirit down in shadows cast by starlight. The Order House's arch is open, leading to domed rooms and *del'ri*-fibre pallets, and to *chiruzeth* chambers below us, where hidden canal waters flow. Doug Clifford sat, hands linked, staring at the ground between his boots. Then he turned his head fractionally, caught my eye, and gave me a deliberately theatrical version of his mandarin noncommittal stare.

I reached down and took his hand, risking the rejection of that touch, not knowing – when he returned the grip – if it would be to move my hand aside. But his fingers closed over mine with such force that his knuckles stood out white. And I love the breathing warmth of him, human warmth not felt for so long a time, and his smile—

Later, in terrible clarity, I thought, *But it should have been Blaize Meduenin.*

The dawn was hazy, heavy with a sea wind; and I stood with Doug outside the Order House. Morning, and an odd mixture of satisfaction and regret. *Now I'll feel awkward in the future, meeting Sophie Clifford again* – and some self-disgust, at self-interest so nakedly displayed.

'I wouldn't want you to think that . . .' Doug's worried expression faded into a smile. 'We understand each other, Lynne, don't we?'

Only powerful embarrassment could provoke such a cliché out of Douggie. I smiled reassurance, hoping for that slight barrier to vanish, for him to be what he was before. I thought, I wish I could walk down through Harbourgate and stand on the docks, and see the wide horizon, and the long morning shadow of the Rasrhe-y-Meluur on the waves, and the first islands of the Kasabaarde Archipelago . . .

A voice from the alley said, '*Shan'tai* Clifford. *T'an* Christie.'

I looked down the steps. A slight figure stepped out of the dawn shadows – masked, and barefoot, and wearing a brown *meshabi-*robe. And it was an *ashiren*, a child.

'I have a message,' *ke* said, in a pure, archaic form of Coast dialect. 'From the Tower. The Hexenmeister says that you may come there and speak with her, *t'an* Christie.'

Doug glanced at me, shaking his head.

'I know,' I said. 'I'm not twenty-six any more. This time I'm not going to enter the Tower just because I've been invited. Not with what I know. Without some better reason, I won't enter it at all.'

Doug turned up his collar against the sea wind. 'I'll go. It's envoy's business. I'll speak with them again.'

The *meshabi*-robe felt too thin for the dawn chill. I'm too old to go barefoot, I'd found a pair of the *del'ri*-fibre sandals that Kasabaardeans wear. An Order House's gift. That niggled. The inner city can't afford gifts now.

'Doug, has it occurred to you – it's all very well to condemn PanOceania and loudly support Orthe. We've still got to work out what we can *do.*'

That lined, round face held a determination unlike his usual urbanity. 'Get Carrick V declared a Protected world. If the Company research in Maherwa is successful, that won't be easy.'

'Nothing's easy. If the Company goes, the Coast's left to starve. If the Company stays, everything changes out of all recognition. Where's the easy answer, Doug?'

Knowing that in Maherwa, facing Calil bel-Rioch – was it blocked Tower-memories that sent me over the edge, then, or the simple impossibility of taking that decision for Orthe? It's not a decision anyone should be called on to take, and we so often are.

He squeezed my arm reassuringly, and, as he followed the brown-robe, called, 'I have every confidence, Lynne. Wait here for me. I'll have an answer as soon as possible.'

A cool wind blew, flapping the *del'ri*-cloth awning.

I waited in that bright dawn – knowing nothing of what Molly Rachel and Calil bel-Rioch were doing, four hundred miles south and east of Kasabaarde; nothing of what was said and thought that same hour by the Hexenmeister. The wave that had been gathering momentum since PanOceania came to Carrick V was about to break, and I didn't know what rough water I would have to ride.

I don't know what I'll do, I thought, I only know that, for better or worse, I've come home to Orthe at last.

Midday in the crowded city, and I saw among the *hiyek*-Ortheans the uniform of a government envoy. Doug and I met at the edge of a stretch of bare earth that lies between the Order Houses and the Tower gardens. He shrugged.

'Lynne, I've talked to the brown-robes again. They say the Hexenmeister won't speak with any offworlder in person except Lynne de Lisle Christie. I don't know what you want to do about this. I believe I would think very carefully—'

—three of us running through the dusty city, under the molten-metal sun. My lungs ache, and my head; adrenalin from the attack of Havoth-jair's assassins. Blaize Meduenin moves cat-silent, alert, glancing rapidly from side to side.

Are there more of them? In alley-entrances, in doorways; the assassin's knife, that sound – like ripped silk – of a blade being torn from its scabbard. Are there more, near us, now?

My heart hammers.

And the third one of us, that slender white-maned woman, stumbles as she runs. Black blood wells out from between her fingers gripping her arm. No more than a child, Ruric's child: Rodion Orhlandis. Who stumbles against me as we cross that stretch of bare earth between Order Houses and the gardens surrounding the Tower.

'There.' No other sanctuary. And as the girl falters, I pick her up, and stagger the last few yards into that one refuge from all attack: the Brown Tower . . .

593

The light of Carrick's Star is still as acid-white, and I saw Doug squint against it. He fumbled for eyeshields. I put that decade-old memory back into my mind. Adrenalin still made my heart pound. The effects of memory? Or this, now?

'Doug, the Tower depends on secrecy. I'm the only one they're likely to let in, because I already know . . . and you're right, it needs thinking about; that's no good reason for going, is it?'

Light glinted off the glass shields covering his eyes. He said, 'It may well be considered unwise of me to pass this on, but I suppose it would come to you in any case. I have a message I was directed to give to you – a *verbatim* message, if the Ortheans who serve in the Tower are telling the truth. From the Hexenmeister. I understand from reading your old reports that you've received such messages before.'

'Douggie, for Christ's sake, *what did they say*?'

'The message is "Come because you remember there was a room in the Citadel, in the island-city of Tathcaer".'

Deliberately I cut off all thought, all feeling, all speculation. The sun beat down like white-hot iron; somewhere a *rashaku* called. The air was loud with the murmur of the *hiyek*-Ortheans a dozen yards away.

'Doug, walk with me as far as the Tower.'

Two pale-skinned and tan-maned Ortheans in brown *meshabi*-robes stood at the entrance. I was conscious of the warm dust, almost ankle-deep here; and the smell of the *lapuur*, and the *kazsis* that spidered its crimson way up the brown brick wall in front of me.

'Give you greeting,' said the male. His shadow pooled at his feet, black as a pit.

The female stood with her back to the slab of metal, ten feet high and seven feet wide, that was the only break in the brickwork. Set back into a plain brick arch, the colour of silt.

Doug touched his wristlink. 'I'll call you at five-minute intervals. Let them know this is patched up to the orbiter, through the shuttle. Lynne, I wish you wouldn't do this.'

His spare comlink was fixed round my left wrist; a permanent discomfort. I put my hand on his arm for a moment, then walked forward. The metal slab slid up, disclosing a smooth-walled corridor beyond. I didn't look back as I entered.

Something in the dry air hushed speech. There was a soft noise as the metal slab sank back down, cutting off the heat and white sunlight. The two brown-robes stood beside me. I put out a hand and brushed fingers across the wall. Dry stone, pale and seamless.

Yes. There are certain places in the Tower that Ortheans sometimes see. And nothing visible there to disturb them.

'Come, *shan'tai*,' the female said. Both of them seemed young, no more than early twenties.

As I followed them, I was conscious of a subliminal hum, just below the threshold of perception. I thought, Have I ever been away from here? The last ten years could be a dream. Oh but this body is not a young woman's body, and as for me . . .

We came at last to a room once familiar. One of the few with windows, and the light of Carrick's Star slanting whitely in to bleach the already pale walls. The room was small, darkened by the shelves that stood in almost every free spot; and the shelves were piled with scrolls, bound books, papers, maps. I moved forward, wondering if there would still be the great table standing before the hearth.

'You don't have to cater to my tender sensibilities,' I said, 'I know there's more technology in the Tower's Archives than pen and ink—'

The world went away. The mind refused belief but the body reacted: dizzy, cold, stunned.

A lean Orthean woman sat writing at the table. She wore a white shirt and black britches, and her high-arched feet were bare. She turned as she glanced up, leaning one arm on the back of the chair. That sleeve was rolled up casually, showing the dusty anthracite skin of her forearm, the long fingers that held a writing-stick. The other sleeve was empty and the cloth tied in a rough knot below the shoulder.

I don't believe –

Her mane fell like a raven's wing across her forehead where (half hidden) the black skin puckered with the scar of an old brand. The mark of an exile. Put on her in a room under the Citadel in the island-city Tathcaer. In her forties now, by that face; that high-boned face. Proportions just slightly wrong: cheekbones that make the face too wide, jaw that makes it too narrow. She brushed the back of her wrist across nose and lips, and her eyes cleared as the nictitating membranes slid back. Sad, unshocked eyes as yellow as sunlight; in that shade almost luminous. This lean and ageing woman; casual, competent, silent.

She threw the writing-stick down on the table and stood up, the chair scraping back, all in one movement. And stood with a crook-shouldered balance, and looked.

'Ruric,' I said. Could only say. *Amari* Ruric Orhlandis. Older; and I would have known her out of ten thousand.

And because I needed to be certain this was no memory, I took

595

a step forward and reached out and gripped that six-fingered hand; dry, hot skin.

' "Ruric" . . .' The Orthean woman shook her head, then. 'Christie, I wish I was – I wish that I were all Ruric, all Orhlandis, but I'm not. I'm Hexenmeister, now.'

CHAPTER 15

A Mirror Seen in Mist and Pearl

There was a plain wooden bench set where Carrick's Star shone whitely in through the window. I sat there. Motes in the sunlight were bright, distinct. The Orthean woman stood beside me, the long fingers of her hand resting on my shoulder, kneading a part of the shock away.

You can't be anyone else and therefore you must be—

'Ruric?'

She moved to the table, hitching one hip up to sit on the corner there and pour the ubiquitous *arniac*-tea with that long-practised and crippled dexterity.

'I'll have to ask you to keep this one of the Tower secrets. It shouldn't be known in the Hundred Thousand who the Hexenmeister is.' The woman put down her bowl, brushed back her mane. The brand was a jagged line from brow to temple, pale brown against her black skin; a raised ridge of flesh. The brand of the exile. For a second the fine web of lines round the yellow eyes smoothed out: she could have been the young Ruric, *T'An* Commander of the army, *T'An* Melkathi.

'You're *supposed* to be dead.'

It sounded querulous. The woman grinned.

'Sorry I can't oblige you. You wouldn't be the only one to feel disappointed.'

'I didn't mean that.'

'Didn't you? You might feel that way yet.'

Noon light made her a shadow, black on black. This lean, forty-year-old Orthean woman, with the youthful grin. How do I know if what's different about her is being Hexenmeister, or being ten years older?

'If you're Hexenmeister—' Then I'm speaking to that old male that I met in the Tower, when Ruric Orhlandis was plotting and intriguing in Tathcaer . . . I remember his voice: *And when she speaks with you, she'll remember this, as I do now, and she will be me.*

597

The woman came to hunker down on her haunches before the bench, and I met that yellow gaze. 'Yes, I am Hexenmeister. Christie, you think you understand what I mean by that. You don't.'

'How can you say that? You know what I know!'

She grimaced, stood, stretched her back. The white slit-backed shirt was open, showing her small high breasts, and the second pair of rudimentary nipples on the lower ribs. She turned, and I saw how that black mane grew in a vee down her spine to the small of her back.

'No *harur-nilgiri*,' I said, surprised. 'You might convince me yet. A *telestre*-Orthean without a *harur*-blade, and especially Ruric Orhlandis—'

She swung round, eyes blazing. 'They exiled me, that doesn't mean I'm not of the land!'

In a room in the Citadel in Tathcaer – 'Ruric Orhlandis, once T'An Commander and now T'An Melkathi, first named Onehand and Yellow-eyes, and now and for ever after to be named murderer, conspirator, and paid traitor to the Hundred Thousand.' – And those words themselves written by a traitor.

I stood, unsteadily, and went to get a bowl of *arniac*. She watched me. The crimson liquid was only lukewarm, and I drank it down in a draught.

'I wanted to speak with you first.' She glanced down. 'I've sent my brown-robes to invite the government envoy here, and the two offworlders from PanOceania.'

'You'll let them come *inside* the Tower?'

'The Tower needs to consult with Earth. I've been planning for that. The problem is you, Christie—' The Orthean woman hesitated, and said wryly, 'That's a name I thought I'd never use again. You're the problem. You're muddying the water. And I can't see any way to solve matters, except by doing this.'

A breath of dry air blew in the open window, rustled the papers on the shelves, set the *kazsis*-vine tapping against the brick arch. Ruric Orhlandis reached out and weighted down the papers on the table with her ceramic bowl.

'And just how am I supposed to be muddying the water?'

'By making known something that my predecessor let you believe – no, I won't lie. Something he made you believe. It was done deliberately.'

All the fear and insecurity that I felt in Maherwa returned in a moment, doubled and tripled; and then slowly began to ebb. I studied her face intently.

'Perhaps I've got stupid as I've got older. Ruric, you're going to have to spell it out.'

I saw her take a breath. It is not a human movement, that sharp intake of arched ribs. Nictitating membrane slid down over her eyes.

'It wasn't my responsibility. I wasn't even here. Christie, I feel ashamed.' She rubbed at her forehead. The claws on that six-fingered hand were neatly trimmed. Then she flicked a sharp, hard glance at me. 'Sunmother! You don't make it easy. This, then. The Hexenmeister who held the title before me . . . Well, there are drugs, as you'd call them. And techniques that sometimes come out of the inner city, that make one see or hear unrealities. Christie, trust nothing of what you thought happened to you when you were here before! He told you the lie that the Tower always tells, about memory; but he made you believe it.'

Ruric paused, then at last added, 'How can I say I'm sorry? I wasn't even here then. I don't know what made him do it, nor whether he knew that it would damage an offworlder as it's damaged you. It's an evil thing to have done.'

I stared at her. 'No. No, I know. I *remember* . . .'

Again, that crooked smile. 'I don't expect you to believe what I say, what anyone in the Tower says. That's another reason why I'm bringing other offworlders in. They'll need proof, too. Proof that you're – misinformed. You've half convinced that man Clifford.'

'For God's sake, I didn't go through the last month just to – I *know* what I know! Ruric, it's been hard enough to work it through. I know; I'm certain.'

And then I thought again of that dark-maned Coast woman, Havoth-jair. Damaged. And my memory of how it happened is sharp and clear – and inaccurate. It *wasn't* I who condemned her to that, it was Evalen Kerys-Andrethe (though I could have stopped it). If that memory is no memory at all . . .

There was no time to think. Ruric turned as a brown-robed servitor came to the door of the room, exchanged a brief word, and nodded.

'I'm told the government envoy is here.'

In total disbelief and confusion, all I could manage to say was, 'How can you let outsiders into the Tower?'

'Because they are outsiders. I couldn't allow my people in. There are things in the Tower, even if they're not what you think is here. And Earth and I have to talk,' Ruric said quietly. 'If I've learned nothing else in eight years, I've learned the nature of the problem.

599

I won't try to solve it with fire or *harur*-blades this time. Christie, it's been a long time, but believe this: I still won't stand by and see your people ruin Orthe.'

It's impossible to take it in, I thought. *He told you the lie that the Tower always tells, about memory, but he* made *you believe it.*

'. . . assure you this is a great privilege,' Doug Clifford said smoothly, as brown-robed Ortheans ushered him into the small library-room. He frowned, then concealed it.

'Give you greeting,' the Orhlandis woman said. 'Strange to meet, *t'an* Clifford, at last. I've had indirect dealings with you and your government for six years now.'

'Hexenmeister.' Barely a question in his voice. Is he familiar enough with my old reports to realize who she must be? Then I saw the curiosity even his diplomacy couldn't hide, and realized *yes, he knows*.

Ruric moved aside to talk to a fair-maned male in the Tower's brown robes. While she talked, her gold-yellow eyes sought mine; veiled and cleared.

Doug muttered, 'Lynne, are you all right?'

'No, but give me time.'

'I wasn't expecting this,' he said. 'I've linked a time-alarm through the shuttle to the orbiter. If we're not out of here within a reasonable time—'

'Warning people we're in here is one thing. Getting out may be another.' Part of me observed that that was a sensible comment, considering the state of mind I was in. The rest was panic.

The brown-robe left, and Ruric turned to face us.

'The two offworlders from the PanOceania Company will be here soon. I've got things to say to you before they get here. *T'an* Clifford, you and Lynne Christie have influence so far as Orthe's concerned; you want a policy of non-interference—'

'May I ask how you come to that conclusion?' Doug's politeness was marked.

'I hear things. The inner city.' She looked at me. ' "I'll act as a source of inside information." And the rest.'

I watched her, waited. She walked across to the window, and reached up to slide a fretwork metal shutter halfway across the arch. Noon glare diminished. The shadow dappled the white *del'ri*-cloth of her shirt. Skin and mane vanished, blended with darkness.

'I know what Christie's told you. It's important we start clean,' Ruric said, 'not believing lies and half-truths. *T'an* Clifford, there *is* Witchbreed science in the Tower. It's *not* what Christie's told you. We have to deal together, for Orthe. We have to believe each other. And so I'll have to show you what the Tower's Archives really are.'

One step took her across the line the shutter cast, into the light of Carrick's Star. Her face showed age in that white glare.

'Whatever I choose, there's a risk. To bring offworlders inside the Tower, tell them truths that my people don't know – it's dangerous. Letting you believe the lie is more dangerous. Especially since we may need Earth's help.' Her face changed when she looked at me. 'I didn't have to have you here, now. I owe it to you. For what the last Hexenmeister did. And for a lie I once told you.'

All I could say, out of ten-year-old memories, was 'How can we trust anything you say!'

Her eyes shone clear and dark as amber resin. 'I don't expect belief from anyone.'

Was it unspoken: *except from you*?

'Come,' she said decisively. 'I'll leave it to you what report you make, *t'an* Clifford. Just don't talk to *my* people.'

Clifford sniffed, raised an eyebrow. 'My government favours non-interference with alien cultures. It therefore follows one wouldn't, shall we say, implement the dissemination of internal information . . .'

I got up off the bench, finding my legs unsteady. The smell of old paper and parchment was momentarily so strong as to make me dizzy. Clifford took my elbow. For all his screen of verbiage, he was nervous; his hand trembled. The two of us followed the Orthean woman out into the corridor. I thought, I know the way . . .

Here there was no sun, only a dim reflected mirror-light. Deeper into the interior of the Tower now, and the colour and texture of the walls changed, to a slick brown substance. I thought it all seemed smaller than ten years ago. But memory plays such tricks. At a dead-end corridor the Orthean woman and I halted simultaneously, only Doug Clifford caught off guard.

He glanced at me, at the Orthean woman, and back to me. There was reassurance in his expression. For a moment, he would rather believe the impossibility: my story.

What can she show us to change that? I wondered. And was so lost in thought that I barely registered the familiar repetition of entrance to the lower levels: the wall that split and slid aside, the small chamber that we stepped into, the pressure underfoot as it descended. Not until it halted, and the wall again parted to let us out, did I concentrate. *Here*, memory told me.

I walked past them, out into a cool high-roofed hall. There was faint light the colour of lilac and lightning. The walls were blue-grey *chiruzeth*. And not six yards from where I stood was the first of a row of tomb-shaped objects. *Chiruzeth* sarcophagi. Large enough so that an Orthean or an offworlder might lie there enclosed . . .

'Douggie, isn't this what I said I saw?'

The small man came to stand at my shoulder. The blue-pink light made his complexion look unhealthy. There were beads of sweat on his forehead.

'Yes. Somewhat reminiscent of a *siiran*. I imagine about the same level and development of civilization could produce this.' He glanced back. 'How can you take the risk of letting anyone inside this installation, Hexenmeister?'

'*T'an* Clifford, I don't want the Tower ripped apart by offworlders looking for Old Technology. I know what PanOceania's doing with the canals round Maherwa. It's necessary they should know there's nothing here useful to them.'

The dark Orthean woman walked past us, to the nearest tomb-like object. The fingers of her single hand moved delicately on its carved rim. A faint iridescence glowed within the *chiruzeth* tank.

But that's not what happened when I—

A voice whispered almost inaudibly in the sarcophagus-tank, and an image grew. Faint, immobile. A still image.

'Welcome to the Tower Archives,' Ruric said sardonically. She again hitched herself up to sit on one corner of the *chiruzeth* device, and glanced round the distant reaches of the hall. 'Not as impressive as it might be, is it? But precious. These devices can't be replaced. Not now.'

Archives?

Clifford moved closer to the *chiruzeth* tank. 'Hexenmeister, I have to confess that I don't quite see the implications of what you're telling us.'

Ruric caught my eye, grinned. Her dark hand moved on the *chiruzeth* surface. The still image changed. The voice whispered.

Without meaning to speak, I said, 'That isn't what these devices do!'

Her head bowed over the tank, black mane falling forward. The image was of *ziku* and mossgrass. They grow in the Hundred Thousand. Unbidden, her hand came up to rub at the stump of her right arm.

'He didn't lie to you in everything.' She raised her head. 'That's why you believe. You can take evidence two ways. The Tower does have Witchbreed technology. The Hexenmeister – anyone

602

who holds the title Hexenmeister – has a more-than-mortal memory. It's stored in these devices. The Tower's been adding to the knowledge held here for sixty generations.'

Doug Clifford stared at the image in the tank. 'Data storage and retrieval.'

'The Witchbreed Empire—' She made a grimace, her distaste plain. 'Now they're gone, these devices can't be replaced.'

She slid down, stood with that swordfighter's balance; and her head came up, and for a moment it was Ruric Orhlandis, the Crown's Ruric, Melkathi's Ruric, the Ruric I mourned as dead.

'*T'ans*, this doesn't change anything. The Tower is still the guard against the rise of another Golden Empire. Our hands aren't clean. What of it? Whose are? All the Hexenmeisters have used every method in their power to keep us from becoming what the Golden Witchbreed became – what your people are. Forgive me, it's true. We have information and secrecy and not much else.' She smiled wryly. 'But I knew that when I agreed to become Hexenmeister.'

Clifford's face was intent, his eyes fixed on that *chiruzeth* tank. Data storage and retrieval. Without looking at her, he said, 'If you were to have contact with a pro-isolationist group, one that has some influence with Earth governments and multicorporates—'

'*No.*' Both their heads turned towards me. I took a breath. 'I need things explained. What are you telling me? That I was – what? – hypnotized, drugged into believing that memory-transfers are possible? And they're not?'

The Orhlandis woman said, 'The last Hexenmeister was very practised in making people believe they hadn't spoken with the Tower. Or that he had powers that do not exist. Christie, he couldn't have known it would damage an offworlder as it's damaged you.'

Too stunned to think, I could only stare at her.

'It wasn't a right thing to do.' She sighed. Then a hardness came into her face. 'But the Tower has only secrecy to protect it and the Tower *must* survive.'

I walked forward and put both hands on the rim of the *chiruzeth* tank. No more than a data-link, a holotank? Remembering how I lay down in one of these slick coffins, and the stab of a mental violation.

Shattered into a million pieces, a million lives—

The air cool, the light a frozen instant of lightning; and cool blue-grey walls . . . and that all but imperceptible hum. A sudden image came to me of the white hall in Rakviri *telestre*, the intent faces of Barris and Jaharien, the iron bowl eaten away in energy-change to *chiruzeth*. The effect that just one relic of the Empire could have. Can I have built up a whole delusional system, just based on alien data-storage archives?

I swung round and faced them, the human male and the Orthean woman.

'What right – how the fuck did he dare do that to me!'

As I spoke, I knew: There is still a doubt. That younger Christie who first came here, she would have voiced her doubts. I looked at Douggie's bland expression, and the ageing features of the alien woman, and I kept silent. Desperate to get out of the Tower and think this through alone.

'Does that satisfy you now?' Ruric asked Clifford. 'Questions later. I'll take you back now. I must talk to the PanOceania offworlders. *T'ans*, you see the risks I take. I can't prevent you spreading this knowledge on the Coast and in the Hundred Thousand. I can only ask you to wait.'

'That would seem to be acceptable.'

Looking at Clifford as he spoke, I couldn't tell what he was thinking. Which means that I know exactly what he thought.

All children who go to the sea pick up pebbles, shining black and red and white from the water. Nothing left later but a handful of dry and salt-encrusted stones. Pyrites; fool's gold.

Memories hard and solid and bright: should they be colourless now?

'Explain the languages,' I said, as we left the desiccated Tower gardens and walked down between Order House domes. 'That's just *one* of the things I know. Explain how I can be fluent in most of the languages of the Coast and the Hundred Thousand.'

Clifford shrugged off the challenge. 'Lynne, for all I know you've spent the last ten years studying Orthe. Don't be angry – I'm saying what others will say. I have to keep an open mind until I'm presented with proof.'

How could you . . . ? Douggie!

Real worlds and hard facts, they tip the balance. I nodded, let him walk on towards the Westgate. Cold bites deep to the bone, and fear is cold. Though Carrick's Star radiates fiercely, and the hot Coast gales blow, and the dust is warm underfoot: such a chill . . .

A six-fingered hand touched my arm. I looked down, saw a thin-faced male in a faded *meshabi*-robe. The nictitating membrane slid back from his eyes so far that a rim of white was visible round the green iris.

'Who cut off your mane and hurt your eyes?' His interest was childlike.

'I'm not Orthean, *shan'tai*, I'm offworlder.'

His head cocked sideways, like a bird's. 'You wear the mask of the Tower. How many masks do you wear?'

Not now, I thought, and rubbed a hand across my bare face. At this precise moment I don't need the inner city and its madmen.

He added, 'I used to have a name and that was a mask.'

I shook his hand off, walked rapidly away. He called something unintelligible. Winding alleys put distance between us, and I made my way between the curving white walls of domes; and the heat of the sun at last made me slow and seek shelter. There was a glimpse of sandstone blocks between white domes, the wall of the inner city; and a massive low arch: Harbourgate.

Some instinct said: In the mental state you're in now, they'll talk to you. All of those who are outsiders, and have no other world to go to. All of those who come here to heal themselves, before they go back and change this world. All those who will never leave, because for them there's no world at all . . .

'Show me your hands.'

A shadow fell across me. I glanced up, saw a woman on the low step of an Order House. Half a dozen Ortheans sprawled there. She had an accent I couldn't place. A mane bleached to colourlessness, a skin like coal; wearing nothing but cords on which pierced stones were strung.

'Show me your hands!' she repeated. 'They're gloved with blood to the elbows.'

She stepped down on to the dry earth. I said, 'I can still defend myself—'

'You are alone, but there's a multitude with you. You think defeat, but victory is only a thought away. I can see you where you stand. Your robe is dirty and your eyes are veiled.' Her dark face shone with a smile, too febrile for comfort. She stepped nearer. 'Let me be your mirror. I show you—'

'What you see.'

'What you think I see.'

Adrenalin hammered. No control in her. The sun's heat made me dizzy.

Do I mirror you? I know how it feels to be you, how you carry yourself; fear raising hackles of mane down your spine, eyes veiled against the white sunlight.

When she spoke again, her voice was soft. 'Why did you come here?'

Was my smile as crazy as hers? I grinned, reckless. 'I came here because I thought I might find – I was about to say, find asylum.

Now I think about that, it's been one, the inner city, and it is one, in quite a different sense!'

The corded pebbles slid against her dark skin. She was a head shorter than I, and that made her look up, and veil her eyes against the light. A gust of warm air caught her mane and wrapped it across the sharp ribs: white on black.

She said, 'Your hands are empty and your eyes weep blood.'

'*Shan'tai*, I don't think you any more reliable than – than any other mirror.'

After a long moment, she turned away. I walked away from the Order House steps, crossing the open ground between there and the city wall. Thinking, Will I become like her?

After Max died, I found that I could believe exactly what I wanted to believe – until the distance between that and the truth widened so far that I fell down the gap, ended up on the floor of hell in a hospital bed. Could I have built up a delusional system here? Alien interference an irritant grit: the Tower-myth the pearl that builds up around it? Surely not—

Not all monsters are of the mind. Not all delusions are totally detached from the truth.

The shadow of the sandstone wall fell cool on my skin. I stood in the arch of Harbourgate, staring out at brightness. Carrick's Star shone on the ceaselessly-moving water of the harbour. The hoop-masts of *jath-rai* flashed in the sun. I put both palms flat on the sandstone surface, rough and dry against my skin. The Order-robed male in the gatehouse looked curiously at me. He wouldn't act unless I showed I wanted to leave the inner city . . .

Where would I go?

I blinked, blinked again at the harsh light. Wanting to do what human bodies can't: bring down a third eyelid to cut the glare. Do I only think I know how that feels?

Now I don't know: did I come to the inner city to learn to control these visions, or did I come because I had learned to control them – to accept them as memories? They still wash over me. Take over. All I've learned is to stop fearing that. And if they're delusions, not memories, does the fear return?

I rubbed my hands against the sandstone, anchoring myself in physical sensation. Stone, and bright light.

Those lost days, I became not just the person to whom the alien memory happened, but Christie-experiencing-the-memory. As one sometimes clearly thinks in a dream, *I am dreaming*. Two simultaneous levels of awareness.

Is that delusional too?

Okay, girl, now you do what you did in those twenty-five lost days – call it up deliberately, and go into it. Only this time, watch. Judge. Does it feel fake? *Does it?*

The reflected sunlight from the water dimmed. I let the sensation carry me. Feeling that deep difference, a self that is not mine, is alien, and is yet utterly familiar.

Dim light, grey and shifting, which I see now is fog. Swirls of mist that move above me, around me. I move six-fingered hands, drawing a robe closer about myself. The cold bites bone deep.

That bright shadow.

And underfoot is broken ground. Shattered slabs. The mist puts beads of water on the blue-grey surface. Bending to touch it, I find the chiruzeth *not broken but distorted, melted, warped.*

A brilliant blackness.

Without volition, I am moving, scrambling across the tilted slabs. It is 'I' who moves, and Lynne who has no control over it. Breath harsh in the throat. The drag at muscles climbing a slope, where the mist thickens to fog again, and so I move in a grey sphere continually shifting, myself at its centre.

A brightness that ends in splinters like crystal, or the edge of cat-ice on a puddle—

A silver glow in the mist. Moving on up the slope towards it. Does the sun, hidden now, cast light enough to shine on something beyond the ridge? Only the fog clings close, dark grey and heavy, smelling stagnant as the floor of the sea.

A wall grows out of the fog, massive chiruzeth *blocks; a wall that as I follow it, one hand trailing along the cold, wet substance, ends suddenly. The surface is rounded, ridged like candle-wax. Beyond are the regular lines of halls, chambers, towers. I climb over the low part of the wall. Walk the* chiruzeth *floor that I have never seen (but I recall Kirriach, over the Wall of the World; great ruined city of that barren land) . . .*

Carrick's Star shines on the Glittering Plain, and a flare of light flashes out even to the western horizon—

I stop, crouch down, touch the mist-damp floor. And something else. It could almost be an inlaid line of glass or silver, this streak in the chiruzeth *paving. But as I follow it with my eye, I see how it widens. Grows. Splinters of silver-glass following the contours of broken walls. See how, beyond the next broken arch, that sky-exposed floor is all silver; pure and bright as the surface of a mirror.*

The infinite sun of Golden rule. The brilliant beating heart of Empire; Archonys, that great city—

Cold makes me shiver uncontrollably; I can hardly walk. The muscles of my legs are weak. To step through that arch takes long minutes. Fog mats damply in mane and robe. Each sound, each footfall, is muffled.

Some trick of air shifts layers of cloud, somewhere in the thousands of feet of space above. The mist begins to turn from grey to white. To the heart of pearl: sea-cold, iridescent.

Walls of mirror rise up round me. Broken silver towers, lost in the earth-touching clouds. Arches clear and brilliant as glass with the sun on it. And I see through those arches distant landscapes of silver; walls, paving, bridges . . .

Remember that what you see is not a primitive but a post-holocaust world. What you see is plain and simple war damage—

White mist swirls and shines. The cold works its way into my body. I reach out and touch the silver-glass wall. Claws slide from its diamond surface.

That touch is obscene, as if I touched fossil-flesh.

An iron bowl transformed to a lacework of rust. And in it, *chiruzeth* grows.

What made this a living city – is dead. Pearls of water hang on the surface of dead mirrors. As I turn, the cloud-cover for one freak moment thins. I am standing at the top of a hill. Below, and stretching out for miles to east and west and south, the broken city lies. Broken, dead, fossilized: turned to glass and silver, mist and pearl. That in an instant, then the light reflected sears into eyes that are agonizingly, irrevocably blind—

—light from the lapping waves of the harbour of Kasabaarde.

For some minutes I could only lean against the hot sandstone wall. At last lifted a hand to wipe the tears away, and stepped out of the arch's shadow. The sun's heat soaked into me.

Is that what lies under the cloud-cover of the Elansiir, the Barrens, the Glittering Plain? Or have I built it up from surmise, words overheard, that brief sunset glimpse off the hills that look west to Eriel? *Is* that what causes climate anomalies, changes a world's weather? I have reason to think it could be exactly what that war damage looks like.

Is it memory, is it delusion?

A gust of wind whisked a dust-devil towards Harbourgate. Masts and sails creaked in the harbour itself. There was the smell of stagnant water. And there's my answer.

There is the source of that vision's blinding light – the sun on the surface of the harbour. There is the smell of the mist – that stagnant smell of the sea. And I have seen the war damage on the Glittering Plain, and seen the ruins of Golden cities in the Barrens; what easier than to put the two together?

And how could 'I' come, blind and lost, at last to the Tower, to give my memories up to the Hexenmeister's Witchbreed devices? The 'I' in that vision was close to death, and far from Kasa-baarde . . . Except that, since it's delusion, there is no 'I'. Only me.

Voices came distantly from the Order Houses, and I walked a few steps in the hot sun, away from the gate and the harbour. Our concern now is that threat of war, not one woman whose mind has been messed about by alien science—

And is that all there is? some child-part of me wailed. I miss the myth of the immortal being in his Tower, holding the living memories of a hundred generations behind membrane-veiled eyes. Mechanically-stored archives are no substitute. But this is the real world, I thought. If there's no immortal Hexenmeister, still, there *are* records of the past.

I do at least know why Ruric Orhlandis says the Tower must survive. Even if my visions of it were false, there *was* a weapon that could turn the very earth on which that city stood to crystalline stasis. The unknown weapon that made those dead wastelands is gone now, gone with the Witchbreed Empire, but there must be no chance of Ortheans ever creating or acquiring such a weapon again. The Tower must stand, and guard against the rise of another Empire – Orthean or *s'aranthi*.

'Doug Clifford said I'd find you here.'

The voice interrupted thoughts that were light-years away. I blinked, realizing David Osaka was standing in front of me. He wiped sweat-sodden blond hair back from his forehead, squinting against the brilliance of Carrick's Star.

'We need your advice,' he said. 'All hell's breaking out in the Order Houses.'

CHAPTER 16

Domino

A storm passed, rapidly, and spring sunlight fell on the inner city with noon brightness. I thought, I didn't realize so much time went by while I was at Harbourgate . . . The shadows of domes seemed black pits on the white earth. Now no breath of air stirred. Coast cities usually cease activity over the hours of noon, but as I walked with David Osaka, we pushed through crowds of *hiyek*-Ortheans in the alleyways.

'Where's the *shan'tai* Rachel?' an Anzhadi male called out.

'Trade for weapons, *s'aranthi*, we'll buy!'

'Feed us, or war—' A tan-maned female's comment was cut short as she tripped over someone's outstretched legs and cursed.

David gave a genial wave, a smile, and kept walking. I sweated, the dry heat making moisture instantly vanish. An iron-blue sky promised heat and tempest. How long now until the monsoon?

'There isn't anyone to negotiate with!' David said, frustrated. He glanced at the plentiful crowds, and I saw no humour on his face. 'No one we can persuade, who'll then tell the rest what to do.'

The old problem with Orthe: no hierarchy. Everybody is talking to everybody, and some decision will arise out of it, but as for what, and when . . .

'Lynne, I'm thinking of advising Molly to let the fighting break out.'

'*What?*'

'Then, whichever *hiyek*-family emerges as victor will be in a position to dictate to the others. They can help us bring in T&A to the Coast cities, without other *hiyeks* being able to object.'

I looked at him, the frown of concentration on that old-young face. 'What about the suffering a war will cause?'

Self-righteous, David said quickly, 'I'm not suggesting it's the *best* way.'

We turned into a wide, *chiruzeth*-floored avenue, between large Order House domes. The avenue was crowded wall to wall. Voices were raised in a dozen Coast dialects. That and the sun began to make my head ache. I shouldered my way through, behind David Osaka, elbows digging into my ribs, mouth dry, gazing over the heads of the Coast Ortheans.

'Wait—' I heard a familiar voice, searched; then saw faces I knew, under the awning of a dome. David stopped, looking where I pointed.

Hildrindi-*keretne* was on his feet, facing a group who sat on benches under the awning. Sunlight threw the planes of the elderly male's face into sharp relief, cast shadows in deep-set alien eyes, so that for a moment it was a skull I saw. Only a month since I saw him in Maherwa, but illness had ravaged him.

'Answer me, *shan'tai* Meduenin!'

Blaize Meduenin sat resting back against the Order House wall. I saw that dusty mane, that scarred face; heard his sardonic answer.

'I know the Coast. I've been here as a mercenary in your bloodline wars. And I've been there when your ships raided the Melkathi and Rimon coast *telestres*.'

A red-maned woman sitting beside Blaize leaned forward, and I saw it was the Earthspeaker Cassirur Almadhera. 'It isn't Anzhadi-*hiyek* that we blame, *shan'tai* Hildrindi, or any other *hiyek*. If the Coast was prosperous, there'd be no cause for raids. Still . . .'

What a music-hall double act, I thought. Carrot and stick, conciliatory and tough. And for a moment, as David and I stood unnoticed at the edge of the crowd on the steps, I hated the red-maned female simply for being able to be where she was. And despised myself, as one does, for feeling so.

The elderly *keretne* leaned on the arm of a stocky gold-maned female – Feriksushar. He raised his thin voice to be heard by all around: 'We live in a wasteland. Tell us about your *telestre*, Meduenin. Tell us about the river Medued, and the *marhaz* and *skurrai* that graze on its banks. Tell us of *ziku* forests, of *rashaku* that nest there, and *hura* in the river whose flesh is sweet, and the *makre*-grain that grows on the face of the earth that She does not burn!'

Blaize stood. The scar that half masked his face was a livid ruin. Roughly, he said, 'Tell *me* what we can do about it! Not *ashiren*-tales, not fantasies – tell me! We can send food-ships to our own *telestres* when there's famine, but not to all the *hiyeks* of the Coast!'

I was about to move on, to get to the shuttle and use the comlink, when Hildrindi said, 'You have the land.'

A silence fell. Cassirur raised her head, eyes veiled, face white and stark against her red mane. She said, 'We hold the land for

611

Her, live under Her sky and return. We care for it and it for us. The land is not ours to give!'

The Coast, to whom location doesn't matter, so long as the *hiyek*-family is together . . . and the Hundred Thousand, to whom the land is a part of themselves, is the *telestre*, is the root from which they draw their source of self.

Blaize shifted his booted feet, balanced as a swordfighter is. He glanced around, alertly scanning the alleys and domes; he did not (ten years ago) like or trust the inner city. *'T'ans*, I'm neither Earthspeaker nor *keretne*. I'm a plain man. I know the *telestres* have been as they are for sixty generations. They're what we return to, when we return from Her. We can't change. That's all.'

A voice from the other side of the steps called, 'What if we act as one, *shan'tai*? What if you don't face *hiyek*-Anzhadi and *hiyek*-Pelatha and *hiyek*-Cuirduzh but *the Coast*?'

David Osaka said in my ear: 'That's what I wanted you to see. They're threatening invasion!'

Dominoes. One goes, and the next, and who can see where it ends? Not the Company, with its data-net predictions of possible cultural change. Not me, with a head full of Orthean memories that are neither mine nor memories. If ever we had need of the Hexen-meister of legend – ! Well, there is no omnipotence in the Tower.

I said, 'Dave, you stay here and monitor the crisis level.'

'Where will you be?'

No reason, if I'm not a target, to stay within the dubious protection of the inner city . . . 'Out in the shuttle. I'm going to contact Molly.'

But there is somewhere else I'll go first.

The Tower entrance remained firmly closed. Eventually I persuaded the brown-robed servants into an exchange of notes: 'The situation between the Coast families and the Hundred Thousand is deteriorating – can't you take action to stop it?'

I waited in the heat and dust, by the brown brick wall, until a male brought me a folded parchment: 'The Tower does not interfere in local squabbles.'

Ruric, for God's sake—!

Then I turned the paper over, seeing what that dark hand had written on the fold: '*S'aranth*, will the Hundred Thousand heed the Tower if they know an Orhlandis is Hexenmeister? I must be secret. And only secrecy protects what is stored here; we cannot risk being attacked. You see I have no choice. But the Tower has its friends on the Coast. What we can do, secretly, we will.'

*

The YV9 shuttle rested outside Kasabaarde's walls, in a rock gully between the city and the last spire of the Rasrhe-y-Meluur. A gleaming white dolphin-shape . . . I plodded up the shuttle-ramp, grateful for the shade inside, flopped down beside the holotank, keyed the dispenser for a drink, and glanced over at Pramila Ishida.

'I'd like to talk to Molly privately.'

The Pacifican girl shrugged. She walked down the ramp, to stand outside in the shadow of the hull. The hot Coast sun blazed in at the entrance-port. I tasted dust, then nutrient-drink.

The rim of the holotank was hard under my palms. It cleared to show the pale moonscape of the south-east Coast, the time there early afternoon. A wristlink contact. And there – I peered into the 'tank. When I spoke to her yesterday did I ask . . .

'Molly, what's your location? Are you still at Maherwa?'

The Pacifican woman's face came into focus as she adjusted her wristlink with her free hand. I got a clear view of the settlement behind her. A scatter of sun-bleached dice: white walls, spider-thread rope-bridges, roof-houses and steps . . .

'I'm at Kel Harantish now,' Molly Rachel said. 'We haven't got back inside the place yet.'

The ground behind her was full of activity. Massive F90 shuttles come down from the orbiter, hulls gleaming palely in the light of Stormsun – six, no, seven of them – and crews unloading cargo. Men and women in Trade&Aid Corps uniform drove cargolifters and groundcars over the rocky earth, shifting terra-forming equipment. And among the Corps people I glimpsed Ortheans with white manes, in the brown scale-mail of the Harantish guard.

'The Emperor-in-Exile did a *volte face* ten days ago.' Molly Rachel's voice crackled, the 'tank snowed for a moment. 'He decided to experiment with Earth tech. Or, I should imagine, his advisors decided for him. The ex-Voice, Calil bel-Rioch, seems to have friends highly placed in the Harantish caste system.' She grinned. 'You should have seen the reaction when we set up the water-purifiers at the edge of the harbour! I've seen it on other worlds. Crop-improvers take time, but drinkable water – that's instant, and it hooks them every time!'

It took me a second to adjust. I said, 'What the hell are you doing?'

'I'm grabbing a chance. Maybe, just maybe, this will lead to us getting back inside the Harantish settlement.'

You still want the Witchbreed artifacts that are in there, I thought. 'Isn't Rashid Akida getting anywhere with the research team in Maherwa?'

Molly scratched absently at the back of her neck with her free hand. Patches of sweat darkened her coverall. She wore a CAS-IV in a belt-holster, and I saw that she had that look we all have after a few weeks on-world, with no trips to the orbiter or FTL. In the Service we called it 'grounding in'. Gravity has a grip on the body, the sky becomes an impossible high ceiling.

'Rashid's people have had no success at all. He keeps *telling* me they're on the verge of a breakthrough.'

Molly squinted – against the Harantish sunlight, but it took me back to a room on the northern continent, how she stared as if into bright light, unseeing.

'Perhaps,' I said, suddenly short of breath, 'it isn't possible to comprehend Golden science without having their world-view. That we caught a glimpse of in Rakviri *telestre*.'

If the Pacifican woman had been an Orthean, her eyes would have veiled over at that moment. She said, 'No. I think that's false reasoning. It's just a matter of time before Rashid comes through. I'd hoped it would be in less than a year, his team have got the whole resources of Earth's data-nets at their disposal – but I'll be happy if we get a result in under two years.'

She shrugged, then, and added, 'If you want to look at the interior of that dome in Maherwa, the maintenance-entrance, I've put it on the shuttle data-net. Oh yes, before I forget, call the orbiter. They've got a blip for you, from your department on Earth. Lynne, about these talks in Kasabaarde—'

'Have you got any idea what's going on here? If we're not careful, it won't be *hiyek* fighting *hiyek*, it'll be the south continent fighting the north!'

The woman shifted, stretching her shoulders that were hunched against the heat. A voice hailed her from the T&A site, and she called something over her shoulder to them, and then turned back to me.

'Lynne, please. Stop panicking. David and Pramila are keeping me advised. No Orthean is going to risk a major war with an Earth presence on-world, and if there are a few minor incidents – well, they'll defuse tension.'

We're talking about casualties here! I opened my mouth to protest, but Molly got in before me: 'I grant you it's not ideal, but I'm taking the long view. If we can keep hostilities to a minimum until harvest season, then we'll have won. Lynne, when these people see what T&A can do to their crop-yield, they're not going to *need* to fight.'

Anything can be a weapon. Isn't that what Sethri-safere told me?

'I've had David's report on the Tower and the Hexenmeister,' Molly added. 'I'm glad we've got that sorted out. That place might be a very useful source of information. Lynne, I want you to shuttle down here to me. If the talks are breaking up, I could do with an update on that; and I could use your advice on dealing with the Harantish caste-system. How soon can you get down here?'

It is four hundred miles and I'm tired – with a weariness not purely physical. I feel overwhelmed by the Pacifican view of this situation. I thought, But there are more *hiyek*-families on the Coast than are present in Kasabaarde now – suppose I were to speak with them? Sethri said also, *the hiyeks have no unity*. It takes a lot of organization to fight a war, and if that could be undermined somehow . . . Get the south-east Coast *hiyeks* to back out of this . . .

Girl, you sound like Kasabaarde. And Kel Harantish. Isn't that the principle they've used to control the Coast *hiyeks*, these two thousand years?

'Not tomorrow,' I said. 'I'll come down to you the day after, Stormsun-20.'

The holotank faded to clear.

I sat back in the seat, the padding coolly enclosing me. Pramila's restless footsteps were loud outside the port. I leaned over to key in the orbiter-comlink, and record hi-speed transmission of the message-blip that Molly mentioned. The systems took so long to mesh that I thought the Freeport infrared must be out – at last I banked it in the shuttle's data-net.

'All right?' Pramila Ishida queried, wiping her forehead as she walked through the shuttle-port.

'Yes. Sorry. I didn't intend to keep you waiting.' I put my version of a security seal on the banked message-blip, and keyed out.

Pramila leaned on the back of the bucket seat. Because I've seen that demure face almost always turned aside, refusing eye-contact, I think of her as a subdued person. Now she raised her head, green eyes direct.

'Lynne, I need you to answer a question. I can't ask Molly or David or – I need to ask *you*.'

Do I want to learn what's preoccupying this young Pacifican woman? I've never seen myself as the maternal, confidential type. I managed, 'What do you want to ask me? Does it have to be now?'

'This is private. The opportunity might not . . .' Determination was plain on her face. 'Your old reports. Your First Contact with Orthe. It's in the records. In north Roehmonde, in a city called Corbek. There was an Orthean male, called Falkyr—'

'Sethin Falkyr Talkul!'

I haven't thought of that name in years. But if I recall anything, it's that panic moment when I first realized: I can't remember his face. Can recall detail, those whiteless and slanted brown eyes, and the texture of bitter-dark mane, but not his face.

And how often over the last two days have I seen Pramila in the company of Sethri-safere? Falkyr . . . too long ago to think about, he and I were *arykei*, in a far northern province of the Hundred Thousand.

'Pramila . . . We used to say, in the Service, that it was better for such things to happen with one of the truly alien species. Hominids are too close, too nearly the same, and not quite ever alike. Like monkeys, a caricature of humanity.'

'He's not a caricature!' She scowled.

'That's you,' I said as I got up from the bucket seat, and stretched. 'And that's partly because you're an empath: offworld personnel are. Nine out of ten alien hominid races will look at you and me and feel – revulsion. Pure and simple. No matter what you feel for them.'

She smiled to herself, and then at me. 'Revulsion isn't what I feel.'

She surprises me, this small Pacifican woman. No protests about it being unnatural, in any sense.

Pramila said, 'I just wanted to know that I, that I'm not a freak. That I'm not the only one ever to have felt . . .'

'No,' I said, 'you're not the only one to feel that way.'

Don't look so pleased, don't look as if it were some great adventure; it's no less troubling than human emotion. And much, much stranger. Or do I mean, as strange, no less and no more?

'But when you—'

The holo-signal cut across her question. She reached down and keyed in reception. The signal was blurred, coming in weakly, and half-drowned by crowd-noise; and I could hardly make out the flustered voice of David Osaka: 'You'd better get back fast!' he repeated. 'I'm in the middle of a riot here—'

The trouble with kids is that they panic. David's too inexperienced, I thought. And found my mouth was dry.

The old, low masonry buildings of the trade-quarter were surrounded by chaos. Bodies pressed against me from all sides. I shoved a way through the crowd by force. *Hiyek*-Ortheans staggered past, loaded with baggage – or is it looting? – and heavy reptilian *brennior*-packbeasts hissed in protest. A riot? Or are they evacuating the city? Or already fighting—?

I caught Pramila's arm, pulling her under the arch of the Westgate entrance to the inner city. Male and female Ortheans shouted, calling across the alleys in a babel of noise. I saw some in the robes of Order Houses at the gate, standing back in despair from the mob.

'—David be at Su'niar—?' Pramila, her mouth close to my ear, warm breath feathering the skin. I nodded, pushed between a Rainbow Cities male (his fox-face painted with a scarlet and blue mask) and a group of south-Coast *hiyek*. Pramila followed. The shadow of Westgate's arch fell across us.

The press of bodies moved me forward, and I staggered; caught an arm to stay upright, and looked into a white face under a wire-tangle black mane. *The Barrens!* I thought, but the nomad male was gone. I pushed through into the inner city. For the first time since its founding, there was no taking of weapons, no ritual of entry.

Silence . . .

White dust in the alley round Su'niar House was trodden down to packed earth. The awnings that had shaded the steps hung in tatters. Rubbish was scattered on the ground. Storm-light shone on two lone figures, David Osaka and Doug Clifford, emerging from the entrance to the underground chambers.

'What happened?' I looked from one to the other. David shook his head. His fair hair was grimy, lines of strain showing on that Pacifican face.

'The *hiyeks* . . . they wouldn't let the Order House ration out food any longer. They just took it. They rioted—'

Doug walked down the steps. As David moved aside with Pramila, Doug said, 'It's likely that messages arrived from down-Coast cities. To say that the *jath* and *jath-rai* ships are prepared for war. The *hiyek*-families are leaving.'

The storm-light brightened, easing to the haze of late afternoon. Our shadows were watery on the white earth. Douggie's eyes were dark with exhaustion, and he swayed slightly where he stood.

'I'm talked out, Lynne. I've said it every way it can be said – the only way my government can get Orthe declared a Protected world is if the Aid situation is taken care of internally. In plain terms, the Hundred Thousand will have to feed the Coast – they won't listen.' His voice wavered on the last word. 'Is it so difficult to understand? This is the perfect excuse for PanOceania to move a peace-keeping force in!'

So it is, I thought. Movement caught my eye. A young male sat in the dust at the side of the Order House steps. Fragments of blue ceramic bowl surrounded him, and with total concentration his six-fingered hands fitted shards together. The complex braiding of his mane was coming unbound. And then I saw that he didn't wear the rags of the inner city's mystics, but the *meshabi*-robe and woven rope-belt of the Order Houses.

Faint daystars littered the sky over the white domes. A thread of smoke rose, growing blacker.

I said, 'Where are the *telestre*-Ortheans now?'

Shouts and calls came from the quayside, echoing under the sandstone arch of Harbourgate. I led the way through the gate. Dazzled for a second by bright lapping waves, the swaying masts of *jath* ships. Beyond the harbour arm, a faint olive-coloured mass was the first island of the Kasabaarde Archipelago. And, blue on blue, the immense pylons of the Rasrhe-y-Meluur faded into haze.

'There's the Meduenin,' Doug said, pointing into the crowd round the nearest ship.

Voices were raised at the foot of the *jath*'s gangway. As I approached, I saw Cassirur Almadhera gesture extravagantly; her back to me, that crimson mane tumbling from its braids. And there, Blaize Meduenin, looking like some shabby captain of mercenaries grown old in service, instead of one of the Morvren *takshiriye*. The warm wind lifted that fair mane. His head was lowered: I recognized that bullish look.

'—according to your experience, the "alliance" wouldn't last,' Cassirur burst out. 'But there'll be no war between *hiyeks*, now they've turned on us instead!'

She was careless of age, or Earthspeaker's dignity.

'And the church offers nothing at all!' Blaize said. 'Tell me, *Earthspeaker*, what wisdom has the Tower given you, to take home to the Wellhouses? What will the Tower say when the *hiyeks* burn the land around us? You and the Hexenmeister, we'll have no help from either of you!'

'That's not important. What matters now is that the *hiyeks* have offworlders as their allies. And where are those offworlders now? Kel Harantish, with the Witchbreed! I tell you we're fighting the same war that Kerys Founder fought, to keep the land-wasters from the Hundred Thousand, to keep the *telestres* alive!'

The middle-aged Orthean woman's voice attracted stares. Now some of the Morvren people had seen us, and were beginning to look in our direction. I would have faded into the sandstone-wall background if I could. Blaize at that moment looked up and saw me. Nictitating membrane slid down over his pale eyes, flicked back; and that burn-scar twisted a smile into something monstrous, anger replaced by ironic amusement.

Cassirur spoke, a warning note in her voice. Pramila Ishida reached out and gripped my arm. Her fingers tightened. A group of *hiyek*-Ortheans watched us from the side of a *jath-rai*, moored a few yards further down the quay. A yellow-maned male was walking down the gangway.

'Leave while you can,' Sethri-safere advised, speaking so as to be heard over the bustle and noise of departure. 'The truce is ended. Even the inner city is unsafe now. Outlanders, your people won't thank you for what you've done here, but they sent you to do the impossible, and now they'll have someone they can blame.'

His Morvrenni accent was atrocious. Are you baiting them, I wondered, or is that genuine sympathy? In an Orthean it wouldn't surprise me.

Without warning, a young male (whom I have seen with Cassirur, I realized) stepped out of the crowd. He swung clumsily. I flinched. It seemed he only struck Sethri a glancing blow, openhanded. The Desert Coast male looked round absently, tried to take a step back, and his legs folded and he fell. Pramila swore. A shout came from the *jath-rai* – one of the *hiyek* males. Jadur? Sandstone chippings flew past me, Sethri called something, and the Ortheans on the ship lowered winchbows. In a dead silence, Sethri got to his feet. I wanted to laugh at this playground violence – laughter choked in my throat, held back by a hammering pulse.

Dazed, I looked for the winchbow-bolt on the quayside, but it was trodden underfoot. The metal dart had scarred the sandstone wall two yards from my side. And then I looked up to see the yellow mane of Sethri on the *jath-rai*'s deck, Jadur complaining volubly to him.

Did we think we could restart the peace talks? Folly. And I thought, God forbid, how can we choose sides between them?

The Freeporters gathered round Doug, and I saw David Osaka speak to Cassirur. Pramila, silent, gazed down the dock at the Coast *jath-rai*. I shook my head. For the moment this is familiar, I stand with Ortheans who have faces I know – from the *telestres* of Kerys-Andrethe and Beth'ru-elen and Meduenin . . .

A hand gripped my arm, a hand calloused with swordfighter's hardened skin.

Mind still running on the past, and forgotten faces, I said, 'Is Rodion here? Or back on Meduenin *telestre*?'

When I turned to him, his half-ruined face had an expression I couldn't identify. He was still breathing rapidly, from the argument and from that swift, anonymous violence.

'I thought you'd know – *S'aranth*. Rodion's dead. She died in her year of exile.'

A decade ago? Rodion, whom I knew as an *ashiren*, called Halfgold for her pale skin and mane and yellow eyes – Ruric's child. Rodion Orhlandis, carrying Blaize's children, condemned to a year's exile after that Melkathi summer . . . Rodion, in my mind always a young woman, as I last saw her. No need now to try to imagine what she might be like in her twenties, no need at all.

God prevent me being – is it glad? – over the death of my friend, Blaize's *arykei*.

Blaize Meduenin, in a quite different tone, said, 'I thought you knew. I would have told you. You and she were close.'

That shaggy yellow mane of his is beginning to grow too long; the whiteless blue eyes are veiled against the dust of the inner city. He wore empty *harur*-harness – and moved as if that left him half complete. And once you came to me, called me kinsister, and asked if I thought the Orhlandis child, Rodion, would ever look at a shabby, out-at-elbows mercenary . . .

I said, 'I'm sorry.'

He frowned, the scar turning into something fierce. 'She died here, in Kasabaarde. She was a mercenary with my troop. Wounded in a *hiyek*-war we had, a few miles east of the city.'

Words desert me: I want to say, I'm sorry you had to come here, to remember, how it must hurt . . . And I would like to know how soon after that it was that Blaize Meduenin left the Medued Guildhouse, and entered Haltern Beth'ru-elen's service. Oh I would like to know.

The acid brilliance of the sun stung my eyes.

'It's ironic,' I said. 'Isn't her mother supposed to have died in this very city?'

Thus I approach, sideways and quietly, the subject of *amari* Ruric Orhlandis. How can I tell the Hundred Thousand that their 'traitor' is Hexenmeister? How can I *not* tell Blaize and Hal that Ruric is alive?

'Hal – I—' Scar tissue made a sardonic curve at one corner of his mouth. It was not a smile. We stood there in the late sun, and he looked dazzled. His voice was unsteady. '*S'aranth*, shall I tell you something about that? The Orhlandis woman didn't die, she was assassinated. Because she might have been a danger to the Hundred Thousand, alive. Hal had her killed. Haltern n'ri n'suth Beth'ru-elen.'

He hit every syllable of the name with a kind of dreamy precision.

'Took him time to tell me about that. Can't trust an exile, you see. She could have raised an army against us. And now it isn't her, it's those Shadow-begotten Anzhadi . . . Hal won't like hearing that.'

He looked at me, and his face twisted. Alien and unreadable, somewhere between grief and laughter. I have not thought, had time to think, what hopes have been destroyed here today for him, and for the other Freeporters.

'What will you do now?'

'I don't know.' And then he did smile: humour and defiance in it.

'Don't tell me you've been in the Freeport *takshiriye* all these years, and don't have any ideas what to do.'

'For a copper coin I'd leave it all. Turn mercenary again. I understand that, Christie.'

He sat down on the quay wall, heavily, and squinted up at the hazy sky. I stood beside him, staring down into the black and green depths of the harbour. The heat kept even the *rashaku* in their burrows. Voices rang, and *jath* creaked, and there was the smell of the sea.

'We should have done better, here.' He looked up. 'Christie. Eight years gone . . . Why did you never come back? That was the last word I had from you, when you left. That you'd return.'

Because it is this man, his face vulnerable, because for some strange reason I have always felt I owed Blaize Meduenin honesty, I tried to find a truth for him.

'There was another life to go to. And – no, I know what it was. I knew that, if I came back to Orthe, I wouldn't leave it again.' Surprised, I added, 'I don't think I realized that until a few days ago.'

He stood, resting his arm round my shoulders. I turned to fit into the shape of him, conscious of how natural it seemed; of his warmth, of the arhythmic pulse of his blood.

'I've thought of you,' he said, 'kinsister.'

That isn't the word I want to hear – but it'll do to be going on with. I smiled to myself, caught an answering humour in his face. A gust of warm air blew along the quay. *Del'ri*-cloth cracked, tied loosely over stacked cargo. Late afternoon light turned the world sepia, as shadows took on an evening slant. I rested back against Blaize's arm and shoulder. Heat sapped strength. Just for a minute, to let someone else carry the weight . . . Yesterday morning,

Stormsun-18; this evening, Stormsun-19; fifty hours, give or take a few, and so much has happened—

I straightened, moved away slightly, and nodded to Cassirur Almadhera as she approached.

'It's simple,' Blaize said. 'We can't feed the Coast families. We can't give up *telestre* land. We can't stop the *hiyeks* attacking us. Give it three or four weeks – the beginning of Merrum – we'll see *hiyek* ships off the Melkathi or the Rimon coast. And what will the *s'aranthi* do about that?'

'That's what I'm going to find out from Molly Rachel,' I said, 'as soon as I can shuttle down to where she is.'

Cassirur said, 'What else, *t'an* Meduenin?'

He eyed the ageing, red-maned woman; hid humour at her formality. As if she had never raised her voice a few minutes before, he said politely, 'Six years ago, the *s'an* Dalzielle Kerys-Andrethe died, and not one of us found it necessary to step forward and take up the Crown of the Hundred Thousand. Isn't that necessary now, *t'an* Earthspeaker?'

Before Cassirur could answer, a young male with Kerys-Andrethe features protested: 'This Midsummer isn't Midsummer-Tenyear.'

Blaize's smile was sardonic. 'The Kerys-Andrethe have always liked formality. The rest of us know necessity when we see it. We need a new *T'An Suthai-Telestre*. And there are a hundred thousand *telestres* a Crown might come from.'

Cassirur chuckled, then nodded decisively. 'As soon as I'm back in the Freeport, I'll get the Wellkeepers to send word out through all the provinces, tell the *s'an telestres* to come to—'

'Tathcaer,' Blaize said.

'The city's empty,' she protested. 'I doubt there's been fifty people in Tathcaer these past five years!'

'It's where the *T'Ans* have always come, when it was necessary for there to be a *T'An Suthai-Telestre*.'

The two of them spoke of *rashaku* message-carriers; but I was taken back in an instant to my last midsummer in Tathcaer, that white city that lies at the mouth of the Oranon River, that has been called (in jest) the eighth province – and that has stood deserted since the plague raged there one summer . . .

'Come to Tathcaer,' Blaize broke in on my memories. 'You, the *t'an* Clifford, any other offworlders. We're running out of time.'

'Midsummer is at the end of Durestha, isn't it?' I touched his hand, the sword-callouses; looked up to meet that pale blue gaze. 'I've got work to put in with the Company. So has Doug. I'll meet you in Tathcaer before midsummer. There ought to be time.'

Time enough to stop the avalanche? Time enough to stop the dominoes tumbling down? Ortheans jostled me, the crowd moving. An elbow caught me in the ribs and I winced, rubbing shoulders with bright robes. Faces were excited. I braced myself to peer over their heads, and heard Blaize call out to Cassirur, and then I realized what was happening.

Two pale-maned Ortheans in Order House robes came from the gatehouse, carrying a *del'ri*-fibre basket between them. They set it down on the quay with a clash of metal, and began handing back to each *telestre* male and female their *harur-nilgiri* and *harur-nazari* blades.

CHAPTER 17

In a Bright Day,
In a Time Of War

Company regulations state that shuttles must not fly with only
one pilot aboard. Looking at the back of David Osaka's head where
he sat at the pilot's console, I thought, Yes, but that leaves me
with nothing to do for the next few hours . . .

Which is an opportunity to read that message-blip from Earth.

I keyed the holotank to exterior-view while I waited for the blip
to decode. Kasabaarde was a brown stain on the earth, already
fading into distance. Pramila elected to remain there, to continue
observation. Not that there will be much to see, except *hiyek*-
families leaving the city.

This morning of Stormsun-20 shone sepia; and flashes of heat-
lightning walked along the southern sky. We flew east over acres
of stony ground. The few strip-fields were soon gone, giving way
to ridges of rock, and to the angular network of canals. Land
flicked past below like stills from a film – wide canals, small
buildings that are entrances to *siiran*, infrequent "pits" that are
cities at canal junctions, the seaports that lie where canals run out
to the Inner Sea . . .

It'll take the *hiyeks* a week or more to get back to their home
cities and *siiran*. It took Haldin and her people a month to bring
me from Maherwa to Kasabaarde. And when it takes me only
hours to fly back across this barren country – why then, in a very
real sense, we don't inhabit the same world, they and I.

The 'tank chimed, cut exterior-view, and began to run the
message-blip from my department.

An image formed of a young man, leaning back in his desk-
console. He had his feet up, and as the holo-record clicked on,
raised a mug of coffee in casual salute. Acting departmental head
Stephen Perrault of the Liaison Office. In the window behind him
the sun shone, deep yellow in a dark blue sky.

'. . . I've commented on the section-heads' reports, this is an unofficial summary, right?' He smiled. It aged him, made this bearded young man into something piratical. Which is not as fanciful as it might seem, considering Perrault's character; and I can be forgiven for hoping he wasn't coping *too* well in my absence, since I may need a job to go back to.

His recorded image continued: 'As far as summaries go, I can give it to you in a sentence, Lynne. While the cat's away, the rats are at play. Nothing personal.'

'Miaow.' Perrault shares my sense of humour.

'The north European Enclave project has had its completion date put back six months, that's because PanOceania's finance department is hooking us about. So the new housing camps aren't going to be occupiable before next spring. I'm negotiating to get the section of the population that's involved into temporary accommodation – but if we *had* any, we wouldn't need the housing camps.'

'Don't let them screw you,' I muttered. No matter that he couldn't hear.

'I'm also putting out feelers to NuAsia and ChinaCo,' Stephen Perrault's image continued. 'I know that technically this office is part of PanOceania, but Liaison has a legally neutral status, and we're European-staffed.'

Meaning that if you threaten to bring in other multicorporates, it may bring PanOceania through with the finance? That's not a safe game to play.

'We got the tariff question settled in the last parliament, pushed the Bill through; so provided none of the other Enclaves reneges, we should have grain prices down by next July. Or October, if we're lucky.

'Nothing new on the fuel situation.

'PanOceania's taking out its linkman with us here in London. Replacing Singh with some kid who's got no track record, so he's somebody's protégé. God help us.

'One problem that's come up after you left. The British government and PanOceania are squabbling over the demarcation lines of this department—'

Damn it, I knew it; it's *not* safe to push!

'—want to put us firmly under Company control. I know this one comes up regularly, but it looks sticky. Hence the rush report. If we're not careful, we'll be eased out of our status as neutral arbitrators.'

Stephen Perrault paused, drank from the coffee cup. By his grimace, it was cold. He scratched through fair hair and beard.

'Sorry about this – late hours for a few nights. We're fighting on two fronts, and if I have to come down temporarily on one side, it'll be the government's. Unless I hear different from you. I ought to redo this tape, I'm too tired to think . . . No time, if I'm going to get it on the FTL-drone. Listen, you notice they waited until you went offworld? They're going to find out they underestimated the rest of us.'

'The last thing you want to do is antagonize the Company,' I said. The department's status is ambiguous enough as it is – and it's useful that way.

Message-blips travel on unmanned drones that aren't restrained by the limits of living flesh. Stephen would have sent this off ten or twelve days ago. I thought, I wonder how he's holding out? Shit, they need me there!

As he reached across to cut off the holo-record, Perrault added, 'I'll send reports regularly, as we arranged. Contact me when you can. Oh – word here is, PanOceania might have found something startling on Carrick V; true? Message ends.'

That other life presses in on me. Memories of blue sky and cold wind and half-derelict office blocks in the London Enclave, and Perrault and the rest of my team; of days on the holo-link to governments in Westminster and York and Edinburgh, and to PanOceania in Melbourne and Tokyo. Does that put what I do here in perspective? Orthe, only a distant world in the Heart Stars, only Carrick V . . .

I got up from the 'tank, blinking against the shuttle's pale-green interior lighting. I have a responsibility here, put on me in a Wellhouse by a woman called renegade and traitor; put on me by my own actions, when I set foot on this world as First Contact. For the moment, Perrault will have to manage on his own.

'Halfway mark,' David Osaka announced. 'Want to take over, Lynne?'

'Yes, I'll take it.'

'There's an anti-error repeat loop on the navigation systems,' he added. 'We're still getting interference on location signals, but as far as I can make out, *that's* where we'll rendezvous with Molly.'

I took over the console. Aware that, however unreal it seems to my imagination now, fifteen thousand feet below us there are *jath-rai* sailing east to Quarth and Reshebet and Nadrasiir, and the other Coast ports; crewed by Orthean men and women who look north across the Inner Sea with ever-hungrier faces.

'The question is, what is the Company going to *do* about this situation?'

Molly ignored the query, steering the groundcar over rough terrain. Balloon-tyres crunched on shale. Here the pale earth fell away in scree-slopes, and Carrick's Star cast our shadows blue-black on the ground, and the mid-afternoon sky held only a handful of daystars at the horizon.

'I don't understand – why Tathcaer?' she said at last. 'That settlement's been deserted for years. So have all the cities of the Hundred Thousand, except for Morvren Freeport. Logistically it would make more sense if they chose a *T'An Suthai-Telestre* in Morvren.'

I leaned forward to key a control, and a panel in the dome of the groundcar retracted. Smell of sun on hot earth, and silence: the silence of a sterile land . . . 'In Tathcaer, there's a *telestre*-house for each one of the Hundred Thousand *telestres*. And there's the great Wellhouse of Kerys Founder; and the Crown's Citadel. That's why they'll go back there. Molly, I want to know what the Company's going to do about the *hiyeks*.'

'This is Reshebet,' the Pacifican woman said. 'This is what I wanted you to see, Lynne.'

The groundcar slowed. Groups of young males and females were squatting outside low-roofed buildings. The wickedly sharp hook-bladed knives that hung at their belts were *del'ri*-harvest tools. Turned to butchery now? As we drove between the groups I thought, They're farmers. That's all. And so are the Hundred Thousand; this isn't a war of *armies*—

Reshebet swarmed like a hive of *kekri*-flies. Molly let the groundcar nose gently through the crowds of *hiyek*-Ortheans. Some took off their masks to stare at us, and younger *ashiren* hung over the rails of the *jath*-ships that choked the canal here and called out to offworlders. Storm clouds massed on the northern horizon, and the sea beneath shone like gunmetal.

Narrow hoop-masted *jath-rai* and *jath* were jammed so tightly together that I couldn't see canal water, only the decks; vessels sheltering behind the sea-lock wall from the coming storm. Shouts drifted up from the canal where it went inland, and I stood up in the groundcar, and saw great dun-coloured *brennior* on the walk-ways. The packbeasts were harnessed by cables to *jath*-ships, straining with all their reptilian bulk to drag the craft northwards. I looked to the south and saw an endless train of hoop-masts and metal-weave sails glittering in the sun.

'The *hiyeks* have been coming from inland for a week now,' Molly Rachel said. 'Same goes for all the coastal harbours. You can see I didn't have any alternative.'

'Alternative?'

'I've sent a request through the orbiter's comlink, asking that the nearest detachment of the Company's Peace Force be seconded to Orthe.'

She keyed power, and swung the groundcar away from the buildings, out on to rough earth again. No roads here, not even a footpath. All travel is by water. The 'car jolted, and a stab of nausea went through me.

'Jesus Christ, Molly, you're bringing *troops* in!'

She frowned, concentrating on driving. 'It's a police action. Nothing more. They happen every day. You don't think the Ortheans will fight each other with the potential threat of military technology hanging over them?'

Carrot and stick. How many worlds have the Companies done this on? And on how many has it worked? And some small voice inside me said, *An enforced peace is better than a freely-chosen war – isn't it?*

Cool air circulated under the groundcar-dome. The exterior temperature reading was something unbelievable. I leaned back in the padded seat, squinting through the polarized plastic. Saw shale and rock, and the dust-plume of our arrival not yet settled. In the distance, moonscape mountains mark the beginning of the Elansiir. I have lived Orthean for too many days to be sped from shuttle-landing, across country to Reshebet, and now back to Kel Harantish in an hour – I haven't adjusted.

'What about Rashid's people, in Maherwa?'

Molly shook her head. Permanent lines marked her face now, incised deeply round her eyes. That black-wire hair was growing shaggy, and I saw she had pinned it down with two of the fragile *del'ri*-wood combs that Coast Ortheans use. Is Orthe beginning to touch her, or is that just for convenience?

'Nothing!' One dark fist hit the console: the groundcar swerved. 'It *is* something we've never met before, some completely alien way of perceiving the universe – if we can't understand Golden science, we should at least be able to reproduce it blindly! But all I get from Rashid is *no*. And none of these natives understand the concepts their ancestors used.'

Now we drove parallel to a ridge, running into a brief strip of shadow, and emerged into level wasteland. The horizon shimmered, wavered, dissolved. Streaks of mirage-water receded ahead of us. The white mesa of Kel Harantish hung in the heat, pulled out of shape like toffee; pocked with black windows like onyx eyes.

'Lynne, do *you* understand Witchbreed science?'

I turned my head, startled. 'Me?'

'If you were to tell me that somewhere in those fake memories that Pramila reported on, you had the slightest idea of how it functioned – I'd listen.'

An octagonal hall in Rakviri: *Whose hand will take the knife, under that radiant shadow?*

'I don't know,' I said. 'Even if these delusions were the implanted memories I thought they were, or even if they're based on data in the Tower Archives; then either way, the Hexenmeister wouldn't pass on any knowledge of Witchbreed science. I don't want to discuss it. I feel incredibly stupid to have let myself be tricked that way.'

'Sorry. Lynne, I apologize; that was unfair.'

The towering heights of Kel Harantish solidified from heat haze. The F90 shuttles grounded on the wasteland before it were dwarfed by the sheer massiveness of the walls. I saw movement: winches hauling rope-platforms up to the city roofs.

'We might have time on our side,' Molly Rachel said. 'I've got the orbiter keeping a close eye on climate changes. It's not long until the monsoon season. Ships won't cross the Inner Sea in that. If that happens, and we sell T&A to the *hiyeks*, and with the Peace Force here . . .'

The groundcar swung to halt by the nearest shuttle in a spray of shale and wheelspin. She grinned at me.

'You're so anxious to get PanOceania off this world. What I've done here will change your mind. I've got some things to see to – I'll want your advice later. Pathrey Shanataru will show you what we've set up here.'

She was out of the groundcar while the dome was still retracting, running up the F90's ramp, hailing the humans and Ortheans there. I got out of the 'car more slowly. Rock was hot underfoot. I stepped into the shadow of the F90's hull. Voices are the only sound here: no wind through *ziku* or *lapuur* trees, no cry of *rashaku* . . .

'*Kethrial-shamaz*, Christie.'

A plump, brown-skinned Orthean left the group near the shuttle. Pathrey Shanataru. He bowed. His ragged *meshabi*-robe had gone, and so had the scale-mail, replaced by swathes of black cloth woven with myriad tiny gold threads. Amused despite myself, I thought, Not only seedy, but flashy too.

Temporary T&A bases were set up here on the rocky earth. Standard issue, featureless metal and plastiglas domes, hardly larger than the shuttles that brought them. I could see, between them, the harbour: its surface like broken mirrors. And hear the lapping of the waves. I turned and walked as Pathrey led me, past the domes to the harbour. The pumps and sealed units of the desalination plants stood black against the glare. A linked series of them ran from the edge of the harbour nearest us, out along the harbour arm to the open sea.

'Congratulations,' I said. 'The last time I saw you, you were in hiding. You and the *shan'tai* Calil bel-Rioch – is she here, too?'

The plump male smiled. His six-fingered hands flashed with jewelled rings.

'The *shan'tai* bel-Rioch has friends.' His shrewd brown eyes cleared. 'All the friendlier now, since she could promise to bring back to the city all the engines and advantages of *s'aranthi*-offworlders . . .'

It came to me that this middle-aged Orthean male was as excited as an *ashiren*, hugging to himself the triumph of their return, his and Calil's. Does that mean an unguarded tongue?

'The Emperor Dannor *agreed* to all this?' I was incredulous.

'Not precisely,' Pathrey Shanataru said. 'But there are those in the city who see the Coast families moving out of our control – their taking *s'aranthi* gifts is inevitable – and think we should seize advantage while we still can. Before we're left a small city and powerless.'

Heat made pale rock waver, and the horizon ran like water, I halted, panting, then trudged on up the rough slope at the edge of the T&A excavations. Dust buried my feet and ankles, chips of stone lodged inside my boots. Pathrey gripped my shoulder, six-fingered hand warm through coverall-fabric to flesh, and helped me to the top of the ridge. From here out to the harbour arm, the excavators had ripped up Coast rock to a depth of fifty feet. Looking between the gleaming machinery, I saw tanks of pulverized rock, the beginning of a system of interconnected chambers.

'They're modelling it on *siiran*,' I realized, wondering if that were one of Molly's more sensitive notions. 'You realize the Company want something in return. Witchbreed artifacts. And Dannor bel-Kurick isn't going to let offworlders back inside the city, is he?'

'He may,' Pathrey said. 'His advisors put it to him most strongly. I have every confidence in his wit, *shan'tai*. He can see advantage, even when it is Calil bel-Rioch who brings it to his attention.'

I peered across at channels, chambers and tunnels, seeing the sites for the hydroponic systems; the connections to the desalination plants. Basic T&A: extract trace elements from the seawater during the desalination process, introduce them back into the soil to grow crops. Companies have terra-formed inhospitable worlds with larger versions of this process. As for long-term effect on climate and environment – has the Company run a prediction-pattern? I wondered.

'If the Company trades these to the Coast *hiyeks*, then that'll be the end of Kel Harantish's controlling monopoly of the canals. It'll leave the Emperor with no power. Just this tiny settlement, and – starvation.'

Pathrey Shanataru scowled. Then he glanced past me, back the way we'd come.

An Orthean female climbed the slope. Her skin with that white-metal sheen, fox-face and yellow eyes; dressed now in Harantish mail, and all the sepia dye washed from her mane, that had disguised her in Maherwa.

'*Shan'tai* Calil,' I said. Seen first here, then in Maherwa, now here again: how the wheel turns, and takes us with it . . .

The white-maned woman halted, looked at me with a certain humour in those yellow eyes. Then her expression changed. She spoke:

'___ __ _____ ___ ____'

'__ _____ ___ _ ___'

My response was automatic, was natural; and then as I slurred and stuttered, I realized it was in a language that no human should know, that no human tongue should be able to form. *Celebrants, we stand. The ritual chant—*

Calil bel-Rioch smiled.

'Give you greeting, exile,' she said. 'How is my sister in the Tower?'

Bile surged hotly in my throat. I coughed, pulled out a rag into which I could spit, and waved aside Pathrey Shanataru's hesitant offer of assistance.

'Sorry – must be the heat—'

I shuddered, almost grateful for the body's revolt. The first time I've seen her since that clouded time in Maherwa, and again . . . Obviously she planned to unnerve me, *has* unnerved me; this gives a respite.

Pathrey's plump brown face showed concern. He offered a flask. I drank and found it tepid water, water with that taste peculiar to desalination. My eyes ran, Calil was a blurred image of white and gold. And then I saw that Pathrey's eyes showed a thin rim of white round them: wide open with apprehension at hearing that tongue spoken.

'Life on the Coast is hard,' Calil said urbanely. 'The heat – that hammer forges us all.'

Do I want to be alone with her questions? Compared to false memories in my head, the Kel Harantish Witchbreed are degener-

631

ate stock, interbred with Orthean bloodlines. If I were to think as a *keretne*, I would wonder if some freak of ancestry could, after sixty generations, produce a true Golden. This woman facing me, membrane sliding back from those chrome-yellow eyes, as much Witchbreed as Santhendor'lin-sandru, called Phoenix Emperor and Last Emperor – No: that's Orthean thinking, not human.

Fighting for self-possession, I smiled. 'Kel Harantish gives an interesting welcome each time I arrive, *shan'tai* Calil. *Shan'tai* Pathrey, thank you for the drink.'

Evening began to put long shadows blackly on the broken earth. Daystars clustered at the horizon.

'As for the Tower, which you mentioned – I'd be interested to know which the Hexenmeister hates more: seeing the Coast *hiyeks* slavishly dependent on your maintenance of the canals, or seeing them abandon you to begin using Earth technology. It's a difficult question, isn't it?'

She sucked in a breath. I thought, Why, I've offended you. Good. A little more of that and I might know what sort of person we're dealing with here.

'My people tell me you were in the Tower,' she said. 'Where else could you get that look of Empire? That's why I spoke as I did. That's why you could answer.'

But the Tower's memory is only historical archives . . . I rubbed the back of my neck, where the evening sun shone heavy on me. *Jath* sails were visible beyond the harbour arm, losing themselves in the glitter of that Stormsun sea. Footsteps were loud on rock, human voices called from the shuttle landing site, and the blank cliff-face of Kel Harantish reflected back the day's heat. I was covered with a thin sheen of sweat.

'The Emperor could stop the *hiyeks* now,' I said, struggling for balance, 'if he threatened to let the canals rot, and the *siiran* harvests fail.'

She shrugged. 'What would that do except make the *hiyeks* turn even more swiftly to Earth? And why should we care for them, or for the *telestres*? They're nothing but thieves. That land is ours, a part of the old Empire – we're only in exile, here.'

Her tone held some intense, all-consuming emotion. Curiosity? Nostalgia? I thought, There's something in your voice when you say *Empire* that even Dannor bel-Kurick doesn't have, and he is Emperor-in-Exile . . .

'That's the past,' I said.

Her chin came up, and she looked me in the eye. 'Is it?'

Her sun-whitened mane blew across her face in the first soft wind of evening. She glanced over her shoulder at the blank wall of Kel Harantish. She looked older now than a bare month ago, when she had been Voice of the Emperor.

I smiled, in recognition. 'Is that what you do – pretend omnipotence, knowledge of the past? You look more of a Witchbreed than even Dannor bel-Kurick, I imagine they fear you for that, even your own people. Don't try it with me. The Empire fell long ago. And it doesn't surprise me that you know there's a female Hexenmeister. How much careful spying does it take, to keep up that "omniscience"?'

'It's true. I do that.' Calil faced me. A young Orthean woman in dusty scale-mail, standing barefoot in the rubble; and then she raised her head again, with such a sudden and total grace that I could only think *Witchbreed*! Her husky voice went on: '*Shan'tai*, don't they say always that the Golden Witchbreed have no past-memories, that that is what marks our race off from the slave race and their "Goddess"?'

She stepped forward until we were almost touching.

'Offworlders have no past-memories either, but you do, I see it in you. And I – I *remember*. I don't know how or why. I only know I see that millennial time, see that great Empire, and the cities that were greater in size than all this Desert Coast! I've seen aKirrik and Archonys of the Six Lakes. And I have seen that disease that the slave races created to be our downfall, so that we bore no more children, and our last generation turned in their fury against each other, and brought those great cities down. Now tell me *you* have not seen this also, in the Tower!'

For a moment I felt only the dislocation of shock, and then I came back to harsh sunlight, and to Calil's dazzled face.

'Or is it a delusion,' the Harantish woman said, 'built up out of scraps and hearsay, and tales told to a child?'

I have thought that the light of logic, harsh as Carrick's Star, illuminated one thing: Whoever witnessed those ancient scenes of terror could never have come living to the Tower, could never have become Hexenmeister, and passed on their memories to others. And so the whole edifice collapses, the 'memories' are fakes. And now I know I'm still ignorant – I don't know if what I experience is based on Tower Archive data, given to me by the Hexenmeister ten years ago; or whether it's gossip, history, speculation; made up by willpower into some synaesthetic vision.

Looking into Calil's yellow eyes, I see that same desperate *don't know*.

Calil switched again to a Coast dialect and said urgently, 'The woman in the Tower. Who is she? What is she? I must talk to you again. I'll send my Pathrey to you, when it's safe for you to enter the city.'

I watched her walk away across broken rock. Company domes and shuttle dwarfed by Kel Harantish's walls, and Calil bel-Rioch a small pale figure, merging into pale earth . . .

Just when I thought I had all the facts (even if I didn't like the answers), I find out there are still things unaccounted for.

Some change in the light made me look westwards. Steel-grey clouds were beginning to rise where Carrick's Star was setting. Cargolifters rolled; T&A personnel shouted. Excavation here will proceed rapidly, now that the day's heat is fading. Sixty miles away the *hiyek*-families are moving – how long, now, until the rains come?

Second twilight, shifting into night: a shuttle dropped down as I walked beside the walls of Kel Harantish. The roar of its landing hardly penetrated my thoughts, though I registered a night-landing as unusual here. I didn't want to go back to the shuttle-HQ just yet.

The rocky earth was warm, radiating back the day's heat. I stopped and looked up at the stars. The early summer sky of Orthe, so full of stars that they run together in blazes of silver, in great flowers of light. When I looked down, black dazzles floated in my vision.

In that second it flooded back into my mind: *T'An* Commander Ruric, Suthafiori crowned in Tathcaer, Haltern meeting me at the docks that long-ago spring; all the long journey north into forest and the Lesser Fens and those mountains called the Wall of the World. If I were free now, what would I do? If I did nothing but follow my instincts—

I took a microcorder out of my belt-pouch and flicked it on: 'Lynne de Lisle Christie to Company Representative Molly Rachel, dated—' I couldn't remember a non-Orthean date '—Stormsun 20, local time. Molly, this is my formal and official resignation from the post of special advisor to the PanOceania multicorporate Company, to take effect immediately. From tomorrow, Stormsun-21 local time, my rank will be advisor to the government envoy; which Douglas Clifford will confirm. Message ends—'

My hand shook as I clicked the microcorder off. *Dive back into your bolthole, girl!* Back to the Hundred Thousand, who know you; back to government Service. Doug will confirm my position. Then—

Lynne, I thought, how long before you're handing in a resignation to the government, too? Because all you want to do is go back to the Hundred Thousand, back home. Inaccurate as that may be, with all the reservations about being an alien in this culture, and ten years a long time. And why do that?

Because it means I don't have to think if Molly's right to do what she's doing here. And because it means, above all else, that I don't have to think about Calil bel-Rioch and that dead Empire.

Sorry, girl, escape isn't that easy.

I stood in that starlit darkness, and on impulse keyed my wristlink into records I'd studied earlier in the holotank. The preliminary reports from Ashida's research people in Maherwa.

I studied the image: small in the wristlink. An identification-grid covered the film, but I cut that out, wanting to see unbiased by Rashid's preconceptions.

That dome, with the pillars set back into the steps, casting a sharp-edged shadow . . .

Then the viewpoint approached the black entrance, cut out for a second, adjusted to the lack of light, and showed a bare *chiruzeth* chamber. Vision improved. Serpentine curves decorated the walls. Carved vines, that seem to form features in peripheral vision. The viewpoint joggled, continuing across the chamber and down a flight of steps leading underground. So like those underground halls in Kel Harantish . . . I scrolled forward, to the point where the steps opened out into a network of low tunnels.

Tunnels with curved walls, and oval openings into yet more tunnels, so that one saw receding perspectives framed by irregular arches. These curves and supports are less like the architecture of men, and more like organic patterns of hive and vine. A maze, below the city.

All the research team's explorations so far have recorded are tunnels like these. With one exception: an underground location that must, by measurement, be under the actual honeycombed wall of the cylindrical pit that is Maherwa. Here the confined and constricted tunnels open into vast spaces. Walls soar up to meet in gothic arches, seventy feet overhead. Squat pillars jut from a floor that, though it has no pattern to the eye, is to the hand's touch carved with vines and skulls and shells. And there are other pillars that seem, from their translucent interiors, to contain a flow of water; but as to how or why . . . the team can speculate about pumps and water-purifiers, but can't be certain. And can't attempt to dismantle, or sample; not with the Harantish guard always there. But that will come . . .

I keyed the wristlink off. Half dazzled and waiting for night vision, I began to pick my way towards the trackways that the

635

excavators had already worn into the rock, going back towards the shuttles. It must have been close on an hour I wasted, walking round the edges of the site and watching the excavators at work. When at last I came back to the shuttle that Molly had designated her HQ, I thought there was an unusual amount of activity inside.

David Osaka passed me as I walked up the shuttle-ramp.

'What's going on?' I called after him.

He tossed words over his shoulder, still moving. 'It's the detachment of the Peace Force – they're here.'

CHAPTER 18

The Heartland of Corruption

Which means that Molly put in the request some time back. It takes time to get here from Thierry's World. Did the Company *expect* to have to do this – or is that question naïve?

I entered the shuttle and walked down the cabin to the rear compartments. I found I was gripping my belt-pouch that held the microcorder, knuckles white.

'—only way I can see to keep the invasion fleet from sailing.' Molly stopped as I entered the rear cabin, looking up from where she and a Peace Force officer sat over the remains of a meal. 'Ah, Lynne. I don't think you'll know Commander Mendez. Commander Mendez, this is our special advisor, Lynne de Lisle Christie.'

'Hello, Lynne.'

'Hello, Cory.' I briefly enjoyed the pleasure of scoring off Molly Rachel. 'Must be, what, six years?'

'Must be.' The woman nodded thoughtfully. Commander Corazon Mendez: a tall, thin woman with cotton-white hair; now in her mid or late fifties. Not looking any different: the same beak-nosed, gaunt face; the white hair cut sleekly round at neck length. She wore a black coverall with the Peace Force logo.

'Does Doug know you're on-world?' I asked.

'Doug? Not Doug Clifford?'

I explained to Molly. 'Cory was seconded to the Service some years back, as military advisor, round about the time that Doug and I were there.'

'Ah. Yes. The envoy's in Tathcaer, I think.' Molly looked blank. 'I was saying to Commander Mendez, the only way I can see to keep the invasion fleet from sailing is to turn the *hiyek*-families' attention to T&A. Once they see what desalination and hydroponics plants can do – but it's going to take them until next harvest to be convinced, and we don't have that much time. The monsoon will only last two or three weeks. Then there's nothing to stop ships crossing the Inner Sea.'

The Pacifican woman was seated on one side of the table, Cory Mendez on the other. I sank down into the seat beside Cory, willing neither of them to see that my hands were trembling. The older woman smiled. She has one of those dark-complexioned hawk-like faces you often see in the old Anglo-Argentinian families, and at the moment I could see on it a contempt for Pacificans that is not uncommon among Anglo-Argentinians; and a contempt for the commercial side of the Company, not uncommon among the police corps.

'What about the other side of the conflict?' she asked.

'That's a reasonable point. Molly, if I can sit in on this, I think it might be helpful.' Thinking, It is ironic. What I do now will take me where I wanted to go, without the abdication that would have been involved. Without anyone seeing, I reached a finger into a belt-pouch and keyed *erase* on the microcorder. A superstitious impulse.

'I think I can see an interim solution,' I said. 'As Cory mentions, there are two sides to the conflict. We ought to talk to the northern continent. Not to the *telestre*-Ortheans – that's where the Kasabaarde talks broke down – but to the Wellkeepers and Earthspeakers. They're the only people that just might let Coast Ortheans share some land, on the northern continent—'

'Land-*sharing*?' Molly said, incredulous. 'Lynne, you know the *telestre* system better than anybody; they'd never—'

'Share *telestre* land, no, I grant you. But there's land north of the Inner Sea that isn't occupied by *telestres*.' I paused. 'Sure, that's because it's wilderness; but even a wilderness there is paradise compared to farming the Coast.'

Cory Mendez nodded. 'You could make what you're doing there well known here. If you can get a result that's halfway positive, it may delay the invasion, or fragment it; either way, it's easier to contain and control.'

Molly Rachel stirred uncomfortably. The Argentinian woman caught my eye, with a smile that never reached her lips. Yes, I thought, I feel sorry for the girl too. Technically she's superior to both of us, as Company representative – age and experience give us a very unfair advantage. And knowing Molly's resilience, I'd better take advantage of her being off balance to get what I want.

'The Company needs to know what's happening in the Hundred Thousand, in any case.' I turned to Mendez. 'Cory, have your people grounded yet?'

She stroked the rings on her bony fingers. 'I've come in advance.

An observer. I'm old-fashioned, I like to see things for myself, not send my junior officers.'

'Then, if Molly has no objections, you could observe first hand in Tathcaer – I say Tathcaer, because it'll be awkward to ground a shuttle on the mainland, and that city has different rules. We can go oversea, stop over on Lone Isle rather than go back up to the orbiter.'

Anything to defuse hostilities here.

Molly Rachel looked at us. Her long fingers clenched into a fist, and then relaxed. While I watched tensely, she keyed a comlink contact to David Osaka, to Pramila in Kasabaarde, and – after some problems – to Clifford in Tathcaer itself.

'Yes,' she said finally. 'The *takshiriye* are moving back into Tathcaer. As soon as they're established, use that settlement as a base. Take a comlink-booster. I want eight-hourly reports. And I want results. The climate's unpredictable here, the monsoon may not arrive, or it may end before we expect it to – so the data-profile says. Commander Mendez, I hope your troopships are here by then.'

The comlink chimed. She answered it, and then said, 'For you, Lynne.'

David Osaka's voice came through. 'One of the locals is here, asking for you. Pathrey Shanataru. Says it's about a meeting the bel-Rioch woman arranged to have with you – inside the city. What shall I tell him?'

I keyed hold and looked questioningly at Molly.

'It's a foot in the door,' she said enthusiastically. 'Even if nothing comes of this meeting, it sets a precedent. And I don't think you have to be too concerned about your personal safety, Lynne, with half the Company on Kel Harantish's doorstep—'

'Okay, okay, I get the message.' And to David: 'Tell him I'll be there in ten minutes.'

Molly nodded approval. I can't very well avoid doing this, even if it does get the Company back inside the city; and besides, it's something to do while we're preparing to go to Tathcaer—

And that is all rationalization. I *must* see Calil bel-Rioch again. To ask her how she can speak a tongue I have only heard spoken in a vision, in a northern land. Ask how she knows a forgotten language. And ask: how is it that I know it, too?

Cory Mendez said, 'How's the research progressing? Are my people likely to face anything more than primitive weaponry here – any kind of alien tech?'

Molly Rachel shook her head. 'This is a used-up world. There aren't the resources for the natives to make Golden technology viable again, even if the knowledge of it had been preserved. I know Lynne doubts the technology can be reconstructed, even with Earth tech. From your viewpoint, I think there's no need for concern.'

'You don't credit the rumours, then?'

Molly stared. 'Rumours?'

'I stopped over several hours on the orbiter,' Cory Mendez said. 'Sometimes it pays to listen to mess gossip. It's unsubstantiated, but I hear that there's now a trade in more than agricultural equipment going on here. That sonic stunners, CAS-IVs, small handguns, are turning up in Orthean hands in some of the Coast seaports. That there's a black-market arms trade on Carrick V.'

'No.' Molly shook her head firmly. 'Nothing comes on-world that isn't checked by my people on the orbiter. If there is any small amount of Earth tech here, it's come in illegally some time in the past ten years.'

Fear distracted me: the thought of Pathrey, waiting. And Calil bel-Rioch. And then I thought, No, not even she would abduct a Company employee at this juncture . . .

'I'll be back in an hour or two,' I said. And left the shuttle, walking out to where the dark night was broken by strings of radiant lights rigged up across the hydroponic site excavations; and by the sound of seawater pumps, and the rumble of rock being pulverized. The earth was rough underfoot. Thunder scraped and rumbled along the northern horizon. I stopped, sweating, and looked up. The monolithic dark of Kel Harantish blocked out all the southern sky. Silhouetted against the Heart Stars, I could see the ropes and hanging platforms necessary for entry to the city.

David was waiting, and Pathrey Shanataru with him. I walked on to meet them.

Pathrey showed me to the city rooms occupied by the Harantish woman. He oozed obsequiousness, standing aside to let me walk down the steps inside the roof-house; and then as I reached the lower rooms, smiled and made as if to efface himself.

'And this time *go*.'

The woman stood with her back to a narrow window. Pathrey spread plump-fingered hands in protest: 'But, Calil—'

'Listen to my conversations again and they'll be the last things you do hear.'

She smiled. It was a threat: blatant, brutal. The plump dark male bowed, and his eyes flicked once to my face. I caught a look in which there was not just fear, but puzzled hurt.

Calil waited until he climbed the steps, and the roof trap door slammed shut behind him. Then she said, 'Come here, Christie.'

I walked across a floor of varnished *del'ri*-wood. Floor, walls and ceiling; all panelled in that pale wood. In this stone and metal culture, wood is opulence. Ceramic pots held oil-lights, and their light glimmered on the *del'ri*-fibre mats and the window-arch. My boots scraped grit on the polished floor as I came to stand beside the white-maned woman and look out of the window. Warm wind blew in a gulf of darkness. Immeasurably far below, I saw the glare of the T&A site.

'I have been thinking about truth.' She smiled again. Some quality in her voice was hypnotic, at once amused and detached.

Double image: she is only a small Harantish woman, in a white *meshabi*-robe. No taller than my shoulder; thin, barefoot. And she is Golden. I thought, When I look at you I see another face, satin-black skin and mane, but the same Witchbreed-yellow eyes.

'One of the great lies they tell,' Calil said, 'is that truth is simple, and is easy to understand. But truth is complex, with hidden inner workings, and outside masks; and understanding it is difficult, or impossible, and most of the world is condemned to dying without ever understanding a smallest part of it.'

She padded across to the low metal-lattice table and sat cross-legged, and began to pour *arniac* into bowls. I could only stare. As if pursuing some thought, she added, 'I have no right to the bel-Rioch name. I assumed it. It's useful to me.'

I must have looked bewildered. She laughed. It was a short, smothered noise. As if in some past-memory or vision, I came to sit down by her on the *del'ri* mat. The *arniac* tasted peppery. The Coast poison *ruesse* has no scent to Ortheans, but to human senses it is obvious. No taste of it here – do I expect it? I wondered. I don't know *what* to expect.

'Have you been made Voice of the Emperor again?'

She grinned. Her features, seen close, are uneven: the corner of her left eye droops slightly.

'I don't need to be. Didn't you tell me, Christie, that I assume a mantle of mystic infallibility? And if people don't quite believe, at least they don't disbelieve; and I have my own "Voices" to keep me informed.'

I thought, If it comes to pretending infallibility, you're not the expert. That sounded bitter. It's the Tower you want to know about. What can I say to you about Ruric Hexenmeister that Ruric would want known outside the Tower?

Chiming in with my thought, Calil asked, 'Christie, it's always been said there's but one Hexenmeister in the Tower, through all the years; is that merely something they'd have us believe, or is it true?'

'I want to know: why must you know that?'

She held her *arniac* bowl cupped in hands that are white, with a gold-dust glimmer in the skin. The surface of the crimson liquid shivered. When she looked up her yellow eyes were clear.

'I have had visions all my life. Only the Hexenmeister could tell me if they are true past-memories – *if* the Hexenmeister is what the Tower claims.'

'Does it matter?' I protested. 'Listen. That's the Company's excavators you can hear. Earth technology here on Orthe. What does the past matter, compared to that?'

She shook the white mane back from her face, watching me.

Fighting not to be indiscreet, I said, 'And what does the Tower matter, really? We have no way of telling if their knowledge is immortal memory, or only archives; and whichever it is, we still wouldn't have any way of knowing if it were *true*. Three thousand years is a long time. Memories distort, and archives get corrupted—'

Calil, trying the thought out to see how it fitted, said, 'Could it be that's all there is? The great Tower no more than a collection of weevil-eaten parchments, and her spies and agents no less fallible than Harantish's . . . Is that what I can believe, now?'

Argue round it how you can. The 'parchments' are Golden tech data-storage, but it comes to the same thing. In that flickering lamplight I was suddenly tired of deception. It surprised me how bitter I felt against the old man, the old Hexenmeister. All that talk of remembered lives. And I *believed* it. So much grief for so many years.

The Harantish woman said cynically, 'It makes little difference to my city. The Hundred Thousand would hate us still, for what they remember of the Empire, and that even without the Tower to tell the Wellhouses how evil we are.' Now Calil sounded bitter. 'If the past didn't hang upon us like stones, why, we'd not be shut up in a city of traps in the middle of a wasteland. They call us "halfbreed Golden". They fear us, that land to the north. And the Coast fears us, also. Christie, I have had visions that show them not so innocent. They claim they were a slave race of the Golden, bred up from fenborn aboriginals – but there were those who were not slave, and who built up the Empire hand in hand with the Golden Witchbreed.'

'No one's innocent,' I said. Hearing her *I have had visions*. And I

642

couldn't stop myself asking, 'How do you know that language, *shan'tai* Calil?'

'Perhaps it's still spoken in my city. Perhaps I learned it in the Tower. Perhaps—'

Cutting across her provocation, I said, 'We've no records of it anywhere. I've looked. Nothing, in ten years on this world; if it was known, I think we'd have heard it somewhere. As for the Tower . . .' Intent on explanation, I said, 'There's always a Hexenmeister. There are always others who could pick up the role and continue it word-perfect. But as for it being one and the same Hexenmeister, over millennia—'

I broke off, regretting it the instant the words were out of my mouth. My tone would have told her, if nothing else. Haven't I just told this consummate Harantish politician the truth about her traditional enemy? Indiscreet. Perhaps more than indiscreet. . . . But traditions count for nothing now. What does that rivalry between Kel Harantish and Kasabaarde's Tower matter when the Coast is attacking the Hundred Thousand, and Earth is bringing technology and troops here? And won't it make Ruric safer if they know she's only one of many, and not an all-knowing authority? Won't it? A little more and I might convince myself, make good excuses for that one unwise word—

All I could think was: Now I owe a debt to her: to Ruric, and to Orthe.

The *arniac* had grown cold, and Calil bent forward to adjust the spirit lamp that heated it. These walls muffle sound. Nothing could be heard from the other cell-hive rooms below and either side of us. Calil bel-Rioch sat back.

'Well,' she said, 'then there's no one to judge the truth of my visions of the Empire – except myself.'

I made an inarticulate protest. She didn't hear. There was a look on that cold Golden face, so that I thought, This is a turning point for her, but how? *Why?* What has she just chosen to do? Could I have stopped her?

Calil, almost under her breath, added, 'And I have nothing to fear from *her*.'

Nothing to fear – and nothing to gain. If I didn't have it implanted in my memory by the Tower, where did that Rakviri vision come from? If Molly experienced it too, was it exterior to us? I don't know. Oh, you can say that when the Hexenmeister messed up my mind, he used data from the Tower Archives—

That is perfectly rational as an explanation: *why can't I believe it?*

I sat sweating, dry-mouthed.

Calil, still with that new deliberation in her face, turned her head for a moment towards the window; looking towards the dark heat-soaked landscape, the bitter sterile sea.

'Have I seen the Golden?' My voice cracked. 'Have you? I don't know.'

Calil bel-Rioch said, 'I have seen. I do see.'

She reached, without looking at me, and her six-fingered hand closed over mine. Scale-dry and warm, and I felt as if that touch went beneath my skin and marked me clear down to the bone.

'When the Elansiir was a garden land, and not a desert . . . I see the City Over The Inland Sea, in a bright day, in a time of war—'

Between one word and the next, vision flooded up; and then I didn't know whether she spoke, or I, or both of us:

'The City Over The Inland Sea . . .'

'*Chiruzeth*, shining . . .'

The sound of the sea, lapping at cyclopean wharfs . . .

Light blooms into colours. There is a sudden scent on the air, heavy, sweet, an odour of summer. Humid heat. The light, that strange radiance, comes from chiruzeth: chiruzeth *that shines with living light.*

Above me, the suspended city blocks out the sun.

Under the gigantic pillars of chiruzeth *that support the city, dark green shadows hang in the sea depths. Great soaring spans, curving over and up and across, their shadow falling on the Inland Sea. And in infinite distance I see a rim of clear water, shining gold: the distant skyline, between the city and the sea.*

The towers of that incredibly-supported cityscape merge with the pale-blue sky, and with daystars that shine in constellations wholly unrecognizable. Small figures move on the towers, thin and intensely bright.

And chiruzeth *shines: blue, blue-white, diamond-brilliant. That light touches deep instincts: a longing for gardens, for isles where darkness never comes; a world quite other than this, shot through with fire and light unbearable.*

And one of us says, 'There is the city of our enemies. Have you the heart to do this?', *and the other answers*, 'I can, and I do, and I will.'

We stand long enough to see the sunlight fade on the city, and the twilight come and go. The light of the sun shines level under the city, in the air between it and the sea. Above, mile upon mile of towers, bridges, streets, battlements, cupolas, fountains. Now the City Over The Inland Sea lies like a dream of stone, under stars so brilliant they fuse together, burn in a sky like white phosphorus. A few sphere-lights cluster under eaves, or gleam as signals for flyers to land. At the foot of one of the great spans, that is also a bridge-way up into the city, we stand: and a faint and living luminescence clings to the chiruzeth.

'Because we have entered the city, a wasteland will grow here. Because we have entered the city, great ones will go to corruption, their flesh will lie unconsumed—'

'—because we have entered the city. We are the bringers of death. How shall we enter?'

And I see her with starlight on her face, that gold-dust skin, that whitefire mane: see her eyes that are yellow as childhood innocence and flowers. She kneels down on the cold earth. The span and the bridge-arch are before her.

'Go and cry: Zilkezra is dead, Zilkezra of the High Lands is dead and come to corruption, and her flesh must not lie unconsumed. And when you come to the first gate, cry this cry, and they will send out the people of Santhendor'lin-sandru to carry me home, and commit my flesh to their bodies. And cry this cry at the second gate, and they will send word into the city that all may see me pass, and all the slave race and beastmen shall be shut within walls, and so I shall pass into the city. And when you have passed the third gate, cry this cry, and Santhendor'lin-sandru, Phoenix Emperor, he himself shall come to do that which is necessary for one of his blood, and so I shall pass into the city, and so the city shall pass away.'

I say, 'Are you determined on this?'

'I am as we all are: I have no kin, and none to follow me. I am determined on the death of my enemies. Will you do this?'

'I can, I do, I will.'

And I walk up the slope of that chiruzeth *span, one of the supports of the city. Nothing beneath me but stone and air. And there are none but slaves at the great arch, that race we bred up from our blood and from night-hunters in the northern fens: claw-handed, rough-maned, with translucent skin across their eyes. They cover their faces, seeing one of the Golden blood. I speak:*

'Zilkezra is dead, Zilkezra of the High Lands is dead and come to corruption, and her flesh must not lie unconsumed.'

In this time of war the gates are shut, no flyers scour the night sky. The wind off the sea is cold. At last comes the guard of the first gate, a woman of Golden blood:

'Enter the city, blood-kin of Santhendor'lin-sandru. Bring that dead flesh into the city, and there shall be done what must be done. Only forgive us that we take from you robes and weapons.'

She calls our people (slave races must not touch flesh of us) and six of them bring a bier, and set upon it the naked body of Zilkezra, that does not move nor breathe nor speak. And I walk naked beside it as they carry it into the city, and to the second gate.

Here there are few sphere-lights, and so massive are the buildings round us, blocking out the sky, that I know I see scarcely a tenth of their bulk.

'Zilkezra is dead, Zilkezra of the High Lands is dead and come to corruption, and her flesh must not lie unconsumed. Let the people of our blood come and see her brought home to the halls of Santhendor'lin-sandru.'

The commander of the second gate is a young man, who speaks to his guards. I see them go forth into the dark streets. Their footsteps call out the echo of an echo: dim memory of that space that lies below us, between the city and the sea. The commander speaks:

'*Enter the city, blood-kin of Santhendor'lin-sandru. Bring that dead flesh into the city, and he will do what must be done. Only forgive us that we bind your hands and shackle your feet: the living and the dead.*'

And so we pass on into the City Over The Inland Sea: six of Golden blood who carry her bier, Zilkezra who does not move nor breathe nor speak; and her hands and feet are tied with silken cords, and my hands and feet are shackled with iron, in this time of war. And as I follow, I see how on great terraces, and flights of steps, and in entrances to wide avenues, and on seven-span bridges, the people come out to watch the procession pass. And these are true Golden, white manes like fire in the night's chill, eyes gold and cold with the sight of death.

At the third gate I cry the cry:

'Zilkezra is dead, Zilkezra of the High Lands is dead and come to corruption, and her flesh must not lie unconsumed. Let Santhendor'lin-sandru, Phoenix Emperor, come to do what must be done.'

And the third gate opens, admitting us to that city-within-a-city where scarcely a light shows, the spider-heart and lair of the Emperor. I follow the bier up a wide and great flight of steps, to a terrace that lies before carved doors and pillars and an entrance all in darkness. There they lay down the bier, and she lies without motion or breath or speech: the colours of corruption already gleaming under the surface of her skin.

'_____ __ _____ __ _____'

'___ _____ ___'

'_____ __ _____ ___ _____'

An echo comes back from those gleaming blue-grey walls of chiruzeth. The ancient tongue of the bloodline of the Golden Empire. I see how the guards step back from the bier, and she lies with her face to the cold stars: Zilkezra of the High Lands, sister to Santhendor'lin-sandru.

'_____ __ _____'

'__ _____ _ ___'

Unwillingly our tongues echo his, compelled to it. And he, Santhen-
dor'lin-sandru: tall and thin and bright, whitefire, and his eyes as yellow
as summer, as yellow as the sun on the Inland Sea. He stands in the
shadow of the pillars.

I raise the cry:

'Zilkezra is dead, Zilkezra of the High Lands is dead and come to
corruption, and her flesh must not lie unconsumed.'

And Santhendor'lin-sandru laughs. He holds up slender hands, gloved
in some substance light and impenetrable. That laughter is soft acid.

'O brave, sister! What, have you swallowed poison for my sake? And
am I to forget our long enmity, and shroud your poison corpse in my own
body? Will you have me go into nothingness, as you have gone? O, sister,
no! For I will not do it. Not a drop of your blood, not a morsel of your
flesh will I eat—'

Shock radiates out from that focal point, his voice. I hear the crowd cry
at this sacrilege, and I hear him laugh again. He holds up one gloved
hand, and in it the knife shines: gleams once against the dark.

'—but I will scatter you, blood and body! See, here, what I do now.
And you have killed yourself for nothing!'

My hands and feet are shackled, I can only shuffle forward; and she –
she! – is shackled and bound before him. I protest:

'She lives! She yet lives—'

Before I can speak again, Santhendor'lin-sandru throws himself down
full-length on her body and slashes wildly. She cries out, face streaming
blood, a cry that thrills through the stone city. His knife slashes the cord
that binds her hands, half severs her wrist. Zilkezra throws wide her
arms and scatters blood-drops. Santhendor'lin-sandru springs back, face
wet with her blood. The guards run; the crowd seethes in panic, and she
– on her feet, face slashed open, laughing – she gives me one look of pure
triumph:

'So: my revenge. So: my love. *So.'*

And then, almost tenderly, to Santhendor'lin-sandru; who stares in
frozen panic at her blood on his hands:

'That will not hurt you, lover, brother. My poison is not for you.
Not yet for you. Zilkezra is dead, Zilkezra of the High Lands is dead
and come to corruption, and here her body will lie, unconsumed.'

She stoops and picks up the knife, and draws the blade across her
throat. The skin puckers as the metal draws it, and then parts: raw flesh
pushes up and out; blood rills down her breast as she falls.

And he looks up at me in bewilderment, Santhendor'lin-sandru.

'What revenge is it – for her to come here and make herself dead meat,
and harm no one else?'

I kneel down beside him, and wipe a little of her blood from the
chiruzeth.

'Not all poisons are for us, you who shall be called Santhen-dor'lin-sandru, Phoenix Emperor and – Last Emperor.'

Her blood, warm and rich, can incubate the virus, the death she and others have created. Could not the slave races create that bloodborne sterility that makes ours the last generation? Well and so: she has made a death that, cancerous, turns things to feed on their own substance and transform themselves . . .

'See.'

Already, the faint shine of the living chiruzeth *has dimmed. He reaches out to touch a mark, a lichen, a flower:* chiruzeth *is turning under his hand to dead crystal. Spreading as rapidly as ice forms on water, as swiftly as a crack in a mirror – spreading to the nearer pillars, the terrace, the towers of this* chiruzeth *city – spreading unstoppably now, until even this earth, even this sea itself, are turned to crystalline death –*

'She brought it. She freed it. She has given you a great gift, brother of Zilkezra. She has given you the death of all cities, the death of the Empire.'

The night air begins to shimmer. As that genetically-engineered virus spreads, multiplying as it causes chiruzeth *to transform to dead matter, the energies it releases will kill almost as many as this plague of stone itself.*

The City Over The Inland Sea will shine, a beacon, a brilliance. Shine as other cities in the Elansiir and the north will shine also – others have their vengeances, too.

'— ——— ———'

I can't name it, human tongues can't speak so; and Calil bel-Rioch, her eyes full still with vision, can only stumble for the name the Last Emperor (his face filled with love of his sister) gave to that weapon, and in poor translation say at last, ' "Ancient light".'

PART FOUR

START FOUR

CHAPTER 19

Recognizable Strangers

How could I have told her?

Ten days later and a weary monologue of self-justification is still playing in my head: sooner or later Calil would have heard, her people listen to Company gossip, they'd hear, 'the first envoy was tricked into believing one of these natives is immortal' . . . oh, she would have heard without me to tell her!

The shuttle grounded. Tact took me out of it ahead of Cory Mendez – a small figure waved a greeting, and even in the dimness of first twilight I could see it was Doug, leaving his own grounded shuttle to meet us.

First twilight smelt of rain recently fallen, the flagstones underfoot slick with damp. Mist began to rise. Light grew swiftly, the east a magnesium flare; and I smelt the wind and rubbed cold hands together and, as Carrick's Star cleared the horizon, began to walk away from the foot of the shuttle-ramp. A full minute later, the echo of my footsteps came back from distant walls.

'Good timing,' Doug greeted me. 'The first *takshiriye* came in on the ships from Kasabaarde yesterday.'

Then his gaze went past me to the shuttle, that was marked with a Peace Force logo.

'Molly's going ahead with this? Without consultation?'

The light grew stronger. I walked on a few paces across the square, seeing the city take shape round me. Mossgrass rooted in the crevices of the paving underfoot, blue-grey fronds tightly curled. The arch of the sky was milky, freckled with daystars, and I could taste on my lips the sweet salt of Orthean waters; could hear the sound of the sea.

'Douggie, come on; it was obvious after the talks in Kasabaarde broke down, the Company would have to do something.'

'You *approve* of this?'

The first time I came to Tathcaer, I came aboard a *jath*-ship, a ship that catches the dawn tide as it sails the barren sandy coast of

Melkathi, and comes to where river meadows of mossgrass are blue and grey, mist still curling where *marhaz* and *skurrai* graze. And there, held between the two arms of the Oranon River, is the island-city of Tathcaer . . .

The air above was cold and vast now; and I wondered, Are there ships up there already? Cory Mendez' Peace Force ships, docked in the Company orbital station? Are they landing on the Coast now? And when they see that threat, what will Sethri and the Anzhadi do?

I said, 'Storms won't keep those ships in harbour forever. What do you plan to do when the *hiyek* fleets sail north to the Hundred Thousand?'

There was a high flush of anger on his round face.

'This is an internal matter. Internal hostilities. The Company has no right to bring its own forces in!' He took a breath. 'I'll see how home office reacts to this. And how people in general like the idea – I don't think PanOceania is going to find itself very popular back on Earth.'

Now the day shone clear, the white gold of early morning, and I stand in the great Square below the Citadel, in the heart of the white city, Tathcaer.

That walkway that zigzags up the sheer cliff-face behind me, up to the top of the Citadel crag, that's where I went with Haltern Beth'ru-elen when he took me to my first audience with the *T'An Suthai-Telestre* – light shines on the rock now, and on the masses of blue vines that have overgrown all the cliff-walk, choking it, that hang out questing tendrils on the morning air; vines that spill down to cover the deserted gatehouse and archway where the Crown Guard stood.

'Douggie, if you're thinking of starting a media propaganda campaign . . . just be sure you're right.'

'I am. I am,' he said, 'and I'm amazed that you can't see it.'

He broke off then, as Cory Mendez left the shuttle and came to join us, be-ringed hands behind her back. Her rings clinked. 'If we're going to go down into the city—'

Doug said, 'I'll do my best to lead you, Commander. I'm afraid it isn't easy to get around in the city yet. Lynne – Lynne?'

Only the deserted Citadel stands unchanged, each tower and balcony and cupola and terrace clear in the light that puts precise shadows on luminous grey masonry.

'I didn't think I'd see the day. Douggie, I didn't ever think I'd see the day.'

I turn one way, and there on the east side of the Square are high walls, and beyond them the dome of the great Wellhouse that imprisoned us when we returned from Kasabaarde: Blaize, Rodion, Havoth-jair and me. The gates hang askew in the wall's archway, and through the gap can be glimpsed a courtyard, and fountains that are now dry.

Cory Mendez tapped her fingers impatiently together. There was a CAS-IV in her belt-holster.

'Are we likely to find native authorities here?'

'They won't be happy about the shuttle landing,' I realized.

Doug said, 'This is the only open space on the island of sufficient size for a shuttle to land. But, as you imply, we're stretching *telestre* custom to have it here at all. If I might suggest a course of action, we should attempt to get down to the harbour on foot. One of the old Dominion consulates used to be there, on Westhill.'

The silence was broken by the raw, metallic cry of a *rashaku*-lizardbird. It was enough: suddenly there was a catch in my throat, water in my eyes. Once I saw a *rashaku* cling to an awning-pole here, the sun bright through its spread pinions, and that on a day when the whole Square was full of *telestre*-Ortheans – *s'ans* in robes and bright tunics, gems and *harur*-blades shining, some with young *ashiren* sat up on their shoulders; city tradesmen and merchants and young Ortheans from the Artisans Quarter, and those in Mercenaries Guild leathers, and Peir-Dadeni riders with their plumed manes . . . And we sat the whole day here and played *ochmir*, Haltern and Blaize and I, at Midsummer-Tenyear, when the new *T'An Suthai-Telestre* was to be named.

Emotion is never less than ambiguous. I am hurt by the desolation of this city, so there is some love for it in me; but this, now, is a city of strangers. Those were the last few days before the treachery of Ruric Orhlandis was made known. I think of her now, in the Tower, perpetrating that massive necessary fraud—

There is a link between vision and memory and the Tower, and I don't know what it is.

'. . . something on her mind,' Cory Mendez was saying. 'For a few days now. Lynne, shall we go?'

'What? Yes, of course.'

We began to walk across the Square, leaving the shuttle secure behind us; moving away from Citadel crag, that is the point of this arrowhead-shaped river-island. It seemed we hardly moved, so large a space the Square is, and so empty. No crowds, no *skurrai-jasin* carriages.

'Who drove these people out of this settlement?' Mendez asked Doug Clifford, as we walked.

'No one. They decided they didn't need it.'

'And now they do?'

'Haven't you realized, Commander? They're coming here to make a new *T'An Suthai-Telestre*, a new Crown.'

Corazon Mendez, all Peace Force, said, 'It doesn't do to allow political unrest when a war-sequence is in operation. We could stop that.'

Seeing Doug's face, I hastily cut in with, 'That might be unwise.'

'It would be an unjustifiable intervention,' Doug said.

Cory smiled. 'Still trying diplomacy, Douglas? Good. Just remember, I have to cope with what happens when diplomacy breaks down.'

I let them argue, and walked ahead. The remaining sides of the Square are taken up with the white façades of low-roofed blocks of buildings. We were coming to the gap between them, that marks the beginning of the one named, paved road in all the city, that runs from here clear down to the harbour: Crown Way.

There is a link between vision and memory—

I should go to the Company, to Molly; but Molly thinks of that experience in Rakviri as a "side-effect" of alien technology. Who else can I go to? When I am desperately, steadfastly trying not to think of a room in Kel Harantish, and the face of Calil bel-Rioch. Who?

At the top of Crown Way, I stopped.

Tathcaer lay sprawled below me in the early-morning sun. The light made a clarity of the air. I looked down the hill at the pale-plaster *telestre*-houses, with their blank outside walls and inner courtyards, and their cisterns now standing dry. I saw no smoke rising anywhere. Only a sprawling confusion of white and sand-coloured buildings, with narrow unnamed alleys between them; and now as my eye grew keener I could pick out landmarks: the Guild-Ring, Wellhouse domes, the barracks on that prestigious district known as The Hill, home of the *T'An* Commander . . .

Silence. No dawn bells. All the alleys are choked with the feather-fronds of *lapuur*, growing unchecked, and the sporeborne red-and-black branches of *ziku*.

Melkathi summer: the smoke from brush-fires obscuring the sun. Orhlandis telestre, burning. And she, cornered, ash-stained; only the harur-nilgiri *bright in her hand. She who had been* T'An *Commander and* T'An *Melkathi; and there is no one now who will not willingly see her exiled –* I wanted, suddenly and desperately, to hear her tell me how she'd survived from then till now; what had happened, what the truth is.

And will that tell me what really happened between Calil and myself?

Looking east, I see the wider and more shallow branch of the

654

Oranon River, sparkling under ten or twelve bridges; and beyond it, blue meadows fading away into the hills of Ymir. And, looking west, there is a deep and narrow channel, once crossed by the Salathiel ferry; and in the distance, mudflats, and the chalk headlands of the Rimon coast. Not an acre of this land but I have memories of it.

As Doug and Cory came up with me, Doug said, 'It will be difficult crossing the city, I'm afraid. I've only just got here myself; I didn't realize quite how bad it is.'

I gazed south, across the dips and hollows of the city and its clustered buildings. Two hills rose up. On them are squat brown forts, pocked with the black shadows of window-arches. On Easthill I once had a *telestre*-house, Easthill-Malkys; but now at four or five miles' distance I can't make out individual buildings. The Westhill *telestre*-houses I didn't often visit.

Invisible from here, over the saddle between those two hills, lies Tathcaer's harbour. The two branches of the Oranon rejoin there at the estuary. It was the harbour I first saw, under a daystarred sky, crowded with all the ships of a trading port, and the young Haltern there to meet the Earth envoy. I don't know if I can stand to see that harbour silted up, deserted . . .

I wonder if, when Ortheans return on Her earth, they feel the same: neither the place nor the person are the same?

'Where now?' Cory Mendez asked.

I put all doubts and problems into that corner of my mind reserved for procrastination. In that moment of searching, I caught sight of what I'd been looking for: 'There.' I pointed to where *telestre*-houses, blurred by distance, went down a long slope to the place where the Salathiel ferry used to run.

A thread of smoke rose up into the bright morning air.

'Mother of God!' Cory Mendez swore, stopping to push away pale green fronds of *lapuur*. Heat-sensitive, the feathery plants coiled with vegetable slowness around her bony wrists. She added, 'Damn all technology embargoes – what I'd give now for a laser-cutter!'

'Depends how badly you want to be in the middle of a forest fire,' I observed. 'Looks like it's been a dry summer.'

The walls of this choked alley were carpeted with bronze foliage of *kazsis*-nightvine; sapling *lapuur* rooted in the earth. A ribbon of blue sky overhead showed noontide stars. I picked black spines of *ziku* out of my sleeve, and was showered with that tree's red spore cases. Two- or three-year growth, most of this; equally hard to push through or walk over. Stems of *kazsis* gave soggily underfoot.

Doug Clifford emerged from the next alley-entrance, beating away swarms of *chirith-goyen* and *kekri*-flies that shone like mica in the hot sun. He wiped sweat from his red face.

'I can't see a thing,' he confessed. 'We'll have to try getting up to a roof-top again to get our bearings.'

How can I cross half the Hundred Thousand and then get lost crossing half a city? I grinned, thinking how I'd asked that question in exasperation ten years ago. Tathcaer has a way of doing that to me.

'Four hours,' Doug added gloomily. His coverall was dusty with *ziku* spores, his boots snagged with the thorn of *hanelys*-tanglebush; he looked as uncomfortable as a ruffled cat. 'I despair of reporting to Molly Rachel that we've spent *four hours* trying to cross a native settlement . . .'

'Douggie, you're cute when you're angry,' I said, quiet so that the Mendez didn't hear; and decided to ignore the explosively obscene comment that D. Clifford made in reply.

Corazon checked her wristlink. 'I'll call in at the end of the hour. The satellites—'

I held up a hand for silence. They waited.

'There,' I said. *Kazsis*-stems crunched as I climbed through to the blocked end of the alley.

The sound of voices grew more distinct.

Two spindle-trunked *ziku* grew up at the alley's end. Their scarlet foliage cast shadows on the sandstone masonry of the *telestre*-house walls, that here stood twenty-five or thirty feet high. I stepped between them, feeling they made a natural entrance to this unnatural clearing. A fire had burned here, perhaps last summer – young *ziku* and *lapuur* sprouted in the blackened earth, mossgrass began to cover the tumbled masonry. Five or six Ortheans were sitting on fallen stones, boots stretched out idly on the flagstone floor, now open to the sky. There was a low Well-house dome beyond. Then a young male looked lazily up at the *telestre*-wall above my head.

'Right, Hana, they're here. You can go back on watch.'

A lithe, yellow-maned male dropped from sound to broken wall, sure-footed, and from that masonry to the earth. 'Shadow take it! Send someone else. I'm tired of baking in that sun.'

There was laughter: the others glanced up from where broken walls and seedling *lapuur* protected them from the heat. Mercenaries, by their dress; by the *nilgiri*-blades and *nazari*-knives, and the *ochmir* board that lay between them on the rubble.

A dark-maned female raised her head. She lay on her back, face in the shade, eyes veiled with translucent membrane. 'I'll go on watch – if you go to the Wellhouse, Hana.' She got to her feet, turning casually to me; 'You *s'aranthi* want the Wellhouse, yes?'

Doug emerged from the tangle of vegetation at the alley-mouth, followed by Cory Mendez, her hand resting on the CAS-IV holster.

'Yes,' I said.

The city had a quiet so intense that, when no one spoke, you could hear the shifting of warm summer air; could almost hear the sunlight falling on the stones. Each small sound was magnified: the creak of leather boots, jingle of *harur*-blade harness as the woman walked across the burnt earth. I heard some heavy animal shift padded feet, and saw the shaggy bronze coats of *marhaz* in the shadow of a wall.

'Who's *T'An* in the city?' I asked a male with braided mane, and northern province dress, whose belt-badges proclaimed him captain. 'Can you tell me who has your contract?'

'I won't answer your questions,' the male said, and his gaze went to each of us in turn. *Three offworlders, all armed, one plainly from the paramilitary forces* – not in those words, but I saw the thought in his face. And something I'd never seen in an Orthean before: that half-ashamed and half-defiant ignoring of hi-tech weaponry. He said, 'Hana, take them to the Wellhouse.'

I saw, across that stretch of rubble and sunlight, the low dome of a Wellhouse. An Orthean stood at the door. The scarlet mane was a flare against the brown brickwork, and she lifted a hand in casual salute, and I recognized the Earthspeaker Cassirur Almadhera.

'One thing occurs to me,' Commander Cory Mendez said. 'The Company must station a detachment here, as well as on the southern continent.' She paused, then lifted her wrist to key in the comlink transmitter. 'I'll relay through to the orbiter and check – my squads should be making hi-orbital docking about now.'

Doug Clifford blinked. 'Out of interest, what size force did the Company assign here?'

'A small force,' the white-haired woman said, 'three squads in fifteen F90s; that's two hundred men. If it wasn't for the ban on anything except medium-tech, I could handle these assignments with a tenth of the manpower. PanOceania abides by home regulations, of course . . .' Here her smile became cynical.

'You don't change, Cory,' Doug said. He couldn't hide his distaste. Corazon Mendez shrugged.

'You and the groundsiders who make "humane" legislation ought to try it, Douglas. Try forcing a cease-fire when you can hardly do more than bluff. These beings here are alien, they don't think like we do, but they'd understand a seismic-nuclear missile if they saw one demonstrated!'

'*Cory*—'

She glanced at me as we began to walk towards the Wellhouse. 'That would put a stop to your "farmers' war", Lynne. As it is, all I can do is threaten – and a little more.'

Inside the Wellhouse, Cassirur Almadhera didn't seem at all surprised to see us. I assumed she'd had word of the shuttle's landing earlier on.

'I'll take you down into the city to meet with the others who are here,' she said, with a slight inclination of the head that acknowledged both Doug and Cory Mendez. 'You must eat first, I think. The *ashiren* will fetch food. Christie, Blaize Meduenin gave me your greeting when he returned from Kasabaarde. I didn't expect to see you again in the Hundred Thousand so soon.'

'You've heard what's happening on the Coast, of course? Yes. We have to talk. Earth and your new *T'An Suthai Telestre*, when you have one.'

'Soon. Soon now.'

Cassirur's children ushered Doug and Cory through into the Wellhouse dining-chamber. I followed. Heat had robbed me of hunger. When I came to the central part of the dome I went on and into it, hardly aware that Cassirur Almadhera followed me.

Midday sun slanted through the roof-slot of the low dome. Where it fell on the mouth of the Well, bright coruscations danced from the water's surface and cast mutable shadows of light on the white walls.

Here is Your daughter from a far world. Receive her name. Words spoken by the Earthspeaker Theluk in a northern Wellhouse, with Ruric as my second; none of us knowing then that one would die and the other be proven traitor, and I – I would forget that naming ceremony, because I never knew what it meant.

'Who's here from the Freeport?'

She said, 'Haltern Beth'ru-elen. Blaize Meduenin. I've had word on the *rashaku*-relay that the *T'Ans* of Melkathi, Rimon, and Roehmonde will be here soon; and even that the Andrethe will leave Peir-Dadeni to come here.'

'To an abandoned city,' I said, still half in the past.

'Ah, that was Suthafiori's death, and the summer of the white plague.' She smoothed her green *chirith-goyen* robe with brown six-fingered hands, and then wiped tendrils of red mane from her forehead; squinting up at the inner curve of the dome with unveiled eyes. 'Tathcaer was never abandoned, Christie. Without Wellkeepers, summer lightning would have razed it. Now we need it again, we come back to it.' She paused, looked at me. 'Different from our meeting in the Freeport, this.'

Just a few months have put us here, I thought. The Company arrives, the Coast goes to war, the Hundred Thousand fears Witch-breed technology, others crave it – and then the Tower . . .

'I said in Morvren that you had the look of one named for the Goddess,' Cassirur said. 'One sick with past-memories. You've lost that – or it's changed. Does She still know your name?'

That abrupt, natural change from politician to Earthspeaker. I smiled to take the irreverence out of what I said: 'Probably not.'

Her dark eyes went cloudy, membrane sliding across them. 'If I were a superstitious woman, I'd wonder if that wasn't because you've been to that abomination, Kel Harantish.'

'You trust one Desert Coast city, you Earthspeakers – but do you know as much about Kasabaarde as you do about Kel Harantish?'

She laughed, a short bark that sent her head back. Then she shrugged. 'Perhaps the Hundred Thousand doesn't listen as closely to the Tower as you believe. We trust ourselves only. Not outland-ers. And not *s'aranthi*.'

She knelt, one knee on the rim of the circular Well, trailing a claw-nailed hand in the water. Her slit-backed robe pulled aside to show the complex braids of her mane, rooted down her spine.

'And when it comes to war, Cassirur?'

Without turning round, she said, 'Many will go to the Goddess. But we meet, and part, and meet again, and we do not forget. And the earth is always here for us again.'

A steep western scarp falls several hundred feet to a plain, desolate as these hills, that stretches out to the horizon. Sun reflects off something – water? snow? No: it ends in sharp edges, splinters . . . I kneel under a daystarred sky, feeling dirt and grit beneath my hands, and there the earth itself changes. Crystalline mirror: each shard of stone or frond of mossgrass transmuted to a fragile, sterile petrification—

I made the hard-learned effort and pulled free. Cassirur looked up at me as I said harshly, '*Is* the earth always there? You ask the Coast families. They'd use Witchbreed weapons if they could, or Earth technology; and you're going to find your only way out is that technology – improve food production here and share land with those who are starving—'

The scarlet-maned Orthean woman got to her feet. Her expression told me I'd miscalculated, broached the subject too soon and too baldly.

'We're not *hiyeks*, Christie. We won't take offworlder science.

659

We won't take that path that leads to a new Golden Empire and a new destruction!'

This untidy, middle-aged Orthean female, with little of the Earthspeaker about her; she spoke now with a hard anger in her voice. It was automatic (but I disliked myself for doing it) to go straight for the weak point and attack: 'Has Barris Rakviri come to Tathcaer?' I asked. 'Or is he still back on Rakviri *telestre*, making Witchbreed relics into functioning technology?'

The Almadhera held my gaze for a long moment. 'Barris Rakviri is dead.'

'What? *How?* When did it happen?'

'A month ago. We gave him *saryl-kabriz* in his food,' the Earthspeaker said. She spoke quite calmly. 'He died. Jaharien Rakviri chose to follow him, and he took the *saryl-kabriz* poison also. And that is an end to Witchbreed science in Rakviri *telestre*.'

Light from the Well rippled across her pale features and green robe, and in the silence I heard *ashiren* in the dining-hall, and Doug and Cory's voices raised in argument, and I could only stare at this Orthean woman that I had thought I might be coming to know. What's more appalling? I wondered. What she says or how she said it?

'You killed him?'

Cassirur Almadhera inclined her head. 'I killed him. I suppose by that I'm the cause of Jaharien's death also, and for that I'm sorry.'

'How can you stand there and say that!'

'I sent him to a joy,' she said, 'that *I* would sooner have than any of the shadows it casts on earth, which are love and ecstasy. I gave him *saryl-kabriz* poison to close his eyes, and death to open them in that bright realm; poison to close his mouth, and death to open it to breathe in the fire of Her world.'

We meet, and part, and meet again, and we do not forget.

I stared at her, and she smiled. It was warm and friendly, and a little humorous. She made a gesture to follow her into the dining-hall, and walked through the archway.

Pain made me aware that I was digging my nails into my palms. What I feel is shock, I thought. Is outrage. It is *not* familiarity, there's no way I can have Orthean memories of what it feels like to have past-lives, no way I can be thinking how different it is from how the Witchbreed glutted on death, fed on cessation, worshipped extinction, but Ortheans love the cycle of turn and return *because that is a delusion*.

I thought I am human, there's no part of me that's Orthean,

660

much as I want that and the light of Carrick's Star sent ripples across the curve of that radiant dome.

It was some while later that the silence was broken by footsteps, and Doug Clifford entered the dome, glancing up at it as he came in.

'I'm going to open up the old government quarters on Westhill,' he said. 'There's hi-tech equipment under store there, we ought to be able to contact the Company and the orbiter. I want to know how they're reacting to Orthe at home.'

I said, 'The people here aren't going to be co-operative. We'll have our work cut out. And it won't be long now before Coast warships can cross the Inner Sea.'

That day was Durestha Seventhweek Nineday, a Fast-day; the next, Durestha Eighthweek Firstday, a Feast-day. It dawned with the clarity of summer, drowned daystars in a mid-morning heat haze, shone warm on the neglected stonework of the Dominion government quarters.

'. . . the department has had to come down on the government's side,' Stephen Perrault's image told me from the holotank. I didn't turn to watch, but stayed looking out of the window. His message-blip continued: 'That means the multicorporates want to close us down now, and open up a new Liaison Department. One that they can control. I can stall them for a few more weeks, but we need you here to fight for us!'

That's my career, I thought. It seemed faint, far away, drowned in the blaze of colour that is Tathcaer: the white city in summer. This was a small *telestre*-house, Westhill-Ahrentine, and from its first-floor windows I could see the ferry and the western end of the harbour. Ships jostled, moored at the docks, and brightly-robed crowds seethed round them. A constant influx of Ortheans and *marhaz*-riderbeasts streamed from the Salathiel ferry. Once on the island, they vanished into tangled alleyways that were rapidly becoming cleared. The city was coming alive again.

And I just want to bask in it, I thought, that long and golden summer of Tathcaer . . . All the while, urgency nagged me. Beacon-forts were manned all along the coast, the *rashaku*-relay and heliographs brought nothing but warnings to watch the sea . . .

Stephen Perrault's voice ceased. I realized I'd paid him no attention, would have to replay the blip. And then as I turned away from the window, for the first time since my return, I heard the harsh carillon of the city's noon bells.

Doug came through from the next room. 'The comlink's out

661

again.' He frowned. 'I haven't heard anything about reaction at home yet. Which indicates either a superfluity of apathy on their part, or that my esteemed masters are failing to ˌ 'horize media coverage.'

Something of the Cliffordian humour in that, for all that his was a genuine concern. I said, 'Could be they're keeping their heads down. My deputy, Perrault, says the Companies are on the warpath again.'

'I have to confess, if I were a national government, *I* wouldn't quarrel with a multicorporate Company whose GNP exceeds mine by several orders of magnitude . . .'

He moved to the window, looking down at the bustle on the quay.

'The Almadhera tells me the church is reopening the big Wellhouse up by the Citadel. You said we should be talking to Earthspeakers and Wellkeepers, Lynne; are you coming up there with me?'

'I'll come,' I said. 'Where's Cory?'

'Our esteemed Corazon. Now that,' Douggie said, 'I would very much like to know. She's Company, not government. I have no authority over her.'

Do I? I wondered. As special advisor? Dubious. Only Molly has that authority; and Molly, damn her, doesn't care one jot about the low-tech Hundred Thousand.

'If we can take a *skurrai*-carriage across the city—'

'You go,' I interrupted him. I leaned both hands on the sill of the window-arch, looking down into the street. 'I'll join you in an hour or two. It was about time some of them started coming to us, instead of us running after them.'

Two Orthean males were plodding up the steep alley to the entrance of Westhill-Ahrentine. One, dark and in middle years, I had a feeling I ought to recognize from somewhere. The other, supporting himself with a staff and his companion's arm, but gazing round with a bright-eyed curiosity, was Haltern n'ri n'suth Beth'ru-elen.

CHAPTER 20

A Visitor to Westhill-Ahrentine

'Give you greeting,' the dark male said. 'We have met, *t'an* Christie. You may not recall. I'm Nelum Santhil, of Rimnith *telestre.*'

Dear God, Nelum Santhil! I covered shock. Haltern was regarding me with covert amusement. I stared at the dark male, with his thin Melkathi robes, and short-cropped mane, and I would not have recognized the man who, ten years ago, had been Portmaster of Ales-Kadareth in Melkathi – who allowed SuBannasen and later Orhlandis *telestres* to ship in illegal gold from Kel Harantish, who then betrayed both SuBannasen and Orhlandis . . .

Haltern's staff tapped on the floorboards as he crossed the room, and sat in one of the couch-chairs by the window. The sun gleamed on his fine, white mane. With deliberate casualness, he said, 'Give you greeting, Christie. Nelum Santhil's newly arrived from Ales-Kadareth, where they named him T'An Melkathi.'

It was a major effort to keep still. *T'An* Melkathi? But that's Orthean politics. I offered herb-tea to both of them, and Nelum Santhil accepted, and as I poured it from a stone jug I thought, Hal, you're a wicked old man! And you've never given up your ambition of having the edge over *s'aranthi*.

'And what can I do for you and the *T'An* Melkathi?' I asked, sitting down beside Hal on the couch-chair, proud of my self-possession.

'As representatives of two provinces – ah,' Hal interrupted himself. With a charming air of apology, he went on: 'That's something else I should perhaps have mentioned. Morvren Freeport has been foolhardy enough to name a Beth'ru-elen as their Seamarshal – that is, myself.'

I looked at him. Lines puckered the reptilian skin round that neat mouth; unveiled eyes were brilliant, pale, and lively.

'Got any more like that?' I slipped automatically into colloquial

Peir-Dadeni, that Santhil wouldn't know. 'Don't think I can take too many shocks to the system – very funny, Hal.'

He gave way and chuckled, resting a claw-hand on my arm. It wouldn't be so bad if I wasn't glad to see the old rogue, I thought, quelling exasperation. There was laughter in his eyes, and that paradoxical Orthean combination of humour and utter seriousness.

'What can we do for you?' I repeated.

'You can help make certain that the right man has a chance to become *T'An Suthai-Telestre*.'

I must have glanced at Nelum Santhil because the dark male shook his head. 'Not myself, *t'an S'aranth*. I only support this.'

It's the *s'ans* who name one of their number to become *T'An* of a province, but to take the Crown one must – in the great Wellhouse below the Citadel, under the eyes of all gathered there – name oneself. So at the heart of all *telestre* politics and intrigue there is this final, public honesty.

'Who? Not you, Hal?' It would be like him to ask.

'Blaize n'ri n'suth Meduenin,' the old male said. 'The Rimon *s'ans* want to name him *T'An* Rimon and he won't hear of it; if he's not *T'An*, he can't take the Crown, and I think – Christie, disagree with me if you can – I think Blaize Meduenin is the best *T'An Suthai-Telestre* we could have now. Christie, we want you to talk to him!'

It stopped me dead. 'Why him? And why me?'

'He's been a mercenary,' Nelum Santhil said. 'We need a Crown who knows how to fight, and who knows how to avoid fighting. All Howice *T'An*-Roehmonde knows is how to keep himself *T'An*; Geren *T'an* Ymir isn't trusted, he's been out of the Hundred Thousand too often; and The Kyre's too remote a province for people to know Bethan *T'An* Kyre – '

'Romare Kerys-Andrethe will be *T'An* Rimon if Blaize won't, and Romare is a fool,' Hal said. He clasped six-fingered hands on the top of his staff, and stared down at the dusty floorboards. When he raised his head, his gaze had all the intensity of a younger man's. 'Why you? Christie, you know him. You crossed the Wall of the World in his company. He'll listen to you because . . .'

'Well?' I prompted.

The old male said thoughtfully, 'Because you and he should have been *arykei*, and he let the time go past. I don't say it lightly, but you're one of the few people that he trusts. If you tell him he should be *T'An* Rimon he'll believe you.'

Hal, you don't change. Always manipulating people, always working behind the scenes . . .

'He'd make a good *T'An Suthai-Telestre*, and perhaps it would be a good thing for the Coast if he were. I'm not convinced it would be the best thing for us.'

Hal looked at me shrewdly. ' "Us"?' Now is that the Company, or your government, or some other faction on Earth that we know nothing of?'

Voices from the street echoed in the silence, and *rashaku* cried. *Kekri*-flies danced in the window-arch, glittering blue and green. There was the scent, faint now, of *kazsis*-nightflower.

'Talk with him,' the old male said, in his own Peir-Dadeni tongue. 'Talk to him, and make up your own mind . . .'

I looked at him. 'Three words occur to me.'

' "I'll do it"?' Haltern suggested hopefully.

' "Devious old bastard . . ." ' I managed to translate the sense of the expression. He laughed. Nelum Santhil looked at us both in bewilderment.

'I'm a little worried about something else at this moment,' I said, 'as I haven't seen Corazon Mendez today—'

'Commander Mendez is with Romare Kerys-Andrethe, in the barracks at Hill-Damarie. Now if that eases your mind,' Hal said drily, 'you can answer my question.'

I said, 'Where will we find Blaize Meduenin?'

Skurrai-jasin jolted across the Square, the squat reptilian beasts treading down mossgrass that had rooted between the paving-stones. Their shaggy coats and cropped, metal-capped horns gleamed in the sun. Like the others, our driver avoided the shuttles that stood locked and silent at the south end of the Square. Across at the cliff-walk, twenty or so young Ortheans with curved knives were hacking back the vines and creepers. Above, the Citadel merged with the cream-blue sky. A warm haze put blurred shadows on the stone.

Haltern signalled the *skurrai*-carriage to pause, spoke to a male leading a *marhaz*, and several yards further on did the same thing, this time talking to a young female who led one of the beasts of burden. As the *skurrai-jasin* halted before the gates of the great Wellhouse he said, 'A week to the naming. We'll be ready. Ah, yes . . . you'll find Blaize in the Wellhouse here.'

I got down from the carriage and then paused, resting one hand on the brightly-painted wood. I studied the unremarkable face of Nelum Santhil.

'The *T'Ans* Melkathi had bad luck when you were their Portmaster, *t'an* Santhil, I wish you better luck with yours.'

The dark male winced. '*T'An* Haltern said you had a sharp wit. Are you still so bitter for your Orhlandis *arykei*?'

Haltern eased himself down from the carriage-step, clattering his staff. He made a gesture to the driver and the *skurrai-jasin* jolted away. Carrying Nelum Santhil to whatever other business a *T'An* Melkathi might now have.

'My Orhlandis . . . *arykei*?'

'The tale's told that way.' Haltern smiled. 'If it doesn't have you and Blaize *arykei*. Or you and Howice *T'An* Roehmonde.'

Ortheans must have a very curious idea of human sexual appetite. *Howice*?

'Ruric Orhlandis won't come back to the Hundred Thousand, Christie, if that's what you're thinking.'

He took my arm, leaning heavily on it. We walked up the steps and into the courtyard, where a crowd was in evidence; some talking, some cleaning, some eating. Many hailed the new Seamarshal of the Freeport with respect.

'Hal, about Ruric.'

He paused, leaning on his staff. The sun gleamed on that wispy, cropped mane. I saw he still wore a *harur-nazari* blade at the belt of his white, slit-backed robe. Haltern Beth'ru-elen: come off the sidelines at last, come out of the political shadows to be recognized as Seamarshal *T'An* Morvren.

'Blaize told you I made her exile . . . permanent.' Those pale eyes were less harassed, more adamantine. Then he said quietly, 'I tell myself she was traitor, land-waster, exile; she would become a leader for our enemies, there was nothing else I could do, and still I don't believe it.' He paused. 'She dreamed no other lives. I often wonder now, will she return from the Goddess's realm? Or had she so much Golden blood that she died as they did, with no rebirth?'

It was a physical pain not to say 'she's alive!'; I have risked her secrecy once, I can't do it again.

I let the silence stretch out. The old male at last began to walk on, turning his steps towards the Wellhouse entrance on the far side of the courtyard. I held his arm.

'There,' Haltern said.

Blaize Meduenin stood outside the arched entrance with a group of dark-maned Ortheans. Five or six young males and females, with chain-girdled tunics, and faces masked in scarlet, ochre, and indigo paint. From the Rainbow Cities, the subtropic lands of the far south. With them was a thin male, mane a black barbed-wire

666

tangle, tanned skin marked at ribs and hip with old white scars. Untanned leather garments marked him as being from one of the nomad tribes that live in the dead cities over the Wall of the World.

Haltern walked through the entrance into the dome-hall, beckoning for Blaize to follow. The fair-maned male excused himself from his companions. As we met, I had time to think how small the dome seemed, how shabby the tiers of stone seats leading down to the Wellmouth, and then the smell of the *becamil*-wax candles hit me; the candles they always used to illumine this dim amphitheatre. I felt as if someone had scooped my chest cavity out hollow.

'*T'An* Morvren, *t'an* Meduenin, give you greeting.' A dark-maned Wellkeeper bowed as he passed us, hurrying down the tiers towards a group of other Wellkeepers and Earthspeakers. Young *ashiren* in Wellhouse robes came respectfully to offer herb-tea. Hal waved them away. Blaize's eyes met mine. He smiled. And then must turn aside to answer a query from a *s'an* in Ymirian dress; reassure him and send him away.

And here we are, I thought. Hal, frail and silver-maned, but with all the dignity of the Seamarshal about him; Blaize, whose Rimon boots and britches and sleeveless jacket were all fine; *chirith-goyen* cloth and *marhaz* leather. Here we stand, deferred to, respected; where Suthafiori and SuBannasen and Orhlandis once stood, when Blaize was a shabby mercenary, and Hal a spy, and I nothing but wide eyes and youthful enthusiasm.

'Would you have believed this?' the stocky male said, and that half-scarred face twisted into the old smile.

Hal eased himself down on to the stone tier. 'Not when you hunted us at Oeth, into the Great Fens.'

'Not in Corbek,' I said, 'when you gave false evidence against me in a Wellhouse trial.'

Blaize grinned at that. Then he stood looking down at Hal, and his expression became serious. 'I was a mercenary then. I was under contract, following orders. That's the way I like it. You must know that through the years I served you in Morvren, I never wanted to be *T'An*.'

Haltern cupped his six-fingered hands over the top of his staff. He sighed, that frail body sagging. 'We've been friends for too many years to talk of "service" – or am I wrong in that?'

'No,' Blaize protested. He looked helplessly at me. 'Tell him, *S'aranth*. Why not leave the *telestres* to deal with the Coast, as they've always done?'

Haltern put in sharply, 'You're a soldier. You know the difference between raiding ships and an invasion.'

'And there's Earth technology to be taken into account,' I said. 'Earth weapons. You've – we've – got to make peace with the Coast. Or else the Company's going to let Cory's troops loose, and their stopping a war can be as nasty as others starting one. Blaize, you're trusted, the *s'ans* listen to you, for God's sake realize you have to take a stand. Be *T'An* Rimon. Be whatever else you have to.'

He looked at me consideringly. Aware of falling into rhetoric, I thought, How do I say what I mean?

'And if what the Hundred Thousand decides doesn't please Earth?' he said.

'I don't give a shit about Earth—'

They both turned startled eyes on me. I felt unprotected. The one still young, the other old: soldier and politician . . . In my panic I looked round to see if I'd been overheard. Doug Clifford was down in the group of Earthspeakers. Cory Mendez came in by the other entrance on the far side, without Romare Kerys-Andrethe. And then I saw Blaize smile, saw a silky humour in Hal's eyes.

'That's a dangerous fence to step over,' Hal said quietly. 'No going back. Your people, if they know, wouldn't let you.'

Blaize cut in with, 'Does it matter?' and embraced me; and then stepped back, and said to Haltern, 'You, Beth'ru-elen. Will *you* name yourself *T'An Suthai-Telestre* when Midsummer comes?'

Those pale eyes veiled. Candlelight and light from the roof-slot put shadows on his face; Hal's face, that I never could read easily. He said, 'If I were a younger man.'

And Blaize, very soberly, said, 'I can't carry the weight of it. I'm a fighter, not a politician. All I've learned from the years in Morvren is that no one knows enough to give orders to all the Hundred Thousand.'

I said, 'No one ever knows, but someone has to take the decisions all the same.'

His scarred face was shrewd. 'You push us into your patterns.'

'Either you're being cowardly,' I said, and saw the flare of anger on his face, that twisted the scar into something monstrous, 'either that, or you know your own limitations. I don't know. You'd better find out soon.'

'Yes,' Haltern said, 'we don't have much time.'

We both push you unfairly, I thought. From our assumed positions of superiority, trying to force you into something we won't or can't do.

And if I were *T'An Suthai-Telestre*? In this my city of Tathcaer, a charmed midsummer circle, and outside it the warships of the Coast, Sethri's hungry face, the dream of Empire in Kel Harantish, and the offworlders who began by bringing knowledge and end by bringing guns—

'Yes,' Blaize's voice interrupted, and I looked up to meet his gaze: he spoke as if he could read my thoughts.

I said, 'I'm sorry we ever came here. To Carrick V.'

He stood with his chin a little raised, claw-nailed hands resting on *harur*-blades. His gaze travelled round the hall – to the men and women in all the different fashions of Melkathi, Rimon, Roehmonde, Morvren, The Kyre . . . to the plain brown brick of the dome, and the shaft of light that plunged from the roof-slot to the black mouth of the shaft of the Well. The hum of voices rose and fell. *Becamil*-wax candles sputtered. A warm breeze drifted in from the courtyard, bringing the scent of *kazsis* and *marhaz* dung and cooking-fires.

He said, 'Kerys Founder marked out the *telestre* boundaries. That was after the Empire fell, when there was chaos. And I love the land. I'm an outsider, I hardly see Meduenin, but it has all my memories, I'd sooner cut off this hand than see it destroyed by outlanders. To change is to destroy.' Then he shrugged, and with all the mercenary's assurance, said, 'Sometimes change *has* to happen.'

Haltern caught my eye. And I thought, Yes, I know, only outsiders have the capacity to see such things. Outsiders like you and I and Blaize Meduenin.

'Be *T'An* Rimon,' I said. 'For no other reason than that I can't imagine Romare Kerys-Andrethe saying what you've just said.'

Blaize broke into laughter that turned heads clear across the dome. For that moment we were as we had been: mercenary, intelligencer, envoy. Hal's wheezy chuckles racked him. I grinned.

'Let's talk more of this later,' Haltern said. 'Come down and speak with the Wellkeeper now. There are Earthspeakers here from all the seven provinces. I want to talk with them, hear what they say about the most distant *telestres*. They've heard of my time in Morvren. I want to know if they'll call it just another Freeport madness – the thought that men and women of the Coast could come here, and share wilderness land.'

I followed him down the step to the next tier. Blaize remained standing, and I looked back and up at him.

The ex-mercenary said, 'When the *s'ans* ask me again – I'll be named *T'An* Rimon.'

*

669

Two twenty-seven-hour days lost themselves in a marathon of talk. Every Orthean in the city (and they continued to come in by the hundreds) heard of 'land-sharing', and wanted to talk about it with the *T'Ans*, the *takshiriye*, and the offworlders. Especially with the offworlders. Their objections were many and violent. Some time towards the late afternoon of Durestha Eighthweek Threeday I staggered back to Westhill-Ahrentine, exhausted. And stopped in the *telestre*-house's inner courtyard to look up at a blue sky brilliant with daystars and think, *Do we have a chance?*

These things have their momentum. Endless pressure, seemingly with no result, and then all in a minute it'll go. We only need the smallest toehold, I thought. If we can get some people from the *hiyeks* to talk here in Tathcaer. But how?

Cory Mendez walked out from the ground-floor rooms. She also glanced skyward. 'Lynne. Will you be travelling back to the southern continent with me?'

'When?'

'Today. Half the force are grounded there. My second in command is sending a shuttle down from the orbiter.' The hawk-faced woman paused. The warm wind scattered *ziku* spores crimson on her black coveralls, and as she brushed herself she said, 'Your association with the government envoy isn't wise. Under the circumstances I'd take the opportunity to put some distance there, were I in your position.'

And this is Company loyalty? Well, yes, I suppose it is . . . I changed the subject: 'What's your assessment of the situation here, Cory?'

'My assessment is that home office will let me down again and insist on "negotiations", until the situation's past repair. Whereas a quick surgical strike . . .' She pushed ornate silver rings up her thin fingers. 'You mean the *native* situation? An outbreak of hostilities. Within a very short time.'

Turning to leave, she added, 'I have no confidence of getting it – that would be *too* sensible for the Company's marketing side – but I've requested from Representative Rachel the free use of coercive power.'

I watched her walk out through the archway and into the city. What chills me is that it's just possible she has a point. If that aborted the Coast's invasion . . .

Here I stand with the hard stones of Tathcaer underfoot, hearing the distant voices of *ashiren*. Under the weight of such normality, I can hardly conceive the reality of what I'm trying to prevent.

'Lynne,' Doug Clifford called from one of the upper-storey

windows. 'The comlink's functioning again. Come and give me the benefit of your opinion on this.'

The holotank-image was intermittent, but recognizable as twelve-year-old stock-footage: the first satellite surveys of Carrick V.

'Which news-WEB put this out?'

'A small company,' Douggie said. 'They're syndicated to most of the inner worlds and, were I to hazard a guess, I'd say that most of their finance originates with the NuAsiaCo.'

'Your people at home know who to talk to, don't they.'

The voice-over fuzzed, then cleared. '—*Carrick V, one of the low-tech, sparsely-inhabited worlds near the Heart Stars. When asked about rumours that a form of alien technology has been discovered on Carrick V, a spokesman refused to comment. He also denied accusations that severe cultural disruption is being caused by the PanOceania multicorporate. The Enclave government with technical jurisdiction over Carrick V also refuses to comment.'* The image altered to the face of a brown-haired young woman, with slanting brows and direct green eyes. '*Roxana Visconti, for the Trismegistus WEB.*'

'That's an end-of-broadcast filler if I ever saw one,' I mused. 'Wonder if there's been anything since that?'

Doug keyed the holotank to Clear.

'If NuAsiaCo can put PanOceania in any kind of commercial difficulties, there's every likelihood that they will indeed do so.'

I went to the table and poured bowls of herb-tea from the half-empty jug, and took one back to Douggie. He put it down absent-mindedly on the edge of the holotank.

'Lynne, one of us will have to talk to Anzhadi-*hiyek.*'

I cupped the bowl, sipping the citrine liquid. 'Yes. At the moment, though, can *you* find anyone willing to let an outsider on to this continent?'

He rubbed at his lined forehead. 'No. You don't change two millennia of history in half a year. Lynne, the Orhlandis woman, I can appreciate she can't have her identity known; but surely she could exert some form of pressure on the Wellhouses?'

'She may be. I have to be so careful asking.'

Late afternoon sun slanted through the window-arches, patching the floorboards. The rooms still seemed disused. Covers remained on half the equipment. The shifting warm air brought the scent of *ziku* spores in, and rustled through old printouts and map-images still pinned to the walls. A rhythmic hollow clop came from the alley where *marhaz* and *skurrai* passed by.

'Call Molly Rachel,' Douggie said. 'You still have a technical right to be kept informed by the Company. I want to know—'

'What the storms are like on the Coast right now?'

He took from the holotank the tab that contained the Trismegistus broadcast, tucking it into his breast pocket. 'Pray for bad weather. We need the time.'

By the time the systems linked up to give me access to Molly, afternoon had passed into second twilight, and mist from the rivers muffled all the city's sounds. The upper-storey room was hot. I welcomed the cool night air.

The holotank began to image Molly Rachel. Her skin seemed blue-black in the interior lights of the shuttle. A soft sound ran in the background, a hissing that, before she could speak, broke into a crackle that split the image. The sound that followed I recognized as distant thunder.

I keyed in a climate profile, superimposed mid-image, and the Pacifican woman smiled a crooked smile when she saw it.

'I was going to ask how weather conditions were in your area,' I said. 'And the rest of the Coast?'

'Same as this morning, and the last three mornings.' Those long black fingers keyed an inset-image. The metal hulls of F90 shuttles shone wetly, rain drumming back inches with the force of its landing; the earth was a morass. Lightning spiked a barren horizon, and the shuttle's exterior sensor momentarily went black. Molly said, 'Storms in a holding-pattern from here, three hundred miles up the Coast. Climatology put it down to the Elansiir range. And the central-continent war damage.'

'What about the *hiyek* ships in the harbours?'

Molly shook her head. The tangled black hair, shaggy now, was pinned back with *del'ri*-wood combs; her coverall was crumpled. She looked as though she hadn't slept.

'The storms block surveillance,' she said. 'That and whatever atmospheric effect it is that the war devastation makes. At least the native ships can't slip away now. I'd hesitate to send one of the Company's amphibious craft out; *jath* and *jath-rai* are helpless.' She sighed. Her brown eyes were keen, but the rims were reddened. 'I seriously think we made a mistake in coming here. The natives are interested in settling old grievances, not in the benefits of technology.'

'Molly—'

'Calil bel-Rioch tells me that the "Emperor" here is threatening to forbid the T&A station, and it isn't half finished yet. She says he doesn't want the Coast families independent.'

Is that what Calil's aiming for, to be Emperor-in-Exile herself? I hate to say it but we could do worse than have a pro-technology leader in Kel Harantish . . . And then I thought of those yellow eyes, that slight droop of the lid; her smile at the imagined death of Santhendor'lin-sandru, who was also an Emperor.

'This isn't a scheduled call,' Molly Rachel reminded me. 'What do you want?'

'I want to talk to the Anzhadi. If I can get some of them over here and talking, other *hiyeks* will follow their lead.'

She said sourly, 'If you can find them. What do you think I've been trying to do? The Anzhadi are mingling in with the other *hiyeks* and keeping under cover. You can look for Sethri-safere in any of the eighty small ports between here and Quarth – my people have.'

I thought, Yes, Sethri doesn't want to fight the Emperor *and* attack the Hundred Thousand and nor do any of the other Anzhadi, they're not stupid. Only they've spent too many years knowing of the Hundred Thousand, looking at them with hungry eyes.

'You've heard from Cory Mendez?' I asked.

'Commander Mendez is on her way here.' Molly's noncommittal expression slid into weariness. She rubbed at her eyes. 'I've told her cultural taboos are too strong for her to station a detachment of the Peace Force with you right now. Lynne, we'd better come up with something soon—'

Because actual bloodshed will make you look bad on Company reports? Or is that too cynical?

'—because I'm running out of options,' Molly Rachel said. 'I can't play soft arbitrator if hostilities break out.'

CHAPTER 21

Midsummer-Eightyear

The next morning, six days before the solstice, they opened up the halls of the Citadel, that great sprawl of stone on its high crag. I took a *skurrai-jasin* up to the Square. Sea mist curled round the white roofs of Tathcaer, and held close to the ground the reptilian scent of the *skurrai*, the slightly overripe odour of the food-collection points. A little after first twilight and already the city alleys are crowded.

I found the Earthspeaker Cassirur Almadhera in the Stone Garden, up on Citadel Crag.

'There was a question I learned to ask when I was on Orthe before,' I said. 'Have the Wellhouses had any communication from the Hexenmeister of Kasabaarde?'

She straightened. The green and scarlet slit-backed robes were gone, replaced by undyed *becamil*-cloth. Her skin and robe were smeared with ochre, and she held a clump of mossgrass in one dirty six-fingered hand. Her eyes cleared.

'Christie. Have you forgiven me Barris Rakviri's death, then?'

I felt uncomfortable. 'That's no business of mine.'

'You judge the action.'

'I haven't the right to judge.'

She smiled the protest away. Morning sun gleamed on the Stone Garden's miniature cliffs and crags, on the smooth and carved rock-beds covered with scarlet, yellow, viridian and blue moss-grass. Dew collected in shallow pools, shadowed pools. Thousand-flower moss tumbled down a flight of steps that ended at Cassirur's feet.

'This could be rerooted,' she said absently, looking down at the moss on the choked stairway. The shadow of the Citadel slanted across this garden that lies between the sprawling building and the river cliff. A sheer hundred feet below the Oranon roared, dividing to pass the island-city. The smell of the river was rank in the air.

'About the Hexenmeister—'

Cassirur settled the clump of mossgrass in a dew-wet crevice. She wiped her hands on her robe, and brushed the mass of red mane away from her face. Clear light showed the lines in that reptilian skin.

Irrelevantly she said, 'Have you heard from the Tower that the Goddess was an invention of Kerys Founder, and Her Wellhouses set up only to put use of the Old Science under ban? That's untrue. She is older. When we lived in those great Golden cities we joined with Her in secret. She is older than the Tower knows.'

'Cassirur, I wish you'd answer a simple question!'

The scarlet-maned woman laughed. She moved away from the thousandflower-shrouded steps, and all of a sudden turned her face up to the sky. The nictitating membrane flicked back from her eyes and she gazed straight into the sun. Then she lowered that gaze to me. Such a radiant shadow I have seen in other eyes, long ago; Orhlandis eyes.

I said, 'What happens when men and women of the Coast land here and burn the *telestres*, kill you? Will you fight and die, or just die?'

'The *s'ans* say we should fight first, and then, if the men and women of the *hiyeks* do not return to their canals, give them what space here that we can.' She paused. Her tone was prosaic. 'We must see if they can be discouraged. The fighting will mean less of us, more food, so we can take them in. And if, as I think, they prove to be land-destroyers – why, then, we can kill them later, when they're divided amongst the Hundred Thousand. And having sent them to the Goddess, hope She brings them back to fertile lands.'

I stared.

'Don't take me for *s'aranthi*,' Cassirur Almadhera said. 'We don't need to hear from the Hexenmeister. We have always planned this, in the Wellhouses, if a numerous enemy should come against us.'

There in the early sun, this Orthean woman; standing in her dirty robe, bare high-arched feet planted four-square on the rock.

'Don't take me for an idiot,' I said. 'That might be the way to deal with an Orthean war. It revolts me, but it might be. These are Ortheans with human weapons. Yes, and who knows, maybe with Witchbreed devices of their own – will you give *saryl-kabriz* to *them*?'

White sun reflected back from the rock, drew curls of mist from wet mossgrass; dazzled me when I turned to walk back into the Citadel, away from that woman silhouetted against a daystarred sky. Cassirur's thoughtful voice came clearly to me:

'Perhaps yes. And perhaps not fight at all. Let them come freely amongst us, and then send them to Her Bright Realm with poison or with hidden knives. If you will hear it, *that* is what the sole message from the Tower these past six years has said. That old man the Hexenmeister would sooner pretend a belief in our Goddess than see a war fought with Witchbreed or Earth weapons.'

I kept on walking. Was it shock, that clarity in my mind, or familiarity, or both? So very Orthean, what Cassirur said, and I remember—

Memories that are the constructs of delusion.

Somewhere inside the interlocking halls of the Citadel I found Doug Clifford, after wandering through silent, dusty rooms, and halls where *ashiren* were setting out braziers to combat the chill in the air. He listened, in the long gallery, while I repeated Cassirur's words of an hour before.

'*No*,' he said. 'I'm fully aware of the principle of cultural toleration, but it does have inherent limitations.' Then, with a bright-eyed anger, 'Haven't they the plain common sense to avoid a massacre!'

'Ortheans look on death differently. As something they'll survive.'

'Corazon Mendez won't see it that way.' Doug halted by one of the slot-windows. '*I* don't see it that way.'

'Neither do I. But I'm not Orthean.'

Something in me wanted to protest that. I didn't let it. Doug and I walked on down the gallery, on the floor newly spread with *zilmei* pelts and matting. Voices called back and forth. There was the sound of heavy objects being moved.

'At least we'll know in advance when the invasion is going to happen,' I said. 'Molly will warn me when any *jath*-ships leave the southern continent. Doug, how can I report back to her on Cassirur? It was bad enough before this happened. Now what are we going to do?'

'Endeavour to ascertain whether it's what one might call a general conviction, or merely the prerogative of Earthspeakers and Wellkeepers.'

Here the long gallery opened into an octagonal hall, without the benefit of a connecting corridor. Other halls were visible through archways. Sun put blue shadows on white stone. No Witchbreed thing, this low-roofed warren. I could see through into a larger hall, where two pale-maned females were putting up hangings and ribbon-banners, and I wondered in which of these rooms I had first met that woman called Suthafiori, Dalzielle Kerys-Andre-the, Crown of the Hundred Thousand.

Doug touched my arm. 'Lynne, was my impression of the Orhlandis woman wrong? Would she use her position as Hexen-meister to encourage—'

'A massacre?' I prompted. That round squirrel-face was a stranger's face, then; Douglas Clifford, who could presume to judge *amari* Ruric Orhlandis. Why should it hurt me, to think she would do that? It's the Orthean way of thinking, and she's Orthean; and yet she's an outsider too. I said, 'I don't know, Douggie.'

There was something of the bantam about the small man as he gazed round, getting his bearings.

'I'll talk to Romare Kerys-Andrethe,' he said. 'He's here, I believe. And representative of some of the *s'ans*, wouldn't you say? Lynne, you talk with the *T'An* Haltern and Blaize Meduenin. We need to know who else thinks as Cassirur does. If *telestre*-Ortheans take that kind of violent action, I'm afraid it could be seen as an excuse for Earth to take over the government of Carrick V – and God knows to what kind of action *that* might lead.'

Which of the *T'Ans* first took up quarters in the Citadel I don't know, but where one went, all followed. I found the *T'An* Seamar-shal's new quarters in a high tower, one of the few rooms with a slot-window. Haltern was looking down at the city.

I saw nothing but upper air, and the flick of *rashaku*-flight against a sky swimming with stars, and then coming to the stone sill, I saw what he saw. *Marhaz*-riders crossing the Rimon hills and the Ymirian meadows: groups of three and four, and *ashiren* mounted on the smaller *skurrai*, and by their dress – only spots of vermilion, green, and gold at this several miles distance – they must be from the furthest *telestres*. North Roehmonde, Peir-Dadeni, The Kyre. The wind blew warm in my face. Humid sea mist began to roll up from the harbour, gradually blotting out *telestre*-houses, blurring the white walls, turning the heat-sensitive *lapuur* from green to ash-grey . . . Here one could look down into inner court-yards of blind-walled *telestre*-houses, see young *ashiren*, bright-clothed adults, *marhaz* in stables, and fountains playing. Roosting *rashaku* rose up in clouds, disturbed, as *telestre*-Ortheans came back to their city.

'The Andrethe of Peir-Dadeni is here,' the old male said. He sank back on a couch-chair. It was piled with grey and black *zilmei* pelts, against the chill of the stone walls.

'Are there more to come?'

'The *T'An* Ymir. Geren has no love for cities.'

The inner bead-curtain swung back, and a male in Morvrenni robe brought herb-tea. His brown mane was intricately braided, and there were gold studs set in the skin between his fingers; and something in the way he hovered over Haltern n'ri n'suth Beth'ru-elen made me move, turn my back to the window, so I had the old male's face under that light. His wispy silver mane seemed thin. But it was the hollows in that wrinkled face that alarmed me.

As the *l'ri-an* left, I said, 'Hal, I haven't suggested this before, partly because we have comparatively little data on Orthean physiology, but one of the Company medics—'

Haltern shook his head.

I asked, 'Why not?'

With no self-pity or melodrama, but with infinite regret, he said, 'It would make no difference. I shall die quite soon.'

Half of me was shocked, half not. Well, I have been with Ortheans long enough to know something of them; that accounts fully for the sense of familiarity. I came to sit on the couch-chair beside him.

'Soon?'

'Soon, *S'aranth*. No,' he lifted one thin hand, and when his pale eyes met mine, they were full of a wicked humour. 'I shall use this, you see. I hope to see Meduenin as *T'An Suthai-Telestre*. Midsummer falls in six days. Now if I tell the new *T'An* Rimon that I stay only to see him as Crown . . .'

A sudden lack of expression crossed his face. He lifted a hand to his mouth. I saw that he chewed *ataile* leaf, that herb that brings both pleasure and eradication of pain.

'Hal—'

'*Ataile* is a small vice. Nor I think, now, shall I be concerned over its addictive properties. No,' he said, quite differently, 'don't grieve, Christie.'

'Hal, do you remember, in Roehmonde; that woman Sethin was ill, and she said she wouldn't stay for the pain? You stay. That's what hurts me now. I wish you'd let me call a medic in.'

'If it pleases you, do.'

The fire in the brazier burned low. I leaned forward to put *ziku*-wood chips on it.

'You mustn't weep,' he said. 'Christie, you were so young when I first saw you, so frightened and so shrewd! I have you to thank if I understand anything at all of offworlders.' He rested a hand on my shoulder, and there was no weight there; bones thin and hollow as a bird's. He said, 'This body pains me. Still, I would live, if I could, any way that I could'

I looked up, startled, unguarded.

'—How can I leave young Meduenin without some guiding hand? And the *telestres*? Your people, I don't trust them, Christie; I never have. To go to Her now—' He broke off. The pale and whiteless blue eyes were veiled with membrane. In the wreckage of that face I could still see him: Crown Messenger, politician, spy, friend.

I said, 'Cassirur Almadhera doesn't regret death, for herself, or for others.'

'Ah.' Hal nodded. 'That's the church. But no matter that we return, it means losing *this* life, *these* people; and it's arrogant of me to think I can't be spared, isn't it, *S'aranth*? Arrogant and true. We have no Suthafiori, no Kanta Andrethe, now.'

He leaned forward to the table to pour herb-tea. The weight of the stone jug was all but too much. I dared not help him. The cold of the stone walls must have got into my bones: somewhere deep inside I was shivering. *You mustn't grieve*, he said. Ah, Hal. That sly, quiet humour of his; now it hurts.

'Let me sit with you for a while,' I said. 'Hal, I don't believe what you do. We shan't meet again.'

He pulled the *zilmei* furs more closely round him. 'We can't afford to sit, Christie, with only six days until Midsummer – I must have people come here, if I can't go to them; you can tell me what happens in the city. I shall be in the Wellhouse on solstice day.'

He paused then, and more quietly said, 'You and she were alike. You and the Orhlandis. If I see her in that bright realm, will she ask me why I've abandoned the land? What will I say to her?'

I took both of those thin, six-fingered hands in mine. I felt a very Orthean humour, some emotion between wonder and melancholy; thinking, Yes, that's Hal, you'd use even your death to find out what you want to know. Isn't that just like you?

I ached to tell him the truth.

'Ruric would have approved,' I said. 'Of everything. Even the manner of her death, perhaps; it came out of as great a love for the Hundred Thousand as she had. Isn't it strange where that can lead. She burned Orhlandis *telestre*, and you . . .'

His hands tightened on mine, but with so little strength that they seemed boneless. 'It's done. I would undo it if I could.'

Droplets of sea mist sparkled on the white stone walls. For all that there was business awaiting the *T'An* Seamarshal, for all that preparations for Midsummer demanded attention, we sat there in the weak sunlight, in silence, until the harsh clangour of the city bells marked out the hour of noon.

*

For three of the next six days I was the only offworlder in Tathcaer. Douggie took the shuttle to the Coast to try and talk with Anzhadi-*hiyek*, but his transmissions reported only failure. Sethri and his *raiku* were missing. On the fourth day Corazon Mendez and a group of her officers overflew the land round Tathcaer, and caused problems by attempting to land in the city; a rocky islet just beyond the estuary, Kumiel, was eventually set aside by the *T'An* Ymir for this purpose. And that made me realize: Tathcaer is a city again, with inhabitants and proscriptions and *takshiriye*, it has a Court and will have a Crown, we can no longer treat it as deserted . . .

And Tathcaer for those six days lay under a sweltering heat. *Lapuur* expanded their feather-fronds, shadowing the white walls with greenery. Passers-by hugged alley walls, where the shadows were coolest. Ortheans, still coming in from the surrounding countryside, slept outside in sun-baked courtyards; and though it was quiet from noon until second twilight, after that a hubbub of voices arose; Ortheans drinking herb-tea and *siir*-wine in brick courtyards, and even the smallest *ashiren* sitting still to listen and ask questions. On long walks from Westhill-Ahrentine to the Citadel and back I heard two topics of conversation. Overt: who is most suited to be Crown? Covert: are the Wellhouses right when they say what we should do when the invaders come?

I talked with them, and with the *T'Ans* of Rimon, Ymir, and Roehmonde; with the Andrethe of Peir-Dadeni, the *T'An* Seamar-shal and *T'An* Melkathi and *T'An*-Kyre.

The last day of Durestha Eighthweek: 'The question is,' I said, 'what will the *hiyeks* do? They must know the Hundred Thousand could be planning to divide them up and then kill them.'

Douggie raised his eyebrows. 'Take hostages from the *telestres*? No, that only succeeds if there's that fear of death.'

Heat reflected back from walls into the courtyard of the com-panion-house, where we sat under feather-fronded *lapuur* and the black and scarlet *ziku*. Spore cases floated down through the humid air. It was a big courtyard, several groups of Ortheans were sitting round tables talking or playing *ochmir*, and shaggy bronze *marhaz* were stabled in a pen on the far side. *Kekri*-flies hovered over heaps of dung. There was a rank smell from the harbour, visible through the archway entrance.

'My guess is that the Coast Ortheans won't split up,' I said. 'Would you? They'll take some land, some fertile land, and try to – well, in effect, build a Maherwa or a Reshebet. Not *hiyeks* taking control of *telestres*, but a *hiyek* province in the Hundred Thousand.'

Doug, about to answer, looked past me at the archway. 'Good grief.'

I looked over my shoulder. A frail, silver-maned male; staff in one hand, the other resting on a younger male's shoulder – Haltern Beth'ru-elen, and the *T'An* Melkathi, Nelum Santhil. While I gaped, Hal limped up to us and sank down on a wooden couch-chair.

'*Siir*-wine, if you please,' he said to Santhil, and when the dark male had gone into the companion-house, smiled at us. 'I feel a little better, I think. Don't tell Blaize Meduenin. I'm still hoping to make him take the Crown.' His pale eyes gleamed.

'Hal,' I said weakly; then shook my head. 'I give up.'

'Very wise, *s'aranth-te*.'

A small child, dark-maned and some six seasons old, followed Nelum Santhil out of the companion-house; and coming up to us, said, 'Will you play *ochmir*, *t'ans*?' and then fell silent, gazing at offworlders. Doug took the board and counters from *kir*. I saw a glance pass between Hal and Santhil, and the *T'An* Melkathi went off towards one of the other groups of players.

All intrigue under the surface, I thought, who knows what's happening? The *takshiriye* hear word from all the Hundred Thousand *telestres*, and not all those words are for others' ears . . .

'—a *hiyek* province in the Hundred Thousand,' Doug Clifford finished repeating our discussion as he set up a three-handed game of *ochmir*. Those small bright eyes flicked up to surprise whatever unguarded expression Haltern might have. He hadn't.

'A Witchbreed province,' Hal corrected. 'Listen to what's said here. The Coast *hiyeks* have the canals, that's Witchbreed science, and the *telestre* people won't see it as a "province" but as a seed of a future Empire.'

'Call it a colony,' I said. 'Call it what you like, I can see it being attacked. If not with *harur*-blades, then with something to starve them out of the land. Hal, could your people be brought to fire the land? Become land-destroyers, as once in Melkathi—'

'No!' His denial was too emphatic.

We played in silence for a time, making those alliances that occur in *ochmir* with three players: Hal and I, Hal and Doug, Doug and I. A shadow fell across the table. When I looked up, it was to see the clear eyes and scarlet mane of Cassirur Almadhera.

She grinned at Haltern. 'Down at the harbour, listening to travellers' gossip? And you so sick you couldn't leave the Citadel! Or so the Meduenin told me . . .'

'You've no business to follow a sick old man.' Haltern, ruffled, hitched his *chirith-goyen* robe round his thin shoulders; more piqued than anything else. 'It seems She spares me for a little time yet – but not for my ease. How did you find me?'

Cassirur Almadhera indicated some *ashiren* who were sweeping the courtyard free of *ziku* spore cases. Two of the children grinned, and I recognized them as hers. Haltern snorted. The light of Carrick's Star shone a pale gold here, slanting down through the feathery *lapuur*, gilding his pale mane; dazzling on Cassirur. It shone warm on the dusty flagstones, and, past the shadow of the arched entrance, on the masts of *jath*-ships moored at that dock. Not far from this companion-house at the foot of Crown Way, I had first disembarked, entering the Hundred Thousand.

'Come up to the Citadel,' Cassirur said. 'It's time for the *T'Ans* of the provinces to lay down their authority. Tomorrow there will be named a *T'An Suthai-Telestre*. Tonight the city is under the authority of the Wellhouses.'

Haltern stood, beckoning Nelum Santhil over from one of the other tables.

'We'll come,' I said. 'Doug, we should speak with the *T'Ans* again before the transfer of authority happens.'

Skurrai-jasin stood outside the entrance of the companion-house. The stocky, reptilian beasts nibbled at *kazsis*-vine with their pointed upper lips while they waited; and the sun shone gold on the fine-fibred shaggy pelts. A cool breeze blew off the harbour. Masts creaked. I gazed along the line of ships – fewer now than when the city was the port for all outlanders entering the Hundred Thousand – and at the cloth awnings of food-sellers' booths on the quay, and at the crowds. Haltern beckoned me to his carriage, leaving Cassirur to follow in the next with Doug and Nelum Santhil. I sat down in the *jasin*'s padded wooden seat. The flagstones jolted us. The driver leaned forward to shout at bright-robed Ortheans to move out of the way. Sun and humid heat blurred their voices, blurred the gleam of gems and *harur*-blades. When I glanced back I saw Nelum Santhil had left his *skurrai-jasin* and was walking across the quay to a Melkathi ship.

'Do you trust him?' I said.

Haltern Beth'ru-elen smiled. 'No. I've known too many *T'Ans* to do that.'

'Hal, you're *T'An* Seamarshal!'

'That must prove them untrustworthy . . . *S'aranth*, he's afraid. We all are. There are rumours that the Coast Ortheans have Witchbreed weapons newly remade.' Here he shrugged, and reached into the sleeves of his white robe for *ataile* leaves; and said indistinctly as he chewed them, 'My *takshiriye* Messengers report that to be false, and I think it so. What may be true is that Earth technology and Earth weaponry is finding its way to the *hiyeks*.'

The *skurrai* carriage wheeled as the driver shouted curses, avoiding a cart piled high with shelled edible *hura*. Then we swung away from the docks, entering the city.

I said, 'Have you thought? If I were Sethri Anzhadi, I know what part of this land I'd try to take and hold . . . Tathcaer. Take this city, and the nearest farming *telestres* in Ymir and Rimon.'

'It makes no difference,' Haltern said. 'If there's such a cancer in the Hundred Thousand we can't leave it, we must cut it away or kill it, even if it is the white city. You asked me, could we become land-destroyers . . . I fear for Tathcaer.'

We jolted through the narrow alleys up to the Citadel Square. The *skurrai-jasin* often stopped, hailed by Ortheans who wanted to question the *T'An* Seamarshal. Peir-Dadeni riders with manes pulled up in plumes on the crowns of their heads, and braided intricately down their spines, leaned six-fingered hands on the sides of the carriage or gestured extravagantly. Plainly-dressed Ymirians put stolid questions, their eyes veiled against the summer sun. They walked barefoot in dusty alleys black with shadow; and in the narrow gap of sky between buildings daystars shone like a scatter of salt.

Must war come here? I thought. War with weapons that Sethri Anzhadi will call 'Witchbreed', that will be black-market Earth weapons, and really where's the difference between them? How can Tathcaer be defended against *that*?

The Square was crowded. Ortheans called comments to the *T'Ans* who passed, going up the cliff-walk to the Citadel. I gave Haltern my arm and we made slow progress up the zigzag walk.

'We shall see,' he said, pausing, 'if tomorrow in the Square the *s'ans* name us *T'An* again . . . And then to see who will be *T'An Suthai-Telestre* . . .'

I let him get his breath. The city sweltered below: Square, Wellhouse, and all. Up on the crag I saw no Crown Guard, but the brown robes of Earthspeakers and Wellkeepers were everywhere. They directed us, with Doug and Cassirur (and where, I thought, is Nelum Santhil?) to a low-roofed hall that was lit only by windows facing into an inner courtyard.

As Cassirur went to speak with an elderly male Wellkeeper, Doug Clifford moved up beside me.

'Dalzielle Kerys-Andrethe held audiences here before she died, the last time I was in Tathcaer.' He kept his voice low, not to be overheard in that crowded place. 'It wasn't often that she allowed offworlders to be present.'

Ribbon-banners hung from the walls, muted by the crepuscular light. Both the great hearths were bare. Two or three dozen *telestre*-Ortheans clustered together in the middle of the hall, their robes and gems rich; and I saw how one fair-maned male wearing the silver circlet of a *T'An* had gold studs set between the fingers of his delicate hands – and is that Khassiye? I thought. A thin, proud face: Cethelen Khassiye Reihalyn, minister to the then Andrethe when I knew him. When he refused me entrance to the city Shiriya-Shenin, after I came down, a footsore refugee, from those mountains called the Wall of the World . . .

'*T'An* Khassiye,' I said, greeting him; and Haltern, leaning heavily on my arm, said, '*T'An* Khassiye is Andrethe of Peir-Dadeni now.'

Khassiye smiled, his thin face looking little older. '*T'an* Christie. *T'An* Seamarshal. You've come to lay down that authority? It's a heavy burden for a man not well.'

'Yours is the heavier,' Haltern said, 'since being adopted *n'ri n'suth* into the Andrethe *telestre*, I think. Reihalyn was a low-river *telestre*, wasn't it, *T'An*?'

Khassiye flushed. Debate from other groups overtook us. That needling rivalry between the *T'Ans* amused me; I didn't need to follow all its finer detail. As I stood and looked at the people gathered in the hall, I recognized many faces, pointing out to Doug those that he might not recognize:

'*T'An* Howice of Roehmonde . . .' A plump male, swathed in *zilmei* pelts and sweating because of it: when I was in the northern province of Roehmonde, it was he who imprisoned me for a Wellhouse trial. '*T'An* Bethan; I never knew The Kyre province well, she's a stranger; that's *T'An* Geren Hanathra—'

Douggie peered at the large, fair-maned male. 'Wasn't he a shipmaster? And mixed up with the Orhlandis woman?'

'He was Ruric's *arykei*. It was his ship that brought me from the Eastern Isles to Tathcaer, the first time I came to the Hundred Thousand.'

That progress brought me to a position from where I could see the far end of the long, low hall. A marble block was set up there. Massive, almost translucent in the shadowy light . . . Two of those young Ortheans who act as *l'ri-an* stood by it, with a male in Earthspeaker's robes. The stone was carved in relief with *marhaz*, *zilmei*, trailing *kazsis*-vines, *hanelys*-flower. On its flat top surface were cut seven circles, Well symbols, that might hold the silver circlet of a *T'An* and were empty now; and an eighth circle cut deep into the stone, that held the plain gold circlet worn by the *T'An Suthai-Telestre*.

'The ceremony's timed for noon,' a voice said behind me. I turned. It was Blaize Meduenin. The light half hid his face, but gleamed on that silver streak in his mane. He still wore plain mercenary's gear.

'Is that the way for a *T'An* Rimon to dress?' I teased.

'We need more than pretty finery now. Christie, if they name me *T'An* Rimon tomorrow, I'll raise up companies of fighters from the Rimon *telestres*. We need a *T'An* Commander of the *telestre* forces, now; the new Crown should appoint one.' His hands fell automatically to the hilts of *harur-nilgiri, harur-nazari*.

Does that mean you'd sooner be *T'An* Commander? I wondered. Or does it sound like a *T'An Suthai-Telestre* deciding policy? Out of all these here, you're the only one that really knows the *hiyeks* and Earth. Other than Haltern; but Hal . . .

'Where's the *T'An* Melkathi?' Blaize asked, running his gaze over the group present. 'If Nelum Santhil's going to be here by noon, he's leaving it late.'

Now there's a man I wouldn't be sorry to see not named as *T'An* Melkathi tomorrow, I thought. Nelum Santhil Rimnith, who once took bribes from Kel Harantish – what would Ruric think if she knew? And she *does* know, I imagine; there isn't much the Hexenmeister doesn't hear.

And I wish she could be here now.

I looked round at the company, the *T'Ans* of the provinces, those who accompanied them; the shaven manes of Wellkeepers and Earthspeakers, and the lively young faces of the *l'ri-an*. All those alien faces. Wide, whiteless eyes; narrow chins. And the thin bodies in scarlet, blue and amber-coloured robes; the delicate high-arched feet and strong six-fingered hands . . . and their voices, a babel of the languages of the seven provinces. *Harur*-blades clashed gently as they moved.

None of them are Suthafiori, none of them are *T'An* Commander Ruric; but still, it's the same land, I thought. Though I saw Cassirur Almadhera talking with Doug, it didn't stop a surge of hope. There's a way through this, if we can find it. Haltern, Blaize; even Khassiye and Santhil and Howice; they're more practised at keeping the *telestres* whole than we can ever imagine, practised over long years and long lives . . .

Because I was watching Cassirur with Doug, I saw the elder of her black-maned children enter the hall and approach her. She bent her head to listen to the *ashiren*, and her face changed. There was a commotion at the door, and then two more people entered. One offworlder – *what the hell is Cory Mendez doing here now?* And the other, half-crippled with the haste in which he'd arrived, was the dark-maned Nelum Santhil. The talking in the hall stopped. Outside, noon bells began to ring. They went unnoticed, except that Nelum Santhil raised his voice to be heard over them: 'There's no time for ceremonies,' he said. 'Tell the *s'ans* in the city. If we're to have a Crown, we must have one *now*. There's no more time.'

He reached out and gripped the arm nearest him, which was Cassirur's, and leaned on that while he struggled for breath. We stood frozen in that twilight hall, waiting. The clamour of the noon bells ceased.

Into that silence he said, 'Warships from the Coast landed at Rynnal and Vincor and Rimnith this morning. They're burning the *telestres*. They're burning Melkathi.'

CHAPTER 22

First Strike

'Why the *fuck* weren't we warned?' I demanded.

Cory's sharp face was livid with anger. 'Surveillance showed nothing. Those vessels must have slipped out of the Coast ports under cover of hurricane conditions – damn Rachel! She should have told me primitive craft could survive that.'

'Where are they now?'

The hum of voices in half a dozen languages almost drowned her out, but I heard her say: '—heat-sensors can't tell one native craft from another. I'm going to overfly the area. It's the only way. Jamison; Ottoway! *Move!*'

Two of her young officers fell in beside her as she pushed through the crowded entrance and out of the hall, head high, that sleek white hair a blazon. I forced my way through the press of bodies to Doug Clifford's side.

'The Peace Force is going to Melkathi.'

'So am I,' he said grimly. 'This will have to be reported. I'll take the government shuttle. I'll send out tapes to every WEB in the Heart Worlds, let them *see* what the Company's doing here.'

'You'll need a pilot, then – I'll come.'

He nodded. The low entrance of the hall was jammed with bodies, and I shoved between Khassiye and Howice *T'an* Roehmonde, aware that Doug followed; ignored a question from Cassirur on the way out, and at last came half-walking and half-running out into the sunlight at the top of the cliff-walk. The light of Carrick's Star was momentarily blinding. I stopped. Doug pointed, and I saw far away pinpricks of light on the Ymirian hills – heliographed warnings.

'The shuttle's on Kumiel. Damn tech restrictions!' Doug's brevity and irritation were uncharacteristic.

'Look.'

As we hurried down the cliff-walk, I indicated the mass of Ortheans in the Square. Nothing but a mosaic of heads and bodies:

impenetrable. In fascination I saw waves of shock travel out from those nearest to the great Wellhouse entrance, heard the buzz of confusion, and realized it must mean news was coming in on the *rashaku*-relay. Then we were down in the hot, humid air at Crown Gate.

I caught a glimpse of black. *Cory?* Before I could call to her, she commandeered a *skurrai*-carriage, and her harsh authoritarian voice rang out, clearing away the nearest crowds. *And the Peace Force shuttles are on Kumiel too* – I had a blackly humorous urge to laugh. Then a pointed muzzle showed between a group of fur-clad Roehmonders. I seized Doug's arm, pulled him into the *skurrai-jasin* and caught up the harness, and as the squat beast heaved the wooden vehicle off over the flagstones a weight made it dip. Startled, I glanced round. Blaize Meduenin swung himself up on the back.

'One of the *T'ans* must see Melkathi, and quickly,' he said. Doug blinked, and then muttered agreement.

We have to know what's happening, have to know if it *is* an attack; how bad, what size force, what damage—

Skurrai-jasin are not fast. As we trotted down between *telestre*-houses in that sweltering noon, I was rigid with impatience; coaxing every advantage from the beast. I caught my face growing heated, aware that we presented a ridiculous spectacle.

'I can't get a response from the Coast base,' Doug said, mouth to wristlink. 'Nor from the orbiter. It must be the storms.'

Will it take us longer to cross the city, to come to the harbour, to be ferried out to Kumiel, than to fly the shuttle a hundred miles down the coast of Melkathi – yes, dammit, yes. And while we're doing this, what's happening there?

I pulled the *skurrai*'s harness and the beast shouldered its way between stalls in the Guild-Ring. Doors were shut here, entrances barricaded; and anxious Ortheans in Rimon and Ymirian dress stood by the wooden display platforms. No trade in this market now.

'They know,' Blaize said softly. Membrane slid over his whiteless blue eyes. He gripped the back of the *skurrai-jasin*, boots planted firmly on the wheel-guard. When Ortheans tried to stop the carriage, he bawled at them with all the authority of a mercenary commander.

Coming down to the docks, the city was in uproar. Arguments, fights, panic-stricken barring of *telestre*-house entrances. Then suddenly it was open sunlight, salty air, as we swung on to the quay. Across the bright water, a *jath-rai* was already tacking for Kumiel.

Cory Mendez? If we could only get through to Molly Rachel –
what will she order the Peace Force to do?

'Damn all proscriptions of technology,' Doug Clifford muttered.

Blaize jumped down on to the stones of the quay. *Harur*-blades
jingled. He signalled to a *jath-rai* moored at steps near us, had brief
words with the shipmaster. I glanced back as I got down from the
skurrai-jasin, but the shoulder of the hill hid the Citadel now.

'This is what we get for keeping to the rules.' I looked at Doug.
'Cory Mendez won't put up with these restrictions now, you
realize that? And if Sethri and the Anzhadi *do* have black market
Earth technology – they won't keep to the rules.'

A moment of stillness. Doug squinted against the brilliance of
Carrick's Star on Tathcaer harbour, scratched at his grizzled red-
grey hair.

'Another boundary crossed,' he said. 'Another restriction
removed.'

There are protections that are intangible, only noticed when
they're gone; and I had time to shiver, quite literally, and think,
How long before there are no rules at all? and then Blaize called,
and hurried us up the swaying plank to the *jath-rai*'s deck.

The small craft rocked in the swell. Kumiel Island hardly seemed
to grow closer. The cool wind left my hair stiff with salt and lips
dry, and I gratefully took the flask of *siir* that Blaize handed me,
and drank as I stood at the ship's rail, and saw the Peace Force
shuttle lift off from Kumiel with a hurried roar. The heat of
Carrick's Star made rocks, sea and craft shimmer.

'Sunmother!' Blaize hit one stocky fist into his open hand.
'For ships to cross the Inner Sea in Stormsun—' and then he
grinned crookedly: 'Sethri Anzhadi. He would have made a good
mercenary.'

'How can you say that?'

'Pride in the skills of war,' Blaize Meduenin said. 'You should
listen to your Corazon Mendez, *S'aranth*. If this is to become an
Earth war, perhaps it should be ended by Earth's ways.'

That scarred face was open, honest; and he met my gaze as if
this was a serious possibility he discussed. *Once a mercenary, always
a mercenary?* Before I could say more, the *jath-rai* scraped Kumiel's
tiny quay.

Doug Clifford spared no backwards glance for us, barely giving
us time to enter the government shuttle before he palmed the exit
shut. Sunlight replaced by green interior light: summer's heat by
cool air, and I fell into the pilot's seat and put the console through
as fast a take-off sequence as I ever hope to, and before the lurch

that announced liftoff, Douggie was halfway to keying in *record* on the holotank and simultaneously opening all channels on the comlink. Blaize Meduenin leaned on the back of my chair, studying the small navigation-holo.

'I'll key us to follow the coastline east,' I said.

'A hundred and fifty *seri*,' Blaize directed. 'Christie, use the Melkathi sandflats to place us.'

Say, a hundred and eighty miles. By the time I'd keyed a recognition pattern, Doug had the comlink at last functioning:

—*visual contact made o1.76.345/97.31.823; repeat, 01.76*—

—*Ottoway, report. Report position. Where is Green Two?*

—*Green Two repor*—

White noise blanked all channels, then faded intermittently.

—*drop into low orbit from the hi-orbit station, form up on latitude 65: stabilize and observe.*

Error-rate on satellite survey equipment up to 83%. Fucking hell, what kind of atmospherics does this world—

Doug keyed the volume low. The three of us moved to the large holotank, studying exterior-image. A haze partly obscured the land beneath us. Blue-grey sea merged with Ymir's blue-grey hills. One highlight from Carrick's Star blazed off the water, following us eastwards. At this low level of flight, no more than two thousand feet, the roads that mark *telestre*-boundaries are visible as white threads; *telestre*-houses are perfect miniatures. They were fewer and further between, now, as we began to fly over Melkathi, that sandy, barren land.

'Keep the heat-sensors trained,' Doug ordered.

'It could be just a skirmish. One ship or two, or—'

'The *rashaku*-relay says fifty *jath* warships,' Blaize said. 'Exaggeration, of course. But by how much?'

The shuttle bucked, kicked in empty air; and I leaned back to the pilot's console, saw we were registering other air traffic – Cory's shuttle and the low-level orbital surveillance craft – and corrected for it. So long as her ships stick to surveillance . . .

'Why don't they answer?' Douggie said, frustrated; and then made an abrupt shift to public voice as Pramila Ishida's face came on the comlink screen. 'Put me in contact with Molly Rachel, please. I must speak with the Company representative.'

'I don't have time for this. We have our own problems,' the Pacifican girl said, her expression somewhere between exasperation and fear. 'Molly Rachel is in Kel Harantish, no contact is possible, I'm afraid—'

I leaned over Douggie and said to her, 'Has Cory Mendez been in touch with Molly? Does Molly know what's happening here?'

White noise cut her speech, the image fuzzed and died. I was still working out whether it was a breakdown or a deliberate cutting of the contact when Blaize stabbed one claw-nailed finger at the main holotank: *'There!'*

Flat land baked under the light of Carrick's Star. Here the coast ran down into mudflats and sandbars, fringed with white surf. Black smoke smeared the eastern horizon. I swung the shuttle seawards, then inland, dropping down below one thousand feet. The black smear became a tower of smoke, billowing up, spreading at the crown; seeping across the sky as we came closer to it, and we entered a sepia light.

'Those are Coast *jath*,' Blaize said.

Hoop-masted metal ships gleamed on the sandflats, and as we came closer I saw how they listed to one side, beached; the sand churned up round them. Nothing moved.

Doug's hands were poised delicately over the sensor controls, his face showing an intent concentration, as if he were a musician or engraver. 'The heat-sensors aren't picking up anything large enough to be humanoid life . . . That fire is some thirty miles inland.'

'Rimnith,' Blaize said.

Even Doug looked up at that tone. I felt how earth is kin to Ortheans, that crumbling warm and fertile earth as close to them as their skin: to hurt it is to hurt them.

I swung the shuttle inland, and the smoke of the burning grew thicker. The root of that dark tower was a spot near low hills, and smoke billowed up thick and black, and at its foot there was a tiny spark of orange. White specks in the air resolved into shuttles on hover-mode: Cory Mendez and the Peace Force. I let us overshoot, skimming the edge of walls of darkness, smoke that rose up and blotted out all light. Even with air-purifiers, the smell of burning leaked through into the cabin.

'I want to go in,' I said.

Doug turned from monitoring the holo-record. 'That would be very unwise, Lynne.'

'Look down there.'

From this height they were only dots, hardly moving on a track that must be (given the speed we were moving) another ten or fifteen miles inland. But there were too many of them. Blaize said nothing, but I knew he recognized that pattern. Refugees.

'I'm taking us down. There might be something we can do.' I looked at Doug. 'Record it. Put it out on the WEBs; this is proof of what the Company's caused here, *it might help stop it before it goes any further.*'

Blaize said nothing as I keyed in a landing-pattern, and the shuttle sank down, drifted in hover-mode to settle astride an earthtrack on a barren and sandy heath. As the power died, he touched the hilt of *harur*-blades.

'We know where the *hiyeks* were,' he said then, curtly nodding at the holo-image of burning land. 'We don't know where they are now.'

We all have our own ghosts. I never thought that I should stand again in Melkathi and smell burning.

Even here, a dozen miles distant, the air was citrine; flecks of black ash drifting down from no detectable source. The earth felt warm underfoot. Here was little but sand, and sparse *hanelys*-tanglebush and *siir*. The heath's dips and hollows made it impossible to see far in any direction. Blaize, stepping from the shuttle-ramp, unselfconsciously bent down to touch the earth, and to sign himself on the breast with the Circle of the Goddess. Doug Clifford joined us, shutting off his wristlink.

'Cory wants to know precisely what we civilians are doing in a hostile area,' he said. 'I thought a communications failure might be tactful at this juncture. After I told her that we had a temporary power-fault.'

'Listen—' And I realized I'd automatically stepped to one side, CAS IV loose in its holster, the old Service training surfacing after all these years. I didn't draw the stungun. Blaize looked perfectly relaxed, and I know how fast he can move.

Because the terrain was so irregular, we heard them before we saw them. The pad of *marhaz* and the jingle of their harness, loud in that noon heat and silence, and voices . . . The first *marhaz* topped the rise, a dozen yards away. A thin beast, black-and-cream pelt eaten by parasites, horns uncropped and gleaming wickedly in the smoky light. Its rider was equally thin and shabby, a fair-skinned and dark-maned *ashiren* some fourteen seasons old.

'Give you greeting,' Blaize called, 'in Her name.'

Two other *marhaz* joined the first. One carried its pad as if lame. A red-maned *ashiren* turned in the saddle and held up *kir* hand, but the straggling procession took no notice, and only gradually halted as they saw us. Young Ortheans, from three-births still in arms to *ashiren* old as the riders, and all ages between. Still they came over the low rise, until there were fifty or sixty of them; all with black or red manes, most with strongly similar faces – all the *ashiren* of one *telestre*? I thought, remembering Blaize's voice when he said *Rimnith*.

The Meduenin said, 'Where do you travel, *ashiren-te*?'

'Keverilde *telestre*.' The red-maned child's voice came harshly. 'If there is Keverilde, still. *T'an*, they burned Rimnith—'

'Where are your elders?'

Ke was silent, but another of the riders, a ten- or eleven-year-old *ashiren*, said, 'Gone into other *telestres* to wait.'

'Wait until we can fight—'

'—they burned—'

'—burned the land—'

'We offered them guest-right,' the red-maned *ashiren* cut in, over the babble of other voices. *Ke* picked absently at soot smears on *kir* thin, tawny robe. 'We offered them guest-right and they burned the land, *t'an*.'

No time for *saryl-kabriz* poison, I thought. Cassirur, what now?

Blaize Meduenin stared back the way they had come. Nothing was visible but that black wall of smoke in the south.

'Keverilde is too close,' he said. 'Eirye, or Beriah . . . *Ashiren-te*, will you be afraid to fly, as offworlders do? We will take you all, in turns – but the beasts you must leave. Will you go, *ashiren-te*?'

'Now wait a minute—' Doug broke off. He watched the Orthean children.

All the Orthean features are delicate on a child: feathery mane rooting down the spine, slender clawed fingers and high-arched feet; the eyes that blur with translucent membrane. Alien, unsexed. The red-maned rider let *kir* beast pad closer to Blaize Meduenin, until *ke* could look down at him.

'Take the youngest of us,' the rider said, with precarious adolescent dignity. 'For myself, I'd sooner ride into Shadow than travel with those who are friends to the Coast.'

'That's foolish. You'll be weary, and in danger,' Blaize reminded *kir*.

The rider smiled, and it was adult, cynical. *Ke* said, 'All of us are in danger now, *t'an*. Now that the Coast raiders have *s'aranthi* weapons.'

Doug, with an exaggerated sigh, glanced from the rabble of children to the shuttle. 'Three trips,' he estimated, 'and God knows we won't get any help from Cory Mendez. I wouldn't take the risk if these weren't children. What in God's name are their people doing sending them away alone?'

A remembered voice in my head said, *Who'd harm ashiren? Who'd dare?* When I looked across at Blaize, I knew he had no faith in that now. The restrictions have broken down.

Two hours later, back on the same spot; nothing changed but Carrick's Star declined slightly from noon.

'Link your navigation-data in,' said the thin, blond man in Peace Force coveralls. His name was Ottoway, I gathered; he had prematurely creased and tanned skin, and in his eyes something of the same look as Corazon Mendez. He said, 'It's funny. They seem more afraid of a ship on their soil than of the actual flight.'

I watched the remaining *ashiren* and *marhaz* file up the ramp and into the F90, whose shining white bulk dwarfed the government shuttle. Blaize Meduenin stood at the top of the ramp, preparatory to going with them.

They *remember* flight, in the days of the Golden Empire . . . and it isn't to reassure them about flight that the Meduenin is going with them. They don't trust offworlders, now.

'Thank Cory when you see her,' I said. 'We'd have been some time taking the last group over to Beriah, and we're getting low on fuel.'

'Just getting non-combatants out of a hostile area,' Ottoway said. 'About yourself, Ms Christie, and the government envoy, Clifford—'

'Yes, of course.' I smiled. And made for the government shuttle, before he should realize I'd reassured him about absolutely nothing. Away in the south there was the sound of shuttles and observer-craft, there where the horizon still was yellow with smoke. I palmed the lock shut, cutting out the faint smell of combustion on the wind.

'We're going to have to do something soon,' I said, taking the seat beside Doug at the holotank.

'Mmm.' He reached out to the console. 'You might find this interesting. I got a signal some few minutes ago that I failed to identify immediately. Eventually I realized that it was being relayed through the Morvren communication-link from Thierry's World . . . Listen.'

'—been requesting permission from the Company to land, but they've refused. I couldn't get in contact with you, envoy Clifford—'

The replay-image showed a young woman's face. I recognized those heavy, slanting brows: the 'caster from the Trismegistus WEB. Doug ran the record forward.

'—there are 'casters from three or four other WEBs on Thierry, but transport to Carrick V is under so many Company restrictions that it's impossible to get through. Envoy, I want to 'cast from the surface of Carrick's world itself. I want to show the Home Worlds and the Heart Worlds just exactly what's happening here—'

Doug keyed out the image. 'I sent her the record of the refugees here in Melkathi. I've authorized the government base on Thierry's

World to finance transport for any WEBcasters travelling to Orthe.'
With uncharacteristic vindictiveness, he added, 'It won't do Representative Rachel any harm to have WEBcasters following her every move.'

'I'd sooner keep friendly relations with Cory's people. We may need them. I was talking to Ottoway,' I said, as I leaned back in the bucket seat, and reached over to key a container of coffee from the supply-panel. 'He says the area round Rimnith is quiet, the fires are dying down.'

And was it a wet spring, a wet summer? I remember when Orhlandis burned the whole countryside was in danger—

'And they've had some success with the observer-craft. No sign of any offshore fleet.' Only the normal shipping you find in summer, in the seasons of Durestha and Merrum, in those coastal waters from Ales-Kadareth to Tathcaer to Morvren Freeport and the Kasabaarde Archipelago . . . 'All they can pick up is a concentration of life forms near Rimnith, and that *must* be the Coast Ortheans. Doug, I'm willing to bet there are Anzhadi there, maybe Sethri himself—'

'For God's sake don't make the suggestion that you're going to, Lynne. You can*not* attempt to make contact with a group of guerrilla invaders.'

'Somebody has to.'

The shuttle's interior was cool, illuminated with that faintly green and soothing light; and the silence was no silence, but only the hum of powered-down systems. I noticed the imprint of footsteps on the floor: the sandy earth of Melkathi trodden in. Doug leaned back and rubbed at his eyes, the light from the imageless holotank casting upward shadows on his features. He sighed.

'We're running out of time.'

'I know,' I said.

'I must talk with Cory Mendez. If storm conditions abate, and I can get through to Rachel at Kel Harantish, then . . . ' He looked up. 'We have just enough fuel to make a landing on the way back.'

For half an hour I let the shuttle stand by the ruins of the Rimnith *telestre*, partly to seem no threat, partly to see if it would provoke attack. I stayed in the shuttle, exterior-sensor and transmitter working, and didn't venture outside, because I'm not stupid. Doug Clifford stayed at the comlink, trying to contact the Coast.

The earth still smoked blackly. In the orange light, angular *hanelys* stood like iron lace. Wisps of smoke curled up from the ground. Even the stones of the sprawling complex of buildings were cracked with the heat.

'I'll move a mile or two south,' I said. 'I can't tell if the heat-sensors are reading body-heat, or hot spots in the earth.'

The shuttle lifted heavily, wallowing south, and I set it down on bare heathland that had escaped the conflagration only because there was so little to burn. And waited. At last the sensors showed a moving body. A small figure appeared, approaching the shuttle. When he got close, I saw the filthy *meshabi*-robe that cloaked him: a male, elderly, with a brown-blond mane. At his belt hung both a hook-bladed knife and a CAS-IV holster.

'Earth tech,' Doug said, leaning over to look at the holotank's exterior-image. 'I want this recorded for evidence. Are there other *hiyeks* here?'

'I can't tell. The heat's still masking the sensors.'

'*Kethrial-shamaz shan'tai!*' The Orthean's voice came through the transmitter pick-up. I saw how he craned his neck, looking up at the shuttle's blank walls. 'Are there *s'aranthi* there?'

'What *hiyek*?' I asked. He glanced round, found no focus for the voice. His bare feet were blackened with ash, and membrane covered his eyes so that they looked blankly white. Alone. And where are the Ortheans with you, who set the fire in Rimnith's sparse fields, put the spark to the tinder-dry reed thatch of the *telestre* buildings? I repeated, 'What *hiyek*? Anzhadi?'

A flicker of reaction. I keyed the image into close-up. Brown-blond mane rooted down broad shoulders; he had a square, stolid face. He said, 'If there were Anzhadi here, *shan'tai*, they wouldn't come in reach of you.'

'Is Sethri-safere with you? He'll talk to me. Tell him Lynne Christie—'

'You talk to me or none. What do you want with us, offworlder?'

One of the Peace Force shuttles split the sky overhead. The *hiyek* male flinched. I heard Doug talking with Cory's officers, but I concentrated on the nameless Orthean male.

'Do you want to bring *that* down on you?' I remember Cory saying: All I can do is threaten. And here am I, threatening. 'It's hardly an army you've brought with you, ten or a dozen *jath*; and it wouldn't help you if all the Coast were here, would it?'

'Can you take us from among these people?'

He let the question stand. One claw-nailed hand was at his belt, close to that incongruous CAS-IV; and the rising wind blew his unbraided mane across his face, and whisked ashes into the air.

'Can you?' he repeated. 'Take the *jath*. There they are. Have them. Take the empty *siiran* on the Coast, and much good may they do you; take the canals, every one of them, and the cities they flow through; take it all, we don't need it now—' His eyes unveiled, they were a striking glass-green. 'But if you want us, you must pick us out from among *your friends* – and if there are few of us, there are still fewer of you *s'aranthi*!'

That clear gaze went past me, he stared only at the hull of the shuttle. In that gaze I saw *siiran*, those plant-filled underground chambers of *chiruzeth*, pictured them empty. Pictured Molly Rachel's research team in Maherwa, the canal system's controls left open to their investigation . . . What's happening on the Coast now, under cover of hurricanes? Do all the *jath* and *jath-rai* wait there, are the men and women of the *hiyeks* beginning to drift back towards their homes, have they abandoned this crusade? Or are there other ships slipping out on to the Inner Sea, a migration rather than an invasion?

'Northerners won't have you on *telestre* land,' I said.

'They will have seen this.' He jerked his head in the general direction of Rimnith.

'That won't work—'

Doug leaned across and switched from outside transmitter to comlink.

'Doug—'

'This is a live transmission. An observer-craft. Lynne, look.'

At first it looked like a repeat image of Rimnith. Then I saw that the billowing black smoke rooted on a shallow hill, and that the burning buildings were only half consumed. No person moved, but two – no, three – bodies lay motionless in the burning *hanelys* and reedbeds.

'Keverilde *telestre*,' he explained.

'Doug, that's thirty miles away from here.'

Another image inset itself over the burning hillside, a close-up of a rocky gully. It was shaded over with the black rods and spines of *hanelys*, and under the vegetation was a gleam of white. Voices over the comlink went wild.

'That's a groundcar!'

'Cory's people can track groundcars, they're energy sources – when they're in use.' He paused. 'They say the *hiyek* people may have as many as eight or nine.'

A lot went through my mind in that silent second. That Sethri must have brought them over, you could load small groundcars on *jath* ships; but what's the black-market connection for Earth

697

technology? That the Peace Force would be able to trace where the *hiyek*-Ortheans moved in Melkathi, and what would they do about that?

I keyed back to exterior-view, but the *hiyek* male had vanished. His body-heat was lost among the deep hidden fires in the peat heathland, sensors couldn't track him now.

'Is Cory herself there? Put her on-link, Douggie, we're going to have to talk to her sometime.'

'As government envoy, I have the right to know what action she plans to take – although if she has a modicum of wisdom,' Clifford added, 'she'll practise some masterly inactivity . . . Lynne, you know the multicorporates, you know them better than I do: how is PanOceania going to react?'

The comlink suddenly formed a clear image. It was split: half showing Corazon Mendez in the interior of a Peace Force F90, that hawk-face and sleek hair immaculate; the other half was the unsteady image of a wristlink, showing churned earth and excavations and black cloud-cover, and then shifting to the dark face of Molly Rachel. The wind tugged at her coverall, blowing that mass of tangled hair.

'—take *no* immediate action,' she was saying. Then: 'Lynne? Is that you? Get out of the area. Is that Douglas there with you?' Her voice was loud, raised over the buffeting of the wind and rain.

Doug, over my shoulder, said, 'I must know what action you're advising. I protest most strongly against any use of force against the local population by Commander Mendez.'

Cory interrupted from the F90. 'Damn all national governments! I can't even get data on the size of the invading force. This may be a raid or it may be a full-scale invasion; and until we can get surveillance working, we're as blind as the natives.' Her attention shifted to Molly Rachel. 'I won't engage in low-tech hostilities on those terms, Representative Rachel. Any action *must* be hi-tech, for the sake of my men.'

The Pacifican woman put a hand up to hold shaggy hair out of her face. Rain starred the holo-image. She smiled, almost snorted with humour, and said, 'All I want you to do is watch, for the next few hours. I need you *here*, Commander. All hell's broken loose in Kel Harantish – there's fighting inside the city. No one's attacked the T&A site yet, but I want some protection for those installations.'

I cut in: 'Who's fighting, Molly? Even the Coast *hiyeks* aren't crazy enough to attack the *telestres* and Kel Harantish together.'

'This is something internal, some factions in the city—' She broke off. In the background, clearly heard, was the whine of CAS weaponry: the side-leakage of Coherent Amplified Sound. She said, 'Some of them have CAS-III and CAS-VIII equipment. When I find out how that got imported . . . '

'I'll send Jamison down from the orbiter with a squad of flyers,' Cory Mendez said. 'That should serve as a warning, to keep your installations safe, Representative.'

Too much of a coincidence. Someone knew the *telestres* would be attacked, decided to take advantage and act themselves, while the Company's too busy to interfere . . . I let Doug talk to Corazon and the Pacifican woman, and I thought of Calil bel-Rioch. Alive still, or dead; caught in the fighting, defending, or its instigator? I can't believe she has nothing to do with this.

Doug said, 'What's the situation on the canals and in the Coast ports?'

'I've sent out a shuttle on visual surveillance; David Osaka—'

The split image was abruptly blank on the left-hand side, reduced to coruscating light; and Cory's image turned to bawl at her comlink officer to restore the link. Molly's face appeared for a moment, soundlessly speaking, and then again vanished.

'Get out of the area,' Cory Mendez cut her link with an equally scant courtesy, and without the excuse of an equipment breakdown. I switched back to exterior-view. In the sepia haze of the sky, specks that were F90s and observation craft quartered the air above Melkathi. Not yet three hours since I'd heard the noon bells ring in the Citadel. Exhaustion had such a grip on me, I felt I could sleep where I sat. And could only then realize that this, this afternoon of Durestha Eighthweek Nineday, is the date the WEB-casters will use to mark the outbreak of war . . .

And what day to mark its end?

'I'm taking us back to Tathcaer,' Doug Clifford said. 'I have to talk to the *T'Ans*. It's likely that they appreciate the implications, but one must be certain.' And then that small-featured round face creased in a smile that held no humour. 'God alone knows what they'll do about naming a new *T'An Suthai-Telestre* now.'

CHAPTER 23

Night Conference at the Wellhouse

Early afternoon sun shone on the white façades of Tathcaer, on pollen-yellow air, and a harbour full of bustle as *jath-rai* put out to sea. The ferry that took us from Kumiel to the city rocked in their wake.

Riders will have gone out, I thought. And *jath-rai*. None of them can have reached the Rimnith area yet. Blaize won't be back from Eirye. And here *we* are, already back. We live in different worlds.

'It's imperative I have some contact with Molly Rachel again, and in the near future.' Doug stepped on to the quay, saying over his shoulder to me: 'Will you go up to the Citadel and endeavour to find out the *T'Ans"* reaction to this – ' He broke off; smiled. 'I'm treating you as though you were advisor to the government. Lynne, I apologize.'

'This isn't the time to worry about that. Yes, I'll see the *T'Ans*.'

I stood for a moment and watched him vanish into the crowds, a small neatly-dressed man, dull among the brilliantly-robed Ortheans, intent on reaching the comlink at Westhill-Ahrentine. Faces turned as he passed. Unfriendly looks for *s'aranthi*? Perhaps. I turned to look for a *skurrai-jasin* to take me up to the Citadel, moving again at the Orthean pace.

And the Citadel, that great sprawling stone building, was empty of *T'Ans*; gone down into the city, or out towards Melkathi by whatever means they could travel; all of them gone, except one. My footsteps were loud, walking through those low-roofed halls. It wasn't until I saw his stricken, immobile face that I made the connection: *Nelum Santhil Rimnith*. Dusty sunlight shone on that sleek brown mane, on the unveiled eyes. Grief dazzled him. He no longer wore the insignia of a *T'An* Melkathi.

'Give you greeting, *t'an* Orhlandis,' he said, no recognition in his eyes, 'tell me how Melkathi burns.'

*

Towards mid-afternoon I got back to Westhill-Ahrentine. The Wellhouse took in Nelum Santhil, and I could find no other *T'An*, mad or sane. Just the steps from the courtyard to the first-floor rooms of the *telestre*-house exhausted me. Twenty-seven hours: a day not to be endured without some break for sleep before evening, the human biological clock demands it.

'Get through to Molly?' I asked, looking in on Doug Clifford where he sat at the comlink.

'Her base at Kel Harantish doesn't answer. Rashid Akida and the research team are being evacuated to the orbiter . . . ' He rubbed red-rimmed eyes. 'Corazon suggests that young Rachel and the other two – Pramila, is it, and David Osaka? – may be in the city itself. Some form of protective imprisonment?'

'She'd get out before that happened,' I protested. 'We've had that once before, she wouldn't . . . Where the hell *is* she?'

The holotank was now showing pictures of a *telestre*-house. Low, sprawling stone buildings, with *marhaz* pens, and in the background the wind-whipped sandflats and the sea. It seemed untouched, and then the lens panned round to the north, and I saw flames, like the teeth of a comb, jagged on the heathland and sweeping towards the sea.

—*Commander Mendez will make an announcement in four hours*, the WEBcaster's voice said.

'Tapping into WEB transmissions?'

'As they go from the orbiter to Thierry's World. I've given the WEBcasters on the orbital station permission to land.' Doug keyed across the board, and a half-dozen other transmissions showed variant images of Melkathi. 'I estimate that within twelve days every NET at home will carry these transmissions. At that point, surely, some restrictions will be imposed on PanOceania—'

'By the other multicorporates, if by no one else.' I touched him lightly on the shoulder. 'Leave the Citadel until evening, no one's there. Wake me for Cory's announcement, hey? If I don't sleep, I'm just plain going to fall over sideways . . . '

He chuckled. 'Lynne, you're getting old.'

'And when I'm awake, *you* can sleep.'

I lay down in the further room on a couch-chair piled with *zilmei* pelts, and the warm air of summer brought the scent of *kazsis*, and the voices of Ortheans in the alley below; all fragile now, all temporary and under threat.

A rough hand shook me awake. Doug's voice said, 'You'd better hear this.'

'What?'

'Corazon Mendez. She's broadcasting to the WEB personnel on the orbital station.'

'*What?*' I sat up, swung my feet off the couch-chair, and the world swam. Light hurt my eyes. Light of early evening, not yet even second twilight. I staggered through to the comlink in the other room, still half doped with sleep.

Doug leaned over the holotank. The image split between WEB-casters, seven or eight of them, clustered in one of the orbiter's cabins, and Corazon Mendez in an F90 shuttle. Adrenalin spurred me awake.

'What has she said?'

'That she's making her announcement before the stated time – listen—'

'I repeat,' Corazon's voice came thinly, 'this announcement is for the benefit of the Wave-Energy Broadcaster nets. This Company has the situation on Carrick V under control. Necessary action to implement this was taken at 22.00 localworld time, when a surgical strike was made on hostile areas, using six F90 shuttles armed with mid-tech long-range weapons. The F90s used their weapons to make a high-level strike on the following Desert Coast ports: Reshebet, Nadrasiir, Mesh-lamak, Nazkali, Saransiir, Psam-nol, Luzukka, Gileshta, Merari, Lakmarash, Kumek-aruk, and Quarth . . . Satellite surveillance now shows the harbours at these locations to be blocked, and thus impassable to hostile craft intending to invade the northern continent—'

'What?' I said. 'She did what?'

Doug moved his hand in an abortive gesture. 'She – I don't – we—'

The WEBcasters crowded the 'link in the orbiter. I glimpsed the face of the Visconti woman, saw it stricken, some faint echo of outrage; then someone asked a question not audible on pick-up, but Corazon Mendez heard, and nodded: 'Yes. Our F90s left from the government base on Thierry's World. They refuelled from the PanOceania orbiter, and left from our Company docking facilities at 21.30. They made three overflights and three forensic strikes—'

'Forensic!' Doug spat.

'—and returned to orbital docking. I'm pleased to say all six craft returned safely.'

I sank down into the comlink chair, too weary to stand. 'Isn't that amazing?' I appealed to Doug. 'F90 shuttles attack *jath-rai* and a population armed with knives and rakes, and the shuttles get away *unscathed* – Jesus, they were lucky!'

He gestured for silence, intently keying through the comlink channels; and I guessed he was searching for the satellite-images.

Corazon Mendez finished: 'This decision was taken in view of the danger of hostilities spreading from the relatively small area of the northern continent to which they are at present confined, and in view of the possible danger to Company and government personnel stationed at present on Carrick V.'

'She can't have—' I tried to key in, found the link restricted.

'What about the Company's commercial representative?' called one of the WEBcasters.

'Full consultations with Representative Rachel took place, and her agreement was given; as was that of the British government for use of refuelling and docking facilities on Thierry's World—'

Doug Clifford's hands froze on the comlink controls. He stared at the silver-haired woman's image, at her self-possessed expression. 'That's a lie. That's a lie on both counts. Oh, that *stupid* woman. How could she do this? How?'

The Peace Force Commander added, 'Provisional consultation took place on Earth before we left, and approval was given for this type of action.'

'*Shit!*' I couldn't key in a contact. Cory wants this between herself and the WEBcasters, I thought, and none of us saying the wrong word; has she really done this without consulting Molly? Has she really done this?

The 'link babbled, WEBcasters vociferously interrupting each other to question her. Blips would already be shuttling back to Earth in FTL drones. I had to stand up, to pace across the room; and at the window I stopped and looked at the sky above the courtyard. At the blue sky and the skeins of daystars. Such a clear sky, and now so dangerous.

'If the *hiyeks* have any hi-tech weapons, they'll use them now. Any minute, any second—' I swung back to face Doug. 'I want to go to the orbiter. I want to go up there and tell them *no*, the Company doesn't have our support, *no*, the government didn't agree to their using the base on Thierry's World, *no*—' Anger, shame, and such outrage it left me breathless.

'Here are the satellite transmissions.'

I went to stand beside him. The WEBcasters and Mendez were tiny figures in the corner of the tank. The main holo-image shone with the acid-white light of the Coast – have the storms gone *now*, of all times? – that light that shone on ochre earth and the far-distant foothills of the Elansiir mountains.

Reshebet, is it? A curve of *chiruzeth* marks the sea wall. Now you can hardly see it for rubble, rock blasted in from the low ridges that used to line the canals; and in that rubble are the tilted hulls of *jath* ships, that metal shining, but dimmed with dust. Hoop-masts are twisted, *jath-rai* driven up one on the other by the force of the blasts. The canal that runs to the harbour is choked with wreckage and all the low shacks collapsed; the waters of the canal flooding out on to the barren land around, and sinking down and leaving no more than a shadow of water on the earth . . . Bodies lie in the incandescent sun: Ortheans sprawled under tumbled rock, or floating face down in water; and now as the image moves a little inland there are crowds (seen from above, foreshortened), some moving, strung out along the track beside the canal; some still and silent; there a man holding an *ashiren*, there two pale-maned females, and there, and there.

'The strike was aimed at purely military targets,' Corazon Mendez said, in voice-over. 'Casualties have been kept to a minimum. I ordered the F90s to make a low pass over these ports at 21.40 and again at 21.50 as a signal to evacuate the local population from the harbour areas.'

Doug's hand closed round mine, unconsciously gripping hard enough to hurt. His face had gone a sick colour between yellow and grey.

'The *civilians* are the only military targets on the Coast—' That from a WEBcaster, the dark-haired Roxana Visconti.

'By this action now we will have prevented greater use of force,' Cory Mendez said. 'Had more than a small fraction of the invasion fleet reached the northern continent, more severe action might have been necessary, which the use of punitive force at this stage has prevented.'

Though I tried, I couldn't get the satellite transmission to show me more than that one image. I wanted to know if the harbours were all as devastated; wanted to know how many *jath* ships had been caught in the destruction. 'How the hell could we do this! The Company *can't* just—'

'They have,' Doug said. He turned away from the holotank, looking at the dusty *telestre*-house room, the brazier and couch-chair and satellite-maps pinned to the walls, and his face was blank with bewilderment. He said, 'They can, because they have the power to do so. And now am I supposedly to go to the *T'Ans* here and inform them, "My government supports what the PanOceania multicorporate has done in attacking Orthean people, and there-fore *I* support it"?'

I said, 'The Company's always bitching about how NuAsia grabs territory, how ChinaCo does; don't they see this makes them look like any other multicorporate?' I abandoned the holotank. 'Doug, you don't have a choice; if you don't go along with the Company, they'll put pressure on at home to have you removed.'

'Then I'm very much afraid that that is what they will have to do.'

Too cold, too shocked, I couldn't take it all in. There is the sky over the roofs of Tathcaer, an evening sky as clean and clear as any other, and the brilliance of Carrick's Star; and now to wake up this one particular evening and find everything changed—

Doug, neatly fastening the cuffs on his coverall, said, 'Some authority is going to have to inform the *T'Ans* and the *takshiriye* what's happening on the Coast now. You're the representative of PanOceania. I'm here on behalf of the government. I suspect that Commander Mendez is well aware that our duty—'

'We weren't consulted, we weren't told, we're not responsible – Douggie, I don't believe even that *Molly* knows. I can't contact anyone on the Coast. This is Mendez acting on her own.'

To outsiders, we will be called responsible. Government envoy, special advisor . . .

'It won't be a great deal of time before *we* hear from the WEBcasters,' Doug said. 'Did it look as though public feeling is going to be in favour of what's happened here? I'm familiar with WEB personnel. If they're shocked, groundsiders will be appalled.'

Outside, I could hear the evening bustle of Tathcaer, smell the smoke of cooking-fires; and I realized, I can't predict now what the *telestre*-Ortheans will feel about this. Which is more terrible, that an enemy burns Melkathi, or that that enemy has suffered the use of *s'aranthi* weapons?

'The government will be called responsible,' Doug Clifford said. He took a breath. 'I want to turn around and say I agree with all your condemnations, I am ashamed to be part of this administration. If there was anything I could do to condemn this, I would do it. All I can do is stand helplessly by and watch the mechanism grind on.'

The thought of crossing six miles of Tathcaer to the Citadel was exhausting in itself, and as for what explanations would have to be made to Howice and Khassiye and Bethan, to Blaize and Hal, Cassirur, Romare Kerys-Andrethe . . .

I said, 'We've got to try and stop this here. Now. We've got to get these people and the *hiyek*-families to make peace *now*.' And then, as we left the room, I said, 'But Douggie, have you thought? How will we react if what Mendez has done *does* put an end to the fighting? Does that make her right?'

Starlight shone down through the slot in the roof of the great Wellhouse. That light of Orthe's summer stars, mixed with the glowing yellow of *becamil*-wax candles, shone on the braided manes of hastily-dressed Ortheans where they stood or sat on the stone tiers, shrouded the entrances to that domed, shadowed amphitheatre. Male and female voices rose in a babble; there was the wail of *ashiren*. In a moment's quiet came the whirr of *rashaku* wings and apprehension became tangible: *what message from Melkathi, now?* The clamour of discussion rose louder.

'Attacked the harbours?' Cassirur Almadhera exclaimed, outraged.

'Bombed the harbour entrances to make them impassable to shipping.' Doug faced the group of *T'Ans* on the lower tiers of that stone amphitheatre. He stood with his head high; he looked beleaguered and defiant and (though no outsider would see it) ashamed. I moved to stand beside him, before that impromptu council of accusing faces – now they had the news, they seemed determined on wringing us dry of facts.

The starlight robbed Cassirur's mane of scarlet, made her face an ashen mask. Her hand dropped to Hal's shoulder, where he sat below her on the next tier.

'Mother of the Wells! To fight, yes, but to destroy—' She stopped. Earthspeakers care for all land. Romare Kerys-Andrethe, dark and self-satisfied, muttered something to her, and then turned aside, speaking with the blunt and soldierly Bethan *T'An* Kyre. That Orthean woman frowned.

'How dare you act without consulting us?' Haltern made to stand and sank back, pale with anger, ill with it; and Cassirur's hand tightened on his shoulder, that Earthspeaker's sensing touch. He ignored her whispered warning. 'Is that a measure of precisely how much your people take note of the Hundred Thousand?'

'Independent action—'

He overrode Doug. 'Taken against *us*. Against Ortheans.'

That got attention from a group of three: Howice *T'An* Roehmonde whose face held a frown of private concern (Roehmonde being far enough north not to worry just yet, but soon); the elegant and caustic Khassiye Reihalyn, *T'An* Andrethe; and Geren Hanathra, Geren Shipmaster, now *T'An* Ymir. That last looked at me with hatred.

'They're *hiyeks*,' Howice *T'An* Roehmonde protested. His plump fingers wound together nervously. '*Hiyeks* and lovers of Witch-breed abominations – what does it matter if *s'aranthi* kill them?'

'Because if they can do that to the Coast,' said Haltern n'ri n'suth Beth'ru-elen, 'they can do it to us. Isn't that right, *t'an S'aranth*? Christie, am I correct? Pardonable violence against hostile local forces, leading to the imposition of a garrison to see that

706

there's no fighting anywhere; Coast or Hundred Thousand; am I right?'

'Hal—'

'Am I right?' The white mane flew, his voice cracked with anger; and those small brilliant eyes veiled with membrane. 'Ortheans have gone to Her at offworlder hands, that's what you've told us; how long before it happens again, in Melkathi, and how will you tell *hiyek* from *telestre*?'

I couldn't tell if he meant land or people; and language being so ambiguous, perhaps his thought was too. He sank back into the *becamil* robes protecting him against the summer night's air. Doug and I stood together on the lower tier by him, and as I looked up I saw how we were surrounded by condemnation: Cassirur and Bethan gazing down, Romare and Howice and Khassiye Reihalyn on the tier above them.

'Tomorrow's the solstice,' I said. 'Naming day. Midsummer-Eightyear. Tomorrow one of you will be *T'An Suthai-Telestre*. Why do you think we've been so concerned to get this news to you? Nothing compels us to tell you. Listen to me—'

'Listen to the PanOceania Company,' Khassiye Reihalyn said, studying the gold studs between his fingers instead of offworlders; speaking with malice.

'*No.*' I took a breath. The *becamil* candles wavered in a breeze from the upper archways, and that yellow light shone on them: picking out gems on the hilts of Khassiye's *harur*-blades, shining on Haltern's white mane, on Bethan's dark skin; making half-shadowed masks of Romare and Howice's expressions. And I remember, ten years ago, a night council in a room in the Citadel . . .

Geren Hanathra stepped down one tier. Light shone on his yellow mane, on that hardly-aged face. He said, 'If I had known what I brought from the Eastern Isles that year, I should have drowned you like vermin. Yes, stand here, *S'aranth*! Stand as she did, *amari* Ruric Orhlandis; betray us as she did—'

'Unfair.'

The voice was weak, but it was Haltern's; looking up with pale and whiteless blue eyes; meeting my gaze with something of the old ironic humour.

'She has been a friend to us, Geren; and the *t'an* Clifford also. And that on occasion when it was not to their advantage, I admit it.' He smiled. 'Better if you hadn't, Christie. It makes it harder for us to see you offworlders as nothing but enemy, all Shadow. Or harder for some of us . . . I am too old to lie to myself, and make anger cover what I feel, although I have tried.'

In the silence that followed, the voices of the other Ortheans in the Wellhouse rang across the stone tiers; and a female in north-province Earthspeakers' gear came over to speak with Cassirur Almadhera; and a Peir-Dadeni rider took Khassiye Andrethe aside. I sat down on the lowest stone tier beside Haltern, and gazed up at the other *T'Ans*.

'You know me. You know Doug and me, and we know the Company. You won't trust offworlders now, and I don't blame you, but I'll tell you this: the only way to stop the Company getting a foothold in the Hundred Thousand is to make peace in Melkathi. Take the excuse for intervention away. You must do that.'

A new voice said, 'Then it's not us you should talk with, *t'an* Christie, but the Coast families that are burning Melkathi.'

It was Nelum Santhil. His face showed strain, but the rationality was back in those dark eyes. He looked as though he'd slept in the crumpled Melkathi robes he wore. One six-fingered hand held a curling strip of parchment: a message from the *rashaku*-relay. Quite deliberately he walked down the stone steps and seated himself on the tier beside me. 'I'll go to Melkathi with you and the *t'an* Clifford,' he said. 'Christie, you don't trust me, but I care more for Melkathi province than SuBannasen or Orhlandis did. I can talk to the *hiyeks*. The Melkathi *telestres* . . . we know about poverty. About failing harvests. About famine, and plague. Help me to get to the Anzhadi and I'll talk to them about peace.' He paused. 'I am not to become *T'An Suthai-Telestre*, I know that, so it doesn't matter if I am absent tomorrow—'

'It's against all custom!' Romare Kerys-Andrethe protested.

Cassirur returned from talking with the northern Earthspeaker in time to say, 'Custom's a guide-rope and not a chain. *T'An* Christie, will the *hiyeks* in Melkathi have heard what's happened today in Reshebet and the other harbours?'

I looked at Doug. He lifted a brow. 'If they happen to have an illegal comlink. As yet I've picked up nothing in the way of unauthorized transmissions.'

'If not . . .' Cassirur's eyes veiled, dark, 'then they will not know until a *jath* ship reaches them, if it ever does.'

'The *hiyeks* will not suddenly become our friends because of this,' Romare said. 'I hold with your opinion, Earthspeaker; best lull them into peace and then send them to Her. Or will that bring offworlder ships down on *us*?'

'It's a possibility,' Doug conceded.

The stolid female in *zilmei* pelts and *skurrai* leather, that I knew vaguely to be Bethan Ivris *T'An* Kyre, said in heavily-accented

Ymirian: 'T'Ans, weren't there new *telestres* founded in Peir-Dadeni, some five hundred years gone? Let these others, these *hiyeks*, go north into the Barrens, over Broken Stair; or west into the wilderness. Let them make *telestres* there by Her will. The *kazsis* flowers where the vine is trained. So in ten generations they will be of the *telestre*, as we are.'

Nelum Santhil looked up at her. 'Is there land, or only wilderness? Can anyone live there?'

Cassirur interrupted: 'The *hiyeks* have lived too long with Witchbreed science. Will you send them into the Witchbreed's ruined cities now, will you have them bring back that Empire? Who knows what lies undiscovered in the Barrens?'

Nelum Santhil and Bethan Ivris ignored her, and I looked at the two of them, this mountain woman, and this male from the arid city Ales-Kadareth. I almost wanted to laugh, seeing how the *T'Ans* of the prosperous *telestres* looked affronted. What would Suthafiori have made of these two outsiders? She might well have overruled Ymir, Rimon, Roehmonde, Peir-Dadeni, if she thought it made better sense . . .

'Word from the *t'an* Meduenin,' Nelum Santhil said, at last holding up the ribbon-message that he had been absently winding and unwinding in those dark six-fingered hands. 'Blaize Meduenin sends word, he has spoken with one Jadur Anzhadi of the Coast, taken prisoner near Keverilde *telestre*. This *shan'tai* Jadur speaks of the destruction of Reshebet.'

Excitement flickered on all those Orthean faces. So the Anzhadi *do* have an illegal comlink, I thought. They know what Cory's done. Is it coincidence that Jadur is one of Sethri's *raiku*? Is he a prisoner or a would-be envoy?

Nelum handed the ribbon-message across to Hal, who peered short-sightedly at the script.

'If we can speak with the Anzhadi *now*,' Nelum urged, 'they and the *hiyeks* back on the Coast have suffered greatly. Let's make what offer we can, while that shock's new. *T'An* Christie's right. There must be no excuse for offworld intervention.'

Geren and Howice and Khassiye broke out into protest, interrupting each other; Cassirur bent over Hal's shoulder to read the message, pointing, speaking excitedly; Nelum Santhil obdurately blocked her objections. Bethan enthusiastically spoke to other *s'ans* who, attracted by the shouting, moved down several tiers to speak with the *T'Ans*. Doug urbanely cut Howice *T'An* Roehmonde off in mid-argument. It was minutes before I realized, in the middle of it all, that my wristlink was signalling for attention.

I stepped aside from the group, on to the Wellhouse floor. A few yards from where I stood, the black Wellmouth gaped, and I felt a chill come up from the water fifty feet below.

'Christie here.'

The distance-thinned voice said, 'Corazon Mendez. I'm sending a shuttle to pick you up from the settlement at 08.00 localworld time.'

'Now hold on just a minute—'

Corazon said, 'I don't have time to argue. You're special advisor to the Company, Lynne. I have the authority to co-opt personnel.'

Cory's an old hand at this, knows not to antagonize Company staff, so why—? And then I thought, *If I didn't know Commander Mendez better, I'd say this was fear.*

The clipped tones went on: 'I'm taking a squad down to the Kel Harantish settlement and I may need an expert on xeno-psychology. That's you, Lynne. Meet the shuttle on Kumiel Island at 08.00.'

The wristlink blurred: empty channel. I stood staring at the black Wellmouth, not really aware of what I saw. *If Cory Mendez is this concerned . . . what has she heard from Molly Rachel in Kel Harantish? What else can happen?*

'I intend to travel down to Keverilde,' Doug said as he extricated himself from the crowd of Ortheans on the stone tiers. He was flushed, slightly ruffled; above all, determined. 'Who was the call?'

'I may have to go down to the Coast and sort things out with Molly.'

He registered my non-answer and smiled. 'That information could be useful, now there's some progress here. It's a good thing that you still have access to the Company.'

Starlight shifted on the floor of the Wellhouse dome. The air near the Wellmouth was cold, dark. Easy to be confident here in Tathcaer, I thought, but there are so many other factors; so many things that can still happen . . .

More soberly, Doug said, 'Ascertain, if you can, what part young Rachel played in authorizing today's attack. I need to have the full facts at my disposal when I enter the protest at home. I think that, despite current events, I shall still protest . . . '

I couldn't hide it: I knew it then, knew it when I stood on Kumiel six hours later in the cold dawn, waiting for the Company shuttle. What drove me to leave was not a desire to find out what was happening on the Coast, urgent though that might be. I left because it would be too humiliating to have to say to Ortheans, in Tathcaer or in Keverilde, Corazon Mendez has succeeded where I have so far failed.

CHAPTER 24

A Mortal Coldness

Corazon Mendez herself led me down the shuttle's cabin to comfortable seats and flasks of coffee. That sleek white hair was immaculate, black coveralls with hardly a crease; and her face showed no strain. She said, 'You're aware, no contact at all can be made now with the T&A site at Kel Harantish?'

The seats were soft. I drank, set the flask back in its socket as the F90 thrummed into flight. The angle of ascent was sharp. Rising up to hi-orbit, then dropping down to the Coast; profligate with fuel, but taking hours rather than the two days flying over the Inner Sea. PanOceania can afford it.

Cory Mendez settled seat-webs across us. Attempting humour, she said, 'I'm sorry your expected disaster failed to materialize, after the strike.'

'Cory, for God's sake! I warn you, I'll register the strongest possible protest at home, and I'll make it stick. When something goes wrong here the Company will want a scapegoat, and I'll do my best to make certain that it's you.'

There was a smile on that lean face. To do her justice, she tried to hide it.

'It's a catastrophic failure of judgement,' I said at last. 'You can stop hostilities temporarily, but – Christ, I sound as though I *want* a disaster. It's not so. Cory, I'm terrified of what's going to happen on Orthe now, and that's the truth.'

She nodded twice, those sharp blue eyes on me; had a smile that might be humour or sympathy. 'I think you underestimate the effectiveness of being brutal. You'd let matters go on until there was no other option but a major hostile incident, and one all the worse for being delayed. I don't deny the strike resulted in casualties. That's cauterization. We can't allow what we would have had – war with an alien population who've got their hands on hi-tech weaponry.' Now her smile was entirely conscious of irony. 'Your Coast farmers wanted to know about CAS and projectile weaponry. Very well, we've just given them an object lesson. It's far more effective than Clifford's diplomatic bleatings. Some situations can only be resolved through fear.'

The shuttle tilted, power roaring, reaching up towards the edge of the atmosphere. Six miles below us that blue globe turns.

'They're not children, to all be scared of fire because one burned its fingers.'

'Lynne, that's exactly what they are.'

As I looked round the cabin at Cory's officers at their consoles, I felt desperately isolated. 'You've acted on your own authority. Will Molly Rachel back you up? If she's been in protective custody in Kel Harantish, she won't necessarily have heard what's happened. Better have a good explanation ready.'

'We have to have order.' Cory's face, that lined face, sharp as a bird of prey, was open and honest now. 'We saw the early years of the Dispersal, Earth falling apart because suddenly there was a universe full of inhabited, reachable worlds. The Companies are the thread that ties us together now. PanOceania can't afford violence on worlds where it has an interest. Lynne, I spoke to some of your Ortheans in Tathcaer. Their attitude is the same: they'd sooner win, as I would, by the wrong means, than not win at all. Do me the credit of believing that when I say "win" I don't refer to military battles?'

The shuttle tilted back to level, slowing, and I knew we would shortly dock and refuel at the orbiter. I didn't meet the older woman's gaze. What now? Leave Doug to mediate in the Hundred Thousand, put some Company man like David Osaka in Morvren Freeport; there's Carrick V settled as another Company market. Research into Witchbreed artifacts can go ahead unhindered. Working towards some hypothetical breakthrough . . . And what happens to me? Self-pity aside, it's a good question; I've messed up at least two careers in these past few months, and it looks as though it's all been for nothing.

'Kel Harantish . . .' Cory looked thoughtful.

'I can give you a considered opinion on that,' I said. 'If Dannor bel-Kurick, the Emperor-in-Exile, has been fighting – it'll be over contact with Earth technology, and I think there are groups there powerful enough to overrule him. Molly won't be in any danger if, say, Calil bel-Rioch is protecting her.'

'The faction in that settlement that supports the Company is strong enough?' Mendez queried.

'I wouldn't be surprised to find Calil as Voice of the Emperor again. Or, in all but name, Emperor herself. All that worries me is that Molly and the others may have been caught in the city when fighting broke out, and handled it badly.'

'It may not be as straightforward as I previously indicated—' She paused. Metallic echoes thrummed through the ship as we docked. Then as we waited she said, 'It was unwise to risk on an open comlink, particularly when the equipment you were using is the property of the government envoy. This is another reason why I requested your presence. Your knowledge of the archeological background.'

'I don't understand.'

'I believe that Representative Rachel *is* in the settlement,' she said. 'One of her last transmissions before loss of contact had to do with the Old Technology. She indicated they might have had a conceptual breakthrough.'

'Rashid's team—'

Cory linked her fingers, and the thick silver rings clinked together. 'That was a deliberate lie. Rashid Akida and several of the research personnel were not among the people evacuated up to the orbital station. There's a high probability they're still with Representative Rachel.'

She loosed the seat-web, preparatory to going to the comlink to authorize the refuelling. 'A conceptual breakthrough on Golden science – all the more reason to protect Company personnel by keeping the peace, if Carrick V is going to be a major market for us.'

I watched her walk across the cabin to speak with her officers. The level hum of power and the shuttle interior's warmth were soothing, too soothing for the couple of hours' sleep I'd had; time began to slip. Half-awake, half-asleep, I expected every chime of the comlink to announce some dream-parallel of Mendez's announcement – was that really only twelve hours ago? – from the Hundred Thousand, Doug Clifford saying how temporary this temporary peace had turned out to be . . .

I sat up, made a mental effort to stay awake. Panic suddenly made me breathless. Is it possible to become too awake? I saw the shuttle clearly, heard the signal of completed fuelling, and at the same time felt the surge of memories – memories resisted because I knew them to be delusion – and in an instant experienced the full force of vision—

The sky is cold; palest blue. Wind cuts like ice. The light on the horizon is silver, as if Orthe's dawn came at once from all quarters of the horizon. The light is silver. Against it, silhouetted, the ramps and towers and terraces of a great city; that great city, Archonys.

'Speak,' she says. 'Do we have the trick of it yet; do we have the secret?'

The language of the slave race falls from those thin lips easily, and it should not, but how else could we comprehend her? And I know that thin and high-boned face, with honey-yellow eyes; that pale gold-dusted skin and floating mane: she who is given the name of Zilkezra of the High Lands, Zilkezra of the Golden, sister of Santhendor'lin-sandru.

She says, 'You have laboured long and hard for it, and for us, and for love of us, and have not yet succeeded?'

'We have that knowledge,' I tell her. 'We have worked, we understand it, we give it to you freely. That ancient light will take Archonys, but that great city will not die alone.'

Her hands on my shoulders are cold. She turns me to face those others gathered here, on the great terrace above the Six Lakes. Hawk faces and golden eyes and slender bodies in metalmesh robes, and I must lower my eyes. Their gaze upon me is a mortal coldness. And they are more beautiful than the silver dawn.

'Now you see,' she says, 'this that we created from the beasts of this world to be Our servant, this has served us well. This child of Orthe has given our revenge into our hands.' And she says, 'Let them in future time grub in the dirt, I will make death their only crop. Let this be a cold world, a sterile world, let it blaze back the sun's light like a star; let nothing move on the face of it but the cold wind, and the dust of cities, and the dust of men.'

The light on the horizon is silver, older than Time; an ancient light, the brilliance of annihilation. Yet more beautiful stand Zilkezra and the Golden of Archonys; we who are but their made children, their slaves, we stand appalled at that beauty which we desire. How many of us, in other lives, will deny all but our slavery? When Orthe is a world of telestres and hiyeks, will we deny that some of us loved the Golden, worked with them, for them; and for love of them created that destruction, as some of us for hate created their sterile deaths?—

Vision gave way to an uneasy calm. I put it behind me, as I put all such experiences behind me now, and tried to think of what might be occurring below, as the Company F90 shuttle raced the dawn-line down to the surface of the Harantish peninsula. Could only think of Corazon Mendez's phrase and the Company research team: 'a conceptual breakthrough on Golden science'. And in what area of Golden science it might be.

Cory Mendez took the seat beside me. 'Jamison reports dry storms in the Harantish area, suggests breathing-gear.'

'What does he say about the base?'

'The excavation site is deserted. The F90s are on autolock.' She steepled her fingers and rested her chin on them; silver rings dented her skin. Her gaze was abstracted. She said, 'I wish communications were – more reliable.'

Windlasses creaked. *Del'ri*-fibre ropes thrummed in the wind as the platform inched lower. White sky blazed over white earth; heat sucked the breath from my mouth. Dust stung the side of my face, particles sharp as glass, and I squinted up through the eyeshields at a robed figure gripping the platform's rail. As the wooden structure grounded, grating on the rock at the base of Kel Harantish's walls, I saw three other figures: guards in brown scale-mail. The first figure stepped forward, peering at us through veils of white dust.

'*Kethrial-shamaz shan'tai!*' called Pathrey Shanataru. He linked six-fingered hands across his podgy belly, that was now swathed in fine-textured black-and-golden robes. He inclined his head in my direction, then included Cory and Jamison: 'You are expected, which I think you may know. Come into the city.'

Cory Mendez slipped the air-tube from her mouth, coughed at the dust in her throat, and said, 'Is Representative Rachel in the settlement?'

Pathrey's dark eyes shifted. Veiled as they were against the dust-storms, their expression could not be easily read.

I glanced at the guards. 'Is there still fighting going on?'

'No, *shan'tai* Christie.' A sly smile spread over his rotund features. 'I am bid, by the Empress-in-Exile, to welcome you, and bring you to her.'

Cory raised white brows at *Empress*. In Sino-Anglic, she said, 'We'll have to go in. It should be safe enough.'

Pathrey Shanataru stood aside to let Mendez and her junior officer Jamison walk on to the lift-platform. I saw Pathrey note the presence of CAS weaponry. He made no open protest. Only, as I joined them, he stood so that his face was not visible to the Peace Force officers, and spoke quietly enough for the wind to mask his words.

'You must be cautious, *shan'tai* Christie. We Harantish are not the same now. I think sometimes—' and he stopped, and said no more.

'Is Molly Rachel in the city? Pathrey—'

'Oh yes,' he said. '*Shan'tai*, it should not be I who tells you.'

Corazon Mendez stood foursquare on the platform as it lifted, no thought for the gulf of air below. Dust whitened her uniform. She towered a head taller than Pathrey when she leaned over to us.

'*Shan'tai*—' the polite term came unfamiliar from her lips '—I warn you, it's ill-advised to procrastinate. The Company is in a position to demand the full facts.'

It is? I thought. The small Orthean male nervously brushed away dust that the wind lodged in his robes. He gazed out at empty air. I knew in an intuitive flash what he would say.

'I am sorry for this,' Pathrey Shanataru said, 'and I should not tell you, *she* should, she will be angry . . . Your Representative Molly Rachel is badly hurt.'

Cory demanded, 'How badly? What is the extent of her injuries? What medical care has she received?'

Fear and intuition together made me look at Pathrey, at those shifting dark eyes. It came to me, that this might be bad enough to put Molly out of action for – weeks? months? *But I need her here, need her to restrain Cory's Force. Hell, I never thought I'd say that!*

'Where is she?' I asked.

'You will be brought to her, *shan'tai*.'

Cory said, 'Make it fast.'

The wooden platform jerked to a halt, hung swaying above emptiness. The Harantish guards dismounted and steadied it as we climbed down on to the city's roofs. Pathrey hurried us without pause across the expanses of white stone, up steps, down ramps; past roof-houses first lost and then disclosed by the whirls of dust. I found the air clearer at this height, slipped the air-tube out and took a breath, smelling dry earth and sun-warmed stone, and somewhere something rank.

Pathrey dropped back a step, letting Cory and Jamison walk ahead between the guards. I said quietly, 'Is it Calil bel-Rioch who's Empress-in-Exile?'

'Calil bel-Dannor.' A smile vanished somewhere in that fat brown face, and his unveiled eyes were small, dark, and brilliant. 'It became necessary to disclose that *shan'tai* Calil is in fact the daughter of Dannor bel-Kurick, abandoned in the lowest levels of Kel Harantish in childhood, and so,' he said with a disarming satisfaction, 'fully entitled to succeed him as Empress, after his unfortunate final, fatal illness.'

'What a fortunate coincidence that it should be so.'

He caught the dry tone, smiled; and there was something in that expression of ruefulness, of bewilderment. 'She's . . . changed. Ah. *Shan'tai*, ignore what you see now. The fighting is not long over.'

He spoke to the guards, and one stayed outside the small roof-house which we now entered. Corazon ducked her head to enter. I saw her speak to the burly Jamison, who checked his wristlink, and remained with the Harantish male. The other guards, pale-maned females so alike as to be a twin-birth, lifted up the heavy trap door.

I preceded Cory down the *del'ri* climbing-web into the chamber below. Despite common sense, I waited to hear the trap slam behind me – it didn't. Cory Mendez and Pathrey Shanataru climbed down. It being comparatively dark, it was not until I had stood for a moment on the stone-tiled floor that I saw the stains. Great patches of black liquid that seeped down into the gaps between the tiles and stained the plaster walls. In the dim light, the smeared print of a six-fingered hand was plain on one wall. Curving smears of black on the floor led to bundled *del'ri* mats in the far corner of the chamber . . .

'*Shan'tai.*' Pathrey Shanataru held open the trap door set in this floor, disclosing a flight of stone steps.

Corazon Mendez walked over to the heap of *del'ri* mats, boot-heels clicking on the tiles. She bent to lift one corner. I saw how her mouth quirked; expectant, sardonic. She let the corner of the matting fall back.

'Knives and swords are messier than CAS,' she remarked, in Sino-Anglic.

'*Shan'tai.*' Pathrey, insistent, at the trap door. I couldn't catch his eye. I was suddenly aware of the heat, of that smell that (to human senses) is not quite rot. Disgust lodged in my throat, sour as vomit. I walked over to him and down the stone steps.

Five levels below, the stone walls changed to *chiruzeth*. My legs ached, and my eyes also, with straining against the gloom. The dust-storms outside dimmed the mirror-reflected light. Black stains spattered the stairway. I saw no more bodies.

'Pathrey . . .'

'Dannor bel-Kurick was not without friends,' Pathrey said, leading us down another flight of *chiruzeth* steps. The air felt cool. The blue-grey walls held a luminosity only seen in peripheral vision. Neither Pathrey nor the guards stumbled as Cory and I did, and when he turned his face to me, I saw his dark eyes were unveiled and deep.

We went down, down steps sharp as if newly cut, for all they must date back to the days of the Empire. Through chambers whose walls were carved with bas-relief images, some glint of light striking from a curve or angle. The air seemed full of swirling, grainy particles; smelled of scorching, and that hidden corruption. Exertion left me panting for breath, heart hammering, muscles trembling.

The last flight of steps ended at the beginning of a wide, low-roofed chamber. I stepped down on to the *chiruzeth* floor. The light was dim. By chance I looked to the left. A pale-maned Harantish male lay beside the wall, face buried in the crook of his arm. The black that stained the floor was not shadow. I took a step in that direction and then stopped: what seemed like movement was the crawling of beetle-like insects on his naked back. They rustled.

'Lynne,' Cory said.

I turned away. That sharp face of hers was calm. You're used to it, I thought. Then: I've seen it before. Yes. I never get used to it.

With something between black humour and hysteria, I caught the black-and-gold sleeve of Pathrey's robe. 'Just how many friends did Dannor bel-Kurick have?'

'Many that one wouldn't have taken to be so,' Pathrey Shanataru said. 'In truth, I think some of them themselves didn't know it.'

Cory raised her wristlink. In the silence, I heard Jamison answer; and after a second, an answer from the orbiter. It reassured me to hear another human voice in this charnel-house.

'Pathrey, did Calil permit this?'

He said, 'You'll see the Empress-in-Exile now, *shan'tai.*'

We walked on. The two brown-mailed guards flanked us. A brighter light became visible at the arched end of the chamber, a yellow glow outlining the curve of *chiruzeth*. Our footsteps sounded loudly, but Pathrey's bare feet were silent.

'Stay here,' he ordered the guards, at the arch. I saw a look of relief pass between them. Then we entered through the archway and I realized, *Dannor bel-Kurick saw us here*. This low, wide chamber; alcoves to either side still crowded with the refuse of millennia . . . We paced down the narrow central passage between heaps of relics, towards lights and clustered groups of people. Light that came from candles on great iron stands reflected back from *chiruzeth* artifacts, from metal belts on shimmering red and blue and viridian robes, from metal combs in unbraided white manes. Heads began to turn at our approach. A young Harantish female laughed, was checked when an older woman touched her arm; three males in black robes whispered together. I looked at their narrow-chinned faces, the eyes that were whiteless brown or black, those manes dyed white; saw how they were imitations—

On the terrace that looks down on the Six Lakes, slender bodies in metalmesh robes; they who walk as dancers, white manes unbraided to the wind.

—but this is Kel Harantish, not Archonys. Kel Harantish, hard and white-shelled; inside, all the soft colours of corruption.

'The sooner we get the Representative out, the better,' Cory said in an undertone. 'Medical care will be on a primitive level, here, and . . .' Her voice trailed off.

Pathrey, walking with his head high, led us between towering stands of candles thick with congealed wax; between the gathered Harantish Ortheans; out into the empty floor between them and the arched end of the chamber. I felt my boot catch, glanced down, saw the *chiruzeth* floor was coated black – for a moment saw nothing else. Candlelight gave way to a light that is pale blue and lilac. The glow of sphere-lights.

'Give you greeting,' said a voice, muffled; a mouth half full of food. I took a pace forward. The black bloodstains were wet on the *chiruzeth* floor. My gaze followed the liquid to where it still sluggishly flowed—

A pile of white, round objects shone in the cold light. The heap was as high as my waist. Two other heaps lay near the dais and the carved *chiruzeth* throne, that I dimly saw now was occupied. White objects, ovoid, speckled with black. Then I saw the slanting, narrow eyesockets; the teeth in broken jaw-bones, the cranial sutures of inhuman, alien skulls. The bone before me was old, dried to yellow; but the stains were fresh, and so—

I fixed my eyes on a level, didn't (couldn't) look at the other charnel heaps, afraid (aware) that they were not old . . .

'Give you greeting,' the voice repeated. Something moved in the air. I flinched. A bitten *arniac*-fruit hit the *chiruzeth* floor and rolled to the edge of that heap of severed bone. I looked up.

She leaned back in the carved *chiruzeth* throne, chewing, and sipping from a carved bowl of *del'ri* wine. That thin face had a grin on it. Her white mane was roughly braided up, and her feet were bare and dirty. Her short white robe was stained on the breast with spilled *del'ri*. The thin copper chains that girdled her waist were green with verdigris. Sphere-lights hung in empty air above that throne, shedding light the colour of lilac and lightning.

She stood, stepped down from the throne, and kicked aside fragments of bone as she walked up to me. Her yellow eyes were sunnily cheerful. She wiped her *arniac*-stained hands down her robe. *A child*, I thought, *little and dirty and brilliant and bad. Calil bel-Rioch. Calil bel-Dannor.* Then her eyes met mine and it was a woman I saw, a Golden woman: Empress-in-Exile.

Pathrey Shanataru stepped past Cory and myself. 'I told them *shan'tai* Rachel was here and injured—'

Her hand struck once, vicious and fast. The blow echoed in the low-roofed chamber. Pathrey's head rocked back, then he touched his mouth and looked at the dark blood on his fingers. Someone in the crowd behind us laughed. I glanced back. Even in that crepuscular light I could see the numbers of Harantish there were growing.

'I'm glad to see you again, *shan'tai* Christie. This will be Commander Mendez? I've heard of you, *shan'tai*; give you greeting.' Calil inclined her head. Her voice held immense good humour. That studied normality chilled me.

Corazon Mendez said, 'I understand you offered protective shelter to Representative Rachel and other personnel. Rashid Akida, Pramila Ishida, and David Osaka.' Cory's voice stayed even, but she looked white round the eyes and mouth.

'Did we? Possibly. *Pathrey*—' This last in a very different tone. The plump dark male bobbed his head, half reached out a hand to her.

'The Representative is in the ninth level, *K'ai* Calil.'

'You'd better conduct the *shan'tai s'aranthi* there.' Calil turned away dismissively. She mounted the low steps to the throne.

Candles hissed, the only noise: bare feet on *chiruzeth* are silent. None of that crowd of Harantish Ortheans spoke. Light cast rounded shadows on the floor from those abattoir piles of skulls that clustered round the throne. I breathed shallowly but the stink of blood still caught in my throat; if it had been human, animal instinct would have made me vomit. Outside the circle of candle and sphere-light, eyes watched, dim figures there. Only *she* stood out clearly. That small figure, now seated on the *chiruzeth* throne, one foot tucked up under her; biting into a handful of *arniac*-fruit and dripping red juice on to the lap of her robe. She reached up to tuck a tendril of mane back behind her ear, and that claw-nailed hand left red smears on her cheek. I met her eyes. Yellow-eyed, that fox-face, bright with humour. Fear cramped in my stomach: *Here is a dream made flesh. Here is the child of Santhendor'lin-sandru and Zilkezra.*

'My Pathrey Shanataru is something of a liar,' she said, still smiling. 'Your Molly Rachel is not injured. She was injured. She is dead now.'

CHAPTER 25

Traitor's Gate

'Don't talk to me about xeno-psychology,' Cory Mendez said grimly. 'That woman's a psychopath!'

She keyed her wristlink as she walked. Pathrey led us down yet more steps, into higher-roofed halls and small chambers. He glanced back at her, worried. She swore under her breath.

'Getting interference again. Lynne, I suggest we act *very* carefully from now on.'

If we'd been a day sooner, half a day, could we have prevented this? I felt exhausted, afraid.

'Here, *shan'tai*.' Pathrey stopped at the arched entrance of a tiny room. He touched my arm, and said miserably, 'I thought to prepare you . . . I know *s'aranthi* are shocked by deaths. That was the reason for the lie.'

His speech was slurred, his mouth swelling from Calil's blow. I pushed past him into the small room. Mirror-reflected light was dim, but bright enough to show the place was empty but for a pallet on the floor.

Molly Rachel lay there, half-curled on her left side. Her eyes were partly open, but only a line of white showed under the lids; and she was too still. I felt the cold, soft skin of her throat for a pulse; her black hair brushed my wrist, and I shivered. She had been dead long enough, I saw, for the blood to pool in those parts of her body nearest the floor. The last act of planetary gravity. A darker flush on that dark skin.

'Knife wound,' Corazon Mendez said, squatting down to touch the ribcage. She picked up the unresisting hand and began to undo the wristlink. Without thought I grabbed at her arm: 'Leave her!'

I stopped. 'Sorry. Cory, I didn't mean—'

'It has to be a job. It's the only way to look at it. And this,' Mendez said, that hawk-face with a flush of anger, '*this*, dying on some stupid backwater world, just because you're caught in the crossfire – it's tragic.'

Sometimes I despise myself for the ability to become detached, but I used it now: looked down at Molly Rachel's body and allowed myself to feel nothing. I said, 'We must find out about the others, Rashid and David and Pramila.'

Cory bent to recover the Pacifican woman's wristlink. 'Records have been made recently. Says here, they're for your eyes.' She handed the wristlink to me. 'I have to abide by that, I suppose, but there may be data here that it's essential I have.'

'You'll see it.'

Cory Mendez bent over the body again, and I left the small room for the larger outer chamber. Pathrey Shanataru would have followed but I stopped him with a look. *One of these Harantish killed her, deliberately or by accident – who?*

And does it really matter now?

The wristlink's holo-image was tiny and clear: Molly Rachel's face. Brown skin, loop-tangled hair, luminous brown eyes. A squint of exhaustion drew her face into taut lines. And now she lies a few yards away, skin smoothed free of strain . . . The dead voice came thin and clear.

'A few points, Lynne, while I'm stuck here inactive – I might as well. Have this sense of *déjà vu*. Regarding Kel Harantish, isn't this where we came in?'

Her image chuckled. Something caught my breath.

'I'm leaving the northern continent as your department, but it must be brought under control. I hesitate to say this, but make whatever deals with Clifford's government that you have to. This isn't the time for the Company to be fussy.

'I . . . might need you here for a short period of time. The Calil woman bothers me. I know it means the risk that you'll react with false memories to Witchbreed artifacts – that's why I let you go north – but I may need your help.'

The dark face was illuminated with mirror-light. What I could see of the background showed a *chiruzeth*-walled room. The deep levels of this city. And is she alone?

'I'm duplicating this part of the report to home office and Cory Mendez. If it wasn't for the atmospheric interference, I'd send it through to the orbiter . . . There'll have to be an investigation but I'm pretty certain, Lynne; the illegal CAS weapons came in on the authority of Pramila Ishida. You know she has a – connection – with *hiyek*-Anzhadi. Sethri-safere. As far as I know, she's with them now. Lynne, she's done what I, God forgive me, always expected you to do: she's gone native. I've put a stop to the illegal arms trade, but as for what's already come in under the guise of agricultural equipment . . .'

The recorded image cut out. Immediately it re-formed. Time had obviously passed. Molly's coverall was rumpled, stained on one cuff with *arniac*-juice. She spoke with strained alertness: 'I've been cut off from contact with Rashid and David. If the damned com-links would only *work* . . . There has to be some way of overriding the radiation from the wastelands, if that's what this is. I . . . assume Rashid and David are unharmed. If I knew how the rumour got about that the Maherwa research is successful, I'd – we still don't know the first thing about Golden science, whatever Rashid says.'

The image remained still for so long that I thought it might have frozen, except that the dark lashes from time to time slid down over her brown eyes. At last she drew a long breath.

'And if Rashid *is* right, that makes being caught in this settlement a catastrophic error of judgement on my part. For that reason, I've destroyed all Company records here. I don't trust Calil bel-Rioch with any technology. If you come here, Lynne, you'll hear it: she calls herself "Empress". Not "Empress-in-Exile" . . . And now I don't know if Rashid or David are still alive, or – you see, I never intended that we should break the cultural restrictions by giving Golden science to *Ortheans*, and you blame me for searching out a commercial interest for the Company but how else can we justify the aid?'

That thin recorded voice paused. I stood in the large, dimly-lit chamber. What would you feel now, Molly; what would you say, if you knew then that you were about to die?

'I can't tell what's possible,' the dead woman said. 'Do you know, I half hoped your crazy theory about Kasabaarde was true, if only for your sake, and then that turned out to be propaganda. How can I judge what's alien? I thought the Harantish only knew how to maintain the canals by rote, by ritual transfer of knowledge they didn't understand. Now I'm not so sure.'

The image flickered again. By the wristlink's indicator, not much of the recording left to run. When the holo-image formed again, Molly Rachel looked tired and filthy, but she pushed back her tangled hair with long dark fingers, and grinned.

'Still can't get a contact out, but I can overhear transmissions. Must mean the interference is waning again. Lynne, I recorded this for you because you're next in seniority; David's here – I've just seen him. Pramila . . . God knows what the Company's going to do about Pramila. I want you to deputize for me formally in the Hundred Thousand. Use this place as a threat, if you have to; not sure quite how, but you'll think of something! I know you. We'll have to make sure Commander Mendez doesn't overstep the mark. I believe we're nearly there, Lynne. The fighting's stopped, the Empress-in-Exile says we're released from protective imprisonment. I should see you within two or three hours – in person, or by 'link. Take care.'

The record ran through to its end.

What happened in that blank time between that and her death? Silence is the only reply. The *chiruzeth* hall was cold, and I shifted my weight, aware of cramp from standing so fixedly to watch the wristlink's image. When I looked up, Cory Mendez was waiting.

'Here.' I handed her the wristlink.

As she activated it, I saw Pathrey Shanataru still at the entrance to that tiny room where Molly Rachel's body lay. Watching me. His black mane hung in sleek curls down his spine, but despite that and his new black-and-gold robes, he still had that indefinable air of seediness.

'*Shan'tai* Christie,' he said softly, and beckoned. When I left Cory Mendez and crossed the chamber to his side, he offered me a metal flask that hung at his belt. The liquid in it had the harsh bite of *del'ri*-spirit. I drank down half of it, feeling the fire.

'How did she die?'

'I don't know. That,' he said, 'is true, *shan'tai*.'

And if it isn't, what can I do about it? I tried again: 'Where's David Osaka? And Rashid Akida?'

He wiped his forehead, looking uncomfortable. 'If *K'ai* Calil says your people were never here, then believe her, *shan'tai*.'

There was fear under his obsequiousness. I glanced over at Cory – lost in the wristlink's record – and then back at this sleek Harantish male. He had to look up to meet my eyes. There was something in the movement that said *Witchbreed!* even of this plump, dark male; the faintest echo of the Golden.

'Pathrey – tell me about Calil bel-Rioch. Bel-Dannor. How long have you known her?'

'All my life,' Pathrey Shanataru said. 'No, *shan'tai* Christie, she's twenty years younger than I, but I think I had no life until I knew her. She was a barefoot brat, then, running the roofs with the other beggars. Traders' *ashiren*, the lowest caste. I come of a science bloodline, my people know canals and *siiran*. Did that bring her to me? I don't know.'

He raised the metal flask and drained it of *del'ri*, looking back at me with vulnerable eyes.

'I remember the first time I saw her. She was fighting another *ashiren* for a scrap of *del'ri* bread. Won it, too. Ate a mouthful and then stamped the rest into the dirt.' Pathrey paused, embarrassed.

'She speaks of you sometimes, *shan'tai* Christie. She would not like it if I spoke of her to you.'

'Is she mad?'

He winced at the direct question. He brushed one claw-nailed hand over his face, an oddly ineffectual gesture.

'You can't judge her, *shan'tai*. She has always seen . . . more. She made me travel with her, we went as far as the Rainbow Cities; and everyone who set eyes on her shunned her as Golden, as Kel Harantish is shunned; and she would tell me how, one day, Kel Harantish would stand alone.'

When he paused, I waited. His dark gaze was far away.

'I remember once we went to Kasabaarde, in the dress of mercenaries. She wouldn't enter the inner city. When she saw the Tower, from a distance, I remember she said to me, "If not for that we could hold command over all the *hiyeks*." So I asked, what about the north? And she said, "They come of the same stock, they would follow us without thought." I remember she looked at the spire of the Rasrhe-y-Meluur as a beggar's child looks at bread . . . '

His soft voice raised hissing echoes, here in this *chiruzeth* chamber nine levels below ground; here in the chill that is never disturbed by the Desert Coast's heat. Mendez still watched the wristlink. Something in the line of her back told me her attention had shifted.

Pathrey's dark gaze met mine. 'Do you lay blame on her? She sees our people prostitute their skills, only to keep us supplied with food and water; which elsewhere all men take for granted . . . I saw her weep, once. The white plague took a hold on the city. It was three seasons before we could bury all the dead – bury them, because they were poison meat. All they gave her was the contempt they had for a trader's child, and yet she wept.'

'That butchery in the throne-room, will she weep for that?' I grabbed his shoulders. The fine cloth robe bunched in my hands as I shook him. 'That's one of my people *there*, dead, will Calil weep for *her*?'

Cory Mendez glanced up. I released Pathrey. It was an effort to unclench whitened fingers. He rubbed his shoulder with a plump hand, looking up at me reproachfully.

I said, 'Pathrey, how long will you survive in Calil's court?'

That soft gaze was suddenly shrewd. The self-justification I'd identified in his tone vanished, replaced by something harder. He said, 'I can talk to her. She strikes out, but – I've always had that privilege. And as she is now . . . *shan'tai* Christie, you can see it, surely? As she is now, there has to be *someone*.'

725

Corazon put Molly Rachel's wristlink into a pocket of her coveralls. She glanced round at that ill-lit *chiruzeth* hall, and finally fixed her gaze on Pathrey.

'I'm bringing a troop in, to escort the body of Representative Rachel.'

She did not add, *And for my own protection*. She didn't have to.

Pathrey looked doubtful. '*K'ai* Calil may not permit that.'

'*K'ai* Calil should consider that a member of the PanOceania Company has been killed in her city,' Cory said. Unconsciously she twisted the silver rings on her bony fingers. '*K'ai* Calil should also consider missing personnel. Rashid Akida and David Osaka. I want them now. Or *K'ai* Calil must consider very carefully the events at Reshebet and Quarth and the harbours in between.'

The dark male made a hurried bow. I thought, Will you go running to Calil? Then Pathrey appeared to come to a decision. He muttered, '*Shan'tai*, I don't know where your people are. They said they would take one of your ships-of-the-air—' he deliberately used the Harantish paraphrase, not Sino-Anglic '—to rejoin you; but I saw no ships leave. That's all I can tell you, *shan'tai*, and that's more than I should.'

He walked hurriedly and silently away towards that level's steps. I began to move in the same direction. This is too close to that small room where Molly . . . and neither Cory nor I are safe in Kel Harantish now. As I walked with the Peace Force Commander towards the stairs, I said, 'You're not serious. There's a qualitative difference between a strike to block harbours and a hi-tech attack on a city.'

The lilac glow of *chiruzeth* made her angular face seem old or ill.

'If I have to threaten to get Company personnel out, then I'll threaten. If I have to take further action, I'll take it. We can't afford to be seen giving in to these tactics, Lynne, we can't countenance the kidnapping of Company personnel!'

'Is it possible there is a shuttle missing? On-world transport records are pretty careless at the best of times, so—'

'It's just possible,' she grudgingly conceded.

'Then there's substantial doubt. You can't take violent action.'

She halted. I paused with her at the foot of the flight of stairs that led up into misty mirror-light. The hollow halls echoed to our footsteps, to our breathing. Some independent part of my mind registered the bareness, the *chiruzeth* walls carved in angles and curves; the rest of my concentration was on Corazon Mendez. I can try to talk your language, Commander. What I want to say is, You don't know what you're doing!

The white-haired woman said, 'The late Representative

extended privileges to you, in respect of what authority you could wield. I'm sorry that I can no longer do that. Not in the present state of hostilities.'

'I don't accept that.' The underground chill made me shiver. 'The Company co-opted me as an expert on Carrick V. I'm best able to judge this situation. Until we find David Osaka, I'm technically head of the trade mission; I have superiority over the research grades—'

'*Not* over Security.'

I know a losing battle when I fight one. If I shut my eyes, I see the light in the throne-room, see it fall blue and lilac on those empty-socketed skulls. And Calil. How she stood barefoot in those black stains, sticky on the *chiruzeth* floor! Talk to me about psychopaths, Mendez.

I said, 'Let's shelve that one for now, shall we? It's Rashid we need to speak with primarily, I think you know why.'

That touch of authoritarianism made her respond. She nodded, and then said, 'You'd better talk to whoever you can, here. We need Rashid. We need to know if there *has* been a breakthrough by his research team.' And then she drew an unconsciously deep breath. 'Can you imagine Golden technology here in this settlement? That woman would have control of the Coast before you could say "Empire".'

We climbed two levels, beginning to come where Harantish people passed on unknown business, whispering as they saw offworlders. A familiar plump figure appeared. Pathrey Shanataru, returning, panting as he hurried to intercept us.

'You may bring your escort—' He turned from Cory to me. 'The Empress wished you to speak with her people – fifth level is a good place – ask what you will—'

'Is there any point?'

Pathrey straightened, getting his breath back, shaking the folds from his robe. Membrane slid back from those dark eyes. 'Don't think me stupid. We have one of your people here dead because we failed to keep her safe. You will hardly trust us now. And there must be trust, *K'ai* Calil needs *s'aranthi* trade, how else can we survive? So she sends you her Voice, to speak with her people.'

Oh, I thought. Realizing only then that I must be speaking with the Voice of the Empress-in-Exile. He looked momentarily smug.

'I'll get Jamison down here,' Corazon said.

I left her, following Pathrey up the stairs to the next level. Then without any warning, I had to stop. I felt exhausted, disorientated by the shifts in geography and time zones; and for a moment I leaned a hand against the cold *chiruzeth* wall. I squinted up the stairwell at the stronger light above and thought quite unexpectedly, *Molly's dead.*

No more of that outspoken honesty, that I've envied even when it was me she hurt. I won't see again that energy, that grin of hers, that unwarranted generosity; and why did I never tell her? To know her for so short a time, and most of that quarrelling. *The risk that you'll react with false memories to Witchbreed artifacts – that's why I let you go north – but I may need your help.* Why should she act as if I'd behaved like a friend to her?

The dark angles and dusty light of that stairwell were blurred, blind, hidden by tears.

'You have this in common with the true Witchbreed.' Pathrey's voice came clear, clinical almost. 'Death for you is final, and no further meeting. Come, *shan'tai.*'

I spent the next three hours on the fifth level of that block, speaking with Harantish Ortheans. Most of that group were science bloodlines, with some ritual knowledge of canal technology – and is it more than ritual? – and a few were traders, and one or two were of that tiny administration surrounding the Empress-in-Exile. It doesn't have to be more than a tiny administration, I thought. Because they're all of one mind. The unanimity is frightening.

A thin, elderly male voiced the general opinion: 'We've been at the mercy of the *hiyeks* and the Tower for too long. *K'ai* Calil will find a way for us to stand alone, free of them. Your *s'aranthi* machines will bring us food and water, and this is all we need. *K'ai* Calil makes a friend of you offworlders where *K'ai* Dannor would not. We follow her now.'

Conscious of the hours ticking away, I said, 'And the *shan'tai* Akida, the *shan'tai* Osaka; what of them?'

The male looked at me with veiled eyes.

'Who?'

Pathrey Shanataru stepped forward to speak with him. I sat back on the metal bench, staring round that low-roofed chamber. Close enough to ground level for the walls to be stone, not *chiruzeth*. There were a few outside traders with this group of Harantish Ortheans – and as I thought that, I felt a touch on my arm.

'*Shan'tai* Christie, give you greeting.'

I almost exclaimed aloud. A narrow face, with brilliant green eyes, and a white mane shaven down to fur; last seen in Maherwa . . .

'*Shan'tai* Annekt,' I said, very quietly.

He smiled. 'So it is I who will give you the message. How strange a coincidence. No, don't look startled, be as you were. This is much safer than meeting you secretly.'

'"Message"?' Thinking: I *knew* you were more than a Coast trader.

'Word has gone with all the traders out of Kasabaarde this season, which I now pass on to you, so. "*Shan'tai* Christie, because what was lost may be found, come to the Brown Tower in Kasabaarde. Come because you remember, there was a city seen in mist and pearl".'

Annekt spoke by rote: the message was not in any of the Coast dialects, but in that thick Melkathi that they speak on the heath *telestres*. *A city seen in mist and pearl* – and what was lost may be found. Rashid, what did you find in Maherwa? Will you give Witchbreed again the use of ancient light? Christ, that can't happen! Can it?

'What does the Hexenmeister want with me?'

'*Shan'tai*, it may be the Hexenmeister has need of a go-between to speak with offworlders. And I have heard rumour that you were in the Tower before?'

There was naked curiosity on his face, but I was too confused to satisfy it, even had that been wise. The Tower is only archives. Only a dead record of the past, and records may lie. And I have fought the false memories that threatened to drown me, have fought them as much as I can, but if I go to the Tower, will I "remember" delusions too strong for a human mind to stand? And for all that she's Hexenmeister now, Ruric was once traitor to the Hundred Thousand. To us all.

Annekt's green eyes veiled. For a moment I hated him, this casual stranger. The Tower cannot be ignored, even if it is only archives; archives may tell us what we need to know, and God knows we need all the help we can get. And there is more to it than that. If I go there, I will (I know) ask her, What did I see at Rakviri *telestre*? What did I experience with Calil? And will she have an answer?

I said, 'You can send word that I had the message.'

Midday came and went unremarked. I felt the heat of it as I climbed back up to first level, and to the open roof, where Peace Force troops stood with the covered body of their Company Representative. As I climbed up on to the roof, I slid eyeshields into place. The dust-storms had died down. Harantish Ortheans were on the roofs, watching us curiously as we passed by; and there were others down at the harbour. I saw the whole panorama as our platform was winched down. There was no movement near the T&A excavations.

With Molly gone, the impetus of the trade mission will just . . . run down. Until the Company sends another representative. It won't be trade now, it'll be peace-keeping, and a desperate scramble after Witchbreed technology. Unless I can hang on in there and keep the T&A going?

The wooden platform grounded, scraping rock. Jamison's troops disembarked, and rested the stretcher on the earth. That dark, shrouded shape. One thinks the ridiculous: *can she breathe in there?* Dust can't hurt her now.

Cory spoke to Pathrey Shanataru again. I took the opportunity, stepped back into the shadow of Harantish's cliff-wall. Hoping that the interference had eased, I used my wristlink to call Doug Clifford.

His image appeared. After a brief greeting, it assumed that prim expression that is Doug's camouflage for self-satisfaction. 'Lynne, I thought I might warn you of one thing. The WEBcasters are on their way to the Coast. They want to see the *hiyek* harbours. And Kel Harantish, I believe.'

'Cory won't give them transport,' I objected.

'They have shuttles through from Thierry's World that they can use. Courtesy of the government.'

You have to admire Douggie. I let it pass without comment. 'I've bad news,' I said; and sketched in the events of the past half day, telling him of David and Rashid's disappearance, of Molly's death. I saw his shock.

'It's a bad business—' He glanced off-screen. 'Lynne, I have to go. I'm taking a shuttle down to Keverilde *telestre* to talk with Jadur Anzhadi. Ah . . . it may be more urgent than even we thought. Satellites show an unusual concentration of shipping in the islands of the Kasabaarde Archipelago, and I grant you it's the summer trading season, but—'

'But we don't know how many *hiyek* ships sneaked out under cover of that storm, before Cory's strike. I'd better pass that on to her, I suppose.'

The small image nodded. 'I'll call you at 19.00. Let me know immediately if there are developments where you are.' He paused. 'Molly Rachel . . . I can't take that in. It's a bad way to go.'

'Are there any good ones? I'll hear from you, Douggie.'

The Peace Force troops picked up the stretcher and began to make their way cautiously across the rocky ground. Cory stood looking up, watching Pathrey's platform being winched higher, squinting through dark eyeshields.

'I've just had word from Ottoway. They've found Osaka and Akida—' She ignored my exclamation. '—in the excavation site over there. I've had both of them put in cryogenic hibernation, the orbiter medics *might* be able to save them both. Rashid Akida's in a bad way. Exposure, heat, dust . . .'

'What the hell were they doing?'

'Hiding? Running? We won't know until they can speak. Lynne, I'm going to put a permanent troop here, garrison the T&A site. Someone has to watch these psychopaths.'

'Is that wise?'

Her hands, that had been twisting those silver rings, fell to her sides. Her voice went harsh. That sharp face came up: eyeshields glinted. '*You* don't have a say in the matter. Lynne, I'm sorry, I have to worry about security now. We have an invasion on the northern continent; now we have the possibility of alien technology in use here. It's a very volatile situation. The Force will have to clamp down until it settles.'

And if I try to contact the Company home office, that will take twelve days. Until then . . . I can't force her to accept my authority. All I can do is continue to preserve my independent status, until I can use it.

I said, 'I want the use of a YV9.'

Corazon Mendez stared. 'What use do you have for a shuttle?'

'We must know about Golden science.' I faced away from her. The rock shimmered in the heat. The sky swam. No daystars, not even on the horizon; this land is harsh as the surface of some forsaken moon. 'Is it possible Rashid's made a discovery – some synthesis of Earth and Witchbreed technology, perhaps?'

'But a shuttle—'

I don't know if that was the first time I consciously admitted it. Did I give a tacit consent by continuing to use the Tower's false memories as a guide? And now that there's Calil in Harantish, I must know from Ruric Hexenmeister how far those dreams of ancient light are to be distrusted. I must ask Ruric if she's lied to me again. Or, if not, what has reached out of the past to touch me.

I said, 'I'm going to Kasabaarde. To the Brown Tower.'

PART FIVE

CHAPTER 26

The Tower

I landed outside Kasabaarde, and disembarked. The spire of the Rasrhe-y-Meluur jutted into the daystarred sky, a towering blue *chiruzeth* pylon gilded on its western side by the light of Carrick's Star. Wisps of dust storms obscured its base. I stared up, craning my neck, thinking, Hard to believe it's still the same day . . .

Midsummer. Somewhere in the hours just past, a new *T'An Suthai-Telestre* will have been named in Tathcaer. *Who?* A Crown in the Hundred Thousand, an Empress in Kel Harantish . . . And yet it's neither of them that are controlling events now. It's the ordinary men and women of the *hiyeks* and the *telestres*. And is there still a truce in Melkathi?

Interference again made comlink contact all but impossible. I lowered my wristlink, turned to seal the shuttle and put it on auto-lock. The road here is indistinguishable from wasteland. Kasabaarde's Westgate is infrequently used, leading only to the small settlement L'Dui and the smaller Lu'Nathe. A hard, hot mile's walk to the gate; it left me sweating.

As I entered the city, I saw few people. I walked down translucent-floored avenues, hearing the rustle of canal water under my feet. Daystars paled above, in the late afternoon sky. Windvanes slowly turned. A few Ortheans in *meshabi*-robes passed. None spared a glance for a *s'aranthi*. The white dust worked down inside my ankle-boots, and the strong, beating heat of the sun made me dizzy. Easy to be lost in Kasabaarde. I walked down avenues and alleys, keeping the sun always at my back. And then I came to an open space, and a high sandstone wall.

Will there be guardians at the gate? I wondered, recalling the last time I'd been here. I had forgotten – I always do forget – that to come to the Brown Tower, one must pass through the inner city.

When I came to a sandstone arch, a white-robed male waited in the shadow of the gate. He was not long past *ashiren*, a brown-skinned boy with a white mane shaven down his spine, and a *del'ri*-fibre robe belted at his narrow hips. He stood with his bare feet slightly apart, rising up on to his toes.

'Go away,' he said. 'The inner city is closed.'

Never in centuries – I gaped; recovered. 'My business isn't with the Order Houses, it's with the Hexenmeister.'

He pressed his lips together. I could see how his hands were shaking.

'Go away. No *s'aranthi* can enter here. No one. The Order Houses are abandoned, there's no *use* in going in.'

'I must go to the Tower.'

Oblivious, he said, 'The Order Houses are all empty. The *hiyeks* rioted—' Membrane slid back from his brown eyes, leaving a rim of white all around. The wild gaze saw me. 'What did the Tower do to stop it? What did the Hexenmeister do to save us? The mob stripped us of everything and what did the Tower *do*?'

'What could it have done?'

His boy's face became petulant. As his attention wandered again, he said, 'The Hexenmeister could have stopped it; they would have obeyed . . .'

He sat down in the dust, resting his back against the masonry of the arch. I saw, half-buried there, *harur*-blades. I was conscious now of the weight of the CAS-IV holster at my belt. When I was certain the young Orthean male no longer noticed my presence, I sidled under the arch and through into the inner city.

Violence and vision. The vision gone, still the violence may remain . . .

I began to walk, as silently as possible in the dust, nerves taut; seeing no movement, hearing no voice. My mouth was dry with tension. All through the alleys, between the dome-buildings, under the awnings, lay the debris of a mob's passing. Overturned stone tables, broken *del'ri*-wood flutes, a bale of blue cloth spilling down steps like a river; broken crockery and glass. All I could hear was my pulse hammering.

I came to a dome that rose up out of the white dust, where the awning over the doorsteps was half pulled down. The late afternoon light shone in through its door, fell on rubbish, broken *arniac* bowls, a cast-off robe. Order House Su'niar. I called out but my voice fell flatly, without an echo. Deserted.

Gone, for how long? How long until they return – if they ever do? Is the inner city something we've lost forever?

At last I came to that stretch of open ground, and crossed it, and entered the gardens of the Tower. Here were stunted ash-grey *lapuur*, the earth between them trodden flat; and their fronds

736

curled in the heat, alternately hiding and disclosing the sun-baked bricks of the Tower's west wall.

Suddenly I was overcome with a strong conviction. *Everything that's important is happening away from here – four hundred miles down the Coast, or a thousand miles away in Melkathi. Not in this backwater. I can only spare a few hours here, and even then, that's hours that are being wasted . . .*

Ah now, hold on a minute. I recognize that refusal to look at the Tower.

Deliberately I dug my nails into my palms. The pain cleared my mind. Again I felt the sharp heat of the sun. Dust caught in my throat. I looked round at the drooping *lapuur* and up at the high dome of the sky, my perception changing: *it is so still here because here is the eye of the storm . . .* And something nagged at me. *If I can put all the pieces of my 'memories' into one pattern, there is something I ought to see.*

But those memories are false. Aren't they?

I thought on that while two brown-robed Ortheans came to lead me into the Tower; a melancholy walk through slick-walled artificially-lit corridors. They took me, not, as I had expected, to the library-room, but up through an elevator to the roof-garden. There, in the sunlight, among the stone tubs that spilled scarlet blossoms of *arniac*, a dark Orthean woman sat cross-legged at a low table.

Ruric Orhlandis glanced up as I approached. Her single hand held a bowl of *siir*-wine. The Tower roof-garden is walled, so I could see beyond her nothing of the city, only the sky and the daystars and the setting sun.

'Good,' she said. 'I wanted to talk to you, *S'aranth*.'

I could only look at that narrow, dark face, at those sunny eyes, and hear what she said to me a month ago: *I wish that I were all Ruric, all Orhlandis, but I'm not. I'm Hexenmeister now.* I saw her smile.

How did I convince myself she meant the duties and responsibilities of the office of Hexenmeister, not that she is less – or more – now than *amari* Ruric Orhlandis?

'I came to ask about – memories? Visions? I'm not sure what they are. Came to ask you, because it seems to me that if it's only fragments of Tower Archives, it's too damn *real*.' I looked at her. 'And now . . . it isn't something I can prove, but I know, now, that you're not just Ruric. I can see it – sense it. But I can't explain it. You're Hexenmeister.'

She said, 'Yes.'

'Then – I need to know why I'm not the only one to experience these memories. I could understand it, I think, if it was just me, because I've been in the Tower. But what about Rakviri, and Calil bel-Rioch?'

She inclined her head. No necessity for explanations: the Tower hears these things.

She said, 'There are still dreams of ancient empires in the world, and they touch you, as if they were not quite dead. They cling to relics, and to places, and to people who desire, with desperation, the days that are past. Because you have been in the Tower, you become sensitive to this.'

'"Come because you remember, there was a city seen in mist and pearl" . . . So that was true, too?' I stood looking down at her. The Tower is the Tower, not an archive; the Hexenmeisters are one Hexenmeister; how else could she know my visions.

'Damn, you lied well! I *did* believe you. I suppose until now—' Or did I know when Calil and I together saw the City Over The Inland Sea? And couldn't consciously admit it, because that means admitting one thing more . . . 'You lied to me again, tricked me again. Except that it isn't you, is it? It's the Hexenmeister. That ought to make it different, but—'

She rose to her feet in one swift movement. All the old sword-fighter's grace was there. She stood in the sunlight, in the Tower garden, and I shivered. This lean, ageing woman, skin like flaked coal; dressed in simple shirt and britches, with bare feet, and mane straggling out of a half-crop . . . is this something wearing the Orhlandis face as a mask?

'Christie . . . ' Ruric Orhlandis sighed. 'Sunmother! For Her sake, don't be so stupid – it *is* me. I may have more lives in my head, but it's still me; and yes, I lied to you again, what did you expect? Do I look as though I'm playing *ashiren*-games here?' That dark, narrow face showed plain exasperation. She hooked the thumb of her single hand in her belt.

'Eight years on and you're still expecting people to act in good faith . . . Sunmother! It's a wonder they let you out without a keeper.' And she grinned, unmalicious, to take the sting out of it.

'You cynical old—' I stopped. '"Old". Ruric, I don't have any idea, do I?'

A gleam came and went in those yellow eyes. 'More than most, you do!' Ruric smiled again. 'It's ironic. There was I, whining that because I'm part Witchbreed I have no past-memories, and now I've more past-lives than half the Hundred Thousand put together. Christie, I tell you, She has a very peculiar sense of humour . . .'

'She isn't the only one.'

'Ah, well. After all, this is too serious to be solemn about.' Ruric turned away, prodding thoughtfully at the nearest stone tub. Then she wiped her hand free of the earth, and in quite a different tone remarked, '*Ziku* spores. A grove of *ziku* would suit the Tower gardens, but I can't get them to grow here. They're *telestre* plants. They don't thrive outside it.'

Del'ri mats were thrown down round the low stone table. The Orhlandis woman sat down, folding long legs, and reached over to grab the *siir* flask, and pour the viridian liquid into her bowl. She hesitated over a second bowl, and looked up at me with only a host's curiosity.

'Ruric, Goddammit! Why am I here?'

'That's my *S'aranth.*' Thin lips curved. She put down the flask, gestured at the mats beside her. I remained standing. She rested her arm across her knees.

'When he—' I hesitated. 'When it was suggested I enter the Tower, eight years ago, and undergo memory-transfer, it was as proof. Proof that the Hexenmeister isn't what you claimed, a month ago – merely the keeper of archives. Now I'm so confused I don't know what I'd take as proof of anything! What you are, what happened to me . . .'

'Same thing,' Ruric said briefly. She leaned her head back for a moment against another stone tub, basking in the setting sun. The black mane fell across her forehead, hiding the scar of branding.

'It takes time to become Hexenmeister,' she said. 'There are always several – apprentices, shall we say? Those who've been through the first stage of memory-implant. That was what I gave you, eight years ago. It was making you unable to speak of it that damaged you, and for that I'm sorry.'

'*You're* sorry?'

The response was automatic, and I saw how Ruric choked back a laugh. My legs ached with standing, so I lowered myself down to sit on the *del'ri* mats. No Tower brown-robes were visible in the gardens now, as I looked round; there was only the light of Carrick's Star falling on brown brick walls, on scarlet *arniac* and gravel paths. Familiar, why? And then I realized: This could be any roof-garden in Morvren Freeport or Tathcaer.

Ruric poured *siir*-wine into a bowl. 'Do you know, I knew you'd come here if I asked? That's why I sent word out with the traders. They'd find you, and you'd come.' She paused, looking at the *siir* and not at me. 'Did you ever forgive me for that summer in Melkathi, and SuBannasen, and Kanta's murder? I asked you to come to me then. When they'd just done this.' Long fingers brushed back that dark mane. The exile's mark: a jagged scar.

I said, 'Thinking back, when you told me you were going into

739

exile, didn't *I* say, "Have you considered Kasabaarde?" Now *that's* ironic.' But I had been thinking, then, of the inner city.

Ruric looked up.

'Now I've called you again, after I've done worse: tricked you into memory-implants, blocked off your own memories from you. Brought you here again, after eight years.'

Chilling, to hear her speak. One the act of Ruric Orhlandis, the other of that old man, the Hexenmeister; she speaks as one remembering both. Like the sun on the surface of a river: one minute all brilliance, all Ruric; and then the light shifts, and under that surface are depths . . . That feeling of frustration came again. On the tip of my mind, as it were: there is more to this than the accumulation of memory, and an ancient being hiding itself in an impregnable tower . . .

Carrick's Star shone on her face, on the lines faintly incised in alien, reptilian skin. She rubbed at her nose and mouth, that gesture utterly familiar from her days as *T'An* Commander of the *telestre* army. She's tired, I thought. And if I know Ruric (*if* I do), would like nothing better than a fight. Simple action. How she must fret, as Hexenmeister . . .

'All right,' I said. 'What am I doing here?'

'In plain terms, you're being kept a prisoner.'

Startled, before I thought better of it, I said, 'You can't hold me here.'

Ruric drank from her *siir* bowl, and set it down with a clink on the stone table. Then she scratched at her mane where it rooted on the back of her neck, and shot a glance up at me from under dark brows.

'Too dangerous to let you loose, with the *s'aranthi* ripping the Coast apart in search of Witchbreed technology. I can't have them knowing what's here. As I said to you once, if you had not been desired to enter, you could not even have passed the gardens. The Tower's defences work both ways, keep people out – and in.'

Not her who said that, but *him*; the old man.

'I could have made certain, early on, that no word about the Tower ever came from you. There are assassins on the Coast. I could have had you killed in Maherwa, by Annekt. Haven't I done all I could for you? But the Tower *must* survive.'

I said, 'Damn the Tower's survival. What use is all your Hexenmeister's knowledge if you never *do* anything with it? Have you seen what's happening in Kel Harantish? The inner city? And in the *telestres*, in your Hundred Thousand? You sit there and whine that all that matters is the Tower's survival—'

'Mine and the Tower's.' She smiled: there was something of pity in it. 'Christie, you do know why. Even if you don't know that you know. I'm sorry. I did you a great wrong, eight years ago, and all I do is compound it further.'

The dome of the sky was ashen now; daystars fading to the Coast's swift twilight. The heat of the day became comfortable warmth. I reached for the bowl of *siir*, drinking cautiously. There was no scent of *saryl-kabriz* or *ruesse*. I looked at Ruric and, as well as human tongues can manage, stumbled out the phrase that Calil bel-Rioch had used to translate ' "Ancient light".'

Membrane slid across those yellow eyes.

'Ruric, is that – it's what I'm afraid of. If the *hiyeks* rediscover how to use the weapon that produces ancient light; if Rashid Akida discovered something in Maherwa, or if it's possible to produce – I don't know – some synthesis of Earth and Witchbreed science.'

'They don't have to,' Ruric said. 'That isn't necessary at all.'

Heat reflected back from brown brick walls, comforting as night began to fall. Because I didn't want to think about what she'd said, I hastily asked, 'And what else am I doing here, besides being a prisoner?'

'I need an offworlder.' Again, that grin, white against her satin black skin; lines crinkled at the corners of her eyes. 'A *tame* offworlder, shall I say? Ah, that ruffles your feathers! Christie, I want to apply to Earth, through the national governments, for Orthe to be given Protected Status. On anthropological grounds. Your WEBcasters are making us so widely known that we might have a chance, now, if we're quick. I can't leave the Tower. I need human support. That's you.'

She put her hand down in a long-familiar gesture to rest it on the hilt of *harur-nilgiri*; found no blade there.

'*T'An* Commander,' I said. '*T'An* Melkathi.'

'I was ignorant then.' She met my gaze. 'One thing I did know enough to fear. That Earth would change us, destroy us. I was more right than I knew . . . If you're to help me, Christie, you ought to remember all the reasons why. You know too much to be safe, and I should send you to Her. I could ask you for that—' she indicated my wristlink '—allow you no contact outside the Tower. But you know what I know, and I'd sooner have you as an ally.'

You know what I know. Fear made my mouth go dry. I moved slightly, the weave of the *del'ri* mat had imprinted on the skin of my hands. The light of Carrick's Star as it set sent long shadows reaching for us.

'Ruric—'

'Now that I am Hexenmeister,' she said, overriding what I began, 'I have the memory of your coming here, eight years ago. And I have the memories the then Hexenmeister took from you. I've *been* Lynne de Lisle Christie. Can you imagine? I'd been four years in exile from the Hundred Thousand, Orhlandis was broken up, Rodion dead, Suthafiori dead. And because you were here before you went back to Tathcaer, and found out what I'd done, I saw myself through your eyes, as you saw me, a friend.'

And by that time I was four years gone from Orthe, on different worlds. Different myself, because of her.

'If I know that my "delusions" about the Tower are true,' I said, 'if I know that it's the Old Science that stores and transfers living memory from Hexenmeister to Hexenmeister; that that memory goes back thousands of years, to before the Golden Empire itself ... Ruric, you *can't* let anyone who knows that leave the Tower.' I challenged her: 'Not if the Tower's secrecy and survival are all you care about.'

She reached across, briefly resting her hand on my arm, where I had half rolled up the coverall-sleeve. Her fingers were dry, hot; the pulse of a different heartbeat felt through the skin. Then she sat back. The western light shone on her high-arched ribs, the small breasts and paired lower nipples, and then as she turned to pour more *siir*-wine, on the mane that rooted down her spine to the small of her back, showing through the slit-backed shirt.

'Christie, some people you have to trust. I *know* you. You love this world, you're *of* it. I did one thing better than I ever knew when I had you marked for the Goddess. That was a true foretelling. This is your home.'

She faced me again, sipping at the bowl of *siir*, and then added, 'It isn't only the Tower knowledge that matters. It never was. You know that.'

'I don't know. I can't quite get there – I do know, but—'

It was suddenly as if there were three of us present: Ruric, myself, and that old male, eight years ago; who had told me what it meant to be Hexenmeister, and in face of my incredulity, said –

' "You *must* believe," ' Ruric quoted softly. ' "Or else you'll believe nothing I tell you. And what I tell you may affect relations between our two worlds . . ." '

' "Kasabaarde is the oldest city in this world, and I am the oldest person. I know this world. So when Orthe comes to deal with other worlds – I am the only one qualified to speak for us." ' I finished the quote. For a moment I was quiet, perceiving the last of the day's warmth; tasting dust on my lips, and the aftertaste of *siir* in my mouth. The *kazsis*-vines began to open their red blossoms, giving off a heavy, sweet scent.

A mile or two away to the west is the shuttle, and my 19.00 hour call from Douggie almost due, outside the city. And here there is the Tower, and all the subterranean levels of it; levels that connect with the first spire of the Rasrhe-y-Meluur, and all that great *chiruzeth* structure that bridges the Archipelago to the Hundred Thousand. I cannot ignore what I know.

'I could put a worse interpretation on it,' I said. 'All that concerns you is that the Tower survive. You must have defences that could make even Cory's Peace Force pause. So when do you decide to take action? When it's possible that the weapon that produces ancient light has been rediscovered. When the Tower's threatened. Am I right?'

The dark Orthean woman put her fingers to my forehead, briefly. I thought suddenly how, long ago, in the north, an Earthspeaker had done the same with water from the Goddess's well. And in that same place *amari* Ruric bears her exile's brand. And was it there that *he* put a six-fingered hand, that old man, the Hexenmeister? I met those yellow eyes that now unveiled. And thought of Calil, and how we had together called up the dead past . . . Ruric took her hand away.

'You *know*,' she insisted. 'Some of the things you said in your delirium, travelling from Maherwa to Kasabaarde – oh yes, I had eyes and ears with you on that journey. That was the nearest you came to an assassin's blade, or *ruesse* in your cup, but you never spoke clearly enough to warrant it. Now I need you to speak.'

I looked at her. Ruric Orhlandis; Ruric Hexenmeister.

'You are what you say you are, but that doesn't mean I can trust you.'

Ruric shrugged, with that old crook-shouldered balance. 'Then you'll have to do without trust.'

Assassin's blade; *ruèsse* in the cup. Yes, I thought. You'd do it. Even as *T'An* Commander you would have done it; it's part of the game. The Orthean game that is too serious to be solemn about . . .

I said 'I don't see *why*—'

The woman rose to her feet. She rested that one hand on the edge of a stone tub; six-fingered, claw-nailed, black against the scarlet *arniac*. She turned her head; those yellow eyes met mine.

'Why? Because there's something I plan to do, and I need your help. It's that simple. Forget that year and Melkathi if you can. Everything I did then, I'd do again. Still . . . I need your help. Christie, please.'

She knows me too well, I thought, and, I have never known Ruric Orhlandis ask anyone for help. As simply as that, I let the world, the Tower roof-garden, the evening sky, all slip away.

Because there was a city seen in mist and silver . . .
I remember:
The darkness is profound, so great that I cannot see how high the walls are, or how far above is the ceiling of this great hall. There is only the blackness of space and the abyss. I feel its coldness on my skin. The floor beneath my feet is a mirror-blackness, made of that rare chiruzeth that only the Imperial bloodline can shape. I see my frightened face reflected: the face of an old woman of the slave race.
I raise my head. There is a little light, enough to show the bases of great pillars; yards in circumference, vanishing up into darkness. And—
He is there.
Steps rise to a dais. On it is a structure both throne and mausoleum, black chiruzeth, shaped over with vines and death's-heads. Blue-and-lilac light from one floating sphere puts a shifting blackness in empty eye-sockets. And he rests back against that tomb-throne. His pale mane shines, his hands are gold dust. I see how he stares up into that infinite darkness: the last, lost heir of glory.
Here is no echoing ritual chant, the ritual is forgotten. Here is no soft corruption waiting the knife. Here is only emptiness.
A young male steps out of the shadows by the throne. His dark skin and mane proclaim him one of the slave race, but his eyes are yellow. He gathers round himself a robe that is all the colours of sunrise, and kneels down on the dais. His sibilant voice hisses in the vast emptiness of that hall:
'Slave, come forward.'
My old body aches. What shakes it is not age, but fear; and I hobble closer, and kneel down upon that mirror-darkness. I bow my head, and say no word.
'___ _____ ___ _____.'

The gold-dust hands clench; his head comes up in one animal-swift movement, and this is He: Santhendor'lin-sandru, Phoenix Emperor and Last Emperor. Speaking the tongue of the Imperial Golden race, that no slave woman should know. If he should think that I . . .
And he stands, Santhendor'lin-sandru, a small, bright figure against the surrounding blackness. As I kneel at the foot of the dais, I see him raise his arms as if he can embrace that annihilation:
'O my sister, my lover, my self! Because she has entered the city, a great race shall come to corruption; because she has entered the city, a cancer eats at the living flesh of it, a plague that cannot be stopped nor stayed! Of chiruzeth that was living, it makes a death. Of life it makes a silence and

a stillness and a light . . . And from the cities it spreads out, irresistible; turns earth to crystal, and will not cease until all the earth is one sterile mirror, and only the wind moves, and blows silver dust across the face of it . . . O Zilkezra, great is thy praise!'

Echoes die. For one moment I fear that power, fear that the old rituals can be reborn. An imminence is in the darkness. And yet the echoes of that ancient power are fading . . . And Santhendor'lin-sandru again takes his place on that dark throne. He signals briefly to the dark slave male. The dark-maned male lifts his head:

'Hear the word of Santhendor'lin-sandru, Phoenix Emperor, in the great halls of Archonys. Hear his word! You are Our children, We created you from the beasts of this world. Now We go down into darkness, and you must follow. Now We go into darkness too bright for mortal sight; a brilliance that swallows up cities and earth and sea.'

He bows his head to the floor, this Voice of the Emperor; and then raises himself again:

'Hear the word of Santhendor'lin-sandru, you who have hidden yourselves away in corners of the world, seeking to end this. That ancient light dawns now upon the world. Once begun, it cannot be ended. Once created, it cannot be cured. Hear his word!'

Fear pulses through me, blinds me so that I cannot see, can only sprawl prostrate on that icy floor. Echoes whisper in the abyss of darkness above. I have thought it was my eyes that watched him, this Emperor of a dying world; and can it be that he knows what we have sought to do?

And suddenly there is a sound, a voice like the wind in dead leaves. It is he, the Last Emperor, speaking that tongue the Witchbreed do not deign to speak: the language of slaves:

'Do you think We do not know you? You who skulk in corners, call yourself Master, passing your feeble memories from life to life . . . thinking that because We do not exterminate you like vermin, We do not know you . . . '

I look up, past the prostrate and terrified form of the Voice of the Emperor. Santhendor'lin-sandru smiles: that hawk-face brilliant and cruel. That rusty voice whispers on:

'Run, little animal, We will let you go. Run, hide. Seek out some lair in the south, in the Rasrhe-y-Meluur or the Elansiir. Use Our works, as you have done for uncounted ages, to pass on your little lives, one Master to another . . . This age is ending, and Our works will not outlive that ancient light. Your age-long life is at an end, little animal.'

Some lair in the south. I am shaking too hard with fear to stand, or to speak. Does he know? Can he know what we are making, in terrible haste, in the south; a last attempt to kill the cancer that has been set in the flesh of this world—

And Santhendor'lin-sandru gazes down from the mausoleum-throne.

Black chiruzeth *gleams in that light the colour of lilac and lightning. I can do nothing but look up at that face. His eyes are yellow, yellow as sunlight, as the eternal noon and infinite summer of Golden rule . . .*

'*Try, little animal. Try to kill that living light. You may even halt it for a time, We will allow that. But you cannot hold it back forever. It cannot be killed. And soon, a few heartbeats or millennia, and you will join Us.*'

Far to the south is that structure later ages will call the Tower. Far to the south, we strive to hold back the devastation that eats away at this world . . .

'*Run, little animal. Run.*'

Now the dark male rises from the floor, gathering his sunrise-robes about him, and steps down from the dais. In his hand there is a flash of brilliance: a ritual knife.

'*Hear the word of Santhendor'lin-sandru, Phoenix Emperor, in the great halls of Archonys. Hear his word! You are to carry Our speech to your companions in the southern lands – but you are not to return to them unmarked . . .*'

'Christie. Christie *S'aranth*.'

The vast dome of the sky arches over me, webbed with light, flowing with the brilliance of Orthe's summer stars. The scent of *kazsis*-nightflower and *arniac* are chokingly strong. I can even look at my dirty human hands, and not lift them to wipe away the nightmares of blood hanging in my eyes . . .

'*S'aranth*.'

'Yes.' A deep breath; some control. 'You – I – the Hexenmeister should never have gone to him; too dangerous!'

Ruric Orhlandis grinned, as she squatted on her haunches by me. 'So long as the body comes living, or newly-dead, to the Tower, the memory-transfer can be made. You *s'aranthi* would say we need "living cells". That isn't accurate, but it'll serve.' She chuckled. 'If I ever die outside, make sure my body gets back here! Wouldn't be the first time that's happened. Now it's too dangerous. I don't leave the Tower. Christie, are you all right?'

Her chatter anchored me in physical reality. The Tower garden, the cold *siir* in ceramic bowls; the night winds blowing from the city. And, distant, blotting out stars, the Rasrhe-y-Meluur.

'You'll have to tell me one thing,' I said. 'How you managed to destroy ancient light—'

And then I could only stare at her.

'That's right,' Ruric said softly. 'You know it. Ancient light can't *be* destroyed. Not once it's created. All we could do was hold it back. We are still holding it back. And, yes, that "radiation" that so interferes with your technology isn't a result of war damage – it's

746

all that holds ancient light at bay. If you like, call it . . .' she was plainly searching for Sino-Anglic terms '. . . a suppressor? Counter-radiation?'

I was abruptly conscious of the Tower, all the levels below me; created from Golden technology that no longer exists, and cannot now be reproduced . . .

'It's housed here,' I said.

Ruric stood up, stretching. She glanced down at me. 'Here. Yes, here. And if that's all you know, that's all I'll tell you. But now you know why, above all else, the Tower must survive. And now you know why I'm afraid.'

CHAPTER 27

Silence, Stillness, Light

Gravel scraped under my boots as I stood up. The night wind was
warm against my face. *Arniac* rustled. I stumbled, unsteady, and
the Orthean woman caught my arm. Above us the sky was a slow
blaze of light; the Heart Stars, silver and crimson and blue; so
thickly clustered that the edges of the Tower roof were a black
silhouette against them. I looked up into that depth, that vastness
. . . and had a sudden, almost physical comprehension of the
thousands of years that have passed since the Empire fell.

'All of it,' I said, 'the *telestres*, the Coast families, the Rainbow
Cities, the Barrens – all of it growing up in those years, whole
civilizations, not knowing what's held back from them; that
devastation . . .'

Ruric let go of my arm, and brushed the black mane back from
her face. There are some expressions unknown to those of us who
live a single lifetime: hers was one. I felt isolated, alien.

I said, 'What about their past lives? Ortheans wouldn't forget
how Golden science works, and they wouldn't forget that ancient
light isn't dead, only . . . quiescent.'

The Orthean woman chuckled, and that was all Ruric, all
Orhlandis. 'Christie, my temper doesn't improve either, when *I'm*
scared . . . Very well, I'll give you an answer, but you know it: the
Witchbreed themselves could barely comprehend the science the
Eldest Empire bequeathed to them, and they never let the slave
races have much comprehension of it. Though it may be that we
understood it better than our masters . . . And as for the other,
they may have assumed that devastation had a natural limit,
reached it, and so ceased.'

Then, more soberly, she added, 'It may be that they do know. I
can't say. There has been nothing they can do about it, except
bury it so deeply they never think of it . . .'

Silence hung over the roof-garden. That gravelled space, filled
with stone tubs and *arniac* and *kazsis*-nightflower, so very like the

roofs of Morvren and Tathcaer: too mundane, almost, for such revelations. And no robed Master to speak of it, only this middle-aged and crippled Orthean woman, dressed in plain britches and shirt, one sleeve knotted up; and with the scar of an exile on her face.

A little whimsically, to gain time, I said, 'And am I Hexenmeister now, or partly so?'

The woman broke into a laugh. It's the first thing I ever noticed about her, in that Residence eight years ago in Tathcaer: how her dark and sober face is illuminated by laughter, how those eyes almost physically glow.

'No, *S'aranth*. You've touched the edges of it. I have a dozen apprentices here like you. Except that, being alien, you may still have some different reactions from ours . . . Still, you have the first stage. Not all.'

Nearly 19.00; Douggie's contact would be due. I stood indecisive, watching the face of *amari* Ruric Orhlandis, Ruric Hexenmeister.

'All I have are memories, and memories aren't always reliable. Ruric, you're going to have to *show* me proof.'

For all I've seen the satellite-images of devastation, the sterile wastelands of the Elansiir, the north Barrens, the Glittering Plain; for all that there *is* an atmospheric distortion that affects Earth technology – and for all that my memories of that crystalline death are so clear – still, I need proof. I will always need proof.

Ruric, quite cheerfully, said, 'You always were a suspicious old . . . now let me see, I have an Anglic vocabulary, what *is* the word I want?'

'Er, I don't think we want to go into that too deeply . . .' Is it possible to laugh and shiver simultaneously? Her knowledge of that language comes from my mind, eight years ago . . . and her use of it is nothing but a smokescreen.

'If you want my help, you have to show me proof.'

'Christie, do you have any idea how hard it is for me to trust anyone?'

I hear echoes in her voice of that old man who was Hexenmeister eight years ago, echoes of the *T'An* Commander of the Hundred Thousand, and of phrases that I myself use. How many others, how many generations, live now in her memory? She watches me, this alien woman: that six-fingered and claw-nailed hand clenching, the starlight bright on sharp-edged ribs and dry-textured skin. I wish I could follow *telestre* custom, groom out that tangled mane where it roots down her spine, comfort her as one Orthean comforts another. But I have only human hands.

The Orthean woman fixed her eyes on my face. Then she

nodded, once, and turned to walk back through the garden. I
followed, almost taken by surprise. She said no word as we came
to the Tower entrance. A brown-robed male ushered us down into
the artificially-lit corridors, down into brown-walled chambers that
I dimly remembered from my time here with Blaize and Rodion.

'Ruric—'

Without turning, she said, 'This may be the most unwise thing I
have ever done. Christie, I owe you a debt, eight years old. Prove
I'm not as unwise in trusting you as you were in trusting me.'

The Brown Tower is, like most things on the Coast, nine-tenths
under the surface. I have myself been into levels that connect with
the complex under the Rasrhe-y-Meluur. Now I expected us to go
far below ground level, but instead the Orthean woman walked
briskly through slick-walled corridors, past the library-room and
its windows, to a chamber that would be perhaps one level below
the city outside. A large chamber, low-roofed, with the same slick-
textured brown walls; and I was about to comment, when I saw
the brown-robe who stood at its entrance.

'Give you greeting,' I said. 'Tethmet Fenborn.'

The artificial illumination struck highlights from his skin, green-
gold, with its fine, waterproof texture. Stick-thin limbs, hands with
hooked claws – he is one of the aboriginal night-hunters that still
exist in the Great Fens. Membrane blinked down over those large,
dark eyes. He glanced at Ruric.

'When you first brought her here, master, I warned you against
her . . .'

'Old friend, you don't let me forget it; and now I'm about to do
a thing you will like even less. See that no one disturbs us.'

Both spoke in the language of the Fens. I had a brief memory
(my own) of fever, exhaustion; mudflats and reeds and fenborn
hunters. Putting it aside, I followed Ruric into the windowless
room.

Soft yellow light came from no discernible source. It illuminated
stone benches, metal shelves, ridges of that wall-material that
jutted out into platforms; blue-grey *chiruzeth* sarcophagi, like those
in the 'Archives', many levels below . . . All the flat surfaces were
swamped with piles of books, parchments, half-finished artifacts of
wire and metal and crystal, earth-trays with plants just beginning
to shoot, *arniac* bowls with a scum of liquid drying in them, broken
mirrors . . .

'Camouflage,' I said. 'Like the library-room that you keep for
visitors. Am I right?'

The dark woman grinned. 'Only partially. I *have* been given to experimentation, over the years, but this is not where most of it was carried out.' And then she became serious. 'One thing I can show you, Christie. I was unwise enough, for a few generations after the fall of Empire, to experiment myself; see if there was not some way, still, of destroying ancient light. It had the result you might expect. I no longer experiment, because I no longer have the science to control what I create.'

She walked between the piles of junk on the floor, to a *chiruzeth* tank not much smaller than those in the Archives.

'I've seen something like this before,' I realized. The resemblance was strong – that octagonal hall in Rakviri *telestre*, where Barris Rakviri activated the growth of *chiruzeth*. About to join Ruric, I suddenly stopped.

She looked up. 'What is it?'

'Something odd. If I were superstitious . . . No.' Briefly, I explained what I meant; knowing she would remember similiar occurrences. 'It's just that there were four of us present at – participating in – that vision. Only a few months ago. And out of those four, three are now dead . . .

'Barris was killed, Jaharien committed suicide – and this morning, in Kel Harantish, I saw Molly Rachel dead. Murdered.' I met Ruric's gaze, held it. 'I *will* find out who's responsible. I can't let it pass.' And thinking of that young woman, her body by now back on the orbiter in cryo-storage, makes coincidences trivial. I walked over to join Ruric at the tank.

She said, 'The past is not always as dead as it should be. And I don't refer solely to "ancient light" – that's the physical manifestation of . . . something quite other.'

Black brilliant light. They fell in love with that bright shadow, Death—

She walked round to the other side of the tank, opposite me. The black mane fell across her forehead as she looked down. Lines of strain showed round her eyes, and membrane slid across that yellow gaze. I at last recognized that strained stillness for what it was: fear.

'I made this,' she said bitterly. 'It took me three generations, and was almost as foolhardy as showing it now to you, Christie S'aranth. Look.'

The *chiruzeth* tank was half full of earth, and stunted shrub *arniac*, and withered *del'ri*. It was the pale earth of the Desert Coast, and that sourceless illumination cast a fuzzy shadow round each pebble and stick. A cluster of *kekri*-larvae squirmed beside a larger rock. A puddle of water glinted—

a mark, a lichen, a flower; chiruzeth is turning under his hand to dead crystal; spreading as swiftly as a crack in a shattering mirror

—no, not water, but light shining from a patch of stones and gravel that is clear now as glass; as crystalline, and as dead.

'See.' The dark Orthean woman put her hand on the edge of the *chiruzeth* tank. The air in the interior shimmered. A wave of heat hit me in the face; faster than the eye could follow came a flash of silver; I cried out – and all was still again.

Shrub *arniac*, *del'ri* stems; rock and pebble and stick . . . now they all gleamed. Silver-glass. I wiped my lip, that hurt; took away a hand marked with blood, where I had bitten down. Now, all the interiors of the *chiruzeth* sarcophagi shone, crystalline; and here splinters of light ran into the *chiruzeth* itself . . .

Ruric Orhlandis reached down into the interior, and picked up what had been a living cluster of *kekri*-larvae. She held a handful of light, that crumbled away into dust, drifted on the air into annihilation. Her eyes were dazed. My palms ran with sweat; heart hammered; I thought I would be violently ill. She lifted her head. She was shaking. A line of white was visible round those yellow irises, in that face that had looked unmoved on the burning of Orhlandis *telestre*.

Unprompted, together, we moved to where we could hold each other in a necessary embrace.

An hour later. We stood in the parchment-odoured library; windows open to the night. A breeze rustled stacked papers, and brought a scent of the city beyond. The Heart Stars cast enough light.

'What do we do?' I said. Then: 'Ruric, it would all have happened sooner or later. With PanOceania, or some other Company. We were called . . . The Harantish planted Witchbreed artifacts where offworlders would find them, knowing it was a bait we couldn't resist.'

Ruric stood by the table. She slopped *del'ri*-spirit into bowls. 'That wasn't the first time that happened, but my agents prevented the other artifacts from being found.'

She handed me a bowl of *del'ri*, and sat down heavily on one of the couch-chairs.

'Kasabaarde has great and wide influence,' she said, 'but not total control. That's as it should be. I think so. Or perhaps I only hope that I think so.'

I blinked at that. Then I sat on the couch-chair beside her. Starlight robbed the room of colour: all was black, silver, grey. I yawned and rubbed at my eyes.

'If I add it up, I've had about six hours' sleep in the last two days . . . I can't even think, never mind come to terms with what

I've seen here.' I paused. 'You're not telling me how the suppressor, the "counter-radiation", how it functions.'

'If you don't know, I don't have the right to tell you.'

Through exhaustion I thought, If I had to guess, I'd say it was some property of the Tower's *chiruzeth* structure. Maybe it . . . I don't know . . . modifies the radiation of Carrick's Star? And my 'guesses' are more accurate than I care to think about.

Chiruzeth; that, when it lived, the Witchbreed shaped by their will alone; that now can't be recreated, their secret being lost . . .

I said, '*Is* all knowledge lost?'

Starlight gleamed on her black mane as she moved her head, drinking from the *del'ri* bowl.

'If there were any hint of Golden science left, the halfbreeds in Kel Harantish would have found and used it; or somewhere in the Barrens there would—'

She stopped and looked at me. Those yellow eyes were luminous, almost with their own intrinsic light.

'Christie, I have searched, for more ages than you can easily comprehend, for some way to undo the destruction that Witchbreed and Orthean together left living on this world. If there was a way, I would have found it!'

'And the Empress Calil? She questioned Rashid Akida, I'm certain of it; God knows what he found. And he's too ill to talk.'

The Orthean woman said, 'Goddess forbid that ancient light should again be used on this earth. I'm not at all sure it would be held back, as the Elansiir and the Glittering Plain and the north are leashed in, held in check – no, I'm not at all sure it wouldn't strain to breaking that restriction, and what then?'

That book-filled room was silent. The light of the Heart Stars shifted on the floor. I lifted the *del'ri* bowl to my lips, wincing at the bite of the spirit; fighting not only exhaustion, but the desire to use sleep as an escape. *I do not want to think about what I have just seen. A world of crystal mirrors, over which moves only the wind, and the silver dust of annihilation . . . No, don't think. Or I will recall what I felt at Rakviri: that the bright shadow is so easy to look upon – and love.*

'And what now?'

'I have to ask you – ' Ruric stopped and glanced up, to where a brown-robed Tower servant stood in the doorway. She beckoned. The male handed her a strip of parchment.

'I can use *rashaku*-relays and heliographs too,' she said, with a smile of amusement. She read, and that sharp-planed face changed: I read amazement, and a kind of wry humour. 'Well,' she said. 'Well . . .'

'What is it?'

'I have eyes and ears in the Hundred Thousand,' Ruric Hexen-meister said. 'Today was Midsummer; they've named a *T'An Suthai-Telestre*. You see how fast word can come to me.'

I leaned over, reading the parchment strip that the long fingers of her single hand spread out on her knee. It was in the curling script of the Hundred Thousand. The name of the new *T'An Suthai-Telestre*, legible by starlight . . .

'"Nelum Santhil Rimnith". I don't believe a word of it!' And then I thought of him in the Wellhouse, with Bethan Ivris; how he had spoken of peace with the *hiyeks*.

Ruric threw her head back and laughed. 'And after he was Portmaster in Ales-Kadareth, taking bribes from Kel Harantish – well, we do change. *How* we do change!'

I tapped a key on my wristlink. Well past 19.00 now, and though Douggie might expect communications to be unreliable, he would be concerned. I said, 'If I can get through, I want to know if Nelum Santhil and Doug are down in Keverilde still, and what's happening about the *hiyeks* – if Sethri's still talking; if there's any fighting—'

'You won't be able to use that inside the Tower, I think.' Ruric bent down and put her *del'ri* bowl on the floor, and then stood up briskly. 'Rest, first. Christie, I have to talk to you again; there are things I must ask you. And you must leave the Tower soon. I'll have my people take you where you can sleep for a few hours.'

And sleep was an escape; a welcome, dreamless dark. No need to think of this ancient Tower, eroded by the ages; the secrets of its creation and repair all lost. No need to think of the bleak devastation miles to the south; or how sunlight had gleamed upon the Glittering Plain . . .

No need to think of that city, four hundred miles toward the sunrise, and a Empress throned on skulls; whose face is the face of the Golden. No need to think: *Is there the slightest chance that, after so many millennia, that weapon might be re-created?*

Sleep is an escape, a dreamless refuge; and a hand shook me out of it, shook me roughly awake: 'We might not have as much time as I thought,' Ruric Orhlandis said. 'I've had word come down from the islands. The Coast ships in the Archipelago waters are beginning to move.'

Dawn wiped the daystars from the sky. A midsummer day on the Coast: sky white as bone, and the wind a breath from an open furnace. I loosened the neck of my coverall, sweating; and swore in frustration as the wristlink showed me only static. I'd thought that on the roof-garden, outside the Tower structure, there might be less interference.

'It's no use.' I thought: What's Cory doing, is she still on the orbiter? Where's Doug? I need to know what's happening in Kel Harantish; I'll ask Molly—

I stopped, taken by that surprise that is not (after all these years) unfamiliar. It takes time to know that someone's gone.

I walked back through the dusty garden to the domed roof-entrance. Ruric Hexenmeister was there. She looked as though she'd slept in shirt and britches, or else not slept at all; the early morning sun cruelly illuminating her shabbiness and exhaustion. She was pacing, bare high-arched and six-toed feet scuffing the gravel; and as I came up, stopped to pounce as a brown-robe brought a message. She exchanged words with him.

Amazing, I thought; still half asleep. Amazing how much there still is in her of *amari* Ruric Orhlandis. She is Ruric. And she is so many others as well. And while she's told me the truth about the Tower and ancient light, she will, if necessary, lie totally about what she's going to do about it. And we both know that.

The Orthean woman paced as if imprisoned; held by the claustrophobia of Tower walls. She stopped as I approached, and stood with her hand hooked in her belt. The dawn wind ruffled her mane.

'Is there any use my stopping on one of the Archipelago's islands?' I asked. 'I could try to contact the *hiyeks* there.'

'Christie, I doubt it. The rumours coming through are confused. Some say the *hiyek*-families are quarrelling now, that they can't agree on whether to sail back to the Coast, or finish what they've begun. I doubt you'd be able to do much.'

A thousand *jath-rai*, scattered among all the Archipelago islands . . . No, I thought. There isn't the time.

'As soon as I can contact Doug or Cory, I'll know what's happening. I *must* know what action Cory intends to take. She's terrified of hi-tech weapons in Orthean hands—'

Ruric grinned toothily. 'So am I.' Then she stabbed one claw-nailed finger in my direction: 'All I hear from you is "Cory" and "Peace Force". You're still in the Company, Christie. *You* restrain her.'

'I don't have the rank!'

'I know,' the Orthean woman said quietly. She took a step forward. 'Try. Because of what you've told me – the Representative dead – there may be some way you can influence events. And yes, I know. I *know*, Christie. What business of the Tower's is a war between the Coast and the Hundred Thousand? None. None at all. My only concern is the Tower's survival, and that, at the moment, means watching Calil bel-Rioch. What happens to the Hundred Thousand is nothing to do with me, it's unsafe to interfere—'

She broke off and turned away, but I saw the pain on that dark face. How could I forget? A decade older than that woman who had been *T'An* Commander, *T'An* Melkathi; but still the same Ruric, that I knew that long-ago summer. Accused, guilty: I still hear her voice saying, *All I've done, even to murder, I've done for the Hundred Thousand. As I love the land – I love it more than life – so I have tried to protect it.*

There is Blaize, and Haltern, and Cassirur; there is even Nelum Santhil . . . I said, 'You know I'll do what I can. And for the Coast, too; Anzhadi and the others.'

She repeated, 'It's no concern of mine. What I can do without risk, I'll do, but it won't be much. I would come with you, if I could; but I can't leave the Tower, can't take the risk of losing this. There are so few who can live with an aeon of memories, and it takes so long to find them . . .'

The dawn breeze began to fail, and the temperature to rise. *Arniac* opened scarlet blossoms. Our shadows fell ink-black on the gravel. I glanced up, not sure if I caught a shimmer in the air, and wondered, *Tower defences?* But it stirred no recollection. There have (I know) been Hexenmeisters too alien, too early dead or driven into insanity, for the chain of knowledge not to have its weak links.

The Orthean woman turned back to me, linked her arm through mine; drawing me to walk between stone tubs of *kazsis*, away from the roof-entrance. 'Christie, I said I'd ask you for help . . .'

'Well?'

Ruric smiled; that quirk that is half humour, half self-mockery.

'Tell me I'm doing it again,' she invited, as we walked in the early sun. 'Tell me I can't be in a place without going against the law of it . . . Listen: you must return here, and this is what we must most urgently discuss – you've said to me, you fear some synthesis of Earth's technology with Golden science? So do I. But I also think this: if such a synthesis were possible, might we not find from it some way to destroy ancient light? Not merely to hold it in abeyance, but to *destroy* that threat that hangs over us?'

'You . . .' The sun struck down like a blow; I wished I had eyeshields. The dry heat exhausted me. And for a minute, I didn't believe what I heard. 'Ruric, you mean letting a research team inside the Tower?'

'They wouldn't come here?'

'Oh, they'd come here, all right! You wouldn't get rid of them. Isn't it an infinitesimal chance that we could understand Witch-breed science?'

Ruric inclined her head. Light glinted from skin and mane: the colour of flaked coal. 'True. And if I were even to suggest such a thing to my people here – the Tower has always been inviolable; I confess I don't quite know what they'd do. If it's to happen, it will take very careful handling.' Membrane slid back from her sun-yellow eyes. 'But it's a chance I can't ignore.'

I drew my arm from hers and stopped, leaning against the edge of a stone tub. It was hot under my palms, and *kazsis*-vine writhed away from my touch. Ruric stood with that crook-shouldered balance, watching me.

'You wouldn't suggest it, if it weren't for the chance that Calil's got there before you?'

'No,' she agreed equably, ' I don't suppose I would.'

'And that's down to us. The Company. We came here; we put a research team in Maherwa . . . Christ, I wish I knew what was in Rashid's report!'

Ruric shrugged. 'There are things even my agents haven't been able to find out. No one's infallible. Not even me.' And she smiled, with that Orthean humour that has more than a little of the macabre about it.

'What we've spoken of – the Tower – I may have to go back to Earth. Talk to the top people in the Company home office and the government. It's not a decision to be made on-world . . . the security clearance must be something phenomenal.' Almost a laugh; and I looked at her: 'You can tell. It's too big; I'm afraid of it.'

'So am I,' Ruric said. 'We do what we can.'

By unspoken common consent, we turned and walked back towards the domed roof-entrance. The sky's brilliance dazzled me. Faintly visible against it was the first pylon of the Rashre-y-Meluur, and its suspended bridge-structure that vanished into sea haze, northward towards the next *chiruzeth* spire . . .

'I'll send some of my people to escort you to your shuttle,' the Orthean woman said. 'If you need names of my people in the *telestres* and *hiyeks*, you can have them. You may need to get word to me.'

'Not a prisoner, then?' I said.

That yellow gaze flicked up, humorous; met mine; and I thought, *Assassin's blade; ruesse; saryl-kabriz.* Perceiving that a threat is sometimes not an insult and not a betrayal.

'Weren't you marked for Her?' Ruric jibed; and then without any affectation or mockery added, 'Christie, I trust you.'

757

PART SIX

Part Six

CHAPTER 28

Ashiel Wellhouse

Summer heat in the Hundred Thousand is mild, after the fierceness of the Desert Coast.

Still, we clung to shadows of *ziku*, the light of Carrick's Star streaming down through red foliage; and to the shadows cast by the walls of Ashiel Wellhouse, as the sun inched its way up to mid-morning. Warm air was full of *chirith-goyen* cloth-flies, dancing over the Wellhouse hives, specks of mica in the slanting beams of sunlight.

'Something's gone wrong.' I stared eastwards, tense.

'You offworlders are impatient.' The skeletally-thin fenborn male beside me smiled. 'You and the *galeni*. Only we know how to wait.'

Galeni is what the aboriginal fenborn call Ortheans. Tethmet Fenborn straightened, shaking the folds of his brown robe across that green-gold skin; and then stalked off towards one of the other groups of people waiting. *Has he seen someone who knows the Tower, someone who'll give him word to send to Ruric?*

The wind brought the scent of fertile earth. Beyond the *ziku* grove, I could see how daystars skeined a milky-blue sky. Carrick's Star shone down on dusty tracks that criss-crossed the hillside below Ashiel Wellhouse, running between banks of brown *saryl-kiez*, now just blossoming into blue flower. There were folds of the Ymirian hills in the north, and heathland to the south, fogged by a blue-white haze; and *there*, three or four *seri* distant, the black scar on the land where Keverilde had burned . . .

'I don't see anything moving down there.'

Doug Clifford appeared beside me. That round face showed strain; he was white round the mouth. He walked with none of his usual elasticity.

'You've been out of contact for forty-eight hours, I hope you realize. Lynne, I have to say, I didn't find that particularly helpful.'

'I would have been here sooner. The shuttle was low on fuel. Cory's people sent a refueller out to Lone Isle; I met them there.'

'Bringing him with you . . .' Doug's gaze followed Tethmet, as the fenborn crossed the crowded yard.

On the shuttle I recorded and re-recorded coded message-blips, sending them through the orbiter to FTL-drones. Twelve days, I thought. Then PanOceania and the government will hear what I heard in the Tower. Meanwhile: 'I do have some new information,' I said. 'I'll be calling a meeting. Cory. Ravi; he's acting head of Research. You. I don't yet know if there should be any Orthean representation.'

Douggie's head came up; he gave me a judgemental stare. With something of his old urbanity, he said, 'I have the distinct impression that Commander Mendez assumes she's acting head of mission. When do you plan to tell her otherwise?'

I'm not telling her anything, let her find it out for herself . . . Before I could phrase that tactfully, Douggie's attention was gone. He stared down the hillside towards Keverilde. Dust was rising, a mile or two distant. Others had seen it too, the crowd began to drift towards the gate-arch. I glanced back at the Wellhouse, to see if any of the *takshiriye* would come outside.

Scarlet mane and green robe flared in the darkness of the door: the Earthspeaker Cassirur stepped out into the dusty yard. A dark-maned male followed. He supported another male, swathed in a dark *becamil* cloak despite the heat, whose mane was a wispy white crest, and who spoke rapidly and quietly and continuously. Nelum Santhil, with Haltern. For a moment all three were framed against the Wellhouse: a sprawling complex, brick walls rising straight and then swelling into onion-domes; smothered with *kazsis*-vine and shaded by *ziku*.

As Douggie walked over to join them, and I was about to follow, a voice behind me said, 'Representative Christie? Can you spare me a few moments?'

A young woman, with dark hair and slanting brows; she stood in the Merrum sunlight, sweating under the weight of WEBcorders. I know you, I thought; not correcting her assumption that I was the Company representative now. Or I've seen you, or—

'Roxana Visconti, Trismegistus WEB,' she introduced herself. 'Ms Christie, I wonder if you'd like to comment on the on-world situation here?'

Dust still rose from the distant track into the summer air. Closer now: possible to make out that it was a group of riders. The Wellhouse yard seethed with activity: Ortheans in priest's skirts bustling in and out of the Wellhouse itself, males and females with

762

the gold crest of the Crown Guard checking winchbows and *harur*-blades, *ashiren* scrambling up on to the low outer wall to point and yell. There were Ortheans outside the outer wall, mostly wearing the thin robes of Melkathi; many with the faces of Keverilde or Rimnith *telestre*. Momentarily I wished I had some control over them.

'It'll have to wait—'

'Is it true that Commander Mendez is launching a full-scale investigation into the death of Representative Rachel? Will you yourself be returning to the Harantish settlement in the near future?'

I thought of Jamison, left to guard the T&A site at Kel Harantish; of Corazon Mendez up in the orbiter. Somehow none of it seems to have any relevance to who Molly was.

'This will have to wait. Look down there.' I pointed towards Keverilde, the lace-silhouettes of charred *ziku* and *hanelys*, the black earth, the tumbled stones – visible even at this distance – of the *telestre*-house. Spirals of smoke went up into the air. Cooking-fires. 'You can't see, but there are two or three thousand guerrilla fighters in that area. What we're trying to do here is talk. Defuse the situation. Ms Visconti, I *will* talk to Trismegistus, but not right now. Not when there's a representative of the Anzhadi about to arrive.'

'What responsibility is the Company taking for this?'

Jesus Christ, I thought, now it's me that has to answer the awkward questions.

I said, 'What does public opinion back home make of this?'

'The response is – unfavourable.'

'Good.'

When she looked sceptical, I added, 'There should be an impartial group here. Look, Ms Visconti, if you want to keep me informed about how they react at home, I might be in a position to help Trismegistus here. How does that sound?'

She eased the strap of the WEBcorder on her shoulder. Patches of sweat showed under the arms of her coveralls. 'I refuse to gloss over what PanOceania's doing to Carrick V, if that's what you mean.'

'You tell it as you see it.' I saw Douggie beckon. 'Excuse me; I have to go.'

Ashiel's outer wall is decorative, only a few feet high; and the gate-arch is a curving hoop of brickwork. Now, in early Merrum, young *rashaku* perched there, their scaled breasts glinting in the sun. Harsh metallic cries rang out: their warning. I walked to join the others at the gate, as the troop of riders came towards us.

'Let them through.'

Nelum Santhil's voice was not loud, but it carried to the male and female Ortheans outside the yard. Some muttered; others stepped back a pace or two. Is it because he's Rimnith *telestre*? I thought. Because he's suffered? He wore plain shirt and britches; there was nothing to mark him out as *T'An Suthai-Telestre*.

Haltern Beth'ru-elen shifted his grip to my arm instead of Nelum Santhil's. Membrane flicked across his eyes; the skin round them crinkled. His grip wasn't strong. 'Are they there, *S'aranth-te*?'

'I . . . yes, I can see four or five people from the Coast.'

Marhaz walked delicately, lifting their split pads from the dusty track and replacing them with care. Their feather-fur pelts glinted bronze and white and black. Most of the riders wore green tunics with gold-crest badges, the mark of the *T'An Suthai-Telestre*'s Guard; and these were war-*marhaz*, both wickedly-sharp pairs of horns left uncropped. Almost lost in the mêlée were four riders in *meshabi*-robes.

After the *marhaz*, and now swinging wide round the group to draw up outside Ashiel, was a groundcar. A fair-haired Peace Force officer whom I recognized as Ottoway got out. He signalled to the foremost rider. I saw the scarred, dusty face of Blaize n'ri n'suth Meduenin, *T'An* Rimon.

The Earthspeaker Cassirur Almadhera said, 'Bring them inside.'

The four Coast Ortheans slid down from the high *marhaz* saddles with obvious relief. Blaize let his *marhaz* pace beside them as they walked to the gate; Ottoway and two officers fell in on the other side. As they approached, I saw one stout and bronze-maned Coast Orthean with a flask dangling from his belt: Jadur, is it? Jadur Anzhadi. And the white-maned female there is either Wyrrin-hael or Charazir-hael . . . Both a head shorter than the *telestre*-Ortheans who pressed close in on them. A taller male, yellow-maned and white-skinned: no mistaking Sethri-safere. A female with him, with a dark mane and sallow skin – no, dark *hair*. In *meshabi*-robe, with a hook-knife at her belt—

'That's the Ishida girl!' Doug stared.

Arrest her on suspicion of hi-tech arms trading? It'll have to come, but: 'Now isn't the time to do anything, Douggie.'

The smell of *marhaz* dung was strong on the air; a complement to the heat. What can happen on such a day? But the tension is still there: stomach-wrenching; settling in the muscles between neck and shoulder.

'Doug, what say you're very understanding, very sympathetic. And then I'll hit them with the *jath-rai* in the islands. Yes?'

He nodded absently, still staring after Pramila Ishida. Nelum

Santhil and Cassirur were closest to the *hiyek*-Ortheans, moving them towards the Wellhouse entrance; and the rest of the crowd followed: Doug with Haltern, Ottoway, the Visconti girl, Tethmet's tall, gaunt figure; males and females from Rimnith and Keverilde. Heat shimmered over Ashiel's low domes. Not a rich Wellhouse – no Wellhouse in Melkathi is – it still had a surprising number of young *ashiren* within its walls. They ran underfoot, under *marhaz*-pads; pointing at the Coast Ortheans and shrieking. No Earthspeaker rebuked them.

I tacked myself on to the end of the group, and then a *marhaz* brushed past my shoulder, and Blaize Meduenin dismounted beside me. In that dusty yard, amid shrieking children and the hum of *chirith-goyen* hives, I saw how the slanting sun illuminated that old scar masking half his face.

Foolish: all I could say was, 'I thought you would be *T'An Suthai-Telestre*.'

He gave the *marhaz* reins to an *ashiren*. 'The Crown? Not me, I'm a fighter.'

'Hal must be disappointed.'

'Haltern Beth'ru-elen finds *T'An* Santhil—' Blaize paused. 'I don't understand Haltern. Eight years ago Nelum Santhil took bribes from Kel Harantish; he betrayed the *T'an* Melkathi. Now he's Crown.'

The stocky male beat dust from his clothing, and resettled *harur-nilgiri* and *harur-nazari*. I thought, Hal will find Nelum Santhil a kindred spirit; *that's* what you mean.

The last *telestre*-Ortheans were disappearing inside the Wellhouse. Groups still sat outside the walls, on the sparse mossgrass. All had *harur*-blades, most had winchbows. I turned to walk into the cool shadowed interior.

Blaize said, 'I think about the Barrens. When we were there. Christie . . .'

'When there was none of this, no fighting, no factions; nothing but to be together and play *ochmir* and wonder if, after all, the Woman Who Walks Far had abandoned us, and we would die – oh yes,' I said. 'I think about it. Or isn't that what you wanted me to say?'

The hazy sun shone on angled ribs, visible through his sleeveless jacket; on paired nipples and skin with a fine reptilian grain. Membrane shuttered those whiteless blue eyes; claw-nailed hands clenched. It would be too easy to bury my hands in that silver-streaked mane where it roots down his spine.

'We have to get inside—'

'You make me envy the past,' he said.

At last, from memory, came the face of that male in a far northern province; eight years ago and very distant now. Who had been, in the Orthean tongue, *arykei*, lover, bed-friend. 'Do you mean Sethin Falkyr?'

'Him? No.' He smiled: the scar twisted pain to mockery. 'Christie, how can I be your *arykei* when you have no thought for any other *arykei* but *amari* Ruric Orhlandis? She's *dead*, Christie. Dead and gone to Her Bright Realm. I've seen your face when someone speaks her name. You won't let her go.'

And as he turned to enter the Wellhouse, he added, 'And will you die here, hope to return when she returns, live when she lives? Take your chance, *S'aranth*. She was Golden-blooded. They don't return.'

Ashiel Wellhouse has no corridors. Round-walled room opens into round-walled room: some are kitchens, some dormitories, some for storage. Slot-windows let in sunlight. It shone on white plaster walls, on the bright manes of *telestre*-Ortheans, picking them out from twilight. In the way of the Hundred Thousand, there was no central meeting, but a dozen or so groups talking at the top of their voices, and Jadur and Wyrrin-hael and Sethri each separately cornered.

I sat down at the edge of the group surrounding Sethri, on a bench beside Haltern Beth'ru-elen. The old male glanced at me. Then he looked again, milky membrane sliding back from those pale eyes.

'They tell me you have been to Kel Harantish, and to Kasabaarde. Christie, I have seen people who looked better for that journey.'

I've long since given up wondering how Hal gets to know what he knows. I said, 'I've just been told something, and I don't know whether it's suddenly crystallized a thought I've had, or whether it's completely wrong . . .'

Sethri's voice came clearly from where he stood facing the Earthspeaker Cassirur Almadhera: 'You give poor choices, *shan'tai-keretne*! Stay where we are, be attacked, driven out and killed. Or else enter your houses peacefully by ones and twos – and be killed. Where's the choice in that?'

He stood with a weary arrogance, speaking a thickly-accented Melkathi tongue.

'Kill all four of them!' called a young male, from the back of the room.

'That won't end this, Anzhadi-*hiyek* has more than we to sustain it.'

Doug Clifford leaned forward, putting a restraining hand on Cassirur's shoulder. I saw how he deliberately avoided looking at Pramila Ishida, where the Pacifican girl sat beside Sethri Anzhadi. '*Shan'tai* Sethri, I assure you that we are fully cognizant of the problems you face. This is a precarious situation, we don't wish it to disintegrate further. If a way could be found for your people to make a tactical withdrawal from this area, then that might ease tensions on both sides.'

Nice one, Douggie, I thought. The sunlight in that pale, domed room picked out crystal beads woven into black and brown and scarlet manes; it shone on the smooth-worn hilts of *harur*-blades, and on faces that now turned to stare at us. I pitched my voice to carry as far as Sethri-safere: 'Before we discuss that, let's talk about the other *hiyeks*. Let's talk about the warships that are only days away from here in the Kasabaarde Archipelago – when they sail back to the Coast harbours, then's the time to talk about getting you out of here, *shan'tai* Sethri.'

Mention of the *jath* ships in the islands made a babble of discussion break out among the *telestre*-Ortheans. Nelum Santhil left Wyrrin-hael to speak with Cassirur. Sethri-safere looked over their heads and smiled at me. That fox-face was thinner now, and the yellow mane straggling; still, he nodded an appreciation of intrigue.

My wristlink chimed softly. I hesitated, torn between priorities; but Doug was handling things well. With a quiet word to Hal, I left the room, looking for a chamber slightly less crowded, to speak in private. Privacy is not a *telestre* concept. I came at last to an archway leading into a larger domed room, where sunlight fell through a roof-slot on to white plaster walls. A black circular opening in the floor marked the Well of the Goddess. No Ortheans were there. I stepped inside.

'Christie here.'

'Mendez.' Corazon's image formed, small and clear. Behind her was one of the orbiter's control rooms. She looked at me, that sharp-planed face uncharacteristically wary. 'I can meet you in two hours, I'm making planetfall again then. What's the purpose of this?'

'Not something I want to discuss on open-channel. Cory, will you do me a favour?' Always ask, when it isn't necessary to order. 'Will you put the Kasabaarde settlement off-limits for the present? No landings, no overflights. Just surveillance. There is a reason. I'll discuss it with you when we meet. I'm at—' I gave the co-ordinates of the Ashiel Wellhouse.

'Yes.' She linked bony fingers, and her thick silver rings caught the light. 'Ottoway reports you're making progress.'

'We've got a lever,' I said. 'The Anzhadi are isolated here, cut off. We're working on that one. A small group in hostile country. We might be able to lever the *jath* ships back to Reshebet and Nadrasiir and the other Coast ports.'

In the interests of co-operation I didn't say: Their having few harbours to go back to doesn't make this any easier . . .

'You may be all right,' Corazon Mendez said, reaching out to cut the link. 'Assuming your Coast Ortheans don't have much in the way of black-market hi-tech weaponry.'

I stared at static: her image gone.

A small *ashiren* with black mane and brown skin padded in. *Ke* looked five or six seasons old. Black-bead eyes glanced up at me, and then the child crossed to the Wellmouth, and dipped a bowl into the water. *Ke* drank noisily.

'*Ashiren-te*—'

The child pushed its mane back from its face, with a six-fingered hand on which the claws were tiny and perfect. Dipping the bowl again into the Well, *ke* offered it to me. I walked across to take it, and drink; and as I lifted the bowl, it came into the shaft of sunlight, blazed white: to drink was to drink liquid light, as cold as the stone from which it was drawn.

'*Ashiren-te*, will you go to your Earthspeaker for me? Ask him to bring the *t'an* Ishida here – the offworlder who is with the Coast people.'

'Yes,' the child said. Then: 'I'll do it if it will make you *s'aranthi* leave this Wellhouse.'

I stared after the child as it padded out on bare feet. *Ke* would not have been born when I was in Orthe before. Would have lived in that eternal circle of turn and return, year and year, land and sea. And now to find a world that we, or the rest of the universe, has made different . . .

Feet scuffed the floor, startling me out of my thoughts.

'I don't have anything to say to you,' Pramila Ishida said, as she walked across to stare down at the Well. Her image reflected in the black water: this young woman, with sallow skin now grimed with dust, brown hair roughly braided up; her *meshabi*-robe torn at the hem.

'I don't know what to say to *you* . . .' It was intended to be disarming, it was (I discovered) true.

'Arrest me,' she invited. 'The Anzhadi will see it as provocation, of course. Or I could just stay here, in Wellhouse sanctuary.' She grinned, maliciously.

'If the Company wants you, it will take you; and where you are or what you're doing won't matter. All I want to know from you is the extent of the arms trade that *you* allowed, and where those weapons are now.' I let a pause occur, then finished: 'Whatever loyalties you have now, some things override that. The prospect of a hi-tech war here is one of them.'

Her head lifted. I saw again those startling green eyes, and that face that now showed what emotion – pity?

'I won't tell you a thing,' the Pacifican woman said. 'That should upset the great Lynne Christie legend. As for threatening me with the Company . . . I intend to see the *hiyeks* get a fair deal, all of them, and you can't do that by talk. At least I've got the courage to fight for what I believe.' Pramila smiled. 'Don't be jealous, Ms Christie. I've done what you always wanted to do, and never could – commit myself to Orthe. I'm with Sethri now. The *hiyeks* are my people. A lot of what I've had to do is wrong, but that's better than doing nothing at all.'

'There might be some truth in that,' I admitted. 'As for what's wrong with it, I despair of explaining that to you – go on, get out of here. Get out of my sight.'

The domed room was quiet when she'd gone. Voices beyond sounded muffled. A scent drifted in: heat and *marhaz* and the lairs of *rashaku*. The sun's light shifted almost imperceptibly towards noon, when it could shine full on the Wellmouth: water blazing with light . . .

I waited those few minutes. But it is only light and water.

Towards mid-afternoon, a groundcar jolted down one of the tracks from the west. Cory Mendez got out. I walked as far as the gate-arch, the air like warm water on my skin; and saw her give orders to her officers before heading in my direction.

'I've been in contact with Jamison, over at the Harantish settlement.' She paused, letting her gaze sweep over the ever-growing number of Ortheans in the Wellhouse yard and the *ziku* groves. Her mental shrug of dismissal was almost visible. She went on, 'I wanted Jamison to inform the local leaders that I plan a full investigation into Representative Rachel's death. Unfortunately, neither that self-styled "Empress" nor her "Voice" appears to be available.' She clasped her ringed hands behind her back. 'I've brought ten F90s down on Kumiel Island.'

'That's two-thirds of your Force.'

'That's right,' she acknowledged.

'If we overreact . . .'

'I can't take risks. This is a highly unstable situation.' She glanced back at the groundcar. A man whom I had taken to be Peace Force climbed out, and I saw that it was the acting head of the research team, Ravi Singh.

Corazon turned back to me: 'Why call this meeting so urgently, and why insist on in-person, not holo-contact?'

Chirith-goyen swarmed noisily round our heads, glinting among the *kazsis*-vine that here swamped the crumbling brickwork of the outer wall.

'It has to be secure,' I said.

Blaise Meduenin stepped out of one of the further outbuildings, talking with an older *ashiren*. Too far off to hear what he said; but I saw the *ashiren* fix a message-scroll to the *rashaku*'s hind claw and let it soar free. They stood gazing after it, until it circled round and flew off westwards toward Tathcaer. I thought, What I know and what I can't say puts a distance now between us, between me and Hal and Nelum Santhil and Cassirur . . . I could find it in me to hate the Hexenmeister for that.

Assaulted on all sides by the Hundred Thousand, how can I remember that cool interior of the Brown Tower? With violence on a hair trigger here, how can I think of that other, sleeping devastation?

Ravi Singh joined us, blinking myopically. 'Lynne, I have some interesting findings.'

'Any news on Rashid or David?'

He blinked again, taken aback, and then said, 'Bad, I'm afraid. They need cryo-travel to Thierry's World. The orbiter doesn't have the medical facilities they need.'

'I'll authorize it.' I looked at Cory. 'Thierry's World can contact us, when either of them can talk.'

Oblivious to all interruption, Ravi said, 'Those new findings I mentioned . . . we have established fairly conclusively that "interference" with comlink and other hi-tech systems here is inversely proportional to their distance from the areas of war damage; that is, taking into account the seasonal tilt of the planet, sunspot activity, and—'

'My navigators and comlink people have been using that as a rule of thumb for the past two months,' Corazon said dismissively. 'Lynne, about this meeting.'

'I want Envoy Clifford present as well,' I said. 'Come inside.'

Making our way through the crowded inner rooms, we at last came on Doug Clifford sitting with Nelum Santhil in a small chamber. The Orthean male glanced up.

'Ah.' He inclined his head to Corazon and Ravi. 'Christie, give you greeting.'

I pondered tactfully getting rid of the *T'An Suthai-Telestre*, or else removing Doug from his company. At that moment the door-arch was blocked, and two more Ortheans entered behind us: Haltern clinging determinedly to the shoulder of Blaize Meduenin. The stocky male eased Hal down on to a couch-chair, by the round window that was choked with the foliage of *ziku* outside. Hal wheezed painfully, and then looked up at me with bright eyes.

'You will be interested to know,' Haltern said unhurriedly, 'that Tethmet Fenborn has made it his business to speak with me – and I with the *T'An* Rimon here, and the *T'An Suthai-Telestre*. He gave me word from the Tower. He said, the *S'aranth* will speak of a past time and a present danger. He also said, the Hexenmeister is unwilling all the Hundred Thousand should go in ignorance of this . . .'

A shadow darkened the entrance. The gaunt figure of the fenborn male, blocking the door-arch. I looked questioningly at him, and he blinked green-gold eyes and silently inclined his head in assent.

Nelum Santhil, dark eyes somehow remote, said, 'We have memories of a past time. Speak, *S'aranth*.'

But how can I . . . ? A kind of relief went through me then, simply to have them there: Hal's sly smile, Blaize standing with half-scarred face in shadow, Nelum Santhil's quiet, corrupt confidence. While I still hesitated, Ravi seated himself on the other couch-chair; and Corazon Mendez and Blaize Meduenin took up identical stances either side of the door.

Yes, I thought, watching Orthean faces. Yes, you have a right to know; if only because, when that great Empire fell, you were not innocent bystanders.

'Normally I wouldn't call this meeting now,' I said. 'We've got all the crises we can handle. Invaders who may have illegal hi-tech weapons; a hostile fleet of *hiyek* ships in the islands. Normally, I'd say why call a meeting about something else, when we could be in for a bad enough time here?'

It was automatic to fall into the Ymirian dialect that serves for common language in Tathcaer; to repeat in Sino-Anglic what Corazon and Ravi didn't understand. I leaned both hands on the back of Ravi's couch-chair.

'Despite what I'm going to say, I have to tell you: I wouldn't discuss this at all now if it weren't for Kel Harantish.'

'We heard of the *t'an* Rachel's death,' Nelum Santhil acknowledged. 'I know the Harantish well, or better, than any person here; and they may now be yours, *S'aranth*, but they're not our enemies. The *hiyeks* are our enemy.'

'Kel Harantish . . .' I paused. 'I'd feel better saying this if there were any proof. There isn't. It may be an unjustified fear; I hope to God it is. If it isn't, Kel Harantish is a threat to you, and to the *hiyeks*, and to the Storm Coast and the Rainbow Cities, and the tribes that live over the Wall of the World. That's no exaggeration. That woman who calls herself Empress—'

Haltern interrupted in a thin voice. 'We have still to rid ourselves of *this* war. Speak.'

Now let me tell you, in this warm and summer land, under this clear sky, how to the north and west and south there is a living destruction, an ancient light. Let me tell you what I have seen in the Elansiir, the Barrens, and on the Glittering Plain. Now let me tell you of the legacy of the past – that is living still.

CHAPTER 29

The Last Nineteenth-Century War

Weather and truce together held: the long Orthean twenty-seven-hour day ticking away, always on the edge of violence, never quite crossing the line. Five more Coast Ortheans came out of the burned heathland under escort, these from *hiyek*-Aruan. And *telestre*-Ortheans arrived, by *marhaz* and by *jath-rai*, as word went out to Tathcaer and south Melkathi and the Ymirian hills – hundreds coming to look out over land that had been Rimnith and Keverilde and now lay occupied . . .

Peace Force 'thopters harried the sky through that long day, scanning. Orbital satellites gave erratic images of the Archipelago, far to the west.

I found Cory Mendez in one of the outhouses that Ashiel no longer used, setting up a temporary comlink-base; she and her officers swearing over the data they processed.

'I'd ban all shipping from the area,' Corazon said. 'Any of these craft could be carrying communications for either side. If there was a way to enforce the ban—'

She pushed a hand through her silver hair, disordering its sleekness. For the first time, she looked as though she carried her fifty years with an effort.

'Don't do what you did on the Coast,' I warned. 'I won't authorize that kind of action.'

Corazon Mendez sighed, and as she turned back to the field holo-tank, said, 'I don't do it for the fun of it, Lynne, whatever you may think. It's a job. I won't do anything, until and unless I'm forced.'

On the fourth day after that, a thick sea mist rolled over the land: hiding heath and shallow rises topped by *ziku* and heat-stunted *hanelys*. I sat with Doug Clifford in a Wellhouse chamber that opened on to the *ziku* grove. Unglazed windows let in humid heat, and vapour droplets, and the smell of cooking-fires. Bethan *T'An*

Kyre sat with us, her *zilmei*-hide clothes and *harur*-blades making her look more like a mercenary than the governor of a province; Nelum Santhil leaned back against the white plaster walls, where he sat on a couch-chair beside her. And Sethri-safere faced us.

'We can't continue with this stalemate,' I said.

Doug pursed his lips. On cue, he said, 'I do have one suggestion we perhaps haven't given due consideration. In view of the PanOceania multicorporate's resources, is there a remote chance of Aid resettlement? That is, resettlement on another world like Carrick V—'

Bethan Ivris spluttered. I caught a very sly look from Nelum Santhil.

'*Shan'tai* Christie.' Sethri shook his head. For all that there was dirt ingrained in that pale skin, and his yellow mane fell matted and filthy, he still by some compulsion could take the room's attention. He smiled ruefully. 'We don't live in *telestres*, *shan'tai*. All the same, take us from this world and we die . . . Offworld-born *ashiren* might live. Still, they'd have no *hiyek*, no family; they'd be Orthean in nothing but body.'

'I know. It's a bad solution to this – but you're not leaving me any good ones.' I could have left it at that and hoped, but I felt uncomfortable with the manipulation. 'Really, I'm giving impossible suggestions in the hope it'll force us into something feasible . . . You can very well say it isn't the Company's concern. We don't have the right to interfere. On the other hand, I *know* the Company has to bear some responsibility for how this came about. And I want to see it ended without bloodshed – screw PanOceania,' I said, '*I* want it!'

Nelum Santhil snorted, black eyes gleaming with that Orthean humour that surfaces at the most serious moments. I felt Doug Clifford wince; he put in hastily: 'Assuming we can reach a compromise here, it should be possible to have Carrick V declared a Protected world. This would mean a slower influx of technology, an assessment of what repercussions there would be from the Aid Programme—'

Nelum Santhil leaned forward, resting his arms on his knees. He glanced at Sethri. The *hiyek*-Orthean stood with his back to the window.

'We won't "share" land,' the *T'An Suthai-Telestre* said. 'It isn't ours to give or yours to take. But as *T'An* Bethan here has told you, there's land north and west of The Kyre that has never been *telestre* land.' And then, aside to the dark-maned female: 'Haltern Beth'ru-elen *T'An* Morvren reminds me, that is how Peir-Dadeni

774

came about. And hasn't the Andrethe of Peir-Dadeni been a friend to us?'

Bethan looked at Sethri. Disgust showed on her blunt features. 'We would be well rid of *you*. Until I saw Keverilde, I didn't know . . . Your *ashiren*'s *ashiren* may shake off the taint of land-waster. But if there were an easy way to do it I would send you all to Her.'

Nelum Santhil repeated, 'Land north and west of The Kyre.'

Sethri's face showed exhaustion, but no loss of control.

'Wasteland,' he said.

'Wilderness,' Bethan Ivris corrected. 'There are few of us in The Kyre, and we are content with mountains; we never needed to move out into the Northern Wilderness.'

Watery sunlight shone in at the window. The *hiyek* male's eyes widened, membrane fully retracted; and I thought of seeing him at the *siiran*, under the Coast's incandescent light. The Anzhadi and Aruan and what other *hiyeks* concealed themselves in that heath to the east of us wouldn't own you as a leader – but they'll listen to you, I thought. The others that have come here will carry their own word; but it's Sethri-safere who'll sway them.

'Free passage,' the *hiyek* male said. 'For *jath-rai*, north up the river. And then passage across the mountains. Can you do that, *shan'tai*?' He jerked his head at the window. 'They won't let us go easily. Can you make them?'

Nelum Santhil looked down at hands that were clenched into fists; relaxed them, and thoughtfully studied the sixfold imprint of nails in his palms. 'When I was Portmaster down at Ales-Kadareth, I found nothing readier to quarrel with a *hiyek* than another *hiyek*. How long will it take you to get word to the *jath-rai* in the islands? And will they listen to that word when it's sent?'

I was conscious of Doug beside me; caught a glimpse of his face that, for all he controlled his expression, told me how hard he was trying not to hope. *In case this is one more false breakthrough.*

In case this is nothing at all . . .

Sethri-safere said, 'You had better find me an escort, *T'An Suthai-Telestre*, or clothes such as your people wear. I must go back and speak with Anzhadi. Your people outside these walls will kill me if they see me.'

Doug Clifford looked up. '*Shan'tai*, I'll go with you.'

'Cory's people can escort you,' I said.

And are we there? I wondered, leaving them and making my way towards the temporary comlink-base outside. *We're moving, but are we there?*

Corazon Mendez grunted assent when I found her, detailing

Ottoway as an escort. She herself remained seated at the field-holotank, studying images that were bright in the gloom of the round-roofed building. She seemed oblivious of the stink of old *rashaku* lairs.

'What is it?'

'Corpse. One of the 'thopters got it, over on the eastern boundary. Local, by his clothes. Being in the hostile area, I wasn't going to authorize a recovery.' She remained bent over the holo-image. I didn't look; could only wonder. Was he Keverilde or Rimnith, could he not stay away from the *telestre* even after the burning?

'I wish I had a clearer image,' Corazon said. 'You can see, here, that's a winchbow-bolt. Probable cause of death. What I'm looking for are wounds that might have been made with a hi-tech weapon.'

Sea mist shifted as the noon hour passed, dissolved on a west wind, leaving Ashiel to swelter under the summer heat of Carrick's Star. I stood in a *ziku*'s shadow, staring into blue distance. Thinking: In Tathcaer now, what are they doing, Khassiye Andrethe, Howice *T'An* Roehmonde, Geren *T'An* Ymir? In Morvren Freeport are they waiting to sight *jath-rai* sails on the horizon?

Satellite-images show only quiet islands, under the sea-spanning shadow of the Rasrhe-y-Meluur.

Below me, all the slope that fell away from Ashiel was covered with temporary shelters of *marhaz*-hide, set up between clumps of the brown and blue *saryl-kiez*. Ortheans walked among them. Some wore the thin robes of Melkathi, others the slit-backed shirts of Ymir and Rimon. The sun glittered on *harur-nilgiri*, *harur-nazari*. Only the youngest *ashiren* played oblivious in the dust. Older children ran from group to group, acting (I thought) as messengers.

'Ms Christie . . .'

Not Trismegistus, I realized as I turned, seeing a man in combat-coverall, WEBcorder slung on his back. A tall, black man, with straight hair drawn back and tied in a horse-tail; with long slanting eyes and a challenging grin.

'Ariadne WEB,' he announced. 'My name's Mehmet Lutaya; I wonder if you want to comment on the absence of the government envoy at this time? Does this have any bearings on PanOceania's actions here?'

There is a certain glaze they have in their eyes. It means they see "Representative" or "Envoy" or "Commander"; not the person. Down in that haze there, somewhere on the heath, Doug Clifford is with Ortheans who are a continent away from safety; nothing to keep him safe but words and luck – and I can't say that to you, I thought. Although I have to say *something*.

'I'll be holding a conference for all WEB representatives in about an hour,' I said. The comlink-centre would be suitably private. Or as private as possible, in the Hundred Thousand.

'When do you anticipate developments?' he persisted. 'I know some of the other WEBs have sent people to the other port settlement – Morvren, is it? Is that where—'

'I hope they know better than to land. Land's taboo,' I said. With an effort, I held back from tongue-lashing this Mehmet Lutaya. No point in taking tension out on him.

'Representative, wouldn't you call that irrelevant now? The invading force here is using groundcar transport, I've got verifiable holos of that. These people have Earth tech on their territory whether they want it or not.'

There was no easy answer to that. 'I'll see you in an hour,' I repeated.

Having no greater desire than to be out of his way, I turned and walked back inside the Wellhouse. Picking a way through the crowds wasn't easy. Some *hiyek*-Ortheans were present in the inner rooms – Jadur Anzhadi lifted a cup in a friendly salute as I passed through one chamber, and I thought, That's not going to make the *S'aranth* popular . . .

Tension twisted in my stomach, so acute it was painful. I felt as if one touch would make me ring like a wine glass, like a violin string tuned up to some unbearable pitch. Worst-case scenarios: Doug used as hostage, murdered out of hand. Desperately seeking consolation, I thought: He's professional, he's done this before, he knows the risks – ah, so do we all. And it doesn't help.

At the entrance to the Well-room I stopped. A male and a female stood together under that dome, by the Wellmouth; she with an untidy scarlet mane, and a green slit-backed robe falling to her high-arched feet; he thin and tall, the brown robe wrapped round his hips not concealing his seamed belly: the pouch of an oviparous species. Cassirur Almadhera and Tethmet Fenborn, talking together. Suddenly I felt very alien.

And why? Because Commander Mendez isn't stupid; she's manoeuvring me towards a position where I take responsibility for PanOceania, but have no authority over it. And that puts a distance between me and Ortheans.

'Give you greeting,' I said, stepping inside the Well-room. 'What news?'

She smiled sympathetically. 'We wait. *S'aranth*, I could almost wish we had acted as the *hiyeks*, and taken your devices for communication – it would be swifter.'

Tethmet Fenborn said nothing. Silence with him seemed, not a lack, but a natural quality.

'Kasabaarde has some spiritual authority on the Coast,' Cassirur Almadhera went on, 'if no temporal authority. Help me convince the *t'an* Fenborn that the Tower should make its disapproval known, influence the other *hiyeks* against Anzhadi.'

I said, 'I understand the Hexenmeister to remain neutral in these matters.' And had a sudden image of that city to the west of us, of Tathcaer, white under the summer sun; and how eight years ago it sent into exile *amari* Ruric Orhlandis. For all her memories, she is Ruric still.

'Did the Hexenmeister say nothing to you about this?' I asked the Fenborn.

Tethmet's green-gold eyes blurred with membrane. If I didn't know his loyalty to the Tower, I'd have taken it for disapproval. 'The word of the Hexenmeister has gone out to the *siiran*, to dissuade the *hiyeks* from war.'

'May She make that not too late.'

Cassirur's inflection made it 'Goddess', but I started; hearing it as plain 'she' – the Hexenmeister in the Tower. I was almost relieved when my wristlink chimed, and signalled a private communication I'd have to take on one of the larger holotanks in the comlink-centre.

'I'll speak with you later,' I said. As I left, I glanced back. Orthean female and aboriginal male: one red-maned and middle-aged and untidy, the other sleek and dark and thin. Memory tells me the one is the child of the other – that, for all we speak with *telestres* and Coast *hiyeks*, it is Tethmet's people who have the prior claim to Orthe. The light from the roof-slot shone whitely down on both of them.

As I crossed the courtyard to the Wellhouse outbuildings, my mind ran half on the necessity for setting up the WEBcasters' conference, half on what this comlink message might be – Douggie calling in? Carrick's Star shone down through *ziku*, and *chirith-goyen* hung in brightness, suspended in spirals of flight. Voices came clearly through the warm air, from the temporary camp outside the wall. Slanting beams of sunlight fell on the trodden earth, on red spore cases fallen in the dust, and I thought of autumn: of the seasons Stathern and Torvern. Strange to think of that in high summer . . .

In a moment of perception, I felt how I stood here: flat heathland stretching out to the east; the sea a few miles south, invisible in haze; the interlocking pattern of *telestres*. Ales-Kadareth far to the east, Tathcaer to the west . . . and, high above, invisible among white daystars, the orbital station and its daisy chain of observing satellites. *Carrick V a Protected world? The inferior is protected from the superior, surely; but here's a world not hi-tech but not inferior either. Orthe has outlived our kind of civilization. How can we aid them?*

And thinking that, I thought also: to the south, there is the Coast, the *siirans*, hunger and disease . . . We created the conditions for this civil war, but how could we not interfere with poverty? Ah, but that's not the whole story. If Calil has rediscovered that ancient weapon, it's only because we came here.

If she can synthesize Earth and Golden science to create that, then we must synthesize our cultures, Carrick V and Earth; survive a little changed, maybe, but survive.

'Christie,' a voice said, as I was about to enter the round-roofed outbuilding that housed the makeshift comlinks. It was Blaize Meduenin. Still in mercenary's gear, nothing to mark him out as *T'An* Rimon.

'Your *t'an* Commander Mendez was just taken up in one of the 'thopters.' His Sino-Anglic was accented, heavy with the inflections of the Peace Force. He grinned, scarred flesh twisting. 'Travelling west. She's had word. So have we – on the heliograph-relay. There are *jath-rai* sighted off Morvren Freeport.'

The third hour past noon, Merrum Firstweek Sixday; and all I could think was, *We're not going to get away with this as easily as I hoped.*

'Blaize, there's always shipping off the Freeport, what makes you sure these are *hiyek* ships?'

He scratched at his blond mane. At last identifiable: the smile was not pleasure, but relief at being able to take action; any kind of action. He said, 'We're not sure. That's why I'm going down there. A *jath* could do it in a day, but I don't have a day in hand. I want one of your ships on Kumiel to fly me there.'

He stood with his chin slightly raised, daring me to challenge that; and I looked at that alien face. Jaw too narrow, forehead too wide; membraned eyes bright in ruined flesh. Old scars. The silver-blond mane definitely needed cutting, and he had braided a twist of it back into the shaggy mass. As he shifted his stance, *harur*-blade harness jingled softly.

'On condition that you report directly back to me, as well as to the *takshiriye* here. I could get word from Hal – but as you say, I don't have the time in hand.'

Blaize laughed. 'I'll do it. If you tell me what your *T'An* Mendez does.'

Ochmir is not the only game Ortheans play to perfection. I agreed, and went on into the outhouse. Two or three Peace Force officers were dividing their time between banks of consoles and field-holotanks, in a round room ill-lit by sunlight. Dried mossgrass crackled on the floor as I walked over to a 'tank, wincing at the stench of *rashaku* that still lingered.

I keyed in for Secure communication, and Cory Mendez's face appeared. Backdraught from the 'thopter whipped her short white hair across her face, and she had to shout to be heard above the engine: '. . . images. Satellites are showing ship-movement in—' she gave a string of co-ordinates, and then added, '—the northern Archipelago islands. I'm ordering an overflight. Four F90s will leave Kumiel Island shortly.'

'I want a report half-hourly,' I said. 'When your people are in the area, I want a report every fifteen minutes.'

The older woman's expression was odd. I sensed how she wanted to handle this herself, on grounds of experience. What restrained her – and would have done more so, had I been Molly Rachel, or officially had Molly's position – is that her people are only, to be blunt about it, the strong arm of the Company's commercial division. How long can I count on that restraint? I wondered.

'Have someone monitor my transmissions continuously.' She signed off.

I called one of the officers over, and as I got up from the 'tank, shadows darkened the door. Haltern Beth'ru-elen walked with the aid of a cane, pulling *becamil* blankets round his thin shoulders; and a pace behind him came Nelum Santhil Rimnith.

'Good,' I said, 'I'd been thinking of inviting you to speak with the WEBcasters, and I'm about to hold a conference here.'

'We have already spoken with them.' Haltern eased himself down on to one of the console seats, and clasped six-fingered hands over the top of his cane. He smiled. 'Most persistent, your young *s'aranthi*.'

Long ago I learned that, though Orthean languages don't have the word for it, you nevertheless don't have to tell Haltern Beth'ru-elen anything about public relations.

Nelum Santhil paced round the block of holotanks, peering with interest at aerial overviews of this part of Melkathi. He seemed preoccupied. His short dark mane was slicked up by the heat, and there was a thin line of white visible round his eyes. Pinned roughly to his slit-backed shirt was a crest badge, such as the

Crown Guard wear; and this was all now that marked him out as *T'an Suthai-Telestre*. The *telestres* love ceremony, they also know when to abandon it.

'Your *t'an* Clifford – no word?'

'Nothing yet.'

Nelum Santhil rested one stubby six-fingered hand on the edge of a holotank. 'The *hiyeks* have means to far-speak, by use of your devices; and I hear also that they have groundcars, to travel. How many?'

No point in concealment. 'Eight, possibly nine,' I said.

'Then the *hiyeks* will know what is happening in the Freeport. Call your *t'an* Clifford,' the *T'An Suthai-Telestre* said. 'Warn him.'

Haltern, who sat resting his chin on his clasped hands, shot me a glance full of amusement. I could guess what he was thinking. *This is the man whom I brought to the Citadel one night, eight years gone; not only a traitor, but a betrayer of other traitors – and now he is Crown. Perhaps the one qualifies him for the other?*

I asked another of the Peace Force officers to make the contact. As I did so, a group of seven or eight young men and women arrived outside the building; and began to come in, talking, and setting down the more bulky pieces of WEB equipment. Lutaya and Visconti were there. As well as Ariadne and Trismegistus, I recognized the sigils of four other WEBs: two of them Pacifican-based (so they would be funded by multi-corporates), one offworld from the Heart Stars, and a homeworld crew who – after some thought – I realized must come from the USSA. With Ariadne from the European Enclaves, and Trismegistus based in the Home Worlds generally, that meant a fair spread of opinion.

The Peace Force officer approached. He said quietly, 'I can't make contact with the envoy, Representative Christie. Shall I keep trying?'

Ironic – that I know what's happening eight hundred miles distant in Morvren Freeport, but nothing of what might be eight miles away, in what used to be Keverilde . . .

Not conscious of a hiatus (but by the officer's face there must have been one), I said, 'Keep trying.' Thinking, What's the connection between here, and the *hiyek*-Ortheans sailing towards the Freeport? What's happened here? Sethri, *Doug*—

'Sorry, people,' I said. 'I'm going to have to put this off for a few hours. I could give you the usual keep-'em-quiet rubbish, but I don't think there's any need to mess you around. I will let you know as soon as I can authorize a news release for the WEBs.'

One of the two Anansi WEBbers raised his voice. 'My colleague in the western coastal settlement says there's a lot of new activity there. Is that connected with this?'

Dissemination of news might hurt the Company, I thought. Can it hurt Orthe? And noted in passing, as one does, how I was now thinking: what order of priorities. It was Nelum Santhil whose eye I caught, where he stood unnoticed behind the group of WEBcasters. When Dalzielle Kerys-Andrethe was Crown, she would have dominated such a group without effort; he, with an equal lack of effort, faded into the background, waiting his moment to move. His black eyes were bright with humour. *How can you?* I thought. And then realized it was personally directed at me. *Here I stand where Nelum Santhil stood before: on both sides of the fight . . .*

I glanced round the outhouse.

'If you want to know what's developing, I should stay around here,' I said. 'I'll arrange a linkup to the orbiter, but I'll want replay facilities for my staff. That applies also to what your colleagues in Morvren send. In return, you can have unrestricted access to Company transmissions.'

At least, I thought, as the group broke into excited discussions, *you can while I'm acting Representative. Cory Mendez will create hell, but by then it'll be too late. And things are moving too fast now. If I can hang on and get us through this crisis – that's all I ask.*

Reports came back from the F90s at thirty- and then at fifteen-minute intervals. I stayed in the comlink-centre. Once during the afternoon, two *ashiren* brought in food for those of us there – the WEBcasters, Nelum Santhil, Haltern, Cassirur; and Geren *T'An* Ymir who'd ridden in from Tathcaer. The small room was full. I became aware that the Ortheans outside had begun to drift into the Wellhouse yard. The hum of their talk was a constant background to the hiss and crackle of comlink transmissions, blurred by Morvren's closeness to the Glittering Plain.

All through those hours, with the *jath-rai* drawing nearer to Morvren Freeport, satellite-images showed no movement at all on the heathland of Keverilde. At one point I took over from the Peace Force officer and tried contacting Douggie myself. It made no difference. There was no answer. I left it, contacted the orbiter: checked on the condition of David Osaka and Rashid Akida, now on Thierry's World; and had words with the acting heads of PanOceania's commercial and research divisions evacuated from Kel Harantish. And then I left the comlink officer to continue trying to contact Doug Clifford, and slept briefly, and woke to find nothing changed.

Dawn was a white blaze in the east: Merrum Firstweek Sevenday. The population of the comlink-centre changed, some of the WEB-casters now (I saw) going off to snatch sleep; Cassirur and another Earthspeaker being joined by Tethmet Fenborn. I pushed the chair back from the 'tank and walked over towards him, thinking, Word could have come from Kasabaarde, but the youngest Peace Force officer intercepted me.

'I've got something here,' she said. 'Commander Mendez told me to notify her too. It's a sat-pic of a body down on the heath; it shows evidence of CAS weaponry being used.'

I bent over the holotank beside her. 'What evidence – visual? That's not usual—'

I stopped, breath cut off short.

The image was small and clear. He lay with the side of his face pushed into the earth, black blood run and congealed from his ears and eyes. CAS weaponry, yes; but it wasn't that that made my heartbeat stutter. The *meshabi*-robe marked him out for a *hiyek*-Orthean; and I knew him. As still as if he slept, Sethri-safere of *hiyek*-Anzhadi lay in a hollow of the earth, dew wet on his skin.

'Get me a heat-sensor reading.'

'He's dead,' the Pacifican woman said. 'Been dead for six or seven hours, by medicomputer estimate. Do you want it picked up?'

'*Yes* – have whoever goes in be extremely careful.'

For a long moment I stood looking at that image, made of clear light. Wild *becamil* had woven thin webs between mane and shoulder and the earth. No movement of ribcage, no flicker of that eye half shut by membrane . . . And once he sat down beside me in the heat and glare of Maherwa and said, *I will be a friend to you, Lynne Christie*. Jesus Christ! I raged internally, senselessly; some *friend*, how could you let this happen now? And my eyes stung.

'*S'aranth*,' Haltern Beth'ru-elen said urgently, at the same moment as the Peace Force officer began to hurry back through the crowd towards me.

'Hal, take a look at this . . . What?'

'There is someone down on Keverilde—' The old male stopped short, recognizing the image of the dead Orthean.

'Sensors are picking up movement,' the officer said. 'A small number of people, at 908-657-867. Estimate two or three, no more; they're not making much progress, but they're heading for this place.'

'Can you identify?'

She said cautiously, 'One of them might be the government envoy. It's difficult to get a visual fix; there's a fog rising.'

'If you – never mind,' I said. 'I'll do it. Find me a driver, armed. What's the distance involved?'

'Six miles. Representative—'

I pushed through the crowd, ignoring urgent questions from the WEBcasters, sidestepped Lutaya; and as I left the outhouse, found the Earthspeaker Cassirur beside me. Cold air hit me, made me shiver. Dawn was drowned in mist that the sun would burn away; that hid the onion-domes of the Wellhouse.

'They may be my people, and if one is hurt, you'll need me,' the red-maned woman said. She signalled to an *ashiren*, who ran into the Wellhouse, and returned almost instantly with a satchel of *marhaz*-hide.

'I – yes, I'm not thinking. I'll take one of the Force medics with us.'

It must have taken only minutes to walk down the hillslope to where the Company groundcars were, but time stretched out; the ground underfoot jolted me, the wet fog dampened hair and coverall, tension snarled into a knot in my gut. I noted that Cassirur now wore at her belt a *harur-nilgiri* blade. Using the comlink, I called a medic; he and the driver were ready to go when I reached the 'car. And then it seemed only seconds while the 'car crept down the dirt tracks below Ashiel, visibility nil, relying on heat-sensors to move at all. Six miles.

'There.'

Cassirur stood, gripping the edge of the groundcar seat. She pointed ahead. Faint light was beginning to leak through the mist. We moved in a shifting circle of visibility some ten yards across; and shadowy figures appeared now at the edge of it. The 'car rolled to a halt. Two people – it *is* Douggie, I thought; knowing him without even having to see his face.

While the 'car driver stood guard, CAS-VIII at the alert, I got down; Cassirur and the medic with me. The fog muffled sound, but I heard one of the two men breathing harshly; and as I walked forward thought there was something familiar about the other – not human, but Orthean – and then I stopped.

Doug Clifford's arm was across the shoulders of the other male, who held him upright. His coverall was darkly stained. One foot was bare and bleeding. His head was hanging down, but as I stepped forward he raised it; cocking his head sideways as if listening. His lips moved soundlessly. A strip of rag was bound round his head, covering his eyes; rag that was soaked red.

'Douggie—'

The Company medic pushed past me, reaching for his kit; and the Orthean male released Doug Clifford's arm with a grunt of pain. I could only stare, until the medic began to remove the blood-soaked rag; I saw a mess of blood and matted flesh—

An Orthean male in black robes, muddy and ripped. Brown-skinned and black-maned. I fixed my eyes on him because I couldn't look at Doug; spoke to cover the sound he was making. 'Who—?' And then recognized him.

Pathrey Shanataru wiped his six-fingered hands on his torn robe. He glanced at the envoy.

'Who did that to him?' the Harantish male said. His voice shook; there was a line of white showing round his eyes. 'It was Calil bel-Rioch. The Empress Calil.'

CHAPTER 30

Turncoat

'If you have any sense of survival,' Pathrey Shanataru added, 'leave here. *Shan'tai*, she may send people after us.'

' "Us"?'

'Take that for good faith,' he said, with a nod of his head at the envoy; and then more urgently: 'I must speak with you, with all *s'aranthi*. To come here, I've risked everything; I've lost everything; you *must* listen to me.'

The medic looked up from where he knelt beside Doug Clifford, who was down on one knee in the dirt. 'This man's in shock. I need to get him to Kumiel, those are the nearest facilities.'

'Drive back to Ashiel.' I stepped forward and took Doug's arm. His head turned towards me, blind behind plastiflesh bandages. My head was full of calculations: how long before the fog lifts? How long before a 'thopter can get him to Kumiel – or an F90 to the orbiter?

'Sethri's dead.' Doug choked: I guessed at the effort of withstanding pain. His other hand came to grip my arm. He said again, 'Sethri Anzhadi's dead. I saw . . . *saw* Calil bel-Rioch have him killed.'

'We know. The sats spotted it. Doug, come on; we'll get you back – for God's sake be careful – that's it . . .'

Doug Clifford stopped. The muscles of his back were hard under my hand. Empathy and revulsion tore me in different directions; I stifled both under professionalism. There will be time to take this in later.

With a studied precision, Doug said, 'You will need to be in reach of orbital communications, therefore Kumiel; take *me* to Kumiel and use the medic facilities there; on the trip, I'll impart some extremely necessary information. *Shan'tai* Pathrey is correct, you must listen to him. What he has to say is important—'

He sagged back against me. 'Painkiller,' the medic said, as he and I manoeuvred Doug into the groundcar, and I sat with him half-supported against me as the driver swung us round in a curve and back up the track towards Ashiel Wellhouse. Cassirur bent forward to speak to Pathrey Shanataru in the front seat, but the dark Harantish male only shook his head.

Minutes ticked past. The fog didn't clear, but it thinned a little overhead; was white, then pearl, then blue, and specked with white daystars. We passed clumps of *saryl-kiez*, grey with *becamil* webs. Pathrey glanced round at the unfamiliar landscape. Only then did it hit me: *the Empress Calil here? But Harantish isn't concerned with this, this is hiyek business* . . . The groundcar jolted. Doug moaned, hardly loud enough to hear, and I put my arms around him and tried to hold him still.

'Doug, listen . . . Can you hear me? You're going to be okay. I'll have you on Kumiel within the hour.' I paused, reluctant, and then forced myself to go on. 'You're telling me to come to Kumiel. What about the peace talks here? What about the other Anzhadi who support – supported – Sethri? Doug?'

His first words were unintelligible. I thought, I shouldn't ask questions. His weight against me seemed so slight; as if he had crumpled into the dirty coverall. There were long scratches on his hands as well as on his bare foot; the one made by *kiez* spines, the other, I think, by hooked claw-nails.

Slurring his words, but still with that precision of language, he said, 'The opportunity for peace talks is over. The *hiyek*-Ortheans no longer follow Sethri, obviously, nor does *hiyek*-Anzhadi have influence now that he is dead. If I put it in plain terms, I would say Calil bel-Rioch and her Harantish Ortheans are now control-ling the invasion of the Hundred Thousand—' He caught his breath, found my hand by touch alone, and gripped it hard. 'Lynne, did that make sense? I have to tell – did I—?'

The groundcar's hum rose to a whine, cresting the hill. Ashiel's wall appeared through the fog. It muffled the voices, half hid the bright robes of Ortheans crowding round: Cassirur stood up in the 'car and ordered them to clear a path.

As I was about to move, my wristlink chimed. The face of a Peace Force officer appeared. I said, 'Can't this wait?'

His voice was tinny in the open air. 'You may want to take this contact in Secure, Representative.'

'If it's that urgent, give it to me now; and for God's sake get a move on—' I moved my wrist and hand away from Douggie, and he slumped back against my shoulder. The miniature holo-image changed: the face of Cory Mendez appeared. Noise and vibration meant she must still be in a 'thopter or small shuttle.

Cory looked at me with a grim satisfaction.

'You wanted updates regularly,' she said. 'Take a look at this. It's live-transmission. The ships in the islands have moved as far north as Morvren Freeport. Now they're attacking the settlement.'

The image was a blur, too small to focus on. In a tone that I hoped didn't show panic, I said, 'Cory, I'm coming down there. Take no action, no independent action, do you understand what I'm saying?'

From blur to vision: the holo-image was clear as some painted miniature. That far west, dawn is just breaking, the sea is milk-pale. It laps the filigree-coast of a harbour island – viewpoint too high to make out people, but there is a *jath-rai*, and another, metal sails flashing in the light; *there* a thread of black smoke blooming . . .

Corazon Mendez said, 'Company regulations say I have to observe, under such circumstances. I'm observing, but I give you fair warning, Lynne; if a situation comes up where I have to take action, I won't hesitate.' She paused, then added: 'If I see signs of hi-tech warfare, I'll have no option but to send my people in to force a cease-fire.'

Eight hundred miles to the west, Morvren Freeport burns.

Do we go by groundcar now, I wondered; risk rough travelling and fog? Or reckon that the fog will lift soon, and take a 'thopter? 'Thopter, yes.

I entered the makeshift comlink-centre, and found Ottoway in charge. He glanced up as I came in, and brushed fair hair out of his eyes. The holotank he watched carried images of Morvren.

'I need transport to Kumiel,' I said. 'Has Cory told you to stay here? Good. I want the closest surveillance of this area. If anyone leaves, either take them or follow them; use your discretion.' *And where is Calil now?* 'As far as you can, keep a cordon of neutral ground around Keverilde and Rimnith.'

He grunted. 'Yes, Representative . . . Ms Christie, there are times when I curse Company regulations. If we could bring new tech stuff down to the planet's surface, half a dozen officers could enforce a peace. But they give us equipment that's twenty years old, and tell us it's to avoid cultural contamination – and *look* at that.' He slammed a fist down on the edge of the holotank.

Is that orthodox opinion in the Force? I wondered. Could be; and does PanOceania know or care?

'You're to continue to allow the *takshiriye* – the local authorities – and the WEBsters free access to all communications,' I shot back over my shoulder at him as I left. I didn't hold out too much hope of it happening that way.

Outside, fog had turned to ground haze. The air was warm and silky-smooth, beaten by the blades of a large 'thopter that rested on mossgrass beyond Ashiel walls; and as I came up to it, I found the tall medic had been joined by another, and both were helping Doug into the cabin. A little distance off, Pathrey Shanataru stood irresolute. He now wore a light *chirith-goyen* cloak, the hood drawn up over his head; he could, in this light, have been from a *telestre*. And down among the *marhaz*-hide shelters there was movement, and I guessed news was being passed round.

'Get in, *shan'tai*,' I said. 'We'll talk as we go.'

The 'thopter swung in the air as if suspended from some sky hook. Ashiel, that had seemed so large, lost itself in brown heath and haze. Cold air blew through the plastiglas cabin; the thrum of the blades was deadened. Now I could smell the sea.

One of the medics sat forward with the pilot, the other stared absently out into void. Beside her, Doug sat with his hands flat on his thighs, and I realized: For the past three-quarters of an hour I have not allowed myself to think the word *blind*.

'I'll tell you what I can,' he said. His face turned vaguely towards me, where I sat with Pathrey. The plastiflesh masked his eyes; left only that prim mouth to be read for expression. We sat cramped so close together that I hardly had to lean forward to take his hand.

'There are small groups of Coast Ortheans scattered all across that heath.' Douggie raised his voice slightly, over the beat of the 'thopter blades. 'Lynne, I don't know if we were as near a truce as I imagined . . . that's irrelevant, now. I knew something was going badly wrong when I saw Harantish men and women with the *hiyek*-Ortheans, and I suspect Sethri Anzhadi did, but we continued to go from group to group, putting forward the *T'An Suthai-Telestre*'s proposals. I think we saw several hundred people; I know there were more there.'

Beside me, Pathrey Shanataru nodded. I gripped Douggie's hand. 'What else?'

'I imagine some of the *jath* that Commander Mendez saw were carrying Harantish Ortheans. Has *shan'tai* Pathrey told you that Calil – that the Empress-in-Exile is there?' His scratched hands tensed. 'Lynne, you don't dispose of Kel Harantish's grip on the Coast in just a few months. They're going to follow her. Obviously she had got rid of Sethri's main supporters while he was with us. She no sooner had him than she ordered he be executed—'

'With CAS weaponry?'

He loosed one hand, moving the fingers to touch the bandage

over his eyes; and I saw how his mouth was a hard line. Quite clinically, and irrelevantly, he said, 'She did this herself, with her own hands; I had still thought there might be a chance of talking so I allowed myself to be disarmed, that was a bad mistake – she has other CAS and hi-tech armoury, yes; but that was mine, Lynne. I'm sorry. I'm talking too much. It's true what they say about shock.'

Does he know about Morvren? Was he able to hear what Cory transmitted to me?

The 'thopter dipped, straightened. Carrick's Star blazed off the surface of the sea, too bright to be looked at; and the coast of the Hundred Thousand was only blue haze.

'She's quite mad,' Doug Clifford said. 'I know Ortheans, by now. There's no rationality—'

'I know,' I said, at the same moment that Pathrey Shanataru said, 'She's ill, *shan'tai.*'

I glanced at the time, reckoned close on twenty minutes before the 'thopter made Kumiel. And then a shuttle down to Morvren; how many hours . . . ?

'Can you add anything to what Doug's said?' I asked Pathrey.

He looked down at his hands, dark fingers bare of the rings he had worn. His hands perceptibly shook. At the one moment I thought of question and answer: *he fears flying more than other Ortheans, why?* and, *the Harantish have Golden blood, and so no past-memories of this when the Empire was here.* And wondered how I had come to take for granted that I think as Ortheans do about the matter – as with most things of Orthe, it all comes back to the Tower.

'I can add much,' Pathrey Shanataru said. He kept his eyes averted from the plastiglas cabin walls.

'I . . . when I last saw you in Kel Harantish, I didn't expect to see you again here.'

'We sailed within hours of you *s'aranthi* leaving.'

Words came from him with great effort. I let silence prompt him now. He raised his head, and I saw there was a bruise on his temple, half covered by the rooting black mane. Membrane slid back from dark eyes. Alien, that expression; and then with surprise I read it for what it was: an aching sadness.

'I shouldn't be here. I should be with her still. After so many years . . .' Pathrey hesitated. 'Is she mad? You *s'aranthi* tell me; I no longer know. After what I have seen her do in Harantish these past weeks, I no longer know. I fear for her, *shan'tai.*'

It was Doug who broke the silence that followed. With a

surprising gentleness he said, 'Tell the Representative what you've told me, *shan'tai* Pathrey.'

The dark Orthean male spoke in a more formal inflection. 'The ambition of Calil bel-Rioch is to be Empress, *shan'tai*, and Empress as it was in the days long past. She would raise up that Golden Empire again, and make this land here a part of it, and all the land that the *hiyeks* have—' He broke off. When he resumed, it was in plain speech. 'You saw her. She would be Santhendor'lin-sandru come again. She has your *s'aranthi* weapons, and now she has those weapons that the Coast has. *Is* she mad? You live as a Harantish woman, *shan'tai* Christie; live shunned and feared and kept penned up in that barren pesthole, and you tell me! All I know is, half Harantish thinks as she does.'

'Is that true? Literally true?'

'Oh yes,' he said. 'There are Harantish now with the *hiyeks* in the Archipelago.'

'Since when?'

'Two days ago. Perhaps three.'

Is he telling the truth, is he lying? Either way, what does he really know; he's one man, and how trustworthy is he? I thought of using the wristlink to contact Corazon Mendez, but hesitated. She would have this man who was Voice of the Empress-in-Exile debriefed, that would take time; nor would it happen soon, with the crisis going on in Morvren . . .

'They do have hi-tech weapons,' Douggie said.

The 'thopter tilted, dipping down towards hazy land that must be Kumiel. Sea glittered; and to the north I glimpsed what might be white *telestre*-houses in morning sunlight. Tathcaer.

'You must stop her, but not harm her,' Pathrey said; his plump face wore an incongruously stubborn expression. 'Nor should you put the blame on her alone, there are many in the city who thought as she did, and who help her now. If it were not she, it would be some other. *Shan'tai*, you must believe me.'

I had no time to analyse that oddly wistful defiance. Doug's hand gripped mine tightly. He said, 'Say what else you said to me, Pathrey.'

The Harantish male blinked, translucent membrane and then eyelids; and reached out to grip a wall-hold as the 'thopter settled towards the earth. 'What else . . . You must understand, *shan'tai*, she speaks with no one now, not even I. Still, there is something more. When that great Empire fell, there was a weapon used, or so tales tell. Now if you talk with my people from Harantish, you will find that they believe that weapon can be used again – that

791

she has discovered the use of it. I have never heard word of this before. I think therefore that *she* puts this rumour among us.'

He opened his eyes. '*Shan'tai*, I have lived these many years. I have some power of reason. I do not believe the ancient weapons of the Golden have been rediscovered, but *she* may believe it. If she does, all Harantish does; all the *hiyeks* will. And that belief in itself may prove as destructive a weapon.'

Now the 'thopter settled down towards the earth. Below us, ranked F90s lined rocky Kumiel; growing as the ground rushed up to meet us. I felt split in two: half of me thinking, Never underestimate ideology; charismatic insanity is not to be ignored, and the other half, without the solace of black humour, thinking, But if Pathrey's wrong and she does have Golden science? The 'thopter touched down on blue-grey mossgrass, between shuttles, with never a jolt.

'I'll have to ask you to stay here,' I said. 'Cory's people will look after you, *shan'tai* Pathrey.'

As he climbed shakily down from the 'thopter he looked back at me and with only the slightest irony, said, 'Call it "protective imprisonment".'

I slid down from the 'thopter, on to Kumiel's sparse blue mossgrass. The air was warm, shimmering over the island's pitted rocks; the white dolphin-backed ranks of F90 shuttles wavered with heat distortion. As the first medic followed me, I drew her aside.

'How is he?'

She glanced back up at the 'thopter cabin. 'We can probably save the sight of one eye if we get him to the orbiter's tissue-regeneration facilities now.'

'I'll authorize it.'

Doug appeared in the cabin door, and I reached up as he put a tentative foot towards invisible ground; seeing how he turned his head in bewilderment. His hand caught mine with so hard a grip it made me wince. Then as I helped him down, I held him, feeling his heartbeat, his warmth; and what I'd meant to say went unsaid, choked in grief and anger.

'I ought . . .' His hands shook. 'I ought to be in the Freeport.'

'I'll handle the government side of things, till you get back. Christ, I ought to know the job,' I said, 'I did it for long enough.'

He opened his mouth to speak, paused; my throat tightened in sympathy. I let the medic take his arm to lead him towards the shuttles, knowing how precariously he was holding himself together. And for a moment I stood there on the springy mossgrass, wanting to do nothing else but go with him up to the orbiter, not trusting others to care for him. And you'll come back before you should, I thought, watching that small figure limping towards the towering hull of an F90 shuttle. Not until then able to realize, *Calil, with her own hands—*

I walked briskly across the island towards their comlink-centre, tasting bile; all but sick with revulsion.

Eight hundred miles to the west . . . I slept for as much of the two-hour shuttle flight as I could, not knowing when I'd get the chance again. Waking, the holotank-images showed bright morning. Shadows of clouds glided across the surface of the Rasrhe-y-Melvur, as we flew past the side of that great *chiruzeth* spire; coming in from the seaward side to overfly the estuary of the Ai River.

The shuttle-pilot said, 'I'm fitting us into the holding-pattern, Representative.'

At fifteen hundred feet, the island-filled estuary lay like a topographic map. Black specks crossed and recrossed airspace above it, and as the shuttle went into hover-mode I identified 'thopters and other shuttles. Sun flashed from the white hulls of F90s – Cory's in one of those, I thought, and reached out to key in a contact. Before I could do it, an incoming message appeared in the holotank.

'Christie here—'

And then I keyed that image to an insert, staring at the main tank. The surface of the sea glittered, pale blue and azure and indigo in the depths. Sparks of light came from the metal sails of *jath-rai*: ten, a dozen, twenty . . . *There were more in the Archipelago, where are they now?* The island nearest the Rasrhe-y-Meluur was as clear as a miniature model; harbour and Watchtower and Wellhouse dome, a movement that might have been *marhaz*-riders – all obscured now, as black smoke plumed up from the *telestre*-houses nearest the docks. Unclear from this height: is that fighting, are those small specks of colour people? – and then the shuttle was over the island, past it; hovering over the channel between that and a larger Freeport island.

'*S'aranth*?' The face of Blaize Meduenin appeared in the holo-insert. 'Sunmother! Will you tell this *t'an* Mendez of yours to land this ship? I must get into the city.'

'Who's there?'

He frowned. 'The river-*telestre s'ans*. *T'An* Khassiye Reihalyn, if the winds favoured him; he sailed from Tathcaer two days ago. But he's Andrethe, not *T'An* Seamarshal; Freeporters won't heed him.'

Knowing Freeporters, they won't take notice of anyone . . . *T'An* Rimon or Company representative, I thought with grim amusement.

'Let me speak to Cory,' I said; and when Corazon Mendez appeared, said, 'Land the *T'An* Rimon on the island nearest to the mainland, will you? I'm going in, too. I intend to speak with the local leaders.'

The white-haired woman blinked, raised an eyebrow. She said, 'How far does your policy of non-interference stretch, Lynne? Just out of interest, you understand. When you yell for a 'thopter to get you out of that mess down there, you want me to send my troops into Orthean territory?'

'Cory, just *do* it, yes?' I keyed out.

In the shuttle's cool, green-lit interior, nothing was audible but the hum of the engines. Hard to believe that outside there is real air, stained with the smoke of burning. My guts ached, my hands sweated: I thought, Is this stupid or is this *stupid*? This is not a thing to get involved in, and it's much too late to stop it now it's started. For God's sake go back to Kumiel and wait . . .

But then, there's no way to know what's really going on without going down there.

River gravel crunched under my boots as I sprang down from the shuttle-ramp. Downdraught from the F90's hover-mode blinded me for a moment in the swirl of grit. I ran for the cover of the quayside buildings. Blaize Meduenin waited under a warehouse archway.

'I'm getting . . .' I leaned up against the pale plaster wall, '. . . getting too old for this sort of thing. And what the fuck I think I'm going to do here, *I* don't know.'

The Meduenin grinned. Wind off the harbour whipped his yellow mane across his scarred face, and brought the rank smell of *dekany*-weed and overripe *siir*-vine. Standing here, at sea level, there was no view in any direction. A windvane towered over this part of the quay, vanes slowly turning; I glanced up and down the dock – warehouses and companion-houses and no Freeporters at all. So quiet you could hear the waves slap at the harbour wall . . . and hear, in the far distance, voices loudly shouting.

'They've reopened the Seamarshal's palace,' Blaize Meduenin said. I remembered seeing it boarded-up, half a year ago. He drew *harur-nilgiri*, holding it in his left hand; and membrane slid down over those pale blue, whiteless eyes. 'Look – there.'

Confused, I glanced round. Then, as he pointed, I saw the hoop-mast of a *jath-rai* not three hundred yards away in the channel between this island and the next. *Meshabi*-robed Ortheans crowded the deck. Morning sun flashed from the metal sail and chains. It was automatic to step back into the shadow of the warehouse-arch, and I thought, Lynne don't be ridiculous and a chip of mud-brick stung my cheek. After a second, my eyes focused on the head of a winchbow-bolt, buried deep in a split in the brickwork.

'Think they'll be lucky, don't they?' Blaize touched my arm. 'Christie – this way; come.'

The sun was hot on my head as we crossed the quay again, slipping into an alley that led away from the harbour. Darkness flicked across the dusty earth and biscuit-coloured walls: the shadow of a 'thopter. I tried to push all thought aside. My stomach churned; I was aware of a sideways glance from Blaize.

The alley opened into a square, crowded with Freeport Ortheans. Over their heads I glimpsed the round-arched doors of the Seamarshal's palace. A crowd in constant movement, men and women arriving and leaving: in the far corner a bronze *marhaz* threw up its head and bugled loudly. I swiftly searched for faces I might know, in that confusion of dark and fair manes; Ortheans in Morvren's slit-backed robes, and the leathers of *marhaz*-riders from the north. There a thin, tall woman whose green-gold skin could only belong to a fenborn; there an *ashiren* no more than twelve seasons old, bearing *harur*-blades . . .

'Khassiye will be in the palace, if he's here,' Blaize observed. With that scar-crooked grin, he added, 'When there's fighting, our *T'An* Andrethe will be well out of it!'

Loud voices rang in our ears; Ortheans calling and shouting. Morning sun shone back from pale walls. Two- and three-storey buildings surrounded this square, windowless but for slots on the top floor. As we pushed through the crowds, I searched for words; at last protested: 'Blaize, this isn't a *game*.'

His eyes looking at me were alien. He doesn't fear death here, how could he, remembering other deaths and other rebirths – but it is not a reality for me. Reality is the sickness, the weakness, the disablement of fear. I can call the 'thopter; I can call it *now*—

'There's Khassiye Reihalyn,' I pointed to the low, stepped terrace that ran along beside the Seamarshal's palace. The tall fair-maned male stood with three or four other men and women; his gold-studded fingers flashed as he gestured, giving orders. He frowned, seeing us.

'*T'an S'aranth*, we have enough Earth devices here without your setting down ships-of-the-air on *telestre* land.'

'Unavoidable necessity, *T'An* Andrethe. But do you mean there are hi-tech weapons being used here? Have the *hiyek*-Ortheans—'

'Communicating devices,' Khassiye Andrethe said. He squinted up in the sunlight as a shuttle glided overhead, casting its shadow down on the crowded square. 'It must be so, *S'aranth*: they act together, though their *jath-rai* are beyond sight of each other. The attack came simultaneously upon our several different islands here.'

Blaize put in, 'This isn't their whole force. What word of the rest?'

A black-maned male in Freeport robes said, 'Still in the islands, *t'an*. Doubtless they will come.'

'And the attack?'

'There's fighting on Southernmost and Little Morvren and round Spire Gate. The fires on Little Morvren are beyond control.' The black-maned Orthean turned to me. 'Do you bring us help, *s'aranthi*, or only fair words?'

'We won't interfere in Morvren – on either side.'

One of the Orthean females chuckled. She had her mane drawn up into a plume on the crown of her head, and braided down her spine; one of Peir-Dadeni's northern riders. With some derision, she said, 'Trust *s'aranthi*? *T'an*, you'll interfere when it suits you.'

A shout echoed. I looked up, and saw an Orthean male on the roof above, leaning over the low wall. He called again, pointing; and I didn't catch the words, but his urgency made me go cold.

'Caveth! Zilthar!' Khassiye Andrethe called two of the Sea-marshal's guard to him, and gave a string of rapid orders.

'Call your people,' Blaize Meduenin said to me. The square emptied rapidly now, Ortheans filing out into the broad avenues of that island. The windvane creaked as it turned, not far away; and under the sound I heard a confused shouting. Coming nearer? The sea wind whipped sound away: impossible to tell.

'Blaize—'

'There's nothing to be done,' the scarred male said. 'Go and speak with the *hiyeks* if you think there is. Go tell your *T'An* Mendez to fire on *jath-rai*. *S'aranth*, if you can't do that, all you can do is leave us to fight.'

'That isn't fair!' I recovered some control. 'I can't – I *won't* – order Peace Force intervention. I will try and make contact with the *hiyek*-Ortheans on those ships, though I don't hold out much hope—'

'Sunmother!' He swore. Then he moved down the palace steps, staring towards the avenues; and the morning sun shone brightly on that dusty silver-yellow mane where it tangled down his spine. *Harur*-blade harness made a soft metallic sound. Without looking back at me, he said, 'Call your people. Leave. And when you leave, let me take that far-speaking device of yours. I need to know if the *jath-rai* in the islands sail.'

I thumbed the recall key, and walked down to stand beside him.

'You're staying here? I suppose this is what I could never imagine – you as mercenary commander. And yet I've been in this position on other worlds, there've been outbreaks of fighting; low-tech weapons . . .'

Straining my ears, listening for the beat of a 'thopter's approach: all I could hear was shouting. Orthean voices; now there was no mistaking it, they were coming closer. Blaize rested his hand on my shoulder and I jumped. And then laughed, shakily; and realized how I looked all the time at the entrances to this square, the alleys and avenues; now empty, but all potential threat. Hot morning sun, and quietness, and distant sounds that must be fighting . . . Deep inside, I went cold.

'Will you go?' Blaize said. There was something in his tone besides exasperation. 'Christie, you were always stubborn. There's nothing you can do here. And you're terrified – I know; I've seen enough raw young fighters.'

'"Young"?' That made me smile, for a second. A distant beat resolved itself into the throb of a low-flying 'thopter, and I thumbed the recall key on the wristlink again, to give a location-fix. The roar of the engines drowned all other sound, and suddenly the sun gleamed on its plastiglas body as the 'thopter seemed to rise up over the roof of the Seamarshal's palace.

'They don't need you here—' I had to shout to make myself heard over the noise. He held out one six-fingered hand, gesturing at my wristlink. I unfastened it. He took it, and I thought, There's so much I want to say. How can I persuade you out of this – ?

The 'thopter grounded in a storm of dust and gravel. At the end of one avenue, a hundred yards away, there was confused move-ment: the momentary brightness of metal. Blaize Meduenin strapped on the wristlink and drew *harur-nazari*, almost in one smooth movement; as if it were choreographed, we ran; he for the shelter of the wall, me for the open port of the 'thopter. I ducked down, running under the rotors; hit arm and knee as I scrambled up into the cabin, realized *I can't leave* and shouted to the pilot to put down. He either didn't hear or chose to ignore me. The 'thopter lurched up a dozen feet into the air and I grabbed the strut by the open port, stomach convulsing. There were ten people in the alley now, more pouring in, bright-maned Ortheans in dusty robes; all of them running together, mouths moving but I could hear nothing over the beat of the rotors.

Hanging there, on a level with the roofs, I looked dizzily down at Blaize Meduenin. The fair-maned male stood in the shadow of the wall. For a heartbeat I thought, They'll all pass him; and all did, except for one male who hesitated after the others had gone, running in a strung-out line towards the quay. My throat rasped sore; I hadn't realized I was shouting. The *hiyek* male stopped, shading his eyes with his hand as he looked up, attention taken by the 'thopter twenty feet above him; his gaze locked with mine. Thin-faced, middle-aged. His mouth moved as if he shouted, and he gestured with the hook-bladed knife he carried in his right hand. A flick of movement caught my eye and then Blaize Meduenin ran between us, one arm outstretched, hardly seeming to brush the *hiyek* male across the midriff; metal gleamed, the male folded over and fell to his knees, and slid down on the earth. The 'thopter lurched again and then rose like an elevator. Fifty feet straight up, swinging round in a curve; I vomited and then spat bile through the open port.

When I scrambled forward and fell into the seat beside the pilot, and got him to swing the craft round and double back over the island, there was no way to spot one fair-maned Orthean male amongst the running crowds. I reached out to key the wristlink contact and then hesitated: *Don't distract him—*

'. . . shuttle?' the pilot mouthed, sparing me a brief glance. 'Observation and . . .'

'Take us down as low as you can!' I had to shout to make myself heard.

The 'thopter dipped and suddenly shot off towards the harbour, skimming the surface, then rising to fifty or so feet above the waves; and the smell of *dekany*-weed mixed with evaporating fuel. An island to either side of us: it disorientated me – had our landing been there, or there, or over there? Looking down on water that is jade green, blinded by the morning sun as the 'thopter swings round again; and I managed to key in an open channel and grabbed for the headphones, hoping to hear the rest of Cory's ships:

—no, repeat negative, no usage of anything above level five technology—

—movement of local ships on the river on the increase. Request permission to extend my flight further up-country; we don't want any nasty surprises from that direction—

—estimated local casualties—

—make contact with the Company representative, and ascertain present location—

The pilot glanced at me and I nodded, and he began to transmit co-ordinates.

'Cory?' I yelled into the pick-up. 'What's the fuel situation; how long can you keep an observation-pattern going?'

'position you over the southernmost of these islands,' Cory's voice rasped. All transmissions had that intermittent failure that must be due to what lay several hundred miles north: the Glittering Plain.

Now the 'thopter circled a small island, and I looked down on tiny *telestre*-houses, roof-gardens thick with scurrying figures; down on alleys in which the shadows were shortening – it must be late morning, close on midday – and on a dock and a harbour arm. The masts of *jath* were foreshortened from this height. One ship shimmered, quivering in the warm air; small figures ran from invisible flames, plunging over the side into cerulean water. My hands were flat against the plastiglas: a wall between me and the world, Not real, I thought; then the rotors feathered the sea into flattened ripples, spreading out from us; one bright-maned head dipped under the water, and never reappeared. The 'thopter swooped up again, high over the island.

'—attempt to force a cease-fire—'

'What attempt?' I shouted. The comlink crackled, and I swore in frustration; and then Corazon Mendez came through with total clarity.

'—I've made attempts at contacting the attacking ships with broadcasts from a low-level flight, Lynne. No, repeat negative, no response. I want your authorization to fire a warning shot. Simply a threat; no loss of life involved. I'll use mid-tech explosive projectiles. These natives can understand that. The threat of force—'

Interference washed out her voice. The 'thopter hung high over Southernmost, and the sun half-blinded me as we turned. Sea and earth and daystarred sky; and the long level line of the horizon . . .

Cory's transmission faded back in:

'—the threat alone will have the required effect: but I want it entered on Company records, Lynne, that I have your authorization for this.'

CHAPTER 31

The Viper and Her Brood

I didn't answer. As the 'thopter steadied, I touched the pilot's shoulder and pointed north. We swung away from the Rasrhe-y-Meluur, that great pillar of *chiruzeth* whose shadow fell on the waves below us. The port was still retracted: cool air blustered in, bringing a smell of ocean, making me shiver – but that was with more than cold. At two thousand feet now, the depths of the estuary made a pattern of deep green and shallow jade below us.

Voices intersected on the comlink-circuit. I ignored them. The thrum of the rotors drowned thought; I felt in suspension at some God-like point of overview – we passed over a *jath-rai*, its white trail fading; decks lined with *hiyek*-Ortheans.

'Cory, I'm considering what you say.' I took a breath, hoping to rid myself of a sick dizziness that was nothing to do with flight. The docks of Southernmost flashed past beneath. Now the flames had a hold: black smoke rolled up from *jath* and dockside companion-houses.

'Yes, I'll give you your authorization,' I said. 'Listen to me – Commander. I'm not trying to teach you your business. I have a contact on Northfast, repeat, a contact on Northfast; that's the city-island nearest the mainland. Co-ordinate it so that he can attempt to pull some of his people back. That might just do it. We might just have our cease-fire.'

'Affirmative. Lynne, put your comlink on-circuit; I'll have my officers co-ordinate the strike—'

I automatically followed her order. When I glanced up from the comlink console, seconds later, the 'thopter was again in the channel between Little Morvren and Northfast. Billows of black smoke swirled in from the west, and the pilot pulled us up another five or six hundred feet. Looking down on the smoke was like looking down on a coral reef or treetops: the same shape, but this lived and moved. A spark burned below. How great a conflagration?

'. . . have to take us out of their air-space,' the pilot called.

I leaned half out of the port as we flew north. *Telestre*-houses, windvanes, wide avenues . . . People lay in the avenues; six, ten, a dozen; arms outflung, or legs twisted. Nothing to be seen but their stillness; they look as if they might at any moment get up and run. Suddenly my heart lurched: *that* is the Residence, *that* is the house of Cassirur Almadhera, *that*, burning fierce as phosphorus, is the Seamarshal's palace – square, flat-roofed buildings; the dry *kazsis*-vine sprouting into flame. Now there were people running, some in small groups, some alone, no crowds; running in the immemorial jerky patterns of street-fighting. It's wrong to look at this, I thought, wrong to be a spectator; and then my stomach and lungs clenched with fear: I might still be down there, no spectator at all.

The 'thopter, running low, no more than a thousand feet, passed over the docks. A shadow flicked us: the bulk of an F90 hung in hover-mode over the harbour arm. Part of its shadow fell on *hiyek* ships there, part on Ortheans running across the quay. I had to lean out of the port and look up to see the sun on that white whale-backed craft; it dazzled me. Then we were past.

Strike co-ordinate at twelve hundred—

—contact made with land forces—

—strike at 057.253.746; repeat, 057.253.746—

Suddenly we were no longer over the sea, but skimming the mainland; the flat and dusty banks of the Ai River. Ferry-shacks were scattered along it; dense crowds gathered round them. *Marhaz*-riders raised dust-trails. Small boats bobbed like woodchips in the mouth of the estuary, their yellow and white sails bright against the muddy water.

A grinding, bass explosion ripped the air. I felt it rather than heard it; felt it in the chest and stomach and bones; couldn't help glancing up at the clear sky – such a phenomenon must be thunder, too fearful to be manmade – and then turned in my seat to stare back. A dust-cloud ballooned up over Northfast, blocking out light and turning the sun sepia. A curious line seemed to be running from the island across the sea towards the mainland – simultaneous to realization, the 'thopter swung into the shockwave and was for long seconds buffeted and pushed sideways. My hands clenched on the siderail, knuckles white. Somewhere below a tidal wave must be hitting the estuary. I clung, eyes shut.

—made successfully at twelve-oh-two—

—no damage sustained by shuttle—

—I'm getting visual damage-estimate; wait—

Carrick's Star blinded me. I rubbed at my watering eyes, tried to focus. A thousand feet below, a river-boat lay on its side in the water. Tiny figures splashed, swimming; no larger than insects. No sooner seen than passed.

'Jesus!' the pilot whistled softly, in admiration. 'Made a mess of them didn't we – sorry, Representative Christie.'

After the fear, the exultation: I tried to repress both. No point now in thinking, Was that the right decision, should I have waited, what else could I have done? And wrong to feel that joy that comes with the use of power, any power, for any reason. I leaned forward as we skimmed the side of that rising mass of dust and grit and rubble turning lazily end over end in the air, only now just beginning to fall . . .

At first I saw nothing. Then I registered that Northfast no longer has a harbour arm. That long mass of masonry gone, and only shattered fragments at the quay end to prove it ever existed.

Smoke and dust clouded the dockside. Metal shone: a *jath-rai* driven up – up the steps that led to the Portmaster's office; it looked ridiculous there. Men and women clambered free of the fallen hoop-mast, staggering; one fell from no cause and didn't rise, and it was whole minutes later before I thought (as the 'thopter crossed the channel between islands) *winchbow-bolt*. I reached out to key in a contact with my wristlink, and found I had to use the console; the world not yet come together again in my head. *Did we really do that*? And: *yes, we did; we really did.*

The 'thopter ports closed, the air-purifiers hummed; dust from the explosion being filtered out of the interior of the craft. That cloud drifted south, dimming the daystars. It hid the pattern of F90s and YV9s, shuttling back and forth across this few miles of coast. How far inland did they hear that? I wondered. What's being said now in the river-*telestres*? How long will it take word to get as far as the nearer Archipelago islands?

'—do we have contact? Lynne?'

'I'm here,' I said. 'Give me your co-ordinates, and have your pilot here rendezvous with your shuttle. I'm coming aboard.'

'Affirmative.'

I closed my eyes, concentrating on the voices on the comlink circuit, knowing better than to interrupt with anything inessential. There was no voice yet speaking Rimon, or Sino-Anglic with a Rimon accent.

The F90 hovered squarely over Northfast, holotank showing a direct live-transmission of the island beneath. Corazon Mendez was standing by the holotank when her junior officer ushered me into the craft's comlink-centre; she glanced up briefly, but continued to talk without pause: '—the extent of damage for Company records. I want a full holographic record, Lieutenant.' She keyed in a different contact. 'Marston, has there been any resumption of hostilities?'

'Some sporadic firing, Commander Mendez. The sea-craft are still keeping their distance. Estimate them fifteen minutes away from any contact with land.'

'Good.' She keyed the channel shut, and straightened. Her hair was sleek, the Peace Force coverall neat. Nothing betrayed tension but that characteristic twisting of her silver rings, of which she seemed unaware.

'The *hiyek* ships have backed off?'

'For the moment,' Cory said. 'The next few hours will be quiet. If we pass the eight-hour mark, I may begin to think we've forced the cease-fire we were hoping for. If not, we're back where we started.'

My legs not only ached, they were trembling. I walked across and sat down in one of the bucket seats. I was suddenly unaccountably thirsty. I said, 'Not entirely back where we started. The Company's used force twice now on Orthe; that's as far as it's going to go. Or were you thinking that, if this hasn't worked, you can do here what you did at Reshebet?'

'That strike was effective,' Cory said mildly. 'May I remind you, Lynne, you're unofficially acting as Company representative. If anything, we share the responsibility.'

Never argue on ground that uncertain. I said nothing in direct reply.

'Is there any news from the orbiter on Doug Clifford?'

'What kind of news?' She was bewildered.

Only a few hours, and communications are confused – I shook my head. One becomes resigned to this sort of thing in the field. 'He was hurt in Melkathi. The Harantish – but you won't know about that either? No. Jesus Christ! Well, so long as you hear about it now . . . You may want to call your senior officers in on this briefing.'

The cool green lighting of the F90's cabin soothed me (as it is intended to do); I became aware of the power-hum, of a low chatter of communication; of other Peace Force officers through in different command-centres.

'Cory, I also want the *T'An* Rimon in on this one. He has local information you could find useful; he's fought here, and on the Coast.' I thought, And for the *hiyeks* and against them – but what will Blaize Meduenin say when he knows that Kel Harantish has entered this war?

'I'll have my people contact him.'

We spoke of other things. I kept up a façade of competence; what I said, I don't know. At last, with no warning, an insert in the holotank resolved into the scarred face of Blaize Meduenin, standing in the sunlight on Northfast; and he spoke with one of Cory's junior officers, in a voice hoarse with exhaustion. Relief of tension made my eyes prickle with tears, but I held them back.

I made no move to speak with him. The resolution of the image was poor, but clear enough to see the stains of black blood on the *harur-nilgiri* held in his right hand. Strain and exhaustion on his face, corrupted by the pull of scar tissue; lines deeply incised near the pale membrane-covered eyes – by being on Northfast for those two hours, he had gone into a place where I could not follow; that place in him I have never more than partly understood.

Eight hours passed with excruciating slowness. I ate, slept; spoke with the Peace Force officers of the death of Sethri-safere in Melkathi, and what that might now mean. F90s and YV9s left to re-power; returned. Carrick's Star beat down unrelentingly, and a heat haze veiled the estuary: heat-sensors patterned the movements of people below, on the mainland, on islands, in the *jath-rai* that lay becalmed off Spire Gate.

Long effort at last got me a clear contact with Melkathi, with the acting head of Company Research, Ravi Singh. His image in the holotank blinked, bewildered: no, nothing was happening at Ashiel Wellhouse; no, nor anywhere in Rimnith and Keverilde.

'I shall move to our base on Kumiel Island,' he announced. 'I don't see any reason to stay here. All the evidence here points to the use of native low-tech, with perhaps some illegal Earth mid-tech weaponry; I see no signs of anything else. If you authorize me to return to the orbiter, I *do* have a research programme I could be getting on with.'

I said something, fortunately in one of the Orthean languages; and cut the contact. What does it take to get through the cotton wool round you? I thought. But I made the authorization. And made another call to the orbiter.

'The government envoy is still in tissue-regeneration.' This medic, Kennaway, an elderly black woman, smiled when she recognized me. 'Ms Christie – I'll let you know, personally, as soon as there's any news.'

I sat at the holotank for some minutes after that contact. Would it help now, to speak with Nelum Santhil, or Haltern or Cassirur? Is what they see at ground level different from satellite-images; is there something to be sensed, there, that can't be detected except through that contact born of the earth?

The small cabin intercom chimed, disrupting my thoughts. When I keyed in, a young Pacifican woman's face appeared: one of Cory's senior officers.

'Commander Mendez wishes to see you urgently,' she said.

Outside the shuttle, Corazon Mendez stood with a group of Peace Force officers. Heat haze faded, though the air was still humid; my coverall clung stickily to me. The smell of burning hung strongly in the air with no wind to shift it, and the island across this narrow channel was invisible in a sepia twilight: Little Morvren blazing without hope of control. Some of the boats used for its exodus still lay beached on the shore below us.

As I walked across to join the group, I saw Ortheans there. Blaize Meduenin's stocky figure, and an elegantly thin male, Khassiye Andrethe, and five or six others in Freeport dress . . . no one in the *meshabi*-robe of the *hiyeks*.

'This is your business, not mine,' Corazon said without preamble. 'I don't discuss compensation.'

'Compensation?'

A Freeport male, older than the others in the group, said ironically, 'There is the matter of Northfast harbour, *t'an*; or rather, the harbour that we had before your Company came lately to the Freeport.'

'I think it may be premature to discuss rebuilding at this stage,' I said. The old male's eyes veiled and cleared. Is that equal appreciation of irony, I thought; or anger, or sadness, or all three?

'You misunderstand me, *t'an S'aranth*—'

A younger shaven-maned male interrupted, 'Not only the harbour! You have put your ships to earth here, and on the banks of the Ai River; you desecrate *telestre* land with the touch of them! What possible "compensation" can you offer for that?'

Heat made me sweat. The back of my neck prickled with what my empathy detected in Cory and her officers: the thought *native superstition* so strong that for a moment I saw the two Freeporters through her eyes – dark reptilian skin, pale manes rooting down their spines; gold and red robes belted with *harur*-blade harness, barbaric splendour.

'I am sorry for the necessity of it,' I said. '*T'an* Earthspeaker, it would not have been done if there had been any other way. Ask the *T'An* Rimon.' The young male's expression altered fractionally, realizing I'd recognized him as a priest of the Goddess.

Blaize moved a few steps over the dry earth and came to stand beside me. It effectively divided us into two groups: Orthean and Peace Force officers – and where am I? Between the two, I thought. Where else?

'I gave my word for the destruction on Northfast.' Blaize spoke leisurely.

'And what else will you give your word for, while there is war in Morvren?'

The younger male's hostility was plain. On the other Orthean faces, I saw at best neutrality, at worst hatred. Now that the haze was almost gone, they stood against a background of sea and smoke; the flat horizon and low islands, and coiling pillars of ash that were spreading to form a ceiling, blotting out daystars and summer clouds. The only movement was a brief sighting of some YV9 or cruising 'thopter.

'We have the use of s'aranthi eyes,' Blaize said, with a laconic jerk of his head at the aircraft. 'It's always said Freeporters know a bargain. That for this—' with a gesture that took in the ranked F90s, Mendez's officers, Corazon herself.

I said, 'Would it please you to come aboard and see that the hiyek ships have retreated south past Spire Gate?'

'Witchbreed trickery!' the Earthspeaker muttered; but the older male gave me a considering look, and bent to listen to a whispered comment from the black-maned female beside him. I've more chance of persuading that Earthspeaker than I have of talking Cory into this one, I thought; and stepped back so that the Freeporters could speak comfortably together.

'Corazon said this is a critical time. What do you think?' I spoke quietly. Blaize shrugged.

'When I fought on the Coast, the hiyeks favoured night attack. S'aranth, I don't know. If I did know, I don't know what I would do.' And then he smiled, mouth tugged askew by the blue-and-red mottled scar of an earlier burning. 'Two questions. What will the ships hiding in the islands do? What will your people do? Can you tell me the answers?'

Oddly enough, it was her memory that came back to me; that exiled woman, Ruric Orhlandis. Who must soon be hearing in the Tower of what happened here – who must feel very much as I do, I thought.

'I can't answer for the hiyek ships. As far as the Company goes – you're on your own. We have to stay neutral. It isn't purely law or policy.' It was instinctive to take his arm, and I felt how that alien musculature tensed; felt the infinitesimal but constant tremor of exhaustion. This the hand and arm of which harur-blades seem

806

so much a part . . . 'Don't tell me I can't understand what happened on Northfast. I can't; I wasn't there. If I had been, I'd have run. But Blaize, you didn't see her in Kel Harantish – see Calil – you didn't see Douggie's face this morning; not his injury, but the *fear*. I've felt it. I saw her butchery in Kel Harantish.'

The pale blue eyes veiled, cleared. He said, 'She makes you incoherent.'

'She – I – yes, she does. And I believe Pathrey when he says there are others like her. Listen, this is a low-tech war here. Don't tell me people are just as dead – I know it's a false classification. But if it escalates, if Calil bel-Rioch *does* have the weapons of the Golden Empire; if she uses them . . .'

Blaize rested one broad hand on the hilt of *harur-nazari*. The westering sun put his shadow on the eroded earth, falling too on the edge of the shuttle-ramp. I remember how in the Barrens I first learned, from Blaize n'ri n'suth Meduenin, how Ortheans carry their dead lives with them: does he now remember how it was in the long and brilliant summer of Golden rule?

'The Freeporters could defend the city well enough,' he said, irresolutely. 'Should I be in Melkathi? You say she's there, this would-be Empress. If this isn't your battle, why are there Company ships here?' Some humour barely showed in his face. 'I should have stayed; I'd at least have *t'an* Haltern to tell me what to do. I don't know, Christie.'

I wanted to hold him, to take away that pain – and what do I know of those two hours on Northfast; what could I say? – but we stood among others: Freeporters in vociferous discussion; Cory Mendez speaking into her wristlink.

'Well, we must keep Witchbreed weapons from use,' Blaize said; blackly humorous. 'I want my part in the battle of Morvren Freeport remembered in past-lives; for that, there must be time enough to turn this into history.'

'I'd like to make the history books myself,' I observed.

'*T'An* Meduenin.' It was the armed Earthspeaker who called. Blaize inclined his head to me, and walked across to the group of Freeporters.

Is it all over but the shouting? No, I thought. Not that easily. This is a lull, how can we take advantage of it? The essential thing is, somehow, to make contact with the Coast Ortheans in the *jath-rai* – how? We've come very close to showing ourselves on the same side as the Hundred Thousand, here. If the Company's lost its neutral status . . .

The sun lay just above the western horizon, flooding the flat estuary with pale gold light. Soon second twilight and the starlit night would come. For now, it made a deceptive peace; filigreed the edges of waves, outlined in gold the low slopes of this spit of mainland earth. I looked south, eyes drawn to that massive tapering pillar of *chiruzeth*; limned with light on its western side. Though it dominates the landscape, the eye refuses the sight of it; can't comprehend it. I kicked the mossgrass underfoot – if I dig down, will I find one of the Old Roads, leading south to the Rasrhe-y-Meluur? And south over all the Archipelago islands to that distant continent, to the garden that was the Elansiir, to that unimaginable creation: the City Over The Inland Sea? All that contained in the sight of this blue-grey spire, whose peak is lost in evening haze: so glassy that it reflects the clouds that pass across its surface . . .

Dead, now, and hollow. They made of the Elansiir, a desert. They made of the City Over The Inland Sea, a desolation seen in mist and silver. They made, of that great Empire, a child-woman in Kel Harantish; throned above the bloody abattoir she has made of her enemies. And if she looses from her hand that ancient light, will it free the devastation that is barely held in check in the Barrens, the Elansiir, the Glittering Plain?

The evening light shines on Morvren Freeport. Each island is clear as glass, walls and *telestre*-houses and docks. Beyond them, the blur of the mainland: the northern continent. And what moves now in the *telestres*, in Shiriya-Shenin that lies nine hundred miles up the Ai River; what in Medued-in-Rimon, and those forested hills? Over the horizon, those blue hills; *telestres* and Wellhouses and Orthean cities – what word goes out by heliograph and *rashaku*-messenger? And far to the east lies the white city, Tathcaer, the heartland of the Hundred Thousand . . . I thought for a moment that memories would overwhelm me, but I didn't know whether they would be of my time there, eight years ago, or memories of others who had come from this land, in centuries past, come at last to the Brown Tower.

It was some while before the thought crept into my mind: If we are not neutral, then the Tower is. And the desperately impractical question: Could Ruric Hexenmeister speak with the Ortheans on the *hiyek* ships?

Lynne, you're crazy; the Hexenmeister can't leave the Tower, Ruric Orhlandis can't leave the Tower—

No, but can she?

The Freeporters were still arguing, gesturing up at the hull of the F90 shuttle. I saw Blaize Meduenin settle back on his heels, speaking with a grim determination; and one of Mendez's officers walked over to join them, bewilderment on every line of her face. Cory had vanished. I walked up the shuttle-ramp and into the cool interior, making my way to the comlink-centre.

The WEBcasters will still be at Ashiel Wellhouse; Cassirur will be there . . . What about Tethmet Fenborn? And is this something I can talk about over open-channel?

I sat down at one of the smaller holotanks, not yet making a contact. It was automatic to key in surveillance, and while I sat thinking, I stared at the holo-image of the estuary: the setting sun, the smoke that at last began to dissipate.

Abruptly, I reached forward and keyed Cory's wristlink.

'Mendez here.' Her image frowned. 'What is it?'

'The *jath-rai* down past Spire Gate are moving,' I said; simultaneously one of her officers cut into the transmission with 'Commander, movement of hostiles at 475.930.756; estimate their present course local-south.'

In the holotank, the images of *jath-rai* raised their thin metal sails in the twilight, catching the wind that springs up at sunset. Cory Mendez came into the cabin as I got up and moved to the larger holotank, leaning over the back of the comlink officer's seat.

'They're moving away from the Freeport,' I said.

She reached down and keyed for satellite-image. After several seconds of interference, the image formed: visual, with heat-sensor overlay. The Morvren coast, the estuary – now enlarging to include all the northern islands of the Archipelago.

'Damn!' Cory pointed. 'That's what I was afraid of.'

The indicators marking *jath-rai* clustered round the islands near Spire Gate. Movement was just visible at this scale of image. As I watched, other indicators detached themselves from islands to the south – a handful, then a dozen, a score; and then like a flood the flecks of light marking *jath-rai* positions began to sift out from among the concealment of island settlements.

I gripped the side of the 'tank, willing the ships to sail faster. 'Cory, the time to be afraid is when we know where the fleet's headed. It could just be that they'll set a course back to the Desert Coast . . .'

The Peace Force Commander bent down to speak through comlink to a YV9 surveillance-craft, ordering it to fly south. Her hand, by her side, was clenched tight enough to drive the silver rings into her tanned flesh.

'You'd better get rid of the locals, Lynne. I don't want any complications.' She glanced up, pale blue eyes brilliant with tension. 'You know your job best; keep them happy, but keep them out of our way. Until we know what's happening here, this could be dangerous.'

Hours crept by. My eyes began to ache with staring into the holotanks aboard the F90. Satellite-images alternated with images sent back from shuttles overflying the islands, fifty or a hundred miles south of where we were grounded. Interference made reception difficult. The satellites gave heat-sensor images – no usage of hi-tech tracked down, only the clusters of body-heat that are the crews of *jath-rai* and *jath* – many *jath*, those deep-sea vessels that can carry three or four hundred aboard. And the shuttles sent back night-images: leaf-shaped silhouettes of blackness on a sea made silver by the blaze of the Heart Stars . . .

'Latest estimate is between seven hundred and seven-ten vessels,' Corazon Mendez said, four hours after the movement of the ships had begun. 'Lynne, does that seem feasible, from your local knowledge? Given the carrying power of the large and the coastal ships, that's about thirty thousand natives on board.'

The *siirans* must be empty. No, more: the islanders must be joining the *hiyeks* . . . I said, 'If you want local knowledge, I'd advise you to bring the *T'An* Meduenin in on this. Cory, you may as well. He still has my wristlink, and I'd be very surprised if he hasn't been following this.'

The older woman opened her mouth as if to speak, checked, and then shook her head. She laughed shortly. 'Yes.'

One of the officers put a call through. There was a hiatus, the shift changing in the comlink-centre; and I took advantage of that to stand and stretch, to wonder if I couldn't find something to drink. The F90's cabin felt changeless: green-tinted illumination, the brightness reflecting up from holotanks on to young, intent faces; the subliminal hum of communications between other Force vessels. This will be the same whether it's night or day outside, whether the Freeport is still standing in the morning, or whether these ships turn for the north to sail and burn it to the ground.

As the new officers settled in, I looked at those young Pacifican faces and wished for some way to move them beyond these holo-images. And then I thought: But what did I really see of Morvren, myself? A few minutes on Northfast, an hour above ground in a 'thopter; the rest by image in shuttles . . . How can we *feel* what's happening here – and if we can't, how can we judge the right actions to take?

Blaize Meduenin came in, inclining his head to Cory. His slit-backed shirt and his britches were ash-stained; and the clash of *harur*-blades was loud in that quiet cabin as he slumped wearily down in the seat next to me.

'Where are they now?'

'Here. Most of them aren't far from land, still. By "land" I mean the islands.'

He leaned forward. The holotank light shone on his matted and filthy mane, and membrane slid down to shield his eyes.

'The different coloured dots represent vessels of different carrying power,' a dark Pacifican officer said. He was hardly more than a boy; nineteen or twenty. 'These figures are local wind-speed and—'

'I'm familiar with the Webster-representation,' Blaize cut him off, Sino-Anglic accented but understandable. 'Some years ago I was briefly on Aleph-Nine and Parmiter's Moon. Christie, have you made any contact with the *hiyeks*?'

Hiding a smile, I said, 'No. It's been distance-contact, so far.' And then I shrugged. 'Cory sent 'thopters down earlier, to try loudhailer-contact. No response.'

'No . . .' The membrane blinked back from his eyes: a flash of sardonic humour. He raised his head, looking across the tank at Corazon Mendez. 'They would probably kill anyone you sent in to talk with them in person.'

Cory attempted a passable formal Ymirian: '*T'an* Meduenin, can you predict what action this fleet will take?'

I saw him register her attempt at courtesy. He had an expression I couldn't place, when he looked at her; and I thought, That's from Northfast. That is the look of one who was there, to one who – quite literally – stayed above the battle.

Blaize Meduenin stared down into the holotank, at dots that moved with infinitesimal slowness. Hard to translate that into the riveted metal hulls of *jath-rai*, cutting the water; thin metal sails spread to catch the falling wind; *jath* loaded to the rails with men and women of the Desert *hiyeks* . . .

'They might attack the Freeport again, if your work on Northfast fails to make them fear.' His eyes veiled. 'They may attack the Morvren and Rimon coast, the *telestres* there.'

'Is there any chance they've been scared into abandoning this, going back to the Desert Coast?' I suggested.

'Chance? *S'aranth*, there are always chances.' He turned that scarred profile towards me. 'You'll know – we'll know, well before morning.'

The night passed. Cory Mendez grew more quiet, withdrawing into her self; and I could appreciate how she felt. All the Company's hi-tech sensors, transport, communications; all of it waiting on the result of *jath-rai* and *jath* and a south-westerly wind. Her officers plainly suffered the same tension.

I made brief communication with the WEBcasters, still at Ashiel Wellhouse; and with the shuttles on Kumiel Island. If it amounted to a news blackout, that is only because, acting representative or not, I didn't know yet how I wanted this handled.

The summer night passed. Before the ten hours were up, a pattern became clear. *Jath* and *jath-rai* drew out from the Archipelago into the Inner Sea, a score here, fifty there; setting courses that would eventually intersect. Plotted, they crossed two hundred miles north-west of Lone Isle. An easterly course that might, if they didn't turn north to the Rimon coast, bring them in a few days within sight of Melkathi.

'I don't care if you can't pick up transmissions,' I said to Corazon Mendez, 'those two groups are in contact with each other!'

Blaize sat, *harur-nilgiri* blade resting its point on the cabin floor, resting his chin on his hands that were clasped over the hilt. He leaned back in the padded seat when I spoke, and said wearily, 'You told me of Harantish soldiers come to the Archipelago, and of the Empress Calil in Melkathi? Then that's where they're sailing, Christie. To Rimnith and to Keverilde, to break the siege.'

I looked down into the holotank, at that firefly-scatter of dots on the Inner Sea.

'I think I should talk with Pathrey Shanataru again.'

CHAPTER 32

The Woman Who Walks on the Sky

The YV9 shuttle, flying east at well below two thousand feet, passed over specks on the sea; some of which must (I thought) be the normal trading ships of summer, others – strung out in line, in many small convoys – Coast *jath* travelling towards their projected rendezvous.

Disembarking on Kumiel Island at about noon, I thought, Given they travel no faster than the slowest coastal *jath-rai*, given they have to raid shipping and the *telestres* for food – or did the Archipelago islanders provision them, willingly or unwillingly? – and then, given good weather . . .

The *hiyek* fleet will reach Melkathi no later than six days from now. Call it Merrum Secondweek Threeday or Fourday. That is a very narrow margin for us to take action in. But it'll have to do.

Daystars glittered round the horizon, pinpricks of light; and Carrick's Star blazed down on the island's rock and sparse moss-grass. North, towards the mainland, sea fog rolled whitely; I couldn't see the coastline, or the roofs of Tathcaer. Temporary Company domes now clustered round the ranked shuttles, I saw. Most stood on the lee of ridges, partly concealed from the city; and I smiled, thinking, Tact and diplomacy from PanOceania? Wonders will never cease, and someone behind me put a hand on my shoulder.

'I was about to contact you. Hello, Lynne.'

'*Douggie*—'

He smiled, almost apologetically. That small, round face was pale; there were hard lines around his mouth. A grey pad covered his right eye. The left eye, bloodshot but clear, could obviously see.

'Looks like they've treated you well – Jesus, Douggie, you shouldn't be back here yet!'

'I find it preferable to have something with which to occupy my thoughts.'

His grizzled red hair was neatly trimmed. I saw they'd given him new coveralls on the orbiter, with the PanOceania logo. That neatness somehow made him seem desperately fragile.

He kept his hand on my shoulder. 'I won't have much depth perception until this heals. Lynne, I've a reason for returning prematurely. I have Pathrey Shanataru at the moment under the aegis of the government, rather than of the Company; forgive me if I would rather it stayed that way . . .'

It was automatic to move with him as we walked across the island. He moved uncertainly, stumbling; as if the dry earth and clumps of mossgrass were dubious territory. Now I saw him in profile, there were white shadows of scars in the socket of his eye. In time it will be just something that happened, long ago, on another world; I sensed that he was not yet free of the shock of it.

'You've been down long?' I nodded at the low dome that housed the comlink-centre; dwarfed by the subwave transmitter bulking beside it. 'You know what's happening at the Freeport?'

Doug frowned. 'There's no guarantee Morvren Freeport won't be subject to another attack. Certainly if I were Commander Mendez, I would expect some *jath-rai* to remain behind in the islands, and cause the greatest possible disruption.'

'Yes. Blaize said that, too—' I broke off, recognizing the pony-tailed black man outside the comlink-dome. Mehmet Lutaya of the Ariadne WEB. Doug's palm was damp where it rested on the shoulder of my coverall, and I thought, I don't want to leave you, I want to talk to you; oh Jesus, I want to tell you about Northfast.

'Envoy,' Lutaya said, striding over towards us. 'Representative.'

Northwards the sea fog was beginning to shift, and Rimon's white headlands gleamed, six or seven miles distant across the straits. Wind ruffled Lutaya's hair and clothing. He had that look that WEBcasters have, a curiosity both avid and totally detached.

'I don't have much time right now,' I said, not breaking stride.

He shrugged. 'Thought I might be doing you both a favour. We're beginning to get feedback through from the Home Worlds.'

Doug Clifford hesitated, letting his hand fall from my shoulder, and queried, 'Feedback on what, precisely?'

'On Carrick V. On the fighting, and how PanOceania's handling the affair.' Lutaya looked at me. 'Nothing's been released here – well, there's no public WEB, is there? Thought I might try to be helpful. Maybe get information in exchange for information? Worth a try.'

Vibration thrummed through the earth as one of the F90s lifted, hovered, and then ripped the air apart as it flew west. Its white bulk faded against the daystarred sky. That'll be on Cory's orders,

I thought. If I can find anything that'll help me curb the Peace Force, I shall be a great deal happier.

'Send records,' I said, 'we'll be——?' and I glanced at Doug.

'In the government Residence, in the city,' Doug supplied. 'On the mainland.'

No, really? But I wasn't about to ask why, not in front of a WEBcaster.

Lutaya nodded. 'I'll bring a full record across. Want to discuss access to information, and to certain areas on this world – that means with Company *and* government, yes? Thought so. About two hours?'

I agreed, and watched him walk away. Doug chuckled. When I glanced at him, he had some shadow of that prim humour in his face; that urbane mask that he loves to wear.

'I imagine he won't be the sole representative of the Earth WEBs to come knocking on the Residence's door,' Doug observed. 'For my part, I must confess, I'm not being over-scrupulous about the rules on data-restriction . . .'

'Who's in Tathcaer?'

The question didn't surprise him.

'In the Residence? As you might have supposed, Pathrey Shanataru. I put him there with Haltern Beth'ru-elen, on his return from Ashiel Wellhouse; and in the care of the *t'an* Cassirur.' Now he had the remnants of that old, sharp gaze; head cocked bird-like and alert, for all the shock still in his system. 'Morvren frightens me, Lynne. Now things have disintegrated this far, I begin to think that we have to take action with some speed. I intend to consult the *takshiriye* now.'

'I'll come with you.'

The summer sun reflected back from the rocks. At my feet, dusty mossgrass was turning brown; and thin stems bobbed waist-high, weighed down by crimson spore cases. Heat made me sweat; the sky was a vast arched dome; and for a second I was back on the Eastern Isles, eight years gone, my first step on to the surface of Orthe . . .

'I'll give you something to think about while we're travelling over there,' I said. 'Douggie, the people we have to talk to aren't the *takshiriye*. We must get in contact with the Desert Coast Ortheans, either the fleet, or the people in Rimnith and Keverilde; *that's* who we have to convince.'

'Impossible.' He rubbed a sheen of moisture from his forehead, and looked away. 'Impossible. Those people are led by fanatics now.'

And what are the chances of making contact with the Harantish Witchbreed?

Mid-morning bells rang a sharp carillon. The shadows of *rashaku-bazur* flicked across the inner courtyard of Westhill-Ahrentine, and their harsh hooting cries echoed; and I came through the gate-arch from the alley outside, and found a game of *ochmir* in progress. Sun shone on the thin white mane of Haltern n'ri n'suth Beth'ru-elen as he raised his head from the board and smiled. A skeletally-thin male Orthean seated at the opposite side of the table also looked up, and I recognized Tethmet Fenborn.

'Give you greeting, *t'ans*,' Haltern said mildly. His pale blue eyes moved to the upper-storey windows, an involuntary movement, soon concealed.

Doug Clifford nodded acknowledgement and didn't break stride. As he went up the outside steps to the upper storey, a young dark-maned *l'ri-an* pulled the bead curtain aside, and he spoke to *kir* as he went inside. I moved across to stand under the *ziku* that shaded the table.

'Do they play *ochmir* on the Coast, *shan'tai* Tethmet? I didn't know.'

'The *t'an* Tethmet learns swiftly,' Haltern said. I thought he sounded a little rueful: when I glanced down at the position of the triangular counters on the hexagonal board, I could see why. The old male went on: 'Christie, this is perhaps the right moment to say to you, you may wish to see the *t'an* Earthspeaker Cassirur.'

'Why is now the right moment, Hal?'

One thin six-fingered hand reached out to place a *leremoc* counter on the *ochmir* board. 'Because the *t'an* Clifford is now absent . . . Cassirur has one of your Company people in the Well-house, up at the Square.'

That Orthean obliqueness. Sometimes I'm plain human and impatient. 'Hal, *who* does she have, and why?'

'The Earthspeaker brought her back from Ashiel,' Haltern said, not to be hurried. 'I believe that her name is Pramila Ishida.'

Now it was my turn to glance up at the top storey of the *telestre*-house. Doug is there, he'll be talking with Pathrey Shanataru, should I be there? But Pramila Ishida will know what the *hiyeks* in Rimnith and Keverilde are doing – if she'll tell me. She may even have information about the Harantish Ortheans . . .

'Why did she – how—' I stopped. 'Never mind. I'll go up there now. Hal, is the woman injured, is that why Cassirur has her up at the Wellhouse?'

Sun through *ziku* spines dappled the low table, and the *ochmir* board. Tethmet reached down to put in a *thurin* counter that completed a hexagon in his colour: the reverberations of that, in the overlapping hexagons, spread right out to the edges of the board.

'She's unharmed,' Haltern said.

Membrane slid down over the fenborn's dark eyes, and Tethmet said, 'She is not whole.'

That's what you get for asking questions of Ortheans. I nodded, and as I turned to leave the courtyard, said, 'Tell Douggie I'll be back before noon. *Shan'tai* Tethmet, please wait; I want to ask you to do something for me. Hal—'

'You will not see the *takshiriye* here; they are largely to be found in Melkathi still. Go. I have said to Cassirur that you will come.'

'Yes, I thought you might . . .'

My footsteps echoed under the arched tunnel-entrance, and I came out from that cool shadow into Tathcaer's hot sun. From outside Westhill-Ahrentine I looked down at the harbour, crowded with *jath-rai*; the sun flickered on the water, and on Ortheans who poled small boats between the shipping, or stood arguing at the quayside booths. Voices came faintly up the hill. And this could almost be any day in the summer trading season – I wanted to walk along the quay and overhear what Ortheans were saying, but instead I hailed a *skurrai-jasin* that was rattling down the slope.

All the way up to the Square, I leaned back in the small wooden carriage and tried to detect some difference in the city's atmosphere. The winding alleys were crowded, Ortheans standing in groups. As we passed *telestre*-houses, I began to see how many had barred and bolted their doors.

'What's your *telestre*, t'an?'

The *jasin* driver tugged at the thong attached to the *skurrai*'s nose-ring before he answered. The carriage swung a tight corner, uphill, and clattered out on to Crown Way; now we were under the shadow of *lapuur* that line it.

'I'm from Temethu.'

'That's – north Roehmonde?' Upwards of eight hundred miles north of Tathcaer, on the way to the Wall of the World.

He turned halfway round in the *jasin* seat. A male, with wideset dark eyes, and an intricately-braided brown mane; if I'd known Roehmonde well enough, I could have told his *telestre* without asking, from the pattern of those braids.

He said, 'Don't misunderstand me, *t'an s'aranthi*, I don't even like the Melkathi *telestres*, and I most surely don't trust Freeporters

817

– if they trade with outlanders, what do they expect? – but since you *s'aranthi* brought land-wasters here, what else can I do but be here?'

The *skurrai* shook its long-skulled head, feather-pelt glinting bronze; all four split pads searching for purchase. Then, as the *jasin* crested the slope into the Square, the brown-maned male turned back to guide us through the crowds that thronged the great open space.

Getting down from the carriage at the Wellhouse steps, I overheard comments about *s'aranthi*. Anger, resentment . . . and more than that: a kind of massive dismissal. The stones of this city so old, that Citadel that crowns the crag there standing for two millennia; and the lives of these people built and rebuilt, like *telestre*-houses, structures of memory. No wonder offworlders seem so transient to them.

Cassirur appeared as soon as I entered the Wellhouse gates. She led me past courtyard and fountains, away from the main dome, to an onion-domed building. I pushed through the bead-curtain, blinking at interior shadows.

'She came to Ashiel at midday on the day that you left here,' the red-maned Orthean woman said, walking through into inner rooms. Her green slit-backed robe was rumpled, travel-stained. At another curtained door, she stopped for a word with one of her *ashiren*.

'Is she hurt? I can't get any sense out of Hal.'

The Earthspeaker Cassirur paused. Her eyes cleared, the bright pale green of sun on *lapuur*-fronds; she was a flame of colour against the brown brickwork of walls and ceiling and floor.

'If you were from a *telestre* I would say to you: the Goddess gave you your twin in her, and she hers in you.'

I stepped through into the small room. Light seeped in through a slot-window; the air was hot. There was a low couch-bed pushed up against the wall, and the Pacifican girl sat up as I entered, and put her feet down on the floor. They were lacerated, bloody; there were deep scratches on her bare arms and legs. She still wore a *meshabi*-robe, and her brown hair was braided in an approximation of the *hiyek* manner.

'Where is he?' she demanded.

'Where's who?' And then I realized. I sat down on the edge of the couch-bed beside her. 'You mean Sethri-safere?'

'I mean his body.'

'They took it up to the orbiter, I believe.' It seemed crass to state that it was for an autopsy.

'I want to see it.'

'Pramila, I can understand that. I'll arrange it, if I can. I'll have to make other arrangements, too; you realize that? The Company will take disciplinary action—'

'I don't care about that.'

She put her head in her hands, pushing her fingers through her filthy hair. So much tension in the line of her back: she was holding herself together by willpower alone. In that dim light I couldn't see if she wept. When she straightened, her expression was stunned, despairing.

'I don't think I even care about what happens to Jadur and Charazir and Wyrrin-hael, and he would call that despicable . . . As for the Company, I—' She gripped my arm. Her nails were bitten down bloody. 'We're always warned not to get involved. Aren't we? Ms Christie, I'm involved. His people are my people, it doesn't matter what I said just now. That's why I'm here.'

'Can you take me to someone who can talk for the *hiyeks*?' I asked. I would have bruises where her fingers tightened on my arm.

'I don't know. I'll try. I – it wasn't easy to get away. There are things you ought to know.' She blinked in the twilight. The heat was making her sweat; when she rubbed her face, it smeared the dust into pale streaks on her sallow skin.

'Cassirur's right. You were right, too,' I admitted. 'I could have done what you have. Perhaps I should have done.'

'Yes.' Not an ounce of regret in her voice. She let go of my arm, and wiped her hands across her face. 'One thing the Company ought to know is the extent of the arms trade. We were able to bring in material from Thierry's World too. I'll give you details. Ms Christie, I'll give you whatever you need to know. His people are my people, and I don't care what I do, I'll stop Kel Harantish and that woman—'

'Calil?'

She stood up. Her balance was erratic, she swayed; and I stood up and took her elbow. She shook herself free. A young woman, barely able to stay on her feet; and she looked up at me with a face that blazed hatred.

'She and those like her. Sethri may have made me part of his *raiku*, but that's one thing I don't have: that ingrained obedience to the Harantish Witchbreed!' And the use of his name visibly hit her, she swallowed; all the Company's training in detachment coming into play.

'Will I find any group I can talk with at Rimnith or Keverilde?'

Waiting for an answer, I felt an empathy almost painful. This young woman, exhausted and filthy and determined, pushing herself to go on, crippled by loss – I might be her, I thought. If I'd ever had the guts to follow my instincts. And I might suffer a loss like that. Still, for all that, is what I feel something like envy?

'Stay away from Melkathi,' she said at last. 'Where are the other ships? If you can find them, there are some Anzhadi *raiku* there.'

Blaize said, *They would probably kill anyone you sent to talk with them in person.* (And is he any safer, in the Freeport?)

'Can you keep going for a while longer?' I asked. 'I'd intended to try contacting the *hiyek* ships myself, but there might be some chance of success if you're there, and they know you. If you can come with me, it'll count favourably on the Company report.'

Pramila Ishida said, 'Shit on the Company, and on all the Companies, and on all of us too. Yes, I'll come with you.'

As we left the small room, the Earthspeaker Cassirur halted me for a moment. She pushed a young black-maned *ashiren* forward. 'Send the child with your messages, *t'an* Christie. I'll be in the Citadel. The *s'ans* are coming to us now – we have to think of defence; of Melkathi, as well as Morvren Freeport.'

That chilled me. I nodded and left her, following the young Pacifican woman out into the courtyards. She moved like an automaton through the morning sunlight, with Cassirur's *ashiren* scurrying at her heels; and heads in the Square turning to stare as we came down the Wellhouse steps. Nothing to do but go back to Westhill-Ahrentine now. There were no *skurrai-jasin* to be seen; rather than attract a crowd, I shepherded Pramila and the child towards the nearest alley-entrance. We could walk down into the city.

Sun reflected back from the upper storeys of *telestre*-houses, shadows shrinking down into the alleys as noon approached; for the moment I was cool. Above, a ribbon of sky was thick with a snowfall of daystars. Ortheans sat on steps, talking, or in the tunnel-entrances to inner courtyards. A hush made me tread quietly, footsteps in any case muffled by the dust; listening to the sounds of the city. The creaking axle of a *skurrai*-wagon, the soft pad of *marhaz* and rider . . . Cities are quiet on Orthe, so quiet you can hear people's voices. And is it because I expect to hear it, but is there a new tone, a new edge, an urgency there?

'I don't mean quantity alone,' Pramila Ishida said suddenly. 'What we brought in – not just CAS handweapons. It's all good Company equipment, seconded from Thierry and Parmiter. I – to tell you the truth, I'm not sure what we did bring in. Not all of it.'

Does it surprise me to hear that? I thought. Knowing the multicorporates – no. Nothing wrong with some semi-official arms trading, so long as you don't get caught; and so long as you by no

820

means allow your on-world staff to know what the fuck you're doing—

I swallowed down anger. 'Give me what information you can.'

'Yes.'

It was the last word she said between there and Westhill-Ahrentine: an hour's hot walking, and the last mile or two by *skurrai-jasin*. Cassirur's *ashiren*, whom I thought to be six or seven, got over its shyness, and chattered solemnly as it walked beside me, pointing out barred entrances and the names of *telestre*-houses. Orthean young seem hardly humanoid, all spider-fingers and curling mane. *No, we are not like them; no, they are not like us: Pramila, how could you think it?*

But I know how.

The courtyard of Westhill-Ahrentine still held table and couch-chairs and *ochmir* board, but no Haltern. I sent Pramila Ishida and the child on up the steps to the upper rooms. And then I walked over to the scrub-*ziku*, beneath which Tethmet Fenborn still sat: gold-green skin shining as if he had just come out of water.

'Has there been word from the Tower?'

That sleek dark head came up, and he fixed me with lustrous dark eyes. What on Ortheans are claw-nails are, on fenborn, indisputable claws: he pushed *ochmir* counters at random across the board.

'Word goes back to Kasabaarde,' he said.

Irritated, I said, 'In that case, you can pass on a message from me. Tell Ruric—' and then I hesitated.

'She is not the Orhlandis,' Tethmet said.

'I know . . . Tell her, if she has any influence over the Desert Coast Ortheans, she must use it. And if she has any influence over Kel Harantish, we need that even more. This has to stop before it goes too far.'

At last, grudgingly, he inclined his head in agreement.

'Lynne!'

I looked up, and saw Doug Clifford at the upper-storey window. A shadow beside him resolved into a black Pacifican: Lutaya.

'Okay,' I called; and then spoke to the fenborn again. 'You can tell her something else. Tell her the Company's compromised. Tell her it's difficult for us to act as neutral arbitrators now, though we will. Tell her, the Tower may be the nearest Orthe has to its own neutral arbitrator.'

'Yes,' Tethmet said.

Tathcaer's white sunlight shone down in dapples through the *ziku*, falling on his sleek black shaven mane, and on green-gold

821

skin that shimmered into invisibility. The *ochmir* board lay abandoned, two-thirds of the minor hexagons covered with white counters: *ferrorn, thurin, leremoc.* How does a fenborn male come to know enough of this *telestre* game to beat Haltern n'ri n'suth Beth'ru-elen? The fenborn live long . . .

'*Shan'tai*, will you stay, please?' I asked. 'I have something to ask of you. Not of the Hexenmeister, of you yourself.'

He said, 'I will stay.'

The steps up to the first floor were steep, and the sun on my head was hot. I paused once, looking back at the fenborn male; and found him watching me. Then I went inside.

Ravi Singh and Chandra Hainzell stood by the holotank in the first room, he looking bewildered, she deep in conversation with the WEBcaster Lutaya, and both turned towards me as I entered.

'I'll be with you in a minute,' I said; and pushed the bead-curtain of the second room's arch aside. The place still had its air of abandoned decay, print-outs and microcorders scattered across the low tables. Haltern glanced up from a couch-chair by the open window. Pathrey Shanataru stood there, staring out over the harbour, and didn't turn as I came in.

And Doug was staring at Pramila Ishida with an expression so complex I despaired of interpretation.

'Lynne. Are you calling Company Security, or shall I exercise my authority as envoy, and have this woman confined and deported?'

'Now hold on just a minute—'

The Pacifican girl put out a hand to the back of the couch-chair, steadying herself. I realized she was on the point of collapse. I gripped her elbow, pushing her over to the other couch-chair, and made her sit down. Then I took Doug a pace or two aside.

'Yes, I'm notifying Security; no, she isn't being deported – not until we know exactly what she authorized in the way of weapons trade. And I may need her for something else.'

'She has to face what she's done.' Doug sighed, shook his head very slightly. 'Lynne, I don't understand you. Regulations aside, what that girl has done on Orthe – the damage caused through her actions – makes *me* furious. You, I imagined, I would have to restrain from being homicidal.'

The small room was hot, close. Harsh bells began to ring outside in the city, the deliberate strokes of midday; drowning out the clatter of *skurrai-jasin* and the high voices of *ashiren*.

'What she's done is more than criminal . . . Douggie, *I* could have done it, in her position.' I went on quickly: 'What I want to do now is get an analysis of satellite-images of the fleet. Somewhere on those ships there are Anzhadi *hiyek*-Ortheans. And then I'm going to take the Ishida girl with me, and fly in, and try to make a contact.'

When he said nothing, I snarled, '*Somebody* has to try it.'

He turned his head momentarily, so that I saw his blind profile, looking over at Pathrey Shanataru; and then his gaze returned from the dark Orthean male to me.

'It may be of little use to speak to the Desert Coast Ortheans. It's the Harantish Witchbreed who have the influence now, and if you plan to make contact with any of them, I imagine you'll find it worse than useless. Lynne, there is a point at which the danger outweighs the possible advantages.'

'We've got maybe four days before that fleet can reach the Melkathi coast, and then we've got a full-scale invasion on our hands!' I became aware of voices silenced in the outer room, and added more quietly, 'I'm also planning to ask Tethmet to come with me, if he'll consent to go. He *is* the Hexenmeister's advisor, and that may just sow some doubt in Harantish minds.'

'You must talk with Pathrey—' Doug broke off as Mehmet Lutaya came through from the outer room.

'I've got the records set up, Representative. Not just Ariadne. Some from Trismegistus, and Anansi.' Lutaya blinked long eyes, waiting.

'We'll come through.'

Haltern rose unsteadily from the couch-chair by the window. He rested almost all of his weight on the silver-topped *hanelys* cane as he walked to stand beside me. The hooded reptilian eyes blinked, lazily; and he smiled that old, sly smile.

'Don't deny an old man the chance of seeing this, *S'aranth-te*. To know how these otherworlds of yours see us, that would be fascinating.' He paused, directing his thin voice at the WEBcaster. 'To know if they see us as requiring a – what is your term for it? A "Protected Status". That, also, will be fascinating.'

And if they don't see it that way, you'll be only too pleased to say whatever's necessary to *make* them see it – Hal, you don't change. For which small mercy, I suppose we must be grateful.

We crowded round the holotank in the next room. Pathrey Shanataru followed us, and Pramila Ishida also, looking as though she could barely stand up. Is this wise? I wondered. Douggie gave me a very quizzical glance. But if there's government and Company here, I thought, aware of Ravi and Chandra and the rest of the Commercial staff; if there's *takshiriye* and Harantish Witchbreed and WEBcasters, what difference can one more make? If I had my way, I'd have *hiyek*-Ortheans here too.

'This is one of mine,' Lutaya said, activating the holotank; and for a moment there was an expression of diffidence on that self-confident face: not so oblivious to comment as I'd assumed. 'For Home Worlds consumption. Summary-update.'

The holotank filled with darkness. In the depths, star-fields took shape and gleamed; and the viewpoint shifted smoothly to a crescent of white and blue:

Carrick V, called by its intelligent hominid species 'Orthe', might have remained merely another backwater world on the borders between the Heart Stars and the Home Stars, if not for one thing – its past. Orthe is littered with the ruins of a vast and ancient alien hi-technology civilization, and with the devastation left by the war that destroyed that civilization, two millennia before humankind achieved space-flight.

Beside me, Douggie said softly, 'Oh dear . . .'

'It's a matter of presentation,' I said, wincing.

The holo-image dissolved into an aerial view of the Desert Coast canal system, that in turn faded to a long-distance shot of mesa-like white walls – Kel Harantish.

Six months ago, Orthe became more than a backwater planet of interest only to anthropologists and academics. Six months ago, relics of Witch-breed technology were discovered – artifacts that are still functional. The PanOceania multicorporate moved in a commerce-and-research team.

The Desert Coast city was abruptly replaced by another image: a wide, island-studded estuary, sky dimmed by smoke, the buildings on the nearest island furiously burning. A metal-sailed *jath-rai* tacked across the channel, the image clear enough to see the rails lined with armed men and women.

Six months later, this is the result.

'I protest,' Pramila Ishida said. She was leaning both hands on the rim of the holotank, supporting herself; and then she caught my gaze, and frowned as if she puzzled herself. 'That is . . . I don't hold a brief for the Company, not any more, but it isn't that simple.'

'It's a summary. Other 'casts have gone out,' Lutaya said, as his own image appeared in the 'tank. In shot with him, against a background of the Freeport estuary and the distant Rasrhe-y-Meluur, stood Cory Mendez.

Commander Mendez, you're in charge of the Security force that Pan-Oceania has brought here to Orthe. Can you comment on this second use of armed force against the local population – the second use of force within three weeks?

In both cases, a small use of force was authorized, not against the local population, but in terms of a warning, against property. Harbour structures, in the main.

Try to look at it as an outsider, I thought; seeing Cory's lined, capable face. Is she plausible? Is she right?

Commander Mendez, the most reliable estimates for casualty figures on the southern continent are: 6 dead at Reshebet, 3 dead at Nadrasiir, 24 dead at Pazramir—

Those figures are open to other interpretations. The essential thing is that, by causing some unavoidable suffering, which the Company deeply regrets, we have put an end to the possibility of an all-out native civil war.

Doug Clifford shook his head. 'Not clever.'

'Sometimes they sink themselves,' the WEBcaster said; and his holo-image went on smoothly:

I understand there is a native force of some seven hundred ships now on a course for the northern continent. Commander, isn't this that 'all-out civil war' you've been trying to avoid?

I have no comment to make at this stage; I suggest that you contact the acting Company representative.

'Thank you, Cory,' I muttered. As the image dissolved into an interior shot, whose curved brown walls I recognized as Ashiel Wellhouse, I glanced up at Lutaya. 'This is a 'cast I've seen and approved?'

'The tidied-up version.'

No Mehmet Lutaya in this shot, only the image of a woman: fair-haired, approaching forty, in coveralls with the PanOceania logo – *that's never me*, I thought. As I always think. She sits on one of the Wellhouse's couch-chairs, face too seriously intent; there are lines of age on that face that I never see in my mirror.

Ms Christie, you're the acting representative of the PanOceania multi-corporate on this world, following the murder of Representative Molly Rachel. Can you tell me what Company policy is in the current war situation?

Firstly, I would like to make it clear that this isn't a war situation – we have had some hostile incidents, which our policy is to contain wherever possible.

Doug raised his head from the tank. 'Now who's simplifying issues? Not to mention a degree of obfuscation . . .'

'I have to get this stuff past the Security staff on the orbiter, you know.'

Now the holotank image showed Lutaya, sitting across from me as I remembered:

In your view, Ms Christie, what caused these 'incidents'?

In my view – purely and simply: poverty. This is a world of people living in the margins. Living in the few areas that weren't reduced to sterile bedrock, thousands of years ago. There have never been many areas of Orthe that could support communities – and in some that have done, in the past, it's just not possible now. The land is exhausted. Particularly on the southern continent, which is where the fleet you mentioned originates.

'Could have done with better editing there,' Lutaya said dispassionately.

And yet there was no war until PanOceania started its operations on Orthe.

Earth technology upset the social system – triggered off what would have happened eventually, as more and more communities reached the poverty line. Yes, that's true. It's also true that Earth technology can put this right – with a properly-funded Aid Programme to the starving areas.

Is that possible now?

'You could hardly ask for a better cue,' Douggie observed.

I watched that image of myself pause, and had time to think, Too pompous, too ingenuous. And hope that what I said carried enough overt support of the Company to pass through intact the covert criticism.

It's possible, if we can halt the fighting . . . Orthe's social balance is so delicate, so artificial – after all, there are very few post-holocaust societies in existence – that it can take hardly any outside contact. We're considering this very carefully. By 'we', I mean the British government, my Company, any other multicorporates in this sector, and of course the Ortheans themselves—

'Of course,' said Haltern, silkily.

—and it may be that some restrictions may have to be made. Carrick V may need a Protected World Status. PanOceania doesn't wish to be responsible for inflicting severe culture shock on an alien hominid civilization.

Too busy thinking, Why didn't I just tell them we've done terrible damage, and we're desperately trying to put it right; I didn't register the image-change until I heard Pathrey Shanataru's sharp intake of breath – he, and Haltern n'ri n'suth Beth'ru-elen. The 'tank snowed with interference, that only cleared slightly, but it was enough to show this for a satellite-image of the wasteland to the west of the Ai River. The silver gleam of sterilized bedrock: the Glittering Plain. Lutaya's voice spoke over the image:

Serious as the situation may seem, it isn't the whole story. The Orthean situation began with the discovery of Witchbreed Old Technology. This is one of the continent-wide areas of submolecular devastation, left by the use of unimaginable alien weapons, millennia ago. I asked a senior member of the research team, Ravi Singh, about the possibility that this technology also exists in a functional state.

'Did you clear this one through me? I don't remember it.'

Mehmet Lutaya shrugged, not looking away from the holotank image. Ravi's dark features appeared, against what I took to be the comlink-dome on Kumiel Island.

Professor Singh, isn't it possible, as other examples of working alien technology have been found on Orthe, that the technology to create this destruction also exists?

One look at Ravi's face made me wince. Why not pick Chandra, I thought; or any other member of the Company team? Why pick the most conservative man in PanOceania?

I'm afraid you have more than one misconception there, as is not uncommon with WEBcasts. A technology cannot exist without its hinterland – without the society that trains its members, so that they can create the industries – mining, manufacturing – that in turn can create the actual technological devices. All of that is gone, on Carrick V.

There was a grin from the aquiline-featured Chandra, on my left, who murmured, 'Once a lecturer, always a lecturer . . .'

Lutaya's image persisted:

Your research team has found artifacts in working condition, that date from approximately two and a half thousand years ago. Why shouldn't weapons have survived?

Even if that were possible, which I strongly doubt, the knowledge to use such technology is lost.

Professor Singh, the southern continent has a functioning canal and water-purification system, dating from at least two thousand years ago, which the local population seem to have no difficulty in operating.

That was never proven.

Ravi's expression shifted from irritation to a kind of smug regret:

Unfortunately, with the tragic attack on Dr Rashid Akida, Company research records have been lost. However, I can assure you, no evidence was discovered to prove that the canal-system isn't operated purely by rote, handed down in that oral culture.

The image changed from Ravi to Lutaya, the WEBcaster standing on Kumiel, a blue and daystarred sky behind him.

That's how the situation stands today, with the—

'*T'an* Christie.'

I looked up from the holotank, half-dazzled by its bright images; and at first couldn't make out who had interrupted me. Then I glanced down, and saw the black-maned *ashiren* standing in the doorway: Cassirur's child. *Ke* gazed up at the group of us with a remarkable self-possession.

'What is it, *ashiren-te*?'

'There is a messenger to see you, *t'an*.' The child looked round at the others who stood in that sunlit, dusty room; the Ortheans and the humans. 'It's the *t'an S'aranth* that the message is for.'

'I'll come down.'

'I've got on-the-spot 'casts from the Morvren Freeport settle-ment.' Lutaya keyed the 'tank on hold. 'I've also got some of the Home World WEBs' reactions.'

'That's what I want to see – I'll be back in a few minutes. Douggie, if you'll excuse me . . .'

He smiled, and inclined his head; and I heard their voices start up as the bead-curtain slid back into place behind me, and I followed the *ashiren* down the interior steps of Westhill-Ahrentine to the ground-floor rooms.

CHAPTER 33

Mutable Shadows

Intrigue in the *telestres* is second nature so I gave no thought to this request for a private meeting, except to run through the names of those *T'Ans* that might wish to gain some advantage from PanOceania's representative – which was all of them. The *ashiren* darted down the steps and through the bead-curtain that led into the ground-floor kitchen. These rooms are slate-floored, cool even in Tathcaer's summer; and I walked through into the main one, past *l'ri-an* busy with preparations for the midday meal. The bead-curtain of the outer door was tied back. Tendrils of *kazsis*-nightflower curled round the wooden frame.

And a woman with skin as black as jet leaned up against the larger table, and reached across it to pick up a sweetmeat which she passed to the child: 'Thank you, *ashiren-te*. Give you greeting, Christie.'

One of Kasabaarde's soft leather masks covered her face. She fumbled at the strings with her single hand, and then pulled free; shaking her head and that cropped black mane. She grinned. Eyes as yellow as sunlight ... Now she stood, and *harur-nilgiri* and *harur-nazari* clashed; both slung at her shoulder for left-hand draw. She wore a plain shirt and britches, that could have been any mercenary's gear. Her feet were bare and calloused.

'Are you out of your mind?' I said.

'Tethmet just asked me that.' Ruric reached across the table again, picking up a handful of *kiez*-fruit and stuffing them in her mouth. She said indistinctly, 'Let's go outside. We're less liable to be interrupted.'

'You *are* out of your mind.'

'Which one?' And she grinned again. 'Let's say, a lot of my past-memories are of your opinion. I think differently. We shall see.'

About to follow her out into the courtyard, I suddenly stopped. 'But Tathcaer – you can't be seen in Tathcaer.'

She stopped in the doorway, turning her head; and the sun

outside made her a silhouette of brilliant blackness. Her face was shadowed. Those ten years lay heavily on her: she is not the *T'An* Commander now, or the *T'an* Melkathi who was named in the great Square below the Citadel, here in the white city, Tathcaer.

'I don't plan to be here long. And I've spoken with the *T'An Suthai-Telestre*. With Nelum Santhil Rimnith . . .' She chuckled. There was a kind of amazement in it. As she turned to go out of the door, she indicated a tray of *siir*-wine and ceramic bowls. 'Bring those, will you? I need a drink, if you don't.'

'But . . .'

By the time I carried the tray out to the table in the courtyard, the dark Orthean woman had seated herself there in the *ziku's* shadow, and was taking no apparent notice of the fenborn male who stood before her.

'—have a responsibility; you should *never* leave the Tower! What if you're killed?'

'I have apprentices in the Tower still.' Ruric Hexenmeister glanced up, staring at the upper-storey windows, and at the daystarred sky; and membrane slid down lazily over those yellow eyes. She leaned back against the *ziku's* trunk. Her mane, that had grown a little longer, fell back from her forehead, and I saw the puckered scar of the exile's brand. As if she felt my gaze, she smiled; and her eyes cleared.

'You think I'm mad to come here? The young *ashiren* and *l'ri-an* won't know me, and I wear the mask in the city. Your *s'aranthi*, of course, won't care who I am.' She gestured with that single hand, and I sat down opposite her. 'Is there anyone here in the Residence I have to worry about?'

Thinking aloud, I said, 'The Harantish, Pathrey Shanataru, he's never met you – or heard you, I suppose. Then – Ruric, Hal's here, Haltern Beth'ru-elen.'

The fenborn male looked at her with as plain an 'I told you so' as I've ever seen on an Orthean face. He turned his back on us, staring at the arched courtyard entrance; disapproval in every line of that skeletal body. Ruric began to pour *siir*-wine. Her face had changed. She said softly, 'I'll see Haltern before I go.'

'Ruric—'

'No,' the Orthean female said. 'If I were Ruric, I wouldn't be here. It's because I'm Hexenmeister, and because, for years immemorial, the Hexenmeister has had some influence over the *hiyek*-families – and even, it may be, influence over the Kel Harantish Witchbreed.'

Sitting here, the noise of the city came plainly to me; and the voices of the young Ortheans in the kitchens, and someone in the distance singing one of the atonal Dadeni songs. Hot, dusty; and I thought how much hotter and barren it is to the east, where Calil's fighters and the *hiyek* guerrillas wait in Melkathi – wait for the ships that sail on a south-west wind.

'When did you leave the Tower?'

'A week past – no, eight days,' she corrected herself. 'My people brought me word of *hiyek* ships in the Archipelago, and rumours that Morvren would be attacked. That I thought might come. Then I had word from Annekt, in Kel Harantish. He said, the city is deserted, the bloodlines are gone, crept out in Coast *jath* in the hours of darkness; Calil bel-Rioch, who would be Santhendor 'lin-sandru, is gone from Kel Harantish . . .'

She lifted the *siir*-bowl and drank, put it down, and wiped her mouth on her wrist. There was a sardonic humour on that dark face.

'I've left the Tower to come and argue with the Harantish Witchbreed – which is the act of a fool, I don't doubt, but what else can I do? I am Hexenmeister. All the weapons I have are words. What weapons Calil bel-Rioch might have – *that* is what frightens me. I suspect she has none, but can I take the chance?'

Something dawned on me at that point. I waited until I caught her gaze, and said, '*I'm* not going to tell you you acted wisely in coming back to Tathcaer. Particularly when four-fifths of the reason isn't that at all, but because the Hundred Thousand's being attacked – am I right?'

That pointed chin came up, and she stared at me with the arrogance of the Hundred Thousand; the look that Dalzielle Kerys-Andrethe used to wear as *T'An Suthai-Telestre*. All humour gone, she said, 'What makes you think you should tell me anything?'

'I don't know. I never could tell you much. Not that you'd listen to, anyway.'

Her mouth, drawn into a tight line, twitched unwillingly; she deliberately looked away, staring at the upper windows, and then she snorted; threw her head back with a bark of laughter, and swore. '*Amari S'aranth!* Of all the Motherless offworlders—'

'You're being too reckless. Taking too much of a risk.'

'No more than anyone else.' The dark Orthean woman sat, shade-dappled: points of light brilliant on the hilts of *harur*-blades. She glanced at Tethmet's stubborn back. He gazed across the small, dusty courtyard, oblivious. She smiled. 'There are others who can take my place.'

'*No.*'

Her gaze fell. Those yellow eyes clouded; cleared; and she shot me a look that made me think, What did she hear me say? And wonder, myself. In the moment's silence that followed, I took a sip of *siir*-wine. Its acrid taste dragged me into the present, out of memories that are eight years gone.

'I'm undecided . . . whether to go back to Rimnith and Keverilde, or to try to contact the *hiyek* fleet. They should be south of the Meduel estuary now. What do you think?'

She reached up with long dark fingers, knotting her empty sleeve more securely. That six-fingered hand paused to rub, as if amputated flesh still pained her after all these years; and the white sunlight wiped all the lines of age from her face.

'Speak with the families sailing *jath* and *jath-rai*. I'll come. I'll want to see your *s'aranthi* records first.' She smiled. '*S'aranth-te*, yes. I would like you to tell me: this is the right action for the Hexenmeister.'

Then the smile slipped, and it was a solemn child's face that for a moment I saw: the *amari* child run off from its *telestre* and come to the white city, thirty years ago. She looked up, yellow eyes under dark brows. On a shaky, indrawn breath, she said, 'Tell me you think it's right, Christie. You might help convince me. There – we – I couldn't *not* come.'

And at that moment, when she should have been most Ruric, I found myself tongue-tied because of those other, ancient memories; the other lives of the Hexenmeister, that I sensed in her. I opened my mouth; could think of nothing to say.

'Master,' the fenborn warned quietly.

Movement disturbed the empty courtyard: the bead-curtain at the top of the outer stairs was pushed aside. The dark figure of Pathrey Shanataru appeared; and with him, Haltern, leaning on his *hanelys* cane, and peering myopically out into the sunlight.

'Is that the Empress's Voice?' Ruric asked. I nodded. She stood, pushing back the couch-chair, that scraped across the paving-stones. Her one hand looped the soft leather mask over her head, hiding yellow eyes behind dark eyeshields. All her attention was on that old Beth'ru-elen male: sleek, stooped, the white wisp of mane. I wished that I could see her face now.

'Talk with the Voice of the Empress,' she said, standing with that crook-shouldered fighter's balance; and at her voice, even kept low, I saw Haltern's head come up. She for a moment rested her hand on my shoulder, and then she walked across the courtyard and up the steps.

Pathrey moved aside. I saw Hal frown, half reach out a hand and then let it fall back; deep lines of bewilderment on that bland face. Ruric reached the top of the steps. They stood for a full

832

minute in Tathcaer's white sunlight. Then, together, they went inside.

Argument with Cory Mendez occupied me for the better part of an hour, through a snatched meal; interrupted by discussion with Douggie, and with Pathrey Shanataru. The comlink-contact with the Freeport proved fuzzy. All I could get from Cory were protests about Company Security.

'It isn't merely hazardous, it's foolhardy,' she said. Her holo-image flickered: a rumpled, white-haired woman in the cabin of an F90 shuttle. 'You'll end up dead, or held hostage; and Company policy with a hostage situation is to refuse any co-operation. Lynne, this is a local situation. It is not one in which the Company should interfere.'

'It's a situation that the Company created.'

Her gaze dropped. Part of the mulish stubbornness faded. She said reluctantly, 'My people will complete an image-analysis for you. Lynne, I wish you'd reconsider.'

'I think it's something we're under an obligation to try . . . I'll take one of the YV9s,' I said, 'there'll be several other passengers.'

I keyed out contact, cutting off her questions. Using the Residence's holotank made my back ache: couch-chairs aren't designed the right height. I stood, rubbing at the small of my back; hearing Douggie in urbane conversation with Chandra and one of the other Company people. Warm wind blew in through the open windows, rustling the bead-curtains. It isn't having too little to do that produces that stasis, but having too much: not knowing where to start.

Mehmet Lutaya walked through from the next room, carrying a bowl of half-burned *kuru* meat. Through a mouthful, he said, 'Tune into the WEB frequency, Representative. Be good to see what's going on.'

'I can tell you what's going on and it isn't good,' I said, Cory's update in mind. I keyed into the channel the WEBcasts would be on, going up to Security on the orbiter; and stopped when I saw a face I recognized:

I'm speaking to you from Northfast, the largest island of the Freeport settlement on the northern continent.

The Visconti woman stood by a curving wall, shadowed by windvanes; Ortheans hurried past her, some in brown Wellhouse robes. She had that hunched look that comes from watching the sky; but she spoke clearly:

The situation here has deteriorated badly in the last two hours. Hostile jath-rai *ships, remaining behind after the main fleet, cruise the channels between these islands. My attempts to establish contact with the attacking forces have failed. I have personally seen low-tech shots exchanged. This is a winchbow-bolt—*

She held out her hand. A metal dart lay on her palm, the point fluted: a black iron bolt.

—and this is the wound that it makes.

The holo-image showed her stepping back, moving along the wall to where three or four Ortheans lay in its shelter. She squatted down by a fair-maned male. His back was towards the camera, splashed with blood like black paint. What I at first took to be torn flesh was the fletching of the bolt, buried deep a handsbreadth from his spine.

'Nice shot,' Lutaya said. He absently offered me the bowl of *kuru*. For some reason, I wasn't hungry.

—Approximately seventy miles to the east of where I am now, the main body of the Desert Coast fleet is coming together. Presumably, this is the preliminary to an attack; at worst to a full-scale invasion—

'That isn't telling us anything we don't know.' I scanned the other transmissions.

'Reckon to put something through every two hours,' he said. 'We're not just sending FTL-blips back to the Home Worlds. Most of us are getting stuff out direct to the WEBs on Thierry and Parmiter and Aleph-Nine.'

And you think it's worth your while hanging round the Company representative, and the government envoy . . . Well, who knows? I thought. You might be right. The next three or four hours are crucial.

Lutaya left, and I got through to Kumiel to make sure a YV9 shuttle was powered-up and ready. After I keyed out, I stood in that small, hot room – half human culture, and half Orthean: print-outs pinned up on the walls together with old ribbon-banners in the colours of Ahrentine *telestre* – and shook with cold; with a fear that made my hands icy and my stomach churn. Eight years ago, on Orthe, I rushed into things that make my heart stop now; rushed in with no perception of how final catastrophe can be. Max, I thought; suddenly guilty that he'd been absent from my mind for so long. *Some things you don't recover from*. And then realized that I had had to reach for that feeling, was not overwhelmed by it, as before . . .

Not caring to analyse that too closely, I walked through into the other room, meaning to speak with Douggie, and Pathrey Shanataru, and, of course, Ruric.

*

834

'I admire your *telestre* fighters,' Pathrey said smoothly. I found him sitting with Douggie and Hal in the courtyard – it is, simply, where one is least likely to be overheard. The dark, sleek Harantish male, mane falling in untrimmed curls; the frail bird-like figure of Haltern Beth'ru-elen, with a *becamil* rug over his knees; and Douggie's urbane poise – almost brothers, I thought. Different origins, but some unmistakable kinship between them.

'Were this an equal fight, I think *telestre* numbers would have it . . .' Pathrey paused and then added, '. . . eventually. There being a goodly number of us aboard the *jath* fleet.'

As I sat down beside him, Hal eyed the Harantish male with polite dislike. Old loyalties die hard: Pathrey is still born of Kel Harantish . . .

'There is one thing more. We have *s'aranthi* weapons.' Pathrey put both hands on the table before him, linking fingers, and stared down at them. His bravado vanished. 'Perhaps more than *s'aranthi* weapons. I've spoken of this before. You gloat that we of Harantish have no past-memories, being Witchbreed-blooded. I do not envy you remembering the use of that weapon, that ancient light.'

'Calil has this?' Douggie pressed.

'Sometimes I believe she does. Sometimes I believe nothing of it!'

'You must have some belief,' I said, 'or you wouldn't be here now.'

The edges of roofs and walls blurred with a faint sea mist, that through the arched entrance could be seen blotting out the harbour. It muffled the sounds of the city. Humid: sweat ran in patches. I watched the plump Orthean male, and saw on his face an aching regret.

'I shouldn't have left her. Half the bloodlines are vying for her ear now, all with dreams of Kel Harantish the new heart of Empire – but that's not what she plans. I know her. No one knows her as I do.'

Douggie, letting him ramble self-pityingly, steered him back with the prompt: 'What's her intention?'

'To strengthen her foothold in Rimnith and Keverilde, I imagine. And before many days,' Pathrey Shanataru said, 'she will say: I have that ancient weapon, that brought the fall of the Golden Empire. And if proof's required, she'll try to prove it – and that may prove the end of us all; if she does have our ancestor's science, that doesn't mean she can control it. But if she can, she will then say: You are again under the rule of the Golden Empire . . . or else you are a land where nothing moves but silver dust and the cold wind . . .'

I said, 'Is it a bluff?'

'*Shan'tai, all* of it may be a bluff. There is something about her now, I hardly know her, I – if she by some mischance has the weapon that Santhendor'lin-sandru used, well, he used it, and she is as he was.'

A young *l'ri-an* came out from the kitchens with *siir*-wine and bread, and the conversation paused. As I helped set out the bowls, I thought, Do I trust Pathrey? Do I even trust him to be a traitor? He was closest of all to Calil bel-Rioch . . . and this could be nothing more than propaganda to scare us.

'Insanity, to hold that threat over our heads,' Hal protested.

'I've known other worlds that existed under just such a balance.' Douggie's unspoken addition was: *if not for very long.* He glanced at me. 'At that point, Earth would intervene, and on such a scale—'

'And with what results?'

Hal cupped his hands, raising the bowl of *siir* to his lips; and when he had drunk, wiped his neat, puckered mouth, and said, 'Calil bel-Rioch cannot live forever.'

Pathrey's protest came too quickly. 'Others have lived her life, in our city. Others have had centuries of shunned persecution, of revilement; have dreamed of the past and the Empire and,' he concluded, with undeniable truth, 'there are others like her. This could not have happened if it were just my Calil alone.'

Knowing the Hundred Thousand (knowing Hal), there have been assassination attempts thought of. I filed that for future thought. My wristlink chimed, signalling the shuttle on Kumiel Island was ready.

'*Shan'tai* Pathrey, if you'd like to come back to Kumiel with me now . . .' Far safer to have him in Peace Force protective custody than left with *telestre*-Ortheans. I stood up, wondering where I'd find Pramila Ishida. 'Douggie, what are you doing about this?'

'I think it is imperative that one of us stay here to co-ordinate government and Company affairs; it could, of course, be you,' he said, steepling his fingers, and looking up at me.

'No, I'll go. If it looks too dangerous, I won't make the contact. There'll be other opportunities. The fleet has at least three days' sailing before it gets near Melkathi.'

Hal turned his face to the misty sky. 'I could wish for the weather to change. If She were kind, a summer tempest might solve this for us.' He blinked, small eyes bright, and inclined his head in Pathrey's direction. 'No ill will to your people personally, *t'an*, you understand.'

'I understand perfectly.'

Douggie's amusement was visible only to someone who knew

836

him. He stepped in smoothly and took Pathrey Shanataru's arm, steering him towards the courtyard entrance, and a *l'ri-an* who stood waiting with a *skurrai*-carriage. As well as avoiding hostility, it would give the government envoy a last chance to speak to the Empress's Voice – I smiled, thinking, Too many years on Orthe, Douggie; it's taught you never to miss an advantage.

Haltern got to his feet. He shook out the folds of his *becamil* over-robe, that was stitched with green and gold thread; and gripped the *hanelys* cane in a thin, six-fingered hand. Droplets of sea mist swirled in the air. The honey-coloured stone of that courtyard seemed almost to glow, taking warmth from the hidden sun.

'You have had knowledge of the Hexenmeister since when?' he asked. 'Since you and the *t'an* Clifford were in the Tower, these two months gone?'

'I couldn't tell you about her, Hal, I'm sorry.'

That round, bland face creased into a smile. Since he'd spoken with Ruric, a few hours ago, some indefinable tension had been released in him; and now he chuckled, and said, '*S'aranth*, we will have you in the *takshiriye* yet! The *T'An Suthai-Telestre* is most impressed . . . But I think it wiser none other knows that the exiled Orhlandis has returned. Or that she lives, and is Hexenmeister. Does she leave with you now?'

'Yes—' I answered before I properly thought; which is what one tends to do, prompted by Haltern n'ri n'suth Beth'ru-elen.

'Be eloquent with the *hiyeks*,' he said. '*S'aranth*, I am too old for such travelling, or I would come with you; and too old for travelling at all, therefore I shan't return to Rimnith and Keverilde – but I shall stay here in the city, and do what I can.'

I grinned, knowing what webs of intrigue among *T'Ans* and *s'ans* are known to the Beth'ru-elen. 'Modesty doesn't become you, Hal.'

He signalled to a pale-maned *l'ri-an*, who ran out to the alley for another *skurrai-jasin*.

'You'll find me in the Citadel, when you return.' And then he fixed watery blue eyes on me, the whiteless eyes of Ortheans; almost spoke, changed his mind, and at last said, 'Christie, I don't know why, after all these years, I should worry about you,' and was across the courtyard and through the archway before I could think of a reply.

Sea fog hides the harbour, and the crowds at docked *jath*-ships; hides the upper slopes of Westhill, and its fortress that I have seen from this courtyard. Tathcaer, clustered full of blank-walled *telestre*-houses . . . still with the overgrown traces of eight years' neglect:

siir and *ziku* and *kazsis*-vine; and this is not the same city that I came to as envoy, and that old man is not the same Haltern Beth'ru-elen. All that remains constant is the bond still existing between us.

I went back upstairs, to find Pramila Ishida sleeping the sleep of the exhausted, and roused her; Kumiel station called in again to say a YV9 was in readiness for flight. Then I looked for Ruric Hexenmeister and was for frantic minutes convinced she'd gone as secretly as she'd arrived – until a masked woman slipped back through the *telestre*-house entrance from the city outside: *amari* Ruric Orhlandis come back from her city, Tathcaer; unrecognized, unknown.

The first *jath-rai* starred the sea four hundred *seri* to the west of Tathcaer. The Company officers crewing the YV9 shuttle regarded me with disapproval, but that didn't bother me. At the moment I'm acting Company representative, I thought. While that lasts, I've got the authority to do this – if it lasts long enough, we're home . . .

'Take us down to eight hundred feet,' I directed.

The coastline to the north of us was invisible in haze. We crossed the *jath-rai*'s wake, coming down low enough to see *hiyek* males and females rush to the ship's metal rails and point up at us.

Pramila Ishida said, 'That's one of the mid-Coast *hiyeks*. Quarth area. Get the data-net on image analysis.'

The young male officer she addressed frowned, glancing away from the shabbily-dressed Pacifican girl; and I nodded, authorizing it. I don't think Pramila noticed that rumours of her part in affairs were obviously circulating among Company staff – and you're past caring about it, I realized.

Ruric leaned down, studying the image in the holotank. The light reflected back from her yellow eyes. When she spoke, it was in the language of the Tower, that she and I alone would comprehend: 'The *hiyek*-families are not the most important thing now, S'aranth. Don't forget: we must speak with Harantish Witchbreed.'

Outriders of the main fleet came into scan. Tall-masted *jath*, made of riveted sheets of metal, their steel sails at once too fragile and too heavy-seeming. . . . First one *jath*, cutting a white line across the ocean; then another, then two more, then a dozen strung out in a wavering line – and *there*, the main fleet. I let the voices of the crew fade into the background, hearing them talk with Kumiel base and with Cory's people at the Freeport; all of that gone, all I could see was the fleet of the *hiyeks* of the Coast.

Jath and *jath-rai*, all sizes of ship; some loaded down so that they

wallowed in the swell. Sails set to catch the strong, steady wind
. . . small boats tacking across the fleet's main course. Sails bowing,
rails crowded, males and females pointing and staring; and Carrick's Star a sunburst on the water. *Jath* wakes crossing, fringes of
foam on a jade-green sea . . .

The YV9's power-discharge ruffled the sea as we came down
lower. One *jath-rai* passed below us, its sails with patches riveted
on, and the deck littered with bundles, with stoves, with sleeping
ashiren, with covered objects twice the height of an Orthean. I
spared a glance for instruments: no heat readings. Yet. And then
the shuttle's speed dropped again as we paralleled the fleet's
course, going down past them. Easy for Cory to say, 'estimated
seven hundred ships'. Now we passed small convoys and groups
of ships, still flying west, still seeing no end to them; ships in
groups that seemed to dot the sea out to northern and southern
horizons – and we at last came on the trailing end of it. Two *jath-
rai* wallowing without sail, furious repairs going on; one *jath* left
abandoned; and on the western horizon, still the occasional speck
of a following ship . . .

Ruric said, 'Not an invasion. A migration.'

I straightened, rubbing the small of my back. 'The data-net will
have processed the images in a few seconds. Then we'll have a
contact.' I turned to the pilot. 'Take us back, please.'

Pramila Ishida had slumped down into one of the bucket seats.
Now she leaned both filthy arms on the edge of the holotank and
stared at the images of *jath* and *jath-rai*, as the YV9 swung round
and flew back across the fleet. She smiled. It was an odd
expression, one could speculate uneasily about what she'd had to
go through, to feel that way.

'A Company representative shouldn't put herself in jeopardy,'
she remarked.

'When I put a voicecast on narrowbeam, I'm going to make it
clear we're armed, and we'll fire if necessary.' And after Reshebet,
I thought, they'll believe me. Ironic, if what Cory did there proves
a protection to me.

The YV9 shuttle switched to hover-mode, some five hundred
feet above the sea. Holo-images showed a daystarred sky, streaked
with high cloud, and a summer haze still shadowing the horizon.
A vast circle of ocean, with innumerable small ships dotting it;
white wakes all curving like an arrow's flight to the east . . . Blue
and gold; and I could almost feel the cool wind, taste the salt.

I switched to data-mode, letting the analysis of the holo-images
appear in the tank; and while it presented alternatives, set up an
outside voicecast on a narrowly directional soundbeam.

'There are Anzhadi on at least three *jath*,' Pramila said.

The cabin's soft green illumination shone on the worn seats, the rim of the holotank; the faces of the Company crew – all four of them barely into their twenties, and not knowing which to regard with greater suspicion: the alien woman, the renegade Pacifican, or the lunatic Company representative. I grinned. When I turned back to the data-images, Ruric spoke from the shadows of the cabin:

'Not Anzhadi, Christie. I'll tell you what I've seen, and that's Harantish Golden on every *jath* and *jath-rai* – a bare handful to a vessel, but is that all *K'ai* Calil needs?' The dark Orthean woman stepped closer to the 'tank. Her long-fingered hand massaged the stump of her right arm, that after so many years still pained her. 'We must speak with—'

The rim of the holotank hit me hard under the ribs, and I gasped for breath. A klaxon split the air. Darkness: either the illumination cut out, or I blacked out for a second. There was a sensation of plummeting, and then I heard urgent controlled voices: the shuttle soared upwards. The klaxon ceased: interior illumination returned.

'—report fired on by hi-tech weaponry at 764.069.546; repeat 764.069.546. Damage report follows.' The dark-haired young officer leaned back from the voice-record, grinned at me, and said, 'We're still flying, Representative. They're not that good!'

'Get me an image rerun. *Now*.'

Ruric's hand was under my elbow, shoving me into one of the bucket seats. Her fingers probed the base of my ribs and I winced.

'Bruised,' she said. 'You *s'aranthi* hurt easily.'

Adrenalin still pumped with every heartbeat, and I let it carry me forward: fear is a good fuel. The holotank showed a rerun image: from one *jath* below us bursts a star of light, analysed as a microbeam-pulse weapon. And there, on the deck, a battered GHD4.

'Put us on an evasion-pattern. I want voicecast-contact with that *jath*-ship. Give me a close-in image.' I bent over the holotank, one hand tight against my ribs, wincing. 'I thought I'd seen that before . . . Pramila, that's one of the ships with Anzhadi-*hiyek* on board. You come here. I want you on voicecast. You tell them, we want a truce, we want a meeting, and if we don't get it – if they fire again—'

'Yes?' And she smiled.

'Then we'll try another ship.' Breath was coming back to me, and a degree of calmness. ' I think it'll be easier, however, to make contact where you and I are known. Even if that isn't essential.'

She hesitantly came to sit down in the seat I vacated, and took the comlink now on narrowcast. There was an expression almost of disappointment on her round face. As if it would have pleased her to have the Company threaten violence against Coast *hiyeks* – to have her worst fears realized?

Kethrial-shamaz shan'tai Anzhadi—

Her voice, magnified, quite clearly reached the deck of the *jath* below us. I saw how pale-maned Ortheans looked up at the hovering shuttle; the image in real-time, and clear enough to show expressions on faces: fear, confusion, hope.

—I was of Anzhadi's Ninth raiku, *and the* shan'tai *Christie has been received in* siiran. *We would speak with you, without the firing of weapons. If you knew Sethri-safere of Ninth* raiku, *then listen; it would have been his will—*

She keyed out the narrowcast, and sat for a moment without speaking. There were bright streaks on her face, hardly visible in the dim green light, and yet she smiled: an Orthean expression on a human face.

As the YV9's equipment picked up and sorted voices from below, filtering out the noise of the shuttle's power-hum, the wind and the waves, Ruric again reached over to touch my arm and indicate the holo-image of the *jath*'s deck.

'Those two? They're Anzhadi, yes, I know them.'

'Not them. There: the Harantish Witchbreed,' Ruric said. 'You must remember, I have had my people in the port of Harantish, and on the canals. That is a face you will not know, but I do, though we have never met. That is Oreys, of the science bloodline Kethalu.'

The pod opened, after what seemed like an hour of darkness and buffeting, and I stepped on to the swaying deck of the *jath*, Pramila Ishida close behind me, and, behind her, the robed and masked figure of the Hexenmeister. Bright sun blinded me. I took a quick squint into the brilliant sky, seeing the shuttle's bulk hovering overhead; and then through dazzles saw *hiyek*-Ortheans on the deck. The *jath* dipped, rose; and I staggered, catching my balance.

A cool voice said, 'Give you greeting, *shan'tai* Christie.' The sound was pitched to carry over the slap of waves on the metal hull, and the chattering of *ashiren* who now flocked towards the pod. They scattered as it rose, drawn back aboard the YV9.

'Give you greeting—' I spoke to the two *hiyek*-Ortheans I recognized: a stocky female, and, leaning on her shoulder, a thin and weary male '—*shan'tai* Feriksushar, *shan'tai* Hildrindi.'

Pramila came up beside me, and said softly, 'Greeting to Anzhadi, and to all *hiyeks* here.'

Ortheans crowded the upper and the inner deck, some in the rigging; dozens of faces all turned in this direction. Their manes were white or yellow, they were small of stature, and thin; and I thought, How can we stop them? This is crazy. For diplomacy to work, it has to work *before* we've got to this stage—

But that won't stop me trying.

Feriksushar said bluntly, 'What do you want, *shan'tai* Ishida?'

The Pacifican girl glanced at me, and then back at the older Orthean female. She let her gaze travel across the lines of Ortheans, and said, 'Sethri-safere of Ninth *raiku* is dead. It was a Harantish woman who killed him. You have Harantish here. Let him speak with us.'

The wind whipped hair into my eyes. I began to get the feel of balance, on that sun-heated metal deck. All the faces that I saw had a stolid impassivity, but I thought there was some reaction at the mention of Harantish Witchbreed, and I said to the thin male, '*Shan'tai* Hildrindi, has the Company now to negotiate with the people of Kel Harantish, about the affairs of the *hiyek*-families?'

His hand was clenched on Feriksushar's shoulder, bunching the thin material of her *meshabi*-robe. The bright sun on his face showed deep lines, and blue shadows about his mouth; and it came to me how few months it must be since I'd spoken with him in Maherwa, and how far his illness had progressed.

'You think to anger us,' he said, smiling. 'Anger speaks unwisely. We took your present approach for an attack on us: that was unwise. Or was it only premature?'

I should know better than to fence with you, I thought. Hildrindi-*keretne*, like Feriksushar, carried a hook-bladed knife at his belt; she had a winchbow slung across her back. It was when I looked over their heads, to the GHD4 beam-pulser now shrouded in patched cloth, that I saw the Harantish male.

'Give you greeting,' I called, '*Shan'tai* Oreys Kethalu. Come down and speak with *s'aranthi*, since you command this ship—'

The crowd parted and let him through. He was tall, loose-limbed, with a feline agility to catch points of balance as the deck dipped and swayed beneath him; and he came lightly down the steps from the upper deck to stand beside Hildrindi. He was pale-skinned, dressed in the brown scale-mail of Harantish; and at first I thought him white-maned, but as he came closer, I saw the roots of it were black. The eyes in his narrow-chinned face weren't golden, but brown.

'These are allies.' Oreys Kethalu's voice was harsh, speaking the common *hiyek* slang. 'Not servants, allies. Allies of the city Kel Harantish, and the Empress Calil—'

842

'Calil killed Sethri-safere!'

The young Pacifican woman stumbled on the metal deck as she stepped forward, face contorted. I half reached out a hand to stop her; then thought better of it. Anger speaks unwisely, as Hildrindi says; and provokes unwise speech in others.

Her human tongue stumbled with the formal speech of the *siirans*: 'Listen, *raiku* of Anzhadi-*hiyek*! How many centuries have the families been slaves to the Harantish Witchbreed? This was your chance to win free – there's land on the north continent that you can have, that isn't *telestre* land; land that doesn't need canals, doesn't need *siiran*. The price is peace, that's all; and you could have it, but what do you do? You invite the Witchbreed to command you again!'

Feriksushar snorted, and over the shouted comments of the surrounding Ortheans said, 'Sethri said he could free us from the desert so we followed him. If the Empress-in-Exile can win us land here, we'll follow her. And if you could win it for us, *shan'tai s'aranthi*, we'd follow you. Hunger's hard on principles.'

Oreys Kethalu held up a blunt-fingered hand for silence. 'We've been shut up in that pestilent city for more ages than you *s'aranthi* can easily count. If the *hiyek*-families were our servants, so were *we* servants to them. Now both our peoples have a free alliance.'

Membrane slid across his eyes as he met my gaze, and then slid back. More quietly, he added, 'Yes, we had from them food and water, that we could not get ourselves. And yes, they had from us our knowledge to keep canals and *siiran* alive. Who was then the slave, *shan'tai*?'

His unexpected honesty stopped me. A moment of stillness in all that movement: the rocking ocean, the wind, the clash of sails, the deep thrum of the hovering YV9. Something brushed my arm then, and it was a robe of coarse brown cloth. The dark Orthean woman stepped forward: Ruric Hexenmeister.

'It's an old quarrel, that between Kel Harantish and the Hundred Thousand. Centuries have not seen the end of it. Now you enter that quarrel and call it an alliance, a hope of gaining freedom – *shan'tai* Feriksushar, do you think you will have freedom, under Calil bel-Rioch's rule?'

The stocky *hiyek* female shrugged. 'The Hundred Thousand doesn't need canals to keep it fertile, so the Witchbreed – your pardon, *shan'tai* Kethalu – have no hold over us.'

Salt was bitter on my lips, stiff in my hair. I suddenly had to clasp my hands together, behind my back, so that no one would see how they were shaking. Delayed, the shock of that attack on the shuttle hit all the harder. I let the fear again fuel action:

'You've got *s'aranthi* weapons, *shan'tai*, we know that. We'd know it even if Pramila hadn't told us—' I registered Hildrindi's ironic amusement '—and that's a matter for concern. Despite all that's happened, the Company's very reluctant to get involved in fighting a war. But now I'll ask you something – has the *shan'tai* Kethalu told you how Calil plans to subdue the Hundred Thousand? Has he told you what weapon she'll hold over their heads?'

Another Anzhadi stepped forward to talk urgently with Hildrindi-*keretne*. The babble of voices drowned all other conversation, all the *hiyek* males and females seemingly shouting at once; and the younger *ashiren* took refuge in the deck-tents.

'*There was*—' Feriksushar's drill-sergeant shout rose over other voices; she added more quietly, 'there was some talk of weaponry, *shan'tai s'aranthi*. What of it?'

Beside me, Ruric reached up to put back the hood of her robe. That tangled black mane rooted down her spine, silvered a little with age; and her narrow, masked face turned, surveying all the *hiyek*-Ortheans. When she spoke, her voice was pitched so that they must strain to hear it over wind and waves: an old orator's trick.

'Let me tell you,' she said. 'You have memories. There are *keretne* among you. Let me recall to you a weapon of the Golden Witchbreed, that made the Elansiir and the Glittering Plain, and that Twilight Shore that lies in the arctic north of the Barrens. There is a weapon that ate like a cancer at the face of the world. There is a weapon that, when the Empire was at its height, when it was of such magnificence that even its slaves must be amazed at such a grandeur of tyranny – a weapon that, in that moment, brought the Empire to its fall. And that is the weapon Calil bel-Rioch claims to have.'

The rhythms of the Coast's semi-formal language lulled them, as much as her Tower robes caught their attention. It was a deliberate piece of theatre, that must now be built upon to reach something real.

Oreys Kethalu, almost shamefaced, said, 'It's a threat, no more.'

With all the Hexenmeister's authority, sensed without their knowing who she was, Ruric said, 'I have seen cities of crystal, dead, and turning to slow dust. That is the threat, *shan'tai* Hildrindi, *shan'tai* Feriksushar. *Hiyek*-Anzhadi, if the Empress-in-Exile has that, it is a threat to the Hundred Thousand, and a threat to you too.'

Feriksushar glanced at Oreys Kethalu with something very like contempt. 'The Harantish are few. We are many.'

I said, 'The Hundred Thousand are many, now, and you *hiyeks* are few. If you can hold a threat over them, the Harantish Witchbreed can hold that threat over you. But this isn't a very fruitful discussion, *shan'tai*. If we could talk of the land to the north of the Hundred Thousand—'

Overhead, the shuttle's hum deepened. The white hull flashed in the sun as it rose, circling slowly to the north; and I was about to make comlink-contact when I realized it was cruising between this *jath* and another that approached us. The second *jath* veered slowly away. I licked my lips, salt-bitter, thinking, If they'd offer us hospitality we'd be halfway to a discussion, but we're talking ourselves out of time and patience here.

Oreys Kethalu stared at the brown-robed Hexenmeister. 'You are from the Tower, *shan'tai*? The Tower is no friend to Kel Harantish.'

Feriksushar said, 'Nor to the *hiyeks*. No friend to the *hiyeks* was ever found in the Brown Tower.'

Ruric chuckled, startling both of them, and said, 'You fired on us just now, and yet the *shan'tai* Christie didn't retaliate. That's one friend you have, and she has the closest connections with the Tower.'

Kethalu, irritated, said, 'That isn't what I meant.'

She sees him as the key, I thought. The Harantish, not the *hiyeks*. And she's keeping him off balance very nicely.

Ruric, in a practical tone, went on: 'Just now, I said that we were slaves to the Empire, and that was true. Neither you, *shan'tai* Kethalu, nor the *hiyek* people here, are slaves. The Coast was *not* slavery and tyranny, but a pattern of survival that you were locked into; the only way you could live in a land that, by all rights, shouldn't support life. And believe me if I tell you, all the Tower has ever done is correct that balance when either of your peoples forgot it.'

Bodies brushed my elbows and my back, and I realized that the *hiyek*-Ortheans had crowded in close. Only minimum sail kept the *jath* into the wind: all other attention was on us. Pramila, myself, Ruric: the Witchbreed male, and the Anzhadi. There was the dirt and musk scent of the *siiran* in that close contact.

Hildrindi-*keretne*, still leaning on Feriksushar's arm, said, 'And now?'

Ruric's face was invisible behind the mask. I sensed them straining to guess her intentions.

She said, 'Now, even you and the Harantish Golden can't make that desolation support life for many more decades. *Shan'tai*, go to the Northern Wilderness. The *telestre* land isn't yours to take, nor theirs to give up. The *T'An Suthai-Telestre* has said he will give you free passage north, to the empty lands.'

'On whose authority?' Feriksushar grunted.

'On his own.'

Oreys Kethalu again put up a hand for silence. Metal sails creaked; heavy water hit and echoed against the hull of the *jath*.

'And on the Tower's authority?' he asked.

'Yes, *shan'tai*.'

'Well, I do not believe you,' he said, and his brown eyes gleamed. 'You are the Tower's messenger, you claim, but *I* do not believe the Tower would loose us from its grip. Not our city Kel Harantish; not the *hiyeks* that serve it. No, *shan'tai*.'

The Orthean woman reached up, pulling at the strings and removing her mask. The light of Carrick's Star was harsh white on her fine-grained skin. She smiled to feel the air on her face; and I could see, as she looked around, her knowledge that no one could recognize the exile's scar on her forehead, no one could name her as Hexenmeister. Only this nameless woman, without authority, to persuade the *hiyeks* and the Witchbreed . . . and yet she has authority, I realized. You cannot carry the Hexenmeister's many lives, and seem unchanged.

'There have been those to whom the Tower deferred,' she said mildly. 'You will have heard of Beth'ru-elen *Ashirenin*, who came to Kasabaarde's inner city, and who founded the province of Peir-Dadeni – and who made our religion of the Goddess real.'

Oreys Kethalu blinked, two layers of membrane sliding down, inner and outer lids.

'The *keretne* here will know what I say is true. Your link with Her is blood and water. In the north, the link is the earth itself, and the wells of Her water; and if you make that link, you are the Goddess and She is you, and you can no more harm the earth than you can cut out your own heart. And the Tower will not go against that.' Ruric paused.

'You were from a *telestre* before you reached the Tower,' the Witchbreed male said contemptuously, speaking under cover of the *hiyek*-families' loud reaction to what she said.

Then Ruric reached out, gripping his shoulder with her single hand. Before he could react, she said, 'Look at me – *look*. Yes. I'm what you are, half Golden-blooded. *Yes*. If the truth were made clear, my Coast mother may have come from Kel Harantish itself. I have no past-memories. All I have is what the Tower tells me.'

Hammerblows of shock opened his eyes: for a second defence-less, he stared at her. 'I don't understand—'

'We're not like them,' Ruric said. 'We have no *keretne*, no past-memory. If the past isn't with us, we're not controlled by it. I've lived in *this* world, not in the days of the Empire. If Santhendor'lin-sandru could love death enough to give it to half a world, that doesn't mean *I* must, or that you can or will do the same.'

He shook his head in bewilderment, this loose-limbed male in brown armour; and his dyed-white mane whipped in the sea wind. I shot a glance at Ruric: saw the wide-set yellow eyes glowing in that dark face.

'Be free of it,' she said. 'What you're doing isn't the only way. If the Tower can change, then so can the Hundred Thousand, and so can the Harantish Golden.'

Almost sulkily, Oreys Kethalu said, 'But I know nothing of northern lands, this "Northern Wilderness" the *T'An Suthai-Telestre* speaks of. It may be no better than the Coast—'

Hildrindi leaned forward and with deliberate irony said, '*Shan'tai*, it could hardly be worse!'

Kethalu rounded on him, dragging him aside and speaking in a furious undertone. Both of them glanced at us from time to time. When I looked to see Pramila, she was amongst a group of other Anzhadi; then I realized our tight little grouping had broken up, was dispersing among the crowd of *hiyek*-Ortheans. The shrouded bulk of the beampulser stood abandoned on the upper deck.

'And if they can change,' the dark Orthean woman said, 'so can *s'aranthi*. Christie, I've got Oreys Kethalu to the point where he'll admit the possibility of change, if nothing more. Can I get you to that point?'

'Me?' I shrugged, then. 'The Company doesn't change.'

Ruric nodded at Pramila Ishida, where the Pacifican woman stood with Feriksushar and the rest of Twenty-Eighth *raiku*. 'What of her? And does your Corazon Mendez think as she once did, now that she's seen the burning of Morvren Freeport? And you, Christie, you're Company. Admit a possibility that things can be different?'

The *jath* dipped, metal prow cutting the ocean and sending up a rainbow-fan of spray. Other ships glided on courses parallel, cutting the bright sea; and the wind came clean from the west. The hull of the shuttle caught the light of Carrick's Star. I kept my footing on the swaying deck, and felt for a second the same sense of release that Oreys Kethalu must have felt. It was nothing that dared to be optimism, and yet – things can be different.

'I admit the possibility,' I said, and saw her grin, and couldn't help but return it. 'This is only one ship, Oreys Kethalu is only one man. It's a possibility, not a probability. Still, I think . . . we've got too much hard work and too little time: I'll tell you what I think in a few hours.'

Ruric Hexenmeister stood with bare feet slightly apart, on that hot metal deck; standing with the old crook-shouldered balance. She looked at the Anzhadi, at Kethalu; and her smile remained. She said, 'It isn't over until it's over. And that hasn't happened yet.'

CHAPTER 34

Waiting for the Morning

'It doesn't happen that easily,' Corazon Mendez said.

She made a shuttle-to-shuttle transfer on the morning of the following day, letting her F90 go on to Kumiel Island to repower. I'd had my YV9 repowered twice now by air-to-air contact. Thirty hours is about the limit for how often that can be done, and the crew were exhausted.

'There's still fighting at the Freeport,' she added.

'I know. There's fighting here. We've been fired on twice.' I didn't look up from the holotank. 'Out of a possible seventeen contacts, we've made six successfully – ah, there; see?'

She leaned over my shoulder. Her black coveralls were crumpled, rank with sweat, as mine were; and there was an unhealthy whiteness to the skin round her eyes. She squinted at the visual image. A multitude of *jath* and *jath-rai*, their shadows cast long on the shifting waters by the rising sun, and here a pinprick of light, and there another, answering: the dot-signals of heliograph messages passing from ship to ship of the fleet.

'And I know it doesn't happen that easily,' I said. 'Nothing's happened yet. Pramila and the Hexenmeister and I have spoken to, what, a dozen people directly, and maybe ten times that many indirectly. Nothing's happened yet. But it still may.'

'Jamison said you had to threaten force to get off one *jath* ship.'

Jamison has no damn business to be monitoring our transmissions, I thought. My temper was short; I'd only managed to snatch a few hours' sleep. The time when I could do that and still remain sunnily enthusiastic is long gone.

Cory pinched the bridge of her nose, blinked, and refocused on the holotank images. 'You've split up, then?'

'It's safe enough, I think; we're each going in with an armed officer from here. Pramila's on that *jath-rai*—' I keyed an inset that showed the broad-built ship wallowing in a deep swell, some three-quarters of a mile to our rear. 'The Hexenmeister is on the larger *jath*, with a group of the Harantish Witchbreed.'

Cory shrugged. 'Gets to the point where it's all names to me, Lynne. All I want to know is, what preparations are you making for when these ships get to the Melkathi coast? I estimate we've got about sixty hours before we're forced into a decision – do we let these natives fight a hi-tech war without interference?'

'It may not come to that.'

She paused, and I looked across at her. Whatever she had been going to say, she visibly changed her mind. 'I'd advise you to go back to Kumiel for a few hours, Lynne, you look half dead. *You* have to be in a condition to make decisions.'

That green-shadowed cabin had begun to make me feel nausea. From shuttle to *jath*, and from *jath-rai* to shuttle – just how disorientated am I? And Cory's right. I can't be at less than peak efficiency. Not now that we have this final chance . . .

'Doug Clifford will travel out to meet you,' I said, 'if you've no objection to working with the government envoy? I've already spoken to him about this.'

'You don't seem to have left me much choice.'

'Molly Rachel used to tell me I could never trust people to do things as well as I can do them myself – even when I can't do them at all! Cory, we've known each other for six years, I've *never* approved of what you do – do you wonder that I'm concerned, now, after Reshebet?'

The white-haired woman tapped her finger twice on my shoulder: a peremptory gesture.

'Lynne, I'll take that from you when you come up with a better idea of how to handle this.'

'Right now this is thistledown, a breath could send it either way.'

She frowned. It wasn't disapproval but consideration. I could see the figures and positions ticking up behind her eyes: so many ships on Kumiel, so many at the Freeport, so many in reserve at the orbital station. This many personnel here, that many in the northern continent, that many on the southern continent . . .

'Lynne, I've been on worlds where the Company's failed. I don't mean a short conflict, deaths, I mean a real failure: the kind of bloody war that drags on for years, for generations, that keeps going by the momentum of its own atrocities, long after all involved have forgotten the original cause. I've always been afraid that I would be responsible, somehow, for one of those catastrophes. The only way I know to avoid it is to stop it before it starts.'

Cory eased herself down into the bucket seat, motioning the crew to continue their duties, with a kind of unconscious arrogance. She added thoughtfully, 'Having said that, I can't know all the factors involved here. Nor can you, nor can the government envoy. We take decisions blindly and that scares the shit out of me.'

Not what she said so much as the weariness in her voice; I thought how Ruric said, *Does your Corazon Mendez think as she did?* I don't have the right to judge.

'I must know what hi-tech fire power these people have. Lynne, Security must have the Ishida girl for debriefing *now*.'

'All right,' I conceded. Could I do it if I had her in front of me now, dirty and exhausted and still punishing herself for Sethri's death? Well, if she's after suffering, Security will cure her of that. And no need to wonder what I'd do, when really I have no choice. It isn't the *hiyeks* that are important now, I thought, it's Calil's Witchbreed, and Pramila isn't a factor there . . . 'When the pod picks her up from the *jath-rai*, have a couple of your officers take her up to the orbiter. And keep me informed, Cory, okay?'

Cory leaned over to the comlink: 'I'll have one of the F90s pick you up here, en route to Kumiel.'

Early morning, and it would still be early when I got to Kumiel. Flight-time between the *hiyek* fleet and the island diminished each time I made the journey. Now it was close on ninety minutes.

'Data-processing facilities are there, Representative,' the F90's lieutenant said as she left my cabin, indicating a small data-tank set into the wall. I nodded; and after she'd gone, stood for a moment rubbing my forehead. The vibration of the F90's power-hum found a correspondence in the tremor of my hands; eyes and head ached. Metal warrens, these shuttles, and they bring out all my claustrophobic tendencies.

I sat, and keyed in the data that Mehmet Lutaya had passed on to me. WEBcasts from Orthe didn't much interest me – but I want to know how they're reacting at home, I thought.

When I tell the Company home office that Carrick V needs Protected Status, I want *some* idea of what public response on Earth will be.

—*Ariadne WEB news update, sixteen hundred hours Pacific Standard Time. This is Evan Kodály on 'cast from the main chamber of the House of Delegates in Tokyo*—

The image in the wall-tank was small, not well-focused. Twelve days, I thought. To get an FTL-drone from Earth to Carrick V. A lot can happen in twelve days . . .

—interview with NuAsia Company's Commercial Delegate, and I asked him his reaction to the escalating sequence of events on Carrick V.

Delegate Chen, you've been making strong protests to the PanOceania delegation here.

Squinting into the small 'tank, I made out the overly-familiar features of Wu Chen; a round, baggy face rarely out of the WEBcasts.

You have only to look at the evidence of commercial exploitation! The PanOceania multicorporate has caused cultural disruption on Carrock V to the degree that a major war is now in progress – a war that their Company has done nothing either to prevent or to stop—

Isn't it also true that on Carrick V— Kodály's slight stress corrected Chen, and I smiled to myself. *—on Carrick V, PanOceania has also invested in a substantial Aid Programme?*

That's merely camouflage, to disguise thinly the blatant exploitation of an alien culture. In the NuAsia multicorporate, our policy has always been to involve the local population at all levels, to provide a guiding hand, as it were—

I skipped forward, knowing Wu Chen's 'guiding hand' far too well to want to hear the routine again.

—news on Trismegistus WEB, Eurotime twelve-midday. Reports are still coming in of casualties in the fighting on the Heart Stars sector world, Carrick V. Nominally, the world is under the authority of the British government, and I spoke to a representative of that government about the actions of the PanOceania multicorporate there.

—I cannot stress too strongly our condemnation of the use of active military force—

Jesus! I thought, and sat up, and keyed back the image. Blond, bearded, and standing against a backdrop of the Department's offices – Stephen Perrault. What the hell are *you* doing as WEBcast representative for the government, I wondered. I'd have to go through his reports when I got back to Kumiel.

—condemnation of the use of active military force; however, reports have confirmed that the local population has access to hi-tech military equipment themselves. PanOceania have therefore been forced into taking action.

Representative Perrault, may I ask whether it's known how the natives of Carrick V got their military equipment?

I regret to say that there is evidence that it was illegally supplied to them, by members of the PanOceania multicorporate themselves. I need hardly add that this was not sanctioned by PanOceania's governing board, and I have no doubt that steps have been taken to remedy this. However, my government feels that the damage has already been done.

Is your government raising the matter of compensation?

Undoubtedly. We also must respond to the public demand for some kind of protected or isolated status for alien cultures, like Carrick V's, that are so susceptible to outside interference.

'Nice one, Stephen,' I muttered. 'When it comes to PanOceania, sink 'em with a smile . . .'

Few of the 'casts added anything to that. I was on the point of skimming through to the end, when one caught my attention. I keyed back and ran it in real-time:

—WEB-Taliessin. Public scandal continues to grow in the matter of PanOceania's involvement on the Heart Stars world, Carrick V. This evening, we bring you comment on the multicorporate's military strike on the harbours of the southern continent of that world—

Faces flicked past in rapid succession. Public-access hour on the WEBs is usually crowded; but now I sat up and stared at the sheer number of calls coming in. And this is only Taliessin, I thought; Taliessin's not the most extensive WEB – I *must* have a rerun of WEB-Marduk and WEB-Tz'u-hsi . . .

It's terrible. Just terrible. I don't know how we're supposed to accept this— A middle-aged man, with flat brown features that for a heart-stopping moment brought back Molly Rachel; he stared bewildered into the imager, *—there are people dead on that world, and we killed them; I don't know how the Company expect us to support them now—*

Background images stayed the same: some street in a southern-hemisphere city. A group of young men and women crowded round the imager:

We want to protest—

What right do we have to do this?

—nothing more than a private army! No Company has the right to that. First it's some little world out in the Heart Stars; next it'll be us, you'll see, it'll be us, here—

All of them wore multicorporate insignia on their coveralls; I judged them part of some Zealand Company. Looking at those young sallow faces, I felt something that might have been regret: for outrage and indignation that I can't feel that strongly now.

—I saw the live 'casts, there were bodies lying in the rubble. What are our people doing there? Why didn't somebody stop them? And it's just going to go on getting worse, more killing—

Frozen image: a shabbily-dressed man on some Pacifican city street. For a second I stared at him with hatred, this nameless man; thought, Suppose you try it, before you criticize? and then keyed out the recorded WEBcast.

The F90 thrummed, jolted with air turbulence, and I sat back in the bucket seat; aware of the small cabin, of the empty space outside, of the orbiter miles above the surface of the world, of the vast distance between here and Thierry's World; of the light years between me and home – a distance incompreh... 'ble. If Orthe's sun were visible now in Earth's sky, it would shine with the light that shone upon the Golden Empire in the height of its power, five thousand years ago . . .

Things can be different. The last thing I said to her, before we split up to contact *jath* separately, was, 'Is it wise to tell the *hiyeks* they haven't been slaves to Kel Harantish? It's all very well you talking about "locked into a pattern of survival", but there was nothing involuntary about the Harantish Witchbreed's grip on the canal system.'

She grinned, membrane veiling those yellow eyes in amusement.

'Lie in a good cause,' she advised. 'If I've learned one thing as Hexenmeister, it's that history is what you remember it to be. Right now I'd like Calil's people to remember the peaceful days of the Golden Empire – and if I had a choice,' Ruric Hexenmeister said, 'I'd wish them to forget Calil bel-Rioch. But we may manage that yet.'

The F90 shuttle began its descent to Kumiel Island.

Doug Clifford met me on the makeshift landing field. We walked briskly across the island, on tracks that had not existed until the Company began to use this land; and Carrick's Star rose higher in the east, a white and silver glare. Already hot: the day promised a heatwave.

'You've left the estimable Corazon Mendez overflying the *hiyek* fleet? Isn't that a trifle . . . how shall I put it? Rash?'

Glancing at him, I thought his urbane manner was a mask over exhaustion. 'I'd have said it was unavoidable. If it worries you, console yourself with the thought that you'll be on the spot – I've committed you without asking you, Douggie, but I couldn't contact you.'

He shot me a sour look. As we were walking, he pointed to the white hull of a government shuttle, grounded near the comlink-centre.

'I've been in Melkathi, and having a problem of contact myself – I know there are upwards of two thousand *hiyek*-Ortheans in Rimnith and Keverilde, but can I speak with any of them? No. I know that there are Harantish in the area, and the same applies. Ride into the burnt area, and it appears deserted.'

'And Calil?'

He halted at a crossroads in the trodden earth tracks. Wind from the mainland hardly ruffled that grizzled red hair, silver over the ears; and he paused and surveyed the blue-grey mossgrass and the granite rock, so different from one foggy morning on a heathland *telestre* . . . One hand strayed up to touch his bandaged eye.

'Who knows where the Harantish Witchbreed go? There are ships moving along the coast all the time. And there's been sporadic fighting between them and ships of the Hundred Thousand.' Doug pursed his mouth. 'I had hoped to cool that situation down, but it seems unlikely now.'

The exhaustion that had attacked me on the F90 was stronger now; I could have fallen asleep standing up. Carrick's Star shone warm on my face. Distantly I heard the sea on the rocks round Kumiel, and the metallic cries of *rashaku-bazur*.

'Will you go out to the fleet? You ought to talk to Ruric, Douggie.'

'Seven hundred ships,' he said. 'Thirty thousand people. Much as I admire Ruric Hexenmeister, I can hardly conceive of her having an effect on them at this late date. Those people are committed. Having said that, of course, I would find it repugnant in the extreme to contemplate leaving any avenue of action unexplored.'

'Does that mean you're going?'

To my surprise, he chuckled. 'Yes.' And then, more soberly: 'The government shuttle is powered-up for approximately six hours. I'll do what I can in that time. When can we expect your return?'

Stephen Perrault's reports want looking at; I've had no reports from Thierry about David Osaka and Rashid Akida; I must speak with the *telestre*-Ortheans and find out what they plan to do when the *hiyek* fleet reaches Melkathi . . . Merrum Firstweek Nineday: we have no more than three days before they do.

And if I continue to rely on stimulants, I'll sleep for six days, not six hours.

'I'll be out with you before noon,' I promised; and he nodded curtly, and began to walk towards the government shuttle. I blinked against the white light of that alien sun, and called after him, 'Douggie, be careful. I hate to say it, but – go armed.'

The next few hours passed in an eyeblink: sleep, a session with the data-tank, and a snatched meal. I conferred with Chandra about evacuating the remaining Commercial personnel up to the orbiter. And I ordered notification, every thirty minutes, of the position of the *hiyek* fleet, and of any change in the local or continental weather patterns.

There were no changes in the hours before noon: the daystarred sky remaining clear, and the wind blowing strongly and steadily out of the south-western quarter of the compass. As Haltern n'ri n'suth Beth'ru-elen said, one summer tempest could end all our problems . . .

I've been in storms at sea. Less sanguinary than Hal, I can't wish that terror on anyone. But (I thought) I could wish for a force of nature to take this decision out of our hands.

The Desert Coast Ortheans have hi-tech weapons, they have at least one GHD4 beampulser. When they reach the coast of Rimnith and Keverilde, are Cory's ships to fire on them? Or are we to watch *telestre*-Ortheans fight hi-tech with *harur*-blades? Christ! I thought, it's ridiculous, the very idea is both ludicrous and tragic. What can we *do*?

Noon came: I found a pilot for a repowered YV9, and flew westwards across the Inner Sea.

'There,' Ruric Hexenmeister said. She indicated the image of the Rimon and Ymirian coastline, bright in the holotank. 'To come to Melkathi anywhere north of the Melkathi Sandflats, they must either change course and sail round the Sisters Islands, or else they must risk sailing in amongst them – Ahrentine and Valerah and Perniesse and the rest. Those are dangerous waters, if not known.'

'They won't risk it, surely?'

This F90 thrummed, flying the decreasing distance back to Kumiel Island to repower. Somewhere in the night outside, Merrum Firstweek Nineday was turning to Merrum Secondweek First-day: time ticking on. Coded images in the holotank showed the long scatter of *hiyek* ships, hugging the shelter of the Rimon coast.

'All the Inner Sea is dangerous, if not known,' Ruric added. 'They'll have *jath* shipmasters who know that, even in summer, to stay this long on open sea is to risk storms. Turn it about: the Sisters Islands are some shelter from that.'

My eyes blurred, and I sat back, rubbing at them. Fourteen hours, and this Orthean summer day not yet over; a day spent airborne above *jath* and *jath-rai*. Of a possible nine contacts, seven successful. I thought: I can't judge, any longer, what "success" might be . . .

Ruric Hexenmeister leaned back from the holotank, one bare black foot coming up to rest on its rim: high-arched and claw-nailed, and worn with much walking. Her single hand went back to scratch among the roots of her mane.

'I've read their heliograph signals,' she mused. 'Plain enough. They're using the canal trade-codes. I read dissension between *hiyek* and *hiyek*, dissension between the families and the Harantish

Witchbreed. If not,' she said, with a crooked smile, 'it isn't for lack of trying! Whatever else we're doing, we're giving them something to talk about.'

I keyed in figures. 'According to this – and I'm not sure I trust it for calculating sailing-ship navigation – the first *jath* will reach that turning point early tomorrow morning. If they *do* go in among the islands—'

'There is Ahrentine *telestre*, and Valerah *telestre*, and the *telestre* Perniesse.'

The comlink chimed. I ignored it for the moment: it was likely to be Doug or Cory, on their way back to Kumiel now night was falling.

'We should talk with Nelum Santhil,' I said. 'With Hal and Cassirur and Bethan, and the rest of the *takshiriye* in Tathcaer.'

She raised her head. In that narrow Orhlandis face, her yellow eyes glowed; and membrane slid down to cover them, hide some unreadable emotion. With a clinical rationality that was all Hexenmeister, she said, 'The Hundred Thousand will not wait long before they send these land-wasters to the Goddess. If the *hiyeks* attack the islands, the islanders will fight. I think it will not matter to them that the Desert Coast brings with it more than winchbows, more than blades – they'll fight. And so we may not have to wait until the *hiyeks* reach Melkathi to see what offworlder weapons your Company gave them.'

'Ruric—'

She overrode my protest: 'If it's shelter the ships need, then we should hold off. Give the *hiyek* quarrels time to spread. You must tell Nelum Santhil that waiting may do our work for us, and he must tell the island *s'ans*.'

' "Our" work?'

She rubbed a hand across her forehead, where the old scar of the exile's brand still puckered that dark flesh.

'Christie, it may be well that I can't be known again in Tathcaer. If I could, I'd be all Orhlandis instead of only a part, all *telestre*, instead of only a part . . .' Her eyes flicked up to meet mine. 'Tethmet will be there when we land, telling me I should go back to Kasabaarde, stay inside the Tower. I believe I'm more use here. I can talk to the *hiyek*-families. But, do you know, even if that were not so, I'd find it hard to stay away from the Hundred Thousand now.'

'Will you come into Tathcaer?'

The pale green illumination of the F90's cabin gave her flesh a sickly cast. An ageing Orthean woman, in shirt and britches, the slung *harur*-blades replaced now by a CAS-IV in a belt-holster; still

857

she is more exiled mercenary in her appearance than she is Hexenmeister – even I see that, who share her memories in part. And it is safer, oddly enough, to be recognizably the exiled Ruric Orhlandis than to be recognizably the Hexenmeister of Kasabaarde.

She turned her attention back to the holotank:

'We have a few hours before we know what they'll do. Time to go into Tathcaer, while we're waiting for the morning.'

Orthe's summer stars blazed, white and blue and red and gold. That light is brighter than Earth's moonlight, and it shone now on the windowless towers of the Citadel, and the rock of Citadel crag, and the many-coloured mossgrasses that grow in the Stone Garden. Dew pools glimmered. Ornamental waterfalls flashed in the starlight, and the noise of running water was a constant background to the talk. A white *rashaku-bazur* clung with all four claws to a rock spire, beating wide pinions and crying harshly. There was the scent of mossgrass, as the sun's heat faded from the rocks.

'Give you greeting, *t'an*.' A male Orthean in Ymirian dress stood as I came down the carved steps beside the waterfall. 'What news? Have you used *s'aranthi* weapons?'

At that moment I saw the *T'An Suthai-Telestre*, and so muttered something conciliatory and uninformative, and walked across the garden to Nelum Santhil's table. Here there was a crowd, mostly *s'ans telestre*. Small children scuttled underfoot, and the older *ashiren* brought herb-tea and *kiez*-fruit. When I glanced round to say something to Ruric, I found that she and Tethmet Fenborn had lost themselves in the press of bodies.

'Give you greeting, *t'an* Christie. What news?'

Before I could answer Nelum Santhil, Cassirur looked up from where she sat beside him and said: 'The Wellhouse *rashaku* bring word, that the *hiyek* ships lie some forty *seri* west of Perniesse.'

Beside the scarlet-maned female sat a hunched male, and he blinked bird-bright eyes and said, 'My people tell me they have *s'aranthi* weapons aboard those ships, and that you have felt the use of them.'

I took the seat beside Haltern. 'Why ask *me* what news? You know as much as I do!'

The remaining person at this table, the stocky female Bethan T'An Kyre, grinned broadly at me. 'We are not fools, *s'aranthi*.'

An *ashiren* put down a bowl of herb-tea on the table before me. These tables are carved from granite slabs. All the Stone Garden is dotted with them, set into hollows, or on slopes, or – as this one –

tucked into an alcove under an arch. And all the granite is coated with a thin film of soil, in which grows blue and scarlet and yellow and viridian mossgrass; and which now was hardly visible at all, for the number of Orthean males and females crowded into this small area. Across dark-maned heads, I glimpsed a black coverall: saw it to be Jamison, and guessed, *Cory isn't far away.* Then I saw her, sitting with Doug Clifford at another table, surrounded by *s'ans* who wore Rimon dress.

Nelum Santhil linked six-fingered hands, leaning back from the table. His dark mane was slicked down and his eyes showed a thin rim of white around the black iris: signs of exhaustion. Still, he wore the *T'An Suthai-Telestre*'s authority easier now.

'Have you nothing to add to that, *t'an* Christie?'

'Only questions, *T'An* Santhil. In a few hours the *hiyek* ships will be in the Sisters Islands – or else they'll turn aside, and in a few more hours be within sight of the Melkathi coast. What are you going to do when that happens?'

His dark head turned towards the Ortheans, gathered in voluble groups in that garden.

'You know the Hundred Thousand, *t'an* Christie. It isn't wholly for me, or my *takshiriye*, to say.'

Cassirur put down her bowl of herb-tea. 'Fight, or wait to kill secretly, that's what I'd say; if not for – no, *t'an* Haltern, I will speak – if not for rumours that go about the city, saying that it is Witchbreed weapons that come with the fleet.'

'That may be true, or it may not.'

'I've questioned the *t'an* Pathrey Shanataru,' Haltern said. His voice was level; it was none the less chilling.

'You haven't—'

'Shanataru is in the Wellhouse,' the Earthspeaker Cassirur said, moving that scarlet-maned head briefly to indicate the city below the crag.

Nelum Santhil said, 'The truth of it is that we have no one mind among us, to be agreed on what we'll do. Christie, that's been our strength, that if any attack us they face not one enemy but one hundred thousand. Now the *s'ans* and the *takshiriye* quarrel, every *telestre* quarrels with its *s'an*; Morvren Freeport is becoming deserted under attack, but the Melkathi coast has riders travelling towards Rimnith and Keverilde from all over the Hundred Thousand.'

I tasted the sour herb-tea. A cool wind began to blow, bringing the sound of the Oranon River, a hundred or so feet below at the foot of Citadel Crag. A priest-robed male came to speak with Cassirur, and she got up from the table and moved aside.

I said, 'I may have to withdraw Company forces from this area entirely. It's possible the fleet would attack Kumiel Island—'

Nelum Santhil raised a brow. 'Even with *s'aranthi* weapons in their hands, *t'an* Christie, I think you overestimate the danger to yourselves.'

'Don't be a fool, Santhil.' Haltern straightened, glaring at the *T'An Suthai-Telestre* as if he were the same Portmaster of Ales-Kadareth still, caught out in intrigue and stupidity; and I saw amusement on Nelum Santhil's face.

'Foolish, am I?'

'She means to withdraw before provocation can occur. Am I right, *S'aranth*?'

'It would avoid the danger of retaliation, yes.'

'And leaves us *harur*-blades to stand against your technology,' Bethan remarked sourly.

'Will you fight?'

Direct questions are not much admired in *takshiriye*. All I got in answer was Nelum Santhil's casual wave at the assembled *s'ans*, and his comment: 'Some may fight. Some may not. You must ask them. Ask each *s'an* of the *telestres* nearest the fleet, and each man and woman of those *telestres*, and then you might know. If they know.'

A female wearing the gold circlet of a *s'an* dropped into Cassirur's vacant seat, six or eight other Rimon-dressed Ortheans with her. She began to harangue Nelum Santhil in thickly-accented Ymirian. Bethan *T'An* Kyre leaned across to join in the argument.

'Walk with me,' Haltern Beth'ru-elen invited.

I hesitated. A glance showed me Douggie had been abandoned by the group of Ortheans at his table. He was speaking in a low tone to Corazon Mendez, who frowned. I thought: We've got no real part in these talks now, these are for the Hundred Thousand . . . And I stood, and took Hal's arm, and followed his lead across a tiny stone bridge, and up mossgrass-covered steps, until we had come almost within the shadow of the Citadel itself.

Small oil lanterns were strung on wires, illuminating what the starlight left shadowed. A tall, thin figure stood up from the nearest table: I recognized the brown robe and sleek black shaven mane of Tethmet Fenborn.

'Where is she?' Hal demanded. I frowned, then realized there was only one *she* he could mean.

The thin Orthean male shrugged. 'She could not wait, *shan'tai*. One of the brown-robes here told her that the Empress's Voice is held prisoner in the Wellhouse, and she went to speak with him if she could. She told me to wait, and tell you this.'

The old male leaned more heavily on my arm. He nodded, smiling ruefully; and when he did, the old sly Haltern Beth'ru-elen was plain on his face. '*S'aranth*, I had thought you should speak with Pathrey Shanataru again, it seems I am anticipated. Go down. My *l'ri-an* will take you. I'd go myself, but I weary easily.'

'Is there any use in my talking to him, Hal?'

'Who knows?' Hal said. 'It's this, *S'aranth*, if it's nothing else – it's a way to pass the hours until the *hiyek* ships reach Perniesse. Go now, *S'aranth-te*.'

He signalled, and a young fair-maned *ashiren* in Peir-Dadeni robes ran up the steps to us. The child had plump features, and something of the Beth'ru-elen face. I followed it, Tethmet Fenborn walked beside me; and I looked back once to see Hal on that lamp-lit terrace. The elderly male was looking down on the tables in the Stone Garden. I remember thinking, eight years ago, that a night spent studying the configurations of talk among the *takshiriye* on such occasions could teach a lifetime of *telestre* politics. Can it tell him what will happen tomorrow?

The low-roofed chambers of the Citadel were as crowded as the Stone Garden, and Hal's *ashiren* led us through a press of bodies. Warren-like, the Citadel, and all its rooms and galleries were full of *s'ans*, and of males and females from the city, and from the country Wellhouses, and from the ships that had come into Tathcaer harbour from everywhere in the Hundred Thousand. Ortheans in Roehmonder furs jostled me, and stared with fear at Tethmet – they have reason to fear the aboriginals of the Great Fens. I blinked in the oil-lamp light that was reflected back from crystal beads braided down spines, and from jewelled *harur*-blades. Dadeni *marhaz*-riders, shipmasters from Ales-Kadareth, farmers from Rimon and upriver Ymir . . . The jostling was rough, and deliberate, and I ignored it. No *s'aranthi* will be popular now.

At last we came out into the grounds again, passing *lapuur* with their fronds curled tight against the night air; walking down the zigzag Crown Steps to the Square below. All the city below was invisible, but for a sprinkling of lights – companion-houses, I thought – and ghost-grey images visible in starlight. Voices came distantly on the wind. The midnight bell had long since sounded, but there was still a smell of cooking-fires: Tathcaer more crowded than at Midsummer, even, and sleepless . . .

'Wait.'

I stood still, at the foot of Crown Steps, and checked my wristlink. The holo-image showed easily-read symbols that were heat-sensor readings. Difficult, standing there on cold flagstones, in the heart of the city, to translate those symbols into *jath* and *jath-rai* on the open sea.

'Any change?'

'Negative, Representative. ETA still 09.00 local time.'

'Keep me informed.' I keyed out. Tethmet's face was expressionless, but the young *l'ri-an* looked up with something that might have been concern or disgust. *Ke* turned, and led us across the Square to the gate of the Wellhouse's courtyard. Those great *ziku*-wood gates were shut.

A hundred and fifty miles to the east, there are Desert Coast Ortheans. On Rimnith and Keverilde. And there are Harantish Witchbreed, and their 'Empress' . . . *Is Calil there?*

When the view-slot in the great gates opened, I said, 'Tell your Earthspeaker I want to interview the *shan'tai* Pathrey Shanataru. He may have information about the murder of the Representative Molly Rachel.'

The slot shut again. I had time to feel the cold – Tathcaer's rivers mean the city has that night chill – and to squint up at the massy stars, and to yawn; and then the great gates soundlessly opened, and Cassirur Almadhera appeared.

'Give you greeting, *t'an*. You keep odd company.'

I glanced over my shoulder at Tethmet, but he didn't speak. 'You could say, it keeps me.'

'Well, we have another of the Tower's friends with the *shan'tai* Pathrey,' the Earthspeaker said. A voice called inside the courtyard, and she glanced back to make a reply, and then said, 'I must attend to the *rashaku* messages. The other *telestres* of the Hundred Thousand wish to know what happens here. Come in if you must, *S'aranth*, but don't hinder us.'

Once in the courtyard, the great dome of the Wellhouse and the lesser outbuildings blotted out starlight. Tethmet walked without stumbling, but I don't have his night vision: it was some minutes before I recognized the small domed building that Hal's *ashiren* led us to. *And are you a prisoner, Pathrey?* I was a prisoner here myself, Blaize and Rodion and I; and that other one of our party, the woman Havoth-jair . . .

'I know the way,' I said, entering.

The main, locked room is small. Lamplight now illuminated the dome of brown brick, and the low tables and benches; and shone too on the shabby, plump figure of Pathrey seated at one of the tables, and on the cloaked woman who leaned up against the wall, speaking to him. She glanced up as we were let in, and her mouth below her mask smiled.

'Give you joy of him. *S'aranth*, I can get nothing useful at all.' Ruric nodded a greeting to Tethmet.

Rooms without doors. That is what I first thought, in Kel Harantish; and now there is this room, with one arched doorway, and no windows at all . . . I pulled a bench across and sat down by Pathrey.

'I want to know how Molly Rachel came to be murdered,' I said. '*Shan'tai* Pathrey, you were the Empress's Voice; if you didn't actually see it happen, I'm damn sure you know how and why it did. I want to know.'

I was conscious that Tethmet had moved aside to speak to the Hexenmeister. The yellow light was oily on the Harantish male's dark skin. He wound his fingers together nervously, and under the sleeve of his robe I saw the edge of a cloth dressing. Hal's people would have questioned him more brutally than I wanted to think about.

'I don't . . . there was no . . .' His head came up. The brown eyes were bright, and it startled me to realize that was anger. 'What must I do to convince you of good faith? I rescued your *s'aranthi* envoy Clifford, I told you all I know of *K'Ai* Calil's plans. I expected to be a prisoner, for a time, but the questions never end! First them, and now you.'

'*Shan'tai* Pathrey—'

His hand slammed flat on the table. 'All I want is to rest!'

I studied him, thinking, How good a liar are you? This small, dark male, still in dirty Harantish robes that had gemmed embroidery visible under the mud; sitting now with his head bowed, lank mane falling about his face.

'You brought us into Kel Harantish,' I said. 'Molly and I; that first day we came to you. Now she's dead and I want to know how it happened. I have to make a report, but that doesn't matter. *I* want to know.'

Without looking up, he muttered, 'Ask *K'Ai* Calil.'

'If I could, I would. Believe me.'

At that, he raised his head. There was nothing sleek or mannered about his expression.

'Yes, I'll tell you. *Shan'tai*, I will. She and your other *s'aranthi* were in the city when the Emperor Dannor bel-Kurick was overthrown, and I put them where it seemed best to me, that is, safe out of the fighting. And then, when Dannor had been butchered, and his head hacked off and made the first of many at the foot of the Phoenix throne – then *K'Ai* Calil went to speak with your *shan'tai* Akida and your *shan'tai* Osaka in their captivity, where I

863

had them safe. And then she went on ninth level, where I had put *shan'tai* Rachel, and she spoke with *shan'tai* Rachel.'

He stopped, half gasping, and the expression on his face was pure malice.

'I'll tell you. *K'Ai* Calil learned something from the first two that she spoke of with the third of my prisoners. And when I went into the *shan'tai* Rachel's room, the *shan'tai* Rachel was dead. It had been done with a small blade, such as the city's beggar brats carry. I think you were lucky not to find *s'aranthi* dead in the throne room, *shan'tai* Christie.'

Calil bel-Rioch, enthroned: little and dirty and brilliant and bad, with the face of a mad child – and yet she's a woman of the Golden, I thought; and whatever she is, the Harantish Witchbreed follow her.

'Why the hell would she do that!'

'You will think that I know,' Pathrey Shanataru said, 'but I don't. All I can tell you is that I believe it was *K'Ai* Calil who murdered your friend, although I didn't see it done. But I know her.'

I went to stand at the door. A breath of cold wind from outside reached me. After a time, I became aware of Ruric beside me.

'Are you all right?' she asked.

'Some of what I saw in Kel Harantish . . . it makes me feel sick to remember it.'

The walls muffled sound. Only the pad of bare feet outside, where Earthspeakers were on guard, came to my ears. Did Molly find out from Akida about research at Maherwa – and if she did, *what* did she discover? And is killing the best way to silence someone? Or was that the psychopath, the woman responsible for the butchery I saw—

'It doesn't get me much further,' I said quietly to Ruric. 'It doesn't give me proof of anything. I do begin to have an idea, though.'

'What?'

'That if I can, at any time, get proof of the person responsible, then I'll have them. If it's Calil herself. Someone'll answer for it.'

The dark woman said nothing, and I was grateful; even if such threats are merely bluster, voicing them is a kind of comfort. She stayed beside me, masked and anonymous, while the brown-robe Tethmet put a few desultory questions to Pathrey Shanataru, and got only the briefest answers. My wristlink signalled an hour past midnight. I checked the sensor readings, but there was nothing there I didn't expect to see – *jath* drawing closer to the mainland. And still no change in the weather.

'You might do well to stay away from the *K'Ai* Calil,' Ruric Hexenmeister said quietly. 'From what you've told me of your experiences at Rakviri *telestre*, you're susceptible.'

It's called empathy, I thought sourly. Mention of Rakviri again brought Molly to mind, and I thought of that odd coincidence again: she and Barris and Jaharien dead, and of all of us in that vision, or whatever that experience was, only me left to tell of it. I glanced at Pathrey, seeing even in him (though I couldn't have told you how) some touch of Golden blood.

'I understand them,' I said. 'And so do you.'

Now that I accept them into myself, the Tower's memories don't torment me – and yet, they're still there. Yes, I thought, I understand them: Santhendor'lin-sandru and Zilkezra and the Golden . . . They fed on death, grew fat on death, glutted on death. Knowing that hour of extinction must come, they felt that knowledge spread back and poison all the hours and years before it, until all life was coloured with this shining darkness. Because extinction is a miracle, they worshipped it. And this is what I have within me now, have had since I came here: visions of that brilliant blackness. Until I can almost see, as Calil sees, how beautiful are all the colours of corruption.

Sleep caught me in the government Residence at Westhill-Ahren-tine, an hour before dawn. When I woke, it was to find Douggie bent over the holotank in the centre of the room, intently studying the images. Bleary-eyed, I got off the couch-chair and staggered over to the comlink.

'Nothing of any great import has occurred.'

'What? Oh.' The light, now that first twilight was passing, shone in at the windows and hurt my eyes. I waited until the first disorientation faded. 'Anything from the Citadel? I thought I'd better contact the orbiter through the comlink-booster, so I left the *takshiriye* to it . . .'

'People are still coming in.' He straightened, walked over to the inner door, and called down to the kitchens for herb-tea. On his way back, he added, 'The *T'An Suthai-Telestre* wishes to have messengers present here, at the comlinks, so that news of what happens to the fleet will be passed back to him without any loss of time.'

'You agreed?'

Douggie brushed ineffectually at his hair. Like me, he'd obviously slept in his clothes.

'I've also notified the WEBcasters on Kumiel Island,' he said. 'I imagine they'll be linked into the communications.'

The first bowl of herb-tea tasted more sour even than usual, but it sufficed to wake me. The *l'ri-an* in the kitchen would be more interested in news from the Sisters Islands than in cooking, I thought. I went down to tell them they could return to their *telestre*-houses in the city if they wished, and on the way back up met Haltern n'ri n'suth Beth'ru-elen coming in. He leaned part of his weight on his silver-topped *hanelys* cane, and the rest on the arm of Ruric Orhlandis.

'Give you greeting,' he said, 'from the *T'An Suthai-Telestre*. I have messengers ready to go to the Citadel.'

By the time we'd settled him in a couch-chair near the holotank, the dawn bells were ringing across the city. Ruric let her cloak fall, and then pulled off the soft leather mask; and turned her face to the open windows. The early sun shone in upon us.

'We passed the harbour, coming here. All the companion-houses are packed, waiting for news; and there are people all the way up to the signal towers on Westhill-Crown.' She abruptly swung round, and gazed into the holotank. Visual image overlaid with heat-sensor readings – I saw her comprehension.

'The leading *jath* and *jath-rai* are here, off Perniesse,' Douggie said, with a touch of pedant in his manner; and the hand that indicated the image trembled slightly.

'Soon, then.'

'It won't happen all in a minute,' I said. I crossed to the comlink, establishing contact with the shuttles overflying the *hiyek* fleet, and spoke with Jamison, who was on an F90. Cory Mendez, whom I'd half expected to find with him, answered my contact from the Kumiel Island base.

Haltern Beth'ru-elen, watching the images as intently as a child does, suddenly exclaimed, 'See! They're turning.'

I pushed between him and Ruric to get a look at the 'tank. Visual image showed the sea, pearl and grey and pink in the early morning, cut with the hundreds of thread-thin wakes of *jath* and *jath-rai*. An inset-image appeared, and in it would be any ship that had made a significant course change, and *there!* I thought; seeing a metal-hulled *jath* tack across, course slowly changing . . .

'North?' Ruric said. 'Sunmother! not Melkathi, then. Or not now—'

'Look.'

Whatever shuttle was sending back this image was flying parallel to the ships, all the strung-out groups and convoys in that great fleet, and now as it approached the leading edge of the fleet I saw one *jath* after another begin to curve away from their previous course . . .

'It may just be one *hiyek*.' Ruric spoke as if she warned herself. 'Quarrelled with the other families, perhaps.'

'No, look.' And I keyed in a closer image, and now the faint blue line in the east became Perniesse; and the *jath* of another group began to move gradually northwards . . . *Changing course as soon as there's light to see. But what are they going to do?*

To speak of "the Sisters Islands" puts them in a close group, really they are several dozen miles apart – Ahrentine not even visible in the image that showed the headlands of Perniesse – and surrounded by rocks and shoals, as well as wide and sheltered channels.

A noise broke my concentration. At first I thought it something quiet and close at hand. Then I realized. Through the open window of this *telestre*-house, I was hearing the noise of the crowds up at the top of Westhill, where the heliograph station stood.

Ruric looked up from the images, a fierce grin on her face. 'They don't attack.'

'They've hardly changed course, never mind got to any island,' I said testily.

Minutes ticked past. Four of us with heads bent over the holotank, oblivious of the sun climbing the eastern sky. I spoke quietly with the shuttles, ordering overflights at a higher altitude – almost as if they could scare off this possibility, I thought, amused; and then thought, Possibility of what?

Wind and tide cannot be hurried. Hal shifted on his couch-chair, easing old bones, and muttered, and sent word to one *ashiren* in the courtyard to go to the Citadel, and then returned to staring at the bright miniature ships. I saw Douggie speak into his wristlink, and realized he was talking to one of the WEBcasters on Kumiel. Figures ticked up, inset into the 'tank: thirty per cent of the *hiyek* fleet now committed to a course taking them into the islands . . .

Ruric Hexenmeister said, 'Can you show Perniesse?'

I keyed in a message to a YV9 – and saw the chronometer and blinked: two hours into the morning of Merrum Secondweek Twoday, and it seemed like only minutes. The shuttle acknowledged.

On Perniesse's blue-grey hills, nothing moved but the herds of *marhaz*. Then the data-net detected readings, the image zoomed in; and we had a shaky picture of slate-roofed *telestre* buildings, and Ortheans who ran purposefully. Too distant and too distorted to see what they carried, but I knew it would be *harur*-blades.

Sixty per cent of the *hiyek* fleet now committed to the course, or already passing into the sea that lies between Perniesse and the mainland of the Hundred Thousand . . .

'They'll never find the islands more unprepared than they are now,' Ruric said, 'and if they mean to attack, they won't give the island *telestres* time to gather their forces.'

In the holotank, the image of a *jath-rai* was momentarily as clear as life. Metal hull, scarred with corrosion; spreading metal sails – and on its crowded decks, *meshabi*-robed Ortheans; some running, some crowding the rails – and then the shuttle's overflight lost the image. In memory I taste salt-bitter lips, feel the swell. The *jath-rai*'s image returned. That's strange, I thought, it looks almost crumpled . . . And then I realized that the metal sails were sheathing, folding into themselves, and the ship itself sliding to anchor in what must be a shallow, sheltered channel.

Not one of the four of us spoke, as we watched ship after ship fold up its sails and anchor in the lee of Perniesse, and other *jath* sail on to shelter near Ahrentine; no vessel close to shore. Even when the noise from the city outside was at its loudest, none of us spoke. Frightened, in case this should be a chimera, and speaking of it break the spell.

At last, when it seemed that all but the stragglers were moored in the sheltered waters of the Sisters Islands, and messengers had begun to come from the Citadel down to the Residence asking urgently for confirmation, Hal raised his head and looked at Ruric Hexenmeister. She nodded once.

'Not an attack. Not *yet*,' she amended hastily. And then grinned at her own caution.

Douggie put his arm tightly round my shoulder. I wiped my face, my hand came away wet. Hal bustled to the window to shout down at his messengers in the courtyard below. The WEBnet blocked, overloaded with transmissions.

That afternoon, as if to mock our fear, a storm blew up from the west, but passed safely south of the Sisters Islands.

PART SEVEN

CHAPTER 35

The Passing of Fire

'The longer it lasts, the longer it *will* last,' Haltern n'ri n'suth Beth'ru-elen observed. 'If I were *T'An Suthai-Telestre*, however, I confess I should wait some hours before sending an envoy to the islands . . .'

Nelum Santhil raised his head from a pile of thin parchment scrolls: *rashaku*-carried messages.

'You're not *T'An Suthai-Telestre*,' he said cheerfully, 'and I choose to send the *T'An* Commander today. If the *T'An* Meduenin is willing to go.'

This morning of Merrum Secondweek Threeday was overcast, humid, and a watery sunlight slanted through the slot-windows. The room, like all in the Citadel, had windows facing on to one of the myriad inner courtyards; and I sat on the narrow ledge, impatiently fidgeting. Hal and Nelum Santhil sat among heaps of reports, half of which they consigned to the iron braziers, the other half of which they let clutter the low couch-chairs they sat on. The stone walls made the room chilly.

'Are you willing?' Nelum Santhil persisted.

Blaize Meduenin turned from the room's other window to face the *T'An Suthai-Telestre*. I hadn't known he was back from Morvren Freeport, and I wasn't certain, now, whether I was glad or not. 'The fighting in the Freeport has stopped. In the main, because the Freeporters have abandoned Little Morvren and Southernmost to be looted. There's little more I can do there. Yes, I'll go to the islands.'

He wore a drab cloak over Rimon shirt and britches, and the fair mane straggled down his spine. *Harur-nilgiri* and *harur-nazari* hung at his belt. Difficult as that scarred face is to read, I thought something was troubling him; and Nelum Santhil paused as if to let him voice it, but the stocky Orthean male remained silent.

'And you, Representative?'

'I want to know what you're going to do about—' I abruptly

remembered, *He's Rimnith telestre* and changed what I'd been going to say '—about Melkathi, and the *hiyek* people there.'

Hal tutted, and tucked his thin six-fingered hands into his sleeves; and then had to give up his irritation to speak with a young *ashiren* messenger who entered the room. Nelum Santhil shrugged.

'When the Desert Coast fighters have gone, the land may be healed—'

'Yes, *when*. It's possible the Empress-in-Exile is there still. I want to know what you're planning.'

Nelum Santhil sat back on the low couch-chair, and looked up at me gravely. 'May I ask, *t'an* Christie, what business that is of the Company representative?'

To me, he is still the Portmaster of Ales-Kadareth who betrayed SuBannasen and Orhlandis, and both of them in a remarkably inept manner; but years pass and people change, I thought, and he *is* the *T'An Suthai-Telestre* . . .

'It's our business so long as there are hi-tech weapons in *hiyek* hands, which I suspect there are, in Melkathi. That's all, *T'An* Santhil. Ideally, I want them recovered, or disabled. Failing that, PanOceania will want some reassurance that they're not about to be used.'

He nodded thoughtfully. 'That must be considered, yes. I'll talk with you later today, *t'an S'aranth*.'

As I stood up, plainly dismissed, Blaize Meduenin said, 'I'll walk down to the city with you.'

There was no opportunity for speech in the crowded grey-stone galleries of the Citadel. Once outside, it was a matter of pushing through the *s'ans* and *t'ans* ascending Crown Steps; and I didn't pause to draw breath until I reached the Square, and looked round for a *skurrai-jasin*.

Here in the shadow of the cliff-wall, that was covered in blue-grey vines, we stood momentarily out of the crowd. A hand grabbed my elbow – as I wrenched free, I realized it was Blaize n'ri n'suth Meduenin, pulling me round to face him; and I left a sharp retort unsaid, seeing the bitterness on that scarred face.

'No word,' he said. 'Nothing! You can trust Haltern and Nelum Santhil and half your Company, but not *me*—'

'I don't know what—'

He put one claw-nailed finger on my shoulder; it rested heavily there.

'I've *seen* her.'

Her? And then it made sense.

'For years I've thought that she was dead, that Haltern was her murderer – however indirectly – and now, without warning—'

I shook him off, turning away; seeing nothing but the Square and the crowds and the wall of the Wellhouse courtyard, and not that accusing face. When I was ready, I turned back.

'It's nothing to do with trust. You were in Morvren, it isn't something I could tell you over a comlink.'

'No?'

'No! Listen, Meduenin, with all that's been going on here these last few days, you think I've had time to worry about your – your pride?'

The wind blew his fair mane across his scarred face, and he looked away, head momentarily bowed. 'If you call it that . . . I suppose . . .'

I have put him on the defensive and done it too easily, *Blaize you're no politician!* It isn't fair to take advantage of honesty: 'No, it isn't pride . . . Anyway, she isn't Ruric now. Or, not only Ruric.'

One hand moved to *harur-nazari* hilt, clawed thumb stroking the sweat-stained guard. His blue eyes veiled, cleared, and then he broke into a loud laugh.

'What's *funny*, for God's sake?'

'You, if you think it isn't obvious she has the mark of the Tower on her now. *S'aranth* . . .' Bewilderment replaced humour. 'She is the Orhlandis, and she is not. I've spoken with her . . . If Hal's people didn't kill *amari* Ruric, then I think that, in its own way, the Tower did. That saddens me. But do you remember what I once said to you, *S'aranth*? Now, the Orhlandis is not my rival.'

'Rival?'

His eyes deliberately sought mine; blurred with nictitating membrane.

'I won't wait any longer,' he said. 'You've delayed and delayed, *arykei*, and I have thought the cause Ruric, alive or dead, or one of your Company men; and now I've done with waiting, and will have an answer.'

Only one day since the *jath* and *jath-rai* came to anchorage in the Sisters Islands: it seems like a year. If I weren't so tired, I thought, if I weren't so shattered, would I know what to say?

'I wish you'd been here,' I said. 'When the fleet got to the islands, I wished you were here with me.'

The white-mottled scar tissue pulled back as he smiled, and his eyes veiled. Again, he rested his hand on my arm. Easy to feel that swordfighter's strength of his.

'Don't you think this is a mistake?' I asked.

'No, *S'aranth*, I don't.'

'I think . . . I think it would be well if they could have been *arykei*: the Blaize Meduenin who was a mercenary assassin, and the Christie who was Christie *S'aranth*. We're not who we were then.'

His eyes, level with mine, cleared; and he grinned like a boy. 'Delay, delay.' And then with Orthean reasonableness, said, 'You've known since Morvren. Since Kasabaarde.'

Out of all that I could have said, I chose: 'You know where in this city to find me.'

A bronze *skurrai* drew up a few yards away, and the driver on the *jasin* leaned down to hear my directions. Watery sun shone through sea mist that blurred *telestre*-houses, and made Blaize's pale mane gleam. Easy to give impulse free rein, to touch that shaggy mane, run hands down the line of jaw and chin and shoulder . . . I stepped back, out of his grasp, and climbed into the *skurrai-jasin*; my hands tingling with that movement.

'Take care,' I called. And then had to smile at myself: Blaize is a fighter of forty years' experience, such men are careful. Before the *skurrai-jasin* had crossed the Square, I looked back to see him conferring with two males who wore the crest of the Crown Guard.

The *skurrai*-carriage jolted down narrow passageways. The sky between *telestre*-houses was a ribbon of haze, and damp heat beat back from the pale walls. Through open arches, I saw crowded interior courtyards; and it occurred to me to lean forward and direct the driver to go by way of Guild-Ring, where I could listen to market rumour. A limp exhaustion, together with the heat, made me heavy-eyed. The humidity kept the city's smells trapped: food and herb-tea and the dung of *skurrai* and *marhaz*. And this is where I began my journey, eight years ago; going north into cold Roehmonde, followed all unknown by SuBannasen's assassin . . . And would she smile to see him *T'An* Commander? Would Rodion have wished it? Rodion Halfgold, who once asked me, *Is he a good arykei?* Yes: but that's not the answer to my own question—

'Christie!'

I started awake, and signalled the driver to halt. We had passed the Guild-Ring's market stalls, and now stood outside one of the companion-houses near the docks. A woman in the mask and brown cloak of Kasabaarde crossed the alley.

'I've heard news from the island *telestres*,' Ruric Hexenmeister said. 'Are you going back to the Residence? I'll tell you on the way there. Is there profit in talking with Nelum Santhil now? –

although if there is,' she interrupted herself, scrambling up into the *jasin*, 'it'll be the first time in my acquaintance with him!'

'Don't underestimate Nelum. He's got Hal with him, remember.'

'I don't forget.'

She leaned back into the corner of the *jasin* as it rocked over the unpaved alley. *Ashiren* scattered out of the beast's way. Wisps of sea fog glimmered round the *telestre*-houses' flat roofs, and there was a faint moisture clinging to her black cropped mane. The mask was disturbing in its blankness: the lines of her mouth gave nothing away.

As we came out on to the docks, and the smell of *dekany*-weed and harbour rubbish hit me, she said, 'There are times when I like to play that I am only Orhlandis.'

The cloak's hood framed that corded neck and lean shoulders; fell down in folds that hid the knotted empty sleeve of her shirt; and I wanted to comfort her – but she is not Orhlandis – or reach her: but the mask is her protection. Still, I wish I could see those yellow eyes.

'What's the *telestre* news?'

'That the Hundred Thousand are safe so long as the *hiyeks* quarrel. Which, they say in the city here, means safe forever.' Her smile faded. 'I hear rumours of offworld weapons – not used, you understand, but shown, when the island *telestres* have sailed out to parley with the Desert Coast ships. So: and we know there are offworld weapons in Rimnith and Keverilde . . .'

'It isn't over until it's over.'

'It isn't over yet. Christie, I've seen – I remember – too much. It makes me fearful. Are we really going to get out of it this easily?'

'There's Calil's people yet.'

The *skurrai*'s pads squished on mud, where fishing boats had spilled their catch that dawn. Wind blew more strongly now, shifting the sea fog. Light danced on the estuary waters. *Rashaku-bazur* wheeled and cried: that cry that is like metal tearing. All the quayside here was lined with *jath* and *jath-rai*, and Ortheans crowded the warehouses and companion-houses and food-booths.

'I want to talk to Douggie and Cory Mendez about this,' I said. And then I looked at Ruric: that dark profile, the sharp lines of her alien face. 'I'm not sure I'm capable of judging a matter when Calil bel-Rioch is involved. Because of Rakviri, because of Maherwa . . . let's say, because of what I "remember". I'd be happier if there was another Company representative here.'

'Frightened?'

'Terrified. Ruric, I'll do it because I have to. It's just that . . . do you remember what you said, once? You called offworlders "Witchbreed".'

The dark face stayed staring ahead. 'I remember. It was in the Citadel, when I was made exile.'

'Because of what we are, because we're human, I think we understand the Golden Witchbreed better than any Orthean can. And you must know that, because you're Hexenmeister, and you know what I know.' I gripped the *jasin*'s rail as we swung away from the harbour, turning up into the alleys of Westhill. 'Even Nelum Santhil thinks this is a war for land, that it's because the *hiyek*-families have lived in poverty and now won't live that way any more. The Harantish Witchbreed know different. What am I supposed to say, Ruric? That even if Calil loses the support of the *hiyek*-families, she's still in Melkathi, and she still has her people with her, and she may – she *may* have a weapon that brought about the fall of the Golden Empire.'

'She may, and she may not. She is not the sanest ruler the Harantish ever had,' the Hexenmeister said, and her lips under the mask curved in a smile.

No, I thought. I can't judge Calil. I remember the City Over The Inland Sea, and that was a vision in a dry and dusty land; and I remember what I saw at Rakviri *telestre*, and how those others who saw it are dead, and – all I know is that fear is irrational, and I am irrationally afraid.

Westhill's *telestre*-houses passed by, and the *skurrai* slowed as the hill became steeper. Sunlight gleamed on its shaggy bronze featherpelt, and on the two pairs of cropped and capped horns.

'And even the *hiyeks* are not satisfied,' Ruric said, 'not yet; that requires negotiation. This is a temporary truce, at best. Christie, I *need* there to be peace here. All else aside, I need to speak with you of what we said before: if offworld science might, given what I have in the Tower, find out some way to cure this world of devastation – to destroy what Calil calls "ancient light".'

'You've no guarantee that our species can analyse Golden science.'

The *skurrai-jasin* drew up outside Westhill-Ahrentine. Through the archway, I saw Doug Clifford in the inner courtyard; he beckoned. As Ruric got down from the carriage, she said, 'I want to speak with him, and with you – and, if it can be contrived, with Nelum Santhil, and with some of the *raiku* on the Anzhadi ships.'

I have thought it over, and this is only a lull; I have thought it ended, and this is only the beginning of that.

'Perhaps the *shan'tai* Pathrey Shanataru tells the truth,' the

Orthean woman said. She reached up to pull off her mask as we entered Westhill-Ahrentine, and those yellow eyes in that dark face were bright and exhausted and full of dread. 'Perhaps all that *K'Ai* Calil and her people have is a memory of ancient light, and a bluff. If we've ended the fighting here, that's good, but perhaps the real war is only beginning.'

Towards noon of the same day, I went out to Kumiel and spoke in person with the WEBcasters there. That kept me busy for several hours. I'd barely finished when Cory Mendez came into the communications-dome, and slumped down in a seat beside me.

'Give me strength!' she said. 'Lynne, your idea of a surveillance operation is – extensive, to say the least. Well, we did it. Now I want to know what Security precautions you want from now on, regarding the situation here.'

I leaned forward as Ottoway pushed past behind my chair. There was no sign of Chandra Hainzell. Must mean they've been evacuated to the orbiter, I realized. Does that mean the only Company personnel on-world are Security? I guess it does . . .

'I want to keep a low profile,' I said, and then as Ottoway came back and hovered, I glanced up at him. 'Yes?'

'There's a real-time contact, Representative. For you, from Thierry's World.'

Cory raised a brow; I excused myself, and went to the furthest of the line of holotank comlinks in that temporary dome.

'Christie here.'

The image in the tank snowed, cleared. Startled, I was about to speak, but I remembered the thirty-second real-time gap in transmissions from Thierry's World. Plenty of time to recognize that sallow, Pacifican face; the rough blond hair, and the young face now white with illness. David Osaka: the shape of a skull sharply visible in his face.

'Lynne? Am I through? I insisted on notifying you myself. He wouldn't listen to me or the medics – Rashid Akida, that is. He said he had to report in person. I'm sorry I'm not making much sense. I've been under sedation.'

'Why is Rashid coming back? Is he fit to travel?'

David stared blankly into the imager: then I saw my words reach him.

'No. The medics say not. It's about the research team's report on Maherwa. He insisted nothing be said on comlink channels.'

'David, can you tell me anything?'

Again that pause, then:

'No. I had no clearance for those records. Lynne, I don't know why he's certain it's important. I thought you ought to know he's on his way.'

Being used to PanOceania, I translated that without difficulty as: Do nothing until you hear what he has to say. And what is it you won't say on open-channel? I wondered.

'Okay, I have the message. You – no, hold contact, David, please. I want you to report to Security while you're on-line.'

In the half-minute before the words reached him, I stood up and called Ottoway over to the holotank.

'David Osaka on Thierry. You wanted a statement about what he saw in Kel Harantish; if he knows anything about Representative Rachel's death. Here.'

Calculating when a ship might arrive from Thierry's World occupied my attention, and so Douggie had to call twice before I saw him walking up the track towards the comlink-dome. The daystar-red sky behind him was milky blue, blending with the mossgrass of the island; and the wind brought the scent of humid vegetation.

'Are you going back to the city?'

I shrugged. 'Came outside for some air, that's all. Douggie, to tell the truth, I don't know *what* to do.'

'There may be a valid reason for that,' he said, absently dusting his sleeve and glancing back at the mainland. Tathcaer was clearly visible: white *telestre*-houses on the rising slopes. 'That reason may be that there's very little any *s'aranthi* – I beg your pardon, any offworlder – can do at this precise moment. Might I suggest we wait until there is?'

'There ought to be a neutral arbitrator between the Desert Coast Ortheans and the Hundred Thousand.'

'I believe,' he said carefully, 'that the fenborn Tethmet and the other person from the Tower are quite capable of fulfilling that role. At least, I understand them to have gone to Perniesse some hours ago with that intention.'

Douggie's care was not for what I might hear, I noted with amusement, but for the comlink officers, who were Cory's people. A figure of six hours came into my mind: as well as I could judge real-time elapsing during FTL travel, the earliest at which a ship from Thierry's World could arrive. And that will be about sunset tonight, I thought. Resolutely refusing to speculate. It may be that there's nothing useful at all in the research team's report . . .

'I intend to put another report through to home office,' Doug added. 'Lynne, if the situation stabilizes here, I plan to go to Earth in person – yes, I know what you're going to say: it takes time.

However, if I'm on the spot, and able to use what connections I do have, I think I have a respectable chance of getting Orthe Protected Status.'

'You're telling a Company representative?'

Humour lifted the corner of that precise mouth. He clasped his hands behind his back. There was a confidence about him now, that had been missing (I thought) since Ashiel Wellhouse and Sethri's death.

He said, 'I'm telling *you*, Lynne. You've seen public opinion on the WEBcasts. I'm going to push from the government side. You're going to push the Company the same way.'

'Am I?' I looked at him. 'I'll rephrase that: I am.'

His attention focused on some object behind me, and I turned in time to see the WEBcasters Lutaya and Visconti approaching. I felt a hand on my arm.

'If I might offer an unsolicited opinion, I suggest that you take a rest before you fall over, Lynne. We're none of us as young as we were, and speaking for myself, I'm ageing by the minute. I don't like to see you looking so strained.'

'I will rest,' I agreed. 'I've got my own report to make out for home office in Pacifica.'

Six hours. And what else will have happened here by then, I thought. We're still so finely balanced I'm half afraid to breathe . . . And why is nothing happening in Melkathi?

Quite irrelevantly, then, as often happens, I thought of both of them: Douggie . . . and Blaize. I *know* Douggie. I know there is a great deal of the poseur about him, and that the small frightened person we all keep inside ourselves is, in Doug's case, not so frightened at all. And what I don't know I can guess, from common shared backgrounds: country, world, species. What do I really know about the humanoid alien Meduenin?

I know that I feel oddly maternal towards this stocky, scarred man; who has fought thirty years as a mercenary and is in need of no one's protection. Who said feeling follows understanding? The heart moves and we, rationalizing, follow after. I know that Blaize has all of Douggie's self-mocking humour and more, and I know that I see myself through his eyes better than I am.

I was preparing to shuttle up to the orbiter and meet Rashid Akida as he arrived, when my wristlink chimed and summoned me out of the F90. As I walked down the ramp to the earth of the makeshift landing field, a darkness blotted out the sky that was pearly with second twilight, and an orbital shuttle sank down with hardly a whisper of noise. I felt the vibration of its grounding through the soles of my feet. It settled on to Kumiel, towering over the smaller craft.

A beam of light broke from it as the port slid up, yellow against the blue twilight. By the time I'd crossed the hundred yards between me and the shuttle, a small figure had left the ramp and was looking round in disorientation.

'Dr Akida?' *Is* it? I wondered. This gaunt Sino-Indian didn't look like the man I'd seen in Morvren. His coverall hung off him, and there were deep lines in his face. His eyes met mine; I saw him sway.

'Ms Christie? Are you the representative now? It's urgent that I talk with you – under Secure conditions, please. I must insist.'

Anywhere on Kumiel, we're recorded; and anywhere in Tathcaer, we're spied on. I almost laughed aloud. You forget what you take for granted. Old training came back to me, and I indicated the track leading down to the shore, half-invisible now in the long twilight.

'We'll cross to the city, the government Residence; tell me as we go. Can you walk that far?'

'Of course I . . . if we could go slowly, Ms Christie, yes I can.'

Now, with twilight, the blue-grey mossgrass released a fragrance as we trod on the fronds. Rock outcrops caught the last light of Carrick's Star, silver in the west, and the slanting light caught Akida's face, and he looked nearer sixty than forty – *If he collapses, what will you do?* I asked myself, and slowed my pace, and quietly checked my wristlink for a rapid medi-call.

At last, when he didn't speak, I said, 'Molly Rachel left a message, in Kel Harantish, before she died. She said she found it necessary to destroy all Company records of research in Maherwa. Why is that?'

'To prevent the inhabitants of that settlement somehow hearing of what I'd – what we'd done.' He stopped, on a small rise, and gazed down the track to the sea. The waters shifted, restless; the air was just on the borderline between warm and cool. He turned his head, and his gaze was direct:

'Briefly, I and my team established no analysis of the ancient civilization's science. I couldn't begin to hypothesize about the basis of it – something so far in advance of our own Paradox Physics that it makes us seem like children. What we *did* discover is the rate of decay of the area's canal system.'

'Decay?'

'To summarize, while the pump and purification systems have been maintained, to a degree, there have been no actual *repairs* to the system for, I would estimate, several hundred years. Estimates are difficult, of course. The *chiruzeth* substance is not at all reward-ing to analyse. However, bearing in mind that it is an estimate—'

'You mean the system's running down.' Even as I said it, I didn't believe it; that is too shocking a thing to be told, on a summer evening and under a clear sky. The Sino-Indian nodded sharply; and began to walk down the path.

'Molly – the late Representative Rachel needed a good deal of convincing. I wish I had my records, but I assure you: given access to the canal system, the research can be duplicated. She felt it might be dangerous for this to become generally known among the native population.'

'But I don't . . .' Believe it, I thought. I remember how long the Harantish Witchbreed have maintained the canals.

I remember that the Golden Empire did not build only for a day or a year or a century, but for millennia.

'Assuming this to be accurate, Dr Akida, what is the rate of decay? How long will the canals continue to function?'

He was quiet, and I could hear the noise of our feet on the earth, and the hiss of the surf. He put lank black hair back from his forehead, wiping away sweat. In pain, I realized; Christ, girl, don't bait him when he's doing this to bring the news personally!

'You push me for definite answers, Ms Christie, and I have only hypothetical estimates. Given that my assumptions are correct, I would say between five hundred and eight hundred years, Earth standard.'

A cool wind blew off the sea, and flared the pitch torches being lit by the ferry, down on the shingle. It brought the sound of voices. Across the water, lights still showed on the island-city; and a *rashaku-bazur* glided silently within a yard of us, and I started violently at that white apparition. Rashid Akida put out a hand and muttered something profane.

'I'm not completely divorced from the world,' he said suddenly. 'Molly Rachel knew how much social and cultural shock some-thing like this can cause, and *I* know, and I've no desire to cause it, believe me. That's why I insist on Security. Do you seriously think that, if I didn't appreciate that fully, I would have allowed Ms Rachel to destroy *all trace* of five months' research?'

'I – no, I'm sorry; I didn't see that.'

'That's five months of my career, of my life. From what I hear, the chances of a research team getting back to that continent are negligible. No, I don't take this lightly.'

Chastened, I put out a hand to help him over the shingle. We came down to the edge of the sea, and a *jath-rai* drawn up to the tiny dock. And then the implications hit me, and I stopped dead. Akida looked back at me with irritation.

'The old civilization, their science – you *can't* analyse it?'

He wiped his forehead again. When he felt in his belt-pouch for painkillers, I could see that his fingers were shaking. He said, 'Negatives are impossible to prove. All I can say is, that with the full resources of Earth's data-net at our disposal, we've failed to comprehend any of it on more than a basic cause and effect level – no, not even that. I don't understand what the cause might be of any given effect. I know the *chiruzeth* canal system somehow circulates pure water, but I don't know *how*. I have artifacts that perform actions, but what their *function* is—' He stopped for breath.

It was as if some knot untied inside me: all I could do was stand on that twilight beach, half deafened by waves, tasting the alien salts of that alien sea on my lips, and think: A synthesis of Earth and Golden technology, is it? Calil, you're bluffing. You don't have the knowledge, there's been nowhere to get it from!

'We'll cross to the city,' I said, and hailed the ferry crew. When I recognized one of the younger Ortheans as Beth'ru-elen *telestre*, I realized I had a messenger. 'Dr Akida, there are people we have to see.'

All exhaustion vanished: I could have raised the *jath-rai* ferry's sails myself. Akida slumped down on a bench, but I walked up and down on the swaying deck, going to the rail to look first at Tathcaer harbour as we approached, then at Kumiel, vanishing into blue darkness. Brilliant clusters of stars began to come out in the high dome of the sky. I used my wristlink for what calls I could, spoke with the Beth'ru-elen *ashiren* to send *kir* to the Citadel; and then returned to gripping the polished *ziku* rail, feeling the seaspray cold on my face.

Momentarily, I thought Artifacts that perform functions and my heart stopped: who knows what relics might survive in Kel Harantish, that treasure-junkheap of the world? Then relief rushed over me. If a weapon was found, I thought, it would have been used before now. The only reason we believe the claim was that possibility that Earth science might restore that lost knowledge. And that possibility's gone. If they can't restore the canal system, I'm damned if I believe they can have Witchbreed weapons!

The *jath-rai* dipped, meeting the turbulence of sunset tide in the Oranon's estuary. Cold seawater soaked my arm. I stood back from the rail as we tacked across the expanse of water that becomes Tathcaer's harbour, gazing up at the dark shadows of Westhill and Easthill against the starry sky.

Rashid Akida's voice came from behind me: 'I'm afraid, if the situation remains thus, that this world is of correspondingly less value to the Company.'

'Is it likely to change – is a breakthrough still possible?'

His voice sounded weary. 'Breakthroughs in understanding are always possible. I should like to compare data on Golden science with that on other Heart Stars and Home Stars worlds. That would mean a five or ten years' research project, and I doubt the Company will fund that now.'

I turned to watch us dock, so that he shouldn't see me smile. Of less value to the Company. Dear me, I thought, what a pity. And yet if I do pity anyone, it's Rashid Akida.

The Beth'ru-elen child scuttled off through the crowd on the quay, heading for the Citadel. It was an easy walk up to Westhill-Ahrentine, but none the less I hired a *skurrai-jasin*; and came to the *telestre*-house shortly after full night. The sky cleared, the stars blazed. *L'ri-an* opened the barred tunnel-entrance to us, and I helped Akida up the steps and into the upper-storey rooms; meeting the stares of first Tethmet Fenborn, then Blaize n'ri n'suth Meduenin, and then – I was equally startled – the *shan'tai* Hildrindi of *hiyek*-Anzhadi.

'I've tried to get in touch with Ruric, and Hal, and the *T'An Suthai-Telestre*,' I said. 'Douggie and Commander Mendez will be here as soon as they can – it's all right, Blaize, it isn't as dramatic as it looks; Rashid, I've also requested a medic . . .' I relinquished Akida's weight on to Blaize, as the Orthean male helped him to a couch-chair.

Tethmet blinked dark eyes. 'She is at the Wellhouse, with the Witchbreed.'

I mentally translated that as *Ruric* and *Pathrey Shanataru* respectively. I crossed the room, checking holotank and comlink; and then became aware that the pale-maned Desert Coast male was watching me with a wry amusement. Hildrindi-*keretne* said, 'I will go, if you wish, *shan'tai* Christie, but I am curious.'

'I'll let you know if you should go in a minute, *shan'tai*.'

Blaize stood up from bending over Rashid Akida. *Harur*-blades rang a dissonance. The Meduenin was still in clothes soaked to the knee with seawater, and I wondered how matters had gone in the *hiyek* fleet. He pushed back yellow mane from his scarred cheek, and looked at me, puzzled.

'All the technology of the Company, and you bring your business in person? Or is that necessary? Christie, what in Her name—?'

I took his hands in mine. They were dry, warm; with that temperature just subtly different from the human.

'I'll tell you,' I said. 'If what I've heard just now is true, we're safe.'

CHAPTER 36

That Bright Shadow

Westhill-Ahrentine's crowded upper chambers grew hot, and smelled – or stank – of *kazsis*-vine, and herb-tea, and human sweat.

'I'll tell you what makes it credible,' Corazon Mendez said, leaning her hip back against the edge of the comlink console. 'My people have been certain Rachel and Osaka and Akida were attacked for the same reason. Now it makes sense. To keep news of the technology fraud from getting out of the Kel Harantish settlement.'

Oh, it 'makes sense', does it; Molly's death and their pain? Christ, I'm glad of that!

'Cory, you—' But the comlink's chime interrupted me. 'Yes. Christie here.'

'Kumiel base, Representative. Lieutenant Ottoway wants to know if you want day and night surveillance kept up over the Rimnith-Keverilde area.'

'Yes, I do—'

Cory leaned down to the pick-up: 'Downgrade it one level. Tell Ottoway he'll need the YV9s to keep up surveillance over the sea fleet. There'll be considerable movement there over the next four days: I want it watched.'

'Acknowledged; will do, Commander Mendez.'

No, I thought. No. This is not the time to quarrel with Cory Mendez. Or anyone else, for that matter.

A thin ceramic bowl of *siir*-wine stood on the console-top, and I reached for it; sipping the viridian liquid and welcoming its bite. Corazon Mendez pushed herself upright, weight on her wrist. The thick silver rings on her fingers clicked against the console.

And what *are* we going to do about Rimnith and Keverilde, and the guerrilla fighters in Melkathi?

This small chamber was crowded: Rashid on one of the couch-chairs, with Kennaway, the black medic I'd last seen up on the orbiter; Doug Clifford in deep conversation with the Visconti woman from WEB-Trismegistus – all of them seeming gross and clumsy beside the frail figure of Haltern Beth'ru-elen, and the two delicate *ashiren* who ran his errands. Through the bead-curtain, in the other room, I could see the *shan'tai* Hildrindi talking to Bethan T'*An* Kyre; and both of them being watched by the silent Nelum Santhil. *How did this place come to be neutral ground?* And then I thought of the comlink under my elbow, the data-tank; and realized *speed of communication*.

The bead-curtain on the outer door clashed back, pushed aside by a fair-maned male and a dark female, both in the shabbiest of Orthean dress; who were, respectively, T'*An* Commander of the Hundred Thousand and Hexenmeister of the Brown Tower . . . Sunlight shone in: this morning far advanced. Blaize nodded a brief acknowledgement, on his way through.

'I've spoken to the Peir-Dadeni *s'ans*, they'll let the fleet travel up the Ai River, but it must be done in small groups—' His voice became muffled as he came up with Nelum Santhil, and spoke to the T'*An Suthai-Telestre* in that familiar accented Rimon.

Ruric, bowing with a studied formality, said to Cory Mendez, 'Forgive me, I must take the Representative from you for a short time.'

I took the hint instantly, and followed Ruric back outside. A table in the inner courtyard had been set with a meal, and we walked down the steps and seated ourselves there. The morning sun was warm, shining on the red *ziku* and the pale sandstone. Haze put a faint bloom on the morning: soft blue.

'I can't spare long,' I said. To be truthful, I could have sat on that wooden bench and gone off to sleep. Avoiding that, I took a drink of the herb-tea on the table; and leaned back and studied the dark Orthean female. 'Not masked?'

She chuckled. Lines showed in the fine-grained black skin round her eyes. 'Officially, I'm not here. Unofficially, there are still those who know me – having been up at the Citadel, that's unavoidable. Khassiye Reihalyn, I beg his pardon, Khassiye n'ri n'suth Andrethe – you remember him? – was appalled. But there seem to be people from Melkathi who still have a kindness towards me.' She shook her head; smiled. 'Strange.'

'No, not really. What about . . .' I looked at the scar on her forehead.

'Truly, yes, I should find myself in the Citadel's prison. Or else the lesser penalty, death. Maybe it's that much is forgiven someone wearing the robes of the Brown Tower. And that,' she said, 'is what I'd speak with you for, *S'aranth*. My Tethmet reminds me constantly that I shouldn't be outside Kasabaarde, and I begin to think I should not; so I've come to beg a favour of you, and that's a journey in one of your shuttlecraft.'

'Of course.'

She turned her head to look across the courtyard, through the entrance archway to the alley outside. The shadow of *ziku* dappled her dark face. Light fell on that narrow jaw, the fine line of her mouth and chin; left her eyes in shadow, citrine-bright.

'When will you leave?'

She smiled. There was nothing of Orhlandis in it; it was an expression I have seen before, in a far southern city, on the face of an old male Orthean, in the Brown Tower. I hardly recognize her, I thought. No, no need for Ruric Hexenmeister to go masked in Tathcaer; who would know her?

'A day or so,' she said. 'Christie, I dare not stay longer than that. If I did, I couldn't leave.'

Humid heat brought out sweat on my face, under my arms; and I leaned back, thinking Why is there always an ache somewhere? and Thirty-eight isn't old. The haze of the morning was creeping down to blur the flat white roofs of *telestre*-houses, and hide the distant view of the harbour at the bottom of Westhill.

And Molly was, what, not quite thirty?

I looked up at the upper-storey windows, hearing voices, but not able to see faces. Doug Clifford, and the Akida: both mauled by this world. And Molly Rachel not going home at all, unless it's in coldfreeze; and that (as we used to call it in the Service) is the short way home to Earth, shipped back faster than living tissue can stand.

Flagstones gritted dusty underfoot, and I leaned forward to reach the jug of herb-tea, and was suddenly conscious of how far, how very far, this hazy courtyard is from the acid heat of the Desert Coast . . . *Have we really done that? Started a war and then stopped it? No: we were only the pebble that triggered an avalanche, and avalanches can be diverted, but – at a cost?*

That's not for me to judge; if there was a price, it wasn't me who paid it. And we will never know, I thought, all that has happened on Orthe in this last half-year. How many lives have changed, on the canals, in the *siiran*. What hurt it is, when you are Rimnith or Keverilde, and smoke darkens the sky . . . What deaths have happened, in cities without walls, in rooms without doors.

'One more thing.' Ruric's voice broke into my thoughts. 'Pathrey

Shanataru comes back with me to the Tower. He being closest to the bel-Rioch child, I wish to know what he knows. You're aware I can discover more than you offworlders.'

I met her gaze, thinking, *Havoth-jair*.

'Last time you asked me that, I consented. You *are* Hexenmeister, aren't you?'

Her long fingers rubbed at the stump of her amputated arm as if it pained her.

'Christie, I said then and I say now: the Tower *must* stand. Any danger to it is a danger to Orthe. I want to know if Calil bel-Rioch heard somehow of that devastation she calls "ancient light", and if she knows that it isn't ended but only held back . . .' She blinked fine membrane down over honey-yellow eyes. 'And if she heard it, I must know where, and stop it being heard again. Or if she remembers, I want to know how it is that a Golden-blood has past memories. You *know* I have to do this. For our own safety.'

'Will the Wellhouse let you take him? Sorry, no. That's stupid of me. When did the Wellhouses ever refuse the Brown Tower?'

The bells for mid-morning rang across Westhill, muffled a little by the sea mist. Small *rashaku* soared up from the flat roof of the *telestre*-house. When the bells ceased, they gave way to a silence in which only the humming of *kekri*-flies could be heard.

'I'll let you have the transport,' I said.

Such a reward for betrayal, I thought. To leave Calil bel-Rioch, to bring valuable information here, to be imprisoned in the Wellhouse; and now to be taken south and have one's mind and memories ripped open . . . Pathrey, Pathrey – and I can't stop the Hexenmeister doing it, because I, also, remember; and know that it's necessary.

And then I sipped herb-tea, and with an Orthean black humour thought: You wanted to help us, Pathrey; you'll be more help than you intended. And who was it told me there's no justice? *Nobody* gets what they deserve, not you, and not Molly Rachel, that's for sure.

Ruric leaned back, cupping a bowl of herb-tea in her single hand. Though she still looked towards the archway, her gaze seemed turned inward. She said, 'A day, or two. Nelum Santhil doesn't fully trust the *hiyeks*, I think, and the past has given him good reason not to, but still, we can't falter at this last stage. It should end well for the Coast, as well as the Hundred Thousand. If there's a way it can be done, I'd have it end well for Kel Harantish.'

I said, 'And for Earth?'

She grinned at me then, raising her bowl in a mocking salute. 'And for Earth, too.'

The comlink dragged me up from a heavy sleep in the early hours of Merrum Secondweek Fourday, the following day.

I pushed back the *chirith-goyen* sleeping-cloths and sat up, half-dazed. Westhill-Ahrentine's rooms are lit at night with *kiez*-oil lanterns, and the yellow light shone on rumpled clothes and my discarded coverall, and on the half-uncovered back of Blaize Meduenin beside me: that line of naked shoulder and hip and thigh, made subtly different by alien musculature, and the tangled roots of a yellow mane. His body warm, dry, against my skin – and then he rolled over, coming awake with less than a mercenary fighter's swiftness.

'Sunmother! what—?'

'Jesus, it's an *alert*.'

I staggered through to the next room, pulling on my coverall, and slapped the acknowledge key on the comlink console. Blaize, behind me, grunted as he banged against the edge of the holotank; and I saw that instinct had made him, all oblivious, catch up *harur-nilgiri* before all else. *Who's here?* I wondered: a reasonable question considering the activity in Westhill-Ahrentine the last two days, *Nelum and Hal at the Citadel; where's Douggie?*—

The wail of the alert cut out. Ottoway's image appeared in the comlink 'tank.

'What the fuck is going on?'

Ottoway vanished, abruptly replaced by Corazon Mendez: 'Lynne, get back here – I'll send a 'thopter in now to pick you up.'

'What's happening?'

The white-haired woman turned her head away, speaking to someone out of comlink range; then turned back: 'Is Doug Clifford with you?'

'No, he's with the *takshiriye* in the Citadel. Cory, what the hell—'

'We're getting sensor readings from the sea vessels in the islands, your *hiyek*-ships, Lynne; they're moving.'

The bead curtain rattled, and Blaize came back dressed and pulling on *harur*-blade harness. He went to the head of the inner stairs, calling, and a wide-eyed *ashiren* came up from the kitchens.

'Send word to the Citadel, *arykei-te*?' he said. 'The child can find Clifford. What message?'

'I don't know, I don't understand – Cory, those ships are going to move. They've got to find safe moorings, reprovision before they can go north. What's the problem?'

'They've been moving for twenty minutes now, and we're getting readings consistent with weapons power-up. Whatever they've got on those tubs, Lynne, they're ready to use it; and goddammit, you ought to be here, there has to be a decision taken about what action we'll take!'

'What course – never mind: I've got it.'

Some moments are frozen, out of time, quite separate from life. Now in this lamp-lit room, among heaped parchments and print-outs, night pressing against the windows; *now* is one of those moments. Blaize with one warm hand resting on my shoulder as he leans over the holotank, its light harsh on his intent, scarred face. And the child-messenger, ten or eleven years old, with great dark eyes in a triangular face; padding across the *ziku*-wood floor to peer into the holotank, claw-nailed hands gripping the edge, scarlet mane rooting down its spine . . .

In the holotank, bright images: the firefly-specks that are heat-sensor readings of *jath* ships sailing out from the shelter of the Sisters Islands. Blue lines that are projected course estimates, and more than two hundred and thirty vessels are moving, and the course estimates are east: all of them east, towards the sunrise and Melkathi.

' "Power-up"?'

'There,' I said. 'Satellites wouldn't pick up CAS weaponry, but those are beam-pulsers; see, there . . . Christ Jesus, what are they *doing*? Cory's panicking – no, no she's not—' I keyed repeat on the comlink. 'Where the hell is Doug, why doesn't he answer?'

Blaize's calloused hand tightened, released. 'How long will it be until your craft comes from Kumiel?'

'A 'thopter? Ten minutes or so – no, wait. Cory,' I turned back to the comlink, 'I'll want the 'thopter for local transport here. I'll keep in real-time contact with you, but we need to know what the response *here* will be. As soon as the 'thopter gets here, I'm going up to the Citadel. We can't take a decision until we see what's happening.'

'Acknowledge.'

The contact snapped to relay, and I keyed it into my wristlink.

'Christie.'

The *ziku*-wood floor was hard under my bare feet. I blinked, still sick with the suddenness of that waking; and reached out to Blaize. The child gazed at us with silent curiosity, *s'aranthi* and Orthean not often seen together. After a few seconds Blaize broke away, and said, 'Go to the Citadel. I'll go up to Westhill-fort; I must see the Crown Guard.'

'Come to the Citadel first.'

He hesitated, and then nodded; and went through into the further room, and came back with two cloaks, and with my boots, and with the CAS-IV stungun in its holster. I belted it on with fingers that shook.

'*T'an*,' said the child, puzzled (and I realized we had been speaking Sino-Anglic, both of us), 'what's happening? What shall we do?'

Blaize said, 'Wake the house, and warn them that a ship-of-the-air will come, and that they should wake other *telestre*-houses here; it may be nothing, but it is better to be ready.'

The child's running footsteps faded, clattering down the inner stairs. I looked at Blaize, that scarred face that was now blank with calculation. As at Northfast, I thought, You've gone where I can't go – where I hope never to be.

'Mother of the Wells,' he said; and then the membrane slid back from those pale blue, whiteless eyes. 'They're fools if they do this.'

A muffled roar grew in volume, rattling the windows in their sockets. The door's bead-curtain lashed inward. The room was filled with the intermittent flash of the 'thopter's landing-lights; descending down into the inner courtyard. The noise was too loud to shout over. I gestured, and with Blaize behind me, ran down into the courtyard and scrambled up into the hovering 'thopter, half-blind with dust raised by its blades.

As he fell into the seat, pressed against me by upward acceleration, I put my mouth close to his ear. 'If they do what? Fools if they do what?'

Blaize Meduenin said, 'If they attack Tathcaer.'

So much confusion on Citadel Crag: I didn't think even the landing of an ornithopter could get the guards' attention. Cory's pilot put the machine down near the top of Crown Steps, on a mossgrass lawn between night-curled *lapuur*. While Blaize scrambled out, I keyed an automatic acknowledgement back to Kumiel, and then followed him: staring up at the multi-towered Citadel, hearing shouts, seeing messengers rushing to and fro between buildings; and then – as we came to one of the main entrances – a voice hailed me in Anglic:

'Lynne! Have you contacted your people? I can't get through to the Residence.'

'There's no one there now. Yes; Douggie, we've got to talk.'

I saw a frown on Doug's face, that lasted for only a second. *Blaize*, I realized. Then Doug glanced past both of us at the 'thopter, idling now; raised his eyebrows, and said, 'The *T'An Suthai-Telestre* has messengers going out for you, and for the *T'An* Commander. We'd better find him.'

It's those ships out there we have to contact, I thought. The Desert Coast families . . .

How?

As if he read my mind, Douggie stopped under the archway-entrance to the Citadel. 'I believe some kind of observation may be in order. Lynne, if I could borrow your 'thopter for half an hour: I want to get to my shuttle on Kumiel.'

'You're not thinking of overflying those ships—'

'One might make a voicecast contact.'

Two Orthean males in Crown Guard uniform pushed between us, and Blaize called them back; stepping to one side to speak with them urgently and concisely. Doug's gaze followed him. That prim mouth quirked a little, and he looked at me, but said nothing. Two *s'aranthi* among so many Ortheans . . . Doug checked his own wristlink again, and his face cleared.

'Kumiel are answering. Lynne, I'll tell the pilot to come back here, as soon as he's flown me to the island.'

'If you overfly, stay out of range. The *hiyek* ships fired on us before.' I shivered. The wind began to blow cold, and though the east was still dark that meant first twilight wasn't far away. Starlight was dimming. Voices of messengers and guards rang in the Citadel's cold stone walls.

'I imagine I'll be back here within two hours or so,' Doug said. 'Convey my apologies to the *T'An Suthai-Telestre*.'

He turned and walked hurriedly away from the arch, across the dew-soaked mossgrass, and I saw him duck under the 'thopter's idling blades and speak with the pilot, and then climb up into the cabin. A siren-blast split the night air. Two or three Ortheans close by moved rapidly back, and the 'thopter lifted, curving away off Citadel crag and out over the city.

Blaize appeared beside me. 'I'll be with you as soon as I've put this troop in order. Tell *T'An* Santhil I'm setting up heliograph-links between here and the forts on Easthill and Westhill. Riders aren't fast enough. Send word if you need me, *arykei-te*.'

I touched the comlink fastened to his broad wrist. 'Send word if you hear anything before I do.'

Hardly minutes that we stood there: still, a dull grey light was growing round us. First twilight passing into dawn. We parted, and I went into the Citadel's low-roofed interlocking rooms. The press of the crowd was even greater here. I caught sight of a male in Wellhouse robes, and began to push through towards him.

Then, bright against the pale plaster walls, there was the scarlet mane of Cassirur Almadhera; and I forced my way through to the Earthspeaker's side.

'Where are the *takshiriye*? Who's here?'

She held a thin strip of paper in those brown, six-fingered hands. A *rashaku* message? When she looked up from reading it, her face was grave. 'Give you greeting, Christie. The *T'An Suthai-Telestre* is in the north tower. I'll accompany you there. I fear . . .'

Cassirur said no more, but drew her slit-backed green robe closely about her, and pushed hurriedly between a group of *s'ans* in Roehmonde dress. I followed. She went unerringly to lesser-used rooms, and then out into a courtyard surrounded on all five sides by high walls, and crossed to a flight of outside steps. I felt the cold wind. The arch of the sky was grey, paling to white; the highest pinnacles of this Citadel just touched with a yellow light.

I lifted my wrist, about to key in a contact to the Kumiel Island base. Before I could do that, the wristlink suddenly emitted a high-pitched squeal.

'*S'aranth*, what—?' Cassirur stopped with her foot on the bottom step.

'I don't know. I – *Jesus Christ!*' I ripped the wristlink off, dropping it on the stone; and the sound rose to a pitch and then shattered: the casing split with a sharp crack. That gunshot-sound echoed back from high walls. Cassirur Almadhera frowned. I knew then what it was: for a minute the implications silenced me. Then: 'Warn the people here. Cassirur, let's move; that means—'

She said, 'I don't understand. You can't speak with your people?'

Blaize, I thought. And then: What's happening to Doug, now? And Kumiel – Christ, what are they doing on Kumiel; what will Cory do!

Cassirur's urgent questions went by me unheeded, I could only stand there, in that deserted courtyard, watching the light of the unseen rising sun gild the high walls; watching and waiting, and – *there*. A sound in the distance, a hollow noise. So very small, for what it is. Another followed, and another; and the red-maned Orthean female turned her head, listening.

I bent down and picked up the useless wristlink and put it in my belt-pouch.

'Pulse-blocker,' I said, not caring that she wouldn't understand. 'Oh, damn Pramila Ishida. Her and Sethri and all the others . . . They've got a transmission-blocker on one of those ships. A CAS-II. That's done us, that's finished us . . .' I looked at Cassirur. 'That's *all* communications out. Ship-to-ship. Ship-to-base. Base-to-orbiter. We're isolated. I can't talk with Cory's people – hell, they can't talk with the shuttles that are already on surveillance – Christ, what a mess!'

That hollow noise came again. Small and soft: only frightening because of how distant it must be, and so how devastating at its source . . .

Cassirur Almadhera pushed the red mane back from her face, intently listening. Then she turned back to the steps. 'Come. I'll hear by *rashaku*. By heliograph, when it's light. We're not in ignorance, *S'aranth*. Come.'

The attack's begun, but where? What's happening? Is it a few ships, is it all of them, is it only here, is it – *what's happening?* We should have guessed they'd have transmission-blockers; if I didn't, Cory should have; what we could have done – what could we have done? What can we do *now?*

Across the six-mile distance between the Citadel and the harbour comes, faintly, the sounds of beam-pulser and projectile fire.

A white fog clung to the land. It shrouded the river on the city's eastern side, blurring the line of the Ymirian hills, far to the sunrise. And it hung in the alleyways, between the *telestre*-houses, so that I could see only a glimpse of flat roofs below. That and the gilded dome of the Wellhouse, and running figures in the Square . . . Almost dawn: river fog turning from grey to white to gold.

'". . . attack on harbour".' Nelum Santhil Rimnith turned away as the heliograph-spark ceased to flash. 'Christie? Give you greeting; I've no time for *s'aranthi* now, unless you've news?'

The lookout post was no more than a flat stretch of the Citadel crag's rock. A low wall had been built on the edge, so that no one could fall down the cliff that went sheer, vine-covered, down to the Square. A handful of Ortheans stood on this pale rock, gazing south over the city towards Easthill, on which the heliograph lately ceased; tall and braided-maned and richly robed – the *T'Ans* of the Hundred Thousand.

'Only that our communications are cut,' I said.

He nodded once, and his eyes veiled. Without another word, he gestured a young male to him; and as I watched them speaking I thought, Yes, you know what it means.

I put both hands on the low wall to steady myself. The pale stone felt cold. Across the fog-shrouded city, the two hills were faint grey lines on the horizon. A brief flash of light there drew my gaze. Two more followed: the *crack* echoed up to us minutes later. I squinted, the sun in my eyes – and realized, that warmth on my cheek, that the sun was rising above the fog: Carrick's Star burning silver, acid-white. And saw also that pale specks caught the light high above. Peace Force shuttles. Not in cruise-patterns, but criss-crossing the area at random. *What will they do when they see –*

See the attack?

Something wrong with the silhouette of Easthill, Easthill where I once had my envoy's Residence – and then I made out that the line of the hilltop was jagged, not smooth. The whine of CAS-weapon leakage reached my ears, and I thought, At this distance? and I should do something and What?

'*S'aranth*, you shouldn't be here,' a worried voice said; and Haltern n'ri n'suth Beth'ru-elen came to stand at the wall beside me, leaning heavily on his *hanelys* cane. 'You can be of no use; go.'

'Hal—'

'Why are they doing this?' He gripped my arm, little strength in that thin six-fingered hand. 'Christie, I never thought I should see this!' He raised his head. 'What will your people do now?'

One of the *s'ans* a few yards further along the cliff cried out. As he pointed down into the city, a Wellhouse male came up with a *rashaku* message; and I leaned out from the wall and stared into the distance – and there: firing to the west side of the city, flashes of light, and now a plume of dust going up into the morning sunlight.

Haltern said, 'Ferries. Ferries and bridges. They will send their *jath-rai* upriver to destroy the bridges!'

An answering flare and *crack!* drowned out his words. Down in the fog, still blotting out the eastern-side river, red and yellow flame billowed up: a black pall rising. Sun glinted on metal sails. *Jath-rai. Jath-rai* and the sunrise tide, I thought stupidly, and: why are they blasting the bridges?

The *T'An Suthai-Telestre* Nelum Santhil strode away, back towards the walls and arches of the Citadel, half the Ortheans going with him. I turned, would have spoken, thought: What can I say? A male in Wellhouse robes padded across the pale rock towards us.

'*T'an S'aranth. T'an* Beth'ru-elen. Will you come? We are to get all who may leave away from the city, while that can still be done.' His eyes veiled, as the sound came of distant explosions. 'If you will come, come now.'

'Hal . . .'

He looked up at me, the morning light sharp on his lined face and wisp of white mane. Those harassed blue eyes had the clarity of a child's. The city lay below and beyond him, mist rising as the sun burned it off, and, rising with it, the smoke-palls of explosions. The air shook. Fear cramped in my stomach, as I knew then: this is happening, this cannot be stopped, they are attacking.

If I can get somewhere I can signal to a shuttle . . .

Such a feeling of isolation gripped me that I clenched my fists, nails biting into my palms.

'There are Beth'ru-elen in the city,' Haltern protested.

People are here that I have known and worked with for the last half-year; some that I've known for far longer – and I didn't, even to myself, think: Where is she? Citadel or Wellhouse or down in the city?

'We're coming,' I said, putting my arm round Haltern's shoulders and urging him towards the Citadel walls. The Wellhouse male nodded and set off in front of us. 'Didn't you always tell me to leave a losing game?'

'This isn't *ochmir, S'aranth.*'

Footsteps eat up so small a distance, compared with what we have to cross: the mossgrass lawns, black with dew; the rooms of the Citadel, the city's alleys, the ferries or the bridge . . .

'Hal, I'm scared, and I'm taking you out of here. What do you think will happen when CAS weapons and beam-pulsers attack people who have *harur*-blades and winchbows? For God's sake, Hal!' And then, seeing his face, I was ashamed of that brutality: 'Please come. There isn't time to argue now.'

Explosions sounded nearer. A *crack!* sounded almost at my side, and I jumped, and then saw how – quarter of a mile away – one of the eastside bridges cleared the mist. Two stone pilings jutted out into the water: beyond that, heaps of fallen stone smoked in the air, and the river-water rose swiftly to choke the makeshift new dam. At this distance, figures no larger than ants ran with ants' seeming purposelessness. The cold east wind made my eyes sting. I had a sudden flashback to another place and time – *what world was that?* – and then realized: Not my Service career, but when I was a child, thirty years ago, caught when they put down the Food Riots in the European Enclaves. The child's fear now bitter as copper in my mouth.

'Hal, come on—'

One hand under his elbow: I hustled him into the shadow of the Citadel's walls, and then – since I must let him rest – called the Wellhouse male back. Two Ortheans in Peir-Dadeni dress left the crowd, and Hal raised his head to speak breathlessly with them. I stared east. The edge of the crag hid the city, and the sky was silver-bright. A deep grinding roar sounded, so that I felt it rather than heard it: the very rock vibrating. A dark speck crossed the arch of the sky. A shuttle – and I'm *here*, I raged inwardly. How can I signal, how can I let them know?

What is Cory Mendez doing now?

I turned to the Wellhouse male. 'Are there *rashaku* on Kumiel Island? Or a heliograph? Is there any way to get a message there?'

He shrugged, alien musculature moving lightly under the brown robe. I wanted to hit him. His fair mane was shaven down to fur, and his eyes were veiled with membrane; and he had the calmness of an Earthspeaker. I thought of Cassirur's Many will go to the Goddess and I wanted to cry.

'*Is* there?'

'If there is, *t'an*, you would have to go to the forts on Easthill or Westhill, or the great Wellhouse here, and I think that impossible now. The forts—'

'I'll go to the Wellhouse.'

The sun is not yet clear of the dawn mist, it isn't ten minutes since the 'thopter landed me here. Ten minutes, I thought. I walked across to Haltern Beth'ru-elen, and said, 'I'll join you as soon as I can. I'm going to try and get word to Mendez.'

The old male looked up. 'What will you tell her to do?'

'I – don't know. Don't wait for me; I'll find you.'

My shadow was long in front of me, slanting into the west. I ran towards the Citadel, found a path that seemed to skirt it, and followed that; breath sawing in my throat. Few people blocked my path. Stopping for breath, I thought, Where? and then heard the shouting of a crowd, and as I came round one buttress of that great sprawling complex of buildings, saw Crown Steps thick with Ortheans. Brown-robed priests kept the cliff-path from being a bottleneck. Evacuation, I realized; bent double, trying to catch my breath, and in that unguarded second thought Blaize and then Buric and then straightened up, throat tight, and ran on.

Flagstones jarred under my feet. A blast of sound rocked me and I staggered, slipping to one knee. The stone was wet under my hands with dew. Roar of sound: a bass rumble that caught in the throat and chest, and *crack!* and I stood up, shaking, and leaned against the wall.

Dust drifted between me and the sky. A spatter of grit stung my cheek, so that I spun round and put my hand up and brought it away bloody: realized that I had the smooth grip of the CAS-IV stungun in that fist and thought What the fuck use is that? and squatted down, back to the wall. Cold stone. The noise went on and on.

Dust, pale in the golden air. It caught in my throat and I coughed and spat, was for one second certain I would vomit; then leaned back again. Sound hit like a hammerblow: I flinched. *I must get up and move fifty yards along this wall and there are the Wellhouse gates. Move!*

The dust-cloud billowed across the Square, that wide open expanse of space. There was sunlight shining on the blue vines that cloaked the cliff, and no one to be seen; jagged beams rising out of rubble that had been *telestre*-houses, those white façades that line the Square, and no living thing moving: only *there* – and I looked down at the flagstones between my feet, and not at the sprawled bodies. *Come on, Lynne, move!* I hauled myself up, the muscles of my legs shaking.

A high-pitched whine pierced the air, making me grunt with pain. Something down the far end of the Square moved, the flagstones shook, and a cloud of stone-dust rolled like a wave between buildings: the surf of it spattered against the Wellhouse wall, fifty yards down from where I stood. *Why can't I see them? Why can't I see who's doing this?*

Easier to run than walk. I kept close to the wall, bruised my shoulder when I knocked against it running; and the air began to clear, blue and gold above me, and the fine dust sifted down and whitened my coveralls, showed the tracks of my feet; there was a silence so abrupt that I heard my own ragged gasps for breath, and then I was through the gates and into the Wellhouse courtyard.

'*Cassirur!*'

Panicked, I thought They've gone and then I saw Ortheans in the arched doorway of the great dome, and slowed my steps as I came up to them. An exhilaration born out of fear began to grip me, and I grinned at the young female Earthspeaker who pulled me into the arch's shelter.

'Where's Cassirur Almadhera? No, anyone will do, anyone who can help me get a message across to Kumiel Island.'

'There isn't time!' She stared out, up at the sky; and flinched back. I shut my eyes in time: the laser-flare was scarlet against closed lids. When I could see through streaming tears, I said: 'What about messages coming in? What's happening?'

'*I don't know.* There is one bridge still, at Eastwall. Go while you can.' She put up claw-nailed fingers before her face, membrane flicking to clear vision; and at last focused. Without another word she strode back into the Wellhouse.

Still on the crest of that exhilaration, I thought, Where else can I go? and moved a few steps into the courtyard. Two Earthspeakers passed without noticing a *s'aranthi*; a third, running, shouting words I couldn't catch. Through the open gates in the high wall, I saw a flash of colour, realized it to be riders on *marhaz*, and ran on suddenly aching legs towards them. By the time I reached the Square they had passed, vanishing into dust and haze.

Weariness caught me. My fingers ached, gripping the butt of the CAS-IV, and I absently put the stungun back into its holster. What is useful for personal protection is no use when – and I lost the train of thought: *crack!* and again, and again; and I pressed back against the high wall. They must be firing from the ships still, and that's the noise down at the harbour. And here? If they've destroyed the bridges, they're turning their weapons on the city.

I wiped my mouth. Dust was gritty in my teeth; thirst an unacknowledged pain. The wind brought the smell of burning. The sun caught the pinnacles of the crag above the Square, and I stood in cold morning shadow, and then without any sense of decision began to walk out into the open. *One bridge still, at Eastwall.* And so to reach the end of this wall and go down into the alleys, down the hill, would take me towards Eastwall (towards the noise of firing), would take me towards a bridge (away from the smoke of burning buildings; how fast does fire spread in a dry summer?) and out of the city.

Blaize, I thought. Ruric.

I stopped, now almost at the far end of the Square, still beside the wall surrounding the Wellhouse. Baked clay bricks cold with this early hour: I reached out a hand for support. Not a hundred yards away, *telestre*-houses made a wasteland of rubble and beams and dust rising into the sunlight; and the sky cleared milky blue, skeined across with bright pinpricks that are daystars, the signs of a hot, clear day. *Is it possible to get back into the Citadel?* The distant cliff-walk stood deserted. *Is there any point?* A few figures, tiny at this distance, could just be seen on the crag's edge.

Ruric, I thought. Blaize.

The ground shuddered. I stumbled away from the high wall. Its shadow was long, blocking out sunlight. Broken bricks littered the flagstones, had in their fall ripped up a tangle of *kazsis*-vine, that wept a clear sap. I stood and stared up, tipping my head back so far that it made me dizzy. *Will the 'thopter come back? That was hours ago. No, not hours; not half an hour* – The daystarred sky blurred. Sound battered my ears: came from behind me, from the banks of the river; came from the distance, down by the harbour; came from everywhere at once. The stink of burning grew stronger, and I coughed.

Quickly, keeping some yards out from the wall, I walked to the end of the Square. I skirted rubble. And then, when I came to the end of the wall, stopped: a few yards downhill, more rubble blocked the alley.

If I stop, I won't move again; I'll be too afraid, I thought, and so I turned without breaking stride and began to walk out across the Square, heading out across that expanse of flagstones, towards the *telestre*-houses on the far side. The white, windowless façades gleamed in the sunlight – untouched? But smoke rose from somewhere.

Another silence: in it, far away, a voice screamed in animal pain – my palms sweated; I was almost glad when a sharp explosion blotted out the sound. *Don't think: move!* A great tiredness weighed on me, and I stopped, and stared round.

Nothing moving but the drifting dust, and the plumes of black smoke that rise over the roof-tops . . . The sun cut through in shafts, slanting from the east; and I walked a step, and looked back, and stopped again. *That* is unchanged – the brown dome of the Wellhouse and, there, the cliff-walk and the pinnacles of the Citadel, high in the morning air, and the blue sky beyond – and I stand here, feet like lead, panting, dazed: *What do I do now?*

Sound blotted out the noise of burning, a roar so deep that I only felt it. It took the breath out of my lungs. I blinked against the flash of the explosion, and felt air hot on my face, and then opened my eyes again and found myself staring up at the grey stone walls of the Citadel. Something is wrong, I thought idly, and the rock and masonry began to peel apart like an opening flower and fall into the air, and part of the cliff began ponderously to slide down towards the Square and I turned to run.

CHAPTER 37

Dust and Sunlight

Vomit tasted sour in my mouth. Something hard dug into my back and I flinched away, blacked out again – again? – for a second; and then I was leaning with my back against something, sitting up, and a thin bile down the front of my coverall. I moved: nausea swamped me, it was some time before I recognized it as pain.

What—?

The blurred light came into focus. I stared up at golden air. Dust hung in suspension, gently drifting . . . blurred again: tears pouring down my face. With my right hand I fumbled for my belt-pouch, got it open, and crammed two painkiller tabs in my mouth: too dry to swallow and so I chewed, bitter froth at last letting me choke them down. Dust moving in the early sun, hazing in gold the heaps of rubble, broken masonry, spilled furniture, smashed glass . . . And my back was pressed up against a great slab of granite. Stone splinters littered the ground. To move – and I yelled: pain sickened me. *But you're not even marked.* Pain settled: my right leg. Coverall torn slightly at the knee and I thought How the hell—? and tried to push myself more upright and screamed.

The sound echoed. All else, silence.

You should be dead, I realized.

Tears poured down my face, and every breath made me gasp. I felt the instant the painkillers began to hit, and opened my eyes (when did I shut them?) and felt sun warm on my wet face. My heart hammered. Even that movement made me feel sick.

I couldn't turn my head. I saw, a few yards to either side, tumbled grey rock like some river ravine, but the sides freshly splintered open; and further off the beginning of demolished *telestre*-houses, and there, beyond a fallen wall, the roofs of the buildings built on the lower slopes of Easthill and *I shouldn't be able to see that from here*. Still breathing as hard as if I'd been running, I looked down, careful not to move; one leg untouched, the other –

the right leg – with only the smallest cut in the beige cloth. Pain burned, centred in the knee. It was a reflex action to try and bend – *no*, I thought, Jesus Christ, don't!

Cautiously, I reached down. There was a tightness, flesh swelling under the cloth. Already? And then I thought: But how long was I blacked-out for? Not more than minutes? I worked my fingers into the rip in the cloth and, centimetre by centimetre, widened the tear. The flesh was puffy. Dare I touch it – and bit back another scream. I bruise easily: a bruise yellowed all the right side of my knee, and it was grazed and weeping blood, and how can that hurt this much? I thought. And knew: the kneecap's broken. I rested my head back against the granite that supported me and swore aloud: my knee throbbed as if a hammer hit it. With shaking fingers I got out the pain-tabs from the belt-pouch. Two taken: six remaining. Without much thought I put one in my mouth and chewed. It made no difference.

Five or ten minutes passed? Fluid thickened my leg so that the knee was hardly visible, and the pain of it brought the sweat out all over me. *How long have I been here?* and then *I ought to move, it isn't safe here!*

'Help!' The effort made me gasp. Mouth too dry: how can I be heard? I gathered strength, shouted in two or three Orthean languages. There was no answer. Nothing moved but the dust and smoke . . . and the faint sound of explosions. No, not faint; Christ, I thought, I can't hear properly! That's close – is it? I can't stay here.

If you try to put weight on that knee, you'll be unconscious, some pedantic part of my mind informed me. Think: you've had Service training. What to do? *Think.* Give it some support. *Do* something.

There is wood in that rubble and wood is splints, is something you can use, can tie round; nothing to tie it with – the belt, that's it. If I can get there, it isn't far—

I put both palms flat on the flagstones and lifted myself, moving sideways. Pain hit me. The nausea faded slowly, and I slumped back; *not* the way to do it . . . A cool breeze blew out of the east, bringing the smell of the river and the alleys; and the acrid taste of smoke. I bent forward and got my hands one under my thigh, one under my calf, lifted; moved the leg inches before pain made me hiss out a breath and rest; and then lifted myself another few inches sideways, to the limit of tension on my knee, and then bent forward and *lift* again . . . Inching sideways, sight blinded with tears; crying out because what does it matter who hears me? I want to be heard. Conscious of cold flagstones under my palms, of

901

grit and rock-splinters; conscious that the stone was now warm, that I must be in the sun, and that I must rest.

A shadow crossed the ruins: a shuttle cruising ! ˙ and I looked up so sharply that the pain made me swear. Sun gleamed on the white hull and then it was gone.

'Bastards!' No more than a whisper: drowned out by the muffled *crack!* of an explosion. Is that near? I thought. No, I'm sure it's not. It's down at the harbour. It is.

The painkillers began really to bite. Is it so short a time? I thought. I won't have much respite, I'd better do what I can now. I rested for a moment, licking my palms where I'd cut them; eyeing the nearest heap of bricks and timber. Too precarious even for someone who could walk . . . I leaned forward, getting my hands round the nearest piece of wood; and then stopped and with some effort tore both sleeves off my coverall at the shoulder-seams. Wrapping them round my hands gave me some protection against splinters. Every tug on a plank or brick jolted my knee; and I doubled up, noises wrenched out of me.

By the time I'd cleared three flimsy slats from the edge of the heap, my hearing was coming back. Every distant explosion made me wince. The sun was hot, even though it was early; and *kekri*-flies buzzed round me in the heat. At last I could turn my head far enough to see the Citadel – and stared: the morning sun shone now on a titanic stump of rock, a few layers of masonry clinging to it here and there. The northern sky seemed bright, seemed *empty*: I have always been used to seeing the Citadel there, and now . . .

I got two hands to my leg and lifted it, laying it down on the stoutest wooden slat – and that's not so strong, I thought; not at all – and rested. Two other slats at the side. And take off the belt, and rip up cloth sleeves, and remember Service training – *no!* I rested. The dust made my lips dry. *If you don't do it now you won't do it at all.* I pushed one end of the belt under the slat, looped it round the two side slats, took a breath, and pulled it tight round mid-thigh. *Where are my blackouts when I need them?* It almost made me laugh: true hysteria. I knotted the first torn sleeve round the splints below my knee, feeling the support bite; chewed another pain-tab; tried to tie cloth *over* the knee and fluid swelling, and screamed. Tied it also below the knee.

You ought to be dead; you're lucky you're alive. Hold on to that thought.

Whatever caught me a glancing blow could have killed me, I thought; and it's done more than break that knee, it's smashed it, I'm sure of it. Jesus Christ, what am I going to do!

Move.

For minutes I stayed still, lying back on the ground, staring up into the depths of the pale blue sky, watching daystars. Not even an hour past sunrise. The light still comes strong and level from the east. Every splintered beam, every brick, every uprooted vine casts a precise shadow. Haze and dust blur the edges of vision, the air still golden with dust that sifted down, and I could taste the smoke of something burning; strain as I might, I couldn't *hear* fire. Not close, then. No, but how close does it have to be, when all I can do is crawl?

I'm not sure I can even do that.

My hands smarted as I eased myself up into a sitting position. You'll be worse cut yet, I thought, staring at the only clear way between sprawls of collapsed walls and buildings. And how *far* is it clear?

Doesn't matter.

I tightened my belt, although it made my thigh throb. Anything to immobilize the joint – and yes, I can ease forward; can drag the leg, and it hurts, but I can do it, I can. *God!* Ah, stop squalling, you little fucker; *move*. That's it: move.

Feeling dwarfed between fallen stone and rubble, I put my hands down and pushed; eased back a foot or so, grunting with pain; and if I had any humour, I thought, I'd laugh at me dragging myself along backwards, can't see where I'm going, but no, I don't feel like laughing. And there have to be people *somewhere*.

The wooden slats scraped on the stone as I pushed myself across the ground, bending double, lifting; trying to ease my leg. The sun was hot on my back. A feeling of sickness swept over me, and I halted; then began again to drag myself slowly across the littered flagstones. The horizon became a shattered wall, jutting up into a blue sky. As I inched on, more came into view – the house split open, exposed to the air; there a first-floor inner window, part of a ceiling . . . Suddenly I looked down, concentrating on my hands. Better not to see some things. Better not to see a crushed arm covered with masonry, a gold stud still set into the skin between each slender claw-nailed finger. Better to look down and see the flagstones, brace a heel and *push* and *lift* . . .

The rumble of fire grew so constant that I ignored it. Only when a shuttlecraft roared overhead did I look up, helpless, and shout and wave; but nothing happened, and I went back to that slow progress. Every few seconds I looked over my shoulder. Tumbled stone blocked one way, and here two or three buildings had fallen together – several bodies lay in the rubble, not moving. And part of a fallen wall.

When I turned my head back, and rested, and checked the splints, my hands left bloody prints on the cloth of my coveralls. Splinters of glass and stone . . . Frightened into effort, I hauled myself forward. The weakened cloth bandages parted. When I could see, through tears of pain, I picked up the lengths of cloth and knotted them together again, tied them, thinking How long will this last? The sun now made flagstones and rubble hot. When I twisted round preparatory to moving, I saw there was no way between the heaps of rubble. No way at all.

I'd like to see this from the air. Cory will report it as 'a simultaneous strike on the harbour and the Citadel' – Jesus, they've flattened everything round here. *How far?*

I leaned forward, resting, breathing heavily. My coveralls were filthy. What I could see of my knee through the torn cloth was a pallid white, swollen with fluid; the bruises turning from yellow to black, and I thought How can it look like nothing and hurt like this? If I could see how far this extends, I'd know what to do: go back, go forward, stay here – no, I can't stay here. Wreckage burns. Well then . . .

Carefully, I lifted myself on to the edge of the heap of fallen brickwork. A house-wall had come down all of a piece here, and bracing my heel I pushed myself up on to it; and then I lifted again and shifted a few inches further up the slope, and felt broken brick under me, cutting sharply. A splinter drove up under the nail of my forefinger. I swore, sucked at it. *Push* and *lift*. Brace heel. Now I was a few yards above ground level, I could see how the Square was devastated – buried under the rock-slide of the collapsing cliff. If I can see where I'm going, I thought, and twisted, moving one hand—

Came down on empty air. Bricks shifted, a kaleidoscope of sky, walls, roofs blinded me; there was a horrible grinding noise and I fell. Plunged backwards and down and *rolled*, throat ripped open with screaming, felt the wooden splints on my leg give – and hit sharp edges with outstretched hands, not able to stop that sickening slide; bricks falling with me, and I hit something that knocked me breathless. Pain convulsed me; I vomited. I was still, but sprawled backwards across the foot of a wall, and splints and belt gone, and leg crooked at an angle. I blacked out.

The pain brought me back to consciousness.

When I felt for pain-tabs, two were gone. A bitterness remained in my mouth. Did I take them? I wondered. And realized that I must have. The white sun dazzled me and I moved my head. The world swung. Nausea made me shut my eyes; when I opened them, I saw my hand lying on the earth in front of me, and realized I must be on my back. Earth, not stone. I raised my head. The rubble-slide had left me on earth, and I lifted myself a little further, seeing that my right leg was still crooked; bruised and swollen.

Reached down to touch my hip, that seemed all hot fire. My leg, lying still partly on broken brick, and the foot and calf turned in at an angle – I shut my eyes, sick; every gasp made pain flare through me, made me sob on every harsh indrawn breath. Which hurts more, the pain or the fear? Fear: I daren't look at my leg, the torn cloth covering swollen flesh, now torn and ripped, and seeping blood and a pale fluid. The sun was hot on my head and the earth warm under my back and I couldn't tell what hurt, myself or the earth; pain too large to be contained in blood and flesh and bone.

Time passing: minute and slow minute. *Dear God let me black out.* Each minute carrying its full weight of hot sun – still just past dawn – and thundering noise. Each explosion made me sob, shake; I shifted, and screamed, and the pain choked me off: voiceless, blinded with tears.

Minute by minute in the hot morning, lips cracking and dusty. *If this doesn't stop I'll die.* And the realization, quite cold and apart, *Yes, I will die.* Not of the injury, not even of shock and pain, but if the fighting comes this way, or the wreckage burns, or this goes on through days and nights without water and food.

Somewhere in those minutes – twenty of them, or half an hour, no more – I put the last pain-tabs into my mouth, and chewed a bitter dust.

The painkillers cut the edge of it, and I lay for a minute and panted, thinking *Pain exhausts* and blinking against the sunlight above me. Now I could turn my head to the side, away from the slope of fallen masonry that loomed on my left hand, and strain to focus . . . into distance.

I lay on broken earth above a slope. A *telestre*-house wall, hit by projectile fire, had dragged part of the hillside when it fell: landsliding down on the alleys and buildings below. Broken earth began three yards from where I lay. I looked down on earth and uprooted *kazsis* and a scatter of kitchen implements and two dark-maned Ortheans. One was buried except for a head and arm. The other – an elderly female – lay face down and motionless. I looked away.

The slope of the hill below me shone in the eastern sun. Pale-walled *telestre*-houses, untouched. Figures ran on flat roofs, scurrying from cover to cover. Beyond that – squinting into the rising sun – the river gleamed. It tumbled and rushed over a fallen bridge. The metal sails of *jath-rai* shone too bright to look at. Faintly through the air came the whine of CAS weaponry, like the hum of *kekri*-flies at this distance. There were people down by the bridges and that cold part of my mind observed *Anyone I can see must be dead; the living will be under cover from the firing* and I turned my head away: pain hammering behind my eyes.

No wooden slats now, nothing within arm's reach or even close, to use as splint or support . . . I caught my breath, eased back – and slumped down: seconds before my vision cleared, and *no there's no point in moving, where can I go?* Better to conserve strength.

I heard voices, close at hand, and without any pause to consider, shouted – voice a dry croak, and taking a breath was agony, but I shouted:

'Help! Over *here*—'

A head rose over the top of the heap of fallen masonry, and I looked up at a brown-maned and brown-skinned Orthean male, hardly more than *ashiren*; and his eyes widened, and he called down behind him, '*S'aranthi!*' and then scrambled over and down – I threw my arms across my face. Grunted with pain – but no slide of fallen bricks came down with him; he stepped lightfootedly down beside me, and squatted down, and glanced first at my leg, and then at this exposed position and the town below.

'Can you walk?' he said in a soft Ymirian accent.

'*No I—*' And what's he to know about it? 'No, I can't move; my leg's smashed.'

'Don't worry.' He flinched as a *crack!* sounded, and on the hillside below, smoke boiled up from a *telestre*-house. 'Hey, Sulis; down here! Quick!'

An older female appeared, so like him that they must be of one *telestre*, and I lightheadedly thought, *I should tell you to get out, it isn't safe here!* and knew I wouldn't. She scrambled down the heap of bricks and masonry and timber, cat-cautious, her gaze on the river below; and without preamble said to the boy, 'We'll have to carry her out', and to me, 'This will hurt.'

She grabbed me under the arms, signalling to the boy. Strong hands gripped my good leg; I felt myself lifted – and screamed: no help for it, screamed and swore at them to put me down for Chrissakes I'm in fucking agony; and the blue sky and the sunlight ran together, and I passed half-in, half-out of consciousness.

And then I lay on the flagstones thinking *Back where I started* with hysterical amusement; this isn't an hour since I stood in the Citadel and talked with Douggie and Blaize and Hal; and I saw the rubble and realized *they must have carried me; how in hell – ?* The woman and the boy stood over me, talking urgently. Then she lifted her brown hand, signalling.

'Thank you – '

The boy squatted down beside me. He put one six-fingered hand up to brush back his mane, and his eyes were on the ruins we were in and not on me. 'Wouldn't have stopped if you hadn't called out, *t'an*. This is our last time through. You're lucky. You – I'm coming, Sulis. Here!'

Wood hit flagstones with a crash; hands lifted me so swiftly that I had hardly time to cry out; and then there was wood under me, something soft jammed into my side; the tail of the *jasin* was fastened up again by the woman, and with a jolt we moved. I raised my head, sick; vomited bile, and then retched. I wiped at the front of my coverall, and the stink made me close my eyes. When I opened them, seconds later, the *jasin* was passing under a grey stone arch, in cold shadow, and out on to a wind-swept quay, and I thought Where? and We can't have come so far in moments.

What lay soft against me was an Orthean female, unconscious and moaning; and I twisted to look back over my shoulder, and saw two more Ortheans in the carriage – one stared at me; her arm was soaked black with blood – and a *skurrai* with the brown-maned boy at its head, and beyond the beast a number of other carts and carriages, and wounded men and women lying on blankets spread on quaystones, and the wind whipped crests onto the river – no, the estuary.

The wide sky was clear, and bright, and the wind brought a fine spray – lips tasting that sweet-salt alien water – and far out, almost to the other side of the water, a ferry tacked into land on the mainland. I shut my eyes, shivered; was hot and then cold; found that I couldn't stop shivering. *They're going to move me, going to lift me off this cart; going to move me again, Christ Jesus!* I opened gummy eyes and stared blankly, and managed to focus on my leg. Swollen flesh: pressing hard against the ripped cloth. The cloth now stained a bright pink. Other leg crooked up, braced against the *jasin* tailboard, *how did I have the sense to do that?*

'—she's an offworlder!'

'I don't care, she goes with the rest. I'm leaving no one here that we can move!'

They came into my field of vision, silhouetted against the estuary, and the morning sun off the water momentarily blinded me. The female, Sulis, and another woman.

'Sunmother, no, I won't take her! Let her stay here and rot.'

'I haven't got time for this!' The dark-maned female swung round, walking away, and threw back over her shoulder: 'Ask the *T'An* – don't bother me – leave her, then!'

I got a hand on the edge of the *jasin* and pulled myself up an inch or two. A small quayside area, a steep hill above; and the sun coming from *there* and so this must be one of the west-river ferries.

Muzzily, I called out, but the Orthean woman was no longer there. The air was full of noise: explosions in the distance, CAS fire much nearer; the crackle of wood on fire, voices shouting, and voices in pain; screams, so that I sank back and gasped and sweated.

A hand touched my hot forehead: the fingers like ice.

'Don't—' And then I focused. Delirium, I thought, quite certain of it; so certain that I didn't speak; and someone called, *'T'An,* there's another boat to load, which lot do we take next?' and Ruric raised her head and called, 'By the steps – there.'

She looked down at me and said, 'What can I do? Think and tell me, Christie. What can we do that will help you, not hurt you?'

'What are you doing here?' Then I thought how urgent it was to move. 'I had a splint, to keep the bone from grating – Ruric, for God's sake! What are you doing?'

She stayed leaning against the side of the cart. The sun shone on her black mane, thick now with dust; and on the sharp lines of her face; and her gaze went to the estuary, watching the half-dozen small ships rocking on the water. 'Getting people out. You should have seen the Wellhouses! They must have moved hundreds in the first hour – anyone who can walk has gone, or if they haven't, they're fools—' She broke off to shout an order down the quay. '—and now it's casualties. The harbour . . .'

'What time is it?'

'About an hour before midday.' She grinned, and the lines in her face deepened. Membrane veiled yellow eyes against the dust. 'That's my *S'aranth*!' And she turned away, giving orders to another Orthean.

The noise deafened me. Vision swam: I was aware that I was fever-hot. Then a sharp pain convulsed me, I sat upright; cried out. There were makeshift splints bound round my right leg with strips of a torn cloak, and in confusion I thought *When did that happen?* and Ruric Orhlandis said 'Better?'

'I – uh; yeah, better.'

'Liar.' She raised her head. The wind blew her cropped mane back from her face. The sky above her seemed hazy, and I realized it was high cloud; daystars barely visible in the milky blue. No shuttles, I thought. The Orthean woman said, 'You'll be on the next boat across.'

The splints felt tight. My knee throbbed; but now at least every breath didn't move it. The *skurrai*-cart being needed, I was lifted off and laid down on the quayside with a dozen other Ortheans. The flagstones were sun-warmed. Intermittently my sight blacked out, and the pain began to bite as the painkillers wore off; I thought, How can I get to a shuttle? to Kumiel? no medics here—

An Earthspeaker who tended the other wounded crossed the quay and examined my leg; but didn't touch it. Glad or sorry? I wondered. Human anatomy is not Orthean: I'd sooner they didn't meddle. Christ, somebody do something!

People still came down on to the quay from the alleys. As the sun rose to midday, the noise of firing increased. A cold sweat came out on my face and neck and back: I thought, No. This is enough. Too much. Not again. All I could see was smoke and dust that hung in the air at the top of the hill. Towards the sea, downriver, black smoke rose and fires raged; and it was a long time before I thought, That's Westhill and heard the sharp *crack!* of a beam-pulser.

I looked down, across the water, fearing to see the metal sails of *jath-rai*.

'—and come back across.'

Ruric's voice, speaking to a dark-maned male in Rimon dress. As he moved off, she came to squat down beside me; where I lay propped up against the wall of the quay steps. The noon sun dazzled on the water. One of the Ortheans with me – the female with the wounded arm – muttered something under her breath; a male grunted and looked at Ruric and spat: 'Orhlandis!'

Ruric ignored him. Her hand moved to rub at the stump of her arm with long dark fingers; and I saw that her shirt was filthy and her britches dust-stained; and she carried a CAS-handgun at her belt. The smooth butt had no Company logo stamped on it. And so it must have come from the *hiyeks*, I realized; and in what riot and confusion – does it matter?

'We'll have to move,' she said quietly, 'they're moving upriver from Westhill. *S'aranth*, crossing over is risky, but so is staying here.'

Her eyes followed the Rimon male she'd spoken to. I saw him supervising the loading of stretchers on to a small boat, shouting at the *ashiren* that was all his crew. The boat lifted and fell: tide flowing down towards the estuary. Ruric lifted her head, looking at the hillside and the *telestre*-houses above us: 'There's more need bringing out.'

'What's happening?'

She shook her head, and was silent. A roar sounded over the noise of explosions and the whine of CAS weaponry, and a shuttle soared high across the city and vanished over to the east. Another explosion rocked the quay: loud and sudden and there was blood where I bit my lip; Ruric stood and gazed east, listening, but the roar died smoothly away. She sank back down. Now I could smell burning again, over the stink of sea and fear.

'Sunmother!' she whispered, 'I'll make them bring the boats back across here.' She threw me a quick glance, and rested her hand on my shoulder. 'Christie, don't worry.'

'The *Citadel*—'

She said nothing, but the membrane slid back from her yellow eyes, fever-bright in her dark face, and she looked up at the city from under dark brows; and my pulse stuttered, a stab of adrenalin cold as ice. Her fingers locked on my shoulder.

'You don't ask what keeps the fighting to the harbour and the rivers.'

Pain making me stupid, I muttered, 'Keeps it?'

'They're fighting offworld technology with winchbows and *harur*-blades. As a diversion.' Her mouth moved in something that might be a smile: ancient and sardonic; and then it was Ruric Orhlandis again, her face sharp with pain, who said, 'Christie, who do you think? The *T'An* Commander, the guard; a handful of mercenaries. They're down there *now*.'

She stood up, shouting across to Ortheans bringing two more loaded *skurrai*-carts out of the alley-entrance; brown-robed Earthspeakers ran to the wounded, and I tried to shut my ears to the noises, the pain. *Blaize*. Confusion muddled me; childlike, I thought T'An Commander, that's Blaize Meduenin and then No, he can't be back there, I don't believe it! and sobbed on an indrawn breath: *yes, he's there; Jesus Christ*—

'Get him out. Ruric, get a message; get him here!'

'What about the rest of them here? If we don't get people out of the city—' She swung round: 'Get them on board! There isn't time for that; carry them if you have to!'

I don't give a fuck about anybody else; get Blaize out; and where's Hal, did he get out early? And Cassirur and Nelum; this is . . .

The raw pain and the fever reached a balance: I thought, with utter certainty, This is a nightmare. It cleared my head. The sun made my eyes water. The sea-wall was hard against my back; and three of us lay propped up against it: a pale-maned female with an arm roughly bandaged and stained bloody; a young male; an older male who cradled a hand smashed and wet. The sound he was making tore at my gut. Sunlight, white and harsh, shattered on the surface of the river; and the wind off the water made me shiver. I hugged my arms across my chest, feeling the sting of cut palms.

Every crash, every loud explosion, made me shake.

Blank-walled *telestre*-houses on the hillside above the quay were quiet, pale in the sun; and I strained to see figures on roof-tops – nothing. *For how long?* The sun blinded me. Ahead, where the river curved, must be Westhill; clouds of smoke rolled down now to the water's edge, hiding the city there. I dropped my gaze and looked along the quay, it was a confusion of people rushing about; makeshift stretchers manhandled down on to the deck of the small boat; one of the Earthspeakers glanced down at a male on the quayside and shook his head; Ruric – *when did she go?* – came back at a run with two males, pointed at the group of us; and they went to the pale-maned female and lifted her, carrying her towards the boat.

'Look.' I pointed. Ruric knelt down beside me, veiled her eyes, and stared downriver against the sunlit water. I saw how my hand shook. Dirt and blood. Then the dark Orthean woman drew in her breath as if she'd been hit.

'I see it.' She straightened up.

A glint of light on metal . . . and then it turned with the wind and was clearly in view: a *jath-rai*, metal sail gleaming, emerging from the smoke that hid the side of Westhill. Staring across a hundred yards of open water, I saw small white-robed figures on the deck. A thunder of explosions made me wince: I shrank back, realized *that wasn't this side of the city* and got my hands to the top of the wall, and hauled myself upright, weight on my good leg.

Another ship appeared from the smoke. The two *jath-rai* caught the wind, prows curving slowly as they came round. For a split second I thought They're going back and then sails shifted, figures ran about the decks, both ships began to head upriver towards us.

'Get them under cover!' Ruric gestured violently; turned to look at the *jath-rai*, then back at the wounded littering the quay. The small boat rocked, was abruptly a yard out from the quay steps and raising its own sails; I saw a spray of water catch the sun. Ruric groaned under her breath; again shouted: 'Under *cover*, get back! Get them out of sight!' Her voice was drowned out by a sharp *crack!*

She turned abruptly, seized my arm and pulled it across her thin shoulders, said, 'Hold on!' and began to half carry me across the quay, towards the shelter of the abandoned companion-houses there. Each step jolted agony through my leg; my vision blurred with tears, the low-roofed buildings becoming only a dazzle; but I got a grip on her shoulder tight enough to make her wince, braced against her: walked; and then as the noise rose to a deafening level, began to half limp, half run, in red agony; and collapse in shadow; she against me; and look out from under a doorway at the quay and the river and the hull of an F90 shuttle as it roared downriver, a bare five hundred feet above.

'—Mendez!' But I couldn't even hear myself over the rattle of explosive fire; a thunder that went on and on.

We lay on the earthen floor just inside the low building. That earth vibrated now, a shaking roar that I thought must be the dockside collapsing into the river; the walls shivered. A hollow *boom!* echoed up from downriver.

'Wait. Don't move.' Ruric knelt up, got to her feet; and shaded her eyes with her single hand, staring out across the water. She stood in the doorway for a moment, then ducked outside. Smoke drifted acridly across what I could see of the dock, there were moans and screams; I glimpsed her and another male and an Earthspeaker, each dragged a stretcher towards the shelter of the dockside *telestre*-houses.

As if there were all the time in the world, I thought, Cory is firing on the Desert Coast ships. I caught hold of the door-jamb, levered myself up on my good leg; and smoke made me cough, eyes streaming. Men and women were dragging themselves away from the quayside in panic; those who were still must be too hurt to move; I caught my breath and then realized, *I can hear them screaming; the firing's stopped.*

Smoke began to thin, from black to sepia to gold. Sun shone down on the quay, on the bricks and timber – I never heard that hit; what did they get? – of a *telestre*-house fired on by the *jath-rai*. One *jath-rai* still remained. It drifted, fifty yards away; the river current beginning to turn it around.

Sharp explosions still crackled in the distance, and there were flashes like summer lightning, and I slid down to the earth, resting my back against the doorframe. It was involuntary. I wanted to move, wanted to get out on to the quay, no matter the ship or the firing; but it wasn't pain that swept through me, it was a weakness as if every tendon had been cut. And then pain made tears run, and I could do nothing but sit and blink and breathe in rasping coughs; and the hard jamb of the door cut into my spine.

*

A minute later and a shadow fell across my closed eyes: 'Haven't you sense enough to be inside?'

I opened my eyes and saw sun on the water and rolling smoke, and Ruric Orhlandis. The dark Orthean woman stumbled through the doorway. She glanced back over her shoulder, winced as a volley of explosions rocked the air; and knelt down, her hand and arm tight across her lower ribs. Her shirt, torn down the back, exposed the wiry roots of her black mane; and as she raised her head the alien musculature shifted under her skin.

'Christie, for Her sake, get in—'

My arms gave under me as I tried to push myself up; I could only lean back against the inner door-jamb. She stayed for a moment, ribs heaving, and then half fell beside me; and the membrane drew back from her eyes, a white line appearing round the yellow iris.

'Hurt – you're hurt?'

She looked dazedly at the interior of this empty companion-house. A tiny white-walled room, with couch-chairs and tables overturned in the panic of flight; dust and sunlight drifting in through the slot-windows.

'Might as well – stay here.' She shook her head as if to clear it. 'Sunmother! Something hit me here—' The arm across her ribs tightened.

'Are you bleeding?'

'No; bruised, I think.' Her mouth twisted. 'It's tight; that's all.'

Pain and weakness went together now: again, it felt as if they balanced. Clear-headed and feverish, all at the same time. I rubbed my hands down my coveralls, then wiped my mouth; tasted grit. Cold wind blew in off the river.

'How bad is it?' I met her gaze. *Can't get your breath and it's a chest-wound* – And I was suddenly cold, mind clear; looking at that narrow face, and the pain. 'Is it bad enough to be a broken bone?'

'Could be.' She twisted, sitting down next to me; let out a grunt of pain; and then coughed and cut it off halfway.

Outside, concussion split the air; somewhere close there was a crash. Someone screamed. Thunder rolled: pounded at the walls of the tiny room. Has to be a shuttle coming in low, I thought; but black smoke swirled across the quay, and I could see nothing. And she sat with her back to the wall, this alien woman; head thrown back and gasping; and the sun faintly shone copper on her black mane and on her shoulders, on the six-fingered hand that clenched on her high-arched ribs. *Humanoid is not human*, I thought coldly, and then *But a rib can pierce a lung, all the same.*

'What's happening out there?'

She caught her breath, that rasped in her throat. 'I can't – there's no telling; you can't see. I saw *s'aranthi* ships over Westhill. I think they were firing.' And she looked at me, and shook her head. 'We're pinned down here.'

She makes too much sense to be injured. I looked up past the edge of the door, and saw the billows of smoke clearing again, and the blue sky beyond, and a glint of light that must be another shuttle.

'You said – said they were coming this way. From Westhill and down that way,' I said.

Her head moved slightly: a nod of agreement. Without opening her eyes, she said, 'An hour. Maybe less. Then they'll be here.'

And what happens to us then – *no*, you don't think about that. And I wondered if, in a few minutes, I could seriously think of how we might move (and go where?); but for the minute just to sit and not cry out with the pain was effort. I reached over, and could only brush my hand against her shoulder.

'We can—'

Her breath caught in her throat again, and her head went back; corded neck stretched in pain. Her arm fell to her side. Abruptly she bent forward, coughing. The harsh sound cut off midway, became liquid; and she put her hand up to her mouth, brought it away black, and spat out a mouthful of blood.

'*Jesus Christ, no*—'

The light from the window shone down on her. A dark woman, cropped mane falling over her forehead; and the lines of pain and age cut deep in her face. Her white shirt was caked with dust. That six-fingered hand pressed on the stone floor, leaving a dark smear; and then she caught hold of my hand in a painful grip. Her eyes opened, amazed; looking at me.

'Where were you hit? Show me.' I kept her hand tight in mine, and she pulled it free; dragged the shirt away from her lower ribs on her left side. The flesh had a pulpy look to it. She let the cloth fall.

'Don't move; don't talk. Stay still.'

What I said was drowned in the roar of falling masonry. Something hit the flat roof above us with a crash. Light flashed on the far wall of the companion-house room: leakage of laser-fire; and I blinked back after-images.

Between gasps, the Orthean woman said, 'Tethmet was right. He said I shouldn't – leave the Tower. Right.' And she made a grimace, trying to smile.

'Don't talk, you'll aggravate it. Stay still.'

She nodded, once, and rested her head back against the wall. I watched her chest rise and fall. Tight, jagged movements. Wondered what it was that hit her and then thought, It wouldn't help to know. Christ, don't let it be bad; don't let it be what it looks like!

Long minutes passed. My mouth was dry with thirst and fear; and it was a fight not to slip into unconsciousness. The noise didn't abate. But in this tiny, pale room, it passed unnoticed. She opened her eyes, frowning slightly. *What can I do?* Nothing but keep her still. If she's got a pierced lung, *if* she has, then the medics will have to get here fast—

She bent forward, spasms wracking at her; and I dragged myself a few inches closer and, half out from the pain, held her shoulders while she coughed, while her head came back; and blood haemorrhaged, ran down her mouth and neck and soaked her shirt.

'—Christie?'

It was a minute before I realized where I was: still leaning against her and against the wall, and acrid smoke seeped into the small room and stung my eyes. My leg and hip were liquid fire. I wiped sweat off my face and couldn't feel it on my hand.

'Christie?'

'I'm here.'

'Stupid,' she said. 'This is – a stupid thing to happen – *ah*!'

'Don't,' I begged, and felt tears on my cheeks; cursed weakness. She gasped, dragging air into her lungs, and it was a wet, frothy sound. I managed to get my arm all the way round her narrow shoulders, supporting her against my left side; her body was heavy, fever-hot, and she coughed again, thickly.

'*Don't* move. Oh, Jesus, *why* didn't you get out on the first boat? Of all the fucking stupid things to do—'

Glass imploded, scattering the floor. I flinched, and then cried out at the pain of the movement. Either the firing was further off or I couldn't hear properly; one loud *crack!* was followed by an almost-silence.

The smoke thinned, and the light of the sun came in through the shattered window, and made an oblong on the stone floor. It shone on her legs, stretched out before her. I grabbed hold of the door-jamb and pulled myself forward, so that I could see through the door; and Ruric slumped against me. I leaned back. The firing started again, closer now.

Coughing shook her; deep spasms, that brought up blood. I wiped at her mouth with my hand.

And this is your Tathcaer, your city, how could you leave it? Oh, Jesus, why didn't you go?

Gently, I leaned her head back against my shoulder. Her weight on my uninjured leg was almost a dead weight. I gripped her shoulders, leaning her back a little on me. Her mane was rough against my arm. I saw her hand in her lap clench, those slender claw-nailed fingers digging into her palm; felt how she tried to hold back the coughing, hold herself still. *This cannot be happening, I don't believe it can happen like this.*

'Stay still,' I whispered. Her skin felt hot, and her pulse hammered.

The light was cruel now, showing her age; showing the skin stretched tight over high cheekbones. Her head moved the smallest fraction. She opened her eyes; and the skin round them crinkled, her mouth moved – the faintest echo of that smile I saw once, in this city, eight years ago.

I said, 'They'll get to us. Don't move; you won't do any more damage. They'll get to us soon.'

So quiet that I hardly heard her over the noise of the firing outside, she said, 'It doesn't matter if I talk. I want to say some things.' And then, all on out-breaths, and with a ghost of asperity: 'I do know – about lung wounds.'

'So do I.'

Now the wind off the river brought the stench of dead weed and garbage, and cordite; and raised chills on my skin. It came to me as a simultaneous perception: all the years that I have spent away from Orthe, all the time between then and now – and all that happened to me then, here in this city: how in the Citadel Dalzielle Kerys-Andrethe sent me out to the *telestres* in this woman's company, and all the long journeying that brought us at last to a room in the Citadel again, she going into her exile and I into mine. It's no use to regret. And she is not *amari* Ruric Orlhandis now, not *T'An* Commander and *T'An* Melkathi; she is Ruric Hexenmeister – ah, but still: how could she stay away?

'Get me back to the Tower—' Her breath caught.

'They – can they heal you there?'

'Take me there anyway.' She coughed, and it was tight; coughed until she bent forward and I held her, and she brought up dark blood, and spat, and coughed again; fighting for air.

She leaned back against me. 'Do you know – in the Citadel? When you came there?' It was obvious she meant her exile. 'I would – ask. Would have asked you to come with me. I don't know why I didn't.'

Eight years ago it wouldn't have been true, I thought, but now it is. And I said, 'If you'd asked, I would have gone.'

She did smile at that, yellow eyes wide and with that intrinsic glow they have in shadow; and the sunlight from the window fell on her hand and hip, and outside the whine of CAS weapons was louder. The minutes passed. She gasped for breath.

My knee and leg and hip throbbed, pain keeping me conscious. Everything in that tiny room stood out with preternatural clarity: the overturned tables, the dust on the floor, the splintered glass. Dust billowed along the quay outside. The sun grew hot. Noise was a constant, no longer noticed. I am thirty-eight years old, she is older; I am holding her here in this empty room and I cannot move.

A few minutes later she coughed again, and this time she didn't stop. I held her while she shook with it, crying out with pain; and my hands were wet with her haemorrhaged blood. Her weight rested against me, heavy and warm; and her black mane was rough against my cheek; her spasms jolted me so that I had to bite on my lower lip to keep from screaming.

A little after noon, her breathing became shallow, and then stertorous. She rested against me, this Orthean woman with satin-black skin and mane; head resting in the hollow of my shoulder, and all my clothing soaked with her blood. The lungs fill and they drown, drown in their own blood; human is not humanoid – but sometimes it is. I looked down at that narrow face.

I held her in my arms until she grew cold.

CHAPTER 38

Past-Memory

'One more here!'

I managed to focus against the light blazing in at the doorway. The voice added something unintelligible, shouting to be heard over the thunder of a shuttle's flight; and then a young Orthean in a priest's robe knelt beside me.

'Just wait, *t'an*, we'll have you safe soon.'

Pain and fever and memory hold me: looking down at my lap, I can see that the patch of sunlight has moved only inches, shines on my human hands that are black with blood and Not more than an hour's passed, I thought, Why weren't you here an hour ago—?

A deep roar sounded, split into distinct successive explosions. The young male's head came up and he flinched, pale eyes veiled; that face narrow at the jaw and wide at the forehead, quick with life. Past him, I saw the river. Light shattered off the water, off the metal sails of a *jath-rai*; and suddenly a great plume of water shot up beside the ship, a shadow darkened the air and passed overhead – and then the roar of the shuttle's passing: I put my hands over my ears.

'—wait, and we'll get you out with the others!'

I found myself alone. I sat propped against the wall, legs out before me; the pain made me gasp with every breath.

An hour is long enough to come to a decision, I thought. And as long as I've decided, I'm okay; I can do it. If it's cowardly . . . that doesn't matter now.

Deliberately and with effort I moved my hand, getting the fingers round her long-boned, cold wrist; and locked them, and thought They won't separate us and began to laugh – caught my breath in pain: laughed so that I shook, and the tears ran down my face.

'Here. Lift her. Help me.' The young male Earthspeaker ducked into the doorway, followed by an older male; and then as he bent over me, hesitated, and then reached down to pry loose my fingers.

918

'You don't leave her—'

He put a dark-skinned hand on her throat, where she lay against me still with her head thrown back. Momentary irritation gripped me: *do you think I don't know how to find breath or a heart-beat?*

'She's dead, we can't help her.'

I tightened my grip on her wrist. Tears ran down my face and in blind panic I repeated, 'You don't leave her here! She comes with me!'

'*T'an*, she's *dead*—' He turned, as the older male whispered something. They stood up, talking in the doorway; and it was irresistibly funny, I thought, To have to drag a lump of dead, cold meat along with me and the pain in my smashed knee flared so that I couldn't help but claw at it; and then scream again when that hurt. I bent double. The body slid down on to the stone floor beside me.

The sun was warm on her face, that sharp high-boned face wiped clean of haemorrhaged blood, but when I put my hand on her, her face was cold and soft. Her mouth hung a little open, and her eyes were closed. The lines in that fine-grained black skin made her seem old, and she will not be old, not now.

I reached for her hand again, where it lay fallen on her breast, and held those long amber-nailed fingers, and again felt laughter tight in my lungs. I screwed my eyes up against the light through the doorway, looking at the distant daystarred sky. *A good joke.* When she should be buried now – and a sharp *crack!* shook the companion-house.

'Bring it, we haven't time to argue,' the Earthspeaker said urgently, 'we can't leave this one even if it is *s'aranthi*; get to the boat!'

He caught my arm and pulled it across his shoulders and I came up onto one leg that twisted and wouldn't hold me. The other male gripped her body under the arms and dragged it out on to the quayside and even with the pain lancing through me, I saw her heels jolt comically over the stones, and laughed on a soundless breath, and retched: part from the pain, and part from the realization, O God, that there should be a *use* even for the dead.

The flat-hulled ferry dipped sickeningly. A rush of spray soaked me, brought me to a semi-conscious state. White wake trailed downriver, a solid wall of sound struck me; and the person next to me screamed, and thrashed, and a hand caught me across the face. I blinked away tears. High overhead the F90 swung into a curve. The sun slid like a silver bead down the length of its hull.

Current turned the boat. Between the gap of deck and rail, Westhill came into view: the slopes hidden now by rolling black smoke. Smashed buildings blocked the lower end of the harbour. A few boats bobbed helplessly in the swell. Dark specks ran on the quay. Dots in the water: the heads of swimmers. A pall of smoke blotted the sky, split by the F90 shuttle's passing; a *jath-rai* listed in the water and men and women jumped from its sides.

The ferry stank of blood and excrement. Cries and screams were loud, over the noise of firing. An Earthspeaker crossed the deck, stepping between bodies laid out on the wood; that rolled as the boat rolled. When I turned my head, I saw that the Orthean beside me was white-maned and white-skinned and wearing a dirt-stained *meshabi*-robe.

The early evening sky . . .

Pale blue and filled with clarity, as a glass is filled with water or light. To lie and look up is to fall into the sky. And no, not quite evening, not more than the end of afternoon, in the long Orthean day.

She rises to her feet in one swift movement, all the old swordfighter's grace still there. She stands in the sunlight, in the Tower garden. This lean, ageing woman, skin like flaked coal; with bare feet, and mane straggling out of a half-crop. That narrow, merry face.

Makeshift tents of *becamil*-cloth are drab against the sky. Ortheans walk between them on hurried errands, walking on dry earth trodden bare of mossgrass . . . I moved slightly, lifting my head; and saw, between the tents that shelter the injured, the wide grasslands that run down to the Oranon River. Acres of flat mossgrass. In the far distance, people trek away from the city against the skyline. Haze blurs distance, the land trembles in this summer day's heat.

She speaks as one remembering more than her own memories. Like the sun on the surface of a river: one minute all brilliance, all Ruric; and then the light shifts, and under that surface are depths . . .

I heard faint, desultory cracks: the distant sound of projectile fire. The noises here drowned it out. Not far off, someone screamed, another voice sobbed with pain; and I rolled my head to one side and saw an Orthean male bent over one of the wounded, feeding him a liquid – *ataile*, to ease pain? – and moved restless to look the other way, and saw a human face. A black Pacifican, hair pulled back into a horse-tail; squatting on his haunches beside me, his gaze fixed on the distant city, and it seemed an hour before I could remember his name.

'Lutaya?'

He glanced at me, then over his shoulder at the camp, and then back at me. 'The medic's here somewhere – don't worry: you're going to be all right. Lie still.'

WEBcast equipment cluttered his back, on a knotted makeshift strap. There were dark stains on the knees of his coveralls. Sunlight on his face showed it strained, eyes with a bruised look to them; and though he tried to sound reassuring, his tone was flat.

Painkillers. I recognize the feeling: that time has slowed or stopped completely . . . My mouth had a sour taste in it. Without thought, I hitched myself up on to my elbows; dizziness blacked out vision and I thought It should have been painful and realized I could feel nothing of my right side: numb from shoulder to hip to ankle . . . The leg of my coverall was cut away. A grey plastiflesh covering encased me from thigh to foot; and I reached down and touched the rigid, warm surface. What damage – *no, that's not important now.*

'I found you.' Lutaya's voice had a touch of child-like pride. 'Didn't know there were any of us caught in the settlement. Thought it was all local wounded here. Came down. Took some good shots. You're a bonus.'

He grabbed my arm as I attempted to sit up, and managed it, and all but retched with a sudden nausea, and he was no more troublesome, no more importunate, than one of the *kekri*-flies that swarmed round. Blue and green and black: *kekri*-flies clustering on wounds, and on bodies that lay motionless a little way off.

'For God's sake!' he protested, shocked. Then: 'Kennaway – over here! She's hysterical—'

I smothered laughter with a dirty hand, rocking back and forwards. Someone listened to me, I thought. The *becamil* blanket that I lay on was large, and its further edge lapped over a still shape: a body of which I could see only one foot and ankle . . .

'This – is – *grotesque*—' And the sun was hot, nauseatingly hot; my face ran with sweat; and all I could do now was roll over, dragging my numb leg with me like dead wood, and reach over to pull the drab *becamil*-cloth. Then it was nothing grotesque, only her face, and her dark body in filthy shirt and britches, and a darker bruise on the skin over those arched ribs. And that face, sunken in repose. The skin indented down round her eyes, so that the shape of the bone is plain . . .

'Broken rib through the lung,' the WEBcaster said, without much interest. 'Is there a story for the WEB in it, do you think, Representative?'

Quite calmly, I thought: You're piqued because I don't thank you for fetching a medic. Puppet-like, I mouthed suitable words.

Now I was sitting up I could see the extent of this temporary refugee-camp. *Becamil*-cloth draped over sticks, small fires, huddled people; it surrounded me, and desultory groups trailed off towards the Rimon hills, and I had been staring for several moments before I saw that a good half of them wore the *meshabi*-robes of the Desert Coast, and mixed with the others unharmed, almost unnoticed.

'What . . .?'

Lutaya stood up, staring across the valley towards the city. His tone was hard. 'I've sent my reports through, Representative. That's all that concerns me. If your Company chooses to fire on that settlement, if—' he broke off. More quietly, he added, 'The locals don't seem much bothered now about who's who. They *all* ran. Don't make much difference when you're under fire, I guess. Here's Kennaway.'

A woman in Company coveralls approached. I recognized the black medic I'd spoken to on the orbiter, when I'd called about Douggie. The woman smiled, and said briskly, 'We'll have transport here in a minute. How do you feel now?'

Now? But the painkillers wouldn't let me feel. I tried to swallow, and she knelt down and held a flask to my lips:

'A sip – that's enough.'

The water tasted tepid, antiseptic, wonderful.

The late afternoon sky . . .

Clear and blue and daystarred: and Carrick's Star an incandescent white light over my right shoulder. Pain pulsed once in my head. I got my left heel and my hands – when did they get bandaged? – braced on the ground, and tried to stand: caught Kennaway and held on to her and stood, while she swore at me: 'Don't put weight on that, you'll damage it even more than it already is! I didn't go to all this trouble to have you mess it up again—'

'Are communications back?'

'*Sit down.*' She lowered me back to the ground. The knee wasn't painful. No more mine than a block of wood: why should I be careful of damaging it?

The earth was warm under my bandaged hands: I could feel it through my fingertips. Only the slightest warm breeze blew. It raised the hairs on my bare arms. A stand of *kiez* scrub blocked off the nearer shelters, and its brown foliage was already spotted with pale blue fruit: summer turning into harvest, into cold days, into the bitter frosts of winter . . . I stared round at all the nameless faces. Where are my friends who were in the city? Where are the people I know? I can't ask at every campfire, at every shelter, at every pile of bodies waiting for the funeral burning – ah God I can't stand never to know! But sheer numbers and time defeat me now.

'Do something for me,' I asked. 'I want to – I need them to bring something from Kumiel Island. Is Kumiel still . . . it doesn't matter. Tell them I'm bringing – a body back for burial. I want . . .'

Some way for her to go home with dignity. Kennaway's face showed incomprehension, impatience, and with a touch of that same macabre humour I thought, I daresay they're busy at the moment.

Manoeuvring my stiff, numb leg so that it didn't get in my way, I eased myself over to where I could wrap the drab *becamil* blanket around her cold body, and sit beside her, and wait for them to come.

Not long now, I promised. And then I can put my decision into action.

'Now that I'm Hexenmeister,' Ruric said, 'I have the memory of your coming here, eight years ago. And I have the memories the then Hexenmeister took from you . . . I've been Lynne de Lisle Christie . . . I'd been four years in exile from the Hundred Thousand, Orhlandis was broken up, Rodion dead, Suthafiori dead. And because you were here before you went back to Tathcaer, and found out what I'd done, I saw myself through your eyes, as you saw me: a friend.'

Friend, is it? I put the brightly-coloured memory away; and with a gruesome humour, thought: Last time I was in the Hundred Thousand I thought travelling with a child slowed me down, that's nothing to travelling with a corpse . . .

'I'll give you a shot.' Kennaway reached for her medic-pak.

'I don't need anything.' You can take laughter for hysteria, for battle fatigue, for whatever you like to think of it as: I see it, simply, as fact. She is dead and she is a damn nuisance—

Kennaway's voice reached me, muffled: 'That's better. You'll do better to cry; best treatment I know.'

Clouds cast their shadows on the sea, and on the hills below, and Carrick's Star shone white on these cumulus, gliding east away from the sun. The waves soughed: a constant hiss on the shingle. Light caught their green crests as they rolled over and exploded into surf. The rock jolted my leg as I was lowered down from the 'thopter. Pain stabbed my hip: the knee had no sensation at all. Kennaway gripped my arm, signalling to the 'thopter pilot, and the craft soared up again, rotors raising dust from the dry earth of Kumiel Island. I heard a distant sound like sheet metal being shaken. The crags of the island blocked my view of the mainland, across the straits to the city . . . I stared up at the evening sky: pitch-black with rising smoke. No wind blew to bring the smell of burning.

'Representative, I'd better get you to the shuttle.'

I glanced at Kennaway, tightened my grip on the metal strut that, tucked under one armpit, made a makeshift crutch, and then realized that two of the young officers who'd travelled in the 'thopter were going ahead now. They carried a heavy, cloth-shrouded bundle between them; treading carefully on the earth tracks of this rocky islet. The sun sent their shadows long and dark before them.

I dug the strut into the earth with every step, swinging my immobilized leg; and the pain in that hip began to sicken me. The setting sun brought sweat out on my forehead. I reached the top of the slight rise.

Two F90 shuttles stood on the landing field, their crews clustered round the ramps; and I looked past their sunlit hulls to the dome of the comlink-centre, saw a distant figure which must be Lutaya rushing to put out another 'cast – the Company representative found – and then two or three more people came out of the dome, and one pointed in my direction. Even at this distance, I knew him. I was conscious of no joy. I could only think, I've nothing to say to you now.

I stood still, waiting, as they crossed the hundred yards between us.

'Shuttle?'

Kennaway said, 'Most base personnel have already been evacuated up to the orbiter. Excuse me, Representative; I'm just going to contact the medic team up there.' She turned and strode towards the dome, calling a few words as she passed those approaching.

A fair-haired Peace Force officer: Ottoway. Another officer that I didn't know, who broke step to speak with the body-carriers, and looked across at me with a frown on his face. Behind them, Douglas Clifford.

'Oh, my dear.' He put his arms round me, and I felt him shake. Then he stood back, and the level sun caught his face, and showed exhaustion on those prim features: there was dirt on his grizzled hair, and the plastiflesh dressing on his eye. His gaze went past me to the shrouded body. 'Who – ?'

Douggie, is there any part of you that for one moment thinks – hopes – it's Blaize? But that's not important now. I dug the strut firmly into the trodden-down earth of the landing field.

'Put her in the shuttle,' I ordered. 'Keep it powered up; and I want a pilot.'

'Lynne, for God's sake, who is it?'

'Ruric,' I said, and saw the beginning of a stupefied shock on his face; turned my head and watched them carry her across the field so that I wouldn't have to see Douggie. What can I say to you? Nothing, I thought.

The pain gave me energy now. I said sharply, 'Where's Commander Mendez?'

A slow flush spread under Ottoway's fair skin. The stocky man opened his mouth to speak, shut it again, and then burst out: 'What else could we do? It was *three hours* before we knocked that transmission-blocker out! We had to fire on them before they got in with the friendly forces or else it would have been indiscriminate massacre—!'

Indiscriminate. I felt a laugh catch in my throat ' "Friendly" forces! Did you hear that Ortheans fired on that 'thopter when it picked me up – oh yes, only winchbows in the camp, but they fired!'

'*We* didn't attack first—'

I shifted, and a stab of pain made me gasp. Doug, with a concerned expression on his face, moved to take my arm; I waved him away. He stared intently at me. Nothing to hear now but the distant surf, the distant roar of engines; the sun is warm on my cheek.

'I don't want to know about it,' I said. 'Where's Cory?'

Ottoway shrugged. 'The Rimnith-Keverilde area.'

'*Melkathi?* What—' Incredulous, I turned to Doug.

It was a second before he answered, that intent gaze still on me, and when he did, it was to say absently, 'There's been fighting in several areas, not just Tathcaer. I believe it's still going on.' He stepped to the right, pointing; and I limped across and stared out to sea, following his gaze. 'And there's that . . .'

The still blue surface of the sea was darker on the horizon, as if it had soaked up ink. Specks reflected back the light of the setting sun, where they cruised far out to sea; and they were metal-sailed, and though I couldn't see properly at this distance I knew them for *jath* and *jath-rai*.

'Are they waiting?'

'Scared to come in – and too badly provisioned to go home,' Doug guessed.

All along that panorama of the sea: dozens of the tiny craft . . . I turned my back on them. *That, also, is not now my concern.* It hit me again: that face of hers, forgotten for whole minutes at a time, so clear in my mind's eye: Ruric Hexenmeister.

'Representative?' Ottoway said cautiously. I looked at him; his expectancy, and shook my head. Did I want to ask you questions? I thought. Did I really? Why?

'See to the shuttle for the Representative,' Doug ordered; and Ottoway shrugged at the dismissal, and walked away across the landing field; and I watched him go without really seeing him.

'I think you're in shock.'

'No,' I said.

'Of course, you realize that this has finished Corazon Mendez's career. The WEBcasters are cutting her to pieces. In twelve days there won't be a Pacifican on Earth who doesn't know her name and revile it.' He watched me narrowly.

'And my name?' That made me smile.

'Yours too, yes, but please don't be concerned. Lynne, I'm certain that it can be put right.' He waited. Then he sighed. 'You haven't the slightest interest in that now, have you? It's hardly surprising. Lynne, you must rest for a short time; even if it's only a few minutes – please.'

A dizzy inconsequentiality touched me. What does it matter what I do now? In a short time – a very short time – it won't matter at all.

'Where do you want me to go, Douggie?'

He frowned, and looked me up and down in the sunlight.

I must present a figure like some WEBcast refugee; hair thick with dirt, coveralls ripped, leg bound rigid in plastiflesh-cast; hands bandaged, and a crutch to walk with . . . And suddenly there was a pulse of pain; the world snapped into focus.

'Christ, yes, let me sit down!'

'Sit down before you fall down,' he advised, the humour no more than reflex; and hovered beside me as I limped across towards the comlink-dome. It towered white in the sunlight. I was almost at the port when I registered torn cables, shattered plastiglas; and realized I was staring at a twelve-foot hole in the side of it. *They did attack Kumiel, then. I thought the hiyeks wouldn't pass us by.* I entered, and faces turned towards me, and I eased down into the nearest seat, leg jutting out in front of me.

'Representative, what—?' One of the young officers stood up.

'The Representative needs medical care,' Doug interposed.

I leaned back, shutting my eyes and letting it pass me by.

The vast dome of the sky arches over me, webbed with light, flowering with the brilliance of Orthe's summer stars. In this Tower garden the scent of kazsis-nightflower *and* arniac *are chokingly strong . . .*

Doug's hands were warm around mine; he clasped them very lightly through the bandages. I opened my eyes. He sat leaning towards me, all the urbanity gone from his manner; and I could see (as one rarely sees with friends) how he comes to be a government envoy.

'I must be sure I have this right. Lynne, you're telling me Ruric is dead? The Hexenmeister? That was her body they were carrying to the shuttle?'

'Yes.'

The Tower garden, the cold siir *in ceramic bowls; the night winds blowing from the city, Kasabaarde. And, distant, blotting out stars, the first* chiruzeth *spire of the Rasrhe-y-Meluur . . .*

'You know it,' Ruric said softly. 'Ancient light can't be destroyed. Not once it's created. All we could do was hold it back. We are still holding it back.'

Douggie swore: his hands tightened on mine so that I winced.

'Lynne, I'm sorry, I didn't mean—' His voice was too quiet to be heard at the half-dismantled line of holotanks and comlink consoles; still, he leaned closer to me. 'I never knew her as you did. All I can think is, all that knowledge lost – the Tower Archives must be priceless; and with her gone, who can understand them?'

'It isn't quite like that, Douggie.'

The sun leaked whitely in through the breach in the dome, and shone on his sparse, tightly-curled hair; and cast a shadow down over one injured and one bright eye. His head came up, he nodded once, sharply, to himself: 'I thought there must be more. Good God, what have we done when we came here?'

And Ruric Orhlandis grins, in that Tower garden; speaking with a macabre humour that is part her, part that old man who was Hexenmeister, and partly a hundred generations of others:

'Wouldn't be the first time that's happened! . . . So long as the body comes living, or newly-dead, to the Tower, the memory-transfer can be made. You s'aranthi *would say we need "living cells". That isn't accurate, but it'll serve.'*

And I thought of her voice not six hours ago saying, *Take me there anyway.*

'I can't stay here long. I'm taking her body back to the Tower.' Now I drew my hands away from his, but only so that I could take a grip on his fingers; try to pass through that touch some idea of how critical this is; and I said, 'Douggie, I want to tell you . . . I – she and I – we owe you some explanation. And what does it matter what you know now?'

Analgesics kill pain but not weakness. Knowing even the smell of food would sicken me, I choked down protein-supplements; buoyed up on the impatience of waiting for the shuttle to power up. Two more F90s came in during that time. I couldn't stand to listen to comlink-nets, but when I limped outside and listened, I could hear distant engines, but no explosions. No firing.

Carrick's Star hung on the rim of the sea.

All the clouds in the vast dome of the sky glowed lilac, and ash-white. I turned my face up to the sky. The line of light is invisible, except where it strikes the upper limits of the pall of black smoke, drifting infinitely slowly to the east; glowing amber in the upper sunlit atmosphere.

I wish that I could see her face. There was a discarded crate on this edge of the landing field, and I eased myself down onto it, leg sticking out straight; and rested the strut on the sparse mossgrass. The F90 shuttle rested on the earth fifty yards away. *I wish that I could talk to you again.*

There is grit on the earth at my feet. Each pebble has its own precise shadow. There are things I would sooner think of than the way you died: choking, in agony, without dignity, without hope. You will have seen such deaths before, being a soldier. And that's no comfort. Something broke in me when you died; and if I hadn't turned my back on this world, I should always have known that it would.

Take me there anyway.

I raised my head and looked past the shuttle, past the edge of the rocks and out to sea. Lines of currents curve to the estuary here; but my back is turned on that devastated city, on the *telestres*, on whatever fighting there still may be. Out there, sea meets sky. And beyond that, far to the south, is a desert coast and a desert city, and a Tower that has stood these five thousand years.

And the Elansiir and the Barrens and the Glittering Plain. Because there was a city seen in mist and mirror-light . . .

And the sea is quiet.

'You should rest,' Doug's voice said from behind me. He walked to where I could see him.

'I have to go to Kasabaarde.'

The sea took his gaze. After a moment he put his hands behind his back, absently tapping his fingers together; and I couldn't help but smile: *that's Doug.* As he turned he saw my expression, and frowned.

'I'd feel easier—' He hesitated. The sun was at his back and I couldn't see his face, and squinting was painful. He repeated, 'I'd feel easier . . . Lynne, you ought to grieve.' That said all in a rush: then he added, 'God knows this is a disaster, but if you go as well, I don't think I – well, it doesn't matter. I know you well enough to know this isn't shock or grief, and I don't like it.'

Blinking into the light, I said, 'I can hold it together – just – because I've got this that I have to do; and then I've taken a decision.'

He came and squatted down on his haunches beside me, this middle-aged man in envoy's uniform; and the sunset put his long shadow on to the crate and the mossgrass. Sparks danced in the air: a handful of *kekri*-flies.

'Lynne, I didn't persuade a Company 'thopter to land out at that refugee camp and fetch you, just to have you commit suicide on me.'

His tone was rallying, serious enough to let me know he thought it a real possibility, and I looked at that round face; no humour at all in it now, and thought how she would have laughed, and said *too serious to be solemn about*. And so it is, I thought, so it is . . .

'In a way, yes. Just that.'

Shock spread over his face. He protested inarticulately.

'Don't, Douggie. I shan't die – but I shan't go back to Earth, either.'

It was an effort to get up unaided, even with the stick, but I made it, and stood sweating for a moment; grinning at the pain. Pain is sometimes the only sensation you can bear. Now I could see him without having to look up at him: Doug Clifford, envoy. And see (however he tries to hide it, out of respect for grief) how much he disapproves.

'You'll stay on Orthe.'

'Yes.'

And once you said to me, *There are so few who can live with an aeon of memories*. But I can. He made me apprentice, that old man the Hexenmeister, though he never intended it for this. Would your Tethmet Fenborn approve, if he still lives? I think he wouldn't. But I *know* I can live with the Tower's memories, I have done just that for the past eight years – if not (and I hear how you would laugh) if not very well.

To Doug, I said, 'It's the only way that I can handle this. Please. Understand that.'

A change to something unimaginable. . . . Is that what it means: to be named for Her, for Orthe, to become all of Orthe? And if, when, I take her memories, will I have Ruric with me again? Can I bear it, to see me as she saw me!

I thought, But I know one thing. If I go into the Tower again, I shall not be Christie after that happens; not Lynne Christie, and certainly not Christie S'aranth.

CHAPTER 39

The Child of Santhendor'lin-sandru

A low hum filled the air. One YV9 shuttle came over the northern edge of the island, hovered, and then sank down on to the landing field; another followed; and then an F90, settling to earth almost silently, and I felt the ground vibrate underfoot. The sunset shone on the white hulls, now stained with smoke and soot. As I watched, the ramps extruded and the crews came out on to the field.

Doug Clifford said, 'There's an hour or so of light left. I'm going to take a 'thopter out to the Oranon River valley . . .' He sighed heavily. 'If the *T'An Suthai-Telestre* is alive – or the Earthspeaker Cassirur – or any of the *takshiriye* . . .'

'How will you find them?'

That urbane self-mockery returned for just a moment. He said, 'Lynne, I shan't, but it eases me to *look*.'

The powering-up must be almost complete, I thought, keeping my gaze fixed on the further shuttle. Pain made a nagging ache in my hip. I clasped both hands on the metal strut and leaned it on the earth between my feet.

'You won't find any of them.'

Cassirur and Nelum Santhil, Bethan *T'An* Kyre, Khassiye Rei-halyn . . . Romare Kerys-Andrethe and Hildrindi *hiyek*-Anzhadi . . . the names bring faces to me: they are suddenly real. *If Hal is still alive* – and I left you by the wall of the Citadel in the early morning light; left you there. It comes to me now that I won't see you again.

Douggie gave me a concerned look: the one name between us is *Meduenin*.

'I'll go,' I said.

'It's several hours across the Inner Sea; the pilots are most unwilling to fly at night without a navigation-WEB—' He broke off, glancing over his shoulder.

Ottoway came out of the comlink-dome, squinting at the level light. It shone on his florid face. Aware only of irritation, I waited until he strode up to us, and said:

'Is the shuttle powered?'

'I'm sorry, Representative. Commander Mendez won't authorize the flight.'

I laughed. Looked at this man in Peace Force uniform and laughed, and then said, 'But I'm going anyway, you know that.'

'Commander Mendez won't authorize it yet.' He shot a glance at Doug that was almost an appeal for help. Run ragged, I thought. It's all fallen apart and even *you* know that. I said nothing.

Ottoway said, 'She's in the Rimnith-Keverilde area. When we reported you'd been found alive, she – Representative, she wants you there, wants you with her; she says a matter of the utmost urgency—'

'Commander Mendez isn't in a position to give orders now.'

Curious, to stand here arguing. This is trivial . . . The warm air soothes my skin, and back-blasts of heat come from more shuttle-craft as they land; and it is easy to look across the earth to the shuttle where her body lies. *I won't be long about it; we'll be gone soon. Tomorrow—*

How do I know that I have a day's grace to get her to the Tower? And then I thought: Listen to the memories. I already know a little of what she knew. That means I know what to do.

'—Representative!'

Ottoway stepped into my field of vision, blocking out the shuttle and the sea beyond. I brought my gaze back from the horizon, that line that is unique in nature, being straight; and stared at the man.

'Commander Mendez has a prisoner,' he repeated. 'She told me to give you the name of *Calil bel-Rioch—*'

That name, stumbled over by this man, spoken with a Sino-Anglic accent – he doesn't know what he's saying, I thought and Douggie's hand closed on my good shoulder, and I felt his tension.

'She's alive?' he demanded; then shook his head. 'It doesn't matter. I don't want to know. Lynne, I'll see you before you leave.' He let go of my shoulder and abruptly walked off.

A precipitate flight . . . he vanished into the entrance of the comlink-dome; a small, neat figure. And Ashiel Wellhouse will always be with him, I thought; and Sethri's death, and a cold heathland *telestre*, and the blindness and the fear.

'I can speak more openly, Representative, now that the government envoy isn't here. Commander Mendez wishes your help in interrogating the prisoner,' Ottoway said, with a kind of self-satisfied pleasure in this remnant of Security routine.

'She doesn't need *me*. The shuttle—'

'Commander Mendez won't pass a message in clear, except that she needs your specialized knowledge. It concerns the discussions you had here two days ago; and the research-report made by Dr Rashid Akida.'

I clenched both hands on the metal crutch; and suddenly realized how fragile a balance I held between control and collapse and I can't take this: Ruric, what do I do?

The sky is blue and daystarred, but I have been where Orthe's sky is acid-white. Where a city stands without walls, where there are rooms without doors; and I remember the Voice of the Emperor Dannor, and how we stood together in Kel Harantish, Calil and I, and called up a vision of the past aeons; and I remember her face in the throne-room saying *Your Molly Rachel is dead*.

Doesn't she know her bluff's been called? I thought caustically. Doesn't she know there's no weapon she can threaten us with now?

Lost, momentarily; I have no grip on the Tower's memories. I was conscious of being worn to the edge of exhaustion. The noise of shuttles landing battered at my ears; on the earth and sparse mossgrass, under a sky still shrouded with the smoke of burning.

'Get the shuttle ready,' I said. As Ottoway protested, I added, 'Contact Cory. Tell her I'll be landing in Melkathi inside the hour – and that I'll be leaving again immediately afterwards.'

In the few minutes before the shuttle was readied for flight, I limped up the slope to where I could look out across Kumiel Island to the north. And I could see across the straits and the estuary, to Tathcaer.

A summer wind began to blow, now that the sun was setting. The stink of burning grew strong enough to catch in the throat, and in eyes; is it possible, across six miles, to hear the crackle and roar of burning?

The silhouettes of the hills were ragged, no forts visible; and on Westhill, Westhill-Ahrentine would be *there* – no, too distant to make out one *telestre*-house. I strained my eyes, seeing alleys choked with rubble, smashed-open courtyards and buildings; half-sunk *jath* in the harbour . . . Smoke rolled down Easthill, obscuring the view. From here you can't see people, can't see the long trails of refugees. The blue hills are quiet, the river valley peaceful, even the pall of smoke hangs still and delicate in the golden air . . . pain and misery invisible now, and I thought *Blaize*.

How could I explain to him what I'm doing and why? I couldn't bear to see the look on his face – *I never want to see you again but I want to know you're living!*

And some caustic inner voice, that is no one else's but mine, observed, *You'll find that out eventually, the Tower has its agents and ways of knowing. You will discover, in the months to come, who has lived and who has died: all of them.*

And by then, maybe I won't care.

A voice hailed me from the field, and I went back, slow and awkward, to the ramp of the F90 shuttle; and went aboard.

Second twilight darkened to night over Melkathi's heathland. I walked from the shuttle to Ashiel Wellhouse, feeling the cold night breeze; and paused on that hill slope to look down to the east – the land was dark. Some things it is better not to want to see. The Peace Force officer fussing at my elbow came back, waiting impatiently; and I rubbed at my hip, at the top of the plastiflesh casing, and took a pain-tab from my belt-pouch. Chewing the bitter analgesic, I gripped my stick and limped across the courtyard – the domed building loud with lights and voices and then I saw why: Earthspeakers went between groups of wounded, lying out on the warm earth; gave *ataile*-juice for sleep; and when *s'aranthi* passed, ignored us as if we had no existence. A child sobbed, over by the low wall, and They'll hate us more for the wounded than for the dead; death is the lesser penalty, I thought. And then, ironically, And when did we become the enemy? One young, still face I didn't recognize until I had passed by; and then thought of a Freeport quayside and Rakviri food-ships – Pellin Asshe Kadareth, all threats silenced now.

'Commander, the Representative is here.'

Corazon Mendez stepped from the entrance of the Wellhouse, out into the torch-lit courtyard. Flickering yellow light shone on her rumpled uniform, on that sleek short-cut white hair; and I saw a CAS-IV holstered at her belt, a comlink held in the hand that now seemed suddenly thin; silver rings loose on those liver-spotted fingers.

'No one else on the shuttle?' Her voice was sharp.

'No, Commander,' the young officer said hastily.

'I'll have no WEBcasters travel on Service ships; I want none of them out here – Lynne, will you come inside.'

As I limped past her, I glanced into her face. It had a vague, almost blurred look; in sharp contrast to her speech. The pupils of her blue eyes were pinpoints; and she shut her eyes and squeezed the lids together, and casually dismissed the young officer.

'Glad to see you made it, Lynne.'

The bathos of that made me stop, in the curved inner room, and stare back at her; my hip ached and my leg was numb and I held self-control on a very fragile thread: 'Is that all you can say!'

'I don't want any of that nonsense.'

She walked past me, heading towards the inner rooms. They looked, through the round-arched entrance, to be deserted; I wondered why, and then saw the armed Peace Force officers there. *In a Wellhouse* – but there are worse things, now, than that.

'I'll see Calil bel-Rioch and then go,' I said.

'I thought . . . she's threatening us with Witchbreed Technology; nothing in it, of course, but one has to cover every eventuality. Seems to know a lot about it. God alone knows how much black-market arms trading the Ishida girl did; don't have to worry about *alien* technology . . .'

Corazon Mendez hesitated. A torch in a wall-cresset flickered, and her shadow shifted on the brickwork; and the wind brought the smell of many people crowded into close quarters: musk and sweat and dirt and sickness, and I tasted pain, metallic in my own mouth. Cory still stood as if she listened for something. Almost inconsequentially she said, 'There's still fighting going on. There'll have to be mop-up operations.'

Not with you, I thought. Anyone involved in this will be crucified at home, because PanOceania will have to make themselves look good; and so there have to be villains to pillory. You, and me if I were here, and *That also is not my concern*; in a way what I'm doing is cowardice.

As I followed Mendez through into the next room, I was suddenly hit by a memory – I have thought of Wellhouses, and of what I once said: to be marked for Her is not a privilege but a responsibility. Not *all* cowardice; I am going where the responsibility calls me. And if there are other apprentices in the Tower better suited, then I'll come back to Earth and take that responsibility there.

But I think I will not leave Orthe again.

'See if you can get anything out of the woman,' Cory Mendez stood back from a door-arch for me to go through. 'I don't – haven't the time.'

As she turned away I realized, *She's given up*. A kind of sadness touched me briefly; and vanished. I know very well that when the shock passes, she will have justifications that even she will believe, for what's happened here – for what we have done.

I stepped through the arch, into the main Wellhouse dome; and without knowing how I thought or sensed it, realized *Danger* and then *is Mendez right; is there nothing to be concerned about?* and a sudden fear twisted in my stomach: *it isn't over until it's over. And it isn't over yet.*

One of the Peace Force guards took my CAS-IV as I went in. The stone floor was hard underfoot, and the metal strut I used as a crutch skidded slightly; I put my weight down on my cased leg, and hissed as pain shot through my hip. I crossed the floor of the inner dome in a few limping steps, and lowered myself down to sit on the raised rim of the Wellmouth.

Light filled the room. Starlight shone in through the roof-slot, and an iron candlestand dripped under the weight of *becamil*-wax candles; that familiar sweet scent. Apart from that the room was bare. Yellow light, and moving shadows. No tables or couch-chairs and I thought, *Cory may not know or care what this place is, but why has the Wellkeeper let her use it to keep a prisoner in?* The Goddess's Well defiled by a Harantish Witchbreed in the inner sanctuary – and then I saw her and I knew . . .

'*Kethrial-shamaz shan'tai*,' said the Harantish Orthean woman, as she walked across the uneven brick floor. She carried a metal jug in one hand, and was chewing; and as I looked up she swallowed and wiped her mouth, and put the jug down on the rim of the Well beside me.

Small, no more than five feet high; and thin – her pale grained skin caught lamp and starlight, almost luminous; and her mane was a white fire drifting round that narrow face; and I sat gazing up at her for a long minute, silent, and realized that this woman was barefoot, and wearing a *meshabi*-robe yellow and brown with dirt; girdled with a verdigris-copper chain; and that she was ash-stained and bleeding from one foot, and none of it mattered – *she is Golden; is Santhendor'lin-sandru's heir, who was Phoenix Emperor and Last Emperor* – and I reached for my stick to try and stand up: pain jabbed hip and thigh as I tried to rise; and it cleared my head.

She is only one Orthean woman; a woman of the city Kel Harantish. And that's all she is, I thought; sinking back down, and reaching forward to shift my leg and try to ease it:

'*Kethrial-shamaz shan'tai* Calil.'

Never underestimate charismatic insanity – but she's a prisoner now. And more than that: the Tower has put memories in my mind – when she lies, I'll know, I thought; and I'll know when, and if, she tells the truth.

The young Orthean woman put a dirty, high-arched foot on the rim surrounding the Well. Starlight shone down into the Well-mouth, gleaming on black water that lay only a few inches down from the rim. There is never a smell of stagnant water in Wellhouses; I don't know why. She looked down at the glittering blackness, and her profile was sharp and unhuman. White mane rooted down her spine, fell forward over high cheek-bones; and she turned her head to gaze at me, nictitating membrane sliding back from sunny yellow eyes.

Why her and not you—?

'So you're living still,' the Orthean woman remarked cheerfully. As if she were perfectly at home, she sat down on the rim of the Wellmouth, rested her foot on the stone, and cupped Well water in her hand to bathe blood from her cuts; adding, 'I want to talk to you. These *s'aranthi* here are fools.'

Disgust filled me. I could rehearse what she's done, these past few months; but what use. I said, 'You're not important, Calil. Can you grasp that? You're not important; I've a few minutes here; if you've got anything to say, then say it. But you haven't, have you?'

Becamil-wax candles hissed in the silence, and burned tall and smoky. The pale plaster roof above them was becoming soot-blackened. The young Harantish woman leaned forward, resting her arms on her raised knee; so close to me that I could smell the musk of her skin. She smiled.

'No, I'm not important, *shan'tai* Christie. I always told you that. You would have it that no one in my city wanted this except myself – well, no matter; my Harantish bloodlines are still out there—' a thin, six-fingered hand gestured to the door; and the land beyond '—in the hills, or on *jath* and *jath-rai* . . . I tell you truthfully, whatever *I* would do if I were there now, there are a hundred Harantish who will do the same. And so no, I don't matter at all.'

Listening to her, I almost believe that she wants to be here. That the Peace Force guards just beyond the arch are unnecessary. That this is, as it was in that *chiruzeth* hall in Kel Harantish, an audience with the Empress-in-Exile . . . What a farce, I thought, half-amused, half-disgusted.

These are the people who would have occupied Tathcaer. And then this Calil bel-Rioch would have threatened the use of a weapon she doesn't have; would have threatened to make the Hundred Thousand into what the Elansiir and the Glittering Plain already are: sterile crystalline devastation . . .

'What do you want to say?'

Instead of answering, she put her arms down from her knee, and lowered the leg to the floor, and began to wipe at the mudstains on her *meshabi*-robe. The tiny hook-nails on her fingers were bitten ragged, and they caught in the cloth; and the skin of her six-fingered hands had in it a gold-dust sheen. She raised her head quickly, as if a sound startled her.

Why, yes – and I couldn't, for a moment, breathe; the realization choked me. *That pale hawk-face is younger than hers, but similarities go deeper than the eyes: that high-boned face is so like* . . . Ruric, didn't you say to me once, *My Desert Coast mother may have come from Kel Harantish?* And so she may, I thought. Is it coincidence, or some distant kinship of a bloodline?

Ah, but it doesn't matter to you now.

Calil bel-Rioch said, 'What have you done with my Pathrey Shanataru, *shan'tai*?'

'Done with—' I bit back amusement, thought, *What have we done with him? Ah, that's a question. He could be halfway to Kasabaarde and the Tower now* – and at that, cut off all thought; *I can't stand to remember yet what we said and did, Ruric and I, before this day.* 'The *shan'tai* Pathrey was very useful in bringing us some information.' *And let her remember* that, I thought; and repeated, 'What do you want?'

'I was not mistaken,' the Orthean woman said.

She rose lightly to her feet. My head swam when I looked up: the room lurched. *Exhaustion* – *I don't have time to waste here,* I thought. *The shuttle* . . .

Candles burned steadily, and then dipped; a night wind blowing in through the roof-slot, where the clustered stars blaze. Her elongated shadow danced on the pale, curving wall. She stood with her cut foot resting on claw-nailed toes; poised, as if she could run. Her robe was torn, and the smell of ash and soot hung in it. And as she turned to look down at where I sat, there was a line of head and shoulder and leg that was all grace, all strength; and the light shone on her floating white mane.

She said, 'I was not mistaken. You have the look of the Tower about you . . . *Shan'tai* Christie . . . have you travelled there, and learned, and learned well? I thought once that *I* would have to come to Kasabaarde. What I know, I do not know from them. *Shan'tai* Christie, have you learned well, and learned of what the Elansiir is?' Those lips curved; the nictitating membrane blinked down to veil her eyes.

'I've learned from the offworlders who were in Maherwa and the canals,' I said bluntly. I got both hands to the metal strut and levered myself upright, resting no weight on my right hip.

As the pain abated, I said, 'I don't know what it is you do. I don't care how close your people think you are to being Golden-blooded; I'm not even sure of what that means. You're threatening with something you don't have, your people don't have, no one has had on this world for thousands of years – and it's immaterial now. If I get one thing out of this, I'll get Cory to make certain you suffer for Molly's death. That girl . . .'

I see her in my mind's eye. Not the woman in PanOceanian uniform, but something I found in her Company record when I made the report on her death – an early image-cube. Against hot sunlight, an aborigine girl standing barefoot and in an old cotton dress; somewhere in her Pacifican homeland. That is Molly Rachel; that's all that's left.

'Her? That was not I; that was my Pathrey. He is something of a liar,' the young Harantish woman said; but her gaze shifted away from mine.

I want to hurt you – if exhaustion and pain weren't confusing me, I thought, I would know what to say; I would damage you so that you *care*. That it's a pinprick, compared to what is happening now on this world, I know and I don't care; and that there are others doing what you've done . . . Rage faded with the realization that quite probably any of the Harantish would have acted as she did.

Calil bel-Rioch turned, walking away from me. She carried one foot lame. When she stopped, it was on the far side of the Wellmouth. Candles gleamed on the black water. Her reflection shone – mirror-perfect: pale mane, gold-dust skin, and that hawk-face with the unveiled yellow eyes . . .

'They make their religion of this,' she said thoughtfully, staring down at the Well water. 'We gave them this, too. When we bred them from animals, bred memory into their bone . . . *Shan'tai* Christie, what did you learn in the Tower?'

To look down into that dark water is to sense the aeons of time past, the millennia that are gone; my eyes dazzled with the darkness. I have forgotten (or chosen to forget) that the past is not dead in me. That memory lives. I shivered, hands gripping tight on my stick; drugs and fever making me light-headed. I looked round at the Wellhouse walls, the pale plaster, and rough brick floor.

'I learned that what is made just for expediency's sake can become genuine.'

'Can it so?' She smiled, shook her head; and then reached down to dip her hand in the Well water, and straightened up again, and put her fingers in her mouth. And it was that simple movement that brought memory back in a rush: the Golden Empire and the dead who are gone, and this half-blooded Harantish woman wears the face that is Santhendor'lin-sandru's.

All I could say was '*Why?*' Blood doesn't compel; the past is not the present, surely?

She stood quite still. There were smears of black ash on her hands. Her robe was dirty. She stood: that whitefire mane taking the colours of candle-flame and starlight. Her eyes met mine, and I saw her exhaustion, her fear; and only then wondered how she had been hunted, captured, this young Orthean woman who now looks at me as if it is me she sees – not the Representative, not the *S'aranth*, but me.

'It's true that I wanted the Hundred Thousand for my people,' she said, 'and that certain things – to be Empress – I have wanted very badly. But that wanting, that desire, wouldn't be assuaged now by the having of it. Wanting things like that somehow awakens the real desire, the *real* longing, of which that is only a shadow or a memory.'

The water of the Well is ruffled, and the night wind is cold. Her soft voice continues:

'I *want* . . . something I had, or saw, or heard of, long ago. And if you ask what it is that I desire, I don't know. I have sensed it sometimes in the way light and haze and shadow fall – they remind me, I do not know how, that somehow and long ago I was disinherited; *we* . . . were disinherited, robbed, sent into exile; and we will always desire something to put in place of what we lost, and there is nothing to match that desire.'

Do the candles flicker, does the starlight fail? Between pain and fever and blindness; I want to call out, there are guards just outside this room. But the dome is thick with shadow. *You have cause to be afraid. We have all cause to be afraid!*

Tower-memories are mine, and at my control. Now, as she walks towards me, reaches up to brush my cheek with her long-fingered hand, I feel how it is to have memory *imposed* upon the mind: recall how eight years ago in the Tower I felt this pain that, if it lasted longer than an instant, would be intolerable agony; but this is not the Tower—

high walls thick with shadow

—Calil bel-Rioch's yellow eyes; and vision:

The Golden have lit fires upon which they cast bone and bread, in the secret places of the city; and speak over them words that should not be spoken; and go willing where – soon or late – the dawn of that ancient brilliance will take them. The thin tang of smoke and the charnel-house stench of the butchery in the lower city comes on the cool air to me now . . .

'Hear the word of Santhendor'lin-sandru! Hear the word of the Golden Empire. In the heart and centre of this city, in Archonys of the Six Lakes, this is Night's Festival!'

The half-blood who is the Emperor's Voice stands beside the Emperor's throne. And his words are hidden now in a great roar of sound, a multitude of voices; for this is the city's last festival, and this is the Empire's last festival, and this is the last that earth will know of us and we of earth.

'Hear the word of Santhendor'lin-sandru of the Golden! He has created in darkness a light that does not die. He has set in the flesh of this world a plague and a canker and a disease of all that is mortal. Now is the last ritual!'

On the vast chiruzeth floor, we raise our voices. Our robes are coloured grey and ash and black; and I stand, moving with my brethren of the Golden – they walk on high-arched feet, whitefire manes electric in the dark air. Our faces are this night hidden behind fantastic masks, painted blue and gold and silver; masks and robes reflecting in the mirror-black chiruzeth floor.

Now music sounds: the only music we will have, and that is our voices, raised in high paean: now one voice and now another, joining, changing, harsh, atonal – the echoes ring back from cyclopean galleries. We sing together, who are the Golden of Archonys.

Here on this timeless night, I have no name. I move alone.

And night comes.

Our hands lift, to scatter handfuls of light-dust upon the night air. Dust that swirls and drifts and glows the colour of frozen lightning. Arms sweep up, long-fingered hands open: light is cast upon the air, reflects in golden eyes, on sharp high cheekbones, drifts to catch in tangling manes . . .

One leads us, in a robe that is black and silver, and he cradles in the crook of one slender arm a globe and ragged staff. He comes to where we are, taking in his cold hand another's hand, leading us out to dance – no choice now but to join the dance – and he takes another's hand, and the chain begins to form. Led away, each of us: Golden and slave, great lords of the Witchbreed made equal now with the beast-born race; all equal in the Dance that ends all pride, levels all ambition—

I hear our voices soar up frail into the dark. Chiruzeth is cold under my feet: time breathes from its substance, darkening the air with the chill of aeons. A slender hand reaches out: I take it and move to the ritual measure.

'—Stop!'

Beyond the pillars I see out into the night, into the city. The walls go up into an infinite dark, that shrouds cornice and pinnacle and balcony and terrace. And in avenues like canyons between palaces and mausoleums, they are holding masquerade and festival—

'Cease!'

Dancers halt: a frieze of shock. Santhendor'lin-sandru on his high throne looks down and sees a slight figure, one of the slave race. It is one

940

of our failures, a child that has remained child although adult: the beast race call it ashirenin. There are a number of them every year, their lives are short.

Ke raises kir head, gazing with membraned eyes at the Emperor Santhendor'lin-sandru on his throne. Kir skin is a rich, burnt-earth brown, and kir mane is gold, flowing down the spine, braided round kir sharp face.

'O did I not say—'

Kir rich, sexless voice; halfway between speech and song.

'—say, your time would come to you, as it came to the Eldest Empire before you—'

Slowly, we gather round. Ke is barefoot on the black chiruzeth floor, and ke stands and gazes, ignoring watchers; kir eyes only on Santhendor'lin-sandru.

'—that your time would come, and you would pass away from the earth!'

Ke laughs. There are small flowers braided in kir mane, and ke puts that mane back from kir lined face, with hands calloused by long years of labour. Somewhere far up in the galleries a flute is being played, up in the tenebrous arches.

Santhendor'lin-sandru stands. His white metalmesh robe trails after him, its collar frames his hawk-face: that face that is all angles; cruel mouth and sun-gold eyes. Behind him are swathes of crepuscular light.

Wearily, he says, 'Take that and kill it.'

'No, you who were called Emperor!'

And he says, 'Why not? You are Ours, We created you, bred you up from the night-hunter beasts of the fens to be Our servants—'

'As you were bred by others.' Ke smiles, head high, alone. 'Emperor of the Golden, we were all created, and what is that to you or me?'

There are knives in the hands of us who crowd close to kir, but ke ignores them. Seems small and dirty beside the pale grandeur of Santhendor'lin-sandru, that white and gold.

And in softest voice Santhendor'lin-sandru asks, 'What comfort have you for Us, who now pass from this earth?'

The ashirenin says, 'None.'

Silence in these halls, so deep that one feels the pressure of it: a sea-bed silence.

The ashirenin looks at him with clear eyes.

'I have no comfort for you, Last Emperor. You have cut yourself off from all comfort. What consolation there is, is ours. Is that of the beast-made, the slave races, the followers in dark cities of a light that does not die – of a light that returns dawn by dawn, and fails sunset by sunset, only to return again.

'We have the comfort of Her face, that brings life from the earth, and

941

quickens death to life again. We have the comfort of that turn and return of the solid world; for we shall come again and walk upon the earth, for we have our knowledge of Her – we meet, and part, and meet again, and do not forget.'

And, sardonic and amused, the Emperor says, 'You have Our permission to believe that. When We made you, We bred that memory into your bone, into the motes of your flesh, so that you recall your mother's lives, and your mother's mother's; but do not ever take it for more than that. We allow you your delusion, little animal, but We mock that belief, for We know whence it came.'

Black chiruzeth reflects them, white and gold shadows in the depths of night; they are dwarfed by the pillars, and by the catafalque-throne, but all our eyes are on them, those two bright figures.

The ashirenin stands, a scatter of light-dust about kir feet, sphere-lights above kir in the tenebrous air:

'This will be remembered, and forgotten, and remembered again, in the ages that are to come – hear me, Santhendor'lin-sandru! We may come to joy by way of an evil act. We may come to truth by way of a lie. Could She not use you, as you have used us? If you made us as we are, still, She made all as it is.

'O hear me, you in the city, you in the darkness! Hear me!'

The ashirenin turns now to face us, to the tens of thousands that watch kir; and ke stands, mane woven with flowers, tunic ragged and earth-stained. Kir eyes are clear as spring water.

'Hear me,' ke says, 'for I have been marked for Her, in the secret places of the earth, and I have drunk from the Wells of Her wisdom, and I see, I know – for our love of Her, we have only this reward: to carry the burden of Her preservation, and that burden we may not set down. You have loosed a death upon the world, but it will not ravage all. I see, I know—'

It is the last word of the ashirenin. Our bodies surge forward and overwhelm kir, we cry out as ke falls, and then there is a sound of bone wrenched from bone and flesh ... A stain upon the chiruzeth, spilled blood; no other sign remaining.

And Santhendor'lin-sandru looks down upon us from his high place, and speaks:

'Let the Dance again begin!'

The stars move in their ritual patterns, and this earth turns towards the dawn.

Pain breaks it.

I felt the metal strut slip on the uneven floor; then my cased leg

942

slid out from under me and I fell, twisting sideways; the leg without any sensation at all – but the red agony that ripped through my side and hip! I struggled, got one leg under me; felt my grazed hands on the floor. And then two hands gripped my shoulders, and I froze: aware of the candlelight flickering on the walls, shimmering on the surface of the Well. And saw, as she knelt down by the low wall, the face of Santhendor'lin-sandru's child.

I opened my mouth to cry out and she said gently, in that language that only the Imperial bloodline have ever spoken:

'___ __ _____'

Be silent, now.

My voice dried in my throat.

The brick floor was painful under me. Her face, close to mine, shone with a light that seemed to come from beneath her own skin. *Santhendor'lin-sandru. Zilkezra of the Golden.* And I have seen through those eyes—

Incredulous, I thought, That's no Tower-memory; how did she – ? and remembered a shared vision, outside Kel Harantish.

'This is Our city's festival,' she said, 'and this is the last night. That ancient light will dawn upon us, in an hour and an hour and an hour. And you have seen that great city; and you have seen the fall of the Golden Empire.'

Her yellow eyes unveiled, clear as water; held me in some fascination or some moment out of Time. Pain throbbed, my mouth was dry; and I saw her simultaneously, Calil bel-Rioch of some dirtwater settlement in a desert, and Calil bel-Rioch who is the last of that ancient race, the Golden Witchbreed.

And why should she not be answered? Ruric left me a legacy of the past, of the Tower; I can answer her now.

'No—' Speech an effort: I forced myself. 'If that's a true memory, what does it matter now? The world didn't end with the passing of the Empire.'

I have the memory in me of those who have been Hexenmeister. With those intent eyes on me, I spoke at last with the full knowledge of that. As if I exist on two levels: this human body, dirty and pain-ridden and weary with grief, that will one day be only another's memory; and the mind that sees, in her face, the past-memories of the Golden . . .

'The secret of its making is lost,' I said, 'and you cannot recover it. If *I* could not, in all my lives in the Tower, then you in your handful of years cannot expect to search out the secret heart of it, no more than Rashid Akida could. You do not have that weapon to threaten us with, Calil bel-Rioch. No matter that your memory of it is clear after three thousand years.'

She said, 'Do you think that We do not know what you do, what you hope?'

Her thin hands knot in the cloth of my coverall; bitten claw-nails scratch the skin. There is a sour stink of dirt about her; her copper belt stains her robe green. And all of this exists with that hawk-gold face, those shining eyes.

' "You may even stave it off for a time, you in the south, with your Tower, and your memories that are of the mind and not of the blood . . ." ' Calil speaking words that are not hers. ' "But you cannot prevent it forever. We can wait the millennia that are only moments. It will come." '

Now she stood, and I could no longer see her face; and it was Calil's own voice that went on:

'There is a Bright Realm that they speak of in the Wellhouse here. The Goddess's fire, that is the sun's fire; and do they know, I wonder, that you built a Tower that holds the sun in its grip; that it is only the sun's radiance holds back the disease of earth, holds back ancient light from their cities and their fields . . . Do they know, or do they choose to forget, or did they never know? Tell me, *S'aranth*.'

The only movement I can make is to shake my head.

'Do they know,' says Calil bel-Rioch, Empress-in-Exile, in that Wellhouse room that is cold with night and silence, 'that their only protection, for millennia, has been the Tower? And do they know that when the Tower falls, all else falls?'

And she says, 'Call a festival, for this is the last night of my people—'

But the Dance is ended.

Dawn comes through the great arches, and I walk towards them. These have been windows opening into depths and darkness, the view from a height, and now – dawn. Warmth falls on my face as I approach, leaving the shadows. The cool of chiruzeth *halls is replaced by fragile heat. The sun glows azure and aquamarine in the edges of the* chiruzeth *arch, a great open archway, and beyond it—*

It is early morning. Pale haze is fading with the sun's rise. I look down, down on terraces of chiruzeth *that fall away below me like cliffs. And all the terraces are crowded with my people.*

Their skins like milk in the morning light, their manes like clouds; and they stand at balustrades carved with vines, all their faces turned towards the east, the east where the sun rises through the mist into a pale blue sky skeined with daystars.

944

They look. O they look, my people, and there is no space in that intense gaze for speech. I see how we stand together, arms interlinked, hands clasped, in embrace.

And as I watch, that pale yellow sunlight is tinged on far eastern hills, with a harsh silver—

Archonys of the Six Lakes, great beyond all cities, your towers in the morning sun, your great halls, your ziggurats and terraces – !

Now all eastern-facing walls are crowded with the city's people, come out to see this last dawn. Come out to stand in warm air that smells of leaves and city dust, come out to stretch in the heat of the morning sun; their faces turning up like flowers towards the light—

On eastern hills: a line of light that is silver, older than Time, bright and deadly.

I walk out on to the terrace, chiruzeth *cool under my bare feet. I hear the soft clash of the metalmesh robe as I lift it from me and let it fall: stand naked to the gold eye of the sun.*

And from here to the eastern hills, all is Archonys; is that great city. And on terraces that face the east, they stand, my people.

Casting aside their metalmesh robes, and raising long-fingered hands to tear their manes, to scratch their cheeks and lacerate their eyes, to raise up their voices in lamentation, to stand naked to the morning that is the last morning that this great city will ever see—

Crying their agony, the long agony of regret, for night passed that will not pass again, for day come that must soon die; for all the years that now will not come to aKirrik and Simmerath, to the City Over The Inland Sea; agony for this heart of empire that beats no more, for Archonys that is fallen, fallen; and for all the days and years and centuries that now we shall not have—

Do I weep the tears of the Golden, the world vanishing in splintered light? Do I see those sunwarmed terraces transmute to silver-crystal death?

Ah, there is no time: no time for regret that pierces sharp as a sword. We have loved the darkness and the light; and now the face of the Sun is turned from us, She has left us, earth's children, now we fade into a dream of ancient time, into a past that holds greater Empires than ours, but no greater death—

'_____ __ _____'

'____ ____'

'_____ __ _____'

Give praise, O praise us; and weep for us who loved that bright shadow, and wept too late; and will not see again sunlight and noon—

'_____ _____'

Weep for Us, and praise the light!

*

'—Do they know,' Calil bel-Rioch says, 'that when the Tower falls, all else falls?'

Her face is weary and exalted and incandescent; as if she has found at last something that will assuage that desire. The shadow of Santhendor'lin-sandru's joy (and, yes, his grief) is in her eyes. And in that ancient tongue she says:

'Did your people tell you, it cannot be created now? Ah, that's true; but it is already there and waiting. And we made our plans long ago for this, and now the Tower falls, and all barriers with it. I could not halt it now, even if that were my desire—'

A moment's aching regret, and then her voice continues:

'—all barriers fall. And we have loosed that ancient light, to dawn upon the world.'

CHAPTER 40

Carrick V

Whatever I would do, she said, *there are a hundred Harantish who will do the same.*

I got to my feet somehow. At the arched doorway, I stopped; one of Cory's officers glanced at me with concern, and looked past me into the Wellhouse room.

'Do you want her moved, Representative, or kept here?'

That small figure is seated on the stone rim of the well, looking down into black water; and one thin hand holds a metal jug with which she scoops up water and pours it out again, in an endless repeating cycle . . . starlight lays a mist of silver above the Well; and her whitefire mane falls down on to her filthy robe; and that hawk-face looks down into the Goddess's Well.

And now the Tower falls.

What I said to the officer I don't know. The Wellhouse's claustrophobic domed rooms passed by in a dream; I limped, and pushed my way between Ortheans clad in priests' robes, and the wounded who lay blanket-wrapped on the floor.

And then the world came back into focus.

'*Cory—*'

Two or three young officers already occupied the room where she was; clustered round a field-comlink. Their voices had a note of hopeless urgency. Ignoring the thin crackle of reports coming in from the F90 and YV9 shuttles overflying the *telestres*, I braced my stick on the floor and limped across to where Corazon Mendez sat.

She sprawled on a couch-chair, legs stretched out before her. That sleek hair was now slicked to her forehead, pale against her liver-spotted skin; and she stared up at me with blurred eyes, and a face looking ten years older.

'You've heard what she says, then? Brought her in an hour ago, and then suddenly she claims . . .'

'What have you done?'

Cory Mendez swung her feet down, and stood up; her silver-ringed hands brushing at her coveralls, and with a touch of her old sharpness, said, 'What do you take me for, Lynne? I've had round-the-clock satellite surveillance on that place, since we were informed how vital it is. There hasn't been a minute in the last few days when I haven't had a sensor reading of the Kasabaarde settlement available.'

And I completely forgot to . . . But relief was swallowed up by apprehension: 'Have you got any shuttles there now?'

'No.' The Pacifican woman's face relapsed into lines of age. 'With what's been happening here? I ordered two F90s out an hour ago, from Kumiel, but they have to repower . . . The Kasabaarde settlement's quiet; nothing's happening!'

'What are we worrying about? She can't destroy the Tower.' But a dread was growing in me. I thought: No matter how long ago it was thought of . . . what arms; what technology . . . *but didn't someone say to me once: Anything can be a weapon?*

Corazon Mendez said, 'There's enough dangerous equipment on that continent to destroy a dozen settlements. It isn't the arms trading I'm thinking of. Representative Rachel had Trade&Aid programmes underway. If you check the records you'll see earth-blasters, automatic deep-mine construction equipment – which T&A trains the local population to use. And that could have been moved. If this has been a long-term plan—'

Outside, the heathland is dark under the Heart Stars' radiance; and a few miles to the south, the sea laps on the Melkathi sandflats; and over the ocean, south and west, lies a desert shore: there is Kasabaarde, there is the broken and deserted inner city, that home of violence and vision; there is the Tower. If will could move me, I would stand there *now*.

'I'm taking the shuttle,' I said. 'You?'

The woman looked over at the young officers round the field-comlink. Her face was blank with bereavement. Stripped momentarily of her role as Security Officer, Company officer; she now turned her face to me, and we both stood in silence. *If we had only known* becomes *too late* in the tick of a clock. She smiled vaguely, painfully; said, 'Yes. I should be there.'

As she left with me, she turned back and ordered one of her junior officers: 'See that government envoy Clifford is informed about where we've gone. I'll contact him from the shuttle. Tell him it's a matter of—' Corazon paused, expression fully conscious of irony. How to make words encompass *this*? She said bitterly, '—a matter of the utmost urgency.'

*

The hull of the F90 shuttle curved against the stars, the light bright enough to show the fire-stains on it; and as I limped awkwardly up the ramp, I smelled in the night air the scent of crushed mossgrass. Cool dew fell. I looked back once at the domes of the Wellhouse, and the flickering yellow lights. A *rashaku* cried, invisible in the night air, disturbed by the noise the wounded made. Hill and heathland stretched silver-grey under starlight, and far to the east there were pinpricks of orange light that might be fire.

The shuttle thrummed into life, and I let the port close, and leaned heavily on my stick as I walked down the cabin and sat by the holotank. Soft green light illuminated the consoles. The pilot, a Pacifican man in his forties, looked queryingly at Corazon Mendez: she leaned over his shoulder to key in a course.

I reached down, lifting my plastiflesh-cased leg and trying to ease it into a comfortable position. Pain throbbed, held back by tabs; and, light-headed, I thought, Here am I in a shuttlecraft of the PanOceania multicorporate Company, on *telestre* land in Melkathi – And not far inland of us now is the place where Orhlandis *telestre* burned, one summer, eight years ago.

If you had seen this then, *amari* Ruric, what would you have done?

The cabin floor vibrated as the shuttle rose. I reached to key in a holotank image. The comlink crackled with transmissions from other shuttles – refuelled at Kumiel, and gone out again? – flying surveillance over the Hundred Thousand: Melkathi and Rimon and Ymir, the city Tathcaer and the Oranon River valley . . .

Land is burning, now. The white city is burning, its pale plaster-walled buildings smashed open; and Citadel Crag is smashed; and what dead lie in the wreckage, and what hurt and unrescued – ? *If we had generations, it might heal.*

Corazon Mendez leaned over to key out the volume of the comlink transmission, and I said, 'Leave it.'

Comprehension came. She didn't speak, and the pilot was silent as he swung the big craft round and set a course to the south-west; and the quiet of the cabin was broken only by the comlink's crackle and hiss: thick with interference.

Don't let it clear.

If that goes, it will be the first intimation that the Tower no longer functions; and that the barriers against the spread of ancient light have been broken down.

*

And the hours of the night pass, this ship racing above the ocean, as the dawn line races at our heels. The stars move in their ritual patterns, and this earth turns towards the morning.

I sat at the holotank, watching the images of night and the bitter sea.

Nothing has happened, nothing is happening—

The seat was uncomfortable, the cabin hot. Cory Mendez sat by the pilot, saying nothing. I leaned back from the holotank, rubbing at my hip.

Half a year . . . Impossible, I thought. Six months ago I stepped on to Orthean soil, outside that city without walls; and Molly with me; what did we think we were going to do? Aid the starving and win profits for the Company? Ah, it seems incredible. How could we have guessed, then, that it would lead to this?

My mouth was sour and dry. I manoeuvred myself up to get a pain-tab and a drink from the console, pausing to listen to the comlink. No words distinguishable now, only the hiss and spark of a radiant interference: *counter-radiation, a suppressor* . . .

I didn't go to the cabin at the rear of the shuttlecraft, where her body lies.

As I sat down, staring into a holotank that showed only blackness, I thought, *But it was inevitable.*

Once such destructive power is created, it will be used. No matter that years pass, and millennia; that is only a hiatus. The universe is older than comprehension and time is infinite. In time, it has been only a tick of the clock since that great Empire fell: this was implicit from the beginning . . .

I thought of Calil's face, drained of all vision. *I want something I had, or saw, or heard of, long ago . . . I have sensed it sometimes in the way light and haze and shadow fall.* And then: *That desire wouldn't be assuaged now by the having of it . . . it awakens the real desire, of which that is only a shadow and a memory.*

And my head is full of visions, hers and mine and history's: the face of Santhendor'lin-sandru, and that great city, and the slave race that gave into their hands the power to destroy a world, and which came first? The power to consume all earth in annihilation, or the desire for that bright shadow?

For a moment I believe that I felt it, that same triumph that Calil bel-Rioch dreams in one of the Goddess's houses, a continent away to the north; and then I had a sudden memory of how, all one long afternoon, we had played *ochmir* in the great square under the Citadel, Haltern and Blaize and I; how Ruric and her child Rodion waited with us, waiting to hear, at Midsummer-

Tenyear, the name of the new Crown of the Hundred Thousand – *which will never happen again*. That is true, whatever happens now. And—

After so much, to lose by so little, when we thought we'd won.

Night passed, clouds blocked the stars and then cleared as we flew southwards; cased in that small craft that sped on, five miles above the surface of the ocean. A speck inching across the face of the world: drawing steadily away from the northern continent, the *telestres*, the outbreaks of fighting; coming closer all the while to a desert coast and deserted canals, and a city that lies in the shadow of the Rasrhe-y-Meluur.

Corazon Mendez moved between the comlink console and the holotank, studying the heat-sensor images that the satellites transmitted from orbit.

'Nothing yet . . .' The black-uniformed woman slumped down into a seat beside me. She rubbed at her eyes. 'I can't raise Kumiel, but I imagine Clifford is following us. The troops in the F90s should arrive at least an hour before we do; I'll have them turn that settlement inside out.'

'If there's anything there, they'll find it.' I checked the course in the data-tank. 'Estimate we'll get there inside two hours from now.'

I looked round the narrow, cramped cabin. The thrum of power vibrated through the metal walls; and figures changed constantly in the 'tank, feeding in navigation-details, bright in the dim light. Tension made a hard knot in my chest, and I thought *Do we dare hope?* Oh yes: in the face of all the evidence!

And I turned my head briefly to look down at the door of that closed cabin, behind which lies the body of *amari* Ruric Orhlandis, Ruric Hexenmeister. *When I am in the Tower, when I inherit her memories with the memories of others who were Hexenmeister, then I'll know – if she ever forgave me for coming here:* s'aranthi, *offworlder,* human. Is that a petty consideration, in this clash of worlds? Yes: but I can't comprehend worlds, only her.

Silence.

Cory's head came up, I had time to think, *What's missing?* and realize that the hiss of comlink interference no longer filled this cabin; and the transmission broke through clearly –

—massive power-discharge! All craft out of the area; repeat, out of the area—

Alarms blared. The satellite-image in the holotank cut out for a split second. It refocused: the pattern of heat-sensor readings leaping wildly. And then all in a minute became still.

Corazon Mendez looked in blank disbelief at the hologram-images.

Lights flashed on the comlink console, and transmissions blared, frantic voices overriding each other with questions, and each voice sounded with no distortion: clear and complete, in the silence.

Earth turns, faster than we travel.

The dawn line raced across the sea, passing us, leaving in its wake fire and foam, and the morning white and gold. The Company shuttle flew low now, at ten thousand feet. The images in the holotank showed storm clouds massing along the southern horizon.

And over that horizon, in the heart of the southern continent that the Witchbreed called Elansiir, weather-patterns are shifting out of constrictions they have endured for millennia, and now endure no longer.

Is it hours or seconds that pass?

The shuttle's cabin grew hot; loud with the transmissions coming from other shuttles, from the base nine hundred miles away on Kumiel Island, from the Company station in its earth-circling orbit. Corazon Mendez left her seat and took the pilot's place; the routine of flight needing all her concentration now; and the officer came to stand beside me where I stared down into the holotank. Visual images: clear and precise.

Flying south, to the Desert Coast.

We came in over the sea, casting a moving shadow on the blue water. The wide dome of the sky was azure, and thick with white daystars; and on the southern horizon clouds began to rise up into the stratosphere.

Some things are too big to be seen: I had been staring for whole minutes before I saw that here there was no skylined *chiruzeth* spire. The blue-grey of the Rasrhe-y-Meluur gone – and then the shuttle dipped low, and we passed over titanic ruins: the deep ocean itself not sufficient to cover them. Deep green water washed over *chiruzeth* that is splintered, tumbled like an avalanche into the sea covering the continental shelf.

A very few minutes after that, the shuttle reached land.

Walls breached, buildings shattered: the floodwater of those vast tidal waves still washes through the harbour of Kasabaarde. We are too high to see more than moving specks, high above panic and terror and destruction. I thought dreamily, Earthquake waves, awed by the magnitude of such destruction; a destruction whose epicentre lay a little to the south. Dust still hung in the stratosphere, dispersing slowly. And below—

Now there is no trade-quarter, those ramshackle buildings are gone, and the *jath* ships driven onto rocks or into deep water. Now there is no inner city, those white domes turned to powder.

And where the Tower stood is a crater, quarter of a mile across and eight hundred feet deep; sensors in this ship perceiving through a haze of pulverized rock no life, no recognizable structure, no stone upon stone left standing.

Because we have entered the city, a wasteland will grow here. Because we have entered the city, great ones will go to corruption. We are the bringers of death. Go you and cry: we are dead and come to corruption, in this resurgence of that ancient light.

By noon, a raw wind was blowing. The sky cleared, bright and daystarred, and the wind blew in gusts that tugged at the grounded shuttlecraft, and shook it where it rested on the rocky earth.

The dome of the sky shone clear above me, and Carrick's Star dazzled from other shuttles a little way off. Dust skirled. The diggers in Company uniforms rested on the haft of the machine, swore, and then manoeuvred it back to carving a slit trench in the ground.

I rested, leaning on my stick, and the wind tugged at me. All around stretches the barren rock and earth of the Desert Coast, a glint of sea there between low hills; and there, in the west, the sky that should hold the *chiruzeth* pinnacle of the Rasrhe-y-Meluur, and that sky is empty now. And at my feet, shrouded for a burial which is not the custom of her people, lies *amari* Ruric Orhlandis, Ruric Hexenmeister. And the wind blows.

No, I thought fiercely, not *your* failure. If this hadn't happened in your lifetime it would have been in someone else's; no one should have to take decisions like these! There *are* no all-knowing, infallible authorities – not my people, and not Ortheans; and no, not even in the Tower.

Southward, the low hills of the Elansiir stand out distinctly, as if they stand out against a raw light.

The Company men backed the excavator out of the grave in a flurry of dust; and as they did so, I saw other people approaching from the shuttles. Corazon Mendez walked ahead of the others, carrying herself stiffly, and at her shoulder came Doug Clifford, speaking in a furious undertone that as he halted burst into speech: 'If not for your ships firing, your provocation, this would never have happened!'

The Peace Force commander swung round on him, her face drawn, and said incredulously, '*Provocation!* I couldn't let Company personnel be fired on and do nothing. Your business is to keep the situation from getting to that stage, *envoy*; why didn't you?'

'Don't—' It isn't right that we should argue over a grave as if it were offal we're burying!

They fell silent. Closer to the shuttles there were guards, and I squinted against the sun, and saw a dark Orthean male amongst them; realized then that Pathrey Shanataru must still have been on Kumiel, and would have been brought here by Doug, and *what does it matter, now*? If we learn the names of whatever Harantish Ortheans brought Trade technology into the city of Kasabaarde; and exactly what kind of equipment it was; does it matter?

Another Orthean walked past the guards, crossing the stretch of rocky earth between the shuttles and this makeshift grave. Walking in the raw air, eyes veiled against noon: a male with a yellow mane, in mercenary's gear, and with *harur*-blades, and with a face half masked by the scar of an old burn . . . Blaize Meduenin stopped, and glanced down at her shrouded body.

'You should give her the passing of fire,' he said, 'it's the custom of the Hundred Thousand.'

Noon shadow pooled blackly at his feet. I reached out a hand but he stepped back. That scarred face turns to the sky, as if he can see past daystars to inhabited worlds, to the worlds of the Heart Stars and the Home Stars, to Earth. As if he can feel urgent voices on WEBcasts, recriminations already beginning . . .

'You can leave worlds behind you,' he said. 'Where can we go, who can't leave this earth and live?' His face twisted with disgust.

Doug Clifford interrupted: 'You're as much to blame for this as any of us, *T'An*; you fought the *hiyeks*!'

The light on the horizon is silver: older than Time.

'No, don't – please—'

The noon sun of Carrick V shines down with a radiance that is fragile and bright and powerless; shines down on Ortheans, Envoy, Representative, Commander; who stand as if this is a ritual that we must conclude.

Our quarrelling voices rise over this barren land, and the unfilled grave where scavengers already gather.

The Crystal Sunlight, the Bright Air

Paul Broderick came to Orthe a haunted man.

You'll have no trouble, the Intendant who briefed him promised. Orthe's a regained world. There were Earth settlements on it before the Insurrection. The natives are used to humans.

Go down, Broderick. Find out if this world needs the Interdict.

Haine's Star scorched down on Orthe, on Kasabaarde's narrow streets, reflecting back from the white domes and ankle-deep dust. The acid light bit into his eyes, even behind the face mask's protective glass. Dust irritated his skin. He quickened his pace towards the wall separating trade district from inner city. If there was cause for the Interdict, it had to be there. Nothing outside the wall was unusual – after the Insurrection. An agricultural society living in the ruins of a high-technology past.

Wind brought the smell of marine life from the harbour, close by the gate. Sunlight fractured off the sea like broken glass. Broderick approached the Ortheans at the gateway.

'You wish to enter the inner city?'

His hypno-trained mind translated the breathy sounds and sharp clicks. He answered as well as he could.

The Orthean who spoke was a head shorter than Broderick. Bleached skin under the city's dust showed a hint of scale-pattern. Masked – as all Ortheans were outdoors – there was only a glimpse of eyes set widely apart under a broad forehead. Under the mask's edge, thin lips curved in a reptilian smile.

'Wait,' the humanoid said. Pale hair was caught up in complex braids; as she turned to consult the others he saw the mane was rooted down her spine to the small of her back. A length of cloth wrapped her narrow hips. Thin ribs were prominent. Small breasts were set higher than the human norm, and a second pair of rudimentary nipples were visible on her lower ribs. He noted the seamed belly. Oviparous.

'It is permitted.' She faced him again. 'Touch the earth.'

He knelt and touched the dry ground, and when he stood she took a bowl of water from another Orthean and offered it to him. He drank, indifferent to infection.

'If you have weapons you must leave them with us. They will be returned to you when you go.'

He carried a knife for just such occasions, and gave it to her. The weapons he carried wouldn't be recognized on a world like this.

'Is there somewhere I can stay in there?' he asked, as they registered his name and possessions in the gatehouse. 'Somewhere cheap?'

'Anywhere.' Her six-fingered hand flicked out, a gesture including all the streets and domes beyond the wall. 'All the Order houses are open to you, Outlander. Open and free. There is no gold in the inner city, not for strangers, nor for us.'

'"Free?"' Broderick said, appalled; and when they had translated it several ways so that there was no mistake: *'free?'*

And then:

What are you doing here, Paul?

No, he thought. No! Not again. Don't think about it—

What right does the Holy Dominion have over this world, what justification for the Interdict? Why, Paul, why?

His haunt was a woman-shaped emptiness visible on the air, distorting the pale sky and squat buildings. Grief and doubt threatened to overwhelm him. He stifled the remembered voice.

Broderick entered the inner city of Kasabaarde.

When Clare Felix died the whole world grieved.

They told Paul Broderick she was dead and he didn't believe it. He heard and smiled: it was a fiction, like the games he and Clare played. A world couldn't exist in which she could be dead.

They thought they made him understand. He understood. The shock blinded and deafened him, but not for long. News of that death would have touched him, he thought mechanically, if he had been dead himself.

He went out blindly into the streets of the megalopolis, into the dust and fumes of a wholly inappropriate summer day. In the crystal sunlight, the bright air, he stood trying to realize it: Clare is dead. Is Dead. Clare is dead but the world's still whole, I still exist, and Clare—

—is dead.

He walked past familiar crowded shops. The news was out by then, satellite-broadcast to the world. On the faces of people he passed, he saw a shadow of that raging grief.

He didn't notice when it began, but after a time he knew that in every shop he passed the tapes of Clare Felix's songs were being played. The music and the words that she had sweated over, snarled at him for interrupting, hummed when they loved – those songs were coming out into the dusty grieving city.

He might have run. He found himself, gasping for breath, in front of a public newsscreen. The dead woman's voice sang out under the noise of traffic, the rumble of the distant starport. People slowed, hesitated, listened; a girl cried. Lines of type formed beside her picture on-screen. Her kind of death would have attracted attention on Parmiter's World in any case: they tended to long lives, not massive coronaries at twenty-seven. Being who she was . . .

Broderick read the customary closing line with a new razor-edged attention. *'She lives in the union of the Holy Dominion; her spirit is with us forever.'*

He waited for the comfort that always brought him. It didn't come. When the weeks turned to months, he realized it would never come.

Wider streets opened here, still with the cloth awnings stretched from dome to dome. The shade was welcome. Sweat tracked down between his shoulders. Few Ortheans moved in the noon heat; they sprawled on the steps that led up to the domes, or sat with their backs against the stone walls and stared into space.

Broderick walked for some time down the avenues. At last, having no better guide, he chose a door at random, pushing through the bead curtain and entering the bright room beyond.

'Welcome to Thelmithar.' A male Orthean paused at the head of a flight of spiral steps. He was darker-skinned than many, his mane receding from his brow until there was only a white crest left. His movements had the carefulness of age.

'Is there somewhere I can eat?' Broderick asked.
'Of course. Will you stay here?'

It was as good a place as any, he thought. 'Yes.'

'Come with me. I'm Surinic,' the old male said. 'Ask for me if you need anything.'

Broderick followed him down the spiral stairs and came into a bright underground hall. Silver light reflected diffusively from mirrors set in the vaulted roof: sunlight directed down from above. A young Orthean played the twin-flute in a corner. The tables round the still pool were mostly empty. Children scuttled past, sparing him curious glances.

He ate what time in the trade district had proved unlikely to cause allergic reaction: breadfungus, *brennoir*-meat, and *arniac*-herb tea. When he left the table, he called the old Orthean.

'I'll pay for a room now,' he said, testing.

The thin lips curved. Surinic weighed the cord of metal beads that passed for money in the trade district and handed them back to Broderick.

'You will be an Outlander, then, not to know there is no payment in the Order houses. Here at Thelmithar – and Gethfirle, Cir-nanth, all the others – they'll feed you, house you, clothe you if you desire it. Freely.'

'For how long?'

'As long as you wish to stay.'

His mind protested, *Nothing's free!* 'If not money, then what? Labor? Information?'

The old Orthean unmasked. Broderick saw his whiteless animal eyes, and the nictitating membrane that slid slowly across the slit pupil. Those hooded eyes held indefinable amusement.

'We're unfortunate,' he said. 'All who travel up the Desert Coast to trade must pass through Kasabaarde, and also all who come down from the north and the islands. All who pass us pay. The Order houses have tolls and taxes, Outlander. They can afford the inner city.'

Broderick shook his head. 'Why give anything away?'

'If you have to ask, why have you come?' The tawny eyes veiled. 'We give only one thing – time. Come here and we free you, feed and house you; but what we give away is time.'

This, Broderick thought. *If anyone can come here, and not have to work – this is why we're considering the Interdict.*

'Time for what?'

' "Idleness breeds violence and vision," the Orders say. There are other values besides what you wear on your back and put in your belly, Outlander. Thelmithar can give you time – what you do with it depends on what you are.'

'Violent or visionary?' It was an involuntary, cynical remark.

Surinc's six fingers linked in a complex gesture. 'I can't tell you what you'll find here. If I could, it wouldn't be the true illumination.'

Reduced to simplicity, Broderick protested, 'People can't just do nothing!'

'No, indeed. Most can't. But those who can . . .'

Left alone, Broderick sat for a while, then felt driven to go back up into the open air. Under the awning's shade, many Ortheans sat on Thelmithar's steps. Come from both continents? Broderick wondered. The concept of the inner city stunned him. It was dangerous.

And will you bring the Interdict down on this city of philosophers?

He shook his head to clear it, but couldn't rid himself of the caustic, loving voice of the dead woman.

Broderick left Parmiter's World a scant few weeks after Clare's death. Her face stared down from newsscreens, her voice followed him in the streets. He left because he knew he'd never hear her songs offworld, never hear her name.

Clare Felix's songs and music were under Interdict.

'How can they do it?' she'd raged. 'I'm good, Paul. All over this planet—'

'Too good,' he admitted. 'Too strong, if you like, for the average mind.'

'Intendant!' She snarled it like a curse. 'What's the Dominion afraid of? Think there'll be another Insurrection if Felix sells offworld, that it?'

She was acid, dismissing his explanations. She didn't want explanations, only justice.

'How can I communicate? I know I can reach them on other worlds – they're different from us, yes, but I can touch them – feel the way they feel, make them listen to me when I sing!'

'How do you think the Insurrection started?' Broderick asked. 'Something in the mind responds, philosophy and religion spread from world to world, psychic epidemics – man tends to chaos. If the Dominion didn't keep the Interdict on that—'

'So you interdict religion, politics, art, music . . .' She sat hugging her knees, knuckles white. Tension drew the brown skin taut over her high cheekbones, sharpened the line of her mouth. 'You've put me in a cage?'

And so he left that cage, Parmiter's World. His fear and hope was that passing under Interdict might wipe out his feelings for her, and the doubt that gnawed him. It did not; it left him more hollow than before.

He went out by way of the Dominion orbital station, travelling on a Dominion ship – there was no other way to travel. The Interdict – a combination of hypnosis and aversion therapy – didn't destroy memory. It implanted a strong disinclination to communicate the Interdicted subject. Perhaps what it did, Broderick thought, was kill the belief in a thing; so that after he left Parmiter's World, Clare glowed bright in his mind, but her music was only noise.

Something with terrifying potential, the Interdict, and so only to be trusted to the highest power: the Holy Dominion . . .

But that was when I believed in the Dominion, Broderick thought. Now who do I trust?

You came here to judge. So judge.

Broderick knew he was hallucinating. Nevertheless Clare Felix followed him from Thelmithar to Cir-nanth, from Cir-nanth to Gethfirle, and from Gethfirle to the Order house Durietch.

The curved wall of Durietch was hot against his back. The scent of *kasziz*-creeper filled the air. In the past week Broderick had heard any number of philosophies, many varieties of mysticism. Any Intendant would recognise at once how dangerous Kasa-baarde's inner city was, breeding such things.

'Outlander,' said a young Orthean near him, 'what do your people believe in?'

The creed came to Broderick's mind: 'I believe in the Dominion, in our immortality in the union of spirit; I believe in the Peace of Mankind, and in the holy instrumentality of the Intendants—'

I believe Clare Felix is dead.

'I don't know,' he said.

'I left the Islands for much the same reason.' The Orthean's skin shimmered, crystalline. 'I thought I might find an answer here.'

'Have you?'

'I don't know. Perhaps.'

Dangerous, Broderick thought. If the inner city's principle spreads. An epidemic of fads, philosophies, cults, heresies. No Intendant should hesitate. *Interdict!*

He missed one ship's pick-up date, and the next one too.

A fight began without reason, and finished as rapidly; a brief scuffle. No one moved to stop it. Broderick, caught in the fringes, rubbed skinned knuckles. Few of the crazies would tackle the Outlander, as a rule. He left Durietch all the same, walking back through dry alleys to Thelmithar. The egg-basket domes of the inner city blazed white against the pale sky.

When are you going back, Paul?

Now it was movement out of the corner of his eye, creeper fronds that mocked the line of her throat, the turn of her head.

You had no business sending me here! This needs an Intendant with faith, not a man who doubts everything!

Clare, Clare, Clare is dead. Known for so long, so familiar; lived with so close (Broderick thought) that you couldn't say I loved her, you'd have to say we were part of each other. So that death is amputation. Without reason. No, no reason. All the Intendant principles: peace, power, and love . . . all of them hollow. Measure it up against her death and what answer's left? Nothing.

Self-pity, Clare jeered. *And selfishness. How many times have you thought of suicide? Paul, Paul, and you always told me you believed in the unity!*

He sat on Thelmithar's steps, among the tranced Ortheans.

Work, Paul – are you going to waste your life?

He retained a lunatic hope that it was a real experience. That it was Clare in communication from the unity. But however hard he begged her, she wouldn't sing. Then he resigned himself to the fact that it was his own mute mind producing her image.

Clare, I miss you. All our lives together wouldn't have been long enough. I miss your touch, your smell, your love. There are so many questions I wanted to ask you.

The last pick-up date was close. Broderick, restless, went from Order house to Order house, questioning those who thought they'd found some illumination, some revelation in the inner city. To any who would listen, he spoke of Clare Felix.

'We're not so intense,' one elderly Orthean woman said. 'We love many times. But you . . . better to have had her a short time than not at all.'

Another, so young he couldn't tell if it were male or female, said, 'The earth is. The stars are. The wind blows and the land grows. What more should there be, Outlander?'

Passionately, he said, 'It doesn't answer her death!'

'I'll die,' the young one said. 'So will you. Does that thought disturb you?'

Broderick laughed at the irony. 'No.'

'If you can forgive the universe for your death, then forgive it for hers. Her death is her own, not yours.'

He left them, unanswered. The ever-present dust worked under his mask as he wandered the streets, irritating his sore eyes. Fury possessed him. Sometimes he shouted aloud. No one took notice of that. He was not unique in the inner city. The short twilight passed, and the fierce stars of the Core blazed in the night sky. Heat radiated back from the stone walls. Broderick kept walking. He crossed and recrossed the inner city, ignoring fatigue. The stars turned in the moonless night.

Dawn found him on the steps of Cir-nanth, dully watching the sunrise. Fatigue blurred his mind. His body ached; he had walked all the long dark hours. Light flooded the face of the dome. A dawn wind blew off the sea. Broderick eased himself down to sit by the bead-curtained door.

It happened then. Between one heartbeat and the next, welling up in him. His eyes stung, wet. He reached out and touched the mortar crumbling between the curved stone blocks, the dead leaves in the dust beside him. He saw the flaring light of the sun and the pale glory of the sky, felt the salt-laden breeze. Felt the breath in his lungs, the beat of his heart, the blood in his body. The pulse, the rhythm . . .

Nothing was changed: Clare was dead. Everything was changed: he was alive.

Broderick drew breath, shook his head in amazement; looking at her death as if it were a thousand years ago, and at her life as if it were a miracle. All the people she had reached out to—!

The inner city said to him: The world is. You are. I am. This is all there is.

And if this is all there is, Broderick slowly pieced together his conclusion, then all that's important is communication. To know ourselves and to know others. Reach out, touch: love. The past and the future don't exist. What matters is us, alive, now.

In Orthe's dawn was a pinprick of falling light, no morning star. The ship. If he didn't leave willingly, they would take him. And take it as further proof that the Interdict was necessary.

'You're our litmus paper,' an Intendant once said to him. 'We drop you in, stir you round, and pull you out, see how you've changed. How else can we judge the really powerful effects on the human psyche?'

On Orthe there are two populated continents where a man might vanish. On Orthe there are remnants of a high-tech civilization, a star-travelling people. Broderick watched the star fall. If a man should build his own ships . . . ?

It would not be the first time someone had gone up against the Dominion. He would most likely fail. Even if there were – as he thought there might be, later – others to carry the word, failure was still probable.

Will you put music in a cage? Clare Felix had asked.

Broderick put on his mask, and walked on into the long morning shadows of that alien city.

THE END

964

APPENDICES
AND MAPS

APPENDIX 1

Glossary

Ai-Telestre – literally the Hundred Thousand, traditionally all the *telestres* existing between the Wall of the World in the north, the Inner Sea to the south, the Eastern Sea, and the Glittering Plain to the west. Unified by Kerys Founder after the fall of the Golden Empire.

amari – 'born of no mother; motherless'. A term used in the Hundred Thousand, referring to a child born of a non-*telestre* mother (and usually a *telestre* father; but possibly adopted *n'ri n'suth*). The child is motherless in the sense that it is not of the earth of the Hundred Thousand; thus the *amari* are always slightly feared or shunned, since a different inflection can make this mean 'without the (mother) Goddess'. It has both a descriptive and a condemnatory use.

arniac – a small shrub that grows in the infertile soil of the Desert Coast. Broad red leaves, black berries, growing to a height of half a metre. The leaf when dried is used to make herb-tea, and the berries are a cure for headaches and fevers.

arykei – literally 'bed-friend', lover, pair-bond (in some rarer cases, a triple or quadruple bond occurs). Given that the care of children in the *telestre* is communal, the *arykei* relationship is not child-based, but depends on mutual temporary or long-term attraction.

ashiren – a child, nominally under fourteen; literally one who has not yet attained adult gender. Diminutive: *ashiren-te*.

ashirenin – one permanently *ashiren*, one who does not change to adult gender at age 13–15 but remains neuter. Change then occurs between the ages of 30 and 35, and invariably results in death. The *ashirenin* are rare, said to have strange qualities for good or ill. Most famous of the *ashirenin* is Beth'ru-elen.

ataile – tough-leafed herb growing mostly in Melkathi and the Rimon and Ymirian hills. When chewed, the leaves produce a mildly narcotic effect, and are addictive.

becamil – the webweaver-beetle, giving its name to the tough multi-coloured waterproof fabric spun from its web. Hives are kept commercially all over the Hundred Thousand.

Beth'ru-elen – called Beth'ru-elen *Ashirenin*, a latent Orthean who died at 35 during late change to female. Reformer and revolutionary. During exile from Morvren Freeport spent time in Kasabaarde's inner city, formulated the philosophical and religious insights that led to the reformation of the church of the Goddess. Later became *s'an* of one of the six founding *telestres* of Peir-Dadeni: the *n'ri n'suth* line is still in existence.

bird's-wing – bush with broad, wing-shaped leaves and edible yellow fruit, common to Roehmonde and border Fen-country; striations of white on green-yellow leaves give 'feather' effect.

brennior – large quadruped used as draught-beast in the Desert regions. Sand-coloured, thick hide, tri-padded foot, tailless. Short flexible snout. Poor sight, good hearing. Omnivore.

Brown Tower – home of the Hexenmeister in Kasabaarde's inner city. Founded some ten thousand years ago on the ruins of an Eldest Empire settlement, for the preservation of knowledge. Most of the underground installations are defunct, though it is still said to have connections with the Rasrhe-y-Meluur and the ruins under the Elansiir. One of the two sole remaining instances of viable Golden technology.

chirith-goyen – or clothworm, the fibre-spinning larvae of the *chirith-goyen* fly. The fibre is woven into a light fabric throughout the Hundred Thousand, and is easily dyed.

chiruzeth – a substance created either by the Golden Witchbreed, or by their predecessors. It has been described as a semi-sentient crystal, manipulated by mental energy; and as a substance in some way analagous to human DNA/RNA. Techniques for altering it from its present inert form have been lost.

dekany – tuberous weed found in shallow waters of the Inner Sea; useful for rope-fibre but not for much else.

del'ri – staple crop of the Desert Coast, a bamboo-like plant with edible seeds in the knobbed stems. Pale green, growing to a height of 2–2½ metres. Harvested twice a year.

Desert Coast – general name given to that part of the southern continent that borders on the Inner Sea, and to the various ports and city-states there. Cut off from the wastelands of the interior by the Elansiir mountain range.

Earthspeaker – sometimes called the Landless. An office held by the members of the church of the Goddess after their training at the theocratic houses. They travel the Hundred Thousand, giving up their own *telestres*, and acting in a multitude of roles which may include priest, agrarian advisor, psychologist, healer, etc. The extent of their authority is impossible to define.

Emperor-in-Exile – hereditary ruler of Kel Harantish, chosen from the lineal half-breed descendants of Santhendor'lin-sandru's imperial dynasty. A tyrant with absolute authority in Harantish's highly-structured society. Claims the ancient right of ruling both northern and southern continents as the Golden Empire did.

fenborn – aboriginal race of Carrick V, now reduced in number and confined mainly to settlements in the Greater and Lesser Fens. Oviparous night-hunters living in a stone-age culture. In the past carried out raids of considerable ferocity on north Rimon and Roehmonde, but have remained within the fen-borders since Galen Honeymouth's treaty with them some two hundred years ago.

Fens – the Greater and Lesser Fens: marsh and fenland covering some two thousand square miles, paralleling the Wall of the World and separating the provinces of Roehmonde (to which it is comparable in size) and Peir-Dadeni. Not least among the dangerous fauna are the fenborn.

ferrorn – see *ochmir* appendix.

galeni – a term used by the aboriginal Orthean species, the fenborn, to refer to that humanoid race now more generally regarded as 'Ortheans' (who are the product of genetic engineering, cross-breeding fenborn and the Golden Witchbreed). *Galeni* derives from the first *T'An Suthai-Telestre* to ensure the Greater and Lesser Fens were regarded as fenborn territory, the *T'An* Galen Kerys-Andrethe, called Galen Honeymouth.

Goddess – sometimes referred to as the Mother or the Sunmother, or occasionally the Wellmother. A sun and earth deity. The church was designed and set up by Kerys Founder as an anti-technology device after the fall of the Witchbreed. It was later transformed by Beth'ru-elen *Ashirenin* into a genuine religious movement. Now more of a philosophical discipline including a reverence for all life, and a recognition of reincarnation. They hold that their spirits pass through many bodies, reuniting in death with the fire of the Goddess ('fire' and 'spirit' have the same root-word in most Orthean languages); the main heresy holds that this is merely genetically inherited memory – possibly why the Hexenmeister is regarded with such deep distrust.

Golden Empire – the five-thousand-year rule of the Witchbreed race, under whose autocratic rule the two continents enjoyed peace, prosperity, and total slavery. Ended by Thel Siawn's infertility virus, which gave rise to a war that devastated most of the southern continent, left the cities and land north of the Wall of the World in ruins, and is still visible in the transformation of Eriel to the Glittering Plain.

hanelys – commonly called tanglebush, a plant propagating itself by runners; 2–3 metres high, stems very hard black fibre with long thorns, yellow leaves during Hanys and Merrum, and small orange fruit in Stathern.

harur-nilgiri, harur-nazari – traditional paired blades, the former a kind of short rapier, the latter a kind of long knife. Used ambidextrously. Common throughout the Hundred Thousand.

Hexenmeister – ruler of Kasabaarde, guardian of stored knowledge, and a sequentially immortal personality. Head of an information-gathering network that spans two continents.

hiyannek – term of endearment on the Desert Coast, 'best blood', that is, best-descended.

hiyek – translates literally as 'bloodline', in the sense of family or lineage. The *hiyek* is the matrilineal-descent family upon which Desert Coast society is structured; and given their dependence on the canal system, it is perhaps not surprising that the root-word can also be translated as 'water'. Blood is understood to be the carrier of past-memories within individual bloodlines. Whether this means that Coast Ortheans assume themselves reborn within the same bloodline, or only allow themselves memories that reinforce this concept, is unclear. A drug used to access these memories, *keret-nen-hiyek*, can thus be translated either as 'Blood of Memory' or 'Water of Truth'.

hura – species of hard-shelled water clam found in rivers throughout the Hundred Thousand.

jath – double-masted, ocean-going vessel, usually with lateen sails; design originating in Morvren Freeport.

jath-rai – single-masted small coaster or fishing boat.

jayante – short weighted weapon similar to quarterstaff, used mainly to immobilize or disable. Originally from the Rainbow Cities, especially Cuthanc.

K'Ai Kezrian-kezriakor – a Harantish term translating as 'Emperor/ Empress-in-Exile', applied to the descendants (or supposed descendants) of Santhendor'lin-sandru, the Last Emperor of the Golden Witchbreed. The *K'Ai Kezrian-kezriakor* rules the settlement Kel Harantish, and the canal system upon which the *hiyek*-families depend for their survival. The 'exile' referred to is from the territory covered by the Golden Empire: the northern and southern continental land-masses. Abbreviation: *K'Ai*, Empress/ Emperor.

Kasabaarde – a Desert Coast city with curious philosophies and influences. Sited at the point between the southern continent and the Kasabaarde Archipelago, gaining wealth from trade and tolls. Divided into trade-quarter and inner city, the latter run by the Order houses; both under the authority of the Hexenmeister.

kazsis – usually called *kazsis*-nightflower, a vine native to Ymir and Rimon. Bronze leaves, dark red blooms, the scent is particularly noticeable after dark.

kazza – carnivorous reptilian quadruped, often trained in the Southland as a hunting animal. Short white pelt with blue-grey markings.

ke, kir – neutral pronoun used for the young of the Orthean species, and sometimes for the Goddess.

kekri-fly – an insect with a short segmented body and triple paired wings; coloured blue, green, or black, with reflecting wing-surfaces. Fond of sewage.

Kel Harantish – once a garrison outpost of the Golden Empire, now one of the smaller Desert Coast city-states. Completely dependent on imports for survival. Home of the last surviving descendants of the Golden Witchbreed, and the Emperor-in-Exile.

keretne – translates as 'eldest blood', 'truthful memory', and refers to those Coast Ortheans, not necessarily old in a physiological sense, who have by gift and training a close access to their past-memories. The *hiyeks*, being mobile, have little use for literacy and records; they therefore rely on this oral culture-store.

Kerys Founder – credited with spreading the *telestre* system that arose after the fall of the Golden Empire, of unifying the Hundred Thousand and founding the Kerys *telestre* at Tathcaer. Led the first crusade against Kel Harantish, and began the Hundred Thousand's long association with the Brown Tower. Set up the church of the Goddess to prevent the rise of another industrial society.

Kirriach – ruined city over the Wall of the World, once known as aKirrik. Part of the Golden Empire's middle province, now called the Barrens, along with Simmerath, Hinkuumiel, Mirane, etc.

kuru – pig-like reptilian beasts sometimes domesticated in Roehmonde and north Ymir. Smooth dark red hides, small eyes and ears, tailless; cleft feet have traces of webs. Omnivores.

labamu – riderbeast of the Barrens tribes. Long-necked quadruped with tough grey hide, solid hooves. Round cup-like ears, hooded eyes, and long muzzles with pointed upper lips; no manes, and flap-like tails. Very skittish and speedy; slender legs and sloping barrel-bodies, with a belling cry.

lapuur – the feathery-leaved tree of south Ymir, Rimon, and Melkathi; pale green trailing foliage, main trunk growing to a height of 3–4 metres.

leremoc – see *ochmir* appendix.

l'ri-an – one who is learning a trade or performing a paid service; usually a young adult or *ashiren*. Literally: apprentice.

makre – a form of double-lobed grain flourishing in temperate areas of the Hundred Thousand; particularly north Ymir, Rimon, and parts of southern Roehmonde.

marhaz – the common *telestre* riderbeast, referred to as *marhaz*-mare, *marhaz*-stallion, *marhaz*-gelding; of reptilian ancestry like the *skurrai*. Cleft hooves, and a double pair of horns. The thick shaggy pelt is composed of feather-structured fibres. Enduring rather than speedy.

marshflower – skin blemish: a dappled pattern sometimes said to resemble the marshfern, and to be more common in those *telestres* that border the Great Fens.

Melkathi – that province distinguished by the Melkath language, comprising the Melkathi peninsula and the Kadareth Islands, the *T'An* Melkathi being resident in Ales-Kadareth. The most infertile *telestres* of all the Hundred Thousand, the most reluctant to accept Crown rule. Mostly comprised of heathland, bog, marshes, and sand-flats. Ales-Kadareth has the name of being an old Witchbreed city, pirate port, and home of strange sciences. Famous for atheists, malcontents, heresy, and rebellion.

meshabi – robe worn by Coast Ortheans, consisting of a length of *del'ri*-cloth belted at the hip; a superfluous fold of which can be brought up to hood the head and back.

moss-eye – preying lizardbird found on the Dadeni Heath, with eye-like markings on wings.

Morvren – small cluster of *telestres* holding land round the mouth of the Ai River; the Seamarshal is resident in the Freeport itself. Freeport has links with the Rasrhe-y-Meluur, Kasabaarde, and the Desert Coast; its language is a south-Dadeni dialect. A great maritime trading centre famous for voyages to strange places, river-craft, false coins, sharp practice, odd visitors, bureaucracy, and general moral irresponsibility. Rumoured to trade with Kel Harantish.

mossgrass – staple vegetation of the Hundred Thousand, a stringy-fronded species of lichen that roots shallowly in topsoil. Seasonal changes in colour.

muroc – shaggy white-pelted beast of the Barrens, tremendously strong but slow; stands 1½–2 metres at shoulder. Short single pair of black horns. Carnivorous quadruped. Sense of smell excellent.

n'ri n'suth – "adopted into the *telestre* of": literally translates as brother-sister. A *telestre* child bears its mother's name, its own name, and the *telestre*'s name.

ochmir – see Appendix 2.

Peir-Dadeni – the newest province, founded five hundred years ago by a group of rebels from Morvren Freeport. Follows the Ai River, bounded on the west by the Glittering Plain, and on the east, stretches from Morvren and Rimon up past Dadeni Heath to the Fens, and the Wall of the World. Keeps the pass at Broken Stair guarded. One founder was the reformer Beth'ru-elen, another the assassin Lori L'Ku, and another was Andrethe, from whom the ruling *telestre* takes its name. Famous for river-craft, trade, dubious frontiers, legends of Berani and the Eriel Frost-drakes; for the Heath's *skurrai*, the river-port of Shiriya-Shenin, and for mad riders. Swears alliance with, rather than allegiance to, the *T'An Suthai-Telestre*.

raiku – the basic unit of the *hiyek*: a group-marriage. The *ashiren* of the Desert Coast families will spend a year alone in the cities of the Coast, forming small groups of four, five, or six, that will become their *raiku*: a lifelong bond of emotional and physical interdependence. This will often include members of the same birth, and stay within one bloodline; though exogamy is not frowned on. *Raiku* are numbered according to the groups formed within one year.

Kei-raiku: one who is outside the *raiku*, either by not yet having joined, or by losing one's group by the deaths of the other members, or – very rarely – by expulsion.

Rainbow Cities – general name given to the settlements in the tropical regions of the southern continent, of which only Saberon and Cuthanc are large enough to be properly called cities.

rashaku – generic term for the lizardbird having the appearance of a small archeopteryx. Feathered wings, scaled breast and body. Four clawed feet, the front pair greatly atrophied; gold eyes with nictitating membrane. Distinctive metallic call. Size and plumage colour vary according to habitat: from the white of the *rashaku-bazur* (sea) to the black and brown of the *rashaku-dya* (hill country). Other varieties include the *rashaku-nai* (fens) and *kur-rashaku* (mountains).

***rashaku*-relay** – the Wellkeepers train a species of *rashaku*-lizardbird in the carrying of messages between Wellhouses. The *rashaku-dya*, with its acute colour-vision, is most often used; they are trained to respond and fly to different destinations when shown different colour-codes.

Rasrbe-y-Meluur – commonly called Bridge Alley, a remnant of

Golden Empire engineering; being a suspended tunnel-structure built on pylons from Morvren Freeport down the Kasabaarde Archipelago to Kasabaarde itself. Still passable, though inhabited.

Rimon – central province, bordering the Inner Sea between Morvren and Tathcaer, sharing the Oranon River border with Ymir. Downland country, lightly wooded, having one main river, the Meduin. Famous for *marhaz*, grain, vines, wine, and border-river disputes with Ymir. The *T'An* Rimon is resident in Medued.

Roehmonde – northern province bounded by Ymir, the Lesser Fens, the Wall of the World, and the Eastern Sea. Hilly forested country, famous for mining, metal-working, charcoal-burning and hunting. The *T'An* Roehmonde is resident in Corbek, a city that never wholly accepted Beth'ru-elen's reformation of the church. There are few large ports on the inhospitable eastern coast. Roehmonde is one of the largest and most sparsely inhabited provinces, a country of insular *telestres*. They guard one of the great passes down from the Barrens, the Path of Skulls.

ruesse – a substance, derived by a method which is unclear, from certain glands of the *brennior*-packbeast. Ingested, it causes paralysis of the respiratory system in Ortheans, death following rapidly. Its effects on humans are similar but much less severe. To humans, also, it has a characteristic scent, reminiscent of roses; this is undetectable by Ortheans.

rukshi – land arthropods, small and segmented with patterned shells and two pairs of claws. Now rare.

s'an telestre – landholder, elected to office by the adult members of the *telestre*, and having unspecified authority. More of an administrator than ruler, having more responsibility than power. The *telestre* is held in trust for the Goddess.

s'aranthi – a human, or humanoid offworlder. This derives from *S'aranth*, a name given to the first contact envoy in the Hundred Thousand, and translates literally as 'one who does not carry *harur*-blades', one who is weaponless. It is ironic that this should come to be applied to hi-tech offworlders as a general term.

saryl-kabriz – an organic poison, fatal to Orthean life, distilled from the bark of the *saryl-kabriz* bush. Has a characteristic sharp scent, difficult to mask. Not to be confused with

saryl-kiez – a similar shrub, brown with blue berries. The sap, unlike that of the *saryl-kabriz*, is not a poison. It can be used as lamp oil; the scent is pungent.

seri – unit of distance, equal to one and one-fifth miles on the standard Earth scale.

shan'tai – 'one outside the *hiyek*, or bloodline', a stranger. This term of address on the Desert Coast can, according to inflection, have varying implicit degrees of welcome or rejection. The respectful greeting *kethrial-shamaz shan'tai* is an invitation to share water/blood/hospitality on a temporary basis.

sidimaat – commonly called 'fire-rose', a large-blossomed bush that flowers once in Merrum and once in Torvern; favours the hot climates of Melkathi and south Ymir.

siriye – the starmoth, a triple-winged insect with poison sting. The wing-surfaces are luminous. Web-weaver. Common on heathland, and at the edge of forests.

siir – a thick-boled vine or creeper, fungoid, growing to a height of several metres, and spreading to cover wide areas of ground. In the Hundred Thousand it is allowed to spore; the yellow spore cases are then gathered and fermented into a green wine-like liquid. The effect on a human is slightly hallucinogenic. The name *siir* derives from a Witchbreed term meaning 'fertile'. The plant was possibly created through their bio-engineering as an all-purpose food crop. A further derivation leads to the *Elansiir*, the 'garden' or 'harvest-field', a name applied to the central region of the southern continent, now made barren by war damage.

siiran – 'shelter'; one of the underground chambers of the Desert Coast canal system, used as habitations, and also used to grow crops in uninhabitable areas. The term suggests a link with the Witchbreed food-crop *siir*, and possibly the canal system was constructed to raise these plants. Climatological changes following on war damage in the central Elansiir means that *siir* itself rarely flourishes on the Coast now.

skurrai – the *telestre* packbeast, referred to as *skurrai*-mare, *skurrai*-stallion, *skurrai*-gelding; double-horned and reptilian; basically a smaller stockier version of the *marhaz*.

skurrai-jasin – the *skurrai*-drawn carriage common in Tathcaer.

Southland – *Suthai-Telestre*: literally the south hundred thousand *telestres*. See: *Ai-Telestre*.

sweet mosseye – plant from which a sour wine is distilled, using the roots; a fern with eye-like markings on the fronds. Rare except in the Kyre.

Sunmother – see *Goddess*.

takshiriye – the court or government attached to the *T'An Suthai-Telestre*, resident in Tathcaer (and Shiriya-Shenin during the winter season).

T'An – the administrator of a province: *t'an*, general polite term for strangers and visitors. Derives from 'guest'.

T'An Suthai-Telestre – in the informal inflection, the Crown of the

Hundred Thousand. Self-chosen from the *T'Ans* of all the provinces, re-elected on every tenth midsummer solstice. The unifier of church and *telestres*.

Tathcaer – capital of the Hundred Thousand, an island-city solely under Crown law, sometimes called the eighth province. Home of every *T'An Suthai-Telestre* since Kerys Founder. The Hundred Thousand have each a *telestre*-house in the city; also there are the Guild-*telestres*.

telestre – the basic unit of Hundred Thousand society, a community of any number between fifty and five hundred Ortheans living on an area of land. This unit is self-supporting, including agriculture, arts, and crafts. The *telestre* system rose spontaneously out of the chaos that followed the fall of the Golden Empire. Given the natural Orthean tendency to form groups, and their talent for making the earth yield, the *telestre* is their natural habitat.

tha'adur – a Peir-Dadeni term for the Andrethe's court and governing officials resident in the city Shiriya-Shenin.

The Kyre – a province of remote *telestres* in the mountains that lie south of the Wall of the World and north of the Glittering Plain. Very insular in character, occasionally trading with Peir-Dadeni. Mostly they subsist on hunting. The province is very sparsely populated; the *T'An* Kyre is resident in Ivris, a market *telestre*. Famous for milk, cheese, wood-carving, mountain-craft, and lack of humour, popularly supposed to be a result of the appalling weather.

thousandflower – mosslike plant growing in woodlands over most of the Hundred Thousand, forms a thick carpet 10–15 cms deep, and varies in colour from light to dark blue.

thurin – see *ochmir* appendix.

tukinna – evergreen tree, thin-boled with black bark, twisted limbs, growing to a height of 10 metres. Foliage concentrated at the crown: scroll-like leaves, small black inedible seeds. Prefers northern climates (like Roehmonde forests).

Wall of the World – gigantic geological slip-fault that has split the northern continent in a northeast-southwest division; being now a range of mountains in which there are only two known passes from the Barrens to the Hundred Thousand: Broken Stair and the Path of Skulls. The barren land north of the Wall is occupied by barbarian tribes living in the ruined cities of the Golden Witchbreed.

Wellkeeper – title given to those members of the church who give up their own *telestre* to run the Wellhouses, sometimes called theocratic houses. These may be places of worship, of philosophy and refuge; working communes for adults or *ashiren*; universities or other places of learning; weapons training houses; or craft workshops.

wirrazu – semi-biped semi-quadruped lizardbeasts found in wooded country; brown pelts, thin horns, run in herds of eight or ten. Herbivores.

Witchbreed – sometimes known as the Golden. Originally the humanoid race brought to Carrick V as servitors to the Eldest Empire – this being an apocryphal name given to the alien settlers who first landed some twenty thousand years ago, but died out soon after that. Nothing is known of the 'Eldest Empire', but it left its mark in the genetic structure of both the Witchbreed and the native race of Orthe. The Witchbreed had great talent for using and developing the technology that was left to them, and made use of both the physical and sociological sciences. They fell to a sterility virus. Sporadic instances of interbreeding took place between Witchbreed and Ortheans, but in general the two species are not inter-fertile.

Ymir – the oldest province, with the most archaic form of language; occupying the land east of the Oranon that lies between Melka-thi and Roehmonde. Good grazing on the Downs, good soil in the lowlands, and the many tributaries of the Oranon make this one of the richest provinces, famous for good harvests. The *T'An* Ymir is resident in Tathcaer. The *telestres* close to the city are famed for ship-building. Ymir is known for its theocratic houses, traders and merchants, beast-tamers, eccentricities of all kinds, and the most convoluted argumentative minds outside of Kasabaarde.

ziku – broad-leaved deciduous tree with edible fruit, grows to a height of 7 metres. Bronze-red foliage, dusty-blue fruit. Common in Ymir and Peir-Dadeni, preferring to grow near water. Hybrid form grown in Rimon with larger and more plentiful fruit, harvested in Stathern.

zilmei – found in north Roehmonde and Peir-Dadeni forests. Black and grey pelts, wedge-shaped skulls, and retractable claws. A bad-tempered carnivore. Distinctive hooting cry.

APPENDIX 2

Ochmir

A game played in the Hundred Thousand, originating in the cities but popular everywhere. It is played on a hexagonal board divided into 216 triangular grid-spaces. The 216 counters are double-sided, the ideogram-characters traditionally blue-on-white and white-on-blue; and are divided into *ferrorn*, which must remain stationary when placed on the board; *thurin*, which may move one space (across a line, not an angle); and *leremoc*, which have complete freedom of movement. The object of the game is to have all the pieces on the board showing one's chosen colour.

This is accomplished by forcing a reversal of the opposition's counters, by gaining a majority of colour in a minor hexagon. The 6-triangle minor hexagons form a shifting, overlapping framework.

The distribution of characters means that a counter may or may not have a duplicate value on its reverse side; it is thus necessary to remember when placing a counter what is on the obverse.

A 'hand' of counters is drawn, sight unseen, from the *ochmir* bag on every sixth turn (a hand on Orthe is six). Only one move or placement can be made per turn, unless this results in a majority in a minor hexagon, in which case all the counter reversals are carried out. Since majorities are retrospective, the turning of one hexagon to one colour will affect the hexagon-frames overlapping it.

There are no restrictions on where on the board a game may begin, and it is usual for two or three separate pattern-conflicts to be set up. It is the *ferrorn* that determines the area of conflict.

Ochmir can also be played with three players (blue-white-brown), in which case the number of spaces that need be occupied for a majority in the minor hexagons decreases from 5 or 4 to 3. In this case there is also the shifting balance of alliances between players; and the game ends when one player gains the 144-counter majority of one colour.

A player may not turn own-colour counters to reverse. In the case of a 3–3 split in a minor hexagon it is left until the shifting framework divides it up amongst other hexagons. The game can be played with retrospective reversals even when all 216 counters are on the board. *Ochmir* is not only about gaining control, but about keeping it afterwards.

The game is based on manipulation, not territory; and on mobility rather than on rank. The value of the counters shift with the game; a player's own counters are also those of the opposition. These themes of interdependence, mobility, manipulation, and control have led some authorities to see a connection between *ochmir* and *Ai-Telestre*, and even to equate *ferrorn, thurin*, and *leremoc* with *s'an telestre, T'An*, and *T'An Suthai-Telestre*.

APPENDIX 3

The Calendar of the Hundred Thousand

Winter Solstice: New year festival.

Orventa: the longest season, 11 weeks. Winter. Favourite season for the custom of keeping *telezu*. No trade, travel, planting, etc., due to bad weather. One of the two main periods of activity for *takshiriye* and *tha'adur* in residence in Shiriya-Shenin. Practice of arts, music, sciences, etc. Usually the First Thaw festival occurs around Tenthweek.

Spring Solstice: festival of the Wells.

Hanys: 3 weeks. Spring ploughing and planting: busy time for the *telestres*. Prevailing westerly winds. Floods. Inner Sea liable to sudden storms.

Durestha: Early summer, 8 weeks. Long spells of hot weather. Travel possible, roads repaired. Guild ships leave for Desert Coast and Rainbow Cities.

Summer Solstice: Naming day and midyear festival.

Merrum: 9 weeks, high summer. Period of great administrative activity in the *takshiriye*, resident in Tathcaer. Favourite season for travel, trade, sea voyages, etc.

Stathern: 2 weeks. Everything stops for the harvest. Culminates in

Autumn Solstice: harvest festivals.

Torvern: 4 weeks, early autumn hunting season; also the time for fairs and markets. The last season for travel before winter weather makes the Inner Sea impassable.

Riardh: 7 weeks. Hunting season. The beginning of winter, preparation of provisions, storing food, weaving, etc. Some late autumn sowing. Usually includes First Snow Festival.

Note: the week consists of nine days, of which every Firstday is a feast-day, every Fiveday a holiday, and every Nineday a fast-day. The day has a length of 27 standard hours. With a 400-day year, this means that in practice the Orthean year is 85 days (12 weeks) longer than the Earth standard year.

ORTHE

CARRICK V
from *PanOceania Company Records*

THE BARRENS

Wall of the World

Shiriya-Shenin

Corbek

The Glittering Plain

SOUTHLAND

Medued

Tathcaer

WESTERN OCEAN

EASTERN SEA

Morvren Freeport

Ales-Kadareth

Kasabaarde

Inner Sea

L'Dui

DESERT COAST

Quarth

Eastern Isles

Lu'Nathe

Psamnol

Kel Harantish

THE ELANSIIR

N

Cuthanc

Saberon

CARRICK V

NORTHERN WILDERNESS

BROKEN STAIR

Ivris

THE KYRE

Ai Garrison

Beth 'ru-e

Shiriya-Shenin

Baharu-Bazuriye

Lei'Eriel

Paranit

Hassichi

PEIR-DADENI

Kepulani

THE GLITTERING PLAIN

R. Ai

Pel'Shennin

Medue

R. Me

Machir

RIM

WESTERN OCEAN

Telerion

MORVREN

Freeport

N
W—E
S

KASABAARDE ARCHIPELAGO

RASRHE-Y-MELUUR

Kasabaarde

0   200 seri (240 miles)

ELANSIIR

Kel Harantish

THE SOUTHLAND